INTERESTING COMMENT OF AN EXPERT

ON "PENNY DREADFULS".
::::::::::::::::::::::::::::::::::

On one of the fly leaves of a copy of "Ned Kelly" (same edit.

as this copy) from the collection of   Mr.Arthur

E.Waite, the famous author of works of Dark Magic,Witchcraft,

Occultism,etc,was written the following interesting

commentary ------------

"A Flatulent Farrago of Fatuous Fiction,

Conceived by G.D.Boucicault. -- Commenced by Borlase,

Continued by Percy B.St.John,Completed by M.Vizetelly,

Cut up generally (under pretext of sub-editing,and otherwise

improving) by G.D.Boucicault.

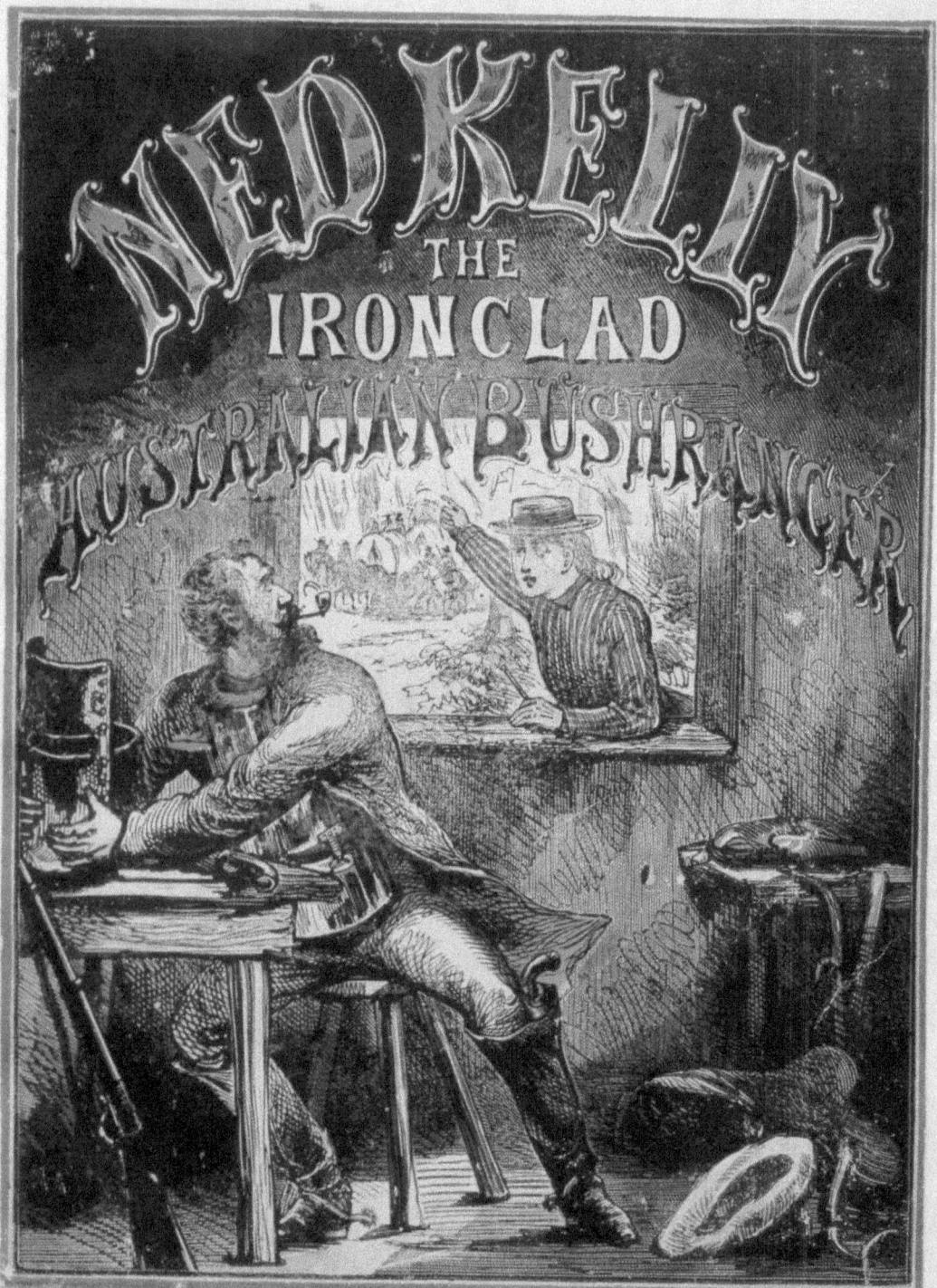

NED KELLY:

THE

IRONCLAD AUSTRALIAN

BUSHRANGER.

COMPLETE.

LONDON :

ALFRED J. ISAACS & SONS, 16, CAMOMILE STREET, E.C.

1881

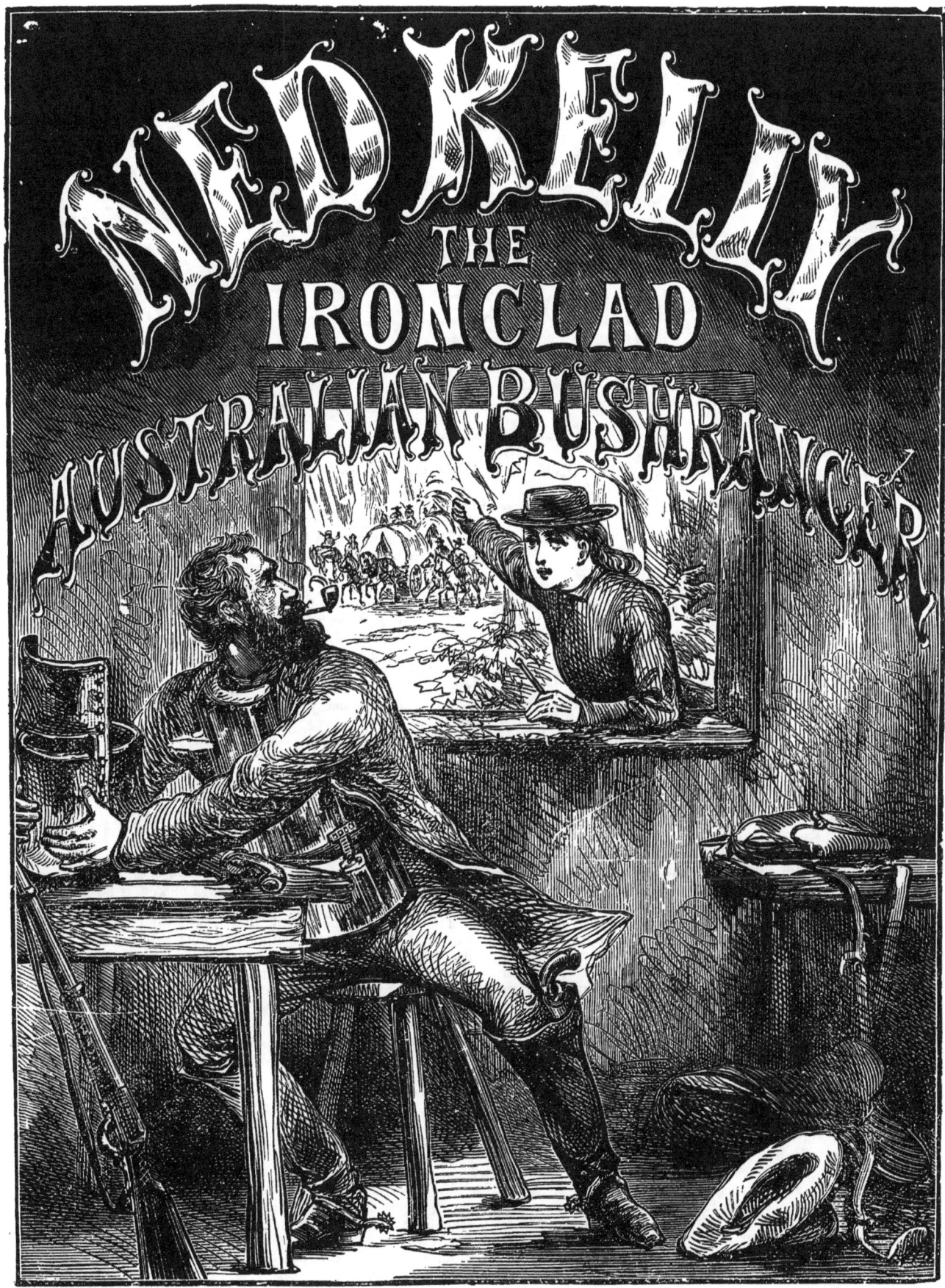

NED KELLY
THE
IRONCLAD
AUSTRALIAN BUSHRANGER

NO 1,

NED KELLY,

THE

AUSTRALIAN IRONCLAD BUSHRANGER.

BY ONE OF HIS CAPTORS.

CHAPTER I.

A GROG-SHANTY AT FOREST CREEK.

FOREST CREEK was the place to *make your pile*, otherwise your fortune, in the year of gold, 1852; and where twelve-months previously the blackfellow, the emu, and the kangaroo had it all to themselves, hundreds of tents dotted the thinly-timbered bush, interspersed with wooden stores and grog-shanties every here and there, whilst down by the water's side the cradles were rocking all day long; not the cradles that add to a man's responsibilities, but the rough, wooden machines in which he washed the refuse away from his gold.

But away with all thought of such labour for the present, for it is knock-off hour, and so the holes are empty and the grog-shanties are full and driving a roaring trade, for a hot wind has been blowing all day, withering the grass, curling up the leaves on the trees, and filling the diggers' eyes and throats with burning dust, so that most of them now feel as though they could drain an ocean dry. This is why the grog-shops are doing such a roaring trade.

Let us look in at the *Emu*, better known as "Mother Maloney's." It is a rickety calico shanty of the shabbiest class, but it is big, and it is furthermore *the fashion*; perhaps by reason that Mrs. Maloney is a buxom widow and is reputed to have been left remarkably well off by "the late lamented," as she invariably called her defunct spouse.

Anyhow, the qualities of her wares could not have been the draw, for her wines might have been labelled VINEGAR, her spirits VITRIOL; and as to her *Stringy Bark*, otherwise Colonial Ale, why, Russian Quass diluted with bilge-water would have been nectar to it.

However, whether because she was fat, fair, and forty, or because bachelor diggers thought she would be a catch in a monetary point of view, her shanty was at all events all the go; and now behold it tolerably full of weary-limbed but light-hearted miners, clad in blue or red woollen shirts, worn *en blouse* over moleskin or corduroy pants, and girt at the waist by a belt or a smart sash of Chinese silk, but covered from the soles of their thick blucher boots to the crowns of their wide-awake or two-guinea cabbage-tree hats, with the clay and mud amongst which they have been working.

Some are sitting on the hard-beaten mud floor, with pewter pots between their legs and their backs propped up against a post of the tent, and others have turned a bucket upside down for a chair, or are balancing themselves on the iron ends of their picks, the handle forming the support.

Picks, shovels, and billies are tossed here and there and everywhere, the confusion is that of Babel, and chaff is flying hither and thither in company with oaths and blasphemy; uttered, however, without malice, but as simple interjections and notes of admiration.

The conversation of most of them would have been as unintelligible as Low Dutch to the freshly arrived out from England.

"Where are you going to mark out your next claim, mate?"

"Guess how many pennyweights I'm making to the tub?"

"I say, Bill Tomkins has had his hole jumped!"

"Is it true that California Jim has sloped to Ballarat with Ned Fletcher's missus?"

"Yes, they did; may I never speak another word if they didn't get thirty pounds weight of gold in less than two days, out of a patch of gravel not more than six inches deep."

"Better luck, that, than happened last week to an old chum o' mine, who paid fifty pounds for a salted claim and found it a *shyser*. It'll be murder, I reckon, if he comes across the cove who slewed him!"

This was the kind of talk that went round and round, varied sometimes by a compliment hurled like a cannon ball at Mother Maloney, as with a face as red as her cap-ribbons, she served her thirsty customers.

Suddenly there enters the shanty a tall, slim individual in seedy black, with a battered bell-topper hat crushed down over his brow. His clothes have evidently seen Regent-street, perhaps even have been constructed by the redoubtable *Poole*; but they are now in a scarecrow condition, and he looks not unlike a scarecrow inside them, so spare and angular is he, whilst his long Dundreary whiskers are full of dust and sand, and his countenance is the colour of a wax-work figure in a Whitechapel or New-Cut penny exhibition.

This strange-looking being threaded his way mincingly between the groups of diggers, until, reaching the bar, he cast a languishing glance at Mother Maloney, and running his long taper fingers through his whiskers, said in drawling accents:—

"Will you cwedit me with a nobbler of rum, my dear good, kind, cwetshur, until I get my wemittances from England to-morrow?"

"It's indade an' I can't, Misther Norfolk Howard, with some folks to-morrow's niver to-day. An' besides it's entirely agin my rules, credit is!"

Scarcely were the words out of her mouth, when some one struck up:—

"Who of Gold don't earn an ounce?
    Loafer seedy loafer. O!
But who can come i en he bounce?
    Loafer, seedy loafer. O!
Who can cut it jolly fat,
Without a mag n Bal arat,
Wear an old bell-topper hat?
    Loafer, seedy loafer O!"

Roars of laughter greeted this sally, whose butt was evidently the seedy individual who had addressed himself to Mrs. Maloney's fond, but *not trusting* nature, in vain.

He did not seem, however, to be a whit disconcerted thereby; perhaps he was accustomed to such treatment.

"Haw, vewy good!" said he, languidly clapping his hands. "Vewy good *for you*; that is to say, I wish I'd such a voice, I do indeed!"

"What would you do with it if you had?" demanded the pleased singer.

"Why, my dear fwiend, I'd take it round and lend it out to the diggers to sharpen their tools on. Grindstones would be nothing to it."

"Oh, you go and be hanged. You've brought your jokes to the wrong shop."

"Just exactly what you've done with your voice. My dear fwiend, you would be worth a lob of gold a day to stand on the summit of Mount Alexander and shout out 'Joey!' to the diggers for twelve miles round when you saw the traps coming. I think you owe me a shout for the idea."

"I'll make you shout in another way if you don't dry up."

"It's because I'm so vewy dwied up that I wequire to be wetted down."

"Pitch us a better stave than that ere one we've just had a werse on, and I'll shout till yer blue in the face, mate," cried a digger, who was hugging a black billy to his rough, hairy breast as affectionately as a young mother could have done her first child, said billy being in truth a quarter full of nuggets and gold-dust.

The loafer didn't require any pressing. He knew that he had a fine voice, and he also knew that a comic song, well sung, was always good for at least a shout in any shanty on the diggings.

"I'll delight your ears with a truly celestial subject," said he. "The words are my own, and I've set them to an easy tune, so that there may be no excuse for not joining in coalbox. 'The Chinaman's Fate,' to the old air of the 'Mistletoe Bough,' gent'men. Here goes.

"The cradles were rocking one fine summer's day,
And the diggers were busily puddling away;
The Chinees were running about in shoals,
Humping the loading that comes from the holes,
Chow Chow his hands with glee did rub,
Cause he'd washed out a halfpenny weight to the tub;
And an old Chinee fossiker to h s mates did say,
'I gettse more go'd dan you wild to day!'

"Now then for the chorus, boys:

"Oh, what a sad tale—Crikey, oh, what a sad tale.

"He took up his pick and he shouldered his spade,
But before he went off to his mates he said,
'Cook a ni c bow-wow, and, mind you, don't fail
To save me some fattee from sucky pig's tail,'
The dinner was cooked, but he wasn't there,
So another old Chinaman ate up his share;
And he wasn't forthcoming at damper and tea,
So that all his mates wondered where Sing-Hi could be.

"Chorus again, boys:

"Oh, what a sad tale—Crikey, oh, what a sad tale.

"They sought him that night and they sought him next day.
And he didn't turn up when a week passed away;
They looked in the gully they poked n the creek,
Yet still he stopped mi-sing for many a week;
They talked of his absence whilst having their grub,
And also when pudding away at the tub;
Till one of his mates gave a hint that Si g-Hi
Had made his blessed pile and sloped home on the sly.

"Now, then, chorus again:

"Oh, what a sad tale—Crikey, oh, what a sad tale.

"Two diggers one day out on Kangaroo Flat,
Whilst driving an old hole came on a queer hat;
And there they found buried right under the dirt,
Some mouldy old bones and a rotten blue shirt
Poor Sing Hi worked there, but he'd put up no prop,
And the top of the drive had come down on him whop;
So when his mates heard that he'd turned up his toes,
They sighed 'Poor, Sing-Hi! *and apportioned his clothes*

"Chorus for the last time, boys:
    "Oh what a sad tale—Crikey, oh, what a sad tale."

Loud were the plaudits that greeted this strange ditty on its conclusion; and the ragged new chum scarecrow was all at once converted into the lion of the rowdy assemblage. Every one wanted to "shout" (colonial for stand treat), and everyone was just as anxious to get another song out of him.

Not much difficulty was there about that. Mr. Norfolk Howard seemed every whit as ready to treat them to song after song as they were to treat him to nobbler after nobbler; but at length the drink he had imbibed seemed to affect him all at once; his words came thick, memory failed him, he merged into another tune, hiccoughed, staggered, and finally subsided between two casks, where he came to anchor doubled up, with his chin on his knees, and appeared to subside into a state of unconsciousness.

When the diggers discovered that flicking small substances at him, and tickling his nostrils and ears with a straw or the end of a tobacco-pipe had no effect in arousing him from the bestial drunken sleep into which he seemed to have fallen, one of them crushed his hat down over his eyes with a blow from his open palm, and five minutes later the very existence of the poor drunken loafer seemed to be forgotten.

With the reader's leave we will keep a sharper eye upon him.

Suddenly, when nobody is looking, he lifts his shaggy hat-brim a couple of inches. Surely those sharp, beady, rat-black eyes that shine so keenly from underneath the heavy and nearly closed lids, are never those of an intoxicated man? They take in everything that passes around, and they twinkle when any miner blows that he has not paid his license.

By-and-by an expression of uneasiness comes into them, however, and he mutters, or rather soliloquises to himself—

"I thought he would have been here by now. Was my information incorrect, I wonder? Curse my ill-fortune if I am to be done this time. If I could cop the three thousand pounds that are offered for Ned Kelly the Ironclad Bushranger's capture, I'd ask M'Pherson for his pretty daughter Lily in marriage at once. Ha! who is this, I wonder?"

CHAPTER II.
MORE VISITORS TO THE "EMU."

AT this juncture of affairs two more diggers came into the shanty, shouldering their tools in true workmanlike fashion, that is to say, with the pick-handle passed through the handle of the shovel, and grasped firmly in the left hand, thus allowing the latter implement to hang pendulous down the back. Over their left arms they carried their upper shirts, that the stifling, breathless heat had caused them to take off, and in their right hands they bore their black billies.

Their faces were wreathed in such broad grins that it seemed to be no easy matter to keep their short black pipes in their mouths.

"Hullo, mateys! blessed if you don't seem in luck," shouted some one.

"In luck enough to shout for the whole d—— lot of you, at all events," rejoined the elder of these new arrivals. "Now, mother Maloney, its fizz and nothing less this time, so out with your boys with the white night-caps on. Twenty bottles of cham, my blooming old Venus. Hang drawing the corks. Off with their heads and pour the contents of their jolly fat bellies into a clean bucket, so that each lad can dip his pannikin in and help himself. That's the way to do business, old girl."

"Sure, an' that's right enough, masther, more especial when the price ov the good liquor is paid down first. Twinty bottles ov fizz will be just twinty golden sovereigns, me honey, divil a stiver less."

"Put in a thumb and pull out a plum, my charmer. Not too big an one though, or you won't get it. Now, then, eyes shut, and fancy that you are feeling for walnuts, not apples," and the speaker took the lid off his billy and held it over the counter towards the buxom hostess.

She dived in her hand, and gave a perceptible gasp as it came in contact with the old tin saucepan's contents. Fain would it have lingered there, had not the digger exclaimed:

"None of your little games, now; take only one and don't be greedy about the size, or I'll have it back, and take my custom elsewhere."

Thereupon the fair and flushed widow heaved a little sigh and took out of the billy a solid nugget of about the size of a plum.

"Now marm, I suppose you'll own the price of your liquor is paid for?"

"Be the powers yes, an' I'm much obliged to ye, Misther Dawson."

A few minutes later a bucket, two-thirds full of seething and hissing champagne (N.B. As good can be purchased in England at two-and-six a bottle) was handed over the bar and placed in the middle of the floor, and tin pannikins being at the same time distributed, the fun commenced in earnest.

The champagne, however, didn't give unqualified satisfaction, and the giver of the treat, presently, himself declared that it was "rotgut," and that three or four bottles of brandy would make it far finer swizzle.

So the brandy was added, and then for the first time lips were smacked with keen appreciation.

"Yes, gentlemen," said the lucky digger then, "we've just made our piles, me an my mate has. We've got seven pint pots full of gold out ov our hole in three days, an that's worth more'n three thousand pounds, or I'm a sinner. We're going on the loose a bit now, down to Melbourne, to see life an look at the gals, and whoever'll bid highest for the claim shall hev it, though there's whole fortins to be made there yet.

"What's that fool blowing about?" asked one of three new diggers who had just entered the shanty unnoticed, owing to the undivided interest of the assembly being centered on the two miners who had made their pile.

"Whoever he is we won't leave him much gold to spend on the Melbourne girls if he and his mate leave this quit alone," retorted the taller of the three new arrivals in a whisper "Hist! let us squat ourselves down amongst the rest so as not to attract attention or suspicion. Somebody will let slip presently the day fixed on for the gold-escort to start. The authorities are keeping it precious close, but it must leak out."

So the three last comers seated themselves amongst the other diggers, whom they closely resembled in all essential aspects, and began to help themselves to the brandy-fortified fizz. They thought that they were unnoticed, and so they were, by all save one man, and that was the scarecrow Lew-chum.

"Very well got up," muttered he to himself, "but if you three disguised coves aren't Ned Kelly and his mates Lanky Jim and Lardy Bill, then I'm not Tom Conquest of the Mounted Police. I'll have you, my lads, and what's more I'll take you single-handed, for I can't afford to share the reward. Big as it is I fear it will hardly win me Lily McPherson."

CHAPTER III.

TREATS OF SELLING AND BEING SOLD.

How could the cleverly-disguised detective have spotted those three men? Their low-toned mutterings he could not have caught from the spot where he squatted hunched up so grotesquely; and their outward appearance was that of nine-tenths of the individuals by whom they were surrounded; for their soft felt billycock hats were slouched well over their brows, and up to their very eyes they were all hair. They were almost as much like gorillas as men.

True, the stature of the middle man was somewhat remarkable, for he was at least six-feet-three in height, and of commanding build as well. He who squatted on his left, sitting on his heels like a Gloucestershire collier, was fat and gross, with a nose that looked as though it had been broken in some grog-shanty, or beer-shop row with a pewter pint-pot; and he who balanced himself on the round of his pick to the right, had a nose of the Napier type, shaped like the hooked beak of some monstrous bird of prey, a nose that you might fancy capable of smelling blood at any distance. This man's form must have been that of a skeleton by the way that his clothes hung about him. He looked like a being who could be twisted and turned into the shape of any grotesque capital letter, from A to Z.

Whilst we have been endeavouring to describe three individuals who are destined to play an important and conspicuous part in this our "ower true tale," Dawson, the lucky digger and giver of the feast, continued to blow about his hole, and what he intended to do with the wealth he had got out of it, with asseverations which his mate backed up with such curt observations as, "Bully for you," "Right you are, old man," "That's the time of day," and so on.

"What a duffer you must be to leave such a good thing not half worked out," suddenly exclaimed a digger with rather more gumption than the rest.

"Not a bit ov it," retorted Dawson. "I aren't a mean, selfish beast as wants to keep every good thing for hisself. I wouldn't be shouting in the way that I am if I was that; nary a bit ov it. Turn and turn about, I say; added to which, I knows of a place as'll turn out betterer even nor this one. I aren't quite a green 'un; and perhaps I knows as much about prospecting as Mr. Hargreaves."

"Whereabouts may this new Tom Tiddler's ground be situated?" asked some one.

"Aye, aye, that's tellings, that is. 'Tis a secret as dear to me as my very life's blood. My matey here is the only man as'll be let into that knowledge. And for why? Because he once saved my life at the risk ov his own, an' I've a 'art as is stuffed as chock full ov gratitude as ever was a calves' with sage and onions. However, this hain't business, gentlemen. Who'll bid for Dick Dawson's claim an' a sartain fortune? Ned, just show the old billy round, an' listen to how their very eyeballs will jingle as they lights on the treasure in it. There's no need for any one to handle the nuggets, Ned, for they're like quicksilver, an'll run down a covey's sleeve before he knows what they're about."

A loud laugh was produced by this elegant way of hinting that the assembled company might not all be as honest as they should be, and it had hardly subsided when Ned began to show the old tin billy round.

Face after face bent over it, and ejaculations of surprise and admiration came thick and fast.

Sometimes a dirty and grimy hand would involuntarily shoot out, but Ned, with some such ironical observation as "No, you don't!" would jerk the billy out of reach, at the same time giving its contents a rattle that sounded like sweetest music to the ears of the listeners.

".. And now for a bidding, gents," said Dick Dawson, when he had once more got his treasure between his legs, which crooked round it as though they had been those of an ape. "Come, take it aisy, don't all speak at once; the hole won't run away, and the gold escort don't start till the day after to-morrow."

At this the tall man gave his fat and his thin friend a nudge apiece.

Even that slight action did not escape the notice of the now loudly-snoring new chum. He saw it between his knees, that now covered his face.

"How do you know the gold escort leaves the day after to-morrow?"

It was neither of the three new arrivals who put the question; they were far too fly. It was a queer little digger on the opposite side of the circle.

"How do I know?" retorted Dick Dawson, in tones of withering contempt. "Don't it strike you werry forcibly that fellows who've got this vast amount ov gold to send down (and here he tapped the outside of his billy significantly) would put themselves to the trouble to enquire and find out?"

"Aye, like enough; but the authorities have kept it precious dark, on account of Ned Kelly and his lambs not meddling with it on the way."

"They've not kept it dark from known honest men like your most humble servant, Dick Dawson. The gold escort leaves the commissioner's tent at six o'clock on Monday morning, and travels down to Melbourne by the Black Forest route. And I can tell 'ee something more nor that, which is, that a dozen troopers will guard it this time, instead ov a paltry half-dozen; so if Ned Kelly and his gang *do* show up, they'll find theirselves in Queerstreet."

Again the tall man nudged his companions slightly, and there ensued a queer sound half-way down the flat-nosed man's throat that sounded very like a death-rattle, though it was in reality nothing worse than a chuckle.

"Now that I've shut up Master Curumosity, let's return to business, mates," continued Dick Dawson. "Look here, I've half a mind to give the claim away. D——ee, I'd do it, but for the fact that a free gift is never vallied. No, what folks git for nothing, they vallies at nothing; so I puts the hole up to auction, an' whatever it brings I hands over to the 'orspital an' the horphan asylum, directly I gets to Melbourne, save, perhaps, a handful for a pretty wench or two."

"Hear! hear!" shouted every one. "Now that's what I calls 'andsome," added somebody.

The bids were started and ran up actively, brandied champagne being a fine stimulant to *spirited* enterprise.

At last, when they reached a sum that caused some of the more sober to whistle, Dick Dawson said—

"That's enough, mates, let it stand at that; I wants a fair price, not a hexorbitant one. Fair play's a jewel, an' 'andsome is as 'andsome does. I won't take a pennyweight more, for it's honest Dick Dawson's boast that no one ever made a bargain with him an' lived to regret it. Now, mate, you as made that last offer, tell me yer name an' where yer hangs out?"

"Jack Hartley. My tent's close down by Brown's store. If you an' your mate don't mind seeing me home I'll give you the price of the claim now. I've got it snugly planted. We can borrow a pair of scales at Brown's on the way."

"Right you are, friend. Come along, then, let us be jogging. We've swilled quite enough to transact business on. Mrs. Maloney, my dear, let the other gents as is here assembled have whatever else they chooses to call for to-night, at my expense. I never likes to disturb harmony, and I wouldn't be leaving them so early but that donty

calls, and that's a voice as never falls unheeded on a true Englishman's ear. Good night all, and God bless ye."

And tipping the wink to his mate Ned, they got Jack between them, and supported him out of the shanty—for truth to say he was rather unsteady on his pins—being followed by the vociferous cheers of the other diggers, whom the prospect of further drinks, at another man's expense, deprived of any desire to quit the "Emu" for a long while to come.

Besides, by this time the flaring naphtha lamps had been lighted, and the place looked extra comfortable.

Mother Maloney was all smiles too, and evidently intended to carry out Dick Dawson's instructions to the letter, the fact being that he had playfully pitched on to the counter another small nugget before going out.

"In for a penny in for a pound," was the motto of one and all, and what mattered it if they were unfit for work next day, for was it not Sunday, a *dies non?*

CHAPTER IV.

TRACKING TO MURDER. PUTTING HIS FOOT IN IT.

Now there are exceptions to every rule, and so when we said just now that one and all had made up their minds to stay and continue the carouse, we must except four of their number. We shall see who they were presently.

Dick Dawson, his taciturn mate Ned, and the half-intoxicated Jack Hartley, were hardly out of the shanty, when the tall man with his two curiously-nosed companions also rose to their feet and re-shouldered their tools.

"Where away? What's the d——hurry?" enquired one or two of the diggers.

"Wife in the straw. Stores to get in. Morrow Sunday," growled the tall man.

"And we've got to take care ov our little brother 'cos you see he ain't big enough to take care of hisself," added the flat-nosed man, with a sly wink.

This observation produced loud roars of laughter, and before they had subsided the strangely assorted trio had quitted the shanty.

Hardly had they disappeared from view when Mr. Norfolk Howard, the inebriate new-chum as every one believed him to be, was observed to stagger to his feet and make a series of short tacks towards the shanty door.

"Hi, we can't spare *you!*" roared out some one. "Glad you've come round, old fellow, for we want another song. A tip-topper like the last."

"Can't sing, be-be-before been sick. Fe-fe-fe-feel as th-th-though my liver wa-wanted to come up. Le-le-let me pass, please."

Several hands had been outstretched to detain him, but this speech caused them to be hastily withdrawn, and as wide a passage as practicable to be afforded him as well. Another second and he also was outside the shanty.

Everything was wrapped in gloom. The hot wind had been succeeded by a southerly buster, bringing rain on its leaden pinions. The trooper took off his hat and allowed the pelting shower to refresh, for an instant, his heated face.

Then his sharp eyes pierced the gloom ahead, and he saw the three men whom he was after about fifty yards in front, whilst the three other men, whom he rightly guessed that *they* were after, showed very indistinctly in the distance.

"Murder and robbery are clearly their little game," muttered the disguised trooper to himself. "Perhaps, however, I'll be able to turn the tables on them. With me on the other side it'll be three to three, for the drunken man don't count for much; and then I must pick out the tall one for myself and the other coves may settle Lanky Jim and Lardy Bill between them, for they aren't worth powder and ball yet."

And as he concluded this mental cogitation the trooper thrust his right hand into the left inside breast pocket of his seedy frock coat, to discover whether the stock of his pistol was handy to his grasp.

Meanwhile, unconscious that they had either a foe in their rear, the tall man, the fat man, and the man with the macaw nose followed the tracks of Dick Dawson and his companions across the Flat.

"This rain is fortunate," said the tall man, "for it has driven every one under canvas. Not that folks are very thick about this part at any time of a night. However, it's best as it is, and there's plenty of light to work by."

"Oh, I feel so soft-hearted," exclaimed the fat man, "I'm in the mood of a sucking dove. Why would the fool flash about his gold so?"

"To tempt better men to possess themselves of it, of course," put in he of the macaw-bill. "We'll put it to a deal better use than he would, eh, Ned?"

"Silence! and listen to me. You see that crooked old gum tree? Curse it, you can't help seeing it, for its trunk looks like a white ghost. Yes, you've spotted it now. Well, the nearest track to the township leads right past it, and almost at its foot there is a deserted shaft close upon ninety feet deep. We must overtake them at that point, overcome them—without using our pistols if possible—for the traps are getting pretty well as thick about the place as the bush flies and mosquitoes; and pitch em in headlong," explained the tall man grimly.

"Oh lor! I feel so soft-hearted," sighed the fat man; "but what is to be must be, and it would be ungracious not to take the good things that Fortune puts in our way."

"Umph, you was always a very taking young man except with the petticoats." retorted Macaw-bill. "See that you do your share of the work."

Meanwhile every minute brought Dick Dawson, Ned, and Jack Hartley nearer to the lonely spot fixed on for their murder.

Three hundred yards farther would have taken them into the very thick of the canvas township, Hartley's tent being about double the distance on the other side.

Arrived opposite the gum tree, however, the intoxicated digger's legs positively refused to bear him any further, and down he went. Dick and his mate were busily discussing how they should get him up and along, when both were suddenly grasped from behind.

"A cry for assistance, and I'll send a bullet through the brains of each of you!" said the tall man of the trio, suddenly showing himself in their front, and pointing a double-barrelled pistol at each of their faces alternately. "Submit to be quietly knocked down and stunned, and your lives are spared!"

"Ha, ha, ha! Ned Kelly, is it thee?" exclaimed Dawson; "Well, this is a spree! Why, the nuggets are all Brummagem ware, specially manufactured and sent out for salting claims* with. They aren't worth their weight in copper or muntz metal. Don't you know Carrotty Larkins, eh, old chum?"

"Why, your hair's as black as a nigger's! and your mate, who is he?"

"Nimming Ned, the cracksman! Well, this is a lark! Not that our get-up is better than yours, and yet it is a feather in our caps to have taken the cappen in. Were you three at Mother Maloney's? I never spotted you."

Before Kelly could make any reply, a voice shouted out:—

"Beware of those fellows you are talking with! They

* A nefarious traffic extensively carried on in 1853. See *Melbourne Argus*

are bushrangers. I call upon you in the Queen's name, as honest men, to help me capture them. I'll account for the biggest. My name's Tom Conquest, and I belong to the Victoria constabulary!"

And the speaker dashed into the very middle of the rascally assemblage, pistol in hand, determined to take Ned Kelly dead or alive.

Had he seen Broken-nose and Macaw-bill let go of their prisoners, which they had done a second previously; or had he heard Dick Dawson's chuckle, he might have been put upon his guard. As it was, he imagined the three robbers had begun to chat in a friendly way with their intended victims, so as to catch them unawares. Hence his shouted warning.

Having given it he lost no time in levelling his weapon at Ned Kelly's face, and pulling the trigger.

But the cap failed to explode, and ere he could discharge another barrel, all five men were on him at once, the pistol was wrenched out of his grasp, and he was absolutely powerless in their hands.

"A Joey in disguise—a wolf in sheep's clothing! And is this great and free country come to this?" exclaimed Broken-nose, lifting up his hands and eyes as though in pious horror at such an act of base deception.

"We will make a stern example of him," said Ned Kelly; "pitch him down that deserted hole. It's ninety feet deep. He won't survive the fall. Well, rascal, have you a bone in your tongue, that you don't cry for mercy?"

"Beg for mercy from cut-throat villains like you? No, thank God! even the terrible position I am in shall not make me lose my self-respect," said the gallant trooper, with a contemptuous glance at his captors.

"Well crowed for a dying speech and confession. You are too good for a trap, you should have been a bushranger. You'd have done honour to the cloth. However, that can't be helped now. In with him, mates!"

The trooper was dragged to the edge of the dark, yawning shaft, the Macaw-beak's great splay hand being pressed over his mouth the while, lest he should cry out and spread the alarm that some devilry was up.

A second later he was hurled over the brink, and fell with a dull, hollow thud, into the awful depths that no eye could penetrate.

"Wouldn't it be wise to serve the other bloke the same way?" suggested Macaw.

"If you did, how should I get his gold? No, no, the poor fellow's in a drunken sleep."

This from Dick Dawson, alias Carrotty Larkins; but Ned Kelly stooped down to assure himself for certain that such was indeed the fact.

Apparently the investigation was satisfactory, for on assuming an upright position he remarked—

"He's tight as a door-nail. You coves had better bring him round by the best means you can, and get him home to his tent as quickly as possible. Yes, get his gold before he is sober enough to wonder whether he has made a foolish bargain, and then hasten both of you to our old quarters in the hills, for Monday night will see me dead or victorious. I will rob the gold escort or perish in the attempt."

"We are with you," said Carrotty Larkins and Nimming Ned, in a breath; and the former added, "It won't be all gold. My Brummagem nuggets will be amongst the treasure. I'll make three thousand pounds out of them, never fear."

"You won't have the assurance to try and pass them off on the experienced professional gold-buyers?" exclaimed Kelly, with something of admiration in his tone.

"Won't I, though? Aqua-fortis nor any other acid has any effect on 'em, nor can they find 'em out by weight. Oh, I'll work the oracle all right, never fear; and directly the thing's done we'll make tracks for our haunt in the ranges. The attack on the escort will be rare fun."

The confederates then parted; and an hour later Ned Kelly and his two companions had left Forest Creek far behind them.

CHAPTER V.

NED KELLY'S HOME IN THE MOUNTAIN RANGES.

SHIFT we the scene from the busy, rowdy diggings at Forest Creek to the summit of a lofty, volcanic hill, some two thousand feet above the level of the sea, covered to the very top with heavy timber, and surrounded on three sides by a dense forest, a spot where one would imagine the foot of white man had never trod.

And yet, behold a hut, constructed of the immense slabs of bark which the monarchs of the Australian forest shed in lieu of their leaves.

Yes, this is a peculiarity of nearly all antipodean trees, that they rid themselves of their bark but not their foliage, which is evergreen, whilst their trunks, clad in their new, tender coverings, are often of a silvery whiteness.

That bark hut is brown enough, however. It is, of course, only one story in height, and possesses a slanting roof of the same material, a door, a couple of windows, and a stunted chimney formed of an old cask.

Up and down its rough, furrowed, outside walls run soldiers and bulldogs. Let not the reader stare; we allude to a couple of species of huge ants bearing those expressive names, the former, we presume, because they are red, and the latter for reason that they are not only white, but also because they bite all who are foolish enough to meddle with them as ferociously as could their namesakes.

Take the primitive habitation for all in all, it was just such an one as Adam might be supposed to have set about constructing when he had been turned out of Eden's garden into the wilderness; and one of Eve's fairest daughters is at all events looking forth from one of its casementless window-apertures at the present moment.

Her eyes are bent on the long white road that crosses the well-grassed plains fifteen or sixteen hundred feet below her eagle's nest on the mountain's summit, looking like a narrow ribbon or a silver-scaled serpent.

It is the newly-made road, leading from Kyneton and the gold fields at Forest Creek and Mount Alexander to the metropolis of the colony, Melbourne; a track, hardly finished though it is, on which many a ruthless and savage deed has been committed; for this heavily-timbered hill and the forests that clothe three of its sides, are the haunt of the bushrangers, and this particular hut is called by them the *Look-out Station.*

It commands, indeed, a wide and extensive range of view, comprising hill and plain, bush and scrub. Northward may be descried with a telescope the square church tower and the shingled roofs of the township of Kyneton, and to the left of it that irregular fringe of wattle trees marks the winding course of the Coliban river. Many a score of miles across the undulating and thinly-timbered plains, and directly in front, rise, with rounded summits, another mountain range behind which is Ballarat; and over the intermediate country is dotted here and there at wide intervals, a white, one-storied, deeply-verandahed squatter's station, with the out-buildings generally at some little distance off; whilst the only signs of life visible, are alternate white and brown specks, which a nearer view would disclose to be sheep and cattle.

This fair landscape is closed in by a sky like a gleaming polished steel shield, from the centre of which the sun glares down like a burnished brass boss.

Having described the view, let us regard the viewer.

That she is a Currency lass, or native-born Australian girl, is perceptible at a glance. An Englishman would have pronounced her seventeen, for she was tall, lithe, and gracefully formed, and the delicious contours of premature womanhood were already perceptible in her bust; but she was in truth only just turned of fourteen, for the glowing sun of Australia brings flowers, fruit, and girls to an early perfection.

This young girl's complexion was that of a brilliant brunette, her eyes hazel, her hair of a rich glossy brown, her lips red as cherries, and the teeth within as white and small as strings of pearls; yet even whiter, if possible, than those teeth, were the bare, plump neck and shoulders, adown which her glossy tresses wantoned, and the arms that were crossed on the rough window-sill over which she leant.

There was no danger of the delicate skin getting sun-burned whilst she did so, for above the hut towered (to a height of full ninety feet before they began to branch off) the stately iron-bark trees; and the foliage of the blue-gum, the peppermint and the shea-oak helped to form a canopy o'er her pretty head whenever she deigned to walk abroad.

Suddenly, whilst she gazes, a horse's hoof-strokes become audible, evidently toiling up a steep and rocky pathway close at hand.

The maiden gives utterance to an expression of mingled joy and surprise, and the next instant, on to the tiny splatch of grassy open space in front of the hut rides a tall, gaunt man, bearded up to the very eyes.

"Father!" exclaimed the girl, "how glad I am that you are come home."

"Well, my bonnie lass, and so am I; but you needn't have been anxious."

"I wasn't *very* anxious. I never am when go out without your armour on, for then I think that you are not bound on a very perilous enterprise."

"No, my girl, you can always depend on that. Come you and take possession of Marco Polo, for I'm dog-tired and have got little time enough to rest in. Short-hobble him, Rose, so that he mayn't stray far, for I shall want him again anon, and then come quickly in and give me some grub."

The young girl rushed at once out of the door, and the bearded man, flinging himself heavily from the saddle to the ground, first kissed her and then placed the reins in her hand, telling her that she looked blooming meanwhile.

"Father," said she, "Marco don't want me to lead him. He will follow me about like a dog. He loves me dearly. Kiss me, Marco Polo."

The beautiful creature, for the animal was a thorough-bred racer, stretched out his long, vein-traceried neck, and rubbed his velvet muzzle first against a cheek and then against a glossy shoulder.

"There!" said the girl, triumphantly, and throwing the reins lightly over the proud steed's neck she just as lightly vaulted on to his back, and with a merry, ringing laugh, trotted him round towards the back of the hut.

The bearded man gazed after her fondly, but a look of sadness came into his great haggard eyes as he muttered to himself—

"What would become of her if anything happened to me? Good Lord! I know her well. She would seek to avenge me, and her devotion would meet with a six foot drop. Would to heaven that I had not brought her up to regard right as wrong and wrong as right; and yet I could not have endured that the only being there is left me to love should regard me as a ruffian and a villain. I am only what circumstances have made me, and why should she be different? My parents were murdered by the law, and her mother was destroyed by a villain. We both of us owe the world nothing but our hate and our scorn, and by heaven, I, at least, never let a chance slip of requiting the obligation."

Thus muttering, or rather reflecting, Ned Kelly—for he it was—strode through the hut into a little lean-to shed at the back, and forthwith commenced to indulge in a thorough good wash, a tired Australian's greatest delight.

When ten minutes later he entered the left-hand room of the hut, which was at once his own bedroom, when at home, the kitchen and the parlour, he was a very different-looking being to what he had been when he dismounted from Marco Polo so short a time previously.

He had taken off twenty years of his apparent age with the false beard and whiskers that had evidently been worn as a disguise, and now, with face closely clipped, all but a heavy, drooping moustache, he looked a very handsome man of no more than thirty-five.

Rose had already spread the rough table—hewn with his own axe—with the materials for a repast, and now she moved up a couple of three-legged stools beside it. The entire room contained no other furniture.

The table equipage consisted of tin pannikins and pewter plates, and a couple of old salmon-tins held the goat's milk and the sugar.

A large flat damper cake had just been taken up steaming hot from the place where it had cooked itself on the hot stone hearth, and Rose threw a fistful of tea into the tin billy, two-thirds full of now boiling water as it hung suspended over the fire, and began to stir it round vigorously with a gum-tree twig, this being the colonial way of brewing the cup that cheers.

Meanwhile, Ned went to a hanging-safe or cupboard of his own manufacture, and took out a portion of a cold leg of mutton.

Fishing a gridiron out of a corner, he cut the meat into thick slices and laid it thereon, and directly Rose had taken the billy off the fire, the gridiron took its place.

A couple of turns to the meat and it was done, and the next instant the bushranger was gorging himself like a half-famished wolf.

"Rose," he said, when he had devoured at least a pound of grilled mutton and two-thirds of a two-inch-thick damper as large as a meat plate, washing the solids down with at least three pannikins of tea, "Rose, this kind of life won't last much longer, my girl. I've nearly made my pile, and we'll very soon leave this wilderness to cut a shine in a big city, where we must see about getting you married well, my Mountain Rose."

"I don't want to get married, father. I'm never going to leave you."

"But, suppose I intend to take unto myself a wife, Rose. What then?"

A look of acute pain crossed the young girl's countenance.

"Father," said she, "you are joking. Is not your child's love sufficient for you? You have often said so. If you give me a stepmother I will kill her, so there."

And the lovely little barbarian looked thoroughly as though she meant what she said.

Ned Kelly laughed in spite of himself.

"You are your own father's child," rejoined he. "And yet, where is the use of keeping up the deception longer," he added, to himself. "For, should a bullet hap to lay me low this afternoon, why should I doom the poor child to toil through life with my sin-branded name clinging to her like a curse? No, the cat shall out of the bag at last."

"Father, what are you muttering to yourself? Is it about this strange woman who wants to rob me of your love? Oh, be sure that she is not luring you on in order to deceive and betray you, to secure to herself the three thousand pounds that the Government has offered for you either living or dead."

"She has never yet seen me, Rose; perhaps has never even read of my existence, for she has not been out in the Colonies very long. Rose, she is the most beautiful creature that God's sun has ever shone on. She is the talk of the world. Sprung from the ranks of the people, she might have been a queen, nay, a crown was offered her, but she would not accept it at the cost of a rebellion. She boxed a king's ears, and the king created her a countess for the honour she had done him. She is a countess now, and she shall be more; she shall be Ned Kelly the bushranger's wife before the world is a week older. He would like the taming of such a splendid tigress."

"Perhaps the tigress wouldn't accept you as its mate, father."

"When the lion woos he does so with a roar, not a purr, child. This woman—this countess—I saw her likeness when last I was down in Melbourne, and its loveliness maddened me to possess the original for my own. Yes, the woman who refused to wed the King of Bavaria shall become the bride of the King of the Bush. All Melbourne is at her feet, Rose, from the governor down to the seediest loafer around Paddy's market. Her latest hobby is to win fame upon the stage, and she has had the pluck to horsewhip, with her own fair hand, at least half-a-dozen of those scrubby fellows who found fault in the newspapers with her performance. Suddenly she has taken it into her head that she would like to see the gold-diggings, and sure intelligence has been brought me that she starts from Melbourne for Mount Alexander by to-day's Cobb's mail. Ha, ha, ha! she won't get quite so far as the gold-fields this time. I mean to win her for a wife in true outlaw fashion, and, if I mistake not, she is a woman who will relish being thus roughly wooed."

"Dear father, what have you to offer a woman such as you have described? Does this hut resemble the palaces she has been accustomed to live in?"

"They say that she makes herself equally at home everywhere; but if she should not like the health and the freedom of bush life, I am rich enough to give her her fling in great cities. I shouldn't wonder, Rose, if I wasn't worth a hundred thousand pounds, or even more."

"She'll make you waste all that on her extravagances, and then she'll hand you over to the law and consider herself well rid of you."

"Rose, your jealousy makes you a bird of ill-omen. Do you think that I could ever love her in the same way as I do you, or in the same way that I loved your poor mother either? Ah, Rose, if your mother had but married me—"

"Had but— Did she not then marry you? Oh God! am I not your child, your own child? What dreadful mystery is this you have disclosed?"

"Rose, listen to me! It's a nasty tale to tell, and I'd sooner be brought face to face with a dozen traps armed to the teeth than have the telling of it, but what must be must be, and I may never have another opportunity.

"Come, my dear, don't blubber," he continued, though there were something very like tears in his own eyes as he spoke. "I loved your mother, my lass, but your mother never loved me, that was about the rights of it. She threw away her affections on an infernal rascal, who, having won the flower, just pitched it aside for any one who chose to trample on. He left the poor creature to want, despair, and abject poverty. Rose, you were born out of doors in the bush, in the most dreadful storm of rain and lightning that I suppose was ever known. Providence, or chance, call it which you will, brought me to the spot just as your poor mother was breathing her last. Squatter Andrew McPherson's baby was the only thing that she had to give me as a dying remembrance; but though I hated brats I loved the giver, and swore to her,

ere she closed her eyes, that you should never want bite
iv sup whilst I lived. An old Irishwoman had the custody of you until you were five years old, from which
time I daresay you can pretty well remember."

"Well enough to believe that no real father could ever
have been half so kind. I hope that you love me as
though I was your own child? Now more than ever will
I endeavour to give you the love and obedience of one."

"You can't improve, my lass; you can't improve in
that way, I mean. I wish though, sometimes, that I had
brought you up differently. I've given you such little
education as I possessed myself, and perhaps that'll be
enough to serve your turn, but I needn't have taught
you to hate all the world. You see the world and I have
been at war for ever so many years, and it's a natural
thing to hate one's foe, especially a foe that murdered
one's father and mother. Yes, Rose, my father and
mother were hanged. I never told you so before, but it's
as well that you should know it now, if only to make you
thankful that you don't bear the name of Kelly."

"I'll never bear any name but that of him who has ever
been a fond and loving parent to one who had no claim
on him as a child," said Rose, coming round from her side
of the table and throwing herself on her knees before Ned.
"I cannot believe that you are a bad man, because you
have been so good to me; but if other people are not so
wicked as you have always made them out to me to be,
why wage such a cruel and relentless war against them?"

"I cannot go into that question now," said the bushranger, hurriedly. "Perhaps, after all, the fight won't
last much longer. I'm pledged to my mates to help them
plunder the next Gold Escort that goes down the road, and
then comes this affair of the countess. Perhaps that'll end
up my lawless deeds. Stay, though; there is one debt of
vengeance that will yet remain! I have sworn to kill your
mother's heartless destroyer, like a dog, whenever and
wherever I meet him. I have been searching for him for
fourteen years—your whole life long, in fact; but I'll find
him yet! Oh, yes, I'll find him, Rose!"

The girl was about to make some reply, in deprecation,
perhaps, of the bushranger's deadly resolve, when, glancing round to get at his pipe, the outlaw descried a cloud
of dust, miles away in the distance.

"My telescope, Rose!" said he, as he sprang with an
oath to his feet.

Rose brought it, and Ned Kelly peered anxiously
through.

"By thunder! it's the Gold Escort," said he. "'Tis a
good twelve miles away yet; nevertheless, there is no
time to lose. On with a high-necked frock and a hat, like
lightning, girl, and away to work the *bush telegraph*. The
boys are close at hand, though I've forbidden them to
come to the hut to worry you, for I know that you don't like
their ways. Kiss me, Rose, and begone. I'll get out my
trusty armour, for, clad in that, I'm a match for half-a-
dozen men."

The beautiful Australian girl obeyed, for she knew that
Ned would brook no opposition to his will in a state of
excitement such as he was now labouring under; but she
was very sad at heart as she departed.

CHAPTER VI.

THE BUSHRANGER IN HIS IRON HARNESS.

THE first thing that Ned Kelly did when Rose had slipped
out through the door at the back of the hut, was to re-don
his shaggy false beard and whiskers; his next to cut up
about half-an-ounce of Barrett's twist, that he carried in a
thick roll in one of his breeches-pockets, and load therewith a short black cutty pipe

When he had lighted this with a common lucifer and
puffed it into a red glow, he leisurely proceeded to the
other end of the room, and fished forth from under a pile
of dirty, frowsy sacks, two most extraordinary pieces of
defensive armour, to wit, a helmet and a breastplate of
thick unpolished iron.

The cuirass he proceeded to strap on, and the helmet
he laid for the present on the rough bush table.

Like that table, both these pieces of armour were of
his own making.

He had fashioned them out of an old ploughshare, and
as the cuirass covered almost the entire front of his trunk,
so the helmet, when fixed on his head, would meet and
o'erlap it, making him invulnerable save as to legs and
arms, unless he turned his back to his foe, a weakness
that Kelly was not at all likely to be guilty of, for he had
at all events the courage of the lion, if he lacked the
jungle monarch's magnanimity.

It is difficult to describe the exact appearance of these
two pieces of armour.

They were heavy and cumbrous, but rifle-bullet proof
There was no attempt at ornament lavished on them, for
they were for use, and not for show.

The helmet had a narrow slit traversing its front to see
through, and in shape was not unlike that worn by the
Knights Templars in olden times.

In lieu of further description, let the reader glance at
them as depicted on our front page, just as they were
sketched by our artist from the originals.

Ned Kelly now looked to his weapons of offence, which
consisted of an American rifle and a pair of long horse-
pistols, with the Tower mark on them.

If this was a romance instead of a true history we should
have made our Ironclad Bushranger more terrible by
arming him with a brace of six-shooters, but we write of
a time when, thanks to Colonel Colt, that weapon was
only just getting known in California, and Dean Adams
hadn't begun to dream of his now famous single barrel
revolving to six chambers.*

Ned had just loaded his rifle, rested it against the
table, and thrust one of his pistols down between his left
leg and his boot, when Rose looked in at the window, and
pointing towards the distant road said—

"It's not what you're looking out for, father. They are
only traders' waggons."

"I know that well enough, my girl. But they are
travelling in the van of the gold-escort for safety's sake.
Like the silly moth, you know, who thinks he's all right
as long as he's near the candle. The troopers and the
gold-cart won't be far behind them, and they'll give 'em the
go-by the other side of the Black Forest. That is to say if
I and my mates let 'em," and Ned smiled grimly.

"Oh, father, isn't it a sin to rob poor men of their
earnings?" asked Rose.

"It's no sin, in my case, to rob a rascally government
who robbed my father and mother of life. The diggers have
already been paid their price for the gold. It's now the
Crown's; and the Crown and I are at open war."

"Well, father, for heaven's sake be cautious. This is a
desperate enterprise."

"The bigness of the prize more than compensates for
the extra risk, my lass. See what luxuries it will procure
us when we become honest folks. But, Rose, should anything happen to me—for there's a chance about everything
—you need never be a pauper, dependent on the cold
charity of the world. You know where the spoil is planted;
few orphan girls have such a dowry. Don't stay here, or
the boys may murder you on account of it. Ay, lass, one
or two of them wouldn't be over-particular. If I do not

* Revolvers were issued to the Australian Police in 1859.

retu... twenty-four hours from the time of my departure, load yourself with as much as you can easily carry, don your seediest clothes, and make tracks for Melbourne."

"Oh, father, why will you think and talk about such dismal things?" sobbed Rose.

"Because you are the only being whom I love, and because a prudent man prepares for *everything*," said Ned, laying a hand caressingly on her shoulder.

"*I* the only being you love? Then you only teased me about this countess?"

"No, what I said was true enough. I'm going to win her for a wife. But perhaps the thought of gaining such a glorious prize stirs up my pride and vanity more than any other feelings. A child loves its glittering toy, but it loves its mother better. So do I love this living toy, this Lola Montez, Countess of Lansfelt. Firstly, because she is beautiful and famous, and secondly, because a king has grasped at her in vain. She will be to me what a first uniform is to a boy ensign, or the Cross of the Legion of Honour to the war-worn veteran: but you, Rose, *you* are part of my life, a portion of my daily existence, the channel that carries the life-current to and from my heart, and without which I should die."

And as he concluded, the man of blood and iron pressed the lovely girl whom he had brought up as his child passionately to his heart for a moment, and then thrust her almost roughly away, to catch up and sling at his back his trusty rifle.

"Is Marco Polo there?" demanded he. "Not a moment is to be lost, Rose."

"Yes, father, he is waiting your going forth as quietly as though he were a dog. I shall follow you at a distance on Swiftsure, so that if you are worsted and hard-pressed you can exchange your tired horse for a fresh one."

"All right, my girl, let it be so; but steer clear of all danger, mind."

"I will father, honour bright; but anything is better than inaction."

"Well, mind what I have told you to do in case I do not return within twenty-four hours. You have your little pistols to defend yourself on the road with, in case you are attacked; not that you will run much risk if you dress as I have told you. When you get to Melbourne take respectable lodgings, give out that your father met his death on the gold-fields, and marry the first honest and sober young fellow who offers you his hand. Never mind his being well-to-do if he's steady and good, for you can make him rich. You can bring him here, and take away between you what you were forced to leave behind when you went forth alone. The boys 'll never find it; no fear of that. To finish up with, your mother's name was Casey, and I *command* you to adopt it as your own if it haps that you are thrown on your own resources."

By this time Ned's second pistol was thrust into his other boot, and now he put down his pipe, and prepared to don his helmet.

"One more kiss, father, ere you do that," exclaimed Rose, almost hysterically.

He gave it her, and then, patting her on the back, said cheerily—

"Come, pluck up, lass. I'll be back all right enough, and bring you a beautiful step-mother along with me, ay, before this time to-morrow."

And stalking out of the hut with his face now hidden beneath its iron covering, he mounted Marco Polo, and without once looking back disappeared in the grim and sombre shadow of the bush.

"Now to ride after and watch over him," exclaimed Rose, as she dashed away the unbidden tears with the back of her hand. "What a history he has told me of our two selves. Fancy his not being after all my father. I'm

sure I love him as much as though I was really his child. His father and mother hung, and undeservedly, so he declares. Oh, how dreadful! I wonder when and how he got his education, for I'm sure he speaks, and has taught me also to speak very differently from those dreadful men, Lardy Bill and Lanky Jim, whom he calls his mates. They often laugh at his fine speech, as they call it. Oh, I wish he could break away from those men and his present perilous life! And then this countess whom he intends to capture and bring here, she will add to his danger. Even Samson was betrayed by a woman! Oh, how I know that I shall hate her!"

And with this concluding reflection Rose dashed through the tree-trunks for a few hundred yards, and then suddenly coming to a halt gave utterance to a shrill and peculiar whistle.

CHAPTER VII
THE GOLD-CART AND ITS GUARD.

THE gold escort and the waggons are meanwhile well on their road.

The vehicle that contains the treasure is four-wheeled, and rough and commonplace enough in appearance. The driver sits on a high box in front, and tools his unicorn of horses by aid of his long whip with rare skill. Beside him is perched a man with a loaded blunderbuss and a brace of pistols in his belt, and the gold is packed in stout, square, iron-banded boxes, whereon are painted strange-looking hieroglyphics known only to the initiated.

There are five thousand ounces of gold packed away in those boxes, and the value thereof, is not far off £15,000, the then price of gold being £2 19s. 6d. per ounce. There is also in the waggon, £700 in specie, altogether, a good haul for our acquaintances the bushrangers, if they only succeed in making it.

The waggon is preceded, at a smart trot, by a couple of troopers with carbine on thigh; on each side of the vehicle ride two with drawn swords, and half-a-dozen more, also with drawn swords, bring up the rear.

Very different looking fellows were they from the Australian mounted police of the present day. There was a great deal more savour of pipe-clay and heel-ball about their attire. They wore bright blue trousers and tightly-fitting shell-jackets (padded and puffed out to the nines) of the same colour.

These were adorned with red facings, and their shoulders were decorated with red woollen epaulettes, whilst their leather stocks were as high, thick, stiff, and uncomfortable as though they had been iron collars, and the peaks of their ugly, flat-topped, glazed-leather shakos came down over their eyes in such a manner that they could hardly see from under them.

They were armed with sword, carbine, and single-barrelled horse-pistol, both the latter weapons being smooth-bored, of course. Revolvers, as we have said, were still in the womb of the future.

In this primitive manner seven tons weight of gold had already been carried down from the different Victorian diggings to the metropolis, and this though they had not yet been worked much more than two years.

The day was a glorious one; the hot wind had departed, and a delightfully refreshing breeze had taken its place; afar off the kangaroo bounded over the grassy plains (an all but extinct animal in those regions now), and sometimes a flock of gorgeously-plumaged parrots or yellow-crested cockatoos (cock-a-twenties, the modern Free Selector frequently names them, on account of their depredations) flashed across the scene like a rainbow-hued cloud, the accompanying screeches being anything but sweet music to the ears.

The entire bush seemed to have assumed its brightest tints. The southerly buster, whose breaking we described in a previous chapter, had freshened up the grass and laid the dust (for clouds of dust often roll over Australia's grassy plains). The vertical, shade-refusing foliage of the gum, peppermint and shea oak-trees, looked less olive-hued and sombre than usual, whilst the emerald fronds and bright yellow blossoms of the golden wattles were as brilliant to the eye as English laburnums, and moreover diffused a delightful, though rather oppressive, fragrance through the air.

The only drawbacks to the pleasantness of the travelling were the bloodthirsty attacks of the mosquitos and bush-flies; but the troopers, who had been much exhilarated by a good dinner and copious draughts of stringy-bark and shandy-gaff at Kyneton, made light of the assaults of such puny foes, and were as hiliariously jolly as the lax discipline of the service allowed.

Presently the half-dozen who rode in the rear of the waggon struck up a song which was very popular with the force about that time—

The diggers, they used to assail us
With taunting, as all of you know;
When for licences once we were hunting,
They always called after us, "Joe!"
Yes, they used to call after us, "Joe!"
They always reviled us with "Joe!"
And 'twas certain to render us savage
Whenever they shouted out "Joe!"

But that epithet's nearly exploded,
The term has received its death blow;
For t'other day, as we came from the races,
They'd the cheek to salute us with "Joe!"
We twigged who they were calling "Joe!"
We rated them for shouting out "Joe!"
We lugged 'em right off to the lock-up,
And that slewed their calling us "Joe!"

There was a momentary pause, and then a deep, rich voice took up the air—

Hey for these glorious golden days!
They will be famed for aye in story;
At hunting coves for licences,
'Tis there I am in all my glory.
The new chums I put in a fright,
To nail 'em I'd jump down a shyser;
But a trifle soon makes 't all right,
And no one ever is the wiser.

Sometimes I don an old blue shirt,
Disguise myself up like a digger;
With hands encrusted o'er with dirt,
I cut a precious curious figure.
To those who sell grog on the sly,
My visit proves a wholesome warning;
A nobbler strong of rum I buy,
And send a summons in the morning.

"A libel on the profession!" shouted one of the troopers, laughingly; while a second exclaimed—

"Hullo, Tom Conquest, is it you, lad? Why, where the d—— have you been, and where the deuce did you turn up from? The inspector has been in a rare way about you. What's your head bandaged up for?"

"Well, I've been under an operation by rather a rough surgeon, mates."

"What for? I thought you were sound as a rock both in wind and limb."

"Was and is are two widely different tenses. I was hurled down a ninety-feet-deep shaft on Saturday night, and I was only got out early this morning."

"Then you must have had at least a thirty hours' fast of it. But how on earth did you escape a broken neck? You've as many lives as a cat, Tom."

"Ha, ha, ha! do you think so? My last life was preserved in a very unpoetical manner, at all events. I fell souse into the body of a dead horse, and the softness of its putridity saved my existence. I wasn't hungry during the thirty-five hours that I was below ground, I assure you. I think the aroma of my defunct preserver prevented my feeling so. The stink was infernal."

"But who threw you in, and who hauled you out, man alive?" asked a trooper.

"Well, Ned Kelly, the bushranger, and four every bit as infernal rascals as himself pitched me down the pit, and as to who drew me out I'm blest if I know. It was a couple of diggers whom my cries attracted to the spot. Directly they had landed me I stank so of defunct horse that they clapped their hands before their noses and ran off, rope and all, without even waiting to be thanked. I walked to the police-camp straight away, stripped, washed, put on my professional togs, had a big feed, learned how long you had started, and came after you. I hate to be out of the game when there's any fun going on."

"Any fun going on? What do you mean?" queried three troopers at once.

"Why, that I'm a false prophet if the escort isn't attacked by the Ironclad Bushranger and his band as it passes through the Black Forest."

"Eh, is that your notion? On what grounds do you found the suspicion?"

"In that he visited the gold fields at Forest Creek on purpose to pick up information as to the day and hour at which it started, the amount of treasure that it would carry, and anything else that might be worth the knowing. I was sitting opposite to him and his two precious pals, Lardy Bill and Lanky Jim, in Mother Maloney's shanty, for more than an hour on Saturday night, in the guise of a drunken new chum, and I watched their every movement."

"By George, hadn't you better ride forward and report all this to Sergeant Fortescue? He rides to the right of the waggon. This is news and no flies."

"Ay, I think it's about time now that I put him up to the outlaws' very probable little game," and Tom Conquest set spurs to his horse, singing at the top of his voice as he sped onward at a hard gallop—

"Oh, stupid folks at us may laugh
And call us Joe and all that;
What the deuce care we 'or diggers' chaff,
We're jolly chaps for all that,
For all that and for all that,
We've our perquisites an all that;
And though we've but eight tob a day
A trap's a man for all that.

What though we have to exercise,
Patrol at night and all that,
We have the chance to nobblerise
At many a tent for all that;
For all that, and for all that
We get precious fresh for all that;
And though we do stick up grog tents
A trap's a man for all that."

The gay young trooper looked a very different individual now to when we saw him attired as the out-at-elbows new chum.

He sat his horse like an English fox-hunter, and, added to a figure that was a perfect model for a light cavalry man was a handsome, frank, open face, with clear, well-cut features, a glossy moustache, and rich brown hair that covered his head with crisp short curls, like those of a retriever dog. Tom Conquest, in short, was a young man of twenty-three, and of a stamp that comrades love and the girls dote on. In return, Tom doted on the girls. Sergeant Fortescue greeted his arrival with a warm welcome, but his face turned grave enough when Tom had given him all his information.

"Are you hurt too much about the head for fighting?" he asked.

"Lord love you, no. There's only a few bits chipped out here and there, just down to the bone, but not through it. I'll fight all the heartier for the smart."

"I'm glad to hear you say that, for you're always game to the backbone in a scrimmage. We will give these cut-throats pepper for their mustard if they do show up, ay, the very strongest cayenne," said the sergeant, cheeril

It seemed strange, the thought of sanguinary strife and slaughter amid a scene of such peaceful beauty as that which still surrounded the rapidly-travelling escort; but that very speed soon brought them to the confines of the sombre Black Forest, and Sergeant Fortescue presently noticed a felled tree lying right across the coach track.

"That looks decidedly fishy," observed he to Tom Conquest.

CHAPTER VIII.

STICKING UP THE GOLD-CART. A BUSH FIGHT.

YES, there was decidedly something inexplicable about the newly-felled tree, for if the gold-cart were to attempt to round it, at either end, other trees grew so thickly around that it was doubtful whether it would be able to regain the track.

"Hadn't the driver better pull up whilst we ride forward to reconnoitre?"

It was Tom Conquest who made the suggestion, and the sergeant fell in with it at once.

"Pull up your cattle, Pat Feeney. Troopers, sheath sabres and unsling carbines. Gather round the treasure, and be on the alert for the word of command," he shouted, and then glancing at Tom, they trotted quietly forward.

Simultaneously they leapt their horses over the trunk of the felled tree, but hardly had the fore hoofs of the animals dented the ground on the other side than six flashes of flame and puffs of smoke directly in their front, heralded the sharp crack of as many rifles, and away was shred one of Tom's red woollen epaulettes, whilst the Sergeant with a cry fell from the saddle.

"Never mind me. Think only of the treasure. Tom, if anybody can lead it and the lads out of this mess you can. God grant I live to see it done."

So gasped poor Sergeant Fortescue, through the gushes of hot black blood that came surging up through his parted, quivering lips.

Tom saw that he was no better than a dead man, and with a glance of commiseration, for there was no time for words, he leapt his horse back over the tree and rejoined his comrades.

"Poor Fortescue's down, boys, and it's our task to avenge him," said he. "Out of your saddles and follow me. This affair will have to be fought out on foot."

"Can't we fire at 'em over our horses' backs?" suggested some one.

"No, a tree trunk will stop a bullet, but a horse's body won't. The fellows are armed with rifles. That's plain enough by the sharp ring of the discharge. So we must look well to ourselves, for the Queen can't afford to lose a single man this day. The rogues shall only seize the treasure over my dead body at all events."

"All serene, Tom. Wherever you lead we're the boys who will follow!"

"Thanks, friends; to the ground, then. Our nags can take care of themselves."

"Why not gather in rear of the waggon, Conquest, and use it as a rampart?"

"Because the bushrangers, lying down each behind his tree, would fire at our legs till we hadn't one amongst the lot of us left to stand upon. Now, lads, no more suggestions. Since I am your leader, I exact implicit obedience. You all of you understand bush-fighting on foot There's a deep gully about a quarter of a mile ahead, and we must try and drive Kelly and his band towards and into it; then for the first time dare we show them our faces. Forward!"

The troopers thereupon made a rush for the nearest trees, but were received by a volley ere they could get under cover that stretched two of them lifeless and wounded a third.

There were only ten of them now, counting the stricken man.

When each trooper had a stout tree in front of him, however, he felt more at home, and began to look out anxiously for the head or shoulder of a foe.

Tom Conquest was well to the front, and within two yards of him, behind another tree, was his particular chum Jack Hogan.

"Jack," said Tom, "if I fall the command devolves on you. Don't show yourself in that way, man. Always *take aim from the right of your tree*, for in doing so you expose a smaller portion of your body to your adversary. Look out!"

"Crack!" went Jack Hogan's carbine, but the ball only sent a strip of bark flying from a tree trunk.

The trooper gave vent to an exclamation of disgust.

"Never mind, old fellow, better luck next time. Duck in your twopenny, or that fellow will draw a line on you. I'll give you a wrinkle, Jack. Shake the powder out of your cartridge into the barrel, then reverse your ball and drive it gently home, and lastly ram in the mass of paper atop of the bullet. You'll make more accurate firing that way, and there will be less recoil, and little windage. It's a wrinkle that I picked up in the Maori war a couple of years ago. Bang!"

And Tom Conquest's carbine rang out in turn, whilst a scream and an imprecation told that *his* bullet at all events, had found its billet.

(*To be continued.*)

NED KELLY

THE
IRONCLAD
AUSTRALIAN BUSHRANGER

NO 2,

The firing now became pretty general. So much so, indeed, on the trooper's side, that Tom had to shout out to them not to throw away their bullets.

"I wish that fellow had an ounce of lead in his tripes," exclaimed the leader on the opposite side, the stalwart and ferocious Ned Kelly, to Lanky Bill and Lanky Jim, who had for shields the nearest trees to right and left of him.

"I never guessed they'd have taken to our tactics. I thought they'd have charged in amongst the trees on horseback, and that we'd have picked 'em off as easy as a, b, c. He's a hawk of the right breed, who's leading 'em on."

"Oh, I feel so faint-hearted. As mild as a sucking-dove," moaned Sandy Bill.

"I'll give you a dove's quittance in lead, if you dare to show an equally *white feather*," hissed Ned Kelly between his set teeth. "Tell you what, lads, we'll retire from these traps in a half-circle, whose termination will bring us right upon the gold cart. In the eagerness of the pursuit they'll never notice this."

"Aye, that notion does you credit, cappen," exclaimed Lanky Jim, exultantly.

"We will fall back then after each discharge, for then our smoke will cover us until we gain the next shelter. That's an Indian ruse, mates."

The ruse, Indian or no, was put into almost immediate execution, and the troopers, guessing from the imperfect, smoke-shrouded view that they obtained of them that their foes were in full retreat, would have broken cover and rushed after them but for the restraining shout of Tom Conquest, who yelled forth:—

"Don't leave the trees unless you want to be shot down like 'possums. Give a rush for those that the bushrangers have just left, before they can re-load, and then play at hide-and-seek with them, as before. They know the game, or should know it well."

So one set of trees was exchanged for another, and the desultory popping whenever a head or shoulder showed itself was renewed for a little while.

"Jack Hogan," called out Tom Conquest, in an undertone to his mate, "when next the bushrangers fall back we must not push *straight* forward, but move at an angle towards the cover they have just quitted. You see, when an advance is made straightforward towards an enemy, he has no occasion to alter his aim; whereas, dodging towards him obliges him to take a flying or a difficult shot. Pass on the order from man to man, but you needn't add the explanation, for this isn't a time for words."

It was, indeed, no time for words. The combat was one to the death, and every one felt that, as though instinctively.

The bushrangers knew well enough that they fought with halters round their necks, and the troopers were equally aware, on the other hand, that the outlaws would show them no quarter if they once succeeded in worsting them.

Two unpleasant facts soon became evident to the latter; firstly, that short-barrelled Government carbines were no match for the American rifles that Ned Kelly and his men handled; and secondly, that the redoubtable freebooter was almost as good a bushman as their own leader.

The way they glanced back to select their next stand, then discharged their pieces, and under cover of the white smoke obliqued and gained it, was a caution to rattlesnakes, as an American backwoodsman would have observed. In vain Tom Conquest threw a hint in one direction and a word of advice in another, the carbine balls would fly wide, whilst the enemies' bullets told with deadly effect whenever a trooper's head was incautiously exposed for an instant.

"Jack Hogan, when skirmishing in the scrub, look for your enemy close to the ground; but in open bush like this, higher up," he muttered to his comrade, as he observed how wildly he was firing.

But poor Jack was not allowed the opportunity to follow his friend's counsel, for the very next moment, as he popped his head round his tree-trunk to get a shot at a bushranger, Ned Kelly discharged his rifle, and sent a bullet through it.

Hogan fell dead without a groan, and Tom Conquest looking round, saw that he had but five men left, whilst the bushrangers appeared to be almost as numerous as ever. Indeed, they had only passed three of their dead bodies.

"We must retreat in turn, we must fall back upon the gold-cart and defend it to the last gasp, aye, to the last drop of our blood," said Tom Conquest.

"A great deal wiser plan to spring into our saddles and ride as though the devil were at our heels, to the police-camp at Curragal for succour," answered a trooper.

But the half-dozen men were allowed time to do neither of these two things.

The bushrangers had either at last grown tired of hide-and-seek warfare, or else they guessed how their fire had diminished the number of their foes.

Whichever it was, they made a sudden rush out of cover, firing as they came on.

Before that discharge three more troopers went down, and the next instant the three survivors found themselves surrounded by nine bushrangers.

They drew their swords and defended themselves gallantly, but again regulation steel was no match for the clubbed rifles of their foes.

Down they were felled like ninepins, and brained as they lay half-stunned on the ground.

Tom Conquest alone managed to effect an escape. He cut one bushranger down, ran a second through the body, tripped up a third, and bolted.

Tom was a capital runner, and he made for the deepest and darkest part of the bush.

Several shots were discharged after him, but by the mercy of Providence he escaped them all.

Soon, however, the bushrangers pursued him in a mob.

Dodging out of their view as much as possible behind the tree-trunks, Tom presently espied a small patch of scrub, into the midst of which he dived as swiftly as a hare, there to "play possum."

CHAPTER IX.

RINGED IN BY FOES. A DARING ACT OF BRAVADO.

TOM'S place of concealment was in deep shadow, and the scrub itself was very thick, but when the bushrangers came on to it and began to beat it with the stocks of their rifles, the fugitive almost suspended his breathing, and even closed his eyes lest their glitter should betray him to his foes.

The man-hunters ended up by firing several shots into the patch of scrub, and some of these hummed by Tom Conquest's ears most unpleasantly close.

Still, however, he made not the slightest stir, and he was amply rewarded for his forbearance by hearing the bushrangers presently move away.

No sooner were they gone than the trooper, after first cautiously looking around him, quitted his place of concealment in turn, and began to move warily through the forest in their wake, reloading his carbine as he went.

Presently he made a slight detour, and approached the confines of the bush as near as it was safe to do so, about five hundred yards to the left of the gold-cart.

As the horses that had drawn it were gone, he concluded that the driver and the man with the blunderbuss had long ago cut the traces and escaped on them.

It was not those horses he wanted, however.

He turned from the gold-cart, around which the bushrangers had already gathered like a swarm of bees, and casting his gaze across the plain, he saw, quietly feeding at a little distance away, the chargers of the unfortunate dead troopers—his own amongst them.

Lying flat on his belly, and wholly concealed from view by the long grass, he placed a hollowed hand on each side of his mouth and gave utterance to a long, shrill, and peculiar whistle

On hearing this, one of the chargers pricked up its ears and, with a joyful neigh, came trotting towards him.

Directly his fine bay horse was alongside of him, Tom Conquest rose to his feet and flung himself into the saddle.

The robbers were far too busy with the treasure to take notice of anything so far away.

Tom looked undecided what to do for a second or two after gathering up the reins, then he ejaculated—

"I'm a darned fool for my pains, and doubtless shall get a bullet through my head as the sole reward of my folly, and yet I can't help it, no, I'm dashed if I can."

As he concluded he drew a large white handkerchief out of his pocket, and fastened one corner to the top of his carbine-barrel and the opposite one to the trigger-guard.

Holding this primitive flag of truce aloft he set spurs to his nag and galloped him gently towards the gold-cart and its pillagers.

He got within hailing distance before he was perceived, and then reining short up he shouted to attract attention, at the same time waving his white flag.

The bushrangers looked round quick enough at this, and seemed to be altogether astonished at the strange vision and what it was about.

"What the d—— is your little game?" suddenly bellowed out one of them.

"I challenge your cut-throat leader to mortal strife, with whatever weapons he chooses. Man to man, out here in the bush, I will fight him to the death."

The bushrangers greeted this challenge with a shout of laughter.

"Look here, you thundering fool," yelled forth Kelly himself, "my cokernut is worth three thousand pounds, and yours is not worth as many brass farthings, so I decline your polite invitation with many thanks. It would pay you handsomely to kill Ned Kelly, though perhaps you'd find it no easy task now that he's got his armour on; but it wouldn't benefit Ned a bit to kill twenty of the likes of you, and he's a man who never fights unless there's money to be made by it. He gets quite enough hard knocks in the way of business not to care overmuch to indulge in them for a pastime."

"Coward!" cried Tom Conquest, "you are a bragging poltroon, Kelly."

"All right, my man; no one will believe that charge but a fool, and what fools choose to credit matters very little to me. Such an insult, however, must not pass unavenged. Bring me down that chattering magpie, mates."

Thereat the other bushrangers began to re-handle their rifles, and Tom Conquest, seeing no fun in remaining there to become their target, hastily levelled his carbine, covered Ned Kelly therewith, and pulled the trigger.

He heard the ping of the bullet against some part or other of the bushranger's iron panoply, and then he wheeled round, and dashed off at full gallop.

The next instant the bullets were flying around him like hail, but again he was fortunate enough to escape being struck.

When he judged himself to be out of range, he again wheeled round, and observing that Ned Kelly was evidently uninjured, he shook his fist at him menacingly, as though threatening his destruction at some future time, and then continued his onward flight.

"Hey for the police-camp at Curragal," muttered he fiercely to himself; "I may be able to take vengeance on those internal villains for the murder of poor Hogan and my other comrades, before sundown, even yet."

The bushrangers now lost no time in bringing up their horses, which had hitherto been piqueted some little distance away in the forest.

Each horse carried across his shoulders two large and strong leather bags attached by a strong strap.

There were thirteen horses in all, and, consequently, twenty-six of these bags.

The boxes of treasure were quickly taken out of the gold-cart, and dashed open with repeated blows from the butt ends of the rifles.

Then everyone set to work to fill the aforesaid bags with the wealth contained therein, until at length they were puffed out to their fullest dimensions.

What remained of the treasure the bushrangers crammed into their pockets and boots, until at last they could hardly waddle about.

Had a posse of mounted troopers descended upon them at that juncture they would have fallen easy victims, for they were as unwieldly as turtles.

Ned Kelly had laden himself with far less treasure than any of the others.

"Now, mates," said he, when the whole had been appropriated, "away with our wealth to the secret hiding-places in the mountain ranges. I shall not accompany you, as I have further business to transact ere I return home. Take mine and our dead friends' horses with you, however, for I will make use of one of the trap's nags for my further journey. Plant my share of the spoil along with your own until I return to the mountain and ask you for an account. We will be quiet for a few days in our dens, until the excitement attendant on this affair is somewhat over. It would take an army to find out all our haunts in the Mount Macedon ranges. Stay; before you depart pile the broken boxes in the cart, and set fire to cart and all. Now then, look lively, my lads."

The deed was done in a twinkling; the red flames shot quiveringly upwards, and then the bushrangers made hasty tracks for their homes in the mountains, Ned Kelly's steed and the horses of the dead being led by sundry of the survivors.

When they had all gone, the ironclad bushranger rounded in the troopers' chargers, and selected the best and strongest of the lot for his own use.

"I want strength and endurance more than mere speed on the present occasion," muttered he to himself, "for I don't intend to play the runaway game."

Carefully re-loading his rifle, he slung it at his back, transferred his pistols from his belt to the holsters, examined curb-chain and girth, and finally vaulting into the saddle, trotted gently into the forest defiles.

"Father!" called to him a voice, as sweet yet clear as the note of the bell-bird; but he heard it not, he was so busy with his own thoughts. He never even glanced in the direction where sat a young girl on a white horse, her face every bit as white as it, not more than a hundred yards to the left of his course.

She would have ridden after him but she dared not, for a river of blood seemed to flow between them. She never before had looked upon a scene of slaughter, never before had beheld the face of a dead man, and three now lay between her and the being whom she had always loved as a parent.

But Ned Kelly thought neither of blood nor death. His reflections were—

"This night the beautiful Lola Montez, Countess of Lansfeldt, shall, instead of a European king, have an Australian bushranger for a bridegroom."

CHAPTER X.

BAILING UP COBB'S COACH—A WOMAN'S PLUCK.

DAYLIGHT has changed to moonlight, a transformation effected in less than a quarter of an hour in semi-tropical Australia.

The heavens have changed from the hue of gleaming steel to the deepest indigo, and are dotted so thickly with stars that our northern skies would seem almost a blank in comparison. Chief amongst them is the glorious constellation of the Southern Cross, and close to it may be observed that strange patch in the sky which has puzzled all astronomers to explain, except by the incomprehensible assertion that it is a void within a void, a yawning chasm in the midst of emptiness, a literal hole in space. That is all that can be got out of the astronomers; and, though the author has gazed wonderingly at that oddly-shaped sky-patch a thousand times, he can broach no new theory.

How bright that full, large, fair Australian moon is! The smallest print could be read beneath its rays. It floods hill and plain, bush and scrub, with its soft white light, and all the creatures that love the night are up and about to enjoy it.

The locusts drone like bagpipes out of tune in the tree branches, and the low, plaintive note of the mopoke, or Australian cuckoo, is answered by the still more mournful cry of the wild fowl from some neighbouring swamp, or the howl of the warrigal, or wild dog, from the deepest recesses of the bush.

But all these sounds together are eclipsed in mournfulness by the rattling of the loose bark against the tree-trunks, which, where their last year's clothing has fallen off, gleam as white as sheeted ghosts on all sides.

Is this a wonderful constellation, or a comet, coming rushing through the trees with the speed of the very wind?

No, it is three great lamps marking the three points of a triangle.

As it approaches nearer a vehicle all ablaze with scarlet and gold, and in shape not unlike a circus band carriage, may be descried, drawn by four long, weedy-looking horses that have the go of the very devil in them.

High up on the raised box sits a tall, slab-sided Yankee, wearing a soft drab felt hat, at least a yard in height from the brim, which is almost wide enough to hold a donkey race on; in his left hand he holds a fistfull of reins, and in his right grasps a whip fifteen feet long in the lash, with which he can flick a fly from off one of the leaders' ears, or give a crack as loud as any rifle shot.

But where the deuce is the man driving? Well may that question be asked, for to the uninitiated there is not a trace of a road visible.

No, it is all grassy bush; ups and downs, humps and hollows, felled trees and standing trees, bushes and huge scattered pieces of bark.

But this is Cobb's royal mail coach, doing its six hundred and nine miles journey between Melbourne and Sydney, and there isn't one of Cobb's drivers who would hesitate to take his gaudy, springless, wide-wheeled and wholly uncomfortable vehicle over the ruts of an earthquake or down the sides of Mont Blanc, if told by his employers that the thing had to be done.

When the enterprising Cobb first started his Yankee coaches in Australia he had to battle against some opposition, but proffering to convey the Government mails to Ballarat three hours quicker than any other coach proprietor, he was given the chance of doing so.

Most people like fast travelling, and so the new Yankee coach was crowded the first day of its run, but it didn't arrive so at the end of its journey. At first it was all very delightful, but when the metal had been left behind (it didn't extend very far in those days), and the driver evinced a decided inclination to reach his destination much as the crow flies—that is to say, on the bee-line principle, with a contemptuous disdain for all intervening obstacles—even the bravest began to feel nervous, if not absolutely terrified.

Matters grew worse and worse. First one side of the coach would fly up in the air and then the other. Next it would be plunging like a ship in a rough sea, and anon seem as though it was contemplating turning a complete summersault.

"For goodness sake be careful!"

Such and many a similar petition was hurled at the driver's ears by the passengers, who every minute were being shaken together, or almost pitched over the sides; but the tall-hatted Jehu paid not the slightest attention to their remonstrances or prayers, so they at last began to let themselves down over the back, an easy feat enough, and anyhow better than remaining where they were to be pitched out and killed.

Suffice it to say Cobb's coach reached its destination without a single passenger aboard, but it won the mail contract, and has kept it ever since, and now hundreds of its coaches and thousands of its horses traverse the four leading colonies of Australia in every direction. People soon took to travelling by them when they discovered that accidents seldom or never occurred—indeed, they are so wide between the wheels that, with the entire absence of top-hamper, there is little chance of a capsize, except through a wheel coming off.

But to return to our story.

On comes the particular coach with which we have to deal, at a pace of about twelve miles an hour, the wheels now and then almost shaving a gum-tree trunk, or the end of a felled shea-oak, as it whizzes along through the moon-lit bush.

The driver might have followed the new road had he liked, but he prefers the old route; all the more as the bush track does not knock his horses' feet to pieces like the metal.

Suddenly a dark and mysterious form spurs a big bay horse out from amongst a neighbouring clump of trees, and plants himself directly in the coach's track.

Cries of alarm ring forth from inside the vehicle, and a passenger who produces a brace of pistols has them forcibly wrested from him and thrown away; for everyone seems to know by instinct that that ill-omened vision in front of them is a bushranger, and the passengers, almost without an exception, are fearful that the least opposition may anger the outlaw into butchering them all in cold blood.

"Bail up, you —— ——!" (both adjective and substantive are too blasphemous and disgusting to be printed). "Bail up, or I'll put an ounce of lead through your brain-pan!" shouts the stranger to the driver, as he draws a pistol from his holster.

"All right, sirree. Job Fairweather's always ready to yield to a convincing argument such as that there!" rejoins the Yankee, coolly; and reining up his cattle he proceeds to light a big cigar.

The man on horseback now rides slowly up to the coach, and, as he draws near, the terrified passengers observe his strange iron head-dress and cuirass.

"It's the ironclad bushranger himself," whispers one in quavering tones.

"Yes, it's that infernal rascal, Kelly, without doubt," echoes another.

"Up with your hands above your heads, every man Jack of you. Up with them, I say. By thunder, I'll brain the man who disobeys my orders. Your pardon, ladies, don't be alarmed, your sex protects you from harm, but I must have your watches and other jewellery as souvenirs of your charms. Hullo, you with the white choker—I like a parson for an assistant—just empty those fellows' pockets of their contents and hand them to me."

"My good man, respect my cloth," pleaded the clergyman, very meekly.

"You are a lying hound, notwithstanding your cloth, to call me a good man, when you know well that I'm about the biggest villain left unhung. Do as I bid you, or you'll never patter from a pulpit again. Turn each pocket inside out that I may be sure you aren't tricking me, and if you find anything of an explosive nature in either of them don't by accident turn it this way, or by similar accident the contents of my pistol will get mixed up with your brains. A wink's as good as a nod to a blind horse, you know."

"But, I—I'm not a horse," faltered the hesitating divine.

"Well, perhaps ass would be nearer the mark, in your case, and had I an ass that wouldn't go, wouldn't I pistol him? By heaven, don't force me to finish the couplet, or I'll end it in d—— unpleasant pantomime;" and as he concluded he thrust the muzzle of his weapon within a couple of inches of the clergyman's head, who thereupon yielded to the exigencies of the position.

"I must turn pickpocket, gentlemen," said he plaintively. "It's a great disgrace to my cloth; but necessity has no law. Pray allow me!" and he proceeded to do his work effectively and well, now and then exclaiming in muffled monotone, "For God's sake, gentlemen, continue to keep your hands up in the air, or the miscreant will murder us all in cold blood. Do, there's good fellows."

The "good fellows" did exactly as they were told, for they had quite as much objection to being shot at, as had the clergyman himself.

When all their valuables had been transferred to the ironclad bushranger's pockets, and every one of their own had been turned inside out, Ned Kelly turned to the womenkind, of whom there were three aboard the coach, and said—

"Now, ladies, I can hardly set the parson to search you, for I daresay the black cloth that he prides himself on would blush as scarlet as a soldier's coat at the mere thought of such a thing. I trust to your honour, therefore, to give me all that you have about you. Chains and watches I know all of you possess, and rings on your fingers as well. Stay, up with your veils in the first place. Ned Kelly don't often look upon a woman's face."

Up went two of the veils at once. The third fair one hesitated.

"The really beautiful are always modest," said the daring outlaw. "Madam, I have heard that you are partial to kings; won't you show your fair face to the Ironclad King of the Australian bush?"

"Ah! you know me!" exclaimed the veiled female, in a slightly foreign accent. "Well, if you want very much to see my face, there!"

And so saying, with two of the tiniest hands, she raised her veil, and revealed a countenance in every way calculated to enthrall even the most impressionless by its rich, glowing, voluptuous Southern beauty.

No twin stars that gleamed down from out the indigo-hued heavens were as bright as those large, dark, melting orbs, which, however, seemed to be equally full of fire.

They were shaded by the longest and silkiest of curved lashes, and surmounted by the most beautifully-arched of jetty brows.

Her hair was brushed back from a low, broad forehead, white and pure as snow. Her features were most delicately chiselled, her rich, full lips were red and pouting, her chin charmingly dimpled, her full, rounded throat as fair as alabaster. She looked a prize worthy indeed of a monarch.

By this time the other women had handed to the bushranger all their valuables, but he took them mechanically, and all the while was seemingly unable to avert his gaze from the enchantress's face.

"Lola Montez, Countess of Lansfeldt," said he, "your destiny is to become the wife of Ned Kelly, the King of the Australian bush. The parson shall marry us at once, and then I'll take you right away to your future home in the mountain ranges. What do you say to my plan, countess?"

"That I haven't so much as seen your face. How can I tell whether I shall like you? I have shown you mine; 'tis but fair that I should behold yours in return."

"Well, I don't know but what it is." And the bushranger dropped his reins on his horse's neck, and raised his ponderous iron head-dress.

Hardly had he done so, however, when the beautiful woman (we have her portrait before us whilst we write) pulled a small pistol from within her sleeve and fired it point-blank at the bushranger's face, accompanying the action with the contemptuous remark—

"Where seven men sit panic-stricken before a single villain, 'tis time for a woman to show what she can do."

Unfortunately, the beautiful specimen of the sex in question had not done nearly so much as she intended.

The little bullet from her almost toy weapon, instead of penetrating the bushranger's brain, had only shorn off a portion of his left ear.

Maddened by pain and rage, he hastily redonned his helmet, and, dashing up to the coach side, hissed between his set teeth—

"For that act of treachery I won't marry you at all. Lola Montez, Countess of Lausfeldt, and some time almost Queen of Bavaria, shall become the mate instead of the wife of the King of the Australian Bush. Come, quit that d—— coach for the crupper of my horse on the instant, or I force you to obey me with a grip on one of those plump arms that'll leave a livid ring for weeks."

"Ruffian, you shall kill me before I will consent to go with you!"

"By heaven, but you shall go with me. Now, you men, keep up those hands, and at the same time keep still. I don't want to ruin the ladies' dresses with the blood and brains of any of you, so take care that you don't drive me to it. If you stroke my fur the wrong way by daring to interfere in this woman's behalf, I'll slaughter the whole biling of you in cold blood, by George I will. Now, madam, look lively. I've taken an oath to have you, and by thunder I will, so make no more to do about it."

He spurred his horse still closer alongside the coach as he spoke, and grasped her by an arm, but no sooner had he done so than his hand was slashed across by the keen blade of an Albacete knife.

"Tiger cat!" he yelled, as he let go his clutch, "throw that knife away, or I'll put a bullet through you, beautiful as an angel though you are."

"Do it, ruffian. Better death than to fall alive into the power of such as you."

Whether Ned Kelly would have shot her, or whether he used the threat merely to intimidate the proud and courageous Spanish beauty into yielding to his will, is a point that was never decided, for at this critical and highly-dramatic position of affairs another pistol rang out, and Ned Kelly wheeled his horse round to confront four well-mounted men, the foremost of whom held his smoking weapon still in his grasp.

"Sheer off, my hearties, unless you want me to give you a swift journey to purgatory," exclaimed Ned Kelly, with an oath. "I don't suppose you guessed who I was, only seeing my back, eh?"

He spoke in sneering accents, but then all in an instant his tone altered to a shriek of vindictive and triumphant rage.

"Squatter M'Pherson as I live! And so the devil at last has delivered you into my hands? Take this from the lover of the girl you murdered, whom you left to die of want in the bush, you smock-faced scoundrel."

As he spoke, he transferred his reins to his teeth, and drawing his pistols from his holsters, fired both point blank at the squatter.

It was very seldom that Ned Kelly's bullets didn't fly true to their billets, and he was, as a rule, equally handy with his left hand as with his right; but on the present occasion the rage and excitement under which he laboured caused both balls to fly wide, and the next instant two of those who were with the squatter fired at the bushranger in turn, and he found to his dismay and chagrin that a ball had penetrated his right shoulder, depriving him of all use in that arm, whilst he was more than suspicious, from its rearing, that the other had wounded his horse.

Not to flee for his very life under such adverse circumstances would have been little short of madness, so, setting spurs to the troop horse, Ned Kelly broke through the four mounted men, who in vain endeavoured to lay hands upon him as he passed, and made off into the bush.

Before they could reload their pistols he was fairly out of range, and though three out of the number were most anxious to pursue him, the squatter, their master (for the others were his stockmen), refused to hear of such a thing, knowing perhaps that, if they did pursue the bushranger, all the shots from the long rifle that he carried slung at his back would, in all probability, be fired at him alone, for, strange to say, not one of them had observed that Ned had been fairly winged in the shoulder.

At any other time the bushranger would have drawn

rein directly he was out of range, to hurl defiance and threats of future vengeance against those who had worsted him; but on the present occasion he was stricken too sorely to do more than mutter them to himself.

That much he did, however, binding himself by the most awful mental oaths to kill M'Pherson ere the year was out, and to possess himself of the lovely Spanish woman whilst she was on her way back to the colonial metropolis.

Thus much resolved on, he determined to make his way back to his bark hut in the ranges with as much speed as possible.

He soon discovered that the troopers were out, however, and patrolling in force between the Forest Creek road and the hills.

He dared not risk running the gauntlet, circumstanced as he was, and so he struck away to the left and rode more than a dozen miles to a deserted shepherd's hut, in which he thought he would hide for a while.

Alighting from the troop-horse, he started it off, for the animal's wound was after all a trifling one, and creeping into the hut sank exhausted in a corner, where he was almost in an instant covered with ravenous fleas, they being the usual habitants of such a place.

Meanwhile Cobb's coach was merrily bowling along again. To the slab-sided Yankee driver the scene that had just occurred was almost a weekly one, and he treated it as one of the ordinary incidents of the road. The pulse and heart of only one of the travellers beat as calmly as did his, and they pertained to the beautiful Spaniard, Lola Montez, Countess of Landsfeldt.

CHAPTER XI.

A SQUATTER'S STATION AND A FREE-AND-EASY GUEST.

CHANGE we the scene to a squatters' station some dozen miles to the west of Mount Macedon—a large, rambling, one-storied weather-board structure, whose roof terminates in a wide, deep verandah, that runs round three sides of the building, and is buried beneath the leaves and blossoms of well-nigh every variety of climbing plant.

Pretentious structures of stone and brick have long ago taken the place of these primitive habitations of the colonial aristocracy, as the squatters indubitably are; but they do not harmonise nearly as well with the characteristics of the surrounding scenery, which requires picturesqueness rather than grandeur for its accompaniments.

That pile of buildings a quarter of a mile away on the left is the wool-shed and its surrounding stables, barns, &c., rough structures built of the native woods, roofed-in with shingles split on the station; whilst just below, near the creek, is the sheep-wash. You may see it glistening beneath the white moonlight; and for the rest behold an undulating grassy plain, sprinkled singly and in clusters with trees, with a glimpse of a white post-and rail fence at intervals; and in an opposite direction Mount Macedon, begirt by sombre eucalyptus forests, that mount its sides and crowd its very summits.

Four or five days have elapsed since the sticking up of Cobb's mail, thirteen miles away, by the ironclad bushranger, and the rescue of Lola Montez, the lovely Spanish adventuress, from his clutches, and now Andrew M'Pherson is at home, where, looking forth from the front of his station, he could have exclaimed, with Alexander Selkirk, that he was monarch of all he surveyed; for his run extended in that direction for no less a distance than fifteen miles right away; and, scattered over that extensive domain, he can count his horned cattle by thousands and his sheep by tens of thousands.

Should he not have been a happy man, more especially as his greatest treasure of all is a daughter who dotes on him, and who is famed for her beauty throughout the entire colony?

Andrew M'Pherson is *not* a happy man, however. He has three reasons for being otherwise. He mourns the loss of a wife of whom he was very fond; his heart has long been stricken with deep, though unavailing remorse, for the seduction and afterwards brutal desertion of a beautiful and innocent girl, whom fifteen years ago he cast aside (as a child throws away a toy it has grown tired of) in order to marry that wife; and to these two sources of grief has lately been added the threat that, for his heartlessness and brutality in the one instance, he is doomed to perish by the avenger's steel or bullet within the year; and he feels that the ironclad bushranger is the man of all others most likely to keep his word.

But away with ill-omened forebodings. It is Lily M'Pherson's fifteenth birthday, and the event is commemorated by a ball at Mittagarra.

Friends have come from far and near (to use the latter relatively, for people living a score of miles apart were considered *near* neighbours in Australia in those days), and this is why the stable-yard is full of traps and buggies; the stalls of saddle and driving horses; and the roomy and well-furnished rooms of guests.

Yes, if the squatter's mansion of the gold-fever era was still of wood, he had at all events learnt to furnish it luxuriously within; and the bullock-drays that brought up from Melbourne all these new requirements to an artificial state of existence, also brought wives and daughters dresses and folderols of the very latest fashion in Collins-street.

Thus it is that, at the present joyous assemblage, the young people can dance to the strains of a ninety-five-guinea Erard's piano, instead of those of an indifferently-played fiddle, which would have been the case a few years before; and thus also it is that the slim and graceful, albeit delicately-rounded, forms of Australia's bright-eyed daughters are arrayed with all the richness, taste, and elegance that could have been found in a London or Paris fashionable *salon*.

Conspicuous amongst them all, ay, as much so as a stately lily would have been with daisies only for its rivals, behold our Lily, the daughter of Andrew M'Pherson, and the sole heiress to all his wealth.

She is attired in simple white; a soft, clinging Indian muslin, trimmed with valuable old lace, and her sole ornament is a spray of silver wattle, intermingled with her golden hair.

There is sufficient of topaz in her eyes, of coral in her lips, and of pearl in the exquisite texture of her skin for her to dispense with the real gems, for in her case the presentment is far more lovely than the reality could be.

Nothing could exceed the whiteness of her smooth and polished shoulders, save cherry blossom or snow, and not one of the forty-five thousand varieties of rose is delicate enough in its tints for us to compare her cheeks with.

She was at once a poet's vision and the bright creature of a painter's fancy, who has just awakened from a dream of the bright and blessed habitants of heaven.

To sum up all, she was perfection's own self in face, form, smile, voice, and movement.

No name but that of Lily would have suited her, for she had the lily's purity, as well as its whiteness and its sweetness.

And yet, why does she look unhappy to-night?

Is it because she would prefer the respectful homage and attentions of some of the young "Cornstalks" with whom she has been acquainted from childhood upwards (in a less fervid clime she would have been but a child still) to that of the tall, languid, and "haw-haw" kind of swell who seems to have almost wholly monopolised her.

Captain Montague Vavasseur has come out to Australia "to see what the demmed infernal place is like," or, at least, so he himself would have described to one of his own sex the reason of his visit.

He had been at Mittagarra for a week.

He had ridden up to the Home Station one evening and, a perfect stranger, thrown himself on the hospitality of the squatter as coolly and collectedly as a man with a full purse would enter one of our great London hotels.

"He had heard tell of the demned hospitality of the squatters, and he'd put himself to the inconvenience of coming up country to see if it had been exaggerated, as he intended to write a book on the demned country."

This was very much the manner in which he had introduced himself to M'Pherson, and, by way of answer, he had been told to "make himself thoroughly at home for as long as ever he chose to stay;" which he had done accordingly, to the very top of his bent.

Captain Montague Vavasseur looked of any age between thirty and forty.

He was tall and spare, with a long, drooping, tawny moustache, and curly hair, which was growing thin in places.

"Demned heavy helmets in the Dragoon Guards—my corps—make all the fellahs' heads bald in no time." Such was the excuse that he gave for that.

But the heavy helmet couldn't have given him those very decided crowsfeet about the eyes, which, in conjunction with the thinning hair and the generally *blasé* manner of the gallant captain, sufficiently hinted to the close observer that not only had he sown a plentiful crop of wild oats, but also reaped tares in abundance.

He had now constituted himself the fair Lily's shadow.

Could it be that the captain was a mere adventurer, who had perhaps run through a fortune in the old country, and then come out to the new one to revenge himself by marrying a squatter millionaire's daughter?

If so, he had sat down to lay siege to the proper citadel, at all events. And has he a chance of success?

Let the young lady's actions answer the question.

See, she escapes from her shadow at last. She, in fact, sends him away to get her something, and whilst he is gone slips out of the ballroom (after all, 'tis but a carpet dance), evades one or two of her girl acquaintances every bit as skilfully as she had got rid of the captain, and a minute later leaves the house by means of a long French window that opens on to the verandah.

No sooner is she out of doors than she looks cautiously around her, and, feeling convinced that no one is watching her movements, she speeds through the garden and the small peach orchard beyond, and three minutes later gains a post-and-rail fence, where she is immediately clasped in the arms of a handsome young trooper.

CHAPTER XII.

LILY'S MEETING WITH TOM CONQUEST.

"I WAS afraid you would not be able to get away, as you had a party at your place, and yet I would not have missed the chance of wishing you many happy returns of your birthday, Lily darling."

"I knew that you would be here, Tom, and I resolved that you should see me by hook or by crook. Well, why don't you compliment me on my appearance, sir? Don't you see that I am *en grande toilette?*"

"I see that you only want a pair of snowy wings, though not a bit more snowy than your beautiful neck and shoulders, to make a complete angel of you, darling," exclaimed the young trooper, in tones of intense admiration; and then he sighed heavily as he added—"Ah! Lily, I very much fear that you are so far beyond my reach as though you really were an angel. There is an awful gulf between riches and poverty."

"A gulf that true love can always bridge over, Tom."

"I'm not so sure of that. Your proud father will never give you to a poor devil of a trooper with a scanty pay of eight shillings a day; and until you are twenty-one you cannot marry me without his consent."

"But I'm only six years distant from twenty-one, Tom, and the time will soon pass by. I recollect my ninth birthday as though 'twere yesterday."

"Small consolation to a man who wishes to pluck the dainty rosebud to be told that he shall have it when it becomes a full-blown rose."

"Will you not love me when I become a woman, Tom?"

"Yes, but I'd like a lovely girl-wife to commence with. It's very hard, Lily, that fate should persecute us in this manner. Now I have tried hard to win the reward offered for the capture, alive or dead, of Ned Kelly the ironclad bushranger. On two occasions I have nearly run him to earth, but he is as slippery as an eel, and has as many lives as a cat. Three thousand pounds would bring in three hundred a year, which with my pay would keep a nice little cottage going full swing at Richmond or South Yarra, without being beholden to your father for assistance. But even then his consent would have to be asked."

"I would not marry you until it was given, Tom. And I should so shrink from owing our happiness to blood-money."

"But I don't know how to get money any other way. It's within the lines of my legitimate employ. I'm bound down to serve the Queen as a mounted trooper for three more years, and I can't desert my flag, you know. If 'twasn't for that I'd precious soon try the diggings."

"Well, Tom, dear, keep up a good heart, for I'll be true to you through thick and thin. We must trust to time, and better still to Providence."

"Lily I will find out a way to make you mine within a year or I will go mad. It is horrible to think how near others can get unto you, and I, who love you more than life itself, obliged to keep at such a terrible distance. Who is that tall, pump-shaped fellow who has been mooning over you the whole evening? He's spoons on you, ay, gravy spoons at the very least."

"Oh, he's a guest, a self-invited one, and I don't like him in the least. Papa didn't like him at first, but he has changed round and been awfully taken up with him the last few days. He is a Captain Montague Vavasseur, an Englishman in search of the picturesque, and in my opinion no end of a humbug as well. But how did you learn all this, Tom? I hope you haven't been a Mr. Paul Pry?"

"Is there any harm in regarding one's pet constellation or over-bright peculiar star through a telescope, Lily? No, I haven't been a Paul Pry; I've been a simple astronomer, studying the movements of a heavenly body, through this tiny but very powerful opera-glass. That must have been the reason that I saw the fellow *mooning* so distinctly. The evening was, I suppose, too warm to have the curtains drawn."

"Warm! I call it melting hot, Tom. I am so glad to get out of the close, stuffy rooms, into the comparatively pure air. But I must not stay much longer, or I shall be missed. How still everything is, Tom. I've read of the weather being like this just before an earthquake."

"Happily, darling, we are not subject to such fearful convulsions of nature in these favoured regions. There's a decided hot wind blowing, though. I wonder your father don't clear away the trees a little on the north, for were a bush-fire to spring up in the ranges I wouldn't say but that a fierce hot wind might not one day bear it on its wings down upon Mittagarra in a sheet of flame. The grass too is as dry as tinder to-night. I have even refrained from smoking my accustomed pipe, rather than that the shadow of a danger should menace my adored one."

"It is not at all kind of you thus terrifying your adored one half out of her life," retorted Lily, with a laugh. But though she spoke lightly, yet the rapid rise and fall of her fair expanded chest, and the sudden flight of the delicate colour from her cheeks showed plainly enough that the trooper's words had really alarmed her.

"Pardon me, darling," said he, folding her in his embrace, "I told you in order that you might give your father a hint on the matter. That the station has stood for fifteen or sixteen years without being so destroyed, is sufficient proof that the danger is not a very serious one; yet, nevertheless, to be forewarned is to be forearmed, you know, and I haven't known exactly such a season as this since my arrival in the colony. Why, the creek has dwindled down to a chain of pools already."

"I'll put an idea of the possible danger into papa's head, Tom. And now good-bye, dear, for I must be going," said Lily.

"First of all, darling, accept the birthday present that I bought you the last time that I was down in Melbourne. A small token of my great affection for you, Lily. Look, do you like them, dearest?"

And, as he put the question, Tom Conquest suddenly opened a little red morocco case that he had for some time held in his hand, and revealed, reposing in their nest of crimson velvet, a pair of beautiful opal earrings.

"Oh, the unlucky stones!" exclaimed Lily, as she clasped her hands, and heaved her plump and milk-white shoulders far out of her dress. "Oh! Tom, what made you buy me them? Don't you know that the opal always blights true love, that, in fact, it is full of evil meanings and omens?"

"Let me fling them away, then," said Tom, though not without a sigh, for the trinkets represented many a self-denial extending long months.

Perhaps the young girl read the meaning of that sigh, and of the somewhat troubled look that accompanied it, for she suddenly rejoined with a laugh—

"What a little silly I am to take notice of old women's tales, and to pretend to put faith in such ridiculous superstitions. They are lovely earrings. I never saw such sweet opals in my life; a rainbow would look dull compared with them. I thank you very much for your kind present, dear Tom, and as a penance for my paining you, which I can see that I have done, I will allow you to put them in my ears."

"If you think they really are ill-omened stones——"

"I think nothing of the kind, Tom; so please do as I tell you."

The amorous and gallant young trooper was nothing loth.

Lily bent towards him over the post-and-rail fence, and with trembling fingers he affixed the beautiful earrings to the still more lovely ears.

In doing so their faces came very close together, and to help stealing a kiss was to Tom a matter of sheer impossibility.

It was received with a scream.

"Lily, what's the matter? You are surely not angry with me?"

"Oh, Tom, I've been bitten. It burns. It is some poisonous thing. Oh, God! there it is again!" and as she spoke she thrust her hand down inside her very low-bodied dress, and, from her bosom dragged a hideous, brown, many-legged centipede.

It was at least nine inches in length, and must have crept into its last soft, innocent resting-place from a hole in the topmost rail over which the young girl had leant.

With a shriek she now threw it from her, and Tom at once trampled it under his foot. Then he exclaimed—

"Is there a doctor amongst your guests? If so, run to him at once, darling."

"Yes, Doctor Roper is there. Do you think that I will die, Tom?"

"No, no; there is no danger at all when medical attendance is on the spot. Run, dear, run. One kiss, and away. Never mind the burn. God grant that your beautiful flesh escapes a scar. That is my chief dread."

So Lily kissed her lover through her tears of anguish, and rushed away; and he, flinging himself into his saddle, trotted off, muttering—

"Why did she, after all, accept the opals? It must be all their doing."

CHAPTER XIII.

CAPTAIN VAVASSEUR OPENS HIS HEART.

LILY M'PHERSON'S re-entry amongst her friends, pale, tearful, and palpitating, stopped the merrymaking in an instant.

She was surrounded at once by an anxious circle, Doctor Roper the foremost of all.

"Off with her to her room at once," said he, directly he was informed of what had happened. "One or two of you girls suck the poison out of the punctures, and be sure that you don't swallow it. I'll be there presently with a bottle of whisky. Queer medicine, Miss M'Pherson; but you'll have to drink every drop in wine-glass doses within the hour. What do you think of that?"

But though he put the question, the doctor didn't wait to have it answered.

"M'Pherson, carry your daughter to her room; her strength is failing her. Now, young ladies, lose no time; away with you! Get as much poison out of the punctures as your pretty lips can, and the whisky will drive out the rest. Cherries dipped in cream the poetical part of the operation, and guzzling raw spirits the practical. I know where the fire-water is kept."

Within an hour beautiful Lily M'Pherson had drunk a quart bottle of proof spirit, in wine-glass doses at five minutes intervals, without feeling it rise in the slightest degree to her head.

"Now you'll do," said the doctor. "Go to sleep, and you'll wake up to-morrow morning almost well."

"Shall I be scarred at all, Doctor Roper?" asked Lily, anxiously.

"In a month's time there will not be the slightest mark of either bite."

Five minutes later our pure and lovely Lily was fast asleep.

Supper was immediately served; but no one seemed to have much appetite, the gentlemen especially, and directly it was over there was a general move.

Horses were re-saddled or harnessed to traps and buggies, good-nights were gravely said, coupled with evidently fervent hopes that Miss M'Pherson would be well on the morrow, and then the birthday party broke up and dispersed in all directions.

   .   .   .   .   .

The following morning found Lily without a trace of either inflammation or fever, but nevertheless very weak and disinclined to get up. She had her breakfast in bed, and then amused herself with reading for a couple of hours, the fierce, hot wind meanwhile shaking the window-frames, and laying a thick deposit of red dust all over her toilet-table.

About noon her anxious father came to visit her for the second time.

"Well, my darling, and how do you feel now?" he asked.

"All right, papa; only weak and tired. Isn't it a dreadful day without?"

"A regular *brick-fielder*, my dear, as we used to call them across the border. The thermometer stands at a hundred and twenty degrees, and the cherries and peaches are actually roasting and frizzling on the trees. The water in the creek, too, seems to get lower every hour, and if it goes on much longer, our loss in sheep and cattle will be tremendous. I haven't seen such a summer since my arrival in the colonies twenty years ago."

"I hope there's no danger of a bush-fire, papa," said Lily, uneasily.

"No, no, my dear. I have enjoined everyone about the place to be most cautious how they light fires and pipes out of doors, and to bury broken bottles wherever they come across one.* But, Lily, I have something more novel than this kind of thing to talk to you about. I have received an offer for your hand in marriage, and I've very nearly promised it."

The beautiful girl felt almost as sharp and acute a pang as these words fell upon her ears as when the venomous centipede had plunged his fangs into her snowy flesh the preceding evening.

"Oh, papa," she gasped, "how terribly abrupt you are. An offer for my hand. Who can it be from?"

---

* Broken bottles frequently cause bush-fires.

"Captain Montague Vavasseur. The Honourable Montague Vavasseur, if you like it better, and heir-apparent to the Earldom of Cassilis. Oh, he has perfectly convinced me of the truth and correctness of his statements. I shall one day see my darling child an English countess."

"No, you will not, papa, at all events if the title is to be won through Captain Montague Vavasseur. He is the most brainless puppy that I ever encountered. Of all men in the world I think I detest him the most."

"An excellent and infallible symptom that you will love him in the future. I assure you, Lily, that he is madly smitten with you, and your mishap last night brought matters to a crisis. By George! there was no pacifying the man, even after he was assured that you were in no earthly danger. When the guests had departed ne opened his heart to me fully, said that he'd come out to Australia in order to select a pure and perfect child of nature for a wife—yes, those were his very words, and that he had at last discovered the perfection of his high ideal in you."

"Very pretty language, papa, I make no doubt. I haven't discovered my ideal of perfection in him, however. Papa, do you want to send me sixteen thousand miles away from you?"

"My darling, I am tired and sick of a squatter's life. Nothing would please me better than to realise my fortune, and return to Europe."

"Oh, papa, I would rather die than marry that dreadful man!"

"Well, I didn't like him at first, as you well know. It takes some time to get thoroughly acquainted with some people's inner worth, and he is a case in point. What think you? He concealed his rank, because he wished to be loved for himself alone! Doesn't that touch you, Lily?"

"No, because it seems to me that he concealed the only thing that he possibly could be loved for," rejoined Lily, contemptuously.

"My child, don't be so truly nonsensical in your ideas. I have set my heart on seeing you a peeress, in allying my wealth to your husband's title; the partnership is not an unusual one in these days. I shall be thankful when the moment arrives to turn our backs on Australia for ever. What with droughts, floods, bush-fires, bushrangers, and the constant smashing of the Melbourne banks, this place is not the paradise that some folks make it out to be. I've twenty thousand pounds now hid away in my iron safe, because there's not a single bank that I can trust with it."

"Well, papa, surely we can make arrangements and go to Europe without this Captain Montague Vavasseur being mixed up with it?"

"Lily, how perverse and obstinate you are. I trust that this dislike to a marriage with the Honourable Montague Vavasseur, is not occasioned by any prior and less worthy attachment! There has been a trooper fellow hovering about the station all the morning, asking some of our people how you are. How could he have got to know that anything was the matter with you, and how would it concern him in any way?"

"It might have been Mr. Conquest, papa, and if it was, you can't forget that at one time he was on terms of close intimacy with the entire family."

"Before they ran a mucker. Circumstances alter cases, Lily. So if this fellow was Tom Conquest the trooper, remember that your father would rather follow you to your grave than take you to church to give you away to a beggarly trap with a pay of eight shillings a day. By-the-by, you've never told me yet where you got that centipede-bite. There are very few in the house—I haven't seen one, in fact, for months. It occurs to me now, that I missed you for a considerable time during the evening, and heard more than one of your young friends enquiring after you."

"Oh, papa, I rushed out of doors to try and get a little fresh air, it was so stiflingly hot within; and now do please leave me alone for a little while, for what you have told me has put me quite in a fever."

And Lily straightway turned her flushed face to the wall to avoid all further questioning.

"Well, think over what I have said as calmly and as quietly as you can, and endeavour to come to a sensible decision thereon. You've heard the saying that young people *think* old people to be fools, but old people *know* young people to be so. Thereon pondering, come to the conclusion that your father knows better what is good for you than you do yourself, and bend yourself to his will as a dutiful and affectionate child should do."

And with these words Mr. M'Pherson quitted the room.

"I wonder if he noticed the earrings?" thought Lily to herself; and then she burst out crying, for, though she loved her father dearly, she was nevertheless not a little afraid of him also, for he could be a very violent man when his strong will was persistently thwarted, and on one occasion, in a fit of ungovernable anger, he had even lashed his beautiful child with a stock-whip.

"I'll be true to you, Tom, as long as mind and flesh can stand it," soliloquised Lily to herself as the painful remembrance of this event occurred to her. "But, oh! if papa beats me into marrying this stranger. I'm sure that I shall give way before very long, for I am such a little coward, and do dread pain so."

CHAPTER XIV.

THE BUSHRANGERS AT MITTAGARRA.

An hour or two later the squatter and his guest are sitting under the passiflora-covered verandah of the house, smoking cigars and drinking cold whisky-and-water.

Captain the Honourable Montague Vavasseur has again opened his heart to his host, and has received a good deal of vague encouragement in return, and now both men, thoroughly satisfied with themselves and with each other, lean back in their easy, cane-seated armchairs, and, shaded from the blood-red sun, whose lurid glare quivers over the yellow-brown plains which stretch away in the distance far as the eye can reach, busy each with his own thoughts of the future.

The cigars are smoked out and fresh ones lighted, but still the castle-building goes on; in fact, it is too hot to do much else. Even the cattle lay under the scant shade of the gums and iron barks with their tongues lolling out for lack of water, the birds of the air shelter themselves in the leafy walks, and nature in a strange unnatural stillness seemed to be awaiting with hushed awe either an earthquake or the blast of the last trump.

All at once, however, there appear upon the scene—one around either angle of the verandah—a pair of bearded ruffians clad in ragged blue jumpers open at the chest, still more ragged moleskin trousers, blucher boots worn all out of shape, and battered and weather-stained billy-cock hats slouched well over their eyes.

The only things bright about them are their eyes and the barrels of the formidable-looking pistols which they grasp in a threatening manner as they approach.

"Good gwacious!" exclaimed Captain Montague Vavasseur, and in an instant he has slipped in at an open window and made good his escape—at all events, for the present.

But the squatter is either slower of movement or else scorns to avail himself of the same ingenious ruse.

"Hulloa! you infernal scoundrels, what do you want here?" he asked, at the same time picking up the empty whisky bottle for a weapon.

"We don't want to hurt anybody. We feels as mild as lambs, don't us, Jim? We only dropped in on a little matter o' business."

"I don't transact business with men who approach me with arms in their hands. Put up those pistols, and then say what you require."

"We requires to know where our Coppen is, for one

thing. It's come to our ears that you and he had a bit of a shindy t'other night, he by hisself, an' you with three to back yer. He aren't turned up since at our usual rendayvoo, and so we've comed to know whether you laid him by the heels or runned him to earth, or what was the upshot on it."

"If you call Ned Kelly your captain, I'm sorry to say he got away from us. I imagine he was badly hit, though, and as he hasn't turned up, I trust that he has died, alone and untended with an ant-hill for a pillow, in the loneliest recesses of the bush, like the wolf that he was."

"Well, those are nice compliments to pay our head boss within the hearing of his two most particular pals. Shall we put a bullet in his crop to teach him civility to his betters, eh, Lardy Bill?"

"Lord! no, Lanky Jim. I feels so soft-hearted, you can't think. Which way did our noble capting ride, Mr. McPherson, Esquire?"

"Towards the ranges at first, and then he turned off at an angle towards the Ten Mile," answered the squatter, savagely.

"Ah, that was to avoid the traps. They was pretty thick over the lower spurs of the ranges about that time. The capting's a 'cute un, and I guess we'll find whereabouts he have planted his blessed self now. His daughter be in a rare way about 'im, reg'lar demented like."

"His daughter? Has the infernal scoundrel a child, then?"

"A 'dopted one, 'tis said. The capting found her a new-born babby in her dead mother's arms. Long while ago it must ha' been, for the gal's fourteen year old now if a day. I've heard tell that the poor woman was trying to find out some infernal scoundrel of a swell squatter cove, who had seduced her with promises ov marriage when her time comed on sudden, an' that Ned Kelly, riding up as she war dying ov exposure an' wet an' cold, swore that he'd be a father to her little 'un, which he hev bin all along."

"This is a strange tale. Did you ever hear the name of the woman who—who died? If not, what does Kelly call her child?" asked the squatter, much paler and more agitated at the bushranger's admissions than he had been a minute before at sight of their levelled pistols.

"Never heard tell of her mother's name. Did you, Lanky Jim?"

"No, nor don't want to either. Just cut this palaver short, Lardy Bill."

"All right, don't be in a hurry, old 'un. Don't know the woman's name, sir but the girl goes by that of Rose, and a handsome, bonny lass she is too, only none of us dare so much as to cast a hye on her."

"Is she tall or short, dark or fair—tell me what she is like?"

"I can't describe a gal. Perhaps if I was to say she was a feminine, juvenile, an werry handsome, a flattering edition of your own self, I'd be drawing the best picter as is possible. You might stand for her father main well, and if you was so everyone 'ud see the likeness atwixt you."

"Come, stow all this rot. Do you want to keep barneying here until the long-legged cove, as slipped through the window, brings half-a-dozen of the station hands down upon us? Come, just you stop it, Lardy Bill. I came to stow the swag, not to yabber yabber about a gal," and Lanky Jim twecked his macaw-bill with angry impatience as he concluded.

"Lord love the man! how impatient he is surely. None of the station hands can be down on us under half-an-hour, an' by that time we'll be far away. Howsomever, as short reckonings is said to make long friends, Mr. 'Pherson will now doubtless conduct us to his iron safe, inside which a little bird has sung to us that there are twenty thousand pounds locked up," and Lardy Bill bowed ironically.

"Villains! would you rob me of such an immense amount, even if I had it?"

"Ay, or double as much D——! if money is the root of all evil, as the parsons preach, you should thank us for delivering you from it. Anyhow, it's your gold or our lead—one of the two; and a fortin aren't so much use to a dead man," growled Macaw-bill.

Andrew M'Pherson saw that the two men were thoroughly in earnest at last, and that it was as much as his life was worth not to yield to their demands.

"Come along with me, if it must be so; but as my daughter is very ill, I will ask you to make no more noise than necessary," said he, therefore.

And, with a bushranger on each side of him, he entered the house.

"Surely Captain Vavasseur will turn up at the right moment, and prevent these fellows from decamping with the spoil," thought the squatter to himself. "If he's wise he'll thrust a weapon into my hand as well, and then we'll be able to fight the rascals on equal terms, confound them!"

To his intense dismay and disgust, Captain Vavasseur did not turn up, however.

The men forced him to conduct them to where the iron chest was, stood over him whilst he unlocked it, and then helped themselves to all the bank notes and specie that it contained.

Having done this they forced him down into a chair, and bound him thereto with the tassels and cords of the window curtains, and, for their better security, locking the room door on the outside and taking the key away with them.

Andrew M'Pherson was in a terrible pucker at the way in which he had been robbed of so much treasure, and the non-appearance of Captain the Honourable Montague Vavasseur.

"The man must be a poltroon and a coward," muttered he between his set teeth, "to desert a fellow in that fashion. I'll tell him a bit of my mind when I next come across him."

Hardly had the words escaped his lips when the object thereof unlocked the door and entered the room, fairly bristling all over with weapons.

"Well, you're a pretty fellow, and no mistake," said the squatter, angrily.

"My dear sir, I rushed where I thought you would naturally have sped also, to defend to the last drop of my heart's blood the threshold of your daughter's chamber. As, however, the ruffians approached not, I at last deserted my post, and came to seek you. Where are the ruffians?"

"Far enough off by this time, and my twenty thousand pounds with them," growled the squatter. "Please to remember, when bushrangers turn up the next time, that they aren't a class of fellows who have any design on the opposite gender, unless, indeed, it happens to be a racing mare. Pillage is their sole object, confound 'em! Just undo me, will you? and I'll get up another bottle of whisky. It's no use pursuing 'em, for they are sure to be well mounted, and their haunts are not a score of miles away.

CHAPTER XV.

REVEALS A BREACH OF HONOUR AMONG THIEVES.

IF we have made the visit of the bushrangers to Mittagarra station rather a quiet affair, we have at all events erred on the side of truth.

Bloodshed seldom or never accompanies such visits, unless there is some grudge to be satisfied.

The author of this narrative was a visitor at Balboa station at the time it was stuck up by Morgan, who popped in as quietly one night as though he had been a friend of the family, requested a good supper to be laid before him, invited the ladies to play and sing to him, enjoyed a prolonged game at chess with his host (moving the pieces with his left hand whilst he held his revolver in his right), locked his entertainers in their respective bedrooms, when the time for retiring came, with a cheerful good-night, called them up to give him his breakfast at early dawn, and an hour later rode away on a three-year-old racing colt worth a thousand guineas, laden with every portable valuable about the place.

Of course had opposition been offered affairs would have turned out very differently, but members of the bushranger fraternity generally pounce down on a farm or station at a time when no resistance is to be apprehended, and then, as long as they are allowed to have everything their own way, they are as amiable as a bear when eating honey, especially after making a good haul.

On the present occasion Lardy Bill and Lanky Jim rode way from Mittagarra well pleased with themselves and the world in general. Their horses they had left concealed in the shrubbery, within a stone's throw of the house, so that, as M'Pherson had told Captain Vavasseur, pursuit (with the wooded ranges so close at hand for them to fly to for shelter and concealment) would have been worse than useless.

"A good job, that," said Lardy Bill to his mate as they headed their horses towards the Ten Mile. "A very fine haul for the two ov us."

"Yes, but not so much when divided between a score," grunted Jim.

"And why should it be divided between a score, mate? We two got the information out of the drunken shepherd who was knocking down his cheque at 'The Bunyip,' and we two did the whole blessed thing thing 'atween us, so why should we go blowing about it, and letting all the world know?"

"Lardy Bill, I won't say as what you haint sensible in the abstract, but you forget the capting. He'd precious soon hev us lynched on to a gum-tree branch if he found out we was a working on the cross, and not on the share-an'-share-alike principle—he would so."

"Now that we've feathered our nests so well, why shouldn't we ha' done with the capting, and the other boys as well, Lanky Jim? Ten thousand apiece! why, what a shine we could cut in the old country with such fortins, if we could only once get clear away from this blasted land of hot winds, moskitters, and sandy blight. We could set up a big pub in Whitechapel and do a roaring trade, my eye, we could.

' Oh, there's something so sweet in the crib I was born in,
And there's no-hing. I'm sure to com are with it here;
How delightful the cry, 'Buy my sprats!' all the morning,
And the voice of the pothov as comes round with the beer.
If here I stop, perhaps I'll be scragged, there's no knowing—
So to Lond'n's crack fakements I'll get back again;
And if I but live till the next wessel's going,
I'll be off to old England and Petticoat-lane.

"Oh, I'd like to drop in now to old Harry Potter's,
Where they serve up the 'slap-bang' so stunning and be—
Oh, could I but get at those sheeps' heads and trotters,
Jumping Moses! I'd walk into them like a shot;
I'd satisfy soon my most craving desires—
Do my penn'orth of pudding again an! a ain;
And slip into the fried fish of old Mother Myers,
The corpilent Jewess of Petticoat-lane."

"Umph! that's quite enough of that," grunted Lanky Jim, "You've got a woice as ud charm the heart of a wheelbarrow, Bill; but then you see I ain't a wheelbarrow, and what's more to the pint, I've got no taste for poetry or music. Whilst you've been a philandering with the muses, one or two werry sensible notions has crept into my pate. I approves ov all your propositions, Bill, an' you may consider that motion as carried. But I rises now to make an amendment. Why shouldn't we add another three thousand to our present fortin, mate, by selling the capting to the traps? Answer me that, Bill?"

"Why, you infernal villin, you vouldn't surely? And yet I'm blessed if it's half a bad idea, Lanky Jim. The capting must be a great plague to all honest folks, and so ve might look upon it in the light of a duty as we owes to society. Society hev bin werry good to us, Jim, and if you really think as ve could square the obligation in that manner, why, as an Englishman an' a Christian——"

"Stow all that rot!" interrupted Lanky Jim, impatiently. "An extra fifteen hundred each aren't to be

sneezed at. Not but what I subscribes to honour amongst thieves, as long as it's observed on all sides But who first broke the code? Why, the capting his blessed self. Vot did he go all alone to bail up the coach for? Why, it stands to reason, to pocket the whole of the swag unbeknown to us. A man who'd serve his pals in that mean way would betray 'em just as lief. We'll be beforehand with him, Lardy Bill, and just cop the reward."

"Vell, Jim, I'm a soft-hearted chap as can't say no to a mate, but I wonder where the deuce we are to look for the capting?"

"Oh, we'll find him, never fear. It's a bargain, eh? No backing out?"

"Criss-cross on it, there!" and, thrusting a very dirty finger into his mouth, Lardy Bill marked a cross on his throat with the wet digit, exclaiming—"Strike me dead if I tell a lie, Lanky Jim."

"That'll do," chuckled Macaw-bill. "I know well that a Lancashire-born man won't break that oath. We must get ourselves up as a couple of swagsmen or shearers, mate, for it'll serve no good purpose our being recognised by either traps or beak, for, though there's a free parding offered to any members of the band as betrays the capting, yet it seems to me as it ud be safer to do it in a private kerpacity; for, as the public characters that we are, something might be remembered agin us, an what we've just a-done might crop up, too, werry awkward."

"If anything did crop up to hinder our making immediate tracks out of the cussed country some ov the boys would assuredly cut our throats for us. I say, Ned sold to the beaks, what'll become ov the gal? A fine lass, Jim, an if I was but a marrying man——"

"Stow that. I say, Bill, couldn't we make sommut out ov the wench as well? She knows where all the capting's riches is planted, depend on it. She'd pint it out with a knife at her throat, maybe."

"It stands to reason as she would, in course it do, Jim."

"Then there's another augermentation on our riches, Lardy Bill. When we hev copped the spoil, we must slit the gal's throat to stop her tongue wagging."

"I puts a veto on that, Jim. I won't have the lass injured."

"Nonsense, beauty's only skin deep. Her blood's the same colour as a sheep's."

"I don't care, I won't have a hair of her head injured, I tell you."

"Then maybe you'll live to regret it, Lardy Bill." And Jim at once sank into a dudgeon, as he ever did when he was crossed in aught.

"Ay, my lad," he muttered, "I'll silence the wench whether you likes or no, when the time comes, and you dare not split on your only pal. And when we gets to England—if we sets up in business together—it strikes me as one of the parduers will die suddenly one night—of appleplexy, mebbe—an' a will will be found leaving all his property to the tother. Ay, Lardy Bill looks just a fit subject for appleplexy, an' I'll make him carry on at the brandy-bottle, doctored a bit it maybe, till grim death carries him off."

These pleasant reflections beguiled another six miles or so of the journey, Lardy Bill being sunk in equally deep thought, when all at once they were recalled to themselves by a voice hailing them with—

"Hi, there, mates! Lanky Jim, Lardy Bill! Hi, there, I say!"

Both men at once glanced in the direction of the sound. A glance was sufficient.

"It's the capting!" exclaimed both in a breath.

CHAPTER XVI

A SCHEME OF DEVILISH VENGEANCE.

IT was indeed Ned Kelly, lying just inside the open door of the shepherd's hut, into which he had crawled for concealment three nights ago.

He looked miserably thin, and hungry and careworn.

"Hullo, governor, we was a-looking for *you*," sang out Bill, as he and Jim rolled out of their saddles and led their horses towards the hut.

"I though that some of you would have been by long ago. I hid here from the traps the night of the gold escort robbery."

"Did you get any tidy pickings aboard Cobb's mail, capting?"

It was Lanky Jim who put the question, and his grey fishy eye gleamed greedily as he did so.

But Ned Kelly answered him—

"What I *did* pick up will be apportioned fairly when I return amongst you. I've not stayed away from our haunt in the ranges from choice. I was wounded in the attack on the coach, and had to fly for my life. Landed here, I started off the horse, lest its presence should betray my whereabouts, and when, the following night, I started off myself to return on foot, I plunged my left leg into a wombat hole, not a dozen yards away, and gave it such a wrench that I was glad to creep back here on all fours."

"I say, boss, it's lucky for you that shepherds and hut-keepers, stockmen, and station hands in general, have most of 'em sloped to the diggings," laughed Lardy Bill. "You'd have been nailed, else, to a certainty."

"And as helpless to defend himself as a sucking-babe," added Lardy Jim, more to elicit information than aught else.

"Not quite that," said the ironclad bushranger, bending on his subordinate a keen and searching glance. "I have a ball through my right shoulder, but my pistols are both loaded, and I can make as sure of shooting a man with my left hand as with my right. But here, I am answering questions instead of putting them. When did you last see my daughter Rose?"

"This blessed morning, and a werry white Rose she looked," answered Bill.

"I'll soon restore her colour to her. Thank God she has not left the Lookout-hut—to, to search for me I mean, of course. She—she might have come to some harm if she had. Well, I'm as hungry as a wolf. Roots and berries don't fill a man much. Whose run am I on? I don't know much about this side the ranges. What station's that over there?"

"Mittagarra—M'Pherson's station," answered Lardy Bill.

"What! Andrew M'Pherson's?" exclaimed Ned Kelly, with almost a shriek of delight. "Is the infer—— is the squatter at home, mates?"

"How the deuce should we know?" responded Lanky Jim, as he bestowed on his accomplice a warning look. "You may be sure that he is at home though, for squatters don't leave their stations at times like these. There'd be a general sloping of all hands to the diggings if they did."

"Do you think this hot wind will blow itself out before night?" was Ned Kelly's next question, as he looked anxiously and eagerly around.

"Not much chance of it, I should say, from the sandy redness on the sky in the direction that it's coming from," rejoined Lardy Bill.

An expression of fierce exultation crossed the haggard countenance of the Ironclad Bushranger.

"Nor do I think it will lull," said he. "Now listen to me, Lardy Bill and Lanky Jim. Ride back to our haunt in the ranges as fast as your nags will carry you, and bid Rose be of good cheer, for that I will be back to-night. You needn't tell her that I am wounded, for it would only cause her to fret needlessly, poor girl," and Ned sighed.

"Lord bless us, capting, aren't you a-going to return with us then?" queried Jim.

"No; I have other matters to attend to first. One of you come back with a led horse at ten o'clock to-night to take me away. Ha, ha, ha! there will be plenty of light to find out the hut by," and Ned chuckled, grinning to himself.

"Not any too much light, capting, for the moon's on the wane," said Bill.

"Well, well, there will be the stars, won't there?" answered Ned, his usual caution having by now returned to him. "See that you bear in mind all that I have said. Make it five minutes to ten to be here, and then you are certain not to be *over* the hour. I don't think we are short of gold watches in the ranges, eh, lads? For the present just leave me a fig of tobacco to stay my hunger and a box of matches to light my pipe with, and I'll last out the day very well; especially as I have pleasant thoughts to amuse me."

"May we make so bold as to ax what those pleasant thoughts are, capting?"

It was Lanky Jim who put the question, but the answer that he got was one that effectually shut him up.

"You needn't snap a fellow's head off, capting," he muttered, apologetically; and, two figs of Barrett's twist and a box of lucifers being handed to Ned, the two subordinates hastened to take their departure, for the Ironclad Bushranger knew how to exact implicit obedience from his men—at all events, whilst they were within sound of his voice or the sinister glare of his eagle eye.

"I wonder what's the natur' ov the little game that he's bent on now?" said Lardy Bill to Lanky Jim, when they'd got a little distance away.

"Blessed if I know, and darned if I much care," retorted that worthy. "One thing, he couldn't be in a better place for us to sell him to the traps. Keep it dark, Lardy Bill; keep it dark from the boys, I caution you."

"No fear of me blabbing. And so you think things are working round, Jim?"

(To be continued.)

THE "ANONYMA" SERIES OF POPULAR NOVELS.
PICTURE BOARDS.   PUBLISHED AT 2/-

NED KELLY

THE
IRONCLAD
AUSTRALIAN BUSHRANGER

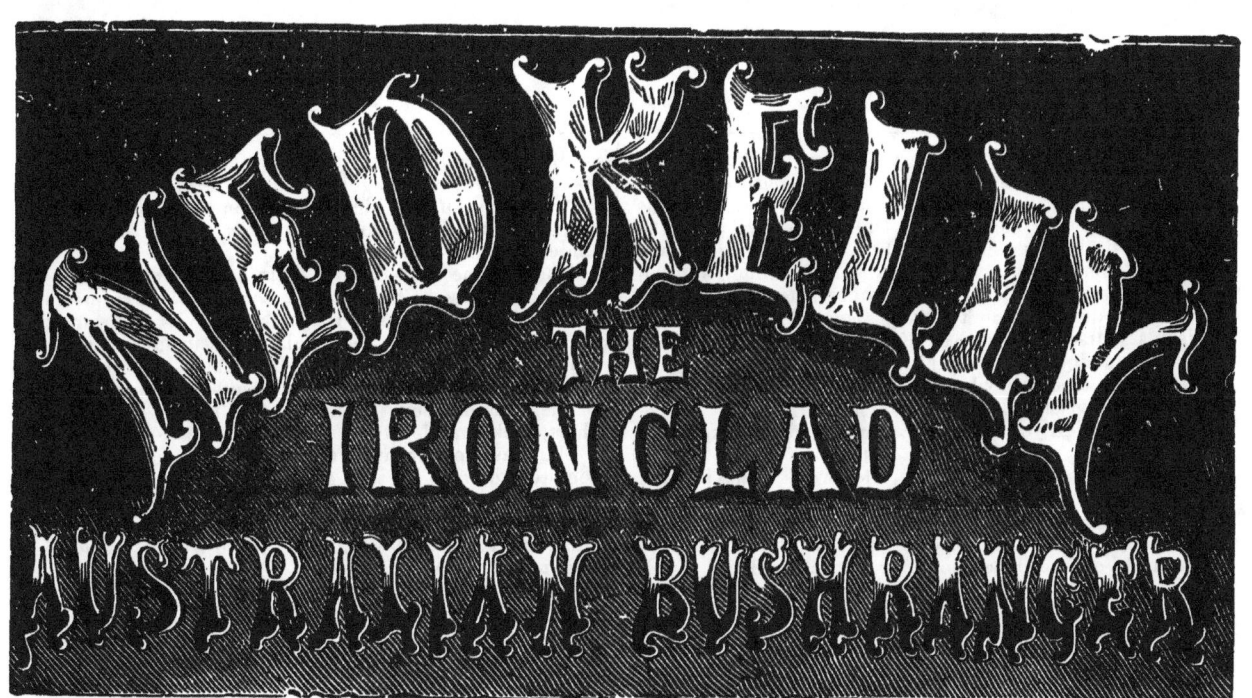

NO 3,

"Working round! Why, they hev worked round already. Well, bring the traps from Carragal up to the hut to-night. But we'll keep ahead on 'em, and settle his hash before they comes up. Did you notice how the weather-boards was shrunk, Bill? We can draw a bead-line on him from the back of the hut through a dozen gaping fissures. You see he's of the same value dead as living, an' dead men can't split on their pals. We couldn't disguise ourselves past Ned Kelly's recognition, an' he'd be wild enough to say anythink about us when once he knowed as twas we who had sold him. We can easily tell the Joeys as he let fly at us first."

"Lanky Jim, you're the devil's own godson," exclaimed Lardy Bill.

"If so be as that's the case, then we're twins, Brother Smut. But there mustn't be any quarrel or disagreement between pot and kettle in this case. We must force the girl Rose to disclose where the capting's spoil is all hid away afore we starts on the expedition, for all the gold and jewels in the world wouldn't tempt me to trust myself up in them ranges when once the deed as we contemplates is done. The boys would skin us alive, or roast us over slow fires, if once they could lay hands on us. That's why we'll hev to cook the girl's goose when once we've forced her to point out where all the swag's planted. What must be must be."

"The gal shan't be hurt, Jim: no, not a hair ov her head."

"Pooh-pooh, man! Don't be a muddle-head."

"I won't have the wench hurt in any way, Jim: so there. No, nor insulted either, as much as by a look. It's bad enough to make the lass a beggar, though her pretty face is a fortin that neither you nor I can take away, and I hope as it will get her a rich husband and a good un. We'll make her take an awful oath not to betray us, and if she won't do that we'll lock her inside the hut—ay, and gag her too, if need be; but nothing more serious—no, not for worlds."

Lanky Jim tried to shake Bill's "cussed stupidity," as he phrased it, but all in vain, and so he relapsed into a surly mood again, nor rediscovered his tongue until they had reached their home in the ranges.

*   *   *   *   *

Meanwhile, Ned Kelly remained in the hut, little guessing that plots were being hatched against his life by the men in whom he placed almost implicit confidence.

There he lay, gnawing twist tobacco to stay the wild cravings of his hunger, and all the while gloating over his anticipated vengeance.

"Ay," he muttered to himself, "if the north wind but lasts, as I feel sure that it will, I'll roll a sheet of flame down upon your homestead, Andrew M'Pherson, that shall give you and yours a foretaste of hell. If you manage to escape, it will yet render you a houseless beggar, and it will take a swift stock-horse to carry you out of its reach with life. Your flocks and herds will be sure to fall a prey. Ha, ha, ha! and I don't believe there's more than one chance in a hundred that anything living except the birds of air will get clear off, for the conflagration will rush onward at the rate of fifteen miles an hour at the very least, if only the hot wind does not lull. Ah, my girl, the one and only love of my life, even though Andrew M'Pherson's victim, you shall be fearfully avenged to-night, and all the devils in hell shall dance with glee."

Little did Ned Kelly guess, as he indulged in this rhapsody, that she whom he loved, at all events as his own child, Rose Casey, was at that very instant sheltered at Mittagarra station.

CHAPTER XVII.

ROSE CASEY A GUEST AT MITTAGARRA.

RETURN we now to Rose Casey, the adopted child of the lawless bushranger; to the fair and lovely maiden who, twenty years later, still looking a mere girl, was destined to pass as his sister; while he, in truth an elderly man of fifty years and upwards, was so wonderful in his strength, his sprightliness, his agility, and his disguises that, to the last moment of his life, ay, even on the scaffold, he was reported in all the colonial papers to be considerably under thirty.

Had anyone half-an-hour after he was cut down but peered into the coffin in which they laid him (a privilege which was extended only to the author of this narrative as his captor), he or she might have imagined the pale, cold corpse lying there to have been the grandfather of the apparently young man who had been standing in the dock of the Supreme Court House on trial for his life but a few short weeks previously.

We must not, however, anticipate. We have only been tempted to do so to this extent lest they who have read the report of the trial in the columns of the colonial newspaper press, or cheap and inaccurate biographies of this remarkable man written by those who know nothing about him, might be disposed to question our data or even our facts, both of which are indisputable.

It will be remembered that Ned Kelly, on bidding Rose farewell ere he set forth to attack the gold escort and Cobb's mail, had commanded her, in case he did not return to the bark-hut within twenty-four hours, to conclude that he was either dead or captured, and to make the best of her way to Melbourne, with as large an amount of treasure concealed about her person as she could conveniently carry.

But Rose did not follow these injunctions. She clung to the hut day after day, hoping against hope that the man whom she regarded and loved as a father might yet return to it and her.

She might not have made up her mind to quit it even when she did but for a dreadful dream that Lardy Bill and Lanky Jim broke in upon her when she was asleep, tortured her by roasting her over a slow, fire until she confessed to them where Ned's own share of treasure was planted, and then barbarously murdered her, so that, as they phrased it, "she should have no chance of splitting on them."

Rose put faith in dreams, for all people are inclined to be superstitious who live in trackless wilds or grim and sombre forests where nature clothes herself with solitude and her immensity.

She therefore no longer dared to remain alone at the *Lookout Station*, and so, as the glowing sun began to sink in the west, she said good-bye to it with many tears, and made her way towards the plains.

She carried a brace of small loaded pistols, concealed about her person, and much treasure in gold and unset jewels as well. She was mounted on Swiftsure, and made up her mind to reach Melbourne, though it was ninety miles distant, without a halt.

Perhaps there are no horses in the world possessed of so much *bottom* and endurance as those reared in Australia. Who would think of riding a grass fed beast ninety miles at a stretch in England? What English horse, in fact, would do it? But such a journey is no uncommon feat in Australia. When on the lookout for bushrangers, the author once rode a single nag seventy miles a-day for five consecutive days, without injuring him in the least degree; but it must be remembered the path was green turf, and not as *Punch's* "'Arry" has it—"'Orrid 'ard roads."

But though Rose Casey intended to make Melbourne in a single stage, she was not destined to do anything of the kind.

In fretting about Ned Kelly and her abandoned home, she did not particularly attend to the path that she was pursuing. The consequence was that she got out of the lower spurs of the ranges at quite a contrary point to that which she should have done, and so for more than an hour she essayed to strike the main road in vain.

At each cast that she made she got further and further afield, in fact, and as the hot wind, laden with fine brick-coloured dust, was still fiercely blowing, she soon began to suffer from thirst.

in vain she struggled against the inconvenience, which soon became a positive torture.

Not a creek or a waterhole was to be seen, and so, catching sight of a white-roofed station, Rose resolved to ride up to it and ask for water, both for herself and nag, and to be put in the right direction for Melbourne as well.

What if they did question her? she could make some evasive reply or plausible excuse for travelling alone at such an hour, and they would not dare to detain her by force.

So she galloped Swiftsure past the woolshed and the dockyard, through the Home Paddock, and right up to the cockatoo fence that surrounded the peach orchard and the little vineyard.

She was quietly rounding this when she heard a voice exclaim—

"What, is that Annie Martin, and alone? Can it be possible?" and at the same moment a slim and graceful figure, clad in white, came forth from behind a tree and approached her.

"I'm not she whom you imagine. I am a stranger and a lost traveller. I've ridden up to beg some water for myself and horse, and to be put in the right direction for Melbourne," answered Rose Casey.

"You mustn't go any further to-night, whoever you are," said Lily M'Pherson. "You don't mean to say that you are travelling down to Melbourne alone? Why, I declare, you are a girl no older than myself, and how beautiful you are too. I hope you aren't a ghost."

As darkness was rapidly veiling the scene and such a lovely and mysterious visitor had never before turned up in that region at such an hour, Lily's doubts may be pardoned.

But Rose Casey put them at rest by saying, "If I was a ghost I don't suppose I should feel thirsty, or be such a simpleton as to lose my way. No, I'm a fellow-mortal, and, I'm sure, look much more earthly than you do."

"Then if you are a mortal you will have to stay at Mittagarra all night. It will be dark in five minutes, and there is no moon. You would have to pass through the Black Forest too, and might be set upon by the Ironclad Bushranger or some of his band. Come, dear, I will go with you to the stables myself, and then take you in to supper, it will be just ready. You don't mind sleeping with me?"

"Do I mind sleeping with a lovely and kind little angel? you should ask. But no, I cannot stay. 'Tis impossible, impossible!"

"But what makes you in such a hurry? No trouble I hope?"

"Yes, yes, I—I have lost a very dear friend, my only friend on earth, in fact. That—that is why I am in such haste to reach Melbourne."

"Oh, I am so sorry. But do come in, if only for an hour, for rest and refreshment. I am sure my father will send one of our stockmen to see you at all events safely through the forest. How brave you must be to dare to travel alone of a night. Come, dear, come along. I will take no refusal. An hour is but a very little while."

Rose Casey was persuaded. She had never been inside a rich squatter's house in her life, nor had she ever been addressed with words of kindness by one of her own sex. The situation had its charm and she could not resist it.

"All right," she said, "I'll stay an hour, if you wish it; but you must not try to keep me any longer."

Lily was over the fence in a twinkling. Her first action was to grasp Rose's hand, her next to pat Swiftsure's snowy hide.

"Come along, said she, "the stables are close at hand. I'd call a man to take your horse, but we've not too many about at present, for they've nearly all run away to the diggings. However, I daresay we can manage."

They did manage very well, and five minutes later Lily M'Pherson led the lovely brunette (whom she little imagined to be her half-sister) into the house to present her to their joint father.

At that instant it was that Ned Kelly, far away in the deserted hut in the bush, struck match after match and threw them, flaring brightly, in amongst the long dry grass and the little patches of tea-tree scrub that grew close up to the unhinged hut door.

The herbage ignited almost immediately, and the flames began to spread and rush down the hill before the wind.

In an hour that conflagration would be miles in depth and breadth, and Ned chuckled to himself at the thought that every inmate of Mittagarra was doomed by it to a terrible death.

CHAPTER XVIII.

MR. M'PHERSON SEES A GHOST.

LILY M'PHERSON was prepared to witness some surprise on her father's part at the arrival of such a visitor at such an hour, but she was wholly astounded at the manner in which he did receive her.

The squatter was deep in his weekly *Australasian* as they entered the large and sumptuously-furnished dining-room, and at first he did not look up therefrom; but as they drew near he exclaimed—

"Well, Lily, I suppose your advent announces supper?" and, throwing his paper down, he peered up beamingly through his gold-rimmed spectacles.

In an instant his ruddy cheeks blanched to the ashy whiteness that distinguishes those of a corpse, his lips parted, his eyes opened to their widest extent, his hands closed around the arms of his chair with a convulsive clutch, and he gasped with accents of horror—

"Lily—Lily! Great heavens! do you see that you are not alone? Lily, I say, do you or do you not see the thing that is clinging to your arm? You have brought the dead in with you, child; the dead that have been buried for well-nigh fifteen years. Or—or—is it my conscience that is brewing this beautiful yet horrid phantom? If so, the hour of my own fate is near. Lily, do you see anything standing by your side?"

"Dear father, what ails you? You must have been asleep in your chair and had a fearful dream. Nay, you cannot even yet be wide awake. This young lady is no ghost; she is a traveller who has lost her way, and is our guest for an hour, that is all."

"No, no, no! It may appear so to you, but she looked just like that before you were born. It is the ghost of Rose Casey, and it has come for me," exclaimed the squatter, covering his eyes with his hands, and shuddering with horror.

"What's your father's name, girl?" asked Rose, sharply, at this juncture.

"M'Pherson. Andrew M'Pherson; did you not know?" answered Lily, hardly knowing what she said, for she could not comprehend the scene at all.

"I think you'd better tend him. He looks as though he was going to have a fit," rejoined Rose, coldly and icily; and as Lily flew to her father's side, her half-sister glided out of the room just as though she was indeed the ghost that she had been taken to be.

Arrived at the door she paused, thrust her hand into her bosom and pulled forth one of her little pistols.

"Would it not be a good deed to slay my mother's murderer?" she muttered to herself, between her tightly-clenched, strong, white teeth; and for an instant the squatter's life really hung in the balance, for the beautiful barbarian was a dead shot.

Happily, ere her finger could curl around the trigger, her true woman's nature asserted itself.

"I can't do it," she half sobbed, and turning round she tore through the passage and out of the house at the back making her way direct for the stables.

Before Lily M'Pherson, in her new-born anxiety concerning her father, was even aware of the fact that she had quitted the room, Rose was in the saddle again, and riding rapidly away from the station

She had not slaked her burning thirst, and yet it no longer oppressed her.

She had not the slightest idea how she should discover the road that led to Melbourne; but she thought little of that either.

Her sole desire was to get as quickly away from the house that held her mother's betrayer and murderer as possible; she felt that she should not be able to breathe freely till such time as her horse's hoofs did not even spurn his land. Oh, her wrath and her hatred were very bitter!

Suddenly, however, whilst looking around for some particular beacon or well-known landmark to steer by, she caught sight of a huge surge of fire, rolling with resistless impetus down the wooded slopes about five miles away, and bearing directly towards the station.

"Good God! If none of the station hands are up and about, and there is no one to give them warning, they will be lost!" gasped Rose.

For an instant she almost exulted at the fate that seemed to be rushing down from the ranges upon her mother's destroyer and all his flocks and herds and other worldly possessions.

But then she thought of the beautiful young girl who had spoken so lovingly to her, and had seemed disposed to show her so much kindness.

"Oh, I can't let her perish without warning. She is not answerable for the sins that her father committed before she was born. I will ride back and save her, even though I lose my own life in the attempt."

Wheeling Swiftsure round, she lost no time in putting her humane project into execution.

The horse had had abundance of water, and was thoroughly refreshed, so that he bore her with the speed of the wind itself.

There was no time to ride round to the side of the house, so Rose put her steed at the garden fence, and thereafter guided him straight across the brilliantly-laid-out flower beds, reckless of what damage he wrought, for she knew well that a far more fell destroyer was near at hand.

And now she had gained the verandah, and was about to shriek out the name of Lily, when a voice exclaimed close by—

"Good gwacious! what a shock you gave me. Oh my! I never!" and Captain Montague Vavasseur rose from out the depths of a cane armchair, in which he had been comfortably dozing 'neath the starlight.

"I want to see Miss Lily instantly. Call her, if you please."

"Oh gwacious! what's the matter? Who are you, my dear? Oh, weally!"

"Will you do my bidding, you gaping fool (we have over and over again declared Rose to be a barbarian), or must I ride right into the house?"

"Oh lor'! oh lor'! here's a go! You are a female bushranger, I do believe. Help! Murder! Fire! Miss Lily! Fire! Murder! Help!"

"That'll do," said Rose, "that'll soon bring her. Go on! go on!"

But the gallant captain, instead of going on, ran off.

He darted backwards through an open French window, much as he had done on the occasion of the visit of Lardy Bill and Lanky Jim, and disappeared.

So Rose now began to scream out the name of Lily with all the strength of her lungs, at the same time giving the information as to whereabouts she was to be found.

To her intense relief, she presently heard the swift pattering of feet and the next instant her half-sister was by her side.

"Spring up behind me on Swiftsure," said Rose, excitedly. "Ask me not why or wherefore, but do as I bid you. Not a moment is to be lost."

"No, no," answered Lily; "I cannot leave my father. Somehow or other, you have frightened him. He is ill. I cannot make it out. I can make nothing out. You have

brought some dreadful horror or mystery beneath our happy roof. Oh, heaven! what can it all mean?"

"Lily, this is no time for explanations. I want to save your life; do not, by delay, render it impossible. A bush-fire is rushing down on the station from the ranges. If you are short of hands you can't drive the fire-plough, and so stop its advance. The conflagration, when it once reaches the grassy plains, will speed on at the rate of twenty miles an hour before this fierce north wind. Lily, I hate your name and race, and not without reason, but I love you, and would fain save you, if you will give me but the chance. So, for heaven's sake, come!"

"What, and leave my dear father behind? Never! Away you! and fear not but that we will follow close behind. Away, away! We will to the stables at once; we have horses enough for all. Good-bye—go, go!"

"Swear to me first that you will be in the saddle in five minutes."

"I do swear it. But why will you think of me more than of yourself?"

Rose made no answer except, "Remember your oath;" and wheeling her horse round again, crossed the garden, leapt the fence, and stretched out across the plain, lighted on her way by the red glare of the conflagration.

She glanced back and was thunderstruck at the headway that the bush-fire had already made.

A dense, lurid smoke spread like a sombre canopy above the blazing bush. Huge trees, like gigantic funnels of steam engines, were belching forth flames thirty, forty and even fifty feet in height, which waved and curled in the wind like the flaunting banners of the dusky legion of hell.

Already horses and cattle, frightened by the glare and roar of the conflagration that was yet miles away, tore across the plains with neighs and bellowings, whilst the poor stupid sheep gathered together in flocks and stared stolidly at the advancing destroyer.

"Oh, God!" thought Rose, "will she escape in time? And yet," she added fiercely, "what is she to me or I to her? I was a fool for my pains. Let her perish with her father, and the fool new-chum who ran away from me, and who doubtless she intends to marry."

CHAPTER XIX.

THE FLIGHT FROM MITTAGARRA.—THE PURSUIT OF A FIRE-KING.

AND now the big bell that is commonly used by the cook to call all hands to dinner is tolling for dear life.

Vain its iron alarum, for the down-swooping fire wants no herald of its approach.

From the huts tumble the men, all making for the stables, whilst already through the swamp of the home-paddock gallop the station-horses, with Jumbo, the black boy, shouting and cracking his stock-whip incessantly in their rear.

There was "mounting in hot haste" indeed, whilst the eagle-hawks fluttered and circled and indulged in harsh and discordant screams of terror high overhead, and lower down flying foxes, singly and in pairs, beat their forked, leathery pinions, and with mouse-like squeaks steered southward, with little thought of the nectarine and peach orchards that are the scene of their usual nightly feasts and gambols.

"Can anything be done, sir?" asks the station overseer, as he touches the brim of his sun-tanned cabbage-tree hat to his master.

"No; we are not enough of us. Let us think of our lives, and our lives only. It would be madness to attempt anything more," answered the squatter gravely. "Stay, don't forget to let the poor dogs loose."

"Jackson, Jones, Jumbo, my horse, you knaves! Why the devil don't you bring me out my horse?" screams Capt. Montague Vavasseur, at this juncture putting in an appearance, with a very pale face and excited mien. "I want my nag at once, my men!"

"Jack's as good as his master in a case like this, Vavas-seur," said the squatter, somewhat sternly. " 'Tis each for himself, and God for us all. You know where your horse is stalled as well as anyone. Now, Lily, my dear, you must ride Sheetanchor and I'll take Yon Yangs. Don't be frightened, there is no great danger, I assure you, at all events for you. For me, perhaps, who have had a warning from the spirit world—ah!"

And Andrew M'Pherson, who had muttered the final remark in an undertone to himself, shivered as he thought of his late visitant, whose wonderful likeness to her dead mother at the same age had caused the squatter to regard her, especially now, as having been her ghost.

But now everyone belonging to the station, womankind and all, are in the saddle.

" Come on!" shouts Jack Fowler, a dandy young stock-rider, as he gives a crack with his whip as loud as any rifle shot. " We've plenty of light to steer by, so the devil take the hindmost, as I think there's every probability that he will on this occasion."

And away go the fugitives at breakneck speed through the bush, following the reckless and well-mounted Jack Fowler as best they can, and stringing out like British fox-hunters.

" Steady, my lads, steady! it's no use bursting our beasts early in the flight. We shall want all their strength, wind, and endurance later on," cried out the squatter, warningly, and then he turned to Lily to cheer her up, and assure her that there was no real danger.

She could tell otherwise by the blanched and haggard look of her father's face; but she pretended to be com-forted, for she was as brave as she was beautiful; and, in truth, she did not look a quarter so scared as did Captain Montague Vavasseur, who rode on her left, and who could ejaculate nothing but, " Demmed country!" which he did continuously.

Already the heat of the conflagration could be felt, though it was still a good two-and-a-half miles in their rear. Already the onrolling smoke had blotted out the indigo-hued heavens and all its gleaming stars, whilst sparks quivered in their stead amidst the sulphurous canopy—quivered and twinkled and perished in countless myriads.

Around, all was horror and confusion; the sheep were clustering in larger and larger groups, facing and stamping at the roaring flames, as though thus they could intimidate them from further approach; whilst the panic-stricken and more rational cattle, amidst a perfect tempest of bellowing, were pouring in long lines into the flats, and rushing along them, instinct-led, towards the nearest creek. Here and there, half-wild horses were pursuing the same wild course, whilst kangaroos "bumped, bumped, bumped" a dozen feet at each leap across the plains, and wild dogs, red as foxes and ravenous as wolves, scudded past the fleecy flocks, for once in their lives without the slightest wish to rend and tear and devour their best-beloved of spoil.

Oh, the horror of their howlings as they tore along !—the wailings of the damned could not have been more awful.

Lily shuddered and glanced back over her shoulder.

What was that that she beheld? A huge fiery serpent hundreds of yards in length, rushing madly through space ! The luminous monster stole on, zigzagging through the grass towards the devoted station as though sentient with life.

" It's the brush fence," explains the squatter hoarsely, and even while he speaks it spreads abroad amongst the grass, advances in the changed form of a sheet of flame, leaps upon its prey, rears its gorgeous crest above the roof and even the topmost chimney, sweeps in at every window. shoots up a mimic volcano through the shingled roof, and in a couple of minutes Lily beholds her child-hood's home reduced to a heap of smouldering ashes.

But there is no time to shed weak, sentimental tears.

The horrible foe is too near.

The rush and roar of his advance are now so loud that they absorb all other sounds.

The conflagration is at present four miles wide and nearly six deep. The brush fences will, in fact, in some directions carry it forty or fifty miles before it can re-ceive a check.

Straight ahead, towards a wide gully with a creek brattling along its bottom, seems to be the only possible avenue of escape, and that haven of refuge is still a dozen miles distant.

Even if the creek is reduced to a string of waterholes the flames will not be able to leap across the wide chasm that, during the countless ages, its wintry floods have worn in the soft alluvial soil, and in its depths there will be coolness and moisture and safety.

How much all three are required none but those can guess who have been placed in a like position.

Already is the hair of the fugitives beginning to crisp on their heads, their throats are too dry for speech, and the horses, despite the heat and the rate at which they are being pressed forward, are as dry as at starting, the sweat having been absorbed by the intense heat of the atmos-phere. Now, too, their tongues begin to loll out, their gallop is not so steady as it was, their eyeballs seem to be starting half out of their sockets, and frequently they utter shrill neighs of terror.

Now and then Andrew M'Pherson still attempts to com-fort and encourage, as best he can, his beautiful child, though he cannot even be sure that she hears him above the roar, ay, almost shriek, of the flames.

Captain Vavasseur has shot ahead long ago, and can no longer be seen. Indeed, presently the smoke grows so thick and dense that it seems as though earth had been left behind and they were winging an aerial flight through dim and lurid clouds.

God of heaven! is the fire heading them?

On *either hand* now they can hear the crackling of the flames, as well as in their rear.

Yes, the dimly-seen trees spout smoke and fire, and seem to change to columns of red-hot gleaming iron.

A minute or two later and these bush giants, still spouting cataracts of flame, begin to fall about and around them, filling the smoky air with sparks and hot ashes.

Suddenly Lily loses sight of her father.

She looks wildly around but sees him not.

She tries to cry out, but her parched throat refuses to utter an articulate sound, and all the while crash ! crash ! crash ! come down the trees around her, happily in this part of the run growing singly and at some little distance apart.

Ah ! a shriek from her horse—for horses can shriek under the influence of either pain or terror. A wave of fire flows beneath them, reaching, however, hardly to his knees, and in an instant past ; but he falls writhing on the scorched and blackened plain, struggles to rise, falls again, and this time a huge flaring bough hurtles through the air, and comes down across his neck and shoulders, pinning him to the earth for ever.

Happily in his first fall Lily was hurled out of the saddle, clear of his frantic and agonised struggles, and there she still lies, with a thick rain of ashes descending upon her, when a horseman, clad in some kind of a uni-form, draws rein by her side.

CHAPTER XX.

NED KELLY BETRAYED AND CAPTURED.

ALL this while Ned Kelly, the ironclad bushranger, lay in the deserted shepherd's hut at the head of the Mitta-garra Run, up in the ranges, rejoicing in the havoc and destruction he had wrought.

There was no chance of the fiery avenger recoiling on himself as long as the wind continued in its present quarter ; and did he not presently expect Lardy Bill and Lanky Jim with his horse?"

Little did he guess, whilst he was so ruthlessly rejoicing over the too probable destruction of Mittagarra and all who were beneath its roof, that perils quite as imminent threatened himself.

Even now, whilst he laughs and chuckles like a fiend or a maniac, or a strong mixture of both, at the awful fate to which he has doomed the man whom he hates, and all belonging to him, his treacherous accomplices in a thousand villainies, Lardy Bill and Lanky Jim, attired as shepherds, are creeping through the tea-tree scrub towards the back of the hut in order to shoot him down and sell his dead body to the police.

The police themselves are close at hand and watching the movements of the two seeming shepherds keenly, for they are not quite convinced that the whole affair may not be a plant to lead them into a very death-trap, and that the hut towards which the two informers are stealing may not hold a dozen hale armed and vengeful bushrangers instead of one wounded and almost helpless one.

Carefully and very cautiously, for the two slinking jackals are in heart mortally afraid of the wounded tiger, Lardy Bill and Lanky Jim approach the rear of the hut, gun in hand.

"Oh, I feel so soft-hearted—mild as a sucking-dove! Don't you, Jim?"

"No, I don't; and if you experiences such darned common-place sentiments, why the d—— don't you leave the deed and its reward to me?"

"Because, since he has to be shot, a brace ov bullets in his vitals won't hurt him much more nor one; and, besides, you forgets the debt as I owes to society along ov him," retorts Lardy Bill, anxiously.

No fear is there of the conversation being overheard, with the roar of the conflagration so near at hand. However, it is prolonged no further, and both the rascals now creep towards the hut in silence.

Presently they reach it, point the muzzles of their pieces through two of the many fissures between the gaping weather-boards, cover their victim as he lies on the ground, almost rolling in his fierce joy at the too probable destruction of the man against whom, for fourteen years, he has borne such an inveterate hate, and almost simultaneously discharge their guns fairly at his head.

Ah! only the caps explode, and it is just the same with the second barrels.

"Treachery has been at work, the police have drawn the charges, so that we should have no part in the taking of him, and that they might cop the whole reward!" hissed Lanky Jim in Lardy Bill's ear. "But d—— 'em, we'll foil 'em yet. Quick, Bill! let us dash round to the front and beat his skull in before they can come up!"

"Oh, Lord! I feel far too soft hearted. He's got his revolver, and we're blowed on. If the traps do us out ov the reward, they'll leave us the gallows for our pains. I don't want any further proof of their ill will. I—I'm a-going to slope, and I hope as you'll have the sense to follow me."

And, turning round, he dashed away at the top of his speed, followed, after only a moment's hesitation, by the Macaw-beak.

Ned Kelly, with the roar of the flames in his ears, and the blood lust against Andrew M'Pherson in his heart, had not even heard the snapping of the four percussion-caps so close behind him.

Neither did he hear the scuddering away of his two faithless allies, or the stealthy advance of the police in their stead, until the latter rushed into the hut *en masse* and threw themselves upon him.

His left hand had almost clutched a pistol as it lay on the ground near at hand, when one of the troopers kicked it out of his reach; and, though he struggled as desperately as he could considering the nature of his hurts, he was soon overcome and bound securely.

With a bitter oath he demanded to know by whom he had been betrayed, for he felt convinced that he had not been discovered by chance.

"Two shepherds brought us the information—leastways, they said that they were shepherds, though some of us had

our doubts on the point. Have you a couple of choice acquaintances with peculiarly-shaped noses—one flat and broken at the bridge, and the other for all the world like a cockatoo's bill?" asked a sergeant.

The expression of the ironclad bushranger's countenance was terrible to behold as the trooper made this explanation.

He had put more confidence in those two men than in any others of his band, and now they were revealed to him as the worst of traitors and sneaks.

"You can easily have your revenge," said another trooper. "They have given us the slip now but doubtless you can tell us where they are to be found. If through your assistance we can capture them, I think I may offer you the satisfaction of having one hung on either side of you."

"I cannot betray their haunts without at the same time betraying that of others who may be true and faithful to me. Besides, I prefer wreaking personal vengeance. Take me where you will, and lock me up where you like, yet I will escape, and kill those two men by tortures such as have never yet been dreamed of. As for hanging! Ha, ha, ha! the hemp has not yet been planted that is destined to make a rope for my neck. No, no, of that you may take your oath."

And, having thus delivered himself, Ned Kelly relapsed into sullen silence. Not another word could be got out of him for the present.

So a horse was brought up and he was lifted on to its back, and his ankles secured by a strong rope under its belly.

Then the half-dozen troopers mounted in turn, and closed in around him, carbine on thigh and quite ready to shoot him through the head should he make the slightest attempt at escape.

Ned Kelly smiled grimly.

"I don't object to all this," said he, "for I want a little nursing and doctors' treatment badly enough. I had a bullet driven clean through my shoulder the other night, and a police surgeon is just the man to put me to rights and set me up for work again. Directly he has done this I shall wish you good-bye and be off again to the ranges."

"I say, Ned, where did you pick up your fine speech?" asked a trooper.

"I had the honour of being educated by an Oxford B.A."

"Ha, ha, ha, ha! at Oxford University in old England, Ned?"

"No, at a Government Establishment in Hobart Town, called The Tench. My worthy preceptor had been sent out because, in a momentary fit of forgetfulness, he signed another man's name instead of his own to some money security or other. Hard, wasn't it? He took a mortal fancy to me, the old bloke did, and made me something more of a scholar than perhaps you even imagine."

"It's a pity you haven't put your learning to better account, Ned," said the sergeant, gruffly. "Thunder take that fire," he added, "what a round we'll have to make owing to it. How the deuce did it break out I wonder? Is it any of your infernal devilry, Ned Kelly, eh?"

"Yes, I wanted to roast out Squatter M'Pherson, and I guess I've about done it," answered Ned, with a demoniac and reckless laugh.

"Roasted out M'Pherson? Had you any down on him then?"

"I've been seeking his destruction for fourteen years and a month."

"Umph! you don't generally leave your debts of hatred unpaid so long. I suppose you didn't care how many innocent people, who had never done you even a fancied injury, you destroyed with him."

"Devil a fear, as long as he went along with them. When a city is bombarded the innocent women and children have to take their chance of hurt. This is a similar case. Who serves old Blazes must beware of scorched fingers," and with another reckless laugh Ned Kelly grew sulky once more.

Not another word in fact could be got out of him until they arrived at a bush township just on the other side of the Black Forest, where, on gaining the police-camp, he was unlashed, taken down off his horse, and locked up in one of the cells, where he was given a good supper, where, moreover, a surgeon came and dressed his wound, by no means a dangerous one, as the bullet had gone clean through him, making only a flesh wound.

CHAPTER XXI.

RIDE FOR LIFE.—SURROUNDED BY FLAME.

LILY M'PHERSON no sooner felt herself lifted off the ground, and placed in front of someone on a great, strong, proudly-stepping horse, than she wailed forth the one word, "Father!" and then fainted dead away.

"Thank heaven for that!" exclaimed Tom Conquest, the trooper, for it was he. "The two of them I could not have saved, yet it's ten to one that she'd have had it so or neither, if she had maintained her senses; so it's just as it should be."

He strained the unconscious girl to his breast as he thus soliloquised, at the same time pressing his lips to the floating masses of her hair; albeit, instead of the "perfumed tresses" that novelists are so fond of describing, it smelt most abominably of fire and sulphur.

Then, surrounded by crashing branches, blazing bark, and sudden whirls of yellow flame, that would continually play and crackle about him from some sappy fern, sheltering Lily's face from the intense heat as best he could, whilst he felt his own cracking and blistering, and his eyes apparently changing into balls of solid fire within his head, dauntless Tom Conquest strove his utmost to get out of the fix into which his love for the fair girl, whom he dimly hoped to save, had gotten him.

And whilst he pushed resolutely on in the direction that resembled a raging hell more than anything else, Tom could not help reflecting to himself, uncharitable as it was to do so at such a time, that in all probability Lily was now an orphan, and all obstacles to their union removed by the fact, for, not a couple of minutes ere he had rescued her, he had ridden past her father lying apparently dead in the middle of a patch of blackened sward, himself almost as black as it.

Tom struggled to quell such thoughts as quickly as they occurred to him, but though a man may combat evil deeds, uncharitable or wicked reflections are far more difficult to overcome, and 'twas so in the present instance.

But much danger and peril had yet to be encountered, and the trooper now began to centre all his thoughts upon the present.

It was almost impossible to decide in what way to lead, and so he determined to leave it in great measure to the instinct of his charger.

Often he felt as though he must fall from his saddle, which he could not but think began to feel crisp beneath him.

The wind every now and then roared and shrieked through the burning waste, carrying with it dense clouds of ashes that obscured everything to the darkness of midnight.

On these occasions he was obliged to pull sharp up, as even his charger's head was hidden from his view.

Several times he almost despaired of escape, for still occasionally a tree fell crashing near them, and frequently in the murky gloom they could almost stumble on to a seeming pillar of fire that lay hissing and sputtering across their track. Then too the heavily-laden horse would often tread on spots where the fire had crept into the earth along the rotten roots of trees, burning his feet and fetlocks and covering himself and double burden with red-hot ashes as he struggled out.

All at once—crowning catastrophe at such a time and place—the horse sprained his fore fetlock in extricating himself from one of these holes, and went dead lame.

Tom Conquest dismounted and lifted Lily M'Pherson also to the ground.

She seemed to be showing some faint signs of recovering from her swoon, and he had begun to feel that his own senses were on the point of leaving him in turn, when his feet slipped from under him, and he slid and rolled by turns down, down, until he finally splashed into water.

It was only a foot or two in depth, but such as it was it instantly instilled new life into him.

He scrambled out of it a different man, and bounded up the bank full of fresh vigour.

A minute later and he had half supported half-borne Lily M'Pherson down the almost precipitous declivity, and having sat her beside the water hole, he ascended the bank yet a third time for his horse, which he had some difficulty in getting down.

This feat accomplished he had time to think and his thoughts told him that they were at the bottom of the gully, which he had been striving so long to reach, and free from all further danger.

CHAPTER XXII.

NED IN LIMBO.—ROSE TO THE RESCUE.

NED KELLY meanwhile lies fretting and fuming in solitary confinement in one of the narrow, dark lockups of the police-station at Boroma.

This is the first time that he has defied the law unsuccessfully; the first time that it has immeshed him in its net, and so he strides up and down the small, confined space with all the fury and restlessness of the tiger that he so closely resembles, stopping every now and then to seize hold of and shake the thick bars of his cell door, more as a vent to his fury than with any hope of getting out by that means.

Since the wound in his shoulder has been attended to, he feels almost free from pain, and his brute strength seems to be almost restored by the hearty supper that he has eaten.

True, his right arm is of little or no use, but he feels that with his left he could do wonders were he only free, and how eagerly he longs to be free no one can imagine whose movements have hitherto been so unfettered as his.

And how fierce and burning are the thoughts that course through his brain. How he longs for vengeance on Lardy Bill and Lanky Jim, and how fearful is his dread that, not content with betraying him, they may have afterwards repaired to the hut in the ranges, and tortured Rose into confessing where all her and his private spoil and possessions were hidden; as likely as not both ill-using and murdering her when the necessary information has been obtained.

It was strange that these fearful thoughts and apprehensions did not turn his brain. They certainly seemed to set it on fire, and caused him to shake the iron door, or rather gate, of his cell with redoubled force every time that his rage got almost too strong to bear.

But the troopers pay no heed to the row that he is making; and, as there are no other occupants of the cells that night, he has no neighbours to rail at him for keeping them awake with the shindy.

Why are the troopers so oblivious of his existence?

Well, the fact is they are entertaining a guest whom they delight to honour, and the like of whom they have never had quartered upon them before.

Hardly had the doctor departed, after doing all that he could for the prisoner, than Rose arrived, mounted on a white horse, in a perfect state of sweat, and herself bearing every token that she had just ridden a desperate race against something or other.

"I would like a drop of water and to be permitted to rest here for a little while, if you please," she had said to the sergeant. "I am a niece of Mr. M'Pherson, of Mittagarra; but in endeavouring to reach the station, where I was expected as a visitor, I have been driven back by a fierce bush-fire, and narrowly escaped with my life. Do you think that my dearest uncle and cousin can have fallen victims to it?" And she put on a most anxious expression of countenance.

"No, miss," answered the sergeant, for W. M'Pherson was a great man in those parts; "I don't think as how you have much grounds for fear. The fire broke out in the ranges far enough off to give sufficient warning of its approach, and your uncle, miss, keeps horses that *can* go, and no mistake about it. Therefore, I don't see as you need be anxious, and I think you'd a sight better let me run across the way to the 'Leichardt Arms' and bespeak a bed for you there. I'm sure Mrs. Jones would be proud to turn out of her own at any hour to accommodate a relative of Mr. M'Pherson."

"But I wouldn't have worthy Mrs. Jones put herself to such an inconvenience at such an hour. What is the use of a bed to one who is far too anxious to sleep; and how could I enjoy comfort in a cosy bedroom when perhaps at this very moment my poor uncle and cousin are homeless and houseless wanderers? No, please to give me a chair to sit in, or a shakedown to lie on, for a couple of hours here; then it will be daylight, and I'll ask you to allow one of your troopers to ride with me over to Mittagarra, for I shall be too nervous to go alone, not knowing what horrors or painful surprises may have to be encountered at the end of the journey, or even on the road."

Here she managed to squeeze out a few more tears, and even to give a convulsive movement to her bosom as though she was labouring under some strong emotion; so the good-natured sergeant granted her petition at once, lifting her tenderly out of the saddle to the ground, and ordering one of the troopers to conduct her steed to the stable.

It was certainly rather strange, agitated as she was, that she should have so narrowly observed in what direction the trooper led her horse, and exactly where the door of the stables was situated, ere she suffered the sergeant to lead her inside the station.

Here she drank off three pannikins of water in rapid succession, thereafter indulging in a copious flow of tears; eventually, however, almost permitting herself to be convinced that her uncle and cousin must have escaped the conflagration, whereupon she became comparatively calm.

The sergeant pressed her to partake of some food, and she did so; also to drink a glass or two of Cawarra wine, and she complied. Lastly, she was pointed out a colonial sofa, and told that she might appropriate it to her own use, and she proceeded to take immediate possession.

Still, every one was anxious to do something more for her, which may be accounted for by the fact that she was both young and lovely; fourteen being the age at which girls born and reared in a hot climate like Australia are freshest and most charming.

But she would not have anything more. She smiled and brought the deadly battery of her bright eye into full play, and then begged everybody to take no further notice of her, as she meant to snatch a couple of hours' sleep if it was possible.

So the sergeant went and got a couple of pillows for her charming head, and one of the troopers threw a horseman's cloak loosely over her prettily-rounded form, and she pretended to close her eyes and woo slumber right off-hand, but did nothing of the kind.

She distinctly heard the sergeant say in an undertone to his men—

"Now, lads, 'tis high time that we followed the young lady's example, bless her innocent heart and pretty face, for we've had a tough night's work, and we'll have a tougher one to morrow in getting Kelly down to Melbourne; for if we don't act promptly some of his band may attempt a rescue, ay, and effect it, too, for he's lots of sympathisers in these parts. So turn in, and snatch what rest you can, and I shall do the same. Tierman, you'll escort Mr. M'Pherson's niece over to Wangaratta as soon as ever she requests you to be astir, only don't

rouse her until she wakes of her own accord, for it 'ud be a pity."

Then the sergeant and the half-dozen troopers all crowded into an adjoining room to the left, and shut the door between the two, and the half-closed eyes of the girl on the sofa twinkled with keen satisfaction as she observed that the key was on her side, and a stout bolt also, both to be used if needful.

She lay quite still, however, and her gaze now that she was alone wandered all round the room that she occupied, and which was dimly illumined by a lamp on the mantelpiece, which the sergeant had turned down very low ere he quitted the chamber.

By its light she beheld whitewashed walls adorned with pistols, carbines, sabres, handcuffs, and here and there a big reward bill, one of which offered "Ten thousand pounds for the taking of that daring outlaw and murderer Edward Kelly, either alive or dead."

The beautiful girl's eyes gleamed brighter than ever as she read this huge poster through. She had often seen it before posted on gum-tree trunks out in the bush, but with its present surroundings it seemed to have a new fascination for her, and when she had finished its perusal she muttered to herself—

"You haven't got him to Melbourne yet, and perhaps you won't. What fools you were not to take him dead."

Having thus given vent to her feelings she took further stock of her surroundings, particularly observing the troopers' jackets and shakos that were hung up on pegs here and there, and some pairs of high, brightly-polished boots, armed with glittering spurs, that stood in one corner.

This and very much more she noticed, especially a second door exactly facing her couch, and, when one of the troopers had opened it a little while previously, she had seen a dark and gloomy passage within, with a narrow grating here and there, and a bunch of huge, formidable-looking keys which the aforesaid trooper had hitched on to a certain hook when he returned to the room.

Having taken all these careful mental notes, Rose Casey, whom the reader has doubtless long ago recognised, listened anxiously for all to grow still in the adjoining apartment, as on the sound slumber of every one of the half-dozen policemen and the sergeant depended the success of the desperate enterprise that she had planned, namely, the rescue of the villain whom she loved as a father.

The reader may wonder how she knew that he was there.

It happened by the simplest means in the world.

By dint of hard riding, and having got a good ten minutes' start of those whom she had so chivalrously, and at such great hazard to herself, ridden back to warn of their peril, Rose had managed to keep ahead of the conflagration, until after a nine-mile race, neck and neck with Death, she had reached a long strip of fallowland, in the centre of which she was safe.

From this oasis of refuge she had watched the whirls of the fire-king rush by on either hand, surge on surge and wave on wave, o'ercanopied by onrolling clouds of dun smoke, and when the tempest of desolation had passed her by with a rush and a swirl she had continued her flight, and shortly afterwards reached the outskirts of Boroma, when she beheld entering the township from another direction a small body of troopers escorting a prisoner.

Instinct almost seemed to tell her who that prisoner was, but she reined back her horse into the obscurity of a small paddock to make sure, and her heart gave a great leap within her as conviction resolved itself into certainty and she beheld Ned bound and helpless in their midst.

Then she rode a little way back into the bush to marshal and array her thoughts.

It took her nearly an hour to make up her mind what was best to be done, but at last she had resolutely decided and this was the result.

At last Rose Casey threw the horseman's cloak from off

her, raised herself on the couch, slipped off it on to her feet, crossed the floor as noiselessly as though she had been a spectre, and listened at the door on the other side of which she fondly hoped that the troopers were all sound asleep.

Not a sound came from within save hard and stertorous breathing, mixed up with an occasional snore, and with a smile of satisfaction Rose noiselessly turned the key in the lock and shot home the bolt.

Then she tucked a pair of the big boots and a sabre under one arm, put a shako on her head, thrust a brace of pistols into her pocket, burdened her other arm with as large a sized uniform jacket as in her anxious haste she could stay to select, took down the great bunch of keys with trembling but deft fingers, and, holding them so that they should not jingle, managed to open the door that led into the dark passage with the gratings here and there, and passed through it.

When she had fastened the door behind her she found that it too was lighted a little way down by a common tallow dip fixed in a dirty tin sconce that was hung against the wall.

The wick had contracted such a cauliflower-top that the feeble rays hardly did more than render darkness visible.

They did, however, enable Rose to peer into cell after cell, and discover each to be empty until she came to the one exactly opposite the light, in the extreme end of which she distinguished a form huddled up in a corner with a pair of keen, dark, vengeful eyes gleaming out from beneath shaggy brows.

Their expression changed in an instant as they lighted on her. The crouched-up form upreared itself to its full height and noiselessly approached the iron grating that served for door.

"Rose!" it exclaimed anxiously, "Good heavens, what brings you here, my girl?"

"I am come either to save or to perish with you, father," she made answer. "Here are disguises and weapons, and the keys to unlock your dungeon door. The police are sound asleep. I know the way to the stables. In five minutes, father, we will be clear off."

CHAPTER XXIII.

THE ESCAPE FROM BOROMA.

NED KELLY had some difficulty in convincing himself that he was not dreaming.

When by dint of rubbing his eyes and grasping Rose's hand through the iron bars of his cage he had assured himself both that he was wide awake and that she was no vision of a distempered imagination, he began to entertain nervous fears on her behalf which never in his life had he felt on his own.

"Oh, Rose," said he, "they will imprison you for years for this assistance that you are trying to render me. Go away, go away; I will escape without your help by-and-bye. I will not have you imperil your precious liberty for the sake of a scoundrel like me. I say I will not."

"It's of no use, father; you are only losing valuable time. I escape with you or remain with you. I am quite decided about that. You could not persuade me to the contrary though you talked for a month, so do not let me incur all the peril in vain. Ah, the right key at last," and, flinging open the door of the cell, Rose rushed in and threw herself sobbing with joy into Ned's arms.

He could no longer withstand her entreaties; the open path to liberty was indeed too great a temptation.

"You are a noble girl, Rose," said he, "and henceforth our lives shall still more be bound up together. How on earth have you managed to work the oracle?"

"This is not the time to tell you, father. We must work now in order that we may have a chance of talking by-and-by. Here is almost a complete trooper's dress. On with it and let us get away as soon as we can."

"But these old moleskin pants, Rose?"

"The high boots and the skirts of the tunic will almost hide them. Be quick, dear father."

Ned was quick. He dragged on the boots, but the coat was too much for him.

"Give me a hand, Rose, I can't get this arm into the sleeve. Bullet through the shoulder the other night. Stiff as the very deuce, my dear."

The lovely girl lent her assistance on the instant. She was as gentle as a young mother could be over her first infant.

The tunic on, she buttoned it up, next strapped on the sword-belt, bidding Ned hold the scabbard in his hand so that it should not rattle.

Then she placed the shako on his head.

"Now follow me as noiselessly as a fly creeps over a pat of butter. Come!"

She had not yet given Ned the pistols, for she could not bear the thought that they might have to be used against those who had been so kind to her.

Knowing his ferocity and impetuosity she resolved that he should only have them in case of the most urgent necessity.

He did not ask her for them.

It was strange how a great, heavy man could step so lightly, but Ned resembled a beast of prey in all things, even in this.

Out of the cell, along the dim, candle-illumined passage, and through the door at the end thereof into the main room of the station, and there was only one door between them and liberty.

Ned was halfway across the floor, and Rose was close up to the colonial sofa that had been given her as a sleeping-place, when the bushranger gave vent to a muffled sneeze.

He could not have helped it for the life of him, but it was sufficient to occasion an alarm.

A step was heard in the next room, and the handle of the door was seen to shake.

"Artifice, not violence!" whispered Rose, flinging herself at once upon the couch.

Ned caught her meaning. Three strides and he was pottering away amongst the miscellaneous articles on the mantelpiece.

At that instant the door between the two rooms was half opened, and a trooper's head and shoulders were thrust partly through.

Seeing, in the dim light, a tall, stalwart form clad in the uniform of the corps, he exclaimed with a yawn —

"Hullo, mate! what's up? You're early astir."

"Don't let me disturb you fellows. I'm out of the weed, and I'm after somebody's 'baccy."

"All right."

A minute later and Ned Kelly had noiselessly unlocked and unbolted the outer one.

As noiselessly he opened it, and then gave Rose a quick and significant glance.

She was on her feet in an instant, and out into the star light.

Ned then shut the door, and tramped somewhat heavily down the little garden path to the water gate, so that the ring of his spurs should be audible.

Rose, on the contrary, crossed it diagonally, so that she might not be seen from the window of the room which the troopers occupied.

Arrived at the fence, she first signalled to Ned which way he was to go, and then scrambled half-through and half-over it.

Presently they stood side by side at the door of the stables.

"Foiled after all!" hissed Ned between his set teeth, as, on lifting the latch, it refused to yield to his pressure. "We might have made up our minds that it would be locked."

"But, father, I was not quite so foolish as to leave my bunch of keys in the cell door. One of them will doubtless undo it."

3

And she produced them from her pocket.

One after the other was eagerly and impatiently tried, but not until the entire bunch was gone through was one found that would properly turn in the lock and open the door.

With fresh hopes then they entered the stable.

"Will you pick out your horse, Rose, or shall I?"

"Oh, I have Swiftsure with me, father."

"But is he used up, that's the question?"

"No he's fresh as a daisy, I'm sure."

"We have a ninety-miles ride before us."

"All right, father, I am ready for it."

Ned said no more, but selected what seemed to be the longest and toughest of the troopers' horses, and began to saddle it.

In three minutes it was harnessed and accoutred, but she was not an instant behind with Swiftsure, for like many a colonial girl she could groom, saddle, and ride a horse fully as well as one of the opposite sex.

"Here father, stick these pistols in your holsters," she now said, giving Ned the long and brightly-polished regulation double-barrels for the first time. "Now then, are you ready?"

"Not quite lass. I'll just hamstring the other nags to bar all immediate pursuit."

"Father, if you do I'll leave you at once and for ever," said Rose in subdued accents of horror. "Poor things! How could you be so cruel?"

"All right, girl, go ahead," rejoined the bushranger sheepishly; and Rose led Swiftsure out of the stable, Ned following her with the troop-horse that he had selected.

Suddenly an idea seemed to strike him. He locked the stable door and tossed the keys to Rose.

"Put them in your pocket," said he, "'twill take them some minutes to force the lock, and a minute saved is a minute gained. Now then, into the saddle my lass, and hurrah for Melbourne city!"

CHAPTER XXIV.

COBB'S COACH AGAIN.—PURSUIT.

ROSE was atop of Swiftsure in a twinkling, and, Ned having mounted the stolen charger with some pain and difficulty, they trotted easily away side by side from the stables.

It was a necessity that they should pass the front of the station, however, and it unhappily chanced that as they did so the restless trooper whom Ned had successfully hoodwinked within doors was looking out of a window and caught sight of the fugitives.

The night, or rather early morning, was clear, and the starlight even brighter than usual, so that a female form and a white horse were clearly visible.

His suspicions aroused, he glanced into the next room, and at once perceived that their fair guest was gone, and, this causing him to smell a considerable-sized rat, he dashed across the floor and into the dim passage beyond, to discover that the Ironclad Bushranger was gone also.

"Hi there! Up mates! Kelly's hooked it! That infernal wench that we gave shelter to has set him free. Curse her!" he yelled at the top of his voice, as he rushed back into the room where he had left his companions.

In an instant they were all of them equally enraged and excited.

They rushed forth pell-mell, and grasped the first firearms that came to hand; but they might just as well have taken it more quietly, for by the time that they got out of doors Ned and his pretty girl-rescuer were out of sight.

"We must saddle our nags and pelt after them, lads," said the sergeant. "It'll be daylight in a couple of hours. Ten to one they'll take shelter in the ranges, for the reason that he'll think it's the last place we'll look for him after what has happened."

"I'd sooner say he'd wing his flight straight for Melbourne. A big city affords twice as secure a hiding-place as a big forest," suggested a trooper.

"It's just possible that he may think of that, especially as he is such a chap for all manner of disguises," said the sergeant. "Tell you what, lads," he added; "we'll divide our forces. Four of us will beat up his old quarters in the ranges, and the other three shall ride on the spur towards Melbourne. And now there's no time to be lost so let us to the stables at once."

Great was the troopers' rage to find the door locked, and while they were breaking it in, Ned Kelly and Rose had gained the open bush on the other side of the township, where, avoiding the metal, they struck across country as the crow flies, in the direction they wanted to travel.

"I'd go back to the hut first to secure some of the spoil but for the risk of the thing. You see, Rose, as Lardy Bill and Lanky Jim have turned traitors, the entire band may be just as bad as they, and I'm not exactly in fighting form at present," said Ned, growlingly.

"Oh, dear father, let us push on for Melbourne, and there disguise ourselves, and take to honester pursuits," answered Rose. "What is the good of living the life of a hunted wolf, with the certainty of being run to earth some day?"

"Perhaps you're right, lass; perhaps you're right; though I don't think I should live long without some excitement. An honest life must be a terribly dry and uninteresting one. By thunder, Rose, here is the Melbourne mail! See the three lamps glinting amongst the trees? Touch up Swiftsure, and come along with you."

"Father, what would you do? For goodness' sake, don't bail up a coach at a time when every moment is of vital importance to us—when deadly foes are on our track, and at any instant may come up with us. I have gold and gems to the value of many thousands of pounds about me. What do you want more?"

"Nothing, Rose, nothing. I won't meddle with the coach. I only want to see who's aboard of her. Come along, lass, I say, and keep on the off-side, so that that infernal white horse don't show up quite so plain. We shall hardly lose a second of time, for the coach is going townward; and, besides, I'm accustomed to gratify my whims at any and all hazards."

Rose made no further objections. Traversing the rolling plain obliquely, they struck right across the coach's course, riding parallel with it as it drew near.

"Hi there, you! Do you know if any of Kelly's fellows are out to-night?" yelled the Yankee Jehu, as he observed Ned's uniform and dangling sword-scabbard.

"Reckon not. A swagsman told me just now that Ned was taken, but I'm blest if I quite believe him," answered the bushranger with a laugh.

"If he is, I hope they'll scrag him without loss of time, or he'll manage to slip out of their hands somehow. Good night, mate."

And the great, gaudy, springless vehicle shot past them like a comet.

Rose had taken little heed of what had passed between her companion and the tall-hatted driver, for all her faculties had been riveted and enchained, as it were, in the contemplation of one of the passengers, on whose face, as she sat inside the open coach, much of the light of one of the lamps had fallen.

It was a woman—young, fair, statuesque and wondrously beautiful. And yet to Rose her loveliness seemed to be that of the glittering-scaled serpent, that repelled whilst it attracted; a comeliness that savoured of the malevolent rather than the beneficent.

She involuntarily shuddered as she continued to regard her, and a kind of presentiment seemed to enter into her soul that their lines of lives would cross, to the shipwreck of her own happiness and to her father's destruction.

"Well, Rose, you see there is no harm done. I have let the coach go on its way," said Ned, turning towards her with a smile.

"Yes, and she is in it who you hoped would be a passenger; and now I suppose there is not the slightest doubt about Melbourne being our destination?"

"Why, my lass, what on earth ails you? And how the deuce did you know that the Countess of Lansfeldt was in yon coach?"

"Through the instinct that any ordinary wild creature feels when it meets the eye of a deadly foe, father."

"She'd better not be a foe to you, Rose, or I'll twist her neck; but you've seen in her Ned Kelly's future wife, nevertheless. Did you say, lass, that you'd great store of wealth about you in gems—in *unset* gems?"

"Yes, father. I've all the diamonds that you have ever to—— brought home."

"That's fine, Rose. We will be able to dazzle the Melbournites in fine style, this proud woman included. I have our future pretty clearly mapped out, I think. A brilliant future it will be."

"Not as long as the gibbet for you and the prison-cell for me cast a shadow over it, father," answered Rose, sorrowfully. "For heaven's sake," she added, vehemently, "don't let the light of that woman's eyes blind you to present danger."

The warning was not a needless one, for at that instant the ring of hoofs became clearly audible at some distance in their rear, and Rose, glancing back over her shoulder, dimly distinguished what looked in the starlight like shadowy forms of men and horses coming swiftly on their track.

"It's the troopers, father," said she.

"Spur up, then, my girl, and we'll soon say good-night to them," answered Ned, cheerily; but even whilst he spoke he inwardly blamed himself for having lost valuable time over the coach.

And now the pursuers sighted the chase, greeting it with a "view hallo!" that would have done credit to a Leicestershire hunting-field.

CHAPTER XXV.

A RACE FOR LIFE.

"This will be a big run, Rose," said Ned Kelly, "so we mustn't take too much out of our nags at first setting off. It's good staying power more than speed that'll win the day. We must try every dodge that occurs to us to throw 'em off the scent, lass."

Rose made no answer save a slight inclination of the head, but she thought within herself—

"Oh, for some big patches of scrub instead of this open bush, and that night were only approaching instead of day."

"I wish your nag was any colour but a white one, Rose. He's almost as good as a lighthouse to tell those fellows which way to steer," growled Ned, presently.

"Shall we separate, father, to—to meet again somewhere near Melbourne?" asked Rose, bewildered and oppressed by the thought that now she was of more danger to Ned than service, a notion very painful to her.

"No, girl, no. You and I never separate any more—whilst, at least, we have the chance left us of keeping together. It'll be daylight in an hour and a-quarter, and then a white horse will be no worse than a brown one. Curse that coach, and the woman inside it also, if they have let us into this mess!"

All the while that the two were thus communing together, they were journeying onwards at that easy, slinging gallop, that is so peculiar to Australian horses, making it no difficult matter to those familiarised with the pace to almost sleep in the saddle without falling therefrom.

Not with such deadly peril close in their rear as Ned and Rose had, however; a peril that signified the gallows for one, and years of long imprisonment for the other, if they were but taken.

So still was the night air (for the north wind had died out and no blustering southerly buster had yet succeeded it) that often they could hear the laughter and conversation of the troopers, and even the jingling of their sword-scabbards and chain-bridles as they came tearing along.

"They seem to make cock-sure of running us to earth in the end," growled Ned.

"Ought we not to strain every effort to shake them off before daylight, father?"

"Ay, ay, lass, but the thing is to get sufficient start. They are too close on our heels for us to play them a trick of that kind. Ah, Rose, if you'd only have let me hamstring their horses this danger would have been escaped altogether."

"Better run this peril than be guilty of an atrocious cruelty, father. Oh, dear, what's that?"

"What's what? Oh, I see, an enemy ahead of us. Where the deuce could he have sprung from now? Out of the earth, one would almost suppose. Well, a bullet will soon send him to earth *again*, that's one blessing."

And Ned plucked a pistol from his holster as there came sweeping towards them, uttering discordant cries, a slim trooper, mounted on a wild-looking horse, and apparently wearing a black mask.

He didn't venture very close, but, keeping just out of pistol-range, eyed them with keen scrutiny.

Suddenly he gave a strange and unearthly kind of a chuckle, threw up his head, and emitted the shrill "Co-o-ee!" that when uttered by an Australian black-fellow can be heard in calm weather at least two miles away.

It was instantly responded to, and with evident satisfaction, by the pursuing troopers, towards whom the mysterious apparition immediately sped, without having afforded Ned a chance of getting a fair shot at him.

"Confound that devil's imp!" said he, as he returned the pistol to its holster, "it will be of little use our attempting to conceal ourselves during the daytime anywhere, now that that bloodhound has joined them."

"Who and what is he, father?" asked Rose.

"Eh, don't you know, lass? Why he's a cursed native chap. There's lots of 'em in the force now. They use them as trackers, and no dogs in the world have such good scent or such keen vision as they."

"Never mind, father, cheer up. Our nags are as fresh as when we started."

"I'm chiefly thinking of you, my child. Don't speak to me for a bit. I've a half-formed notion in my head, and I want to ponder it out."

So Rose relapsed into silence, and for some five minutes naught was to be heard save the thud, thud, thud of their horses' hoofs upon the green turf, the humming of the locusts in the tree-branches o'erhead, the sharp trumpeting of the bush mosquitoes, with the occasional shrill cry of "More pork! more pork! more pork!" from the Australian cuckoo, answered perhaps by the jocund "He-haw, he-haw, ha, ha, ha, ha, ha, ha; he-haw, ha, ha, ha," of the laughing jackass; each one of these sounds mingled, however, with the thud of other and more distant hoofs, and the faint chink and rattle of military accoutrements.

"Rose," said Ned suddenly, "We must risk all on a chance. Yes, by George, we must. If we can't shake off those d—— traps before day-dawn we'll have a hundred enemies in our rear and many a foe in our front as well, and be taken to a dead certainty. We must strain every nerve to get out of their sight whilst darkness lasts, and if we can succeed we'll double on them, cross some of the ground that the bush-fire raged over last night, strike across country to Ballan, and gain Melbourne to-morrow night by the Bacchus Marsh instead of the Kyneton-road, which latter will be safe to be covered with Joeys on the lookout for us. That's my scheme, Rose."

"Pray heaven that it may be crowned with success, dear father. Shall we spur on now?"

"Ay, at racing speed, lass. Keep your eyes on my horse's head and handle your own nag to correspond. Now then, away!"

The pace was now increased to almost railway speed, and to Rose it seemed as though, instead of their progressing, the green turf was flowing under their horses' feet like a ghostly river, and the white-trunked gum and iron-bark trees reeling past them in a drunken or maniacal waltz.

With their heads stretched well forward and their ears cast sharply back, their thin nostrils quivering, and the veins in their glossy necks swollen out to the size of whipcord, Rose's white mare and Ned's stolen police charger pelted away neck and neck through the gloom.

They could hear at first their foes urging their steeds on in pursuit, but the sounds seemed to grow fainter as they tore ahead.

Well was it for them that the darkest hour is that immediately before the dawn, for it served them well in the present instance.

"By Jehoshaphat, we've given them the go-by after all," suddenly exclaimed Ned as, after traversing the open bush at breakneck speed for half-an-hour, he drew rein to listen if he could still catch the sounds of pursuit.

"Now, Rose, we must swoop round to the right, and double on them with a wide sweep. Come along."

"All right, dear father, I'm ready for anything."

And away they went again like the wind.

Another half-hour and the air became pungent with the aromatic odours of burnt gum-leaves, which plainly enough told them that they were rapidly approaching the arena of last night's conflagration.

Presently hundreds of red-hot stumps of trees gleamed like so many danger-signals out upon the plain in front of them, and ere ten minutes had elapsed they were traversing a scorched and blackened desert where their horses sank fetlock-deep in ashes at every step.

"This'll puzzle the black tracker," laughed Ned. "See, the ashes are so light that even this gentle breeze fills up the slight indentations of our horses' hoofs as soon as they are made. We will skirt it for a league or so, and then cross a creek that I wot of, and steer straight towards Mount Buninyong, which will bring us into the Ballarat and Melbourne road about midway between Ballan and Bacchus Marsh. Are you tired, Rose?"

"No one could feel tired mounted on Swiftsure."

"And I dare say, if Swiftsure could speak, he'd return the compliment by saying that no horse could feel tired with such a feather-weight as you upon his back. So come along, for a backfellow can see a devil of a way across such a bare plain as this, and the dawn is coming up fast. Another hour, and I hope we'll be able to take it a deal more easy."

CHAPTER XXVI.

THE ASSASSINATION OF MR. M'PHERSON.

IT was trot, trot, trot, now, every step of their horses sending a cloud of black dust and ashes eddying around them.

Red-hot tree-stumps were all about, and every few minutes they would pass a blackened and half-roasted bullock, around which the eagle-hawks were already clustering, for it was not often that they had their meals cooked for them in this fashion.

They were the only signs of life; all other birds had flown far away; the kangaroo and long-legged emu had also fled; even the wild warrigal, smelling roast beef afar off, stood on the margin of that ebony desert, uttering his wild, unearthly howling, and afraid to cross it.

All at once an object that Ned had taken to be the scorched and blackened carcase of a sheep, rolled over on to its back, and an almost inarticulate voice exclaimed—

"Water—water—I thirst, I burn! Water—for the love of God!"

"It's a man, and he's alive!" said Rose. "How dreadful it is that we can't give him what he asks for."

"He'd die directly he'd drank it, I expect; and, besides, we have no time to think of anyone but ourselves. Come along, lass, and let the old buffer be."

"Oh, father, how can you? Let us, at all events, bestow one word of kindness upon him in passing."

She spurred Swiftsure towards the strange-looking object as she spoke, but was suddenly greeted with an apparently half-choking cry of—

"The spectre again! The spectre! Keep off, Rose Casey! Keep off, I say! Torment not a dying man! Oh! don't come nearer—don't come any nearer!"

"Eh, who the devil have we here?" exclaimed Ned Kelly," pushing his big, powerful horse in between Rose's white steed and the prostrate man. "What name do you answer to, eh?"

Catching sight of the uniform of one of the mounted constabulary, and the ghost, as he supposed Rose to be, being at the same time hidden from his sight, the apparent log of burnt wood said feebly—

"I am Mr. M'Pherson of Mittagarra, and I don't believe I'm so badly hurt as what I look. I was more suffocated with the smoke than scorched by the flames. I shall live, oh I shall live!"

"I don't think that you are likely to live."

"Oh yes I shall. I shall get over this. A drop of water and I shall be a new man."

"Rose," said Ned, "there's water at the bottom of that gully, a couple of hundred yards to the left. Go to it, my lass, and bring a little in your hat."

The young girl immediately started on her humane mission; the squatter, whose face and hands were every whit as black as his charred clothing, shuddered as she passed him by.

"Well enough you may tremble at the sight of her, M'Pherson," said Ned Kelly, in the low and terrible accents of suppressed passion. "That girl is not the ghost of your victim, Rose Casey, but her daughter. Would you know who I am?"

(To be continued.)

NED KELLY

THE IRONCLAD

AUSTRALIAN BUSHRANGER

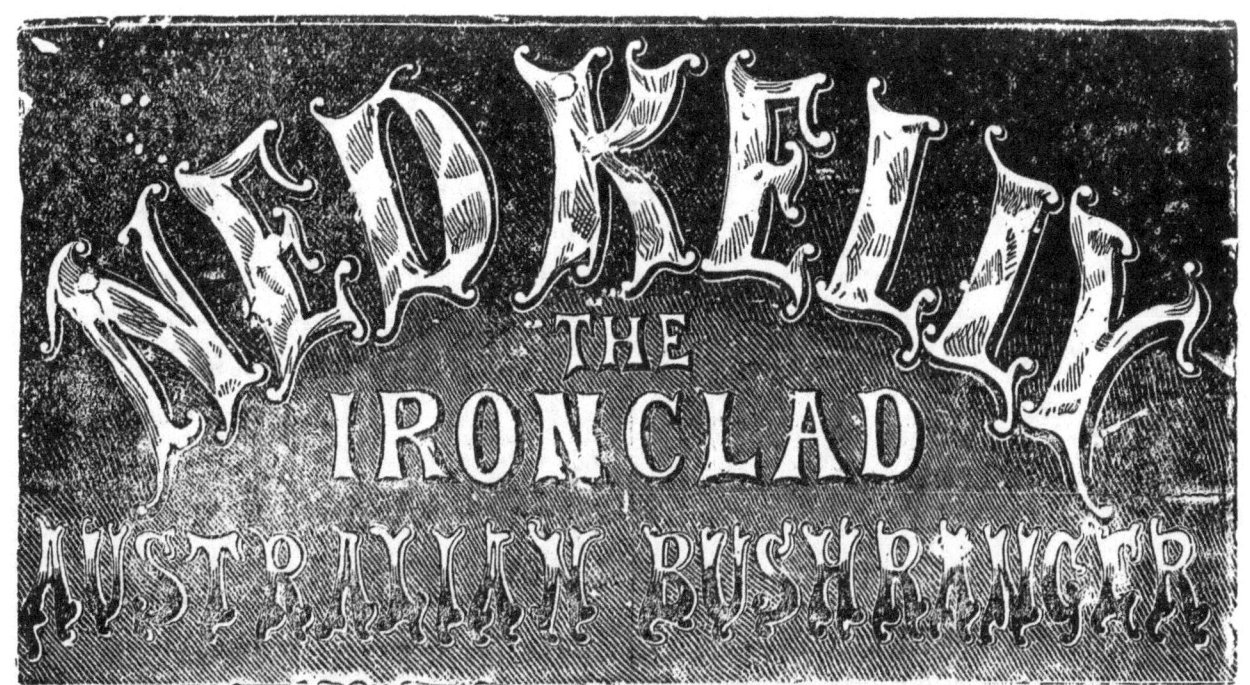

NO 4,

he squatter did not speak, he only glared.

"I see you are afraid even to guess. Well then, I was the boy lover from whom you stole her. I was with her when she died. I adopted her child as my own, though her father was a villian, and I swore as I did so that the day should come when I would avenge both the dead and the living by taking that villian's life. And Andrew M'Pherson, you have another child, born under happier auspices than poor Rose Casey. Well, I hope that the fire I kindled last night in the ranges will make her a pauper, as surely as this knife is about to make her an orphan."

And as he concluded Ned Kelly flung himself out of his saddle, whipped a knife out of his pocket which the police had overlooked when making him a prisoner, opened the blade with his teeth, threw himself upon the prostrate squatter, and, heedless of his faintly-gasped petition for mercy, sheathed it thrice in his body up to the very hilt.

As he withdrew it for the third time he espied Rose hurriedly retracing her steps with the water that he had made a feint of sending her for; and anxious that she should know nothing of the dreadful deed that he had just committed, he shoved the open knife under the body, and, leaping into his saddle, laid hold of the bridle of Swiftsure, who had stood quietly by the whole while, and trotting towards her with both horses, headed her off, as it were, from his victim, and, as he came up with her, said cheerily—

"No good after all, my lass. Hardly was your back turned when he went off like the snuff of a candle. So now jump into your saddle again."

"Oh, father, are you quite sure he is dead?"

"As sure as I am that you're alive. Didn't you see me dismount and bend over him? It was to make sure that his heart had stopped. Oh, he's as dead as a door-nail."

"Father, how comes that blood on your sleeve?"

"Blood? Oh, ah, yes, to be sure. He coughed it up just as the death-rattle took him in the throat."

"Oh, father, mayn't I go up and look at him?"

"No!" thundered Kelly. "Get into the saddle; we have lost more than enough time over him. Do you forget that the bloodhounds of the law are upon our track—that a much worse death than his threatens me, and years of wearisome imprisonment yourself? Mount—mount, I say, and don't be a fool. Do you hear?"

"Yes, father," said Rose, obeying his command with something very like terror, for never had she known him to speak so crossly to her before.

The next minute the prostrate form of Andrew M'Pherson was left far behind; but little did Ned Kelly suspect that not one of his three stabs had touched a vital part, and that the squatter was destined to live, to his (Ned's) no inconsiderable peril in the future.

Suddenly Rose exclaimed, "Look, father, we are not the only travellers across this terrible desert of fire and ashes. Over away yonder I can see two other mounted forms. They look to be our very duplicates; a trooper, and a lady with him."

Ned glanced in the direction that Rose's outstretched hand indicated, and the sight filled him with uneasiness and apprehension.

"Let us get down into the gully before they spot us," said he, "I don't think they've seen us yet."

Happily they were close up to the aforesaid gully now, and the next instant both of them were on their feet, and carefully leading their horses down the almost precipitous bank.

How the poor creatures drank of the still pools when the bed of the creek was presently reached, Ned and Rose greedily following their example, for the latter had been too anxious about the apparently dying man out upon the plain to gratify her own thirst before.

Their parched throats relived, Ned said to Rose—

"You mind the nags, whilst I climb up the bank again to take observation. I want to be assured that that trap hasn't really espied us, as our future movements must depend on that."

Placing both reins in Rose's hands, he swarmed up the bank easily enough, even though his one arm was still of no use to him; and when his eyes were above the level of the plain, for he did not deem it prudent to reveal a single inch more of his person, he took a wary but comprehensive glance all round.

The two riders were considerably nearer now, but he noticed two things—

Firstly, that they rode very slowly and in zig zagging fashion; and secondly, that their faces were continuously turned earthwards, as if looking for something.

"It's the *legitimate* daughter searching for her father's body," he muttered between his teeth. "Hang it, she can't very well miss finding it, or that trooper chap fail to discover that something more than the flames has been at work upon it. Thunder! if Rose wasn't here I'd ride out into the plain and pistol them both, for it would be far the safer plan. But there, I can't bear my bonny lass to regard me as a demon, and so I must stay my hand while she's in my company."

And having thus soliloquised, Ned descended into the gully again, and said to Rose—

"We'd best ride down the creek for a mile or so, for if we were to scale the opposite bank hereabouts, it's very likely they would see us, and then they might come across our pursuers and tell them which way we had winged our flight. Come, my girl, to horse!"

A minute later they were riding along at the bottom of the gully, with the banks rising to a height of twenty feet on either side of them.

The winter torrent of yellow water, that doubtless at seasons of flood filled the whole gorge, having shrivelled up under the fierce summer heat to a string of shallow pools, this was no difficult feat, and when they had journeyed about a mile and a quarter in this fashion, they scrambled with their horses up the opposite side of the chasm, and found themselves on another wide, sparsely-treed plain, with a curious conical mountain rising skyward at a great distance away, which Ned informed Rose was their steering point, Mount Buninyong.

CHAPTER XXVII.

A MEETING WITH OLD ACQUAINTANCES.

THE horses were much refreshed by the water they had drunk, and also by the wetting of their hoofs as they journeyed down the creek, and now they cantered easily along as spry as though they had just come out of the stable.

Half-an-hour later the sun rose up out of the eastern heavens, surrounded by a cohort of rosy clouds. The distant mountains blushed every shade of blue—from royal purple to the softest ultramarine, and the entire face of nature was revealed, looking calm, tranquil, and in every way most beautiful.

The route of the two fugitives lay across a gently undulating country, well grassed and watered, dotted thinly, and in park-like clumps, with the graceful pencil cedar, mingled with dogwood and native walnut trees, whilst the strongly-scented wattle-blossoms filled the air with fragrance, and the low rich notes of the thrush, the sweet warble of the magpie, and the boisterous cadence of the laughing jackass reverberated through the still atmosphere.

All through the morning they encountered hardly a soul, which is scarcely to be wondered at, inasmuch as they kept clear of the ordinary lines of travel, and about midday they drew rein on the margin of the Bandy Jim Creek, whose banks were almost carpeted with wild flowers of rich and varied hues, but, with one or two rare exceptions, affording no perfume.

Above them, here and there, cropped up picturesque rocks of bluestone, half hidden by the blossoms of the clematis and ranunculus, intermingled with the creamy petals of the dwarf banksia, or native honeysuckle, and the silvery and golden bloom of the wattle.

They short-hobbled their horses so that they might recruit their strength with a feed of the sweet rich grass, only to be found at this season of the year growing near running water; but how to fill their own stomachs was a much more difficult problem—in fact, a complete puzzle.

Necessity, however, being the undisputed mother of invention, and Ned Kelly discovering that there were some shoals of fish in the creek, conceived the notion of spearing some with his sword as they wriggled their way through the shallows.

It was no easy job this, but he at last succeeded in nailing two, and, having killed them, he and Rose devoured them raw, for they were fearful of lighting a fire lest the smoke should attract the attention of any scouring bands of troopers on the lookout for them.

Nothing but fearful hunger could have tempted them partake of such a repast; but they were surprised to find the fish really delicious eaten in that manner—a discovery which, however, had been made by many before them, for in the north of Asia there are entire tribes who would declare that cooking fresh-water fish in any manner entirely destroys the delicacy of their flavour. *Chacun à son goût*, we say.

After an hour's rest the two fugitives again betook themselves to the saddle, and they had not ridden very far when they descried two individuals tramping along in front with shouldered swags, at whose appearance, as they drew closer to them, Ned uttered an oath that seemed to be one more of delight than of rage.

"What's the matter, father?" asked Rose.

"Don't you know those infernal scoundrels?"

"They look to me like Lanky Jim and Lardy Bill; but I could not swear from a back view."

"They are the very men, though. Rose, it was those two rascals who betrayed me to the traps."

"Are you quite sure, father, that it was them?"

"By George, yes! One of the Joeys told me all about it, and also how they tricked them out of the reward offered for my capture. They fired at me, Rose, through the back of the hut in which I lay concealed, the treacherous Judases! They dared not face me living, so they determined to take me dead."

To such high tones had Ned raised his voice as he concluded that one of the men heard him, and turned round to see who it was.

"It's only a trap an' a gal," said he to his companion. "They won't take no notice of us, matey."

"Oh Lord! won't they, though?" exclaimed that individual, looking round in turn. "Why it's Ned Kelly's gal on her white hoss. Oh, what can it mean? I feels so soft-hearted over it, Jim."

"Don't be a mean-spirited cuss. She won't notice who we be in this rig-out; and if you're afeard as how she will, veil yer ugly mug with a good cloud of baccy-smoke as they rides past."

This was very good advice, no doubt, but the ruse didn't avail them in the present instance.

"Bail up, you ruffians!" was suddenly thundered in their ears; and the next instant one was hurled to the right and the other to the left by the buffeting shoulders of the trained police charger.

Both went to grass, half-stunned, wholly bewildered; and, before either could rise, he was covered by a levelled pistol, one of which was grasped by Rose Casey.

"Well done, lass!" cried Ned. "Don't let the scorpion get a chance of turning his sting towards you. If you see his hand moving towards shirt, belt, or pocket, put a bullet through his head. Now, Lardy Bill, I think I'm in your debt. Am I, or am I not?"

"Lord, capting, who'd have thought it would have bin you? Now, this is what I calls onhandsome ov you—first entering the perlice, an' then 'unting down a couple ov old mates as was always true as steel to you."

"Liar! you know that I'm no trap well enough, ay, as well as you know that you and your mate tried to sell me the other night, and made a nice mull of it. Your gun hung fire, didn't it? Ha! ha! the Joeys had drawn the charges so that you shouldn't cop a penny of the reward. It strikes me that they've been done brown in turn. But that's no matter. You shall never play the character of Judas any more. I'm going to turn a mongrel beast, half fox and half wolf, into a dead jackass."

"Oh, don't shoot us, capting! We don't deserve it. You've been told a pack of lies about us—nothing more. I'll take my solemn affidavey to it."

"Not only did you betray me, but I'll bet that before you decamped you robbed the general community right and left, you oily-tongued sneak and traitor," answered Ned, severely. "Turn out your pockets, dog!"

Lardy Bill at once did so. They were empty.

"Off with your jumper, and fling it here."

"Lord love you, capting, and what for?"

"Do as I bid you, or I'll blow your brains out."

Lardy Bill obeyed the order with a groan.

Ned caught the jumper jacket, and whistled as he discovered how very heavy it was.

He banged it against the pommel of his saddle, and it gave out the dull ring of gold.

"Pretty well padded, 'pon my word," said he. "If the rest of your togs are quilted in like fashion, you must be a walking mint."

"Oh, Lord, capting, it's only our own little savings and gains. Don't rob us, capting, pray don't."

"Rob you? I expect I'll only be getting back my own gold, and if it should happen not to be so of what use will it be to two dead men?"

"Dead men? Oh don't go for to kill us, capting!"

At this moment crack went a pistol, and Rose uttered a faint cry of pain.

Involuntarily, Ned Kelly wheeled his horse round to Rose's assistance, and no sooner were his eyes diverted from Lardy Bill than he in turn plucked forth a pistol from inside his open shirt, and took a cock-shot at Ned.

"Are you hurt, dear?"

"No, father, no. Look out for yourself. That man's got another pistol."

It was true that he had, but before he could discharge it Ned's horse was tramping him into the dust.

Seeing his comrade's danger, Lanky Jim endeavoured to push by Rose, concluding that a levelled pistol in a girl's hand was most likely of little account; but he had not got three yards when Rose fired at him, and brought him down with a ball through the hip.

She might have killed him had she liked, for Ned had taken great pains in teaching her pistol practice, but she had a woman's natural horror of taking human life.

"Bravo! lass, we have scotched the old serpents finely," laughed Ned. "What made you cry out?"

"A bullet grazed the tip of my ear, father."

"It's lucky it didn't take it off. You ride on a little way now, Rose, and I'll overtake you."

"Don't kill them outright, father. Oh, don't!"

"Ride on, girl, I tell you. Ride on at once."

"Not until you promise me you will spare them."

"Rose, obey me, and don't be a fool."

"Father, you shan't take human life whilst I have the power to save you from a crime," and she looked superlatively lovely as she spoke.

CHAPTER XXVIII.

A TERRIBLE REVENGE.

LARDY BILL and Lanky Jim, with their weapons discharged and no chance of being allowed time to reload them, writhed in their agony and despair upon the ground, whilst Rose pleaded with Ned for their miserable lives.

They had little hope that she would succeed; but for all that she *did*, for wonderful is the influence of woman over even the most fierce and rugged natures.

"I'm an infernal fool to listen to you, but I never could

deny you anything for long, and you know it; so you just ride on, and I'll grant your desire," Ned was fain to mutter at length.

"But—but you will not break word?"

"Did I *ever* break a promise to you, Rose?"

"No, no; and since you have promised me so faithfully I will trust you. And yet why should I ride on? Why do you want to remain behind?"

"To force these fellows to strip, so that I may be sure they have disgorged all their plunder."

Rose made no further objection, but rode on; and directly she had got a little way off, Ned, again turning towards the grovelling men, commanded them to strip and throw him each of their articles of attire in turn.

It was no easy command to execute, sorely injured as they were, but Ned vowed that he would pepper them with bullets if they did not, and trample them beneath his horse's iron hoofs as well; and so they were fain to make an effort, and as each garment was in turn tossed to him he shook it, and, if it gave forth the chink of gold, spread it across the pommel of his saddle, and if it did not, dropped it contemptuously on the ground with an oath or a sneer.

When the two men were reduced to an Adamite state of simplicity and coolness, Lardy Bill quivering in his fatness and Lanky Jim shivering in his leanness, Ned uncoiled the long trail rope that hung at his saddle-bow, and throwing it at, rather than to, Lardy Bill, said sternly—

"Get up, you dog, and bind your companion firmly to that tree."

"I—I can't get on my pins, capting. Your horse has trampled all my bones out of jint."

"He shall trample you into a shapeless heap of blubber if you don't obey me."

"Oh, lor', don't talk like that. Which tree?"

"The one just behind you, that the white bull-dog ants are running up and down so lively. They've got a nest just at its foot—see?"

Lanky Jim looked round as well as Lardy Bill, and uttered a shriek as he beheld his doom.

"Oh, mercy! capting, mercy!" he gasped. "The devilish things will cover me all over in five minutes. They will devour me alive. In an hour I'll be a skelington, a hideous, grinning skelington. Oh, you promised not to murder us."

"Nor will I. The ants may eat you or leave you alone, just as they think fit. I'm not responsible for *their* actions. Now, Lardy Bill, hurry up. Now, Jim, look lively. The ants will thank me if I have to puncture your tough hide with a bullet-hole or two so that they may creep into your intestines, but you hardly will."

Lanky Jim shrieked at the mere idea of such a thing, and without further spoken objection walked up to the tree and planted his back against the trunk.

"Bound to do it, mate, though it goes sadly agin my grain," said Lardy Bill, as he followed him up with the trail rope, and then he added in an undertone, "I'll do it so that ye can slip out again as soon as his back's turned on us."

But Lardy Bill was not allowed the opportunity of carrying his amiable intentions into execution, for Ned Kelly watched the operation a great deal too closely to give him the chance.

A dozen times at the very least he found fault with Lardy Bill's method of operations, but at last Lanky Jim was bound tightly and securely enough to satisfy even him, and then he commanded Bill to give the ant-mound (a hillock as large as a bee-hive) a good stir with the iron lynch-pin that was at one end of the rope.

"But if I do they'll be all over me, capting!"

"Well, and what do I care about that?"

"They're as big as bees, and they nip for all the world like the cussed quadrupeds they're called after."

"And aren't you in a fine condition for nipping?"

Lardy Bill groaned aloud, but he dared not disobey the commands he had received.

Standing as far away from the ant-hill as ever he could, he stretched out an arm and hand, and gave it a thorough good stir.

The terrified and ferocious insects the next instant covered it in their countless myriads, some of them making straight for Lanky Jim with wide-gaping jaws.

Lardy Bill, with fear-rolling eyes, and his mouth screwed up into the shape of a monstrous capital O, was on the point of beating a hasty retreat, quivering all over like a giant blanc-mange cast in a particularly ugly mould, when he was brought to a halt by Ned exclaiming—

"Go back and sit down on that mound."

"Oh, lor', capting, I'd rather die a hundred times! It would be worse than being kicked to death by spiders, that would," answered Lardy Bill, trying to convince both himself and Kelly that they were both joking, but with lamentable ill-success.

"Do as I command you, scoundrel! Did you fancy that I was going to let you off easier than your mate, or do you want my horse to knock you down and dance over you again first?"

"Oh, capting, this is awful, *this* is!" moaned Lardy Bill; and he went and plumped himself down where he was bidden, hoping, perhaps, by sheer weight to squash a few hundred of his foes ere they could attack him in turn.

In an instant, however, he sprang to his feet with an awful shriek, and was in the act of rushing away at all hazards, when Ned Kelly levelled a pistol at him, and put a bullet through one of his thighs, thereby causing him, with a shattered howl, to fall backwards right across the ant-hill.

In the twinkling of an eye he was covered with the ferocious insects.

He tried to break away from them again, but his perforated leg refused to support him.

He fell down once more among his diminutive foes, rolling, writhing, shrieking, and endeavouring, but all in vain, to scrape them off his naked body with his hands.

In vain we say, for even when they were torn limb from limb, the gaping mouths, with the heads only attached thereto, clung firmly to the flesh whereon they had so grimly fastened.

Ned Kelly stayed for a second or two to watch and keenly enjoy the agonies of the two scoundrels who had sought to earn three thousand pounds blood-money (ultimately raised by successive additions to ten thousand pounds) by betraying him to the police; and then, giving utterance to a bitter laugh, he set spurs to his horse and galloped after Rose.

He overtook her about a quarter of a mile on, coming back to meet him

"What did that pistol-shot mean, father?" she asked.

"Only a bullet through Lardy Bill's leg, so that he should be no better off than the fellow whom *you* winged," answered Ned, with a laugh.

"You have kept your word, father?"

"Of course I have. Why these doubts? I ask you again. Did I ever break my word to *you*?"

"Never, father. Forgive my mistrusting you, even for an instant; but I know how you must hate these two sneaking sordid wretches. What are those clothes across your saddle-bow?"

"Some of the rascals' togs. They are heavy with gold pieces and other treasure that is sewn up inside the lining. We have not time to rip them open now. We must push ahead, Rose."

Ned Kelly would have been still more anxious to push on rapidly had he only suspected that the pistol shots that had been fired had reached the ears (for sound is borne to a great distance in the clear pure air of Australia) of a posse of mounted troopers who were on the keen lookout for him and his fair companion.

And now, arrived within a close distance of where the ironclad bushranger's hideous revenge had been perpetrated, the agonised shrieks of Lardy Bill and Lanky Jim ed them on to the exact spot just in time to prevent that vengeance from being wholly consummated.

They gather round and deliver the men, who in another five minutes would have been as dead as Hamlet's ghost and Queen Anne, and Lanky Jim has just strength and venom enough to gasp, " Ned Kelly an' his gal gone that way, towards Buninyong," ere, with a groan and a gasp, he faints dead away.

So two of the troopers remained to tend the apparently dying men, whilst the remaining three spurred sharply on the fugitives' track, presently holding a brief council of war, and deciding to make somewhat of a detour with the object of heading them, and planting themselves in ambush in a secure place where they could quietly await their coming, and pop off Ned Kelly from behind a tree without allowing him the slightest chance of escape, or of injuring any of them in turn.

CHAPTER XXIX

ROSE GRADUATES FOR THE GALLOWS.

NED KELLY and his beautiful adopted daughter rode as gaily along through the sunlit bush as though grim death wasn't lying in wait for them (in the guise of three well-armed troopers sheltered snugly in ambush) a matter of three or four miles ahead; and sometimes the ironclad bushranger, ironclad now no longer, would laugh and chuckle to himself at the manner in which he fondly imagined that he and the bulldog-ants in partnership had polished off his late treacherous allies, without the breaking of the promise he had made to Rose.

Little did he imagine that Lardy Bill and Lanky Jim had quite as good reason to laugh at him, and the Squatter Andrew M'Pherson to join in the chorus. The axiom that threatened men live long was fated to be exemplified in all three instances in a most remarkable and extraordinary manner.

Rose could not imagine what Ned was chuckling about so frequently, but she was unfeignedly glad to see him in such good spirits, and sometimes smiled for company.

Both smiles and chuckling were to receive a check before long, however, for as they drew near unto the Melbourne and Ballarat road the usual array of bills and posters on the smooth bark of the blue-gum trees became, a distinguishing feature in the otherwise romantic scene; and suddenly, just above the by no means modest flourish of trumpets of Doctor L. L. Smith, appeared the familiar lion and unicorn fighting desperately as usual for the crown, the lion having for second and backer a huge dumpy capital V, and the unicorn an equally dropsical-looking capital R.

This imposing heading proclaimed a police reward, to Ned Kelly the most engrossing of all literature ; so he pulled rein for moment to read the proclamation calmly through, the more so as he saw his own name in very big print thereon.

The first little discovery that he made was that he had increased in value to the extent of a thousand pounds since the Gold Escort Robbery : for the immense sum of FOUR THOUSAND POUNDS was now offered for his capture alive or dead ; but this fact did not alarm him half so much as a supplemental reward of £500 that was offered, lower down in the bill, for the arrest and safe custody of a young girl who was stated to have personally taken part in the attack on the escort, and to have fired at the driver and his companion as they were making their escape from the scene of slaughter.

Then followed her description, and it was so exactly like Rose that she might have been recognised therefrom as readily as from a painted portrait.

Ned swore a terrible oath.

"Never mind, father," said Rose, calmly. " I ask for nothing better than to share your fate, whatever it may be. Government has anticipated my wish."

" But it has been humbugged with a lie. You took no part in the gold robbery ; you never fired at the two cowards who cut the traces and galloped off on the cart-horses before the traps and my boys came to blows, did you, Rose, eh?"

" You know, father, that nothing would induce me to attempt to take human life except the most desperate extremity, such as in defence of my own or your existence. The two men you speak of galloped close by me as I was waiting with Swiftsure for you to escape on in case you were worsted in the fight, and Marco Polo hurt so that he couldn't bear you away. They both looked at me very hard as they shot past, and I think would have been up to some mischief had they not observed a pistol in my hand."

"The venomous rascals! And so they thought that they would sting you at a safe distance ? Should I ever lay a hand on them, I'll——"

"Don't fret, father. Let them be," broke forth Rose, interrupting him. "See, I am not angry ; no, nor frightened either. Let us think only of present dangers, for I can't believe we are out of the wood yet."

"Well, lass, I would be more satisfied myself if darkness was only a couple or three hours nearer. We daren't strike the Melbourne road until dusk has set in ; the risk would be too great."

Scarcely had these words escaped Ned Kelly's lips than forth from behind rather a big patch of tea-tree scrub that bordered the faint bush-track that they were pursuing, came spurring the three troopers who had planted themselves there in ambush to await their coming.

The fact of Rose riding between them and Ned had alone prevented their discharging their carbines at him from behind their leafy cover, and in all probability bringing him down without the slightest danger to themselves.

They cursed her for the coincidence, but still, as they were three to one, they did not anticipate defeat.

They didn't regard the young girl in the light of a possible combatant, and so they gallantly swooped around the strangely assorted pair, brandishing their sabres and calling upon them to surrender themselves peaceably.

Ned's answer to this was to pluck forth a pistol from his holster and shoot one fellow through the midriff, who at once dropped from his horse, writhing in the agonies of death.

Then, had he only been able, he would have drawn the sword that hung at his own side, and tackled the other two.

But his right arm being still next to useless, he hurled the discharged pistol at one of the troopers' heads, and then made haste to pluck forth the second.

Ere he could do so, however, both were upon him, the sword of the first raised to cut him down, and that of the second shortened to run him through.

Rose saw with horror the imminent peril that he was in, and thinking only of saving his life, nor pondering that to effect that she would have to commit an act that the law would regard as murder, and punish with the gibbet, she drew forth one of her own handy weapons, took quick aim, fired, and saw a second trooper drop from his charger to the ground.

At the same instant the third and now sole survivor made a slice at Ned's head, but the bushranger ducked it suddenly and avoided the blow, seizing his assailant in turn by the throat and compressing it with such force that he dropped his weapon and looked as though his eyes would follow suit.

Had not Ned's horse suddenly edged away he might have succeeded in throttling him outright, but as it was he was obliged either to let go his hold or part company with his steed.

He chose the former alternative, and the trooper took advantage of his sudden liberation from that awful clutch to beat a precipitous retreat.

"We must pursue him—we must kill him, or your own life is sacrificed, Rose," said Ned, with his face as white as that of a corpse

The lovely and now trembling girl had never seen him look so pale before. On his own account he never would have turned so, but he saw that she had committed *murder* in his defence, that the trooper was stone dead whom she had fired at, and that if the third man was allowed to survive his evidence would suffice at any moment to clasp that fair, round, full throat with a collar of hemp 'neath the awful gallows.

Determined, therefore, to slay him at all hazards, Ned Kelly spurred his horse in pursuit; but what was his horror at discovering that he could only get a limp out of the good steed that had hitherto borne him so well!

He dismounted, to find that it had run the point of one of the dropped swords into the soft part of the off fore-hoof, the weapon having fallen into a deep wheel-rut, leaving the point and some three inches of the blade protruding.

"Dismount and lend me your nag, Rose," said Ned hoarsely; "that fellow *must* be account d for."

"I won't have any more blood shed, father."

"Nonsense, your own safety demands it, child."

"I won't owe my safety to more crime. I know what I have done—I did it to preserve your life."

"And now I want to preserve yours in turn."

"It may not be, father; I will not have it so. I will gallop away from you if you do not desist."

"Rose, are you mad? But what's the good of further talk? Your hesitation has given him already too great a start I could never overtake him now. There is a police camp not five miles away, and in an hour we shall have a whole pack of them at our heels. Now what the deuce is to be done?"

Ned had never been so nonplussed before.

"We must both ride on one horse," said Rose.

"Yes, for those of the two dead troopers have followed their mate at a gallop, confound them. But Swiftsure's nearly used up as it is, Rose."

"There's several horses in yonder paddock."

"By George! we're close upon a station then. I have it, Rose—we must play a bold and desperate game. 'Tis our only chance. I'll jump up behind you. See, there I am. Thunder! but I'm twice the man that I was yesterday. There's the Home Station, Rose. I can see it between the trees. Spin towards it like wildfire, my lass."

CHAPTER XXX.

TAKING THE BULL BY THE HORNS.

ROSE did as she was bidden, and would fain have asked Ned on the way what he intended to do there, but that she knew he would not thank her for disturbing his thoughts in such a way.

Presently he enlightened her somewhat of his own free will, and this was the programme he submitted for her guidance:

"Rose," said he, "Ned Kelly's band have stuck up the Melbourne and Ballarat day coach between Ballan and Bacchus Marsh, and murdered every passenger aboard of it except yourself. Of three troopers who came up to the rescue two were served in like manner, and I, the third, had my horse shot under me and only escaped a like fate by shamming dead. When they had gone—the bushrangers I mean—I brought you on here as being the nearest human abode to the scene of the inhuman butchery. You are in the greatest anxiety to reach Melbourne to receive the blessing of a dying mother, and I am of course in the same eager hurry to convey the news to the nearest police camp—which lies in Melbourne direction, mind you—of the outrage Kelly's rascals have committed. With such a yarn we shall both of us win the sympathy of the good folks at the station, no matter who they may be. We'll get a hasty meal—of which we both stand in great need—the loan of horses to help us on our way, a change of clothing—oh yes. I'll manage that—and whatever else we may require You've some blood on your face, Rose— don't rub it off—and lots of it on your dress, better still.

You must look very pale and frightened, but determined on continuing your journey, and I shall talk of escorting you to Bacchus Marsh, where you can catch the night coach. That's the outline of my plot; I may improve on the details as they are demanded of me. Don't go forgetting your assumed character and calling me father. Be very careful about that, my lass."

"What shall be our respective names then?"

"I'm Mr. Lanyon, and you're Miss Delancy."

"Very well, I'll try my best to sustain the character."

"Right, girl. Try, and you'll do it, never fear. We are close up to the station. This nag was lent us by a woman, whom we encountered on the way, to bring us hither as soon as possible, and I am to say that it would be sent for. Stay, no, that will hardly go down, for they will wonder why we didn't push on for the nearest township instead. We must abandon Swiftsure, and do the rest of the journey on foot. I'm as right as ninepence, and all my stiffness has passed away. I only wish that my arm was as good as my legs, and I'd be precious well content."

Ned was on the ground by this time, and Rose speedily dismounted in turn.

"Now then, off with saddle and bridle. The grass will hide 'em long enough for our purpose, and there are half-a-dozen other white horses about, so that one more added to their number will attract no suspicion. As to the traps, they'll never suspect us of taking refuge in such a place."

"What are we to do with these jackets and things?"

"With all the treasure in them? Oh my!" and Ned gave a low whistle, expressive of embarrassment.

Suddenly, however, he began looking intently along the ground close under the outside fringe of scrub, and presently espying a wombat-hole, he signalled to Rose to toss him the things, which he commenced to twist up into small compass, and then to ram down into the hollow funnel.

"There's a plant!" he said, "a hundred to one I'll find it again though I don't come for it for a matter of six months; and I'll wager that no one will find it but me. Come along!"

"Must I say farewell for ever to poor Swiftsure?"

"No fear. I'll bring him safely away when I come for the treasure. But let us hurry up."

Rose obeyed, after once rubbing her soft cheek against Swiftsure's equally velvet muzzle.

The horse uttered a low whinney, and would have followed them had not Ned driven it back.

There is no need for us to give a description of another squatter's station, for they were all pretty much alike at the period of which we write. When our story leaps over a period of some years, as it is destined to do ere it closes, we may be tempted to give a word-picture of what such a residence and domain is now.

The supposed trooper and his lovely girl companion were received with the hospitality that distinguished the Australian squatter of that day, and Ned Kelly's tale was listened to with a mingling of sympathy and horror.

The squatter was an old white-haired gentleman, who had landed with "Johnnie Falkner," the lately well-known Collingwood, J.P., in 1838, and had helped him to build the first habitation ever erected on the site of the now magnificent city of Melbourne.

He and his matronly, silver-ringleted spouse and two middle-aged spinster daughters all gathered round the trooper and the girl to listen to the thrilling account of the bushranger's fabulous misdeeds, Mr. Fairfax bemoaning meanwhile the fact (Ned was delighted at it) that his three stalwart sons and most of his station hands were cattle-mustering that day far off in the ranges, so that they could afford no help.

Ned told his tale most plausibly; and Rose wept over her dying mother, and shuddered at the horrors she had just been the witness of, in capital fashion, so that, as Kelly had foreseen, horses were immediately offered them, and food and wine pressed on their acceptance.

Both were nearly famished; but, as eating ravenously under the circumstances of their visit might have excited suspicions of the truth of their story, Rose required a great deal of pressing ere she could be induced, as her entertainers phrased it, to "force something down to keep up her strength."

Even Ned ate as though his natural appetite had been much impaired by what he had just taken part in; but he got through a very tidy picking for all that, and made up for lack of solids with plentiful libations of the rich red hermitage that was the produce of Mr. Fairfax's own vineyard.

"Might I ask you to increase the obligations that you are placing us under, by lending each of us a new rig-out, Mr. and Mrs. Fairfax?" said the bushranger, as coolly as possible, when he had finished his repast. "I see Miss Delaney shudder each time that she involuntarily glances down at her blood-stained apparel, and as for myself, I feel convinced that I should reach the police-camp with much less chance of being murdered on the way, were I dressed as a civilian instead of as a trooper. I have every reason to believe that the police post is watched by some of the wretches, so that no intelligence shall be borne thither of their infernal doings. Indeed the rascals stripped and carried away the uniforms of my two unfortunate companions, so that if two seeming troopers should call here during the afternoon or evening, don't forget that in all probability they will be a couple of those awful miscreants disguised as such."

"Oh, dear me! can't you send me some protection from the station, Lanyon? My sons and the stockmen may not be back until to-morrow night; before then we may all be murdered in cold blood."

"I will send you aid directly I reach the police-camp. I shall drop Miss Delaney at Bacchus Marsh, there to wait the evening coach. It will be all in my way. You will know the troopers I will send by a white band round their sleeves, so I advise you to close and barricade your doors and windows, and fire upon all others who may approach the place, without holding any parley, for they will naturally tell any amount of lies to gain admittance. Now for these togs that you are going to lend us, and if the fresh mounts could be ready for us by the time that we are ready for them, a good quarter of an hour might be saved."

"A very sensible remark. I will tell Sammy, the black boy, to round in and saddle for you the two fleetest steeds that I've got in the horse-paddock. Maria, my dear (this to his wife), will you instruct the lad to that effect. Jane and Fanny, do you take Miss Delaney to your room and see what you can do for her; and you, Lanyon, come along with me. I fancy that a suit of my eldest son's clothes will prove an exact fit for you."

As it happened, the fit could not have been a better one, and Ned being left alone in the old squatter's bedroom to dress, he first locked the door, and then, taking off his bushy false beard and whiskers, made free with Mr. Fairfax's shaving materials to make a clean scrape of what had before been only a close crop.

This done, he redonned the mass of false hair for the present, completed the transmogrification of his general toilet, little heeding what pain his wounded arm gave him in pulling off one coat and lugging on another, and in ten minutes he was all ready to depart.

CHAPTER XXXI.

THROUGH STILL FURTHER PERILS.

NED didn't say no to another glass of wine, as it was pressed upon him, but he was very glad to see Rose enter the room just as he was on the point of laying it down empty.

She was clad in a light grey cloth habit and a low-crowned soft felt hat decorated with a plume of cock-feathers, white cotton gauntlets, and so forth, and looked a very different girl from what she had done half-an-hour previously.

She could hardly help smiling at Ned's change, who had purposely picked out the most dandified suit of all that had been laid before him; so that, arrayed as he now was, he would have cut a very passable figure in Great Collins-street at promenade hour.

The squatter and his wife were most anxious to know what they could do more for them, but Ned declared that there was nothing more left to be done, and Rose said that she only wished that she had a pair of goggles to save her eyes from the dust, which had tormented her terribly coming along.

At this remark Ned bestowed upon her a glance of approval, and there happening to be a pair of that species of spectacles about the house, they were hunted up and promptly found, and when Rose had donned them, they added very materially to her disguise.

And now the horses were seen, in the custody of the native boy, being walked up and down just outside the window; so Ned declared that no time had better be lost, and Rose again pleaded her anxiety to reach her dying mother's side as soon as possible, and as all the Fairfaxes were anxious for some troopers to arrive for their protection as soon as might be, they offered not the slightest opposition to their immediate departure.

Consequently, a couple of minutes later, after a warm shaking of hands and no end of good wishes on either side, the bushranger and his girl-companion trotted away on a couple of the best horses that the old squatter possessed.

"We gammoned the flats well, and no mistake," observed Ned, when they had done looking back and waving adieux to their late kind entertainers. "If the traps do ride up to the station now to make enquiries, they'll be taken for disguised bushrangers, and receive bullets in lieu of explanation. What an infernal lark it'll be!"

Rose smiled as in duty bound, perceiving that it was expected of her; but she wished from her heart of hearts that the need and occasion of such larks had passed away for ever.

No sooner had they got out of sight of the house than Ned pulled off his false beard and whiskers, and shoved them well under his saddle-flap.

"What do you think of me now, Rose?"

"Oh! father, it improves your appearance wonderfully."

"Would you have known me, had we met by accident?"

"Not in the least. You look a languid swell of the first order. I saw just such a one at Mittagarra station the other night, but you cap him altogether. You look like one who would faint at the mere sight of blood. It's a wonderful transmogrification!"

Ned didn't take much heed of this. A portion of Rose's speech had alone struck him.

"What the fury took you to Mittagara?" he asked.

In as few words as possible Rose told him.

"But you took nor bite nor sup beneath that accursed roof?" and he looked at her almost fiercely.

"No, father, I did not," and she told him briefly why.

"Rose!" exclaimed Ned. "'tis a wonder that I did not destroy the one solitary being whom I loved on earth, amongst those whom I had good reason to hate, and for your and your mother's sake, my lass," and he proceeded to tell how that it was he who had created the bush-fire, with the intention of destroying Mittagarra and all whom it contained.

His narration was interrupted, however, before he had got very far with it by the sudden vision of four mounted troopers riding directly towards them.

"Oh, father, we are doomed to ill-luck," said Rose.

"Well, I can't say that we are very fortunate."

"One thing, we are in fine racing condition. I am sure both our nags would go like the very wind if put to it. We'd best not let them get too near."

"Rose, our best plan will be to put a good face on the matter and confront them boldly. It would be bad policy to allow ourselves to be chased too close up to Melbourne so as to give the entire force the cue that we were playing 'possum in or about the city. They'd be on the eternal lookout for us there, and we'd be in hourly danger of arrest. I want, whilst we are ruffling it in full feather at Melbourne, for everyone to suppose we are somewhere else."

"Well, father, your will is my will also," said Rose.

"All right, put a good face upon it then. I'm a nephew of old Fairfax, and you are my daughter. We are making a short visit at the station—confound it, did you pick up what 'twas called?"

"Yes, father; its name is Tarramea."

"Good! That's fine. We are going to—to—to Bacchus Marsh for evening vespers. This is Sunday, aren't it?"

"Yes, but vespers have commenced long since."

"Well then, to meet some friends who are journeying to Ballaarat by the evening coach. That'll do."

"That'll do; and our names, father?"

"Roger and Edith Fairfax, but they won't ask them."

"Should they do so it is as well to be prepared."

There was no time for further colloquy, for the four mounted troopers were now close upon them.

Ned and Rose were on the point of passing them by with careless nods when he who seemed to be in command, though none of the four wore a sergeant's stripes, reined up his horse and said—

"A couple of words with you, sir, if you please."

"All right, my man," said Ned. "What is it?"

"Have you seen anything of a gal on a white horse, and a man on a big brown one?"

"No, we haven't met anyone since leaving Tarramea."

"But I saw two such people, papa," interposed Rose, "or at least I think so, for they were too far off for me to be quite sure about the matter."

"What way were they riding, miss?" asked the trooper

"I saw their horses' heads and necks on the other side of yonder brush fence as we were coming out of the home paddock. The man's horse was behind, and seemed to be going lame. They were heading towards the gap between the Black Hills."

"Do you hear that, mates?" exclaimed the trooper, turning towards his companions. "Ten to one they are making for the twelve-mile patch of the Mallee Scrub that lies between Deep Creek and Burnbank, but I guess we'll overtake them before they reach it, especially if Ned's horse has gone lame. Thank you for your information, miss. It's that murdering villain, Ned Kelly, and his young savage of a gal that we're after. A rare chip of the old block that wench is turning out—couldn't have been worse if she'd been born a boy. However, she's committed murder at last, and Jack Ketch is waiting to clap the white cap over her bold, handsome face. Thank 'ee again, miss. You're quite safe riding in that direction, if so be as you aren't mistaken in the parties," and, touching the brim of his shako, the trooper wheeled round and, followed by his companions, galloped away in the direction that Rose had indicated as that taken by the fugitive.

"You did that capitally, my dear. By the time that they have discovered the wild-goose chase that they have been sent on we shall be in Melbourne safe from all pursuit," said Ned, approvingly, as they renewed their journey.

Rose made him no reply. She was weeping bitterly. For a long while she managed to restrain her sobs, but at last, when her bosom was almost bursting with its pent-up emotion, she was forced to give way to them, which she did unrestrainedly.

"Why, lass, what on earth's in the wind now?"

"Nothing, dear father. On my word, nothing."

"Tut, tut! folks don't blubber for nothing."

"Yo—yo—you don't think that the hangman is really waiting for me, do you, father?" sobbed Rose.

"No, no, child. I'm very certain he is not."

"Oh, father, such a terrible, such a disgraceful death! The muffled head—the horrid drop—the hooting crowd! I'd sooner be gored to death by wild oxen. Father, promise me a present directly we get to Melbourne. Say that it shall be the first thing that you will buy me there?"

"All right, Rose, it shall be so if you wish it."

"Good, kind father, purchase me then a bottle of the most deadly poison—a phial so small that I may easily conceal it in my bosom. I will only have recourse to it to save myself from a death of ignominy and shame. Indeed I will, father. Why can't we leave the country altogether, and lead different lives elsewhere?"

"Silence, Rose, or you will drive me mad."

"Not another word after you have promised me."

"Well, well, there! I promise; but, Rose, there isn't the slightest danger. Our detection will be impossible. I see nothing but a career of affluence, splendour, and absolute safety before us. I do not, indeed. Tut, tut! my bonnie girl, dry your tears. In four hours' time we will be in Melbourne, gay, glittering, joyous Melbourne, and all our troubles will be over. We will be as 'big bugs' as any people there."

Thus did Ned try to cheer Rose up, and he in part succeeded, little fancying himself, meanwhile, that the perils of the journey were far from being over, that the deadliest was, in fact, yet to come.

CHAPTER XXXII.

SOME OLD ACQUAINTANCES.

SHIFT we the scene to a spot some twenty miles nearer Melbourne than that whereon we left Ned Kelly and Rose—a piece of thick scrub about three miles in length and one in breadth, situate between the Mount Alexander and the Ballaarat roads just as they unite in one, and so continue all the way to the metropolis.

In the midst of that patch of scrub, yet so situated that they can hear the rumble of heavy or the rattle of light vehicles proceeding along either road, is pitched a camp; and around it are gathered a group of seven as ruffianly-looking fellows as any nation under the sun could manage to produce.

The full moon shines down upon a dirty ragged calico tent, on a huge cauldron of savoury broth that hangs suspended from three crossed props over a big fire; on the woolly-headed, bare-armed buck nigger who superintends the cooking; on the dark, gipsy-looking sentry, who stands grasping the barrel of his rifle and intently listening for the slightest sound a little further off; and, lastly, on the five remaining rascals, who sit or stand eagerly discussing, and occasionally laughing over, deeds of violence, bloodshed, and murder, in close proximity to the aforesaid ragged tent.

Are they honest miners, journeying to or from the Ballaarat or Mount Alexander diggings?

Well, they are got up as much as possible to look like it, but their ferocious countenances give to all honest labour the lie.

The least ruffianly-looking of the group wears an old bell-topper hat cocked rakishly on one side of his head,—albeit it has lost its brim a long while ago—and a red belcher handkerchief twisted loosely around his neck.

With one hand thrust deep into the side pocket of his rusty jumper, and the other balancing a dirty clay pipe in such a manner as to give point to his arguments, our old acquaintance Dick Dawson, alias Carroty Larkins, harangued his cut-throat-looking band as pourtrayed in our engraving.

"Pals," said he, "we must all stand true to each other. We are but seven of us left, but seven has always been a lucky number, and I don't see as why it should prove an unlucky one now that you've done me the honour of electing me as your capten. All I can say is that I'll prove as true as steel to your interests, an' that without showing favoritism to one more nor to another."

"Like our old capting with his precious Lardy Bill an' Lanky Jim," growled the man who sat on his left, grasping the handle of a big woodsman's-axe with both brawny hands.

"Hear! hear! Well said, Nimming Ned," growled a chorus of voices, and then a single one added, "Ned

Kelly took too much upon his blessed self. He war a tyrant, he war, divil a doubt of it."

"Which I will never be lads," ejaculated Carroty Larkins quickly; "no double allowance of spoil for me just because I've the honour of being your leader. No such thing. Share an' share alike, I say. You see I aren't hampered by the petticoats."

"Blow the petticoats!" came a unanimous chorus.

"Well, they are at the bottom of every mischief," assented Carroty Larkins. "The capten, I means to say the late capten, allays thought a deal more of that gal Rose nor he did of any of us, and, wither his vitals! we was none of us considered good enough even to cast a glance upon her. I'll bet that he desarted us all along of her—desarted us without so much as a good-bye or a Devil-take-ye. He never knowed no manners, did Ned."

"I wouldn't say as how he hadn't made up his mind to betray us to the traps. If that wasn't his little game why need he have slipped off so sly after the gold escort affair, eh, pals?"

It was Nimming Ned who put this question; and some replied to it with dubious grunts and others with nods of more than half-approval.

At this juncture, however, the sentry out beyond the camp-fire held up his hand to impose silence, and everyone began to listen intently.

"Riders—two of 'em!" ejaculated Nimming Ned.

"Shall we stop them?" questioned everyone with his eyes, though not a word was spoken.

Then Carroty Larkins, after a moment's consideration, said—

"Ay, on course we will. All's fish as comes to the net, lads. Come, let us look sharp."

The other men at once sprang to their feet, and, grasping their weapons, stole after their leader through the thick undergrowth, ready for any deed of villainy as long as it brought them in gold.

.   .   .   .

Ned Kelly and Rose were riding quietly along the road Melbournewards, when all at once three shots were fired out of the close scrub on their left, and down went both their horses, writhing and kicking in their death-agonies.

Ned was on his feet in a twinkling; but, seeing Rose lying apparently unconscious on the ground, and within a likely distance of having her brains kicked out, he flew to her aid without ever bethinking himself of what the character of the danger could be that now menaced them.

As he was in the act of lifting her up, however, both were surrounded, laid roughly hold of and torn apart, whilst Carroty Larkins shouted out—

"Prig his barkers, if he's got any, and empty his pockets afterwards. Not that he's of much account, only a lardy-dardy swell. We'll pluck him and let him go, and keep the young woman for ourselves. Ha, ha! that's the little game."

"Larkins, you're improved in villainy since we last parted company. Don't you know me?"

"Jehoshaphat! The Capten! Leastways I should say Ned Kelly, for he ain't capten no longer, having ov course been sacked when he sneaked away without so much as a good-day to his old pals."

Carroty Larkins tried to speak defiantly, but as he was a cur at heart, there was a something that *would* creep into his tone that gave the lie to the independence of his words.

"Who dares to say that I deserted the band?" exclaimed Ned, as he struggled fiercely in the hands of his captors. "I was betrayed into the hands of the traps by Lardy Bill and Lanky Jim, and my daughter helped me to escape from the Booroma lockup only last night. We have been pursued hither and thither by the Joeys almost ever since, and our retreat is now cut off in every direction except that of Melbourne, which is alone why we are journeying thither. So how do you make it out that I've *sneaked* away?" and the bushranger looked around him fiercely.

"Well, it looked werry like it, didn't it mates?" rejoined Larkins, glancing eagerly round for, at all events, the moral support of his pals.

"Ay, werry," let out Nimming Ned. "And if Lardy Bill and Lanky Jim betrayed you, as you tell us they did, what became ov 'em after? Just you answer that Ned Kelly."

"What became of them? You'll have to ask a certain nest of bulldog-ants, far up in the bush, that question," broke forth Ned Kelly, fiercely. "They should have taken more care to keep out of my way. Ha, ha! search for them if you like, and you'll find Lanky Jim's skeleton bound to a tree, and Lardy Bill's stretched across the ant-hill at its foot, with his right thigh bone shattered with a pistol-bullet, so that he could not crawl away. So perish all who would dare to play me false!" and as he concluded he cast a terrible look around upon his late followers.

Carroty Larkins, quailing before it, slunk away, but Nimming Ned, who had more brute-courage, exclaimed with a wolf-like growl—

"Which way is it to be, mates—the old capten or the new un? I'm for Carroty Larkins, I am."

"And I'm for Ned Kelly, still!" at once spoke up another bushranger; whereupon Larkins, coming back, exclaimed heartily, "I'm for Ned Kelly as well, and as I expect are we all. Ned, I was opposed to you as long as I thought you'd used us mean and shabby, but I accepts your explanation as a true un; indeed, I've no doubt whatever of its being so, and I therefore resigns the command and beseeches on you to take it up again. There, I've said it."

A cheer from all parties concerned greeted this speech, in which Nimming Ned faintly joined.

Thereafter he walked across to Larkins, and whispered in his ear—

"Our hailing him as our capten *now*, don't stop us cutting his throat when he's asleep by-and-by. His carrion's worth as much as his living body remember, and I'll eat my head if both he and she haven't a precious lot of spoil hidden away about, 'em," and here he chuckled grimly.

The rest, however, seemed heartily glad to have got their old leader back again, and conducted him in triumph through the belt of scrub to their camping-ground, where the soup was just done to a nicety and all ready for eating.

Rose had by this time quite come round, and great was her horror at discovering by whom she was surrounded.

Ned's rage and mortification were every whit as great, but he dared not show it. All that he could do was to make the best of circumstances and patiently abide his time.

CHAPTER XXXIII.

PLANS FOR THE FUTURE.—MELBOURNE.

YES, Ned Kelly was really annoyed, almost beyond all patience and endurance, that his lot was again cast amongst this set of ruffians.

He had made up his mind to have gone to the neighbouring colony of Sydney—to have introduced Rose to the respectable world, and somehow or other secured her a brilliant marriage."

Yes, he had determined to be a political refugee (a class of men that all romantic women love), an Irish noble with a price set upon his head for endeavouring to emancipate his unhappy country from the rule of the heretic Saxon.

And now here was a dead weight cast upon all these brilliant plans and prospects, a dead weight that he dared not cast off. But in the meantime what should he do with this disreputable-looking tail in Melbourne? They would never pass muster as Irish refugees, they looked a deal more like Neapolitan brigands, and the chances were that they would find themselves totally unable to keep out of mischief, whilst the odds were at a hundred to one that if one got lagged he would seek to slip his own neck out of the hangman's noose by substituting those of all his comrades, his (Ned's) and Rose's included.

And yet Kelly felt that to shake them off now was impossible. Having re-elected him their captain, an honour that it would have been as much as his life was worth to have declined, they would stick to him as tightly as barnacles stick to a drifting piece of wreckwood, expecting him almost daily to plan out schemes of villainy that would enrich the entire commonwealth, which riches would be quickly dissipated in women and wine, two sources from which betrayal was about equally to be expected. Could things possibly have happened worse?

How Ned now regretted that he had revealed himself to the bushrangers, for he felt sure that not even Carroty Larkins would have recognised him else.

True, he had done so in order to save Rose from their ruffianly hands; and when he reflected that the revelation certainly had saved her, he became convinced that after all he had acted for the best.

So the question was reduced to that of making the best of a bad bargain. What was already done could not be recalled. He must make what use of these men he could, controlling them so that they should do as little harm as possible.

Rose guessed pretty nearly what were the subjects of his thoughts, and so did not interrupt him even by a word.

The bushrangers, however, soon showed themselves to be more impatient; and when supper was disposed of and pipes lighted, they nudged each other as to who should be spokesman, and presently Carroty Larkins made bold to speak up—

"Well, capten, since I've given up the command to you with a werry good grace, I suppose as I've a right to consider myself your leftenant; and in the character of that there indiwiddle I now axes you the plan ov our future campanes."

"May I first enquire of *you* what you intended to have done in case I hadn't rejoined you?"

"In course you may, capten, an' in the present instance easy axed is easy answered. You see we've a tidy little covert here, right atween two roads, and them the main roads to and from a couple ov rich diggings, so that we couldn't be in a better spot for filling our pockets at other folks' expense. Ain't I right, boys? If so, speak up."

"Ay, ay! a fine place," echoed several rangers.

"The best place that I ever saw," echoed Ned.

"Come, I'm glad as you agrees with me, capten."

"Yes, it's the best place I ever saw for the traps to hem you in on all sides and catch every mother's son ov you without a possibility of a single one breaking cover. How long have you been here?"

"Arrived just six hours ago," said one.

"I thought you could not have been much longer than that at work," laughed Ned. "Well, another twenty-four would probably have seen you all in a much securer place, namely, inside Pentridge Stockade. Why, you could not have chosen a more favourable spot for being entirely surrounded, cut off, and destroyed."

The men looked perfectly astounded and bewildered.

Larkins scratched his round bullet-head and looked both silly and sullen; whereupon Nimming Ned bent forward and whispered in his ear:—

"Three inches of cold steel will atone for all this. 'Tis a poor return for what you've just bin and gone and done for him, to show you up in this manner, Carroty, darned if it isn't!"

The remaining five men, however, seemed to be remarkably thankful that their old leader had turned up in time to preserve them from the catastrophe that he had pointed out as threatening them.

And now they demanded, as in one breath, what were his plans for the future.

"Wait a bit, my lads, and I'll tell you. Rose, my dear, just walk out of earshot, will you?" I have that to say to these brave fellows that it is not fitting that you should hear. Keep a sharp lookout for deaf adders, though, for this used to be a terrible place for them, and come back when I whistle."

Rose raised no objection, but did as she was bidden.

"Now, my lads," continued Ned, "are you ready for great things? and to accomplish them the more surely, can you keep for awhile from drink, sweethearts, and *blowing?* and it'll be worth your while."

Thereupon some of the bushrangers remarked that if 'twas *very much* worth their while they might manage. At all events, they would try, they said.

"It's no good only trying," retorted Ned testily. "Before the enterprise is commenced I'll have to bind each one of you by the most solemn and awful oaths to remain sober, and give the fair sex (*foul* sex would be a more correct term, when applied to some of your sweethearts) a wide berth, until we are clear away at sea."

"At sea?" echoed two of the bushrangers, almost joyfully; for they had once been honest, sturdy, British sailors. "At sea, did you say, capten?"

"Ay, at sea!" reiterated Ned, "and in possession of a stout craft laden with golden spoil, and bound for the old country! What think you of that, lads?"

"That the thing's a deal too good ever to come off, that's what I think ov it," growled Larkins.

"Tut, tut! nothing's impossible to brave and determined men. But there's a hard nut to be cracked first—the nut that the golden kernel is inside of. What say you, lads, to robbing the richest bank in Melbourne city and decamping with the spoil? Don't speak all at once!"

But they did speak all at once, the scheme was so exactly to their taste.

Even Nimming Ned was won over.

Larkins alone was obdurate, for he hadn't forgiven Kelly for so severely criticising his generalship, and out of sheer spite he felt disposed to oppose him in everything.

In reply to a host of questions—all poured in upon him at once, and mingled with Carroty Larkins's clearly audible asides of "The thing can't be done. It stands to reason as how it can't be done. A short road to the gallows, that's all that it'll prove," and so on—Ned raised a hand to impose silence, and then said impressively—

"Listen, lads, to my scheme. The Bank of Australasia is on the right-hand side of Collins-street, a few doors from the Criterion Hotel and the *Argus* Office. Opposite are some fine shops, and it's not very often in these times of everybody sloping off to try their luck at the diggings that one of 'em isn't to be let. I shall take one of those shops and open it, say, as a wholesale drug store, or a merchant's of some kind. The upper portion I shall appropriate as my private residence, whilst the entire ground floor and the cellars will be devoted to business. Do you follow me?'

There was a general shaking of heads, and looks of quite comical bewilderment.

Not one of the assemblage understood him in the least degree.

Ned smiled grimly, and then continued—

"In my business I shall require many hands—warehousemen, and shopmen, and carters, and indoor and outdoor porters. They will live somewhere or other about the basement premises, and talk and dress and act like other folks. They will make no friends in or about the city, but be sober and orderly and civil to all customers and others, and work by night as well as by day.''

"Oh, that be blowed!" at this point remarked somebody.

"Yes, they will," said Ned Kelly, fixing the speaker with his eye; "for at night each man will be working for his own future. He will be wielding spade and pick to make himself a millionaire."

"A milliner! What the deuce do we want to make ourselves milliners for—a trashy trade as is only fit for women?" growled Carroty Larkins.

"The capten don't mean that kind; he means the sort as is rolling in wealth, numskull. Millioners and millingers hain't the same thing either Go ahead, boss, and don't mind him."

"Well then," said Ned, "at night, to speak more plainly, we'll be driving a tunnel right under Collins-street to—can anyone guess where?"

"Ay, close up to some bonnie craft as is lying alongside the quay at the bottom ov Flinder's-street, which we'll board and carry on, then put to sea in," hazarded one of the ex-sailors wildly.

"Fool's game, fool's game!" muttered Larkins.

"I should think it would be," laughed Ned Kelly. "The tunnel will be into the bullion vaults of the Bank of Australasia, where each one of us will be able to enrich himself to the very top of his bent. Ha, ha! you seem to grow suddenly interested. What think you of my plan, lads? Do you fall in with it, eh?"

Fall in with it? There wasn't a bit of doubt about that. The seven men suddenly changed into seeming maniacs in their greed for gold. Their eyes almost started out of their heads, their hands clutched the air or the grass; they gasped for breath, the scheme seemed to them such a grand one, and the success thereof so extremely probable.

"And when we've copped the gold, if so be as we *do* cop it, what then, capten?" asked Larkins.

"Ere that time comes I shall have chartered a sloop or small coasting schooner to convey some of my merchandise to New Zealand. The gold ingots, and bars, and nuggets, and dust, once on our own premises, we can pack them away into boxes and barrels bearing the name of our usual wares. At dawn our carts will convey them aboard our vessel as she lies alongside the wharf; a few minutes later the remainder of her crew will go aboard of her, to wit ourselves, decked out in true nautical fashion. A steam tug will be ready to take us in tow, and we shall be fairly outside the Heads, with a blue above and a blue below, as the song has it, by the time that the city clock strikes ten, and the lazy bank clerks are just settling at their desks."

"Capten, it's you that's got the head for contriving, an' no mistake," exclaimed a bushranger who hadn't before spoken. "The scheme's a beautiful one intirely. Faith, an' whin I gets back to old Oirland wid my share ov the wealth, I'll buy a castle, an' marry a beautiful young colleen, an' drive a bright yaller chariot drawn by six spotted coach-horses, wid a post-boy in scarlet on each ov 'em. 'Dade an' I will that."

"Ye'll never get to Ireland, man, for the capten's mite ov a coaster will go down in the big seas off the Cape of Good Hope," growled Larkins.

"Why, you chuckle-head," exclaimed one of the ex-sailors, on hearing this, "who'd think of sailing to England that way? It's round the Horn we'll have to go; and for the mountain billows that one meets with in those regions always and for ever a-rolling before the brave west winds to the east'ard, give me a light-heeled craft as 'll dance over them, far before a huge monster as will wallow down souse between every wave and feel as though she never meant to rise again. I know what it is to take aboard one ov they icy green billows, I can tell you, m tes—ay, and what it is for a big ship to broach to in 'em also, and perhaps have her poop cabins wrenched from out of her, and scattered all over the sea like shivered matchwood."

"So you see, Larkins, that a small, light, well-built craft, that answers her helm quickly, is as safe as a three-decker," said Ned, turning to the in every way discomfited ex-captain. "Now let me put it to you at once and for all time, do you cast in your lot with us heartily and of your own free will? Answer like a man."

"I do, capten, hand and heart. There's my fin upon t," retorted the party addressed, who knew well enough that if he attempted to back out now he would most assuredly be murdered as one who knew far too much for the safety of the rest, leave alone his power to compromise the success of their daring enterprise

Ned Kelly accepted the offered hand, and gave it a wring that caused the proprietor thereof to wince. Then all the other bushrangers crowded around him, eager to shake hands in turn.

When Kelly had gone through the ordeal, he said—

"Now, I and my daughter had better continue our journey to Melbourne at once. You will have to give us two of your horses in place of those that you have shot. Take the harness off the dead animals for our use, and drag them out of sight into the bush, for should some trooper come across them ere you are well away from here their suspicions would be sure to be aroused, and you might precious soon find yourselves in Queen-street. Now my final directions are, that you all get well away from here before dawn, leaving your horses and all weapons that can't be readily concealed, behind you; that you enter Melbourne singly, or at most in pairs, and from different directions; that you get yourselves shaved and looking decent as soon as possible, and even before you think of reassembling, each in the kind of dress that was the badge of his calling or pursuit before he took to a fierce and lawless life, for there are slop and second-hand clothes shops everywhere, and that you await my coming in the employment office that you will find in Great Bourke-street, nearly opposite the Horse Bazaar, at noon, on Tuesday, all pretending to be strangers to each other. You understand me?"

"Yes, yes!" exclaimed everyone in a breath.

"Make haste with our horses, then," answered Ned.

No objection was raised. Two of the men immediately set off to catch and equip a couple of steeds, and Ned whistled to Rose.

In a minute she was by his side, and looking up anxiously into his face.

"We are about to continue our journey," said he; "shake hands with our friends, lass, for when next you see them we shall all of us be engaged in honest and legitimate trade."

"I am so glad to hear it," answered the lovely girl, and she held out one hand to Carroty Larkins and the other to Nimming Ned at once, who each laid hold of the tendered article as gingerly as though it was a piece of valuable waxwork that without tender handling would be very likely to break off in their grasp.

The others copied their tactics exactly, as presently did the two men who brought up the horses.

Ned lifted Rose into the saddle and then mounted himself.

The bushrangers would have raised a cheer, but Ned stopped them, as it would not have been altogether safe, and after reiterating some of his cautions and directions they rode away.

"We are well out of that mess, dear," said Ned.

"Yes," answered Rose, "but I'm glad we fell across the men, both for their own sakes and that of others, since you have really persuaded them henceforth to turn over a new leaf and lead an honest life."

Ned Kelly looked keenly at the fair girl. There was no suspicion or irony either in her expression or tone. He had never seen her look so bright and happy before, and so he had not the heart to undeceive her as to the honesty of his and their future career.

"Yes, Rose," he said, "with the capital that I have in hand I am going to open business as a merchant, and take all these men into my employ."

"Oh, father, I hope none of them will betray you."

"I have no fear, girl."

"Well, you know them better than I do, and if you feel certain that you can trust them I shall feel very happy in the thought that you have done them good."

"Be happy, then, for I am quite safe."

And then he changed the conversation to other topics, for he dared not dwell longer on that one.

Melbourne was now only fifteen miles distant, and scattered villages and townships soon began to enliven the way.

Now and then a coach would flash past them, going one way or the other, and frequently they would meet or overtake a heavily-laden tilted waggon; those approaching the metropolis laden with bales of wool, or perhaps a stinking cargo of green hides, and those proceeding up country filled with provisions, wares, and clothing for the shops and stores of far-distant bush townships

Troopers, too, were encountered, with jingling chain-bridles and clattering sword-scabbards, and diggers on horseback and on foot, all pressing forward towards the golden El Dorado of Ballarat and Forest Creek, to find, very probably, after months of toil, mares'-nests instead of nuggets.

By-and-by the dark grey walls of the formidable prison of Pentridge frowned upon them, causing Ned, brave as he was, an involuntary shudder; and shortly afterwards they rattled through the pretty suburban township of Brunswick, to be quickly succeeded by that of Fitzroy, when for the first time the gas-lamps of Melbourne spread out before them in long glittering lines of light, and ten minutes later they drew rein at the already famed Albion Hotel in Great Bourke-street.

Here Ned ordered the very best accommodation that the house could afford for himself and daughter, who gazed in awe and wonder at the to her sumptuously-furnished room to which they were immediately conducted, wondering in her own simple mind whether anything in a king's palace could be finer.

Poor rooms, after all. Gaudiness and execrable taste was all they then could boast of.

CHAPTER XXXIV.

MESSRS. BELLAMY & CO., WHOLESALE MERCHANTS.

A WEEK has passed away, and a new and extensive place of business has been opened in Great Collins-street, exactly opposite the Bank of Australasia, under the designation of "Bellamy & Co, wholesale merchants."

The warehouse is, however, apparently crowded with great bales and boxes and articles of merchandise, done up in every form and shape; and clerks and indoor and outdoor porters and warehousemen, all clean and business-like, are eternally pottering hither and thither; and carts and waggons are continually being laden and unladen before the doors; and sailors, with a fresh and wholesome smell of the briny about them, visited the premises hurriedly and darted away again with equal speed, hitching up their unmentionables, and squirting tobacco-juice about the pavement, as sailor-men are proverbially supposed to do.

Had anyone looked at the upper windows of Messrs. Bellamy & Co.'s, he would have observed those of the drawing-room floor to be draped by cloth-of-gold curtains, decorated with heavy bullion fringe and tassels; and at one or other of them he would have frequently seen the face and form of a young and lovely girl, the face framed by a mass of glossy clustering curls, that gleamed with almost the brilliance of jet as they rippled over full, fair, creamy shoulders that would have put to shame the whiteness of Carrara marble; and the form, that was just swelling into the rounded contours of womanhood, draped in the most expensive stuffs that the whole world was capable of contributing to its adornment.

After business hours a couple of thoroughbred horses, held by a natty groom, or a high dogcart and tandem, might be frequently beheld in front of the side private door, and presently that young girl would trip forth, attired for riding or driving, as the case might be, and attended by a gentleman who was supposed to be her father, but who might almost have passed for her elder brother—said gentleman being always faultlessly attired, and neatly gloved and booted—and bystanders would remark, as the comely and aristocratic-looking couple dashed off—

"There go the rich Mr. Bellamy and his only child. Dear, oh, what a roaring trade that firm's doing!" Whilst some of the deeper thinkers, who had lived in Melbourne for some years, would be apt to mutter to themselves—

"I wonder who the deuce that fellow is, and where he turned up from, and whom he transacts business with? No one recollects his coming out," and so on, ad infinitum.

Of course the reader is better informed, and has long ago recognised, in Mr. Bellamy and his daughter, Ned Kelly and Rose Casey.

And how happy is Rose. She believes that the man whom she regards, and notwithstanding all his crimes venerates as her father, is really leading an honest life, and, furthermore, has induced others to do so. She recognises at least half those clerks and porters and sailors and warehousemen as former members of the bushranger band up in the Mount Macedon ranges, and the new hands who are strangers to her, and about equal them in numbers, look to her equally honest and respectable.

How changed would have been her feeling had she but known that the whole lot of them were the biggest set of villains ever left unhung, that the subterranean tunnel was already commenced whose termination would be the bullion vaults of the opposite bank, and that one and all, her stylish-looking companion included, were ready to commit any and every crime rather than be foiled in their undertaking.

Behold them of a night in a large room on the basement-floor of the mansion, that has been given up to them for their sole use, and you would not suppose this

There sit Carroty Larkins and Nimming Ned in the foreground, pipes in hand and a great pewter pot of gin and ale standing between them on the rough table, looking as respectable as two working men could well look: at another table sit our sailor friends, similarly engaged (our artist has drawn them to the life), whilst a couple of younger and more ardent spirits are doing a double shuffle in their heavy hob-nailed boots, and three or four of their fellows look admiringly on.

NED KELLY

THE
IRONCLAD
AUSTRALIAN BUSHRANGER

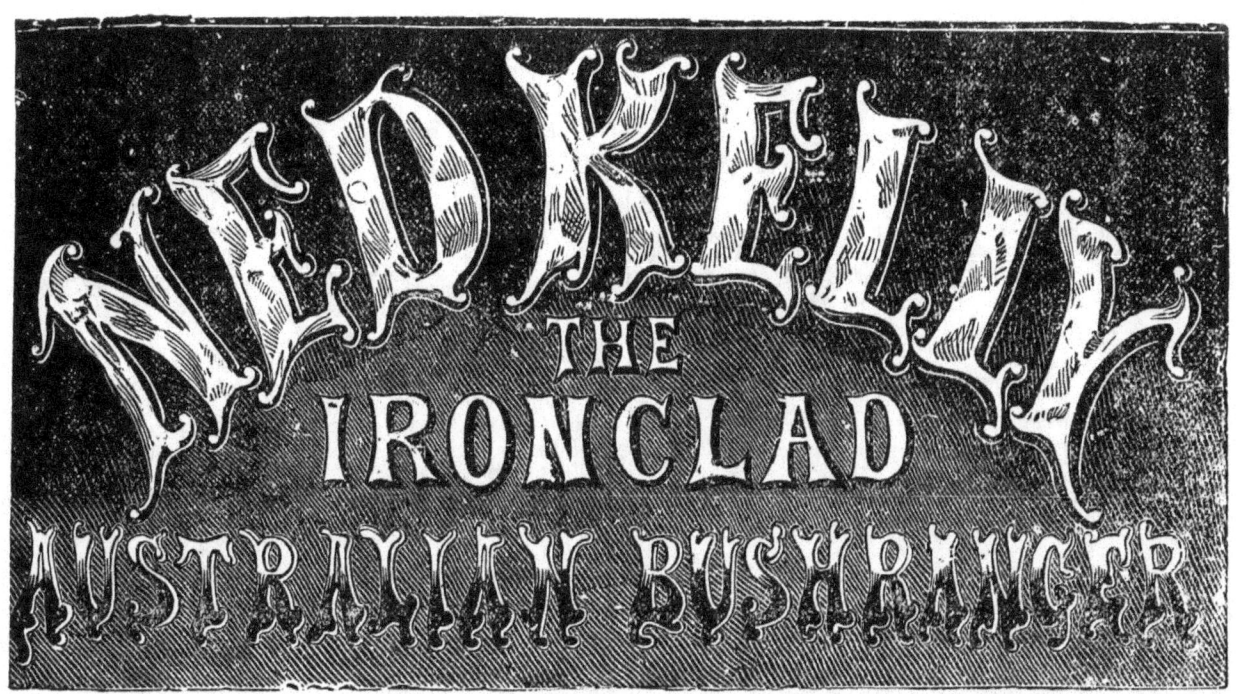

NO 5'

CHAPTER XXXV.

AN UNEXPECTED APPARITION.

In the last chapter the select company therein depicted sat with open eyes and mouths, expecting the promised vocal display.

"Go it," shouted Nimming Ned, taking a pull from a flask and handing it to Carroty, who plentifully wet his whistle and then struck up the following ditty:—

"What a difference exists between London and here,
For there things are cheap, but here things are dear;
There's a shilling goes further in value, though small,
Than a sovereign out here, which goes no way at all.
At home aristocracy seems all the go,
On the diggings we're all on a level, you know;
The poor man out here ain't oppressed by the rich,
But dressed in blue shirts you can't tell which is which.

"Now for the chorus, boys:—

"So this is the country, with rich golden soil,
To pay good reward for industrious toil;
There's no masters here to oppress a poor devil,
For out in Australia we're all on a level.

The swell that in London rides through Rotten-row
Is admired and bowed to by many, you know;
But if he thus rode down the Ballarat-road,
I rather guess he would be jolly well "joed."
Lucky diggers in cabs you may frequently meet,
In blue shirts, being driven in Great Collins-street;
If they dressed so in London and drove about there,
Good gracious! how all the Cockneys would stare.

To the Church of St. George's in Hanover-square,
To get married, the great folks of London repair;
In phaeton the bridegroom and all his friends ride,
And a fine carriage then dashes up with the bride.
Full of fashion and beauty the church is that day,
And how sweetly the bride weeps when given away;
To the breakfast they hasten, and then, light of heart,
The happy pair off to the Continent start.

But a wedding out here is a different thing;
No carriages drive up, no marriage-bells ring.
To the church here the girl and her lover they start,
And if they don't walk they ride in a spring-cart.
The bride takes a bottle of brandy, chock-full,
And to keep up her spirits imbibes a long pull;
She don't faint away, nor yet get in a funk,
But when married goes home, and gets jolly well drunk.

In London the swells in the parks drive all round,
But the diggers drive here with a pick underground;
And the props that they use, surely, everyone knows,
Aren't like those used in London for hanging out clothes.
The women use fans there, the men use 'em here,
Though to Cockneys that statement may sound very queer;
And the fellows that frequently hang round hotels,
Out here are called loafers, at home are called swells.

In London, the gas is lit up every night,
But the thing that's called gas here don't give any light;
The gutter at home and the gutter out here
Are things widely different, to all is quite clear.
In London two trotters you get for a penny,
Which you pay a bob here for, or else can't have any;
All kinds of provisions are high in price here,
And taturs and greens is most awfully dear.

In London you go to a threepenny hop,
But here it's a bob if the weasel you pop;
At home there are workhouses, here none at all,
So, of course, here the weakest must go to the wall.
In London the peelers down aries will go,
To make love to the cook and the victuals, you know,
But here there's no aries down which to intrude,
So, of course, the Australian bobbies are slewed.

The gals that come out in Australia to roam
Have much higher notions than when they're at home;
And you'll find precious quickly they don't care a pin
For a digger unless he has plenty of tin.
Lots of gals from an offer that would be debarred
If they togged up in Hoyle's prints at fourpence a yard,
Find it perfectly easy a husband to fix,
Dressed in a score yards of satin at seven-and-six.

"Now, chorus for the last time, lads, and in good vollum—

"So this is the country, with rich golden soil,
To pay good reward for industrious toil;
There's no masters here to oppress a poor devil,
For out in Australia we're all on a level."

Just at this moment their mirth was somewhat damped by the sudden entrance of Ned Kelly, whose looks were furious, and his words no less so. He scowled upon the revellers with ill-suppressed rage—

"Idiots! dolts! confounded asses! What are you about? Do you want to rouse the whole neighbourhood, and call down the attention of the police? Curse you all!

*A fan is a machine for pumping fresh air down a mine shaft.

Am I always to be in danger from your infernal stupidity, by which you risk your own necks and mine too? Clear out of this, the lot of you! Such pals as you are, are not to be trusted. I'm only safe because I've got your necks in my hand, and down you must go with me if I go to the 'drop.' I shut up this crib to-night and leave it. We don't work together any more. I'm done with this job. Now vammus!"

The men expostulated, but they might as well have tried to move the pyramid of Cheops.

Out they went.

Ned locked up the place, and, to baffle his crew, he arranged to meet them in a week on the ranges.

He appointed another meeting with Carroty and Dawson, and removed the same evening with Rose to an hotel.

He began to fear that so many cooks would spoil the broth, and that their want of caution would betray them and him too.

They had nearly "knocked down" the "spoils" they had in their possession when arriving in town; and if they required fresh supplies they must return to their old bush practices of robbing, and perhaps murdering, lucky diggers.

This was of daily or nightly occurrence at Gandhurst and Ballarat.

The ground was honeycombed with pits from twenty to fifty feet deep, and nothing was more easy or common than for half-drunken or perfectly-sober diggers being, like Joseph, "cast into the pit," there to remain and rot.

Many a lucky digger has entertained his assassin, and, when asleep, been murdered and thrown into the nearest hole in the nearest "claim."

Ned's band were most practised in this style of "foraging," as they named it, and always knew how and where to replenish their exchequer.

Consequently the most of them cleared out of Melbourne the following morning at daylight.

To deaden suspicion Ned removed the same night to a third-rate hotel.

He gave orders to have all his merchandise and furniture sold (as he was about to proceed to England), paid a quarter's rent, and gave up the premises.

But nothing was more foreign to his intentions than to abandon his bank project.

Rose did not know whether to feel alarmed or pleased at being an inmate of what seemed to her too public a residence, but, keen and observant, she followed Ned Kelly, and maintained a cool demeanour.

Graceful and ladylike by nature, and not being too demonstrative in manner, she passed muster for the daughter of a gentleman who was visiting the land of gold for amusement, while the sight of so many gaily-dressed people and waiters, flitting about in hot haste, brought all her self-control into action.

Ned seemed to know the hotel as well as if he had been its oldest inhabitant, and, bringing Rose into the dining-room, he ordered a plentiful rather than elegant repast, which was quickly served, and as quickly despatched.

"Rose," said Ned Kelly, as he pushed away his plate and leaned back in his chair, "it is time that you went to bed. The long journey is too much for you. You look thoroughly done up—washed out; but a good long 'coil' will bring the bloom back again. Listen to me. Keep up the name of Bellamy; show no surprise at anything you may see or hear, but keep your ears and eyes open, and let me know all you see and hear."

As the unfortunate girl rose with a sigh to go to the room appointed to her, she stooped and kissed the fierce bushranger.

The caress seemed to produce a saddening effect upon him; he leaned his elbows upon the table, and shaded his face with his hand as if striving to conceal its expression from Rose.

"What is the matter, father?" she asked. "It is you

who require sleep. Your eyes are sunk deep in your head. Rest, father, or you will be knocked up."

Ned laughed bitterly as he pushed back the hair from the girl's brows and looked fixedly into her eyes.

"I have no time to be ill, Rosa," he said. "This place and all about it call up strange recollections. I am rather downhearted at times, and particularly so to-night. I've something to think of, so be off to your room."

She obeyed without uttering another syllable, but was evidently depressed by Ned's manner and words.

Ned sat staring for a long time at the gaudily-decorated walls.

His eyes were fixed upon vacancy, his thoughts evidently concentrated upon some important project.

At last he sprang to his feet, and, giving himself a shake, as if to dissipate unwelcome thoughts, he put on his "billycock" and rushed out into the open air.

He was in a restless mood, and paced nervously through the streets, stopping now and then to scan the faces of the passers-by, for, like all criminals, "he feared an officer in every bush."

Some had only just arrived in the colony, and exhibited all the curiosity and interest in surrounding objects, of "new chums."

Activity and ardour seemed the characteristic of everyone. Busy about business or pleasure, "the world before them where to choose," as Milton says of our first parents—no downcast labour-worn faces—plenty reigned round and about—and every man had that look of independence and hope so absent from the careworn faces of our working population.

The women, too, had less of the "drab"-like and slattern aspect so characteristic of our female "lower orders."

And no wonder. Beef and mutton were and are twopence a pound, and wages from twelve to fourteen shillings a day.

The poor man's paradise, it's no wonder if the inhabitants of this modern Eden felt and looked "as jolly as sand-boys," whatever that may mean. But with a splendid climate, easy work, good pay, and plenty of food, content and something more irradiated the faces of "the working classes" of this marvellous colony.

The night was beautifully fine; but this is a cold and inadequate phrase to convey a picture of an Australian night.

A sky of burnished silver, studded with stars as bright as harvest moons, flooded the atmosphere with a rich light even when there was no moon to dwarf them; and small print can be read by starlight in these regions. Moonlight is as unlike anything of that name in England as electric-light is to a farthing dip or the speck in the back of a glowworm.

In Australia she is seen in her full glory, and makes a second day of the night.

Her disc presents the surface of burnished gold which one sees when regarding her through a powerful telescope.

Such a thing as "the pale moonlight" spoken of by Sir Walter Scott does not exist in the Antipodes. It is soft, mellow, with the effulgence of fifty-power European moonlight, and almost rosy in tint.

The very stars were almost as bright as northern moons, the sky was studded with them as with diamonds, and might have suggested to the reflective where the real "diamond diggings" were to be found.

As Ned Kelly was returning to the hotel, bent on "turning in," he thought how peaceful everything looked, and what a contrast the calmness above presented to the restless fears of every kind that encompassed him here below.

His rugged nature was somewhat softened, and just then he noticed a very "seedy" looking young fellow glancing wistfully into the open door of the hotel.

The expression of his face was so woebegone and ex- ... spoke to him—

"Down on yo' luck my lad, eh?" he asked.

"Luck!" was the sullen and sad reply—"I and that word parted company long ago. Work I can't get, as they say I'm a 'swell'; and as to begging, well, I couldn't whine or cringe even if I was on the brink of starvation. I'm big and strong, and willing to work; but somehow I don't know how to begin. Ha! ha! Well, after all, this sort of thing makes up one's life, but it can't last for ever, and that's a comfort. I must either do or die."

"Been to the diggings?" Ned asked

"Yes, and parted with every shilling for a salted claim." the young fellow replied. "If I ever meet the man who sold me, this world will be too small for both of us."

"What is your name?" Ned Kelly demanded. "You seem to be a fellow of pluck. Can I be of any help to you?"

"My name, if it's any use to you, is Harry Marston."

A sudden thought flashed through Kelly's brain.

"I'll use him," he muttered; "just the man I want—unsuspicious, young, and respectable. He's the ladder I'll climb out of danger on.

"There's a sovereign for you; you can repay me when you can, and, if you follow my advice, you won't long want tin. Give me a look in at the Bush Inn to-morrow morning—Mr. Bellamy. Humph! we don't do the swell business with cards here; but you'll remember the name."

"Remember the name," Harry Marston said, his face blazing with hope and gratitude; "by Jove! I won't forget it in a hurry. No angel of light could be more welcome than the sight of you."

"I am not quite one of your angels of light, yet," Ned Kelly said, laughing; "a little darkness suits me better at times; but I don't suppose who or what I am matters much to anyone. Enough," he ejaculated, with some bitterness, "we shall meet and understand each other better in the morning, I dare say."

He turned away abruptly, and, entering the hotel, strode up the staircase towards his bedroom.

He had nearly reached the top, when he stopped and clutched at his hair. His blood, which seemed to suddenly stagnate, in another instant coursed madly through his veins, for right in front of him stood "Sandy" M'Pherson, or the "fetch" of the squatter.

"Death and furies! speak if you are a man," Ned Kelly growled between his teeth.

Even as he spake, the figure vanished, and Ned, with all his powerful strength and iron will, felt as weak as a child, and clutched the ballusters to save himself from falling.

"Am I mad?" he muttered. "Has my brain turned? Come back, and if you can be grappled with, let me place my hands upon you, and I will finish the work I thought I had done before."

There was no reply to these ravings, and after a moment's hesitation, Ned Kelly entered his room and glanced wildly and ferociously around.

"It was my fancy," he said; "but I'm not a fellow given to that sort of thing. Pshaw! when Ned Kelly's 'nut' fails him and he goes wild, some of the lot hereabouts will have to look out; but I'll get out of this right off, and cut the road. I've enough, and Rose must be looked to."

He threw himself on the bed, but could not sleep. Whenever he closed his eyes the figure of Andrew M'Pherson rose before his heated imagination. He certainly saw a man he thoroughly believed to be as dead as Adam. His knife had dived three times into his body, and if he lived after that, more than Ned Kelly would have been astounded. He tumbled and tossed about all night. At last he fell into a troubled heavy sleep, but was evidently greatly disturbed by his dreams. His whole career, as well as its probable end was vividly pictured by the nightmare that oppressed him. Day dawned, and found him awake but restless and feverish. He was weak, trembling, and continually glancing over his shoulder. He did not leave the room until he had swallowed a pint of brandy to restore his shattered nerves. The fiery spirit put nerve into him. His eyes glistened as of old, and when he went down to join Rose at breakfast, the girl saw no signs of the miserable night Ned Kelly had passed, or of the "shadows that struck more terrors to the soul of Richard" than the forms of fifty ordinary enemies.

"Oh, father," said Rose, "just before you came down such a funny thing happened. I was sitting by the window, when a tall, dark man stopped and stared at me —not impertinently, but as if he had seen me before. And, stranger still, I think I have seen him, but I cannot tell where. But, if he did once know me, I don't know how he could have recognised me in this disguise;" alluding to her hair, which no longer curled over her head like the wool of a Newfoundland dog, but was now worn Madonna-like. The whole character of her face was changed.

"So she, too, has seen him," Ned muttered, compressing his lips, and grasping the edges of the table. "This must be a visitation from the dead. No man could live after the way I handled him with my knife. I couldn't be such a botch as to do my work so badly. I don't generally leave much to finish when I'm on the war-path."

"You need not pay any attention to strangers, Rose," he said aloud. "People just arrived in the colony are always looking out for others they have met in Europe, and strange mistakes are often made. However, its not worth bothering about, so we'll talk of something else."

As soon as breakfast was over Kelly went into Collins-street and opened an account with an obscure bank in the name of Mr. Bellamy. He didn't want to parade himself too much, but he knew the police would never look for Ned Kelly in the Bush Inn.

Considering all circumstances he played the part of a gentleman fairly well. Rose acknowledged him to be an actor of no mean merit. Ned had observed that another house opposite the Bank of Australasia was to let. His thoughts immediately reverted to the apparently abandoned scheme of robbery. Like many people, robbing a bank did not seem so criminal as robbing an individual, and, although the crime had little weight with Kelly, the thought of plundering a company was more to his liking.

Kelly reconnoitred the premises and saw they would do well for his purpose. They were furnished, which would save him a great deal of trouble. He took note of the agent's address, lost no time in possessing himself of the key of the house, and made a close examination of the rooms, but especially of the underground portion. There he was for some considerable time inspecting. He left the place with an expression of satisfaction on his countenance. He immediately took the house, and then sought Rose, to whom he communicated the fact of his having become the tenant of the premises in question.

"Now, Rose, make yourself at home as soon as possible. We shall be very comfortable there."

He told her of his rendezvous with Marston, and then went to fulfil it. He was sure the young fellow would keep the appointment, the sovereign lent him would ensure his punctuality.

He found Harry Marston waiting for him, and it leaked out in conversation that the young fellow had been brought up to the medical profession.

"So you understand the use of drugs and their prices?" said Ned Kelly.

"Pretty well," Harry replied.

"Then as I am about to open a drug store in Collins-street you may as well come and manage it for me. We won't talk about wages now, as you can agree on that matter another time. You will find me as good a boss as any in or out of the colony."

Harry Marston was delighted, and took a great liking to his free-mannered and free-hearted employer. Little did he dream of what was coming, or, poor and miserable is he had been, he would have shrunk from the service as from an engagement in the infernal regions.

"When am I to commence work?" he asked.

"At once," Ned replied. "Of course I shall want you to see that the shop is properly fitted, so you may as well come along now, and I must introduce you to my daughter, Miss Bellamy."

Harry Marston looked uneasily at his rather dilapidated clothes, which Ned Kelly, ever observant, understood in a moment.

"Never mind your togs," he said, jovially. "It isn't the feathers that make the birds here. We'll rig you up to-morrow in first class style, and in such a way as will make you think you've never left England, and you shall yet 'swell it,' as finely as any 'big-wig,' in the colony. Rose is not the girl to judge a man by his coat."

Harry Marston sighed. He was then thinking of a quiet little village, and an ivy-covered cottage, with a lawn running down to the banks of a stream ever making music as it hurried to greet its parent ocean. He was thinking of the garden-gate where he parted with some one inexpressibly dear to him, and the words he uttered were imprinted on his memory.

It was the old tale—never to forget her—that hope would buoy him in his efforts to win that which would enable them both to realise the dreams of their youth. Alas! what sad awakening have most of those dreams! Little do either party know the influence of time and absence. Love, like death, appears to make an impression that never can be mitigated, much less effaced; but, alas! both have their poignant impressions lulled by the great physician, time. However, in lovers' eyes there's no such thing as time or change, and Harry's last words were, "Rich or poor, we shall meet again."

He remembered how she turned away slowly and sadly, and how he watched her with a choking sensation, and a feeling that he must call her back or go mad. He had always written hopefully to Amy Melville, until the day came when he found himself robbed of his little capital, and a homeless outcast in the streets of Melbourne.

But now there was a chance of retrieving his fortune, and in his gratitude he could have embraced Ned Kelly.

"Rose, my lass," he said, after he had introduced her to Harry Marston, "what do you think of him? He looks as if he was from the right stock, eh?"

"I think I shall like him very much; especially, father, as you seem to be quite taken with him."

"But you musn't be falling in love really, Rose, for that would spoil all my plans for your future."

Rose laughed merrily, and said she was not one of the falling in love sort.

"Love him, indeed!" she said. "Why, father, what nonsense you talk. When I fall in love with anybody, I think the sky will fall—there's not much danger of that."

"But I want you to fall in with my little plan. You must gain his love if you can, it will be most necessary to our future plans. He is an instrument I must use. All men are vain and weak, especially where women are concerned. When a man thinks a woman—especially a pretty one—is taken with him, he's half-captured, and already started on the road to meet his fate. So, exercise your influence over him, Rose; make him your slave, and when the time is ripe for action, we can mould him as we wish."

Rose nodded her pretty head, and displayed her white pearly teeth as she smiled, but still she did not relish the task placed before her.

"I told Marston that he was to be my assistant," Ned continued; "but you must find means to impress him with the idea that I have taken a great liking to him, and am thinking of setting him up in business—to give him a start in the world."

"And he is to pay you back when he is prosperous," said Rose.

"That's the style, girl," Ned replied; "I see your part will not want much rehearsing. We will have his name over the door, and so throw the Joeys off the scent."

He here revealed to Rose his intention to rob the bank, and the means by which he intended to do it.

Rose seemed greatly agitated, but knew it was useless to expostulate. Besides, it must be confessed, her moral sense had not been improved by her relations with Ned; but he assured her this would be his last *coup*, and then he'd be off to South America and lead a different sort of life.

CHAPTER XXXVI.

HOW THE DRUG-STORE FLOURISHED.

IT took some time for Harry Marston to believe in his good fortune, or to thoroughly appreciate it.

His patron, Mr. Bellamy—as Ned Kelly called himself—interfered but little, save in the employment of a porter or two, and, as the reader may guess, Dick Dawson and Carroty Larkins were not long in establishing themselves on the premises.

One evening, as Harry Marston was writing a letter full of hope and good tidings to Amy Melville, Rose entered the room, and looked over his shoulder.

"Writing home?" she asked. "Pardon me, I am sorry that I disturbed you."

"Don't apologise, Miss Bellamy," Harry Marston said, as the colour mounted in his cheeks. "I am writing to those who are most dear to me in the world. I was telling them of my good fortune, and that I could not make out why Mr. Bellamy and you are so kind to me."

Rose sighed, and cast down her eyes.

"My father is a peculiar man, and he acts on the impulse of the moment," she replied. "It is no vain boast to say that he is so enormously rich that he does not know what to do with his money, and if he has given you a start, perhaps it was for—for my sake as much as your own."

"For your sake, Miss Bellamy?" Harry Marston said, opening his eyes in astonishment. "I fail to comprehend your meaning."

"Do not question me," Rose said, turning her head away shyly. "My father desires that I shall become the wife of a worthy man, but he has left me to follow the dictates of my own heart, and——"

She ceased speaking, and with hurried footsteps she turned and left the room. The fact was that she was not playing a part. She was evidently attracted by the handsome person and amiable manners of the "manager."

"What is the meaning of all this?" said Harry Marston, pressing his hand to his brow. "Can it be possible that the girl has taken a fancy to me? Pshaw! I must be a vain madman to think of such a thing, and yet why was she so disturbed?"

The thought troubled him, and impressed him more than he cared to own. There lay the unfinished letter to Amy, but he had been three years in the colony, and the long, weary absence might have sickened her heart and estranged her affections.

All this he argued and more. For a moment he almost wished he was free—love, beauty, and wealth before him!

"If I do not write," he said, "she may think that I am dead, and in time, with the last ray of hope, she will perhaps forget me." But he felt he was a traitor as these thoughts flashed upon him.

Rose's beautiful form and face was vividly depicted in his mind as he spoke, and he advanced towards the table with the intention of tearing the letter into fragments, but as he touched it, a thrill went through him, and the chord vibrating on his heart brought back all the old memories.

"What a coward and villain I am," he cried, passionately. "To thus return evil for good, to encourage the love of my benefactor's child with the knowledge that I cannot accept or return it, is a base return for their generosity in my hour of peril and want. No, I will yet have to repel her. I know not——I will confide my secret to her. I know she is good and generous, and will esteem me all the more for my loyalty to Amy."

He finished the letter, and then, as if fearing that his good resolutions might break down, he ran out to post it, and felt delighted to know that in a couple of months it would be in his darling's hands.

Rose watched him from a window, and as she did so a peculiar light flashed into her eyes.

"So," she murmured, "you do not take the bait so well as I expected, but time will show. If a woman's wit and a woman's cunning ever conquered, I will bring you to my feet, Harry Marston; and I would in truth be nothing loth to see you there."

The evening was cool, and Harry Marston strolled quietly along the street, enjoying the cool breeze that had succeeded a blazing day.

Two men talking rather thick and loudly attracted his attention, and hearing Mr. Bellamy's name mentioned he stopped.

"Well, Jack," said one, "our new boss is cutting a fine shine with his money; and did you twig the girl? Why she's dressed like Queen Wictorey."

"And yet he ain't no gentleman, I'll swear," Jack replied. "See here, Bill, I was in a swell's service for many a year, and I can spot the real thing as quick as you can a diamond from glass. Why this feller don't brush his teeth in the morning as all the swells do, and his hands are as hard and coarse as bullocks' hoofs. And as for the girl, I'll tell you what she is——"

"What is she?" demanded Harry Marston, losing his temper and striding up to the fellows. "Keep a civil tongue in your head, and don't be talking of people you know nothing about, or you may get into trouble, my friends."

"Who in thunder are you?" the man demanded. "If this is not a free country I should like to see one. A man may say what he likes here."

"But he must take the consequence," said Harry Marston. "I happen to be the keeper of the drug-store, and to be on good terms with Mr. Bellamy and his daughter, so I won't hear their names bandied about by such scum as you."

The men looked at the well-knit muscular figure before them and felt abashed.

"Don't rise your dander," Jack growled. "When a man comes into such a place as this and flings money about as the wind scatters chaff, it is only natural that people should wonder where he got it from."

"That is his business and not yours," Harry Marston replied hotly; "and it is like your confounded impudence to mention his name in any way but with respect."

"Well, you have a right to stick up for him," said the man called Bill, "especially as you are the young fellow he has taken under his wing. But don't be above taking a bit of advice. Keep your eye open; mind who you're working with. We knows a thing or two."

Harry Marston was too indignant to reply, and, turning sharply on his heel, he left the two men staring at him.

The conversation did not add to the ease of Harry Marston's mind.

Why should Mr. Bellamy be suspected by anyone, and suspected of what?

The want of cleanliness about the teeth and the hard hands had never impressed him before; but he thought of all now.

But what were such trifles to the gratitude he owed the man who had lifted him from the mud to a state of prosperity?

Filled with thought, he was nearing the shop, when a man slipped a piece of paper into his hand and glided away like a shadow.

The paper was a printed bill, offering ten thousand pounds reward for Ned Kelly, dead or alive; and Harry Marston, after reading it carefully, folded it up and placed it carefully in his pocket.

"I am not likely to fall across this celebrity," he said, laughingly, as he entered the house, "and if I did I think I should give him a wide berth rather than risk being made a target of to his sure aim. Besides, by this morning's paper he's far enough off just now."

He was thinking of an account of a "bailing up" of a bank-manager which appeared in that morning's paper, and in which the name of Ned Kelly prominently figured.

The fact was, some ruffians belonging to his former band traded under his name, and caused it to be supposed the ubiquitous Ned was always the chief of that party, and the head and front of their offending.

This suited his purpose well, and directed suspicion from his person when residing in the city.

He was not quite so prodigal of showing himself now until after dusk. He became more cautious as the great aim and end were approaching.

But to return to Harry.

"Hulloa! What are you waiting for?"

He addressed Dick Dawson and Carroty Larkins, who were hanging about in the passages.

"Mr. Bellamy told us to wait,' Carroty Larkins replied "He says that as we are sometimes late in the morning he will have us sleep in the house."

Harry Marston made no reply, but the intelligence astounded him; and he was puzzled to know what motive Mr. Bellamy could have in keeping two such fellows under the same roof.

"Very well," he said at last, "I will see Mr. Bellamy and have the necessary arrangements made for you. By the way, you are a couple of strong fellows, why don't you go into the bush and earn ten thousand pounds by catching Ned Kelly?"

"Eh?" said Carroty Larkins, starting back. "Who put you up to that dodge?"

"A notice issued by the Government." Harry Marston replied. "Here it is, and you may make what use of it you think fit."

Carroty Larkins and Dick Dawson exchanged glances; but Mr. Bellamy's voice calling for Harry Marston put an end to all further conversation on the subject.

"I have sent for you," said Ned Kelly, "to ask you a few questions. I may be right or I may be wrong, but I fancy that you have been casting sheeps eye's at my daughter Rose."

"I give you my word of honour that such a thing has never entered my head,' Harry Marston replied hastily, and he blushed up to the roots of his hair. "My dear sir, I would not dare——"

"Tut, tut!" said Ned laughingly, "boys will be boys, and girls will be girls. Hear me out. I rather suspect that Rose has been drifting in the same direction. You have acted squarely with me, and I will be honest with you, and I tell you plainly that if you can win her, I will throw no obstacle in the way."

Harry Marston drew a deep breath, a mist gathered before his eyes, and the room seemed to swim.

"Mr. Bellamy," he said, "I am at a loss to understand why you continue to shower favours on me. You picked me up a beggar, knew nothing about me, and yet overwhelm me with kindness, and would even sanction my marrying your lovely daughter!"

"My dear fellow," Ned interrupted, "I haven't travelled round the world half-a-dozen times without knowing when I see a real good fellow—one of the right sort! Well, of course, I come of a good family myself, so you see I am able to judge. And as to knowing little of you, perhaps I know more than you think. Well, think over what I have said, and keep the matter a secret."

"I will be plain with you," said Harry Marston; "instead of having any thoughts of your daughter, who is far removed from me in point of worth and wealth, I am engaged to be married to a lady in England."

"So are many young fellows here," Ned said; "but they have left others behind them who may take their places. But I don't want to throw cold water on your hopes, and as I have said before, I suspect that Rose is getting fond of you; you had better sleep out of the house, and see as little of her as possible."

"But, sir," said Harry Marston, "I hope you do not think I have taken any mean advantage of my position here?"

"On the contrary, I think you have acted like a man, in telling me the truth," Kelly replied. "Well, there is an end of the matter for the present. Look out for a suitable place in the morning, but in all other respects you will be master here as usual."

As soon as Harry Marston left the room, Ned rose and walked hurriedly to and fro.

"What am I doing?" he said aloud. "I am tampering with the girl's happiness—she fancies him already, that's clear, and what sort of a mate am I preparing for him? My example has not been of the best—but there, it's no use preaching; she must take things as she finds them, and if they are a little against her grit—well, I can't help it. I've done my best for her, and I love her as a father —ay, better than half the fathers and mothers in the world—and ought she not to serve me? Of course she ought. Yet I would not be sorry if she could marry Harry Marston; he's a decent, good chap, but he's booked in England he says. Well, that takes off some of the regret I should feel at his being bagged for the little affair that's coming off. But what does it matter when we're all off with the bank's gold? He'll be nabbed as a party to it, because his name is over the door. I can't, however, sacrifice us all to him—nor Rose neither. He belongs to another woman; more fool he, that's all I've got to say—good chance for him lost here."

He started as the door opened, and Rose softly entered the room.

"Father," she said, "am I to continue this deceit with Harry Marston? I assure you I don't like it, only you tell me it is necessary to your plans. I have had an interview with him, but he is gloomy and silent."

"I hardly know what to say, lass," Ned Kelly replied, knitting his brows, and speaking in a low tone of voice. "I begin to wish I had never set eyes on him, or brought you into it. You ought to be away from me altogether; I'm bad company, my girl, for you."

"Do not heed me," Rose said earnestly. "What can I do to repay the love and gratitude I owe you? I fear but very little, and yet in my poor way would sacrifice my life for you, as I ought to do, if necessary; and I would do so to the last."

"To the last!" Ned Kelly repeated. "What do you mean by that last?"

"I have strange fancies at times," Rose replied—"daydreams, some people would call them, for I lose myself, and seem to wander into the future, where I have more pleasure than in the present, which is saddened by apprehension for you. There is something telling me that my career will not be a long one in this world. I have indefinite apprehensions, I don't know of what. When I try to think of the future, a sort of mist comes over my thoughts, but most especially when I think of you, dear father, then I become doubly uneasy—I feel I am losing my nerve."

"Come here, lass," said the bushranger.

He placed his hands on the girl's shoulders, and gazed thoughtfully into her eyes.

"I fear another feeling is stealing into your heart, and that is altering your nature. You fear something, and you don't know what you fear, unless it is, as you say, for me. Well, the track I am in now will carry me out of the path we have both followed for some time, and lead us to money and a quiet life, far away from the scenes I shall not wish to recall; far from the land that saw the ignominious death of my parents, and the destruction of the only woman who ever really had the heart, such as it was, of Ned Kelly."

CHAPTER XXXVII.

THE GHOST SPEAKS.

"COME! look sharp there; I want a nobbler, and so would you, miss, I can tell you, if you had ridden and walked the number of miles I have."

The speaker was a smart young fellow, booted and spurred, and as he stood at the bar he hummed in a rich manly voice a tune to the time he impatiently marked with his whip on the counter.

The pert and pretty barmaid who was spooning on a young and good-looking man just returned from the diggings, and probably doing her best to fix him in a matrimonial sense, did not seem pleased at the stranger's manner. But his good-tempered face and handsome appearance brought back her good temper, and she added a smile, gratis, to the drink.

"Phew!" said the stranger, as he put the empty glass down and smacked his lips, "Tom Conquest feels something like himself again, but whether I continue to feel in the same frame of mind depends on whether the news I have got is true or false. I've heard funny facts about Kelly. It is too good to be true."

"What have you heard?" said the digger. "From all I have heard of him there isn't much against him. He's shut up only a bank or two, and it's only the rich that he makes shell out. Whoever heard of Ned's molesting a poor or a working man? Why there isn't a shepherd in the colony who wouldn't give him his last pipe of negrohead and every bit of mutton and damper left in the hut."

"Oh that may be," said the trooper, "but robbery is robbery and nothing else, whether it be rich or poor. I suppose if you made a pile worth £1,000 you'd be rich, wouldn't you? Well, if Kelly stuck you up and took the savings of your life's work how would you feel? Do you think that would be only robbing the rich? He don't rob where he can get nothing, that's about it, and he wants the shepherds to keep him fly to the movements of the police. I hope my suspicions about Ned Kelly are right. My information ought to be good if those two fellows I rescued from the ants can be believed, and yet it seems hardly possible that Ned would have the audacity to come here."

Tom Conquest called for another "nobbler" and lingered some time over it; standing with his back to the counter he could see the people passing to and fro in the street.

Suddenly he gave a start, and uttered an involuntary cry, much to the astonishment of the young lady and her half-enamoured swain, and rushing out of the saloon he reappeared dragging a man with him.

"Is it you, Sandy M'Pherson?" Tom Conquest cried, "or have you come on earth again to tell us what you think of the other place?"

"I am thankful to say that I am still in this sphere," Andrew M'Pherson replied, "but what in the name of wonder brought you here?"

"My horse's legs and my own strong determination to accomplish what I have taken in hand," Tom Conquest replied. "But sit down, for I want to have a talk with you. Who healed those gashes Ned Kelly gave you?"

M'Pherson smiled as he sat down and toyed with the straw of the sherry-cobbler which had been meanwhile served to him.

"It is not a long story," he said, "but as it may bear telling, perhaps you would like to hear it?"

"I should," said Tom.

Both were speaking low, so as not to be overheard, and as the bar was almost deserted, they could converse without fear of interruption.

"It so happened," said M'Pherson, "when Ned Kelly dug his knife into me that I had a thick bundle of papers, just delivered by the mail, in my pocket, and they saved my life. The would-be murderer was too infuriated to stop and ascertain what turned the point of the knife, and

I received only one flesh wound. Blood spurted out on his hands and coat, and he left me fully satisfied that I was thoroughly done for."

"Wonderful!" said Tom Conquest. "Well, how is——"

"Do you mean Captain Montague Vavasseur?" M'Pherson, interrupted. "Oh, he is very well, and I hope to see him married to my daughter, Lily, before the year is out."

"The devil you do," Tom Conquest muttered under his breath, and then aloud, "It was about your daughter I was going to ask."

"Oh, she is all right," M'Pherson answered carelessly; "a little paler than usual. I believe the silly girl has formed an attachment somewhere, but she must learn to get over that. She shall not throw herself away on any fellow who chooses to crop up with a good-looking face and empty pockets."

Tom Conquest winced, but he had too much good sense to make any reply, and he broke away from the subject abruptly.

"You asked me what I am doing here," he said; "may I put the same question to you?"

"Certainly," said M'Pherson. "I have just lodged the gold and specie I intend for Lily's dowry in the Bank of Australasia, where it will be safe from the clutches of such rascals as Ned Kelly and his wolf-like gang."

"What would you say if I told you I strongly suspect that Ned Kelly is in Melbourne?" said Conquest.

M'Pherson's face went as pale as paper.

"In Melbourne!" he repeated. "Then every hole and corner ought to be searched, and the scoundrel hung on the tallest gallows. Stay! By Jove! that accounts for the strange vision I had the other night at the Albion Hotel, in Bourke-street. I was going to my room, but hearing footsteps I turned, and saw a man glaring at me with such a furious look that I was glad to get out of his way, and lost no time in doing so. I thought at the time there was a look of Kelly about him."

"Did he appear to be alarmed at the sight of you?" Tom Conquest asked.

"It did not strike me so then," M'Pherson replied. "I thought the fellow was mad and with delirium tremens, so I made myself scarce; but now I turn it over in my mind, there was wild surprise in his eyes, just as if he had seen a ghost. Could it have been that ruffian Kelly?"

"Thank you," said Tom Conquest, closing the book in which he had been making notes. "The plot thickens, and somehow I fancy that I shall touch Ned Kelly on the shoulder before many days are over."

"If you do I will give you anything you ask," M'Pherson said, eagerly. "You shall name your own price; anything I have shall be yours."

"I shall be satisfied with the reward offered by the Government," Tom Conquest returned. "Mr. M'Pherson, I will ask no money from you; still, if I succeed I should like to ask you for a present."

"What is it?"

"You won't be offended if I speak plainly?"

"No. Go on; out with it. What the deuce have I to give better than money?"

"Your daughter."

Had a dynamite explosive fallen at the feet of Andrew M'Pherson he could not have been more taken aback or looked more astounded and vexed.

"What!" he cried, "you marry my daughter Lily? Pooh-pooh! This is nonsense. Rubbish! Come, Tom, be serious, talk sense. You know that's coming it rather strong. I've no right to give away what does not belong to me. My daughter is not my slave, to be bartered away at my pleasure, or exchanged for any equivalent I may select."

"I was never so earnest in my life," Tom Conquest said. "I love Lily with all the strength my heart is capable of, and if she consents. I don't see the difficulty."

"And so you are the fellow who has been hanging about my place?" said M'Pherson beginning to bluster,

"This is taking a very unfair advantage of a casual observation. All the Kellys in the world are not worth sacrificing Lily for. No, my boy, Lily must not marry a pauper, or even (with a sneer) a Government mounted policeman. I must put a stop to this little game. It is too preposterous."

"I love her too well to mind the covert insults you would convey by your words. You would give her away to an adventurer and a mountebank," said Tom, "without an enquiry as to his means or even his character. There is as much of the captain in that fellow Vavasseur as there is life in Julius Cæsar. Give him my compliments, and say that I happen to know he is a swell 'cracksman' from London, and he had better skedaddle before he is laid by the heels for that small jewellery business in which he was implicated twelve months ago. You don't seem to like this, Mr. M'Pherson?"

"You are telling me a pack of lies," Andrew M'Pherson said, "I don't believe a word you have uttered."

"It is well for you that you are Lily's father," Tom Conquest said. "Well, time will show whether I am a liar or you a fool for entertaining a fellow who has the gift of the gab and a heart as black as midnight. I have no wish to quarrel with you, M'Pherson. So now to business, I'll yet make you think very differently of me and your sham captain. Where are you staying?"

"At the Albion."

"Then don't mention my name, if you wish to see Ned Kelly laid by the heels," said Tom Conquest. "You see I am disguised; would you have known me if I had not told you who I was?"

"No, you have dyed your hair and altered your face somehow."

"It altered itself from the hour I was pitched down that hole by Ned Kelly and his ruffians," said Tom Conquest, "but there's a good deal of life in me yet, as I hope to let my friend Ned find out to his cost."

CHAPTER XXXVIII.

A PASSAGE TO WEALTH.

HARRY MARSTON was not long in noticing that Ned Kelly was anxious to get him out of the house each evening as soon as the premises were closed. He saw Rose at times, and she continued her part of the love-smitten maid, but Harry avoided her as much as possible.

Rose was determined not to let him slip through her fingers so easily.

"Mr. Marston," she said, one day, "I am very lonely here in the evening. My father has much correspondence, and, preferring to be alone, often writes far into the night. So you see," she added, with a musical laugh, "'I stoop to conquer,' and I want you to act as my friend and companion."

"Most willingly, Miss Bellamy," Harry Marston replied. "It has ever been the impression that friendship, pure and simple, between a man and a beautiful woman could not long endure without degenerating into love, degenerating, I say, because in friendship there is no element of selfishness, whereas love is the sublimity of selfishness on both sides. Each party loves because each party gratifies him or her self by so doing, whereas friendship has nothing to gain but the gratification of its object, and that friendship I feel for you, and I do not fear misconstruction."

"That is almost saying that you are incapable of falling in love," said Rose, coquettishly.

"Far from it," Harry Marston rejoined, "I am helplessly heart and soul in love already."

"Indeed," said Rose, with something of disappointed irritation in her manner. "I am not inquisitive, but I should like to know who the lady is."

"You may see her sooner than you expect" Harry replied. "I am about to write and ask her to come out to Australia."

Was it perfect acting that caused the blood to fade from Rose's cheeks? No, she had overdone her part, the play was becoming a reality, and although she struggled against her own feelings, she confessed that she was more than half in love with Harry, her own and Ned Kelly's intended dupe.

Her reluctance to play a part that might imperil the future of Harry was rather weakened by the avowal she had just heard from his own lips.

Rose felt that she could not stay in Harry Marston's presence. She was trembling with jealous anger about a girl she had never seen and perhaps never would, and the sensation was novel to her.

"I would have saved him in some way," she said, "but not now. Let her come to the rescue if she can; he has despised my love, for he must have seen that I am not indifferent to him. His avowal of his passion for another was intended to stifle all evidences of love on my part. Why did my father ever bring him here? But she may never come out—I'm too hasty. I feel that he really likes me, and were it not for this boyish love —— but here he is"

It was evening, and Harry approached her to enquire the whereabouts of her father. She proposed to accompany Harry to seek Ned, and away they went, a very handsome pair, it must be admitted.

No sooner were they out of the house than Ned Kelly, throwing aside his town clothes and jewellery, adopted a labourer's suit, and went, lantern in hand, down to the cellar.

The place was almost blocked up by empty barrels, designed to be very shortly filled with débris, the work of Ned and his assistants Messrs. Larkins and Dawson.

"Here we are, Ned," said Carroty Larkins. "and ready to go to work with a will. The tools in the box labelled 'Soda' are splendid, and the only difficulty will be in getting to the bank too soon."

"What are we to do with the earth as we dig it out?" Dick Dawson asked.

"Fill the casks with it," Ned Kelly replied; "the cellar is too small to hold all the stuff we dig out. I will take care that nobody has the key but myself in the day time. Now then, lads, clear away and let us go to work. We have plenty of time, but I want the work to be done quietly and without loss of time."

The men went at it with a will with pick and spade.

Ned took his turn, and at it they went; not a word was spoken.

The tunnelling was easy work through the clay-soil until they got to the bank foundation-wall. The rattle and rumble of the vehicles overhead all day long prevented the noise the picks made against the stone foundation being heard, even had the vault been inhabited at the time. The work of making a cavity here was speedily accomplished.

Ned Kelly swung the instrument over his shoulder and struck the cellar-wall with a skilful and powerful blow. A dull sound, like the booming of a muffled bell, came from the wall, and Ned Kelly looked askance at his comrades.

"What is the meaning of that?" he asked, under his breath. "I never heard such a sound come from solid earth."

"It sounded like a death-bell," Carroty Larkins said. "I don't half like the sound."

"Peace, you ass!" Ned Kelly hissed. "Omens are for children and frightened women, not for men with gold within their grasp. Go in and win, you fools, while you've got the chance."

Thus encouraged, they worked silently on, and succeeded in accomplishing their object.

They postponed their entry into the vault until such time as the bank officials would be absent on a public holiday or the Sabbath.

Kelly took care the men should keep sober, and prohibited any "liquoring up" until they had got clear out of Melbourne.

They growled a good deal at this prohibition, and would

have disobeyed but for the glorious golden prospect before them. Once successful, they could bathe in brandy.

After their work, Kelly, enjoining silence, told his worthy assistants to be off to their "flea-traps"—*Colonice-beds*—while he remained behind to examine the progress made, and test the tunnel.

Apparently satisfied he turned away, but sprang sharply round as he thought he heard a voice. So he did, but only the voice of a Bank clerk in the Bank vault stowing away raw gold.

Ned Kelly's hair bristled and a death-like hue appeared through the swarthiness of his cheeks. Clenching his fists and assuming an attitude of defiance he hissed out—

"Man, goblin, or devil, Ned Kelly is ready for you."

But it must have been fancy after all, for who should be in the tunnel? There was not a living creature but Ned Kelly in the cellar, and at last, convinced that he had been labouring under a delusion, he turned away locked up the cellar, and went to the sitting-room, where he found Rose.

"Well, lass," said he, "have you any news to tell me? Our work proceeds merrily, and all will be ready in a few days."

"That is well," Rose replied; "but I am rather troubled in my mind, father."

"What about, my girl?"

"I went out with Harry Marston, as you know," Rose replied, "and we were followed all the time by two strange men. One of them was the man who stared so hard at me as I sat at the hotel window; the other was younger, and although he endeavoured to conceal it, I knew from his gait, as well as seeing him recognise some troopers, that he was one of the force."

"Hulloa! that looks dangerous. There's smoke somewhere," said Kelly; "we must get out of the fire. That infernal reward is enough to make a man sell his own father, and is almost enough to make Larkins or Dawson peach—or any of the mob, for the matter of that. I don't like it, though, girl; it has a queer look. However, cheer up, my lass; after the haul, we're off to enjoy a little quiet for the rest of our lives. I'm sorry to leave Harry in the trap to be caught, but self-preservation and yours, too, Rose, require a sacrifice; and I don't know but Miss Melville's lover is as good a stopgap as anyone else."

He touched a tender chord in this hit at Harry's indifference to Rose, but she only sighed.

He recognised the meaning of her dejection, and comforted her by saying—

"He'll be in no danger, as his remaining after our departure will shield him, if not from suspicion, certainly from being convicted, if tried."

Rose concealed the true state of her feelings, and said—

"I am only too anxious about your safety, my dear father. What should I do if anything happened to you? I would rather die a thousand deaths than live to see you come to any harm!"

"You are a brave, good lass," Ned Kelly replied, placing his coarse, rough hand on the girl's pretty head. "Well, talk no more to-night. I'm tired as a costermonger's donkey after a race-day, and you don't look too fresh."

CHAPTER XXXVIII.

THE TRADE-MARK OF VILLAINY.

WHEN Harry Marston left Rose he walked slowly back to his own lodgings, and had reached the door when he felt a tap on his shoulder, and turning sharply, found himself confronted by a broad-shouldered, stalwart young fellow about his own age.

"You have made a mistake, I think; but as it is getting dark, it is a very excusable one, although you 'tap' rather hard upon the shoulders of your friends if you claim their recognition often in this fashion."

"I don't think there's any mistake, my friend. I took the liberty of following you some short time since, and

will be pleased if you can spare me a few minutes of your time, which I suppose is not too valuable."

"You're devilish cool, my friend! What the deuce do you want with me? I'm not accustomed to be pulled up like this in the street or anywhere else," said Harry; "and as I never take liberties, I never allow them, especially from strangers. What do you want with me?"

"Don't lose your temper, I don't mean you any harm," was the reply; "but I do not wish anybody to hear what I have to say, which is for your good and for mine."

Harry gazed fixedly at the stranger, and being impressed by his frank, manly bearing, and having no possible grounds for apprehension of any kind, followed him.

Scarcely a word was exchanged until they reached a house in a by-street. The stranger tapped sharply at the door, and in another minute Harry Marston found himself in a room filled with constables and troopers.

"What is the meaning of all this?" Harry Marston demanded, as, amazed and alarmed, he recoiled towards the door, which had been promptly locked and bolted as he entered. "For what reason have I been lured to this place?"

"Patience, my friend," said the man who had brought him to the house. "You will know the reason presently, and admit that it is a good one. My name is Tom Conquest, and I am on the track of that murderous villain, Ned Kelly!"

"Well, what has that to do with me? Surely you do not take me for that notorious scoundrel?" said Marston, in an amused tone of voice. "For my own part, nothing would please me better than to see him dangling from the gallows."

"You are the keeper of the drug-store in Collins-street, I believe?" said Tom Conquest.

"Yes; but what right have you to cross-question me?"

"No strict right as yet; but I think you will prefer answering a few quiet questions here, to the exposure of going before a magistrate, who will make you answer what he likes. Your patron goes by the name of Mr. Bellamy?"

Marston saw the force of his interrogator's representation, so replied—

"Goes by it? Why, of course, his name is Bellamy!"

"You think so, but I think otherwise," Tom Conquest observed quietly. "I daresay it will cause you some alarm when I tell you I suspect that this so-called Mr. Bellamy has a strong likeness to Ned Kelly."

"Why, you must be cracked," said Harry, "or he must be, to venture into such a place as Melbourne. Bah! He's a kind, good, generous fellow. I know him well; to him I owe my prosperity, and I won't hear a single word said against him. He's as much Kelly as you are."

"I don't blame you," Tom Conquest returned, "but listen to me, and drown all sentiment. I saw you with a lady to-night, and I'll swear in any court of justice that she is Rose Casey, Ned Kelly's adopted daughter."

"Nonsense," said Harry Marston, "her name is Rose Bellamy."

Tom looked perplexed, and stroked his chin thoughtfully.

"I seldom forget a face, especially when it belongs to a woman," he said. "Well, we will say, for argument's sake, that I am mistaken in the young lady, but if Mr. Bellamy, as you call him, has a bad scar on the back of his left hand, and wants a piece of his right ear to make it complete, Ned Kelly is as good as in the meshes of the net which the law has been weaving for him."

Harry Marston's heart beat high, and the colour in his cheek faded away. He had often wondered why Bellamy generally wore a glove on his right hand, and his hair over his ears in so hot a climate. Yet he could not credit that the man so highly worthy of gratitude could be the man whose hands had been steeped in crime of every kind.

The whole colony was on the alert for the villain who had wrought so much mischief; the blood of Kelly's victims, and the wholesale, daring, daylight robberies he had committed cried aloud for vengeance; his name was used as a taunt to the police, and the influence of his courage, success, and example was most pernicious and dangerous in a population so leavened with new and old crime, for the jails of the neighbouring colonies had been silently emptied into Victoria.

"If Bellamy is the man I want," Tom Conquest continued, "he bears the trade-mark of villainy stamped upon him in the very signs I have mentioned. Test him. my friend, and let me see you again to-morrow evening, here and at this time. If you are an honest man, you will be as anxious to prove the truth or falsehood of this suspicion as I am."

"I am sure that I shall disappoint you," said Harry. I admit he always wears gloves when he goes out, but not in the house. I have noticed a scar, that any man might get."

"We're on the track, believe me. At all events you will keep this meeting a secret?"

"Yes, because I would not wound so good a fellow by the bare mention of your suspicions," Harry replied.

However, he was glad to get into the open air, and away from the keen-eyed man who scrutinised him so closely, and now the light and almost contemptuous demeanour he had assumed gave way to a whirl of conflicting emotions. His brain throbbed in unison with his heart, and he turned faint at the thought that he might have taken service under the greatest scoundrel unhung.

Marston was early at the store in the morning, but did not see Kelly, who was not visible till the evening. When he did appear he was restless and uneasy.

They were having a pipe together in the back-room, and were keeping up a constrained conversation. Both were evidently not thinking of the subject of their talk, and at last both relapsed, with abstracted air, into semi-silence.

This was suddenly broken by Kelly, who said—

"I was wondering what brought you out to this country without plenty of capital."

"Oh, many men of first-rate family have come out beggars."

"Oh, you did not need to tell me that good blood ran in your veins, for any man with an eye in his head can see you've got the points of breeding—foot, hand, and ear. These are thoroughbred marks that don't escape me any more than they do a woman."

"Well," said Harry, forcing a laugh, "I see you have two of the points, but let me see the third, your ears."

Kelly started to his feet as Harry Marston approached, and showed evident signs of apprehension and dislike to the investigation. He was obviously most reluctant to undergo the examination. He was more angered and confused than the circumstances warranted.

"Harry," he said, with an awkward attempt at dignity, "I never take liberties with others, and never allow them to be taken with me."

"I meant no offence," Harry Marston said. "If I have offended you, I am sorry for it; but I think you have taken me up rather sharply for nothing."

"I allow no man to trifle with me," Kelly said, striding up and down the room in a towering fury; and then as if recognising the suspicious violence of his own conduct in visiting with such animosity, Harry's movement to uncover his ears, he seemingly calmed down, but felt rather nervous and suspicious that "something was up" or why this attempted scrutiny? He left the room without a word, leaving Marston pondering over his conduct and the allusions of Conquest. Harry did not well know what course to take, so was content to await his next meeting with the trooper. He liked Kelly personally, and even if satisfied of his identity would hesitate to denounce a man from whom he had received nothing but generosity. Had he not saved him from starvation, lifted him from the streets, fed him, clothed him, and paved the way to prosperity? But a murderer and a wholesale thief!—his kindness must have a motive. If he were really

the notorious ruffian, Kelly, so savage a beast and reckless a robber could not be actuated by honest feelings towards a stranger like him. "If he were Kelly!" The thought fully possessed him, he could not shake it off. "Better the streets and starvation than to eat the bread of charity from the blood-stained hand of such a merciless, dog," he suddenly exclaimed.

Meanwhile Ned Kelly was not idle.

As soon as he was clear of the room, he sought Rose and stood before her with troubled aspect; her face was pale and rigid, and he walked up and down the room like a caged beast.

She could not imagine what was the matter with him. and her first thought was that some dire calamity had or was about to happen. She was in constant fear and trembling, not knowing at what moment the thunderbolt might fall.

"Father! father!" she said, placing her hands gently on his arm, "what has happened? Don't look so wild, you alarm me!"

The clouds were lowering on Kelly's brow, and his face was almost purple with perplexity and annoyance; but with a great effort he recovered his self-control.

"The game is up," he said; "we are sold! That accursed whelp, Marston, knows who I am! I saw it in his eyes, though he endeavoured to conceal it. You must fly, Rose; take the first vessel for Sydney, and when there go to the post-office, and ask for a letter addressed to Rose Jennings. It will be for you, and will contain instructions when and where to meet me. By that time I shall have matured my plans, and will be either a man or a mouse."

"Oh, father!" Rose cried in a sudden agony of fear, "fly at once. Do not hesitate, or think of me, or all is lost! There has evidently been treachery. Someone has given information. I thought you were too bold. You have been recognised. Marco Polo will carry you thirty miles before midnight, and then you can laugh at pursuit. Get back to the Ranges, where you are safe."

"You don't want money, I think?" Kelly said.

"No, I have sufficient to last for a long time yet."

"Well, you ought to have, as I drew out the rest of my balance at the bank, and gave it into your charge, Rose. Keep it and use it, my girl, until we meet."

"Kiss me, and begone, before it is too late; my heart grows cold," Rose replied, "at the thought of what will happen if you remain here."

"You must stop in the house for another hour," Kelly said; "by that time I shall be out of Melbourne, but first——"

His chest heaved, and again the terrible evil light flashed from his eyes.

"What are you thinking of?" Rose demanded

"Thinking how I should like to be in the cellar with Harry Marston just now. I know he's the traitor—I saw he suspected me. How I should like to clutch him by the throat, and feel him growing weaker and weaker under my hands. But I suppose I must reserve that luxury for the future. There's life in Ned Kelly yet, as those who try to nab him will find to their cost."

CHAPTER XL.
UNWELCOME VISITORS.

"AND so," said Tom Conquest, "you are satisfied I am right, and that you have been made a fool and dupe of?"

He addressed Harry Marston, who stood with his back against the wall, looking gloomily at the young trooper.

"Yes," Marston replied, "and yet it goes against the grain to turn informer. If I could give back the favours the man has showered on me I should feel satisfied."

"Favours!" Tom Conquest repeated, sneeringly. "The murderer of men and helpless women and children deserves no mercy. You ought to think yourself lucky that you have escaped so easily, and proud of having done society so good a turn I and my men will make the raid in two hours' time. Now go, and use your time as you think fit. We shall not want you."

Little dreaming of what had happened, Dick Dawson and Carroty Larkins were waiting as usual for Kelly.

"I wonder what keeps the gov'ner?" Dick Dawson growled. "He's mighty particular about keeping the key of the cellar. We might have made the haul by this time."

"And the girl has shut herself up," said Carroty Larkins. "I don't like the look of things, Dick—I don't, I tell you. What if Ned has heard something, got scared and cut off by hisself, and left us to stand the racket?"

"No fear," said Dawson. "He wouldn't leave the girl. Come, Carroty, tip us a stave just to pass the time till he comes. Strike up, old man. don't be downhearted."

An uproarious shout of applause followed Nimming Ned's song, and scarcely had the sound died away when Rose, plainly dressed and wearing a thick veil over her face, appeared on the scene and was passing out, when Carroty cried—

"Here, stop a minute. "When are you going, miss?"

"How dare you ask the question?" Rose returned. "Are you my gaoler? Out of the way, or you shall answer for this to my father."

"Where's Ned?" Carroty Larkins demanded. "It's past his usual time, and we don't want to waste the whole night in hanging about and hollering ourselves hoarse."

Rose did not deign to reply, but sweeping haughtily past him she reached the door. It was opened for her from the outside by a vigorous blow which splintered the stout panels and sent the lock flying

There was no back way out of the house, and as Tom Conquest, with a score of police at his heels, appeared, Rose and the bushrangers knew they were caught like rats in a trap.

"Very sorry, miss," said Tom Conquest, raising his cap, "but you must consider yourself in custody. I arrest you as Ned Kelly's accomplice in murder and robbery."

He handed her over to a stalwart officer, who took her gently by the arm and led her back into the house.

"Keep a sharp watch on the windows," said Tom Conquest, "and scatter the brains of the first man who attempts to escape. Now, lads," he added, drawing a pistol and levelling it at Dick Dawson's head, "the game is up, so you may as well submit to having the bracelets put on without trouble. Hold up your hands. I'll shoot the first man who resists." Dawson did not seem very much afraid of Tom's pistol.

"But what's the row? What have we done?" Dick Dawson whined, while a wink passed between him and Conquest.

"Stow you yabber, and tell me where Ned Kelly is!"

"We don't know no such a party," Dick Dawson replied, with a look of injured innocence on his face; "Mr. Marston is our master, and a very nice gentleman he is."

"That's a lie!" Tom Conquest said, as he clicked the handcuffs round Dick Dawson's wrists. Where is the man you call Bellamy?"

"Gone out," was the reply, "and when he comes back he'll make you smart for this 'ere outrage on our liberties."

"You'll be   to tell your story to the magistrates," Tom Conquest said. "I happen to know all you rascals by name and reputation."

One by one the bushrangers were handcuffed and taken away, Tom Conquest and six men remaining behind.

The young trooper did not send Rose with the first batch of prisoners. He kept her in the sitting-room above the shop, and endeavoured to question her, but not a word would she say for a long time.

"Come, miss," said Tom Conquest, impatiently, "I don't wish to be hard on you, and I'll give you the chance of turning Queen's evidence. You are much too young and pretty to die, but if you continue your obstinate conduct you will surely be hanged. as I have ample proof of

who you are, and what part you have taken with Ned Kelly."

Inwardly trembling, yet outwardly calm, Rose assumed a look of surprise and indignation.

"If you wish to speak of my uncle, Mr. Bellamy, I will give you all the information that lies in my power," she replied haughtily. "He is dining with some friends at the Albion Hotel."

"That tale won't do for me," said Tom Conquest.

"Then find a better one, and act upon it," Rose returned. "This is some infamous plot. I don't know what you mean by associating my name with that of a bushranger, but you will have to pay dearly for this outrage upon innocent people. Where's your warrant?"

"Hulloa! warrant indeed! What does 'Miss innocent' know about 'warrants?'"

Tom Conquest and his men glanced knowingly at each other.

The time passed away, and as the American clock struck the hour of midnight, Rose burst out laughing.

"You are a strange girl," Tom Conquest said. "What is the reason of your mirth?"

"My own thoughts," Rose replied "Take me away, or lock me up here, I am sleepy."

"That thundering villain Kelly has given us the slip," Tom Conquest muttered "Marston has evidently let the cat out of the bag too soon. Kelly smelt a rat and has bolted. Well," he added, turning to one of his brother officers, "I don't see the use of keeping the girl here; she has made up her mind to keep her lips closed against the truth."

Rose laughed again, and so loudly and scornfully that the room rang with the sound.

"I am quite ready," she said; "give my compliments to Mr. Marston, and say that I should like to see him in the morning."

"Take my arm," Tom Conquest said. "there is a crowd in the street, for the news has spread like wildfire; but we may be able to slip away unobserved. Clear a way for us men."

The fair prisoner, however, did not escape unobserved. As she appeared the motley concourse of people sent up a shout, and Tom Conquest felt Rose's arm tremble on his arm for the first time.

"That's Ned Kelly's girl," roared a fellow. "I wonder how she'll like the change from gold bracelets to iron ones. She don't look much up to the stone jug and floor-scrubbing."

"She's a woman after all," said another. "Don't jump on her now she's down on her luck."

"But she's worse nor Kelly," shouted the first speaker, "she's a very devil in petticoats."

A rush was made at the man, and it would have gone hard with him had it not been for the interference of the police, who huddled him into a side street, in which he made the best use of his legs.

Rose felt somewhat relieved when the prison gates opened to receive her, and when placed in a cell she sat down on the edge of the poor pallet.

"Father is safe, and that is all I care about," she said. "I would rather have my tongue torn out than utter a single word against them. Hasten, good Marco Polo for each stride takes you master further away from danger."

Sleep of course was out of the question. Her brain was   itself   discover who the traitor could be. She thought of Harry, but she knew nothing of his attempt on Ned's ears, and concluded it was the work of Carroty or Dick.

In the morning the female warder entered the cell.

"Am I to appear before the bench, to-day?" Rose asked.

"Yes, but not before you have had something to eat and prepared yourself for what's before you. I've been in a mess myself, and know what it is," the woman replied with something of sympathy in her voice. "Keep up your pluck. I daresay there's nothing against you. There are lots of swells want to see you."

"I will see nobody," Rose said, almost fiercely. "It is bad enough to be here, without being stared at like a wild beast. It ought to satisfy them that they will soon see me in the dock.

CHAPTER XLI.

NED KELLY MEETS WITH HOSPITALITY.

CHECKING his horse for a moment, Kelly turned his head and looked at the lights of Melbourne, now far away in the distance, and then leaning forward he patted Marco Polo encouragingly on the neck.

The horse pricked up his ears, as if knowing what was required, and, in answer to a word, swept along in a swinging canter, covering mile after mile untiringly, and seemingly without exertion, but Ned Kelly knew better than to over-tax the willing creature's strength, and drawing rein proceeded at a moderate pace.

Kelly was armed to the teeth, and was resolved that he would never be taken alive.

He branched off the main road into the bush, though he had little chance of encountering anyone at that hour of the night.

After leaving Melbourne behind, he had not met a single human being. After travelling two hours, he suddenly brought Marco Polo to a standstill and listened.

Was it the wind, or did he hear the sound of voices? He was not mistaken; for as he sat as motionless as a statue, and under the shadow of a large tree, a fragment of a song, followed by a burst of laughter, put him on the alert.

"A party bound from the diggings to Melbourne," he muttered; "I must have a look at them."

Not far away he came to a tent pitched under some trees, and the sound of the horse's hoofs brought out four men in hot haste.

"Who are you?" one demanded.

"A stranger to you, at any rate," Kelly replied. "Put up your barkers. What do you take me for? Surely you don't think I'm going to eat the lot of you, do you? I've missed my mate—have you seen anyone pass? I've ridden a long way, and both myself and my nag are done up. Give me a pipe of tobacco and a drop of tea; a mouthful of damper wouldn't poison me. So, mates, I'll join you."

"Oh, you're as welcome as the puppy dog on the chain," cried the wit of the party; at which there was a guffaw of laughter.

"But who the devil are you?" demanded the speaker. "No tricks must be played with Sam Clinton. If I bark I bite as well."

"Well," said Kelly, "I have something to do with the police, and my name's Tom Conquest."

"We have heard of you," said Sam Clinton; "so welcome to what we have and a share of what's going."

After a hearty meal of mutton, damper, and tea, Kelly went out to see that Marco Polo was safely tethered, and, returning to the party, threw himself down on his side, and apparently went to sleep; but no weasel was more wide awake than he.

He noticed that the men wore broad belts, filled with nuggets and gold-dust, round their waists, but they were not to be caught napping, as they took turns at sentry duty.

"I wonder why they did not employ the Government escort," Kelly mused. "Perhaps they thought they were strong enough in numbers to do without it, but if I had another man with me, I'd make them go a little lighter in their pockets to Melbourne."

But they had sheltered and given him food in the hour of need, and, remorseless villain as Kelly was, he banished all thoughts of robbing the men.

Before the sun rose the party of diggers were astir, and after breakfast Ned Kelly bade them adieu and went his way; but his horse had not taken many paces when he heard a shouting after him.

"What's the row?" he demanded, wheeling his horse round, and clapping his hand on a pistol. "There's no good luck for anybody in turning back."

"You have left something behind you," said the digger. "What is it?"

"One side of your whiskers,"the man replied, laughing.

Ned Kelly cursed as he touched his cheek and discovered the truth of the assertion. The whiskers had fallen off during the night, and as Ned Kelly rode up to the man who held it he said sternly—

"A man in my line has need of some kind of disguise. Take care that neither you nor your mates say a word about this."

"I don't see anything to get your dander up, Mr. Conquest," said the digger. "I'm jiggered if I'm quite sure you're as square as you look."

"Just mind your own business, and don't bother about mine, I'd advise you."

As he spoke he saw something resembling a cloud of dust in the distance, but his practised eye convinced him that it was a scouting band of troopers, and, giving the reins a shake, he swerved Marco Polo round, and set off at a fast gallop.

"Show them the way, my lad," he said, patting Marco's neck; "those cocktails would be stumped in half an hour at such a pace as this."

(To be continued.)

NED KELLY

THE IRONCLAD

AUSTRALIAN BUSHRANGER

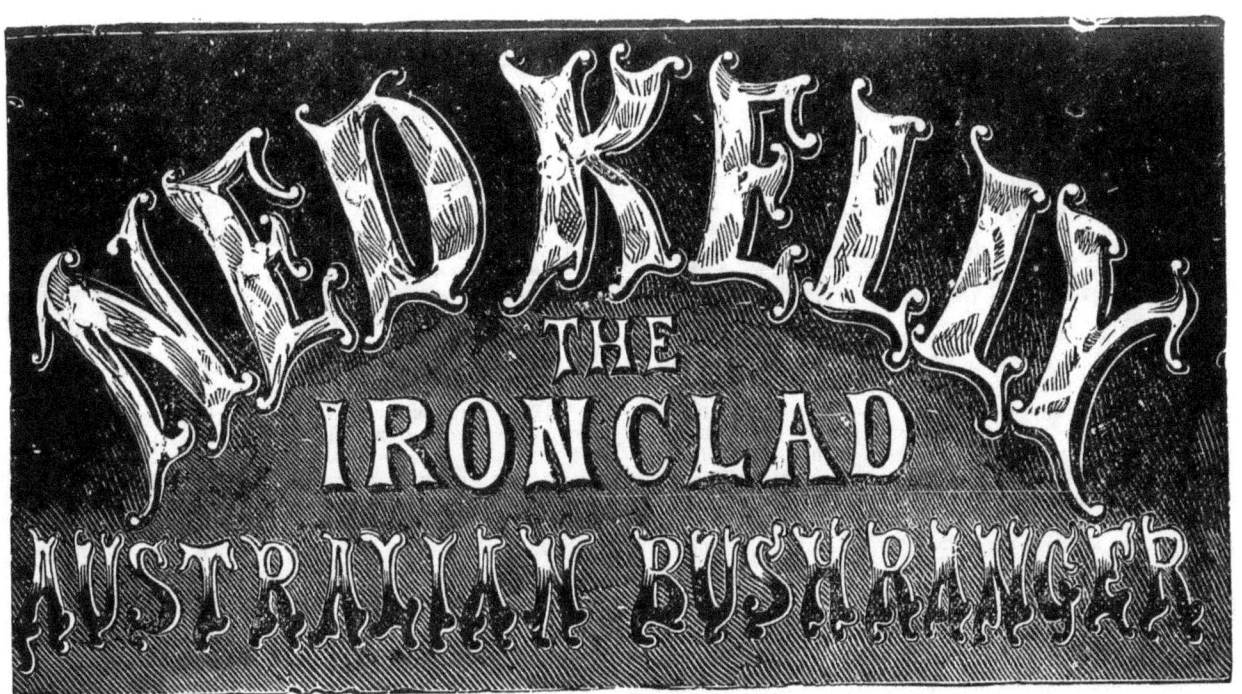

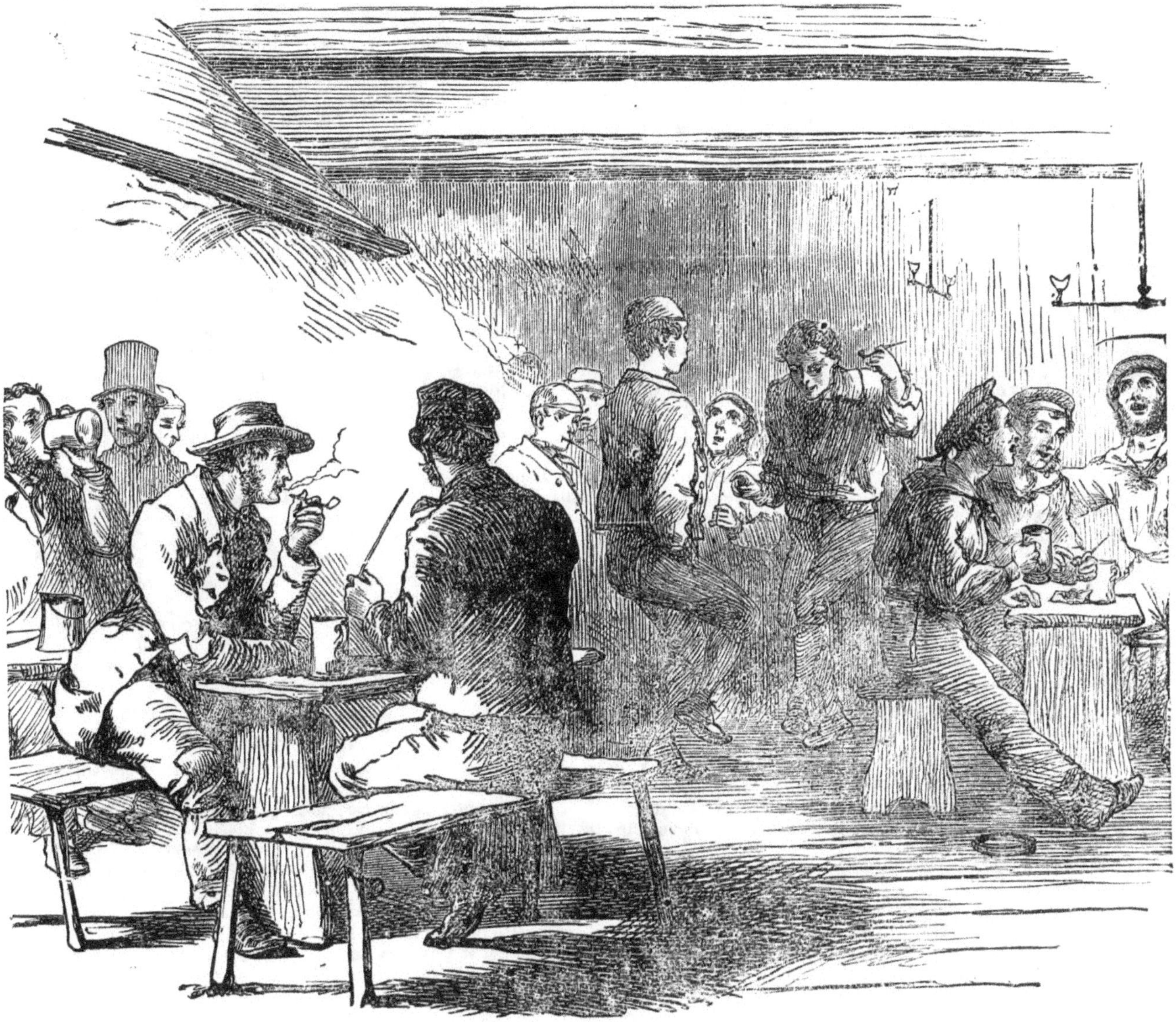

NO. 6

CHAPTER XLIII.

A RATHER UNCOMFORTABLE CONVERSATION.

It took Ned some weeks to traverse the distance to Sydney, seven hundred miles as the crow flies. But he had no adventures on the road worth mentioning, and only awaited the arrival of Rose, to quit the colony for some safer abode. He anxiously read the local papers to see if anything of his doings was known, but beyond the announcement of his departure for Adelaide (as was given out), little else was said.

Conquest, who suspected Mr. Bellamy's identity, called at the Melbourne newspaper offices and requested silence upon the subject, as likely to further the ends of justice. Almost the first person he met in George-street, Sydney, was the black-eyed Lola, who was playing at the theatre.

Mr. Bellamy paid her great court, and the countess received his advances with pleasure; perhaps because she was struck with his bold, manly, devil-may-care bearing.

There was the opera and the theatre, and bazaars and fêtes, and picnic parties up the Paramatta river, and it was upon one of these latter occasions that Lola Montez said to Mr. Bellamy—

"You are not very colonial. Do you *never* take off your gloves?"

Ned started at the question and a flush of evident confusion rose to his face.

"What a strange question!" he exclaimed, looking at her keenly.

"Oh, I am an acknowledged eccentric, and as such am privileged to ask whatever comes into my head. *Have* you a reason?"

"Yes, I have; but I would far sooner not confess it."

"Ah, a mystery! Do you know I hate mysterious people."

"Is it because you don't care for a rival in that line?"

"No, but I believe all women hate puzzles that they can't unravel."

"Very well, since to be hated by you would be worse than death itself (there he bent upon her an amorous glance), I will no longer allow this little habit of mine to remain a mystery to you. I wear gloves for the most unromantic of all reasons, namely, because my hands are red and coarse. Are you satisfied with the explanation?"

"No, because I do not believe it. What nonsense you talk."

"Truth is often considered nonsense, for the reason that we are so little accustomed to its sound. I wear gloves because I am too colonial. I find my men (and I employ a good score) work better for a master who is not too stuck-up and who is now and then not above doing a little manual labour himself. Such things are not expected of employers in old and long civilised countries, but out here they always are, and at all events it establishes a bond of unity between employers and employed. Still one can't touch pitch without being defiled, and so, though my hands are always clean, I can't give them the delicate look of gloves."

"I would like to see a hand that had been embrowned by honest toil. It would be a novel sight to me. Pull off your right-hand glove."

"And why particularly my right hand glove?"

"Because people work more with that hand than the other."

"And it is more apt to meet with accidents also, such as cuts and blows?"

Ned felt that the present moment was one of deadly peril to him, and that perfect coolness and nonchalance could alone carry the day.

He laid a hand lightly on Lola's arm, at the same time saying with an easy laugh —

"Now it is *you* who are growing mysterious. You are really driving me to the most commonplace and unromantic explanation. I will be frank with you, however, if you have the patience to listen. I was one day holding a chest of merchandise steady for one of my men to split

it open with an axe, when the instrument slipped in his hand and descended on the back of mine, inflicting the most unsightly gash. Behold the direct testimony of the truth of my words," and pulling off his right-hand glove he held up the scar for her inspection.

The lovely Spaniard looked at it closely, and then suddenly raising her superb eyes scanned still more narrowly his face.

But he stood the keen, searching gaze with an easy smile and without the quiver of a muscle.

"Forgive me," she said, "I *must* be mistaken; and yet 'tis very strange."

"What is very strange if I may make so bold as to ask?"

"Was that on more than one occasion you have reminded me of a bushranger who attacked the coach in which I was journeying to Forest Creek, and whom I slashed across the back of his right hand with a Spanish knife that I carried, because he was rather too demonstrative."

"Happy man even to receive such a remembrance as that from the most lovely woman who ever trod Australia's golden soil. Do you know I almost wish that I was he," answered Ned, with a glance of admiration.

CHAPTER XLIV.

NED KELLY IS SET A STRANGE TASK.

'Twas evident that the countess's suspicions were at all events allayed if not entirely dissipated.

Nevertheless, Ned Kelly felt that for a few minutes he had been standing on the brink of a precipice.

If with her known impetuosity she had denounced instead of questioning him he might have found himself in a particularly awkward fix.

Lola Montez having shown her cards, however, he now played out his trumps in such a manner that by the time the pleasant picnic was over and they had all got safely to Sydney he felt quite assured that ere very long he should be able to score game against his fair antagonist.

"That woman *shall* be mine!" he over and over again muttered to himself, as he grew more and more enamoured of the lovely foreign adventuress. "If my supposed wealth and devotion should, united, fail to win her, then when the proper time comes, she shall be seized upon and carried aboard the treasure ship by force, where I will make her mine without affording her the consolation of a parson's pattered prayers. Hang it! 'twill not be so difficult a matter to run away with a woman as with a bank full of gold."

Thus often ran the current of his thoughts, whilst his passion grew more intense and ungovernable day by day, until soon he found it absolutely impossible to miss one of her performances at the theatre, and almost as impossible to restrain himself from kicking up a row with the multitudinous admirers who besides himself were always fluttering about her in the green-room.

"There will be blood spilt if this goes on much longer," he would sometimes mutter to himself fiercely, and to make the probabilities of such a crime more remote he one night won the privilege of escorting her home to her suburban residence at Potter's-point, close to the large and commodious Police Barracks, and delayed taking his farewell in so pointed a manner that she could not very well avoid asking him indoors; the very thing that he was driving at.

He did but small justice to the little recherché supper that was so daintily laid out by an elderly Spanish Jezabel, who seemed to be half servant and half companion; but a few glasses of wine warmed him up pleasantly for what he was firmly resolved should follow after, and so when the countess significantly observed that it was getting very late he refused to accept that or her yawns either as a hint that it was high time for him to depart, and instead of rising to his feet he sank on to his knees, and seizing hold of both her hands gripped them until she almost winced with the pain, whilst begging her to accept his love.

She heard him through to the very end of what he had to say, merely interrupting him once to request him to remember that her hands were not of cast-iron; but when he had done she said, with an arch smile—

"You had better get up and sit down now, for I'm sure you must feel exhausted after all that exertion. Is it not the case?"

"I will never rise from my knees until you grant my prayer."

"Oh, but I don't mean to grant it until you have done something to prove yourself worthy of it, and you can't perform that in such a foolish attitude."

Ned Kelly was on his feet in a twinkling, and regarding her earnestly.

"Pour yourself out another glass of wine, take a seat, and look like a reasonable being. I hate to be stared at. I get so much of that kind of homage at all times. Now drink your wine, and listen to me."

Her admirer instantly vowed that he was all attention.

"Then I'm going to say to you almost the exact words that I've said to at least a dozen others who during the past week, have made of me the same complimentary request that you have just done."

The glass was at Ned's lips, and he almost bit a piece out of it at being thus coolly informed how many rivals he had.

"Don't excite yourself," exclaimed the countess, who had remarked the action. "Besides, those glasses are rather expensive. I will not say yes, to a single Australian admirer—and I assure you again that I have a host of them —until I am avenged for a terrible insult that I have received in their colony."

"Tell me the name of the rascal who has dared to offer it to you, and, if it will give you any satisfaction, I will shoot him down like a dog."

"There is no need for such extreme measures. The man who insulted me is a common criminal, with a price upon his head; a brutal bully who could threaten a weak woman, and even maltreat her; a monster who could clutch my poor arm" (and here she stretched forth a delicately-rounded arm, white as milk, and bare to the very shoulder) "and, whilst he poured forth the most infamous and revolting threats, squeezed it in his iron grip until it bore the marks of his vile and ruthless fingers for days. To win my love, you must hunt to the death the man who has so grossly ill-used and insulted me. The day that the bushranger Ned Kelly is lodged in gaol I will affiance myself to you, Mr. Bellamy, and the day after he is hung I will marry you. There is the answer to your petition." Ned almost thought there was a malicious twinkle in her eye, as she imposed those conditions.

Had a bombshell dropped through the ceiling at Ned's feet, with the fuse all alight, he could hardly have been more startled than he was by this speech of his inamorata.

It was not pleasant, the thought that he would have to be hung before he could marry her, and he regarded her with almost a scowl, as wondering whether after all she had pierced his incognito, and was availing herself of the occasion to tell him pretty plainly what she thought of him— a preliminary step, perhaps, to ruthlessly handing him over to the police and the gibbet.

"But no," he reflected, after a moment's anxious doubt, "she would never have the pluck to sit smiling there if she really thought herself in the presence of a man who would think little of strangling her if he suspected she knew him. It is not in a woman's nature to be so bold."

"Ah! you're a coward!" said the countess, with a sudden petulance. "You are either afraid of this outlaw or you think I am hardly worth the winning at so great a hazard. You are like all the rest. No one has closed with my offer—not one. You colonials are a set of poltroons, and I see very well that I shall have to go and seek him myself. I won't leave this colony (would to heaven I had never come here) until I am avenged on that man, more

for the insulting words that he dared to utter to my face than the mere hurt he did me, for that was but a trifle. I will seek him *myself*, since heaven will not raise me up a champion, and with my bare breast opposed to his iron-cased one I will fight with him a duel to the very death!"

Those who know anything of the daring, reckless, and masculine doings of this woman, will not be surprised at her determination. She faced the enraged population of Munich with cool and mocking threats when they, aroused by her intolerable insolence and bad influence over King Louis, tumultuously sought her life.

As she concluded, she plucked a pistol mounted in solid silver, with an ivory stock, from inside her low-corsaged dress, and, apparently in a fit of absence of mind, pulled the hammer back to full-cock, and deposited the weapon in her lap.

Again Ned looked at her suspiciously, for this action placed him far more in her power than she was in his.

True, he also had a pistol about him, but he would have to unbutton his coat and dive into the depths of an inside breast-pocket to get at it; before he had effected which, if she but suspected his design, she would have plenty of time to shoot him through the head.

Besides, how could he hurt her as she lay there looking so beautiful?

Her broad white chest, palpitating with violent emotion, was in its loveliness a far stronger defence than his own thick iron corselet had ever been.

But what should he say—what do?

He could not sit there looking like a fool (though he felt quite as big a one as ever he looked), without making some kind of a proposition likely to please her.

"I would not have you risk your life for worlds," he therefore contrived to gasp out. "I—I will go and unearth this Kelly, wherever he may be; and—and when found, I will either shoot him dead or hand him over to the tender mercies of the law. Of course, if he resists and I *have* to shoot him you will marry me equally as though Jack Ketch had the final disposing of him."

"Well, yes, I will; but there must be no doubt about his death. His corpse must be recognised and sworn to by at least a dozen people."

"Of course, of course. But suppose I strive my very utmost to bring him to book, but cannot? Is my case then hopeless?"

"Ned Kelly once really dead, you having done your very best to be the instrument of his death, and failing through no fault of your own, your case will be still more hopeful." And she smiled upon him brightly.

Ned despairingly wished that he could see matters in that light.

"Is it absolutely a necessity that this fellow should be defunct before you marry me?" he half groaned.

"Absolutely; I have taken a most solemn oath to that effect. You do not know how revengeful is a blue blooded Spanish woman."

"Then I'll hunt all Australia over for the miscreant," said Ned. "I will start in search of him the day after to-morrow. Will that satisfy you?"

"No; I shall only be satisfied when he is dead," answered the countess. "Thanks to you, however, I have little doubt that that event will come to pass ere long. Good-night, Mr. Bellamy. It really is getting very late."

"Then I will take an immediate farewell. One kiss to seal the contract."

"No, I never pay beforehand for work that's to be performed. Good-night, Mr. Bellamy. Don't trouble to come round the table. None but the brave deserve the fair. Show me that you are brave, I am yours."

CHAPTER XLIV

NED'S DISCONTENTED TRUDGE MELBOURNEWARD.

So Ned Kelly left the presence of the beautiful Lola Montez without a kiss or even a hand-shake, and departed to kill himself or hand himself over to Jack Ketch before he could even hope to obtain for himself such favours—an odd position to be placed in.

"The woman's as whimsical and capricious as a child; and, by George, how bitterly she can hate, to be sure. By thunder, its fortunate she has never taken it into her head to inspect my ears. The curls hide 'em pretty entirely, but if she was to poke them on one side and find the top of one ear nearly gone altogether she might remember her pistol-shot as well as the slash she gave me with her knife."

He stalked along in moody reverie after this self-colloquy; but soon he broke forth again, for his mind was very ill at ease:—

"If she found me out after she had married me—I say 'if,' for I don't consider it at all likely—she'd not dare to split on me then for very shame's sake, for I know she'd die rather than the world should know she had become the wife of a bushranger. Ha, ha, ha! I should be sure of her then. But how the devil am I to get her? Well, at all events, I must set out in search of myself, and glad enough shall I be to enjoy the freedom of the bush again for a while. I only wish that some lucky chance would throw in my way a man closely resembling my bushranger self, and I'd soon provide the carrion she wants, and swear till my eyeballs started that he was Ned Kelly himself!"

All the while that Ned, according to his regular custom, was thus muttering his inward thoughts and resolutions half aloud, he was striding along the road in the direction of the city, whose myriad lights covered the slopes about a mile and a half in front of him.

A full moon looked down from the star-spangled heavens upon the still and tranquil scene, but Ned frowned as he presently passed the dark and gloomy pile of Police Barracks on his left, for therein dwelt the men with whom he had waged war for years, the "bloodhounds of the law," as he was wont to designate them.

For a minute he paused, folded his arms across his chest, and, regarding the flint-stone pile sternly, muttered to himself between his set teeth, whilst his bushy brows almost met—

"I wonder if the day will ever come, as I have again and again resolved that it should do, when I and a chosen band will gather around you, carry you by surprise, and put every rascal inside you to death, and then, clad in their togs, mounted on their horses, and armed with their weapons, bail up half the swells and rob all the banks in the colony. Ay, that would be a glorious raid, but then I'm on another tack now, and I don't see how the two things could be worked together. By thunder, though, if my present scheme fails by any chance I'll relieve my feelings and put myself into a good temper again by having recourse to the other. My track shall be marked by fire and blood, and then I'll see if I can't frighten the New South Welshmen out of their gold as easily as I have done the Victorians."

Again he strode doughtily on. Never before had he felt so excited and ill at ease with himself as he did on that particular night. Was it that "coming events threw their shadows before," the awful shadows of the condemned cell and the gallows-tree?

And now the rambling, wooden, one-storeyed Emigration Depôt is abreast of him on the right, and at the foot of the gentle descent that appears beyond lies the beautiful Sydney Harbour, like a moonlit lake, beyond which a gas-lit street stretches up the opposite hill, with a square-towered church, and shops long since closed.

Far to his left, on a rounded eminence, glittered in the moonlight the calico tents and shanties (mingled here and there with a corrugated-iron building) of New Town, the abode of lucky and unlucky diggers, newly-arrived emigrants, and *mauvais sujets* of every description, now the Camberwell of Sydney, and called the North Shore, it is presumed for the reason that there is nothing North about it. a lovely peninsula, a limited but exquisite specimen of country scenery. The "North Shore" is a gentle elevation, and is a well-known "bit" to all artists.

Sounds of jollity, merrymaking, and fighting are wafted across the hill by the fresh breeze from the bay, as far as Government House, but Ned Kelly takes no heed of them.

What he does take heed of, however, is that there is a trooper coming up behind him on foot, with his sword tucked up under his arm and his long bright spurs clinking as he strides along.

Another minute and he passes Ned by with a cheery "good-night."

"Good-night to you," responds the bushranger, well aware that prudence would dictate a courteous answer; but though the words are as polite as they need be they are involuntarily snapped out like the half-bark, half-snarl of an angry dog.

The tone induces the trooper to regard the speaker keenly, and as he turns his face round Ned recognises in him the sole survivor of the gold escort, the young trooper who afterwards rode close up to the cart with a white handkerchief on his sword, and challenged him to mortal combat.

Nothing would have pleased Ned better than to have granted him the favour then and there, for he was terribly riled by the events of the evening; but far too great interests were at stake for him to risk the gratification of the whim, especially where pistol-shots would be clearly heard at the Police Barracks.

CHAPTER XLV.

MYSTERIOUS PERILS GATHERING THICKLY ROUND.

HE trudged along therefore, and so also did the trooper, for a matter of a hundred yards or more, but then the latter came to a halt, seemed to stand irresolute for a second or two, and eventually crossed over the road to Ned, as he arrived almost parallel with him, and asked him for a light for his pipe.

Ned produced his match-box (fusees and vesuvians have, strange to say, never met with any degree of favour in the colonies), and handed it to the trooper without a word.

But he was quite conscious that whilst the trap was lighting his pipe he was favouring him with many a furtive glance.

It seemed to be an operation of some difficulty, kindling the contents of that pipe, and Ned was getting out of patience altogether, when suddenly it glowed red all over, and the trooper, returning the match-box, observed—

"We are old acquaintances, I fancy. Your face seems very familiar to me."

"Well, you've looked at it long enough for it to be, at any rate."

"Oh, no offence, I hope? Only everyone likes coming across old friends."

"I don't recognise an old friend in you. I don't fancy I ever saw you before."

"Don't you? I feel pretty well convinced, mate, that I've seen *you* before, but when and where I'm blest if I can exactly remember."

Kelly was now clean shaved, and the absence of beard and whiskers had metamorphosed him completely.

"It don't much matter. I've been pretty well all over the colony in my lifetime, and so, I expect, have you," rejoined Kelly, sullenly.

"Oh, you are colonial-born then?" said the trooper, suddenly and sharply.

"No, far from that, but I've been out here some years, nevertheless."

"The colony seems to have served you well at any rate. Made your pile?"

"Almost. I've prospered on the gold-fields at Ballarat, and since then equally so in trade. Yes, I've no reason to speak ill of the colony."

"Ever been at Forest Creek or up Kyneston way?"

"No. I don't know those parts. I made my pile at Golden Point, Ballarat."

"Ah, many fortunes have been made there. Carrying on business?"

"Really, I don't see by what right you put to me all these questions."

"Oh, I don't know exactly about the right; but when two fellows are walking along the same road side by side they generally enliven the dulness of the way by conversation. I'm just as ready to answer questions as to put them."

"Very well then, just for a change I'll ask you who you are?"

"Corporal Tom Conquest, of the Victorian Mounted Constabulary."

"You are rather young to be a corporal, are you not, Mr. Conquest?"

"Well, you see, capturing bushrangers leads to quick promotion in these times, and shooting them down is almost as good. I hope to be a sergeant before long."

"Allow me to congratulate you on your prospects of speedy promotion. I suppose you have no scruples of conscience at winning it through bloodshed?"

"What! scruples of conscience at shooting two-legged wolves, who have twice the ferocity of their honester brethren who run on four? I should think not. Why, destroying vermin like that gives me very considerable pleasure."

"And I don't suppose you object to the pecuniary reward that is generally attached to their capture or destruction? Wouldn't you like to lay that infernal scoundrel Ned Kelly by the heels, and pocket ten thousand pounds, and win every honest and upright man's gratitude by the deed, eh?"

"I believe you, mate; and that's just what I intend to do."

"May you succeed. But there's many a slip 'twixt cup and lip."

"Not when the holder of the cup's hand is steady. I have taken a solemn oath to bring this villain Kelly to the gibbet, and I'm on his track now."

"On his track at the present moment? The devil!" and Ned's hand involuntarily stole towards the pocket that contained his loaded pistol.

"Oh, I don't say at the present moment exactly," retorted the trooper, with a laugh. "But I am on his track for all that, and I'm bound to run him to earth in the end. you'll see. Do you know why I stopped you to ask you for a light?"

"Because you wanted to pump me for some reason or other, eh?"

"Say rather because I had more than half an idea you were Ned himself."

The bushranger thought that a good laugh would be the best answer he could make to this remark, and he managed to laugh with a great deal of boisterous vehemence, as though it were really an excellent joke to be mistaken for so bloodthirsty a miscreant.

The trooper laughed too, and to Ned's intense relief added—

"I soon found out my mistake, though I was convinced much against my will, I can assure you. Still, there is a likeness between you, especially in your build."

"I'm certainly very much obliged for the handsome compliment you pay me," said Ned, bridling up. "Some people perhaps would feel their vanity tickled at being told that they resembled so celebrated a character, but, as an honest man who never wronged anyone of a penny, I assure you that I do not. However, I must be jogging on, so I will wish you good-night. I hope you will catch the scoundrel soon."

"I'm safe to do that, for I have secret advice which I can absolutely rely on that he was in Melbourne for nearly a month, and then left for Sydney."

And with a cheery "good night" the trooper passed down in the direction of the shipping, whilst Ned walked just as rapidly in an opposite direction, feeling that perils were fast thickening around him.

He couldn't shake off this growing feeling of uneasiness. He dared not go straight home for fear that Tom Conquest, his suspicions not quite allayed, might track him thither; and thereafter, hovering about the place in the daytime, recognise some of his underlings.

So he walked up one street and down another, often fancying that he heard stealthy footsteps in his rear; but when he looked round he invariably saw nothing calculated to arouse his suspicions, for the hour was a very late one, and there was hardly anyone about.

At last he felt that before he dared venture home he must fortify himself with at least one glass of spirits and water; and so he turned in at the private side-door of a "public" in George's-street, and passing through the bar into the snug little cosy beyond, only made use of by a favoured few, he dropped the heavy curtain that shut it off from the general public, who at the present moment were represented by emptiness, and giving a poke to the embers of the expiring fire, for the night was rather chilly, he called out for a strong glass of hot brandy and water.

It was presently brought him by Lady Knott, the land-lady, for the "public" could at that time boast an English titled lady for landlady, and a French marquis for a billiard-marker, sufficient proof in itself of the topsy-turvy state of society in the colony.

Ned (beg pardon, Mr. Bellamy) paid for his grog and was thanked for his order with a civility that the ordinary scum of barmaids would not have condescended to show to a customer, and then the hostess, a very finely-made and good-looking woman, moved into the outer bar again, where a second or so later Ned heard the chink of spurs, and peeping forth from behind the curtain beheld the very trooper who had been the cause of his present great uneasiness also in the act of giving an order.

At the sight Ned uttered a muttered curse under his breath.

CHAPTER XLVI.
NED GETS A FEW ACCEPTABLE WRINKLES.

How thankful Ned was that he had dropped the curtain between the "cosy" and the bar; for he felt that he might hear something important while he remained unseen, since he was well aware that young men of all types and professions had a weakness for boasting of their achievements, and bragging generally of what they could do and did do and intended to do in the future, before the divinities of the bottle-ranged shelf and mahogany counter.

So Ned softly stirred and sipped away at his hot grog, toasting his feet over the hot glowing embers of the wood fire meanwhile, and with the stock of his pistol resting most handy to his grasp, in case it might be required.

"Why, Mr. Conquest, you are a complete stranger. I don't think I've seen you twice these six months!" the landlady was heard to exclaim.

"No, I don't care for town much. I've only just come here from Melbourne; in fact, only arrived to-day. I'm on the scent of a remarkable character, and think I shall run him to earth. I prefer a more active life up country. I'm off again to-morrow night at nine o'clock or about," answered the trooper.

"In pursuit of your favourite hobby, hunting bushrangers, I suppose?"

"Well, something in that line. Small fry, though. Precious small fry."

"I thought you had made up your mind to fly at higher game, and that nothing would satisfy your ambition but the capture of the famed ironclad bushranger, Ned Kelly, the King of the Australian bush, as he calls himself?"

"Ah, but you can't imagine what a slippery game-bird he is. He has as many lives as a cat, and is here to-day and gone to-morrow. However, I don't think he'll be able to keep out of my clutches for very long now. To-morrow I go back to Melbourne to nab a couple of his old mates, who he believes to be dead. Ha, ha, ha! he left 'em wounded in the bush, to the mercy of a nest of bulldog-ants, and, egad! those industrious little insects would soon have made skeletons of them if some of our fellows hadn't trotted up in time to save them. They are as well as ever now, I hear, and shearing on the run of a Mr. Fairfax, somewhere up Ballarat way, past Bacchus Marsh. It seems that Ned robbed them of every stiver before he left them, so that if I can induce them to turn Queen's evidence, and help me to hunt Kelly up—a job that I guess they'll precious well enjoy after the trick he's served them—they'll get a free pardon.

"Wherever do you pick up all your information from, Mr. Conquest?"

"Ah, that's a mystery of the service, and must never be let out."

"But when these two fellows see you coming won't they take to flight?"

"Why, bless your heart, I shall not venture near 'em in these togs. There's an awful clever shearer, who's the talk of the whole country round, and whose nickname is Fleecy Jim; in fact, I very much doubt if he's known by any other. The cove is rather like me, and so I shall in due time turn up at Tarramea, under his name and character."

"But if you are set to shear sheep what will you do—eh?"

"Why, shear 'em, to be sure. I assure you I'm a dab at it."

"I hope you won't come to any harm. Aren't you rather too daring?"

"Not I. Nothing venture nothing have, you know. Set these two fellows and one Dick Dawson on Ned's track, and I'll nab him in less than a week. They'll know all his tricks and disguises, you see, which I do not, and with them for my allies, I'll cop the whole of the ten thousand pounds that are offered for his apprehension; for they will have a quittance in full, and far more than they deserve, in the shape of a free pardon for all their past offences. Do you see that?"

"Yes, and I hope that you'll be successful. That such a villain as Ned Kelly is left so long unhung is a positive disgrace to the colony. I declare we all shudder here at the mention of his name."

"You would shudder more, perhaps, were I to tell you that he was in Melbourne for nearly a month, bolted to Sydney, and has now gone back again; his daughter is with him, but we have no evidence against her as yet. I'm sorry for her, as she is very pretty, but she has blood on her hands as well as her father, and such a crime as the taking of a human life must not pass unpunished. By the way, did you ever hear of a Mr. Bellamy, who has arrived in Sydney about a month ago?"

CHAPTER XLVII.

NED MAKES A DESPERATE RESOLVE.

THE hostess felt somewhat bored whilst the trooper was propounding his last query; not so the subject thereof concealed in the cosy.

"A highly-respectable man, I believe," said she.

"Do you know that of yourself, or only from hearsay?"

"I know what I have stated to be a fact, and so does all Sydney. Handsome, middle-aged gentleman. He is, or was, in business, I hear. Bellamy and Co. in Melbourne."

"Oh, is that all. Who and where is the Co., then?" asked Tom.

"Very probably in London, I should say, indeed most likely."

"Ah, shouldn't wonder. I only asked out of idle curiosity. I don't suppose you ever observed whether Mr. Bellamy had a gash, a healed scar, I should rather say, across the back of his right hand, and a portion of his ears

gone? If 'tis so I should know the firm to be a respectable one."

"I don't believe I ever saw Mr. Bellamy without gloves on his hands. He often pays me a visit, but I am sure I should have noticed his ears had anything been wrong about them. Dear me, how inquisitive you troopers are."

"All in the way of business, madam. All in the way of business, I assure you. Well, you look tired and bored, and just a trifle sleepy, so I'll say good-night. When next you see me I'll be ten thousand pounds the richer, I hope, through being able to inform you that Mr. and Miss Kelly are sojourning at Wintles Hotel * on their route to Gallows-place," and with a cheerful laugh at his own somewhat ghastly joke, Tom Conquest politely raised his shako and then took himself off.

A couple of minutes elapsed, and then a voice was heard from inside the cosy calling in husky tones for another glass of hot grog.

It was at once brought him, for at the season of which we write colonial hotels were kept open all night long, barmaids and barmen relieving each other every eight hours, three sets being required for the labour. The landlady had not recognised Mr. Bellamy when he entered, for the very good reason that when he left Conquest's company he donned a pair of false whiskers, but omitted the beard. He also mounted a pair of blue spectacles.

When the landlady took Mr. Bellamy in this second glass of brandy-and-water she could not help noticing how deadly pale he was, and how his hand shook as he raised the tumbler to his lips.

The lady withdrew, and some five minutes later Mr. Bellamy quitted his retreat and stalked out through the bar, wishing her good night as he passed.

"Odd gentleman in his ways and not over amiable, I should say," thought she, when he had gone; and as she was that moment relieved, she betook herself to bed, there to dream that Mr. Bellamy was the ferocious iron-clad bushranger Ned Kelly, and that with his outlaw band he had entered Sydney and set the hotel on fire, giving her the death of an Indian Suttee atop of the largest four-post bedstead.

Meanwhile the sham merchant's thoughts were almost as horrible as the landlady's nightmare-ridden slumbers.

He could see clearly now how perilous was his position

That Lardy Bill and Lanky Jim, brought to Melbourne and assured of forgiveness for all their past crimes and offences, would hunt him up with the ferocity and unremitting energy of a couple of bloodhounds, he could not for an instant doubt, and that they would be able to recognise half his servants as their former companions was equally clear.

The subterranean passage that was to open into the bullion-vaults of the bank would not be completed for nearly another week, and there was nothing to prevent the trooper being back in Melbourne with these two men in the course of two or three weeks. So he resolved on a bold stroke.

He knew his work in the cellar was unfinished; that a little more work would place wealth within his grasp. He would return by the steamer at once, disguised, to Melbourne, leave Conquest in Sydney to follow when too late, get his pile out of the bank, and slope (via Adelaide) for South America and England, where he was totally unknown.

He left the next morning undetected, and in three days trod the streets of Melbourne.

He timed his arrival to take place at night. Larkins looked almost frightened when he presented himself.

It should here be mentioned that when Rose, after her arrest, was brought before the bench, there was no evidence against her of any offence, nor indeed, against those arrested at the same time. The bird wanted had flown. Consequently all parties were discharged, if not without

---

* Nickname for Melbourne prison.

any stain upon their characters, at least without any proof of the reverse.

Rose then confined herself to the house, with the intention of taking the first opportunity of joining her father.

As we have said, when Ned entered, he found Larkins in charge. Rose was lying fatigued and asleep.

"They must *never reach* Melbourne—no, nor that meddlesome trap be permitted to return to it either," he at last muttered fiercely to himself. "I must take the bull by the horns if I would escape being gored to death by them. I must overtake Master Tom Conquest on the road to Tarramea, and put either a bullet through his brain or a sabre-blade between his ribs. Ay, and then I will just continue my journey, and put an end at once and for ever to the careers of Lardy and Lanky. A little bloodletting will do me good; it will rid me of the megrims and blue devils."

CHAPTER XLVIII.
ONCE MORE ON THE WAR-TRAIL.

NED was very glad to find on reaching home that Rose had gone to rest.

Strange was it that there should be one soft spot in this man-wolf's nature.

All his cowardice, all his fears, all his tremblings were for her. Until she had brought her soft round throat within throttling distance of the hangman's noose, and all in his defence, he had never known fear, and now he almost wished that he was able to pray for her safety, and certainly he would have laid down his own life willingly to have secured it, so inconsistent is human nature.

He even took off his boots and crept softly into her room to look at her as she slept, but he did not dare to kiss even her hair for fear of awaking her.

As he gazed at her he murmured to himself—

"How much she is like her poor mother when she was the same age. I almost wish she was with her mother. I must try to pack her off to England, under the promise that I will soon join her there."

And having made up his mind to this, Ned stole out of the room again, closed the door noiselessly behind him, and repaired to the underground workings to see how the tunnelling operations were getting on.

He found them in the same state as he had left them. Larkins found Carroty the next morning, and he was quietly introduced into the house. The whole party were soon at work again. The ground was hard, and the picks had to be used very gently so that no noise of excavating should reach the ears of anyone who might be traversing the street above, which a police constable patrolled all the night long, at half-hour intervals.

"Larkins," said Ned, "do you think the job's three-quarters done?"

"Quite that, I should say, Ned. I guess we are almost under the pavement on the opposite side of the street, to-night. I'd bet heavy on it."

"I'm exactly of the same opinion, for I've paced the street and I've paced the tunnel. The pavement is twelve feet wide. Why in two more nights we'll be right under the place that we want to get into, the bullion-vault of the bank, and in a week at most we'll be sailing for old England."

Carroty Larkins spat in his hands and then rubbed them vehemently together, which was his way of expressing delight.

"Capten, you're a mas in," said he. "I was jealous of yer once, but I aren't so no longer. 'Taint in man's nature to bear a grudge against another bloke as is about to make a milliner, a golden milliner I mean, of him."

"I am glad to hear you say so, Larkins, as I shall have to leave you in sole charge to-morrow, whilst I go to see about the vessel that is to bear us away. Be sure that you make no more noise than usual, and don't commence your labours a second earlier. The next day is Sunday, and the

next after that St. Patrick's day, so of course no business will be done on either, and ere Tuesday morning I shall be back again. But whilst I am away keep indoors and sober. The loss of such a prize isn't to be lightly risked. Why, once in England, every man Jack of us will be able to live like the best of the swells. I heard only to-day that the vaults were almost bursting their sides with gold, all awaiting the departure of the next mail steamer, which sails Wednesday week."

"Oh, Lord, capten, suppose they sends the big steamer, or perhaps half-a-dozen of 'em, to chase our treasure wessel, eh?"

"Well, we shall have a good seven hours' start before one can be despatched; the great southern ocean is rather wider than a bush road, and I shall choose a craft carrying such a press of canvas and of such a build that it won't be a very easy matter to overhaul her. The Marco Polo and two or three other sailing ships have beaten the mail steamers all to bits, lately, in the voyage home, as I daresay you've heard tell."

"I believe I have heard summat to that effect, now that I comes to think on it. Well, well, cap, we leaves it all to you, for if there's anyone who can safely lead us through this 'ere job, the devil a doubt but you're the man, and you may depend on me for carrying your instructions into effect, and for backing yer up in all things as well."

A few minutes were gone into by Ned Kelly and his second in command, and then the former retired to partake of the rest that he was so much in need of to recruit his exhaustion both mind and body, and to brace him up for the performance of those terrible deeds that he was so firmly bent on.

At breakfast the following morning Ned was a new man, but it was in vain that he urged Rose to leave the colony before him, and set sail for England at once.

Ned had informed her that he would have to go to England and he gave her many reasons, all in fact that he could think of, but the real one, why she should start at once and leave him to come on after.

"Neither in safety nor in danger, adversity nor prosperity will we be ever parted, father," said she. "I suppose this is that woman's suggestion? She has consented to marry you, and she wants you all to herself on the long voyage, but I have a prior claim on you, and I'm not going to relinquish it at a stranger's bidding."

Ned assured her that such was not the case, and brought other reasons forward, and prayers and entreaties to back them, but it was all to no purpose, for he still dared not tell her that the near shadow of the gibbet o'erhung her and that was why he wanted her to get away, for he knew that she had hardly regarded it as a crime, shooting a man to save his life, but rather as a justifiable act.

As she was not to be moved, he resolved to abandon his own fears.

He convinced himself that their danger would not after all be very great when once the troublesome trooper, Tom Conquest, and the treacherous Lardy Bill and Lanky Jim were put out of the way, and he had hitherto been so successful in all his crimes that he did not for a single instant anticipate failure in either of these.

That Conquest had imparted his suspicions to any of his brother constables Ned thought most improbable, as he would naturally be desirous of copping the whole of the reward that was offered for his (Ned's) slaughter or apprehension to his own cheek, and so all the evidence and information that he had raked up and scraped together would perish with him.

These reflections made Ned Kelly at length able even to laugh and jest, and then he told Rose that he was that night going up to Tarramea to get the treasure-stuffed jackets that he had concealed in the wombat-hole, and if possible to regain her pet mare Swiftsure also. He advised Rose to keep the blinds down and keep out of sight till his return

At first Rose warmly combated this resolution, but on Ned's convincing her that there could not be the slightest danger attached to the expedition, she at last yielded a reluctant assent, being partly persuaded thereto by the conviction that he would have gone all the same, whether she accorded or withheld it.

So he told her when he should be back, and adduced the most excellent reasons for being absent so long, and charged her to remain indoors whilst he was away; and at nine o'clock that night, just half-an-hour after the lamps were lighted all down Great Collins-street, he loaded his pistols, and, carrying a saddle on his head and bridle in his hand, he quietly took the road to the police paddock, where he knew several good troop horses were to be found. He placed his saddle upon the best he could find "by the pale moonlight," led it gently out, mounted, and was off.

CHAPTER XLIX.

FOURTH MEETING OF TOM CONQUEST AND NED KELLY.

NED KELLY had set out on his present hazardous, though to him pleasantly exciting, enterprise a very different looking man from what he had ever appeared before.

He had studied a coloured glass photograph of Fleecy Jim, the shearer, in a Bourke-street shop window, and had got himself up as much like unto it as possible.

He had when leaving Melbourne shaved clean, presenting a bare upper lip, but he had made up for its loss by donning a false sandy-coloured whisker and beard in one, that fastened by springs over the ears, and he had dyed his hair and eyebrows of a still warmer and ruddier hue.

Not content even with this amount of metamorphosis, he had by the use of walnut juice given his complexion a brown tint, while his throat, hands, and arms were red enough from a life of exposure, as though they had daily had their scorching in the sun all through the long torrid summer, and in short made himself up in every respect so like unto Fleecy Jim that, had that worthy chanced to have encountered him he would certainly have been considered as like him as two peas.

The garb of a shearer he didn't require for the present, for he felt sure that Corporal Tom Conquest would be got up immaculately in that respect, and he intended to trouble him for the clothes.

And now the disguised bushranger is clean away from the dwellings of men, and his spirits rise wondrously as he feels himself once more to be the monarch of his old domain, the king of the Australian bush.

'Tis a dark, gloomy, and tempestuous night; the wind is coming up from the distant bay in puffs, whistles and shrieks through the tree-covered ranges; the shadows flit fast and furiously across the surface of the moor, in short spurts like race horses struggling vainly to defeat time; the birds have long ago retired to their nests, the native bear to his favourite branch, and the 'possum to his hole in the hollow tree; the dingo or native dog howls dismally from the deeper solitudes of the bush, sometimes answered by the shrill cry of the blue crane from some neighbouring swamp, as he diligently searches for a recherché supper of tender young frogs; a few drops of rain fall at intervals, making splatches on the metal road as large as shillings, and sometimes thunder rumbles in the distance like the devil muttering his curses in the air, preceded by a flash of white forked lightning, that zig zags across a pall-hued cloud and appears almost to hiss as it disappears.

It seems to be exactly the night for deeds of bloodshed and horror, and Ned hails all these tokens as good augury of the success of his mission.

He holds the road just at the point where it branches off in one direction towards Ballarat, and in the other towards Forest Creek. No one can pass on either track without being challenged by him.

A couple of troopers rattle along the road, laughing and smoking, but he slinks back into the bush out of *their* sight and hearing, muttering a curse upon their entire race as he does so.

He waits yet a little longer, and then he hears a solitary horseman coming along at a spanking trot.

"That must be my man," thinks he, and he emerges on the road again and rides forward at an easy pace with the intention of being overtaken.

That's just what presently happens.

"Good night," calls out a cheery voice.

"Good night to you. Whither away, mate?" is Ned Kelly's answer.

"Tarramea, Fairfax's station, shearing job," answers Tom Conquest.

"You ride an uncommon good nag for a shearer."

"Think so? Bought him at a Wangaratta stock sale, an unbroken colt, for half-a-crown. Flatter myself I have made something of him."

"I fancy somebody made him a troop-horse before you had anything to do with him. I arrest you on suspicion of horse-stealing, friend."

"Ha, ha, ha, a good joke that. Why, don't you know me, mate?"

"How the devil should I, when I can hardly make out a feature of your face? Do you think I've the eyes of a Tom-cat that can see in the dark? I can judge of your horse by his step and the way he carries his head, but I can't say the same for you. Anyway you are my prisoner."

"Tut, tut, man! I thought everyone in the force could swear to Tom Conquest's voice, though, truth to say, he don't recognise yours."

"I know Tom Conquest's voice well enough, but *he* would have declared himself to a brother trooper at once. Yours sounds to me a deal more like Ned Kelly the bushranger's, and I'm d—— if you aren't Ned, too."

Almost 'ere the words were out of his mouth he whipped a pistol from his holster, and at the same instant spurring his horse down upon that ridden by the disguised trooper, rolled it right over in the mud.

"You infernal ass!" roared Tom, as he disengaged himself from his fallen steed and struggled to his feet. "What was that for, eh?"

"To get the better of you, of course. I don't care for a fight upon equal terms where it can be avoided. I want good health to enjoy the ten thousand pounds that I shall win for this night's work. Now don't move a hand towards your pockets, for I know what that means well enough, and I'd put a bullet through your brain before you'd time to pull it out again."

"You thundering blockhead! just listen to reason, will you?" ejaculated Tom, almost foaming at the mouth with passion. "I'm no more like Ned Kelly than I'm like the man in the moon—no, nor so much."

"I haven't the honour of that last-named gentleman's acquaintance, and I don't feel in any humour for arguing the point with you, for I'm as sure that you're Ned Kelly, as I am that the man in the moon is at present behind a cloud. I've been on the lookout for you along the road for more than an hour past, for, from information received, I knew where you were bound, as well as on what errand and how rigged out; so you see, Master Ned, there can be no manner of a mistake, though where you stole the troop-horse I'm blest if I can guess. Now, inasmuch as you're just as valuable dead as living, see that you keep your potato-trap shut, and that you obey my commands quick and sharp, without cavil or question, or, by gum I'll shoot you as dead as Moses."

The muzzle of the bushranger's pistol was within a yard of Tom's head, and the bushranger's horse stood as firm as any rock for its rider to deliver his fire, whilst his own had scrambled to its feet and started away at a gallop.

"Hold! I'll convince you—" Tom Conquest had sputtered out so much when he thought he observed his antagonist's right-hand forefinger curling with gentle pressure around the trigger of his pistol. "All right, I obey," Tom therefore hastily finished up his sentence with, for he knew that to get at his own barkers ere he was shot dead would be a matter of impossibility.

"Strip!" roared the disguised bushranger. "Off with your jumper, your hat, your boots, trousers, and shirt. Come, look slippery."

"But——"

Tom had got as far as that, when a bellow of—

"Dry up, or take the consequences, d——n you!" in conjunction with the advancing of the pistol-muzzle still nearer to his face, convinced him that silent obedience was the only way of preserving his life.

So he did as he was bidden, in a minute or two standing upright in only his under-flannel, drawers, and stockings.

Both his pistols were now on the ground inside his jumper side-pockets, for not a chance of handling them had presented itself.

The bushranger laughed grimly as he looked at the discomfited Tom Conquest, and called to mind their very different *rencontre* of the night in Sydney, and the vaunts the trooper had afterwards indulged in.

"Now, you hound," he exclaimed, "I think I have clean bowled you over. So you were going to Tarramea to join your old pals, Lardy Bill and Lanky Jim, who are already engaged there in murdering the poor old squatter and all his family, and then to plunder the Home Station, were you? A mightily clever-contrived scheme, I'll admit, but you see, we lads of the Victorian mounted police are sometimes one too many for you."

"I swear——" began Tom.

"Ha! would you, though?" thundered forth Ned. "A single word, and you're a dead man. By George, on second thoughts, I'll make you a stiff un anyway, for you'll be easier to get down to Melbourne that way. Dead men can't play tricks upon travellers."

"Crack!" went Ned's pistol, and Tom Conquest felt himself unwounded; but, turning sharp round, he was off the metal road in a twinkling, into the scrub where no horse could follow.

"Bang!" went the bushranger's second pistol, and the trooper felt himself hit.

He was still able to dive into the scrub, into and through which he crept for some distance, until he reached a spot where Ned lost sight of him.

Ned swore bitterly to himself because his shots had not proved more deadly ones.

He wasn't going to leave the man whom he so intently hated with one spark of life in him, so after looking up and down the road and listening intently for a second to make quite sure that no one was approaching the spot from either direction, he rapidly re-charged his pistols, and, setting spurs to his horse, made after his crippled adversary.

He tracked him to a spot where a flash of lightning had revealed him diving into the scrub as a hare darts into her form, but there he drew rein, sorely puzzled how to proceed.

He saw clearly that his horse could not push its way through the dense tea-tree branches, and yet were he to dismount and explore them on foot, the trooper, if not desperately wounded, might double round till he got to the horse, and then mount it and ride away, in that manner making good his escape.

So Ned scratched his head and resolved to have recourse to a ruse.

"Come forth and I'll spare your life," said he. "Better go with me to Melbourne and chance it than be helpless there till the wild dogs gather round you, and, hungry as wolves, tear you limb from limb."

"You *beast*," called Tom, faintly, out of the scrub. "I believe that you knew who I was all along, and shot me because you wanted to nab Ned Kelly all to your own hook. You possess the same information as I do."

"Ha, ha, ha! I hear that he's in Melbourne, and I want to secure Lardy Bill and Lanky Jim, who are shearing at Tarramea, under promise of a free pardon from Govern-ment, to enlist themselves as my bloodhounds and help run him down. Ha, ha! perhaps that *is* my little game, who can tell? If so, I shall find the shearer togs that you have cast aside very handy to work the oracle with. Ten thousand isn't much when it comes to be divided between two."

"You wretched brute, you! who are you, and where do you come from?"

"It won't do you any good to have those questions answered. I haven't been in the Victorian police long, though I've served in the New South Welsh for some years. I won't hurt you any more if you'll come out."

"I won't trust you. You're a would-be infernal assassin," moaned Tom.

This conversation was rather a loud one, as the men were a hundred yards apart, separated by, to a horse, an impenetrable scrub

At this moment the moon shone out for a brief second from behind a rift in the thickly-scudding masses of leaden cloud.

It was what Ned Kelly had been waiting for.

Straining his eyes he saw the topmost branches of the dwarf tea-trees shake at a certain spot, and knew that the movement must be caused by a motion of the wounded trooper beneath them.

It was a guide to his aim.

He jumped off his horse, and, revolver in hand, rushed into the scrub after Tom to make his work sure, but apprehending this move Tom tore off his coat and hung it up as a "dummy." The night was very black, and in the darkness it might be supposed the coat was not an empty one, at least so thought Ned, who, in his fury, excitement, and haste just stopped to put two bullets through it, and, satisfied his work was complete, bounded back to his horse, upon whose back he sprang lightly.

At that moment a deeper, pitchier darkness than ever suddenly shrouded bush and sky, a tremendous peal of thunder sounded as though it were splitting the very firmament into fragments, a sheet of blinding lightning struck Ned's horse full in the face and crackled fiercely all round and over it, whilst the maddened brute plunged and reared, and lashed out furiously behind, finally break-ing into a wild gallop and defying all its rider's efforts to control or curb it.

Ned kept his seat, but the terrified horse had borne him a good mile away from the scene of his crime before he could bring it to a standstill.

Then he rode back to the spot where Tom Conquest had dropped his shearer's rig-out, and dismounting he carefully rolled up the clothes, with the stiff, narrow-brimmed straw hat in the middle, into as narrow a com-pass as possible, and strapped them on to the saddle in front of him.

This done he remounted, reflected for a moment whether it would not be as well to penetrate into the scrub to make quite sure that the trooper was dead, and decided in the negative when the probability occurred to him that another flash of lightning might terrify his horse and start it away past recovery, whilst he was pottering about amongst the Septospermum bushes, looking for what he might never be able to find in the almost opaque darkness.

"The skunk's bound to be dead," he muttered to him-self, "and I'm blest if I'll waste any more time over him, for I've still a longish ride."

And thus resolving he set spurs to his horse and dashed along the metal road at a swift gallop in the direction of Bacchus Marsh.

About midnight he passed through the township, and a couple of hours later he was in sight of Ballan.

Hereabouts he left the metal and struck into a bush track on his right.

When he had followed this for about three miles he rode into a patch of scrub on a hill, and about five hundred yards from a head station, and dismounting and tying up his horse—for the thunderstorm had by now passed away

— he exchanged his own for the shearer's dress, concealed the former toggery in amongst the thick undergrowth.

He now started down the hill for the woolshed, where shearing was in full swing and where he had ascertained his two "blood-money" friends were engaged—cocking his hat rakishly on one side of his head, and lighting up a short black cutty pipe, he continued his journey, as dandy a shearer, to all outward appearance, as could have been found between the Murrumbidgee River and famed Hobson's Bay.

He chuckles as he reflects how well he has rid himself of the troublesome trooper, but perhaps he would not have felt quite so comfortable and cocksure that he would never be in danger from him any more, had he but known that *neither of his last-fired bullets had as much as touched his supposed victim*, and that the shrieks, the groans, were all put on. The first shot inflicted a slight flesh-wound.

CHAPTER L.

FLEECY JIM AT TARRAMEA. SHEARING EXTRAORDINARY.

EVERY country has its special products. England has its manufactures, America its cotton and sugar, and Australia its wool.

The production of this latter article has called into existence three very distinct Australian characters—the shepherd, the bullock-driver, and the shearer.

The two former varieties of the Antipodean *genus homo* we may hear of on a future occasion, but we will deal with the shearer now.

The shepherd may be said to grow the wool, the shearer to gather it, and the bullock-driver to carry it to market. There you have the avocations of all three.

As shearing only comes for a few months in the year, every class of impecunious men become shearers for the time being, and the money earned at shearing-time contributes greatly to help people to start a little farm.

But there are regular as well as amateur shearers; professional hands who start in the warm parts and finish up on the table lands, and who rest during the remainder of the year, or, at all events, until they have accomplished that thoroughly Australian feat called "knocking down a cheque."

These shearers are generally called "dons," so it don't hold true at the Antipodes that only in universities can "dons" be found.

Of this class the "don" shearer was Bill Topper— "Slashing Bill," as he was generally called.

It was universally allowed, in the districts where he hung out, that he had no equal, and everyone was ready to swear that no one knew how to open a sheep, or run down the *whipping shoulder*, or put an edge on a shear like him.

The sheds where he worked were commonly crowded with learners, known by the name of *stonebreakers* and *tomahawkers*, anxious to become acquainted with Slashing Bill's new dodges, for Bill, like all geniuses, had various methods that were peculiarly his own, and known as Slashing Bill's "opening blow," "new ribbing blow," "right and left cut," and other wondrous cognomens.

Bill was a sort of boss in all the sheds, for no squatter dared offend him. He looked with withering contempt on anyone who tried to shear as well as himself, or to head him in a pen; and like a cat playing with a mouse, he would let him go ahead, and then, putting on a spurt, he would overtake and pass him ere the other had recovered from his surprise.

All competition, however, soon ceased, and after a few desperate battles with the "old dons," he was declared best in all the districts where he worked.

Slashing Bill bore evidence of being something superior to the general run of shearers.

His close-knit cabbage-tree hat had even a very smart ribbon on it, and was always rakishly cocked on one side of his head. His clothes were always clean and smart, and, according to his ideas, both professional and fashionable. He spoke, of course, authoritatively, and his decision, like that of race stewards, was always considered final. In fact, Slashing Bill was an important man, in his particular line, all over Victoria—a man talked of and envied in his little world. And even the children grew up with his name in their mouths, as is often the case with heroes.

But, as honest Andrew Fairservice observed, "Ilka dog has his day," and now in this fourth year of Slashing Bill's reign, and just in the middle of the fifth season, there come rumours from the borders of his kingdom that there has suddenly turned up a fellow who bids fair to beat him, or at all events, as the shearers express it to each other, "give him such a tying up as he never had before."

Bill was at the time in Ballan, the head township of the immediate district, drinking and flashing about, trying to create a sensation with the last of his money, just as an expiring candle gives a great flare up before it goes out.

He was, in fact, playing the part of the heavy swell, before he began the sober comedy of the shearer.

Bill was a great man amongst the ladies, as he called the barmaids and servant-girls of the township, and he lavished half his money on them, and in showing off before them.

Since his fourth season he had been losing his heart over a pretty barmaid; but after taking nearly all his money from him in presents, she told him very plainly, when he popped the question, that she was "onkommon sorry, but she'd been engaged for months to Flash Ned, the boundary rider."

This answer finished Bill slap up, so he set to at once at the drink, and never cried crack till the fat Irish landlady of the "Currency Lass" had handled his last sixpence and turned him out of doors.

He even became so sentimental on an incipient *delirium tremens*, that he began to talk of drowning himself in the creek; but, after duly considering the extreme dampness of the water, and that it was wholly unmixed with rum, he gave up this idea, and, with a penny still his own out of a £30 cheque, made off with his horse and swag on another perambulation, and in the course of a few hours duly arrived at Tarramea Station.

He had hardly sharpened his shears, tied his handkerchief round his head, and put his saddle alongside of him, when the talk commenced about the new shearer, Fleecy Jim, who was surprising the natives all along those parts.

The younger operators began to talk with almost wondering awe of his new method of opening a sheep, and his quickness in running down the whipping-shoulder; and even hinted that he'd been known to shear a hundred and forty sheep in a day.

Slashing Bill listened to all these mutterings with great contempt, and silently set to work to surprise the gossippers.

But no one praised him now but his old pals; all the rest only "blowing" about Fleecy Jim and his wondrous doings, until at last Bill, after trying in vain to convince them that he was the best of the two, threw down his shears in disgust, and made the following speech:—

"Tell 'ee what mates, I'm darned if I'm afraid to meet this here cove any day of the week, and shear agin him with one hand tied behind my back. I baint afraid on him, or any other man, and I guess I'd know how to get the *cobbler*, even if the devil was shearing agin me. Tell 'ee what 'tis. Some o' they flash youngsters do fancy as how they've got it all their own way, but I guess I'd show 'em precious soon how many blue beans made five; an by this an' by that, if they wouldn't take the lesson quietly, but got warm over it, an' wanted cooling down a bit, why I'd say, 'Come out an' make a ring, an' show fair play, an' then I'll polish you off one by one up to a round dozen!'"

And having thus delivered himself, Slashing Bill wheeled himself round, caught hold of a sheep, and took off its fleece in less time than many a man would have taken in considering where to begin.

Then as he gazed at the shorn animal as he let it go, he declared with a good round oath, that—

"If Fleecy Jim shore his sheep in that style, he must be summat most extraordinary."

And thus encouraging himself, he set to again, vowing with a whole host of sanguinary adjectives and powerful noun-substantives coupled ingeniously together, that—

"If Fleecy Jim dared to show up in that shed, he'd take it out of him, not only with the shears, but with his two bunches of fives afterwards." And he certainly looked as though he meant it.

The opportunity was destined not to be long in arriving —in fact, it arrived so soon as to suggest the idea that the old gentleman down below had had a finger in the pie.

Work had hardly been commenced on the following morning when a flying rumour flew round the shed that Fleecy Jim was approaching on a brown horse; and fast on the heels of the tidings came the apparently veritable man himself.

Slashing Bill glanced at him, and then eyed him with open contempt.

That a shearer, indeed, for him to knuckle under to! Why, he wore tweed trowsers, a plaid crimean shirt, and a stiff, narrow-brimmed straw hat, with a simple black riband around it, and was, besides, fresh and sober-looking, and seemed as though he was in the regular habit of washing himself!

Bill muttered to a pal that "he didn't care a straw for that there milk-and-water chap, with all his new flash togs. He'd precious soon show him what an old, tried hand could do; and when he'd given him a wholesome lesson, maybe he'd kick him into the creek."

Well, Fleecy Jim rolled up his sleeves and commenced work at once; but neither of the don shearers seemed inclined to show what they could do at first start.

They kept up blow to blow, sheep to sheep, until breakfast spell.

It was on returning to the shed that Slashing Bill hit out, and passed his opponent with ease.

There ensued cheers from Bill's party, and Fleecy Jim's backers began to look downcast.

But just as Bill had got two sheep ahead, Jim let out his hand and the fleeces rolled off his sheep like the froth off a pot of porter swept by the hand of a thirsty and impatient digger, when he's been working ten hours and the thermometer stands at 114° in the shade.

Sheep to sheep was kept up for close upon an hour, the sweat rolling off the two men like rain the while.

But the struggle for precedence was not of much longer duration.

Fleecy Jim had passed his opponent in another five minutes with ease, and not all Slashing Bill's frantic and despairing efforts, backed though they were by the cheers and encouragements of the old hands, could bring him up to the scratch.

When he saw his adversary three sheep ahead, and perceived that he was thoroughly beaten, he threw down his shears, and, springing to his feet with a face as red as that of an angry turkey-cock, vowed he had had enough of it, and that, though "he could shear against any man, he'd be danged if he'd try it any longer agin the devil;" for his Satanic Majesty in person he certainly took Fleecy Jim to be.

CHAPTER LI.

FLEECY JIM DENOUNCES LARDY BILL AND LANKY JIM.

So comical did Slashing Bill look in his half-terrified discomfiture, that roars of laughter arose from the assembled shearers, in which all alike joined.

Fleecy Jim laughed as heartily as any of the rest; but all in an instant his manner changed, his merriment dried up, seemed to be frozen on his lips by a single wave of some invisible enchanter's wand. An expression of horror crept over his ruddy countenance in its place, and, stepping back, he pointed to two of the shearers, and exclaimed—

"Hullo, mates, did you know you'd two murderers in your midst?"

The laughter was all over now with everybody, and all eyes were turned upon the two men, the one fat, with a broken nose, and the other thin, with a macaw-bill-shaped smeller, at whom Jim was pointing.

And the worthies in question did not conduct themselves in a manner that was at all calculated to convince the bystanders of their innocence.

Horror and terror were in their eyes as they turned tail, with the evident intention of making tracks, but a couple of shearers promptly collared them, only to be fiercely struck at by the sharp-pointed shears with which the fellows were armed.

Noticing the cowardly action, however, half-a-dozen were quickly upon them, instead of two, and against such numbers the precious pair of rascals had no chance.

Fleecy Jim, alias Ned Kelly—for it was he—smiled grimly to himself, for his victims could not have behaved in a manner to please him better.

By their very actions the fools had admitted the truth of his charge.

"Who are they, mate?" asked a lot of the shearers, as they clustered around him. "What have they done? They've stabbed Bouncing Bill, anyhow."

"He's not the first by a good score," answered Fleecy Jim. "They are a couple of Ned Kelly's lambs. I've good cause to remember them, the scoundrels! seeing as how they murdered my wife and three young children. Let me get at them, boys, let me get at 'em!"

And Fleecy Jim pretended to struggle desperately with those who now began to lay hold of him, and beseech him to "draw it mild."

"Not until those two villains are lodged in a devilishly hotter place than Australia. No man's life is safe whilst they exist—no, nor woman's or child's either, the cold-blooded villains!"

Immediately there was the roar of many voices, furious, excited, and revengeful in tone, striking terror into the souls of the panic-stricken men. Their limbs trembled, and their faces assumed the ashen hue that pales the features of those who stand on the drop.

"Lynch 'em! lynch 'em!" was the universal cry—or, rather, scream—from every mouth.

"Hold up your hands, all who are for it."

Every hand was raised in an instant, except those pertaining to the two culprits and to Slashing Bill.

The latter personage thrust his deep into his trousers-pockets and exclaimed—

"Lynching be jiggered! How do you know as this flash cove be speaking the truth? He's a perfect stranger to all ov us, bain't he?"

At any other time old Bill's words would have been listened to attentively, but now all that he said was put down to being spiteful utterances against Fleecy Jim because he had worsted him with the shears.

The disguised bushranger knew a hundred ways of ingratiating himself with the mob, and there were but few things that he could not do well. He afforded a most lamentable example of talents and courage misapplied. In the present instance he had laid his plans so artfully that they were almost certain to be crowned with success, and at no risk to himself.

As to Lardy Bill and Lanky Jim, their terror and agony were truly awful.

Already they perceived the fools they had been to try to run away instead of boldly giving Fleecy Jim the lie, and challenging him to prove his charge.

The young fellow, too, whom Lardy Bill had stabbed with his shears turned out to be a general favourite, and his wound, a deep but not dangerous one in the arm, had incensed the other shearers against them almost as much as Fleecy Jim's statements had done.

In vain both of them now loudly protested their innocence. Their conduct no words could extenuate.

"Lynch 'em!'"

"Ay, ay, try 'em by Judge Lynch!"

"String 'em up!"

Such were the shouts that rang all round them.

But in the midst of the din old Slashing Bill's bull's-bellow of a voice shouted out—

"Listen to me, lads. Hanging those two chaps may be very good fun, but what sort of a lark will it be when it comes to your turn to be hung, eh? The law'll make what you're about to do as nothing more nor less than murder; for you see Judge Lynch has no colonial appointment, and I for one say, 'Thank God for it.' We're a law-abiding people out here, and gives the greatest criminal fair play."

"Listen to the parson," cried out some of the shearers at this, but the majority looked grave, for the old man's words had somewhat frightened them.

Ned Kelly saw that his project of vengeance hung fire.

"Don't be afraid of scragging 'em, my lads," said he. "There's a reward offered by the Government for their bodies, either dead or alive. Five hundred pounds each man, and the description of them is so exact that a five-year old child wouldn't mistake. The reward bills was being stuck up, wet from the hands of the printers, all over Melbourne yesterday afternoon, so you can have your fun out now and the worth of the dirty corpses to-morrow. I don't mean to touch a penny of the money; avenging my poor wife and children is enough for me."

"We never murdered no wives nor children," roared Lardy Bill.

"Never hurt a female or a kid in our blessed lives," echoed Lanky Jim.

"What did you try to run away for then when you was charged with the crime, you brace of ruffians?" demanded Bill Jenkins, whose wound had been by now bound up; "you'd have plunged your blooming shears into my liver if I hadn't put my arm in the way, wouldn't you? and now I won't be able to work agin for a week of Sundays."

"Hanging is too good for 'em; but since it baint in our power to give 'em anything better, and since Fleecy Jim's made it as clear as mud that we can't be pulled for it, let's clap a couple of halters around their necks and swing 'em up to the beam in the woolshed. What do you say, mates?"

So spake Bill Jenkins's chum, Harry Ward, and his proposition met with unanimous approval.

Suddenly, however, someone exclaimed—

"Let's take 'em off to the other woolshed, lads. It's further from the Home Station, and we're not so likely to be disturbed by old Fairfax, or his son-in-law, M'Pherson, there. No one knows when they may pop into this un."

Kelly was not at all averse to this move, it was in the right direction, as this second woolshed was at the foot of a hill and nearer where he had planted his horse.

On hearing the name of M'Pherson Fleecy Jim might have been observed to start in a most peculiar manner, and become almost livid; there was one man present who *did* notice it, namely, Slashing Bill, for hatred has sharp eyes, and he hated the man who had beaten him in shearing, in no small measure.

"I'd give something to be even with thee, lad," he muttered to himself, and then he began to persistently look out for that something.

Meanwhile a rough stretcher was brought out, such an one as a lame sheep was not unfrequently carried on, and the two condemned men, almost dead with fright, were placed thereon, with their ankles secured together, their arms strapped down to their sides, and the halters all ready adjusted to their necks.

Then four of the shearers laid hold of the stretcher and the execution party set out for the other woolshed, that was situated a mile further down the creek.

CHAPTER LII.

LARDY BILL AND LANKY JIM HAVE A RISE IN THE WORLD

THE path to this second woolshed was across a narrow valley, through the centre of which flowed the creek, and about half the journey had been accomplished when Lanky Jim, who for some minutes had been regarding his denouncer intently, suddenly exclaimed in a shrill voice:—

"I'm blowed if it ain't Ned Kelly himself! That man's Ned Kelly, I say!" he roared out.

"So he is, by the living Jingo, Jim!" almost screamed Lardy Bill.

All eyes, upon this, were, of course, instantly centred on Fleecy Jim.

But instead of looking in the slightest degree confused, Fleecy Jim burst into a contemptuous laugh, and then answered the accusation with—

"And couldn't you really think of anything better to say than that?"

"Ah! I'm blowed if you ain't Ned Kelly, though. We mated with you for two years, and saw you every day all that time, and so if we aren't able to swear to you we don't know our own names," said Lanky Jim spitefully.

"Just listen to the fool, mates!" laughed Fleecy Jim "He calls me Ned Kelly, and says that he's served under me for two years, and seen me daily during all that time, and so must know me; and though I've bin working by his side all day, and drawn his attention pretty considerably on me during the last quarter-of-an-hour, I reckon, and yet he never lets out his grand knowledge until now!"

(To be continued.)

NED KELLY THE IRONCLAD AUSTRALIAN BUSHRANGER

NO 7,

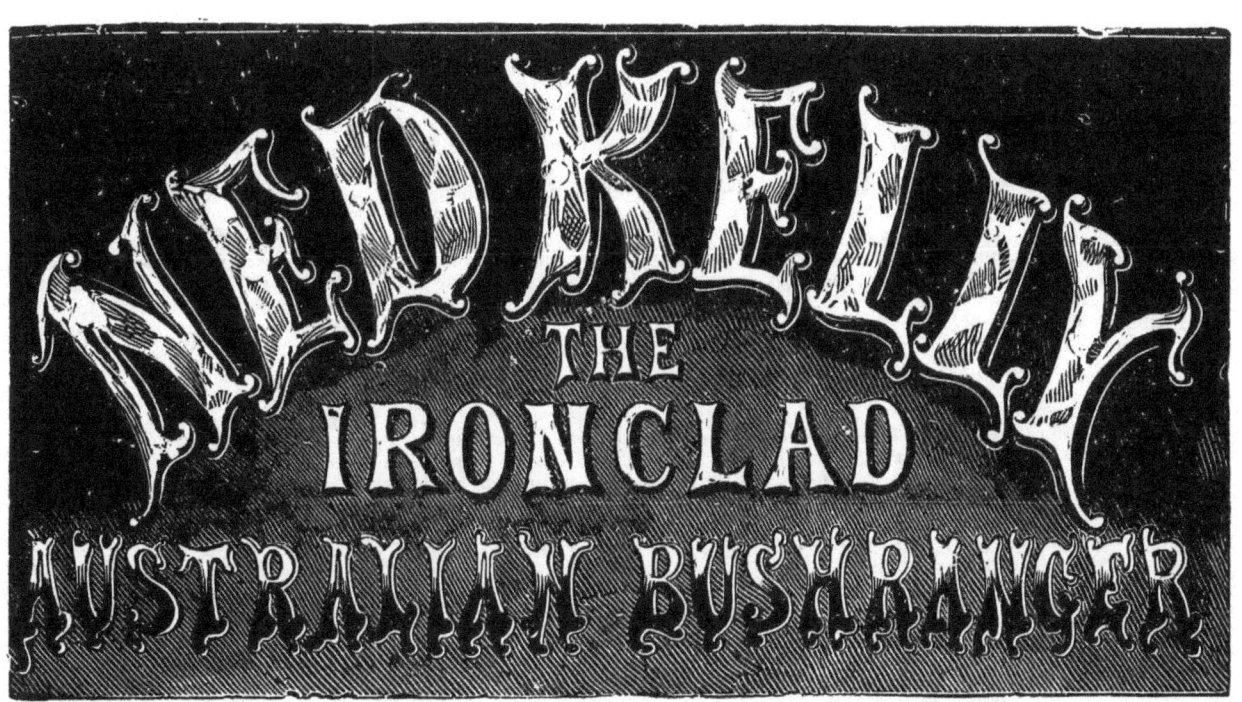

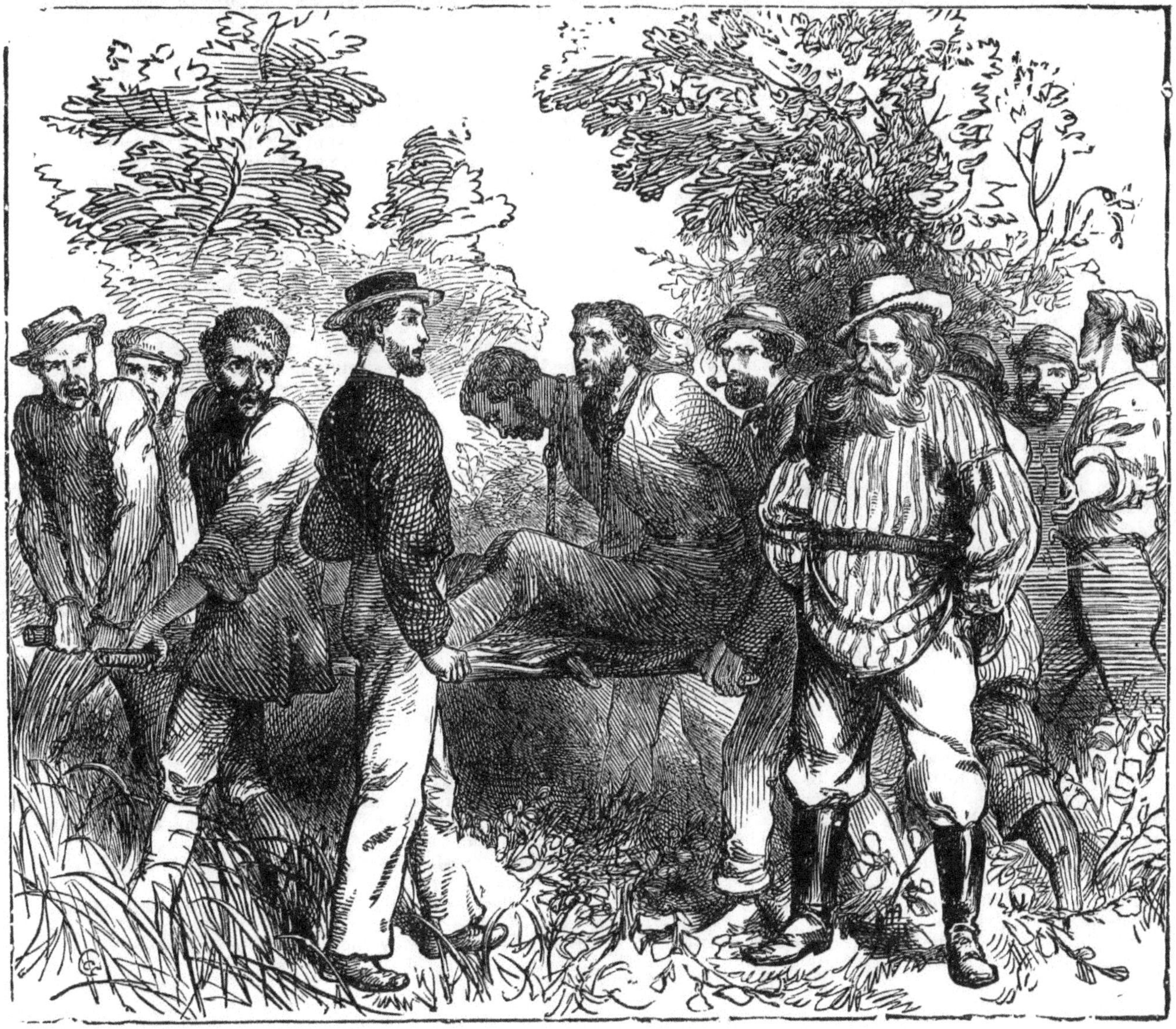

" I shouldn't wonder if you was Ned Kelly, for all that," said Slashing Bill, doggedly, as he thrust his hands deep into his breeches-pockets under his striped blue shirt, which was worn in true bush fashion outside of all, and confined around the waist by a broad and particularly greasy leather belt. " No, I shouldn't wonder a d—— if you was Ned Kelly," the old man repeated, spitefully stamping his foot upon the ground, although, of course, he thought nothing of the kind.

" I think I've given you very good reason for knowing that I'm more shearer than bushranger, old cock," laughed Fleecy Jim, good-temperedly, thereby provoking a perfect outburst of merriment at Slashing Bill's expense. " Why, you old duffer," he added, " do you think as how Ned Kelly, the ironclad bushranger, need ever be reduced to take to sheepshearing for a livelihood? Why, everyone says that he's rolling in tin, and I daresay it's true."

" He came here to have his revenge out on us. We was too honest to serve him any longer—we was altogether too soft-hearted, we was, to do his murderous bidding, and that's why we left his band; and that's why he's got this down upon us, and has hunted us to our destruction," roared Lardy Bill.

" Oh, very likely, Fatty; very likely indeed it is that Ned Kelly would have run his own neck into the halter, just on the chance of noosing yours. Why, you precious brace of skunks, if I was Ned Kelly, you'd have split on me the instant I entered the woolshed, for you know well you'd have won a free pardon from the Government, had you done so, for all past offences, and been granted a considerable portion of the swag offered for Ned's arrest as well. Your yarn won't wash, you rotten dogs, won't wash in the least, I say, except such parts of it as refer to your two selves, for you clearly admit that you are what I charged you with being—a couple of bushrangers."

" D—— it, you are Ned Kelly, spite of all your bounce. No wonder we didn't know you at first, disguised as you are," screamed Lanky Jim.

" Disguised? Well, I rather like that," retorted Fleecy Jim, with another laugh. " How the deuce can a fellow be disguised with his face almost as bare as a blessed baby's? Do you mean to say I wear a mask?"

" No," answered Lardy Bill, " your hair was your mask. We never clapped eyes on you afore except you was woolly up to the very eyes."

" Come, come," said Fleecy Jim, " this patter has lasted long enough. If half the coves present thinks as how I may be Ned Kelly, I'm quite willing to stay amongst 'em until the police has been sent for to inspect me, and I'm sure no man can say fairer nor that."

" No, that I'm beggared if one can," called out Bill Reynolds. " But," he added, " I'm precious sure that not one on us believes what these two rascals say, no, not even the old Slasher, though he do lay it on precious thick out of spite. So bring 'em along, lads, and we'll soon stop their tongues from lying an' slandering any more."

The suggestion was at once put into practice, and in a few minutes the woolshed was reached that was to be the scene of their execution.

But, previous to this, Slashing Bill had quitted the cortége, vowing that he would be no party to a cold-blooded murder, but that " he'd run up to the Home Station an' tell Squatter Fairfax an' Mr. M'Pherson all about it."

" Hurry up, lads, an' we'll get the job over before the 'bloke' can turn up," was now the cry; and long ropes having been attached to the short halter-cords, their ends were thrown over the beam of wood that stretched right across the great woolshed from wall to wall a considerable height above their heads, and the doomed men being placed to stand side by side immediately underneath, four men tailed on to the end of each rope, and calmly awaited the signal for running the miserable wretches aloft, which signal was to be given by Fleecy Jim.

" Well, you precious rascals, have you any messages to send to your friends?" he cried tauntingly.

Lardy Bill was too nearly gone with terror to be able to make any answer, but Lanky Jim, with eyes aflame, even though his face was as blanched by terror as that of any corpse, hissed through his clinched teeth—

" If I have any wishes to give, it is that you may have a hotter place than is waiting for us two; and as for last messages, I'll haunt you waking and sleeping. I shall be with you night and day, I'll never leave you more. Your run of luck is over, for the dying curse you, and the dead will be always with you—ay, when you are hunted like a wolf in the bush, when you see your daughter hung, when you are hung yourself, and all through the long days and nights you will pass in the stone jug. How like you the prospect?"

" So that your beastly ghost hasn't got a tongue, I shan't care very much where or how it haunts me," laughed Fleecy Jim.

" Up with them!" he then shouted to the men who were tailing on to the ropes. " It'll be more fun to see them dance upon nothing than to hear them speechify. Now, altogether with a yo, heave, ho!"

The shearers required no second bidding.

Lanky Jim had just time to shriek forth curses, when up went he and his companion, with a quick, jerky run.

It was an awful sight to witness the contortions of the pair, as they swung and wriggled and twisted about in mid-air, like hideous punchinelloes; their legs and arms working all at once, their tongues lolling out of their mouths swollen and bloated, their eyes leaping almost out of their sockets, and a strange rattling issuing from their compressed throats.

But these struggles for breath and life did not continue for very long.

Lardy Bill was the first to stiffen out, being by far the heavier man; but Lanky Jim was not long in following him, and the two wretches were dangling quietly enough when into the woolshed there suddenly came Mr. Fairfax, Andrew M'Pherson, and Slashing Bill the shearer.

CHAPTER LIII.

TAKING A BULL NOT BY THE HORNS BUT THE TAIL.

" Cut down those men instantly!" exclaimed Mr. Fairfax. " How dare you to take the law into your own hands in this fashion? Do you know you're all murderers? Down with them at once, and cut through the cords that are around their necks! Do you hear me, men?"

Not only did they hear, but they also immediately obeyed their master.

As he moved forward to examine into the condition of the two men, who by this time lay stretched out upon the ground, Andrew M'Pherson (who was, in truth, Mr. Fairfax's son-in-law, and for the present a visitor at Tarramea), exclaimed—

" Which is the man who accused them of their crime, the man who says that his wife and children were murdered by them? Where is he?"

Then at once a dozen outstretched hands pointed towards Fleecy Jim, whose face had suddenly grown blanched, whilst he edged away towards the gentle rise leading up the hill towards where his horse stood.

" That the man?" gasped M'Pherson, stepping backwards. " He is the miscreant who stabbed me thrice as I lay helpless on the plain, when the fire had passed over and spared me. I would swear to him amongst a thousand!"

Nothing daunted, Ned cried out laughingly—

" Why the bloke is clean mad. Who do you take me for? I'm as good and honest a man as any here, and I tell you you lie. I'm well known. Fleecy Jim ain't no new chum, is he mates?"

" No, no!" was the response. " We know him, master —he's right enough."

" I say he's Ned Kelly!" frantically roared M'Pherson, as he rushed to seize him.

But Ned had already marked the programme of his campaign.

During the accusation he had sidled away to the base of the hill, where some young bullocks were grazing.

The identification of Kelly by Lardy and his mate occurred to the recollection of the shearers, and, backed by M'Pherson's earnest accusation, induced them, after a moment's hesitation, to follow the rush made by M'Pherson to secure Ned.

M'Pherson was close on the bushranger, when the latter, with hate and rage in his face, thundered forth an oath and flung with all his force his shears at M'Pherson's body, and struck him in the abdomen. The weapon penetrated the part, and the wounded man fell to the ground, while his assailant, turning rapidly to face the hill, knowing he was more active than those present, and that, therefore, he could "blow" the lot in the up-hill race, found himself among the frightened steers, who, of course, always fly from the object of their fright.

Seizing one of them by the tail, the animal took fright, dashed up the hill, and drew Kelly up after him, with no effort on the part of the latter, who, by this novel locomotive, soon outstripped his pursuers, and was on the back of his horse and off like the wind before his enemies could catch horses to follow him.

He—like the old song—

"Upon the hill he turned
To take a last fond look ;"

and, shaking his hand defiantly, roared out loud enough for all to hear—

"Not yet, I tell you ! And look out, Sandy M'Pherson. You'll swing before Ned Kelly."

He then speedily galloped off like mad towards the spot where his police disguise was hidden.

CHAPTER LIV.

HEMMED IN BY FOES AGAIN.—A DESPERATE LEAP.

HALF-AN-HOUR later the shearer was transmogrified into a trooper once more.

If Ned had been a prudent man he would at once have made the best of his way back to Melbourne, and have thought only of Rose's safety, the quick getting at the treasure in the billion vault of the bank, and then as speedy a flight from the colony as possible.

But, unfortunately for Ned and for his adopted daughter, the wolf's nature in the man was now thoroughly roused ; the fierce lust for blood was upon him, and after a headstrong will had thrown itself into the scale against prudence for a few seconds, prudence kicked the beam, and the bushranger resolved to ride back to Tarramea, to make sure that his vengeance was consummated.

Nothing would have induced the man-tiger to have quitted Australia leaving Andrew M'Pherson, Lardy Bill, and Lanky Jim with a single breath of life in their bodies ; and he had no positive assurance that either one of the three were dead, for the two traitors might have been cut down ere life was quite extinct.

"In this costume," muttered the bushranger, "I can suddenly appear upon the scene as a trooper who has casually heard of the occurrence, and has ridden up both to offer his services and gather information concerning the triple crime for his own use. I don't think old Fairfax is at all likely to recognise me as the trooper who was at his place a month ago, for I was bearded and mustachioed like a bard then, and had a very differently coloured complexion and hair as well."

And thus reflecting, he once more turned his face towards the station.

On his way he met a stockman, galloping like mad, who at once reined up his sweat-reeking horse, and exclaimed—

"You are the very chap I want. Come along with me to Tarramea, for heaven's sake ! There's been the devil to pay, and no pitch hot there, this afternoon. Murder has been committed."

"What, the squatter the boss? That's a bad job. Good master, aren't he ?"

"No, he ain't the master. Mr. Fairfax owns the station, but Mr. M'Pherson married his youngest daughter many years ago—who's been long dead, poor lady—and since Mr. M'Pherson has been almost ruined by a bush fire that destroyed his own station of Mittagarra, an' thousands ov sheep, an' hundreds ov head of cattle, an' scores an' scores of valuable horses as well, an' the growing crops, and everythink else almost. Mr. Fairfax, his father-in-law, have offered him and his daughter a home until he has taken time to look around him an' to start afresh ; that is to say, if he ever lives to do it ; for Ned Kelly has sworn to do for him."

"Ned Kelly! What, has that fellow cased in iron paid you a visit ?"

"Well, everyone do think now that it was ne, though some do still swear that it was Fleecy Jim, and driven mad by sunstroke. Fellers do run amucker when taken that way sometimes. If it was Kelly he's bin the death of two of his old pals. He had 'em hanged, and now they're as dead as pickled pork. If they'd bin cut down sooner it might hev been different."

A glare of fiendish satisfaction lighted up Ned Kelly's eyes as he thus learnt that at all events one debt of vengeance had been paid in full. He was settling scores with his numerous creditors finely before quitting the colony, he thought to himself. Tom Conquest, the trooper, the wild dogs had already feasted on, he made up his mind to that ; then, secondly, here were Lardy Bill and Lanky Jim, the men whom he had so trusted, and who, in return, had tried to sell him to the traps, made food for either crows or worms, he didn't care a rush which ; and now there only remained Andrew M'Pherson to be disposed of.

"I suppose Mr. M'Pherson has been taken up to the house ?" said he.

"Not yet," answered the stockman. "He's so main an' bad, the stab being so deep in the stomach that they're afraid to move him before the doctor comes. Doctor Birch, of Ballan, has been sent for, but I reckon we'll be there first. They've got 'im outside, propped up with cushions an' such like, on the shady side of the woolshed, down close agin the water"

"Come on, then," said Ned, impatiently. "It's necessary in the furtherance of justice that I should extract from him what information I can whilst he's the strength to give it." And he set spurs to his horse as he concluded.

* * * * * *

Half-an-hour later Ned Kelly, in company with the stockman, trotted gently down the hill which so short a time ago he had ascended as a mere appendage to a steer's tufted tail, and rode boldly up to the spot where Mr. M'Pherson lay, surrounded by a sympathising crowd of shearers and station hands.

We forgot to mention that, ere meeting with the stockman, Ned had stuck on to his upper lip a good full moustache, cosmetiqued into a stiff upward curl at the points. It and the dashing police uniform made him look a very different man to a casual observer from Fleecy Jim, the shearer.

Everyone made way for him to approach, and no one observed him in the act of unbuttoning his holster-flaps as he came swiftly up

"I'm glad you've arrived, officer," said Mr. Fairfax, "even though, truth to tell, I'd still rather it had been the doctor. However, I daresay he'll be here presently. Ned Kelly, the bushranger, has been executing wholesale murder amongst us. He is disguised as a flash shearer. and rides a brown horse not unlike yours, that he re-joined in that clump of trees far away yonder. However, he has got clear off, and the best thing I think that you can do would be to ride after him. From the direction that he seems to have taken, I fancy he means to head to the Salt-bush region, to the north of Ballarat.

"Indeed !" answered Ned. "And what does Mr. M'Pherson think about the matter ?"

There was something in the tone of his voice that instantly attracted every eye.

"'Tis him! He has come again! It's Kelly himself," moaned the doomed man.

The bushranger laughed, for with his brace of reloaded pistols he felt that he didn't care a fig for the dozen unarmed men opposed to him.

"Yes, it is Kelly," said he; "and he has returned to finish the job that some officious fools stopped him from completing an hour-and-a-half ago. Don't come near me any of you, for I've more than one life in these little barkers, remember. 'Tis fifteen years ago, Andrew M'Pherson, since I swore that I would be the death of you; but vengeance postponed aren't vengeance abandoned. Come, you skunk, own that you deserve death at my hands."

"Spare me for—for—for my child's sake!" murmured the wounded man, faintly.

"For which child's sake? The one that was born in the pitiless rain, and amidst the thunder and the lightning, pressed to a dying mother's breast? The thing that would have perished but for me! Is that the child you allude to?"

"No—no—no! My daughter Lily."

"I have no time for further talk. You shall die. So take this from the girl you destroyed, and this from the man who, but for her loss and your villainy, might have been something better than he is."

As he concluded, Ned Kelly fired both his pistols in rapid succession at the prostrate form of M'Pherson, and each bullet plugged into his writhing body.

With a double scream he rolled right over, writhing and kicking, and plucking up handfuls of grass in his death-agony.

On perceiving that both his pistols were discharged, the shearers and station-hands, headed by Slashing Bill, would have thrown themselves upon the bushranger like a pack of wolves, but he made to ride them down and escape.

They recoiled before the horse like a flock of timid sheep, and Ned was in the act of getting off, when there suddenly swooped around the northmost angle of the immense woolshed five mounted troopers, spread out like a fan, and coming straight down upon him.

Ned almost tumbled out of his saddle with half real and half superstitious terror, as he recognised in the foremost horseman of them all Corporal Conquest, whom he had made so sure he had left dead in the scrub.

The shearers and station-hands raised frantic cheers of joy and exultation at the sight of the five troopers, and Ned saw that in all directions save one his retreat was entirely cut off.

"At him, lads! Show him no mercy! He is worth as much dead as alive!" yelled out Tom Conquest

But Ned Kelly shouted back defiantly—

"You haven't got me yet!" and wheeling his horse round he rushed him at the Creek, and landed him safely on the opposite bank; though the leap was a clear twenty-three feet breadth of rolling yellow water.

CHAPTER LV.

A DUEL IN THE BUSH.—THE DESCENT OF A MOUNTAIN.

THE daring and the success of the bushranger's leap caused ejaculations of surprise, not unmixed with involuntary admiration, to escape the onlookers; but these exhibitions of opinion changed into frantic cheers as Tom Conquest, the trooper, yelled out at the top of his voice—

"If it's to be a game of follow the leader, my lads, here goes!"

And hardly were the words out of his mouth when his horse in turn had cleared the watery barrier, and landed itself firmly on the opposite bank.

His four companions would fain have shirked following so daring an example, had not the menaces of Mr. Fairfax, who was mounted on a cob that could neither swim

nor gallop, and the jeers of his shepherds, shearers, and stockmen, in a manner forced them to try it.

The first trooper who essayed the leap went souse into the middle of the creek; the horse of the second gained the opposite bank, but, landing on the extreme edge, the ground gave way under its hoofs, and a desperate scramble only making matters worse, it finally fell backwards on to its rider, immersing him in the yellow flood, from which he was rescued with more water stowed away in his internal economy than he had treated it to during the course of long years.

The other two troopers availed themselves of the confusion to trot their horses a few score of yards down the stream, where the banks were not so precipitous, then cross.

But it was no use urging the beasts, they would not take the water, and the current was so strong that any but practised hands would have been carried down the stream and very probably come to grief. So they quietly stopped where they were, in full view of the duel, secretly enjoying it and sympathising with Ned, whom they admired with that vulgar sympathy the ignorant have for such heroes.

Finding himself followed by a single foe, Ned Kelly scorned to continue his flight.

Wheeling sharp round, he rode straight at Tom Conquest, shouting—

"I'd like to know how many lives the devil has given you, and by thunder there couldn't be a better opportunity of lopping off one of them, at least."

"You infernal ruffian. He seems to have given you a jolly good number, at any rate; by Jove, I'll get rid of a few of them if I've the chance."

And as he thus returned Ned's challenge, the trooper reined up his horse as stock-still as a post, and handled his shooting irons with a business-like air.

The onlookers on the other side of the creek saw that a duel to the death was about to ensue, and whilst some were dumb in the keenness of their anxiety, others yelled out some such encouragement as—

"Go it, Tom!" "Keep cool old man." "Drop him." "Pot him." "Shoot down the ——," and so on.

Happily the bushranger's one weapon was empty, and only five charges remained in the other. The trooper, therefore, had one shot to the good.

Tom, too, was as cool as an ice-floe, whilst a perfect tempest of stormy and revengeful passions filled Ned Kelly's breast.

He had hanged Lardy Bill and Lanky Jim, he had settled (at all events, so he fully believed) M'Pherson, and now the irrepressible trooper was the only foe that he had remaining to wipe out old scores with; but if he was the sole one, he was at the same time the most dangerous.

So he was resolved that he would kill him, come what would of it.

"Pop, pop, pop," three misses in succession, whilst his shako was torn off his head, and he felt the warm trickle of blood coursing down his face.

How he cursed the restiveness of his own steed, and the steadiness of that of his adversary.

How could he make sure aim with his horse plunging like the very devil?

Ha, another hit—no, no, only a graze, though the burn was like that of a red-hot iron, causing the outlaw to gnash his teeth in very anguish.

He would settle the trooper, however, though he sacrificed his own life too.

Once his revengeful passions were aroused, he was quite ungovernable, prudence vanished, and the ferocity of the wild beast took possession of him. He was, in scriptural phrase, "possessed of a devil." Like Samson, he didn't care to sacrifice himself so that he destroyed the Philistines who were mocking him. "True foes," says the poet, "once met, only part in death." And so felt Ned.

He spurred his unwilling horse right down upon him, and

when within a dozen feet, levelled his pistol afresh, resolved that his one remaining charge should not, at all events, prove a fluke

In all probability it would not have done so, had not his horse, after standing as still as a marble one for a couple of seconds, suddenly commenced to hump its back, and buck like the very deuce, just as Ned's forefinger curled for the last time around the trigger.

How he regretted the noble steed that bore him seven hundred miles through the bush, and upon grass feed too, and never caved in.

The result was that the bushranger scored another wide, whilst a ball from Conquest's weapon at the same instant furrowing up the glossy flank of Ned's stolen mount, the spirited animal left off dancing the "Cure" with all four feet off the ground at once, and its head tucked between its knees, and swerving to the left dashed off at a tangent across the plain, perfectly indifferent as to whether its rider coincided with its views or not.

Perhaps, however, 'twas fortunate for Ned that his steed did thus take the law into its own hands (or shall we say in the present instant, hoofs?), for Tom Conquest, having fired his last charge, drew his sabre with the amiable intention of exploring therewith the exact position of Kelly's vitals, an investigation that he would have had considerable difficulty in preventing, with a weapon in his hand that he had never learned the use of.

So, the duel harmlessly ended, the game was changed to a steeple-chase once more, and Ned cursed his delay when, glancing back over his shoulder, he observed that two out of the other four troopers had rejoined Conquest; so that now three horses were entered for the ten thousand pounds stakes, whilst he had staked his safety for a mere flash in the pan, and, by the act of rash and suicidal folly, considerably lessened his chances of coming off first chop.

Happily, his steed had still lots of strength and endurance left; its hurts were mere scratches, calculated rather to increase than diminish its speed, and Melbourne once reached, Ned congratulated himself that he would be in comparative safety, at all events for the brief time that he intended to remain there, ere he quitted the Australian Colonies for ever and a day.

How he wished that darkness was an hour nearer; but wishes were no good, and he had to make the best of circumstances as they were.

Death was most certainly behind him; and whatever chanced to be in his front he must encounter and overcome, or else fall struggling to the last.

He now took closer and keener observation of the steed that bore him, for it was now to him what a stoutly-built bark is to its crew in a raging hurricane—the sole connecting link between life and eternity.

With thankful complacency he took in all its points one by one—its small square head, finely-arched neck all traceried with swelling veins, long oblique shoulders, great breadth of chest, ample quarters, well-bent legs, and long elastic pasterns.

Its muzzle was as soft and black as velvet; its eyes as brilliant as polished jet, and its length of stride left nothing whatever to be desired.

Buck-jumping was due to its bad breaking in, but did not detract from its strength or fleetness.

"It's lucky I'm not an ounce over twelve stone," muttered Ned to himself, and then he added, with a frightful oath, "No, I'm not exactly run down yet, and if ever a horse's heels saved a man's neck, this nag's will save mine to-night."

He spoke of night as though it had already arrived, so anxiously did he desire its coming, but in fact the sun's entire disc was still above the horizon.

And now the chase stretched across the great tree-dotted plain, not at headlong and break-neck speed, for Ned was too old a hand to burst his horse at first start, but at that easy, slinging gallop for which Australian horses are so famed, cautiously and carefully avoiding all obstacles, such as felled trees, stumps, and the likely neighbourhood of wombat-holes, for he knew that if his good steed came to grief, he would assuredly do so in its company.

In this manner on they sped, pursuers and pursued, neither gaining nor losing on the other, until seven miles of plain were scudded over, and more rough and hazardous ground was entered upon.

Ned had now to observe greater caution than ever, and keep eye, head, and heel ever on the alert, for the trees began to grow much thicker, wombat-holes and honey-combed ground were together dangerous traps for his horse's legs, and patches of impenetrable scrub to be dotted here and there.

One minute thick copse had to be dashed through, with many scratches to face and hands, and sundry rendings of clothes in the rapid transit; the next the prostrate trunk of a huge tree had to be taken at a flying leap, or swirled round with a comet-like eccentricity of flight.

Then, in a twinkling perhaps, the fleeing bushranger had to throw himself straight along his horse's back, or to duck his head forward almost as low as its withers to save his brains from being dashed out against some low-hanging tree branch, that stretched like a white and ghastly skeleton arm right across his track.

Presently he came to a hill, up which he had to go, although the ascent was nearly as steep as the roof of a house; and even as his horse dashed up it in a succession of goat-like springs, he could hear the resounding hoof-strokes of his enemies not a couple of hundred yards in his rear.

Was he now on an extensive table-land, or what?

He could hardly tell where he was, for he had been headed away from the proper bush-track to Bacchus Marsh, and could not tell with any positive degree of certainty whither he was steering.

Presently, however, his doubts were set at rest by coming almost instantaneously upon a nearly precipitous slope, leading down into a deep, black, sombre valley at least two hundred feet below.

He tried to wheel round to the right, but was headed off by a trooper. To the left the same thing occurred.

He had no time to reload his pistols, his sword was a weapon he felt no confidence in because he did not understand its use, and every trooper was carefully trained thereto so he felt that he must risk the descent at all hazards.

At it he went, therefore, speeding down the declivity at a pace that was truly terrific, for his horse soon lost all power of stopping itself, and Ned rightly guessed that the effect of hauling on the curb would be to cause the creature to turn a complete somersault.

Each moment the velocity of his progress increased, and he could hear the three troopers on the summit of the hill, laughing at his dilemma; which was presently increased by the sharp cracking of their pistols, and the buzzing of bullets past his ears that sounded like angry hornets on the wing.

At last there was a mighty crash, owing to his horse running full tilt against a tree-trunk, without the possibility of stopping short at the bottom of the descent, and down steed and rider went in a writhing heap.

Ned was on his feet in a twinkling, but saw, with a mingled horror and despair that it was impossible to describe, that his gallant steed's course was for ever run.

The near foreleg was broken, and the animal unable to raise himself.

What was to be done now?

Ned looked back, and saw his three foes cautiously descending the hill that he had come down like a thunderbolt.

Ah! he would reload his pistols and stand at bay!

It was his only chance.

CHAPTER LVI.

A BATTLE WITH STONES.—OFF AND AWAY AGAIN.

NED felt a grim satisfaction in the thought that he might be able to settle two of his enemies, at all events, ere he

NED KELLY.

was overcome by the third; but he gave utterance to an oath, and the devilish grin of exultation that had o'erspread his countenance changed into an expression of the most unutterable dismay when he discovered that somehow or other he had lost all his ammunition.

Death or certain capture, which would mean exactly the same thing in the long run, now seemed to stare him in the face; but, noticing how dark it already was down in that deep valley all amongst the close-growing trees, it suddenly struck him that he might be able to hide from his pursuers. for a while at all events, by dodging behind the trunks.

He immediately put this plan into execution, looking about for stones to use as missiles.

Nearer and nearer come the troopers.

They are at the bottom of the descent, but they seem rather chary of entering in amongst the trees, for neither of them, of course, guesses how utterly defenceless Ned is.

They call upon him to come out and surrender himself, promising him that they will spare his life.

"You mean to say that you'll leave the job that you are not game to try to Jack Ketch and the drop," answered the bushranger from the deepest recesses of the wood. "No: if you want me you'll have to come and take me."

"The beggar isn't going to crow over me. Come along, mates. So many thousands of pounds are worth running some risk for," said Tom Conquest, enraged and excited by Ned's vaunt.

They could not follow Ned into the impenetrable scrub on horseback, so they dismounted, hung their nags up by the bridle on a neighbouring tree, and, cocking their pistols, plunged into the thicket after Ned.

Surely the end had come! Surely the wolf was run to his lair at last!

The troopers' eyes are as sharp as hawks'. They advance with the utmost caution.

Kelly had knowingly led them on step by step until he had placed some distance between them and their horses.

A stone is hurled, and whizzes past one of their heads.

They greet the unsuccessful throw with shouts of derisive applause, for the act tells them as plainly as words could do how helpless the hunted felon is.

"Be cautious!" yells out Tom Conquest. "It may be but a trick, mates."

Hardly has the caution escaped his lips, when a better-directed missile strikes him full in the face.

He reels, half stunned, and before he can recover himself, Ned Kelly has commenced to practise the ruse he had soon seen might be practicable. The troopers had been twenty minutes in the scrub and were completely astray as to the points of the compass. Kelly still drew them until he escaped altogether from their sight. He had worked round to where the horses were hooked up. He was not long in springing upon the back of one, and, leading the other two off with him, started off at a gallop, the bush ringing with his defiant loud laughter.

Yells and shouts, the crack of whips, and the trampling of many hoofs at this juncture, however, betoken that numerous reinforcements are at hand.

The sound strikes ominously on the bushranger's ear.

"If he's playing 'possum in there, we had best surround that patch of thick bush and completely hem him in," Ned hears a voice cry out, which he immediately recognises as that of Mr. Fairfax the squatter.

So that even now if he escapes it will be by the bare skin of his teeth, and the waste of a single moment may mean the loss of his life.

He would have liked to have bestowed on Tom Conquest one more crack on the head just by way of making assurance doubly sure; but self-preservation is the first law of nature, and he would have to ride back several yards to carry his fierce whim into execution.

So he heads straight in an opposite direction to that where all the noise and turmoil comes from and forces his horse (having let the other two go) on as fast as ever

he can through the trees and thick patches of Septo-popermum scrub.

How glad he feels when he gets clean out into the open, after some five minutes of the most difficult navigation conceivable.

The gloom of night is coming on now, and no mistake, but he sees a broad level valley lying before him, and in the distance a few lights, which he fancies are those of the township of Bacchus Marsh.

Choosing them as a guiding star, though never for an instant intending to go near them, he starts off at an easy gallop, for he does not know what his new steed can do yet.

He hopes to get away unperceived by his foes, whom he imagines still to be on the other side of the timber; but he isn't a clear five hundred yards out into the open, when a regular "View halloo!" sounds in his rear, and looking back he sees that now he has a score of enemies on his track instead of three.

There are four troopers (he can make out their snow-white shako-covers plainly enough), and the rest of the pursuing force is composed of stockmen, boundary riders, and two or three young fellows whose superior style of get-up suggests to him the idea that they must be Mr. Fairfax's sons.

"What a formidable pack of hounds for the hunting down of one poor, badgered fox!" mutters Ned to himself bitterly. "And yet, not exactly a fox either," he adds. "By the Lord Harry! they shall find me considerably more of a wild boar when they come up with me--if they ever do!"

And he increased his speed by a sharp application of the spur, a few seconds later being gratified to find that his new mount had both speed, wind, and bottom.

"Ha, ha!" thought Ned, "the race is not over yet, and perhaps midnight shall, after all, see me enter Melbourne town!"

CHAPTER LVII.

THE RACE FOR THE TEN THOUSAND POUNDS STAKES.

THE "view" was breast high, the hounds were in full cry, and the stockmen rode lighter, at all events, than did Ned, for their costume was little more than Crimean shirt and moleskin trousers.

It was a second Dick Turpin kind of an affair.

A backward glance showed Ned all his foes, stringing out and urging their mettlesome steeds forward with crack of whip and dig of spur;—a kind of from London to York ride, and a dead horse and half-dead man as a final tableau.

But there would be no *alibi* to save him, and there's no turnpike-gate in Australia to stop him; and there was the difference.

He ripped off his coat an threw it away, his shako followed suit, and then his boots. How he wished that his nag could be freed from its heavy semi-military trappings. Well, perhaps in time even that could be effected; but not just yet.

His best plan, he thought, after a minute or two's reflection, would be to out-distance his foes as soon as possible, and then play some of Reynard's many tricks in order to get rid of them.

Away, away with a sudden spurt darts Ned, his heels and his hands both at wackwork. His horse shoots on like an arrow, it is a killing pace; but then, if he can't get out of sight of his foes, how can he play them any such trick as doubling on them, or otherwise throw them on the wrong scent? No; his present is the right dodge, he is convinced.

His horse begins to roar

Confusion! is he a broken-winded beast? Anyhow, he must go on like the very devil, should he even burst his gall. There's another belt of thick timber three miles ahead, opening out to the left, and Ned thinks he knows a short cut through this to a bush shanty known as the "Bounding Kangaroo," kept by a pal of his, where he may be able to obtain concealment and shelter for a few hours at the least.

As he goes ahead like a very sky-rocket, Ned thinks of the many ruses he has read of in highwayman tales for confusing and puzzling pursuers when hard run as he is now.

A sharp quarter of an hour's burst has put him at all events out of sight of his foes, and given him at all events a chance of eluding them.

He knows his surroundings and his way far better than he thought he should have done, and strikes straight through the timber for the "Bounding Kangaroo," which he recollects to stand on the sou'-sou'-west angle, and close to the boundaries of a sheep-run called Coolwomurra.

While he is thus heading, a dissertation on bush inns will not be amiss.

The bush inn, then, is a peculiar characteristic of Australian life, and there are two varieties, namely, those that border on some track leading from one important town or city to another, and which vehicles and horsemen and pedestrians pass daily, and secondly, those that stand beside less frequented paths and by whose doors a solitary traveller does not journey perhaps more than once or twice in the course of a week.

The former class of hotels sometimes do a rattling trade, for once or twice a day a coach disgorges its passengers into them for a hastily-snatched meal; and a dinner of weak tea, bread, potatoes, and fried beefsteak, at half-a-crown a head, yields a good profit in a country where beef costs only twopence a pound, and the wheat and vegetables are raised on land for which, most probably, not a tittle of rent is paid.

Then the horses' feeds are charged high in proportion, and those who feel inclined to patronise the bar, as nine-tenths of the male passengers invariably do, have to pay through the nose for whatever they imbibe, for a shilling for a nobbler of wine or spirits, sixpence for a glass of ale, and a bob a bottle for lemonade are the lowest sums ever charged for drinks. These inns too are not very expensive establishments to keep up; and being generally long, rambling, one-storied structures of wood—three-fourths stable and one-fourth house, a couple of female servants, and as many male, with perhaps a black boy thrown in, can get through the work very comfortably, and £150 or so would amply cover the value of the entire stock-in-trade.

These are the reputable Bush Inns. Now let us regard the other kind.

Far back in the grim and silent bush they stand, close to dim and uncertain tracks that lead, at best, to some miserable cluster of huts, dubbed a township, and very probably miles distant therefrom. Be sure, however, that there is a squatters' station not very far away, for from the squatters, shepherds, stockmen, boundary-riders, and other station hands does mine host derive four-fifths of his entire profits.

These men are paid their wages half-yearly by cheque, and being all of them single (squatters won't often employ married men) and there being no other way of spending their money they resort singly and in couples to the Bush Inn, hand Boniface their £20 cheques, and ask him to inform them when they have drank the value thereof, which he does not hesitate to do, and after keeping them gloriously drunk for about six days, he generally kicks them out on the seventh, and when the chill night air and the dew have made them sober—if an attack of delirium tremens does not intervene—they usually return at once to their respective occupations for another half-year, when the spree that we have just described is repeated, and the process of sweating down a cheque gone through once more.

The landlord derives four-fifths of his profits from these drunken station-hands; and he also gains a trifle from wandering shearers, overlanders and swagsmen, but for a score of years at least his secret patrons have been the numerous bushrangers that have over-run the colony.

At the lonely and disreputable Bush Inn they often feast and carouse with little fear of interruption, paying for everything with gold and notes, and scorning, or, perhaps through motives of expediency declining, to accept of change.

Here at this kind of places they are also kept au courant with the affairs of the outer world, the movements of the police, &c.; and the landlord and his men, ay, even his womankind too, are at all times their most effectual and efficient scouts, safeguards, and bush telegraphs.

The reader must imagine that this brief, but necessary, digression has brought Ned Kelly up to the door of the bush shanty, a long, rambling wooden structure, with an old creaking signboard representing the festive kangaroo aforesaid swinging from the low-hanging branch of a venerable gum-tree that stood immediately across the way.

It had evidently once upon a time been an important place, for it was surrounded by ranges of stabling, and the road that ran past the door had plainly been both a coach and a waggon track, though that it was so no longer was plainly evidenced by the way in which the grass and bush flowers had grown in and filled up the wheel ruts.

The house, too, bore an aspect of age and neglect; the paint was blistered and burnt on the closed doors and shutters, revealing a gaping crack here and there; whilst many of the windows were broken, and others awkwardly boarded up.

Only one light was visible in the house, and that gleamed forth through a cracked casement close to the front door.

"Umph! no customers! All the better," ejaculated Ned Kelly, as he drew rein and hammered away at the door with the hilt of his sword.

He had to repeat the summons thrice before it was answered. But at last he heard heavy, slouching footsteps coming along the passage, bolts and bars were withdrawn, as though under protest, and then a brawny, sinister-looking man of middle-age appeared in the doorway.

No sooner, however, did he catch sight of Ned's dangling sword and the semi-military equipment of the horse that he bestrode, than with an oath he darted back and slammed the door shut again, and the next instant Ned heard the bolts and bars being shot back into their places.

"What's the d—— matter with you, you blessed fool?" roared Ned, incensed beyond measure at this apparently unfriendly action. "Show up again, and look lively about it, or, by thunder, I'll set your old ramshackle place alight, and roast you alive inside for all the world like a crab in its shell!"

"What's that you say?" growled a rough voice; and, looking up in the direction from whence it came, Ned beheld the landlord on the top of the low shingled roof, surveying him critically and at his leisure from his post of vantage.

"Come down, you old fool, and attend to my wants," roared out Ned. "Do you take me for a d—— trap, you timberhead?"

"Good Lord! why, it's ten thousand pounds Kelly!" retorted the man.

"It's death to you, Jim Bent, if you don't lend a hand."

"Say, man alive, what do you want done?" And the landlord wriggled about on the roof like a lively eel.

"A quart of ale for my nag, and a stiff glass of grog for myself, powder and lead for my pistols, and a something by way of disguise."

"What'll you stand if I do all this?"

"I'll stand 500 ounces of raw gold. You'll only have go and dig it up like potatoes."

"All right, Ned, I'm your man. You stay there. I'll collect what you want, and be with you in a brace of shakes. Always you trust to Jim Bent."

But the precious rascal was all this while thinking within himself—

"A bird in the hand is worth two in the bush. His

talk about buried treasure may be all a yarn. When I went for it it might be gone. I'd sooner trust the Government of the two, and so with moderate blessings I think I'll be content. I can shoot him down from a window, as he is unarmed. He was a d—— fool, sure enough, to admit that."

So the next salutation that the bushranger received from his friend and ally of years' standing was a shot from the window above the door, a shot that was quickly followed by another, and then by a third.

"You infernal scoundrel!" roared the bushranger, who felt himself struck in two places. "You rascally Judas, I'll burn you out as I said I would. A single lucifer will set your tinder-dry crib alight."

"Ay, sheer off, I've an old world blunderbuss here that'll lodge as many slugs in yer carcase as there are to be found in the heart of a spring cabbage," retorted mine host of the bush shanty, half in fright and half in bluster, and rushing away from the window he, in a second or two, returned and thrust out through the rickety open casement a huge bell-mouthed weapon, that looked as though it had once belonged to the guard of an English mail, which it indeed had, in the person of Jim Bent's grandfather.

"Now," said he, pot valiantly; "attempt to set fire to my crib, and I'll blow you to smithereens. You havent got your iron pottery on now, remember."

"Curse you!" yelled Ned. "Yes, curse you, you treacherous hound. By thunder, if I but live over to-night I'll do something more than threaten."

"But you won't, my tulip," retorted Jim Bent; and, as Ned Kelly wheeled his horse round to gallop away, the traitor discharged the blunderbuss—or, at all events, attempted to discharge it—full at his back.

Luckily for Ned, the cap missed fire; and he would assuredly have returned to the inn to carry out his threat had not the neighing and trampling of horses and the wild uproar of many voices informed him that the noise of the firing had served to lead his pursuers in the right direction.

The landlord of the shanty laughed aloud as he saw Kelly check up his horse, and then wheel it round once more, and, having by this time pressed down another cap on the nipple of his mediæval-looking weapon, he treated himself to another potshot at the bushranger's retiring form, and almost foamed at the mouth with fury as he discovered that he had scored another fluke, his amiability being by no means restored to him by Ned hurling back the taunt—

"The blood money's not for you, at all events."

It looked very like as though it was for somebody ere night had again changed into day, however, for Ned's wounds, though they were not severe, were at all events sufficient to confuse him and render him giddy.

The moon had come out too, a full moon, which in Australia answers every purpose of daylight, so clear and effulgent is its silvery radiance, and, far as the eye could reach there seemed to be no covert or shelter.

Ned felt that he was almost on his last legs, but still as hope springs eternal in the human breast, he continued his headlong flight.

Hour after hour the moon, gleaming from out the indigo-hued heavens, revealed the fleeting shadow of one poor haggard and despairing wretch being hunted to the very death by at least a score of hooting, jeering foes.

At length his horse began to reel, and blood to mingle with the foam spumes that he had of late been freely scattering over his glossy coat, like wintry snow-flakes. The end was near at hand.

Agonising was the thought, for Melbourne was by this time hardly five miles distant, though it might as well have been a thousand leagues away as far as there was any possibility of his living to reach it.

Out upon the metal and he can see still clearer how weak his horse has grown, his roaring might have been heard a quarter of a mile away.

Ned glanced back. The "field was pretty well weeded."

Out of the full score of men who had started in pursuit of him, only eight or nine still hang persistently on his rear, but those eight or nine are a full half dozen too many.

And now he reaches the point where the Mount Alexander road joins the one from Ballarat, and conducts a splendid specimen of Macadam all the way to Melbourne. Without for an instant relaxing his speed, Ned reflects whether it would be any good attempting to double back on the Mount Alexander road and seek his old haunts in the ranges.

The question is almost at once answered in the negative by his horse coughing up a volume of blood, and then going to earth as dead as a doornail, pitching Ned heavily over on to his head in the act.

For a couple of minutes the bushranger lay on the road stunned. Then he staggered to his feet and in a confused kind of way looked around.

He saw rearing horses and scowling or contemptuous faces on all sides. He drew his sword with a kind of dimly-defined resolution to defend himself to the last gasp; but it is stricken from his hand as easily as though it had been a child who had grasped it, and the next instant he is hurled on to his back and the handcuffs are fastened around his wrists.

CHAPTER LVIII.

A WILD BEAST SAFELY CAGED AT LAST.

IT's all over with him now. He has to be lifted on to his feet and placed on a horse, to which he is secured by a rope attached to each ankle, and which passes under the animal's belly.

Yes, it is assuredly all over with him now, for the excitement of the chase over, and despair at his heart, he is a very child.

His captors taunt him and jibe him, and not a few curse him for all the mischief he has wrought, and some think it good fun to chaff him about the black cap, the condemned cell, Jack Ketch, and the gibbet.

"He rode very nigh home of his own accord, didn't he, mates?" chuckled one, pointing towards the flint-grey walls of Pentridge Prison that upreared themselves not more at most than a mile away on the right.

"Ay, it was his father's and mother's place, waren't it? They died there, didn't 'um, universally loved and respected—as the papers say—and was a-buried in their own grounds like the high nobs, not in no common cemetery?" grinned another, as he gave Ned a nudge to attract his attention.

Ned glanced at them, but he could do nothing more. Yet, if a look could have killed, his assuredly would have done it at that instant.

The moon still shone brightly, and as the cortége slowly wended its way towards the great prison—one of the strongest in the world—a distant church clock could be heard tolling midnight.

Though he still shook with apprehension, Ned would not suffer any more outward expressions of alarm to escape him, and so the cortége continued on its way until the prison gates were reached, which speedily rolled open to admit so illustrious a prisoner, and Ned soon found himself surrounded by all the gaol officials in a group, some of whom bade him a jeering welcome.

"It don't require much pluck to laugh at a fellow when he's got his teeth drawn," said Ned Kelly, in low deep tones of concentrated passion. "But bear it in mind, you Pentridge fellows, that the tigers in a menagerie sometimes kill their keeper."

Ned didn't intend his words to be prophetic, nor, at the time, did he or either of the men who laughed at them guess how terribly the weird threat was destined ere long to be fulfilled.

"Where shall he be lodged, sir?" asked one of the warders of the governor.

"Give him number 18. His father tenanted it last

You can show him his name that he wrote on the wall the night before he was hanged."

Ned bent upon the gaol governor a glance that intimated as plainly as words could have done, that *his* days would not have been very long in the land had Kelly senior's son the power to clutch him by the throat at that moment. But the despot could afford to smile at a glance.

Ned's ankles were released from their lashings, and he was lifted down off the horse. Two warders then laid hold of him to walk him away.

He did not attempt to resist, for he knew it would have been futile, but, looking around upon those who had brought him in, bound and fettered, to this strong and terrible place of durance, he said scornfully—

"The game mayn't be played out even yet. You may be four by honours, but I'm blowed if you have yet scored the odd trick. You can't touch a penny of the Government reward until I'm hanged, remember that, and the rope aren't round my neck yet, even though the darbies are on my wrist.

This was Ned's parting greeting, and he said not a word more.

Another minute and the inner prison walls encompassed him round about.

He stood in the centre of a large paved hall, with a skylight in the roof at least sixty feet overhead, through which the white full face of the moon looked down as though with bitter mockery upon him.

This hall was a kind of guard-room, and was hung round with weapons and staves, handcuffs and fetters. There were two great iron stoves in it for diffusing warmth around in the winter time, but it being now summer no fires were lighted therein. From it seven gloomy stone passages branched off in different directions, and, on one of the two warders who guarded him taking down a bunch of keys that hung in company with many others against the yellow-washed walls, up one of these passages he was forthwith conducted for a considerable distance.

Cells were to right of him and cells were to left of him, and from the little tiny square iron grating let into the door of each, many a wild and despairing face looked out upon him as he passed them by.

But Ned had no desire to recognise old acquaintances or for old acquaintances to recognise him at such a time and in such a place, and so he kept his eyes directed straight forward.

At last his guards came to a stop, and, whilst one maintained his hold upon him, the other inserted a key into the huge lock of a door, and, turning it therein with evident difficulty, pushed against the door and thus opened it.

"Your dad's library and study," said he, as he disclosed the gloomy interior to view. "Splendid place for calm reflection, Ned, and delightfully cool at all seasons of the year. Added to all that, there's no fear of burglars. We've got fine stout walls to maintain the place select by keeping all bad characters outside."

And with this time-worn joke the once ironclad and dreaded bushranger was pushed roughly inside, and the laughing warders hastened to close, lock, and bolt the door upon him.

CHAPTER LIX.

IN PENTRIDGE JAIL.

IT was indeed a change for the hardy bushranger to find himself—he, used to freedom in the bush—a prisoner in Pentridge jail, in the same cell, they told him, once occupied by his late father before he was hanged.

They were careful to tell him this ere they left him to himself.

Anyone who has seen a caged tiger or hyena in a moment of fury, may conceive what Ned Kelly was like.

Though heavily fettered, he moves up and down easily by reason of his giant strength.

Is this to be the end of his career—to be hung in the ime of his life?

And what was to become of Rose?

If he could only see Rose! Of course her coming to the prison could not implicate her, as she had already been "had up" and discharged for want of criminating evidence.

Above all, he must put off being placed in the dock, as there was abundance of witnesses to give evidence against him, and ensure his conviction without loss of time.

To this end he must feign to be more ill than he really was, and so gain time.

There was another scheme well known to all his fraternity—to pretend sincere repentance.

This would make the chaplain friendly and ensure him comforts.

Still, he did not wish to overdo his sickness, as he might be removed to the infirmary.

The sickness he was too clever an actor not to keep up when visited some hours later with food.

The governor of the jail himself, curious to see this notorious malefactor, came with the warders.

Kelly seemed utterly subdued, and spoke in a respectful tone.

The worthy head of the prison was quite taken by surprise. The man was a craven after all.

He promised him such extras as his situation required, and left him.

Ned Kelly was apparently so weak that his irons were actually removed.

He then asked to see the chaplain.

He came readily. He was an old man of most benevolent appearance, and no doubt simple as a dove.

Kelly began in low and apparently earnest tones.

He manufactured some story about his wrongs, and the bitter sufferings he had endured.

Still he was rather glad that his career had been suddenly stopped before he could do further harm to society.

The good man congratulated him on his repentance, which, if sincere, would procure him pardon in heaven if not on earth.

"One of my great sorrows is that I should have caused an innocent girl like Miss Bellamy annoyance," he said. "I wish I could see her to ask her pardon."

"I daresay that could be managed," replied the simple pastor. "I do very much as I please in this place."

Kelly thanked him.

"Unfortunate man," he then continued, "are you aware that is the cell in which your father passed the night before his execution?"

Kelly gave a violent start.

"Oh!" was all he appeared able to say in his supposed excitement.

"Yes; and have I passed many a day in conference with him," continued the chaplain. "I cannot say he was repentant; but he made a sort of confession, which I took down in brief and wrote out."

"Indeed!" said Kelly, gasping.

"Yes; I have kept it ever since. Such things are not made public," he went on, "but you can read it if you like."

"I should be most thankful to know all about my wretched father," replied Ned Kelly, in a whining tone.

"You shall have it," responded the good clergyman, and went out.

He had some difficulty in obtaining permission for the visit of Miss Bellamy, but at last the order was given.

The chaplain, however, was to be present at the interview and hear all.

Then a message was sent.

Meanwhile Ned Kelly was examining his cell with keen anxiety.

It was oblong, and the lower part consisted of masonry. Above six feet it was oak planking.

The light came in from the roof.

At the side below the window he could make out four round holes, about an inch and a half in diameter.

But, though given time and tools that might afford room for hope, yet still what could be done without either?

6

Ill or well, he would soon be taken up before the magistrates

His dinner was brought, which he ate slowly.

Then about an hour later came Rose, who looked her part well. She was grave, but pitiful in her manner.

"You want to speak to me?" she said, approaching where he lay on a rough couch.

The chaplain seated himself on the one stool in the cell.

"I have asked to see you," he went on, "to express my deep sorrow that you should have been subjected to annoyance on my account—that, in fact, you should have been taken for the daughter of so notorious a malefactor as myself."

"It is of no consequence now," she replied—both were talking with their fingers all the time. "I have, with the permission of the worthy chaplain, brought you this Bible; I hope you will study it well, and that it will profit you."

"I will study it well," responded the man with a wicked and cunning leer.

"Take the advice of the good chaplain," she continued, and handed him what looked like a small thickly-bound Bible.

It was a box full of the very finest and best burglar's instruments.

"Farewell," she now said, "and may you repent sincerely."

"Amen," responded the hypocrite.

And Rose went out. She knew at once why she had been sent for.

In case of accidents, Ned Kelly had long had this cunning contrivance prepared.

It was devilish, but it was highly characteristic of the man.

Rose went out. The chaplain then approached the culprit.

"This is the MS. I spoke of," he said, handing him a roll of paper, "you can read it at your leisure. I am going away until to-morrow," he continued, "you can then return it. I will see you before you go before the bench."

Kelly could only bow his head. He was really too overcome to speak.

Then he was alone.

He opened his box. It contained saws of the finest tempered steel, which, though fine and small, would almost cut iron. There were also files and a chisel.

Rose had expected to find him ironed, and hence had forgotten nothing.

Then concealing his precious instruments, Ned Kelly opened the roll of paper.

It was headed thus:—

"THE DYING CONFESSION OF THOMAS KELLY, alias Red Kelly, No. 135, a lifer."

It consisted of about 144 closely written sheets.

"I can read that at my leisure," he remarked sotto voce; "I have other fish to fry now. Who knows" (with a laugh) "mayhap, I may add a chapter or two?"

And then he leaned back on his couch and relapsed into deep thought.

Should he escape?

That was the all-important question now. All was haphazard.

True Ned Kelly knew many men who had been confined in Pentridge prison, and they had given him a pretty good idea of the inside.

He had every reason to believe that this cell, which was separate from the others, and used as a condemned cell or for dangerous prisoners, overlooked the governor's garden.

If so, his chances were great indeed.

There never had been an escape from Wintle's Hotel, and therefore no provision had been made for so remote and apparently impossible a contingency.

It was a matter not to be considered.

Ned Kelly, the more he reflected, the more hopeful he became.

What did he not owe to Rose?

He had ever loved her for her mother's sake, how much more for her own?

She was really no relation to him, and already a finely-developed woman.

Why not marry her?

The idea flashed through his mind like a ray of sunshine, but he knew she regarded him as a child does a father.

At all events it would link her to him, and was at any rate a more sensible idea than that in relation to the countess.

The thought passed away never to return.

But Ned Kelly was down in the mouth now, and not inclined to be vainglorious.

Evening came, and with it the last meal of the day. A cursory examination of the prison was made, and then he was locked in for the night.

The condemned cell had no trap in the door, as when occupied by one about to die two warders watched him day and night.

Ned Kelly was glad to find it was not a truly Australian moonlight. It was rather dark than otherwise.

So much the better for him.

Placing his stool on the table, he was just able to reach to the four round holes twenty inches apart.

Kelly was not so stout as he was doomed to be afterwards, and it might be done.

The holes had an iron lining. These he easily removed with his chisel.

Then the saws began.

The planking was stout, and about an inch thick, stout and strong enough for any malefactor without superior tools.

But these tools were manufactured in London by a man who understood his business.

Kelly knew that he must escape that night or not at all.

A half-finished job would sure to be discovered by the keen eyes of the warders.

Kelly worked with a will.

He found, to his rapture, the instruments worked admirably.

Rose had taken from her pocket—she had not been searched coming in with the chaplain—a flask of strong brandy and a phial of oil.

He drank the former, and used the latter freely when required.

He had begun at eight. He heard the clock strike twelve.

The square of wood was out.

He peered through, and saw that it did look over the private gardens.

But he saw another thing. There were grand goings-on at the governor's house.

It was lit up, and soft music was heard. He had made this out before, but thought it afar off.

Now, to get out.

Below the orifice was a shed with a sloping roof.

Now Ned had to wriggle through the hole as best he might, his hands as it were pinioned behind him.

As soon as they were through he could help himself somewhat.

The house was some distance from this part of the prison, so that a slight noise would scarcely be noticed.

He stood on his stool and thrust his head and shoulders through with difficulty.

It was a tight fit.

Still, at last his arms were free, and he prepared for a fall.

It was only three feet, and he was not bruised, only a little shaken.

He then rose to his feet, and took a keen look around to examine the situation.

Then he came to the conclusion that his only chance of escape was through the governor's house.

Here was a situation.

The garden was luxuriant, and he was able to approach the residence unseen.

The music still went on.

Soon he came upon two persons talking—a male and a female.

He peeped

One was a footman in gorgeous array, the other a pretty parlour-maid.

The footman was a tall fellow, about the height of Ned Kelly himself.

"I can't stop no longer, Mary," he said, as he gave her a last kiss; "supper will be wanted."

Kelly coughed.

The girl ran away, and the indignant flunkey, cockney and ex-convict, turned to see who had had the audacity to interrupt.

He saw a stranger before him.

"Who are you? You ain't no right here. I'll call the steward," said Jeames.

Ned Kelly simply felled him to the ground like an ox.

He then carried him back to the tool-house, where he found plenty of cord.

Whipping off the man's clothes, he then secured him with a gag made from the end of a mop.

He then changed habiliments; but this was not all.

He must be careful.

Doubtless on such an occasion as this there were many extra waiters.

This was his safeguard.

Creeping up to the house, Ned, peering about, found a back kitchen, with soap, towels, and all requirements for the toilet of the attendants.

The clothes had not fitted the man he had felled to the ground.

Hence he was certainly an extra.

Kelly examined himself keenly, and washed every sign of dust and heat off.

He then put on the podgy white gloves, and prepared to enter the house.

There was great confusion.

The guests were hurrying to the supper-room to the tune of the "Roast Beef of Old England."

The servants were also hurrying in with the various dishes.

Ned Kelly caught hold of a large dish indicated by the cook.

"Roast beef," said that functionary, "to be placed before the governor."

Ned Kelly knew him by sight of course, but also because he was at the head of the table, which was profusely ornamented.

The guests, nearly forty in number, were soon seated and the signal was given.

Ned Kelly took off the cover for the governor to carve, and held it while he did so.

The man confessed afterwards that it was one of the most trying positions he had ever been placed in.

His only hope was that everybody was laughing and enjoying him or her self.

When the cover was on, Kelly watched the others and began going round with wine and other drinks.

He thus gained the door, and slipping through was soon in the passage.

There was a buffet near the drawing-room door. It was deserted now.

He drank a tumbler of raw spirit, and then advanced to to the front door. It was open.

The sentries were even enjoying some refreshment in a room close at hand.

It was one o'clock when Ned Kelly was outside and making his way back to Melbourne.

When the truth became known, the guests were astounded by his audacity and good fortune.

CHAPTER LX.

IN MELBOURNE AGAIN.

Free!

Such was the thought that surged through the man's brain and made his bosom heave.

Now, of course, his wisest line of conduct would have been to obtain a horse and ride away.

But two reasons militated against this.

His love for Rose and his greed for gold led him towards his possible destruction.

But Ned Kelly was one of those kind of men who never diverge from a resolution.

He knew many men in the back slums who were more to be trusted than one of his own gang.

They were receivers and worse, many of them ex-convicts, and not likely to split on the man who was looked upon more as a demi-god than anything else.

He procured a disguise of an elaborate nature, and then, mounting a big cigar, sauntered along the streets of Melbourne with his hands in his pockets.

In this way he reached the house opposite the bank.

The blinds were down, and not a sign of life was visible.

But the owner had contrived a very simple signal, known only to himself and daughter.

A simple-looking nail-head, pressed very hard, rang a bell in Rose's room.

He waited four minutes, and then knocked in a peculiar way at the door.

It opened at once, and Rose stood before him.

She was too astounded to speak, but took him into a comfortable sitting-room.

Here she placed brandy before him. Evidently she knew well, and acted in accordance with his well-known tastes and instincts.

He drank a stiff draught.

"What news?" he then said. "Where are Carroty Larkins and Dick Dawson?"

"At work in the cellar," she answered.

Ned Kelly simply nodded, rose, took up his pistols, and descended with a light.

He was soon in the cellar, and was about to enter the tunnel, when he saw Larkins and Dick Dawson come out of it with scared faces.

"What's up?" cried Ned.

They started back with an astonished look.

"You here?" said Dick Dawson; "we thought you was in the jug——"

The pair had heard of Ned's capture, and had returned to Melbourne to carry out Ned's intended bank robbery.

"Escaped," he answered, in a dry tone; "but what's up—you seem frightened?"

"Not a red cent in the bullion-room," was the reply; "all the red store has been shipped."

What Ned said need not be repeated. His words were not blessings.

They returned to the house, and plans were now laid for their dispersion.

Ned insisted that all should travel separately, as being safer.

He proposed that all should make for Adelaide, which is 600 miles from Melbourne, and in the seaboard of Australia, where they were personally unknown.

Arrived there, he would propose a scheme. He would not even hint it now.

Ned Kelly gave the two men some money, and bade them lose no time in getting out of Melbourne.

"Don't go drinking, my lads," he said, significantly, "but get away straight."

They promised and were let out.

"Now, Rose, get ready," the self-dubbed father said; "we must not delay. But that no one would believe in my coming here we should never be free to leave now."

Rose hurried at once to obey her father.

They had money, both in notes and gold.

"I wonder," said Ned Kelly, in a sad and kinder tone, "when we shall meet again?"

"Don't be downhearted," answered the girl, kindly. "Soon, I hope."

Little did they suspect what was really to happen after that night.

Then they went out, and until they were at a considerable distance from the house remained perfectly silent.

"Rose, my darling, I noticed as I passed along that a vessel will sail to-morrow for London," he said. "Hence you can take the mail-boat for Adelaide. Go to the Ballarat Hotel, and enter your name as Mary Parsons."

"Yes, father," she answered. "I have always obeyed you, and always will as long as I live."

Poor girl!

And so they parted at a sailors' boarding-house, where the captain of the sailing vessel was staying previous to his departure.

Ned now, with a deep sigh, as if anticipating coming evil, advanced on his way.

He was so cunningly disguised with a wig worthy of the London stage that he did not in any way fear detection.

The bar of a celebrated hotel was open, though it was four o'clock, and Kelly sauntered in.

He had consumed a hasty supper which Rose had prepared for him.

But he was fevered from thirst.

Besides, the man was possessed of a devil. It was the love of notoriety.

Many of his most daring crimes were committed to be talked about.

He wanted to hear if his escape was as yet a matter of conversation.

The bar he entered was at the back of the hotel, and was kept by two men who were adepts at the knife and pistol.

They had a rough lot to deal with.

But they would stand no nonsense. If the man refused to pay they would leap across the bar, knock him down, and then with pistol and knife defend themselves against any confederates he might have.

Ned Kelly took a keen glance around. Loafers were the chief denizens.

Recollect the bar was behind the real hotel, and almost unknown to its regular customers.

It was kept by one of the most successful enterprisers in the world in that line.

Ned Kelly took a second glance.

There were some police off duty congregated in a group.

But it was clear that there was no one personally known to himself.

"Don't believe it," were the first words he heard as he entered within the unhallowed precincts.

"Don't believe what?" asked our hero with a rowdy shake of the head.

"Who's who?" was the response.

"That ain't any matter," answered the other. "I only wanted to know what it is you did not believe—that's all, my pippins."

"That Ned Kelly has escaped," the man continued in rather a sullen tone.

"No!" was the gaping answer.

"Ask the traps."

But the police knew these men too well to be enticed into a wordy encounter.

Then Ned threw down some gold and stood drinks to his immediate neighbour.

He drank nearly a bottle of champagne.

After this a mad idea came into his head.

Slipping out, he went to a livery stable close by, and depositing a fair sum, obtained the loan of a really good horse.

Mounted on this he returned to the Royal Hotel, and paused at the door.

It was a hot night, and the doors were open wide.

"Another drink, boys," he said, and handed a ready customer gold.

The drink was consumed, and then Ned Kelly, the ironclad bushranger, spoke—

"So you think that Ned Kelly has escaped?" he said, in a musing kind of way.

"We do—we do!" was the cry.

"And it's true, for I am he," shouted the excited and half-drunken bushranger. "Good-night."

And away he sped into the darkness of the night, with an exultant foolish laugh.

The astonishment of all was great.

The police affected to disbelieve the statement of the drunken ruffian.

"That was Kelly himself," said a cool-looking loafer smoking a cigar of large dimensions the celebrated bushranger had given him. "Knew him the minute he came in."

"Why did you not speak before?" irately cried one of the few police who remained.

"'Cause such as me takes no share," was the grim answer, "in that there reward. The traps keeps it to theirselves."

At which there was a general laugh on the part of the brotherhood.

Meanwhile, Ned Kelly, well aware that he had by his own vainglorious imprudence set a frightful nest of hornets at his heels, rode like a madman.

Luckily he knew the way well, and could avoid dangerous thoroughfares.

He was determined to ride the whole way to Adelaide, a distance of six hundred miles.

This man was one who never threw a chance away.

He would avoid all very well known regions where bills might be issued.

He had dyed himself, and this dye he determined to wash off at the earliest opportunity that offered.

He slept that night in the hut of a shepherd, who, having an unlimited supply of whisky given him, was not curious.

(*To be continued.*)

NED KELLY

THE
IRONCLAD
AUSTRALIAN BUSHRANGER

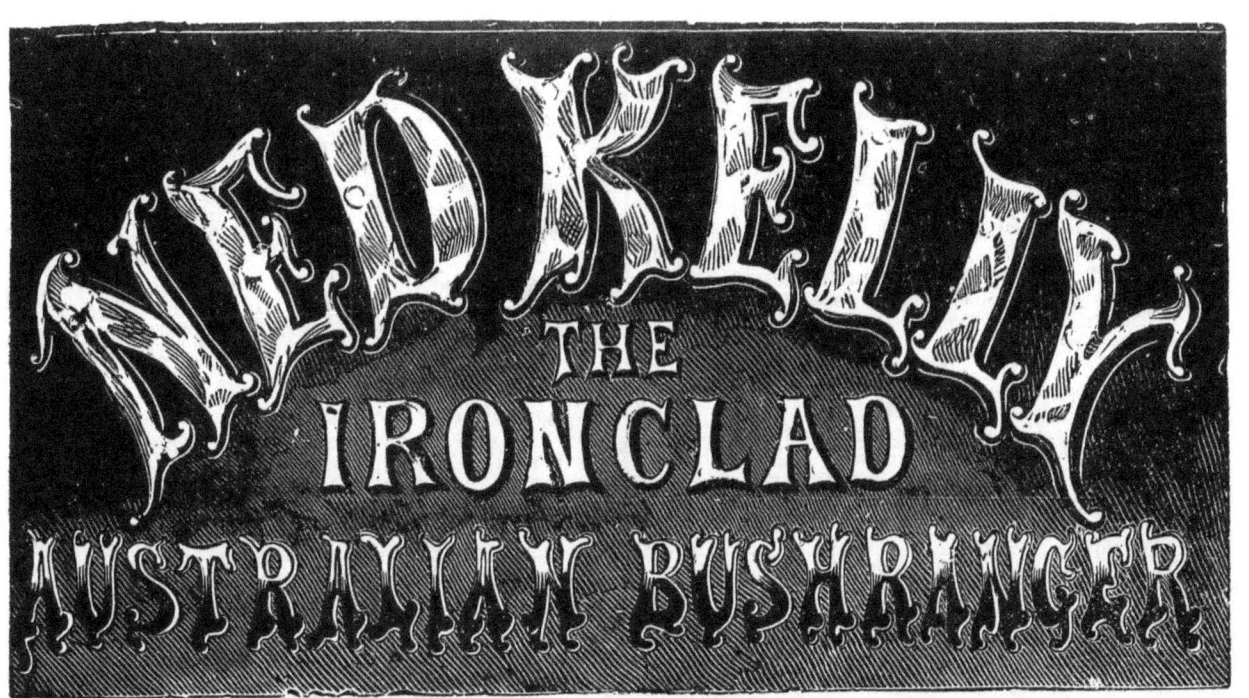

NO 8,

His guest was very swarthy at night, in the morning he was ruddy and fair.

But he asked no questions.

Ned Kelly had, as the girls said, a way with him that was irresistible.

After a hearty meal, Ned thanked the man for his hospitality, and once more started on his road.

He was in high spirits, had a good horse, and congratulated himself on his wonderful escape from prison.

A few hours ago he had never expected to breathe the air of freedom, and he laughed to himself as he thought over the way he had outwitted the police and gaolers.

Not one feeling of regret or remorse entered his mind. The outrages and crimes he had committed were, he considered, matters to exult over rather than regret.

He had always been a bad unscrupulous man, and gloried in it, depraved villain as he was.

The law had no terror for him; he was brave and feared nothing, and openly declared that he cared neither for God nor man.

Ned of course expected to be pursued, and knew there was every chance of being captured.

But he had been in so many dangers and desperate situations that he did not despair of eluding his pursuers, in fact, he had begun to believe that he was protected by Providence, forgetting that a man's crimes are not always punished swiftly, and justice if slow is nearly always sure.

The daring recklessness of the man often saved him, when a more timid man would have been lost.

He had not proceeded far on his road along the rough highway, when he was startled to hear horses' hoofs behind him.

As they came nearer and nearer, Kelly glanced round as if seeking a hiding-place, but after a moment's hesitation decided to face it out whatever the danger might be.

Without once glancing back he continued to advance although he felt curious enough to know what the horsemen were.

At last they came up with him, and Ned Kelly saw that they were two young policemen evidently in pursuit of himself.

They pulled in their horses to give them breath, for they had been hardly ridden, judging by appearance.

"Good morning," said Kelly as he too reined in, with a pleasant smile, as if highly delighted at the prospect of company for a few minutes. "You seem in a rare hurry. Going in search of sheep-stealers, I suppose?"

"We are going after bigger game than that," replied one of the policemen, "we are looking after Ned Kelly the bushranger."

"Ned Kelly!" repeated our hero. "I thought he was safe in prison. You don't mean to say he has escaped?" This in a horrified tone. "He ought to have been shot when first captured. The news you have just imparted to me will fill hundreds of people with alarm and dread."

"Yes," replied the young policeman who had spoken before and was evidently a more communicative man than the other; "but if I am not mistaken we shall soon capture him again."

"You think so?" casually remarked Ned.

"Yes," the other replied. "I am certain."

"He is very cunning and clever, from what I hear," responded Ned Kelly; "and, if what I hear is true, two men would stand a very poor chance with him. He can fight like the devil, and the knife and the pistol are weapons which he knows how to use better than any man in the colony."

"We know all about that," cried the policeman, rather angrily, for his pride was hurt at Kelly's insinuation that they were no match for the ironclad bushranger; "but we have no reason to be afraid if we come across him. We are well-armed and well-mounted, and besides have the feeling that we are in the right. Kelly fights with a rope round his neck. He is the biggest scoundrel that ever and must be hunted down like a rat. The highway-

men in England in the old days were saints to the man who has made his name the terror of Australia."

"If every man got his deserts, few would go unpunished," said Kelly, with a laugh, turning away his face to hide the hideous look of rage that disfigured every feature.

For one moment he felt inclined to draw his pistol from his belt and shoot the policeman through the head, but he conquered the impulse, reflecting that it would do no good.

These two policemen might not be by themselves, others might be following close behind. If Kelly was a bad man, he was not a fool. No one could accuse him of that. Besides, he was afraid that the report of his pistol might attract attention.

Nothing in his manner evinced that he had any hostile feelings against his companions.

He spoke craftily of his own escape, trying to find out how much they knew, and keeping a keen watch upon them without appearing to do so.

The police seemed in no hurry to part company with him, and presently Kelly fancied he saw them exchange significant glances as much as to say, "This is our man."

But not a muscle in his face betrayed the conviction that was in his mind, that they had discovered his identity.

He talked and laughed pleasantly enough, and wished them every success in their undertaking.

"If I were you I should not like the job," he said, presently, "but perhaps after all folks exaggerate about Kelly's power and pluck."

"We do not underrate his powers," said the policeman, significantly, and then, as if by accident, he pulled his rein, and Kelly found himself between the two horsemen.

"The rascal will not surrender without a desperate struggle," observed Kelly, with a look of menace in his eyes.

He saw that they were rapidly approaching a police-station, and there was no time to be lost, and suddenly pulling out a short black pipe asked one of his would-be captors in a nonchalant way for a light.

"Oh, I'll get you one close by," was the reply, as off No. 1 went to the police-station, which just hove in sight, to get more than the light required.

No sooner had he disappeared than Ned, drawing a pistol from his pocket, swore he would scatter No. 2's brains if he did not at once dismount.

The persuasive eloquence of the muzzle of the pistol had the desired effect, and down jumped the lad (for he was nothing more), and allowed Kelly to take hold of the bridle.

"Good-bye, my friend," he coolly said. "The prison isn't made, or the traps born, that are a match for Ned Kelly."

With a loud laugh, he rides rapidly away, leading the trooper's horse with him, to "keep him," as he said, "in good company."

When No. 2 arrived at the police-station, great was the chagrin and rage at the success of the ruse. The police, on hearing of his escape, rose with loud yells of anger and disappointment, and, mounting their horses, started in pursuit.

They were not only eager to reap the great reward, but they now had a personal grievance against Ned Kelly, and wanted to be revenged upon him for the success of his "dodge."

In fact, they were cruelly mortified.

Kelly, now perfectly calm and self-possessed, urged forward his horses as he heard the shouts of his pursuers behind him.

He necessarily rode blindly along the first path that presented itself.

It was a race for life and liberty once more, and all caused by his own folly.

The policemen fired more than once, but the bullets whizzed over Kelly's head, and he gave a shout of derisive and laughing defiance as his horses dashed forward at mad and headlong speed.

The men, as can be easily imagined, did not spare the

steeds, and Kelly hearing another shout of triumph, looked back and saw that his pursuers were gaining upon him. He resolved to keep the second horse with him, and change steeds when his weight began to tell upon that he rode.

He made up his mind instantly that if they came much nearer he would turn and fight.

A sinister light gleamed in his eye as he listened to the yells and oaths of the enraged men.

His position was desperate indeed, but he did not despair; he never did—the secret of success.

He was flying along at full speed, without following any particular direction, when he glanced ahead, and a smothered cry escaped from his lips.

Just in his path, just before him, was a wide gully, cutting off his retreat, and he must turn and face the policemen, or take this awful, this terrible leap.

In an instant his mind was made up.

There was only one thing to be done. He would not attempt the leap.

The pace had been a killing one. His horse was distressed, and those of his followers were not much less so.

He resolved, as he said, to "burst the lot," and so pressed his animal still more with spur and hand. He had the satisfaction of gaining on his pursuers. He saw they were flagging, and that the men were somewhat done up from excitement.

He avoided the leap, and turned sharply towards the scrub, and for a few minutes was hidden from view. He rapidly changed horses, and mounting the led one, felt he now really had the foot of the field. The time occupied in the change had allowed his enemies to gain on him, and a loud howl of delight pealed from their lips as they thought they had him at last.

They were quickly deceived, for they now felt he was leaving them at every stride.

Seeing further pursuit useless, they moderated their pace, upon which Kelly likewise "drew it milder," and, mocking his friends with what the French call a *pied-à-nez*, begged them to go and get the reward and drink his health.

"Never saw such a thing in all my life," said the first policeman.

"Faith, and it bates Bannager Biddy," replied the second, who was an Irishman, "and Biddy bates me."

And they rode away.

Kelly gave a deep sigh of relief, and laughed mockingly as he continued on his way.

At present, at least, he was out of danger—but for how long?

He did not allow his horse to relax his pace, but rode hard till night came on, looking back every now and then to convince himself that he was not being followed, until it was too dark for him to see any object distinctly, when he allowed his steed to take it easy.

He had entered the wild scrub, and was slowly moving through the long grass, when he suddenly saw a faint light in the distance, and knew that he was nearing some habitation.

CHAPTER LXI.

THE INN IN THE BUSH.

HE soon found that the light proceeded from a lonely inn, one of those places frequented by roughs, ex-convicts, and shepherds, and Kelly's face brightened as he alighted from his horse, and, pushing open the door which happened to stand ajar, entered without ceremony.

"Supper and whisky," he said laconically, and the landlady, on hearing the order, hastened to set a good meal before him. It was served in a private room, and presently her husband came lounging in and looked at the stranger with some curiosity.

They were a well-matched couple—the man, a tall herculean fellow of about thirty, and the woman a fine strapping wench of five-and-twenty.

"I thought it would be more comfortable for you here," observed the landlady, as she and her husband sat down at the same table to discuss their own evening meal.

"Thank you," said Kelly curtly, but against his will he found himself drawn into conversation.

He did not wish to appear churlish, nor had he any desire to arouse the suspicions of the man and woman.

The name of the couple was Marsh, and they were evidently natives of the Emerald Isle.

It needed little inducement to persuade them to speak of the country they had left.

The woman at first tried to ply Kelly with questions, but after briefly stating that his name was Jones, he changed the conversation, and began to talk of Ireland, a subject which appeared agreeable to his companions.

They appeared to be rather free and easy people, but they were none the worse for that in the eyes of the celebrated bushranger, who began to ask questions in his turn.

"Why did you leave Ireland?" he asked bluntly, as he refilled his glass.

"We were given a free passage by the Government," returned the man, with a wink. "A pig-headed jury found us guilty of participating in a murder that took place at Balla, near Castlebar, and we were shipped off for change of air. When we were discharged from the Tench by order of that same paternal Government, we settled down here to try and turn an honest penny."

"Balla, near Castlebar?" said Kelly, interrogatively, looking at the woman with new interest as he spoke; "is that where you came from?"

"That same," responded the man.

"Was your father named Kelly?" asked the bushranger, addressing Mrs. Marsh, who sat with her plump elbows resting on the table, and her eyes fixed upon his face.

"That was her father's name," interposed the husband, before she could speak; "and who might you be, to know so much about us?"

"I am Ned Kelly, your wife's brother," was the quiet reply.

"My brother!" cried the woman, in astonished surprise and delight, whilst her husband warmly grasped the bushranger's hand.

He was evidently regarded as a great hero by the interesting pair.

They had heard and gloated over the bloodthirsty and daring deeds of Ned Kelly, and were glad to welcome him to their shanty.

He felt now that he was indeed amongst friends, and could rely upon their truth and honesty as far as he was personally concerned.

They regarded him with undisguised admiration.

That which appeared revolting to other people became in their eyes manly courage and heroic bravery.

His sister clapped her hands with delight, and, throwing her arms round his neck, gave him a hearty kiss, which he took in very good part, congratulating himself upon having found such a comfortable and secure hiding-place.

He was no longer compelled to behave with caution, and could show himself in his true colours.

"This is the strangest thing that has ever happened to me in the whole course of my life," said Mrs. Marsh.

The husband assented to this remark, and produced a bottle of real whisky, in which the bushranger and his relatives pledged each other.

"I drink to our better acquaintance," cried Marsh, lifting his glass on high. "I think we shall find it a very pleasant as well as profitable connection."

"No doubt we can put business in each other's way," agreed Kelly, tossing off his glass and looking significantly at Marsh.

Marsh put his forefinger to his rather rubicund nose and winked solemnly at his brother-in-law.

The two men were ready to swear by one another from that moment.

That night was a jolly one indeed for the two, and long after the shanty was shut up they drank and talked and laughed, and thoroughly enjoyed themselves; Marsh and his wife swearing that Kelly was the most wonderful fellow they had ever met or heard of.

"I have done many things that have astonished Australia," said Kelly, before retiring to rest, "but I am not yet old, and intend to do many daring deeds which will put my past exploits completely in the shade."

This was no idle boast; Ned Kelly meant to keep his word. The notorious bushranger was a man of iron resolution, and seldom made a promise that he did not carry out.

He had been in the saddle all day, and consequently soon fell into a sound sleep, his powerful frame stretched out to its full length, and his massive head resting on his brawny arm.

Sleep, which is often denied to the innocent, came always at his bidding, and he could have dreamed away till daylight had not the silence of the night been suddenly broken by an ominous sound—a loud knocking at the door.

In an instant Kelly was wide awake and on the alert, and lifting his head he listened intently.

He was joined a few minutes later by his sister and her husband.

"Come," said the woman, anxiously, "there is no time to be lost. The policemen are at the door and must be admitted, but there is a hiding-place in which you will be quite secure from all fear of discovery. Come at once."

Kelly unhesitatingly obeyed. He knew intuitively that he could trust these people, and his instinct seldom played him false.

"My horse?" he said, anxiously.

"Has been hobbled out down in the gully. Have no fear," was the reassuring reply of the woman, who was in a curious state of déshabillé.

The police, impatient at being kept waiting, hammered ceaselessly at the door, swearing that if it was not at once opened they would break it in, and Kelly was hastily conducted to the hiding-place beneath the floor of the shanty.

It was a very awkward and cramped position, but anything was better than falling into the hands of the police —of the hated traps.

"What the deuce is the matter? Has hell broke loose?" enquired the landlord, in a sleepy voice, as he threw open the door with such suddenness as to send the foremost policeman sprawling in on his hands and knees.

"We have received information that Ned Kelly is concealed in this house," said the man, sulkily, as he rose to his feet.

"Ned Kelly?" repeated Marsh, still in a sleepy voice, putting on a stupid look, and glaring vacantly at the police officers.

"I have said so once," said the man, looking at him suspiciously. "Why didn't you open the door? We have been making enough noise to wake the dead."

"You've half-frightened me out of my life," retorted Marsh. "What with the old woman clinging round my neck, and declaring that the bushrangers were upon us, I did not know whether I was standing on my head or my heels, and felt half-inclined to fire a pistol right into your midst."

"It is well for you that you thought better of it," said the policeman, grimly. "How much longer are you going to keep us here? We want to search the house."

"Search my shanty?" cried Marsh, indignantly. "You are up to some games, boys, and want to help yourselves to my liquor."

The police waited to hear no more, but impatiently pushing him on one side they entered the shanty-inn.

"Search away as much as you like," cried Marsh, "as long as you keep out of my wife's bedroom I don't care. Keep out of there, and I shan't make the least fuss if you pull the whole place about my ears."

The policemen, half inclined to laugh, immediately made a rush for the apartment alluded to, expecting to find Kelly there, followed by the injured husband loudly protesting against the unwarrantable and improper intrusion.

"Why, he isn't here, they cried, on entering the room with very little ceremony.

"Who said he was?" retorted Marsh with a provoking grin. "Nice fellows you are to come dragging decent females out of bed at this time of night."

The men looked at him suspiciously but made no reply, eagerly searching every nook and corner.

But Ned Kelly the bushranger was not to be found, although they lingered for some time unwilling to believe that they had been baffled.

"What have you gained by dragging a poor man out of bed, and disturbing his well-earned repose?" enquired Marsh, angrily. "But to show that I don't bear malice, I'll stand drinks all round."

This offer was well received by the police of course, who who were tired and thirsty.

"Death and destruction to Ned Kelly," shouted the leader, and the bushranger smiled, as he heard the words in his secret hiding-place beneath.

"That's it," assented Marsh, "and what I say is, I wish you may get him."

A few minutes later the landlord had the supreme satisfaction of bolting the door on his unpleasant visitors.

He waited until the sound of their horses' hoofs had died away in the distance before he released Ned Kelly from his place of confinement.

Ned had great difficulty in rising from his place of concealment. His legs were cramped, and he almost gasped for breath as he stood upright.

"I could not have stood it much longer," he said, as he stretched himself. "I should have had to cry out if they had not taken their departure in the nick of time."

"It was the best we could do for you," returned Marsh, apologetically, "and now let us consult as to what is to be done. You can't leave the shanty to-night, it is not to be thought of for a moment. Although to all appearances the police have taken their departure, I know you are too old a bird to think of venturing out so soon."

Ned saw the wisdom of these words. He therefore decided to remain where he was until darkness should once more veil the earth.

He knew that it would be madness to think of remaining at the shanty for any length of time, but it would be equally absurd to venture out too soon.

"Their suspicions will be lulled by to-morrow," he said, "and the best thing I can do is to take your advice. I will keep dark until night comes on."

Nevertheless the bushranger found the hours pass but slowly, and was more than once tempted to venture out in defiance of all danger.

He grew snappish and sullen, and his relatives scarcely found him so agreeable as he had been on the previous night.

It was a relief to all parties when darkness came on, and the bushranger's spirits rose and his temper consequently improved when the hour of departure drew near.

The forced confinement in the shanty was torture to a man of Kelly's disposition. He longed for some kind of action, and gave a sigh of relief as he bade his sister an affectionate farewell, and followed Marsh to the spot where the boy was waiting with his horse.

There was a smile on his fierce and brutal countenance as he bent down to shake hands with his brother-in-law.

"You have done me a good turn," he said, "and Ned Kelly won't forget it," and without another word he left Marsh where he stood, the echo of his horse's hoofs gradually dying away in the distance.

CHAPTER LXII.

IN THE SCRUB.

OUT into the darkness rode Ned Kelly, his heart swelling with a pleasant sense of freedom, in spite of the dangers which might encompass him on every side.

Il's talents and perseverance were indeed worthy of a better cause.

Well directed, he might have been a hero, or what the world so calls.

The bushranger did not keep the high-road more than he could help.

He rode at some little distance from it, keeping it tolerably in view.

All that day he travelled with few rests, nor halted until night fell on the scene.

Then he looked round and saw a wood at a great distance. Towards this he made his way. Suddenly he became aware of a small crackling fire.

Kelly at once approached and saw that a fellow-traveller had halted and made a fire.

"Good night, mate," said Kelly in his most cordial manner, "making yourself comfortable?"

"Yes; come in and join," replied the other.

Kelly needed not twice telling. First seeing to his horse's wants he joined the other.

He was a fine young fellow of about seven-and-twenty years of age, a gold digger, but of a superior sort.

Kelly had cold meat, bread, and whisky, but no cooking utensils.

The stranger was making water boil for tea, the universal drink of the Australian.

The two fraternised, and for some time nothing was thought of but eating.

Then they filled their pannikins with whisky and water, loaded their pipes, and talked.

John Morney had come out to seek his fortune, and, having succeeded tolerably, was going home.

"I left a mother, a sister, and one dearer still, to seek my fortune," he said, with a pleasant smile, "and now am going home by way of Adelaide.

"So am I, mate," replied Kelly, and told some story invented on the spot.

The other listened and believed.

He was a straightforward young Englishman, without any guile, and ready to believe any plausible tale that was told him.

And so, with laughter and joke, the night passed until it was time to retire.

They had their blankets, and, each seeking his spot they wrapped themselves in them and sought refreshment in slumber.

At least, John Morney did.

But not so Kelly.

An infernal idea had entered his head.

If this man was able to return to England he must have made a pile.

"Sized his pile, I fancy," said Kelly to himself, "pretty well."

Money, and the brutal gratification it procured him, was all he thought of.

Why should he not take advantage of this windfall that had come in his way?

So he lay under his blanket, watching for the unfortunate and trusting traveller to sleep.

Kelly was armed with pistol and knife.

The latter he carried in a sheath, and it was a bright and glittering blade.

Presently the man whose evil genius had brought him in contact with Kelly, gave unmistakeable signs of being asleep.

With the caution and cunning of a panther, Kelly put aside his blanket, and crept towards the poor young man.

Relentless as the most ferocious of wild beasts, the bushranger raised his deadly weapon, and struck at the other's breast.

A cry, a gurgling sound, and all was over. The blow was, indeed, well and surely struck.

Then Kelly coolly proceeded to search the body of his victim.

He found a rather heavy belt and a pocket-book which he appropriated without hesitation.

Then he caught his horse and rode off to some distance, until he reached a dense part of the scrub and wood, where he again camped.

He drained his whisky flask and then slept as soundly as any innocent child might have done.

At early dawn he examined his plunder, found the belt full, while in the pocket-book was a draught given by the Union Bank of Melbourne on Adelaide, for £1,100.

Any sense of remorse that might have arisen in the mind of Kelly was set at rest by this momentous discovery.

Kelly put away his plunder, and then rode on until he came to a small shanty inn, where he procured breakfast.

Then mounting, he once more started on his way, eager to accomplish his journey.

Kelly took care to avoid all except solitary travellers, which, by keeping a good look-out, he easily did.

He did this all the more that express messengers had placarded a new reward for his own apprehension.

That night he found himself near a small inn of the rougher kind. This he resolved to enter, though determined not to stay.

If his hand was against every man, every man's hand was against him. The reward was stupendous.

While he was eating his supper he suddenly heard horses' footsteps.

His own steed was in a rude stable at the back. Quick as thought—his knife and pistol ready—he concealed himself behind a partition.

"House," said a familiar voice, appearing on the scene.

"Here," replied a gaunt old woman, appearing on the scene; "what's your will?"

At the same time there entered Dick Dawson and Carroty Larkins, who at once ordered supper.

The woman retired to obey orders.

"So you've come along, my hearties?" said Kelly, with a gruff laugh.

The men were delighted to see their chief. Questioned by him, they declared that they had had no adventures by the way.

It was now resolved to travel together.

Eating heartily, and securing tobacco and spirits, they once more started for the woods, where they passed the night.

As they approached the seat of population they were very careful.

Police stations were carefully avoided, as a matter of course, by these unparalleled ruffians.

The troopers were keenly on the alert. The whole colony was ringing with the daring and impudent escape of the bushranger.

His cool audacity was only equalled by his villainy and bloodthirsty recklessness.

They might be sure, therefore, that a good look-out would be kept.

As, therefore, they approached the town, they were doubly cautious, and when in sight concealed themselves in a rather wild place, and waited for night.

Then, after some arrangements as to meeting, they separated, each to take his solitary way into the town.

Kelly looked around keenly, and at last, making a virtue of necessity, rode into the town.

He had disguised himself admirably, and had little fear of being recognised, except by someone who had seen him.

At all events he must risk something to carry out his plans.

CHAPTER LXIII.

ADELAIDE.

NED KELLY was not known in Adelaide, though he had "mates" and correspondents there.

The confederacy of crime is something marvellous all over the world.

But among bushrangers and convicts it is a thing really wonderful to contemplate.

They have their signs and passwords, which enable them to recognise one another anywhere.

It is said there is honour among theives, but there is nothing of the kind.

They betray one another every day openly and secretly, as is very well known.

But where an organisation is powerful, and those left behind are always ready to punish the betrayers, men think twice before they enter on a course of treachery.

Ned Kelly knew this, but he was too much of a cynic to trust anyone further than he could help. He had had some experience of late.

Ned Kelly went straight to a small inn and put up his horse.

This inn was in the purlieus of the town, and was very quiet and tolerably respectable.

He dined, drank a glass or two of whiskey, smoked a pipe, and then sauntered down the town.

First he went to the post office to ask for letters for James Fairfax.

There were no letters.

Then he sauntered to the Golden Nugget, a house of call for sailors.

Here he had made an appointment with Dick Dawson and Carroty Larkins.

He was roughly enough attired now, and not likely to excite suspicion.

In those days the system of photographing prisoners was not known, at all events in the colonies.

He was, therefore, in no immediate danger.

He sauntered into the place, and looked around with his usual scrutinising eye.

It was a saloon such as has never been seen except at places possessed with the gold fever.

The costume was rough, but the faces and the language was much rougher.

Kelly sauntered through the group until he came to where a knot of men in a peculiar style of dress attracted his notice.

They were half sailors, half diggers.

Most had plenty of drink before them, which they tossed off freely, while their more unfortunate brethren came in for a share.

Kelly thought he had never seen such a villainous lot in his life.

They were six in number, while he occupied a table to himself.

Apparently they did not notice him.

"I hate work!" said a thin, mean-looking fellow, with sallow complexion and pock-marked face; "I allays did."

"How did you come out here then?" asked a burly ruffian, known as Salmon Roe.

"Well, you see, they sent me, and I got more work nor I wanted," was the answer.

"And now," asked Salmon Roe, in a tone of contempt, 'what do you think on, Poacher?"

"S'pose I must work," was the disgusted answer; "go and dig in those gold mines."

"Work!" laughed the leader of the sailor party. "Work's for fools. I know a trick worth two of them things."

"I should," groaned the man known as Poacher, a fair specimen of the low, loafing, idle English peasant—they are not many, but they beat anybody when yon find them; "like to know what to do to keep from work."

"Dig for gold!" said Salmon Roe, amidst universal approval. "Bosh! let flats dig and wise men gain by it"

"How?" asked the Poacher.

"There must be no flies," answered the burly ruffian, "no flies here. I'm up to a big thing, but no man joins me without I knows something about him. I've done Newgate and the Tench."

"I've been once in Clerkenwell, twice in Millbank, and ain't long kicked out of Pentridge," added the Poacher.

Each of the men gave some such satisfactory answer.

Our hero had, seemingly, after a heavy drink, fallen asleep on the table.

"Listen," said Salmon Roe.

Now we may as well premise that a large number of vessels were at this time lying at Adelaide waiting to go so England.

Thousands of pounds of gold were piled up in the banks seeking a ship.

Some ships, unable to find a crew, were paying demurrage at the rate of £200 a day.

Sailors ran away to the diggings as fast as they landed.

They did not come back.

Many passengers were waiting to go home, but not the highest terms offered could get a crew.

The harbour was choke full of vessels of all sizes, and not a sailor to be had for love or money. The agents were in despair, and the loss to the owners enormous. The very captains, in some instances, caught the infection and left their ships to take care of themselves, while they bolted to the "diggins."

"Now, mates," said Salmon Roe, "this here is my idea. Supposing we finds out a ship as wants a biggish crew—it must be a ship as carries raw gold—well, we can ship before the mast.

"Yes, yes," was the universal cry.

"I can find twenty fellers," went on the cold-blooded rascal, "agents ask no questions—we ship. On we go—gale of wind comes—ship goes down."

"She springs a leak, and we are obliged to abandon her off the coast of South America. We man the long-boat, and don't take no provisions—oh, no!—and no liquor of any kind, not a drop—or no, no brandy, no wine, no 'bacca, no nothing. We reg'lar starves ourselves! Now, what do you think on this little game?"

"Right you are," was the comment. "You've got the game marked out pretty. I'm blowed if we ain't just the chaps to make you win it. Who'll lead? Who's the cove as is game to be boss in this here business?"

"I'm your man," said Kelly, jumping up from his recumbent position. "Here's the cove who'll lead you to swim in tin—to make you as rich as lords."

"Hold hard, mate," said Salmon Roe. "You're mighty ready, but we must know our pals. Who the devil are you and where do you hail from?"

"May be you've heard of Ned Kelly," that worthy replied, with a gleam of almost pride in his eyes as he spoke.

"Rather, but you don't mean to say that you—you—"

"I'm Ned himself, just out from the Pentridge Stockade, and ready to lead you all to glory if you'll follow me. I like your plan—it's easy as melting butter over a fire. Now say the word, and we'll go to work like men."

Ned's fame was enough to give him a good appointment, even "down below," and he was elected managing director of the new company by acclamation.

"Sham and brandy," cried Ned, casting gold on the counter.

The order was obeyed.

As soon as some considerable drink had been imbibed, the audacious outlaw ordered a private room.

He was flush of cash, and bade them bring the most luxurious supper for money.

The astonishment and delight of the others to find themselves in company with Kelly was something scarcely to be conceived.

In the eyes of these bullies and ruffians he was a hero—there have been worse heroes!

No resistance was made to his taking the command. He was, they thought, a king among men.

It was settled that the men should keep as quiet as possible, procure themselves a respectable kit, and be ready at a moment's notice.

Salmon Roe was to remain where he was in communication with all his gang.

Ned Kelly, as Mr. Preston, was to put himself into good clothes and look respectable.

Then they were to look out for a ship.

Thus they parted

Next day Ned Kelly dressed as a respectable gold-digger presented himself at the bank, and, handing in the draft, was at once paid.

The audacious bushranger had now a fund of nearly three thousand pounds.

It struck him now that he had better go as a passenger, and thus be useful to his confederates.

He waited until evening and then communicated his idea to Salmon Roe.

That worthy highly approved of it.

The good ship Lenore, a fine vessel, had a cargo and passengers, and was only awaiting a crew.

Next morning Ned Kelly called upon the agent, Mr. Lawson, and booked a cabin passage in the Lenore as Mr. Henry Preston.

The agent thought his client a very agreeable sort of man, and when he had paid his money readily went out to have a glass of champagne.

He in this way came to notice the bushranger's face, and also that he had his left-hand glove on.

An hour later Salmon Roe, as Joe Perkins, very well made up as a mate.

The agent, Mr. Lawson, received him very courteously, though him rather rough and peculiar-looking man.

"Me and some of my mates are tired of this digging work," said Joe Perkins; "a passage back to England with good pay will suit us better than work."

"How many are there of you?" asked the agent.

"Twenty-two, sir," said Joe.

"When will you join?"

"Daybreak to-morrow," was the answer.

"You will sign articles to-night?" continued the surprised and delighted agent.

"Sar in sure," replied the obliging mate.

And so it was settled.

The gang of murderers, plunderers, and robbers were all engaged as able seamen.

Mr. Henry Preston that evening, dressed in swell style, with plenty of luggage—rather new, it is true—occupied a room in the Royal Sydney Hotel.

He had dined elegantly and well. He was up to everything, and was doing the grand.

The waiter brought him the special evening paper.

He opened it languidly.

"Shocking Accident at Melbourne," he read; "loss of the brig —— with all hands."

Ned Kelly leaped wildly to his feet. Then he sank down again and read—

"On board was the daughter of the notorious Ned Kelly, who, now it is well known, aided his escape with such extraordinary pluck and cunning.

"She was a worthy scion of her father, and society has probably escaped from a great danger.

"A girl who at the age of nineteen could have displayed such consummate astuteness, might have developed into a Lucrezia Borgia, or any other feminine monster in history.

"It is believed that the deplorable occurrence was caused by the drunkenness of the captain and crew.

"All that has been found of the ill-fated vessel has been her figure-head, which was of cork and floated ashore."

Kelly poured himself out a very strong glass of brandy and drank it off.

He was ghastly.

Literally the only being he had ever loved had gone to her account.

His fancy for Lola Montez was a mere craving animal passion, as far removed from love as heaven from the other place.

CHAPTER LXIV.

ON BOARD THE LENORE.

Let us give an account of the Lenore and her inhabitants, on board of which was to be perpetrated one of the most awful and gloomy crimes ever even brought to the charge of Ned Kelly, the ironclad bushranger.

The captain, named Elton, was an excellent and superior old salt.

The second officer, Mark Reynolds, was also an admirable sailor.

The crew, beyond those brought on board by Joe Perkins—and they were sailors—were a poor lot.

Broken down seamen, foreigners, Lascars.

Then came the passengers.

There were no less than eleven families going home to England.

Alas! amongst them were three young wives and some dozen or more grown-up girls.

Could there be no warning angel to give them a hint of the awful fate to which they were apparently doomed?

On board that ship there were three-and-twenty of the most unmitigated scoundrels who ever disgraced this earth by their presence.

They had doomed the ship.

To what fate would they doom these innocent members of the other sex?

It may be said as a trait in his favour, if it be true as he asserted in his last moments, that when he sat down to dinner with the passengers he shuddered at the sight of so much youth and beauty.

"I would have retreated if I had dared," he said, and it is to be hoped it was true.

Mr. Henry Preston at the dinner-table was very quiet and unobtrusive.

He sat at the lower end, and though he played his trencher very well, he did not seek in any way to obtrude his conversation.

He listened.

He wanted above all to take the tone of his associates before he spoke.

Thinking him diffident, one of the passengers who sat next him, a rich wool merchant, spoke—

"Glass of wine?" he said.

"With pleasure," replied Mr. Henry Preston.

The ice once broken, he conversed freely, but was careful not to go beyond his depth.

He knew all about sheep, cattle, and so on, and was therefore in no danger on these topics.

He was excessively polite to the ladies, and they soon found it out.

Then came the card table.

Ned Kelly was clever at that; even when it did not suit him to cheat, he played well.

"I have been up in the bush," he said, modestly, "and know a thing or two about cards. It would not be wise for anyone to play against me who was not sure of himself."

"We'll risk it," cried Colonel Taylor, laughing. "Here we are, three good hands. Let us try."

And they did try.

All saw at once that Mr. Henry Preston was a dabster. He never made a mistake. He always played the right card in the right place.

He won, but no one grumbled. He had good cards and good play on his side.

There was usually a light supper on board these ships—in those days it was Liberty Hall—and at the meal Colonel Taylor introduced Mr. Preston to his daughter Ellen.

She was a most charming girl, fair, happy, and full of spirits, returning to beloved England.

She felt interested in Mr. Henry Preston and chatted with him freely.

His heart smote him. He was not a poor man, and then came qualms of conscience.

Why should he not expose the whole conspiracy, and throw himself on the mercy of all?

No! He must die if he declared who he was, and death was not a pleasant prospect for Ned.

Matters must take their chance.

After they had been out some days, Mr. Preston need

to take a fancy to go and smoke a cigar at night near the bowsprit.

He would walk carelessly on until he met Joe Perkins, the second mate.

Then they had frequent talks.

Ned Kelly knew that to talk to any of these men of foregoing their purpose was impossible.

There was nearly a quarter of a million on board, sufficient for these men to look forward to an unending orgie.

But Ned proposed that they should secure the genuine crew and passengers, take the money, and let the ship go.

"Dead men tell no tales," was the brutal answer; "we don't mean to kill the young females—till we're tired of them."

And the low, brutal ruffian would say no more in answer to the other's proposition.

And so time passed on.

At table the captain often spoke of their course, and gave reasons for their approaching the coast of Brazil.

One day he indicated that they were not more than three hundred miles off the coast of South America.

"We shall go no nearer," he said, "and if the winds keep as they are we shall get a better offing."

That night Ned Kelly and Salmon Roe came to an understanding.

The ship had been riddled all along the garboard strake and elsewhere, the holes being stopped up carefully afterwards.

The plan was this.

While the cabin passengers were at breakfast, the honest crew were to be secured.

Then the mutineers were to rush in to kill and slay all who resisted.

The treasure was then to be captured.

The launch and jolly-boat would carry all they required, and they could easily reach the coast of South America and represent themselves as shipwrecked mariners.

Next day the mutiny took place.

The noise excited the alarm of all on board. The villainous gang rushed into the cabin and shot down several of the elder men.

All knew at once what would happen—a rush was made for deck, men fought desperately, girls tried to leap overboard, and lovers even shot them down, rather than leave them to the awful fate which awaited them.

What followed it is utterly impossible to describe in these pages.

There followed an orgie of the most fearful kind, and then some hours later, the Lenore went down with her dead and living freight, while the mad and drunken crew started with shouts of glee and triumph for the shore.

The Lenore was reported in due time as lost with all hands.

She was only one of dozens who at that time met the same terrible fate.

The mutineers with their gold and provisions now made for the coast of South America.

Salmon Roe was a good sailor even to being a navigator, and he and Ned studied the map.

Ned advised that they should land on some uninhabited part of the coast, where they could conceal their treasure, and then play the part of shipwrecked sailors.

Of course, their future course depended entirely on circumstances.

The whole party were agreed that after what had happened the safest place was England.

There could be no possible chance of their being suspected as concerned in the loss of the Lenore.

Not a soul on board would be alive to tell the tale—of that they were well aware.

The wind was fair, and soon the coast of South America was in sight.

Luckily they had not been able to put on board a very large amount of spirits.

The men were therefore tolerably sober.

A good lookout was kept, and the boats were careful to approach land without being seen by any of the inhabitants.

They were about thirty miles below Rio de Janeiro, the capital of the Empire of Brazil.

The coast was high, rocky, and wooded.

Salmon Roe carried the vessels into a small land-locked harbour, where there was at the bottom of the bay a cavern.

"I fancy, my friend, said Ned Kelly, in a low aside to the mate, "you've been here before."

The other winked, that was all, but it was a very meaning and voluminous wink.

It said a great deal.

It was decided on landing to hide away the treasure in the cave, to conceal also the long boat and launch, and start on a walk.

Every man was to secure a certain amount of money in his belt. Their destination was to be Rio.

What they were to do there was a question. The solution was left to the two captains.

The idea was to run away with some taut and safe vessel, and make for England.

It would be just as easy with care to land on the English coast as on that of South America, and disperse, each man with his pile.

Both Ned Kelly and Salmon Roe would have liked to defraud their comrades out of the whole of the treasure, but it was not possible.

So that night they passed their time in the cave and slept, oblivious of the hideous and fearful crime which had been committed on the high seas, and hopeful it would never be brought up in judgment against them.

Perhaps not in this world.

Ned had no wish to be the only passenger saved, so he simply was to appear as second officer of the lost City of Leith, a vessel which had sailed a few days before.

The crew marched seven miles along the coast, until they reached a large straggling village, where their appearance excited a considerable amount of astonishment.

Several, however, of the men could speak every lingo under the sun, and were able to explain. Their story was believed.

Though they were all sailors, they were also fortunate gold diggers, which made them none the less welcome.

They were entertained at their own expense at a large wine-shop, where the leading inhabitants condescended to join them.

Before the meal was over it was hot enough to take a siesta, and so they arranged to stop until evening, dine, have a dance, and start at early dawn.

Before they laid down Salmon Roe made a short but expressive speech.

"Messmates, at this here dance be careful about the girls," he said, impressively; "no nonsense and no knives. If we rouse suspicion before we reach Rio it is all UP with us. Drink as little as you can help."

It was indeed terribly hard lines; but the men knew that it was wise advice, and resolved to abide by it as far as possible.

Then they slept.

After which they dined in the best way they could on fruits, vegetables, and a scanty supply of meat, such as a true Briton very properly turns his nose up at.

Then they smoked and waited until the music began, which announced the tertulia or ball.

The Brazilian women are half Spanish, half savage looking, with fine eyes, but sallow complexions and heavy figures.

This is usually derived from the circumstance that they do the hard work.

But there were lots of young girls not yet spoiled; and then sailors are not very particular.

Knowing the fierce jealousy of the race, Salmon Roe was careful to warn his men again.

Then he left them to their chance.

The native women who knew the white men, as they

called them, had plenty of money, were very gay, pleasant, and cordial.

Several pedlars with jewellery accidentally came in, and Jack was very ready to buy anything that a *senorita* desired.

They were liberal too in the way of cool and pleasant drinks.

For themselves they chiefly stuck to *aguardiente*, a vile strong kind of brandy which poisons more than it intoxicates.

Soon the fun became fast and furious, and the shouting and laughing were tremendous.

Some of the younger Brazilians began presently to look ominously dark.

They didn't mind the girls accepting presents, dancing, and consuming cool drinks.

They objected to the English sailors being too demonstrative.

Arms round the waist they did not care for, but when kisses were ravished there was a row.

Jack Mulligan, one of the younger of the sailors, a hot Irishman, with a handsome but villainous countenance, was dancing with a superb girl.

She was flirting tremendously, and had already got a necklace and a pair of bracelets out of the fellow.

He was very excited with drink, and in the conclusion of a dance behaved to her in a way that excited the jealousy of a tall young Brazilian.

This individual, mad with fury, flew upon the Irishman with a long and pointed stiletto.

Salmon Roe levelled a pistol, and, speaking in Spanish, cried—

"Caraio—stop; justice shall be done!"

Everybody stood still.

"Jack, apologise to the lady and her friend," said the mate in English, with a withering glance, "or I'll shoot you through the head. If you think we shall ever get *to* Rio like this you are mistaken."

Jack hesitated.

The mate put his finger on the trigger.

"I can speak gibberish," said Jack suddenly.

Then Salmon Roe turned to the young man, said his companion meant no disrespect to the young lady and her friend, but had had too much *aguardiente*. The lover was satisfied.

A moment's reflection, however, must have satisfied the Brazilian that to cope with twenty-three well-armed and stalwart Englishmen would have been a slight mistake.

They accordingly cooled down, and the remainder of the evening passed off well enough—the sailors being careful.

Avarice for once overcame the lust for drink and its consequences.

They contrived to collect early on the morning, bought up all the cheap coloured stuffs in the place, and gave them to the children.

This, with a distribution of drinks and sweets satisfied all, and the Brazilians and the pirates parted very good friends.

They were careful to avoid further adventure by the way, and when the hot part of the day came halted in a wood, and there rested and took their siesta and meal.

They had provided themselves with food and drink, wallets, and gourds.

They enjoyed themselves thoroughly, smoking their pipes, sipping grog, and playing cards.

When the heat of the day was over they started again, and soon after dusk entered the great town of Rio de Janeiro.

CHAPTER LXV.
JACK ASHORE.

THE mercantile capital of Brazil is situated on a large, wide-spreading bay, like an arm of the sea.

It covers a large amount of territory, and has a very great number of inhabitants.

Its manners and customs are peculiar, and many of them not by any means savoury.

But as our visit to Rio is only an episode in the history of our hero, we have no time or place to go into particulars.

The men were well received, but on intimating to the acting British Consul that they had money of their own were not interfered with.

They scattered themselves over several sailors' boarding-houses, with arrangements as to meetings.

Mr. Henry Preston and Mr. Joe Perkins, second officer and mate, went to an hotel of the kind frequented by persons of their rank.

The men went to an inferior class of house, arranging for communication.

Next morning after breakfast they went out to see about passages for England.

In consequence of the gold fever, the shipping interest was affected even at Rio.

Most ships had gone to Australia in search of freight and passengers.

It would not be easy to find a passage for three-and-twenty men.

"What a nice-looking craft," suddenly said Salmon Roe, nudging Ned Kelly, as he pointed out a handsome two hundred ton schooner yacht to their English guide from the inn.

"No bad judge," replied the guide with a smile; "that belongs to Lord Barton, who has brought out a party of friends in search of sport. He has gone up the country with his friends."

"Yes—a handsome vessel," said Salmon Roe.

"The crew live on shore on board wages," said the interpreter; "it is cared for by the steward and shipkeeper."

The two men exchanged glances, and turned away as if quite indifferent.

"That is the ticket," whispered Salmon Roe.

"Just so," replied Ned Kelly.

And they went quietly back to their hotel to lunch and think.

Both had made up their minds.

On further inquiry they found that Lord Barton would not return for a month.

There was no hurry.

It was arranged that every man should have his fling for a day or two before anything was carried out.

Ned Kelly and Salmon Roe agreed to do the respectable, and to keep within bounds.

To excite suspicion might have proved fatal then or at a future time.

They lived quietly, played billiards, went to the theatre, and then adjourned to the *monte* and other tables.

Some of the games were new to Ned Kelly, but with that native and marvellous shrewdness native to most Irishmen, he saw through them at once.

Of course he knew that luck will beat the best man, but Ned Kelly was one of those never to be tempted into "risky" play.

He lost freely and won warily.

It is a perfect truth that one may ruin himself by caution, another by recklessness.

In gambling there is such a thing as luck, which is accident, but wariness is best.

Ned Kelly was always on the study.

He became quite a celebrity in the second-class billiard and gambling rooms where a certain celebrated gentleman now enjoying the hospitality of one of Her Majesty's jails is said to have graduated.

But he never lost sight of business.

Salmon Roe studied the "Nautical Almanack."

"The moon wont rise before to-morrow morning," observed Salmon Roe; "that' its the time."

"All right," said Ned Kelly.

It was not necessary to say any more.

Now, Salmon Roe had found out two things.

The first was that John Jones, of the yacht Lightwing, was very fond of his glass and very proud of his master and his yacht

Salmon Roe had found Mr. John Jones' favourite house, and had met him several times.

Salmon Roe pretended to admire his master very much, having heard of him everywhere.

"I tell you what I'll do," said the supposed Joe Perkins; "show us over the yacht, and I'll stand the biggest supper as ten pounds will fetch."

John Jones had agreed; and when he did so, signed his death-warrant.

Salmon Roe had given him money to find all necessaries for a feast.

It was to be indeed a grand one.

In due time the two villains went on board, and, seating themselves in the owner's cabin, began the evening.

It was uproarious.

At length the steward and ship-keeper were helplessly drunk.

The villains had heavily drugged their liquor, and now proceeded to gag them.

Then they were pinioned, heavy weights tied to their legs, and silently they were dropped overboard.

Then a signal was made, and like shadows in the night, the rest came on board, all provided with seamen's bags and other requisites in which to conceal their treasure.

Then the yacht was quietly hauled out of the harbour, no sails being hoisted until they were a good distance off.

"We must keep out of the regular track of vessels," said Ned to Salmon Roe, "as we dare not go into harbour."

"Just so," answered the mate.

"We must scuttle her off the coast," continued Ned, "some dark night, and land on boats. Then each man with his plunder will make for Liverpool."

"Yes," continued Salmon Roe, smacking his lips with anticipated glee.

"My friend," said Kelly—they were alone—"take my word for it, and do as I shall do. I mean to give all save you. Larkey, and Dick Dawson the slip."

"Why?" asked the mate.

"Rely upon it, the moment they get to Liverpool they will cut it flash," replied Ned. "They will show their gold, dress up their wenches, and excite suspicion. The moment the robbery of the yacht is known, the loss of the Lenore will be connected with it."

"Right you are," said the mate.

"So ware hawks!" continued Ned, "a nod is as good as a wink to a blind horse."

The mate agreed.

All sails were cracked on, and the hiding-place of the treasure soon reached.

The yacht was amply provisioned with every luxury that could be thought of.

Of course there was no difference between the cabin and the forecastle.

Jack was as good as his master.

Still Ned was too wide awake not to keep up good discipline. There were plenty of smart seamen's clothes on board, and they were freely used.

A smart young seaman was dressed up as valet, the mate as the sailing master, while Ned Kelly assumed a garb suitable to the owner of the yacht.

Of course this was only in case of any unexpected accident hardly on the cards.

Ned had a good lookout kept aloft, and whenever a vessel came in sight, the topmost sails were hauled down and the course altered.

But it is a long lane that has no turning. They were off England at last.

But they waited before proceeding to action—waited for a dark and tempestuous night, which soon came.

Then they ran in under bare poles, put out the boats, well-appointed as life-boats, and left the vessel scuttled.

Fortunately for them the night was so dark even the coastguard was less vigilant than usual.

All landed, and then even the boats were destroyed in the same way.

"Disperse," had said Ned; "we shall meet in Liverpool."

And every man turned off in the direction of the great seaport not very distant.

The four leading ruffians now determined to act with extreme prudence and caution.

They would do nothing to excite suspicion, but proceed warily.

Salmon Roe was a native of the neighbourhood of Liverpool.

He told them they were sixteen miles distant, near to a cross-country road.

There was a village about a mile inland, where there was a small inn. There was no railway station for seven miles, but a coach passed this inn twice a day for the station.

Their plan was to go to the inn, say they were passengers for the coach, and give no account of themselves whatever.

At all events they might say something vague—been visiting friends, were due in Liverpool.

They would have to reach the inn about an hour before daybreak.

Ned Kelly agreed to be guided in all things by his companion who knew the country.

They started across the fields and soon gained the highway and the inn.

No questions were asked.

Customers were tolerably scarce in those parts, and only too welcome to the Dun Cow.

Ned and Salmon Roe played the part of masters, Dick Dawson and Larkey of men.

Supper was ordered, and the two heads seated themselves in the parlour to enjoy it.

Fresh meat and vegetables were a rare treat to these long-voyage mariners.

Then they lighted up their pipes and joined in the general conversation.

Both were careful to eschew any topic connected with the sea and the colonies.

At last the coach came, and four places were found, two outside and two in.

They thus reached the junction, and shortly after took the train for Liverpool.

The men, who kept quite aloof, went to a small inn while the other two established themselves at an hotel.

Ned Kelly determined to be very wary. He knew the character of his comrades, and was perfectly well aware how they would act.

He determined therefore to avoid those quarters frequented by sailors.

When in their cups, the crew of the Lenore would be just as likely as not to speak of Australia and the bushranger herd.

He and Salmon Roe, now assuming the names of Parker and Grey, took the character of captain and mate, which they could very well keep up.

Of course, they could not keep from drink and some mild sort of dissipation, but they were very careful.

"I don't think," said Ned Kelly the next day, "I can put up with the old country much."

"Why?" asked Roe.

"It's too blessed slow for me," replied Ned. "The bush for me, my boy."

The other laughed.

"Still one might do a stroke of business even here," he said. "The traps don't seem up to much, except cold meat and gab."

Ned grinned.

He did not, indeed, think much of the police, who really do seem, in too many instances, to be more for ornament than use.

"We'll try the old park for a week or two," continued

Ned, "and then I shall hark away for the diggings once more."

After a late breakfast the two chums went out, seeking the better part of the town.

They were not far from the custom-house when they suddenly came upon two gentlemen.

"Come out to Bellevue to-morrow, Lawson," said one. "Dinner at two sharp. I want to talk more about this affair."

"I will come," responded the other. "Something must be done to check this fearful state of things."

Ned and Roe both recognised the man.

It was the shipping-agent of the Lenore, with whom one had engaged himself as an A.B., the other as a passenger.

Mr. Lawson gave a start as he came face to face with them.

He evidently recognised the men as having shipped at his office in Adelaide—one as seaman, the other as passenger—on board the Lenore.

He looked thunder-struck.

If the Lenore was lost, how did these men survive?

They passed on, however, without moving a muscle.

But Roe looked back presently.

The shipping agent was pointing at them.

"He either knows us or suspects us," remarked Salmon Roe; "we'd better move on."

"By Jingo, that's the Adelaide fellow, agent for the Lenore. Hang him, what brings him here just at this time, to spoil our little game?" said Ned.

"He musn't spoil it though," replied Roe; "we'll spoil *his* game first. He spotted us certain. If he has time he'll put the police on our track, and then it's all up, and scragging is pretty sure here."

And he turned down a side street, round through certain passages, and entered a rough but busy public-house.

They ordered refreshment.

"There's a pretty game," said Roe, speaking in a kind of slang unintelligible except to their own lot; "what's brought him over?"

"Our business, I fear," replied Ned Kelly, with a self-satisfied grunt, "you heard what he said?"

"Yes," replied Roe.

"Well, we'll find out where Bellevue is," growled Ned, "and we'll silence a man who is so very clever."

Salmon Roe grinned all over his face.

That evening they spent in a music-hall, to them a kind of earthly paradise.

They contrived before going there to discover who Lawson's companion was.

He was Mr. Compton, a rich ship-owner, and Bellevue House was situated near a rural and romantic village in the suburban districts.

That was enough.

Kelly's character was a peculiar one. He actually revelled in the thought of crime.

He would commit one, almost for the fun of the thing, without hope of reward.

In this instance there was a motive.

Lawson, the agent, might at any time betray him.

If he could in any way connect them with the Lenore, their identity would soon be betrayed.

Therefore—*ergo*—his life or theirs.

Salmon Roe was quite of his comrade's opinion, and so the matter was settled.

Next day at breakfast in a quiet and cosy room, the murder of the shipping agent was arranged.

They took care to ask no questions at the hotel, but after breakfast went out.

Their first visit was to the house of a man who dealt in sailors' rough dresses.

They indicated a desire to have a spree among the roughs of the place, and borrowed a couple of suits of Jack Tar togs.

They dressed in these and left their other clothes behind them.

The Hebrew merchant let them out the back way, which was his custom with his friends.

To trace them would not be very easy.

They took an omnibus to the extremity of the town, and then walked.

It was quite a rural district even then, but now very much built on.

They as a matter of course made for the first rural inn they saw.

It overlooked the highway.

Mr. Lawson probably had done the same as themselves, for he soon appeared walking.

They allowed him to pass, and then followed slowly in his track.

He took no notice.

Presently they reached a spot where only the local church was visible. A few ancestral oaks stood here and there.

Salmon Roe had provided himself with a pistol, and now hurried forward and placed himself behind a tree.

Mr. Lawson was walking slowly.

Ned Kelly contrived to head him.

"Good morning, Mr. Lawson," said the bushranger, in a mocking tone.

The shipping agent stood back astounded.

"You know me!" he gasped.

"Yes; and seems to me you know me," was the sarcastic reply.

"I'll take care the police do," was the angry and very injudicious answer.

"It is rather unfortunate to have a good memory," said the bushranger quietly; "one more word with you and I have done."

"Say the word, you fearful ruffian," retaliated Lawson; "I have no time to waste on such as you."

"Indeed!" replied the other; "I think your time is limited indeed, in this world; for when I tell you I am Ned Kelly you know your fate."

The agent made a dash at the audacious outlaw, who with a mocking laugh disappeared.

Then the villainous countenance of Salmon Roe might have been seen from behind a tree, taking aim.

With a wild despairing cry the shipping-agent fell to the ground.

The assassins moved away as soon as they became convinced that the man must die.

He, however, lived long enough to speak a few words to those who found him

Next day the ruffians read the following in the Liverpool —— :—

"EXTRAORDINARY MURDER.—Mr. John Lawson, who was sent to England to investigate the loss of the gold-ship Lenore, was yesterday murdered at Elton, near Liverpool."

[Here followed details.]

"Before dying he made the following extraordinary and almost incredible statement:—

"'The assassin I know not, but he was one of the men, I believe, who shipped as A.B. on the Lenore.'

"'The instigator, who shipped as a passenger under the name of Harry Preston, declared himself just before the shot was fired to be Ned Kelly.'

"'The deceased was able to say no more, and so we are in this position:

"We have the notorious and bloodthirsty bushranger in our midst with no clue to his identity.

"Mr. Compton, however, states, that did he see them he could identify the two men who had been pointed out to him by Lawson."

"This won't do," observed Kelly mildly

"No, it won't," replied Salmon Roe. "It's my idea, Lunnun's the place for us."

"Just so," continued Ned, "and we'll start by the midday express."

Orders were given to that effect.

So cautious, quiet, and circumspect had been their coduct that no one suspected them, except perhaps the Hebrew dealer in old clothes.

But it did not suit him to put the bloodhounds of the law on the track of any of his customers.

It would have ruined him in the opinion of a very large class of the floating population of Liverpool.

The two men drove off to the station after a copious breakfast, and secured seats.

They sent an enigmatic message to Dick Dawson and Ned Larkins.

They were not particularly anxious about them, but it was necessary to be cautious with regard to those who knew too much.

CHAPTER LXVI.
LONDON-TOWN.

NED KELLY and Salmon Roe arrived in London in good health and spirits.

They had plenty of money, and meant to enjoy themselves in their own peculiar way—with caution.

Parker—as Kelly now called himself—was so well disguised that it would have been almost impossible for anyone to recognise him, however familiar with his appearance under ordinary circumstances, and Salmon Roe had also made a complete change in his attire.

Ned had now a good opportunity of beginning a new life in England, if he had liked to take advantage of it, but he was such an unmitigated scoundrel that he enjoyed and gloried in his bloody and immoral deeds.

Murder, robbery, and all kinds of wickedness were his delight. He was evil to the very core.

There are some natures so evil and depraved that not one redeeming quality can be found; conscience is deadened by a long course of crime, and the power of discriminating between right and wrong no longer exists.

Romance writers will doubtless describe Ned Kelly as a brave, noble-minded, chivalrous man, driven to his evil courses by the force of circumstances; but we, who have promised to make a plain statement of facts, according to the best of our ability, cannot disguise the truth that he was one of the most unblushing villains in existence and a disgrace to humanity. Despising danger, defying the written and unwritten laws of God and man, he has made an unenviable name which will be remembered for many generations to come.

Of course Kelly's gigantic stature and broad shoulders attracted universal attention, as he swaggered along the London streets with his congenial companion by his side.

People constantly turned to stare after him in the crowded streets, little thinking that they were gazing at a murderer whose hand was against every man.

Mr. Parker gave out that he and his friend had determined to make London their headquarters for a time at all events.

The bushranger made up his mind to continue his old life, and he wanted to give the great city a turn.

"My name will be as notorious here as it is in Australia,"

he had said to his friend Salmon Roe, or Grey, as he now called himself; and, needless to say, he meant to keep his word.

At the present moment they were indulging in the harmless amusement of looking for lodgings.

"It must be in a respectable neighbourhood," said Kelly, with a grin. "Near church and rail. They shall have money down instead of references."

The neighbourhood they had chosen for their temporary abode was St. John's Wood.

Grey would have preferred a less respectable locality, but Parker had spoken and he must obey.

He was not quite so reckless and brave as the so-called Mr. Parker, and thought, not unnaturally, that they might attract attention in that quiet and respectable locality.

"Here we are," said Parker, at last stopping before a house with a small garden in front. "Looks the kind of crib that will suit us. A trifle dull, perhaps, but then you know we can always go out in search of amusement."

Grey muttered something under his breath as he followed Parker up the gravel path.

On knocking at the door it was opened by a trim servant girl who looked at the two men with considerable surprise.

"You have apartments to let," said Parker. "Can I see the mistress of the house?"

The servant was about to comply with his request, when a lady, evidently a widow, came forward with a smile.

"Yes, I have apartments, sir," she said. "Do you want them for yourself and friend?"

She instinctively guessed that the men before her had money; at the same time she instinctively knew they were not gentlemen.

"We should like to take them at once if they are suitable," said Parker; and the gracious landlady led the way into the parlour.

Parker was not the kind of man to be long about making up his mind.

"These will do," he said, addressing the landlady; "I'll take them for a month."

"What about references?" said the landlady, in a half-hesitating tone.

"References?" cried Parker. "Unfortunately, I am a stranger to London, and can give no references. But I'll give you a month in advance, money down. Will that suit you?"

And he took out his purse, which was literally packed with gold.

"This is very unusual," said the landlady, looking, however, with longing eyes at the money in the purse: "I am always very particular."

(To be continued.)

NED KELLY

THE
IRONCLAD
AUSTRALIAN BUSHRANGER

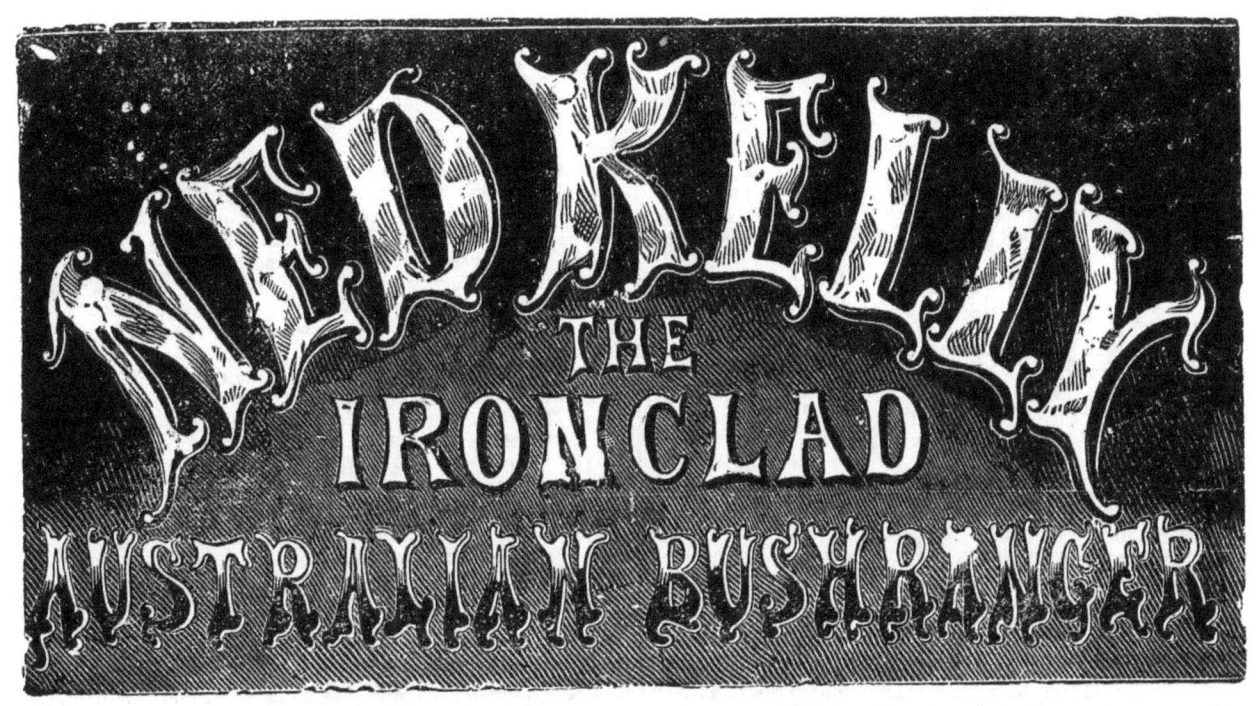

NO 9,

"Take it or leave it," replied Parker, rudely, "I have no time to waste. We are both tired, and have no desire to stop where we are not wanted. There are plenty of other people who will be glad to receive us. Come on, Grey."

Grey without a word, followed Parker out into the passage.

They had got to the front door and had just opened it, when the landlady, having recovered from the surprise Parker's eccentric conduct had caused her, came after them.

"You are too hasty, sir," she said. "I shall be very happy to take you as lodgers if you will pay a month in advance."

"I thought you would alter your mind," said Parker, with a loud coarse laugh, as he walked back to the parlour. "Now take your money and go, we want to be alone," and he threw some sovereigns on the table, which the landlady was not slow to pick up.

Then with a curious glance at her new lodgers she withdrew, leaving the two men alone, Parker comfortably seated in a large arm chair.

"Here we are in comfortable quarters," he said. "You see what you can do with money. No enquiry as to character as long as the tin is forthcoming."

"I wish you hadn't settled down in such a respectable place," said Grey, gloomily. "I don't like it. We can't do what we like here. It may suit you, but it doesn't suit me."

"I've an object in what I have done," replied Mr. Parker, with an unpleasant, sneering smile. "We can live like gentlemen here without attracting the least suspicion. The landlady seems a very respectable woman, and, of course, the neighbours will think that she had references with us."

"Perhaps you know best," said Grey, still keeping to his own opinion, but not wishing to arouse Parker's fiendish temper.

"Of course I do," said Parker; "we will stop here until London gets too hot for us. This is the richest capital in the world, and I mean to share in its prosperity."

"Most men would be satisfied with what we have got," said Grey, "and retire from business before it is too late."

"I never could settle down," said Parker snappishly; "I must have excitement at any price. You ought to know me by this time."

"It's my belief that you will never be satisfied till you are hanged," muttered Grey to himself; but he said aloud, "You know I am always ready to do anything you ask, I'll stick to you through thick and thin."

And the conversation ended, for the landlady entered the room on some pretext or other.

She was a curious woman, and wanted to get into conversation with her lodgers.

But finding they were very uncommunicative and rude, she retired in disgust, feeling that she had done wrong in allowing them into her respectable house; but then she was a poor widow and the money came in very handy indeed.

Mr. Parker was by no means mean in money matters He threw gold about as if it were of no more value than dirt. He had not worked for it honestly, and when it was all gone could get more by adding crime upon crime.

That evening Mrs. Daniel was horrified to hear loud sounds of laughter mingled with dreadful oaths, which made her tremble in her shoes.

She dared not go into the room to remonstrate with them, for she was afraid, poor woman ; and so they smoked and drank and continued to enjoy themselves in their own way, unmolested by the mistress of the house. At all events they paid.

Their mirth was so unearthly and diabolical that the old woman and her servant shuddered involuntarily.

The old lady was anxious about her furniture, too, for it was being knocked about unmercifully by the two men who were now red-hot with drink

More than once the two women thought that the men must be quarrelling and fighting, so harsh and savage were their voices.

"Who can these men be ? " Mrs. Daniel asked herself.

It seemed to her almost as if hell had broken loose in her quiet home.

Presently the bell rang violently, but the two women were too frightened to move, and sat on their chairs as if turned to stone ; so Parker came out and put his head over the banisters, and cried out in his loud stentorian voice, which was rendered hoarse with drink—

"Mrs. Daniel, you are a quiet, lonely woman, we have come here to wake you up a bit. Come up, we want to see you. Don't be afraid, I wouldn't hurt a kitten. I am the softest-hearted man that ever lived."

"Ha, ha, ha!" laughed his companion, who was in a more intoxicated condition than Parker. "Come up, Mrs. Daniel, and give us a tune ; there's a piano in the corner of the parlour."

The house was a detached one, so there was no fear of the noise attracting the attention of the neighbours.

"A good idea," cried Mr. Parker. "Come upstairs, Mrs. Daniel, and we'll make a night of it."

But there was no response from the room below to this mad request.

Mrs. Daniel commanded the servant girl to answer, but she was, if possible, more frightened than her mistress, and took no notice of her mistress's words.

"I'll come down and fetch you," cried Mr. Parker, and he rushed down the stairs four steps at a time, shaking the house with his heavy tread.

The two women, uttering a cry of terror, made a rush for the back door.

But they were too late.

The two men-lodgers were upon them, and dragged them back.

"Don't run away," cried Parker, with a fat chuckle "Don't be afraid of good company."

"Mr. Parker," cried the landlady, "your conduct is most disgraceful."

The two men only gave a hoarse laugh in return, and compelled them to follow them to the parlour.

Mrs. Daniel began to see that it was no use to resist the two lodgers, and resolved to submit to them.

Drunk as Parker was, he had no intention of doing the women any injury, but he wanted a bit of fun.

Had they been in the bush it would have been different, for the servant girl was pretty and young.

Mr. Parker did not wish to be driven from London until he had done something which should make his adopted name known throughout the great city.

The landlady was forced to sit down before the piano and play a lively dance-tune, Grey holding a red-hot poker over her head, threatening to do for her if she stopped playing.

Then the gallant Mr. Parker seized the servant girl round the waist and danced about the room, his ferocious face red with excitement, and perspiration standing out on his brow in big drops.

He was, as we know, far from an agreeable object, and the girl shrank and shuddered in his close embrace.

The furniture had been piled up in one corner of the parlour and many articles were broken, but Mrs. Daniel did not venture to utter a word of remonstrance or complaint.

"Play faster," cried Parker, whirling the girl round the room as if she had been a feather, and the exhausted landlady fearing violence did her utmost to comply with this request.

It seemed to the two women that he would never stop ; and the girl would have sunk exhausted on the floor if Parker had not held her up with his strong arm.

But all things must come to an end at last, and Parker released the girl and allowed her to sit down.

"You both look hot and tired from your exertions,' said Mr. Parker. "I'll give you something which will make you all right again."

The two women, terror-stricken by the ferocious appearance of the two drunken men, offered no objection when a huge tumbler of whisky and water was placed before them.

It was nearly boiling and the two poor women drank it down with tears in their eyes, much to the enjoyment of the two men who were only too happy to see the comical misery of the others.

Then they were allowed to leave the room, Mr. Parker having pressed half-a-dozen kisses on the unwilling lips of the servant-girl, who would have slapped his face had she dared to have done so.

The skin was taken off the roof of her mouth, and she felt scorched all down with the fiery liquor, and her heart beat painfully with the fatigue she had undergone.

Parker, fearing they might go and alarm the neighbours, took the precaution to lock them in their room.

Then he returned to the parlour, and threw himself on the floor, not taking the trouble to go up to his bedroom, and in a few minutes the two men were fast asleep, and their loud snores resounded through the house.

They had left the lamp burning on the table, and it cast its subdued light on the disordered room, and on the faces of the two men who lay in a drunken slumber on the floor.

CHAPTER LXVII.
SEEING LIFE.

IN the morning Parker and Grey felt very much annoyed with themselves for having been so imprudent on the previous night.

"It is all up with us now," cried Grey; "they will split on us directly they get out of the house."

"No they won't," replied Parker, coolly; "I am going to speak to them. If they do not swear to keep still tongues in their heads, I will cut their throats. You must have seen how frightened they were or they would have thrown up the windows and called for help when I locked them in their rooms."

"Won't they swear anything, and then, directly our backs are turned, go and split?" said Grey, rather doubtfully.

"What a fool you are," cried Parker, impatiently. "We haven't done any great harm to them. If you like, I'll set fire to the house and burn them alive. That will put them out of the way."

"No, they might escape," said Grey, dolefully. "I like your first suggestion best."

So the two women, who had not closed their eyes all night, were released, and Parker, holding a knife to their throats, made them swear to hold their tongues.

"If you repeat a word as to what occurred last night, I'll cut your throats," he said, looking at them with his bloodshot eyes. "It isn't the first time I have cut a woman's throat; remember what I say, if you are false to your oath, I will kill you; so don't trifle with me."

The women looked at him in speechless terror and were only too eager to swear anything, and Mr. Parker put his knife away, much to the relief of the two unfortunate beings, who had thought their last hour had come.

"I'll pay for the things I smashed last night," said Parker, who felt himself master of the situation; "I'll give you your own price, I am not mean in money matters, having plenty to spare."

And so matters having been arranged to the two lodgers' satisfaction, they sat down and ate a hearty breakfast, after which they left the house, having procured latch keys so that they could go in and out when they liked.

"Do you think it will be safe to return to that house again?" said Grey; "women are very treacherous creatures, and they may betray us after all."

"Let them—that's all," said Parker significantly. "I know a thing or two!"

Grey was curious to know where Parker was going to, but did not ask questions.

He would find out soon enough, he thought.

Birds of a feather flock together, and Parker, who had heard a good deal of London, instinctively made for a part where he was sure to find men who were answerable to the law for many evil deeds.

But he knew that night was the time to see the worst characters, for as a rule your true criminal avoids the light of day.

He comes out in the night like an unwholesome reptile.

Parker was unlike most criminals, who are very often cravens and cowards. He shouldered his way through the crowded streets in the broad daylight, without the slightest fear.

How they amused themselves in the course of the day is of no importance; suffice it to say that when night came on they found themselves in one of the lowest slums in London, a place avoided by respectable people; the streets and courts were dimly lighted, and evil smells came from the gutters.

The place is bad enough now—for improvements are made very slowly in London—but it is a thousand times better lighted, and smells a thousand times sweeter than it did a few years back.

There were gin-palaces with wide-open doors, and women with sodden, expressionless faces drunk at the bar, some of whom had babies in their arms.

Ribald songs were sung, and the language was simply disgusting.

The drink in these bright gas-lit places was poison for both body and mind.

And the landlords of these horrible places could laugh and smile as they took the poor deluded wretches' money and dispersed their filthy thirst-producing liquor, and could go to church on Sunday with a calm conscience

If the drink were pure and wholesome it would not matter so much, but death and crimes are produced by filthy adulterated compounds which are drunk by the ignorant poor.

There is plenty of work for Christian men here, without going abroad to convert woolly-headed, naked heathen. The money that is spent in African missions might save many poor English children from worse than death.

At last Mr. Parker arrived at the entrance of a court and turned down under the narrow archway, still followed by his friend.

This place had such an evil reputation that the police gave it a wide berth, only venturing up it when obliged.

"I suppose you wonder how I knew of this place when I have never been here before?" said Parker to his friend.

"I must confess it puzzled me slightly," replied Grey in his usual dry manner.

"Well, the fact is, I was told of this crib when I was in Australia," said Parker, stopping before the door of a very old and dilapidated house, which looked as if it would topple down at any moment. It was shored up by two stout beams which appeared very inefficient props to keep up the building.

"How will you get in? Do you know the signal?" said Grey.

Parker nodded, and gave three peculiar taps on the door, which after a minute had elasped, a wicket was opened, and a very old man with dirty iron-grey hair put out his head.

"Who is there?" he asked.

"A friend," said Parker.

Then followed certain words in some strange slang only known to the initiated.

The door was flung open at last, and the two men were allowed to enter.

The old man, whose age must have been nearly ninety, held a candle on high as he led the way up the long, winding passage. The walls were damp and clammy and the paper hung in ribbons. The ceiling was low, and the plaster having fallen on the mouldy floor, the bare rafters were exposed.

The air was foul and fœtid, and the candle burnt dimly, casting but a faint light along the close, vault-like passage.

They followed the man in silence, and soon came to a steep flight of stairs, rotten and wormeaten.

The light was greatly needed now, for the banisters had gone, and one false step would mean death or deformity.

The old man, in spite of his advanced age, displayed great agility in ascending the rickety stairs, and the two men cautiously followed in his footsteps until they arrived on the landing.

Here the old man stopped to take breath, and gave vent to a hollow cough which echoed through the house.

"You are strangers to the place," he said, speaking to Parker, suspiciously. "How came you to know the sign? Are you one of us?"

"How should I know the sign if I were not one of you?" said Parker, impatiently showing the cloven foot as usual.

"One of our chaps might have split," replied the old man speaking almost as if he regretted having admitted them "I am afraid I have done wrong in admitting you without the chief's order."

"You have done quite right," said Parker, slapping him on the back. "Introduce me to the gang."

"You are not a detective?" said the old fellow. "If you are, I warn you it will be certain death."

"I am not a detective," said Parker. "I will undertake to say that I have done as many jobs as any man living in this country."

He said this proudly, for he was, as we have remarked before, proud of his crimes.

Somewhat reassured by Parker's words, the old man opened a double door, one of oak and the other of green baize.

A flood of light shot out on the landing and almost blinded the two visitors. A moment ago all had been as still as death, but now the door was opened the noises that saluted their ears are almost indescribable.

Before Parker and Grey had time to look about, they were hurried into the crowded room.

"Who have we here?" cried a burly sandy-whiskered man who was seated on a small barrel which was placed on a larger one. "How dare you bring strangers here, Grassy, without consulting me?"

"They gave the right signal," replied Grassy, looking frightened. "What was I to do?"

"What was you to do?" cried Bob Lively, the captain of the gang, "you ought to have announced newcomers, not gone for to bring in strangers on your own responsibility."

"I didn't mean any harm," said the miserable old man, looking frightened, while Parker stood in the centre of the room, an amused spectator of the scene.

"You didn't mean any harm," said Bob Lively, sarcastically; "you're getting in your dotage, Grassy, and the sooner the daisies grow over you the better. You ought to have been in your wooden surtout long ago; you ain't no use in this here world, and ought to be under ground. Let the newcomers come forward and explain theirselves."

Parker stepped before the captain.

"What do you want me to explain?" he asked, with insolent politeness "You speak as if you had a right to bounce everyone here, and I for one won't put up with it."

"I'm boss here, I'll have you to know," cried the man who sat on top of the barrel, with an air of great importance. "And I'll have you to know, also, that I am the swell of this place, and will put up with no nonsense. If you don't own up who you are, I shall have you turned out neck and crop; so speak up quickly."

"I'll show you who I am," cried our hero, defiantly; "and what I think of you and your brag."

And without another word he rushed at the man, and, giving the barrel a shove, sent him sprawling on the long table round which the men were gathered, spilling the drink they had before them.

Bob Lively rose pale and white with anger, and bounded towards Kelly with the intention of doing great things.

But that powerful miscreant was ready for him.

Drawing back his huge sledge-hammer fist he hit out from the shoulder, and the next moment Bob Lively fell upon the floor, with an ugly crack on the temple, stunned and bleeding.

Then arose a hideous shout of rage from the nondescript crowd.

"Down with the man who has floored the captain," they cried, as they rose from their seats, and angrily surrounded the audacious bushranger, who stood before them perfectly calm and collected.

They looked at him in surprise, utterly amazed by his dauntless bearing.

Not a muscle of his face moved, not an eyelid quivered.

"Stand back."

As Ned Kelly spoke he produced a six-shooter and pointed it at the yelling mob.

They hesitated.

To attack him meant certain death and destruction to some of their number. He had climbed on the table and surveyed the crowd of upturned excited faces with a cool, collected smile.

"Ned Kelly's your captain," he cried. "The first man who yelps 'No' shall have the contents of my pistol. Let him stand out and front me if he dares."

The crowd of desperate men looked at him in fear and admiration as he sat quietly toying with his "shooter."

Then by general consent a loud shout came from every throat, shaking the rafters of the old house.

"Three cheers for Ned Kelly the swell bushranger!" they cried. "Hip! hip! hurrah!"

"Drinks round," yelled Kelly, who was now in his element.

The suggestion was received with acclamation, and he was already as popular as he had been unpopular five minutes ago.

The nobblers were soon brought in, and everyone drank health and long life to the new captain, who held his glass on high and drank to their better acquaintance.

"Now bring in a pail of water," said Ned, with a grim smile, and his order was unquestioningly obeyed.

When it came he threw the contents over the prostrate Lively, who still lay on the ground stunned and bleeding

"That will bring him to," he said, coolly, as the beaten bully picked himself up, and looked wildly around.

Lively saw at once that his reign was over, and resolved to eat humble pie for the present.

When the opportunity came he intended to revenge himself upon the man who had achieved his downfall.

The uproarious roar of laughter that rang through the room did not abate his wrath, and he resolved to keep his word at any cost.

Ned Kelly had made an enemy, and he knew it; but with his usual recklessness he despised the danger.

"You own that I am the best man?" he said, looking insolently into the face of the man he had punished so severely.

"Yes," said Lively, sullenly, who was drenched to the skin, and whose face still bore marks of the bushranger's sledge-hammer fists.

"Then down on your knees," said Kelly.

None knew better than Kelly the value of the applause which greeted him. He was the monarch of the moment.

The crew of evil-doers are generally ruled by their fears, although there are many exceptions, and Kelly resolved to make the most of his opportunity.

"You have struck me; is not that enough?" cried Bob Lively, who looked very dejected at that moment

"Down on your marrow-bones and beg my pardon roared Kelly, seeing his advantage, and determined to abide by it.

Still the man hesitated, while the brutal crew looked on with unalloyed satisfaction, delighted at the degradation of the man who had been their leader.

"Down, I say!" cried Kelly, pointing his pistol at the man's head. "Down or die!"

The man, seeing no alternative, complied.

The rough and brutal men laughed and jeered as they beheld the discomfiture of the man who knelt at the feet of Kelly, thoroughly cowed. He had lorded it over them too long, and they were glad to witness his debasement.

However bad an Englishman may be, he likes to witness a display of courage, and the gang rallied round Kelly to a man.

They felt annoyed and mortified, when they found out what a craven Lively was, that they had submitted to his rule so long.

Had he showed one spark of manhood they might have pitied him; but as it was, they regarded their late leader with utter contempt. He had lost all claim to their respect.

Kelly now had time to look about him.

The room was lighted by a large oil-lamp which hung from the ceiling, and cast a yellow gleam over the surrounding objects.

There were cunning faces, stupid faces, repulsive faces; the pickpocket, with his narrow forehead; the professional burglar, with his thick-set figure and beetling brow.

Every man in that room was ready to do anything but earn an honest living.

The yellow light made the faces look even more repulsive than they were; and Kelly saw that he had fallen among congenial companions.

So far as the others were concerned he had nothing to fear; but he knew that Bob Lively was his bitter enemy, and resolved to keep an eye on him.

Looking round the long room he was surprised to see one familiar face.

He recognised an ex-convict whom he had known in Australia.

Unobserved by the others he beckoned to this man, who, obedient to the sign, came forward and shook hands heartily with the bushranger.

He was a thick-set, coarse-lipped man, and had a cast in his eye. His teeth were jagged, and his forehead was low and protruding, and he spoke through his nose with a peculiar twang.

He had lost two fingers on his right hand, and dragged one leg after the other when he walked.

"Who would have expected to meet you here?" he said. "To tell you the truth, I am heartily glad to see you. I have a bit of business on which will bring grist to the mill; will you assist me in a good lay? You are a man who, when once he puts his hand on a thing, will do it without backing out."

"I am on," said Kelly. "I am not under the necessity of doing anything just now, for I am flush of coin, but to oblige an old friend I will be in the job, whatever it is, and there is Ned Kelly's hand upon it."

He seized the other man's hand in his iron grip, and he nearly yelled with pain, but he controlled himself by a violent effort, by clenching his teeth together.

"Do you know what I want you to undertake?" said the ex-convict.

"Haven't the slightest idea," said Kelly. "I promised to help you, thinking you would not lower yourself by engaging in any petty transaction."

"Neither would I," replied the ex-convict, who was known by the name of Joss. "It is a burglary job I am on—lots of diamonds and gold, and all that sort of thing. We shall get a mint of money if the job is well carried out."

"It shall be well carried out," said Kelly. "When we get away from here we will talk over the subject quietly. There are too many present to share profits."

"Too many cocks spoil the broth," replied Joss, with a hideous leer, as he put his tongue in his hollow tooth and made a disagreeable noise.

"You have expressed yourself very clearly," said Kelly, with a grin.

And then suddenly looking round the room, he gave vent to a loud oath.

Captain Bob Lively, taking advantage of the general uproar, had slunk away.

"Your late master has gone," he said. "He means to betray us. Rush to the door and stop him before it is too late."

All the men obeyed, but in a few minutes returned with blank looks on their faces.

He was nowhere to be found.

"We shall have the police on us before we know where we are," cried Kelly. "What does Bob Lively deserve if we ever catch him again?"

"Death!" they all cried.

"You are right," said Kelly, and when we catch him we will carry out the sentence you have all agreed upon."

"We will, we will!" they all answered in wild excitement. "Death to the traitor and spy!"

"Discretion is the better part of valour," said Kelly. "Let us leave this shop before it is too late. He has been gone longer than we think. I do not care to stop here like a rat in a trap."

They were all about to follow this sensible advice, for, in the general excitement, they had not noticed how long it was since their late captain had left the house, when there came a long and prolonged knocking at the front door.

"The police are upon us," said Kelly, looking at the excited crowd.

Some were pale with fear, others seemed almost indifferent, while a few boasted loudly that they feared not the police.

"Is there no way of escape?" asked Kelly.

"Yes," whispered Joss, "I know a way. Leave the others to their fate. We must look after ourselves. Follow me. In this case every man must take care of himself."

All was confusion now.

CHAPTER LXVIII
THE BURGLARY.

NED Kelly and Salmon Roe followed Joss without a word. The others might fight it out as long as they escaped.

Joss led them into a room adjoining the apartment in which they had spent the evening, and, throwing open the window, jumped out upon the leads, still followed by Kelly and Grey.

"I was determined that if danger ever threatened I should not have my retreat cut off," cried Joss, pointing to a plank which was put across from the leads to an opposite window.

"A very wise precaution," observed Kelly.

Greatly complimented by these words, Joss began to cross the frail plank, which shook violently with the weight of the three men.

Joss tapped at the window, and, receiving no answer, dashed his fist through the pane of glass, and, putting aside the catch, opened it himself.

They now found themselves in a room which was in complete darkness.

At this moment they heard loud shouts, and saw a number of men swarming on the leads.

They were all shrieking with terror, and the three men saw to their surprise that the opposite house was in flames, and that the poor wretches were trying to escape.

With a loud derisive shout Kelly seized the plank and prevented the miserable crew from escaping. Rather than jeopardise his own safety he would leave them to perish in the flames.

It was a grand but awful sight. The house was old and burnt like tinder, and the flames seemed to lick the sky.

Some of the men desperately flung themselves from the roof, alighting with a dull, sickening thud on the flags below.

Kelly and his two friends waited to see no more.

They had no time to lose if they wished to get away in safety; there was no pity in their hearts for the poor crime-stained wretches who had met with such a terrible and unexpected fate.

Groping his way to the door, Joss found it locked; but Kelly, flinging his broad shoulders against it, exerted all his strength and hurled it open, and they all rushed headlong down the stairs.

They then entered another room, and found half-a-dozen painted and bedecked females, who manifested not the least surprise at their intrusion.

Joss explained in a few words what had happened, and Kelly threw them a sovereign or two, which were accepted with the greatest show of gratitude.

They then left the house, and found themselves on the banks of a canal, and coming to a bridge they crossed it, and Joss, knowing the neighbourhood well, led them down divers streets and turnings.

Kelly and Salmon Roe, feeling every confidence in Joss, asked no questions, but trusted implicitly to him.

After a time they slackened speed, and, looking back, saw that the sky was red with the reflection of the fire they had just left.

"We are safe now," said Joss, with a sigh of relief. "I am sorry for the poor devils, but we must look arter ourselves."

"We had a narrow let off," said Kelly. "Had it not been for your having that board placed across from the leads to the window we should have perished in the flames."

"It struck me that it might come in handy," said Joss, with a smile. "We never know what may happen, you know, and it is better that you should be prepared. I took that advice from a clergyman, 'be prepared, and have no fear,' he said, and he was quite right. I have never had reason to repent of the advice he gave me. He was the prison chaplain, and a nice young man he was; you had only to pretend to be converted, and you got off werry easy indeed. Be converted first, and then pretend to be ill. Win the chaplain's good opinions, and then have the doctor to see you. Give two or three heavy groans and say you have a pain in your left side, and you'll find yourself all right. Prison hain't half so bad as some people think, if you only do the artful. Cry and whine, and you have no reason to complain. I believe I should have died long ago if I hadn't a-been locked up. My liver was that swollen and my heart that bad that I didn't give myself three months to live, but when I was in prison my grog was stopped, and I was compelled to live a very regular life, which was very unpleasant, but very conducive to long life and good health."

"You don't seem in a hurry to get back to quod," said Salmon Roe.

"Not exactly; I like my liberty," said Joss. "Them officials with their brass buttons and tight coats are so conceited and overbearing, and the oakum-picking is such an uninteresting pursuit, and besides, no man likes to be under lock and key. It isn't natural a bird should like being shut up in a cage, even if it is made of gold. A lark will beat himself agin the bars and nearly always dies, and the wild animals in the Zoo look restless and dissatisfied as they walk up and down a-grumbling and a-growling.

Ned Kelly did not take much interest in the long-winded speech of Joss; but, not observing the disapproval with which his words were received, he continued—

"The job is to come off very soon. All my plans are made; it is at the West-end. I ain't got to rob a duke or a lord only a plain mister who is worth about two

millions of money, who has got a large place with I don't know how many rooms."

"Can we do it to-night?" asked Kelly.

"There is nothing to hinder us."

"Then it shall be done."

"It shall!" cried Joss excitedly. "I have got a kind of partner who takes all the goods I bring him and keeps them snug enough. He is considered to be a respectable chemist, but that is only a blind. He has a back entrance to his house, and a lot of very convenient outbuildings. We can take his pony chaise and drive to our place in quick time. I am in with the butler, and we shall have no difficulty in entering the house."

Kelly was agreeable. The idea of the adventure pleased him greatly.

Salmon Roe had a presentiment that they had been through enough of late, and would have liked to retire to rest, but he never said a word. He was not quite so strong as his leader, but was afraid to aver that he was thoroughly dead beat and tired out.

They walked along at a rapid rate, and soon came upon a more salubrious neighbourhood, with rows of shops on one side and private houses on the other.

Joss pointed to a green lamp, and signified that they had arrived at their destination.

"I'm glad of it," said Salmon Roe. "I never did like walking. I'd sooner ride than trot on my legs any day."

They stopped before the door, the green light from the lamp casting a ghastly tinge upon their upturned faces.

Joss rang the night-bell, and then holloed through the tube.

The door was opened in a very short time by a tall thin man with red hair, whose face was white and death-like.

He appeared rather startled on seeing three men. He had evidently only expected one.

Joss observing that he looked uneasy hastened to explain that they were friends of his who had offered to assist him in his little undertaking.

Somewhat reassured by Joss's statement he allowed them to enter the house, and, leading them through the passage, took them to a stable in a back-yard, where they found a horse ready harnessed to a light trap.

"You see I am all ready for you," said the chemist with a sickly smile.

"Yes, I see that," said Joss, somewhat impatiently. "Are the tools in the cart?"

"Yes."

"You think that butler is to be trusted?"

"I am sure of that," replied the chemist. "You have nothing to fear. If we get a good haul this time I shall retire from the business. It is too dangerous to please me. Every time anyone enters my shop I look up and expect to see a policeman."

"Your nerves is in a bad state," replied Joss, as he climbed into the cart and seized the reins. "You have plenty of doctor's stuff about. Why don't you strengthen your nerves by taking a gorge of quinine every now and then?"

And, having delivered this elaborate pleasantry, he drove off with his two friends, all ducking down their heads to avoid the top beam of the stable door.

The yard gate was opened and they left the place noiselessly enough.

Before they had proceeded a hundred yards the rain began to pour down in torrents, soaking the men to the skin.

But they were inured to hardship, and took no notice of the heavy rain which beat down upon them, making it difficult to drive safely.

It was just the night a burglar would have chosen—dark and threatening, the lamps hardly having power to light up the streets even for a few yards round the lamp-posts.

Very few people were about at that hour, and the cart continued on its way, passing every now and then a policeman who had found shelter under some doorway.

But the police did not look upon the three men in the cart with suspicion, or, if they did so, were unwilling to leave the friendly shelter and venture out into the driving rain.

And therefore the three strange companions drove along unmolested until they reached their destination.

Salmon Roe was left with the vehicle, which had been driven on some rough building ground, and was sheltered a little from the inclemency of the weather by a newly-erected house and a high wall.

"Follow me," said Joss, laconically, and Kelly obeyed unquestioningly, never doubting the honesty of his friend, so far as he was concerned.

They cautiously made their way along a narrow lane, which was so dark that they had to advance with great care.

Joss had not exaggerated in describing the house he was about to rob as a mansion.

Not a light was to be seen in any of the numerous windows, and, after looking up and down the lane, Joss knocked at a side door.

They had not long to wait, for the door was opened almost immediately, and they found themselves standing in the grounds of the house.

"You are late," said the butler, who appeared to be in a great state of trepidation as he led them towards the house. "I have been waiting here so long that I had given you up."

"Better late than never," muttered Joss. "Is everything quiet?"

"As the grave," said the butler, with a shiver.

He was evidently a weak-minded man, and half repented of his compact with the burglar.

They were now inside the house, and Kelly looked about him curiously.

"What next?" he whispered, as they paused on the landing.

"We shall have to beard the lion in his den," observed Joss, with a grin. "The master of the house sleeps with the keys under his pillow."

"I'm game," said Kelly, coolly; and kicking off his boots he quietly opened the door of the richly-furnished apartment, in which an old man lay calmly sleeping, with a shaded lamp burning on the table near the bed.

Kelly advanced with extreme caution, and thrust his hand under the pillow, his fingers closing on the keys.

At this moment the sleeping man stirred uneasily, and in another moment he sat up in bed, staring at Kelly, with a wild look on his face.

"Curse you," hissed Kelly, and he struck the old man a heavy blow with the butt end of his pistol.

It descended with a terrible crashing noise, and all was silent in that chamber from that moment.

The wretched butler, who stood outside the door, shivered in his shoes.

The old man, though rather harsh in his way of speaking, was a very good master.

The bushranger felt not one atom of compunction. It was matter of indifference to him whether the man died or not.

All he cared about was the plunder, and this the treacherous servant soon indicated to them.

It was indeed a haul.

The old man—we may as well say that he did not die—was a great amateur in diamonds and precious stones generally.

He had a most splendid collection.

Next day all England rang with the news.

The mansion of the well-known millionaire, the great traveller and explorer, had been broken into, and his splendid collection stolen.

He himself had received a fearful blow from the butt end of a pistol, but it luckily had not any serious result.

The police had been called in, and were making enquiries in all directions.

Of course, with the usual result

Long before bills were printed, the missing articles were on the Continent.

There was also an account of a fire in a thieves' den in Whitechapel.

"Several persons perished, but the only noticeable part in connection with the wretched affair was that one of the survivors has set afloat the absurd *canard* that Ned Kelly, the Australian bushranger, was present.

"It says a good deal for the reputation of this unmitigated ruffian that even the assumption of his name should have led to such scenes as those described by our reporter."

The reading of the paragraph gave considerable satisfaction to Kelly, who felt himself tolerably safe.

CHAPTER LXIX.
NED MEETS HIS MATCH.

NEXT morning at breakfast-time Ned, elated with the grand success of his burglarious experiment, treated himself to an extra grilled kidney, with a bottle of champagne.

The landlady, Mrs. Daniel, had found out that though her lodgers were rather rough individuals they paid well, and to her that was the one great consideration.

She therefore determined to put up with their eccentricities so long as their money was forthcoming.

But Kelly was too well acquainted with the female character to risk anything.

He knew that if the scene of the other evening were too often repeated it would be talked about.

He therefore agreed with his companion that they should at home lead as quiet a life as possible.

Joss came about twelve o'clock to see them. He had disposed of all the plunder, and brought the results.

He was dressed as quietly as was consistent with his nature. He, however, was too cunning and cautious to do anything to attract attention.

"What would you like to do to-night?" he said, when he had settled down to a smoke and a drink.

"Don't know," answered Kelly. "What's slap?"

"Care about theatres?" asked Joss.

"Not much."

"Try Cremorne," suggested Joss.

Joss gave a fervid and rather eloquent description of the place, and it was agreed that they should go after a late and sumptuous dinner.

They then hired a vehicle and drove far away into the country.

To men of Ned Kelly's calibre quiet is almost impossible. They must be doing.

After the drive came the dinner. It was the best that to their ideas could be got for money.

After this the three started for the well-known gardens, then about in the height of their popularity.

We presume that few of our readers require to be told what Cremorne was like.

A nobleman's park and mansion had been turned into an hotel and gardens.

There was a large ball-room, open-air dancing places, refreshment bars.

The company was usually more numerous than select, though many persons were in the habit of going solely for the fun of the thing.

To Ned Kelly it was simply paradise.

Though his coarse nature was not susceptible of enjoying high-class music, he was sensual enough to appreciate the sort that was played at the gardens.

Joss led them to the high-class refreshment bar, and there induced Kelly to spend money.

This Kelly was quite ready to do. There was nothing the man liked so much as to be admired and talked about.

They then adjourned to the ball-room.

Here a difficulty arose. Except a rough kind of jig—such as is often danced in the diggings—Ned Kelly knew nothing about dancing.

Still he was one of that kind of men who never, under any circumstances, own themselves beaten.

"You dance, Parker?" said Joss.

"Yes," said the Red Bushranger, with the utmost coolness.

"Then allow me to introduce you to my friend Mrs. Cora Grant," resumed Joss, "one of the most charming widows in London."

Probably she was a widow, very likely she was not. It matters not to us.

She was very beautiful, of that subtle order of beauty which enslaves men so easily.

Dark, with violet-blue eyes—a dangerous colour be it known—petite, with a charming figure; she was also beautifully and elaborately dressed.

There was a look of innocence in her smile that was something terrible to see.

Such women it is who ruin families.

She accepted the invitation of Mr. Parker to join their party, with the greatest of pleasure.

"I am very much of a rough traveller," said Ned Kelly, as he walked round the large ball-room, "and not much up to dancing. I do not known even what that tune means."

"That is a waltz," replied the fascinating widow, with a seductive smile, "it is not very difficult."

Ned Kelly at that particular moment would have gone up in a balloon at the request of his angel.

But Cora Grant was an experienced lady. She knew the more vigorous sex well.

Herself a very clever dancer, it was not difficult for her to pull her partner through.

But she was also quite aware that to be seen dancing with such a man more than once would excite ridicule.

So she took him round the gardens, showed him all that was worth seeing, and made the time pass lightly and pleasantly.

Of course, during the evening, questions arose as to supper, which appears to be the end of all these festivals.

In those days, as a matter of fact, suppers were the aim and object of the owners of the place.

But it was not the aim and object of Cora Grant to sup there.

"I have a pretty little cottage in South Hampstead," she said, "and should be pleased to see you and your friends to supper. It is rather late to get it ready."

"We'll order it as we go along," replied Kelly, in his rough way. "I suppose money will do anything, even in this stupid old country?"

"Yes," she answered, with a great affectation of indignation. "What do you mean?"

"In my country the gentlemen always treat the ladies," answered Ned Kelly with a laugh.

And Mrs. Cora Grant condescended to accept the candid and easy explanation.

Ned Kelly, like very many other clever men, was easily led away by a woman.

About an hour before the closing of the gardens, a party of about nine started for South Hampstead, calling on their way at a celebrated hotel and restaurant, where a most extravagant supper was ordered.

The little house at Hampstead was of the usual style, glaring finery, but no real comfort, but quite good enough for the Red Bushranger.

Only from hearsay had he known anything of such places, he was used to the bush.

Now, wary and cunning as Ned Kelly was, he had on this occasion over-stepped the bounds of prudence.

He had drunk too much.

This may happen to any man, but let the evil-minded and wicked beware most.

Then is the old proverb realised, and the nature of the human being revealed in all its nakedness.

Ned Kelly, the dreaded bushranger, the man of many crimes, the assassin, and the thief, succumbed.

The supper was something wonderful. The Australian mad said no expense was to be spared.

The supper over, the whole party, now increased to over a dozen, began to play cards.

Here Kelly was as a rule at home.

Few men could beat him.

Whist was one of the games which required too much from him.

It demands highly superior faculties and memory, coolness, judgment of character, rapid calculation, and the strategy of combined movements.

Cora Grant placed them all at a table and herself sat behind Ned Kelly.

He was doubly intoxicated with drink and passion.

She looked over his cards. They were playing one of those games that depend perhaps more on luck than skill, but where sometimes a card, properly selected, may influence the game.

Kelly sipping his wine from the hand of his charmer, took her advice, and the money began to flow.

Ned Kelly did not care.

With the death of Rose the last manly relic of good feeling had died out.

Had that strange but eccentric girl have lived, he might like many another, have been saved by a woman.

Perhaps had the bushranger have noticed the way in which Joss played, after looking at Cora Grant, he might have been aware how he was being cheated.

But like Samson he was in the hand of a Delilah and and he succumbed.

At last Ned Kelly got rusty.

"I have lost twenty quid," he said, "and a little over; now come let us have a drink and a smoke."

And all present took the hint.

Ned Kelly was free and easy enough, but he did not like being cheated.

And he had a very strong conviction that he had got into a rather hot trap.

Green indeed is the man who thinks he can cope with London rogues and vagabonds.

We need go no further into the details of that specimen of London life.

Kelly felt the loss of his twenty "quid," as his funds had been much reduced owing to his reckless extravagance. He must soon replenish his purse somehow or other. So that he succeeded in accomplishing this object, the means were not matters of import; any method, "from pitch-and-toss to manslaughter," would suit him

CHAPTER LXX.

A LONDON HELL.

Joss knew the ins and outs of London, and Kelly wanted to be shown about. In the great city, which is really the capital of the world, not nearly one half the crimes that are daily committed are ever brought to light by the police.

Witness the multitude of people who inspect every corpse recovered from the Thames, to identify the bodies "found drowned."

We boast of our police and detective force, but they seem to be utterly powerless to stem the tide of crime.

Undiscovered murders are daily on the increase and every man in the community must shudder when he reflects how many miscreants are at large carrying their awful secrets in their heart, and haunted by the remembrance of their wickedness and fearful passions.

It is to be regretted that so many men who deserve to suffer on the scaffold for their hideous crimes should escape and breathe the air of liberty.

The sun shines on good and bad alike, and it is a wonder that these awful miscreants can walk about in the light of day, and talk and laugh, and eat and drink, as it they were no worse than other men.

While so many fiends in human shape are still loose upon the world we have no reason to pride ourselves on our police organisation.

We are heavily taxed, and the stolid policeman treads

the pavement with his thick clumped boots. He is generally a stupid individual, very often a mere boy, with no more intelligence in his head than a Dutch doll. He principally distinguishes himself by arresting drunken people, and never on any occasion except when obliged does he attack a desperate ruffian.

There are exceptions, but they all serve to prove the rule.

Our detectives are a very intelligent body of men, but recent events and disclosures present to us that they can be, and are often, bribed, and gold with them seems to cover a multitude of sins.

"I propose to take you to a gambling shop," said Joss to Kelly; "they are supposed to be shut up in this here moral city, but I can show you a place where lots of the stuff changes hands in a night."

"Go ahead," said Kelly, "let's have a go at 'em."

And so it was agreed that they should venture into the gambling house that night.

English people are very often too fond of holding up our country as the place which is most purely governed in the world. To hear them talk you would think that English prisons were empty, that men never kicked their wives and starved their children, and that the workhouse was a very comfortable place indeed, where you dined off roast beef every day and had a servant in livery to stand behind your chair.

You call Paris immoral, but let us look at home. We denounce the Russians as barbarians, but do not many horrible atrocities occur at our own doors? The Greek brigand is called a monster for cutting off the ears of his victim, but in a country where people throw vitriol and set fire to houses and burn people in their beds, in order to pocket the insurance money, it would be as well to hold our tongues, remembering the old adage.

There is more vice, more misery, more charity, and more wealth in the great city, than in any other capital in the world.

Kelly, with his usual keenness, saw that there was something to be picked up, and resolved to prolong his visit.

Joss and Salmon Roe took a cab to the West-end, and discharged the cabman in a quiet street.

Then, after proceeding at a rapid pace, they stopped before a house the windows of which were in complete darkness.

"Here we are," said Joss. "They have got padded shutters, which deaden the sound and hide the light."

"I should think the police must know of the existence of such a place," said Kelly.

"Perhaps they do and perhaps they don't," replied Joss, evasively. "Perhaps they find it worth their while to hold their tongues. The police are very obliging gentlemen if they find their interest to be identical with yours."

Kelly looked surprised.

He had always considered London to be a place where such things as large gambling houses would not be allowed for a moment, but he found out his mistake when he entered the hall of the gambling house, a spacious and well-lighted place, with a grand staircase, and handsome marble pillars.

"The place is supposed to be a club," whispered Joss, "but it is nothing of the kind; anyone can come here if they only have money."

Kelly made no answer, but followed Joss into a large salon crowded with excited men.

The bushranger looked about him with idle curiosity.

It was a mixed company, but there were few in that room who would not have started back in horror if they had known the name of the man who was quietly standing in their midst.

They were gambling, it is true; but the low and vulgar vices of the atrocious criminal Kelly would have made them avoid him like a pestilence. He knew this well enough, and a grim smile passed across his harsh face as he strode up to one of the tables and offered to take part in a game which was about to commence.

The men who were playing baccarat made no objection, and he took his place at the table.

Kelly won at first, and soon had a good pile of gold and notes before him, greatly to the satisfaction of his companions who stood looking on.

But at last luck changed, and Kelly began to lose as fast as he had won.

The game required no skill whatever, and the bushranger frowned as he saw his sovereigns swept away. He felt half inclined to draw his pistol and make a clearance, but he remembered where he was and prudently resisted the impulse.

There was a lantern-jawed, unwholesome-looking man at the table who seemed to be making a pile of money, and this individual attracted Kelly's attention. The bushranger gave him a keen glance and mentally set him down as a flat who had had a sudden run of luck.

The game played gave him no mental occupation, and he had, therefore, plenty of time to watch the man by his side, and to observe how his winnings increased.

The stranger was the only man there who did not appear to be the least excited by what was going on. He played calmly unconscious of the envious eyes fixed upon his lean face. His features never brightened, nor did he appear in any way moved by his wonderful good fortune. He seemed to take everything as a matter of course, and Kelly, fuming over his losses, could not help feeling amused at his behaviour.

He made up his mind that the fellow was an idiot, as he saw the dull eyes carelessly resting on the glittering gold before him.

"He is as innocent as a baby," thought the bushranger, and then turning to the stranger, he said aloud, "You seem to be in luck's way."

"I calculate I have made my pile," returned the Yankee, fixing his light, thin lashed eyes upon Kelly's face, and softly rubbing his bony hands together as he spoke.

"You don't seem, however, very pleased over your success," said Kelly, feeling puzzled.

"I came here to be amused," replied the Yankee. "It don't matter to me a red cent, if I lose or win. I only want to pass the time, and mean to give all I win to a charity. I win money from the bad and give it to the good."

"You don't keep a penny for yourself?"

"Oh, dear, no," replied the American stranger. "I don't touch a farthing of the money that I win; it is all for the poor."

Kelly looked at the man again, and a new light broke in upon him.

The man was not such a fool as he looked. There was more in him than met the eye.

He was doing the greenhorn for some purpose or other —that was what Kelly believed.

The man's luck now attracted universal attention, and everybody gave him threatening glances.

But the man was blind to the rage that was manifested on almost every face.

At last Kelly was compelled to give up the game. He had no more money in his pockets, and left the place with his friends.

"Cleared out?" said Salmon Roe.

"That there tallow-faced Yankee was a 'cute sort of chap, I should venture to say," remarked Joss. "Never saw such a run of luck in my life."

"You are right," said Kelly; "but before long he will not have a farthing left. I'll have all the money he has won, if I have to pot him for it."

"You can't do that in the London streets," said Joss. "You forget that you are not in the bush."

"I forget nothing," replied Kelly. "I have told you my intention, and mean to keep my word."

And he abruptly left his companions, and returned in the direction of the gambling-house.

He concealed himself in a doorway and waited. He was not kept long.

The successful gamester presently came out and walked away.

He took a keen look around, and then moved off rapidly towards the city.

The night was quiet, and the hour one at which few people were about.

Kelly glided after him until he entered a narrow street. The hour was late, and the street as silent as a grave-yard. Putting on a false nose, which he always carried for the purpose of disguise, he crept up stealthily to the Yankee, and, plunging his knee suddenly into his victor's back, proceeded to garrot him, exercising great strength and great brutality in carrying out his purpose. The wrench he administered was so powerful, and the pain inflicted so severe, that the man fainted, upon which Kelly robbed him of every shilling, and left him apparently lifeless on the pavement.

Kelly slipped away just in time to avoid being seen by a policeman.

He walked some distance, and then calling a cab was driven to the hotel.

Joss and Salmon Roe asked no questions, but when they read of the robbery in the papers they were what they called in a "blue funk."

Both began to think their comrade rather a dangerous character to associate with.

"Ain't pleased?" said Kelly, with a loud laugh, as he watched their countenances.

"Dangerous," replied Joss; "we'd better keep close for a day or two."

"Let's try Wapping," suggested Kelly.

But Joss would go nowhere until they had shifted their lodgings and changed their dress.

The robbery had excited much excitement in London and a large reward was offered.

"Better get back to the diggins," observed Salmon Roe in a growling tone, "you'll make it too hot for us here."

Kelly laughed, but he had no desire to affront his comrades, as they might prove dangerous.

They intimated to their landlady that in consequence of important news they had to start at once for America, and taking their belongings easily found quiet lodgings in the City-road.

All agreed to be very careful and do nothing to attract particular attention.

The mate, however, secretly determined to seek a ship, as he was afraid of the wild ruffianism of Kelly getting them into trouble.

But at all events he determined to stick to him while he could.

CHAPTER LXXI.
WAPPING.

THAT night the three friends started to the rough part of London frequented by seamen of all classes.

The two men Joss and Roe begged Kelly to be careful and to avoid exciting any undue attention, as there were many persons who would be looking for the robber of the Yankee gambler.

They went down to Thames-street in a cab and walked the rest of the way.

Their destination was one of those free-and-easy dancing houses where the returned sailor spends his hardly-earned wages in drink and debauchery.

Cooped up in a ship for perhaps many months, limited in his drink, and never seeing one of the other sex, it can scarcely be wondered at that the Jack Tar should, once he puts his foot on terra firma, launch out wildly.

The public-house they entered was a very low one.

Passing through the bar they entered a long low room, where to the sound of a scraping fiddle dancing was going on.

The trio were dressed in a half-and-half sea fancy dress, so that they looked like merchant captains in their best garb.

As all classes are in the habit of frequenting these cribs their appearance excited neither surprise nor astonishment.

They went to a table in a corner and at once ordered drink and tobacco.

The attendance was motley indeed. In addition to the English sailors present there were French, Italians, Lascars and others, while the feminine gender was represented by a very mixed collection of gaudily dressed females, who had a free run of the premises in consideration of their inducing "Jack ashore" to squander his wages in poisonous spirits and adulterated drinks of every description, which were so manufactured as to create the thirst they were purchased to slake.

Ned Kelly was in his glory.

He at once invited several to drink, and soon his table was crowded by guests as well as covered by bottles of drink.

Kelly as a rule was boisterous in his mirth and made very coarse jokes.

Both Joss and Roe were excessively nervous, as their comrade's loud talk attracted attention.

Besides, his allusions were so very colonial that any keen-witted man must have noticed them.

Fortunately the great majority were too much occupied with their own affairs to take much notice.

Suddenly, however, a man pushed through the crowd and sat down.

He was a queer-looking fellow, with a burly form and merry head and countenance.

"May I drink, boss?" he said, looking Ned Kelly full in the face.

"Fire away," replied the bushranger, recognising one of his own gang, Stingo Bill.

The man did not require second telling, but poured himself out a full glass.

Ned Kelly was luckily sober, or he might have done something rash in his temper.

As it was he was cool and collected, and, while the man was drinking, exchanged a meaning glance with his friends.

They knew at once that danger was in the wind.

Kelly now bustled about with the drink, and then sent a few shillings to the musicians with orders to strike up an extra lively tune.

Kelly then selected a partner. As he did so he made a sign to Roe, who followed him.

"Keep your eye on that fellow," he whispered to the other; "he's a sneak, and will betray us if he can."

"What will you do?" asked Roe.

"Be off as soon as I can," was the answer; "he don't know you, so get him in tow as soon as you can, and I will give him the slip."

Roe nodded his head, and Kelly joined the dancing mob.

Roe began talking to Stingo Bill, whom he at once attacked about Australia.

This was a subject on which the man was at once ready and willing to talk.

Still his eyes fixed on the bushranger.

"Seem interested in that feller," observed Salmon Roe, in a sneering tone.

"Yes," said the other, "know'd him in the diggins; his mug is worth money."

"Who is he?" asked Roe.

"That's tellings," was the man's answer.

And Roe at once knew that he intended to betray his old associate.

He looked around in search of Ned Kelly. He was nowhere to be seen.

Stingo Bill himself seemed engaged in the same keen examination, for suddenly missing the bushranger he darted for the door.

But Ned was nowhere to be seen.

With a loud imprecation Stingo rushed into the street, and finding a policeman told his story.

It was not believed, and only considered the yarn of a drunken sailor.

Meanwhile Ned Kelly had left the neighbourhood and gone to some other place of the same kind lower down the river.

He began to find that he had to pay the penalty of his notoriety.

Even in London he was known, and his presence could not be kept much longer concealed from the police.

Once it was believed in he would not be safe a moment.

That evening over supper a long consultation was held, and the trio came to a decided conclusion.

To leave England as soon as possible was the decision come to.

"We won't go direct to the Colony," said Kelly, who could be as cunning as he could be reckless, "but ship as A.B. on an Indiaman. We can then work back to the diggens."

His friends agreed with him, and next day they went straight off to the docks and made enquiries about a ship.

They were decently dressed, and, though their countenances were not very favourable to their behests, they seemed fit subjects, and all three were successful in obtaining places on board the Revolta East Indiaman, bound for Bombay.

She would sail in a fortnight.

For the present she was in the hands of the stevedores, and the actual seamen were not required.

Joss proposed a visit to the little house at South Hampstead.

Ned Kelly was quite willing, but he was determined not to be taken in again by Mrs. Cora Grant.

Meanwhile, the police, putting one thing and another together, began to believe that the notorious criminal was in England.

The loss of the Lenore, the audacious carrying off of the yacht, the murder of the agent, Mr. Lawson, were things which seemed to concide rather strangely.

Besides, Kelly was missed from his old haunts in Australia.

Still his presence in England was so stupendous a fact that few cared to believe it.

The colonial authorities had communicated to the British Government the fact of Kelly's absence from Australia, and their suspicions that the notorious outlaw was in the Old Country. The English police duly received this information.

Still, on the extreme quiet, the police set inquiries on foot, and it was lucky for Kelly and his associates that they had changed the venue and gone to live elsewhere.

But it could not last for ever.

The party at Mrs. Cora Grant's was always more numerous than select. Some of the most heavy swells in London went to honour the cottage with their presence.

Men with more money than wit.

Ned Kelly, even at his best, was not an agreeable or pleasant man. but he did all he could to conceal his shortcomings.

It is easy enough to play the part of the horny-handed son of toil who has been fortunate enough to make his mark and win money.

On this occasion Kelly was very careful at cards, and though he did not win much, was able to avoid losing.

"Do you know, Cora," observed a rather fast specimen of the press tribe, "that it is going about that Ned Kelly the Australian bushranger is actually in England?"

Not one of the trio moved a muscle.

"Indeed," replied Cora; "don't you think the idea very absurd and far-fetched?"

"Well," continued the pressman, "one never knows. He escaped from prison under wonderful circumstances, and has not been heard of in the colony ever since. Of course it is rather improbable, but one never knows."

The three men drank in every word, though all the time appearing to be wholly engaged in card-playing.

Kelly made up his mind that he would get out of England as soon as possible. He did not feel quite so safe as in the bush.

But he was careful to show no interest in the matter, though at supper he got into conversation with the literary gentleman, who thought him a fine specimen of the lucky gold-digging class.

It was late when the party adjourned, and the three men went home.

"We'd better look out," observed Salmon Roe to Ned Kelly; "the police are clearly on the lay."

"Yes, but before I've done with them," retorted the bushranger, sneeringly, "I will teach them a thing or two."

Joss and Roe exchanged glances,

They were terribly afraid of Kelly doing something rash and foolish which would bring them into serious trouble.

Next day, while seated at breakfast near an open window, Joss suddenly drew back.

"There goes Limber, the detective," he said; "he seems to be very intent on business. He's a dangerous character, and, if he is on our track, will find us."

"What's to be done?" asked Kelly, who had no desire to have anything to do with a first-class English detective if he could help it.

"Get out of this," replied Joss; "I tell you what, we'd better clear out and get in a poor quarter. This is likely to be hot enough to roast us."

"I leave it all to you, Joss," said Kelly; "but mind and be careful."

"Well the quarters what some folks calls is poor but honest," continued Joss; "brickeys and bargees—and that sort."

"Anything for a quiet life," drily replied Ned Kelly· "your Mr. Limber is not the sort of man for me to make acquaintance."

As Joss was personally known in London, he was the first to clear out of the apartments.

After all, the life of a criminal is but a hunted life—hardly worth living.

As soon as the three had made an appointment they went out, agreeing to meet in the evening.

Ned Kelly was very careful to avoid any places where suspicion might be aroused.

In the evening he started off to the rendezvous which Joss had made with him.

It was truly in a strange district where the poor rather than criminal class lived.

In such a human bee-hive as that selected by Joss, it was possible for them to hide.

It was quite a new life and a new experience of existence for Ned Kelly.

CHAPTER LXXII.
PRICE OF A WIFE.

THE White Elephant was a large old-fashioned public-house situated near the banks of a canal, and was frequented by bargees, and a very rough lot they were.

It was close to the towing path, and next door to the dirty-looking inn was a general shop which sold everything, from a pair of braces to an ounce of shag, and it was at this store the men laid in provisions for their journeys.

They were a sturdy lot were these bargees, ruddy-faced athletic men, as strong as lions, and very fond of showing off their strength.

The public-house was kept by a retired prize-fighter, whose nose was broken, and whose face was battered in such a hideous way that it was painful to look at him.

He was regarded as a wonderful man by his customers, and they worshipped him as a great hero.

Bargees are as a rule not a very select class, although there are among their number many decent fellows enough.

They are not much given to conversation, and as a rule only open their mouths to eat or drink or give vent to some blood-curdling oath.

Brant the boxer, the landlord of the White Elephant, was a middle-sized man with a broad chest and a width of shoulder which would have been ample for a man six feet two high.

He served at the counter with his shirt-sleeves tucked up to his shoulders and displayed a pair of arms which a blacksmith would have been proud of.

It was his delight to tell of his fights and adventures over again, and the buyers found great amusement in listening to him.

He had been a soldier, had served in the fore and aft regiment, and of course had much to talk about. His adventures were all the more remarkable, perhaps, because half of them were not exactly true. He invented them on the spot, and, having a ready wit, always managed to get up a hearty laugh.

Beer with a dash of gin in it was the favourite drink at this establishment, and the men seemed to thrive on it, for they were a robust set of fellows, and when they got drunk they slept themselves sober again, the only ill effect being a splitting headache.

Sometimes they would be in a playful humour and kick their wives and thrash their children; but, as a general rule, they liked to fight among themselves.

The reason we have been at such pains to describe this house and the landlord and the customers is, because Kelly is about to appear there.

He had made a solemn promise to Joss, who was beginning to get frightened that his recklessness would get them all into trouble, that he would be very careful in future, but he had made this promise so many times before that Joss felt very doubtful about his really keeping it.

The three men entered the place dressed in a very rough style, for had they been attired in better clothes than the other customers they would have instantly attracted too much attention, and would have been regarded with distrust.

As it was they did not attract much notice, for the men who were at the bar were listening to one of the landlord's everlasting yarns.

The place was unusually crowded on that evening, and loud shouts of laughter were heard on all sides.

As usual, the landlord's story was well received.

Kelly, having called for drinks, seated himself on a bench with his two companions, their drink standing before them on a barrel.

Joss felt pretty comfortable now. He could breathe more freely, for he thought it extremely unlikely that the police would track them to this house.

"It was the hardest fought round I ever had," said the landlord. "I felt that Jim Rogers was getting the better of me. I was that punished that I felt quite groggy, and my little holder advised me to throw up the sponge, but I did nothing of the kind. No man will ever get the better of me, not while I lives, I thought, and I rushed in, hitting out with all my might, for I felt kind of spiteful.

Yes, I hit out with all my force, catching Jim a litter in the face which broke his jaw. He fell to the ground covered with blood, and I was declared the winner. He goes about now with his mouth on one side, and speaks so indistinctly as you can hardly understand, and he actually bears malice agin me, when it was done in a fair stand-up fight."

Kelly and his friends liked the game for they joined in the laugh with the others, and Kelly pulling out a sovereign offered to stand drink all round.

None were too proud to accept the offer, and Kelly was as popular as a man could be.

It is extraordinary how a man is looked up to among a certain class, if he only stands treat freely in a public-house.

The landlord was not left out, and related many more tales; the one that gave the most amusement was that of a native who for treachery to the English had been blown to pieces at the cannon's mouth.

Kelly's liberality increased as the drink went round, and he ended by making everyone in the place tolerably intoxicated, landlord and all.

Then the landlord got quarrelsome and wanted to fight, as he always did when he was in liquor, but the bargees treated it all as a joke, for they did not like the risk of an encounter him.

"Ain't one of you got pluck enough to come forward and have a round," cried the landlord presently. "are you all a set of curs and cowards?"

No one responded, but Kelly's eyes flashed and he would have rushed upon the man had it not been for Salmon Roe, who begged him to come away and be quiet.

Brant caught sight of his enraged face, and coming forward asked Kelly if he was a man, and had pluck enough to have a fight with him, just, you know, to see which is the best man.

Kelly made no reply, but with a growl like a wild beast seized the landlord round the waist and lifting him on high hurled him out of the open window with such force that he lay upon the flags almost stunned. True, the window was not very high as it was on the ground floor.

When he entered his house again there was a subdued look on his countenance, and he did not offer to have another friendly round with Kelly.

He had met his match for the first time in his life, and stared in wonder at the man who had so easily beaten him.

(To be continued.)

NED KELLY
THE
IRONCLAD
AUSTRALIAN BUSHRANGER

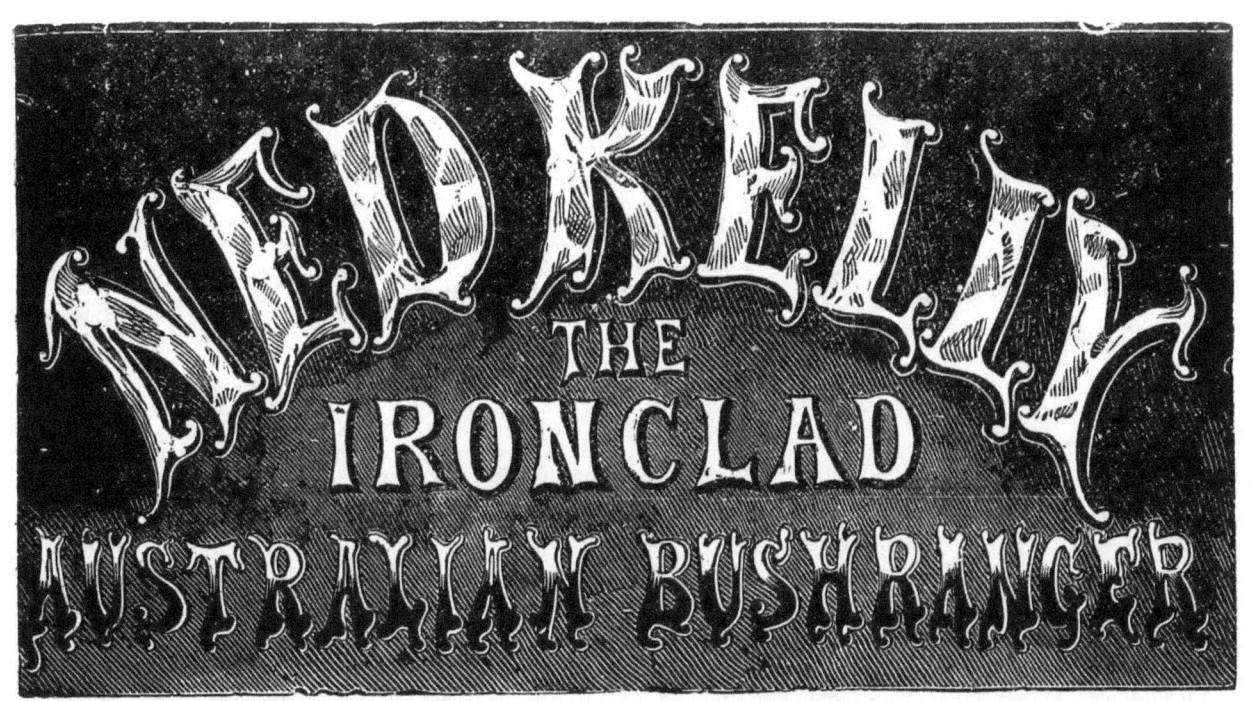

NO 10,

"You are the first man that ever served me in that way," he said, as he wiped his face. "I didn't seem to have no chance with you at all."

The bargees were delighted with Kelly's feat of strength, and crowded round to shake hands with and congratulate.

At this moment a very poorly clad woman entered the public-house looking about her timidly. She was a healthy, handsome young person with a fine complexion and a bright pair of eyes. Her figure was very well proportioned.

Kelly eyed her with sudden admiration. She was just the sort of woman he liked.

"Hulloa, here's Bill's wife," they all cried, "she's come to fetch her old man," and she was offered drink, which she refused.

"Bill," said the woman, pleadingly addressing one of the men who was more intoxicated than any of the others, "do come home, I am sure you have had quite enough to do you good. Don't waste all your money."

"Go away," cried Bill. "I don't want you to come after me. Get back, or it will be the worse for you if you do not obey me."

But the woman still begged of him to leave the drunken crew and come home.

"Get home," cried the man, clenching his fist. "Get home, or I will strike thee."

The woman hesitated, but, glancing up in his face, she saw that he meant to keep his word, and so she left him with a deep sigh.

"I wish I could get rid of her," muttered the man to Kelly. "I'd sell her for half a sovereign, and think it a good riddance."

"Do you really mean that?" said Kelly, looking at the man in a strange sort of way.

"I do," said the drunken bargee, with a stupid look. "Why should you doubt me, mate?"

"I will give you a sovereign for her," said Kelly, who could hardly believe that the man was in earnest, for the idea of selling one's wife seemed such a strange one to him. He had never heard of the sale of such "cattle" in Australia; perhaps because "wives" were not so plentiful in the market as in England.

"Hand over the money and she is yours," said the man. "I tell you afore you give me the money that she is a bad bargain."

"That's my look-out," replied Kelly; and so the money changed hands.

Soon after this Kelly, Salmon Roe, Joss, and Bill, and two bargees left the public-house.

Kelly left his companions on board a barge, promising to be with them presently, and went with Bill to fetch his recently-acquired property.

The man was very intoxicated, and staggered from side to side, Kelly having great difficulty to help him along.

At last they reached a small cottage, and after flinging open the door he staggered into the room, Kelly following him.

The woman was seated in a corner, and rose and thanked Kelly for taking the trouble to bring her husband home.

"He has comed to fetch you," said the drunken bargee, with a vulgar leer; "I have sold you for half-a-sovereign, and you are his property—he is your new lord and master."

"Don't be stupid, Bill," said the woman, smiling at what she considered a mere joke.

"A bargain's a bargain," replied Bill doggedly, "and you now belong to him."

"You see that your husband is tired of you," said Kelly, with an ugly smile; "I have more money than he, and will make you very happy."

And he put his arm round her waist, Bill having, in the meantime, fallen asleep.

"Release me!" cried the woman, and exerting all her strength she gave Kelly a push and ran away from him—disgusted.

Kelly recovered himself in a moment and rushed after her in a furious passion.

She entered another room and, slamming the door, double-locked it against him.

Kelly put his broad shoulders against it, and burst the door open to find the room empty.

She had climbed out of the window, which was not very far from the ground. Kelly was after her in a moment, and lifting her in his arms, carried her along, taking the precaution to place his hand on her mouth.

She struggled and kicked but all in vain. She was a strong and powerful woman, but Kelly only laughed when she tried to escape.

The place was totally deserted, and Kelly had no fear of being molested as he walked along the towing path.

He soon reached the barge where he had left Salmon Roe and Joss. They were greatly surprised when they saw him with the woman.

Everyone laughed when he related what had happened to him—buying a wife.

Then more drink was consumed, and the woman looked on in fear and trembling. She knew very well that her husband was intoxicated and would regret what he had done when he woke up sober, but that did not make her position any the better.

It was night now, and Kelly walked up to the woman and seized her by the wrist.

"What are you going to do with me?" asked the woman in her abject terror.

"You are my wife now, so come along," said the brutal ruffian, dragging her along by the hair of the head in his rage, for she had dared to resist him, which with Kelly was unpardonable.

"Never!" cried the woman, and rage giving her strength, she struck Kelly with her fist.

With a savage oath the ruffian lifted the woman in his arms, and, mad with rage and disappointment, hurled her over the side of the barge; and the next moment she was struggling in the water.

No one in the barge offered to give her any assistance. Had they wished it they would not have been able for they were too intoxicated.

Kelly looked on at the drowning woman with a cruel smile as she glanced up at him imploringly. But Kelly did not notice, and stood there with folded arms.

At this moment a dark figure came rushing along the towing-path.

It was Bill, who had woke up and remembered that he had sold his wife.

Regretting that he had done such a foolish thing, he was now in search of her, half mad with fear that something awful had happened.

Kelly recognised him at once, and uttered an exclamation of surprise when he saw the man, without a moment's hesitation, plunge in to the rescue of his wife.

He was always at home in the water, and was soon by his wife's side, and, being an expert swimmer, brought her to the bank. Then shaking himself like a dog, he menaced Kelly with his fist, and Kelly only returned a shout of defiance.

The man would have rushed upon Kelly, but his wife, fearing for his safety, persuaded him to go away, and the man took her advice, feeling very much ashamed of himself for the way he had acted, and vowing that he would never again take too much drink as long as he lived.

After a good sleep Kelly and his friends left the barge. The Red Bushranger had again found his match in the person of a bargee.

CHAPTER LXXIII.

THE DERBY DAY. THE "WELCHER" DODGE.

As a matter of course, after the events recorded in the last chapter, Ned Kelly moved out of that neighbourhood.

He resolved to be more careful for the future, and not do anything to excite marked notice or attention

It was the end of May, and England was at its brightest.

The great racing carnival of the year approached nearer and nearer every hour.

It was not likely that Ned Kelly would miss seeing the Derby, as he happened to be in England. He had heard so much about it that he felt curious to see the sport, and had arranged to go down in a wagonette with Joss and Salmon Roe and a few men he had picked up God knows how.

The wagonette was punctually waiting at the Spotted Dog in the Strand, at the appointed time, and Kelly, who had made up his mind to enjoy himself, was seated beside the driver.

Everything being ready the wagonette started and soon joined the crowd of vehicles all going in one direction.

Kelly gave a sinister smile as he reflected that he was running a great risk. He was riding through the streets of London in the broad daylight after perpetrating so many hideous crimes.

The man was perfectly reckless, and the thought of the risk he was running gave him unalloyed satisfaction. It added to the luxury of the hour.

He did not really know what fear meant, and, having no conscience, felt as happy and light-hearted as any one of the thousands who were going to the Derby.

Kelly had not forgotten his crimes, but they did not interfere with his selfish enjoyment.

The day was a hot one, and the dust blew in heavy, choking clouds.

The road to Epsom has been so often described by so many able pens we have no desire to go over the beaten track, and will simply say that they arrived safely at the race-course.

They took up a position not far from the grand stand.

Ned Kelly was, as a matter of course, fond of the good things of this life, and had taken care to bring down a large hamper full of eatables and drinkables.

He had an Australian appetite, and could always do justice to a good meal.

The party laughed and talked, and ate and drank, and enjoyed themselves to the utmost.

The bushranger was an inveterate gambler, and although he did not understand horse-racing, determined to have something on the race.

He was guided by chance, and selected a horse haphazard, not caring much whether he won or lost.

His friends thought him a fool for risking so much when he knew so little of horse-racing, but they wisely held their tongues, and did not express their opinion, except by slily winking at each other.

There was one false start, and then the horses dashed away, everyone craning their necks.

It was a very good race.

Ned felt his blood run furiously hot through his veins as he watched the horses, which came towards him like the wind.

The jockey in the orange jacket was in front. He was riding the favourite.

A crowd of horses all together came behind so close that it was impossible to tell who was the second.

There was a confused Babel of shouts.

"The favourite! the favourite!" was roared by a thousand voices. "The favourite has won!"

It was an awful and cruel moment for many of the spectators. How many hearts beat with hope that must be dashed to the ground! How many men looked on with haggard faces, panting for breath, their hearts beating wildly and painfully—dishonour, ruin, and death stared them in the face! It was a moment of agony for many, almost equal to the tortures of hell.

On came the favourite.

The crowd of horses behind began to thin out, and come along in a thin line.

It looked as if the favourite had it all her own way, but at this supreme moment a rank outsider driven skilfully came up to the scratch, coming up with the foremost horse hand over hand.

The excitement was intense.

The noise died away and the people looked on as if turned to stone.

"Scarlet wins," cried Kelly, "the horse I backed has won."

And he was right. He had won by a fluke. He had won by luck and went and got the money.

He was returning to his friends in a very jubilant frame of mind when he was surrounded by a crowd of men.

One of the "dodges" of the blacklegs and blackguards who frequent race-courses is rather a remarkable one and not generally known. These ruffians watch some unknown repectable or disreputable party who wins from the bookmakers who swarm in the ring. When the lucky individual gets his money he is immediately spotted by the sharks who surround him, and, shouting "A welcher! a welcher!" proceed to hustle and otherwise attack the astonished stranger, who immediately becomes an object of hatred and contempt to the sympathising crowd, who join the pack that seems ready to tear the unfortunate man limb from limb. The noise and shouting effectually drown the frightened wretch's remonstrances, and in the end he finds himself bruised, and stripped of his money and perhaps his coat and hat into the bargain. His watch most certainly is *non est*. Under the welching accusation which finds universal credence he becomes the typical dog on the race-course, and every hand is against him. Lucky if he escapes with sound limbs. Kelly was singled out by the fraternity, who had seen him win a pot of money, and nearly came to grief.

"A welcher! a welcher!" they cried, and stones were hurled at the astonished Kelly, and he was struck with sticks.

His first impulse was to draw a pistol and shoot among the crowd, but he was not a fool, far from it. No, he would only fire when obliged; he had no desire to be arrested at that moment, so he resolved to run for it, and took to his heels followed by the mob.

"A welcher! a welcher!" they cried, following close on his heels, and throwing all kinds of missiles after him.

Kelly was a good runner, and bounded along at the top of his speed.

He rather enjoyed the chase than otherwise. On, on he flew, never once looking behind him at the mob, which yelled and howled, panting for his blood.

Ned soon came near a police-station, and a good-tempered policeman standing at the door beckoned him. Kelly was surprised, thinking that he must have guessed his identity, but he did not hesitate and rushed up to the policeman.

"Get inside, you'll be safe there," said the policeman.

Kelly, without a word, obeyed, and the door being shut was indeed perfectly safe. The crowd outside gave two or three spiteful kicks, and soon went away.

"You was chased on account of being a welcher?" said the policeman, "but I dont blame you at all. If fools will part with their money, serve them right."

"I am nothing of the kind," said Kelly. "I came down with a party of friends, and was attacked for nothing."

"You all say that," said the fat policeman with a chuckle; and two or three other policemen present, seeing the joke, laughed too.

Soon after Kelly left the police-station, but not without giving the fat policeman half-a-crown for himself.

When outside he burst into a loud laugh.

"If those men knew that there was ten thousand pounds offered for my apprehension," he muttered, "wouldn't they be mad for letting me through their fingers!"

He returned to his friends, who could not understand where he had got to, and explained what had happened.

It was now time to think of returning home, and they all climbed into the wagonette, noisy, rollicking, and flushed with drink—a well-matched company, with all their faults, follies, and crimes.

Indeed, it would have been difficult to find a more ruffianly set of blackguards.

They were all innately coarse and low, and even people with low notions of morality and probity must have shuddered to see their brutal faces, seared with evil passions and unrestrained indulgence in all the wild excesses which made up their daily life, and rendering the shortcomings and delinquencies of ordinary trifles light as air in comparison.

Kelly was in high spirits, an sing ribald songs as they rode through the gathering dusk, the air sweet with perfume, and the stars twinkling in the pale blue sky.

Surely such an evening might have suggested solemn thoughts even in the minds of the most hardened offenders ; but Kelly sang on untroubled by the still small voice of conscience.

He was utterly depraved—a disgrace to the human species.

His almost herculean proportions loomed up against the clear sky, and his companions looked at him with the admiration which brute courage and brute strength almost invariably create in the vulgar mind.

Kelly was worthless, base ; but in the eyes of his boon companions he was a hero.

It was seldom indeed that he was in such a sociable mood, and they were delighted to find him so complaisant.

His songs were applauded to the echo as he drove along, not unmoved by the flattery—men of his culture seldom are—and his stentorian voice once more rung out in some rude ditty, more lively than select.

The driver, who had been well primed, lashed up his horses, making them dash forward at their utmost speed, but Kelly sung on, unheeding the warning even of many a well-intentioned pedestrian who paused to look after the swaying vehicle in surprise and dismay.

"Hullo !" exclaimed the bushranger, "where the deuce are you going ? Stop, I say !"

More easily said than done. The horses had their bits between their teeth and were tearing along the hard road at break-neck speed.

"Good Lord !" ejaculated Joss, "there is safe to be a spill. Confound it, you fool ! can't you stop 'em ?"

The driver made no reply. All his attention was centred on his horses ; and perhaps in that moment of peril even Kelly remembered his million vices.

It is hard to say. Who can judge such a man or understand the secret workings of his heart ?

On dashed the horses, now thoroughly beyond control, and the driver tried in vain to pull them in.

"Sit still, as you value your lives !" he cried ; and Kelly and his companions obeyed.

The bushranger writhed on the tenter-hooks of his own imagination, and felt the crash before it came.

He knew that this wild ride must end in a spill, and trembled for the safety of his own precious neck.

When they arrived at the foot of the hill there was a loud crash and one of the front wheels coming off, everyone was flung out.

They all had a severe shaking and a few bruises ; but the only one who was really injured was Joss, who lay on a pile of stones, stunned and bleeding.

The others had been pitched on to the grass which grew on the side of the road.

It was to be regretted that Kelly had not been killed. The world would have been well rid of such a scoundrel.

But the ruffian seemed to bear a charmed life.

"Is he dead ?" asked Kelly coolly.

"Not quite," replied Salmon Roe, who was bending over him.

Kelly drew out a flask containing brandy and put it to his lips ; but the man could not be resuscitated.

"Let's take him to a doctor, poor devil," said Salmon Roe.

"Don't let's bother about him, but leave him here," said Kelly heartlessly ; "we can't trouble ourselves about him."

"No," said Salmon Roe ; "he's our pal, and I don't mean to leave him here to die if I can help it. There is a village at no great distance."

"You're getting precious soft-hearted all at once," said Kelly, sneeringly. "I don't think it's much use taking him to a doctor. We had better take him to an undertaker's shop and get him a suit of timber, he looks as if he'll want one soon. He'll be dead before an hour."

And having delivered himself of this brutal and unfeeling jest Kelly subsided into sulky silence.

They bore the injured man along the lane, Kelly leading the way and holding the wagonette lamp in his hand.

The village was soon reached, and a crowd of people came round them to see what was the matter. It was explained to them in as few words as possible, and inquired of the villagers where the nearest doctor was to be found.

"That's the doctor's" said a man, pointing to a handsome house with a carriage-drive.

The doctor was at home and saw to the man at once.

He was not so bad as Kelly had thought, and under the skilful treatment of the doctor soon came to his senses and stared wildly round the room.

"Where am I ?" he said, and then glancing at the doctor he gave him a look of recognition.

The doctor looked at him with a puzzled expression on his face ; he evidently remembered seeing Joss before. In fact he had reason to remember, for that gentleman had committed a burglary in his house, and had struck him down and left him for dead.

"Villain !" cried the doctor. "You are the man who tried to murder me. I will send for the police and give you into custody."

And he went towards the bell with the intention of ringing it.

But Kelly laid a detaining hand upon his arm.

"You must be mistaken, my dear sir," he said. "That man whom you accuse of such an awful crime is a pal of mine, and I'll swear would be incapable of hurting a child."

"If he is a friend of yours, I am sorry to see you in such company," said the doctor drily.

"It is a case of mistaken identity."

"If it is a case of mistaken identity, it can be easily proved," said the doctor, and he would have rung the bell.

But Kelly hit him behind the ear with all his might, and the doctor fell without a groan.

"Come away," said Kelly, "while there is yet time."

Joss still felt weak, exhausted, and ill, but he managed to follow Kelly and Salmon Roe out of the room, and noiselessly opening the front door, they walked softly down the carriage drive.

"A narrow escape," he remarked, when they arrived at the nearest railway station. "A very narrow squeak, indeed."

They took the first train back to London, and arrived there without further adventures by the way.

CHAPTER LXXIV.

COUNT ANATOLE RICHE.

WE need hardly say that when men live in the reckless and spendthrift way that was adopted by Ned Kelly and his associates, that money maketh to itself wings.

They began to find it necessary to pull in their horns.

They were not exactly impoverished, but had to look to their purses.

One evening Ned Kelly paid a visit to a well-known restaurant and billiard-room in the neighbourhood of Leicester-square.

His friends had gone off on the spree to an East-end theatre.

Ned Kelly played with tolerable luck, but the betting was slow and he lost interest.

Several times he had heard a sepulchral voice give him a hint during the game.

It was like a shadow whisper.

"No, zat is not ze game—just a little higher—and you pocket—ze ball—fools' game—give me ze cannons."

Ned never moved a muscle. He knew the man whoever he might be, was right.

His advice was admirable.

"No, *mon ami*, not ze pocket zis have—ze cannon first, and you vins."

And Ned Kelly did win.

After the game was over he turned and looked at his mysterious adviser.

Short, podgy, with a thin cadaverous face, hollow cheeks, one might read in his countenance recklessness and crime.

He bore the unmistakeable signs of having been a gentleman.

It is said that even sin and shame cannot extinguish the last relic of birth.

Just as no amount of money or tasty culture can turn the low-born into the mere semblance of high birth.

Of course it comes in course of time, but it requires a generation or two to effect the change.

Lord Chesterfield said it required three generations to make a gentleman.

The Frenchman was shabbily dressed, but he wore his clothes with a grace that was wonderful.

"My good fellow," said Ned Kelly, "I really thank you—you are a dabster at the game."

"I no comprehend vat you say," answered the other; "but I know vot you mean. I can play."

"Then why not play?" asked Kelly.

The Frenchman gave one of those inimitable shrugs of the shoulders which few but subjects of his country could copy.

"Ze *argent*, ze money," he said.

"Well, I owe you one," retorted Kelly. "Will you feed and drink?"

"Vid plaisir," answered the other.

And they at once removed to a *cabinet particulier*, as the Gallic stranger called it, a private room as we designate it.

"Such accommodation is getting more common than people believe in London.

Ned Kelly had a vague idea that every Frenchman was a professed cook.

He acted accordingly.

"Order what grub you like," he said, "and drink—only I want drink—whisky."

The Frenchman's face was a study.

He had been literally starving for nearly two days, a crust or two excepted.

He had spent money in the Reredo, and of course was admitted.

But genuine food and he had been strangers for some time.

It was almost a ghoul-like glance he gave at the waiter as he ordered the supper.

It was what Kelly called "gollopsious."

Even the rude bushranger recognised the superiority of the Gaul.

He had never tasted such supper before.

"Down on your luck, mounseer?" he said, when the supper was cleared away, and they were smoking and drinking punch.

"D—— low," was the response of the Frenchman; "and you no believe me Count Anatole Riche, of von of ze—von of ze biggest *familles* in France."

"Oh," said Ned Kelly, slightly taken aback, "a real count?"

"I inherit von big *fortune*," the man went on; "I go ze pace as you say. I go at last to Homburg, and I lose all —every Napoleon I have. I come to *Londres*, but my *mauvaise fortune* come vid me. I am ruin."

"Sorry for you," said Kelly. "A few weeks ago I was flush, and could have helped you; now money is getting low. I should like to earn some."

"*Hein!*" cried the Frenchman, "we are alone. If you see von safe there full of ze gold and ze *argent*, you no turn your—vat you call it—back to it."

"Count," said Kelly, "I'll trust you. I'm game for anything to make money."

"Zen you is my man—ze chap I look for ze long time," said the Frenchman. "I tell you zometing you not know."

"Fire away, mounseer," replied Kelly. "I say frankly, I'm game to cut a throat or blow up Buckingham Palace, if there is money to be made by it."

"*Saperlote!*" cried the Frenchman, in a tone of inimitable affected surprise.

"Yes—we I've heard is the word you use," replied Kelly. "I'm ready."

It is not essential to our purpose to tell the whole story of what Count Anatole Riche proposed. It is sufficient that Kelly assented.

But it is necessary the reader should know what the count exactly proposed and which was righteously carried out.

At this time Homburg, near Frankfort-on-the-Maine, was celebrated as possessing, in addition to unrivalled scenery, a Kursaal or gambling-house, or, rather, fairy palace, surpassing any monarch's residence

The rooms in which rouge-et-noir and roulette daily (Sunday included) took place were immense, lofty, and decorated as highly as the most lavish expenditure and highest art could suggest.

The beholder, on entering these halls of Eblis, was struck dumb with astonishment at the magnificence that surrounded him, and which he was entitled to enjoy—gratis.

The gold room, thirty feet high and one hundred and fifty feet in length, was imperial in luxury and more gorgeous than Eastern magnificence can depict.

Curtains of ruby velvet, edged with rich gold lace, terminating in heavy and immense bullion tassels, draped the numerous and immense windows.

The ceiling contained scenes from the amorous poets, representing myriads of goddesses and Cupids floating in azure fleecy clouds—the said goddesses and Cupids clothed —or rather unclothed—in a manner suitable to the atmosphere they appeared to revel in.

The halls, sheeted with glass and panelled in pink with gold frames, and crystal de roche chandeliers studding the room, and shining in the day like rippling water, and at night like millions of diamonds.

Soft music, proceeding from the Austrian band (composed of the first musicians in the world) ravished the ears, which promenaders, generally fancifully but beautifully attired (for *La Toilette* reigned supreme in this Arabian Nights' palace), both inside and outside the rooms, enjoyed to their hearts' content.

The silver room, where la roulette was played, was equally splendid in its appointments, and the stakes permitted were from two shillings to the maximum of £320.

When the bank lost to one player £8,000 it was closed for that day.

The orange and other rooms were simply all that unbounded wealth and the highest art could make them.

The grounds were like all we hear of Paradise—serpent, woman, and everything else to lead poor man to his fall.

These charms, less the serpent and his female friend, were *à discretion*, as the bread is at French restaurants.

The rooms were crowded day and night by foreigners of distinction, by cads from English counties, and *calicos* from French ones.

Swindlers from every nation—the oppressed Poles in particular—swarmed.

Pickpockets were as plentiful as blackberries, and a little murder or two often diversified *les distractions* and *ennui*, occasioned by an empty purse and pressing claims.

For instance, a fortunate player goes out for a stroll in the adjoining woods. While contemplating the beauties of nature somebody else is quietly contemplating him, and is cautiously stealing upon him, much as a panther creeps upon the unsuspecting antelope.

A sudden blow on the back of the head from a heavy life-preserver—a fall—a silence—and the player has lost his last stake—his life.

8

His assassin hastily plunges his hand in the dead man's pockets, which are rifled of their contents, and the whole affair kept a profound secret by the Administration, as if it it transpired the *scandale* would be prejudicial to the tables, and to the Principality of Hesse Homburg, which drew an enormous revenue from the tables.

Another favourite way of replenishing the purse was to "stalk" a winner in the aforesaid woods, pot him through the head, and leave a pistol in his hand or just within reach of it on the ground, suggesting that deceased had committed suicide.

When Kelly went home that night he took Count Anatole Riche with him.

His companions were rather surprised to be introduced to a "furriner," but they were well aware that Kelly always had a motive for what he did.

They thought they knew a thing or two about cards, but the Frenchman astonished them.

It was agreed that they should travel comparatively as strangers.

Next day Count Anatole Riche went to a swell West-end tailor, and rigged out in first rate style.

It was arranged beforehand that he was to be the big-wig of the party, the others to play the part of rough but honest citizens.

That evening they went to the opera, the most novel sensation in which Kelly had ever indulged.

Next day they started for Homburg.

No one who has not been on the Continent can realise, even in the faintest form, the beauty of those places of resort.

They are now suppressed by the Prussians, and the passion for public fair and open gambling has relegated itself to private (plundering) circles.

Hundreds of men and women, too, who have succumbed to the attractions of what are popularly called hells—casinos in polite parlance—have been drawn into the net by their captivating beauty.

The house itself was a wonder, but the gardens were simply unique.

Well might an enthusiast have cried with the poet Moore—

"*Oh, if there be an Elysium on earth, it is this! it is this!*"

Nothing, perhaps, was ever done more correctly to imitate Paradise than was done to make grounds at Homburg, Wiesbaden, and Baden attractive.

As a matter of course, everything eatable and drinkable was of the most exquisite quality.

"*Jamais!*" said the Frenchman, as he introduced his friend, "have you *regardez a jardin* like diss?"

"It's pretty jam," observed Joss, who was one of those men who never appear astonished. "I likes Cremorne better."

"*Ze barbare,*" exclaimed the count, holding up his hands.

Of course our Englishmen knew nothing of the games played at the tables of Homburg.

The first evening, therefore, in accordance with the advice of the count, they simply sauntered about, staked a trifle, and looked on.

Then they retired to their hotel, and after supper went into the full details of their nefarious plot.

Let no one fancy we are romancing. What we are about to relate is positive fact, well known to everyone who has frequented any of the great gambling shops on the Continent.

Of course, to Ned Kelly and his rough associates the place appeared fairyland.

The count took his boon companions out for a drive next day.

Above all things he wanted to steady their nerves, and was careful about drink.

"Ze *champagne* and ze grog is de *diable* if you want to do von little bit of business," he said; and, then grinning, he went on, "I see von day a *piece*—a farce you call him—cool as ven cucumber. Dat is vot ve be——"

"Who taught you English?" suddenly asked Kelly.

The Frenchman—scoundrel, gambler, robber, thief—turned pale and shivered.

"No ask me zat qvestion again," he growled. "My sisters Engleesh governess. She dead now—jamais! I von't be asked qvestions."

All guessed his meaning, and the subject was never alluded to again.

It was seven o'clock in the evening when they started for the gambling-house.

Sooth to say, Homburg was the favourite resort of those rich foreigners who were and were not bitten by the insane mania for gambling.

Kelly and his comrades felt awed almost when they entered the room.

The bushranger had been careful to save money enough to keep up appearances.

The room in which roulette was played was brilliantly illuminated by gas.

Some eight croupiers sat at as many different stations to pay out and rake up the money.

It happened that at that time a man had been very lucky.

He had broken the bank.

People crowded in to see him.

Breaking the bank is a very simple process. The owners of the casino will never go beyond eight thousand pounds.

When that sum is lost the head croupier cries—"*La banque est fermée!*" and proceeds to cover it over with a green cloth.

This had happened that afternoon.

Ned Kelly and his companions sat down on one side of the table.

Next to Ned Kelly was a lady of rather talkative disposition.

She was American.

"That's the big boss," she said, pointing to the other side of the table, "who's broke the bank three times."

Kelly looked, and saw before him the man he thought he had killed in London streets.

He shivered all over, but made no sign.

In these places there are four rooms—orange and blue the golden, the other the silver.

Our adventurers had selected, as a matter of course, the golden room.

Bullion and bank-notes were scattered in rich profusion on the table—coin enough to tempt a saint.

Count Anatole Riche played with care, but he was watching the table all the time.

The entire stranger was winning at a great rate.

But to return to the plan of the Frenchman's campaign.

The rooms, brilliantly lighted with gas, were always crowded with company.

The bank was always at the centre of one of the long sides of a parallelogram-shaped table—a mammoth dining-table in fact. This bank was administered by a "pay-master."

Behind him, perched on a high stool, sat a *chef de parti*, watching the paymaster and overlooking the whole table, *croupiers* and all, and on each side of the said paymaster sat an assistant croupier to rake in lost and pay out won money.

On the opposite side to the *chef de parti* sat another *chef* doing exactly the same thing, and flanked by similar assistants.

Every employé was watching every other employé. The bank contained a large amount of money always exposed, in gold or bank-notes, ready for distribution amongst the winners.

This money was the prize the Frenchman proposed that he, Kelly, and his band should bag, and on this wise—

They were to assemble in the rooms on a given night, one of the gang was to be placed at each gas-lamp, and, at a given signal, the whole were to be simultaneously extinguished, and the contents of the bank grabbed and pocketed. Kelly stood sentinel behind one *chef de parti* and the Frenchman over the other.

Joss was to be seized with a violent fit of sneezing as the signal for operations.

All were at their posts. Ruffians and hardened villains as they were, the moment was a trying one; something like that felt on the battle-field before the first shot is discharged to open the battle.

Their hearts beat, and their hands trembled a little.

Kelly was like steel; no nerve, no heart, no conscience. Born bad, he kept bad; he was morally *dead*. He stood firm as a rock, awaiting, with stern determination and nonchalance, the supreme moment.

The table was fully occupied, the players eager, the money piled up beside the bank, when Joss's violent sneeze resounded through the room.

In a moment the lights were out, the room in utter darkness, and dismay amongst those present as if another Belshazzar's Feast had been interrupted by handwriting on the wall.

Women cried out, men swore, petty robberies were committed and pockets picked, but the great haul was accomplished. The bank was robbed of £5,000 and the robbers got off easily in the dark.

When lights were re-introduced and the gas turned on, blank surprise, coupled with consternation, sat on every countenance.

The croupiers and officials looked dazed, while the impecunious lot of semi-scoundrels, titled or plebeian, rejoiced that someone had done the bank.

Old Blanc, the proprietor, simply smiled, ejaculating, in reply to the violent commiseration of his visitors—

" *Doucement, doucement, mes amis. ça se remettra bientot, ce n'est rien; allez, continuez, amusez vous; mais il faut changer le gaz contre l'huile.*"

And this was the reason why oil-lamps for the future illumined the Homburg rooms.

The coin had vanished, and so had a good many of the habitués.

Fortunately for Kelly and his friends, a good many others took advantage of the darkness to take their departure richer than they came.

As soon as the *coup* was over the conspirators went quietly away to the hotel.

They were five thousand pounds richer for their little game, but Kelly was not satisfied.

" Count," he said, " I know a thing or two."

" Vat is von ?" asked the Frenchman.

" That infernal Yankee has sized his pile pretty big," was the answer. " I think we might relieve him."

" *Ma foi!*" remarked the Frenchman, " I fancy zat he have too much money."

" Well, we'll put an end to that," answered Ned Kelly " He lodges in this hotel."

" *Cre-Nom!*" cried Count Anatole Riche, using his favourite exclamation.

When the waiter came in to take orders after supper they found that the American gambler was a certain Elijah Buccles, celebrated for his luck.

He was said to have won seven thousand pounds.

Probably, like a good many other speculators of this kind, he kept it among his luggage.

If so Kelly and party determined to have it.

CHAPTER LXXV.

THE ROBBERY AND ITS RESULT.

FORTUNATELY for Kelly and his party no one suspected them. Count Anatole Riche was so perfect a gentleman that all looked up to him.

His English friends were rough and ready, but so highly respectable.

There were a good many *chevaliers d'industrie* about, but though the police watched them carefully none of them appeared more than usually flush of cash.

So the thing blew over.

Meanwhile the French count and his comrades kept very quiet. They looked in at the saloon soon after it was opened, and risked small sums of money.

Nothing was done to excite suspicion.

Kelly was no less reckless than usual, but he submitted to be guided by the more wily and cautious Frenchman.

The American continued with varying success, sometimes making great hauls, and at others losing small sums.

Whenever he stayed there was great excitement. People crowded round to watch.

Late in the evening of the next day the man began with a run of luck.

He had broken the bank in several establishments, and was regarded somewhat with dread.

His luck was singular.

It was clear he was in vein. The colour on which he staked turned up continually.

The excitement was great.

At last, as before, the croupier declared play over, and a green-baize cloth was thrown over the table.

He had broken the bank.

" You are lucky, Mr. Buccles," said Ned Kelly as they went out together.

" Well, pretty fair," was the calm reply. " I generally am."

" You are staying at the same hotel with us," continued Kelly.

" Yes," answered the American, who spoke with scarcely any nasal intonation.

" Shall we shuffle the cards to-night ?" continued the bushranger.

" Don't care if I do," replied the stranger. " You'll sup with me first."

This was agreed on, and a supper was served such as is only to be found in such places.

Everything was of the best.

Expense was no object, and all was delicate and delicious in the extreme.

They supped in Elijah B.'s rooms.

Then cards, with cigar, spirits, and wine were produced. All were keen, shrewd players.

Kelly and the Frenchman played against Buccles and Salmon Roe.

There was no thought of unfair play. With such hands it would have been folly.

Kelly soon found himself losing money and equally his temper.

At last he threw down the cards.

" One might as well try and play against Old Nick," he said, half laughing.

Elijah laughed, as he rose and put his money away in his desk.

After drinks all round they parted.

Kelly was sullen and moody.

" Seems hard," he muttered, " for that fellow to have all the swag."

" It is," said Salmon Roe.

All exchanged glances. There was a murderous look in their eyes which all understood.

The man's winnings were principally in notes, for convenience of carriage.

" I'll do it," said Kelly.

A long conference ensued.

Kelly would take all upon himself. He would commit the robbery and fly.

In his portmanteau was a favourite disguise of his. I included a false nose and whiskers, which entirely change the appearance of his face.

All the others went to their rooms, locking themselves in.

Kelly opened his portmanteau and took from it a bunch of keys.

He had noticed that the room preceding the bed-room of the American was unprovided with bolts, but had a stout lock and key.

When all was still he went out in his stocking-feet. In his hand he carried the keys, while he was provided with a knife and some chloroform.

He soon unlocked the door, which, however, he again secured before he entered the bed-room.

The door of that was unlocked.

He listened with intense interest and attention. The man breathed heavily.

Kelly had a handkerchief over his nose and mouth.

With a sponge saturated with chloroform he applied it to the man's nose.

The desk was now rummaged, and the contents secured. It was a considerable sum.

Kelly now went out, and locking the door after him took away the key.

There was a train at daybreak, and by this Kelly would go.

The difficulty was to get out of the house; there was a night-porter in the hall.

Carrying his bag in his hand, he crept down the thickly-carpeted stairs.

The porter slept soundly in an armchair, Kelly had his boots off.

Stealthily and warily he approached, opened the door, and in a few minutes was in the street.

He was dressed like an ordinary tourist, only his nose, whiskers, and wig so utterly disguised him, no man could have recognised him.

It was broad daylight, and the station was open, so that he excited no attention.

Half-an-hour later he was whirling along in an express train, with nothing to identify him by.

Even his carpet-bag was taken from inside a portmanteau, while he had secured a second passport.

In this way he reached London.

His companions were to join him by various and devious routes.

Their plan was then to visit America, where they could spend their money without exciting any suspicion.

On reaching London, Kelly, as Mr. Desmond, went to a quiet hotel.

The robbery made a great stir, and one day Kelly heard it said that the police had a clue to the thief, who they believed had gone to London.

He at once decamped, procured a fresh disguise, and went to a sailors' boarding-house.

Here he was in his element.

But his usual luck here deserted him. The second evening of his arrival, when under the influence of drink, he showed a lot of notes.

That night his room was entered by four men. He was stupidly drunk, and they made a clean sweep of all save a few pounds and notes in a pocket-book under his pillow.

The rascals, doubtless, were astonished at the amount of their haul.

They were no more seen in that part of the world.

The rage and mortification of Kelly may be more easily imagined than described.

Of course, to state the facts would have been madness.

His comrades who, except the count, all duly joined him, could scarcely credit the news. Their crime had been done for nothing.

Still, they had plenty of money, and for several weeks led a roaring life; and then, finding funds running low, again looked out for a ship and easily found one.

CHAPTER LXXVI.

AGAIN AT SEA.

At last the time came when they were to join their ship.

To Kelly it was a matter of rejoicing.

He had had quite enough of England by this time, and would only feel too glad to be on the high seas once more.

His scheme was to get to India and thus put the limbs of the law off his track.

As soon as he got to Bombay or Calcutta he would lie quiet for a short time, and then make his way again to Australia, where at all events he knew what to do for a living.

The vessel they had found berths on board was the Earl Russell East Indiaman.

She was a fine large sailing vessel, roomy and well provided.

Her crew was numerous and as usual of a mixed order, good, bad, and indifferent.

Some of them were excellent sailors and trustworthy men.

The cargo was of great value.

The three men joined in the docks the day the Earl Russell dropped into the Thames.

The passengers were numerous, and as usual with vessels of her calibre, of high character, officers and civilians, ladies and gentlemen.

Some were returning to their posts, others going out for the first time.

There is a mighty amount of confusion at first starting on board ship, but soon all settles down into regularity.

The three men easily contrived to be in the same watch. They could thus keep together, and enjoy the amusement of conversation.

One evening— they had been about a week or more— Kelly—the men seated around in the bows, the sky clear and the wind fair—told them some rattling adventures in the gold fields.

"Shouldn't I like," said one of the men, "to go and pick up the chips."

"It's fine," retorted Kelly. "Better than working," he added, with a grin.

"Why did you leave it?" asked the other, a fellow known as Sandy Sam.

"'Cos I had made a lot," continued Kelly, "so came to England to spend it. Mean to go back some time."

"I should like to try it," the sailor remarked with something of a sigh.

"We could run away with the ship, sell her, and then make for Australia," observed Kelly, with a bantering laugh.

Several men looked at him with something of surprise in the expression of their countenances.

"It's not wise talking mutiny," said one, drily.

"Only joking, mate," laughed Kelly.

"It's bad joking," the other continued.

Kelly made no response. He was satisfied. He had laid the train.

Time would show if it would come to anything.

The three men had determined, if they could get adherents enough, to mutiny and seize the ship. There were many places where they could run in and sell the cargo.

Piracy is not quite so extinct as many people imagine and many vessels never heard of are captured and destroyed by these pests of the ocean.

They lurk about certain obscure islands, and hide in places almost unknown to ordinary cruisers.

Meantime, all went merry as a marriage-bell in the cabin.

There was the usual flirtation, card-playing, and amusement. People become intimate under such circumstances who, perhaps, are fated never to meet again.

There were several young ladies, but the belle of the whole party was a Miss Liston.

She was about eighteen, and all the young men were in ecstasies about her.

Among her most devoted admirers was Captain Frank Armstrong, with good connections and a fine position.

Miss Liston was going out to join an aunt, she herself having lost her parents at an early age.

She was under the chaperonage of a Mrs. Colonel Warden, who, however, was not very severe in her style of government.

So that the young lady behaved with propriety she had no wish to interfere.

So before the voyage was a third over, it became clear Captain Frank Armstrong would be the winner.

On one or two occasions when Kelly was at the wheel—he was not at all a bad sailor—he had seen the beauty, and admired her in his coarse way.

That evening he again broached the subject of running away with the ship.

He, Joss, and Roe had sounded a good many men and found them not at all unwilling to join in

During his campaign on board while beating up for recruits, one of the sailors confided to him the plot, and he had it from the third mate, that there was a quantity of dynamite on board which was labelled "hardware" and not declared or entered at the Custom House when shipped, which rendered the captain and owners liable to a heavy fine. As he heard the news Kelly's eyes brightened with a fiendish glare. Here was a chance of sending the whole "boiling" as he styled it "up in a balloon" whenever he chose it. He induced the man to show him where it was stored. This was easily done, as the casks of "hardware" were piled just close to the foot of the mainmast and covered with a tarpaulin. All right, thought Kelly, who determined to murder every "human," as the Yankees say, if necessary, lower a boat well provisioned, place a good fuse in the "hardware," and haul off to safe distance and wait for the blow-up of ship and cargo.

Satisfied at this safe conclusion to the enterprise, he became not only contented in mind, but positively jocund.

Like a man who had made a grand and successful "coup" in the Stock Exchange, he felt a placid content and feeling of certainty.

But they had to use great caution and discretion, as some of the men were good and true—right loyal British sailors, who would not be tempted to commit any act of treachery and murder.

Still incited by the cunning ringleaders, a very powerful body was recruited.

The men who could not be induced even to listen to such a proposition, would have to be secured and put out of the way.

The mutiny must take place at night, when the passengers would be asleep.

Even if the cargo was not available, the goods belonging to the passengers would be something, while they were well aware that there was a good assignment of bullion on board.

It was determined by those in the scheme to wait until they were in the neighbourhood of some islands, said by Salmon Roe to be much frequented by Malay and other pirates.

They have every requisite for enjoyment, as it is understood by sailors.

Dutchmen from Batavia have houses there supplied with luxuries. They make enormous fortunes.

Salmon Roe made Ned Kelly's mouth water with the description of these islands.

At last the time approached.

Ned, as a matter of course, was to be the ringleader and give the signal.

The crew were not very far from forty in number, and twenty were in the swim.

A fearful crime was being as coolly concocted as any ordinary business arrangement.

It was evening.

A splendid night, and the passengers were chiefly on deck—all who were not playing cards.

The man at the wheel was a steady-going fellow, and well up to his work.

Suddenly there came a darkness on the sky to the south and east, and the captain became aware that a cyclone was about to attack them.

All hands were at once called to shorten sail, as the signs of a storm increased every moment.

Everything was bustle and confusion for a moment, and then all were ready.

The captain stood, trumpet in hand, on the quarter-deck, ready to give orders.

Before he could speak the blast was upon them.

It shook the vessel all over, and she went down almost on her beam ends.

"Let go everything," was the cry.

The sailors swarmed up the rigging as the orders were obeyed.

Halyards and all other ropes necessary to the fulfilment of this order were let go.

The sailors who were ordered to go aloft ran up as swiftly as possible to furl the sails, and were intent on their duty.

Mutineers or not they valued their own lives.

Almost everything was snug and taut when suddenly there was a great cry—

"Man overboard!"

On board a ship there is no more horrible cry than this.

The passengers and crew were as it were paralysed.

Then young Captain Armstrong threw off his coat, heeled off his boots and leaped into the sea.

The head of the sailor who was overboard was just above the water.

Captain Frank Armstrong made for him, shouting aloud all the time—which was scarcely audible—and caught hold of him by the hair just as he was sinking.

He held him off, aware how dangerous it was to allow a drowning man to clutch you.

The sea surged awfully high. The young officer scarcely hoped to live through it.

Still he held on the man.

Then came the welcome sound of a boat being dropped into the water.

Then the young officer was dragged into the long-boat with the half-drowned sailor.

It was a heroic act, but little did Captain Armstrong guess the result it would have.

The two were soon on deck, and the sailor being much worse than the captain, was attended to first, in the cabin by the surgeon.

"Narrow escape, my lads," said the surgeon, when the seaman, a good-looking scapegrace of nineteen, "very sharp squeak."

"Who saved me?" asked Jack Mathers, in a sharp, hurried tone

The young officer was pointed out.

"Sir," was the reply, "may I ask as a favour to speak to you and the captain alone? I have a terrible secret to reveal."

All thought the youth mad, but his wish was gratified at once.

He looked carefully around.

"Nobody can ever hear?" he asked.

"No," answered the captain, rather harshly.

"To-night at twelve, sir, there will be a mutiny," he whispered, "twenty of the men are in it and Ned Kelly is the leader, so you know what you have to expect."

The two men were unable to speak.

"It is true, sir, continued the young man very earnestly, "I am one of the mutineers, and would never have spoken had not this gentleman here have acted as he has. I was led into it, sir, from no wish of mine."

"Boy," said the captain, "you shall be rewarded not punished; but really you must be mistaken—Ned Kelly is in Australia."

"No, sir, there are several who know him by sight," was the answer.

"That will do," continued the captain in a firm tone; "the fact of the mutiny is enough. Now, Captain Frank, get all the passengers ready. Can I trust you?" to the half-drowned sailor, whose name was Jack Palmer.

"Sir," was the astonished reply, "did not that gentleman save my life?"

"Yes, at the peril of his own," responded the captain earnestly, "it was a brave deed."

"It was a very lucky one for him and you sir," continued the man, who was tolerably fairly educated.

"How so?" asked the captain.

"It will save all your lives, I believe," responded Jack, "the men mean to mutiny to-night at twelve—you know what will follow."

"Great heavens!" cried the captain, "are they all in it?"

"No, sir, about twenty are in it; I am lost. I swear I was over-persuaded, threatened like ——," he went on.

"How to get at the men who are not in it?" said the captain, turning to the cavalry officer.

"Sir," put in Jack Palmer. earnestly, "that I am alive is thanks to this gentleman. I will risk my life freely to save you—let me go aft and I will speak to the boatswain. He will speak to the men, whose names I will give him, or you can send for him here."

"All right my lad," replied the captain, "you shall go scot-free."

And he passed the word for boatswain and carpenter to come aft.

Of course this excited no suspicion.

Jack Palmer fully explained matters to the boatswain, and gave him the names of all the good men and true.

This was rather a hard nut to crack, but somehow Jack was able to impress their names and characteristics on the minds of the boatswain and carpenter.

The mutiny was to take place at eight bells, when the watch was changed.

The mutineers were as a rule, only armed with knives, and few only with pistols.

They depended wholly on a surprise.

This matter settled, the boatswain and carpenter returned forward.

The captain now contrived to summon all the male passengers under some pretence or other, and let them know what they had to expect.

It was settled that the ladies should receive a hint that some of the crew were inclined to be rebellious, and be advised to retire to their state rooms at eleven.

The men would then arm themselves and be ready for immediate action.

The loyal crew would come aft and be armed to resist the others.

Meanwhile the wind continued.

The vessel even under bare poles was managed with difficulty.

There were two men at the wheel, and two spare men waiting to relieve them.

The captain scarcely ever left the deck. Dinner was was very nearly a farce.

It was not only the storm that affected everybody, but the anticipation of what was to come.

A long discussion ensued between the captain and some of the passengers as to the best course of action.

Some were in favour of letting the mutineers know that their intention was known.

But the majority thought it wise to give them a strong and wholesome lesson.

And this opinion prevailed.

After dinner the usual routine went on. There were card-tables set and music.

At eleven the ladies retired, and the gentlemen crowded round the table with grog and cigars. Not a word was said in reference to the expected raid on the captain.

At half-past eleven the lights were all extinguished except in the steward's cabin.

All were armed with either pistols or guns of some kind or other.

A good lookout was kept.

Then eight bells was sounded.

All were ready, and then the loyal part of the crew made a rush aft and were at once handed arms.

"Death to the mutineers!" was the cry which met the ears of Ned Kelly and his followers as they made a rush for the cabin.

A deadly volley repelled them.

"Sold!" shouted Ned Kelly, with a fearful imprecation. "Somebody shall suffer."

"Who can it be?" asked Salmon Roe, who was severely wounded in the left arm.

"That confounded young shark, Jack Palmer," hissed the bushranger; "but I'll settle him."

Meanwhile, all had fallen back to the forecastle to consult.

The surprise had been a failure.

What was to be done? The passengers, with the loyal crew, were nearly as many in number as the mutineers, well-armed and provisioned.

It was indeed a terrible sell.

"What's to be done?" asked Salmon Roe, while the others growled in an inaudible tone.

Luckily for them, Ned, Roe, and Joss were armed with pistols of the very best make.

They carried a good many lives in their hands.

"Don't know," surlily cried Ned.

At this moment one of the sailors from the other end advanced with a white handkerchief on the end of a cane.

"Now then, messmates," he cried, "a word with you all—don't be foolish."

"What do you want?" asked one of the mutineers. "Speak up at once, Jim."

"The captain offers these here terms," the man went on, "free pardon and no questions asked—if you give up the ringleaders."

"What of them?" the other asked.

"They will be given up at the first port and tried for mutiny and piracy," was the answer.

"Come back in ten minutes," answered the man, "and then you'll get an answer."

The man retreated.

Ned, Roe, and Joss had heard all, and stood aloof with their pistols ready.

Give up they would not. They would slaughter right and left rather.

When the man who had been spokesman approached, they waved him back.

"Lower a boat and set us adrift," said Kelly, "with what grub you can find and some water, then make your own terms."

The storm was abating rapidly, and the men thought that perhaps this would be the best plan.

There was a boat outside the bows.

Food and water could not easily be obtained without the connivance of the steward, so the amount was rather small.

Still, a certain amount of biscuit and some tin bottles with water were put in the boat.

The night was still very dark, and the sea ran high.

But Ned was determined not to be handed over to the officers of the law.

Somehow he might be recognised.

The boat once lowered, the three men had their belongings lowered into it.

They had some small useful boxes, and in these were certain luxuries not usually to be found in the impedimenta of a sailor.

These chiefly consisted of bottles of spirits.

Just as the boat was ready to start, the man with the handkerchief returned.

"Have you decided?" asked the man.

"Yes; we throw ourselves on the mercy of the captain," was the answer; "the others have taken to a boat and escaped."

He approached the emissary of the officers, and explained that the three ringleaders were armed heavily with pistols and other weapons, and that they were afraid to attempt their capture.

"Return to your duty," said the captain; "they cannot hope to live in such a night."

And the men returned to their duty.

CHAPTER LXXVII

ON THE WIDE WATERS.

THE three men who launched themselves, as it were, in a cockle boat, at the mercy of the waves, must, of course, have been desperate.

To Ned Kelly and Salmon Roe it was not so much; they were used to the sea.

But to Joss it was intolerable.

He was a very poor seaman at the best, and in such weather it was awful and terrible.

"I wish I'd never seen the sea," he groaned, as they pitched and tossed on the top of the waves. "We shall all be drownded."

"Not if we're born to be hanged," said Ned Kelly. with grim prophetic humour.

Joss made no reply, but sank his head between his knees and groaned.

It was not a pleasant position.

The boat was both for sailing and rowing, but at present all they could do was to ship the mast and bide their time.

The wind had expended its force. Clearly they had only had the tail of the cyclone.

But the waves were very high.

Presently, however, Salmon Roe intimated that it would be better to hoist a sail.

This was done, and the boat did not pitch and toss nearly so much.

The night soon passed.

But not one of the men in that boat had the least idea of where they were, or what would be their fate.

They might be cast away among savages, or picked up by a passing ship or drowned.

But the weather moderated still more towards morning.

Then the heat of the sun became intense and they were compelled to quench their thirst.

But their supply of water was very short, and they knew that on this their life depended.

They blended it with some spirits and thus allayed one of the most painful wants of nature.

Ned and Roe had to take it in turns to steer, as Joss was of no use in that way.

They were in a decided fix. If they were picked up by a ship, their story would be a difficult one to tell.

After considerable hesitation, they determined to tell a part of the truth should the vessel be outward bound.

They would assert that the Russell had foundered, Earl and that some of the crew and passengers had taken to the boats.

They had cast loose the one in which they were at first, thrown in their luggage and had only just time to push off, when the vessel went down.

About an hour later, Joss and Roe being asleep, Ned Kelly sighted a sail.

It was that of a tall ship and was coming directly in their path.

He woke them up, and all three at once indulged in the luxury of a drink of water.

Then they kept a sharp lookout on the approaching ship, They all knew that their story would appear fishy, but they could not help themselves.

At all events they would secret their pistols and bottles of spirits.

On came the ship, it seemed to them with singular slowness, but they kept direct across its bows, and a little after mid-day were sighted.

As a matter of course they were taken on board, and their story listened to.

They were also admitted as supernumeraries with the crew.

"Roberts," said Captain Hammus to his first officer, "I don't like the look of those fellows. Odd lot—very."

"Well, sir," replied the other, "I am very much of your opinion. I will keep my eye on them."

But the three men were very wary. They took care to do nothing to excite suspicion.

They were very free in their talk about ordinary matters, but very reticent as to their antecedents.

The vessel, the Prince Albert, on board which they were was bound for Calcutta.

This was awkward, as their own vessel was the same.

They must contrive to get on shore as soon as possible after their arrival, as, if the captain who had saved them once learned that their own vessel was safe, explanations must follow.

They were all of them tolerably flush of money, so that they cared nothing for their pay.

At last the time came when they were in sight of Calcutta, which, as everyone knows, is situated on the Hooghly a branch of the Ganges, about a hundred miles from the sea.

From a small fishing village it has in about a century, under British sway, grown into one of the greatest and most flourishing cities in the world.

The minute the vessel cast anchor, Salmon Roe went aft and spoke to the second officer.

"We want to go ashore," he said, gruffly.

"When there is leisure," was the answer.

"We ain't signed no articles," replied Salmon Roe, "and don't want no pay. Stop us, if you dare."

The second officer shrugged his shoulders, called them idle skulkers, and bade them to a very warm region, but not to bother him.

The men were in mortal fear, for not a hundred yards off they had recognised the vessel from which they had deserted.

There was too much bustle and excitement for them to be noticed, so they got a boat and went on shore without drawing much attention.

Salmon Roe was an old salt, and had been in Calcutta before.

He no sooner was on terra firma than, handing their packages to the native porters, he bade them lead on.

He at once avoided the English town, which consists of houses built of brick in a handsome style, and covered with white plaster which takes a fine polish, and made for the black town, on the borders of which the sailors' boarding-houses were situated.

Ned Kelly and Joss had perforce to trust to Salmon Roe. They knew nothing whatever of the place.

Every temptation that a sailor can dream of teems in Calcutta, and the three soon found themselves enjoying themselves thoroughly.

But all three were well aware that there would be considerable talk about them, and that they would be looked for.

The best thing they could do would be to find a ship and get back to Europe as fast as they could.

But man proposes, and Providence disposes.

That night the temptations of the so-called boarding-house kept them up late.

The place was crowded with men belonging to ships in the harbour, amusing themselves as best they might— dancing, smoking, and drinking.

Suddenly Salmon Roe gave a great start as he saw several sailors come in at the door.

They were men belonging to the crew of the Earl Russell Indiaman from which they had escaped.

He made a sign to his companions, and led the way into the interior of the place.

They all understood that the better part of valour was discretion.

If recognised, there would be very little hope of their escaping scot free.

There had been so many ships missing under suspicious circumstances that they would, if caught, be certainly made an example of.

They procured sleeping quarters and retired to rest

Next day they would try and contrive some way o getting out of Calcutta, if they shipped in a coaster.

There seemed to be no safety for them there.

In the morning, after a meal, they took care to close quarters.

Salmon Roe having made some alterations in his apparel, knowing the town was then sent out to try his luck.

He went to the quarter where the shipping agents were to be found, and visited several.

But no ship was to sail for several days.

Now what they wanted was to get out of Calcutta as rapidly as possible.

At any moment they might fall in with the officers and crew of the Earl Russell.

But nothing could be done.

Salmon Roe thought he would go out and consult with his friends before deciding anything.

He stuck his hands into his pockets and set out on his return journey.

Suddenly he jostled against a man of powerful frame and of tall figure.

He wore a semi-Oriental, semi-European costume, but, though swarthy, he was no native.

"Zeph!" cried Salmon Roe in amazement.

"Sal!" was the other's cry.

"Yes; what are you doing here?" was the first speaker's demand.

"Let us go where we can be private," responded the other.

And he led the way to one of the many refreshment places provided for the thirst.

"In the name of wonder," asked Zeph, when they were provided with their favourite stimulants, "what brought you to Calcutta?"

"A ship," replied Salmon.

"Of course, but we parted in London, and you were bound for the gold diggins," said the other.

He was a huge, herculean man, evidently of the seafaring persuasion.

"Well, I didn't like it," growled Sal; "too much hard work for me, so I cut it, and you——"

"We'l, you know," said Zeph, "I was some years in Madagas:ar, and speak that and many other lingoes. I went out there, joined a fellow who called himself an Arab prince—pirate he was—and became his first officer. To cut a long story short, we quarrelled, I had my party and he is, and he and his party went by the board. I am up here recruiting."

"Where's the vessel?" asked Salmon.

"She's hid away safe enough," answered Zeph. "But what I want is real good fellows, these Arabs ain't much use. I want men who will side up to a gold-ship and cry, Stand!"

"I'm one," said Salmon, "and I've got two other prime ones quite ready."

"That's your sort," observed Zeph; "but there must be no nonsense about them. I've got a native vessel close handy—a dhow they call it—and pretty spicy crew. Four more would make things look ship-shape."

"We're ready," said Salmon. "When do you sail?"

"To-morrow, if I have my complement," returned the her.

"We'll ship," returned Salmon. "Where are you hanging out?"

"Grogan's, in the Black Town," answered Captain Zeph, as he was called.

"So are we," exclaimed Sal; "dine with me and my pals?"

"Done," said Zeph.

And a rendezvous was appointed for the afternoon, where in the cooler part of the day men could venture to allay the pangs of hunger.

They then separated.

Among the many islands inhabited by Orientals of various heads, pirates have existed from time immemorial.

They are sometimes designated by the name of slavers, but in reality they are sea-thieves.

They are gradually being extirpated, since swift, small, steam cruisers are able to hunt them up, but many mysterious disappearances can only be accounted for in this way.

By open violence or cunning they surprise ships and leave no clue to their foul deeds.

About the time of which we speak, several underwriters were convinced that many of the missing vessels they had to pay for were the victims of foul play.

On the voyage home from India the vessel had passed near so many uncivilised and savage places, where small vessels could be perdue, that it was not easy to obtain a clue.

When Salmon Roe informed his companions of the singular adventure he had, they were delighted. It was just the thing for them.

The greater part of the visitors to the place they resided at, were sailors belonging to the ships in harbour.

A great many did not live there, and for money they could be as private as they liked.

Ned ordered a dinner regardless of expense. He intended to impress Captain Zeph as well as he could.

He was just the sort of man after his own heart he expected.

Certainly in addition to his Herculean proportions, Captain Zeph had the quality of ugliness to a most marvellous extent.

Coarse features, huge sandy whiskers, a nose flattened to his face, and little piggish eyes, did not make an attractive-looking man.

But there was an affectation of frankness about his manner which with some would pass for blunt honesty.

(To be continued.)

NED KELLY THE IRONCLAD AUSTRALIAN BUSHRANGER

NO 11,

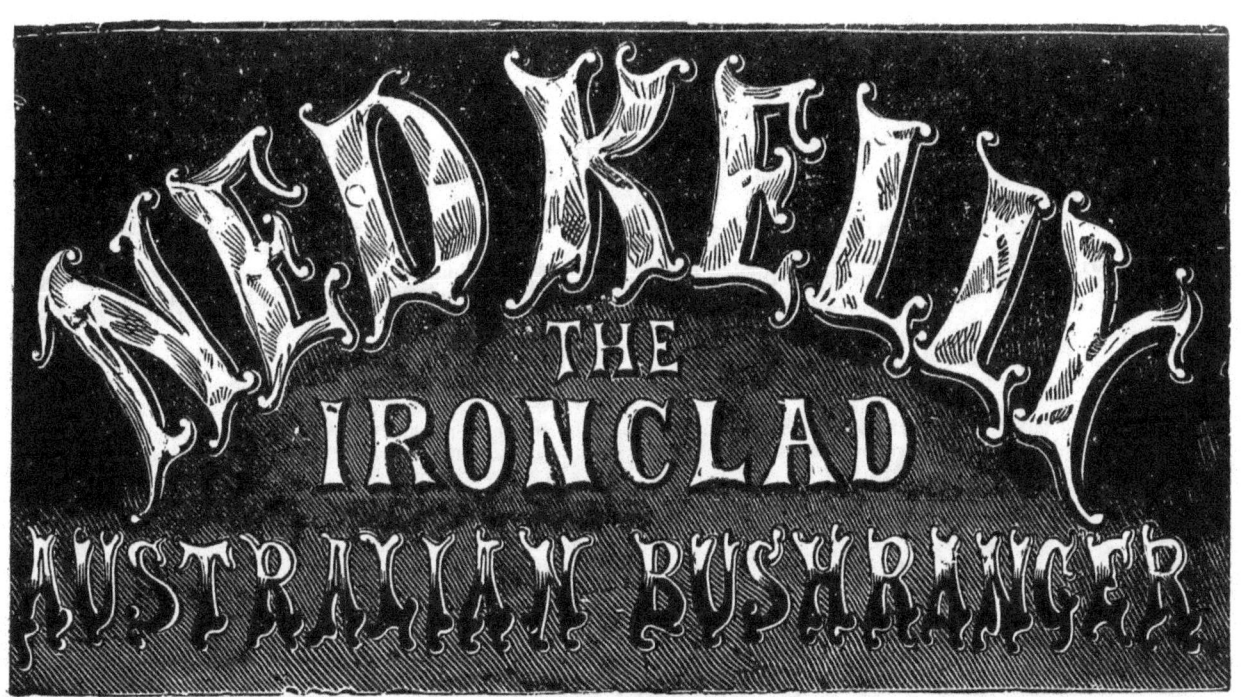

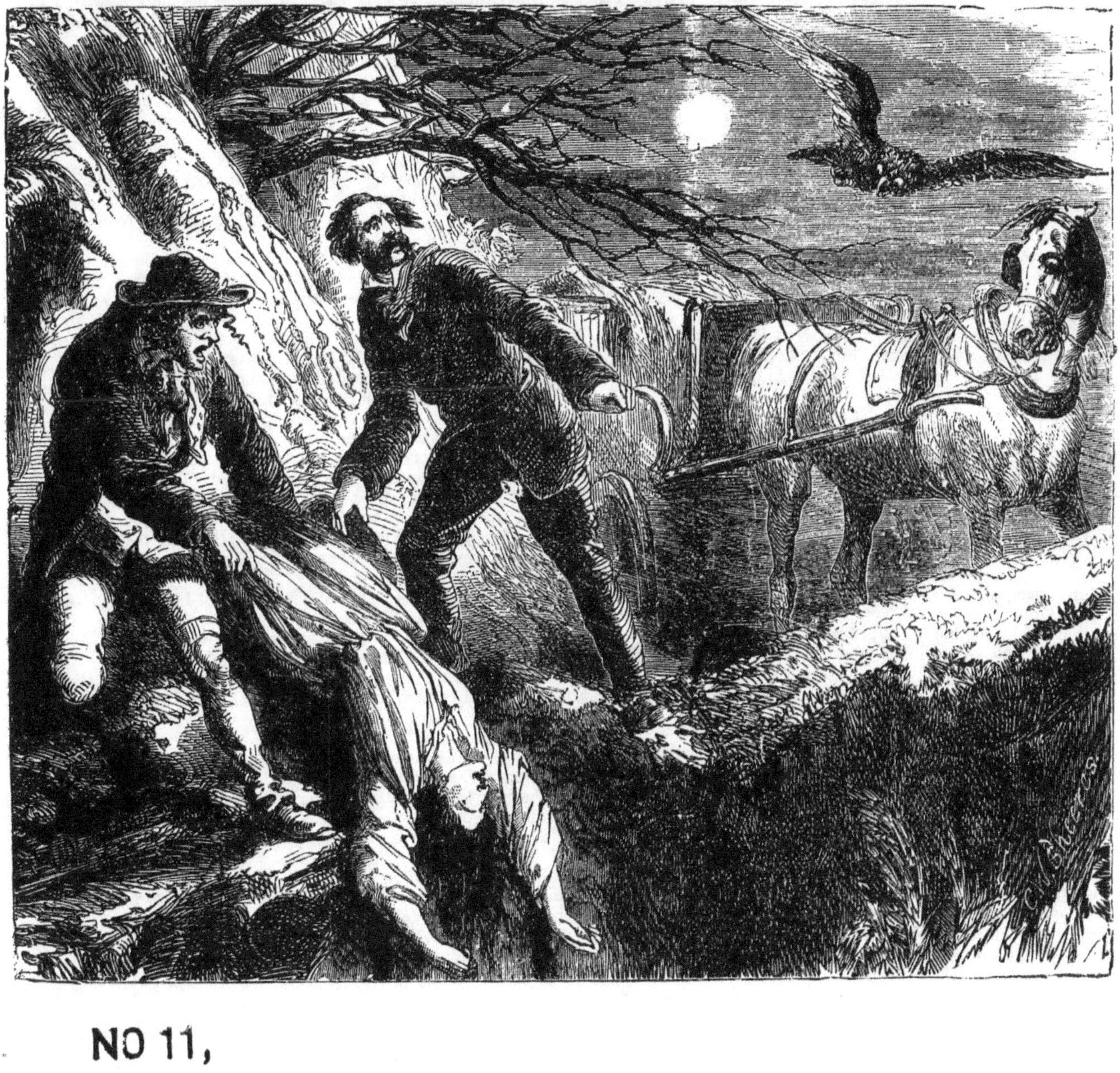

But Ned never believed in a man's honesty. It was not a commodity he gave any one man credit for.

Still he thought this specimen of the human race would suit his book very well.

When dinner was over and they were smoking and drinking their plans were talked over.

The great majority of the crew were Arabs, with enough Europeans to command them.

"I aint partikler fond of playing second fiddle," said our hero, "but I don't mind shipping."

"The whites will share and share alike," replied Captain Zeph.

"Yes, I know," continued the other. "I suppose you've heard tell of Ned Kelly?"

"Yes," answered the other.

"Well, when I tell you I'm that cove," the bushranger responded, "you'll think I deserve to be toasted."

Captain Zeph stared at Salmon Roe.

"It's a fact," said that worthy.

"My hand on it then," cried Zeph "then we'll be heard of."

And so the unholy compact was made.

It was at a late hour when, accompanied by bearers with their luggage, the four men went to a landing place, and were taken on board a native boat, which before daybreak glided down the river.

Late the same night, they were on board of the pirate.

It was a well-built brigantine with every requisite for speed.

It was made more for running than fighting, as it could not venture to contend even against the smallest man of war.

But still it carried one heavy gun carefully concealed from observation, and a crew very disproportionate to its size

The plan of Captain Zeph was to sail up to some unsuspecting vessel, with a very small crew to be seen, ask some question as to longitude and latitude, and then contrive to run aboard.

Sometimes he had been beaten off, at others he had triumphed.

Indiamen on the voyage home were not tempting enough prey now.

The gold ships of Australia were the great temptation, and on their track they agreed to go.

Captain Zeph saw at once that Ned Kelly was a master mind and at once promoted him to be his equal.

The lieutenant nominally was an Arab named Ali, but that was only in the sailing of the ship.

These natives were to be paid wages—very liberal wages.

The European crew—English and Dutch—were seventeen in number, and when an attack was to be made were the only ones who were seen on deck.

CHAPTER LXXVIII.
THE JAMES STIRTON.

AMPLY supplied with olives, and well appointed, the vessel, commanded by Captain Zeph and manned by his villainous crew, made goodly way.

They took no notice of any vessels they came in sight of.

What they wanted was to secure a large amount of treasure at one haul, and then to run for some safe place and enjoy the results.

Ned Kelly proposed they should run to within a hundred miles of Adelaide, and then, furling all sail, look out for a homeward-bound vessel, which would be sure to have gold on board.

Then they could set sail, keep it company at a distance, and watch their opportunity.

Captain Zeph was quite agreeable to anything that his worthy friend proposed.

So after a very favourable run they reached the spot, and at once proceeded to lie to.

A good lookout was kept.

Two days passed, however, and not a vessel was to be seen except of a character such as was of no use to them.

The third day broke, and then the welcome sight came of a fine vessel, with all sail set, bound on her way for home.

Doubtless she had a goodly crew and the usual numerous passengers, happy to return to their native land, where anxious friends awaited them.

The Arab Chief, as the pirate called his vessel, had sail put on, and steered in the same direction as the ship.

The day was fine, but the weather looked rather threatening.

On board the homeward-bound vessel there happened to be a very numerous body of passengers and a rather fair crew.

The first immense excitement of gold-diggings was going down a little, but still large fortunes were being made.

As in everything else, there will always be discontented people; and a good many men who had not found their expectations answered began to leave for home.

The suspicious losses of so many vessels—far beyond the usual average—had made owners and captains more careful in selecting crews.

The James Stirton was rather fortunate in this respect, and had a crew that could be depended on.

There were, of course, some scarcely worth their salt; but still, as a rule, they were better than usual.

The captain was named Lascelles, and his mate Newton.

The passengers were not very numerous—about twenty—but the cargo was valuable.

It consisted of gold and wool.

It was midday, and most of the passengers were on deck, merchants, travellers bent on seeing Europe, and a few ladies.

The captain is standing near the bulwarks, looking through his glass.

"What do you make of her, Newton?" he suddenly asked, after a good look at the Arab Chief.

"She looks a rakish kind of craft," responded Newton, "can't make her out."

"We'd better be careful," the captain continued, "a pirate in these parts is not a very likely event, but some mysterious disappearances have taken place which I really cannot account for."

"Yes," said the mate, gravely, "something must be wrong somewhere. That letting loose such a lot of vagabonds on the colony, has a deal to answer for.

"No—what with bushrangers and sham sailors, one does not know what to do," said the captain, in a musing tone. "Good job the Rosario has come on the coast."

The Rosario was a very sharp sailing sloop of war, which had been sent to cruise about and try and solve the mysterious disappearance of so many ships.

"In my opinion," said the skipper, "she wont do much good, the missing ships have been scuttled and destroyed by their crews. Look what a lot of duffers have been shipped."

"True," responded the mate, "but still I believe there has been other foul play too."

The captain nodded, and then turned to answer questions put by some of the passengers.

Still both he and his officer kept a sharp lookout on the other vessel, which was apparently going in the same direction.

Night came on.

The sky was very cloudy, and it was quite likely that the weather would be nasty

A sharp lookout was kept, and the strange vessel was almost forgotten.

Soon the wind rose, and they were compelled to make all snug alow and aloft.

Not a sign of moon or stars was to be seen. This continued until about midnight, when there was a break in the sky and light fell on the face of the deep.

The strange vessel was close on board of them, and hailed as if angrily.

"Ship ahoy!" shouted a stentorian voice in rather an angry tone. "We're short of water, and want you to spare us a little. We'll round to under the leeside and jump on board to lend a hand."

This was a proposal that embodied some danger to the smaller vessel, as a collision in the then state of the sea would have been dangerous to the pirates' craft.

The weather lulled and the wind fell with the suddenness that it rose.

The captain of the homeward-bound told the chief mate to give the water supply wanted, whereon the latter shouted to his new friends to "come abroad" and lend a hand to tranship a couple of water casks.

The pirate stood off, lowered a boat, filled with a demon crew, armed to the teeth, who were soon seen swarming up the sides of the ship.

Springing on to the maindeck, they quickly rushed into the poop where the captain and chief officer were standing.

Zeph and Kelly, leading, presented their resolvers at the heads of these two men, and swore a blasphemous oath that they would send their souls to the shades below if they didn't order all hands below and allow themselves to be secured.

Stunned by the suddenness of the attack, and seeing how utterly the ship was in the hands of the numerous marauders, they stood paralysed, but eventually passed the word to go below, which, indeed, was not very necessary, as most of the Jack Tars (who on these Colonial lines are anything but the heroes of romance they are popularly represented to be) had already "made tracks" into the forecastle, not caring much what became of the ship and cargo so long as they were pretty safe themselves, while some of them had sudden thoughts of joining the piratical band.

Amongst the passengers great consternation prevailed, and the ladies were almost in a state of catalepsy from fear.

The captain and officers had grand apprehensions of what was coming, but kept their fear to themselves.

The first thought of the pirates was, of course, the gold, which Ned Kelly and Salmon Roe knew was always secured in certain lockers.

Of course no difficulty was found in securing it and conveying it on board the Arab Chief.

"Now my friend," began Captain Zeph, "what passengers have you on board?"

"A sail close at hand!" cried one of the pirates.

"The Rosario sloop of war," shouted Newton. "Up, lads, and at them."

A blow from the butt end of Kelly's revolver floored him; but all saw a smart-looking vessel, evidently a cruiser, at no great distance, and no time was lost in getting on board their own vessel and steering off.

"We must run for it," said Captain Zeph, who was not at all pleased with the turn affairs had taken. "The Rosario is a fast sailer."

Every stitch of canvas the vessel could carry.

Whoever had built the Arab Chief had thought before all things of speed.

She could outsail almost anything.

Still the Rosario was, it was well-known, a vessel which, having been a year on the station, was by no means a craft to be despised.

There was nothing for them to do but escape or sink.

To fight the cruiser was out of the question.

The English man-of-war, having communicated with the James Stirton, at once started in pursuit.

The Arab Chief was indeed a prize worth having, and the officers of the Rosario determined to chase her, if it was round the world.

On board the Arab Chief the crew were in a terrible state of anxiety.

The wind was pretty stiff, and she bent to the breeze.

Her sails were good, and every rope of the best.

An hour passed and there appeared to be but little difference in the speed of the ships.

They were about three miles apart.

"What do you make of it, Zeph?" asked Kelly.

"There is little difference," responded the pirate; "but she sails better than I like. I wish I could give her the slip."

"How is it to be done?" asked Kelly.

"I should like to know," mused the other; "I am afraid we must make for land, beach her and scatter."

Still they kept on for some hours, and still there appeared very little difference in the speed of the two vessels.

Salmon Roe's brow contracted.

"She's gaining on us a little. It'll be a long time afore she comes up," he said; "but she'll do it in the end."

"Then we must give up our craft," remarked Zeph with a sigh.

The gain was so small on the part of the cruiser, that they had a good time before them.

They made direct for the coast of Australia. Salmon Roe undertook to direct.

He knew of a bay where they could run in and anchor close inshore.

It was their only hope.

Morning came, midday, and still the cruiser came on.

The gain was very small, but still it was sufficient to indicate that in the end they must come up.

But now the coast of Australia is clearly visible, and all depends on time.

The wind is steady, and the Arab Chief keeps on her way steadily.

On board the Rosario they begin to guess what the scoundrels are about to do.

"They will beach her and escape," says the officer in command to his lieutenant.

"I'm afraid so," replied the other. "It is a splendid craft. I wonder where on earth she hails from."

"Some of the Malay Islands," answered the captain. "They have hiding-places somewhere. Would that we could catch her."

Meanwhile everyone was preparing on board the Arab Chief for the finale.

All secured their share of the plunder, weapons, and ammunition.

None sought to overload themselves.

It was three in the afternoon when they approached the shore.

The vessel was directed into a small bay, surrounded by low land, grass, and trees.

All sail was taken in, and the boats put out in haste.

Not a moment was lost.

The Rosario was coming up hand-over-hand, and they all knew it.

As soon as a landing was effected, everybody dashed into the bush.

It was not their plan to keep together. Most would strive to reach a port, and there enjoy themselves while their money lasted, when they could make for the diggings or get a ship.

There could be no one to identify them,

Kelly determined, however, to keep to the bush for the present, as he had no wish to have his return to the colony suspected.

They were some distance from any village or town, only shepherds' out-station huts being scattered here and there, and miles apart.

But Ned Kelly knew they would not travel many days in the direction of Port Adelaide without falling across a bush inn.

They dropped it at many a solitary shepherd's hut, who was but too glad to share his mutton damper and tea with his visitors, who gave him the "news," or what he thought to be such.

As to danger from any quarter, he never dreamt of it, as he had nothing to lose, and thus realised the Horatian lines of the impecunious traveller laughing before the robber.

The variety of costume adopted at will by the denizens of Australia is so common that if one were to appear in the dress of Elvino, or Somnambulo, or Robert the Devil in the opera of that name, it would scarcely excite a passing remark.

So our vagabond party, though dressed half-and-half sea and land costume, attracted no attention on that head, except that "some fellows passed here in rummy togs," and there the matter ended.

Thus Kelly, Zeph, and Roe steadily progressed towards the capital of South Australia, and were not displeased to hear that "diggins" had recently been discovered in that colony as well as in Victoria, which adjoins it.

CHAPTER LXXIX.

THE TEMPLE STATION.

THE three "pals" journeyed for some hours, guided by landmarks known to Ned.

His eye was keen and unerring, and he never was known to miss his way.

It was quite evening when they reached an inn, which was nothing but a one-storeyed rambling building, with deal counter and seats.

All men were tired, thirsty, and hungry, so that their first task was to obtain refreshments, which, though coarse, were abundant.

They enjoyed themselves heartily, and then found an outhouse where they could rest

They were asleep in a very few minutes, and did not wake until late in the morning.

After breakfast the four held a conference as to future proceedings.

They had money and could afford to enjoy themselves.

Ned Kelly had disappeared altogether from the ken of colonial people, and might have been killed in some obscure quarrel for what people knew.

The question arose—should they venture into a town or should they make their way to some populous gold-digging locality, where they could amuse themselves and perhaps do a stroke of business?

After spending some time and much money in Adelaide, an irresistible inclination to return to the scene of his former atrocities came over Kelly.

But he thought the Adelaide diggings ought first to be visited, and something made out of them.

So off they set, determined to get plunder somehow.

Kelly was totally unknown there, but shortly after the arrival of the three villains robberies were plentiful, and the bodies of some miners, known to be successful, were found in strange places.

But how did they get there? the reader will naturally enquire.

Perfectly easy.

But Kelly and his companions must have horses to take them to the diggings.

Well, there was an easy way of obtaining these. They would help themselves.

At the inn they heard that a squatter had recently established himself at a place called Temple Station.

He had gone in for wool on a large scale and had a very extensive run.

He had built himself one of the usual rough-and-ready residences, where he lived with his family.

He had, they said, erected wool-sheds, with the usual barns, &c.

He necessarily would have many horses.

These worthies proposed to help themselves to three without any consent on the part of the owner.

They started after breakfast for Temple Station, which they found without difficulty.

It was a very extensive one, and a number of men were employed as stock-keepers, shepherds, and the like.

These squatters lived in a rude kind of splendour, and, above all, were hospitable.

The three men declared themselves bound for the diggings.

They had concealed their wallets with their plunder in a thicket at some distance from the house. They did not care to excite suspicion.

Mr. Temple asked no questions, but gave them the usual hospitality.

This they frankly accepted, and after a rest they went off, but concealed themselves in the thicket, whence they could see all that went on.

At various times during the day men came riding in and put their horses in the paddock, going to different work on the establishment.

But it was not until quite evening that all labour ceased.

Then they all went to the final evening meal

The paddock was quite away from any of the occupied buildings, and this the villains had noted.

Two kept watch while one went in and selected three animals, the best of course.

These they saddled and coolly led forth.

The saddles and bridles, when taken off the horses, are usually thrown into a wooden shed near the paddock, and often left in the woolshed.

Kelly and his fellows waited, of course, for night before starting.

All walked quietly until they were a good distance from the station, when they mounted and away as fast as they could make the animals go.

The anger of the defrauded squatter may be imagined when the morning revealed his loss.

Still, he sent word to the nearest police-station and described the three men.

At all events they should be hunted out of the locality. No doubt they were bushrangers.

By this time the news of the outrages at these diggings was circulated through the colonies, and reached Melbourne.

They were quite of the "Ned Kelly" series, and the moment Conquest read of them he shouted out—

"By Jupiter, that's Kelly! I'd swear to his play anywhere. I'll have him yet, or he shall make cats'-meat of me. I'll get myself sent off to Adelaide to help the authorities."

And he was off by the next steamer to Adelaide the following day.

He was soon on the road to the scene of Kelly's little game, and saw Mr. Temple.

"By heavens!" he cried, "it is that unhanged rascal Ned Kelly."

Mr. Temple was terrified.

He had particularly noticed the scar on his hand by which Kelly was known far and wide.

Hope resumes its sway in Tom Conquest's breast. He will yet win the reward.

He at once rides off, and again is the patient and energetic officer on the track of the renowned bushranger

Ignorant that his presence is known in the colony, the man goes forward for the diggings.

He has been there before, but people come and people go, so that he is sure to find no one who would know him personally.

He and his companions do not ride into the diggings; they get rid of their horses before, as they might excite suspicion.

The diggers are very much scattered, some claims being rich, others poor.

Just to do as every one else does the men take up a deserted claim.

They selected one out of sight of others, and then pretended to work.

But it is all pretence, an excuse for being in possession of gold which they freely spend in the evening in the grog saloons.

Here they find plenty of ready gamblers, and pass many a night in the wild excitement of cards and dice.

Ned Kelly is fortunate enough to meet no one whom he has ever seen before.

He finds himself, in fact, strangely forgotten. His absence of nearly a year has brought other names into notice.

Ned Kelly is delighted for the time, but he soon determines that the colony shall ring with his name once more.

His egregious vanity cannot let him rest.

But he will have his fling first.

There is a police-station at this place, but Ned Kelly and his companions are careful not to go near it. They keep very quiet and are careful not to drink and be quarrelsome.

The police are careful not to interfere with those who keep themselves quiet.

The three men live in a hut alone, where, unless someone comes in sight accidentally, they smoke, and play, or sleep.

Should a stray passer-by appear they at once appear to be very busy.

Their gold they have found a snug hiding-place for.

Occasionally they take a stroll round and look at the others washing.

Strangely enough, they are unfortunate at cards. Cheating is too dangerous with men of the class of the gold-miners, and their luck is very much against them.

What with their extravagant expenditure, champagne and other luxuries, their ill-gotten gold is disappearing rapidly.

One of their favourite resorts is a sort of low music hall, where white men drink, smoke, and play, dances and songs amuse them.

The songs and dancing are not of a very refined character it will be imagined readily, but with rough natures it is sufficient.

At the same time, some of the diggers are highly educated and refined gentlemen.

The society they move in just rubs off a little of the finer edge, that is all.

One night at the grog saloon, Kelly is playing for self and partners against a man whose luck has been extraordinary.

Kelly's dander is up.

He will break this lucky gambler or he will lose his whole pile.

His companions back him up in his opinion and agree to stake any amount.

The stranger is a cool and collected Yankee who is imperturbable.

Kelly loses his temper, and the game goes very much against them.

He cannot quarrel, as the man makes no bragging or boasting, but simply wins.

"I can't understand it, hanged if can," presently says Kelly.

"Do you mean to say I ain't straight?" asks the Yankee, coolly.

"No," replied Kelly, dashing down the cards, "but I risk no more."

And he and his companions moved away. They could not play any more.

They were very nearly ruined, and something must be done to replenish their exchequer.

Should they work?

"Work be blowed! It's only chicken-hearted muffs that work."

No, they would see if something else could not be done here or elsewhere.

CHAPTER LXXX.

HOW TO KEEP IT DARK.

FORTUNES are made and lost at the gold diggings, but the best paying game is that of store-keeper.

John Abrahams' store was one of the most extensive.

He sold everything, and turned his money over and over again.

Money was plentiful and people did not object to pay through the nose.

Abrahams had a daughter, whom he loved very dearly and it was for her that he was scraping money together. He had made up his mind that she should, when he died, be left with a large fortune, and worked ceaselessly to carry out this idea.

He was never satisfied with his gains, went on accumulating wealth at a surprising and rapid rate.

The old fellow scarcely ever left his store. Things didn't go so well when he was away, he would often say, "I must be there to look after my interests."

His daughter often begged of him to take life more easy. They had money enough, why not retire from business and spend his declining years in comfort and quietness?

But the father only shook his head and said—

"If I left off business I should die. Some people are content to be idle, but I am not one of them. Without work I should be the most miserable man in the world. I should rust, and the rust would eat into my life as it does into metal, until it cuts it in two."

The mind ought to be employed and not allowed to rest.

Abrahams' daughter had many admirers—a few for her beauty, a few because she was good-natured and pleasant, and a great many because of her money.

But the man who had succeeded in making an impression on her heart and winning her father's good opinion was a young German of the name of Fritz.

Sober, hard-working, plodding, and industrious, he saved what he earned, while the other miners as a rule spent their hard-earned gold in dissipation.

He had been as successful as he deserved to be, and left what he saved in the hands of Abrahams for safety.

The old man was very glad to see that Rachel's future husband was steady and saving, for he knew he would not squander the money he had scraped together.

Ned Kelly, Captain Zeph, and Salmon Roe, were out of luck, and hearing of the old man's wealth determined to rob the shanty.

"It's better than digging for gold," said Kelly. "It will be easy enough to break into the store and carry off the money."

"Serve him right," growled Salmon Roe. "Why does the old fool tempt one like that? A man that keeps his money hid away like he does deserves to lose it."

Ned Kelly, having once come to the determination of relieving the old man of his gold, made up his mind to carry out his intention at once.

Nothing could be gained by delay.

He might get frightened and hide his money in a safe place.

So the first dark night was taken advantage of, and the four scoundrels made their way to the store.

All was still.

Unsuspicious of danger the old man slept soundly, tired out by his day's work.

It was a long rambling building, not very strongly built.

After some time and trouble the bushranger succeeded in forcing open the door, making some noise over the job, but not enough to attract notice.

The tents of the miners were a little distance off.

They all entered the store after looking about them to see that all was right.

They had their reasons for not wishing to be interrupted by the miners, who would have shown them scant mercy.

The store was crowded with goods, and Kelly, stumbling over something, awoke the old man, who slept under the counter.

"Thieves!" he shouted.

The next moment Kelly's hand was on his throat.

"Tell me where your gold is hid and your life shall be spared," said Kelly, who was not actuated by humanity, but wanted to know where the old man kept his money.

If they killed him they might search the hut in vain for the concealed gold.

To allow the old man to answer he loosened his hold on his throat.

"Never!" said the old man: "you shall not rob my guild."

"Do you not value life?" cried Kelly, mad with passion. "I swear that I won't harm a hair of your head if you are not a fool."

"You shall never know from my lips where it is concealed," said Abrahams.

Then suddenly releasing himself from Kelly's hold, he cried out desperately—

"Murder! murder! Help! help! help!"

"Fool," hissed Kelly, through his clenched teeth.

Then there was no subdued cry of agony, a dull, sickening thud, and all was over.

When entering the store stealthily Kelly armed himself with an axe (he had prohibited the use of firearms, unless they were attacked), and this more for the purpose of breaking open any locked box than for the object of murder; but when he saw the whole scheme likely to be frustrated by the Jew's outcry, he did not pause to smash in the head of the unfortunate man by one blow from his powerful arm.

The corpse fell without a groan to the ground.

Kelly had added another murder to the list of his crimes.

"Now for the gold, boys," he cried. "We must find it, if we pull the old hut down."

They had a lantern with them and began the search.

The men cursed and swore as they looked about, turning over boxes and packets.

"It will be daylight if we don't find it soon," said Kelly. "Look alive, or we shall have come here for no purpose. The obstinate old ass has died with the secret, and the game will be lost."

And in his hideous rage he kicked the corpse again and again.

"Hush!" said Zeph. "You'll wake the girl."

"Perhaps she knows where the gold is," said Kelly. "Let's wake her up and compel her to reveal the secret."

"Women shriek so," replied Captain Zeph. "It would be safer to leave her alone. She might alarm the diggers, and I don't want to dance upon a tight rope yet a-bit. Them miners are up to lynching as if they was born to it."

"How she has slept through all the racket I can't make out," remarked Zeph. "But them girls do sleep sound."

"Perhaps she is awake and afraid to cry out," observed Salmon Roe, looking about him with the lantern; "them women are so precious artful."

"Hullo!" said Kelly, throwing open the lid of a small barrel which apparently contained flour, and, diving down his hand in the white stuff, he pulled up a handful of gold.

The cunning old man had just put a coating of flour over his treasure, thinking that it would effectually prevent robbers from finding the money; but he had not prevented Ned Kelly the bushranger from reaping the benefit of his labour.

They soon secured the gold, and were about to leave the hut, when a door of the closet in which Rachel slept was flung open, and she stood before them, looking pale and beautiful.

"Murderers!" she shrieked, catching sight of Abrahams' body, "you have killed my poor father, but shall not escape unpunished. I will alarm the diggers. My father's death shall be avenged!"

Her cries were terrible to hear, and Kelly, with a fearful oath, rushed out of the hut, followed by his companions, who shut the door of the hut in the girl's face.

When the diggers arrived the bushrangers had got clean away.

They found the girl kneeling beside her father's dead body, her face white and marble-like, her eyes wild and dilated.

"My father has been foully and cruelly murdered," she said, her voice clear and distinct; and many a rough digger turned away to hide a tear, affected by the sight of the poor orphan kneeling beside the remains of her father.

He had been mean and avaricious, and had cheated and lied to get his money, but he had always been good to her.

"And I swear by heaven and earth to seek out the murderer until I die. I will not rest till he is punished."

She knelt beside her father in her grief, with one hand pointed up to heaven, unconscious, in her agony of sorrow, that she was only clad in her night-gown, and that the rude eyes of the diggers were upon her.

They left her to her sorrow, not wishing to intrude longer upon the young and beautiful girl who had forgotten everything in her wild, ungovernable grief.

The diggers were rough men, but such a scene could not but touch a soft place in their hearts, and they swore to assist the girl in her just vengeance.

On the following day the murder was the talk of the place, and the news was known for miles around.

It was not that murders were uncommon in those parts, but it was the brutality of the crime that aroused general indignation.

Rachel was known and liked, and it seemed a foul deed to rob her of her father.

"That wench means mischief," said Salmon Roe, with vague uneasiness. "It is astonishing how these women will stick to an idea when it once enters their head. She swears to avenge her father's death, and it's my belief that she will keep her word."

"Will she though!" cried Kelly, with an inexpressible accent of rage and menace in his voice, while his thick lips parted in an evil smile. "The girl is playing with edged tools, and had better have a care. If we allow her to play with our lives and liberties, whose fault will that be d'ye think, pals, eh?" grinning a devilish and meaning smile, while he drew his hand significantly across his throat.

Any other man than his boon companion might have looked at the bushranger with repulsion at that moment, but his fierce and threatening gesture seemed to inspire that worthy with sentiments of the deepest admiration. Salmon enjoyed himself a reputation for bravery, but he felt that he was nowhere in the presence of Ned Kelly.

"You mean that she must be put out of the way?" said Salmon Roe.

Ned Kelly nodded.

"She will swear to the murderers anywhere," observed Salmon Roe. "It would be rather awkward if she came upon us unexpectedly and denounced us to the traps."

"The job must be done without loss of time," said Kelly. "We have only to wait till night comes on."

This they did, and then sallied out of the deserted hut in which they had taken up their quarters.

Their very temerity in lingering so near the scene of their crime had averted all suspicion, and it seemed only natural to the diggers that these men should have established themselves in the forsaken shanty of an unsuccessful miner who had departed for parts unknown.

Resolved to remove all trace of evidence against them, they determined to make away with Rachel. Consequently about ten o'clock that night, when all was prepared, and a horse and cart borrowed (nominally to fetch some flour from a neighbouring store), the villains approached the dead man's residence, and saw by the light reflected through the window that someone was up.

This they soon discovered to be Rachel, whose lamentations were loud and incessant.

Roe knocked at the door, and begged her to step out and speak for a moment to a friend of her late father, who was most anxious to see her for a few seconds, as he had something important to communicate to her.

She, bewildered with grief and half-stunned by her terrible loss, rose and tottered outside the store, when she was suddenly garotted by an iron grasp and rendered instantly senseless.

Kelly was the ruthless executioner, and he chuckled as he squeezed the breath of life out of the fair form which quivered with a few convulsive struggles ere her spirit returned to Him who gave it.

The body lay almost passive in Kelly's grasp.

His pals looked almost frightened, and certainly they trembled with nervousness and admiration.

" Ain't he a rare un ?" muttered Zeph.

" Why, the Old Un is nothing to Ned. He'll put him out when he gets there, mark my words. But, come on; don't let us be jabbering here when some bloke might wake up and spoil our game."

" Without uttering a word Kelly bore the still-warm body to the cart, and, with his brother fiends, sprang in and was off.

They drove quickly and cautiously to the outskirts of the diggings, to one of the numerous abandoned pits with which the ground was honeycombed, and on the bottom of which lay many a murdered corpse of those whose return with fortune was anxiously looked forward to by many a fond mother and friend in the far-away home.

Here the body was removed from the cart and launched head-foremost into the abyss—for the pits, fifty feet deep, can truly be so described.

A dull thud, the rattling of the stones as they accompanied the falling corpse, all in a few seconds.

The moon shone serenely upon the resolute but murderous countenances of the three fiends, who now felt the only evidence against them in this world had been safely disposed of.

" That job's settled," ejaculated Kelly, with a grunt of satisfaction, as he told his friends to " light up," and the three smoked their pipes with a calm feeling of contentment and satisfaction, much in the same way as, about thirty years ago, Mrs. Manning, who murdered her visitor, O'Connor, cooked a goose in the kitchen wherein, with her husband's aid, she dug a hole and thrust the body, found there subsequently by the police.

CHAPTER LXXXI.

FLIGHT.

THE murder of John Abrahams and the disappearance of his daughter excited great commotion in the Adelaide Creek diggings.

Ned Kelly and his comrades fancied that they were looked at askance.

On the second evening after the murder they were leaving the saloon, when passing round at the back they heard a man say—

" Tom Conquest is coming up from Melbourne. He swears Kelly's here. He knows his style of game—leastways that's Tom's opinion—expect him every minute; he'll soon make these fellows out."

Kelly at once determined to leave without a moment's delay.

He explained the character of the man to his companions, and should they come face to face with this trooper, he would be sure to know him.

" I propose we get horses, ride away direct to Melbourne," he continued; " there we can get disguises and hide till the hue and cry is over, and perhaps do some business."

The men agreed. They had no desire to be caught by the police.

An hour later they were on their way out of the diggings, but not by the main path followed by the gold escort, but by the scrub.

They left without beat of drum and moved as rapidly as possible.

After going some distance they heard horse's foot steps, and peering out from some bushes saw a body of mounted police riding up.

Sure enough they were headed by Tom Conquest.

Ned now made up his mind to strike off in the wilder regions, making his way to inhabited districts only after a time, when they would again have to " hobble " horses.

But that must not be too soon, or it might set the dreaded foe on their track.

It was easy to procure food from the shepherds scattered over the country, many of them ex-convicts.

With these men it was best to be on friendly terms.

The third night they ventured to approach a station and repeated their horse-stealing feat in a very simple manner. Salmon went up to the Home Station looking for work, while his chums lay *perdu.* He spotted where the saddles and bridles of the stock-keeper were often huddled together, so that when night came he could steal out of the hut where strangers were often allowed to turn in, and carry off to his companions the saddles, &c., required. Nothing is easier than to rob any station of such articles.

They now hurried to put a long distance between themselves and the scene of their latest crime.

On reaching Melbourne they sold their horses to a dealer for a trifle, saying that they had no need for them any longer and entered the town at night.

They easily obtained fitting disguises, after that they took up their residence at a decent hotel.

Now they had time to look around them and to calculate what was to be done.

Ned Kelly thought, after amusing themselves for a day or two, they might try and get together some of his old followers whose haunts he knew of, and attempt some great robbery of gold from an escort, and perhaps attack and rob one of the local banks, which often held large sums of money.

There was a bank at a place called London, the centre of a district.

It was a strong brick-built building, with a station not half a mile away.

His plan was to rob the place in the open day by means of an armed band.

The bank manager, his clerk, his wife, and servant alone lived there, while there were but two houses in sight.

The others considered the plan a most audacious one, but were not to be outdone in daring by their associate.

In the hotel there was a large dining-room, billiard-room, and coffee-room.

Without making any very great display, they lived well, and having exchanged their gold for specie, spent it openly.

In the same hotel was a man of the name of Rintoul.

He was a diamond merchant, and was spoken of as a very successful man.

This man they made friends with, and found him accessible enough.

He had a kind of office in the hotel, where he carried on the trade of bullion dealer as well.

He bought gold, and intimated his intention of shortly going to England with his treasure.

The three men occupied two rooms in the same passage as himself.

He carried up his treasure at night and locked it away. He was very careful, they knew.

But they at last hit upon a plan. In the daytime it was easy enough to enter his room.

Salmon did so, and examined it carefully.

What appeared the door of a locked closet was in reality a door of communication with the next room, occupied by them, too.

They easily contrived to remove the bolts which were on the other side, and then to make it look as usual.

Salmon kept in his room all the evening so that no one should enter.

Then at midnight all went to bed.

They were collected in the one room, and listened keenly.

The man, Rintoul, moved about for some time, and then all was still.

They pushed the door and listened.

The man was sleeping soundly, b   slumber could not be relied on.

They must silence him for e

There was a dim light from the window. Ned Kelly approached the bed and placing a slip-knot quietly and cautiously round his neck, coolly strangled him. He then lifted the body out of bed, and tying the rope to the head-rail of the iron bedstead, threw the body forward on its face, to make it appear a case of suicide.

Scarcely a gurgle was heard, scarcely a sound, and there he lay dead.

Of course these men found no difficulty in ransacking his boxes, the contents of which they transferred to their own.

Then they left the wretched corpse and returned to their own rooms.

They were to leave next day very early, so none were surprised when they came down to breakfast, and, hastily consuming it, went out with each a heavy carpet bag.

Going some distance in a car they hired another vehicle to drive them to a given point. The man had good horses and drove them rapidly.

Suddenly he received a severe blow on the head, was hurled into the road, and Kelly took the reins.

Some distance off they left the carriage, and made off by devious ways known to Kelly.

Avoiding all habitations, they travelled incessantly until they were a considerable distance from the seat of their crime.

They obtained food at out-of-the-way places, nor stopped much until they were in a wild and almost inaccessible country.

After leaving the haunts of civilisation and entering the scrub they determined to be in hiding some time before they ventured to do anything to throw the police upon their track.

They selected a hiding-place at no great distance from a shanty inn, where they ventured to procure food and drink, but always took care to visit when it was untenanted by others.

But happening to fall over, in the person of stockman, one of his old associates, Kelly let him know that he was about to do a daring exploit and wanted a dozen well-armed and mounted men to join.

The whole country was now in a state of terror and alarm.

These atrocious crimes, attributed by public opinion to one man, caused a universal feeling of dread, and people asked themselves—what next?

The police were urged by the Government to find the miscreant, but his cunning was too great.

Besides, in those days there was such extent of bush that, with a population scattered about sympathising with crime, he had many accomplices.

Still Kelly, on this occasion, determined to be quiet for a little while.

When he had accomplished his next raid he would go off to a distance and where he was not known at all, and, contemplated removing depredations to the colony of North Australia, and its capital—Queensland.

To do this he must abstain from crime, so as to attract no attention to himself.

Ned Kelly, in the district where he had concealed himself with his associates, had made himself a rough hut

It was so situated that anyone could be seen at a quarter-of-a-mile off, when he could get into inaccessible hiding places.

But his comrades were always ready to give him warning, and the owner of the hut where liquor was sold was not one to betray a customer.

The time fixed on for the attack on London, as the spot where the bank was situated was called, rapidly approached.

Kelly had made an appointment with his men at a point six miles from the place.

It was a very wooded spot on the banks of a small river.

It was in the centre of a number of sheep runs, and was accounted rather a populated place.

Kelly had provided himself with a moustache and wore a wig of grey hair.

No one who did not know him would have for one moment believed in the deception.

One young man had gone forward as scout and when they got within a short distance from the spot came and told them that the coast was clear.

In a few minutes more sixteen heavily armed men surrounded the bank, Kelly and five others alighting an entering.

A country town in the colonies is not unlike the same place in remote districts in England.

Being Britishers, it is only natural the colonies should reproduce the localities they left in the old country.

The bank in both places is a quiet, private-looking house, and, with the exception of the word "bank," might be taken for the village doctor's residence.

A few loiterers are always at the cottage doors; and the apothecary's is always full of gossips. The arrival of anyone is an event. His appearance and business are soon ferreted out, and form interesting topics of discussion for days. The locality is generally characterised by a stagnant calm, and generally remains in profound repose.

About mid-day several horsemen were seen quietly riding down the High-street, smoking short pipes, and quietly regarding the inhabitants.

They passed the bank and approached the police-station, where two of the mounted force were also engaged in the arduous duty of "blowing a cloud."

Suddenly pulling up in front of the officers they suddenly presented their revolvers at their heads, desired them to remain still, sent Salmon inside for the arms, desired the men to retire inside the station, and left one of their gang to mount guard over the prisoners.

This operation was performed very quietly, and the horses' heads turned towards the bank

Kelly, Zeph, and Salmon dismounted at the door. Kelly entered first, and, presenting a piece of paper which the clerk took for a cheque, suddenly drew his six shooter—an operation imitated by his assistants—and swore, if the astonished clerk did not deliver up his cash and the keys of the safe, his passage from this world would be more speedy than he would desire. The manager at this moment came out from the inner office, upon which Zeph pointed his revolver at the midriff of the electrified banker, and desired him to "look sharp and cash up" without delay.

Binding the clerk and the manager and placing them in different rooms, the doors of which they locked, the band rode off quietly with their booty.

Of course, in a short time the victims made known the robbery, when the consternation was at fever height.

"It's Kelly; no one but Kelly would chance it," was the universal cry.

The police, who had also been similarly locked up, looked very small and very vexed.

The instant they were gone the terrified wife and daughter of the manager appeared and liberated the two unfortunate men, one of whom, the clerk, rode off to the police station, where he learned how the occupants of that building had been treated.

Returning to the rendezvous the plunder was divided and the band broke up.

Kelly returned to his place of concealment, and making appointments with his immediate companions in a fortnight started alone to a shanty inn kept by his sister and Joe Marsh.

Kelly's sister had been some time in the Colony of Victoria, and married to an ex-convict who was doing a good business in a bush "pub." Here he knew he could be quiet for some time.

He was doubly cautious now, as he had a good bit of gold with him.

He travelled at night, resting in the day, and going by devious ways.

He at length reached his sister's house but before he

entered he concealed the greater part of his treasure in the hollow of a tree.

He would not even trust his relations too implicitly.

Still he was very liberal with his money, and expressed a wish to stay a few days. He had resolved to return for a time to Adelaide.

This they readily agreed to, and then he requested Marsh to go to the nearest store and buy certain things for him.

These were a complete suit of clothes of the well-to-do squatter class, a square portmanteau, and some clean linen.

Also a pair of spectacles.

Marsh laughed, but next day rode off to the store, a considerable distance, to make these purchases.

He was further to buy a good stout horse that would carry a good weight.

It was only the next day that Marsh returned with the requisites.

Marsh had been very careful, and the things were a fairish fit.

Next day, after a copious breakfast, Ned Kelly, presenting a very respectable appearance, started on his way.

He had no hesitation in seeking the high road. He had got rid of the carpet-bag and put his things in a large rug, which was strapped behind him on his horse, a powerful big-boned thing which could bear even a greater weight than Kelly.

He did not, on reaching the highway, show any hurry. He was satisfied that his disguise would defy detection.

He, however, was well armed, and prepared at a pinch to defend himself to the last gasp.

He travelled quietly, stopped at roadside inns, and was treated with all the respect due to his supposed position.

He was pleasant and agreeable.

When he met a trooper he scarcely looked at him, he was so respectable.

In this way in time Adelaide was reached. He went to a quiet commercial hotel, giving the name of Caleb Jones.

His first act after going to his room and ordering dinner was, to look at a file of the *Melbourne Argus*.

Ned Kelly could scarcely spell his own name, but he could read print.

He easily found the account of the murder, and of the bank robbery.

Both were ascribed to Ned Kelly.

He was delighted, especially as the police were severely blamed, and spoken of in terms of bitter reproach.

Kelly chuckled, and, having dined, went out and walked about the town looking at the big bills which were everywhere posted up in regard to himself.

He was delighted.

He returned presently to the hotel, and joined the guests in the public room.

One after the other Salmon Roe and Captain Zeph came, and all met as strangers.

Gradually they made acquaintance and became great chums and companions, going out together, and dining at the same table.

They were free but not lavish with money, spending it like men who had plenty, but who were not reckless.

CHAPTER LXXXII.
TOM CONQUEST IN ADELAIDE.

THE three men, as we have said, were very careful to do nothing to excite attention.

The colony was ringing with the news of the awful atrocities committed by the arch fiend and his associates.

Everybody seemed to believe that these crimes were the outcome of Kelly and his gang.

Every honourable man wished to put an end to their monstrous iniquities.

Their disguises were admirable.

The one great danger was that of getting intoxicated and talking too much.

Kelly, or Jones as he called himself, was tolerably on his guard, for, with all his brutality and coarseness, he was shrewd.

The others were very inferior in intellect.

"Boys," he said one day when they were having a rather rich and copious breakfast at some restaurant of repute, "whatever your little game may be, don't take too much drink, except at night."

"I can't turn sniveller all at once," replied Captain Zeph; "it ain't salubrious."

"No more can I," added the other.

"Well," continued Kelly in a stern and commanding way, "the first time I catches you drunk I'm off. My neck is my own property."

"Who talks about getting drunk?" was the answer of Captain Zeph. "Can't a fellow enjoy himself?"

"Yes, in reason," was the dry reply, and the breakfast proceeded and the subject dropped.

In those days, when money was so rife, of course every amusement that could be thought of was provided.

Dancing saloons, gambling houses, theatres, and questionable music-halls were established and tolerated.

After breakfast the four men adjourned to a billiard-room kept by one of their own kidney, though he never suspected that these three gentlemen who spent their money so freely were of the fraternity.

The man had seen too much of colonial life not to be aware of the fact that they were "swells," but not gentlemen.

Australian men of the educated classes are as refined and polished as anyone.

Still, the audacity of the conduct of this trio was of itself enough to throw people off the scent.

Over the fireplace in the billiard-room was the usual police bill offering the £10,000 reward for Kelly.

James O'Connor was too anxious to be on good terms with the police to decline putting up such a poster.

The three men were too used to this sort of thing even to notice it.

They secured a table and called for champagne, after which they began playing.

The game was of no particular interest to them because the betting was among themselves.

Money was pretty well in common, though Kelly was very much richer than his associates suspected.

Presently some other people came in and began playing at another table.

One of these Kelly knew by sight.

He was one of the largest wool-growers in the colony and seemed to have a charmed life.

Whether he speculated in one thing or the other, he, like the character of ancient days, found everything turn to gold.

His name was Marsden.

If he had one fault—it was his belief in his luck.

In business this was very well, but he carried his confidence into cards and billiards.

An almost imperceptible sign passed between Kelly and his confederates.

It meant, "Game to be stalked."

The three lazily finished their game and then laid down their cues.

They professed to be greatly interested in the game played by Marsden and his friend.

After the game had gone on some time and Marsden had made some good points, Kelly spoke.

"Something like play," he said to Roe.

"Back your opinion," cried one of the players, a man of the name of Black.

"Certainly," responded Kelly; "twenty to four on the striker."

The striker was Marsden.

"Done in fives," the other continued.

And Kelly won.

"You seem a dabster at this game," observed Mr. Marsden, when the game was over. "Will you play me?"

" It would be robbing you," coolly rejoined Kelly. " I could give you twenty out of every hundred."

Now Marsden, though a decent fellow and a gentleman at heart, was awfully proud of his prowess at billiards.

The room was filling, and a great many friends of Marsden were present.

" You think so ?" was the sarcastic reply.

" I am simply certain," was Kelly's cool rejoinder.

" I will lay you a thousand to five hundred," exclaimed the rather exasperated citizen.

" Done," responded Ned Kelly.

The excitement was great.

The bushranger ordered a cup of coffee with a soupçon of brandy in it.

He lost the toss.

His adversary had to begin. We are not going to enter into the details of a billiard tournament.

Marsden played a goodish game, but Kelly was too much for him.

He won the thousand pounds, and a good many odd bets besides.

" You are too much for me," said the wool-grower, a little sulkily. " Shall we play another game ?"

" Level betting," cried the bushranger.

It was agreed ; and, after an interval for refreshments, the tournament was renewed.

Kelly won easily.

His power of calculation was something wonderful. He scarcely ever missed a stroke.

He won again.

" I presume," remarked Mr. Marsden, with a sneer, " you are a professional."

" Professional what, may I ask ?" asked Kelly, in a bullying tone.

" I mean no offence," was the reply, " only you are a most remarkable player."

" Have I cheated ?" was the next curt question, put with assumed dignity.

" No—no," the other said. " You couldn't if you would. Let us dine at —— Hotel, and try our luck at the cards."

" Anything to oblige," coolly replied Kelly, " only—few men can beat me at the pasteboard."

" Frank confession is good for the soul," laughed the wool-dealer.

" Have you a pack of cards," asked Kelly, " and do you play piquet ? "

" Yes, and our friend the marker will let us have a pack." said Marsden.

" Well, I will just play you one hand at piquet," continued Kelly, " your friend shall look on, and I will beat you right off——"

" How ? " was asked.

" You shall see," said Kelly, seating himself at a small table.

The cards were produced.

" I will not play for money," drily remarked the bushranger, " unless you particularly wish it."

" A hundred quid," answered the millionaire.

" Gentlemen looking on," then observed Kelly, " will say nothing. I will explain after."

All nodded.

The cards were dealt. To anyone not understanding the game of piquet any explanation would be useless.

Suffice to say that Marsden got as good a hand as a man could wish.

Kelly had dealt, talking all the time, telling rather a good story in his rich Irish accent.

Marsden held four aces and a run of eight.

Marsden turned to a friend to show him the almost unparalleled hand.

Kelly went on talking, telling a comical story of a very warm character.

" I'll bet a hundred to ten on my cards," cried Marsden.

" Don't," drily answered Kelly, who had learned the trick of a Frenchman in the Tench, " look at your hand."

Marsden did look, and found he had the worst piquet hand possible.

Kelly while they were talking had changed hands with him.

The audience roared.

The feat seems impossible, but the writer has seen it done.

" You could not do that again," cried the discomfited wool-grower.

" Try me," said Kelly, drily.

" You shall come to the Scrap to-night," responded Marsden, " and if you can do that again—I'll stand supper round."

" Done," answered Kelly.

The trick is not at all an uncommon one, but it has a load of historical interest. It was played upon the late Emperor Napoleon before the Empress and his whole court.

After this they went to the Scrap.

CHAPTER LXXXIII.

THE SCRAP.

WHAT was familiarly known in Adelaide society as the Scrap was a private gambling-house.

It was on a tolerably large scale but not select, as money was the only entrance fee required.

The large room was crowded with men, women, and young girls, and having indulged in a few pleasantries with the female portion of the company, Kelly walked over to his friend the wool-grower, and tapped him briskly on the shoulder.

" Well," he said, " here I am to give you your revenge I am a man of my word, and never break a promise under any circumstances."

Marsden was quite willing, and the two took their places at the table, Kelly commencing to talk, as he so well knew how to do, and rattling out anecdote after anecdote, to the great amusement of his companion, who, however, watched him as he shuffled the cards, with the determination not to be taken in this time.

" You won't catch me napping twice," he thought, looking excessively cunning.

It was a picturesque scene, and would have made a fine subject for an artist who wished to point a moral.

No one looking at the faces of that rough company could doubt that crime leaves an unmistakable mark upon the human countenance.

There were those present who knew nothing of the character of the men and women with whom they were associating, but they were in the minority.

" What's the row ?" cried Marsden suddenly, attracted by a noisy discussion going on in another part of the room.

Quick as lightning, Kelly saw his opportunity, and was not slow to take advantage of it.

He deliberately substituted his own cards for those Marsden held in his hand, and this done sat calmly waiting for him to continue the game. The furious fight in the room had diverted attention from the card party.

" Confound it ! " exclaimed the wool-grower, looking at his cards with a bewildered expression. " Why, you have never done me again—it isn't possible."

There was a loud roar of laughter from the group who stood watching the players, and Marsden was reluctantly compelled to own that he had lost his wager.

" Nobblers all round," he cried, to cover his annoyance, and all those in the immediate neighbourhood were supplied with glasses of whisky straight, which effectually put an end to the laughter and chaff he so much disliked.

Marsden was very watchful when they commenced the next game, fearing that Kelly might try to play the same trick again ; but the bushranger reassured him on this point.

" Enough is as good as a feast," he observed, " a repetition would make the joke too stale. I have done you twice; I am perfectly satisfied. This game's on the square, but I mean to win it just the same; so keep your eyes skinned and mind what you're about."

Marsden obeyed the injunction, but soon found that the luck was all on Kelly's side, and, after losing a considerable sum of money, rose from the table and declined to play any more,

Kelly was leaning back in his chair taking great gulps of raw whisky, and rapidly becoming intoxicated, when a fine strapping wench came up to him with an impudent smile and challenged him to a game of écarté.

Kelly was agreeable enough.

He was rather partial to the society of females, and did his best to make himself agreeable to his companion as the game proceeded, fixing his bold bloodshot eyes upon her with evident admiration for this remarkably fine and rather coarse-featured young woman.

She seemed bent on encouraging him to drink, and he certainly needed very little persuasion, gulping down the fiery liquor with a perseverance worthy of a better cause.

He began to play rather knowingly in consequence, actuated by old habits and instincts, and forgetting his gallantry towards the sex.

Suddenly a very trifling incident occurred, but it had a wonderful effect upon the bushranger.

He was sober in an instant, although he was careful to feign drunkenness.

The girl who faced him had an expression of countenance and a tone of voice that strangely startled him.

Where had he witnessed these peculiarities? He looked keenly and enquiringly at his *vis-à-vis*. A thought suddenly flashed across his troubled mind.

Could it be possible? Yes, the voice was certainly not that of a woman. The truth suddenly flashed upon him

He was playing écarté with Tom Conquest, the detective!

His only chance was not to betray the discovery he had made, but to quietly wait his opportunity and make a bolt of it, leaving his companions in the lurch.

His dismay was great, and he hardly knew how to act, being doubtful as to the detective's next move.

He felt like a hunted animal at bay.

He no longer tried to win or make use of any of his old tricks

His one thought was how to get out of the room.

"Stop a bit, old girl," he said, as he rose from the table, leaving a pile of gold behind him. "You've been having all the fun in your own hands, but I'll be back in a minute. Just look out for a turn of luck. You have won the last three games, and it is now my turn."

He tottered unsteadily to the door, and the moment he was out in the open air drew himself erect, as sober as if he had been drinking nothing but water all the evening.

Kelly had escaped from the danger that menaced him —the Damoclesian sword which had been suspended over his head, and he troubled himself very little about his companions.

But he had scarcely had the time to warn them if he had desired to do so, and the attempt would have only brought himself into danger, and he was not the man to risk his own safety for the sake of others. Every man for himself was his motto.

"They will get along all right," he thought. "I do not believe that Tom Conquest knows them by sight; but at any rate it is not my fault if they are taken. They must look after themselves."

To tell the truth, Kelly was heartily sick of his associates, and glad to get rid of them for a time at least.

He was not one of those criminals who shrink from solitude and tremble at the thought of solitary communion with their own heart. Perhaps this was because he was so thoroughly case-hardened, so lost to all shame and compunction.

It is hardly possible to sympathise with such a man, and yet it is most probable that he was scarcely conscious of the extent and magnitude of his own villainy.

The rain came down in torrents, soaking him to the skin, and the bushranger, enraged at having been compelled to evacuate his comfortable quarters, swore a savage and blood-curdling oath that he would be revenged upon Tom Conquest.

He felt, indeed, that he had a narrow escape, and but for that chance movement on the part of the detective he would have never seen through his clever disguise.

"Curses on him!" he muttered between his clenched teeth, as he looked at the sullen sky. "The meddling fool shall live to regret what he has done this night. I swear that this night has sealed his doom Ned Kelly will give him his death-blow."

While he was thinking of the vengeance he would mete out to another it never occurred to him that the guilty must some day meet the doom of guilt. He never reflected that there must be a terrible recompense for all his revolting crimes.

Every action of his life gave his guilt a blacker dye; he was always on a new scent for blood.

Ned Kelly's was a strange and incongruous nature.

He considered that he had a right to prey upon his fellow-men, but when they tried to hunt him down it never occurred to him that he deserved to be hounded and killed like any other cruel and inhuman beast.

"A bitter curse go with him—a scathing curse!" muttered Kelly, still thinking of Tom Conquest.

It was a dark unhealthy night, and it was a toil to breathe in the black air.

Ned heeded not the rain. He was red-hot with drink, and his blood ran through his veins like liquid fire.

Some people have frightful dreams, but the most imaginative person could never dream of the horrible atrocities Kelly had committed during his past life, and was yet to commit before the close of his strange eventful history.

It was waste of breath, but in his fierce frenzy of rage and ungovernable passion it gave him relief to find vent for his venom in words.

His cankered heart was full to overflowing with bitter wrath.

"A debt repaid ceases to be a debt," muttered Kelly, "and I shall never rest satisfied till I have paid Tom Conquest in full."

So thought this fool who had blundered through the book of guilt, spelling his villainy—a slave to his own vile passions.

All the fiends in hell would have had more tender scruples than he.

The bushranger must have had a constitution of iron, or else his wild life and fearful temper would have wrecked his body.

He would roam earth for vengeance upon those who dared to cross his path.

We wish that we had a less ghastly and revolting tale to tell, but this is no work of fiction—every word set down is the simple truth.

Kelly went through the blind elements intoxicated with rage, and longing for someone upon whom to vent his evil passions.

It is difficult to determine how a man differs from the brute creation.

The bushranger knew that he could hazard no delay. He must get to some place of safety where he could hide for a day or two.

He would of course be searched for in all directions, and must hide until the hue and cry were over.

Most men half as guilty as he would have found a fiery whirlwind in their conscience, but nothing could equal the hell within him.

"Sold! sold! sold!" he cried exultingly. "Ned Kelly has yet to find his match. Tom Conquest or any of his crew shall never get the reward. Sooner than get into their hands I'd give myself one leaden pill, or go over a precipice—do anything to balk them of their blood-money."

He strode over the soddened grass making no sound

his keen eyes on the alert to catch the first glimpse of a pursuer, and his ears strained to take in the slightest sound; but all was still, not a leaf rustled on the trees, nothing was audible but those faint murmurs of the night which can be so distinctly heard by a sensitive ear at such an hour.

He found himself in a small green dell built all round with high sloping hills, and paused as he became aware that he was nearing a small hut, hesitating whether to turn his footsteps in another direction, or advance boldly and demand shelter for the night.

He was not long in coming to a determination, and walking quickly towards the door of the hut knocked repeatedly until the door was opened, and a man in a slouched hat looked out at him with an angry frown.

"Hush!" said this individual, warningly. "Do you want to disturb the uneasy slumbers of a dying man?"

Kelly responded that he had no desire to do anything of the kind, but would be glad to find shelter from the rain for a few hours at least, and after a moment's hesitation the man stood aside and allowed him to enter the hut.

Kelly gave a glance at the haggard face of the sleeper, and it seemed to him that his features were not altogether unfamiliar; but he soon dismissed this idea from his mind, having something else to occupy his thoughts.

He smiled, as he wondered what the man who stood near him would have thought if he had known who he was—for Kelly was feared by some people more than the most ferocious wild beast, and he was rather proud than otherwise of this distinction.

There was a sinister smile on his lips as he sat listening to the heavy rain as it beat upon the roof of the rough hut, occasionally glancing at his companion, who volunteered a remark now and then, and seemed disposed for conversation if Kelly had given him encouragement.

But the bushranger's hurried flight had made him feel moody and sullen, and his short answers soon made the man relapse into silence, which remained unbroken until the sleeper turned uneasily in the bed, and presently opened his heavy eyes, staring hard at Ned Kelly, and passing his wasted hand over his heated brow, while an expression of utter bewilderment stole over his pale features.

"What!" he gasped, sitting up for one moment, and then falling back breathless and exhausted, "Ned——"

Kelly knew the man now, and made a warning gesture.

"I know your friend," he said, turning to the other man, who was looking at the two in surprise.

Truly he knew him only too well.

They were old companions in crime, and had been partners in many a vile and cruel deed, which surely must haunt the guilty sinner on his dying bed.

At the sick man's request, Kelly seated himself near the bed, and, seeing that he had taken notice of his warning, breathed more freely, for he did not care about reposing confidence in too many people. It is a great mistake, as criminals have found to their cost.

The rain had ceased, and, at the sick man's request, the door was thrown open, for the night was hot and close.

Saunders—for such was the name of the friend who had remained at the hut to nurse the sick man—stood looking out into the darkness out of earshot of the two who were conversing in whispers.

"Do you remember the time when I saved your life at the risk of my own?" said William Donovan, feebly, looking up at the dark, harsh features he remembered so well.

He had a strange kind of liking for the bushranger, and perhaps his devotion to the man so unworthy of it was the one tender point in his dark career now drawing to a close.

"Yes," assented Kelly, "you did do me a good turn on that occasion, and I haven't forgotten it; but why remind me of that now? You have some motive, of course, or you would not waste your breath?"

"I have," said Donovan, faintly. "I have a motive which I will explain at once, for there is no time to be lost. You can see, of course, that the hand of death is upon me?"

"You look devilish queer, but doctors tell us that while there's life there's hope," returned Kelly, evasively. "Let's hear what you have to say. Perhaps it will be as well to get it over. Is it anything that concerns me?" with quick anxiety on his own account. "There is no plot hatching against me, is there? You have nothing of that notion to reveal, I hope?"

The sick man shook his head.

"No," he returned. "It is something very different. It does not concern your safety in the least; but after saving your life, I think I have a right to expect your assistance in this matter."

"Well?" asked Kelly. "Get to the point, can't you? What's the use of beating about the bush? What do you want me to do?"

"What I want you to do is, to take the money I have saved to my wife and family. Don't mistake me, you will find it worth your while. I don't expect you to put yourself to all this trouble for nothing. Saunders would do it—he has been a true friend to me—but he is afraid to go to England, and I therefore look to you to carry out my last wishes."

"It shall be done," said Kelly, now thoroughly interested. "How did you obtain the money, and where is it to be found?"

Donovan briefly explained how he had obtained possession of the treasure he wished to divide between his family and Ned Kelly. It is enough for the reader to know that he had waded through blood to obtain his ill-gotten gains.

(To be continued.)

NED KELLY

THE IRONCLAD

AUSTRALIAN BUSHRANGER

NO 12,

But such men are not necessarily without natural affections for their own kith and kin, and the thought of leaving his family well provided for soothed his dying moments.

He told Kelly where he had hidden his gold, and received the bushranger's solemn promise to attend to his last wishes.

What was an oath to such a man as Ned Kelly? He did not care how often he perjured himself if it suited his purpose. All he wanted was to get possession of the gold.

He would have left the hut at once, but thinking it better to keep dark for a few days, made a virtue of necessity, and expressed his willingness to remain with Donovan until the end if he desired his company.

The dying man was truly grateful for this proof of Kelly's friendship, and never thought of doubting him for a single moment.

He had no misgivings, and believed that Kelly would carry out his wishes at the earliest opportunity.

"You will keep half of the money," he stipulated, and Kelly smiled covertly as he agreed to the arrangement.

It was amusing to find a man who knew his real character credulous enough to believe any promise he might make.

He would not have been such a fool as to trust Donovan if their cases had been reversed.

"Good," thought this shrewd and cunning villain looking at the pale features of the dying man, for whom he had not the slightest spark of pity.

Donovan lingered longer than they expected, and it was fearful to hear him swearing and yelling in wild paroxysm of fever.

Saunders often put his hands to his ears to shut out the terrible sounds, but Kelly paid very little attention to these ravings of a disordered brain but calmly smoked his pipe and stared at the raver. He thought it rather a bore, but it would soon be over.

He would have been glad to leave the hut, it is true, but as he could not do so he behaved like a philosopher—a very easy thing to do when it is someone else that suffers, and not yourself.

Suddenly the wild cries ceased, and the dying man lay calm and still.

"Ned," he whispered, opening his heavy eyes, "it is growing dark. I cannot see. Come nearer."

The sunshine was streaming into the hut, but Donovan grasped blindly for the bushranger's hand.

"Here I am," said Kelly, bending down. "What do you want?"

"You will keep your promise?"

"Yes."

"You swear it?" asked the dying man eagerly.

"I do," returned Kelly, without the slightest hesitation. "Make your mind quite easy on that score."

The dying man, satisfied with this promise, sank back upon his pillow and fell into a heavy slumber, from which he never awoke. When the sun once more streamed into the hut, it shone upon a dead face, and Kelly turned away from the sight not in pity or grief, but because it suggested unpleasant thoughts.

CHAPTER LXXXIV.
COMING TO TERMS.

KELLY had no intention of making any of his friends a confidant in the confession made to him by the dead bushranger.

He would find and carry off the treasure of the miner, and whether he sent any to England or not would depend very much on circumstances.

He knew the spot indicated very well. It was near one of the wildest parts of the heights.

In the dead of night he crept into Adelaide and went to the house of a Jew well-known for buying and asking no questions.

He was always to be seen day and night by his customers. Knocking, he was at once admitted.

He was a little, wiry, sallow-faced Englishman, doubtless, if his antecedents were known, an ex-convict like so many others.

"Rather late for business, sir," he said, with a smile, rubbing his claw-like hands together.

"Never too late for that," laughed Kelly. "I should like half-an-hour's chat, so pull out some first-rate swizzle."

The old man led the way into a small sanctum, filled with all sorts of goods.

But there was a table and two chairs.

Dick Pond opened a cupboard and brought out a bottle and two glasses.

Kelly poured himself out one, smacking his lips as he did so.

"Good stuff," he said, "and now to business."

Opening his waistcoat he unloosened a belt from around him.

His gold was in his box at the hotel, but his share of the diamonds he carried about him.

"What do you think of these?" he asked, as he showered the diamonds on the table. To provide against contingencies, Kelly had changed the produce of his many robberies into diamonds. He was a shrewd judge of their value; nearly every shilling he had plundered was thus invested, and it was only when he required cash for his current expenses that he drew upon this novel Bank of "Exchange" by selling a precious stone.

The man snatched at them with the avidity of a vulture securing its prey.

"What do you think of them?" Kelly asked with a quiet chuckle.

The man looked up rapidly and fixed his eyes with a meaning glance on Kelly's.

"Will you truck?" was the cool reply.

"At a price," said the other, drily.

"Speak out," continued Kelly.

The man fetched some scales, and examining each one separately weighed a number together.

He then named a price, upon which Kelly with a rough oath proceeded to return them to his belt.

"Don't be in such a hurry," said the trader, looking a little white about the gills.

And filling a glass each the bargaining was renewed.

At last they came to terms.

Kelly intimated his wish to remain concealed in the trader's house until the next evening, when he would want an outfit, arms, and a good horse.

Mr. Pond readily agreed to let him have a room and all requirements, after which, it being very late, Kelly retired to an upper room, where he locked himself in.

He slept heavily, and it was late when he awakened, and opening his door called out.

The man soon appeared, and ushering him into a sitting-room on the same floor, gave him breakfast.

After the meal was over, Kelly asked his host if he could send a letter for him by a trustworthy messenger.

"Yes," said Pond.

"You must write the letter," laughed Kelly, "my education has been neglected."

"Mine ain't much," replied the other, with a grin, "but I can manage."

"Only a few words," continued the other. "'Going on a journey. Home in a few days,' with the address."

The man having procured materials, wrote as directed, and sent the letter by a girl.

She was acute and cunning.

There was no fear of her being followed or cross-questioned by anyone.

Kelly was not disposed to go out in the day-time, so he found time hang heavy on his hands.

The man, in the intervals of business, kept him company, smoking, drinking, and playing cards.

Thus night came.

Pond now produced a complete miner's outfit, with high boots, Kelly being further disguised with bushy whiskers and a shock wig.

This, and a slouched hat, altered him so much that no one could have recognised him, except, perhaps, Tom Conquest.

Having paid his host very liberally, he went out into the street and mounted his horse.

Kelly had no intention of lingering, but rode hard that night until he reached a wild and rough district, where, however, he found a stock-keeper's hut and a small out-house.

He had with him whisky, tobacco, and a wallet of food; so after fastening his horse, he aroused the man.

"Who the —— is there?" presently cried a sleepy voice. "Be off, or I'll drop you."

"Two can do that, my friend," sarcastically replied Ned Kelly. "I'm a traveller lost my way—got tobacco and schnaps—will pay for a shakedown."

The man made no reply, but presumedly, having peeped out, was satisfied.

The hut was a small square building, with a fireplace, some stools, a rude couch, and a pantry-cupboard.

The man growled out something as he showed Kelly a stool.

Kelly first produced a flask of whisky, then some tobacco, and finally some food.

The man was glad of the drink and smoke, but declined the food, of which Kelly partook freely.

The fellow then, who saw that Kelly had a blanket and cloak, showed him a shakedown, and the tired traveller retired to rest.

Sleep to him was the one necessity of all others.

In this place, at all events, he would in all probability be safe.

He slept rather late, and found the stock-keeper abroad when he woke, attending to his business.

Kelly went out and saw to his horse, after which the man, who was a rather superior person, returned.

"You've a fine animal there," he said in an admiring way. "Going far?"

"To seek my fortune," replied Kelly, with a laugh.

"I've had a snack," the other went on, "but waited breakfast for you."

So he led the way into the hut and soon cooked some mutton, made a damper and some tea, which meal Kelly enjoyed very much.

His constant exercise and his life in the open air gave him a gigantic appetite.

The man tried to learn something of his guest, who was unusually reticent for a gold digger, but Kelly could always spin any yarn; and James Sinclair could make nothing of his guest.

But he liberally paid for his accommodation and rode off, himself and animal well fed.

"Strange fellow," said the stock-keeper to himself; "can't make him out at all."

He guessed afterwards who he was.

Meanwhile Ned Kelly, who knew the country well, hurried forward in the direction indicated by the dying miner.

When once his greed of gold was excited Ned Kelly knew no hesitation. Money was his god.

It was but little out of his way to visit the shanty inn kept by Marsh and his sister.

He thought he would have one quiet evening there before he adventured among his fellows.

Still he avoided all places where he might fall in with his fellow-creatures.

It was towards night when the outlaw reached the neighbourhood of the tavern.

He rode up and, dismounting, fastened his horse to the post.

Mr. and Mrs. Marsh were in the bar, and a number of rough customers were present.

Ned Kelly walked up in his most swaggering way and called for a drink.

It was supplied.

He then asked if he could pass the night, as he had travelled far that day, and would want to travel further the next day.

He was told to come in.

The woman had recognised him at once, and he was quite welcome.

When they were in the private room they shook hands. Both had heard of him since his departure, and, like all depraved natures, were more proud of him the worse he acted.

They got an assistant, an active Irish girl, to attend to the bar, while Maria herself cooked some supper for her brother.

Ned Kelly and his brother-in-law at once drank and smoked together, such being about the sole amusement of such people.

An hour later a supper was laid before him, which he enjoyed.

"People about here safe?" asked Kelly.

"Stock-keepers, stray travellers, bullock-drivers," replied Marsh. "Nothing to fear."

"I'll go in the bar and stand drinks," replied the outlaw, laughing; "can spare a little coin."

And he did so, asking the men to drink for the good of the house.

It was the custom of the country, and none refused to accept the stranger's hospitality.

Presently Kelly proposed a quiet game of cards for a mere trifle, and, all agreeing, was soon the king of the castle.

His merriment was infectious, his stories were broad and exciting, and well calculated to win the admiration of the rough-and-ready crew he had to deal with.

After the house was closed, he spent an hour with his sister and brother-in-law, and then turned in.

He had a good bit of ground to cover before he reached Golden Point, but Kelly could bide his time.

As he rode along he communed with himself, and tried to think of some great coup by which to satisfy his lust for gold and add to his nefarious reputation.

The man was desperate and yet cautious, fond of notoriety and yet reckless.

After breakfast, making a handsome present to his sister and promising to return soon, he started on his way.

For several days he met with no adventures and so neared Golden Point.

It was in the height of its prosperity, and exhibited a heterogeneous mass of tents, huts, and a still more heterogeneous mass of people—diggers, dealers, and store-keepers.

They were a rough lot, all intent upon one thought—that of making money.

Everybody went armed, everybody drank, everybody played cards.

Ned Kelly rode up to one of the rough-and-ready houses which gave entertainment to man and beast, and made himself at home at once.

He was in no hurry. He would look about him.

He had not been half-an-hour in the house before he recognised one or two of his old comrades, but was careful to keep out of sight. They might be inclined to earn the reward.

He determined, as soon as he had rested and refreshed, to move away.

He easily secured a position where he could see without being seen, and enjoyed his meal, his pipe, and his glass.

As night came on, the inroad of miners became greater, and Kelly thought he would make a move.

Pay on delivery, was the maxim of these places, and he had no bill to settle.

Rising, he moved quietly away, went out and procured his horse from an ostler.

It was dark, and Ned Kelly had to discuss with himself how to spend the night.

As he prepared to mount, a hand was laid on his shoulder. He started round.

"Ain't you a word for your old pal, Joe Long?" he said, in a low tone.

"Why, who'd a-thought of seeing you, Joe?" replied Kelly, recovering himself.

"Prospecting," growled Joe; but it ain't a bit of good. Work never did agree with Joe Long, and it don't do."

"Out of luck here?" said Ned.

"Yes."

"Got a crib of any kind?" asked Kelly.

"Yes, a quiet sort of place," said Joe Long; "only prog's scarce."

Kelly gave him gold and bade him get whatever was wanted. He'd wait by a tall tree which he pointed out.

Joe Long took the money and soon came out with supplies.

He then rejoined Kelly and led the way.

In the thick darkness that clothed the scene that night the human figure was almost lost and confounded with the outlines of huts and stones and trees.

But Joe Long knew the way as well in the dark as by daylight.

Presently, quite out of sight of the other huts, Joe Long halted by a hollow tree, and took from the inside a lantern.

This he lighted and again led the way until they came to a hut.

The vague horizon of darkness that a few feet from the lantern still encompassed them until their feet actually trod the ground in front of the cabin.

It half-burrowed in a small hill.

All was lonely, silent, motionless, uninterrupted, basking in the cold light of the stars.

Joe Long entered and hung the lantern upon a hook that dangled from the rafters.

He then proceeded to light a fire by which to cook some bacon and other food.

After a while Joe, having given his old pal a supper, began to enjoy himself.

"What are you doing up here?" he asked Joe presently. "Last place should have thought of seeing you."

"Looking around," answered Ned carelessly. "Town's rather warm. But I mean to do something big soon, and you shall have a chance."

"Thank you," said Joe, and, producing an old pack of cards, they proceeded to play.

Then Kelly rose and, leaning against the doorway, looked out upon the night.

In front was profundity and blackness; above the vault was serene and tranquil.

He came in and prepared for bed.

After one glass and one pipe he wished the other good night and retired to rest.

CHAPTER LXXXV.

THE TREASURE.

THE man Joe Long was plump and short, rather closely cropped and shaven.

He was not a man to manifest any very great activity, but on the next morning he was very busily engaged in preparing breakfast.

As a rule all men who connected themselves with Kelly were faithful and devoted.

He was summary in his jurisdiction; but, though firm, he was just.

"Joe," he said, when the other placed a breakfast before him, more copious than refined, "I think I shall start the band again and do something big."

"That's the style!" cried Joe.

"I've got some important business in Adelaide," continued Ned Kelly, "where some friends of mine are staying. I must go there, and then, let me see, a fortnight hence exactly we'll meet at Blackwater Gully."

"All right, guv'ner," said Joe, "you'll let me have some rhino?"

"Certainly," was the answer. "Try and get a dozen of the best men together. Have you seen Mike Bawn lately?"

"He's in camp somewhere," replied Joe Long. "Seed him two days ago."

"Well, after breakfast," continued Kelly, "I'll take a look round. Find such of the boys as you can trust, and let 'em know I'm about. Know a safe place for supper?"

"Jim Wilkins keeps a saloon," responded Joe; "he's all right."

"I suppose he is," drily remarked Ned. "I'll even trust him. Invite 'em all to a feed. Call me Captain Crisp."

The other laughed.

Few men, even to the most innocent, called themselves by their right names in Australia in those days.

So it was arranged.

After breakfast Joe Long went back to the diggings, while Kelly made for the scrub.

It was a very hot day, and as a rule everybody suffered, except the placid orange-coloured Chinese and the snakes, the weather apparently making the latter more vicious and their bite more deadly.

The rivers in many places had dried up in their beds, in some places cattle perished, while the pretty, graceful shell parrots dropped dead from their perches among the burnt-up foliage.

In the distance ran a fine range of hills, towards which he made his way, a shimmering, hazy white-heat hanging like a cloud over the flat.

An hour later he entered the scrub.

He began to look around him. The man had described the place where he concealed his treasure minutely.

Soon he came to a clump of trees.

He got within their shade, and began to study every one in turn.

On one were several notches.

This one he examined keenly, and found that it was hollow. A lot of dry grass and moss had been thrust into a hole.

This he removed, and found, as the other had told him, a wallet of gold.

He at once fastened it to his horse's saddle-bow and prepared to return.

He had no intention of letting Joe Long know anything of this "find," so determined to conceal in some safe place near to the hut.

It was midday when he got back, and, tired by the heat, lay down.

An hour later Joe came with provisions, and the two had a meal and a sleep.

Towards evening it got cooler, and so the two ventured out to join their friends.

Mike Bawn and about a dozen more of the old ones had been found.

They were only too glad to see Kelly and to enlist under his banner once more.

Joe Long went down first to arrange matters with Jim, and Ned Kelly slowly followed.

His associates, however, had been warned not to be too demonstrative.

He sauntered in, and was soon shaking hands with many of his old pals, as "hard nails" as any in the colony.

But no names were mentioned, and after several rather exuberant drinks the guests were ushered into a private room, where a copious rude supper was provided for them.

The diggers in those days thought more of quantity than quality, either in eating or drinking.

Jim Wilkins had heavily laden his board, and everything was in profusion.

Enigmatical enough was the conversation between Kelly and his friends, but they all understood.

The meeting at Blackwater Gully was arranged for that day fortnight, and all were told to be there armed and prepared for action.

Then the tables were cleared, and the whole party devoted themselves to one of the usual gambling orgies, which were the delight and pleasure of the diggers.

When at last all were tired and exhausted, Jim Wilkins closed the Red Lion Hotel, and the inmates dispersed.

Mike Bawn accompanied Joe Long and Ned Kelly to their hut.

Mike was a dark, terrible desperado of powerful, almost gigantic frame, with a countenance at once fierce and brutal.

He was, however, a fit lieutenant for the desperate Ned Kelly.

They reached the hut.

"Seen Tom Conquest lately?" asked Mike Bawn of his chief.

"Yes," was the dry remark, "I have."

"I hope I shall have my turn," continued Mike Bawn; "only let me capture him. He caught and hung my brother——"

"I know," said Kelly.

"Tit for tat's allus been my motter," grinned the giant. "If I ever gets a chance and let that chap escape, then I expect Sol's ghost will haunt me to my dying day."

"Wait," continued Kelly. "When you bully boys meet me again, I shall have something to say about Tom Conquest."

The giant growled.

His was not a nature to have any patience.

He thirsted for the other man's blood.

But he knew that Kelly was right, and that they must bide their time.

So the subject was dropped, and something else spoken of.

As a matter of course they drank and played cards, after which they sought refuge in sleep, that sleep that knits up the ravelled sleep of care.

Kelly, early in the morning, after acting with extreme generosity to his associates—the golden link was the most potent of all—bade them farewell.

Their rendezvous was arranged, and it was also settled that time was not to interfere with their arrangements.

Then Ned Kelly mounted his horse, and starting from the city of tents, headed once more for Adelaide.

He had his treasure all safely secured about him, and was prepared to be circumspect and careful.

Ned Kelly was under the impression that, apart from his own old associates and gang, he was utterly unknown to anyone save Tom Conquest and the father of the girl whom Tom Conquest loved.

He was, therefore, rather reckless with strangers.

In fact, so far as he was personally concerned, he feared no man.

He determined to take his return journey to Adelaide extremely easy.

Something might turn up.

This monster without—since the death of Rose—a redeeming quality within his soul, started.

He was well armed. The road to him was well-known.

Between the diggings and Adelaide was, however, a considerable ride.

Kelly was ready to believe that because he had already escaped so often with impunity, he might continue to do so.

Therefore, except the most ordinary precautions that a man takes under the circumstances, he took none whatever.

He wished to get back to Adelaide as quickly as possible, so that he might rejoin his companions and then make rapidly for the Black Water Gulley, and carry out some audacious plan of robbery.

He had determined to outdo himself in some act of audacity, cruelty, and impudence.

His disguise was a very good one, and then there was his keen self-possession and cunning.

The first thing he did was to "swap" his horse. This was a very common thing in the colony, and nobody thought anything of it.

Then he started.

Kelly was careful whenever he could get hold of a colonial paper, to read what was going on—generally with a view to what was said about himself.

As a rule, however, he heard enough conversation on the subject without reading.

Well mounted, and well supplied in every way, Ned Kelly started on his return journey to Adelaide.

Distances in the colonies are not counted as they are in the Old Country.

Men think nothing of hundreds of miles in the colonies, and a hard ride of seven hundred miles—which has been done on a memorable occasion by a very well-known person—did not excite astonishment.

But Kelly was in no hurry.

As soon as he was clear of the diggings he made for the high-road, and for the place where it diverged on one side for Melbourne, on the other side for Adelaide.

The bushranger now was particularly cautious.

He wished to excite no attention, to do nothing to draw notice on him.

For this purpose, he had to restrain in every way the exuberance of his character.

Despite the great success of the gold-fields and the money spent by the diggers, hotels were on a very rough scale except in towns.

The road-side inns remained barbarous, though with expensive accommodation.

Kelly, who knew every inch of the way, travelled slowly and as if in no hurry.

He spoke freely to those he met, and inquired the news of all ordinary comers.

More frequently than was agreeable he heard his own name coupled with every possible and impossible crime committed in the colony.

An evil spirit pervaded the man.

He desired to be heard of, but he chose to select his own character of crime.

It annoyed him to have some petty charge laid to him, something mean and contemptible.

One of his chief sources of disguise was dyeing his face, and this he practised with great success.

All the first day he travelled without finding any place of public entertainment.

He had at night to find himself camping out in the woods.

It was no hardship to a man like Ned Kelly, or to anyone else eleven months in the year. It is more agreeable to camp out at night than occupy a feather bed.

When the hour for repose came, he simply withdrew into a thicket.

He was careful on such a day to secure a supply of water.

He had some cooked meat, damper, and tea, with a rough blanket.

Into the scrub he went.

There is nothing disagreeable to a strong and energetic man in passing a night thuswise.

Only to natures like his, the mere fact of loneliness means misery.

What man of evil cares to be left with his own thoughts, to his own devices?

No matter! it had to be done.

Kelly was always careful of his horse for his own sake, and saw to his steed.

Then he located himself in a grove of gum trees, where, without a fire, he contrived to make a very tolerable supper.

After this he lighted his pipe, and passed an hour or two in the disagreeable task of reflection.

What had Ned Kelly to think about?

His own evil deeds, and his own evil origin.

No pleasant reflections; and yet, like many another so-called hero, he complacently thought of the many audacious deeds he had done, and which had excited, in some disgust, in others admiration.

"They shall talk of me more," he said to himself, as he rolled himself into his blanket.

Such a determination would be all well enough if in an honourable cause; but, with those of the outlaw bushranger, they were simply terrible.

Night passed.

At a tolerably early hour the man was on the move, and by night got into a main-road, where he met travellers, and once now and then, a terribly rough stage coach.

For him, however, there was no society until, at least, he reached, towards evening, a kind of hamlet, where the coach changed horses.

Here he determined to pass the night.

He could be sure of an excellent supper, and probably of a certain amount of company and amusement.

As soon as he had thrown his reins to a rude kind of ostler, he intimated his intention of passing the night there.

He then walked into the public room, which no matter how rough, was amply provided for.

"Supper!" was the first order, and then bowing to some four or five strangers, "Drinks—if the gentlemen will allow me?"

Amongst a certain set this sort of introduction is the right sort of thing, and those present were not of a kindred to refuse.

They nodded with a laugh, and the usual drinks popular in the colony in those days, were brought in.

Kelly said little, being satisfied to pay and then eat his evening meal as ordered.

After that he became more social and joined very soon in a game of cards.

It was "spoiled five," which indicated that the players were Irish.

Ned Kelly was very clever at this as at every other game, and put money in his purse.

Still he was careful not to do anything to alarm his new acquaintances, and the night's festivities wound up by a stiff bowl of punch.

"You're a broth of a boy, and know what cards is," remarked a rather curious customer, as they rose to leave, "come to my room, and let us go our level best for a fiver or two."

Ned Kelly never refused these sort of challenges, and the usual adjuncts being sent to the room, the two adjourned.

The man was an enthusiast and rather reckless, consequently suited Ned Kelly.

They played for several hours, consumed a considerable quantity of whisky, and finally retired very much satisfied with themselves.

Kelly was as usual the winner, but not to a very alarming extent, and Simon Gordon the traveller, was not at all annoyed.

"I'm off to Adelaide," he said, "I've business there, perhaps I shall take a trip to the Old Country. Some think the murderer of my brother-in-law," mentioning the deceased merchant, "has gone there, for I'll be bound to follow him up."

Ned Kelly stared with a look of real and unaffected astonishment.

"Hadn't heard," he said.

Then he had to listen to the details of his own fearful crime told with bitter emphasis.

This rather sobered Kelly, who for a moment thought it was what is vulgarly called a plant.

But he presently saw that the other was perfectly genuine, and accepted the proposal to travel the rest of the journey together.

"My traps is gone on," said the traveller, "and we can ride together."

Thus sheltered under the protection of his victim's relative, Ned Kelly made his entrance into Adelaide, going direct to the hotel where his colleagues awaited him.

They were by this time big men at the hotel, and Kelly was proud to introduce his new friend to them.

Simon was a shrewd man of business, but also fond of pleasure and his ease.

He enjoyed any kind of relaxation. He was therefore glad to have anyone who was well acquainted with the means of revelry.

There was no ship quite ready to start for England from the usual cause, and the traveller had to wait.

Kelly smiled grimly as he suggested to his friends another voyage to England.

But none were prepared for such a contingency just yet. They had considerably broken into their money bags and must replenish.

The "how" now arose.

Mr. Simon Gordon was not a man out of whom much was to be made. He was an easy-going pleasure-loving individual, but by no means a man to lose all his substance very easily.

He was hospitable, spent money freely, but was no easy fool to be fleeced.

They soon found this out.

But he was ready and willing to pay his share in all amusements.

A friend of his had a villa in the outskirts of the town. He was a successful merchant of the rough-and-ready sort, and was always glad to play the hospitable.

Gordon took the whole four out there and introduced them to Mr. Stanton and his family.

There was a buxom wife, a son, and several daughters.

Kelly always did make himself agreeable with the women, and singled out one girl, Mary Stanton, to whom he paid marked attention.

She was a merry, light-hearted girl of seventeen, buxom and healthy.

Kelly, despite his roughness of nature, could put on a great deal of the Irishman's blarneying ways when he liked.

He could tell capital stories of the Old Country and elsewhere.

In his rough way he could sing a capital song without the need of accompaniment.

Mary Stanton thought him a wonderful man. Simon Gordon spoke of him as a rich and independent gentleman.

But of course on the two occasions on which Kelly visited Laurel Lodge he made no attempt at any serious manifestation of feeling.

About a week had passed, and Kelly began to think of his rendezvous at Black Water Gully.

He was in the bar of the hotel at a window overlooking the street when he saw Mr. Simon Gordon coming along the side walk towards the house in conversation with a stranger.

Opposite the hotel the two halted, and the stranger looked over.

He was conversing earnestly with Simon.

Kelly knew him now in a moment, though he was not in uniform.

It was Tom Conquest.

Kelly lost not a moment, but joined his companions who were in the billiard-room.

He gave them a whispered direction and then left by the back way.

He at once went to the man who had bought the diamonds, where he procured a rough dress and where he also remained until night.

He then started to walk out of Adelaide, which he decided to give a wide berth to for the present.

He made for a small roadside inn, where at a later hour he was rejoined by his companions, who had also swopped their better clothes for the rough garb of working men.

Conquest had come into the hotel and been closeted with Simon Gordon some time.

The man was a human sleuth-hound, and one of the few whom Kelly feared.

Still he felt himself pretty well a match for him, and took a singular pleasure in foiling and defeating him.

He determined at a future time to show him his mastery over his acuteness and intelligence.

Hitherto they had been equally matched, and Tom Conquest in the deadly contest had nothing to boast of.

CHAPTER LXXXVI.

TEMPORARY RETIREMENT.

KELLY, however, felt himself growing rather tired at times of his life of constant anxiety and watchfulness, and felt half resolved to find out some means of putting an end to the annoyance for a while.

He would not submit to being hunted from place to place like some ferocious animal whom the police had determined to exterminate.

"I can't stand it much longer," he told his friends. "I shall do something desperate if this kind of thing continues.

"It ain't a pleasant sort of caper," assented Joss.

"A confounded shame," growled Captain Zeph. "But how are you going to prevent it?"

"Ay," said Salmon Roe; "the reward is high, and it seems to put them on their mettle. We can't dispose of them all, you know—that isn't possible."

"Do you take me for a fool, all of you?" asked Kelly roughly.

They were sitting on the banks of a stream, resting after a hard day's tramp, and the bushranger was not in the best of tempers.

His companions were well aware of this fact and exchanged glances, but they did not venture to speak.

When in one of his sullen humours he was dreaded even by his associates.

It was impossible to say why they attached themselves to him, unless it was for motives of mutual interest, and because he possessed more brains than the whole three. He was certainly most remarkable in thus winning adherents and awing them into obedience of his slightest whim.

He could often read the secret thoughts of those with whom he was brought into contact, and he observed that his companions were not well pleased at his behaviour.

"Can any of you advise me?" he asked with a sardonic smile. "Perhaps some of you may have a good suggestion to offer, by which I may rid myself of those bloodhounds for a time?"

"We are waiting to hear what you have got to say," said Zeph apologetically.

"You haven't half-an-ounce of brains in your three heads!" said Kelly contemptuously. "I suppose you know that there is a price upon my head?"

"We do," they returned meekly, answering the unnecessary question as Kelly loaded the pistol, but if they thought he had any intention of using it against them they were utterly mistaken. The bushranger knew the value of friends too well for such an act of folly.

"We have managed to live a long time without 'em," added Salmon Roe, trying to make himself pleasant and agreeable. "People can't be all alike in this world, but I wouldn't change positions with you for all that. I shouldn't feel very comfortable if I knew that there was ten thousand pounds reward offered for my nut."

"I've often wondered why you fellows don't round on me," said Kelly with a reckless laugh. "I shouldn't hesitate if I were in your place. It is a great temptation, boys, you must allow."

They laughed, glad to see that Kelly was recovering from his ill-temper.

"You have trusted us," said Joss, "and we shouldn't think of selling you for twice the money."

"How do you know I have trusted you?" retorted Kelly. "I trust nobody, and I believe in nobody but myself. A man is his own best friend."

Kelly relapsed into thought for two or three minutes, while the others lazily reclined on the grass.

"I have hit upon something," he said, suddenly. "It is a grand idea, and will put the police completely off the scent. What put it in my head I can't make out."

"What is it?" they asked in one voice.

"Listen," replied Kelly.

"Fire away," remarked Salmon Roe.

"We are all anxious to hear what you have to propose," said Captain Zeph.

"It is bound to be something 'cute," observed Joss, raising his knees, as he gazed at Kelly with real or pretended admiration.

"Don't interrupt," said Kelly, angrily.

"No offence," said Roe to himself, taking a good pull at the black pipe in his mouth.

"Well, then," said Kelly, "you all know that at this time of the year squatters and wool-growers are short of hands."

"What's that to do with us?" asked Zeph.

Not condescending to reply to Zeph's question, Kelly continued—

"They are short of hands, and will be glad to get them, however inexperienced, if they are strong and handy."

"I daresay they would, but where are they going to find them? This is rather an out-of-the-way part, this is," said Salmon Roe.

"We must offer ourselves," said Kelly.

"Ourselves!" repeated the other.

"Yes, offer ourselves," returned Kelly. "As farm-servants we shall never be recognised; the police will be completely baffled."

"It will be a rather quiet life for us," said Zeph, thoughtfully; "but I suppose it won't last long?"

"Not longer than necessary," replied Kelly. "I only want to fool the police for a week or two. They will get tired of searching for me, and will be thoroughly shunted."

"There is no station about here, is there?" said Salmon Roe. "There isn't a house for many miles."

"There is only one shanty about here, and that is about ten miles off," replied Kelly. "It is owned by a very rich man, who has no occasion to work for his living at all, but can't bear to be idle. He has got lots of stock, and a thundering pretty daughter."

"You seem to know all about him."

"I have been in this part before. Let us start for the place without delay."

The other men who were very comfortable where they were, for they had camped for the night, did not feel inclined to move, but they got up reluctantly and followed Kelly who had leaped the small stream.

They were all strong and active fellows, but they had great difficulty in keeping up with Kelly who walked at a rapid rate.

Before they had done half the distance they were perspiring in streams. The heat was intense.

Ned noticed their discomfiture but this increased his enjoyment, and he redoubled his speed.

Zeph grumbled to the others, but the grumbling did not reach Kelly's ears.

They soon arrived at their destination, and at once addressed the master of the place.

He was a man in a loose jacket and a large straw hat, and was in the act of smoking a well coloured pipe when Kelly accosted him.

"Well?" he said laconically, surveying Kelly, and then, turning his attention to the others, looked at them up and down with great coolness and deliberation.

"We are in want of work," returned Kelly, "and I know there is always plenty to do at this time. Will you give us a job?"

"I think it can be managed," said the squatter, unsuspiciously satisfied that they were all stout strong fellows, a great recommendation in his eyes. "If there is anything I do dislike it is to see hearty active men out of employment through no fault of their own."

"It's hard lines certainly," said Kelly. "We are all truly grateful and will take care that you do not repent your kindness."

Mr. Stephens nodded, being a man of few words, and showed them what they would be required to do.

He was not displeased at having secured such men, little knowing their real character or dreaming that he was standing beside the notorious bushranger.

They all acted their parts with excessive cunning and a coolness which nothing could move, having been well drilled by the astute Kelly, who desired to keep quiet for a few days and knew no other way to secure his object.

A more observant man than Mr. Stephens might have been struck by the bushranger's harsh and marked features, but he employed a number of men and did not think it necessary to trouble himself about their peculiarities of manner and appearance.

All he desired was that they should do his work as speedily as possible, and do it thoroughly while they were about it, and if they satisfied him on that point he asked no more being an easy going man, who took life as it came and was careful not to give himself more trouble than was absolutely necessary.

He was just the man Kelly would have picked out for his purpose if he had been given the choice. The bushranger hated the inquisitive and curious like poison.

"I hope this won't last long," said Joss, discontentedly, when they were alone after the second days work. "Hard work goes against the grain. It ain't often I have tried it, but I'll be—— if it ain't enough to make a fellow wish himself in the stone jug."

"You've got good grub and a bed to lie on," returned Salmon Roe, with a grin. "eat and thank your stars."

"Thanks be hanged," said Joss. "I'd sooner be in jail than stand this life much longer. There you know you are obliged to do work; but there is no need for this slavery as far as I can see. Is Kelly getting funky—"

"What's that," asked the bushranger, clapping his hand on the speaker's shoulder, to his great dismay for he had not known that Kelly was so near.

He commenced a lame apology but Kelly cut him short at once.

"Dry up." he said, "there is no need for excuses, I am as sick of this life as you can possibly be and am only waiting till I see a way out of it. Have patience for a little while longer boys."

"Oh, you are thinking of cutting it then?" said Joss, with an air of relief.

"Did you think I was a fixture here?" asked Kelly. "We'll be far away from here before long never fear."

And with this assurance they had to be content, well knowing that Ned Kelly would remain where he was as long as he thought proper, unmoved by any remonstrance they might make.

Kelly found it very difficult to continue steadily to fulfil his self-imposed servitude in the station, but the necessity of lulling all suspicion and throwing the authorities off the track made him submit for a time to the irksome yoke. It could not last much longer, for his "company" were beginning to get rebellious and restless under the decent discipline of labour.

The bushranger was becoming a great favourite with the master, having managed to take every duty, however slight, off his hands, and it soon became evident that Kelly could soon, if he liked, be promoted to the post of overseer.

This of course created no little jealousy amongst the other men, and Kelly himself scarcely knew how much he was disliked, until one day he had a little difference with the man who had been everybody before he made his appearance, when he found that the sympathy was decidedly not on his side.

"Why should you be put over my head?" said the man as they stood in the stock-yard after the day's work was over. "What the deuce brings you here to interfere with an honest man's work? Its—— tramps like you that gets us the sack. You crawling crackman, that's what you are, its my belief. I wouldn't leave an old knife in your way, if I wanted to keep it."

"Hold your jaw," fiercely howled Kelly, "or I'll make an old knife of you. Why, the marks of the darbies aint off your arms yet, you old lag!"

"They ought to be on yours, I believe, if the truth was told," was the reply, "and I'm blowed if I don't think

you've had the 'Irons' on your heels already. Let's see you walk, do. Why you've got the 'lifer's' stroddie—nah! hah! Get up. You aint game. Well, I'll help you. You'll get used to have the metal off your ankles in time," and approaching Kelly, he roughly pushed him off the rail of the stock-yard upon which he was sitting.

The man, whose name was Jim Shute, put his ugly face close to Kelly's and spat at the bushranger, who was utterly taken aback by the insult.

Shute, thinking that he was thoroughly cowed, then struck him across the face, much to the delight of all the spectators with the exception of Kelly's three friends, who expected to see the man stretched lifeless at the bushranger's feet.

Kelly, with a roar like a wild beast, felt for his pistol, but some friends of Jim's, knowing that a row was coming off that night, had taken the precaution to remove it from his belt.

"Don't feel for your barkers," said Shute, "but have it out fair, like a man."

Before he could utter another word he was seized in the powerful grasp of the enraged bushranger, and hurried towards a small stream, in spite of his protestations and struggles.

He was like an infant in that powerful grasp, and none of his friends offered to interfere, although they had only been too eager to get up the row.

There was something about Kelly which made them respect him at that moment.

He did not look like a man who would be trifled with, and they therefore contented themselves with watching the proceedings from a respectful distance.

Ned, with a mocking laugh, forced the man's head under water, holding it there till the blood ran out of his nose. Had not Mr. Stephens appeared upon the scene the man would most certainly have been killed.

He had been a witness of the whole scene, and his verdict was, "Serve you right!" when Shute came to make a formal complaint, but he privately lectured Ned for thus giving vent to his temper, however much provoked.

His little lecture made Kelly grin when his back was turned, but he took it in good part, promising not to let his temper run away with him again.

"Look here," said Joss, shoving the bushranger on one side, "don't look startled by what I am going to tell you. I know that this is a rather useless caution, but it is best to be careful, situated as we are."

"Cut along," said Kelly; "I prefer anything to suspense. Out with it, man!"

"Well, I'll tell you what it is," said Jim, "that Shute suspects who you are. I saw him looking at you with a nasty smile a few minutes ago. I believe he means mischief."

"Curse him," said Kelly; "why didn't I smother him? If he suspects me, how is it he does not speak to Stephens?"

"Because he thinks that trick won't pay. Some of the other men would want to go halves with him. He has got some other idea in his head."

"Well, all we can do is to keep our eyes on him for the future," returned Kelly, and then the subject dropped.

But that night, as the four friends sat talking together, Jim Shute crawled close up to them and listened attentively to every word they uttered.

What they said fully confirmed his suspicions, and rising, with a smile upon his face, he slowly stole away, vanishing without the slightest sound.

"What's that?" asked Kelly, suddenly lifting his head as the thunder of horses' hoofs fell upon his ears. "Hulloa! look out! Shute has gone off to set the traps on us—the ruffian!"

"I told you so," said Joss, while the others looked at each other with consternation. "Our best plan is to slope before it is too late."

"Yes, let's clear out," cried Captain Zeph and Salmon

Roe in a breath, "This is no place for us now. We have stopped too long."

"Not so fast," said Kelly. "I've got a dodge worth two of that. My idea is to rouse the house and denounce him as a horse-stealer. It will give us breathing time at all events, and we can easily find some excuses for not joining in the pursuit."

"That's trumps," said Jim, admiringly. "What a out you have got."

Mr. Stephens was soon aroused, and great was his anger and indignation to find that two of his best and most valued horses were missing.

Several started in pursuit of the supposed thieves, and Kelly and his associates remained behind with others to protect (?) the women. Mr. Stephens was at the head of the pursuers.

The bushranger laughed grimly as he watched their departure.

"Now, boys," he cried, when the sound of the horses' hoofs had died away in the distance, "Let's go and prepare Miss Stephens for a little journey. I'm going to take her away in pledge, and I expect that the old man will offer a very handsome ransom for his pretty daughter. In any case we shall find her useful in keeping the traps at bay, and if the worst comes to the worst she'll be a pleasant companion."

"But where shall we take her?" asked Roe, not displeased with the idea, but fearful that they would find a petticoat rather in the way.

"The Grey Scrub Flat is the place," returned Kelly as he went up to secure the girl, who was quietly slumbering unconscious of the terrible danger that menaced her.

Kelly, showering blows upon the door, aroused her from her sleep, and she sprang up in bed startled and alarmed.

The bushranger soon made her understand what he wanted her to do, and, fearing that he would carry out his threat of entering the room if she hesitated, hastily attired herself, shivering with horror, and longing inexpressibly for the sound of her father's voice.

Several horses were nearly saddled when Kelly led the trembling girl out into the open air.

"Stephens will wish he had not been in such a hurry to go after his stolen horses," said Kelly as they rode away.

He led the horse upon which the unhappy girl sat, pale and trembling, and motionless as a statue.

She was almost paralysed with grief and horror at this outrage.

She looked at the long, rambling structure, and wondered if it could be possible that they were indeed taking her away from her home where she had lived for so many happy years without dreaming of danger.

Who shall picture that poor creature's unutterable sickness of heart!

She was not a fainting woman, and was fully alive to all the horrors of her position.

If she could have lost consciousness she would have escaped much misery.

"Cheer up," said Kelly, consolingly. "We would not hurt a hair of your head, so there is no occasion for you to look so frightened. My comrades and I are devoted to the ladies, eh, mates?"

"We dote on 'em," said Joss with a leer.

"Literally adore the ground they walks upon," said Captain Zeph, while Salmon Roe smiled approvingly in chorus.

"Oh, if you have the slightest spark of pity, restore me to my home," said the girl, finding voice at last.

"All in good time, my dear," said Kelly, unmoved by her distress. "You will have to exercise a little patience while your father is making up his mind how much you are worth. You cannot expect that we shall part with you for nothing, after all the trouble we have had to carry you off during the absence of your worthy father, for whom we shall always have a great personal friendship. But business is business, and we cannot part with you until we get something in exchange."

The girl looked at the dark, forbidding face, and saw how impossible it was to move him to pity, but she made another wild appeal, another vain and fruitless attempt to move his stony heart.

"My father will reward you well," she cried, "He will ask no questions if you will only take me back at once. In the name of heaven take me back if you are not fiends in human shape."

The tears of anguish rolled down her fair cheek as she spoke, but these guilt-stained men witnessed her distress unmoved, and felt no pang of conscience.

It is not true that conscience makes cowards of us all. These men were utterly without mercy, and could laugh with careless mirth at human misery.

Death never comes to those who wish for it, or poor Kate Stephens would have fallen to the ground a lifeless corpse.

She began to sob bitterly, not to move their pity, but to relieve her overcharged heart, which seemed full to overflowing.

"Those tears are scarcely complimentary," said Kelly. "Do you know who I am, my pretty lass?"

Kate made no reply, but continued to sob bitterly.

"I am Kelly the ironclad bushranger," said Kelly, with some pride of manner.

He was proud of his unenviable notoriety.

The girl gave a low startled cry of horror and dismay.

She had heard that name before, and knew that a man like Kelly would shrink from nothing, however infamous.

How blind her father must have been to employ such men.

It seemed to her now that everybody ought to have seen through them at first.

They were riding swiftly through the black darkness, and with desperate strength she suddenly tore her horse's bridle away from the bushranger, and, turning her horse's head, galloped in the direction of home.

It was a bold stroke, and for a moment the men were taken utterly by surprise.

"Curse the young hussy!" cried Kelly, angrily. "We must lose no time, or we shall lose her after all. She knows how to sit her horse."

They turned their horses' heads and followed in pursuit of the unhappy girl, who shuddered as she heard the horses' hoofs.

Closer and closer they came; but she urged her horse to the top of its speed, and managed to keep a little in advance, hoping against hope.

Suddenly Kelly determined to put an end to the chase, and, drawing out his pistol, fired recklessly, caring very little which he shot, the woman or the horse.

The girl gave a wild cry as the poor animal fell to the ground wounded.

Kate herself was uninjured, and struggled to her feet to find herself in the grasp of the terrible bushranger.

"A pretty dance you have led us, girl," said Kelly, angrily. "You might have known that a wench could not outwit four men. It would have been better for you if you had taken things quietly instead of putting us out of temper."

"Fiend!" cried Kate, indignantly, and her black eyes shone like stars, "do your worst."

Kelly looked at her with undisguised admiration in spite of his anger.

He liked a woman with some spirit.

She shuddered as he placed his hand on her arm, shrinking from him in very evident disgust.

"Come," he said, "you will have to ride on my horse since you were foolish enough to compel me to shoot down your own. As I said before, you have gained nothing by your foolish display of temper."

"I wish that I could strike you dead," said Kate clenching her little fist in impotent rage. "Why are such wretches as you allowed to live in this bright and beautiful world?"

Kelly scowled at her savagely.

He felt that Miss Stephens was going a little too far. He didn't mind a display of temper, but he objected to personal abuse.

"Come!" he said again, rather harshly this time, and picking her up unceremoniously, placed her before him on his horse in spite of her wild struggles.

The girl could not bear to feel his strong arm round her slim waist, and shrank from him in unutterable horror and loathing.

She did indeed regret her attempt to escape. It had done her no good, but only made her position infinitely more disagreeable and unpleasant.

Kelly looked at her half-averted face with a smile, and held her closer as he felt how she shrank from him.

"It would have saved us a great deal of trouble if we had done this at first," he said. "We ought to thank you for suggesting the idea."

Kate made no reply.

She was too indignant to be able to command her voice, and she knew that those evil men only sneered at her tears.

It was a terrible position for a young girl, sweet and innocent, and poor Kate longed for death in her misery.

She felt that she had very little mercy to expect from these men, and her only hope was that her father would return home, and finding her gone, immediately start in pursuit of his lost daughter.

"Where are they taking me to?" she thought, as they rode along, the deep silence unbroken save by the clatter of the horses' hoofs.

"This must be a very romantic ride for you," said Kelly, breaking the silence. "It will be something to remember when you are old and grey, if you should live so long."

"I shall remember it as the greatest degradation I have ever endured," she returned with an indignant blush.

Before Kelly could make any reply he heard the sound of men, and hastily clapped his hand over the girl's mouth as she was about to cry out.

Then the four men drove their horses behind some bushes, which effectually concealed them in the darkness.

Hardly had they done so when a party of horsemen came in view.

It was the party that had gone in search of Jim Shute. Stephens was at their head.

They had evidently come up with Jim Shute, for there were two horses with riders being led along.

Jim Shute was nowhere to be seen, and the bushranger felt no doubt that he had been hung or shot.

The young girl's feelings may be easier imagined than described.

To see her father so near and not be able to make known her presence to him, was terrible.

If she could only have given one cry.

She struggled so desperately that Kelly had the utmost difficulty in keeping his hand over her mouth.

The horsemen were soon out of sight again, and gradually the sound of horses' hoofs died away in the distance.

"You little she-devil!" said Kelly, when he thought it safe to speak; "you nearly spoilt all with your tongue. I'll teach you to defy Ned Kelly!"

And with these words the brutal ruffian struck her in the face with his open hand.

"Coward!" cried the girl, her eyes flashing with indignation and mortification. "Coward! to strike a woman!"

"You had better be careful," said Ned Kelly, significantly. "Remember you are in my power, and I can do what I like to you. If I had not got an object in view you should be my wife for a week or two; but I want to get a price for you. If your father thinks you worth paying for, you shall be returned to him safe and sound. If not, I'll keep you here till I am tired, and then turn you adrift as a warning to those who trifle with Ned Kelly."

"Monster!" cried Kate; "why not kill me at once? I ask you in the name of mercy to put me out of my misery!"

The girl was not afraid of Ned Kelly's fist, but she felt a dread that the licentious bushranger would never let her return before he had accomplished her ruin.

She had heard tales of women being insulted and cruelly used by bushrangers.

How could she defend herself from them? She was a poor weak girl, in the power of men whose deeds were so notorious.

The country rang with tales of their misdeeds.

All that night they galloped on, and Kate knew that she was leaving her home farther and farther behind.

At last morning broke.

Kate looked about.

The country was unfamiliar, and she knew she must be far from home, for she had often had long rides with her father.

The sun shone upon the level scrub-land, and upon the face of the terror-stricken girl and the villains who had torn her from her home.

She was as white as death and exhausted with the long ride.

Grey Scrub Flat was reached at last.

This was their destination.

Kelly and his pony stopped before the door of a tumble-down shanty.

A man came to the door.

He was a shepherd. Kelly knew him well, he had often done the bushranger a good turn when that gentleman had made it worth his while.

"Hulloa," he said, looking in surprise at the girl, "been wench-stealing? Why, I'm blessed if it isn't old Stephens' daughter," giving her a pitying glance. The two had met before.

"We want to stop here for a day or two," said Kelly.

"With the girl?"

"Yes."

"Couldn't you go somewhere else?"

The man was not all bad. He had helped Kelly to escape from justice often because he had done him a good turn once, but he had never joined him in his crimes.

"Shut up," said Kelly, roughly.

And the men dismounted from their horses, much to the annoyance of the shepherd.

"It ain't safe to stop here."

"Why not?" asked Kelly.

"Because Stephens will search high and low for his daughter," replied the shepherd.

"He'll never think of coming here," said Kelly, and pushing the girl before him, he entered the hut.

The girl, who had seen the shepherd before on her father's land, threw herself at his feet and begged him to take her back.

The shepherd would only have been too glad to comply with this request, but he could do nothing against four men.

"You have some feeling," cried the girl, "you will not let them ill-use me, you will take me home and my father will reward you."

"He couldn't take you home if he wished to, you little fool," said Kelly, with a grin. "You forget that we are four to one, and the first move he made against me would be his last."

The girl saw that Kelly was right.

She would not waste her breath in idle pleading, it could do no good.

The rough owner of the hut felt his heart bleed for this defenceless woman in the power of these men.

He was afraid she would meet with a fate ten thousand times worse than death.

Ned Kelly could have brought her here only for one purpose, and that purpose was so horrible that the shepherd shuddered.

The girl was doomed.

The shepherd resolved to defend her with his life, if

Ned Kelly tried to treat her with indignity. He gave a sigh of relief when Kelly told him of his real intention, and asked him to go off at once to negotiate with old Stephens.

He was only too glad to consent to this, for he knew that the old man would pay any sum for his daughter.

"You shall have your share," said Kelly, in conclusion, and the shepherd started off at once. Before leaving he was warned that if the party were betrayed, Ned would shoot the girl on the spot, and that scouts would be placed on the lookout for all comers.

The girl was locked in the hut, and, worn-out with exhaustion, fell into an uneasy sleep.

Kelly and his men, the weather being fine, laid themselves down under the bushes.

Presently Joss, who had taken a great fancy to the girl, sneaked away and made for the hut.

Opening the door quietly he crept softly in.

The girl was lying with a happy smile on her face, innocent and beautiful.

Joss looked at her with delight.

He muttered, "I don't see why Ned should not allow us to touch her, because he doesn't want her himself. He is a dog in the manger, that's what he is."

He stooped to kiss her, and the girl awoke to see the hideous wretch gloating over her.

She gave a wild shriek.

"Shrieking won't do no good," said Joss.

Again her shrieks rang out.

In another moment Kelly came rushing into the hut, red with passion.

He seized Joss by the collar and hurled him out of the hut.

"Keep your ugly carcase out of that hut," cried Kelly. "Do you think I have run away with her for your pleasure? She is to be returned to her father unharmed, providing he pays the money for her."

Joss muttered something, but he did not molest the girl again.

He knew better.

Kelly did not care much what became of the girl, but he guarded her from Joss, because he enjoyed keeping that gentleman in check.

In the evening the shepherd returned with a handsome amount.

"This is half of what you are to get," said the shepherd. "When she is returned to her father you will get the other half. Old Stephens is a man of his word."

Then Kate was given back to her father, uninjured and unpolluted by the bushranger, and her joy was great, and she returned thanks to God upon her wonderful escape.

CHAPTER LXXXVII.

BLACKWATER GULLY.

KELLY and his companions now knew that to remain in that neighbourhood would indeed be the height of folly.

He must put hundreds of miles between himself and the enemy.

They rode hard and fast, nor halted until they had reached a wild and desolate district, miles away from the scene of the late outrage.

They stopped only to rest their horses, nor halted anywhere except in wild and almost inaccessible districts.

Several days after leaving Gray Scrub Flat they came to a small glade belted by strong-limbed trees.

They were within an hour of Black Water Gully. Here Kelly proposed to halt.

It was a beautiful spot.

How peaceful the sun fell through the trees! How beautiful was the forest green! How happy and unconcerned the birds flew in and out of the branches!

But the bushrangers took no note of this. They had no eye for nature.

Having hobbled their horses they supped, and waited for night to set in.

Then Kelly led the way in the direction of the wild valley of Black Water Gully.

Approaching carefully, Kelly soon found that it was tenanted.

Under the shelter of some lofty trees were collected a ruffianly band, among whom Kelly at once recognised Mike Bawn and others.

A whistle brought them all to their feet, and soon the gang was revealed, all very delighted to welcome Ned

Some hours were passed in revelry, and then all sought much-needed repose.

Early in the morning Kelly held a council of war, to which his immediate associates and Mike Bawn were admitted.

"My notion," said Kelly, "is to go up to Ballarat, and watch our chances. We can either see what turns up, or do a great stroke—rob the escort, and follow it into Melbourne."

"Better tackle it on the road," replied Mike, "if we're strong enough."

"If we make a big haul," continued Kelly, "we can be off to the ranges, where all the troopers in the world, black or white, would never hunt us up."

So it was agreed.

To go to Ballarat in a body would, of course, have been the height of folly.

They would have to disperse, appoint a rendezvous, and meet as if casually.

That day, however, they journeyed together, halting at night at a shanty, where they found a rude and motley group.

This was just their style, and they added to the rioting and noise.

They were all bound for the diggings, except a few who were stock-keepers or shepherds.

At the end of the day's march the band separated, Kelly retaining with him his three inseparables.

They would not excite any particular suspicion.

They camped in a wood by the wayside, and enjoyed themselves as usual.

Suddenly they heard horses, and peering out saw six troopers led by a guide, a man whom they had passed during the day.

He had, doubtless, in some way recognised some of them.

Everyone flew to his gun, and then rushed for his horse.

The police came bounding on.

"Spread!" cried Kelly.

"On! on! men!" exclaimed the officer in charge. "We have the ruffians now," and he fired a pistol in the direction of Kelly.

The bullet whizzed harmlessly away into the forest, but the bushranger was more fortunate, wounding the other severely.

He then rode away; swerving his horse round, he dashed into the forest.

The flight of Ned Kelly was taken as a signal by his men, who, scattering instantly, followed his example, hoping to find concealment in the forest or different gullies, with which they were well conversant.

Two of the men gave chase to Kelly.

Swiftly the bushranger rode, his body bent low in the saddle.

The track he had chosen was evidently known to him, and the police found it extremely difficult to follow.

The trees seemed to open and to close upon the fugitive, like a green sea, making shooting uncertain.

Twice the pursuers tried it, the balls *en ricochet* from the tree-trunks.

Soon it was apparent that the fugitive was distancing them. They saw him turn back, and heard his taunting laugh of defiance.

Suddenly he threw up his head and shouted to them over his shoulder.

"I know the place!" cried the astonished officer to his trooper. "We are approaching One-tree Gulley; it crosses our path. He'll never attempt the leap, no horse could do it."

"I don't know, sir," answered the man. "If that man is Kelly, he may, if the horse is sound; he's done it before—it is known as his leap."

"Then he has escaped us," ejaculated the officer, as he perceived the splendid horse rising to the jump.

The trooper levelled his pistol and fired at the horse.

But in his anxiety he did not touch him. The animal reached the opposite side.

Neither of the men dared to follow. It was a desperate leap, only to be taken by an utterly desperate man.

The troopers gazed after the retreating form in admiration It was a daring deed indeed.

Kelly rode off at a rapid pace. He knew that the mounted police would have to go a long way round, but he determined to give them no chance of molesting him.

The rendezvous was in a deserted claim, which had been given up some time as exhausted

He rode hard until about twelve and then halted.

He had come by devious ways, and knew that he could not be pursued.

He halted, took a pull at his whisky-flask, and then slept soundly, his hobbled horse feeding within fifty yards of him. The grass was so plentiful that the beast did not require to roam in search of food. His hard day's work and Kelly's weight had told somewhat upon his inclination to ramble.

At about an hour after dawn he rose, chewed some tobacco to keep off the hunger, and started on his way.

Bushell's Creek had once been a popular digging, but it had long since been exhausted.

At all events better claims turned up, and it had been deserted.

Still two or three half-ruined huts remained.

Yet it was very still and quiet.

Had it not been for the windlass of a shaft, a coil of rope, and a few heaps of lime and gravel, which were the only indications of human labour in that stony field, there was nothing to intercept its monotonous dead level.

Kelly reached it about nightfall, and made himself at home in one of the huts

He sat waiting for his fellows.

They came in about an hour, and none of them had seen anything of the police.

They had given them the slip.

The question now arose as to whether it was a wise thing to go to Ballarat.

Kelly insisted that in that motley city of canvas they were safer than anywhere else.

The crowd, the ever-changing crowd, the places of entertainment and refreshment were all means of hiding themselves.

And as usual the rest of the gang gave way to their leader.

Next morning early they started for Ballarat, which they reached towards the evening.

A general dispersal took place, all agreeing to meet at the Big Nugget in the evening.

It was a notoriously large digger restaurant, known all over the colony.

Though roughly built, a mere huge shanty, it was a wonderful place.

Already people were finding that fortunes are made, not digging for gold, but by food, luxuries, and necessaries for the really hardworking diggers.

Men earning money in such an easy and precarious way as gold-digging, are ready to pay any price for what suits their appetite or fancy.

At the back of the huge canvas caravansari were some rude stables, and to these Ned Kelly committed the charge of his horse.

He then swaggered into the Big Nugget and ordered supper of one of the waiters.

It was at once provided.

It was indeed a Babel of voices, and even of languages, for few were unspoken in that place.

Kelly got into an obscure corner. Except when excited he did not care about attracting too much attention.

It was not at all a wise thing to do under the circumstances in which he was placed.

While he was supping the others dropped in, and joined their chief at his table.

The scene was one as picturesque as it was wild.

In the canvas city they found on the outskirts a hut which had been left by a recent tenant, rudely furnished.

This they hired with its rude furniture, and late at night retired to its protection.

It was solitary, and they could consult without fear of being overheard.

There were so many people at the gold diggings at that time, that nobody thought of asking anyone about their business.

Diggers were accustomed to idle for days together, and it excited no surprise when men spent days and nights in the saloons.

They were never closed. When people came in the morning they generally found the sleepy-looking "all night" bar-keeper on the point of withdrawing for the day, on a mattress in an out-house.

A Chinese or other porter would be seen washing out the stains from the bar-room and verandah.

No one could believe, unless he went at that time, in the existence of so much lemon-peel and cigar-stumps.

But Kelly and his friends were not of those who cared to show early.

(To be continued.)

NED KELLY THE IRONCLAD AUSTRALIAN BUSHRANGER

NO 13,

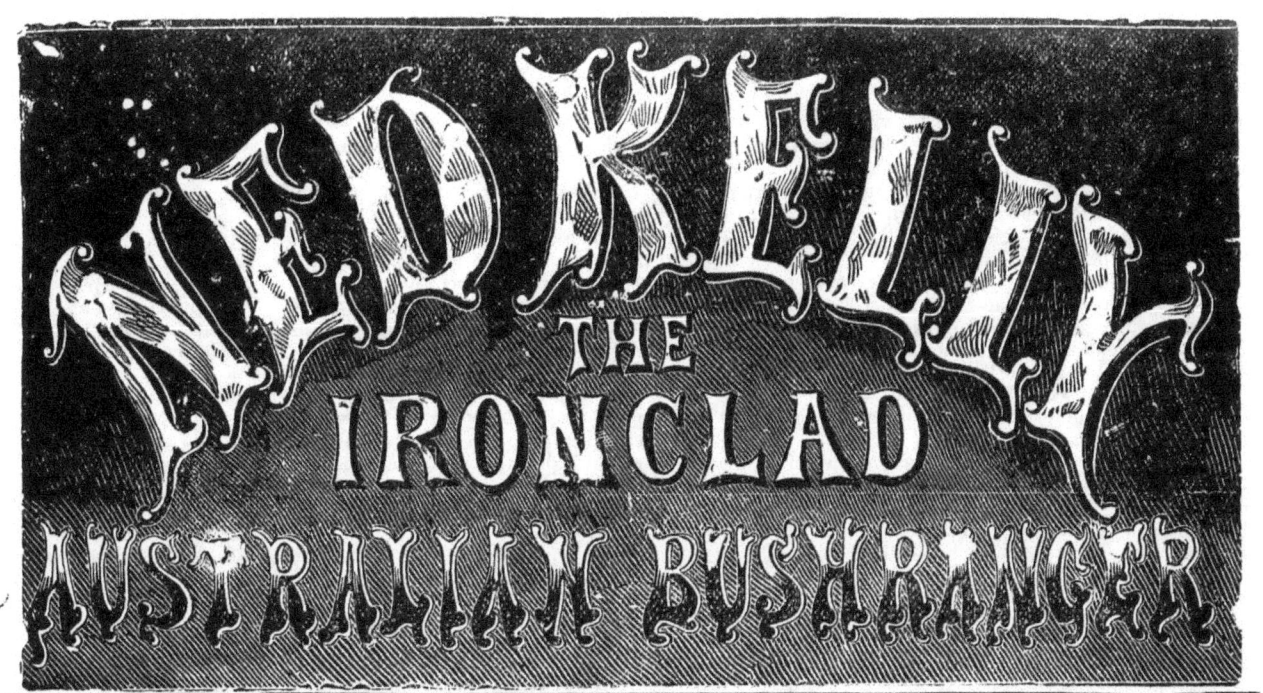

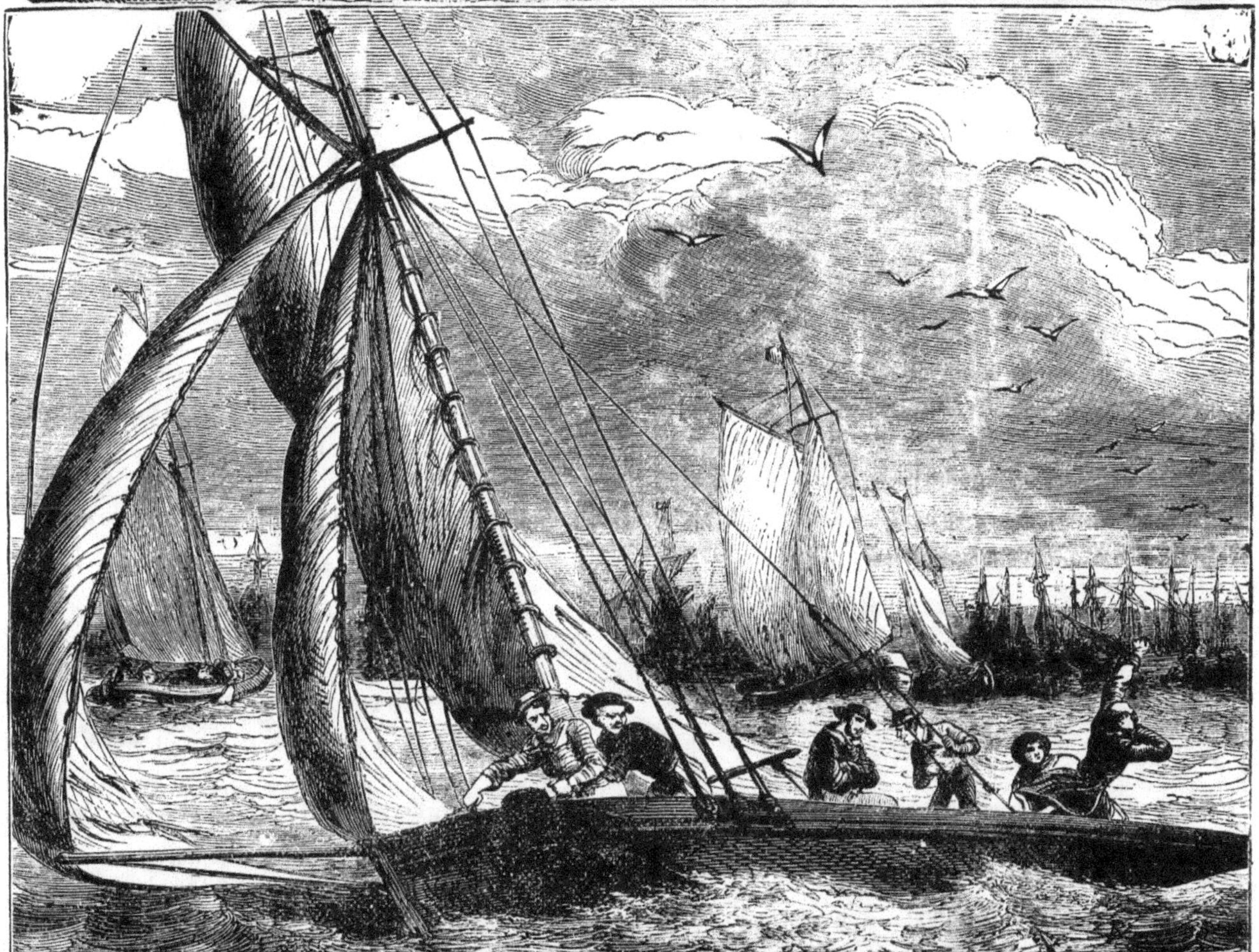

They preferred to have their breakfast comfortably and wander round.

Their object was to learn when the gold escort would leave Ballarat for Melbourne and then organise their forces.

About midday they went to the Big Nugget and found some of the others had arrived.

Ned Kelly found the Ballarat gold escort would depart in five days for Melbourne.

The Big Nugget was waiting for the escort.

That night he ordered a meeting in a gloomy and retired gully, a mile out of Ballarat.

It was known as Dead Man's Hole.

There was some terrible tale connected with it at the time, but which is now forgotten.

It was in a wild and desolate region, where few were likely to penetrate of their own accord.

A fire was lighted in a sort of hollow at the side of a hill, and round this the band collected, one of the party keeping a good watch on the hill-side.

Kelly counted fifteen heads.

He then made them a little speech, in which he laid out his plans fully.

They were astutely arranged, but required determination and resolution to carry out.

Any failure would involve very serious result.

The gold escort would, in addition to twenty mounted troopers, have returning diggers, men who, as a rule, would fight desperately.

The whole thing would have to be a surprise and a well-organised one.

Kelly gave his orders, and then the gang dispersed and returned to their different locations in and around Ballarat.

Kelly, though not personally known to any but his own associates at the diggings, was described with such minuteness on the bills, that had he not have been most careful with his disguises he must have been recognised.

Not so much, however, had been heard of him lately, and it was generally suspected in the colony that he had made himself scarce.

This was very much in his favour, as people ceased to look out for him, and other topics of the day cropped up.

Kelly was in reality very much annoyed, as his great and crowning defect was vanity.

Not to be spoken of at all was to him a great source of disgust.

Of course he dared not obtrude the subject for fear of exciting suspicion.

But they should know he was alive in a day or two, succeed or not.

On the fourth day, that before which the escort was to leave, Kelly fetched his horse, paid for its keep, and started with the mate.

They were to go in couples.

About two days' journey from Ballarat was a place known as Troy, where there was one of the roadside inns.

It was situated near a very dense centre of bush, through which the road passed.

In consequence of the previous attempts to rob the escort, the leaders had adopted the plan of having scouts abroad.

They went in front and examined every inch of the ground, which was thus rendered tolerably safe.

Kelly was at his wits' end to concoct some way of circumventing the troopers and their convoy with the least danger to himself and party.

Meanwhile all preparations were being made in Ballarat for the journey.

The waggons were ready, the gold was ready, and the troopers were ready.

"I should like to be safe in Melbourne," observed the officer in charge, one Johnson, to a successful digger about to accompany them. "Never feel safe as long as Kelly is unhung."

"I've been in the colony a year," responded the other with a sneer, "and I've hear tell till I'm sick of this man Kelly. What's he ever done?"

"He's the biggest blackguard England, the colony, or America ever produced."

"That's pilin' it up," was the dry response. "I've been in California and heard of a man named Slade, a man whose heart, and hands, and soul were steeped in the blood of offenders against his dignity—a man who awfully avenged all injuries—affronts, insults, a slight of whatever kind—on the spot if he could, years afterwards if lack of opportunity compelled it; a man whose hate tortured him day and night till vengeance appeased it, and not an ordinary vengeance either, but his enemies' absolute death, nothing else; a man whose face would light up with a terrible joy when he surprised a foe."

"Never heard of him," said the officer.

"A high and efficient servant of the Overland, an outlaw among outlaws, and yet their most relentless scourge. Slade was at once the most bloody, the most dangerous, and the most valuable citizen that inhabited the savage fastnesses of the mountains."

"Curious character," said the officer in rather a doubtful tone. "Can hardly believe it."

"True as fact," was the answer of the successful digger. "I'll tell you one of him. He was train master of one of the Californy-bound emigrant trains. One day on the plains he had an angry dispute with one of his waggon drivers, and both drew their revolvers.

"But the driver was the quicker artist, and had his weapon cocked first.

"So Slade said it was a pity to waste life on so small a matter, and proposed that the pistols should be thrown on the ground and the quarrel settled by a fist fight.

"The unsuspecting driver agreed, and threw down his pistol, whereupon Slade laughed at his simplicity and shot him dead."

"Pretty sharp that," replied the officer; "but I could tell you stories of Kelly quite as warm. He is a hot member if there ever was one."

"We must look out for this fiery gentleman," continued the traveller. "I for one do not mean to be robbed with impunity."

And so the time passed.

The day came for the start.

It was to be early in the morning.

Captain Johnson, the leader, had selected twenty picked men, while the travellers who would accompany them were seventeen stout fellows.

The bullion was extensive, being worth about sixty-three thousand pounds.

The captain sent forward a vanguard to feel his way as it were.

They were to peer into the bushes, sound thickets, and so on.

The roads in the colony are not like those in the old country, but cut right through the woods, very rough, except the main roads between large towns, which are well kept enough.

All the first day was passed without adventure. They were amply supplied with food, and when night came they camped in the wood.

Sentries were placed, fires lighted to cook with, and then each amused himself as best he might until the hour of repose came.

Captain Johnson had men carefully posted, with order to challenge any attempted intruder.

But that night passed away without interruption, and was an early hour they started on their march.

As they advanced on that day they came to some very thick forest, through which a road had been made.

It was very dark here, the roadway being somewhat narrower than at other places.

"Eh—what is that?" suddenly cried Captain Johnson.

And no wonder the exclamation was made. Kelly had planned a novel mode of attack. He first of all made such a barricade across the road the escort would have to pass, as would arrest their progress for some time, and bring the whole party under the range of the "firing party," as we may fairly style the bushrangers, who were planted in trees of thick, almost impenetrable foliage, and had time to take deliberate aim at the unsuspecting escort.

At the moment the captain made the above exclamation, a volley from the muzzles of twenty guns saluted the travellers, who, seeing themselves attacked from all quarters simultaneously, and not knowing but that their enemies were much more numerous, were seized with instant panic, and bolted off into the bush.

Two of the troopers lay wounded on the ground, but, fortunately, though Kelly had "marked him for his own," Captain Johnson was untouched.

The horses reared and plunged, but could not get away from the escort waggon.

The harness was good and tough, but more than one trooper was *non est*, it being supposed (charitably) that his horse bolted. At least, one of the force was heard to exclaim—

"This is hot enough for me, and to protect other people's gold too."

At a preconcerted signal from Kelly, down dropped the gang from their perches, and, with guns levelled, threatened the remaining troopers with death if they moved hand or foot; and, to tell the plain truth, they didn't seem inclined to test the sincerity of the threat.

What did the safety of the escort matter to them? If it arrived safe, they got no more pay than if it was lost. But it was otherwise with their captain.

Calling in his unwounded remnant of troopers to follow him, he singled out Kelly, who had dropped from his hiding-place close to him, and, rushing forward, revolver in hand, fired, but missed his aim.

Kelly sprung upon him with a yell of a wild beast, and threw him on his back.

His gun and pistols had been emptied in the contest, and he now relied on his knife.

This was uplifted to settle the mortal career of his opponent, when the loud tramping of horses was heard, accompanied by shouts in a ringing voice—

"Keep it up," it said, "I'm all there! Skewer the scoundrels!"

It was Tom Conquest at the head of a patrol, who had been scouring the neighbourhood.

Ned Kelly did not stop for his arrival, but made off, with all his belongings.

"We'll meet at Barber's Creek."

CHAPTER LXXXVIII
BARBER'S CREEK.

As soon as they had escaped from the scene of conflict, Kelly and his friends decided to disperse, making a rendezvous at Barber's Creek.

The bushranger sullenly spurred his horse, which bounded on, leaving his associates to take their separate ways. He was in one of his vile humours and seemed determined to take it out of the unfortunate animal he bestrode.

The horse, maddened with pain, dashed onward at a headlong pace, snorting with rage and agony.

The poor animal was covered with foam, and more than once tried to throw Kelly, but he was an accomplished horseman and stuck to the saddle.

Kelly was wounded, but he fought against the pain with all the fierce energy of his nature which gave him a kind of fictitious strength in spite of the loss of blood.

He looked like a ferocious and terrible demon in his wild paroxysm of ungovernable rage.

He urged the horse forward, flying along at full speed, without following any settled direction.

It was a magnificent sight, the struggle for supremacy between horse and rider.

Kelly justly prided himself on his horsemanship, it was an accomplishment of which he was very vain.

"You won't try to unseat Ned Kelly again in a hurry, you ——?" he cried, at last, with a savage smile.

He was beginning to find the amusement rather fatiguing, and his face looked drawn and haggard, affording a striking contrast to his broad shoulders and muscular frame, but although suffering intense pain, he never gave a single groan, so great was his strength of will. He set his teeth hard and swore occasionally, and this was the only outward sign of the bodily anguish racking his giant frame, with the exception of the ghastly pallor which showed through the bronze of his dark skin.

The cruel, burning pain of the wound, however, increased rather than diminished as he rode on, and he found it difficult to arrange his ideas, and soon began to yell and blaspheme, gnashing his teeth with impotent rage, while a patch of red on his cheek bones made the ashen hue of his face appear even more startling than before.

His throat was parched with thirst, and his voice became hoarse and cracked, as he raved on, swaying from side to side, until at length he fell from his horse and lay motionless on the long grass.

So he lay face downwards as he had fallen, until a man walking briskly along with a gun on his shoulder, and followed by a couple of kangaroo-dogs, stumbled over the prostrate form.

"Hullo!" cried this individual, bending down before Kelly, and lifting the bushranger's heavy head upon his arm, while he tried to force some spirits, from a bottle he carried about him, between the tightly-clenched teeth.

The man had noticed the horse feeding near, and naturally came to the conclusion that Kelly had been thrown.

"Is he dead, I wonder?" he thought, looking at Kelly's pale face with solicitude, but he uttered a second startled exclamation when he lifted his hand to find it covered with blood.

He saw that Kelly was insensible from the effects of a gaping wound, and that the life-stream was slowly welling away.

The man had some slight knowledge of surgery, and at once set to work to staunch the blood.

By the time this was accomplished, and he had succeeded in forcing a few drops of the spirit down Kelly's throat, the white face began to look less terribly suggestive of death.

Perhaps if his preserver had known who it was that he had saved from death, he would scarcely have felt so much relief when the wounded man opened his eyes and asked abruptly—

"Who the —— are you?"

It was rather an unceremonious way of addressing one who had just acted the part of the Good Samaritan, but the stockkeeper merely smiled as he returned—

"I am Bob Don, if that will make you any the wiser."

Ned looked at him suspiciously for a moment, wondering if he had saved his life merely to obtain the reward offered for his apprehension.

He had no faith in disinterested kindness, but Bob Don's face was frankness personified, and after glancing at his merry twinkling eyes, Kelly gave a faint sigh of relief.

The man might be a fool, but he was not a rogue.

"You want to know how I came here?" said Kelly, seeing that Don was ready to swallow any explanation he liked to offer.

Don assented.

He did consider it rather curious, he admitted, but Kelly had better defer all explanations until a more favourable opportunity, as he must be still weak from loss of blood.

Kelly caught eagerly at this large hole.

He wanted to invent a good lie while he was about it, and he did feel giddy from the effects of his wound and the rather heavy fall.

"Can you manage to get into the saddle?" asked Don the unsuspicious. "If so, I'll take you to my hut and let you have a spell of rest. I see that it won't take you many days to get up your strength. You look better already'"

"How ye?" asked the bushranger, laconically.

"Three miles," returned Don; "and it's my belief you could walk it if it came to the push. But there's no need for that when you have got the horse handy."

He looked at Kelly's huge frame with admiration as he spoke. He was not a very big man himself, but admired well-developed limbs and physical strength in others.

"I'm blowed if I ain't quite unsteady on my pegs," said Kelly, as he rose with the assistance of his new friend, who helped him to climb into the saddle, and led the horse quietly along, little thinking of the "big prize" he had within his grasp.

Bob Don was not a man who cared particularly for money. His chief satisfaction would have been the knowledge that he had been able to rid the land of a brutal ruffian.

He had not the slightest idea, however, that he was addressing the terror of Australia.

He volunteered the information that he was a stockkeeper, and owned a large run, as he walked along at the horse's head.

He had been a shepherd, but when, in 1841, sheep fell in price from 40s. to 1s. a head, his wages bought him the sheep-station and stock of his bankrupt employer.

He seemed to be a talkative individual, and rambled on for some time without waiting for an answer.

"By Goles! he is an innocent," thought Kelly, with a grim smile, as he looked down at Don's broad-brimmed hat, and listened to his ceaseless flow of talk. "If I had a tongue like that, I should have been nabbed long ago. It's a regular misfortune, and if Mr. Don don't look out, he'll get knocked on the head some of these fine days for letting it run on too fast."

"How on earth did you come to be riding along on this 'ere hoss, without having your wounds attended to anywhere?" persisted Don, unconscious of the fact that he was giving offence to the person addressed. "It was regularly courting death, and so I tell you, mate."

"Perhaps so," said Kelly, feeling strongly tempted to bring his knife down on the back of his new friend's head, and thus put an end to his curiosity, "but I had my reasons for acting as I did. It's a confounded disagreeable story to tell, but you must know, me and my brother ain't cousins, and we had a slight rumpus about a girl, which ended in a free fight."

"Well?" asked Don, as Kelly paused.

"Oh, well," said Kelly, "I got the worst of it, and cleared out of the building, so that he shouldn't be tempted to finish me off to save further trouble. When people can't agree it is best to part, say I; and he was jolly well glad to see my back. He was determined to get me out, dead or alive. So I thought it best to slope."

"He must have been a strong sort of chap," said Don, without sarcasm. "I'd like to see that brother of yourn."

Kelly made no reply.

Perhaps he thought an answer to this remark superfluous.

"I've got a wife and one kid," continued the communicative Don, placidly.

"They won't be surprised or put out," he added quickly, as if in reply to some objection his companion might have been about to make. "I often bring folks home. They are used to it by this time, bless your heart."

Kelly laughed noiselessly, wondering if the stockkeeper's family had ever entertained a visitor of so much importance before.

He felt that he was in luck's way when chance threw Mr. Don across his path, for although death troubled him so little when he was merely a spectator, he placed a most extraordinary value on his own life.

Therefore, thinking it as well to conciliate Don, and not knowing how he would be affected by his display of ill-temper, Kelly made some rough jest, brightening considerably when he found that his rude witticism was received with every mark of approval.

He knew that the person who talks little is often accredited with having something to conceal, and was deeply anxious not to arouse the suspicions of Don if he could possibly help it.

Don had often listened with a shudder to the stories of Kelly's atrocious deeds, and he little thought that he was conversing amicably with that notorious bushranger.

The mere idea would have made him jump out of his shoes.

The bushranger feigned even more faintness than he really felt when he reached the station, and artfully parried all the questions of the stockkeeper's womankind.

Mrs. Don was a comfortable woman, and her daughter a remarkably pretty girl.

Kelly admired her from the first.

But he had very little opportunity of improving his acquaintance with his host's daughter, who had a fair face, with a delicate peach-like bloom, large blue eyes, a pretty rosebud mouth, and a figure which looked almost too slight for real strength.

The bushranger's pale face was covered by a sudden flush as he looked at this vision of loveliness, blooming in the solitude, with few eyes to admire her delicate beauty.

He wondered how Don and his wife came by such a daughter.

His wonderful reserve of strength enabled him to recover from his weakness in an incredibly short space of time, but he still feigned illness, feeling that it would be better to keep dark for a little longer, and old Don's daughter was a powerful attraction to chain him to the spot.

On more than one occasion he had tried to make himself agreeable to her, but the girl rejected all his overtures.

For some reason which she could not explain, Lucy Don did not like the man her father had befriended. There was something in the expression of his eye which made her recoil from him with instinctive dislike and distrust, but she said nothing of this to her parents, fearing that they would chide her for her folly.

Mr. Don was in the habit of leaving home early in the morning, while his wife attended to the work at home, and his daughter made herself useful in a small garden, which was her especial care.

Kelly, utterly without gratitude to the man who had prevented him from going to the devil before his time, resolved to take advantage of this.

He was tired of the society of Bob Don, but he found it impossible to leave his pretty daughter behind.

"Morning," said Bob Don, as he left the station, looking back to nod at Kelly. "You are getting quite strong and will soon be thinking of leaving, I suppose?"

"Yes, I shall have to leave here soon," returned the bushranger, with well-simulated regret, thrusting his tongue in his check as Don walked away, without the slightest idea what would occur during his absence.

Kelly waited until he had been gone some time, and then, having ascertained that Mrs. Don was busily engaged inside the hut, went in search of Lucy.

The girl was attending to her garden, and singing like a bird from very lightness of heart.

Kelly looked at her with unbounded admiration as he stood watching her, himself unseen.

It was very early, but the sky seemed to promise a magnificent day, and the sun shone down on the girl's fair young head, making her light-brown hair look like threads of gold.

All unconscious of the bushranger's presence, the girl sang on, happy in her youth and innocence, happy in her own pure thoughts.

Even if she had known he was so near she would not have dreamed of danger.

She disliked him, without having any suspicion of the truth. She would have been frightened out of her wits if she had known who it was her father had rescued from death.

She had a sweet, clear voice, and even Kelly, who was no judge of harmony, listened with pleasure, and waited in silence until the song was at an end.

"Brayvo!" he said.

The girl gave a start of surprise and looked about her. To her idea there was nothing in Kelly's appearance that spoke greatly in his favour; but, above all, she disliked his voice.

"Brayvo!" he repeated, coming forward with a smile on his lips. "You thought you were singing for your own amusement, and didn't expect to find me a listening behind a hedge. Why don't you give us another tune—a more lively one this time? I like your voice, but I don't like your song."

The girl looked confused, and perhaps a little annoyed, as she coldly declined to sing again.

"Do now," said Kelly coaxingly.

"The songs I know would not please you," she answered with increasing coldness.

"I am the most easily pleased man in the world," returned Kelly with an admiring glance at her pretty face. "Don't be obstinate."

"I do not wish to sing again."

"It's always the way with the women," said Kelly; "they want a deal of coaxing."

And he put himself in her path, seeing that she was beginning to get alarmed, and looked wistfully in the direction of the station.

"Let me pass, please," said Lucy.

Kelly gave a hoarse chuckle.

"Don't try to get away," he said, looking down at the girl with a smile which frightened her out of her wits. "I've got something to say to you, my gal, I tell yer. I suppose you guess what it is? You women always pretend to be innocent, and all that sort of thing; but I am an old joker, and understand your whims, and ain't to be taken in by you. I have taken a liking to you, my gal, and want ye to cut away with me—slope sounds better, perhaps. Will you come of your own accord, or shall I have to bring you?"

The girl gave a shrill cry of terror, as he seized her in his strong grasp.

"Father!" she shrieked.

"Come with me!" hissed Kelly, dragging her along by the waist.

"You beast!" said the girl. "Let me go, or it will be the worse for you! My father will punish you for this!"

"Blow the old cuss!" retorted Kelly. "I ain't afraid of Bob Don, my lass. I could crack him in my thumb like a flea if I had a mind."

"He saved your life," cried the girl trying to appeal to his better feeling. "What would have become of you if father had not bound up your wounds, and given you a shelter when you were recovering from the loss of blood and gaining strength? Surely you will not act with such base ingratitude as to steal away his only daughter?"

"Jaw away," said Kelly, "I like to hear your pretty prattle."

"Oh!" she cried with emotion, "have you no heart? Is it useless, quite useless, to appeal to your gratitude and your generosity?"

"I must put an end to this," cried Kelly; and clapping his hand over the girl's mouth, he drew a stout handkerchief from his pocket and securely gagged her as she was about to give a piercing scream, a loud and despairing cry for help.

He then mounted his horse, placing her before him, and as he did so Mrs. Don came out of the shanty shading her eyes from the sun.

She gave an angry cry on beholding her daughter and Kelly riding away together.

"Infernal luck!" he ejaculated. "Here's a pretty fix. The old woman will kick up a devil of a row, and Don will be after me in less than no time. I shall be lynched if he gets hold of me. He will be sure to get plenty of coves to help to hunt me down. Those quiet good-tempered men are not pleasant when roused. If ever I do come to grief it will be all on account of these confounded women."

He urged his horse forward as he heard a faint sound in the distance, rightly judging that Don had not allowed the grass to grow under his feet, but had already started in pursuit. He did not care in the least for Don himself, but what if he had companions?

"—— him!" he muttered. "If he comes up with me I'll put a bullet through his lungs and let daylight into him, the —— fool!"

The pursuer or pursuers, Kelly was not sure which, had the advantage, for his horse had a double burden.

Kelly found great difficulty in retaining his burden, as she used all her strength to embarrass her captor. He held her like a vice, and at last he was so exasperated that he swore he would quiet her effectually if she gave him any more trouble. Still she struggled, and told him death was preferable to his brutality.

The bushranger looked back over his shoulder with a frown that promised nothing very pleasant for Don if he should be alone.

At first he saw nothing; but after glancing back over his shoulder several times he became aware that a large body of horsemen, headed by a woman, were coming up in hot haste.

He recognised the woman at once. It was Mrs. Don, followed by her husband, and, to Kelly's consternation, the mounted police.

Nearer and nearer they came, but still Kelly did not drop the girl.

Kelly saw that without something extraordinary happened all was indeed lost.

Suddenly an idea flashed through his brain, and a fiendish smile lit up his evil face.

The girl should purchase his safety. If they refused to let him go on his way unmolested she should die.

He saw that his horse was gradually losing ground, and knew that he stood no chance in the open country. He therefore turned into a wood, his horse making no sound on the soft grass.

It was with great difficulty that he avoided being swept from the saddle by the heavy branches of the trees.

He was well aware that nothing could be gained by hurry now. He never lost his presence of mind for one instant. We do not wish to take away the only quality in Kelly's character which deserves admiration. His courage and coolness when in danger were wonderful.

Kelly looked about him in every direction in search of a hiding-place, but none presented itself.

He heard his pursuers crushing through the wood behind him, and resolved to turn and face them.

He knew he could not escape. His horse was thoroughly blown from carrying double weight. Kelly himself was a heavy man.

So he resolved, as we have said, to face his foes—but to make a shield of the fair form he carried.

Suddenly pulling up and facing round, he awaited the approach of his pursuers, who were yelling like a pack of hounds at some wild beast.

"Drop, you black-hearted cur!" cried the distressed mother, who saw her daughter still struggling to free herself.

"Not if I know it," said Kelly. "I know a trick worth two of that. Come on another foot, and I'll cut her blessed throat before the whole lot of you. Stand back, I say, old woman and all of you, or I'll rip her up, and no mistake. Ned Kelly ain't to be bagged by such as you."

While so speaking he had drawn his knife, and most certainly would have sacrificed the girl's life if his pursuers had attempted to "rush" him.

By this time the girl had got the gag out of her mouth, and cried to her mother to save her.

The mother, of course, thought of nothing else, and whether Kelly did or did not escape justice was no consideration when the life of her child was concerned.

Knowing the furious passions of the man, and also recognising the desperate condition of the bushranger, and seeing that his threat was his only safeguard, his opponents paused, and finally agreed to his proposal that they should retire a couple of hundred yards, give him a fair start for his freedom, and he would leave the girl where they should find her safe and sound.

He indicated a small hill about 500 yards distant, on the other side of which was the forest, almost impenetrable, and effectually shrouding any intruder from pursuit.

To this the mother, with natural apprehension, demurred.

"Don't trust that villain, don't lose sight of him," she screamed.

"Shut up, you idiot," he replied. "Ain't my wizzen more use to me than your filly? I tell you, you may make your choice. If I'm taken, your daughter has my knife into her. I'll stick her as I would a sheep; so don't lose time, make up your minds. I haven't any time to bother with the lot of you. Yes or no, that's your game."

The unfortunate girl who still writhed in Ned's Herculean grasp, simply uttered the magic appeal—

"Mother, mother, save me!"

Consequently the arrangement was made. The force retired the prescribed distance, when Kelly, seizing his horse's bridle, led the brute off, his hostage accompanying him, sooth to say, with no very great confidence in her captor's keeping his word, but reassured when she thought of the inability of the outlaw's horse to carry double weight with sufficient speed to out-pace the party still in sight.

His departure was watched with mingled feelings of apprehension and curiosity by his enemies, but as they knew his only chance of safety lay in the fulfilment of his promise, they became reassured as to the safety of the girl, and began to look upon the episode as an amusing one.

"Blowed if he ain't a rare un," ejaculated a trooper.

"He deserves to get off, in my mind, for he's a rare pluck'd un," said another.

And admiration for successful villainy was the predominant feeling amongst the unreflecting men who were on his track.

He fulfilled his contract, arrived at the mount and left the girl on the top of it, in view of her friends, but warned her if she turned her head to watch the path he took, he would return.

In a few seconds, Kelly, who knew the ground better than his alphabet, doubled under the slope instead of entering the forest, and was absolutely in the rear of his pursuers, and off in an opposite direction to his supposed path, when they rode up, restored the girl to her mother, and then rushed after the bushranger in the wrong direction.

He arrived at Barber's Creek without further adventure, and found his companions already waiting for him.

Next morning they broke up into small parties agreeing to meet in a month.

Kelly kept with him Zeph, Joss, and Salmon Roe.

CHAPTER LXXXIX.
BLUE RIDGE STATION.

As we have already stated, the stations of even very wealthy men, were rough-and-ready places, with every rude comfort and some luxuries, to which, however, now they have generally attained.

Blue Ridge Station belonged to a man named Clarence. He had a number of men scattered over the run in his employ, while his family consisted of his wife and sister, a girl of eighteen.

She was handsome, showy, and attractive. Several of the young men around admired her very much, but above all James Powers, a very smart young fellow of seven or eight and twenty.

The Blue Ridge was on the road to Sydney from Ballarat.

Ned Kelly now assumed, with his companions, a very plain dress, suitable to honest miners. But they could not conceal their countenances which were to say the least, not of the most amiable character.

The four had travelled hard and fast two days, without visiting any houses save a store near Barber's Creek, when they had changed the appearance of the outward man.

They carried no open weapons save pistols, but not one of them ever went without a long clasp-knife.

As James Powers was jogging along the road in the direction of Blue Ridge Station, he was overtaken by our four estimable worthies.

He started as he turned, for they were rough, and strangers were looked upon with distrust in that quarter when so many terrible tragedies were being enacted by the desperadoes spread over the country.

"Good evening, sir," said Kelly, civilly enough, "we've had a hard ride and would like to know if there's any 'grub' to be got near here."

"Well," answered James Powers in a half-hesitating kind of way, "I have got a friend round here, ten miles off, who'll give you what you want."

And he rode on.

"Come from the diggins?" he asked.

"Yes—pretty well tired of it," answered Kelly; "ain't done much—mean to work our way—to England."

After a hard ride they came to Blue Ridge Station and here James Powers was welcomed by Clarence, while the others were handed to the overseer, with orders to supply them with everything they required.

Food is plentiful and the hospitality of the inhabitants boundless.

Their horses were attended to, and then their wants were seen to very profusely.

Mutton, tea, and damper were the principal ingredients of a meal, though in such houses as this there was sure to be a drop of something stronger than whey.

The bushrangers were on such occasions very cautious in their conversation, and though they were careful to steer clear of dangerous subjects, they told many a rare story of the diggings.

After supper, an out-hut was pointed out to them where they could sleep if they liked, and the hospitable offer was accepted.

"Must be rich people, plenty of tin," observed Joss; "should like to try a haul."

"Don't keep much pewter in the house in the Colony," answered Kelly; "folks mostly take it to the bank—besides its too risky."

At this moment one of the men returned. He was a short, ill-looking fellow, who squinted and looked to the right and left.

"What is it?" asked Kelly.

"Don't you know Fiery Dick?" asked the man, with a leer.

"The devil it is!" said Kelly, and he drily added, "And you know me?"

"The moment I seed you," continued the other.

"What are you doing here?" asked Kelly.

"Working, worse luck!" retorted Dick with supreme contempt.

"Do you want to join?" asked the bushranger.

"Yes—but I can put yer up to a job first," was the other's reply.

"What's that?" asked Kelly, curiously.

"Master's made a big swap, bought a run from Master Morgan—close by," continued the other, "some of the ochre is in the house."

"Ah!" said Kelly, with greedy eyes, "where does he keep it?"

"In his bedroom," answered the other. "I was a listening—and he did not see me—when he locked it up in the black box.

"Rather risky work," said Kelly, musing. "Who sleeps in the house?"

"The master and the missus, at the back," he continued, "and the sister in a small room hard by."

"And this cove who brought us?" asked Kelly.

"He stays here the night," answered the other.

Kelly now took the man out to show him the means of entering the house by the window.

There was no shutter, and the window was only shaded from moon or sun light by a muslin curtain. It could be easily opened, and was big enough to admit a man's body.

The great chance was that these people, leading a healthy and open-air life, would be very tired and sleep soundly.

Kelly determined to risk it.

The man told him they always slept with a lamp in the room.

On the occasion of the visit of Miss Ann's sweetheart, they would take something extra.

A long consultation was held, and Fiery Dick promised to have the horses outside the station.

They would be ready on the main road, which was a quarter of a mile distant from the station.

Then Fiery Dick left them and returned to his duties.

In the colony the class of people to whom we are alluding retire early and rise early.

Most are in their saddles the greater part of the day.

Kelly always carried his tools in his wallet, so as never to throw a chance away.

His companions were quite prepared to second him.

They all waited until midnight.

Kelly had examined the scene of action.

The hut was low and rude.

Kelly approached and keenly examined the window.

The hinges were held in their places by rusty screws. These Kelly attacked with his usual extreme caution, and in a moment or two the window was open.

Kelly peered in.

Two people were lying on the bed, evidently in a heavy sleep.

Still Kelly's heart beat wildly.

The position was a desperate one, as the persons employed at the station were numerous.

The window opened inward on hinges, with nothing but a latch to keep it in place.

Still Kelly heard no one move.

He crept in with all the caution of a snake and the cunning of a fox.

He was in the room.

On one small table was a black box, on another, between the window and the bed, a large oil lamp, lowered to a very low focus.

Kelly clutched the box. As he did so he heard someone move.

He accidentally gave the table with the lamp on it a kick, and at the same time a pistol shot was heard.

Then he was through the window.

The oil caught fire, and a loud cry was heard from the master of the house.

"Stop thief! Fire!" he roared.

Kelly darted away in the direction indicated by Fiery Dick, and soon joined his companions.

Those at the station were in too great confusion to follow.

The Home Station hut was on fire.

Reaching the rendezvous, Kelly, mounting, rode off. Fiery Dick had by this time joined the party.

We may as well say that, except the destruction of the house and the loss of the money, no harm was done. The money loss was not great, as it was only ten per cent. of the whole amount of the purchase.

Mr. Clarence was a rich man, but the impudence of the outrage and the recklessness it displayed left little doubt that it was Kelly's deed.

Another was added to the list of his infamies, and the public wondered at the impunity with which this atrocious criminal was able to carry out his nefarious plans.

It caused much discontent, and the colonial press was very severe in its comments.

Meanwhile the gang were determined to put a long distance between themselves and the scene of their misdeeds.

There was one thing which caused them more trouble than anything, and that was the continual necessity of assuming disguises.

On the present occasion they determined to camp in a dense bush, at no great distance from an inn.

There were numerous huts of stock-keepers about, but their own spot was rough, wild, and almost undiscoverable. Here they agreed to remain until the hue and cry was further away from them.

Food was easy to get. A sheep or two would not be missed, and the roadside inn would supply them with everything else.

Rude as they were, they were well provided, having to supply a population which, since the gold discoveries were made, was always on the move.

An open space was found under some lofty trees, where a very little fire could be made without exciting suspicion, as the smoke was lost in the upper boughs of trees.

Fiery Dick, who could easily give himself out as a shearer, would go down and obtain provisions.

Knowing the character of the people in the neighbourhood, the owner of the shanty inn would not be likely to ask any inconvenient questions.

Money was the one idea of this class of men in the colony.

The inn was three miles from the camp, and Fiery Dick had to come by devious ways.

Not that he was suspected or watched.

Still, he might be, and they were entitled to take every precaution.

As a rule one of them accompanied him to the skirts of the wood and watched for his return at a safe and cautious distance.

Now it happened that on the morning of the fifth day Kelly accompanied him and watched for him in the scrub. Kelly had good eyes, and as Fiery Dick went on he saw a tall, handsome young man, in trooper's uniform, with a frank, brave, fearless face, spring from his horse.

It was Tom Conquest, and behind came eight mounted troopers.

Kelly at once determined to be even with him.

He watched carefully, and soon saw him come out in company with Fiery Dick, who placed himself at the head of the troopers.

He had betrayed them.

Kelly took to his heels at once. He had never run faster in his life.

"Mount for your lives, men!" he said. "Tom Conquest is after us. Dick has split."

No one required twice telling, though the volley of oaths and other strong language which ensued was fearful to listen to.

They, however, lost not a moment, and soon the summer stillness of the bush was abruptly broken by the clatter of horses' hoofs.

They were all in a furious rage against Fiery Dick, though in reality he was probably not to blame.

Tom, who knew Mr. Clarence, had recognised him and compelled confession.

Still, it was lucky they had commissioned one to watch Fiery Dick on his daily excursions.

Passing through the dense forest and bush they proceeded to cross some more open country, leading to what were known as the ranges.

Here they could hide in defiance of all the colonial police until it was safe to move once more.

And such proved to be the case.

When the police and Fiery Dick reached the scene of action they found the camp empty.

But they did not blame Fiery Dick, who was, however, sent to prison to be tried for having assisted Ned Kelly in robbery and attempted murder.

After a halt of several days, Kelly and his party determined to make their entry into Sydney without beat of drum in the night.

They intended to appear as sailors for awhile, so as to have time for reflection.

For this purpose they would get rid of their horses as having no further use for them.

Then they could adjourn to a crimp, a sailors' boarding-house, and mature some scheme for their future guidance.

Kelly was dreaming of some great and extraordinary coup that should be talked of.

As the horses were good and sold cheap no questions were asked, and that trouble was over.

Then with their wallets and small bags they started for a sailors' boarding-house, where they easily obtained one large room for the four.

Early next morning the coarse miners' suits were exchanged for sailors' clothes.

The money stolen from **Mr. Clarence** was soon got through in the low gambling shops of the town, besides which the reckless extravagance of the scoundrels and their frantic liberality to vicious companions aided the depletion of their purses.

CHAPTER XC.

SYDNEY.

SYDNEY, the capital of New South Wales, is a wonderful town. Those who have not seen it can scarcely believe in its wonderful development since its first foundation in 1798.

It is built upon the most beautiful site in the world, and much more beautiful in every respect than the vaunted Genoa the superb. It lies on the edge of a bay unsurpassed by beauty and convenience in the world. The water is sixty feet deep at the natural wharves.

At the time of which we speak the city was infinitely busy, while pleasure was rife everywhere.

There was no amusement that could be thought of that could not be found in that place.

In the daytime the four sailors kept indoors, amusing themselves as best they might.

At night time they furbished themselves up to look like captains and mates, and went about.

In those days, except in first-class hotels and clubs, everybody was admitted everywhere who had plenty of money.

The four selected a house where billiards were allowed and cards not objected to.

It was also a place where money could be spent without stint, as the *menu* was expensive.

Kelly and Zeph were very good hands at billiards, and therefore played continually.

The other two preferred cards, or drinking and smoking.

After the quartette had been in the habit of going to the place—the Eastern Casino it was called—for two or three nights, they found themselves observed by a young man, who, though neatly dressed, looked otherwise seedy and miserable.

His spirits seemed low, and he seldom played or even took a drink at his own expense.

Kelly made inquiries about him.

He was a clerk in the Union Bank, where he had a good situation, but, spending money and time too freely, was always without cash.

Ned Kelly had an idea.

It was prodigious the amount of ideas that struck him.

Gold was pouring in very freely to this bank awaiting transmission to England.

The sum total must be very large.

"You seem interested in billiards my friend," said Kelly, suavely, on the third night, putting on his very best quality airs. "Why don't you play?"

The young man flushed and looked round slyly ere he made any answer.

"The fact is, I pretty well lost my last quarter's salary on the board of green cloth," explained the other. "I cannot afford it."

"Will you liquor?" said Kelly. "I'm not going to play any more. Come I'll stand a supper."

The man, whose name was Temple, and who belonged to a very good family, was only one of those too easily led away.

"Very happy," was the jaunty answer of the seedy one.

So they drank, and then John Temple went off to a private supper-room with the four respectable sailors, captain and mates.

John Temple had not had such a feed for a long time.

It was with particular relish and enjoyment he ate his meal.

After supper there was the flowing bowl and the weed, which all delighted in.

The punch flowed round freely. There was no stint of that commodity.

"Let's have a game," said Kelly.

"I have no money," was the answer.

"I'll lend you five quid," said Kelly. "Anything for amusement's sake."

And he thrust the gold into the other's hands, whose face became at once flushed and excited.

It was to him such an exceedingly novel sensation.

He was a poor fool, and not much of a player.

But they let him win.

And then, as he had too much to drink, they made him up a shakedown.

Next day was Sunday, and during that day Kelly had made up his mind to propose a big scheme to the bank clerk.

He could see at once that he was weak and easily led by evil counsel.

John Temple was rather surprised to find himself in a sailors' boarding-house the next day, with money in his pocket, and a luxurious breakfast awaiting him.

It was hard to understand what had passed; but with him the present was everything.

After breakfast his new friends proposed a drive to one of the places frequented on high days and holidays by the people of the town.

John Temple was delighted, and was equally glad not to have had to go home and dress.

He would have had to face his mother and sister at home, where they were nearly starving.

He was glad to avoid this.

Suddenly, however, a better feeling prevailed, and, remembering he had money, he sent them a sovereign by a messenger, telling them he had met some friends with whom he was going to spend the day.

This duty performed he started to enjoy himself, and this can be done in the colony if it can be done anywhere.

It was the dark of the evening when they returned to dine at the boarding-house.

They had a private room, in which after dinner they locked themselves.

Kelly had provided plenty of drink, but he was careful not to let John Temple go beyond a certain amount.

He had much to do and to say to him before they parted that night.

"You do a lot of work at that bank," he began when he thought the young man primed.

"Yes—for very bad pay," cried Temple.

"It's a tarnation shame," observed Kelly in a commiserating tone of voice.

"Yes; but what's to be done?" sulkily answered Temple, "the big-pots get all the money."

"It's the way of this here cussed world," growled the bushranger; "and sometimes you have big piles?"

"Pretty good size now," said Temple with a grin "something likely."

"That's your ticket," urged Kelly in a low, persuasive voice; "now why don't you help yourself, make for England, and live like a fighting-cock?"

John Temple turned very pale, and looked both excited and astonished.

"It would suit me to a T," he answered, speaking in rather a tremulous tone.

"Can I trust you, my young chicken?" asked Kelly.

"You can; I'm sick of this life—poor, in debt, deeply involved," he said. "I will do anything to get out of it."

"Do you ever sleep at the bank?" the other continued, who had got all this out of him before.

"Twice a week," replied the weak-minded youth, "the manager makes us take it in turns."

"Can you get the keys?" Kelly went on.

"Yes," faltered the other.

"Well, to-morrow I'll look up some friends," continued Kelly, "and we'll do the job. I'll have a craft ready to put out to sea in—and then away for such a spree as you never seed."

John Temple nodded idiotically and was soon put to bed, as they wanted him to go sober to business the next day."

But he agreed to meet them every evening at the Eastern Casino, when they would report progress.

"Found a flat!" said Joss, "a rare good un. Hope he won't get light and peach."

"I don't think so," responded Kelly, "he's all there when the rhino is concerned. Bit like anything."

So next day, freshened up, with clean shirt and everything correct, the bank clerk went to his duty.

He was quite exhilarated with hope. He wanted to give up the life of honest drudgery he had been leading, and by which he might have become an honourable man, for the sake of making money suddenly by nefarious means.

Except with exceptionally wicked natures, bold and audacious, crime carries its own punishment. Kelly was not of those.

Le jeu ne vaut pas la chandelle.

It brings sorrow, sleepless nights, and sometimes that madness which incites to suicide.

But now the unfortunate John Temple saw all through roseate spectacles, little dreaming what the dread future would bring forth.

CHAPTER XCI.

THE BANK CLERK.

NEXT day Kelly made inquiries as to chartering a coasting vessel, a smart craft, in which he could trade in "notions" and other things.

Salmon Roe had gone off to the rendezvous to collect together the whole of the band.

They had come in twos and threes.

Kelly meant them to go on board secretly, and when once on the high seas they could decide what was to be done.

Every man could secure arms and ammunition.

As so many of them were seamen they got anywhere they pleased.

There are plenty of places in Sydney, as elsewhere, where everyone is welcome who brings money, and no questions asked.

But, of course, they must avoid places where English cruisers are very much in the habit of calling. They are apt to be rather inquisitive.

When Kelly called, under an assumed name, at a shipping agent's, and offered to charter a vessel to trade down the coast in general goods, he found no great difficulty in obtaining what he wanted, the more that he also intimated his desire to purchase a good many of the goods required.

He secured the White Eagle, a good-sized schooner, in the course of the day, paid his deposit, and began to treat for goods.

He said he should find his own crew.

As this was only reasonable, no objection was made.

Next day, the charter money being paid, the vessel was formally handed over to Kelly, who began his preparations.

Salmon Roe returned in a day or two, and then some of the quietest of the men were told off for loading.

They were busy all day, and in such a port as that no one took any particular notice.

They easily carried on board their arms and ammunition, with tobacco and such liquids as they required.

At last the day came to carry out the most nefarious part of their plans.

John Temple was to be on duty on Friday. His office was to remain after banking hours in a small counting-house adjoining the apartments of the head manager.

This gentleman generally went out of an evening, but always returned before midnight, and shortly afterwards retired to rest.

The junior clerk then paraded about, saw to the fastening of the doors, after which he returned to his chair.

All the keys were kept in the head manager's room. but John Temple knew how to get at them but too well.

On more than one occasion during his nocturnal vigil he had availed himself of this knowledge to help himself to certain small sums.

He had been very cautious, being a very petty and nerveless thief, and had contrived hitherto to escape detection.

The key of the outer doors of the bank he had managed to secure while pretending to put them in their proper place.

He sat now waiting the half-dreaded signal, with his heart in his mouth.

Did no thought of his mother and sister and one dearer still check him in his headlong course? No, indeed. Conscience was silent and dumb.

The manager, who had two rooms en suite, retired to sleep the sleep of the just.

A neighbouring clock sounded one.

Then there was a discreet tapping on the outside in a peculiar way, and John Temple went and with beating heart removed bolts and bars.

The thing was done and he was at the mercy of the robbers, four in number.

Closing the door they put on rude masks, so as to be unrecognisable.

"Secure the manager first," whispered John Temple, leading the way. "He might be dangerous."

Kelly had no wish to push things to extremites if he could help it, so came provided with the means of securing the man effectually.

They went in, John Temple leading, and found the manager, Mr. Benson, fast asleep.

Three of them caught hold of him, and, before he could make the least resistance, gagged and had him effectually.

His struggles were terrible, but at last finding that they were useless he lay quiet and still.

John Temple now secured all the keys which were in his possession, and then he led the way to the vaults.

As it happened the actual quantity of bullion in the bank was not very large, a heavy sum having been sent to England that very day; still there was a good haul enough for these rascals.

But one bitter disappointment was reserved for them. The safe containing the notes was one of those only to be opened by one who understood a secret combination which John Temple did not.

Kelly was savage in his expressions of rage, but it was clearly not John Temple's fault, so that they had to put up with what they had already obtained.

They therefore ascended to the upper regions to make off as quickly as possible. John Temple had, of course, to accompany them.

The manager would too surely recognise and denounce him to his employers.

Such was Kelly's second successful bank robbery, one of many he was yet to commit.

They had carpet-bags with them, and it now became a serious question as to how to reach their inn without being suspected by the police, who, if they saw them about at that hour, would certainly make enquiries.

But John Temple knew of a place close at hand, of not very reputable character, where they could pass the time until daylight, when they could hurry on board ship and be off.

They were fully cleared and everything was ready for a start at a moment's notice.

The difficulty was to think of a place where they could go and spend their ill-acquired earnings.

John Temple found them the shelter they required, and at daybreak they immediately went on board their ship, which lay in deep water alongside the wharf, and worked down and out of the beautiful harbour. They had a good start.

A more villainous crew never perhaps was collected on one ship.

The great thing was to get away from Sydney as fast as possible, and so far that no cruiser would have any idea in which direction the White Eagle had sailed.

All sail was cracked on; long before business hours in Sydney the schooner was out of sight of land.

Everything depended on their putting the authorities at fault.

Meanwhile, in the capital of the colony the excitement was indeed intense, while indignation was profound.

When the hour came for the bank to open, the door remained closed despite all the knocking.

The principal was immediately sent for. He came in hot haste to give authority to open.

He had a key to a side door, so that he could obtain admission when he liked.

He entered rapidly, and soon became aware of the misfortune which had happened to the manager, and the treachery of the clerk.

The first thing was to release the unfortunate prisoner, then rushing off to the police-station, information was given.

The house of the wretched family of John Temple, his mother, sister, and cousin, was first searched, but no trace of him had been seen.

As the news spread, it reached the ears of the police that he had been lately seen a good deal in the company of sailors, and the boarding-house inhabited by Kelly and his associates was visited.

They were at once on the track. A man resembling the one the police described had that morning gone on board the White Eagle schooner, which had sailed soon after daybreak.

Minutely interrogated as to the character and description of the men, the police came to the startling conclusion that Kelly and his gang had been in their midst.

The news was astounding, but the chief question that arose was what was to be done.

The authorities were applied to, and at once granted a small but well-armed and swift cruiser to go in pursuit.

It was a wild-goose chase, but they were safe to be heard of somewhere.

Such unmitigated villains could not possibly remain idle wherever they located themselves.

But where would they go at first?

They had plenty of money, and would be sure to seek some place where they could spend it.

It was a tangled web to unravel, but Captain Redknap, of the Snake Revenue cutter, determined to persevere.

It would be a slow process. He had an excellent description of the White Eagle, and must question every ship he sighted.

He was to hear of her sooner than he expected.

That night, after dark, fire was seen at a considerable distance, for which they made at once.

It was a coasting brig that had been boarded by the White Eagle, which took from them water and biscuit.

They then scuttled the boats, and wantonly fired the vessel, hoping thus to prevent information of their whereabouts being given.

Making off in a great hurry they failed to do it effectually, but the crew were already driven into the bows, and must have perished but for the welcome succour they had received from the man-of-war.

CHAPTER XCII.

ON BOARD THE WHITE EAGLE.

WHERE Ned Kelly was there was very little question as to who should be leader.

The stupendous energy and self-assertion of the man always carried everything before him.

The ex-captain Zeph was, as a matter of course, appointed second in command.

He was a clever and experienced navigator, and on him they had chiefly to depend for their safety.

As soon as they were fairly out at sea, Kelly asked Zeph to produce a map and decide on some place where they might go to spend their ill-gained earnings in, of course, riot and debauchery.

In company with Zeph was one Jennings, a very shrewd and clever seaman.

Zeph spread the chart out, and at once clapped his finger on a certain spot.

"That's the crib!" he said.

"Spit out the name," cried Kelly.

"Singapore, in Torres Straits," was the quiet answer of the man: "fine place."

"Never heard of the shop," said Kelly.

"Time you did," continued Zeph. "Rare jumping off place—niggers and Chinee; plenty of fun, from arrack to tiger-hunting."

"Go for Sing'pore," answered Kelly.

The vessel was well-built and a good sailor, well appointed with provisions and even luxuries.

So they started for the desired haven, with every prospect of success.

Kelly was very strict in his discipline on these occasions, as it was their only hope of safety.

Of course there were certain laxities that would not have been tolerated either on board of a merchantman or a man-of-war.

That is, more drink was served out than was wise.

But a restriction the men would not have submitted to.

All went well until the next day.

The breeze had been fair until then. It now began to freshen into a gale from the eastward, and blew with some violence, but after a while it died away into a perfect calm, leaving a heavy swell in which the vessel rolled incessantly.

About midday the sky began to blacken, and before an hour more had assumed an appearance of the most dismal and foreboding darkness.

"Dirty," said Kelly, with a grim smile.

"Very," answered Zeph; "we shall have a buster, and no flies about it."

There could be no doubt that something like a hurricane was coming upon them.

The warning, however, was not lost upon them. Most of their sails were taken in, and then even experienced sailors thought they could defy the storm that was fast approaching.

An hour later it came on them with sudden and terrific violence.

The noise the wind made was horrible.

The wind was from the eastward, and the water as it ran on deck was warm as milk; the murkiness and closeness of the air was in a short time dispelled, but soon the ship heeled over dangerously.

Every article that could move danced to leeward, but worst of all the topmasts went by the board.

The men looked at one another aghast, waiting the end with frantic fright.

Curses flew round like carrion crows, or rather white sea-gulls.

No voice of command could be heard, and no orders were given.

All discipline was suspended, and every man was equal to his neighbour.

Luckily these hurricanes are of short duration, and just after nightfall the fearful gale ceased.

But the vessel was doomed. A tremendous sea smashed her rudder. She lay like a log, wholly unmanagable. She shipped tons of water, and was rapidly becoming water-logged.

There were no skilled carpenters on board, and they could not stop the leaks.

All looked round desperate and moody.

For these men there was only one resource, and that was the boats.

Fortunately they were stout, and able to accommodate the crew.

"We'll have to get back to the colony," growled Kelly, "worse luck, I say."

"Mate, it might be wuss," said Zeph.

Orders were now given to lower the boats, and to put water and food within.

Each man was to take a limited kit, in which, of course, would be contained his share of the plunder.

All took care to see that their weapons were cleaned and loaded.

As they pushed off from the nearly-sinking schooner the wind almost ceased, and a thick damp and misty haze settled on the waters.

It was impossible to see a hundred yards before them.

Still they pulled steadily, aided by a small compass which Zeph could just make out.

Suddenly they heard a bell sound upon the waters, and the men by one assent ceased rowing.

They then heard eight bells sound clearly on the night air.

Kelly and Zeph exchanged a wolfish glance.

"If we could only swop vessels," said Kelly, in an undertone to his companions.

"Should like to see what's her size, mate," replied Zeph, "before we do anything."

And he guided the leading boat until they came in sight of the strange vessel.

Then Zeph lifted his head.

"It's the cutter Snake," he said. "She's on our heels, and means to nab us."

Kelly swore rather hard and fast about his luck.

"She's a biter," he observed. "Got too many teeth for us to draw."

"No," whispered Zeph. "She's like a ship at anchor watch, or a nigger sloop where the boss, in a storm, takes in sail and goes below."

"Is it likely," continued Kelly, "we could get alongside and try it on?"

"All serene. We can hardly make her out there. She can't see us at all down here," answered Zeph, and his whispered order went round.

As Zeph said, from the boats the cutter Snake, a fine vessel of about a hundred tons, could easily be seen, while from the deck of the small man-of-war the boats, in that haze, would not have been easily visible."

After the severe storm, from which the cutter had come out intact, all were tired on board the Snake, and a poor watch was kept.

Besides, they were n a time of intense peace, and a night surprise was the last thing to be thought of in Australian latitudes.

Zeph soon showed the men how to fix their oars in the rowlocks so as to row without making a noise.

In this way they reached the side of the cutter unnoticed.

The man at the wheel was half asleep from fatigue, while the rest of the watch were nestled in the waist talking or sleeping.

The officer who should have been on the look-out, had just gone down into the cabin for a cigar and a glass of spirits.

Nothing suspicious was anywhere in sight, while the weather was all that could be desired.

None suspected what a foul and treacherous foe was lurking near them, nor thought they were close at hand.

Just at this moment a breeze sprung up, and the Snake began to feel its force.

She yielded gracefully to the pressure, her canvas belly'd, and away she crept from the boats to the tune of an eight-knot breeze.

Curses, not loud, but deep, followed her course.

However, in a few moments the wind lulled again; but it had served to wake up the attention of the officer of the watch, and stirred up the crew, who were soon moving about on deck.

Kelly's boat followed close.

It could easily do so, as the Snake was only forging ahead about four knots an hour.

She made for a small port north of Sydney, and evidently would snug up there for the night, as the weather was intensely hot, and semi-cyclones not improbable.

Besides, daylight was necessary, as coral reefs abounded here.

Standing off at a safe distance, Kelly watched the vessel into port, saw her made snug for the night, and a boat carrying the captain and twelve hands pull for the shore.

Waiting until all was quiet on board, Kelly's gang worked up silently to the side of the schooner, and found the companion-ladder had not been hauled up, so that an easy means of ascent was offered.

The ruffians crept up the side of the schooner as silently as flies into a sugar-basin.

They soon secured the watch (one man being considered sufficient in harbour), and then proceeded to batten down the hatches.

On board men-o'-war the crew are not as a rule armed until the beat to quarters is heard.

Kelly and his gang were in possession of one of the finest cutters in her Majesty's service.

What was to be done now became the next important question.

Even Kelly revolted at the idea of putting a whole crew like this to death.

"As a general rule," he said, "quarts of blood don't matter, but this ere job is a big one; what's to be done?"

"Don't know," answered Zeph, "except set 'em afloat.

How to get up the anchor was the difficulty.

Working the windlass would possibly be heard ashore, and up it must be hove before the schooner could be moved a foot.

Accordingly, the windlass was worked very slowly and gradually, and, as the anchorage was light, and the anchor did not bite in this calm land-locked berth, it was just hoisted off the sandy bottom, and half of the gang manned the boat, attached a tow-line to the schooner and with a long pull, and a strong pull, and a pull altogether, soon got her outside the harbour.

In the meantime the battened-down crew were making furious efforts to get on deck, and Kelly swore the first man that showed would have his skull split.

Still the noise continued, and, resolving to stifle it and show the utter uselessness of opposition, he determined to let them know who was aboard.

"Look here," Kelly growled down the hatchway, "stow your row, or it will be worse for you. Don't make any mistake about it. NED KELLY'S ABOARD! and you know what that means. Any more of your —— bellowing, and I'll send the lot of you for crabs' meat."

Consternation went to the heart of his hearers.

They knew what an unscrupulous villain the man was, and that shedding blood was rather a pastime than otherwise to him, particularly if it furthered his ends.

They could not guess what their fate would be, and almost feared it would be walking the plank with most of them.

The first lieutenant, who was in charge of the schooner, thought it was some practical joke of the middies, and that the whole thing was pantomime, but he could scarcely reconcile with this thought the movement of the vessel.

Zeph walked to the quarter-deck and stood over the skylight of the cabin, beneath which was a framework of iron bars.

"Hilloa! what's up?" he cried, hoarsely.

"Who is playing this foolish trick?" said a stern and commanding voice. "Open at once, unless you would be punished for mutiny."

"It ain't no mutiny, governor," answered Zeph, in a sneering tone; "only your crew is prisoners, and we want your ship."

"I don't believe it," was the resolute answer; "it's a deuced bad practical joke."

"Come on deck and see, my lads," answered Zeph, "but if anybody fires a shot don't blame me if you all walks the plank."

By this time the cabin hatchway was removed, and the officers, four in number, came out. The men were still kept below.

They found themselves confronted by between thirty and forty desperadoes.

"What is the meaning of this?" asked the lieutenant. in an indignant tone.

"Its no use doing the big boss here," said Kelly.

Now the lieutenant at once knew the class of men he had to do with.

If he had had a crew behind him he would have tried the dignified and commanding, but he was utterly helpless.

Such a gang as that he saw before him would have no mercy whatever on him or on his followers.

"So that my men are fairly treated," he said, "I care not. Share their fate I will."

"All serene, my jolly swell," responded Kelly. "Get into our boats," he added.

Presently the officer and deck-watch were allowed to enter the boats. Biscuit and a little water was given them.

One of the men was now ordered to summon the crew, and inform them of the change of ownership in the vessel

As a matter of course these were unarmed, and could therefore make no resistance

They were ordered at once to go over the side and join their ill-fated companions.

Resistance was madness, and they therefore obeyed in silence.

Soon they disappeared in the haze and mist.

There was a change in life for these consummate rascals, a change scarcely to be credited.

A splendid English cruiser with every comfort and luxury that money could procure for the officers, and excellent quarters for the men.

It was indeed a change to be on board a well-appointed vessel, armed and well provisioned.

But it now became a matter of consideration what precautions must be taken before they ventured into an English port.

The names of officers and men would of course be found on the ship's books, but they might meet with a consort.

Zeph, who before commencing his nefarious career had been in the Navy knew everything about signals and all that.

Still, as a British man-of-war, they would not enter any English seaport.

They would change the name and rig and call themselves American; but what about the uniform? That was unanswerable.

She must profess to be a yacht.

Fortunately Zeph, in his portmanteau, had the ship's papers of the White Eagle, which, by judicious manipulation, might be made to serve as those of the armed yacht bound for the Solomon and other Cannibal Islands.

Young Temple was good at any kind of writing, and, besides, the papers of yachts are not closely overhauled.

So it was decided that this should be their plan.

After a hearty supper the watches were set, and all those off duty went below.

Sleep was very much needed, and even few of those on deck could not resist its temptations.

But the night was fine, and there was a good man at the wheel, so it did not matter.

Next day paint brushes and pots were procured, a platform slung, and every vestige of the Snake effaced.

There were several men able to carve a figure-head on board, so that before night every trace of the vessel's indentity had disappeared.

Plenty of good plain clothes were found, and as Captain Higgins (Kelly) intended to play the part of a *nouveau riche* there was not much fear of detection.

He had no pretence to pass as a native-born American. That would have been beyond even his powers of mimicry and disguise.

So all appeared plain sailing, and the vessel with a fair wind.

(To be continued.)

NED KELLY
THE IRONCLAD
AUSTRALIAN BUSHRANGER

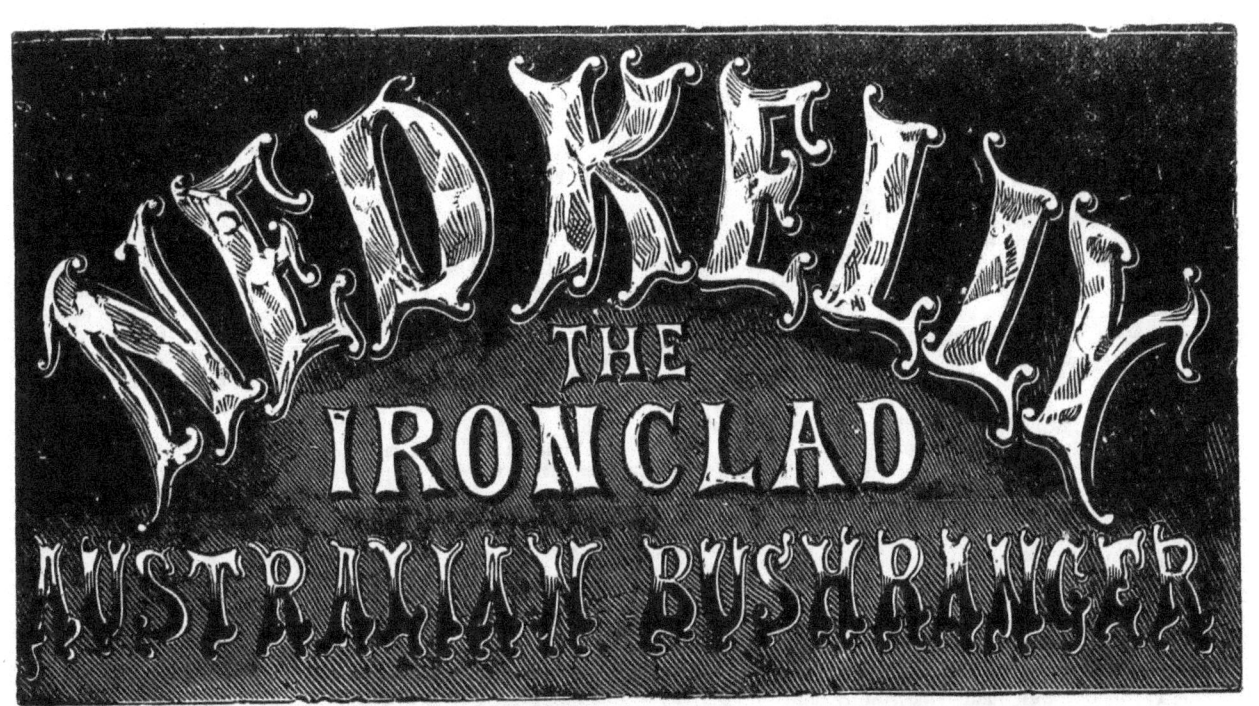

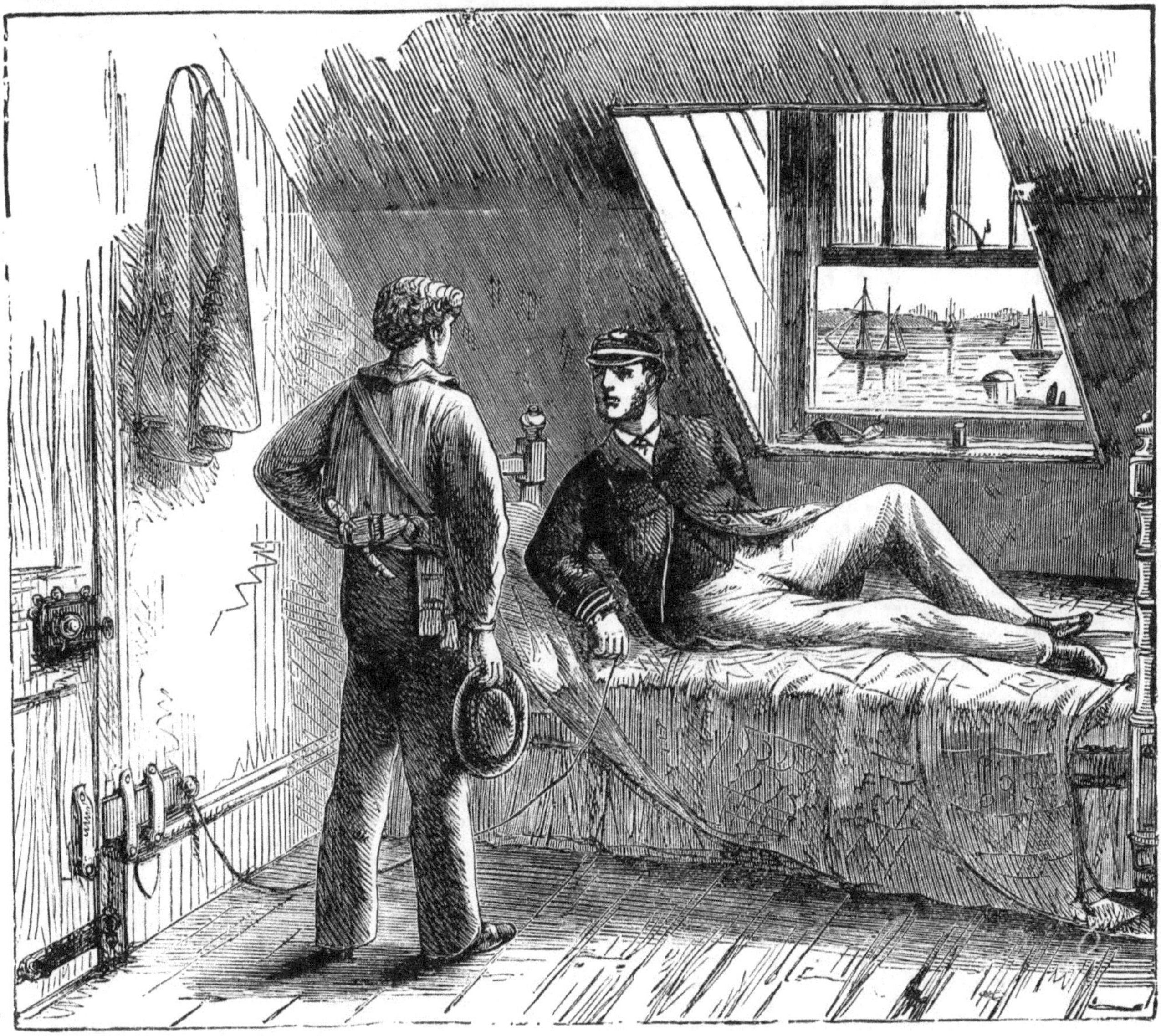

NO 14,

CHAPTER XCIII.

CATCHING A TARTAR.

NEXT day was equally fine, and the rascally crew were looking forward with delight to an easy and rapid journey.

The cutter was under all canvas, with a fine breeze and smooth water, when there was a cry of "Sail oh!" on the larboard quarter.

"What do you think of her, Zeph?" said Captain Kelly, examining the stranger through a glass.

"Some stray merchantman, chucked out of her course by the storm. We'd best, if you mean to speak her," he added, with a wink, "put yer head towards her under easy sail, so as to near her about sunset."

"Look out!" said the man at the wheel, a 'cute youth of some two-and-twenty summers, "if e'er I saw wood and sails, that there is one of John Bull's calves of the ocean, and a forty-four gunner at that!"

Zeph made no reply. He ran up the maintop, and remained for ten minutes in absorbed attention of the cut of the stranger's sails.

"We're done," cried Zeph, as he came down, "if we don't mind. We must show our heels."

"All right," said Kelly, "give your orders."

The vessel was well manned certainly, and all sail was set upon her like lightning.

"Heave the log!" cried Zeph.

He was obeyed, and she was found by their measurement to be going about nine and six.

"What is the other feller doing?" asked Kelly.

"Ten," whispered Zeph, in an alarmed tone. "She's about nine miles off. She'll be up before dark. She draws up. I can see her bowsprit when she lifts, and half-an-hour ago I only saw her foreyard."

Kelly was appalled at this ill-timed news.

The word foreyard made him think of the yard-arm.

Still he determined to run as long as he could, and then to die fighting.

Surrender on his part was folly. It was simply suicidal madness.

So everything was done that could be done—that art and cunning could devise.

An hour passed, and then those who knew the real danger could see the water-line of the frigate.

Dull dismay took possession of all; and there was poor discipline on board the pirate.

As to the bank clerk, he was sick of the whole business.

He saw he would be robbed of his share of the bank robbery, and be cast in the world a penniless vagabond, unless he could continue in a course of crime and blood, for which he had neither taste nor nerve.

He trembled at all that was going on.

He resolved to abandon his companions on the first opportunity, and even had thoughts of turning Queen's evidence if he could secure his own neck.

He almost longed for the opportunity.

Some suggested the boats, but Zeph stood out. He still had hope of ultimate escape.

The sun had sunk some time below the horizon, the cloud of small sail coming up astern of them began to be indistinct, and at last disappeared altogether in a black squall.

Zeph was perfectly prepared for this emergency, which he had expected.

He shortened sail, kept on as much as he dared, and reversed the course of the ship. At the end of four hours the squall was over, and it became lighter.

Though they scanned the sea in all directions, the frigate was nowhere to be seen.

They, however, were in dangerous proximity to a coral-bank, to which Zeph proceeded to give a wide berth.

But they did not venture to start until daylight came and made them aware that none but a few coasters were in sight.

They at once cracked on all sail, and resumed their voyage.

A strict look-out was kept, as none had any wish to catch such a Tartar again.

There was always someone at the mast-head, with keen eyes and a glass.

Two days passed without any further adventure, the White Eagle going on her way rejoicing, with her villainous crew.

But on the third day two things occurred. The look-out sighted a sail, which Zeph declared to be the same they had just avoided.

He also sighted another black squall to the southward.

"What in the name of —— is to be done now?" said Kelly.

"Shorten sail, and haul dead on a wind right into that dark squall yonder," replied Zeph.

"I suppose it's all serene," growled Kelly; "and so I leave it to you, mate."

"Shorten sail there!" shouted Zeph, in a stern, firm voice.

All this was done with surprising speed.

A good many of the fellows had been deserters from men-of-war, and fled to the diggings; but all worked with a ready will.

"Haul in the larboard braces, brace sharp up, put the helm and bring her to the wind," cried Zeph, continuing his orders.

"Port it is," said the man at the wheel, and the vessel was close hauled upon the starboard tack.

She had on her a square mainsail, boom mainsail, and a jib.

The distant vessel was clearly visible, as she was so much taller than the cutter, while her top canvas was kept on much longer.

The White Eagle moved with graceful ease, running right at the squall, which soon burst on them with thundering force.

But all was snug below and aloft, so that when the wind struck her, everybody was ready.

It was a heavy tussle, and necessitated the taking in of more sail, but the cutter lived through it.

Once more she had been fortunate enough to escape, for when the heavy storm was over, the frigate was nowhere to be seen.

But now came the question, what were they to do? Their pursuers might be bound for Singapore, as well as themselves.

A consultation was held, and Zeph proposed that they should run to within some ten or twelve miles of the settlement, and cast anchor in some unfrequented place.

It would be easy to find a native boat, and Zeph who spoke most of the lingoes of those seas, could go in and learn the news. So it was agreed.

All the time they were proceeding on their way keeping a strict lookout.

A third meeting with the cruiser might prove more fatal than the two others.

Singapore is a British settlement on the Malay coast. Its surface is generally undulating, with round jungle-covered hills.

In some parts it is exceedingly swampy and unhealthy.

The town of Singapore is situated on the south side of the island.

By rivulets it is separated into three distinct divisions, the west inhabited by Chinese, the central and best part by Europeans, and the east by Malays.

The central part of the town is laid out in regular streets with a parade and carriage drive.

The western division comprises the warehouses of Dutch merchants, as well as the dwellings and shops of the Chinese, who have a splendid pagoda in this quarter

The *Kampong Glam*, a Malay quarter, is indescribably filthy and squalid.

Many of the dwellings are erected on posts. Bridges, chiefly of wood, unite the three divisions together.

The retail trade of the town is chiefly carried on in the open streets, even to the money-changers.

Finding that the cruiser was not in the harbour, Zeph ordered the men to return to the vessel, which then came in with flying colours.

Captain Higgins and his mate reported themselves to the American consul, who was very gracious, and not at all particular about papers. He asked them to dinner and the captain said he would give a grand banquet to all the Americans.

He would accept the hospitality of the consul on that day, but he would like a quiet day or two to repose and look about.

The supposed Americans took rooms in a private hotel, where they brought some luggage.

They dined with the consul, who thought Captain Josiah Higgins a curious customer, rather reticent and sparing of speech, while his sailing master was both pleasant and agreeable.

After dinner the consul returned to his business, and they to their hotel.

Here they expressed a wish in the evening to see some of the sights of the town, and asked if there was any singing and dancing going on.

"I should like to see where the jolly tars go."

"Rather rough, sir," said the attendant waiter, smiling and gracious.

"We'll put on rough togs," laughed the owner of the yacht, and so retired to smoke and drink in a room overlooking a garden full of marvellous fruit trees.

When night came the guide presented himself. He was a Malay, and was going to take them to a kind of drinking shop with a garden, where the sailors danced with such girls, native and others, whom they found there.

It was a low quarter of the town, and rarely visited by the English.

It was a Malay Cremorne, with bowers and tables, and was lit up by Chinese lamps.

Presently, shaded by some creepers and evergreens, they saw some of their own men come in and begin to foot it in the usual way.

They did not make themselves known to them, there being no motive.

Presently a waiter came up carrying a tray, which he placed in the adjoining arbour. He was followed by two sailors.

They had not observed that the next arbour was occupied by Kelly and his companion.

"You'll never guess why I brought you out here, Bill—never," said the other.

"Ain't good at guessing, Jack," was the answer.

"Well, do you see, if I'm right, and I'm sure I am, we'll arn a lot of dollars," continued Jack, "blowed if we don't."

"How so, my hearty? I know we're two pals, and allays divides, so spit out."

"What do you think I see outside the pagoda, just now, Bill?" whispered the other. "Why a wessel they calls the White Eagle; well, there's some big swindle about, for she's the Snake. I know her like my own father. I served aboard of her for five years."

"No, Jack!" cried the other.

"But I say yes, Bill!" persisted the first; "and as soon as this drink is over, out I goes and I peaches."

"No you won't! collect some men!" whispered Kelly; "follow—secure them—and bring them aboard. I'll teach him to put a finger in my pie."

The other went round, spoke to the men, warned them there was danger in the wind, and that they must follow.

They obeyed.

Presently the two men came out and made at once for the English quarter, where all the Government offices were situated.

As they entered a dark passage, they were set upon, gagged, and hurried down to a boat, as if they had been drunken sailors.

The supposed yacht lay well out.

An hour later, when it was quite dark, they sailed, and were far away at sea before morning.

Kelly gave the two men a severe rope's-ending, and then cast them adrift in a small open boat without oars, food, or water.

"Sink or swim, and be d—— to you!" was his brutal cry; "that'll teach you to make and meddle with Ned Kelly."

And so he left them.

CHAPTER XCIV.

STOWED AWAY.

THE great object now was to keep dark for a while and do nothing to excite suspicion.

If they could only find some place where for a little time they could be quiet and enjoy themselves out of the way of English cruisers it would be wise and prudent.

A consultation was held in the cabin.

Zeph declared that Batavia in Java was about as jolly a place as he knew of in the world.

It was a Dutch port, but was very much frequented by sailors of all kinds.

Ned Kelly on the sea, from pure ignorance, was not like Ned Kelly on land, and he had to submit to the advice of Captain Zeph.

The man since he had been disgraced in the Royal Navy had served in various capacities in ships of all nations.

He knew these particular seas better than he did almost any others.

So it was resolved to make for the Dutch colony and spend some time there.

Zeph keenly examined the map, and at once fixed on their course.

Anything was better than remaining in those immediate seas and running the risk of meeting the dreaded cruiser.

Of course a good and careful look-out was kept both night and day.

The men all knew that they sailed with ropes round their necks, and didn't wish to give anyone the chance of hauling the other end of it just yet.

For several days nothing whatever occurred and they were within twenty-four hours of Java and in sight of a small island, when a sail was again announced as in sight.

Zeph went up and after ten minutes came down with a blank face.

"It's that infernal cruiser again; she sails like lightning," he said, "we must hide. I know there is land close yonder."

The island is not on many maps, but is well known to sailors in those parts.

It is not inviting to ordinary seamen, but it has often been seized as a refuge, a place of concealment for pirates.

On the side on which they viewed it it presented to the view a precipitous and rugged-bound coast with high and pointed rocks groaning defiance over the unappeaseable and furious waves which broke incessantly at their feet and recoiled to repeat the blow.

For them to land was impossible on that side, but Zeph told them he knew of a cove where they could take shelter.

It was to leeward of the island, and was soon found. Its entrance were indicated to the memory of the sailor by a rock here and there covered by verdure but swarming with sea birds, of which there were myriads.

The sea beat quietly against its base; the feathered tribe, in endless variety, had been for ages the almost undisturbed tenants of this natural monument.

It stood out by itself in the wide ocean, like a pyramid in the desert. It was not, and never had been inhabited, but wild fowl of every description made it their home.

All its jutting points and little projections were covered with white guano.

The water was very deep, and they easily ran into the bottom of a land-locked cave.

Here they agreed to remain until they could decide on their future movements.

On landing they found the remains of a very old wreck and two or three huts that had been built out of the fragments.

They contained a few benches and tables composed of boards roughly hewn out and nailed together.

Around were bones of goats and wild hogs, which was a pleasant discovery, as they were always anxious for fresh meat.

As soon as they were safely moored a look-out was sent to the summit of a rock to watch for the suspicious vessel.

Zeph went up with a powerful glass and saw her approach presently within two miles of the island, when she steered, strangely enough, a course which would take her straight to Batavia.

"Hang me, if she ain't picked up those two fellows," said Zeph; "that's the Spitfire. Could any fool have said anything about Java?"

"I wanted to scrag 'em," said Kelly, in a sullen tone; "who was right now?"

"Well, it can't be helped," replied Zeph, coolly. "I tell you what we'll do—we'll leave the White Eagle here, and start you and I and six men for Batavia in the captain's cutter. I know a place close to Batavia, a little fishing village of natives, where we can leave our men, and in the evening walk into Batavia."

"Rather dangerous, mate," mused Kelly, who when not the leader exhibited less recklessness than usual. "And a ten mile pull ain't much in my way."

"My friend, in Batavia there is a Jew, Joel by name, who has been agent for us lads of these seas for years," said Zeph, "he buys and sells under the very nose of the authorities. He will find you manifesto, ship papers, passports, anything. We will go to him."

"Useful lot of acquaintances you've got mate," said Kelly in rather a dolorous than laughing tone.

"Want friends in this part of the world," replied captain Zeph, with a laugh.

"Seems so," replied the bushranger.

They now descended from the height, and on approaching the huts found a very fragrant smell of cookery.

The goats and hogs were very tame, as this island, a rock in the sea, is rarely visited, and they had plenty of fresh food, including eggs, of which there were innumerable quantities about.

It was only one mile long by half-a-mile wide, and exhibited curious phenomena.

There was a valley close to the land-locked bay, with thousands and thousands of trees, each of them about thirty feet high.

But every tree was dead, extending in leafless boughs to another—a forest of desolation, as if nature had at some particular moment ceased to vegetate.

On the lowest of the dead boughs the gannets and other sea birds had built their nests in numbers unaccountable.

So unaccustomed did they seem to man that the mothers brooding over their young only opened their beaks in a menacing attitude at them as they passed.

As night approached the men returned to their quarters.

Zeph and Kelly had a long conversation.

The former having by far the better education of the two, could easily play the part of a planter from the interior, Sourabaya, or elsewhere, while Kelly could do the overseer.

So it was settled.

At midnight the weather was set fair, and the wind in the proper direction.

The boat was provided with everything necessary to the short voyage.

Salmon Roe was to command while the two principals went on shore and into the town.

Plenty of provisions were stowed in the longboat, and all were armed to the teeth.

At midnight they started, and Zeph, with a small compass, began to steer.

They had a short voyage before them.

The ship's boat had been painted out of all recognition by anybody, besides having been slightly otherwise altered.

So time went on until they were within four miles of Batavia, at one of those marshy points so common on that shore.

The entry into Batavia is up a wide river like a canal, the waters of which are level with the land.

It was formerly styled the European's Graveyard, and was, and is so unhealthy, that a new township has been formed twenty miles higher up where the land rises, and a very handsome city has supplanted the old one.

The summer retreat from the intolerable heat is at Beitenzorg, a city built upon a mountain about 2,000 feet above the level of the fen. It may be called the Sanitarian of the Island.

A fishing village lay at the bottom of the little bay, and into this place Zeph ran.

At certain seasons of the year the rich merchants and residents in Batavia would come out to this place to indulge in fish dinners, and Mein Herr Hermann therefore kept a Lust-haus, where people could be seasonably entertained.

This Zeph knew, and leaving the boat in the marshy entrance to the river, where fever and ague always reign supreme, started with Kelly for the capital.

Here they tried to hunt up Hermann, but learned he was at the village aforesaid, and immediately returned thither for an interview.

However astonished Herr Hermann might have been to see his old friend Zeph, he showed nothing of it.

No more mistaken notion can be conceived than that piracy is done away with in that part of the world.

It is not so terrible in its results as of old, and yet many a missing ship, supposed to have been lost in a cyclone or a typhoon might have its loss traced to human agency.

Having satisfied their appetites, Zeph and the Dutchman were closeted.

After a very few explanations the owner of the house agreed to look after the boat and its crew, while the others went to Batavia in a native vehicle provided by him.

This was just what was wanted.

A little after sundown the vehicle was ready and the two men started, and were driven direct to the house of Herr v. Joel.

He was a merchant of what might be called all-sorts.

He dealt in anything, from a sack or coffee to a ship.

During the time of the celebrated pirate Van Arden, whose atrocities and audacity are still remembered in those seas, he often entertained him openly at table, and introduced him to his friends.

He was never even suspected.

Batavia is a strange place. Its characteristics are exceedingly peculiar.

It is composed of two portions, the old called Jaccatra by the natives, situated in a marshy flat near the sea, and intersected by the great river and sundry canals.

The new suburban portion, extending over the higher grounds to a distance of several miles inland, contains the houses of the Europeans who have left the old town, as we have already said, because of its great insalubrity.

Fever is often caught in it by sleeping in it one night. But Kelly was hard.

Still it is the business part of the town, though in consequence of the desertion of the Europeans it presents a very dilapidated appearance. Still it is the business town.

The suburbs inhabited by the Europeans present more the appearance of a garden than a town, with cocoa-nut trees, bananas, &c.

The streets of Batavia have footpaths on either side for the use of the Javanese and Chinese.

Slaves must either walk on the unpaved centre, or if on he footpath, they must get out of the way of every freeman they meet.

The Dutch are notoriously the most cruel taskmasters and slave-holders in the world.

Europeans, as a rule, never walk.

In the olden time if they did, etiquette demanded that a carriage should follow.

Batavia is the great depôt for all the Dutch possessions, and is very rich.

Such was the place the pirates had reached.

The residence of Herr Joel was of the usual semi-native, semi-European style.

A long verandah ran in front, with creeping plants, and it was low, of one story.

He was at home. He was not one of those who, because he was rich, assumed a right to a country and a town house.

He lived at his office. But it was provided with every luxury money could provide.

Herr Joel was a man who denied himself nothing. He had no objection to work, but he also was very fond of play.

He was very polite and condescending to Zeph. He had made money by him before and was prepared to make money by him again.

Introducing Kelly as Jacob, the overseer of his friend, Mr. Lionel Wells, an intending purchaser of a coffee estate. he explained that they had come to Batavia on very important business.

The fact was a large coffee plantation was in the market privately, and probably, if sold before it was put up to auction, might be privately purchased at a very much lower rate.

His friend, Mr. Lionel Wells, had plenty of money; but still he wanted to get the property as cheap as possible

They had, therefore, come to Herr Joel to ask him to help them. All they wanted was a handsome suit of clothes, a diamond ring or two, and an introduction to one of the best hotels in Batavia frequented by the English.

Now the Dutch Jew, receiver, merchant, and what not, could believe just what he thought proper about the statement.

All he cared was about making money.

He found them clothes, jewellery, luggage, and what was of much more importance, names—Mr. Lionel Wells, of Salpha Farm, Sourabaya, and his overseer, Jacob Jones, of the same place.

He then sent them off to a good hotel of the place, where they were, as a matter of course, received.

But not without a little hesitation.

A Hindoo waiter, speaking in a mixed lingo of Dutch, English, and native dialect, explained that they must put up with inferior rooms for a day or two.

"Him English Majesty officers, Spitfire, have taken rooms, sah!" he cried, in a patois only understood by Zeph; "want to find, sah—a pirate—tink him come yah!"

The idea was so comical to the Hindoo, and waiter at a respectable hotel, that he chuckled immoderately.

"Beg pardon, sah—sahib"—he went on, "but de ideah too comic."

The very respectable Mr. Lionel Wells, of Sourabaya, condescended on the part of himself and overseer to accept inferior apartments.

They indulged in mild refreshment, and then, habited in white linen suits, with straw hats to match, sauntered into the billiard-room. The light was kept out by venetian blinds, which, however, helped to keep the place cool.

As this hotel was very select, and only persons of acknowledged repute were admitted there, no one made enquiries.

There are rough English in Java, as elsewhere; but the planters, as a rule, are rather superior characters.

Some may be a little uncultivated, but vulgarity is the exception.

There was little fear, therefore, for Zeph and his companions being noticed.

Zeph, whose real name would have astonished some of those present, could be the gentleman whenever he liked.

It may take three generations to make a gentleman, but it takes more to unmake one.

The appearance in the billiard-room of Mr. Lionel Wells and his overseer excited no particular attention.

The commander of the Spitfire, Captain Charles Montressor by name, was a rather pompous individual, but a very keen and clever officer.

He was playing a game when Mr. Lionel Wells and Jacob Jones entered the room.

"I believe," he said, sipping a cup of very genuine, good coffee, "that the rascals who stole the Snake must be a set of flying Dutchmen, with a Cape fly-away ready for them at every turn. It's a most remarkable fact."

"Yes, sir," replied Lieut. Dallen, "the rascals are cunning. But take my word, for it—we'll have them yet. Such a set of unhanged rascals cannot last long."

"It would be flying in the face of Providence to believe it," replied the captain.

Lionel Wells and his overseer, who looked as humble as Uriah Heep, stood listening attentively.

"I am from up country, Sourabaya, sir," said Lionel Wells, deferentially. "May I ask, sir, what you mean?"

"You may, sir," said Captain Charles Montressor, politely. "I've been sent in chase of a gang of as vile cut-throats as ever lived—men only fit to be lynched at sight."

"Indeed!" cried Zeph.

"Yes, sir—murderers, robbers, bushrangers, and now pirates," exclaimed the captain, indignantly. "Yes, sir; they have had the temerity to lay their hands on one of her Majesty's vessels—to steal a sloop of war. Only let me catch them."

"I hope you may, sir," replied Zeph, calmly. "Such insolence should not go unpunished."

"No fear," said the captain, hotly. "I've got two fellows here who know them by sight, and if I chase them round the world I will have them."

Kelly gave a peculiar glance at his comrade.

"Knows them by sight?" remarked Zeph.

"Yes, the unhanged rascals who have run away with the Snake," cried the captain, irately, "had the impudence to take her into Singapore as an American yacht. But I am losing my game. Just have a broiled bone presently, and I'll tell you all about it. I'm losing my game, I say."

And so Ned Kelly and Criss Zeph were invited to sup by a post captain in the British Navy.

It was really too astounding, and tickled the rascals' fancy excessively.

The game continued with varied success, and then the officers threw down their cues and gave orders for supper.

"Residents, I presume?" remarked the captain.

"Yes, sir," replied Lionel Wells, bluffly. "I have a plantation at Sourabaya, and have come down with my overseer to make purchases. It is my habit once a year."

"Grand country," said Captain Montressor. "Pity our people ever gave it up to the Dutch."

"Yes," answered Lionel Wells—who was certainly amazed that England having once owned such a prize should have given it up—"quite so."

A planter, though he may be rather rough, sometimes belongs to the aristocratic class in these commercial communities.

They are usually the hosts, with the merchants, who entertain our roving guardians.

The supper was jovial, and Lionel Wells, in the exuberance of his enjoyment, actually invited the captain to visit him in his place up country.

Captain Montressor graciously accepted; a day was fixed, and entered in the captain's notebook.

11

Then the conversation continued.

"You were speaking just now of pirates," remarked Wells. "I thought, except among the Malays and the Arabs, they were things of the past?"

"No, sir," cried the English captain, warmly; "we have them in our very ports—the biggest unhanged scoundrel in all creation, one Kelly the bushranger."

"Up here we get little news," said Wells.

The captain gave a brief but eloquent outline of the outlaw's career, to which Kelly listened with a perfectly stolid countenance, but keen, merry eyes.

"Well, sir, this villain, this cut-throat and his desperadoes, actually, during a haze and a dark night, boarded H.M. cutter Snake and surprised the confounded sleepy crew," continued Montressor, angrily, "turned them adrift and took possession."

"You astonish me," cried Wells.

"Yes, sir," the irate officer continued, "they did, and then they painted, altered her rig and name, and went into Singapore as yachtsmen, Americans going round the world, they had the impudence to say. But at Singapore, two of the old crew of the Snake recognised her, and decided to give information to the authorities. Unfortunately, they were overheard by some of the gang."

"Unfortunate, indeed, sir," said Zeph, stolidly.

"Yes, because they were overpowered, kidnapped, and taken on board," the captain went on. "The pirate then sailed, and, once at sea, put the two men afloat without any oars. Fortunately, we sighted them and took them on board.

"While in the cutter, they had heard enough to become aware of the character of the crew," the captain added; "they took particular note of Ned Kelly and his lieutenant. Besides, they learned that the yacht was bound for Batavia. Here we are ready for them, and may I never be an admiral if I don't string the rascally lot at the yard arm, if I get within sight of them."

"I hope you will succeed, sir," said Lionel Wells earnestly. "The impudence of the scoundrels is something beyond conception."

"It is; but the two lads we picked up owe them a grudge, and swear they would know them in any disguise," added the captain. "So no more tricks upon travellers."

"We are deeply indebted to you for your hospitality," said Lionel rising, "and for your extraordinary and interesting narrative. I think we will return now. We have business in the cool of the morning."

The quartette parted after shaking hands, and the planter and his overseer retired to their double-bedded room, where they for a quarter of an hour indulged in unrestrained laughter.

"I thought I should ha' busted," said Kelly. "It was too scrumptious, shaking hands with a post-captain."

And again he roared in a low, underhand way.

The other did the same, and then proceeded to discuss some punch, and cigars, which they had ordered into their bedroom.

At a very early hour in the morning they paid their bill and went out.

They had stated at the hotel that they were staying at a friend's in the upper town, but, for convenience of business, would pass the night there.

As they descended the steps from the front verandah two sailors presented themselves.

They were ex-men-of-war's men of the Snake, turned afloat on the ocean, and picked up by Captain Montressor.

The two desperadoes moved not a muscle of their faces, but the Jack Tars ran up the steps in a curiously eager manner.

"This way," said Mr. Lionel Wells, darting down a small alley. "The sooner we're out of this the better."

And he took to his heels until they were in some winding alleys, which soon brought them to the house of Herr v. Joel, the merchant.

Without arousing him they procured the car which had

brought them, and the driver, and drove off as fast as they could to the little village where they had left the long-boat.

Meanwhile the men rushed up to a waiter, a negro, who spoke English.

"Who are those fellows?"

"Don't know, sah; never see 'em afore. Gemmen sleep yah last night, sah, sup with the officers in the ebenin'."

"Show me to the captain's room."

The Hindoo obeyed. The room commanded a view of the shipping.

Going along the nigger told him the names of the strangers.

In answer to a second knock the captain, in a sleepy voice, bade the waiter come in.

On shore he liked his ease, but was always ready in case of business.

"Sailor man, sah, want see you, sahib."

"Show him in," cried the captain. "Well, what is it, Jack?"

"Please sir," said Jack, touching his foc'lock, "Ned Kelly and Bill Zeph have just left the house. I'm told you supped with them last night."

Swearing is not the ordinary fault of officers in the British Navy, now-a-days, but Captain Montressor gave vent to a round oath.

"Go rouse the first lieutenant," he said, "and bid him come to me as soon as dressed."

He then leaped out of bed, and dressed rather quicker than he had ever done in his life. It was too marvellous to believe.

Then the lieutenant came to him.

"What's the matter, sir?" he asked. "War declared with France and America?"

He was a near relative of the captain, or he would not have dared to speak to him in such a jocular tone.

"Worse, sir!" cried Montressor. "We supped last night with Ned Kelly and Bill Zeph. Yes, sir, and they asked us to their plantation, and shook hands with us."

"Surely, sir——," began Lieutenant

"I am neither mad nor drunk," said the captain. "What I tell you is a positive fact. Away to the British Consul, ask him to communicate with the authorities, and have the town searched.

The captain then descended to the lower regions and communicated with the manager, who explained that on arriving and giving their names, they mentioned Herr Joel, a very respectable merchant, as their introducer.

"Send for him, with my compliments," said the captain, in a dry and irritated tone.

The lieutenant soon returned, having roused the consul, who promised his personal attendance to the matter.

But nothing came of it, while Herr Joel almost told the exact truth as to his transaction.

How the rascals had found him out was a profound mystery. One of them spoke excellent local Dutch.

There was nothing left for it but to put to sea and pursue them.

Meanwhile, the two outlaws had reached the fishing village, and at once put to sea.

The mast and sail were taken down, and then the long-boat was rowed swiftly down the stream, until they came to a cove distant from any habitation.

The vegetation was luxuriant, and the trees grew to the edge of the water.

Here they intended to remain a while. A look-out was arranged on a tree whence the open sea could be clearly seen.

They had not long to wait.

The cruiser was soon visible sailing along at a moderate rate, a mile from land.

They had concealed the long-boat in a creek over-arched by trees, but was much more effectually hidden when worked into the tall reeds, which, like the tea-tree scrub in the rivers' mouths in Australia, are so close and so flexible that they bend like standing corn, and once in amongst them all trace is lost of the fugitive. Just such cover the pirates availed themselves of, and there they remained until their pursuers, like the Levite in Holy Writ, "passed by on the other side."

The look-out came down next moment in great trepidation.

The ship's launch with a strong crew was coming along close on them.

The pirates withdrew on board and lay still. All were heavily armed and prepared for the worst. If the launch came in they must fight hard, and run up country.

It was a desperate matter, as lose their boat they must, while, even if they got another, there would be a stout blockade kept up.

The launch was near the mouth of the little cove, when the order was given to back water.

"Couldn't hide a dingy in there, sir," said a young and pert voice, that of a midshipman.

"I expect you are right, Walters," replied the lieutenant, "and we know their boat was a large one" (they had called at the village and made enquiries). "Go ahead."

The pirates once more breathed freely, but remained still until the sound of voices was no longer heard.

Even then it was decided to keep close until night.

This they did, and, when darkness had covered the deep, pulled out—still having no mast—to where their ship awaited them.

Between Kelly and Zeph it had been determined to put oceans between them and the British cruiser before they again made a halt.

CHAPTER XCV.
ANOTHER AND A BETTER WORLD.

AFTER long consideration the next scene which they selected for their labours was California, where they could not be known.

They would put in at the Cape for water and provisions, and then make boldly round the Horn.

Their vessel was stout, had a broad beam, and could stand any amount of rough weather with any other Queen's ship in the service.

The men grumbled, but Kelly explained that they were in serious danger while the baulked and enraged captain of the cruiser was near them. He would make short work if he caught them.

He promised them a day ashore each at the Cape if they would be cautious, and then at San Francisco unlimited leave of absence.

They set sail, and duly reached the Cape, where, aided by the politeness of the American Consul, they were able to get ample supplies.

The men had their run on shore, but were careful to do nothing to excite suspicion.

They drank, fiddled, and danced to their hearts' content, spending money lavishly.

Then they began their arduous journey.

Luckily the weather was fine, and with the exception of an inevitable storm or two, they found themselves in the Pacific.

The voyage to San Francisco was very smooth and fortunate.

The locality has been described as nauseous. Kelly and his crew found it the very place to their taste.

But the chiefs sought adventure, and after two days, leaving the vessel in charge of some of the safest men, started up country, promising to return with a good swing for the party left behind.

The travellers for up-country were Kelly, Joss, Zeph, and Salmon Roe, with a fellow named Stewart whom Kelly had recognised.

He had fled Australia, being looked after for more than one atrocious murder.

He was one of the criminals amongst the thousands the "paternal" Government of England has secretly freighted to Victoria from V. D. Land to get rid of the expense of their keep.

He was a man after Kelly's own heart, a miscreant of the deepest dye.

These banded together to plunder up country, and procuring horses, miners' clothes, with tools, started for Scotch diggings.

Of course this was only a blind, as we are well aware they had other views.

Having reached the desired spot they looked about them, found a digger who was about to leave, bought his house and claim, and thus obtained a footing.

Then they determined to look around, and see what the country was made of.

They entered the scattered town—it being evening—found plenty of saloons, one of which they entered.

A motley scene presented itself. The visitors to these "saloons" were as many-coloured in feature and garment as Joseph's coat. Every nation had its representative there, and some in their national costumes. All were gambling and drinking.

Everything was enormously dear, but none of the imbibers seemed to think the price asked by the Hebe behind the bar was too much for the winning smile that accompanied the demand.

The place was brilliantly lighted and the noise something bewildering.

But the most reckless gambling was carried on in the Chinese quarters; and as more fun and most plunder would be found in the house of "the childlike and bland," and less resistance offered to violence, our party resolved to resort thither in search of prey.

CHAPTER XCVI.
THE JOSS-HOUSE.

THE house which Kelly and his party had selected was kept by a very worthy Chinaman named Sing-Wang.

He supplied the best of coffee, fiery liquors, and provided numerous other ways of passing the time.

The house was nothing more than a shed with a bar, and behind the landlord's private room, where he kept his stores, and probably his money.

Sing-Wang was a stupid-looking, inoffensive Chinaman whose one only ambition was to make money enough to return to his native land, and live in comfort.

Kelly and his friends felt quite at home in the joss-house. They were fond of drink, no matter what its quality, and bad company.

The bushranger swaggered up to to the bar, followed by his friends. Kelly was for a wonder not sober.

"Now, then, look sharp, you sneaking-looking cuss!" he cried, looking at the Chinaman. "Don't stand skulking about; but serve round your poison."

"That's right, old smutty, look alive!" said Captain Zeph.

"What is it to be?" asked the immovable Chinaman in broken English, which we cannot pretend to imitate.

"Whisky, you pig-tailed monstrosity!" howled Joss; "bale it out quick, you infernal heathen! if you are not as sharp as greased lightning I'll make a hole through your head!"

The Chinaman seemed accustomed to these polite and affable remarks, for he grinned from ear to ear as if he had been complimented on his personal appearance.

"Don't grin at us!" shouted Stewart; "shut up that gash, or I'll cut out your tongue by the roots!"

The man was used to this sort of thing, and was well aware he would be paid.

In less time than it takes to tell, the liquor was placed on the counter, and the Chinaman demanded two dollars.

"Two dollars!" cried Kelly, "grin and be blowed to you, do! Can't you trust me for a moment? Do you want to jump down my throat? Do you think I am going to sling my hook without paying you for your cursed poison?"

"Money down—no slate kept at the bar," said Sing-Wang, pointing to a placard behind his back.

"Go and be smothered!" roared Kelly. "If you are not more civil I'll turn you into a dead Chinaman, and send you home in a plank suit. You are fretting to find yourself between four deal boards. That's what the matter with you!"

The patient Sing-Wang still held out his hand. It was the rule of the house, he said.

"Two dollars!" he repeated.

"Take that!" cried the enraged bushranger, throwing the hot whisky in the Chinaman's face. "I hate the sight of you pig-tailed gentry, and should like to drive you out of the country!"

Sing-Wang wiped the tears from his eyes, while those in the joss-house jeered at him, for Chinamen are not popular in California, however much they may be tolerated.

"Me poor Chinaman, and want my money," he cried. "Can't give whisky for nothing."

Kelly was in an obstinate humour, and still declined to pay, and furthermore stated that he would drink as much as he liked without spending a penny.

"Dat not fair," cried the horror-stricken Sing-Wang, who began to see what his customer was like.

"Fair or not, I shall do what I like," replied Kelly, ferociously, and as he spoke he pulled out a pistol. "Fill up the glasses again, or I'll make short work of you, you ugly, yellow-faced, old dried-up parchment-skinned thief!"

"Me give no more drink for nothing," said the Chinaman in a dreamy voice.

"Look sharp!" cried Kelly. "Will you trust me or have a bullet through your nut?"

Sing-Wang hesitated a moment, and then reluctantly brought the drink.

"I'll trust to the honour of Englee genl'man," he said, trying to look easy in his mind, for he felt sure that the whisky would never be paid for.

But Captain Zeph, who did not want a row, called him on one side and paid him, and Sing-Wang was made happy.

The joss-house was almost empty when Kelly entered it, but it gradually filled up and soon became crowded.

They were a rough lot, and seemed very thirsty, for they drank like fishes, and seemed to enjoy the fiery spirit.

Some smoked, some swore and talked, some sang, and some gambled.

Sing-Wang was evidently doing well, for most of the miners spent their money as soon as they earned it. In fact, they would work hard for a couple of weeks and then never leave the joss-house until all their money was in the Chinaman's till.

When drunk they would not be very particular in seeing after their change, and Sing-Wang was not the sort of man to insist upon their accepting it.

The subject of conversation that evening was a man, Peleg Oswald by name, who had struck a good lead, and was declared by everyone to be the luckiest fellow in creation.

He was a tall, gaunt-looking fellow, spare and hollow-eyed, with lean cheeks and a large mouth, on which there was always a disagreeable grin.

He spent his money freely, swore and chewed, and was very fond of fighting.

"Is any critter ready to take a hand with me, or are you all afeared?" cried Peleg Oswald, throwing down some money on the rough table. "Are you all cleared out, or ain't you got enough grit on yer to run your chance? There's the money, boys."

To the surprise of Kelly and his friends no one came forward; they did not know that Peleg Oswald had hardly ever been known to lose as yet, and almost always succeeded in clearing out his men.

"I'll take anyone," continued Peleg. "Don't stand back. I'll put down double the amount any other chap likes to put down if he'll only stand forward."

"No," replied a seedy-looking man. "None cares to play with you, you make it too lively for 'em. You always win, I guess."

"Always win," cried Peleg; "you mean, I guess, to insinuate suthin' wrong. What are you a-crowding up to me and a-hinting, and a-throwing out agin my credit? I'm straight, I am. Don't try to sneak out of it, you blatherskite. You insinuated afore strangers that I cheated. You're a nice old figger-head to come here a roaring and howling for a fight. Why don't you say suthin'? Speak your mind if you dare. A cussin' and yelling at a man because he happens to have the luck. You're mean, downright mean, you aint got pluck enough to have it out between man and man."

"I didn't mean no harm," the other said.

"Didn't mean no harm," yelled Peleg Oswald, "s'posing I pulls this yar pistol out of my belt," suiting the action to the word. "S'posing I pints it at you and it goes off of its own accord, would it make any difference to you, you sucker, if I didn't mean no harm? I think I must do for you, I don't see why a sneakin' cuss like you should be allowed to live. If I does it's all on account of good nature."

"I knew you was a-joking," said the man who had given offence, with a sickly smile, making for the door with more speed than dignity.

"Joking be blowed!" cried Peleg, and the next moment he fired, but to his annoyance missed the man.

"Missed!" he muttered, and made a rush after the unfortunate individual, "I'll make dead sure of him this time."

"Don't be in such a hurry," said Charles Stewart, getting in front of him. "You challenged anyone in this here company to a game, and I am ready to accept."

"I'll be back in no time," said Peleg, with a savage grin. "Let me clear out the vermin and play Euchre afterwards."

"Now or not at all," said Stewart doggedly; "are you my man or not?"

"It wouldn't take long to settle his hash," remarked Peleg, "I'd be sharper than Jersey lightning, that I would."

"You can settle your dispute with that coward another day," said Stewart, "but if you want to shuffle cards with me, you must do it at once."

"I ain't a quarrelsome man," observed Peleg Oswald. "I'm a man as likes peace and quietness; but when a man puts my back up, I'm a demon—a regular ring-tailed coon. The American eagle don't fly over a chap who is more full of grit than the cuss who stands afore you, stranger, you may bet your pile on that."

"You have proved your manhood, and that poor frightened, trembling cuss is about a mile away by this time," returned Charles Stewart.

"And I guess is running still," said Peleg, spitting out a large plug of tobacco on to the grimy floor.

"He may run to a warm place for all I care," cried Charles Stewart. "Are you going to play or not?"

"I'm on," replied the gambler.

"Order liquors before we begin."

This was done, and then the play commenced.

The Chinaman looked on at his customers with as much expression in his face as a barber's block.

He only thought of the money that came to his mill.

It was nothing to him if his customers killed each other as long as they did not interfere with him.

There was one man in the company who was known by the name of Swearing Joe.

The Americans were the first to institute the spelling bee, and it was in California that the swearing bee was first invented.

The man who was modest in his language had to stand drinks all round.

The game had been very popular until Swearing Joe had presented himself.

But that hero was so strong and fluent in his language

that the others owned that he was the best at the business, and it was given up.

"By Jerusalem!" cried Swearing Joe, "if old Oswald hasn't gone and found a man soft enough to play with him. I bet a square dollar that he'll go away from the table with his pockets turned inside out."

"You'll be turned inside out, I guess, my friend," said Oswald. "I can't bear to hear bad language. I shall get old Shiny Face to put up a notice, 'No swearing allowed. All those who want to use strong language are requested to go outside.'"

Everybody laughed heartily at this sally.

"Who's a using strong language?" said Joe, in an irritated tone of voice.

"Don't interrupt the game," cried Stewart, speaking in his usual snap-dragon tone.

"To ensure fair play," observed Oswald, "I'll put my pistol on the table. You are a stranger, and I warn you before I begin that if I see anything that ain't square I shall let fly."

Stewart gave a hideous scowl, and produced a knife and a pistol as well.

The two men soon became interested in the game.

Their flushed faces were unpleasant to look at, and they poured down the brain-destroying drink with avidity.

The Yankee played a good game, and played fair.

He had never cheated at cards, but Stewart tried all sorts of tricks, and Oswald, who was a rare old stager, saw through him in no time.

But he kept his temper, grinning to himself.

"He thinks I am only one year old," he thought, "but I'll bet that he'll soon find out his mistake. I calculate that this child is not to be done by no Britisher on airth. Ther'll be a muss afore the evening's done. I can't stand such goings on much longer, I calculate."

The luck has changed.

This was the verdict of the crowd that gathered round the players.

They had not been so observant as Oswald, and did not see that Charles Stewart was undoubtedly chiselling.

At last the Yankee could stand it no longer.

His blood boiled over with rage and indignation at the foul conduct of the other.

"No you don't," he cried, clutching hold of Stewart's arm as he was about to sweep the gold off the table. "Just stop a minute, my friend."

"What do you mean?" cried Stewart angrily, with, however, a startled look.

"I've had my eye on you all along, and know what sort of a cuss you are," cried Peleg, looking for his pistols, which Kelly had quietly removed from the table. "You had your hands too full when you tried to take me in. It ain't easy to get on the blind side of old Oswald—'cute old Oswald. He's got his eye skinned, he have."

"Take my advice, and hold your —— tongue," retorted Stewart. "Look here, if you don't shut up there'll be the devil to pay. Take my advice, and step outside to cool off. You're carrying matters a little too far, so be advised."

But Peleg declined to budge an inch.

He knew nothing of his man, and was in one of his most aggravating fits of obstinacy, and began to yell and blaspheme, while Stewart listened quietly, but with rather an ominous glitter in his eyes.

"Will you quit?" he demanded at last, as Peleg paused to take breath. "Will you take a friendly warning and walk your chalks while you have got the chance? I don't want to be disagree'ble, but if this goes on much longer I shall cut up rough."

Peleg's answer was an oath, and an instant later Stewart sprang forward, plunging his knife in the man's heart. He deliberately pulled a handkerchief out of the man's breast-pocket, and wiping the knife calmly, returned the weapon to his own belt.

These little episodes occurred so often in these quarters that it excited little comment.

The victim was dragged out of the room by the heels and thrown outside.

"Let's liquor," he said, and not one of those present declined the invitation, the general impression being that "the darned fool had brought it on himself."

Stewart did not again allude to the trifling episode, but spoke of other things, and his companions followed his example.

He resumed a conversation he had been carrying on with Kelly, as if nothing out of the way had happened.

"I tell you what it is," interrupted Swearing Joe, "if you don't d—— well cut your lucky you'll be sorry for it. There are some people in this place who are so infernally particular, that they'd think nothing of lynching you right off for that little bit of fun. I know 'em, and my advice is, clear out. There have been a good many rumpusses in this 'ere place, and a body of men have been and organised themselves to put a stop to it altogether."

Stewart perhaps thought it would be prudent to take advantage of this friendly warning, for he soon after disappeared.

Kelly and his companions looked for him in vain. He was nowhere to be found.

CHAPTER XCVII.

SHORT SHRIFT.

THAT a man should blow a hole through another or stab him in the vitals was no very uncommon occurrence in that part of California.

The Chinamen who had carried the dead body of Peleg out of the joss-house had taken the precaution to empty his pockets, but having performed this kindly office, they speedily forget that such a man had ever existed.

The man who had hurried another into eternity so recklessly had not gone far, but after passing the scattered Chinese huts near the joss-house concealed himself behind the friendly shelter of some bushes to watch and wait.

It had occurred to him that Sing-Wang, the placid Chinaman, was saving money, and, being of an envious and avaricious nature, he came to the determination of possessing himself of the gold so carefully hoarded by the unhappy Celestial.

He had not taken his friends into his confidence, for the simple reason that he desired to reap the whole profit himself.

He never cared to go halves with any man if he could possibly help it, preferring to act on his own hook, as he eloquently expressed it.

So he waited until the guilty night was far advanced before he ventured out from his retreat.

The wind moaned through the dark tree tops as he crept along as a thing of evil.

All was very quiet and still as he passed on, pausing every now and then to listen, with his hand on the pistol in his belt.

He scarcely knew what he feared, but something in the deep silence of the whole place made him feel strangely uneasy.

He shook off this unusual feeling, however, and became himself again in another moment.

"Just the sort of night for a job like the one I have in hand," he muttered. "That old Chinaman's money-bags shall soon be in my possession. I know I am running a great risk, but it's worth it. I hope that Sing-Wang lives by himself."

He soon arrived at the joss-house and tried the door, which he found was firmly fastened.

"How the deuce am I to get into the confounded place?" he thought. "I could easily break the door in, but it would make a confounded row and wake up everyone within half-a-mile. Eh? The window. I must get through that way."

The night was a warm one, and the unsuspicious Chinaman had left it open, never dreaming for a moment that anyone would try to break into his place.

He had been there some time, and no one ever tried to rob him of a farthing.

Thus he was lulled into false security.

After much difficulty—for the window was a small one—he succeeded in squeezing himself through the narrow opening and landing on the floor.

The interior of the joss-house was as dark as pitch, and the man groped his way cautiously, making as little noise as possible.

He softly struck a match and looked about him. It was a risky thing to do; this he knew, but he could not help himself.

He was in the drinking-saloon, and partitioned off was a small room where the Chinaman slept, doubtless with his money.

A lamp was standing on the counter, and he lit this, turning it very low, and, taking down a bottle of whisky, fortified himself with a stiff draught to steady his nerves.

The silence was oppressive, and Stewart tried to hold his breath, fearing that the sound of his heavy breathing would awake the Chinaman.

For a moment he stopped before the door of the inner room, and then softly turned the handle, making no sound.

A flood of light poured through the half-open door, and Stewart, to his surprise, saw that the Chinaman was wide awake.

His back was turned, and he was evidently in ignorance that he was watched. He was gloating over a pile of money before him, and chuckling to himself.

Stewart pulled out a long knife and crept close up to the unfortunate Chinaman.

At that moment Sing-Wang became conscious of his presence, and, looking over his shoulder, saw the man with his bright uplifted knife, and the look of murder in his deep-set, blood-shot eyes.

He gave an awful piercing shriek

At the very moment he was about to make short work of the Chinee, a sound like rushing waters smote upon his ear. The noise gathered force every moment, and the roar of many voices awoke the echo of the night. Onward it came, like the roar of the rapids, and the angry bellowings of a multitude struck terror for the moment into his heart.

"Lynch him! lynch him!" he heard springing from the excited throats of the mob.

He rushed from the house, while the Chinaman continued to scream his loudest. Stewart was not quick enough; the crowd was upon him, and there stood the Chinee, who gasped out the particulars of the attack.

Twenty strong arms seized the fellow and carried him, yelling and shouting to the jail.

The authorities resolved to try him, and there was small chance upon two grounds of his escaping the gallows. Firstly, he was a "darned Britisher," and, secondly, he was caught red-handed. The crowd did not disperse; they surrounded the prison, and distrusting the authorities, resolved to anticipate the duties of a jury. "Lynch him!" was again the shibboleth that resounded through the tumult. "Lynch him!" was the universal chorus.

Stewart heard it and trembled. The warders even looked pale and troubled.

Presently a mighty rush was made by the surging crowd outside—the door of the prison was forced, and Captain Freeman, the chairman of the Vigilance Committee, followed by the mob, rushed into the room where Stewart stood, pale, firm, but dauntless.

It was the work of a moment to seize him, which was done with needless violence. He was dragged outside, a rope put round his neck, and, with a momentary return of mercy, Freeman cried—

"Out with a prayer, you darned human panther, if you ever knew one, for your time's up."

Firm as a rock, and as dauntless as ever, Stewart scowled at his assailants. His hands were still free.

"Look here," shouted Stewart, "I've got something to say. It's only a few words. Let any three of you ——

Yankees stand out, and I'll tackle the whole three. If I lose I will consent to be hanged, but if I win you are to let me off. Ain't that a fair bargain? Three Yankees to one Englishman, and I'll undertake to come out the winner."

Everyone in the settlement thought that a riot was taking place, and turned out under the impression that the Chinese were being massacred; but when the state of the case was explained, there was a shout of universal indignation as all eyes were turned upon the murderer, who was white as a tombstone of marble.

He was removed to the jail, and everybody retired to rest after cursing him heartily for having disturbed their repose.

Next morning the affair was the talk of the whole place. Nobody could think of anything else.

"Curs and cowards," he yelled at them, "I wish I had a chance at any of your yelping lot single-handed; I'd show you an Englishman is a match for any of you—yes, any half-dozen of such a tallow-faced, lank-jawed——" But his words were stopped by the rush of half-a-dozen of his tormentors, who struck him in the face.

Here his indomitable pluck sprung out. With a few well-directed blows from his brawny and muscular arms down they went like ninepins, which so enraged the Yankees that they proceeded at once to wreak their vengeance and Britisher hate upon their helpless victim.

Fifty hands caught hold of the rope which had been thrown over the branch of a tree, and up went Stewart with a rush that crashed his head against the branch, literally smashing in his skull, so that he was dead before hanging could end his guilty career.

His executioners then quietly dispersed. The laws for public security were so supinely, and, in many instances, corruptly administered, that the public were compelled to take the matter into their own hands.

The country was the rendezvous of the greatest ruffians, convicts and others, from all countries, so strong measures were absolutely necessary for the security of the lives and property of the inhabitants.

Kelly and his friends did not much like the prospect held out by these summary proceedings, and thought they had had enough of that locality for the present. Fine as the climate was generally believed to be, *they* thought the atmosphere getting rather too warm for their personal comfort.

They had contemplated an attempt to rescue their comrade, but soon saw that it was utterly impossible.

CHAPTER XCVIII.
KELLY SKEDADDLES.

KELLY and the rest were stunned at the scene that had taken place, and determined to make the best of their way to San Francisco, whence they would pay their promised visit to Tahiti.

They determined to make tracks for San Sacramento, whence they could go by steamer.

That night very little was done but drink and gamble, while one man, half drunk, with bowie-knife and revolver in belt, kept singing—

> O! O! high and low of all degree,
> A tale I will unfold,
> And tell you where, across the sea,
> You may get lots of gold,
> In the land of Yankee Doodle.
> Make no delay, but haste away,
> To California, O!
>
> So we're told there's lots of gold
> For all who choose to go
> On board a ship, and take a trip
> To California, O!

Next day they reached San Francisco.

It was a lovely day. Winter is by far the best of the year, though when they begin the rains are heavy, but ten days or a fortnight after follow with a delightful sunshine, and temperature never under forty degrees during the day.

The evenings and mornings may require a little fire in the grate, but no one attends to it through the day, so it goes out.

The worst of the winter is the mud; knee-deep is a trifle in the vicinity of the town.

Those of the streets not planked were impassable. All is changed now.

The drinking and gambling saloons were something terrible in those days; the drinking has not decreased; perhaps the saloons have.

The hotels were then extremely bad—the bed-rooms nearly all two beds. In many, hardly any furniture at all.

Kelly and his companions secured two rooms, and then agreed to hold a council of war.

At last they came to the decision to stay awhile, to make for some other diggings, and try their luck.

They communicated with the ship, found all was right, and determined to start up the country once more.

They determined to make for Maryville by steamer and then start for a place called Volcano Diggings, of which they had heard a very good account. Men were making large fortunes, in which the bushranger determined to have a share.

Cards were a very good medium, but, after the fate of Stewart, they felt very dubious of trying their fortune by any but fair means.

Maryville is on the junction of the rivers Feather and Yaba, both large streams merging their united waters into the Sacramento, about forty miles below, as it is the head of the navigation for steamers in this direction, and is the depôt from which the more northern mining districts are supplied with all the necessaries of life, which are conveyed on mules into the mountain region which commences about fifteen miles from the city.

From the lowness of the place and the contiguity of rivers, the vicinity is rendered unhealthy during the extreme heat of the dry season when the temperature often reaches one hundred and ten degrees in the shade.

There are stages—as covered waggons are called—traversing the country for more than a hundred miles into the mountains, but they are most comfortless conveyances.

Kelly and his companions procured horses and mules so as to travel independently.

Two days later, they halted at one of those little caravanserais which sprinkle the road to the mines.

Slumberers lay all around them. On the bar and behind the bar, across the doorway and behind the barrels, they lie thickly stowed away, while from the rafters above them a sick man swings in his bamboo hammock and dolefully groans at each puff of air which stirs his pendent couch.

Outside there are others who cannot find room inside, and whose inclination prompts them to sleep in the open air.

Near one of the trees which surround the tent, a pair of rough-bearded Germans have built a large fire and have stretched themselves on their blankets with their feet to the flames, in true bivouac style.

Their guns are stacked close at hand, and one or two who have mules have tethered them in close proximity.

A little further off some Mexicans have chosen their resting-place. The fire burns brighter than that of any other party, for two of them are yet sitting playing mente by the flickering light.

The others are curled up in their penchoes like so many dogs, and, probably, with about just as much thought of to-morrow.

A merry life the vagabonds seem to lead, for though often hungry and always dirty, yet in their worst afflictions a greasy pack of cards will cause them to forget all their trials, and they will be as happy as though rolling in every luxury.

Though almost everyone was asleep, silence was not wholly prevalent.

Occasionally there was the breaking out of a discordant laugh from the gambling Mexicans, or the tread of the tethered mules as they now and then rose to crop the scanty grass, the mingled cries of wild cats and other animals.

There was not much sleep to be obtained under these circumstances, and the whole party were not sorry to rouse at an early hour and start.

They took a square meal, provided themselves with provisions for the day, and then they started, leaving their companions behind them.

They always travelled as much as possible by themselves, being by no means fond of creating new acquaintances.

The journey to Volcano Diggings did not take them a long time to accomplish.

On the third day they reached it.

It was a wild place, and very much scattered.

Kelly and his party while looking around made a pretence of building a small cabin on the side of a crevice, roofed it with canvas, leaving a corner open to serve as a chimney.

Then they of course adjourned to the tavern.

The usual crowd was there of idlers and hard-working men. Several had been very successful, as the mines were rich, and hard work was rewarded by the usual result.

Among those whom it was said had been specially lucky was John Rutherford. Kelly and his gang noted him keenly.

The man was plump and short. Unlike the other natives of the locality he was close-cropped and shaven, as if to keep down the strong blue blackness of his head and hair, which nevertheless asserted itself over his round cheeks and upper lip like a tattooing of Indian ink.

He drank his glass, smoked, and did not object to a game of cards, but he was reserved and taciturn—if not sulky.

He was a man of iron frame—a *multum in parvo* of thews and sinews—a small edition of the Farnese Hercules—one of those prodigies in which nature seems at times to rejoice.

There are "men and men." As the French say, there are "*Fagots et Fagots.*"

The writer of this history once saw Mr. Dalmahoy Campbell, of Melbourne, Victoria, carry his horse sixty yards; and what the horse must have been may be judged from his owner's weight, which was seventeen stone.

Kelly, who listened carefully to the talk going on around, soon became aware that this man was believed to be rich, though he never bragged or flashed his money.

He lived in a gulch by himself near his claim, which he worked steadily.

Volcano Diggings had a good name, though it was full of people; there were no rumours of murders or robberies of late.

Judge Lynch had been considerably busy at one time, and had rather terrified men into good behaviour.

It was now for Kelly's gang to find out where Golconda Gulch was.

As it happened it was about half-a-mile beyond their own location.

At a sign from Kelly they "humped" a bottle of Bourbon whisky along with them, and returned to their hut.

It was to a remote corner. As soon as they had squatted around the arch fiend Kelly, he advised them to "light up" and listen. There he sat, like Milton's Satan in council. He proceeded to unravel his plan.

"Now, pals, this cove smells of money, the most beautiful scent I know of in the world. Well, he don't use it, and he won't use it, so we must set him a good example and use it for him."

"Three cheers for Ned," was the response to this homily.

"Stow all that just now, at all events," said Ned. "Wait till we can cheer without bother. These diggings were made for men of pluck like us; besides if we don't have the tin these muffs dig up, somebody else will. So I propose to go home to supper with our new friend without waiting for an invitation, and then——"

"Yes," replied Zeph, " I'm on the track ; go ahead, Ned, and then—yes—and then ——"

" Why, assist him to ' turn in ' where he won't ' turn up' in a hurry."

A congratulatory guffaw greeted this refined specimen of wit, and Ned seemed highly gratified by the tribute to his comic powers.

They had just finished speaking when they heard the miner gaily singing one of the sprightly and jocund ditties of his native land, as he merrily trudged along, evidently well satisfied with his day's or night's work.

He was following a beaten track that would soon take him out of sight round a knot of trees.

They waited until they could see him no more, and then prepared to stalk him.

They crept on. Still the man sang merrily and vigorously as he trudged along, his mind full of happy thoughts.

He entered a narrow gully, and soon after a hut built against the rock.

Then there was a light in the window.

The four ruffians stole cautiously up and peered in through some crannies.

He was lying down on his side reading and smoking. He had a large open book before him. There was a smile on his face.

The door of the hut was latched.

" Good evening mate," said Kelly, in as hearty a voice as he could assume, while the others kept in the background ; "got e'er a drop to lay the dust in my throat ? "

" There's plenty down at Malony's, unless you mean water," said John Rutherford

" Water ! good enough for a man whose throat's like a hot frying-pan with no grease in it," replied Kelly, as he lifted up the latch and entered.

The man, who had a gun hanging up, and a pistol in his belt, pointed to a pitcher.

" Well, I can't say as you'd give your liver away to a hungry mate, anyhow," was the sullen answer. " A pull at your water-can ain't much."

The miner felt the rebuke, and that his reception of the stranger was not first-class.

So he jumped up, on hospitable thoughts intent, and went to a cupboard.

Just as he turned his back to Kelly he received a bullet from the bushranger's shooter, which passed through his neck.

He fell, and remained conscious long enough to see the clan rush in on hearing the shot and begin to ransack the place

" Finish the job," shouted Zeph. " While he's above ground we have the noose round our necks ; and when that's the state of the case the white night-cap and the fellow as puts it over your neck ain't far off."

The victim had meanwhile fainted from loss of blood.

" It won't do him no harm," continued Zeph, " lodging another ball in the poor man's body. " He don't know nothing about it, he don't ; and we've saved him a good deal of trouble and hard work in this sorrowful world," he drawled out in a nasal, conventional drawl, winking one eye knowingly for the amusement of his friends.

The murderous cad chuckled and looked round for the approval his charitable sentiments excited.

" Don't let us do nothing by halves," said Kelly. " We'll burn the whole building. We won't let a stick stand. The flames will make short work of that little lot," pointing with a grin to the still and immovable body.

They now continued their search, and found some rough gold concealed in a small box, but not until they had rummaged the whole place.

Before starting they set fire to the hut, and then made tracks for pastures new.

But, as Burns tells us, " the best-laid schemes of mice and men oft gang agee," and so it was in this case.

John Rutherford, though dreadfully wounded, had not been done to death.

He returned to consciousness just in time to crawl out from the blazing remnants of his hut, and, though dreadfully weak from loss of blood, felt that he was not mortally wounded.

When Rutherford was found by friends it was late next day, and he was not for some time able to explain.

By this time the robbers were far away.

CHAPTER XCIX.
MINBREY.

The next diggings to which Ned Kelly and his gang determined to remove was Minbrey. Moving about was convenient in the position in which they were placed. Their conduct wherever they went was so marked that it was likely to arouse suspicion.

Minbrey was not very far from Volcano Diggings, and the four men determined to take it easy.

They were after the first day's journey very tired, very dusty, and very much disgusted.

To men of Kelly's calibre there was comfort and excitement in the leathern bottle slung over the *mantillas* of their saddles.

But they burst into a tempest of fury when they found that the bottles did not contain *aquardiente* as they expected, but had been filled in by a rascally Irishman with bad American whisky.

Still they drank it. It was better than nothing.

All around was a sterile waste, bordered here and there by arable fringes and *valdas* of meadow land, but, in the main, dry, dusty and forbidding.

On they went continuing the scent.

(To be continued.

NED KELLY THE IRONCLAD AUSTRALIAN BUSHRANGER

NO 15,

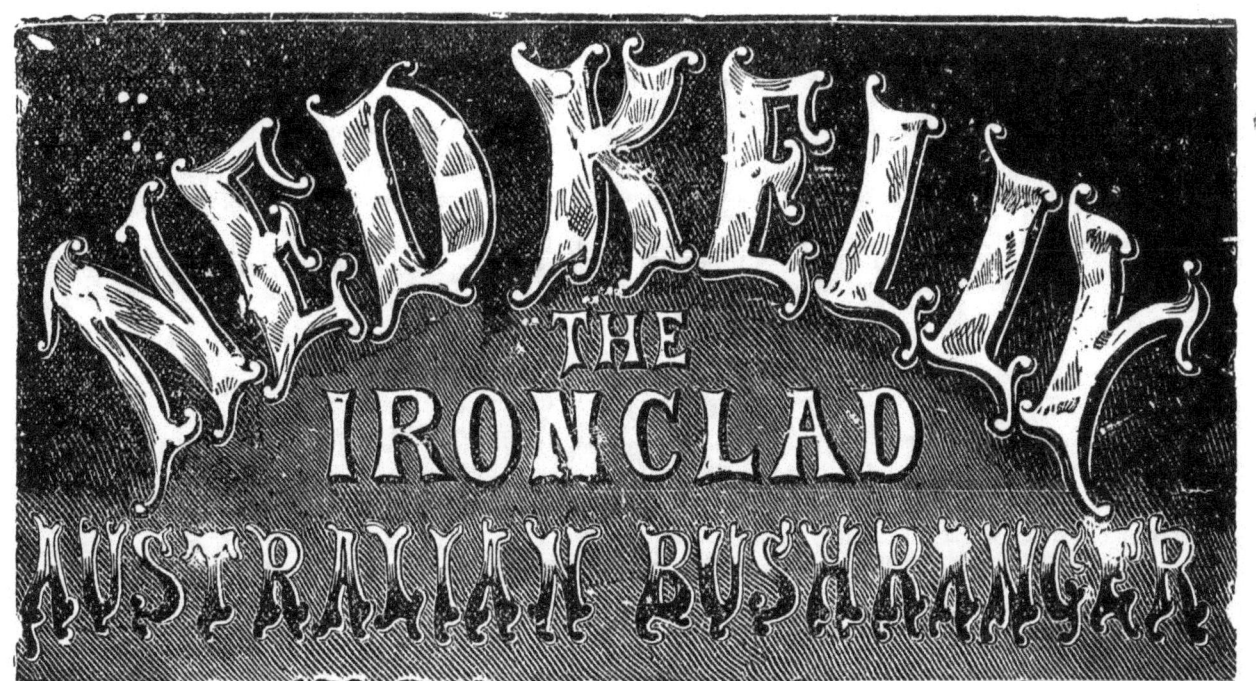

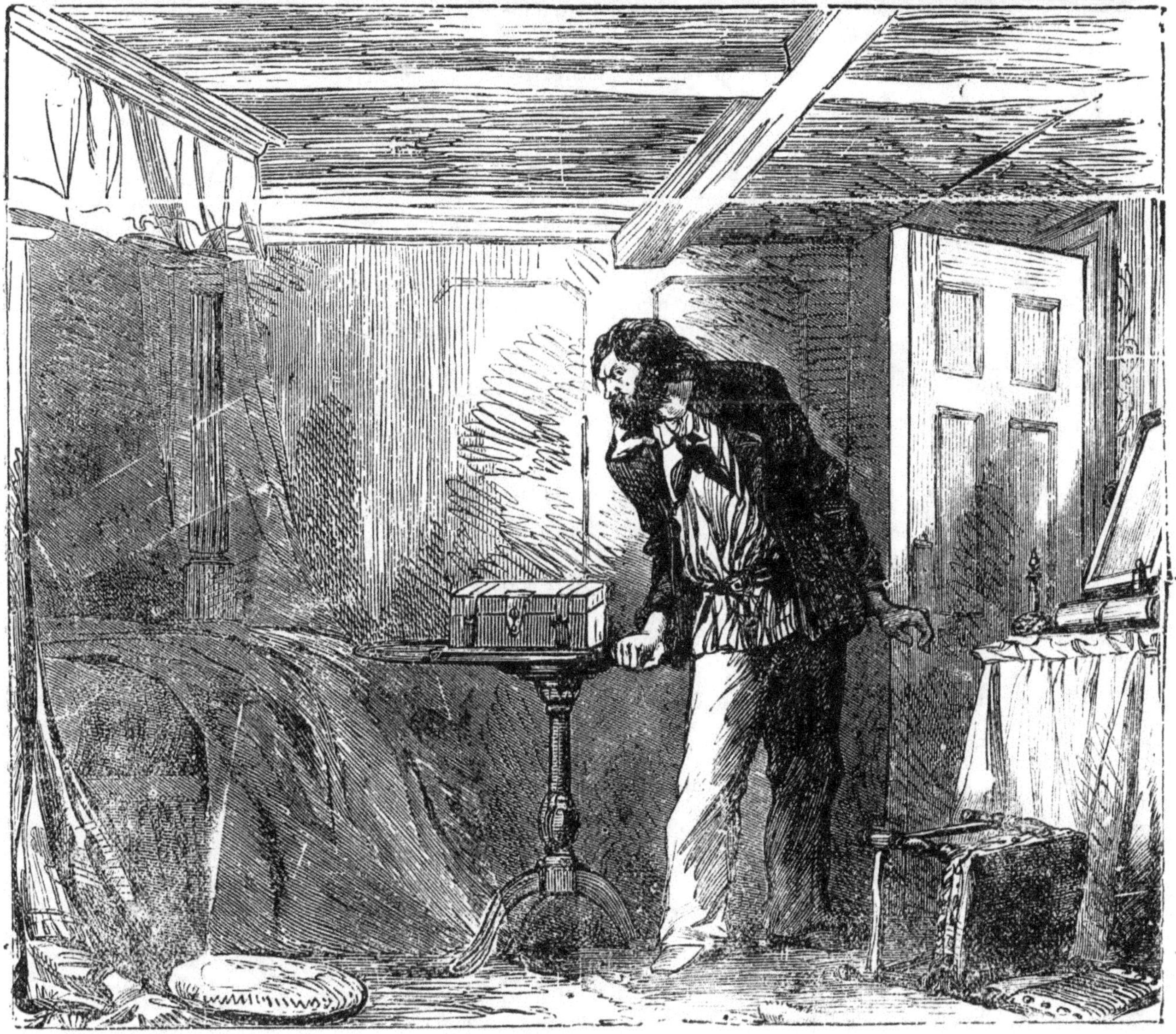

At times the half-worn, half-visible trail became utterly lost in the bare black out-cup of the ridge, but the sagacious mules they had hired soon found it again.

When they had ridden a mile along the ridge they began to descend. Vegetation now sparingly burdened the trail, clumps of *chemisal*, an occasional Manzanila bush, and one or two dwarf buckeyes, rooted their way between the interstices of the black-grey rock.

Now and then crossing some dry gully, worn by the overflow of winter torrents from above, the greyish-rock gloom was relieved by dark red and brown masses of colour, and almost every overhanging rock bore the mark of a miner's pick.

The fog had already closed in on Minbrey, and it was now rolling a white, billow sea above, that soon shut off the blue breakers below.

It was high noon at Minbrey. The pines which abound, in the dusty road and hot air, seemed to smoke from their balsamic spires.

There was a glare from the road, a glare from the sky, a glare from the rocks, a glare from the white canvas roofs of the few shanties and cabins which make up the village.

No Britisher can form an idea of the crushing heat of these latitudes. It is as if one were living in a cauldron out of which the water has evaporated, but the heating-fire still kept burning. The heat positively strikes you from on high and from below and from all around. Only lizards and snakes can live in it. Sometimes the very birds fall exhausted from the trees, and the fruit (as in parts of Australia) are parched and half burnt up while on the trees.

There was even a glare from the unpainted red wood of Jones's grocery and tavern, and a tendency on the warping floor of the verandah to curl up beneath the feet of the intruder.

A few mules near the watering trough had shrunk within the scant shadow of the corral.

The grocery business of Mr. Jones, though adequate and sufficient for the village, was not exhausting or over-taxing to the proprietor.

The refilling of the pork and flour barrel of the average miner was the work of a half-hour on Saturday nights, but the daily replenishment of the average miner with whisky was arduous and incessant.

Jones spent more time behind his bar than behind his grocer's counter.

The hotel was chiefly under the surveillance of his wife, Mrs. Jones, strong, truculent, and good-hearted.

Mr. Jones had early adopted the theory that most of his customers were insane, and were to be alternately bullied or placated, as the case might be.

Nothing that occurred, no extravagance of speech, or act ever ruffled his equilibrium, which was as dogged and stubborn as it was outwardly calm.

When not serving liquor, and in the interval while it was being drunk, he was always wiping his counter with an exceedingly dirty towel, or indeed anything that came handy.

Miners noticing this perfunctory habit occasionally supplied him slyly with articles inconsistent with their service, fragments of their shirts and under-clothing, flour-sacking, tow, and once with a flannel petticoat of his wife's, stolen from the line in the back yard.

This was the place at which the four men put up preparatory to commencing operations.

They had no very clear idea of what they would do, but they had vague ideas of plunder and robbery.

The miners were scattered in all directions, but every now and then a small party was made up to return to Sacramento or San Francisco, and it would be easy to join one of these parties.

Of course they made a pretence at working, or at all events of prospecting, so that they found out who were the lucky diggers and miners

At night they returned to Jones's restaurant and amused themselves after their usual fashion, gambling and drinking.

They lived an easy, idle, but purposeless life, waiting for prey, or rather hunting for it.

Kelly was somewhat anxious to remain abroad for some time, to allow his doings elsewhere to be, if possible, forgotten.

The whole clan were often on the ramble.

It happened that in one of these excursions they came upon a wild and desolate valley, very small, with a few trees.

As they had rounded the curving flank of a mountain, from the rocky beach below them a thin ghost-like stream of smoke seemed to be steadily drawn by invisible hands into the thin ether.

Towards this, being tired, they made, with the hope of getting a hearty meal.

As they neared the camp and stood behind some thick bushes they heard voices.

"It's almost time we got out of this here country, my lads," said one. "We've made a good haul, enough for all four, and the sooner we get away the better."

"I think so, too," said another; "we've been careful—we've got good stout horses and mules, and I say make tracks while we're safe."

"Should our luck be even suspected, it would go hard with us," responded another.

And the subject dropped as Kelly and his party made a motion and coughed.

"Come in. What's up?" asked one of the men, a fine stalwart-looking Englishman.

"We're out prospecting," said Kelly, "and are a little tired, so we thought as perhaps you'd give us a rest and a bit of grub."

Everywhere in the wilds hospitality was general, and the miners asked their less fortunate neighbours to come in.

There was a meal of *tortillias*, *frijoles* (beans), salt pork, and chocolate, and a fresh supply was speedily obtained for them.

Then they being at no great distance from the diggings, thanked their entertainers and went away.

The miners were four in number, like themselves, and stout fellows.

They had four horses, and a small waggon with a couple of mules; this contained their traps and doubtless their gold.

The villains exchanged glances as they moved away.

Doubtless these men would make a good fight but if they could only surprise them and carry off the plunder, it would be doubly useful.

They could secure the waggon.

Kelly proposed that they should follow them at a distance, keeping clear out of sight, and waiting until an opportunity occurred for a sudden rush upon their victims.

So they spent the night at the restaurant as usual, rising early in the morning to watch what might happen.

The head of the party of four men who had made such a successful haul was a young man of great energy.

He and his party, all English, worked steadily for two years, and had all along been tolerably successful.

His name was William Maxwell.

He and his companions had been sober and steady, and had forwarded large sums to England to their account.

They now felt an irresistible inclination to return to England themselves.

At first they had been, like many others, unlucky, and had given up claim after claim in succession.

On one occasion they found themselves, when at the Digger goldfields, after several vicissitudes of fortune, what they call out there "dead broke."

Their credit was very nearly exhausted at the neighbouring store, and they were almost in want of bread.

"Let us have another try," cried William Maxwell; "never give in, is my motter."

And, advised by him, in their desperation they began digging for gold in a very unpromising locality.

It seemed a very hopeless task, but they worked on steadily, standing close to one another.

Maxwell plied his pick on some hard brick like clay, around the roots of an old tree breaking up fresh earth, and tearing away the grass from the surface of the ground.

He aimed a blow at the clear space between the roots, and the pick instead of sinking into the ground rebounded as if it had struck upon quartz or granite.

"Confound it!" he exclaimed, "I've nearly broken my pick. I shouldn't have minded if it had only been a nugget."

A minute later he called to his companions and asked them to tell him what this was, pointing to a mass of gold cropping several inches out of the ground, like a boulder on a hill.

As each successive portion of the nugget was disclosed to view, the men were lost in amazement at its size.

It was about a foot long, and apparently nearly the same in breadth.

Its weight was very great, but they carried it to their hut and proceeded to examine it. It was completely covered with black earth and so tarnished in colour that an inexperienced person might have supposed it to be merely a mass of auriferous earth.

But the weight dispelled all doubt on that point, for it was more than twice as heavy as a piece of iron of the same size.

A fire having been made the nugget was placed on it, and for hours they sat watching it burning the quartz which adhered to the nugget.

The gold was weighed next day, when quite clean, and turned the scale at a heavy figure, no less than two hundred cwt. It was worth ten thousand pounds.

From that hour the four young men stuck together with almost uniform success.

"I don't like the look of those roughs," said William Maxwell, when the others had taken their departure. "I've a strong notion that they were skulking around a good while before they spoke to us."

"Well, we're good enough for them," replied his chum Peterson; "still, if the chief did come too near me, I'd be apt to use my six-shooter."

Meanwhile Kelly and his party had returned to the restaurant, as we have said, where they spent their evening as usual.

It was almost time they left, as men who go on prospecting about and do not work, and yet have an ample supply of money, usually excite suspicion at the diggings.

But though they were continually watched and even sounded by the police and others, there was nothing against them.

By what stretch of imagination could anyone have conceived anything like the truth?

Still Kelly judged that the wiser part of valour was discretion, and next day, mounting horse, started on the lower journey. About midday they reached a two-storey hut on a small knoll near a sickly river.

It was not a very eligible place, swearing, drinking, and card-playing being the ordinary programme, with a free fight thrown in occasionally.

It was a halting place for teamsters, and the amount of dirt and vermin was simply utterly unconceivable.

The *morale* of the old and new comers was about on a par, so after receiving a hearty welcome and the necessary supplies for their commissariat they started off again.

They had been very minute in their enquiries as to the road, and obtained every information, though that was not very necessary. The marks were very clear and distinct.

Towards evening they tethered their horses and camped in a wood of moderate sized trees and safe bushes.

They made no fire and kept off the regular track, where there was a grove of trees evidently often used for a camping ground.

Kelly was only too glad to be satisfied with cold meat when his avarice was concerned.

They were simply banditti on the look-out for victims. Miners were of course the game they wanted to bag.

All took their turn at watching, but that night their patience was not rewarded, and they had at considerable inconvenience to pass all the next day in the place.

Joss, however, went out prowling, and got some provender from the many rude shanties on the road, and thus the day passed.

Just before evening came on the four young men came in sight.

Their little waggon was driven by a negro, while there were several other men in their company. They were bitterly disappointed.

Kelly, with a loud oath, declared that nothing could be done that night and that it would be wise to retire to a greater distance from their intended victims.

CHAPTER C

EXCHANGE NO ROBBERY.

THE bushrangers had taken up a concealed position where they could observe the others without being seen.

It was useless keeping watch that night, as the travellers were of course too numerous for them to manage.

Kelly was not in the best of humours, but he solaced himself with whisky and tobacco, after which he slept.

At early morn he was up, and saw the small caravan proceeding on its way.

He followed at a safe distance, beginning to be rather fearful that they would escape him after all.

If they kept together with the others—and this indeed would be very probable—they would escape, and Kelly's worst ferocity and avarice were both aroused.

He swore at himself heavily for not bringing up more of the gang from San Francisco.

But it was too late to repine. Nothing whatever could be done but trust to the chapter of accidents.

It was absolutely necessary to keep at a considerable distance as the roads were hilly and the air so airified that people could be distinguished a very long way off.

A halt was made by the caravan of the travellers at a refreshment house, and then again they went on, preferring like most people to camp in the open at night.

The spot selected by the English on this occasion, was a small plain shaded by some tall trees, and beneath them they made a fire.

Their casual companions had left them in the course of the day, and there remained only the four men and the negro driver.

Kelly determined under these circumstances to make his way at once.

He first placed the horses at a safe distance from the camp where they could find them when the affair was over.

He had no compunction whatever. Rather than miss the plunder he expected, he was quite determined to kill the lot.

There was no hesitation in his soul.

As soon as the horses were safe he and his gang crept forward with snake-like caution.

It was a very fine night, but rather dark, and the villains were able to approach pretty near to their intended victims.

The small waggon was placed near the fire, the horses were hobbled securely.

Round the fire sat the four men smoking and talking, and occasionally sipping the favourite beverage of the wilds.

The negro was nowhere to be seen. He was probably eating his supper under one of the trees alone in deference to the white men's prejudices.

On crept the murderous villains, their bowie knives and pistols ready for action, their eyes glaring with greedy expectation.

Each man as he advanced picked out his victim.

At this moment there was a great and sudden cry.

"Oh golly, massa," roared the negro, "hoss tief—um shoot—golly——"

The negro at the same time fired into their midst, and the four stalwart fellows leaped to their feet with their short rifles in their hands.

"Scoundrels, come on," roared William Maxwell, "we are ready for you—black, red, or white."

Kelly had selected his retreat with judgment. It was down a narrow gully, that turned short to the right.

Several shots were fired but they were of no avail, as the bushrangers were far too wary to be caught napping.

But Kelly's ferocious rage was something fearful and wonderful to hear when they were out of reach of the foe.

Even his fierce and reckless companions were awed into silence.

He was more like a wild beast than anything else. He raved and swore.

But the first thing they had to do was to think of their precious safety.

Kelly had concealed the horses cleverly and had soon regained the spot and started off in the direction of the hilly country, where there were hundreds of places to conceal themselves for a time.

To have attempted another open attack on these four young men and their watchful negro, would have been simply utter folly and madness.

But Ned Kelly was not without hope, that by some means or other, he would still be able to compass the possession of the successful gold digger's "pile."

As soon as they were out of reach of pursuit, they determined to put their horses to the push, and reach some out-of-the-way ranche where they could pass the night.

They are to be found in abundance on the route, and though the accommodation they offer is rough, it is always welcome.

As soon as one was discovered, the bushrangers easily selected a room in which to pass the night. It was crowded and dirty, but it was a roof over their heads.

They were, however, careful to start off early in the morning. They wished to reach Sacramento city before the others.

There was no knowing what might happen, if they could disguise themselves and make another attempt on the gold.

They reached the city, swapped their horses, resumed their respectable clothes and went to an hotel.

There was no boat ready to go that day. A great many passengers were expected from the diggings, and it was the custom of the boat to wait for them until the latest moment.

Kelly did not much relish the idea of travelling to San Francisco with the four stalwart young Englishmen.

He trusted, however, to his disguise, his impudence, and his unvarying good luck, in case he should go down in the same boat as those he had sought to rob.

As it happened, the miners did come on board the same vessel as themselves, but the boat was crowded, and while Kelly knew William Maxwell and his party, the case was different with the others.

The cabin, saloons and decks were crowded, and the usual amusements we have already alluded to were indulged in.

Kelly and his party were careful to keep as far apart from that of William Maxwell as possible. The latter had evidently a keen and far-seeing eye.

But there was another individual on board, on whom Kelly kept a very strict watch, and that was Sambo Jones the servant to the four Englishmen.

He was a shrewd, clever nigger, and one of those men who never throw a chance away.

Still it was very unlikely that during that hurried scrimmage in the wild country, the black fellow could have re-

cognised any one of those who had attacked them in such a stealthy way.

But Kelly determined to be on the safe side, and do nothing to excite any suspicions.

He preferred to examine carefully the small and inconvenient state room and cabin in which the four Englishmen passed the night.

There probably would be the box which contained their treasure.

But how was it to be got at, was the question the hitherto baffled ruffian asked himself.

Of course it was locked all day, and at night guarded by four pair of stalwart arms, besides the Argus-eyed negro.

It did not seem likely that they could do anything under these adverse circumstances.

They must give it all up until they got to San Francisco, when an infernal idea came into Kelly's head.

He would wait and have patience.

To carry out his new scheme he must try and scrape some sort of acquaintance with William Maxwell and his three companions, and then go to the same hotel.

In those days of the gold fever, classes were very much mixed, and few people asked who was who as long as they behaved themselves.

William Maxwell and his party were not hardened or professed gamblers, but they had no objection to join in a game of cards.

He therefore at night entered the saloon where most persons present indulged in fluttering the flimsy pasteboard.

Whist was not much of a game in these places. They preferred games of chance to those of nerve, skill and cunning.

But an old-fashioned rubber was to be had for the asking, if anyone really wished it.

Poker, euchre, and such like games were, however, the favourites, with brag and even sometimes solitaire.

The four friends generally played with their own set, but sometimes joined a more general table.

At this Kelly contrived on one occasion to be seated next to William Maxwell.

"You play a good game, sir," observed Kelly, in as soft a tone as he could possibly assume.

"Pretty fair," answered Maxwell, looking at a rough customer who was playing beside him, "but it does not require much art. It's purely luck, and nothing else."

"Perhaps so," continued Kelly, "most things goes pretty well by luck, but I've done pretty well. I didn't have much, and now I have a fair pile."

"Some are fortunate, others are not," was the dry remark of William Maxwell, who did not like the style of the speaker.

But Kelly was careful not to be offensive; he thought he knew his man. A little respectful familiarity would not be resented, but too much would be.

So the game went on and Kelly was content to win and say no more.

But he watched Maxwell and his friends with the keen eye of a hawk.

There seemed to be no suspicion lurking in his eye, though Kelly every now and then thought the other looked at him keenly.

But still there was at all events no suspicion shown, and Ned Kelly determined to go on to San Francisco and try his grand coup there.

He meant to have that treasure if it were in any way possible.

It was enclosed in a square box tied round with ropes, and sealed with large seals.

Now Kelly's idea was to have one made exactly like it, but full of rubbish, heavily weighted, which he would on some pretence introduce into the hotel, and then by a bold and dashing stroke seek to change them.

It took Ned Kelly a good many hours to figure out this scheme, but he thought it a good one, and determined to carry it out.

He spoke of it to Zeph and that worthy agreed to join in it with all his heart and soul.

He believed it to be a very probable thing to be done.

"At all events it was worth trying," he said.

"As well be hung for a sheep as a lamb," growled Zeph.

"Perhaps better," grinned Kelly.

Never say die was the reckless motto of these desperate men.

Next evening they would reach San Francisco, and commence operations.

Kelly kept up the habit of occasionally playing cards with William Maxwell, but never tried for too much intimacy.

He was rather humble than otherwise, and William Maxwell began to think he had very much misjudged his character.

He was simply an honest, rough customer after all, with no particular harm in him, he thought.

"Where have I seen him before, though?" observed one of Maxwell's friends. "His confounded face seems familiar to me, somehow."

"I thought so at first, myself," remarked William Maxwell, "but I can't place it. These rough sort of fellows are often very much alike."

"I suppose so," answered the other, rather thoughtfully, and the conversation dropped for the time.

When the steamer stopped at the quay or wharf, Kelly was careful to hear for what hotel Maxwell and his friends were destined.

It was the President Jackson, and Kelly immediately ordered his luggage to be taken to the same rather aristocratic locality.

It was somewhat of a dear place, but the bushrangers had still plenty of command of money without showing gold dust.

Kelly always carried a considerable number of notes about him in the belt with his gold.

Of course, in those days all were welcome, so that they had plenty of coin.

That was about the only question thought of.

Money was what made the mare to go then, as at most periods of the world's history.

All were able to secure rooms, as a good many people had recently started for Europe.

It was before the overland route had been invented.

There was of course a table d'hôte, and this they all sat down to as soon as they were comfortable and settled.

Kelly and his companions were no fools. They were careful to examine other people and do as they did. Thus their solecisms were not very great

Still no one could mistake them for anything approaching to gentlemen.

They were looked upon as lucky nouveaux riches.

After dinner they dispersed to the billiard-room and smoking-rooms, to divert themselves as best they might.

Kelly and Zeph, however, went out to look about them, and their first visit was to a cabinet-makers.

They wanted to know about the gold boxes.

To Kelly's surprise he found that except in difference of size the gold boxes were all made of about the same material.

They could, therefore, easily have a box made the same size exactly as that of the Englishman.

Then it could be sent him, strapped and sealed, with heavy weights of lead inside.

The only difficulty, and it was no easy one, was to ring the changes.

It was no easy task, but Kelly fully believed that he could succeed.

The vessel for England would not start for several days, so that they had time to arrange everything.

During the hurry and bustle of the day, a box wrapped round with black glazed cloth was easily introduced into the hotel. Nobody noticed it but one of the darkey waiters, and it was taken to Kelly's room.

There they proceeded to fix it up to look exactly like that of the successful gold-diggers.

Now remained the opportunity of making the exchange which was not easy.

In times like those, everybody was particularly careful of his own belongings.

Every bed-room had two keys, one carried by the occupier, the other kept by the owner of the house, and only trusted to the servants for a short period of the day.

It was rather hard work to get one of these keys out of the custody of the faithful domestics.

To try that would have been folly; there remained nothing for it but to try the efficacy of Joss's keys.

He never travelled without them, and they had often stood him in good stead.

Well, he would try if he could be as successful here as elsewhere.

Of course it could not be done at night, as then the owners would be in their rooms.

How was it to be managed.

The suit of apartments occupied by the four young Englishmen was next to that occupied by the bushranger.

Now, between them they had managed to make their own box look so exactly like the other, that once in different rooms, it would have been almost impossible to see the difference.

One or the other could have been openly conveyed on a truck to the vessel without exciting the slightest suspicion.

After lunch most of the gentlemen, as everyone is called in the gold regions, adjourned to the billiard-rooms or elsewhere.

Joss and Zeph retired together to the garden attached to the hotel, to quietly mature their plans. After having done so they went to their own rooms, and entering, closed the doors carefully behind them.

Now came the difficulty, the arduous tug of war. They once or twice opened their door a little, and listened for every sound in the hotel.

Presently all seemed perfectly calm and quiet. Not a soul appeared about.

Zeph lighted up a big cigar and approached a window overlooking the port.

Then, tools in hand, he came out and began to apply himself to the door.

In ordinary cases the thing would have been easy, but in a large hotel they were so liable to interruptions.

"Golly!" suddenly cried a well-known voice, "What am de genl'm'n up to!"

Zeph and his pal looked thoroughly scared as they heard the voice of the nigger. They looked round for the black, but saw nothing. They heard the chuckle—the yah, yah, yah! of their black detective, but the sound appeared to come out of the floor. They could see nothing, but understood at once that the game was up, and that in five minutes the attempt to enter the Englishman's room would be divulged.

They hurried downstairs to the billiard-room, where Kelly and Salmon Roe were awaiting them.

At one sign from Captain Zeph they understood, threw down their cues and went out.

Their luggage was the least part of their valuables, and not one stopped to take anything but his hat and coat.

They were only too glad to be off before the negro succeeded in giving the alarm.

Instinctively this class of men know how to leave such quarters.

On leaving the hotel they dived into a district where from third to fifth-rate inns were to be found in abundance.

After plunging down some lanes and alleys they found not only what they wanted, but some boxes and clothes suited to their wishes.

Humility was now their game, and it behoved them to be as little ostentatious as possible.

Having procured what they required, they soon found

lodgings at a quiet hotel where, of course, they told what story they liked, and then, by their profuse expenditures of money, satisfied all parties.

In rude and vulgar places mon   of course, the only consideration.

At the Blue Nugget this was thoroughly the case. Gold was the landlord's idol.

Of course the whole party were well aware that the attempt to rob the Englishmen would put the police on their track.

It behoved them, therefore, to be very careful, and do nothing to attract especial attention to their movements.

With this view the four men secured a private room to themselves where they could eat, drink, and smoke without fear of interruption.

The landlord was a quiet man of unassuming manners, particularly regardful of the comfort of his customers when they paid liberally.

He found Kelly and his party to his taste, as they often asked him up to sup and join them in their whisky guzzling, old sludge, and other amusements.

On the second evening of their arrival a man—a meek apparently well-meaning sort of fellow—came up and closed the door.

They stared at him.

"Now, mates," he said in a low tone, "fair is fair you know. I'm English like yourselves, and I like to serve a countryman."

"Well," asked Kelly rather uneasily, "and what is the matter now?"

"Have you any reason—I only ask from curiosity," he went on "to think you are being asked for—wanted, you know?"

"What makes you ask such a question?" replied Kelly, while the others crowded round.

"Well, you see, Mr. Jacob Pegrem, a officer of the city police, has been peering around," continued Smith, "and he's been asking questions. Luckily I was there, and when he axed about you, I just didn't know."

"Did he particularly mention us?" asked Kelly.

"He asked if I'd seed anything of four chaps as had been staying at the hotel," continued Smith. "Now as you've been fair and square with me, I thought I'd up and tell you."

"We four gents certainly wish to be private just now, to keep dark just a bit," said Kelly; "so if you can help us, we don't mind doing the liberal."

"Well, I've got," in a whisper, "a little place of mine, where chaps can be in private just as long as it suits, and if you like I'll take you there."

They agreed to shift their quarters for a day or so, and, terms being agreed to, about an hour later they were going out at a back entrance to the inn, carrying their own boxes, as if going to join their ship.

Smith guided them with apparently a perfect knowledge of the ins and outs of the town, already very large and straggling.

He brought them at last to a region tenanted by sailors, boarding-houses, Chinese huts—a mixture of all sorts.

Among these he stopped at a small two-storied house, which he entered as if he were its master.

A woman sat on a stool in the front room, which was not very clean or well furnished, but that mattered not to these outcasts of civilisation.

"Brought you some lodgers, Bridget," said the man; "want to be quiet, you know."

"Quiet enough for me," the woman answered, "so as they pays and don't fight."

"All right, old gal; we're your sort. Everyone knows we're just lambs," laughed Kelly.

The man took them up a narrow staircase to two rooms, which would just accommodate them on a pinch.

"I'll bring you bub and grub," said the man, "and let you know the news. Jacob Pegrem won't look for you here."

"All square, my friend," said Kelly meaningly.

"I never peaches on friends," was the dry reply. "Send round all you want presently."

And he went away, leaving the men whatever they might say, anything but easy in their minds.

The police of San Francisco were particularly sharp.

Besides, vigilance committees were very active, and crime was not allowed to go very long unpunished.

Still, in such a seething mass of beings, all intent on money-making, all influenced by the demon of avarice, many crimes did remain undiscovered, the perpetrators getting off with impunity.

In their case there really had been nothing perpetrated, and they had every hope that the matter would blow over with the departure of the four travellers for England.

All they had to do then was to eat, drink and be merry, and bide their time.

Smith kept them well provided with everything needed, not forgetting to charge accordingly.

The names of the four Englishmen were known to Kelly, and with cautious inquiry Smith found that they had taken passage in a vessel, and were about to start immediately for England.

They had, therefore, nothing to fear from them, though still the police might prove officious and dangerous.

So they were careful.

Through Smith he made inquiries about the yacht, and found that she was all right, though many of her men had got tired and deserted.

This was a bad look-out.

CHAPTER CI.

JOSS MEETS A NEAR RELATIVE.

FOR several days they accordingly remained in the small out-of-the-way hiding-place where they had concealed themselves.

They were all afraid of William Maxwell while he remained in town; he was moving heaven and earth to bring them to justice.

But his time was up.

Kelly was anxious to see after his craft. It would have to be provisioned before they started on another journey.

The men had been advised to frequent as quiet drinking shops as they could, but of course it would be too much to expect they would keep away from drink altogether.

On the third day they determined to go down to the Red Plain Hotel, where many of the sailors congregate, and there look up some of their men.

As soon as they could get on board Kelly was determined to take his leave of California.

It had not proved a very paying game. They had rather spent money than earned money.

Still, stowed away, Kelly and his immediate companions had a good supply of money.

Kelly knew that, if he could not collect his own crew, it would be difficult to get hands at such a time, when everyone was suffering from the strange disease called "gold fever," but he must try at all events, and do the best he could.

The bushranger was fond, to a certain extent, of being on the sea, for there he felt himself the monarch of all he surveyed.

He was the king of his ship, and no one dared there to gainsay his authority.

He was the scourge of the land and also the scourge of the ocean, and many people had no doubt obtained the credit of committing crimes for which he was wholly responsible.

This man, whose evil actions had cast a disastrous lustre on his name, had often chuckled on hearing that some innocent person had suffered for his sin, being the victim of circumstantial evidence, and his lips had often curled when he read that they had to be carried to the scaffold more dead than alive.

He might be called everything that was bad, he told himself, but nobody could accuse him of being a coward

always makes the road easy for his follow-
ght, with a grim smile.

...ess cold ruffian, a little peril, a little diffi-
...arding off suspicion, might have inspired salu-
...c, but Kelly went on recklessly, undaunted by any
...cle.

Never once did he cast back a look of regret on his past
life. He was equally indifferent to the future, and only
lived for the present hour.

Kelly had never known fear; but, as he grew older, he
grew fiercer and more bloodthirsty, and many brave men
had been known to stand in awe of him—men who have
fought with wild beasts and savages, and charged uphill
to the cannon's mouth. True he was not wholly dead to
some feelings or rather family instincts, for a good deal of
his determination to visit California, and subsequently New
York, was his desire to hear something of a brother, who
had been acquiring some notoriety as half-smuggler and
whole pirate. His name was Christopher, abbreviated by
his friends to "Kit," and as "Kit, the Cruiser," we may
yet hear more of him.

He subsequently took the most active part in the "resurrection" of Stewart's body from the grave, in expectation of extracting a heavy reward from the very wealthy
family as the price of its restitution. The enormous wealth
of the family fostered this expectation.

Whether "Ned" fell in with his brother's plots, the
sequel will show.

Men declared that they could face anything but that
fiend in human shape, and the words were repeated in
Kelly's hearing, much to his openly-expressed delight.

He knew that there were some people who regarded him
as a hero in consequence of such rumours, and was tempted
into blacker guilt in order to obtain a more world-wide
notoriety.

The poet has said, "Virtues are dead to no man; that
even in the assassin's heart there can be found some pity—
some soft spot."

But, as the reader knows, the bushranger had no redeeming point in his soul like that.

It is a curious study to contemplate this man's life, and
reflect what he might have been had he not been born of
convicts, and nurtured in crime.

With the exception of the mild exhortations of a sleepy,
weak-minded parson, he was accustomed to hear nothing
but blasphemy and beastiality. His mind and morals were
warped by the force of his associations.

Such men as he always pretend to believe in fate; an
easy way to dispose of the matter, and a good excuse for
any career of crime.

Kelly was a restless nature, and never remained long in
one spot, although this was, perhaps, not always his own
fault, for, as a rule, the places he visited speedily became
too hot to hold him.

He had determined, in order to procure the requisite
men to man his ship, that he would offer double wages
and a double allowance of grog.

Even then it was doubtful whether this temptation
would have any effect, but at all events it would do no
harm to try, even if he did not succeed.

"We must take care that we do not ship aboard a lot
of muffs," said Salmon Roe, as they entered a low drinking shop to while away the time until it was time to go to
the Red Plain Hotel, "who won't be any use to us. We
want chaps like ourselves, that don't care a tinker's curse
for anything, and wouldn't be squeamish about a drop o'
blood."

"Trust me," cried Kelly. "I know the sort of customers to pick out; but if we should happen to get
hold of a rotten Jack Tar, who might round on us,
why all we have got to do is to chuck him overboard to
be eaten by sharks, if any of those cursed ugly fish happen
to be about."

"That's your sort," cried Captain Zeph. "Send the lot
to blazes if they ain't the right lot; don't make no bones
about it, but chuck them overboard, bag and baggage."

"I'd give 'em four dozen on their bare hides with the
cat-o'-nine-tails, just to give them time to think over their
latter end," observed Joss, who was in rather a sulky
humour, having been considerably brow-beaten by Kelly
of late."

"Since you have put it into my nut," cried Kelly, with
a grin. "You shall be tied up to the grating first, just
to show the others a good example. It would be a treat
to hear you howl, old man."

This remark, although probably intended for a mere
jest, did not appear to meet with Joss's approval in any way.

"Perhaps I shan't sail with you," muttered Joss to
himself, as he looked askance at Kelly with a rather vicious
expression in his bloodshot eyes. "You ain't a-going to
ride roughshod over me, mate, so I tell yer."

This was a mistake on Joss's part, as he had never told
Kelly anything of the kind, and was very careful not to
let him overhear what he said to others.

"What are you a-growling and a-muttering about?"
demanded Kelly, seeing the man's lips move. "If you
have got any complaint to make, spit it out."

"I should like to smash you up," thought the person
addressed, but he said aloud—"Whose a-complaining,
who is a-growling and a-grumbling, I should like to know?
You seem to have made a dead set agin me, and I can't
please you nohow. Directly I open my mouth you jump
down my throat."

"You are a peg too low," said Kelly, sneeringly. "Go
and drink, man, go and drink."

"I'll drink starvation to you," muttered Joss, with another furtive glance at Kelly's dark face.

The bushranger was making a mistake in his treatment
of Joss, who grew more sullen every moment, brooding
over his real or imaginary wrongs.

Even when Kelly stood treats all round, the man's face
did not clear, and he contrived to spill his liquor instead
of drinking it, ordering another glass at his own expense
in which he mentally drank "hell and confusion" to his
enemy.

Kelly was not blind to this little bit of by-play.

He wheeled round suddenly, and fixed his glittering and
bloodshot eyes upon Joss's face.

"Why did you throw away my drink?" he asked. "I
like to know the meaning of that 'ere trick."

Joss made no answer, but took another sip out of his
own glass and looked sullenly down at the ground.

"Do you hear?" howled Kelly, going up close to him
with a threatening gesture.

"A deaf man 'ud hear you through the roar of Niagara
Falls,"—of which he had heard enough in America—returned
Joss, trying to look at his ease, but the onlookers noticed
that he was unusually pale, and trembled so violently that
he could hardly hold the glass.

"Why do you throw good liquor on the sawdust?" cried
Kelly, in a louder key. "You'd best answer up if you
don't want to rouse the devil in me. Curse you! Why
can't you open your mouth, you confounded fool? Did
you do it to insult me, I say?"

"No."

"Then what was your object? I say again, what was
your object, you whisky-loaded idiot?"

And Kelly stamped his foot, clenching his huge brawny
fist.

"The glass was dirty."

"That is a lie. Did you think I put poison in the glass?
Do you think I'm such a d———n coward as to want to
destroy you in that mean way? Why, I could crush you
like an insect, and have a good mind to."

"Very likely you could," was Joss's answer; "but I
ain't afraid of you, Kelly," he added, looking very
white indeed and trembling from head to foot, "but
I should like to be friends just for the sake of all we have
gone through together. Give us your hand, old pal, let's
have a feel of that good old paw what never was raised
agin a friend. Give me another drink and I'll toss it down
in two twos. Just give me another chance, that's all."

"You'll drink with me this time," said Kelly.

"Only too happy," returned Joss, cheerfully. "There wouldn't have been no row if that infernal landlord hadn't given a dirty glass. Why don't you give him a piece of your mind? It 'ud do him good, and make him look alive another time."

Kelly made no reply to this, but said something in an undertone to Salmon Roe, who grinned all over his face, and disappeared for a few moments, while Kelly contrived to keep Joss in close conversation.

"Ah! here's your liquor," he said, suddenly looking round. "Toss it off, man; drink it to the dregs, just to show you've no malice."

Joss hastened to comply with this request, but the expression of his face changed after he had taken a good gulp.

"Ugh!" he yelled, dashing the glass against the wall, and shivering it into a thousand fragments.

This done, he commenced to dance about like a bedlamite, blaspheming horribly as he did so, much to the amusement of the few spectators present, who roared with laughter, shouting and jeering at the unlucky victim of Kelly's practical joke.

"Show me the man as tampered with that there liquor!" cried Joss. "Only let me see him, that's all; he won't have a minute to live. He had better say his prayers, for I mean to lay him out. Who did it, I want to know?"

"I did," said the bushranger, calmly, standing before him with folded arms. "Why don't you carry out your threat, mate, eh?"

"Oh, it was you, was it?" said the crestfallen Joss, mildly. "What a fellow you are to be sure. It is a good job it was you, and not somebody else. I allows my friends to take liberties with me, but don't stand no nonsense from nobody else. Landlord, let's have another drop to take the taste of the persecution out of my mouth. The stuff did taste uncommon nasty, but I ain't a man to bear malice; there ain't a bit of ill-feeling or ill-will in me, only, another time when you wants to play off any of your larks, Kelly, just give some other cove a chance; turn and turn about. I don't see why I should be let in for everything, it ain't fair. I feel racked with pain, and for all the world as if my blessed inside was being stirred up with a copper stick."

"You look uncommon green about the gills," said Kelly, consolingly. "But don't go and sit down on that bench, we have got to be moving; so come on all of you."

Joss rose with a dismal groan, and followed his companions out of the place.

"I shan't forget that little joke as long as I live," he muttered, shaking his fist at Kelly's broad back.

He kept behind the others with his hands deep down in his trousers' pocket, and occasionally a deep groan would escape his lips, and on all such occasions Kelly turned round to smile at his discomfiture.

Rendered desperate by pain, Joss at last flung himself down on the ground.

Even a mild dose of antimony, which Zeph had procured at a small chemist's next door, not enough to kill, causes intense suffering, and any man but Kelly might have hesitated ere he inflicted such torture on a comrade.

But Kelly, who made every human duty, tie or belief, a theme for ridicule, was not to be debarred from carrying out anything that suited his fancy, even at the expense of his friend.

Joss howled and writhed on the ground, and his fantastic contortions sent Kelly and his companions, who were half-seas over, into paroxysms of mirth.

"I'm a'most dead," whined Joss.

"I'll 'dead' you if you don't get up at once," cried Kelly, who began to feel tired of the entertainment, and wanted an excuse to indulge in his propensity for brutality.

"Get up," said the terror-stricken man. "You've poisoned me, that's what you've done. I shall never rise again. I'm as good as a dead man."

"Lie there and rot then!" retorted Kelly; but the more merciful Salmon Roe kindly kicked the prostrate man up behind with his heavy boot.

"That's it," cried Kelly approvingly; "kick in his lights if he doesn't move his dirty carcase when he's told."

"I never desert a friend in need," observed Salmon, as he again kicked Joss in the small of the back. "Get up, if you don't want the toe of my boot to go through your body."

"I want to be let alone," moaned the suffering Joss; but they lifted him up by the arms and dragged him along in spite of his protestations.

It was the best thing they could have done under the circumstances, and he soon felt the beneficial effect of the exercise.

His gratitude, however, was not very great, for he knew that they had not been actuated by motives of humanity.

He was simply brought along because they did not dare to leave him behind.

By the time they reached the Red Plain Hotel he was almost himself again, and appeared to have completely recovered his good humour.

His only anxiety seemed to be to conciliate Kelly, who did not utterly reject his overtures of friendship.

The bushranger flattered himself that he had brought Joss to his senses, and convinced him that he was the better man of the two.

"I shall be all right after a drop of brandy," Joss declared. "I never had such a turn out in all my life, and wouldn't go through it again for love or money; but its over now. Let bygones be bygones."

"I am quite agreeable," responded Kelly, who was not the injured party, and they shook hands amicably enough to all outward appearance, and the bushranger dismissed the matter from his mind as unworthy of a second thought.

"The lark was a good one," remarked Joss; "but I should have enjoyed it better if you had played it on somebody else."

Kelly made no reply, but entered the Red Plain Hotel, followed by the others.

The place scarcely deserved the name of hotel, but the proprietor found that a big name went down with his customers.

It was crowded to excess, and the company appeared to be of rather a boisterous nature, judging from the sounds which saluted the bushranger's ears.

He looked around at the motley groups, and formed his own estimation of those present, and saw with satisfaction that he could pick out just the men he wanted.

The four friends sat down at a table and ordered drink.

Kelly saw that a good many of his own hands were present, joining in the noisy merriment; and he soon, seeing him there, beckoned Morgan, the boatswain, across to where he was sitting.

He came at once, being one of the few sober men in the room—a man always to be trusted.

"What is it?" he asked in an undertone.

"There are a few likely chaps here," said Kelly, "can't you contrive to get them to join our crew? Make any promise you like, so as you get them to join. I want everything on board early, and all ready for a start."

"Ay, ay!" returned the boatswain.

And then Kelly suggested that he had better return to his mates and secure as many as possible of suitable men.

"Stand drinks all round," he cried; "give them anything they like to call for, at my expense."

"Let them have a little money in advance," suggested Morgan. "It kind of opens their hearts, and makes them feel friendly. But I believe I can find most of our own men."

"Do as you like," returned Kelly; "as long as you get the men together I ain't particular. Don't enlist any men who you think will be likely to stick at a trifle or be soft-hearted."

"I know what I'm about," said Morgan, confidently "leave it all to me."

"All right," answered Kelly.

"I run all the risk," replied Morgan, cheerfully, as he turned to rejoin his friends, who wondered, some of them, what he was up to.

There was not much amusement to be derived from watching the drunken sailors, who were swearing, laughing and talking, playing cards, and enjoying themselves generally in a tipsy fashion; so Kelly and his comrades left the place, after having had two or three drinks.

They were dressed like swells of the vulgar order, and, after strolling about for some time, entered an oyster-shop.

It was rather a showy place, and behind the counter sat a stout woman with a pleasant-looking face, dressed very smartly. She had smiles for everyone.

There were several barmen and Chinese waiters, and they served, while her sole occupation seemed to consist in taking the money. The place was crowded, and she evidently did a roaring trade, taking care to keep a sharp look-out to see that her assistants were not wasting their time.

"Snug and comfortable place this," observed Captain Zeph, as he swallowed his oysters. "I say, Joss, you're in luck's way," he added, "that rather prepossessing female seems to have taken a fancy to you."

"I don't want any of your say," growled Joss; "can't a man eat a dozen of oysters without being bothered."

"She's a-staring at you with all her eyes," observed Salmon Roe.

This was the truth, Mrs. Flynn was looking at Joss keenly, with a puzzled look on her face.

"What the devil is she a-staring at?" said the aggrieved Joss. "I hope she'll know me again; blest if everybody in the world ain't in league to make me uncomfortable."

At this moment the lady beckoned to the astonished Joss, and asked him if he and his friends would not come to a private room.

Joss would have refused, but Kelly, his curiosity having been aroused, advised Joss to acquiesce.

Hardly had the door been shut, when she threw her fat arms round Joss's neck and kissed him repeatedly.

"Let go," cried that injured individual. "Do you want to choke me. What are you thinking of, woman. Just let me alone, I tell you."

"Hold on to him," cried Salmon Roe. "Don't let him go. Keep him tight while you've got him."

"Joss," cried Mrs. Flynn, "dear Joss, I am so glad to see you once again. I never expected to see you again in this world."

"How did you come to know my name?" said the puzzled Joss.

"Don't you remember me?"

"Never set eyes on you before, as far as I know," replied Joss. "Who the devil are you, and why do you go on in this way. I don't like it. so just leave go."

"You are cruel," said Mrs. Flynn.

"Don't take any notice of him," said Salmon Roe. "Stick to him like wax."

"He is the most unnatural husband I have ever heard of," cried Mrs. Flynn. "Do you mean to say that you have forgotten me?"

"Completely," said Joss.

"Forgotten your wife, Nancy!"

"Nancy! You can't mean that."

"Yes, I do It's many years since last we met, but I recognise you at once," said the forgiving wife.

"You have got so precious stout since last we met, that I did not remember you a bit at first; but now I come to look at your features they do seem familiar."

"Then you do recognise me at last?" cried the woman, still clinging to her new-found treasure.

Joss nodded, and as his eyes roved over the comfortable little spot, the thought occurred to him that the meeting might be a lucky one for him after all.

"You seem prosperous here?" he observed.

"I am doing well," said Mrs. Flynn.

"Then I'll never leave you again!" he cried; becoming most affectionate as his glance took in the comfortable and substantial arrangements that met his gaze. "Never leave you again, so help me!" he cried. "How I ever came to do it puzzles me. You, who was so good! Thank you, my girl. Just a taste more of the stuff to spoil the water (as he tendered the glass she had filled for him). Yes, it fairly puzzles me, now I think on it, how I ever could! I'm blowed if I can make it out; but here I am, old woman, and here I'll stick, and we'll be just as 'appy as rats in a cornbin."

He threw his arms round his wife's ample figure as he spoke, and they embraced each other, while Kelly and his companions looked on, amazed at the unexpected and dramatic scene.

"You mean what you say?" she asked rather doubtfully; "you won't leave me again?"

"Never!" he returned, well pleased to have found such comfortable quarters.

"I hope you will keep your word," she said with a faint sigh, as she hastened to place the best the house afforded before her unexpected guests.

After drinking to the health of the re-united couple, Kelly and his companions left Joss with his wife to talk over old times, and went to their hiding-place.

CHAPTER CII.
HOW KELLY AVENGED TREACHERY

THE bushrangers had a good laugh over Joss's matrimonial adventure.

They never, however, for one moment believed he would give up his roving life to sit quietly down with a wife, and help her to keep a shop.

They believed it to be a mere frolic more than anything else, of which he would soon weary.

After breakfast, Kelly, thinking that one person would be less noticed than three, arranged to go down to the "public," and meet Morgan, his boatswain.

He was flashily dressed, while he had assumed a new pair of whiskers, that completely changed the expression of his face.

He knew his way about, and soon found himself once more within the walls of the low-roofed saloon so dear to the sailors' mind.

Morgan, the boatswain, was there, and several other members of the crew.

Morgan had gone round to all the drinking places in the locality, and by telling them that Kelly was about once more to take to the seas in search of plunder and adventure, easily persuaded nearly every man of the old band to join. It was unwise to trust new hands.

The moment Kelly was at their head they were ready for anything.

Of course it was easy in such places to talk over business without being noticed or suspected. There is an argot almost peculiar to Australia.

Kelly stood drinks, and then bade the men be on board in the evening.

To Morgan he left the charge of getting on board all that was necessary in the way of provisions.

Morgan was an astute fellow, and an excellent sailor.

Dissipation and one sudden unpremeditated crime had driven him from respectable life, and no more daring robber of the land or sea existed than William Henry Morgan.

Anywhere but with Kelly he would have been the undoubted leader; but the iron will and brutality of Kelly overmastered everything.

Kelly told them that he might wish to start at any moment, so begged them to be all ready and on board soon after nightfall.

He then, secure in his disguise, wandered about the city and made some purchases, which were carried up to the hotel kept by Smith, whence they could be sent on board.

After finishing his business, he strolled along, and presently came near a police-station. He had no fear there. Too many crimes were committed in California for them to bother about those committed in Australia.

He nearly betrayed himself, however. Coming down the steps of the station was Joss, in conversation with an officer.

"This night, at eight, master," said Joss to the man, "and you shall make a fine haul."

"I'll get the men together," replied the officer, "so don't fail to be here in time."

"Never fear," answered Joss, with a savage scowl on his countenance. "I'll teach him to play his dirty practical jokes on me. But before I place the lot in your net, I must know something about my part in it. I must have an agreement that I am not to be quodded with the lot, a bit o' paper making me safe, if I give evidence against Kelly and his gang. You want 'em, and shall have 'em tight enough. Only you must make me safe."

"All right," replied the policeman, "come with me to the chief, and he'll give you a clean bill of health for the future. Come along; you won't bust yer boiler at that pace."

In a few minutes they were in the presence of the chief police boss, who did all Joss wanted.

And so they parted company.

Kelly's passion was something terrible to witness. He could scarcely restrain himself, but he knew that he must do so if he would have vengeance.

All was clear to him. In return for the brutal practical joke played upon him on the previous day Joss was about to win immunity for himself by betraying his comrades.

Doubtless he was going to give up the ship and all to the local police.

For this purpose a large force would be required, and the officer would probably collect them quietly for an evening surprise.

What was to be done?

Kelly knew where to find Morgan. He would hasten to him first, and bid him hurry up the preparations for their final departure.

This he did, with a strong hint to get everything ready as quickly and quietly as possible. Morgan promised strict obedience.

Kelly then went back to the den where they had been concealed by Mr. Smith.

He watched the place keenly and saw nothing suspicious. No, Joss wanted to have the luxurious enjoyment of witnessing their capture.

He went in, and found his two companions playing a friendly hand of cards.

"What's up?" asked Zeph, who saw that the bushranger looked black as night.

"That villain, Joss, the cowardly sot, is going to betray us," he replied, with a fierce and terrible oath; "he's been to the trap already."

The two men rose hastily, looking haggard and pale at the astounding news.

"We must run for it," said Zeph.

"We must leave here at once," replied Kelly; "come. There's lots of dolly shops about here, where we can talk."

And they hurriedly left the house with their more valuable articles in wallets.

Everywhere in San Francisco there are drinking shops of all shapes and sizes.

They selected one to which a garden was attached with several arbours.

In one of these they seated themselves and ordered dinner.

It was necessary to keep cool.

Believing Kelly and his friends to be wholly ignorant of the treacherous conduct of Joss, the police were of course preparing a net in which to catch the whole gang.

What a triumph for the Frisco police would be this extensive capture!

To do what had been the hope of all the colony forces for years!

The English government would of course ask his extradition, and the reward would be claimed in California and not in Australia.

"I'd sooner run my —— neck into a noose," said Kelly, when they were alone, "than let that white-livered cur crow over us."

"But what's to be done?" asked Zeph. "The traps are on the lay."

"I tell you that they mean to make a big haul, and won't be ready until eight," said Kelly, "when the mean hound is to meet the police. Meet the cuss—never. I'll brain him in his own den first. Listen to my notion."

They did, and with perfect awe.

The plan proposed by Kelly was a daring one indeed, but the most dangerous part he took upon himself.

It required great command of face and temper, and the utmost cool courage.

His comrades admired and agreed.

Towards six o'clock then Kelly went to the oyster-saloon kept by Joss's wife.

He found it busy as usual.

Mrs. Flynn sat behind the bar, presiding over all as usual.

Joss was fussing about generally, smoking big cigars and making acquaintances.

His sallow complexion flushed a little at sight of Kelly, but he invited him to have a drink with almost exuberant hospitality.

Kelly did not refuse.

"Forgotten all about our lark yesterday, eh, old man?" he said, grinning.

"Of course," replied Joss, grimly.

"Going to tie yourself to your wife's apron-strings after all?" laughed Kelly.

"It's safe," responded Joss; "and then, d'ye see, there's no work to do. I'm the perfect gent; all I has to do is to eat, drink, and do the swell."

"Ah!" said Kelly, with a grin, "that life 'll suit you to a hair, my friend."

"Yes," said Joss, who did not like the way in which Kelly spoke.

But Kelly was careful not to excite his suspicions too greatly.

He conversed in a bantering way with him, called for drinks, and smoked another cigar.

Mrs. Flynn seemingly took no notice. She appeared absorbed in the multitudinous ramifications of her business.

Presently the clock marked seven.

"Well, Joss, darlint, about that whisky?" she said, with an odd glint of the eye, which Kelly carefully observed.

"You rampagious she cat!" he thought to himself, "if I only had you safe!"

But he simply watched Joss.

Kelly's object was to induce Joss to walk a few yards with him—to accompany him to a rendezvous, but how to do this had puzzled him sorely.

Morgan, however, suggested the means.

He wrote a letter from the "trap" with whom Joss had been in communication, and whose name he managed easily to learn, requesting Joss to meet him at the police-station upon important business.

Kelly managed so that the missive was delivered while he was at the bar, and chuckled with devilish glee as he saw him leave the house in answer to the letter, and walk blindfolded into the pit prepared for him.

"I shan't be long, Kelly," said Joss; "will you wait until I come back?"

"I don't care," answered Kelly, and reseated himself for a moment.

As soon, however, as the other's back was turned, he

hastily rose and followed him; he took his way down a narrow street which led to the station.

Kelly followed him closely, but cautiously, until he came to a doorway at no great distance from an oyster-shop.

Kelly whistled, and out darted a party of seamen, who threw a horse-cloth over Joss's head.

Before he could shriek he was secured, and hurried along by his comrades.

It was quite dark, and by exercising great caution they managed to reach the boat that awaited them, into which Joss was bundled, far more dead than alive.

Meanwhile, at the police station, several officers and some forty policemen had been selected for the expedition.

At first the officials refused to believe in the possibility of such audacity.

That a common bandit and bushranger should have the audacity to seize a vessel and sail round the world with his gang appeared in these modern times incredible.

(Let our readers who doubt this wait until they see what Kelly's brother did in this line, and the correspondence between Victoria and the British Government upon the subject, vide *Times* July, 1881.)

Great was the joy, therefore, of the officers and men, at the prospect of such a wonderful capture.

Eight o'clock came, but no Joss, and the officers became very uneasy.

One of them determined to go down to the oyster-saloon and make enquiries.

Mrs. Flynn was very much alarmed. Her husband had gone out soon after seven.

The chief of the "robbers and thieves" was in the saloon, and he had gone after him.

"The scoundrel has had some hint!" cried the officer, and dashed back to the police-station.

Then all rushed to the shore, to see the supposed yacht in the act of sailing out of the bay.

The officers were frantic with humiliation and rage. There was not a single steamer available for the chase ready.

All the men-of-war on the station were absent, cruising at sea.

It was determined, however, to send out a sharp revenue cutter to give warning.

But all felt bitterly disappointed at the failure of their well-laid scheme.

Meanwhile, Kelly and the whole of his band had got on board.

Joss was cast into the hold very tightly secured.

Kelly was determined to exercise a bitter vengeance upon the traitor.

It should paralyse even his own crew.

Now his principal object was to escape from his enemies.

That he would be hotly pursued he could well imagine, and safety was the first law.

A sharp look-out was kept, and then he and his men held a consultation.

Kelly determined to try him by court-martial, condemn and hang him.

His associates were enraptured with the idea.

It was an idea suited to their ferocious natures. But for the timely action of Kelly they would all be lying in San Francisco jail.

Had the police but had the sense to keep Joss a prisoner all would have been over with them.

Death, or prison for life, would have been their portion without a doubt.

But they would soon have their revenge on the cowardly traitor who had turned upon his pals.

As soon as breakfast was over Kelly called those who acted as officers together, and bade some of the men bring Joss in.

A court martial on board a regular ship is a very solemn thing.

If the weather be fine the ship is greatest nicety.

The great cabin is prepared with a with a green cloth.

Pens, ink, and paper, prayer-books, an war, are placed round to each member.

"Open the court," says the president.

In this case Kelly, Zeph and Salmon Roe the court, while pipes, tobacco and spirits are fore them.

The prisoner was brought in. He was dead and his legs shook under him with fright.

"So, you white-livered cur, you blooming son of a sea-wolf," cried Kelly, in a hoarse voice, "you sold us to the traps, did you?"

"I did not," retorted the trembling caitiff. "I never peached on a pal."

"You lie, you skulking hound," cried Kelly, as he drank off a glass of brandy. "I saw you come down the steps of the station; I heard you tell the trap you'd meet him at eight; I saw your look at your wife, you snivelling cur, going to see about the whisky."

"I tell you, Ned, it's false," faltered Joss. "My wife told me to be civil to the police, and tell 'em to look round; being civil to them don't do no harm."

"You spawn of —— fire, you hell-fire cat, you skunk," answered Kelly, and for the benefit of the men who were listening he told the whole story.

Groans and oaths emanated from all sides, execrations of the most fearful character.

"Now, boys, it's no use having no more palaver," he continued. "Guilty or not guilty?" he asked.

"Guilty!" was roared on all sides.

"And the penalty for peaching is——"

"Death!" replied all who were near.

Joss tried to speak, but he was dragged off to the deck, where during the brief trial all the needful preparations for the fearful execution had been made, but they fell far short of what Ned thought the merits of the case demanded.

Kelly, with a brutal laugh, went down into the cabin, and tossed off a glass to his swift passage to a warm place.

Of course, according to these men and their villainous code, the deed was a just and retributive one.

He had been a traitor to his pals.

Kelly had for some days pondered over the form of death he would inflict upon

> "Yon trembling coward who forsook
> His master,"

as "My name is Norval" has it.

The yard-arm was too common, shooting was too sudden.

He must be done to death in a way to

> "Make the world grow pale,
> To point a moral and adorn a tale."

To make him an *auto defé*, to burn him on a pile like an Hindoo widow, to impale him and hang him "alive and kicking," up on the end of the yard-arm like a skewered kidney, there to linger out his days and nights in hopeless agony.

Each of these plans recommended themselves to the bushranger's idea of vengeance and justice.

But each had their objectionable points, and as the trembling caitiff stood before Ned he gave him his choice of the fate he would like best.

"Look here, you miserable, skulking, sneaking viper, I'm kind to you, I am, so we all are. You'd have handed us over to the traps. They wouldn't have been as kind to us as we are to you. They wouldn't have given us the choice of how we'd be scragged. No, not they. Now make your choice. Which will you have—blazes, wood, or water? Look sharp, your time is short. We can't be nice about a hound that would have bitten us all and lapped up the blood-money. Speak, Joss, or I'll give tongue for you, and you'd better not leave that to Ned Kelly, I tell you."

" Roast the traitor who would have murdered us all—who sold his mates! Roast him! Roast him!" rattled and roared out all the enraged men, who encircled the pallid, trembling, half-paralysed wretch, whose frightened eyes and quivering frame clearly photographed the apprehensions that convulsed him.

He knew the men he stood before.

Their eyes were gleaming with vengeance—their hands eager to wreck it on the body of their would-be assassin. They stood glaring ferociously like wolves upon the shrinking wretch, while Kelly, like a presiding Satan, looked calmly and maliciously on, enjoying the torture that racked the frame of the victim.

Truly it was a scene where

> "Hope withering fled,
> And mercy sighed farewell."

"Now, then, Joss, speak up; tell the truth now if you never did before. Which shall it be—fire, wood, or water?"

"Mercy—mercy, Ned!" gasped the horrified man. "Mercy for old times, Ned Kelly!"

" Yes, the mercy you'd have shown to Ned Kelly, when you thought to shunt him into the hands of Jack Ketch. Mercy—yes, the mercy you showed to your mates. What did they ever do to you, Joss—eh? Did they deserve to be murdered by their pal—eh? Answer me that."

The only answer was a groan.

" Finish the brute!" screamed the excited voices of the more excited listeners. "Lynch him! roast him! scrag him!" were the cries that raged like a tempest round the doomed man.

"Hold!" roared Kelly. "Listen to me," and all were silent as the grave. " He's not good enough for any of those forms of death. True men have been hung, brave men have been burnt, but dogs like Joss don't deserve the cost of a rope or a fire. No, my lads, he shall have a death only fit for such as him. We will lower him over the side and tow him after us as bait for the sharks, whose snouts are now, with true scent, following in our wake, knowing their dinner is preparing, and that death's aboard. We'll just dip him a bit, so that he shan't be gobbled up in a mouthful, but let him lose a leg first, then an arm, just to give him time to enjoy it."

This pleasantry was answered by a terrified shriek, and the poor devil fainted.

In the meantime everything was prepared.

A stout rope was tied round the upper part of his body, his arms and legs being left free.

When he came to, Kelly lifted the man in his powerful arms and carried him screaming to the side of the vessel.

The victim struggled all he knew now, with instinct of self-preservation, and without any hope of release. He felt his last terrible hour had come ; and, what was more, he felt he deserved it.

His whole previous life passed in review before him; he suffered the pangs of death fifty times over. Verily, "The pains of hell gat hold upon him."

"Ain't I gentle, my baby?" mocked Kelly, as he quietly lowered the shrinking, quivering, trembling body, over the side, by which the white-bellied sharks were coursing along, their noses rising every minute above the water, as if anticipating the repast that was to fill their open jaws.

Shriek upon shriek issued from the unfortunate victim, as he turned his horrified gaze upon the formidable jaws of the huge beasts, who almost sprung from the waves to snatch the man from the arms that were lowering him to such a fearful and certain death.

Kelly held him with mock tenderness close to himself, laughing wildly and maliciously, as he almost cuddled Joss in his Herculean arms.

Those looking on, almost felt compunction, until the thought of the fate he had prepared for them re-awakened their vengeance, and stifled all human feeling.

Suddenly they were startled by a loud and furious curse, and Kelly was seen to grasp the man's throat.

Joss, in his despair and agony, had fixed his powerful teeth in the flesh part of Kelly's arm, and held on like a tiger.

It was only when almost choked, that his bite relaxed.

Maddened by the pain, Kelly resolved the wretch's fate should not be postponed any longer, and crying out to those holding the tow-rope to " slack off." Joss was flopped into the water, which was soon reddened with blood, while half-a-dozen sharks soon obliterated all earthly sign of the once stalwart Joss.

All felt relieved when this interlude was over; Kelly intended it to be a lesson to those around him.

And no doubt it was so, but it was not the last or the least that Kelly practised upon those who, in his parlance " rounded " on him.

The deed of blood done, there was a general carouse ; and Joss's name was dismissed from the minds of all.

Zeph told capital stories of Tahiti and its beauties, both local and human.

Zeph made it out to be a kind of terrestrial paradise. He had been there several times, and only regretted having ever left it.

So, keeping a good look-out, avoiding anything that appeared suspicious, they wended their way towards the happy islands of the South.

Zeph, and one or two real salts, made considerable alterations in the rig—shortened the masts, painted her sides of a different colour, did everything they could to avert suspicion.

And so the days passed, until one evening just before sundown, they sighted the hills of the ancient Otahite, modernised into Tahiti.

(To be continued.)

NED KELLY THE IRONCLAD AUSTRALIAN BUSHRANGER

No 16,

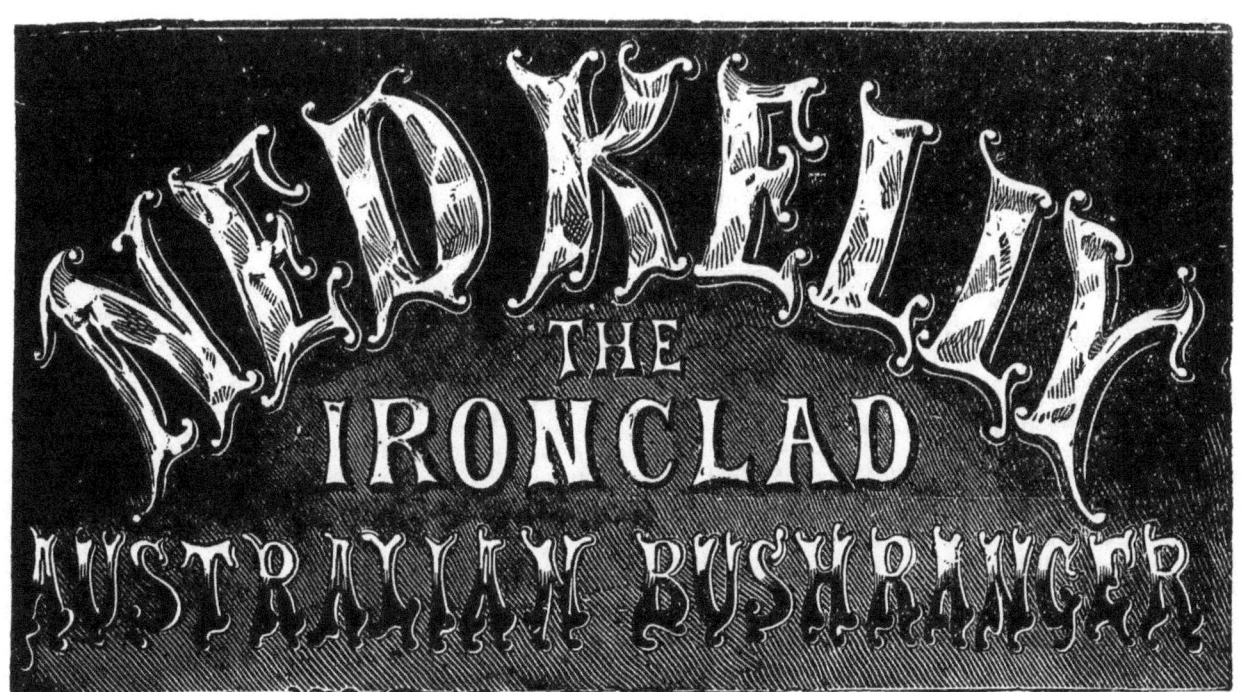

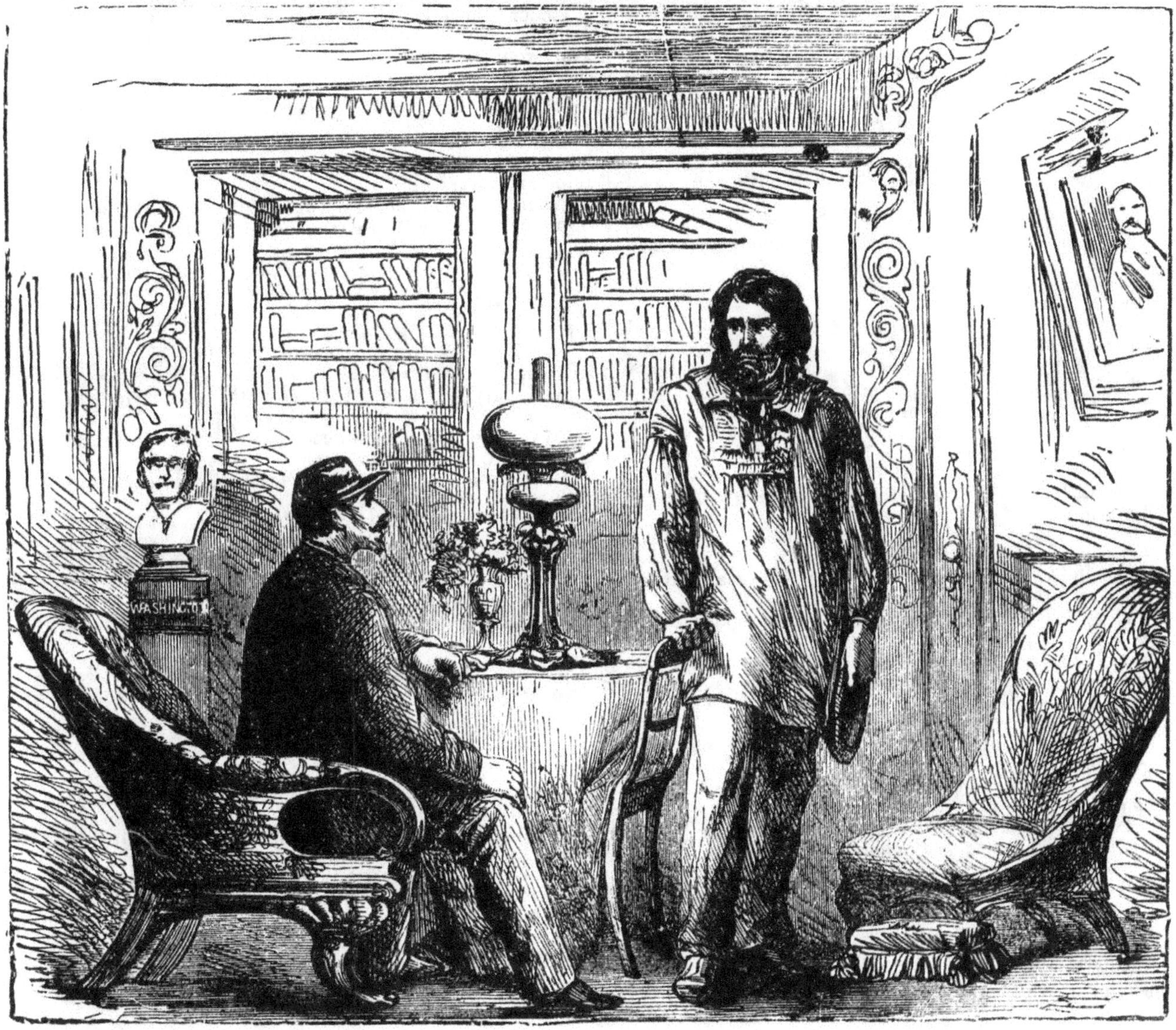

Discovered by Captain Cook, they should have certainly been annexed and kept by England as a truly valuable possession.

But wisdom does not always attend our councils, and the island belongs, *de facto*, to France.

It is almost impossible to exaggerate the beauty of these Pacific islands.

CHAPTER CIII.

NED KELLY IN TAHITI.

New Caledonia is an island in the Australasian seas, in the South Pacific ocean. It is surrounded on all sides by coral reefs, connecting numerous islets and banks of sand, rendering the navigation so intricate and dangerous, that the island can be approached by two openings only.

In physical aspect the island greatly resembles New South Wales, consisting in the interior of barren, rocky mountains, interspersed with fertile valleys.

The sugar-cane and banana, cocoa-nut palm, bread-fruit tree, taro and mangoes are cultivated, and sandal-wood is found to some extent. The inhabitants live mostly on yams and fish. Trepang is fished on the coast.

The natives are of a deep black, with curly hair, robust, active, and well made. Some tribes of them are known to be courteous and friendly to strangers, while others are treacherous, merciless and cruel man-eaters.

In 1849, the station at Balase was attacked, and some of the Europeans killed, and the same year the captain and cook of the ship Mary were murdered, cooked, and eaten.

They speak a language distinct from that of the neighbouring islands. New Caledonia was discovered by Cook in 1774, and called Balase by the natives.

The French, in 1851, sent an expedition to survey the island. Several of the officers and men were massacred.

The Government at once determined to annex the island, and make it a convict settlement. No sooner said than done.

A barrack and all necessary buildings, were at once erected, though the natives were very troublesome at first.

Even the rascals on board the White Eagle, when roused at daybreak and told that they were entering the port of Papiete, were astounded.

Great mountains of every shade of blue, pink, grey, and purple, torn and broken in every conceivable fantastic shape, with deep, dark, mysterious gorges, showing almost black by contrast with the surrounding brightness, precipitous peaks and pinnacles rising one above another like giant sentinels, until they were lost in the heavy mass of clouds they had impaled, while below, spreading from the base of the mountains to the shore, a forest of tropical trees, with the huts and houses of the town peeping out between them.

It was a glorious scene.

The men stood as if enthralled.

The descriptions of Zeph had fired their imaginations, but they little expected to see anything like this.

Kelly was careful that before landing all the men should be steady and sober.

As we have before said, Zeph had a smattering of all tongues, and had a pretty fair ability as to French, the official language of the islands, which had recently assumed the protectorate of France.

When the officials came on board he coolly told them his story, and, as a matter of course, was believed.

Then the supposed officers, and such of the crew as could be spared without exciting suspicion went ashore.

It was a revelation to these men.

Everything was so unexampledly free and easy.

The town itself was nothing wonderful, though it was extensive and well built

But the natives were simply, in the eyes of these sensual and coarse individuals, a revelation.

The women!

Perhaps nowhere on earth are to be seen more lovely creatures than here are found.

Their forms are simply perfection.

No whalebone or steel disfigures their forms, while their dress is nothing but a long white or red chemise, according to the taste of the wearer. In fact the old English sacque.

The men were little men, and were chiefly remarkable for their habit of nodding to strangers and crying, "*Ya rann!*"

Zeph and Kelly were walking side by side smoking cigars in that languid kind of way which men adopt in hot climates.

Suddenly two girls, with almond-shaped eyes full of fire, stopped before them.

Kelly looked at Zeph, who simply grinned.

Then the girls deliberately took their cigars out of their mouths, took a good pull, and then, with a laugh, smoked about five minutes, returned the weeds, and ran away.

"Kangaroos and butterflies!" exclaimed Kelly the bushranger, utterly astonished out of his usual assumption of equanimity, "what does it mean?"

"Custom of the country," drily remarked Zeph. "But you mustn't presume too much. Most of the female persuasions are easy enough, but not all. Be careful."

And he led the way to a noted hotel, known to all English, American, and French visitors as *Le Grand Casuel.*

Here they secured lodgings, dined, and remained in consultation for some time.

It was decided to be very cautious while at Papiete.

Under French laws the government was rather severe, and any open or violent encroachment against the regulations would be resented.

As a matter of course, except under peculiar circumstances, any idea of committing any startling robbery was out of the question.

The port would very soon be too hot to hold them.

But these men were always alive to the fact that something might turn up.

When evening came round they sailed forth in "longshore togs," and went to one of the innumerable grog-shops.

It, like all its compeers, was crowded with French and other sailors, and a very large mass of the other sex.

"Well I'm darned!" cried Kelly.

"What's up?" asked Zeph.

"Look at them two spoonies," responed the bushranger, laughing. "Ain't it fine?"

Well, it was a lesson perhaps in the art of courtship not usually visible to the naked eye.

Presumably, they were sweethearts—at all events, they ought to have been.

The male, a stalwart young Frenchman, was in company with a Tahitian girl.

As Lord Pembroke says, in "The Earl and the Doctor," he had his arms round the girl's neck, while she had hers round his waist, and hung upon his breast in a simply affectionate manner.

Zeph laughed.

He had seen that sort of thing before, and it did not even amuse him.

Kelly seated himself and looked around

The scene was utterly new to him.

No barmaids.

No, nothing but French barmen, with the sleeves of their dirty white shirts rolled up—brawny, bull-necked, black-haired, and shaven.

There were also Yankee skippers to be seen among the mob, and English Jacks.

Presently there was a fight, in which neither Kelly nor any of his comrades was concerned.

The owner of the place interfered between an Englishman and a Frenchman.

"No fightee in my house," he cried "Call de police out.'

The two drunken sailors made some very strong objurgations, and then proceeded again to blows.

Then some native police were called in.

Their attire was of the simplest.

But they were not even respected. They begged, prayed, entreated, commanded the crowd to disperse.

Someone twitched the sticks out of their hands, which caused a roar of laughter and a fresh torrent of eloquence from the brown boobies, which lasted till the mob good-humouredly did as they were told.

Having duly arrested the criminals, their next duty was to carry them off.

Strangely enough, one of the most common articles belonging to modern civilisation was utterly unknown—the handcuff

Rope made from cocoa-nut fibre was substituted, and after a terrible fight the unfortunates were borne away.

"Rum country," growled Kelly; "but what's all this here bunting about?"

"Fête Napoleon," answered Zeph.

"What in the name of —— pepper does that mean?" asked the truculent bushranger.

"Well, mate, the country belongs to the Emperor of the French," replied Zeph, "and this is his birthday. That bill mentions a big thing in the shape of a fête, as they call it, at Government House."

And he pointed to a large poster.

It mentioned that this, the sixteenth of August, being the anniversary of the fête day of Napoleon the Third, a grand garden-party would be given.

The Queen Pomare would be present, it said, and tickets of admission to strangers could only be obtained by reference to their local consuls.

"Let us go," said Kelly.

"Can't get in," replied Zeph.

"Bounce!" coolly responded the bushranger.

And so they wended their way towards Government House, the gardens of which are simply fairy-like.

We have already alluded to the loveliness of the Halls of Eblis, but even the author Vathek could scarcely have conceived anything to equal this place under such an atmosphere.

"Can't get in," said Zeph.

Kelly had been watching.

The man who took the vouchers was a grinning little ape of a half-caste.

The bushranger watched him keenly.

He noticed that he was extremely deferential to some and haughty to others, and his quick wit made him soon aware that the difference consisted in *palm oil*.

"My good fellow," said Kelly, walking up with an awful imitation of an aristocratic strut, "I've left my voucher at home—too much trouble to go back."

And he handed him a sovereign.

The man hesitated, and then, of course, yielded.

The Government House is a very handsome structure of white free-stone, in the Elizabethan style, and finely situated among well-wooded grounds on a height overhanging a cove.

Once inside the grounds the two men swaggered about without hindrance or stint.

The *élite* of Tahitian society was present, but that did not prevent many odd things from occurring

  the Fête Napoleon, and, as a matter of course, there were religious ceremonials.

The religious ceremonials were accompanied by music and dancing.

The hymns were sung to the tune of noted music-hall songs, and the dance nothing else but the notorious *can-can*.

"Look out!" suddenly whispered Zeph, "that is the queen—ain't she a wonder!"

"That there a queen!" cried Kelly. "Why I've seen a better-looking one in the bush."

She was not a beauty and was very fat.

Still she was a very quiet, dignified, and good-natured old lady.

But she seemed much amused at the scene, and was very friendly and gracious to all.

It was indeed what is commonly called a swell ball. Nothing so wonderful had ever been seen by such a man as Kelly.

It was simply like a view out of the Arabian Nights, and reminded him of Homburg, of *trente et quarante* celebrity, on fire-work nights.

He crept up as near to the chief swell party as he could.

The local governor, whose name was General Viscount Dubois, offered his arm to the queen, by whose side was, perhaps, one of the most lovely girls any man ever gazed at.

Kelly was one of those men incapable of love in the real sense of the word, as poets and authors say, but strongly capable of the passion in Montaigne's sense of the word.

He was an animal and nothing else—a coarse, and particularly vulgar animal.

The reader must recollect that we have to describe the man as he was, this being no romance, but the history of an actual (then) living individual.

"Who's that?" he asked Zeph, pointing out the brown beauty to his comrade.

"No idea," responded Zeph. "I'll ask."

Which he did, and found that the lovely creature was the left-sided daughter of the queen.

Kelly, wild, wicked and passionate, at once took a mad fancy for the lovely damsel.

There was not much chance of an introduction, and he knew it well.

At this moment a young man, in semi-naval costume, an undoubted Englishman, stepped forward and joined the group.

He was "only a sailor," but he was unmistakably a gentleman.

He was introduced to the queen by the British consul, and by the queen to the girl.

Then Kelly saw this young man take the arm of his inamorata and lead her out.

He at once joined in a waltz, in which dance the voluptuous natives excel.

They appear rather to float in space than to dance, so aërial are their movements.

Kelly followed the pair with greedy eyes.

On inquiry, he found that her name was Lenee Bena, and, though known to be the queen's daughter, was spoken of as a distant relation.

After this dance was over, there was a great rush to a kind of enclosed meadow, where stood eight girls in very light and airy costumes—more airy than light.

At a given signal, and on the playing of a sprightly tune, the whole eight girls cast themselves on the sward, throwing themselves on their left elbows, and began wriggling about in the semblance of a dance, scratching their right legs.

Having continued this fashion for a considerable period of time, they reversed positions, leaning on their right elbows and scratching their left legs.

It was more energetic than decent, but it made Kelly scream with laughter.

The natives roared, but Zeph explained that their laughter was caused by the outrageous coarseness of the song with which they accompanied the dance.

With rare exceptions, decency and morality are things unknown to the female sex.

As Lord Pembroke says, the girls are not moral.

"It would be thought strange in Europe if a young lady whom you had seen scarcely ten minutes, and had not spoken ten words to, were coolly to propose deserting her kindred and friends, and accompanying you, bag and baggage, to the other end of the world; but in the South Seas, is is but an ordinary occurrence, scarcely deserving of notice.

"I remember at Samoa, two ladies of high degree, fat, brown and forty, paying their court with such irresistible ardour, that after telling most shameless lies about a ferociously jealous wife in England, by way of making a polite excuse for not taking them. I was fain to bolt ignominiously, for fear they should win their end by sheer persistency, like the widow and the unjust judge in the parable."

After a time it became clear, even to the dull intellect of Kelly, that to attempt to scrape acquaintance with Lenee Bana was out of the question, though win her he would.

The sailor-chap who had been introduced was the second lieutenant of an English man-of-war, Lord Westport, and he contrived very cleverly to work into the good graces of the maid of honour.

This so exasperated Ned Kelly, that he determined to relieve him of his companion.

His was a fierce and dogged nature, not easily made to swerve from its purpose.

When he made up his mind to anything, he seldom failed to carry it out.

But this affair, another rape of the Sabines it would have to be, would require care and attention.

Having left the gardens of Government House, they wended their way to a grog-shop also liberally supplied with gardens.

Here they found all the men who had leave dancing away with native girls.

In another department gambling was going on at a furious rate.

They take life easy in these parts. A man earns perhaps five or six dollars, and loses it at cards.

He simply walks off to wherever he is in the habit of sleeping, and at day-break goes up into the mountains, gathers fruit, sells it, and begins again.

But easy and indolent as is the habit of life caused by the climate it is not conducive to morality or even decency.

It is nothing uncommon to come upon a group of damsels *in puris naturalibus*, swimming and diving in a marvellous manner.

There is not the slightest affectation of offended modesty at the sight of a male looker on.

They are taught to swim when mere infants, by the simple expedient of throwing them into the water, and then calling them to the bank, by tendering them their natural nourishment.

Kelly found his men thoroughly enjoying themselves.

The bushranger on seating himself at a table, found himself near an Englishman. There were signs of good origin about him, but he had, though not badly dressed, the unmistakable " vagabond, dry rot," about him.

Kelly noticed that he had no glass before him and at once accosted him.

" Take a drink stranger if it ain't an impertinent question? " he said.

" Thanks—hard up—can't cash cheque," responded the individual in a voluble tone.

Kelly summoned a waiter and ordered a bowl of rather strong sangaree and some of the best cigars.

" Know this crib? " asked Kelly.

" It ain't any account," said the stranger, " been all over the shop—but nothing to be done here. I'm an unlucky mortal."

And he told his story, which was a strange one.

" Seems a change would do you good, my buffer," said Kelly; "a few notes wouldn't be unacceptable."

" Try me man," was the response.

" Well, can you do the big boss? " asked Kelly of the stranger.

" I was bred and born a gentleman," the man answered with a deep sigh; " what is it you want? "

" With plenty of tin and togs," continued Kelly, " you could rub noses with the upper crust."

" So? " said the other.

" Scrape acquaintance with a nob like Lord Westport? " asked Kelly.

" Yes," was the dry response.

Kelly now explained that he was owner of a splendid yacht, but a stranger to the island and its inhabitants.

He wished to give a grand lunch on board to a few of the better sort.

He particularly wished to invite Lord Westport, and some other gentlemen of position, but they must all bring a lady with them.

He had an idea that a dance would be acceptable, and had music.

The man, whose name was Evelyn Hastings, said it could be easily managed, as he had plenty of good introductions, which he had failed to deliver from want of money.

Kelly at once asked him to join him at the hotel the next day, giving him money with which to procure a rig out.

Loose fish as the man was, he looked as if he could be trusted.

CHAPTER CIV..
ON BOARD THE YACHT.

NEXT day, very sprucely dressed, and looking a jaunty, devil-me-care sort of gentleman, Mr. Evelyn Hastings called on Captain Higgins, at the Queen's Hotel.

The bushrangers had waited breakfast for their new guest, who sat down to the meal with a self-satisfied smile.

After breakfast he went out to purchase further necessaries, including some luggage, and to release others detained for rent.

He then returned to the hotel, where for the present he had taken rooms.

Then, when the heat of the day was over, he went out to make calls.

He was away for some time, and then when he reported progress found that he had been very well received.

A day or two passed, and then Mr. Hastings sent out certain invitations to his numerous acquaintances, to lunch on board his friend Captain Higgins's yacht.

There would be music and dancing, and every gentleman was expected to bring a lady.

After sending out the invitations, Mr. Hastings called on a good many of the invited guests, especially on young Lord Westport.

He graciously accepted, and promised to bring Lenee Bana, who was reported the best dancer in the country.

Kelly chuckled. Thirty couples and more had accepted the invitations.

What was the villain's intention? To get rid of all the men and keep the women.

But how was it to be done?

As to that he had not made up his mind.

To murder thirty odd gentlemen in cold blood would be unexampled folly.

Such a fearful crime would rouse a natural confederation against the arch-fiend.

He had quite enemies enough already, without making a host of unnecessary ones.

He determined, therefore, to be wholly guided by circumstances.

It would be impossible for him to abduct Lenee Bana unless he allowed the same latitude to his crew.

What to do with the women before they entered another harbour was another consideration.

They could easily set them on shore on some uninhabited part of one of the many islands, and thence escape.

Captain Higgins, as he called himself, now began to make great preparations to entertain his guests.

Every kind of Parisian shop was to be found at Papiete.

The upper-class ladies dressed in true Parisian style though this was, to say the least, a trifle gaudy.

He gave unlimited orders for the lunch and refreshments, with a select band of music, and everything that could conduce to the enjoyment of his guests.

At twelve o'clock next day the yacht fired a gun, and then was covered from deck to truck with bunting.

Soon after, barges and other boats put out in the direction of the yacht.

There was only one English man-of-war in port, a sloop, while there were several Frenchmen.

Mr. Hastings, who spoke French fluently, had invited one or two of these.

Captain Higgins had deputed Hastings to do the honours, himself standing on one side, trying to look bluff but honest.

As the ladies and gentlemen came on deck, and were introduced by Hastings to their host, they thought that if he were bluff but honest, he was confoundedly ill-looking.

Still he was very humble, said little, and was most profuse in his hospitality.

As soon as all were on board, the guests and supposed officers seated themselves.

The ladies were all young, beautiful and natives.

Hastings had particular instructions on this point, which he had faithfully fulfilled.

The whole deck was covered by an awning, and the tables laid beneath.

Beside were a number of boats, belonging to the guests, the caterer, and the band.

The lunch was thoroughly enjoyed, and then the decks were cleared for dancing.

As Kelly danced only in a very rude way, he had no care for this part of the entertainment.

The band struck up. All who cared for dancing selected partners, and the fun began.

Kelly went below and gave instructions.

None of the guests, naval or military, were armed while the crews of the boats took their refreshments in the different craft.

As the dance ceased, every male guest was suddenly seized from behind, and his arms pinioned.

Then the terrified women found themselves confronted by a band of armed sailors, looking more like satyrs than men.

A Babel of voices arose.

"Bundle the fellers into their boats," cried Kelly; "overboard with them if they ain't quick."

At this moment, Lord Westport, who had noticed the suspicious look of the men coming up from below, and who had the presence of mind to evade capture, rushed at the supposed captain of the White Eagle, and clutched him by the throat.

"Villain, what means this outrage?" he cried "speak ere I brain you."

At that moment Zeph felled him to the ground with a blow from his powerful fist.

"Chuck all the rest into the boats," shrieked Kelly, in a towering passion. "I'll deal with this mighty swell."

"What's the meaning of all this?" gasped Hastings, pale and terror-stricken.

"Mind your eye," said Kelly, furiously, "or it may go bad with you."

Officers, cooks, waiters, musicians, were bundled into the boats.

The scene was simply indescribable. What with the oaths and objurgations of the men, the shrieks and cries of the women, the hideous blasphemy of the crew, the scene was awful.

The women stood still in blank dismay. They guessed the truth.

Not in any way fastidious, yet not one but looked with horror to the prospect of falling into the hands of these wretches.

Zeph, with a body of men armed with rifles pointed at the boats, stood near the bulwarks.

"Steer off pretty sharp," he cried, "or my men will fire into you."

What could they do but go ashore and institute a rapid pursuit.

"Now then for this insolent cub," said Kelly, as the young lord arose.

He was firmly held by two men.

"So, my cheeky young nob," exclaimed Kelly, "you tried to strike me, did you?"

"I wish I had killed you," responded young Lord Westport, to whom Lenee Bana clung, lovely in her abject terror.

"Overboard with him," cried Kelly; "let him walk the plank. Drag the girl away."

He was obeyed, and Lord Westport was taken to the sally-port.

Lenee Bana stood still, dazed and shivering with horror Then she leaned over the side.

Lord Westport, despite his clothes, light and suita to the climate, was swimming in the direction of shore.

He was a very powerful athlete in every way.

But Kelly knew the waters to be infested by sharks who swarmed in that spot.

The yacht was outside the eastern point of the bay.

It was half-a-mile to the shore.

No man, unguarded by a boat, could swim that distance without falling a victim to the voracious robbers of the deep.

Suddenly Lenee Bana gave a wild shriek as a shark slowly lifted himself and made for the swimmer.

He was close at hand, in the act of turning on his back to aim at its prey.

Lenee Bana snatched a knife from one of the sailors, darted into the waist, and leaped clean overboard.

A shout of applause burst from the lips of the astonished and applauding ruffians.

"Man a boat!" shrieked Kelly.

Everybody knows what swimmers the natives of these islands are.

Lenee Bana went down out of sight, and then, rising, swam hand over hand towards the marine monster.

It was close on to Lord Westport, but the brave girl caught one of the beast's fins and plunged her long knife into the stomach in the direction of its heart.

There was an intense wriggle, a spurt of blood, and the shark turned over.

Lenee Bana simply dived, and again attacked the animal.

By this time the boat was out and approaching the girl, while Lord Westport was making frantic efforts to join her.

The boat was first.

The girl who swam easily with one hand, pressed the knife to her bosom.

"Take him in first," she said in very fair and intelligible English.

The men obeyed, and the two were dragged in just as the shark, furious and savage, turned to renew the attack.

Soon they were on deck.

"Now," said Kelly, as he ordered Lord Westport to be secured, "now boys, the girls are all your own."

And he clutched Lenee Bana by the arm with a ferocious grin.

"Stop!" thundered Hastings, who was wild with excitement and horror. "Look!"

And he pointed to the old Semaphore telegraph, which was exchanging rapid signals with the Semaphore tower in Government gardens.

"Do you understand what that means?" he asked in a loud tone.

"No," sullenly responded Kelly.

"Those on yonder tower have seen all, and are telegraphing the news. In a quarter of an hour two men of war will be after you."

All were startled at this intimation.

Escape was certainly the one thing needful for these unhanged villains.

If caught, any fresh outrage would tell against them in case of capture.

"Take the prisoners below, and crack on all sail," cried Kelly. "Zeph, see it is done smart."

Their necks were virtually in a halter, and the men worked indeed with a will.

The cutter, as we already know, was a quick sailer; but Zeph had heard that both the Royal George and Reine Pomare were very sharp vessels.

As soon as they were loose from their anchors, a look-out was sent aloft.

He reported at once two vessels in chase; they were both men-of-war.

Of course they would pick up their officers as they passed, but this would only cause a very brief delay indeed.

Every stitch of canvas that the vessel could carry was clapped on, and every act resorted to that clever seamanship could devise.

The vessels, however, that pursued them, were well-manned and admirably appointed.

Zeph and Kelly sat in the cabin alone.

"Curse Eve, and all her daughters!" said the bushranger. "I wish I'd never spotted one."

"We can swear it's only a lark," observed Zeph.

"What about that Hastings fellow?" responded Kelly. "He's a cursed muff."

"Can't we talk him over?" asked Zeph. "He's poor as a church-mouse."

"Ah! he don't mind a trifle, but he's not up to snuff," cried Kelly. "He'd do a man with a bill, or swindle a tradesman or anybody else, but he'd get nasty nice about a job like this."

Zeph made no reply, but, after drinking off a stiff glass and lighting a cigar, went on deck.

Kelly, after thinking over the matter for some time, followed him.

"Well, mate, what's the ticket?" he said to the other.

"Looks like a dark and dirty night," was the answer. "I tell you that's our only chance give 'em the go-by."

"Leave that to you, Zeph," surlily replied Kelly.

"Well, we'll wait until it's quite dark, then take in all sail, furl up everything," continued the sailor, "and lie to. If they can't see us, it will be spiffing."

This was agreed to, and when darkness fell upon the face of the deep, they suddenly changed their course, put out all lights, and then took in all sail.

The two men-of-war, one French and one English, kept on their course.

All they knew was, that the so-called yacht was in reality an audacious skimmer of the seas, a blot on the escutcheon of humanity.

As for any inkling of the truth, no one could, by any stretch of imagination, believe in the monstrous idea that Ned Kelly was in Tahiti.

On board the English sloop that evening, just before eight bells, the captain and first lieutenant were talking, before the former turned on for his watch below.

"Captain Crowder," suddenly said the subordinate officer, "I see it all!"

"In what way?" asked the superior.

"Don't you remember my reading you that amazing story about the Snake being stolen by bushrangers, and turning up at Singapore and Batavia as a yacht!" exclaimed Lieut. Crofton.

"Yes, but ——"

"That yacht is the Snake, and the rascally cur who entertained us was Ned Kelly," was the startled and amazed answer.

"By Jove!" said the captain.

Then putting things together, this and that, they came to the conclusion that they were right.

Only the more eager were they to capture the suspicious vessel which had carried off the girls.

"That Hastings must have been a confederate," mused Captain Crowder.

"I don't think so, sir," remarked Crofton, "he's not very particular, but he's not in that swim, I think."

"Come down and have a glass of wine," said the captain, "and then keep a sharp look out. This darkness is unfortunate."

And so it proved for them.

Early the next morning, on board the White Eagle, a good look-out was kept.

"Sail on the weather-bow," was shouted.

Zeph went aloft and saw that it was a large vessel under all sail.

"'Bout ship," said he, as he descended to the deck.

As soon as the White Eagle tacked, the other took in her topmast studding-sail and hauled her wind.

The pirates had no stomach for fighting. Their only hope was flight.

"But I mean not to be taken alive," said Kelly, who however, little thought his identity was suspected.

At the first trial of strength between the vessels there was perceptible difference.

On board the Frenchman—for it was that vessel, when the first lieutenant examined her sextant, he could not perceive that he had gained a single cable length.

"We will keep away half a point," said the captain to his lieutenant, "we can afford that, and still hold the weather-guage."

The Reine Pomare was kept away, and at once increased her speed. She neared the pirate a quarter-of-a-mile.

"They are gaining on us," said Zeph, "we must keep away a point."

Away went the White Eagle, and would have recovered her distance, but the Frenchman was again steered more off the wind.

"They'll come up to us, and be cursed," said Zeph, "it's only a question of time."

Kelly swore blasphemous oaths, but prepared for the worst.

The vessel was well armed, and at a distance would make a good fight.

They still cracked on, for so slowly did the foe gain on them, but it might be night before they come up, when by some stroke of cunning they might escape.

But every preparation was made for a fight. The men were well supplied with arms and ammunition.

Towards night, the Reine Pomare seemed to gain on them considerably, and they knew that the end was near.

The Reine Pomare fired a gun, but of this no notice was taken.

Still, after a consultation, it was determined to trust to a long gun they had on board.

Their only chance was to disable the other's masts, and then again seek safety in flight.

Zeph had it hauled out and carefully loaded. He and one or two old men-of-warsmen undertook to work it.

He put a good man at the wheel, and stood by to give his directions to him and to the sail-trimmers.

He took steady aim, and then at an opportune moment fired.

All watched the result, but it was null, except that it set a few ribbons of canvas flying.

"Better run," growled Kelly.

But it was too late. The Reine Pomare was splendidly handled, and soon came near enough for a broadside, which tore several of their sails to pieces, and sent the main topmast by the board.

They must now surrender or die fighting. They fired a broadside as well, and kept up a constant discharge of the long gun.

They certainly did considerable damage, but that did not prevent the other vessel from coming up hand-over-hand.

The pirates were ready, well-armed, and desperate. They fought with halters round their necks.

Soon, amid a cloud of smoke and the roar of artillery the vessels collided, grappling irons were thrown, and then a mass of men darted on the pirate's deck.

The defence was of a formidable character.

Kelly fought with desperation Firing off his revolvers he drew his cutlass and fought against odds manfully.

Several times the Frenchmen were driven back, and many hurled into the sea.

The deck was slippery with blood.

Suddenly from below rushed Lord Westport, and with a drawn sabre rushed at Kelly, whom he cut down, wounding him severely.

The rest surrendered, and a few minutes later, the delighted ladies being set free, the two vessels were being refitted.

Next day they entered Tahiti harbour in triumph, and the audacious pirates were lodged in the local prison.

Such a sensation had never been known in that generally peaceful island.

CHAPTER CV.

THE PRISON.

KELLY was not seriously wounded, but still he required care and nursing.

As chief and ring leader he was more watched than anyone else.

Still on all hands it was determined to make a signal example of him.

Such a daring action as the abduction of the girls and the defence against a man-of-war was unheard of.

Then an examination of the vessel proved her to be the Snake.

The whole mystery then came out.

The English representatives demanded that the vessel and the pirates should be given up to them.

The French authorities demurred, and finally the decision of the knotty question was referred to the home government.

This gave the pirates a long respite, which Kelly determined to make use of.

He resolved to feign great weakness.

He was not chained, but fastened in a strong room with a bed, a small table, and a chair.

All the money that remained to the villains had been secured as prize money, but the persons of the prisoners had been only hastily searched.

Kelly had round his waist a girdle full of valuable diamonds, which he had always ready to put on when in danger or likely to be compelled to "make tracks."

This knowledge gave him courage.

He was visited twice a day by the doctor, and once by a sister of charity, while his meals were brought to him by an odd character enough.

His name was Jean Goujon, a marine, who in the course of his voyages had picked up a small smattering of English.

As the jail was confined to French, English, and Americans, as a rule, this sufficed.

Jean Goujon was a thin, wary fellow, with a cunning, greedy face, and Kelly thought he might venture an experiment with him.

"How do you like this beastly hole?" asked Kelly one day, as the other gave him his breakfast.

"Cochon hole," said the man, with an expression of deep disgust.

"Why you stop?" continued Kelly.

"I have to excest, you know," with an inimitable shrug of the shoulders, "and ven I pay of z y poot me here."

"I suppose you miss your France?" observed Kelly.

"Ah! la belle France, ze beautiful country dat I lofe," said the man, clasping his hands; "and my famille, and ze beautiful Jeannette."

"You could go back to the old crib, if you lik d," said Kelly, in a low, meaning tone.

"How you mean?" cried the jailer, anxiously.

"You'll never peach?" observed Kelly.

"No, nevare," said the man.

Kelly now told him in a few slow, plain words that h had with him a valuable lot of diamonds.

If he would help him to escape he would divide them with him.

If he refused, he should tell the doctor of them, and he would lose all.

The jailer's face was a picture, his hands convulsively.

"Show me ze diamand," he said, in a thick voice.

Kelly withdrew the belt from under his clothes.

It was admirably made and padded, the trousers being made in a particular way to hide it.

He opened one end and took out a fine stone, which he handed to the Frenchman.

He caught at it with delirious agitation of manner, and devoured it with his eyes.

"Is dis mine?"

"Yes; you just take it to some diamond bloke, and he'll tell you its worth. Mind, it's a tip-topper," he added.

"I knows Samuels Levy—he ask no question," replied the jailer, taking his leave to try and get an hour or two out.

Kelly's eyes sparkled with hope. The man was evidently greedy and covetous.

He sat wrapped in deep thought for a long time.

Should he escape alone, or should he let loose all his fellows?

A grand idea flashed across his mind.

He would liberate all, and once again seize the cutter and put to sea.

In the evening the jailer returned and announced that he had received thirty-three pounds for it—a little over eight hundred francs.

The man had questioned him much about it, but he was careful to give no information.

He wanted to know if there were any more, and his answer had been, he believed, yes.

As the man had brought him his supper, with a small bottle of whisky which he had smuggled in, he offered to stay awhile and discuss matters.

Kelly, who saw the man was bound to him body and soul, now unveiled his plan.

He proposed that at midnight next day he should let the whole party out.

Of course he must go with them.

He fully explained his plan of seizing the ship and being far away before they were pursued.

The man listened to him with amazed horror, the impudence of the thing was so intense.

"Bigre!" he cried, "but dat is von fine stroke of vat you say—pisness. Where you go?"

"To a land where gold peeps out of the ground like 'tatoes," said Kelly.

And he described the gold-diggings, of which Jean Goujon had certainly never heard.

The man was enraptured and agreed to everything.

Discipline in that country was rather lax.

There was a guard-house and sentries outside, but scarcely any watch was kept in the interior of the prison at night.

He could with his key unlock the rooms and cells in which the prisoners were confined. Then they could make their way to the garrets and on to the roof.

He would contrive a good stout knotted cord, which would enable them to reach the exercise-yard.

Jean Goujon declared that to ensure success he must have a confederate, and the only one whom he could trust was a woman.

She was bound to him body and soul, and could be trusted.

Ned Kelly did not relish the proposition, but the jailer declared it must be.

Ned Kelly reluctantly gave his consent.

Jean Goujon further offered to make enquiries about the cutter which lay in the harbour.

He then left his new pal and retired, leaving Ned Kelly in the seventh heaven of exhilaration and hopefulness.

He had, after long research, found on board the cutter a secret locker, in which he had concealed a considerable part of his plunder.

He had every hope that this had been spared.

At all events he could but try his fortune.

It was the midday meal which Jean Goujon brought him, and with it news.

The Snake had been refitted, but, pending finding a crew for her to be taken back to Australia, she had a few native sailors put on board her—in fact, what is known to sailors as an anchor watch.

Kelly grinned as he heard.

She had been cleared, well supplied, and of course there was plenty of provisions on board.

Kelly was flushed and excited.

He longed for the night to come, and for it to be over.

The warder bade him be very cautious about the whisky, and not to drink it until the last visit of the doctor and nurse.

They would be sure to smell it, and that would spoil all.

There was no fear of Kelly disobeying his injunctions.

There was by far too much at stake.

Then Jean Goujon retired, leaving the bushranger alone, very much elated, but still filled with suspense and anxiety.

As the prisoners detained in the Snake case were only accused, they wore their ordinary dresses.

The night came at last, and of course Ned Kelly neither went to bed nor undressed.

He was in a feverish state of excitement.

Meanwhile, Jean Goujon had not been idle.

He had been round to all the prisoners, and informed them that they were to make ready for a start.

"Ned Kelly" was enough.

Then he went up to the loft, and opened a window, above which was suspended a crane.

To this he fastened the rope.

To use the chain would have been madness.

He was very methodical in his proceedings, and prepared everything with calm decision.

Then he went to his own room.

The patrol passed every two hours, after which all was safe for that length of time.

He waited until the twelve o'clock patrol had gone, and then joined Kelly, who awaited him with fierce and fiery impatience.

He could even now scarcely believe his good fortune.

It seemed really too good to be true.

Then he heard the key cautiously turned, and the bolts quietly withdrawn.

The jailer entered with a lantern in one hand, a brace of pistols in the other.

Kelly convulsively clutched them, and prepared to follow.

The jailer impressed the necessity of strict silence, and then Kelly found that the corridors were full of men.

Up the stairs they went, treading cautiously and carefully, until they were in a huge loft.

Kelly peered out, lowered the rope, and was soon in the yard, followed by the jailer, and presently by the others.

Once in the yard, the jailer gave a low but distinct whistle, which was answered from the outside.

He then produced a thick, knotted rope, to which a stone was attached, which he cast over the wall.

After an interval of two minutes there was another whistle, and trying the rope it was found to be fast.

Then Kelly led the way in silence.

Soon all were in the street, a narrow lane running at the back of the prison.

Zeph, too astonished to speak, had received his orders from Kelly.

The jailer explained that the Snake was only about twenty feet from the shore. The night was intensely dark.

Kelly and Jean moved away to where the diamond merchant awaited them.

He had sat up by directions of Jean. He stared at the rough figure of Kelly, but went to business at once.

He offered to buy a certain portion of them, which he would pay in gold, and French and English notes.

If they would wait for a day or two, he would purchase the rest, as Queen Pomare would like to have some set for her.

Kelly said he'd think about it and went out. Once in the street, he made up the jailer's money to a hundred pounds as he had promised. He owed life and liberty to him.

Meanwhile, Zeph had made for where the Snake lay, and found only an anchor watch kept on board.

Not a sound was heard.

She was only warped to piles, and when seizing a boat they crept on board, they found three men sleeping on the deck.

These were at once secured.

If there were any sentries about, or custom-house officers, they slept under the heavy night air. At all events they were nowhere to be seen.

A couple of boats were put out after a most noiseless fashion, and every preparation made for towing her out of the harbour.

Once clear of that they could hoist their sails and have several hours start of their foe.

After this escapade they could surely expect no mercy from English or French.

Presently Kelly and the Frenchman came hurrying on board, the vessel was unmoored and slowly and cautiously she was towed out.

The scene was one that would have singularly impressed a thoughtful mind. The beautiful—though rather dark—night, fleecy clouds, myriads of stars, and the vessel as it swept along in dark shadow actually touching the trees as it passed.

Everything was lazy in that fortunate clime, and no one as a rule bothered themselves about other people's business.

The Snake was a mile from shore before an hour, with all sail set.

The astonishment of the crew was something stupendous. Their belief in Kelly when they heard all, became a coarse, vulgar kind of hero-worship.

There were few of those who expected to escape the gallows on board, and their relief was naturally very great.

The wind was fairly fresh, and at two o'clock they had made a good stretch.

Five minutes later, a rocket went up, and the boom of big gun was heard.

"What's the row?" asked Kelly.

"They find out you have escaped," cried Jean Goujon, with a shrug of the shoulders.

"We must crack on a buster," said Kelly, addressing Zeph. "If they see us at daylight we shall be gone coons."

Zeph gave his orders, and then the leaders went below to smoke, and drink, and sleep.

They were to be called at daybreak.

They were, and came on deck at once.

Neither of the dreaded cruisers were to be seen, but almost in the wind's eye was a merchant brig.

"Might hold something useful," said Kelly. "All is fish to our net."

"Nothing comes unwelcome," replied Zeph. "We'll steer for her."

And, altering their course, they did so.

The vessel took hardly any notice of the supposed warship which was coming up.

The brig was Yankee, owned by a man who was going around with notions to sell in the islands.

He was a straight up-and-down sort of a chap, with an inordinate opinion of himself and his country, which is not an uncommon failing with our transatlantic brethren.

As soon as the pirates were close to her they fired a gun.

The brig came to, wondering what was the matter.

The cutter put out a boat, and Kelly and Zeph, with a crew, started for the brig.

They meant to play a practical joke of a kind not likely to prove very pleasant to the sufferer.

When they, in the dress of officers, leaped on the deck, they found the master sitting on a hen-coop.

He was a short, thick, paunchy-looking fellow, who never offered to salute them

"You're Britishers I guess?" he said

"I guess we are," replied Kelly, imitating his twang.

"Thought it was one of the old country sarpents. No harm meant," grinned the master.

"Oh no; only we wanted to know if you had seen anything of a rascally pirate just escaped from Tahiti. He's about our build."

"Seen ne'er a one," replied the other in somewhat of an anxious tone, "and don't want to nuther."

"Is your cargo so valuable, old horse?" asked Kelly of the master, who, used to rough customers in his own navy, was not surprised at the other's roughness.

"We've sweet oil, raisins, and what we call notions," he went on.

"Don't notion what you mean," said Kelly. "Ain't got the rarest idea."

"Well, notions is, you see, a little of all sorts, sir-ee," he answered. "So e like some things, some another. Some likes sweet almonds, and some likes silk; and some likes opium, and some," he added with a cunning grin, "likes dollars."

"Them the kind of notions yo 're loaded with?" said Kelly in a bantering tone.

"Yes, I guess we are."

"Got any good whisky?" asked Kelly.

"Sartin sure," cried the master.

And a boy was at once sent in search of a bottle and glasses.

The two drank freely.

By this time the White Eagle was close at hand, and, to the surprise of the Yankee skipper, showed her teeth.

"What's up?" asked the ma ter, whose face became the colour of one in the jaundi e.

"Hand over them dollars," cried Kelly, "and what spirits you can spare or, by thunder, I'll sink your —— craft."

The man fetched a sigh from the waistband of his trousers as he answered—

"You're only piling it on."

"You'd better be pretty sm rt," said Kelly, as he pointed to two boat loads of armed men.

The unfortunate trader went be_ow, opened a locker in which were thirty thousand dollars— he had been trading round the world for a year—and allowed them to be taken, not without many a sigh and groan.

He gave out a good lot of brandy, whisky, and Hollands, which the pirates secured.

"If you're overhauled by the British skunk," then remarked Kelly, "give my compliments and hope he's ell."

They then started, leaving the owner of the brig to mp, rave, and curse.

As Kelly put his foot on deck there came a cry of—

"Sail oh!"

Ze h went up, and at once declared it be the English ruiser, but hull down.

Zeph at once gave his orders, and soon the White agle stood under press o sail to the northward.

Zeph knew that nothing n would save them but a ght pair of heels.

The wind was one just suited to the craft, and soon they were again out of sight.

Meanwhile, the American had taken care to cross the track of the cruiser, and to put up signals of distress.

The cruiser at once backed her mainyard and lay to.

The skipper went on board and told his story in exasperated tones.

"My in ards is took out," he began.

He'd been imbibing whisky all day.

"Hail Columbia, happy land '
If I ain't ruined I ll be d—d."

The officers heard him with astonishment.

They, however, soon got rid of the drunken Yankee. and started in pu suit.

Zeph now examined the map keenly.

There were not only charts, but there were also "Memoirs of the Sea," which minutely described every island.

The number of inhabited islands was considerable, but there were also some that were quite uninhabited.

Zeph proposed to make for one of these islands, which lay under the lea of Tahama, and there remain concealed until the first hue and cry was over.

Kelly at once acquiesced.

He was, while at sea, completely in the hands of Zeph in whom, however, he had the greatest confidence.

It was not so many years before that the island to which Zeph was about to make his way was the refuge of pirati al vessels, the reefs and shoals by which it was surround ed affording them protection from their larger pusuers, t passages through this dangerous navigation being then only known to the pirates who frequented there, proved an additional security.

The largest of the three islands forms a curve like an open horseshoe to the southward, with safe and protected anchorage when once in the bay on the southern side.

But previous to reaching the anchorage there are extensive coral reefs through which it is necessary to conduct a vessel.

This passage was extremely intricate; but there was amongst the ship's charts a very good one of this island, made by a well-known American.

Zeph felt that he could, with the aid of this, conn her in.

When they were close to the dangerous channel, Zeph put two of the best men at the wheel, and others as sail trimmers.

He himself went forward and placed the chart on the capstan.

The chart was carefully prepared, with every point marked out clearly.

The islands themselves had been originally composed of coral rocks, a few cocoa trees raised their heads where there was sufficient earth for vegetation, while one part was a tall rock.

But the chief peculiarity of the islands, rendering them suitable to those who frequented them, was the numerous caves with which the rocks were perforated, some above high-water mark, but the majority with the sea water flowing in and out of them, in some cases merely rushing in, and at high-water falling into deep pools which were detached from each other when the tide receded; in others was a sufficient depth of water at all times to allow you to pull in with a large boat.

It is scarcely necessary to observe how convenient the higher and drier caves were as receptacles for articles which were intended to be concealed until an opportunity occurred for disposing of them.

They were soon in the channel, and Zeph quickly showed of what seamanship he was capable.

He carefully evaded anger.

He had, however, to be careful, as the breeze had freshened, and the water was in strong ripples, so that they could no longer see the danger beneath her bottom.

Half-an-hour later the wind had considerably increased, and the breakers now turned and broke in wild foam over the coral reefs in every direction.

The sail was still more reduced on board the White Eagle, and her difficulties increased from the rapidity of her motion.

A storm-jib was set and the other hauled down, yet, even under this small sail, she seemed to fly before the wind.

"Sail ho!" cried the look-out, the young sailor who had recognised the frigate on the way to Singapore.

Zeph went up with him, and by means of a powerful glass they made out the Royal George.

But there was little chance of their being seen. They would have to attend to themselves.

Zeph stood at the bowsprit giving his directions to the helmsman.

More than once they grazed the reefs and then were clear again.

Spars were towed astern, and every means resorted to to check her way.

They had now no guide but the breaking of the wild water on each side of them.

"Starboard a little," suddenly shouted Zeph. "Starboard yet. Steady so," and he pointed to some smooth water between the breakers. "Port a little—steady!"

And a few minutes later they were safely at anchor in a sheltered haven under the lee of the tall rock we have spoken of.

They were for the present safe.

Then a look-out was sent to the summit of the tall rock, and he, two hours later, reported the cruiser in sight, bound for Tahama.

The ruffians knew themselves safe for the present.

They took in all sail, lower'd their spars, and then went into one of the old piratical caves to enjoy themselves, which, under the circumstances, meant smoking, drinking, and gambling.

There were no nymphs or naiads to beguile the time in those diggings, not even mermaids.

CHAPTER CVI.
KELLY MAKES A DISCOVERY.

EARLY next morning Kelly, who liked nothing unless it was audacious, proposed that next night after dark a select party in various disguise should visit Tahama, and hear what was said.

He proposed four sailors in the captain's gig, himself, Zeph, and Jean Goujon.

He of course must be carefully disguised. But the marine was not a Frenchman for nothing.

To him to make up as an English sailor appeared the easiest thing in the world.

How he was to carry it out was to the vainglorious Frenchman a mere trifling question.

Of course he must avoid speaking, though for that matter he might be a Jersey man, even a Frenchman.

Such things had happened.

The island of Tahama was about two hours distant.

It was not their intention to go into the harbour direct, but to land somewhere up the coast, hide the boat, and walk into the town.

Kelly had a straw hat, a loose cotton blouse, trousers ditto, and loose boots, the dress of European cotton planters.

He further had a pair of spectacles and a riding-whip, and looked eminently respectable.

Zeph had a similar disguise, while the rest were to represent sailors, while Salmon Roe was made up as an overseer.

On reaching the coast they found a small fishing village, where they could leave the boat and the crew.

It was about a mile from the harbour, and the walk was a pleasant and shady one.

The three walked along leisurely in conversation, smoking as they went.

They passed several natives, who nodded and laughed, but luckily did not speak.

Thus they reached Tahama.

They did not care about making a grand entrance, but worked their way into the town towards the port.

Here were the public buildings, and among others a grand hotel of two stories high, covering a large space of ground, and surrounded by gardens.

In these were several tents.

One of these the three took possession of. They were bell-shaped, and did not reach within three feet of the ground.

Close at hand was another one much larger, which was occupied by a party of English naval officers.

There was Lieut. Crofton, Lord Westport, and the captain they had bamboozled at Batavia.

Kelly knew them in a moment.

"Yes, sir," said the latter: "the unhanged rascal actually supped with us, and invited me to spend a day or two at his plantation."

"The scoundrel!" responded the young lord; "never shall I forget his impudence. To invite her Majesty's officers to a breakfast!"

"The villain must be awfully cunning," resumed the other; "while his impudence is something beyond comparison."

"Nothing would astonish me," said the young nobleman.

How Kelly chuckled. This was all nuts to him. His gross vanity was tickled.

Half his crimes were the effect of his inordinate conceit and vanity.

He was in rapture and when the waiter came—he spoke some sort of English—ordered a most gorgeous lunch.

His companions were afraid he would do some rash and dangerous deed. When exhilarated he was very reckless and daring.

They resolved to watch him carefully, lest he should do anything rash.

But Ned Kelly was too glad in heart to be as mad as he sometimes became when under the influence of drink.

He whistled and crowed, but did nothing at all outrageous.

Zeph and Salmon Roe kept a constant eye upon him; but he merely cracked a joke or two.

He was even cautious not to raise his voice too high. He knew it was a peculiar one, and might be recognised.

Presently, the heat increasing, the officers went in, leaving the bushrangers to their devices.

Kelly laughed grimly. He had never enjoyed anything so much in all his life. It was a splendid joke, and he appreciated it.

"Blow me if I don't keep it rolling!" he said with a hoarse laugh; "we dine at that there *table dot*," he added, pointing to a bill.

"Be cautious, Ned," urged Zeph.

"I value my neck as much as any bloke," growled Kelly, "so don't you do the blue funk."

"All right," responded Zeph.

They went into caravanserai and secured rooms for the night.

They reclined on luxurious couches, and drank sangaree and smoked.

It was unmitigated luxury; such luxury as is not given to such villains often to indulge in. This indeed was living in clover.

Presently they fell asleep, nor woke until the first gong sounded for dinner.

There was no severe etiquette at that time of year as to dress. The two supposed planters found no difficulty in obtaining seats at table.

They kept at a respectable distance from the officers as their voices might awaken unpleasant memories.

Kelly revelled with delight. There was an immense fund of humour in the man; of course, rough, vulgar humour.

He chuckled over what the officers would say if they knew their fatal foe, Ned Kelly, was actually in their midst.

The dinner passed off very well, and then the whole party adjourned to a large coffee-room and saloon, much frequented by the *élite* of the native and European population.

Kelly and his party sat at a window looking out the lively scene.

At eventide all turned out, and the sound of laughter was contagious.

Presently Kelly noticed a familiar voice ; it was that of Jean Goujon.

"Bigre ! mais cela est bien, vera fine, bootiful," he said.

"Hope the cracked idiot won't be found out," growled Ned.

At this moment another voice close at hand startled the bushranger.

It was that of the Yankee skipper.

"Tarnation snakes !" he said, "but that Ned Kelly's a 'cute cuss. Freed me, by gum. Airthquakes and apple sauce, but he's tall !"

"The vilest vagabond that ever broke the bread of life," responded the English captain. "There's ten thousand pounds, sovereigns, offered for him."

"No more !" was all the other said.

"Yes, the daring ruffian has committed more crimes than any other bushranger in the colony," continued the irate captain, "his carcase is worth its weight in gold."

"Jehoshaphat !" cried the skipper, "and the mean cuss cleared me out of thirty thousand dollars !"

"All's fish to his net, Mr. Caleb," laughed the English captain ; "he's not particular."

"So I reckon," answered Caleb, with a growl. "I wish I had the varmint by the scruff of his neck."

"Pretty stiff chap to deal with, I think," retorted the captain, and moved on.

Caleb approached the window and seated himself at a small vacant table, where he was soon joined by his mate.

"Sawdust and gingerbread !" cried Caleb, "ain't that cuss, Kelly, a wonder ?"

"What's up ?" asked Sol Jackson.

Caleb told him all he had heard from the Britisher, and Sol Jackson listened in amazement.

Kelly laughed in his sleeve. This notoriety was almost too good for him.

He ordered up champagne, and then, assuming a very broad Irish accent, spoke—

"Faith, and you'll join us ?" he said ; "shure and something's upset yer."

"A blamed vagabond has," cried Caleb ; "but I'm a ring-tailed roarer, I am, and mean to be even with the alligator."

"To his confusion, may he never die under a blanket, but dance upon nothing," proposed Kelly.

"And me hanging to his heels !" cried Josh Caleb, "that's the right grit. I reckon I'd give a few cents to be thar tu see."

And Josh Caleb told his story, to which the three bushrangers listened with deep interest.

Later on the board of green cloth reigned supreme, and Kelly adjourned to the table.

The play was free, but not very extravagant, yet it was easy enough to win or lose a good many dollars.

Kelly went in for the highest stakes, and won a goodish pile.

His luck was something wonderful.

This drew rather more attention to himself than he liked.

But he had confidence in his disguise, and went on cool and unabashed.

Presently, however, as the luck changed, he quietly withdrew, and looked on smoking.

He then sauntered away to where the English officers and some of their local friends were playing whist.

He stood gazing at them with a sardonic smile as they laughed and joked.

He seemed to stand in a bad pre-eminence over them, as a fallen angel might have done over the true.

Then he and his comrades moved away once more to where the American notion-monger, or ocean pedlar, was holding forth to some of his countrymen as to his wrongs.

"He was darned if he war a-goin' to be streaked by a beef-eatin' Britisher," he said, "and no mistake. He'd bet snakes that he'd be even with him yet."

And many such a brag and a boast did he utter, which were equally foolish and blatant.

"I suppose," said Kelly, "you're not dead on all Britishers ? I'm blowed if I don't half think you are a Britisher."

"Me !" ejaculated the Yank with a look in which surprise and indignation struggled for the mastery. The accusation seemed to almost choke him. "Me a Britisher !" he rather yelled than asked.

He rose hastily to his feet, and, staring with suppressed fury at Kelly, cried in livid and angry accent—

"Me a confounded pumpkin faced Britisher? No, sirree, I ain't. I'd sooner go to —— and pump thunder —I would—at three cents a clap, than be a confounded Britisher !"

His patriotism, or rather his mode of proclaiming it, caused a general roar.

"Well, old horse, you are a screamer, and no mistake. So come along and have a taste of something better than salt junk and ration rum."

"Slide !" ejaculated the denizen of the stars and stripes. "I'm after you as the pinna said to the rabbit."

Kelly ordered a very recherché supper, and for a couple of hours feasting was the order of the night.

Then the bushrangers retired, as, indeed, did all in the house.

I was late.

Kelly was up, however, at a tolerably early hour, and sat down to a breakfast that would have surprised most people.

He was a devourer of unconsidered trifles.

Chops and steaks were nothing to him and his friends.

They determined to keep quiet all day, intending to stay to dinner once more.

Their object was to try and discover what would be the future movements of the English.

This was a matter of life and death to them, as they could scarcely hope to give both of them the slip.

They were in what truly might be termed a quandary.

It would require all their audacity and luck to get out of the difficulty.

The day passed in visiting various well-known places of amusement.

As is the case in such latitudes, the night fell suddenly.

The gang hastened back to dinner, and by some manoeuvring got near enough to the British officers to hear their conversation.

The English had a separate table, but they were close to the one occupied by Kelly and others.

Next the captain of the cruiser sat the British consul in plain clothes.

"I think you are right, captain," he said. "You had better start on the backward track, while the Frenchman cruises about. The fellow is sure to make for Australia."

"Yes ; he'd never be happy out or his old den," remarked the English captain, "so to-morrow we'll start early, and the Reine Pomore can cruise about and search all the islands. The fellow may lie perdu for a few days."

Ned Kelly and the other two exchanged glances.

As soon as dinner was over they rose and went to their rooms.

"We'd better hook it," said Kelly.

"No fear of searching those islands," said Zeph ; "better keep quiet. If a stray craft should see us, they might dart back."

"I trust in you, mate," urged Kelly.

"Do ; let the cruisers get right off, and then we'll make tracks for New Zealand, stop there a few days, and then make once more for the colony."

"Seed nothing like it," cried Kelly ; "a feller feels as if he can breathe there."

And so it was decided to take Zeph's advice, which Kelly did the more readily that he had a special object in view, which he did not confide to any of his fellows.

That evening they heard there would be a kind of hop,

attended by anyone who chose, but not by the higher classes.

Still it was good enough for Kelly and his accomplices, so they went.

It was the usual free-and-easy kind of affair, and the three men enjoyed themselves.

About an hour after their entrance, they noticed Jean Goujon and the others of the boat's crew come in.

They looked very shaky, as if they had made a night of it.

They entered an inferior saloon, and Kelly determined to keep an eye on them.

If Jean Goujon got drunk, he might talk, and in the exuberance of his good fortune it was a very likely thing for him to do.

Kelly followed him into the room, and stood close behind Jean, who, with the others, was standing at a gin and whisky bar.

"*Saperlote!*" cried Jean Goujon, "ve veel **drink ze** visky—vat you call *à la santé* of ze Engleesh."

And he threw down two or three dollars.

"I always cypher'd," said a looker-on; "you Johnny Grenouilles didn't cotton to Britishers."

"Zat is all change," cried Jean. "Ze Engleesh and le Français best of friends. since Boug Johnny time, *à mon vieux* Veel you drinks?"

"I reckon that's Johnny Gudgeon," whispered a man close to Kelly. "Darn my old stockin's, he's worth a pot. Let us off."

And the two men moved away.

Kelly hurried up to where Jean Goujon stood with his friends.

"They've spotted him," he whispered to an English sailor of the boat's crew, "make your carcases scarce, or you'll be copped. Take him with you."

The man nodded, and two minutes later the party took their leave.

Kelly and his companions followed their example, and returned to the hotel.

The English officers had all taken their departure, but the American colony were all there.

Captain Josh Caleb, as he called himself amongst his own people, had come to Tehama under the escort of the English sloop of war.

He thought he would thus be safe.

The bushrangers dined as usual at the *table d'hôte*, and then went to the board of green cloth.

Ned Kelly and Zeph had a long conference, over which they laughed heartily.

Again they supped with the Yankees, who stood treat this time, and a crowded affair it was.

They played cards, they drank, they sang, they shouted, and then the three bushrangers saw Josh Caleb up to their rooms.

Having put him in safety on Kelly's own bed, Zeph pinned a card to his coat, on which he had written a few words.

Then the three men went downstairs, paid their bill, and took their departure.

It was late next morning when Josh Caleb awoke, to find himself lying full-dressed on a bed in the hotel.

Parched with thirst, his mouth white and hot, he rang the bell and the waiter came.

"Water and straight whisky!" he cried.

The waiter gave him both, and then did a perceptible grin.

"What's up, you yaller cuss?" asked Caleb.

The waiter, a Mexican-looking card, pointed to a white card fastened to a button.

Josh Caleb snatched it and read.

The card was written, or rather printed, by Zeph.

"You skinny old curse! don't brag so much, old nutmeg! You've supped twice with Ned Kelly, and you paid for it."

Josh Caleb leaped from his bed with a roar, and, hastily making his toilet, went downstairs, whence he went off to the American Consul.

That individual was at first incredulous, then appalled. But what could be done? There was no man-of-war on that station, but a swift revenue cutter, which was at once despatched.

The fury and indignation of all who heard of the audacious deed, may be imagined better than it can be described.

The impudence of this cosmopolitan ruffian was beyond all bearing.

It thrilled people with astonishment and dread.

CHAPTER CVII.
KELLY PLAYS ANOTHER TOUCH.

MEANWHILE, the chuckling bushrangers had made off; they knew that the only two vessels they had to fear were conspicuous by their absence.

They, therefore, did not hesitate to hire a conveyance to the village, where their boat awaited them.

Dismissing the driver at a small inn frequented by sailors; they found it just open.

It was nearly daylight.

Their own crew was there, quiet, and ready for orders. Not a moment was wasted; a rapid breakfast was consumed, and then they went to their boat and hoisted sail.

No one had the slightest suspicion that anything was wrong, and no notice was taken of the escape of the nefarious gang.

As soon as they reached the cave in which the vessel was concealed, a look-out was sent to the top of the rock to keep a sharp look-out.

One of these was Jennings, the shrewd young man-of-war's man, a sharp, clever fellow.

(To be continued.)

NED KELLY THE IRONCLAD AUSTRALIAN BUSHRANGER

NO 17,

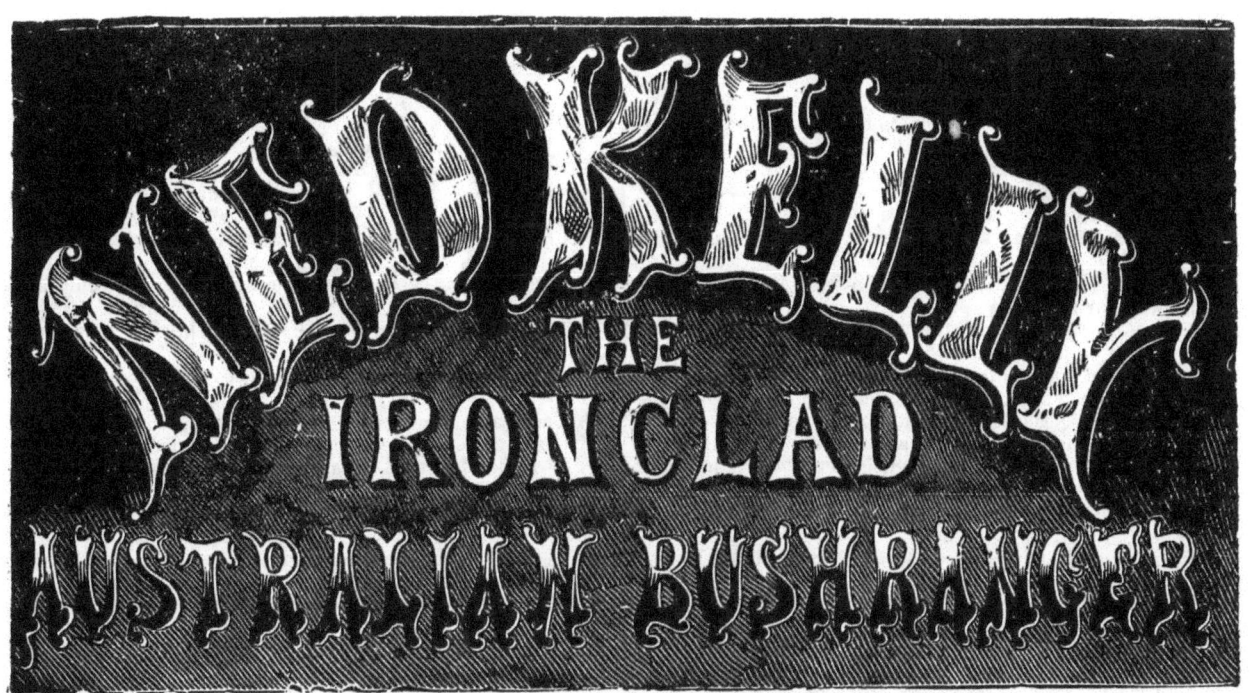

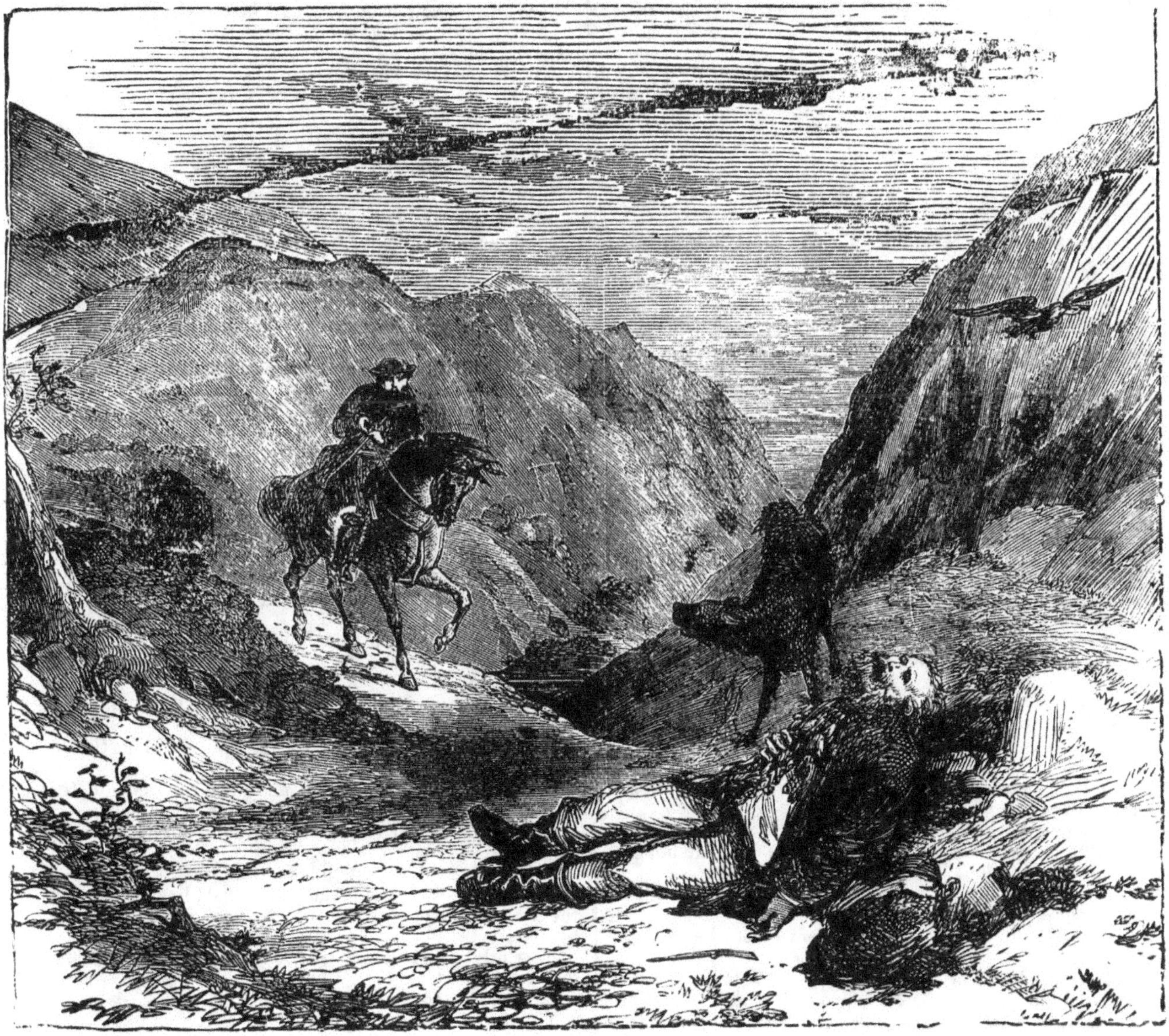

About twelve he signalled Zeph, who at once went up, and saw a sharp-looking schooner dashing through the channel under heavy press of sail.

"The revenue cutter," remarked Zeph.

"Yes, sir," replied Jennings.

And the two went below to report to Kelly. His advice was to haul out at once, and be ready to start as night fell.

"You're right, mate," answered Zeph. "But not just yet; wait for the tide."

Of course that was a matter of which Kelly understood nothing, so he acquiesced.

They spent the day in the cool caves.

"Ned Kelly," suddenly said Zeph, "do you know that somewhere in these caves are hidden lots of tin?"

"One of our sort was took and offered, if his life was spared, that he would show them where over a million, in plate, jewels, diamonds, and money, was concealed."

"And the duffers refused?"

"Yes."

"And what did they do with the bloke?" asked Kelly, with a slight show of interest.

"Hanged him," replied Zeph.

"A very stupid thing to do with a cove," philosophically remarked Kelly; "seems to me about the silliest thing yer can do with a fellow."

And the bushranger unconsciously said in other words what a great author had said before him.

"I tell you what, Zeph, do you think it's true?" asked Kelly, after a pause.

"I do," was the answer.

"Now, look you here, my shaver," said Ned Kelly, in a low voice, "tare an' ouns—what do you think we'll be after?"

"I don't know," cried Zeph.

"Get away slick and straight to the Colony—do a good stroke of business and then back here," exclaimed Kelly; "is this the spot?"

"I believe it is," continued Zeph; "all I know is that not one, but twenty, old salts have told me the treasure is here or hereabouts."

"Then, curse me for donkey's father if we won't find it," exclaimed Kelly; "we must hook it, keep close for a time."

After some further conversation orders were given to be ready.

The men were treated with excessive liberality and then put on careful rations.

"Safety before everything," urged Zeph, and the men were compelled to own that he was right.

The cutter was slowly warped out by boats, and before daybreak was all-a-taunt-o.

The morning was bright, clear, and hazy. The cutter got clear therefore without difficulty.

An hour later, with every stitch of sail on, the White Eagle was steering direct for New Zealand.

Except on rare occasions, the peaceful ocean keeps true to its name. Storms are of rare occurrence, but when they do come round they are excessively severe.

The White Eagle soon lost sight of land. Not a sign of hull and sail.

The pirates felt considerably relieved in their minds, and were to give themselves up to enjoyment.

Several vessels passed them, but none of them were, to all appearance, worth going out of their way for.

Ordinary merchant vessels were not of sufficient importance to take them out of their track.

It happened at this time two of the South American republics were at war—what about nobody knew and nobody cared.

The simple fact existed, and the consequence was both issued letters of marque.

The two same republics are at war at the present moment.

Zeph had heard of the circumstance at Tahiti.

He had determined, before making his way direct to New Zealand, to make a call on the western coast of America.

There are worse places than Callao and Peru, in which to spend a sailor's orgie.

So Zeph determined to make "a slide" for Callao, before steering direct for New Zealand.

There was plenty of time, plenty of money, and no hurry.

Three days passed away and then a sail was sighted. She looked a suspicious looking customer, and Zeph, recollecting what he had heard at Papiete, thought he would be careful.

The White Eagle was well manned, but her crew was not quite strong enough for a man-of-war.

As soon as the vessel hove in sight, Zeph examined her keenly.

As she came nearer he guessed at once that she was a privateer in the service of one of the republics.

She carried fourteen guns, and seemed through the glass to have a very large crew.

She seemed to have taken notice of the White Eagle, for as soon as she perceived her she bore down.

The two vessels then spoke, and the cutter found that the Pride of Lima was in the service of Peru, manned by Americans chiefly, but strangely enough her chief officer was an Englishman.

The supposed yacht made signals and suggested an interview.

The privateer, the Pride of Lima, at once agreed, and the White Eagle put out the captain's cutter.

Kelly, Zeph, and Salmon Roe went in the boat and boarded the privateer.

On the deck of the vessel, which was wonderfully well manned, stood a host of officers in deference to the British flag.

The first man who leaped on deck was Zeph. There was something of the real naval officer about him, despite his fall.

"May I ask what vessel is this?" he asked hotly.

"Pride of Lima," answered one of the officers, an Englishman, "letter of marque under the republic of Peru."

"Happy to have the pleasure of making your acquaintance," replied Zeph. "Ours is the yacht White Eagle, this Mr. Higgins our owner"—pointing to Ned. "We are doubtful about our longitude and latitude."

"We will give you every information," was the polite answer of the officer. "In the meantime, pray let me offer you lunch."

As a matter of course, this was an offer not to be refused, and they politely accepted.

From the moment that Zeph had spoken, a young officer had fixed his eyes upon him in surprised amazement.

He looked, and looked, when he disappeared, with a thoughtful countenance.

Before lunch was put on the table, the young officer went down, making some excuse to speak to the first lieutenant.

He fixed his gaze on Zeph all the time.

That worthy noticed it, and began to feel very uneasy and uncomfortable.

Then the young man went out, and the lunch was ready.

Everything was excellent, and the pirates did justice to all.

Presently Zeph looked up, and saw the face of the young officer peering through the skylight.

He began to feel very uncomfortable and anxious for departure.

But of course they must abide their time.

Presently the captain bade the first lieutenant give them their reckoning, after which he showed them over his ship.

Presently Zeph found himself close to the young officer.

"Uncle Alfred," said a pained voice.

The man known as Zeph staggered back.

Silence!—who spoke?—I cannot think what you mean," gasped Zeph.

"Uncle Alfred," was the calm response of the other, "I knew you at once. Deny me, do with me what you think proper, but do not attempt to deceive me."

"Where are you bound for?" asked Zeph, hoarsely.

"Calloa," was the answer.

"It is well; meet me there in a week," replied Zeph. "You shall tell me all."

"I am second lieutenant," said the young man, "and its an easy enough berth—but will you really meet me?"

"Yes," was the hurried answer.

The letter of marque was a brig of fourteen guns, and with a goodly crew.

Zeph at once re-entered his boat and rowed back to his own ship.

He was very much upset.

The man had been a very different person from what he was now.

Some folly, some imaginary wrong, had changed him, and made him a being of crime.

He was deeply moved, but he made no remark to anyone Who knows what memories of the past had been evoked by this extraordinary meeting—what strange feelings, long since, he believed, dead, were aroused within the bosom of the man of blood and crime?

He afterwards volunteered some explanation to Kelly, but entered into no particulars.

He seemed a changed man, his brow being overcast with thought.

The two vessels parted company, each going its own way, and then Zeph proposed that they should visit Callao.

Kelly was in his hands.

If he had said go to China, it would have been all the same.

Several days passed away, during which they kept aloof from all vessels.

Once more they assumed the characters of Americans, as more likely to ensure them popularity where they were going.

Lieutenant Charles Warner, of the Warspite privateer, had given Zeph an address at an hotel named the Lima.

Dressing himself as much like a gentleman as possible, and looking a rough one at all events, Zeph went to the place.

He inquired if the young officer was in, and was at once ushered into a room where he awaited him.

"So," said the young man, gravely, "we meet again. But how?"

"Charles," replied the other. "Though how you could know me after all those years I cannot tell."

"Remember, we met in London some years ago, after your——"

He hesitated.

"Crime," was the other's response.

"Yes, I remember. I was then a mate on board a vessel bound for Australia," the other went on.

"But why did you leave the navy?" asked his nephew. "What could have possessed you to do anything so foolish?"

"My boy, my captain was a fiend." replied Zeph, "with the exterior of a quiet gentleman. He could torture anyone. There was no galling insult that imagination could devise that he would not indulge in. When under the influence of drink he taunted me—told me I was not worth my salt.

"But would you like to hear my story, boy?" asked Zeph, huskily. "Give me wine—and do not interrupt, above all."

The young officer carried out his uncle's suggestions, and then shut the door and locked it.

CHAPTER CVIII.
CAPTAIN ZEPH'S STORY.

The ex-officer's narrative was rather discursive and interlaced with expletives.

We will not, therefore, tell it in his own words, but give a summary of the narrative.

Zeph was the third son of a country squire, with more pride than purse.

His estate was worth about two thousand a year, and was strictly entailed, and all would go to the eldest son, while the second was provided for by his mother's portion.

Alfred and his sister were dependent on what their father could save, and that was not likely to be much, with the father's habits.

He lived well, kept a good table, and was fond of a-hundred-and-twenty shilling port.

He was liable to gout, and when under its influence was hot, fierce, and irascible.

Alfred, as we shall for the present call him, was of a fiery disposition himself, as was shown by his constant trouble at school.

He was frank, generous, quick and mischievous, and had a large portion of what sailors call devil, which was openly displayed, while a much larger portion was deposited in his brain and bosom.

His ruling passion was pride, accompanied by a great deal of obstinacy.

He was quick at learning, but up to all sorts of tricks and mischief.

In the robbery of orchards he was great, and immense at the stealing of eggs.

He was cunning, and contrived to carry off the new-laid eggs with practised dexterity.

At home he was the plague of his sister. Without intending it he was cruel.

When fourteen years of age he went home for his holidays. His father was ill—suffering from his periodical accession of gout.

It was very fine weather, and cherries were ripe. The father strictly prohibited any fruit from being plucked except by the gardener, a cannie old Scotchman.

But when the cat is away, the mice will play; and these orders were not strictly obeyed when the father was ill.

Alfred and his sister went out one afternoon when luncheon was over in search of an al fresco dessert.

They put a ladder to a cherry-tree, and began their feast.

Just as they were enjoying themselves to the full, the cannie Macdermott came in sight.

"Mercy! the world's coming to an end," he cried. "Did you ever see the like o' that?"

Lucy, the sister, lost her presence of mind and fell with a sharp cry.

Alfred rushed to her, tried to lift her up, and found her ankle sprained.

"You hulking brute!" cried Alfred, and hit the Scotchman a smart blow between the eyes.

He then turned to help his sister, leaving the Scotchman furious.

Half an hour later, Alfred was summoned to his irate father's presence.

The parent was furious.

His cherries had been consumed, his daughter's ankle sprained, and his trusty gardener assaulted.

A violent scene ensued. The father was foolish enough to strike his son with a crutch, upon which Alfred declared he would run away to sea.

"All you are fit for, you thievish rascal!" roared the infuriated father.

Alfred turned to go, but the father rang a bell violently, and Mac appeared with suspicious alacrity.

"Lock Master Alfred up," was all he said.

The Scotchman, a wiry and powerful man—he was very vindictive, and had many tricks played on him by Alfred —caught the other by the arm.

Alfred was too proud to resist uselessly, so he was taken to a room from which escape was impossible, and locked in.

Next day he was taken by the gardener to a rather severe school, were lads were prepared for the navy.

At Christmas he came home, and nothing was said of the past, but the father and son were never cordial again.

In due time Alfred passed his examination and entered the service.

He distinguished himself by his activity and general good conduct.

At last he was promoted, and went home on a visit.

Though always rough he was ready and courteous, especially to his sister.

But his parent was not disposed to have him at home long.

He applied to the Admiralty for employment.

Two days later his father had a big bouncing official communication, announcing his son's appointment to the Digby brig of eighteen guns at Portsmouth.

He was told to join his ship at once and take up his commission.

Alfred started next day, and, on his arrival at Portsmouth, put up at Billing's, as a matter of course.

It was the resort of all the naval aristocracy, and near the admiral's office.

Alfred was now above putting up at the midshipmen's favourite resort, the Blue Posts.

Perhaps this arose from modesty, and a desire to spare his old comrades the trouble of touching their hats too often.

He then made inquiries for his captain.

He did not put up at the George, nor did he mess at the Crown; he was not at the Fountain, nor the Parade Coffee-house.

After considerable research he found that he patronised the Star and Garter.

To the Star and Garter he therefore went, and asked for Captain Ledley Gordon.

It seemed to Alfred a strange place for a captain, as it was a notorious resort of warrant officers, mates and midshipmen.

But there he was, and sending up his name he was told to go upstairs, where he was introduced to the presence of his aristocratic chief.

Captain Ledley Gordon was seated in a small room, with the remains of a glass of brandy and water before him; his feet were on the fender, and several official documents lying before him.

He rose as the other entered, and let him see a short, square-built frame with a strong projection of the sphere, or what the Spaniards call *barriga*.

The abnormal rotundity of corporation was, however, supported by a pair of legs that might have honoured a Bath-chairman.

He was rather good-looking, with a pleasant smile upon his lips and a deep dimple in his chin.

His eyes were peculiar; they were small but piercing.

"Happy to see you, sir," said Captain Sedley Gordon; "proud that you have joined my ship. Sit down lieutenant."

Alfred was delighted. This was the sort of man to be comfortable with.

"I always take care to know something beforehand about my officers," he went on. "I look for good officers and gentlemen, one 'scabby sheep' can spoil a ship. Above all no coarse manners, execrations, or abusive language. I have taken the liberty to make inquires about you—and everything I hear is to your advantage."

What could the other do but bow and thank the kind speaker?

The captain then continued that he should sail in a few days.

"You had better meet me on board at nine o'clock, when your commission can be read, and after that I beg you will consider yourself your own master for a few days, as I presume you have some little arrangements to make."

The young man bowed with a flush of pleasure.

"I am aware," continued the urbane captain, "that there are many little comforts which officers wish to attend to, such as fitting their cabins, and looking to their men, and other nameless things which tend to pass their time and break up the monotony of sea life."

"You are very good, sir," replied Alfred.

"Not at all," replied the captain graciously; "forty years have I trod the planks, man and boy, and not with any great success, as you may perceive by the rank I now hold, for I here sit over a humble glass of grog instead of joining my brother captains in their claret at the Crown."

Alfred could only bow.

"I have sisters to keep——" he went on. "But never mind. To-morrow at nine o'clock."

Alfred went back to his inn thinking how fortunate he was in having such an honest, straightforward, bold British tar of a captain.

He then ordered dinner at the George, and afterwards strolled out to make his purchases, and give a few orders for a few articles for sea service.

He then fell in with some old messmates, who congratulated him on his promotion, and insisted he should wet his commission by giving a dinner.

This he did.

At seven o'clock next morning he went down to breakfast in a speck and span new uniform, with an immensely large epaulette stuck on the right shoulder.

Presently he sallied forth, in his own conceit, as handsome a chap as ever buckled a sword belt.

He skimmed with a light and joyous foot down High-street, and on reaching New Sally Port was hailed, but made no answer until he came to the point.

"Where to, sir?" asked the waterman, as soon as Alfred had secured a boat.

"Brig Digby," he answered.

The waterman simply heaved a sigh and said not a word, at which Alfred was rather pleased than not. He preferred his own thoughts to anything else at that moment.

The brig proved to be a beautiful vessel. She mounted, as we know, eighteen guns.

Alfred's astonishment was great when he found the pennant was up for punishment.

Of course he took it for granted that some aggravated offence, such as mutiny, had been committed.

Seeing Alfred was an officer, he was at once admitted alongside.

So he paid the waterman, who went away.

As Alfred went up the side he saw a poor fellow spread-eagled up to the gratings, while the captain, officers, and ship's company stood round witnessing the athletic dexterity of a boatswain's mate, who, by the even, deep, and parallel marks of the cat on the white back and shoulders of the patient seemed to be perfectly master of his business.

All this did not surprise the young lieutenant, but, after the mild conduct of his captain on the previous day, he was amazed to hear him using language in direct violation of the second article of war.

Execrations and curses pour out of his mouth with a volubility equal to that of the most accomplished Mott on the Point.

"Boatswain's mate," yelled the captain, "do your duty better, or by —— I'll have you up, give you four dozen, and then disrate you. One would think—your- you were flapping flies off a cat's back instead of flogging a scoundrel with a hide as thick as a buffalo's."

While the captain was delivering this elegant speech the victim had received four severe dozen, which the master-at-arms had counted out and reported duly to the captain.

The wretched creature turned his head over his shoulders with an imploring look, but it was utterly in vain.

Alfred all this time, appalled and horrified, watched the countenance of the captain, and the peculiar expression he had not been able to decipher at his first interview he now read most clearly—it was utterly malignant cruelty, and supreme delight in torturing his fellow-creatures.

He appeared to take a diabolical delight in the hateful operation which they were compelled to witness.

Now the second boatswain's mate* commenced operations with a fresh cat, and gave a lash across the back of the prisoner that made Lieut. Alfred start.

"One," said the master-at-arms, in a droning voice, beginning to count.

"One!" roared the infuriated captain. "Do you call that one? it's not a quarter of one. Hang you, you are only fit for a fly-flapper at a pork-shop. I'll disrate you, dang yer. Is that the way to handle a cat——?" and then losing all presence of mind in his blind fury, "I'd show you how how to do it—if I dared. Where's the boatswain?"

"Present," said a stout, gigantic, hulking ruffian, a left-handed fellow, who wore a blue uniform coat and a plain anchor button, holding his hat in his left hand, and stroking his hair down his forehead with his right.

"Give that fellow a dozen, sir," said Captain Gordon, "and if you favour him, I'll put you in irons and stop your liquor."

Tom Best was the boatswain's name, and singularly enough the last part of the threat with him was worse than the first.

He began, as the saying is, to peel. Off came his spacious coat and other garments followed. Then he rolled up his shirt sleeves above his elbow and showed an arm and a back very like the Farnese Hercules, which no doubt all our readers have seen at the foot of Somerset House.

The mild and elegant commentator on the articles of war, seized the cat.

The handle was two feet long, one inch and three quarters thick and covered with red baize.

The lashes of this terrible weapon were three feet long, nine in number.

Tom Best, whose scientific display in this part of his art had no doubt procured him his warrant as a boatswain, handled his cat as one who knew it well—looked at it from top to bottom, cleared all the tails combing them out with his fingers, stretched out his left leg, and measuring his distance with an accurate eye, raised his cat high in the air with his left hand, his right still holding the top of the tails as if to restrain their impatience, when, giving his arm and body a full swing, embracing three fourths of the circle, he inflicted a tremendous stroke on the back of the unfortunate culprit.

The captain nodded approbation.

The poor fellow lost his breath from the force of the blow, and the lash of the cat coming from an opposite direction to the first four dozen cut the flesh diamond-wise, bringing blood at every blow.

It is not necessary to harrow the reader's feelings by continuing to describe a scene now happily impossible.

When the sickening spectacle was over Alfred went up and touched his hat to the captain.

"Oh! you've come," he said; "pipe belay there—send everybody aft in the quarter deck."

Alfred's commission was then read, after which the captain ordered his gig to be manned and prepared to go on shore.

Remembering his promise the day before Alfred went up to him.

"You were kind enough, sir, yesterday to say I might spend a day or two on shore," he said, "with your permission."

"Shore, sir, he cried, "and who is to carry on the duty if you go on shore. Shore! no, sir, you've had enough. The service is going to the dogs now. No, sir, stay on board, or I'll break you like an egg-shell before you've taken the shine out of your brand-new epaulettes. Stay on board and do your duty."

The young officer mildly suggested that he had promised him leave; he retorted—

"Perhaps I did, but it was only to get you on board. I'm up to all your tricks—when you get on shore, there's no getting you on board again. No—now I've got you I'll keep you."

And turning his back he went over the other side with a malicious scowl on his face.

Alfred now took the opportunity of making acquaintance with the first lieutenant, who readily told him that the skipper was the most notorious tyrant and bully in the service.

"But keep your weather eye open," said the other, "and he can only annoy you."

And Alfred determined at once to look out for squalls.

Three days later they sailed for the West Indies.

Alfred seldom came into contact with his captain except on duty.

He was cold, distant, and respectful, and avoided all contact more than he could help.

They reached the Kingston, Jamaica, where they were to remain some time; and here, under the eye of the port-admiral, Captain Gordon had to be careful.

The officers got leave in turns, and availed themselves of it freely.

The first lieutenant, Arnold, introduced Alfred into several families.

Shortly after their arrival they were invited in common with most of the officers to a good ball.

Here Alfred danced with a young lady named Celestine, a Creole, a daughter of French parents, herself born at New Orleans

She was a very beautiful girl. Alfred had met her once or twice in society and been very much struck by her.

While dancing they came almost face to face with Captain Gordon.

Alfred saw a fearful scowl on his face.

The girl shivered.

"Are you not well, miss?" asked the young officer. "Will you rest?"

"Yes, it was only that horrid man," she answered. "I detest him. He persecuted me with his attentions a year ago, and when I refused him, threatened me awfully. Do you know him?"

"He is my captain," was the grave reply.

"I am sorry," she said.

And the subject dropped for the time.

"He is coming this way," she whispered presently in an agitated tone. "Secure the next dance; it is vacant. I can then refuse him."

Of course Alfred did not hesitate.

"Miss Laferl," said Captain Gordon, in his most urbane manner, "may I ask for the next dance?"

"My tablets are full," she answered putting her arm in that of Alfred as the music began.

"But this gentleman has just danced with you," he continued. "Surely he will resign you to me."

"I must decline the exchange," she answered, and drew Alfred away.

Captain Gordon stood petrified, quivering with rage.

But he was helpless.

He was not on his own quarter deck now.

Still he bided his time.

He would be revenged.

He, however, made no more advances to Celestine Laferl that evening.

This incident naturally made the young couple more intimate, and before they parted they were affianced.

Early next morning Alfred went on board and returned to his duty.

The captain took no notice of him.

At length came, in routine, his turn for going on shore.

He was refused in language more energetic than refined.

"You've had your answer, sir."

"I have, sir," retorted Alfred; "but it is unusual, sir, to alter the routine arrangements."

"Mutiny, by heaven!" cried the captain. "I stop your leave altogether."

"Then, sir, I shall write a letter to the admiral," said Alfred respectfully, "which I shall trouble you to forward."

"I shall not send it."

"You have said that publicly, sir," Alfred went on calmly, "in the presence of the officers and ship's company. I shall forward it myself, asking why my leave is stopped."

The captain, who was an arrant coward, at once toned down.

It was not his wish to have an official inquiry into the state of his ship.

He knew that officers and men would all testify against him.

He went below, and presently sending for the first lieutenant, bade him let the second have his usual leave.

"Be careful," said the first. "I never saw such a devil's gleam in a man's eye!"

Alfred went on shore and called on the parents of Celestine.

They were plain, simple people, thinking only of the happiness of their daughter.

Alfred asked for time, that is until he made his next step.

This was agreed to, and they were regularly affianced.

Celestine had a small fortune, which at the death of her parents would be doubled.

This important step settled, the young lieutenant asked the girl to show him something of the town.

It was a cool and pleasant day, and Celestine readily acquiesced.

Presently they passed an hotel, on the steps of which stood Captain Gordon and other officers of similar rank.

Alfred saluted, and the captain returned his salute with ironical politeness, at the same time nudging the man next to him, and saying something which aroused a roar of laughter.

Alfred's cheeks burned.

He knew the coward had said something derogatory to the girl he loved, but he was powerless.

Celestine had simply turned her head with indignant scorn when she saw the other.

"Has that man much power over you, Alfred?" she asked patiently.

"He can do nothing as long as I do my duty strictly," he answered.

"There is a snake look in his eye," she went on, "which makes me shudder. If he can do you an injury he will."

"I fear him not," was the answer.

They spent some happy hours together.

Alfred returned and dined with the parents.

He spent several pleasant hours, and then, fearing to outstay his welcome, left.

Strolling about, he entered an hotel where there was a large billiard-room, much frequented by the officers of the fleet.

The first lieutenant was there, and with him Alfred shook hands.

The captain was playing at a neighbouring table. He was very excited, evidently from drink.

When he saw Alfred he chuckled, and said loud enough for everyone to hear—

"What flats young fellows are to be picked up by a Creole girl. I never knew one worth having by a respectable man."

"Liar!" exclaimed Alfred, mad with rage and passion, drawing his dirk and stabbing him.

He then, in the confusion, fled.

The night air partially restored his senses.

Recovering his coolness, he obtained a boat, went on board, secured his money and plain clothes, and again went on shore.

Ere daybreak he was on board an American vessel bound for Galveston, in Texas.

"I was reckless," he continued. "I was reckless and desperate. I joined a slaver, and so on from bad to worse.

"I did lose the girl, and her loss turned my heart to stone. Then I committed another desperate crime, and was sent to prison. From there I escaped.

"I am an outlaw, and I have been a wanderer ever since.

"He did not die," said Charles Warner, "but expecting death he exonerated you in every way. You might have got off with light punishment."

"But, my boy," replied Zeph, whose real name we need not give, "all that is ancient history. I have become a wild man; everyone's hand is against me, as mine is against everybody's. Forget me; never say to any that we have met. I could not if I wished it return to society."

"You will think better of it, Uncle Alfred," continued the warm-hearted young man. "There are other careers open to you besides the navy. In some obscure country retreat you might outlive all this."

"No, my choice is made," hoarsely cried Zeph. "I am not sorry we have met, because it shows me there is some good in this world."

And he would talk no more of himself, but asked questions of others, of those he had known in happier days.

The cutter had not entered the port and an hour after the meeting was over was again upon the high seas on her way to New Zealand.

After a prosperous voyage they reached a small and insignificant port on the Australian coast.

Here they agreed to remain a few days to take in water and fresh provisions.

But the great question now arose as to what was best to be done.

Kelly was tired of the sea. He was eager for shore once more.

Their plunder fairly divided would give them a good start.

But what about the vessel?

Could anything be done to retain it as a last resource in case of future complications?

Zeph thought not.

There was no place where it could by any possibility be secured.

Besides, its discovery would compromise them.

Their return would be known.

"What's your game, then?" asked Kelly.

"Scuttle her and land in boats," was the answer, and as there was no better thing to be done, Kelly sulkily agreed.

After a few days' rest and recreation, that is of orgies in sailors' drinking saloons, it was agreed to start next day.

Zeph and Kelly had stayed on shore during the whole time, and kept aloof from the men.

They occupied rooms in a boarding-house, and here lived several clerks and others.

Few had cared to inquire who the two strangers were who spent their money so lavishly.

They paid their way and were quiet, which was all the landlady cared about.

At dinner two clerks were in conversation.

"Russell, up at the custom house, is in a fidget about the strange vessel," said one; "he strongly suspects her."

"In what way?" asked the other in a low tone, but quite audible to Kelly.

"Thinks she's the missing Snake," answered the other. "He has telegraphed to Hobart Town for a man-of-war."

"Good thing for Russell, if he's right," responded his companion; "lucky dog."

Kelly and Zeph exchanged glances. There appeared to be some good fortune on their side.

They went on with their dinner quietly; when it was concluded, sat as usual for a few moments.

Zeph, however, slipped out and had the luggage sent down to the boat.

An hour later the two men left.

"Mr. Bene," said Mrs. Jones, the landlady, when they were gone, to one of the speakers, "you've lost me two good lodgers—they've gone away in a huff."

"What do you mean?" asked Bene.

"Your talking about the ship in that way sent them off," she continued; "paid their bill, saying they were in a hurry."

"What do you mean?" cried the puzzled man. "I do not understand."

"That was I believe, the captain and first officer of the vessel yonder," she answered. "I watched them while you were speaking, and they exchanged queer looks."

"Oh, Lord!" cried the man. "What a fool I have been," and he rushed out.

He went at once to the customs, and from there he and the discomfited Mr. Russell had the satisfaction of seeing the White Eagle making seaward, with all sail set.

"Comes of jabbering," said Kelly, with a laugh, "might have jugged us up if they'd have held their tongues."

"Just so," remarked Zeph, who since the meeting with his nephew had been very much changed in manner. He was subdued, and appeared to have that strange feeling which sometimes prevades the human frame—that something is going to happen.

"Cheer up, old cockalorum," said Kelly; "a cup too low; take a stiff one," and he mixed him a very stiff one.

Zeph took it with a sigh then, and then another, and before an hour was over all his good resolutions were gone.

After a prosperous voyage they came within sight of Port Macquarie heads one dark night.

The boats were put out, and every man took his kit, which was necessarily restricted.

The carpenter and others had been at work. Holes had been bored in various places. As soon as all but three were on board the boats, the plugs were pulled up, and the water rushed in rapidly through the leaks.

Then away for the joys of shore.

CHAPTER CIX.

AT THE TREMONT.

The whole gang landed at Port Macquarie, and here the boats were subjected to the same treatment as the ship.

They then separated, making an appointment to meet at Kelly's old hut that day month, by which time probably they would find a city too hot to hold them.

The three inseparables, Kelly, Zeph, and Roe, found their way into Sydney, and went first to a rough sailor's boarding-house, where they hired rooms.

Here they sent for a hair-dresser, and had their frightful wigs and beards trimmed to more civilised dimensions.

They then sent for a ready-made clothier, and selected good but not too flashy clothes.

There remained some further disguise. To go to a theatrical costumier, if there had been such a thing in Sydney, would have excited suspicion.

But Jews and other fences are always in possession of such things to oblige their customers.

So the three, having got their boxes packed to be handed over to a porter, went out.

They easily found the man they wanted, who was a clever manipulator.

When they came out they not only had very fine heads of hair and beards, but their skins had been bronzed a little more than Nature had done it.

Kelly had recourse to his false nose only on rare occasions, but he always kept it about him.

Two vessels had come that day into harbour. They hired a truck, sent for their goods, and then ordering the man to follow them, went to the Tremont, where they intimated that they had not been comfortable at the Continental, and so had moved.

They were, of course, warmly received.

The Tremont, though, not a first-class hotel, was an expensive one. It was a good deal frequented by actors and other class, drawn by the gold fever.

Wherever there is money there will flock adventurers of both sexes.

The Tremont had several of these now, men of rank in their own country, but chevaliers d'industrie all the same. There were many of the opposite sex who called themselves by big names, and some were very fascinating.

The three men were determined to be very wary. It was useless to play the fine gentleman; but they could do the nouveau riche with ease.

After dinner Kelly induced Zeph to come into the reading-room, which at that hour was deserted. He got him to look over a file of the Melbourne Argus since the day of their departure.

There was enough and to spare about Kelly and his gang.

All that was known of their misdeeds in California and Tahiti was recorded.

Both the cruisers had been some days in Sydney, and they read the following in the papers:—

"It is not believed that the villains will venture back to the colony, so that we have doubtless seen the last of the detestable gang.

"The general idea is that they will run aground in some quiet cove, disperse, and spend their ill-gotten gains.

"The colony is well rid of the scoundrels, who will doubtless get hanged elsewhere."

Kelly laughed, and it was not a pleasant laugh to hear

"We'll show them a thing or two, I calk'late, as the Americans say," remarked Kelly; "oh—what's the matter —what makes yer so white about the gills?"

"Listen. Second edition:—

"'The Snake has been found in an almost sinking state She had evidently been imperfectly scuttled. She is being towed in, a powerful double gang working at the pumps.

"'Doubtless the nefarious crew is again amongst us, ready for new acts of villainy.'"

"That's a hoss of another colour," said Kelly, grimly; "we must look out for squalls. The cursed reward will set every gaping fool looking out for Ned Kelly."

"Just so," said Zeph, "but I ain't afraid of many, unless it be Tom Conquest. That fellow has got an eye to business."

"—— him!" hissed Kelly, in a ferocious tone. "He'd better not meddle too much with this cove. I mean to tree him yet."

"Be careful," continued Zeph. "Don't shove your hand in a wasps' nest."

"I'm no fool," blurted out Kelly. "Let's liquor, my boy, I'm thirsty."

Which it appears he always was.

They went now to the grand salon, where music, flirtation and cards appeared to be the great attraction.

There was another room supposed to be "strictly private," in which the game they so well remembered as having learned at Homburg, baccarat was played.

They strolled in, determined to try their luck.

Imagine their astonishment when, in the head croupier, they recognised Count Anatole.

They resolved, however, to keep themselves incognito for the present.

They played with varying luck, not much either way, until the croupier was replaced by another.

Then Kelly followed him, and tapping him on the shoulder, whispered a few words.

"Count Anatole," he said, "have you forgotten our little job at Homburg?"

"Mortbleu!" replied the other, with a frightened look round the room. "What does you mean, sare?"

"Don't you remember me, and our meeting at the Little Rag in London?" answered Kelly.

"Oui, yes—ah! my friend—I lose all again—my moneys zay go like what you call von o'clock," he said, with his old, inimitable shrug; "and zare is noting for me but to come out yar."

" How d'ye do here ?"

" Pretty bad. I have noting to begin vith," he sighed. "If I had ze moneys I start von roulette table, and make my fortune."

" How many chips do you want ?"

" Just a few hundreds," was the answer.

"I'll find the tin if you'll go halves," replied Kelly. " I've shoved some ochre in the bank."

" Victoire !" cried Count Anatole.

" Let's sup by ourselves," said Kelly.

The Frenchman at once acquiesced, and went to secure a private room.

The meeting was a jolly one indeed. The rascals grinned and roared over the memory of their misdeeds.

They roared, chuckled, and laughed until at last they were actually tired.

Then over a bowl of punch they talked business.

All that was necessary was to have a suite of furnished rooms, which could be done with ease, as Kelly, as Mr. Fellowes, had a banker's account.

The count knew where to get a roulette table.

Then cards of invitation would be printed, as the affair was to be select and private.

All that much money was wanted for was to provide for a run against the table.

"Dere is no such ting as lose," said the count confidently.

Another bowl of punch, and then the quartette of conspirators separated.

It was rare fun.

Not that Kelly meant to keep it up long.

It might serve to hoodwink the police for some time, but finally might attract attention.

Occasionally these private hells were treated with scant ceremony.

But Ned Kelly insisted that all at first should be fair, square, and above board.

The count promised.

Next day they easily found what they wanted.

A gentleman had left his apartment vacant for three months while he went to the diggings.

All was at once settled, the place was taken, and the cards printed.

The count wanted it to be " Mr. and Madame Fellowes present their compliments," offering to find a very eligible Mrs. Fellowes at a moment's notice.

But Kelly declined.

It was his policy never to trust a woman. His disguise would be then at the mercy of one of the frail sex.

Count Anatole resigned his position at the hotel—of course, it was only during the height of the gold-fever that this anomalous state of things existed—and went round to several haunts frequented by professional and other gamblers.

The programme was seductive. A select dinner party, followed by a game of chance.

The apartments were extensive, and, by the aid of an hotel, they contrived to dine forty.

They were an odd assembly. There were newly-arrived miners, wool merchants, roués, foreign and native adventurers. There were a few pigeons, but a great many more rooks.

But the game was fair.

Kelly and his companions played for the excitement of the thing. It mattered not to them who were winners or who were losers.

As Kelly sat down he found himself next to a very handsome woman.

She was rather masculine, slight, and had a moustache, such as is commonly the case with Frenchwomen.

But she had fine eyes, full and handsome mouth, and an expression that was bewitching.

She fixed her eyes on Kelly with a look of bold admiration.

" You are English, sir," she said with the slightest accent in the world. She had lived nearly all her life in England.

" Yes," responded Kelly, colouring.

This style of woman was rather a novelty to him.

" I may say that, though I was born in the colony."

" Wonderful place," she went on, taking an admiring glance at the herculean proportions of Kelly.

French women, as a rule, admire brute strength far more than regularity and delicacy of features.

" It is," responded Kelly.

And then the game began, which slightly checked the conversation.

But the Frenchwoman contrived to keep the ball rolling.

She talked between the events, and leaned towards Kelly in a most seductive manner.

She wore an evening dress, exposing to view very fine shoulders.

Kelly began to return her admiring glances. She only smiled all the more.

And this lasted all the evening.

During the course of conversation he found that her name was Madame la Comtesse de Paradis, and that she lived at the Tremont.

" We shall meet again," he said in a fervent tone that to anyone else would have been ludicrous.

" You will sup with me this evening ?" she said with a fascinating smile.

" I had promised one of my p—friends, I mean," he answered.

" Bring your friends. The Count Anatole will come too."

Kelly, of course, could not refuse, and so the evening ended.

It would not do to keep it up too late.

It would excite the suspicions of the neighbours and of the police, and Kelly had no desire to have dealings with the latter.

Madame la Comtesse de Paradis had a small carriage waiting, and in this she returned to the hotel, Kelly accompanying her.

He had not been used to this sort of thing—a fashionable carriage and a pretty woman.

Kelly felt like a fish out of water.

He was very pleased, but he was conscious of a difficulty in keeping up conversation.

But the countess, really a governess discharged for misconduct, did the talking.

Since her disgrace she had lived in certain demi-monde circles, where a varnish is acquired, a little too much for Kelly.

He was bewildered.

On reaching the hotel, they at once adjourned to the rooms occupied by the countess.

She had sent to her dame de compagnie to have a luxurious supper ready.

Madame la Comtesse had only been in the colony four months, and she had made a victim or two.

She was irresistible, and, like another Danäe, was wooed in showers of gold.

Her jewel-box was a wonder.

And yet nothing could be substantiated against her.

She could not help people loving her.

Her secret life, at all events, was well kept. It might be shady indeed, but no one knew anything.

To Kelly the reception in the Frenchw n's rooms was simply a revelation.

Covers were laid for eight.

Kelly, Salmon Roe, Zeph, and the Count Anatole were the men ; the Countess de Paradis, her dame de compagnie, and two bright-eyed French girls were the females.

The repast was exquisite.

The viands and the wines were simply perfection itself, and the champagne lovely.

At the Tremont there were no tricks upon travellers, it was real and genuine.

Kelly was in the seventh heaven of delight.

Next day, when in the seclusion of his own chamber, r

reflected rather grimly on the evening before, or rather, morning

He had made Madame la Comtesse—she called herself Hortense—promises of presents.

He smiled grimly. Well, it couldn't last, and he need not be too extravagant.

There was a mean corner in Kelly's soul.

He went out after breakfast and purchased a rather handsome pair of bracelets.

They particularly attracted Kelly's attention, and though they were more expensive than he intended he did not retract.

He returned to the hotel, and shortly after presented himself at the entrance of the apartments allotted to Madame la Comtesse.

He was at once admitted.

The countess lay in a very studied déshabillé on a couch. Kelly approached, trying to seem at ease, and to do the grand.

But he was so utterly *gauche* and awkward that Hortense very nearly laughed in his face.

But she had a very powerful command of countenance, and smiled.

After a very few words Kelly produced his present.

"I've taken the extreme liberty, Countess, to bring this trifle to offer you," he began.

"*Magnifique!*" she cried, as she matched the bracelets—she knew the value to a penny—"Oh how kind of you."

"Highly pleased," retorted Kelly. "Ain't much judge of jimcracks, but thems right."

"Lovely," answered the woman, and beckoned him to her side.

The ironclad bushranger was completely at her feet. A vulgar Antony utterly prostrate before an equally vulgar Cleopatra.

After a stay of some duration he joined his comrades.

The *coup* of the night before had been a good one, and Kelly saw his way clear to extending instead of decreasing his capital.

That night was but a repetition of the night before, only Kelly paid the expenses of the luxurious supper.

Then there was a run against the bank. A lucky speculator broke it one night.

Ned Kelly was furious.

"This will not do," he said to the count, "we shall be ruined."

"*Certainement oui!*" cried the Frenchman, with his usual shrug.

Ned Kelly had been thinking deeply. At last he propounded a plan.

His proposal was to extend their operations. The count would remain in charge of the tables, while Kelly, Zeph, and Salmon Roe would play elsewhere.

But first they must carry out a desperate undertaking. They would buy up every pack of cards in Sydney.

That very day this was done, and for hours the four arch fiends were engaged in marking them.

They were then deftly put together.

Meanwhile, there was a rush for cards all over the city.

Then Zeph made his appearance in one of the stationers' shops and announced that he had a job lot to sell cheap.

The shopkeeper was too glad to close with his offer and the transaction was concluded.

Next day, Zeph and Kelly went to a private room where introductions were regained.

They were taken in by Senor Mendez, the lucky schemer who had broken their bank.

They seated themselves, and found that the cards were those which they had cleverly and secretly manipulated.

Mendez was not at first in a humour to play, but presently he began.

The stakes were not very high, but you could win a good bit of money.

Kelly began to show a large pile. It increased at every stroke.

Mendez left off playing and seated himself behind Kelly.

"*Demonio!*" he suddenly cried, "you are a cheat These cards are marked."

There was awful confusion.

Mendez had seized the cards and pointed out slight marks invisible to any but a keen eye.

The confusion was awful, but no one thought of examining the other cards.

"You are a liar," said Kelly; "and if they are marked I did not know it."

"*Sangre de dios!*" roared Mendez, "I like that. Refund the money, or——"

Kelly rose and faced his antagonist.

"You're an infernal scoundrel," he said, "but it's ten to one on you and your pals. I'll never enter your cheating den again."

And he went out, leaving his gold on the table. But he had a large portion of his winnings in his pocket.

No one in the room cared about exposure, so no attempt was made to stay them.

They were not in one of those saloons where bowie knives and pistols decided quarrels.

"That plot's stumped," he said, when they were outside.

"He'll blow the gaff!" said Zeph.

"Not he," answered Kelly. "He's up to snuff himself. But oughtn't I to call him out?"

Zeph laughed.

"Not unless you could get him in the bush," he continued. "Those dons are toppers at shooting."

"Ain't I a shot?" asked Kelly indignantly.

"Well, if you like a bullet in your carcase," quietly remarked Zeph.

"I'll have my rights, mate," insisted Kelly with pigheaded obstinacy.

"All serene," laughed Zeph.

And so it was settled that he should next day call on Mendez and demand satisfaction.

Zeph tried next day to alter his determination, but Kelly was obstinate.

One of his savage fits was on him, and he would not be advised

"You'll be sorry," said Zeph.

"—— me if I care," insisted Kelly. "If he turns tail, I'll shoot him in the streets."

Zeph went to the hotel where Senor Mendez was residing, and sent up a card he had written as a stationer's.

It had on it his real name and rank.

He was courteously received, though the Spaniard looked rather cool.

Zeph told his story, which the Spaniard listened to with nonchalance.

He spoke English perfectly, though with a slight accent.

"Tell your friend that he is a low blackleg and thief," was the cool reply. "If I hear from him again, *I will hand him over to the police!* Good morning."

And he bowed the astonished Zeph out of the room. He was dumbfounded.

The rage of Kelly was as fierce as it was impotent.

The threat of the police completely humbled him.

"I'll be even with the beggar yet," he growled, with sundry savage oaths.

But Mendez was careful not to throw himself in his way, and soon after sailed for Havana, in Cuba, there to pursue his varied fortunes.

Would they ever meet again? That only time could show.

Kelly, with dogged obstinacy, would have liked to follow him, but he had other matters to attend to.

"If ever I meet that sneak and coward again," he said, "I'll make cold meat of him."

"All right," replied Zeph. "Good riddance of bad rubbish."

Kelly muttered something, but he was in no humour to quarrel with Zeph, so he changed the subject.

Their stay in Sydney was getting protracted, and might prove dangerous.

Still Kelly was not prepared to leave at once. The countess held him in her thrall.

One morning after breakfast Kelly was taking an early walk. The kind of life he was leading was making him fat.

This would not do at all, as he might at any time have to return to the bush.

He was sauntering along when he gave a sudden start.

It was not surprising that his heart gave a great bound. He had recognised one whom he cared for more than any human being.

A mounted policeman was passing, and he rode Marco Polo.

Marco Polo, a horse which performed exploits quite equal to anything done by Black Bess.

Lest our readers should think we are romancing, we refer them to the (London) *Telegraph* of the 7th July, 1881:

"It is well known in England that for many years the province of Victoria was the scene of unparalleled outrages committed by the most lawless and desperate gang of ruffians that ever attacked a gold escort on its road from 'the diggings' to Melbourne, or 'stuck up' a bank in some lonely little town on the edge of the bush. At the head of these desperadoes, the 'ironclad bushranger,' Ned Kelly, had made himself notorious and formidable by a series of such crimes as appear to be wholly incompatible with the much-vaunted civilisation of the nineteenth century in the last quarter of its existence. In contemplating, however, the atrocities with which we have lately been familiarised in every quarter of the globe, we are tempted to ask with a melancholy American querist, 'Is the Caucasian played out?' Given such opportunities as the wild and tangled fastnesses of the Wombat and Strathbogie ranges in Victoria afford, it seems but too probable that the 'Kelly gang' or other similar associations of fearful marauders will from time to time cause their names to be mentioned with terror even at the other end of the earth. Australia is a land of natural horsemen, and Ned Kelly's celebrated steed, Marco Polo, is as well-known at the Antipodes as Dick Turpin's Black Bess is in these islands. It was not unnatural that, when month after month passed without the arrest of Ned Kelly and his three daring associates, upon whose heads a reward of two thousand pounds each had been set, murmurs of complaint should have been heard in Melbourne against Captain Standish's management of the force under his command. The remonstrants, however, captious from terror, little knew the character of the country in which the bushrangers had established themselves, and where for years they were as safe as runaway negroes who in the slavery days had sought shelter in the Dismal Swamp of Virginia, or in the cane-brake of Alabama."

Kelly then stood still and watched him.

The horse was in magnificent condition.

Kelly stepped up.

The policeman was quite a young man.

"Fine animal that, my man," he said, feeling his shoulder. "Splendid creature."

"You may say that," replied the other, with an Irish accent. "It's a beautiful baste."

"It is," replied the bushranger. "Will you quench?" pointing to a drinking-saloon.

It was a quiet neighbourhood, and the trooper had no objection.

A boy held the horse.

They entered the shop.

"Seems strange such a beauty should be in the police," observed Kelly. "No offence."

"Shure an' it's like this," continued the man. "The baste belonged to that thief of the world, Ned Kelly; and Captain Tom Conquest, when he grabbed the animal, swore he'd keep him."

"Oh, that's it?" replied Kelly. "Well, all I can say is, I hope he may keep her."

"Maybe not," continued the open-spoken young policeman, "as it's said that that eternal rapparee, Kelly, is about again."

"The devil he is?" cried Kelly.

"Yes, and Captain Tom, he's after him. Shure, and he'll get him after all," the man said, "and then won't we all have a beautiful "wake" over his body"

"I hope you may," said Kelly, with a queer expression which the young trooper afterwards remembered.

Now, Kelly had a new ambition in his heart, and that was to recover Marco.

"Do you often ride this here horse?" asked Kelly, as he finished.

"Every morning, sir, I pass this way," the man answered, with a wink at the public-house.

"All right," said Kelly, "I'll have another squint at the critter to-morrow."

And so he went away.

That he would have the horse he was determined; but it must be only at the last pinch.

It was nearer than he expected.

The usual evening occurred.

The table was in luck this time, and Kelly revelled in the delights of winning.

He was in the seventh heaven of delight.

Madame la Comtesse was kind and gracious in the extreme.

Kelly could go into her room whenever he liked.

No need for knocking at the door.

He seldom went of a morning.

But next day, intending to ask her to go for a drive in a buggy, he went up to her rooms, and entered unannounced.

He was in the vestibule.

He heard voices—the voices of Madame la Comtesse and Tom Conquest.

"I tell you, sir, that the man who makes me presents, who is in love with me, is the robber Kelly," said Madame, la Comtesse. "I cannot tell you how I know—but I do know. How about the reward?"

"Half to you, the other half to me," replied Conquest, "but I can hardly think it possible."

"You wait; if he is in the house he shall come here."

Kelly at once started, and met Zeph as he went downstairs.

"Tom Conquest is in the house; that infernal Delilah has betrayed us," he said. "Your purse—meet me at the old Oak Ridge.

"All right," replied Zeph.

Kelly wasted no time. It was about the hour to meet the young Irish policeman.

He started off, and after waiting a few minutes saw the man coming.

He touched his hat.

Kelly patted the horse, which at once neighed in a peculiar way.

"Horse seems to know you."

"Animals always like me," was the retort.

And he invited the policeman to drink. Nothing loth, he not being on duty but only exercising the horse, accepted.

Kelly paid a boy to take care of the horse.

"Walk him up and down and keep him cool," he said; "feed of corn—bait him?" he asked of the policeman.

"No," said the Irishman.

And they went in. Kelly now proposed a lunch such as is taken in the colonies.

A big dinner in England.

There were all sorts of delicacies, and a bottle of whisky, the whole laid in front of the bar.

Ned Kelly presently filled the police-officer's glass again, and the genial Irishman continued the conversation. He was as communicative as most of his countrymen.

"Of course you take care of the beauty at night?" remarked the bushranger.

"As a mother does of her first baby, my jewel. Sorrow, one of us has half the dressing, and feedin', an' coaxin' of that dumb baste. Bedad, he's almost a Christian already, only he's too 'cute to spake—I believe he could if he chose."

"Well, what would he say if he could 'spake,' as you call it?"

"Why, avourneen, he'd just say to you, 'Pat Logan's mighty dry about the throat.'"

"Oh, I see," said Kelly. "Come in then and have a liquor. But where is this wonderful 'hair trunk' your talking about?"

"Snug as Father Murphy's cat forenenst the fire on a winter's night Sure, he's up to his nose in straw in the stables behind the Station."

Kelly had heard all he wanted.

After a final drink, he and the garrulous officer parted.

Kelly retired to an obscure part of the town, where he easily found a hiding place until night came on, when he procured the costume of a superior class of digger, which he donned, and sold the other dress.

Then he got another man to write a letter addressed to Captain Zeph, under an assumed name, with these simple words inside—

"Ware hawks. Sold by the Count Wagga-Wagga."

This he posted, satisfied that Tom Conquest would not betray his knowledge until his presumed return to the hotel.

It was midnight when he left the place of shelter he had selected.

He had no luggage. A brace of pistols, a knife, and an ample supply of money was all he carried.

The police-station was in rather a conspicuous position, but the compound in which the stables were erected overlooked a small open space surrounded by outhouses.

All was silent and deserted, but the wall was ten feet high.

How to get inside, and then with Marco Polo get outside again, was a difficulty not easily overcome.

But the ruffian was fertile of resources, and unscrupulous in his carrying them out.

He resolved to scale the wall, and thus he did it.

He had a rope with him, and at the end of it was a powerful iron hook.

This he threw up and fastened on the top of the wall.

Once fixed on or in the brick-work, he soon pulled himself up to a level with the hook, which was easily done, as the rope, being knotted throughout, afforded foot and hand hold.

Once on the top, he silently descended, but was awfully disgusted when, creeping up to the stables where Marco, the "friend of his youth," was "in clover," he saw a trooper asleep on the ground at the door of the stable!

What was he to do?

He never could lead Marco out without awaking the sleeper.

And no time was to be lost, as daylight in these latitudes comes, as the song says, "so early in the morning," namely, about three o'clock.

Well, now or never something must be done.

So, quietly, he first inspected the gateway, which was, with the carelessness of colonial discipline, unbarred.

Seeing this, he softly entered the stable.

The beast turned his head, and appeared by his movements to recognise his old master, as he gently whinnied.

But as the stable was almost in darkness, he could not have seen Kelly

So some other sense must have led him to prick forward his ears, and, as Kelly subsequently said when recounting the matter, rubbed his nose and head against Kelly's hand as gently as a favourite Tom-cat.

Putting a bridle on Marco, and adding thereto a saddle, he loosened the horse from the stall and turned his head towards the door.

Kelly then deliberately lit a match, set fire to the straw in the neighbouring stables, and saw the whole place in a blaze before five minutes had elapsed.

Immediately the inmates of the station were rushing about the place, when confusion reigned supreme, and fright almost paralysed everyone.

The troopers rushed to save the horses.

Kelly made himself very busy as a "help," and in the tumultuous confusion led his friend Marco in o the open.

He was quickly on his back, and as quickly out of sight.

He had made up his mind that the police should have no clue whatever to the route he had taken.

He would pass through no inhabited districts, keeping wholly to the Bush, and trusting for food to shepherds and stockkeepers, who were only too glad to harbour the popular freebooter.

He certainly did not want to tire his horse, as there might be occasions when he would have to depend upon his pluck and endurance.

Kelly always had his wits about him, as, unlike most of his kind, he never drank when on the "road," or when he had any little game on hand.

A long night's ride tired both man and horse, so he resolved at the first quiet spot to pull up and give himself a "coil" as he called it, and Marco a feed of grass, of which there was plenty about.

Just as he mounted the top of a hill and daylight had fairly broken, he saw a small volume of smoke quietly ascending.

"Hullo!" he mentally cried, "there's breakfast there, and I'm going to have some, and chance it."

He grasped a pistol in his right hand, and rode as bold as brass up to the spot indicated.

Here he saw four men, Squatters, sitting round a large fire, frying chops and preparing the morning's meal.

Seeing the men were gentlemen Squatters, he knew he would be hospitably received, but he was so cautious that though he dismounted to partake of the breakfast offered him, he kept tight hold of the bridle.

His searching glance also revealed to him that there were no firearms about. Indeed, travellers very rarely carried them, as the blacks were harmless, and people seldom carried on their persons anything worth robbing.

After having refreshed himself Kelly thought of Marco. So he bid his entertainers a bluff good-bye, and when out of sight shunted off into the bend of the nearest belt of timber, where he lay down, but not to sleep.

He hobbled Marco, who was soon filling himself with the nutritious grass that was half-way up to his fetlock joints, and watched him feeding.

Here he stopped all day, as he feared an officer in every bush."

It was not known he had "cleared out" from the police stables with Marco, who in the great excitement and terror of the fire was not missed, and, even when so missed, it was supposed had simply got out of his stable in the midst of the general confusion and was, no doubt, quietly grazing within a mile or two of the station.

It was expected that Marco would be found in the next Pound, but, as day after day went by, and no news of the "Government" horse turned up, the matter passed out of the public mind, excepting that the mention in the advertisement of the missing horse having once belonged to the notorious Ned Kelly made it certain that the animal (whose description was given in full) would be recognised if ever seen, the more especially as he had a white star in the centre of his forehead.

When thoroughly refreshed Kelly remounted to pursue his path, which was a long one indeed.

He was making for the colony of Victoria, six hundred miles distant, and prudently avoided the beaten track, as he felt his own company would be about the safest he could indulge in at present.

It was tiresome work, from daylight to sundown, jog, jog, jog, about five miles an hour, startling an occasional long black snake basking in the sun, or putting to flight myriads of white cockatoos, who congregate in thousands, and, when disturbed, make a screaming, jabbering tumult, boisterous enough to wake the dead before their time.

Ned did not feel his own company on reflection, very enlivening.

Reflection was "not in his line." He panted for action —but not the action of a six-hundred-mile ride through bush with houtebted or board.

The latter he got at out-station huts, the former à la belle étoile—Anglicè, under the sky, the superb climate rendering this sort of " beading-out " not disagreeable.

For two days neither man nor beast had tasted food or water.

Ned had lost the track, and in taking a " short cut " had made the usual mistake in such cases.

Towards the third sundown he approached a deep ravine called the Great Sydney Pass.

Still no sign of water, and he listened in vain for " the honest watch-dog's bark."

The bark of the shepherds' dogs when the sheep come homewards is often, in this still-aired climate, heard a mile or so off.

For the first time Ned began to feel that he was in a predicament.

The great pass or gully seemed to be " the Great Divide " between him and the living world.

Hungry, thirsty and fatigued, he was dispirited. The ravine was two hundred feet deep, and, in the exhausted condition of Marco Polo he was afraid the noble animal must succumb at last. The white foam already fell in flakes from his parched mouth ; nevertheless he carried his burden stoutly and willingly.

Both had just turned a bend in the path of descent, when Kelly's quick sight detected a form stretched upon the grass.

Fearing treachery he pulled up. Then, cautiously approaching, he beheld the dead body of a man, who had evidently been lost in the bush, and perished for the want of food or water.

By his side Kelly found a small leathern pocket filled with rough gold, which he speedily transferred to his own pocket.

Here he beheld the picture of what his own fate might be—one by no means uncommon in Australia.

Hurrying out of sight of the corpse he managed to cross to the opposite side of the pass. It was all he could do.

Marco began to show signs of giving in. This perplexed Ned.

What would he do without the gallant steed? If he could have lived on the blood of the animal he would no doubt have made a repast on it—but after!

Thoroughly beaten by fatigue, hunger, and thirst, as well as the awful prospect of death by starvation, he jumped off the back of the poor beast and exclaimed—

" The game's up Ned! pay your stake like a man, and don't flinch. Well if I must go, that's no reason Marco should suffer too. He's done his best, poor devil! One of us shall have a chance for life: so here goes, old fellow, the best, if not the only friend I ever had."

So saying, with a sigh, he took off the saddle and bridle, and turned Marco " loose " for his life.

He lay down himself, and listlessly looked up into a sky that has not its rival for beauty and splendour.

What his thoughts were God knows, but before he was long in the clouds he heard a whinny, then a second, and springing to his feet, saw Marco, not twenty yards distant, with his nose thrust under a lot of reeds.

He knew at once what it was.

Marco had found water, foul and stagnant perhaps' but nectar to him and his master.

Both drank as only the parched with thirst do drink To Kelly, whose lips, palate, and throat were as dry as hot iron, the liquid seemed delicious.

He recognised in it the breath of life, his resurrection from the grave, and absolutely embraced Marco, who was too busily engaged in having his fill to show any recognition of his master's affection.

No wretch reprieved from the gallows felt more rejoiced. He had escaped a dreadful fate and a lingering one.

He remembered the body he had just left, and from which a carrion crow lazily rose as he came in view, showing clearly the unholy repast he had been making.

" Ned's himself again," he soliloquised, attributing his deliverance to no higher influence than chance.

After resting until daybreak he remounted his resuscitated horse and pursued his way towards the township of Wagga-Wagga, which was in his route, and where he was totally unknown.

Yes, at grey dawn, he was in the saddle once more, having by a miracle escaped a fate he shuddered to think of.

That lone corpse in the forest haunted his imagination.

He was rather faint and exhausted, but his horse was thoroughly refreshed, and that was the great point for him.

On the springy, ever-verdant turf Marco went along easily and almost gaily.

He soon discovered at some distance a man looking after a huge flock of sheep, and rode up to him.

" Well, mate," said Ned. " I'm just the chap as has rid through the Great Sydney Pass, without no grub or water. Can you help a lame dog over a stile ?"

" All right," the man replied, laughing, " you're welcome to what I've got, and that ain't wild duck and champagne, you know. There's the hut about half-a-mile off. I'll leave my colley with the flock and go along with you."

Ned Kelly was too tired to talk, so he followed the shepherd, who had built his hut in a sheltered spot, near a small spring.

He had, as usual, nothing but tea, but the restorative effect of this beverage is well known. For this purpose it beats alcohol " all to pieces.'

However, there was an inn no great distance off, which Kelly intended to visit, and to reconnoitre before doing so.

(To be continued.)

THE " ANONYMA " SERIES OF POPULAR NOVELS.
PICTURE BOARDS.   PUBLISHED AT 2/-

NED KELLY
THE
IRONCLAD
AUSTRALIAN BUSHRANGER

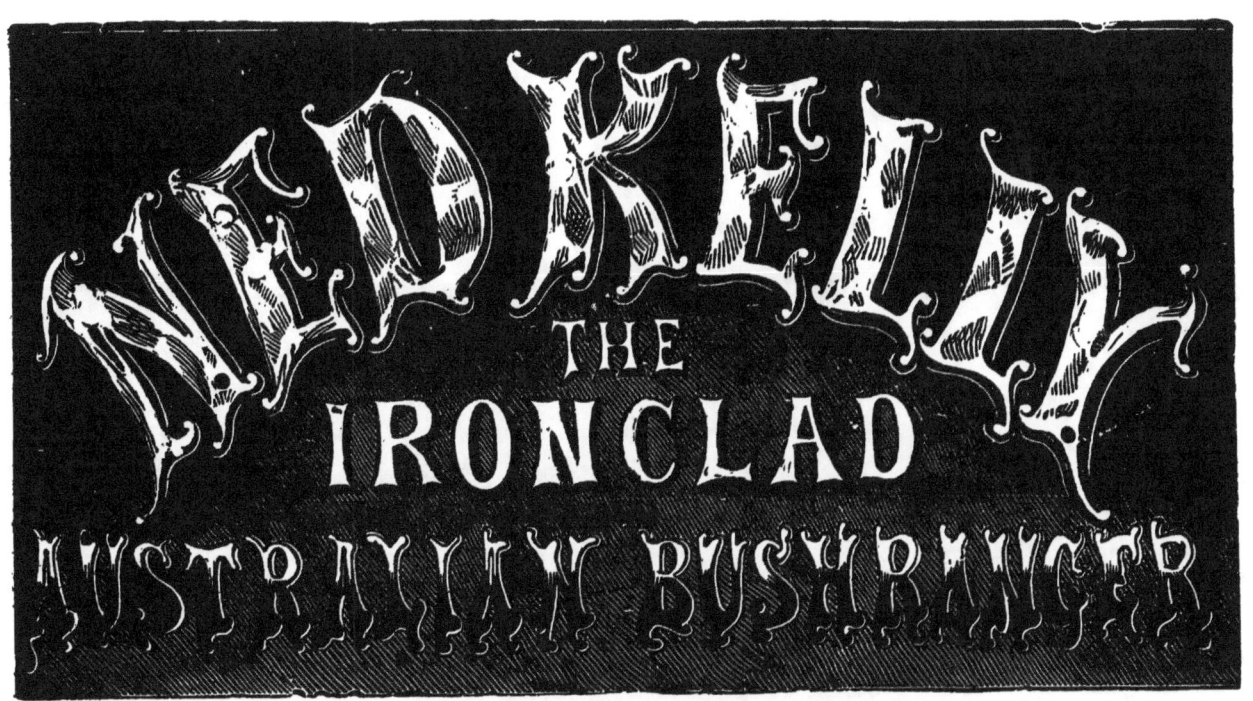

NO 18,

NED KELLY: IRONCLAD BUSHRANGER.

well known that for many years Ned Kelly had made himself notorious by a series of crimes wholly incompatible with the civilisation of the nineteenth century. Ned Kelly's celebrated steed, Marco Polo, is as well known at the Antipodes as Dick Turpin's Black Bess in these islands." *Ned Kelly*, illustrated, Nos. 1 to 11, already published at 44, Essex-street, Strand, price One Penny.—*Telegraph*, 7th July, 1881.

"It is notorious that the robbery of Mr. Steward's corpse was mainly performed by the assistance of NED KELLY'S BROTHER, the Captain of what was neither more nor less than a pirate ship."—*Times*, July.

"The history of NED KELLY and his celebrated black horse, Marco Polo, will ever live in the recollections of the Australian public. The deeds of Dick Turpin, and the performances of Black Bess, are tame beside those of 'NED AND HIS NAG;' in addition to which Ned's history is true, and Turpin's is pure fiction."—*Press*, July.

CHAPTER CIX.—*Continued.*

"What sort of a crib is the whisky-shop?" asked Ned Kelly.

"Roughish sort of den," replied the man; "but the liquor ain't bad. Swells don't patronise it much."

"Well, after our feed can you spare an hour to fetch some more 'straight tip'?" asked Ned, pulling out a sovereign. "I should like to rest my carcase till it's cool."

"All serene, my lad," said the man, as they sat down to a meal which though rough was indeed welcome.

Ned soon felt himself again, and. after lighting a pipe, lay down to sleep, while the shepherd started off to a general store where he could usually get anything he wanted.

These storekeepers are not allowed to sell spirits, otherwise every shepherd and stock-keeper in the vicinity for twenty miles round would be perpetually drunk, and the publicans lose the valuable custom of these men, who will "knock down" a year's wages in a week in drink.

The shepherd returned without anything but tobacco.

Kelly had given the man a sovereign, and refused the change.

After an hour's rest he was up and off.

His host regarded him earnestly, and. as he mounted Marco, said to himself—

"Ned Kelly, or I'm a duffer! He's one o' the right sort, too. I wonder where's the swell who would hand out a sovereign and not ask for change. I wish there was more Ned Kellys, I do."

And back to his sheep he slowly walked. the solitude of his life having been agreeably varied by his strange visitor.

"No business of mine," he muttered as he walked along.

CHAPTER CX.

KELLY'S INTERVIEW WITH THE CLAIMANT.

KELLY rode on without meeting any adventures of moment.

He met a few travellers, but none apparently he had any reason to dread.

Of course, unless Tom Conquest had some inkling of the course he had taken, he had little or nothing to fear from him.

He was far from Sydney—hundreds of miles away.

The moment Captain Zeph and Salmon Roe received his letter they would make themselves scarce.

His absenting himself for a night would excite no suspicion until the discovery was made of the loss of the horse.

So he pressed on, determined to enjoy himself in compensation for the hardships he had gone through.

Early one morning he found himself in a rather wild district of scrub.

Nothing was to be heard save the song of birds.

Suddenly there arose on the air a cry which no one can ever mistake, that of a horse in extreme pain.

Kelly looked in the direction, and his surprise was great when he came upon a scene which for a moment he was at a loss to understand.

A horse was tied to a tree, while a stout, heavy, ponderous man, with heavy cheeks, and a butcher's blue apron on, was standing beside him with a fryingpan, red hot, which he had just applied to the poor animal's flank.

The horse reared, plunged, and uttered a strange, shrill cry.

"What's up, mate?" asked Kelly.

"What's that to you? Can't a feller brand his hoss without having someone hasking himpertinent questions?" surlily replied the big man.

"Dry up, you darned fool. D'ye think I don't know your game?" said Kelly, laughing. "I'm up to your dodge. The frying-pan brand is as old as Adam."

It was a common one.

In the colony most horses bear the brand of the owner, and the first thing a thief does is to efface that compromising mark with the frying-pan.

The fat man looked knowingly at Kelly, and seemed to read him like a book.

"Well, it ain't your hoss, is it?" he asked, with a broad grin.

"Not likely," answered Kelly, "and not my business neither. Am I right for Wagga-Wagga?"

"Wagga-Wagga?" the other went on. "Yes; it's a good fifteen mile yet. You seem a right sort; won't you wet your blowpipe?"

And he threw his frying-pan in the direction of a thicket.

"Right you are," laughed Kelly, alighting and following his new acquaintance to where he found another powerful horse carefully tethered.

Looking at Kelly suspiciously, Orton (for it was that unscrupulous villain *in propria persona*,) said—

"I think I've heard of you before, mate, and of your black hair trunk, eh?"

Kelly's hand played with the handle of his pistol.

"Don't be gallied, lad." replied Orton; "I ain't likely to split."

"Look here, mate," said Kelly, "I'm not curious myself, and don't like those who are. I don't ask you whose horse you're nobbling, and so don't you ask me what you needn't know, but you may know this, that we may be able to work together, d'ye understand?"

"I'm fly," returned Orton. "You're one of my sort. Some has money and no brains, some has brains and no money. Now I'm one of the last flock, but I mean to have the money somehow, and I'm on a heavy lay just now."

"Blow your lay!" said Kelly, "I'm as dry as a hot wind. Is there ne'er a 'public' in this tarnation dry-looking desert?"

"Yes, at Wagga-Wagga, about five miles off."

"Then I'm on for Wagga-Wagga," said Kelly. "Not a big place, eh? Not too many police about?"

"Not one, just now," said Orton. "If there was I can square the lot. But, I say, just look here, mate, I'm fixed in that village, and mind, if I turn up, you've never seed me before, mind that."

"Mum as a dead man in a worked-out pit," said Ned.

Then receiving minute directions from his new acquaintance he rode off.

Such was the first meeting between Ned Kelly and Arthur Orton, which was to lead to such marvellous results.

After leaving his new comrade, the bushranger, who had no motive for haste, rode quietly along.

The day was warm, and with his pipe in his mouth Kelly rode along as quietly and contentedly as if he were a second Wilberforce.

Arrived at Wagga-Wagga, he beheld a small village with nothing remarkable about, except the extraordinary silence that reigned everywhere. One might almost hear the buzz of a bluebottle-fly from one end of the High-street to the other.

The butcher's shop was a conspicuous point, and its occupant equally so.

It very much resembled some newly-built English country village.

There were houses of various sizes, chiefly cottages, with verandahs; there was an iron church, a brick police-station, and the usual one-storied wooden shops.

The first inn he came to, the Wagga-Wagga Arms, was a rather straggling wooden-looking building, making up in extent for the want of height.

Towards this, by natural attraction, Ned Kelly gravitated.

Alighting, he took Marco himself to the stables and attended to him, saw him have a heavy feed of oats, and made snug.

He then sauntered into the bar.

After having secured a room and taken the dust out of his windpipe, he returned to the stable.

He was not a little astonished on entering to see his strange friend in close confab with the ostler.

His suspicions were aroused, but the first sentence he reassured him.

"Werry fine hanimal. He'd carry a mountain, and run away from Heclipse."

"Yes," said a voice behind him, "he's a rare one, and as good as he looks. You know something about horses?"

"Rather!" the other went on, "been used to 'osses halways. New chum, eh?"

They, as agreed upon, did not recognise each other.

"Yes," said Kelly, "green, very, as yet."

"You look jolly green, I must say," laughed Orton, until his fat sides shook like a plate of jelly. "You've just come from the old country, hain't you?"

"Landed a fortnight ago, and don't yet know nothing."

"Hinnocent as a hangel," said Orton, "and you look it. Well, come over to my diggins, and I'll show you the ropes of this here colony."

Kelly accepted the invitation, and followed his friend.

They went over to a butcher's shop, which the fat man entered with the air of the proprietor.

Over the door Kelly read—

"THOMAS CASTRO. Butcher."

On returning to the Wagga-Wagga Arms, Ned Kelly, who gave his name as Wilson, engaged a room and ordered dinner.

An hour later the fat butcher came in and asked for the guest.

The landlord pointed to a back room.

"Going for to try his palaver on him," said mine host with a grin, as he prepared a drink for the ponderous butcher.

Castro went across and seated himself in a huge arm-chair, which appeared to be cut out for him.

He gave a deep sigh as he seated himself.

"Prospecting," he asked, "like most folks? It's too 'ard work for me, and I oughtn't to work at nothing, as I'm soon going to get back my rights."

"Your rights? What's up?"

"I mean I'm a Barrownight in my own right, with lots of tin hanging to it, that I'm kept out of."

"Whew!" was the exclamation that came from Kelly's lips. "Drunk or mad, which, old man?"

"Neither one or the other, as I mean to prove. I've got all the hevidence cut and dry, and a lawyer free gratis to work the job."

This was before his fraudulent intentions were known or his game suspected.

He had lots of audacity, and was profoundly ignorant. This latter quality was subsequently construed by the shallow into "cleverness."

His cleverness was sheer bold lying, and the only "cleverness" he exhibited was in simply and calmly sticking to his falsehoods—the consequences were beyond the reach of his mind.

His whole career showed pigheaded stupidity.

Had he been a clever plotter he would never have given as the name of the captain of the Osprey that of the captain of the Jessie Miller, in which he originally went in 1862 to Tasmania, and years before the Osprey was heard of

How could Roger Tichborne have learned the name of the captain of the Jessie Miller?

However, he was so persistent, that Kelly began to think there might be something in it.

He had heard that someone in the colony had claimed to be a long-missing baronet of high degree and large estates, for whom his family had been looking for years.

He also knew, however, from what he had heard very lately, that he was generally regarded as an impostor.

At all events, he had not found as yet the means of going to England.

"But go I will," said the Claimant. "Rights is rights, and they ain't a-going to do me. I've led a rough life, 'cause I choosed to, and I've heerd Robinson Crusoe was a gent at home."

"Why," said Kelly, "what a howling swell you will be; you won't then forget an old pal will you?"

At this moment the baronet was called to serve a couple

of pounds of chops, and while the knife and steel were performing a duet, Kelly re-entered the Wagga-Wagga Arms.

"Rum un over yonder," said Kelly addressing mine host. "Any truth in his yarn?"

"Can't say; he's been known as Thomas Castro here a goodish bit; says he's a married man," and the man hesitated. 'But that's nothing to you or me. She was a decent sort of a gal. She was for some time in my service; her father was Paddy the Plasterer."

"Hah! hah!" laughed Kelly, "your slavey's a right down lady—well I am——"

"Many a slavey and wuss has married swells here, I can tell you; them as have had the iron bracelets on, have had diamonds on the same place afterwards. Some coves hawked advertisements for Sir Roger Tichborne and say Castro's the man."

"It's a queer yarn," said Kelly, "he seems no fool, and ot a bad judge of hossflesh."

The man looked with a sly wink at Ned Kelly; it was a : evelation however.

"That's it," cried Kelly, and ceased as Thomas Castro came in again.

"It ain't hoften," said the butcher, "as we sees strangers down here. You've been in hold England lately?"

"Some months ago," replied Kelly.

"Never mind, you're a man hafter my own 'art," continued Castro. "My missus is cooking some supper. Will you make one?"

Nothing loth, Kelly followed Orton and was introduced to a good looking, sweet-faced young woman. She was of course utterly uneducated and consequently looked up to her husband with intense admiration.

She considered him one of the cleverest men in the world.

She was very civil to Kelly and made him as comfortable as she could.

There was a really good supper so far as plenty was concerned. With beef and mutton at twopence a pound a bountiful feast was always at hand.

More Colonial constitutions are broken down by over eating, than drinking or smoking. The digestive organs are prostrated by "bursters" of meat.

Mrs. Castro retired leaving pipes and whisky on the table.

Two of the greatest villains on the globe sat down to enjoy themselves.

"And you think you'll pull through," asked Ned Kelly, "and prove your case?"

"I ain't a going to funk it," said Thomas Castro. "If that lawyer in Sydney ain't going to do the right, I'll get to London, if I've got to swim for it and hold on by the tail of a shark."

"Money!" observed Kelly, with a peculiarly significant glance.

"Hem! well that's it," said Thomas Castro; "of course I've been a blessed fool to keep dark all this time. But you see, I'd got used to this rough life, the other never was my style."

"If this here lawyer does not turn up," continued Kelly, "what then?"

"I'll get it somehow. Money I must have. If ever I put my foot in England, I'm all right."

He was not aware that the gobe-mouches of Sydney already believed his strange story, and were already subscribing funds.

But the most singular feature was, that men of standing and education could not see through the swindle and the impossibility of Orton being Tichborne.

One fact alone was sufficient—how could Tichborne have acquired the argot of Wapping?

But Johanna Southcott, at 70 years of age, received from the British public £100,000 to pay for the expense of her lying-in of the new Messiah. Royalty even sent a cradle for the use of the expected Godhead, worth £5,000.

Little wonder then that the sympathy of the masses

(or, as *Punch* has it, "them-asses") should be enlisted for this Wagga-Wagga "Bloater," as "the long-lost heir" of the House of Tichborne.

"If you want money," said Kelly, "you know how to get it. Your little game of the fryingpan ought to fill your pockets."

"Look here, mate," said the Bloater, "as you know my private banker is in the bush" (here he chuckled with glee) "and how my checks is paid, I don't mind trusting you a bit. Will you lend me a hand? It will be all the better for you; you shall be in it, and no mistake."

"Just in my line. Out with it—no secrets amongst pals, or we can't run in the same harness together. You've told me a secret, now I'll tell you one. Can you keep it as well as I can your horse-stealing job?"

This hint was given to prove that Kelly had him in his power in case of treachery.

"Keep it? as the ocean keeps a lump of lead dropped into it. Own up; what is it?"

"Do you know who you're talking to?"

"No, I don't, and don't care much either, if he's true to his pal."

"Ned Kelly never sold a pal yet," exclaimed the bushranger.

"Ned Kelly!" exclaimed the Bloater, in a tone of almost fright.

"I'm the bloke; so now we both toe the line."

"Ten thousand pounds for his capture," rushed across the Bloater's mind. The blood rushed into his face when the thought occurred to him.

Kelly saw the prodigious effect his imprudence produced, and shrewdly guessed the cause. Orton alias Castro was silent for a moment; his eyes positively glared at Kelly, as the £10,000 reward opened up prospects of a capital for the prosecution of his intended swindle. But he soon recovered his calmness.

Kelly read him like a book. The sudden flush and the eager glance, were not lost upon him; but that any man seeking to establish his claim to a baronetcy should turn informer was a thought that simultaneously struck the two men, and all apprehension vanished.

By way of interlude Kelly related the little incident of the manner in which his friend Joss expiated his good intentions, and dwelt with apparent pleasure upon the part the white-bellied sharks played in that little drama.

Castro winced as he mentally placed himself in Joss's uncomfortable position.

"No" he cried.

"Fact," said the other, "and what's more he's the chap to find you the money, when the time comes, if these lawyers don't."

"You?" exclaimed the Wagga-Wagga butcher.

"Yes," gasped Kelly. "I've a goodish bit of tin put away—here, there, and everywhere; show me its the correct card, and I'm fly."

The Wagga-Wagga butcher then told him a story which, as Kelly never repeated it, we can give no version of.

Whether he stuck to his claim, or whether he told the whole truth and elaborated his plot, can never be known now.

Then they made arrangements for the event of the next day.

As Kelly was not known in these parts, he was to sell the horses, though Thomas Castro was to direct the stealing.

The programme was this. They were to travel to the station where the horses were that Thomas Castro had his eye on.

Near this they would halt, and contrive somehow to steal the cattle.

Thomas Castro knew the station well, and would direct the pilfering.

He was to return to Wagga-Wagga in order to divert suspicion, while Kelly would start for Albury, where a market was held for sheep, horses, and cattle.

There Castro would make purchases as a butcher while Kelly rid himself of the horses.

This was one of the curses of the colony. Where so many horses were in the possession of such a large number of owners, it was difficult for anyone to swear to any one particular animal.

And yet horse-stealing was regarded with almost as much anger as in the outlying districts in America.

Scant chance for one found red-handed. A bullet or a rope was the response, and in regions frequented by such people as the colony was, by a paternal Government what else can be done?

The routine of a trial might end in nothing besides the expense.

When Ned Kelly returned to the Wagga-Wagga hotel all the company had cleared out, but the landlord was waiting up.

"Rather late, mate," cried mine host, who was far gone in liquor.

"Not too late for a drink," laughed Kelly, throwing down a coin.

Mine host rose, and at once procured the materials for a "corpse-reviver."

Having consumed his glass, which was a stiff one, he was shown his bed by the landlord.

"I say," said Kelly, as he prepared to fasten his door, "if anyone calls me before I want to be called, look out for squalls."

And he was soon sleeping the sleep as of the just.

CHAPTER CXI.

THE BARONET SHOWS THE WAY.

NED KELLY was accordingly not called early, though the fat butcher had been over once or twice to inquire for him.

Mine host repeated his orders of the previous night and waited.

About midday, Ned Kelly opened his door and shouted for whisky straight.

When this was brought he asked for water and ordered breakfast. The pump was the general resource of visitors to that hostelry, but few would have liked to disobey Kelly's fierce and peremptory summons.

Some men have a knack of being obeyed, and Ned Kelly the bushranger was one of these.

He was attended to, and went down looking particularly spruce.

As soon as he had partaken of a copious breakfast he lighted his pipe and walked over to where the Wagga-Wagga butcher was cutting up his joints and serving his customers.

Thomas Castro nodded, and bade him walk into his parlour, where he would join him shortly.

He did so; and, the business being attended to by Mrs. Castro and the assistant, Kelly and the coming Claimant had a long talk.

They were to start that night when dark, and reach the station by paths well known to Kelly.

After this was all settled Kelly returned to the hotel. He wanted to see his friends and hear the latest news of Tom Conquest.

But they did not turn up that day.

After dark, Thomas Castro came over, and there was a regular merrymaking. Many of the butcher's friends were there, several of whom believed in his monstrous assertion.

No human credulity ever went further. It was a blot on common sense.

Nothing else was talked of. Ned Kelly listened and made no remark. He was no fool, and had very strong opinions on the subject.

About ten, Ned Kelly and his new associates had their horses brought out and started on their way.

Their object was to reach the station about twelve, when all would be in a tired sleep, and then bide their time.

Thomas Castro was well acquainted with the station, where he had been on business—

He knew where four favourite horses were placed and had studied the station with his keen and ready if vulgar art.

Reaching the neighbourhood, Thomas Castro left Kelly in a safe quarter and then crept on to the station.

Good horses were worth money, and would always fetch a price from colonists.

The station was a scattered one, and belonged to one who owned immense herds of sheep.

Kelly remained on the edge of the bush, quiet and watchful.

He was amused by his new associate, but he scarcely knew what to make of him. He appeared shrewd enough, and yet the undertaking in which he was engaged was to all appearance the height of folly.

Still it mattered not to him. He could wait and see more of his new acquaintance and judge better as to helping him.

Presently he heard sounds that indicated the horse-steala, had succeeded and was approaching, with the four horses driven before him.

No time was wasted. It was mount and away without loss of time.

Castro knew every inch of the country, and after a hard ride they were in a secure hiding-place where they could safely rest for a few hours.

Then again they were one the road, and at an early hour parted, Thomas Castro taking the route to Wagga-Wagga, while Kelly made for Albany, where a market was held for the sale of horses, cattle, and sheep.

The place consisted only of a few scattered houses, and an extensive enclosure for the cattle-yards.

It was attended by large numbers of squatters, and small cattle jobbers.

Immediately on his arrival, Kelly rode up to an inn which the other had described as frequented by horse jobbers and others.

Here he found a good many more hagglers than buyers, but engaging a tout, a man who cares for nothing but his commission, he put the horses forward, and after some delay, succeeded in getting rid of the animals at a fair price.

He had very many offers made for Marco Polo, but these he curtly declined.

Having disposed of his merchandise, Kelly went into the saloon and satisfied his thirst.

He had not been at the bar many minutes when he saw the tout making signs to him.

"My boy," said the fellow with an ugly leer, "you've got me into a hot place."

"What's up?" asked Kelly.

"Some fellows say as they knows them horses," continued the tout, "and are looking around for the chap as sold 'em. It ain't no business of mine. I'm a agent; but you twig."

The man's manner was vulgar and impertinent, but his meaning was evident.

"Time for a drink?" asked Kelly.

"Oh, yes. I shoved 'em on the wrong track; but you'd better make tracks pretty soon," the fellow went on.

In truth, the go-between did not want any trouble, but to make money both sides.

While the drinks were being made, Kelly felt in his pockets and brought out some gold, which speedily disappeared in some private corner of the other's garments.

This transaction over, Kelly mounted and made a hasty retreat to the back of the inn, and guided, by the information given him, easily got once more into the bush.

The only course now to be adopted was to work back to Wagga-Wagga and lie *perdu* for a while, until this matter blew over.

It was dangerous work, as the colonists were more furious at horse-stealing than at anything else.

On reaching Wagga-Wagga, Ned Kelly found that Zeph and Salmon Roe were there awaiting him.

They had cleared out at once, on receipt of his warning,

with their valuables, and had neither seen nor heard anything of Tom Conquest.

A conference was now held. Their return to the colony was known, and the bush would be scoured in every direction for them.

It was to be a new precaution to remain very quiet for a time.

After some conversation Kelly proposed first a visit to Melbourne, where, after remaining some time, they could tack back to Sydney.

Kelly hankered to be revenged on the treacherous Count and his associate, the Frenchwoman, who had betrayed his identity to Conquest.

The other desperadoes had no objection; anything was their game.

But their plans were doomed to be upset.

The second evening after the return of Kelly from Albany, the butcher informed him that his presence in Wagga-Wagga was being talked about.

His identity was not suspected, but he was thought to be the stealer of the four horses belonging to Mr. Horsfall.

Kelly at once determined to depart without beat of drum.

He and his two comrades accordingly started into the bush, promising to revisit the Claimant at some future period.

Kelly's plan was to make for the Murray river and go down to Adelaide by a flat steamer, whence he could again take the mail boat for Sydney.

Finding himself on his way thither in the neighbourhood of his sister's shanty inn, Kelly thought he would pay her a visit.

To his great surprise, he found her a widow.

Her husband had fallen in a scrimmage with some impecunious customer.

The widow had made money, and was ambitious. She wished to try her hand at something larger in one of the towns, and was delighted to see and consult with her brother.

Now, Kelly's sister was a fine handsome young woman, one of those peculiarly attractive in a bar; and Kelly, when he found she had a good purse saved, advised her at once.

"Sell your sticks to the first comer," he said, "and get down to Sydney; you'll do fine in a bar, and maybe, lass, we may both work together."

Kate Kelly, as we shall now call her, at once caught at the idea.

Her ideas of meum and tuum were on a par with those of her brother, to whom it may be observed she was sincerely attached.

A customer was easily found, and with a few clothes and her money she prepared for a start, making an appointment in Sydney with Ned.

He and his friends then left her, to make their own way to the river.

After some hard riding they reached a small hamlet whence the flat bottomed steamboats started.

Now came the question as to Marco Polo.

The other horses could be sold, but Kelly would not part with his favourite.

After some reflection and inquiries he found a man who took horses in to grass at so much a month.

He had a large paddock for the purpose.

Kelly paid him a month in advance, saw the shoes knocked off so that he should not be worked, and then rejoined his comrades.

The steamer was to start in a few hours, and in due time reached Adelaide, where they heard that Tom Conquest had just married, and had been appointed chief constable of Melbourne.

This was important news in two ways.

It made their visit to Sydney tolerably safe, as there was no one so well acquainted with the person of the bushranger as the persevering trooper, while they would no longer have him scampering all over the country after them.

CHAPTER CXII.
WHERE KIT THE CRUISER APPEARS.

LEAVING Ned Kelly and his desperadoes for a while, we transfer our readers to pastures new, that we may introduce characters essential to our narrative.

We are in sight of a bay on what may be the shores of a continent or of an island.

It offers nothing to the view but a shelving beach of dazzling white sand, backed with a few small hummocks beat up by occasional gales.

In this place the soil is arid and without the slightest appearance of vegetable life.

The inland prospect is shrouded over by a dreary mirage.

The water in the bay is calm and smooth as the polished mirror, not the slightest ripple is heard on the beach to break the stillness of nature.

At the entrance of the bay, in about three fathoms of water, floats a schooner.

What is she doing in that remote region? for we are on the shores of New Caledonia, the convict settlement established by France, and to which so many desperadoes, who had fired Paris and committed other almost unheard-of atrocities, had been sent.

The schooner is well manned.

Its skipper was a young man of stout build, a man with a countenance soured by misfortune, but remarkably handsome, of the brigand type.

He was a man reckless and daring, and if his life had been laid bare deeds would have been made known at which humanity might have shuddered.

His crew were men used to hardships and ready for anything.

In various capacities he had been everywhere, in the east and the west, the north and the south, leaving some track behind.

He was standing now under an awning in conversation with a Frenchman.

The latter was a short, bullet-headed fellow, with a face of little expression but that of cunning. He had no whiskers, and a short, stubbly moustache.

A word here about the French convict settlement of New Caledonia.

Nothing more atrocious can be conceived than the treatment of the convicts, male and female, by their jailors.

Torture, shooting, villainies of all kinds, were of constant occurrence, and connived at by those in high places.

No wonder the most desperate attempts were made to escape.

Most attempts, however, were frustrated, and repressed with ruthless cruelty.

The only successful escapes were those which were connived at by venal jailors.

There was a permanent committee sitting in France to collect money and organise escapes, which were generally carried out from Sydney.

Sufficient had been collected to tempt some of the officials, and the schooner Kate had been chartered to aid in the escape of a party of Communists, Socialists, and Petroleuses.

"When shall we get the signal?" asked the skipper, Jack Leary by name.

"I expect every moment," replied the Frenchman; "but vraiment, I tink it will come at the nuit—ze dark."

"Well, the sooner the better," continued the skipper. "I don't want to run into the jaws of one of your snappers —they bite pretty sharply."

The Frenchman shrugged his shoulders with an expression of contempt.

"Nevere fear. Ve will vaz you call snap ze fingere at zem," he said.

And drawing out a cigar, he lighted it, and, walking up and down, gave occasional glances at the shore.

This man, Jean Ribault, was himself an escaped Communist, and occupied himself in aiding the escape of others.

He had an agent on the island who was completely in his power.

Besides this, he knew the island well.

Some hours passed, and then night fell on the scene.

The schooner still lay quite motionless.

A boat was put out ready for action.

Then came the flash of three muskets from the shore, and away went the boat.

It ran upon the beach, where a party of eight awaited them, besides a jailor.

With this man Jean Ribault went on one side, and they had a brief conversation.

Money then passed, and they parted.

"*Allons, mes enfans*," cried the agent, as soon as the business was settled, "no time to lose."

The escaped victims gladly obeyed.

Re-capture meant much worse than death.

The boat was ready.

All clambered in, and away they went, the men bending manfully to their oars.

The schooner was ready to slip her anchor at a moment's notice.

She had been selected for her swiftness.

The beautiful model and elegant tapering spars seemed to indicate American origin.

Anyone on board that day could have seen in what perfect order she was.

Her raking masts were clean scraped; her topmasts, her crosstrees, caps, and even running-blocks were painted white.

In every point she wore the appearance of being under the control of seamanship and strict discipline.

As soon as the order was given the crew were immediately on the alert.

The awnings were furled. She slipped her cable, for the noise of weighing the anchor might have been heard ashore, and was quietly towed out of the harbour by a boat lowered for that purpose.

Her canvas was soon shaken out, and in the steady soft breeze "she walked the waters like a thing of life."

The breeze freshened, and the schooner darted through the smooth water with the impetuosity of a dolphin after its prey.

The incessant jabbering for which our Gallic neighbours are so famous was as loud and discordant as that of the white paroquets of Australia when disturbed in the bush.

Gladness and excitement lit up every countenance, and a cargo of the greatest ruffians, men and women, fit only to people the infernal regions, made night hideous by their singing, dancing, and tumultuous joy at escaping from that "Ocean Hell," the French penal settlement of New Caledonia.

Women who had long been dead to every sense of shame, men who would have murdered the twelve Apostles for five centimes, and burnt a church with everyone in it to light a cigar, jumped about and howled with frantic delight.

They were now free from what they had so righteously earned—the whip and the forced *corvée*, and the scanty, wretched food upon which they had to sustain a life doomed to incessant labour under a broiling sun.

Hardly had they made a good offing when they heard three guns fired, and knew the escape of prisoners was discovered.

All convicts were allowed to move about in the day, but unless they presented themselves at a fixed hour in the evening were considered as absent.

As the punishments were too horrible to be risked for a trifle, the officials knew that absence meant escape.

At once the alarm was given, and two swift vessels, always kept ready, were sent in pursuit.

Daylight had wholly disappeared, and the question was, had the schooner been seen by any but those who were looking for her?

This was an important question.

Still she kept on her way, knowing all chance of escape depended on the swiftness of her heels.

They had no means of fighting the well-armed and well-manned brig in pursuit.

She carried too heavy metal, and was by far too well manned.

They must depend on their racing powers, and at a pinch on some cunning trick.

The victims who had escaped from New Caledonia were eight in number—four men and four women.

The first were of the loud-speaking, blatant sort so common France, while three of the women were of the common class of those who helped to fire fair Paris.

The four was different—*petite*, with a soft youthful face and sweet eyes.

No one could have suspected her of crime, and yet sometimes there was an expression of her countenance which betrayed that *moitié Singe, moitié Tigre* which is so often to be found in the French character.

"So, Marie Franconnet," said Jean Ribault, laughing, "you have escaped at last?"

"It was time," she answered, with an ineffable look of sorrow and pain. "But what for?" she asked dreamily.

"You'll do anywhere," he answered gallantly, "with your face and talents."

"I cannot re-enter La Belle France," she continued plaintively; "where else can we live?"

"Anywhere, *ma fine*," was the laughing rejoinder, "if you have money, and you know *la bas* they have a small fund for you."

"But, then, I must earn my living," she continued. "Your money will not last for ever."

"You have accomplishments. You sing, play, and can teach your language."

"I know no English," she sighed.

"No matter," said Jean Ribault; "I know in Sydney a lady who finds situations. Your want of knowledge of English will cause you to be taken into some high family."

At this moment dinner, most welcome to the escaped, was announced, and the conversation became general.

The escaped convicts, by whose friends the schooner was hired, had all the best accommodation to themselves.

Provisions had been taken on in abundance, and the ex-prisoners revelled in them.

After dinner they hastened to perform another duty; that was to get rid of their prison dress and assume other habiliments provided by the agents, thus getting rid of the last signs of New Caledonia.

Meanwhile, Jack Leary, the skipper, was on the look-out. He had a man in the crosstrees, while he himself examined the chase by means of a night glass.

She could be plainly made out, and, it was clear, sailed well.

"It won't do," muttered Leary, "to get caught. It means losing my light little craft."

And calling his first officer they held a long consultation, which terminated in the keen examination of the ropes and sails.

At this time the wind increased.

"That's the ticket," cried Jack Leary; "we'll show her a clean pair of heels after all."

Again an hour of deep anxiety passed, and then once more they examined the chase.

The hull, which an hour before was plainly to be distinguished, could now no longer be seen.

When dawn came not a trace of her was in view. The victims of their own crimes and the harshness of others had escaped.

The next thing to be considered was how to land them in Sydney.

The Kate was chary about showing herself very openly. In Sydney she would decidedly attract too much attention.

Besides, they wanted to keep the mystery, if possible, of their organised escape from New Caledonia. That some English and American vessels had a hand in it was known, desirable to keep the individuality of the secret.

After some consideration it was resolved to waylay a Sydney-bound vessel, half a day from the port, and say these eight foreigners had been picked up in an open boat without luggage and with very little money.

Of course they would not be refused.

And so matters came about.

A vessel was hailed, the escaped convicts taken on board, their story believed, and pitied.

Of course they were taken on without the slightest hesitation. A collection even was made for them.

Thus they landed in glory and in clover. They were evidently not aware that they would be free the moment they landed on British soil, and would not be surrendered.

They went to a quiet hotel, and began to purchase what they required.

There seven of them disappeared from our view; most likely they got mixed up in the seething vortex of crime which at this time swept like a torrent over the colony.

Marie Franconnet, after making her toilette one morning with more than ordinary care, went to call on Madame Ribillard, the agent for governesses.

She received Mademoiselle Franconnet with great cordiality. Her friend, M. Jean Ribault had spoken of her, and she would do her best.

After some conversation, Madame Ribillard examined her books.

"I have a very fine situation," she said, "but what about papers and references?"

Marie assumed a dejected air.

"All lost upon that unfortunate ship," said the girl in a plantive tone.

"Well, the situation I recommend is at Government House," she continued. "Lady Belmont has two daughters who speak French a little, and who want someone to perfect them. I will lay the case before her ladyship, and you shall hear from me."

And so Marie Franconnet went away rejoicing. Thus Marie Franconnet, really Françoise Benoit, the petroleuse, was promised a situation in the house of an English nobleman!

The Earl of Belmont was governor of the colony, a high and mighty personage.

Next day Madame Ribillard wrote to Marie to attend her to Government House.

Meanwhile, of course, the girl lived in the house of the governesses' agent.

The residence of Madame Ribillard was in the old part of Sydney, which in no wise resembles the magnificent capital erected on Port Jackson, one of the finest natural harbours in the world.

The houses are chiefly built of wood.

That of the Frenchwoman was of a superior class, and had been improved by its more recent owners

It had three storeys, and Marie Franconnet's room was at the summit.

After a long talk about the future, the girl retired.

She had been in bed and asleep some time when she was awakened by the smell of smoke.

Hastening to the door she opened it, but as hastily closed it again, for she saw that the stairs were in flames.

Her only hope was the window, but looking out, she knew at once that to leap out would be to expose herself to certain death.

The flames were bursting from the lower windows, and the tenement must soon fall a prey to the raging element.

Marie believed her last hour had come.

But as she appeared at the window, a loud shout from below informed her that she had been seen.

This was true. The fire had soon collected the usual crowd.

The engines had not yet come, but as soon as it was known there was someone in the upper room, a ladder was fetched by a number of men.

Marie, who had dressed herself and secured her small stock of valuables, looked out with feverish anxiety

Would they be in time?

The floor of her room was quite red hot, and the flames must come through before many minutes could elapse.

Then she was lost, all her scheming was over.

No prayer came to her lips, but the old teachings of youth are not to be smothered.

A prayer came to her heart if not to her lips.

Then there was a great shout, and she saw that a ladder had been placed against the house.

Again she looked out and saw that flames and smoke obscured the view below.

She had no courage to clamber to the ladder, which, moreover, was too far from the window for her to reach.

Then again a roar came, and she saw a man emerge from the clouds of smoke and flame.

As he did so, he yelled to the crowd below some orders she did not understand

At the same moment she became dizzy, and fell.

The crowd pushed the ladder nearer the house, as directed by the man, and he was able to enter the chamber.

Clutching a blanket, he wrapped up the semi-insensible form in it, and, being of powerful frame, contrived to reach the ladder with his burden.

Once on the ladder, he kept a firm hold with both hands, one to his burden, the other to the ladder.

He was half blinded with the smoke, while his hands and face were much scorched by the flames.

But he kept on, and finally reached the street, with his still insensible burden, amid loud and ringing cheers.

As these arose the roof of the house fell in, and all knew what would have been the fate of the girl if he had not had the courage to save her.

"This way," said several voices, and then they took him though the dense crowd, which made way without hesitation to where a shop had been opened for the reception of Madame Ribillard.

The good woman had been terribly alarmed for her lodger, and it was her cries that had first drawn attention to her existence.

She received her from the arms of her saviour with delight.

Under the influence of restoratives, Marie soon recovered, and then tried to thank her brave deliverer.

But Madame Ribillard had to translate.

The rough-and-ready individual who had risked his life to save Marie Franconnet, was no other than Ned Kelly.

Though coarse, his was a manly physique which the petroleuse admired.

As she thanked him with tears in her eyes, the bushranger thought he had never seen anyone so beautiful.

He resolved to renew the acquaintance, but now took his farewell.

When he went out, greatly to his annoyance he received an ovation.

A neighbouring drinking saloon had been opened on the strength of the fire, and was driving a rare trade.

Here Kelly was taken, and forced to imbibe several drinks before he could get away.

Such was the first meeting between Ned Kelly and Marie Franconnet, which was to lead to so many and such notable results.

Kelly and his pals had been passing at the time and had stayed to witness the scene.

When it became known that a girl had appeared at a window above, the bushranger was forced by a desire to distinguish himself.

Zeph and Salmon Roe would have held him back, but opposition always roused him.

He would ascend, and ascend he did, to the great advantage of Marie Franconnet.

The house was gutted and several others were injured, but Madame Ribillard was insured, so it mattered little to her.

Kelly returned to his lodgings and when he went to sleep, found himself dreaming of the beautiful French girl.

CHAPTER CXIII.

AN EARTHLY PARADISE.

GOVERNMENT HOUSE, Sydney, is one of the most beautifully-situated palaces in the world.

It is placed on a height overlooking lovely grounds, styled Hyde-park, and a bay only equalled for beauty by that of Rio.

When we say "bay," we should rather describe a succession of bays, one opening out of the other, dotted with fertile islands covered with timber.

Out of these bays start coves of equally deep water—sixty feet in depth—penetrating into the forests, and overhung by the branches of almost primeval trees—a scene of sylvan beauty unrivalled in the world.

Government House is built of white stone, and is a superb residence for any potentate.

It is said that the noble earl, the Governor aforesaid, was almost dumb with astonishment when he entered the capital of a colony not a hundred years old, and founded by successive cargoes of the vilest of England's criminals.

It is no longer a penal settlement.

To this place Madame Ribillard took Marie Franconnet in a vehicle.

The history of the girl was never exactly known, nor how she came to be mixed up with the ferocious group of coupe-gorges and other wretches who did their utmost to ruin Paris.

Her origin remained a myth. That she was well-nurtured, well educated, and gentle in manners, was very clear.

Probably like many others, carried away by a wild and false enthusiasm, she had made an idol of one of the red Republican leaders, and had fought by his side.

Lady Belmont had already given orders, so that when M. Ribillard sent in her name she was at once admitted to a small reception-room, where Lady Belmont, a fine, aristocratic-looking woman, soon joined them.

She received Madame Ribillard, whom she knew and esteemed, graciously.

She then turned to Marie Franconnet, who, on being questioned, stated that, having lost her friends and her small fortune, she had been advised to try Australia, where there was a demand for her qualifications.

She had numerous letters of introduction, all of which had been lost in the unfortunate vessel which had been wrecked.

She remembered only two names, Monsieur Jean Ribault and Madame Ribillard.

M. Jean Ribault had spoken to madame, and she hoped she would give her a fair trial.

"I will," said the countess most graciously, "give you a fair trial. You will live with us, and be the constant companion of my girls."

The salary was exceedingly liberal, and Marie Franconnet went away delighted, and inwardly thinking how easily these insular ladies of rank and title were hoodwinked.

She went out, bought a couple of boxes and some very simple necessaries, and then, putting on a very plain dress and wearing a veil, took her walks abroad.

She was quite surprised at the sight of a city so well built, so different from anything she had seen, except that one she had done her utmost to destroy.

She went down towards the shipping.

She noticed that many turned to look after her neat and dainty figure, but no one attempted to speak to her.

Once or twice she remarked that a man well-dressed passed her.

He was a bold, handsome man, with a rather forbidding countenance.

But he was of those who command, and Marie Franconnet admired that sort of man.

Still she was not going to give him encouragement.

She knew her place too well, so that when his assiduities became rather too annoying, she hastily returned to her hotel.

The good-looking, though rough, stranger followed close on her heels, took note of the name and situation, and retired with a self-satisfied and somewhat sardonic grin on his lips.

It was Ned Kelly, now domiciled in Sydney, carefully disguised, who was determined, before he ventured again into Melbourne, to hear what report was true about Tom Conquest.

He had met his sister, who, partly by his aid and the influence of her own sharpness and good looks, had got a position as barmaid in an hotel, the luncheon-bar of which was frequented by numerous swells, among others, by the officers of the constabulary, who had been in the army.

As the pay is good and the service active, many dashing young fellows had volunteered.

Among these was one Captain Lionel Henshaw, who had already taken some notice of Mary Meadows as Kate Kelly called herself.

"Stick to him, my girl," cried Kelly; "who knows what may happen? Anyway, you can pump him."

And Mary promised.

Fascinating young women are the ones to worm secrets from susceptible young men.

Kelly chuckled excessively.

Happening to get a glimpse of the face of Marie Franconnet, whom he did not as yet recognise as the girl he had saved, and believing, like many ignorant Englishmen, that French girls are ever ready and willing to speak to anyone, especially if well-dressed and rich, he had tried to make her acquaintance.

He had failed, but he in no way felt faint hearted.

That one glance had inflamed his rather peppery imagination, and he determined to follow the matter up. He would scrape an introduction in some way or other.

He followed her home, and soon found means to ascertain her name.

His plan was to get his sister to call, make up some story and thus strive for her acquaintance.

But when Miss Mary Meadows called next day, rather gorgeously arrayed, she found she had flown. She had flitted to Government House, where Mary could not follow.

The daughters of the Earl of Belmont were two, Blanche and Violet, sixteen and eighteen.

They had music-masters, drawing-masters, everything that could be thought of to make them accomplished and lady-like.

Marie Franconnet was only to speak French. She would accompany them in their walks, and except on public days take her meals with them.

The earl and countess liked to practise French, and found no great opportunity in the colony.

There were a great many public dinners and dinners to large families.

These she did not attend.

Now there was in the family the Honourable Percy Boyd, private secretary, nephew, and heir to the earl.

He was a young fellow of about two-and-twenty. He was very good-looking, very impressionable, and very foppish, and not overburdened with brains.

The first dinner at which he sat, he was opposite Marie Franconnet, and that 'cute young lady at once saw that she had made a deep if not a lasting impression.

But she was careful to show no knowledge of the other's evident admiration.

Marie had to play a waiting game, to ingratiate herself with the family, and this could only be done by playing the part of a modest and retiring girl.

It was almost too ludicrous—she, the petroleuse and the mistress of the late Louis Jambert, shot on the barricades, to be looked on as fit to associate with young ladies of rank.

But this Honourable Percy Boyd might be worth winning.

Her first duty to herself, she said, was to learn English. She would never be able to get on without that.

Her employers all spoke French, but she did not wish to confine herself to associating with them only.

Some day English might prove useful. But she had an idea it was very hard work.

Still she would persevere.

Marie Franconnet had great liberty. She had to be present at all the meals of the young ladies, to walk certain hours with them, to drive also. The rest of her time was her own.

She would remain in her room and do as she thought proper.

It was not difficult to get out.

At the back of the Government House were the grounds, and at the extremity of these was a double turnstile turning both ways.

This Marie knew and determined to avail herself of it.

Next day, after breakfast, the young ladies went to take their music and drawing lessons, which would occupy them until lunch.

Marie Franconnet selected a book from one of her boxes, a novel of rather a *prononcé* character, which she took with her to a shady part of the grounds.

Here she seated herself in a position where she could see anyone approaching before they could get close to her.

She then opened her book and was soon deep in its contents.

Presently she started.

She heard footsteps, and saw the Hon. Percy Boyd approaching

She at once concealed her book in a capacious pocket, and assumed a half-sleepy, half-languid attitude.

Percy Boyd saw her flushed face with pleasure, and approached hurriedly.

He was no roué, no profligate—he was deeply respectful to all women.

He spoke French perfectly, and when Marie looked up she saw him bowing with polished grace.

"You are indeed a welcome addition to the colony," he said, after some brief courtesy.

"You flatter," she answered. "I thought you English never condescended to do so."

"We never flatter, we tell the truth," was the response.

Marie laughed, and said nothing when he seated himself close to her.

The young man had seen a little of the world and that was all.

He was scarcely more than a boy, but he was warm-hearted, and the sprightly French girl, with her smattering knowledge of French literature, delighted him.

She was a revelation—a something he had never seen before.

He was delighted, and Marie Franconnet, who saw through him as if he were transparent, was not ill-gratified.

She might win this glorious prize in the matrimonial lottery perhaps, if she were careful.

Suddenly the young man started and looked at his watch. He leaped up.

"My uncle will be wondering what I am doing," said the young man; and shaking hands and bowing, he took his departure, leaving Marie Franconnet in the seventh heaven of delight.

Then, when alone, she continued the reading of her book until the gong sounded for lunch.

After lunch she talked French in the garden for an hour, and then went for a drive through the best parts of Sydney, and out to the beautiful suburb of Parramatta.

After dinner there was a small reception, and one of the girls asked if she would mind stopping and playing.

They had heard her practise and sing.

Marie of course acquiesced with pleasure, and then Percy Boyd gave a grateful look.

Marie Franconnet went to her room to make some little change in her toilette.

Where was she born and where was she bred, that she looked so much like a princess in mien, though so *petite* in size and make?

The Hon. Percy Boyd was expected to marry his elder cousin, Violet.

It was an old family arrangement.

But nothing had been formally decided.

Violet was too young, her parents thought, while her cousin was in no hurry.

Still Percy Boyd knew what was expected of him, and could not make love to Marie before his semi-affianced cousin's face.

Still he could be polite and attentive.

All were surprised at the playing and voice of the young Frenchwoman, who, though only looking eighteen, was twenty-three.

"Where were you taught, my child?" asked the Countess of Belmont kindly.

"In the College of the Sacré Cœur,"* replied Marie lowering her eyes.

"Indeed," said the countess, well pleased, as she must, in that case, have been of good family.

And so the evening went on.

Marie went to her room very vain and triumphant.

Next day she had another hour in the grounds with the Hon. Percy Boyd, the nephew, who was very tender.

Still he did not say anything to alarm the most fastidious mind.

The young man, heir to an earldom and to a high position in society, had to think the matter over very seriously.

He had no father or mother, but he had a guardian in the shape of an uncle.

He felt that such a marriage as he contemplated would never be allowed by the latter.

Still he was young, and determined to win this peerless girl if he could.

What he heard the night before had helped to give him hope.

She was of good family, if poor.

And that goes a long way, even when the person spoken of is French.

Marie Franconnet determined to be very cautious.

She would excite no suspicion in the eyes of any of the family.

She begged the Hon. Percy Boyd not to make a point of meeting her every day, as that might excite comment.

"No one comes here of a morning," he said laughingly, "and I am not to be defrauded of my morning's lesson."

And he again wished her good morning.

After lunch Lady Belmont intimated her intention of taking her daughters out for a drive, so that Marie had her time for a stroll.

Again she put on a simple dress, and a veil that did not wholly conceal her beauty.

She went out, determined to see as much of Sydney as possible.

In the course of her walk she noticed that the man she had already remarked was following her again on the arm of a rather handsome female. She was tolerably good-looking, but coarse.

They were evidently bent on speaking to her, but Marie was determined they should not.

She saw a kind of tea-garden attached to an hotel.

Seeing a female waiter, evidently French, Marie Franconnet ordered tea and entered an arbour.

Kelly and his sister—for it was they—followed, and took up a table close at hand.

The woman tried to speak, but Marie, with a haughty look, shook her head.

Then the waiter came.

---

* A pious convent or school for young ladies. A *petroleuse* was an member of this society.

"Tell those people I do not speak English, and do not want to be talked to," she said, rather sharply.

The two exchanged glances, but bowed politely, and ordered refreshments.

Marie laughed to herself.

Then she stepped out, with a look out of the corner of her eye that electrified Kelly

"She's a stunner," cried Kelly as she left. "I should like to know more of her."

"Not while she lives at Government House," replied Kate Kelly, "you can have no chance."

"She's only a paid governess," retorted Kelly. "Nothing so very wonderful."

"You'll marry her, I suppose," sneered his sister— "that useless creature?"

"If she'd have me," answered the man, hotly. "But I'm a bit too rough for her. I want a wife as can work—like you."

"More your sort," replied Kate, laughing.

And shortly after she returned to her hotel, and made her appearance in the bar, where Ned Kelly was a constant visitor.

He was soon at her stand, and Kelly was there in conversation with Captain Lionel Henshaw.

They were mere casual acquaintances, and Kelly was very chary of what he said to him.

Besides, he needed to disguise his voice, which was peculiar, and to keep that up constantly was hard work.

Still, they drank and smoked together, and spoke of the news.

They even alluded to Kelly

But Captain Lionel Henshaw was new in the police, and knew very little of him as yet.

"I've been told to communicate with Tom Conquest, the new Chief Constable of Melbourne," he said. "I have written to him, and shall know more about the fellow soon"

Kelly and his sister exchanged glances. Such information was well worth picking up.

And then, with a nod to the barmaid, he went away, leaving the field clear to the captain of the mounted police.

"Hope to catch Kelly, sir?" she asked presently, in a careless kind of way.

"I joined the force for no other purpose," was the reply. "I mean to see him hung; besides, £10,000 is a good stake to run for."

"Many have tried," she remarked, "but none have succeeded."

"Yes; but it can't go on for ever," he said. "And then, besides ridding the colony of an accursed fiend, I get enough to start me in matrimony."

And he looked at Kate Kelly with a peculiar glance, which meant "chaff," nothing more—and so she read it.

And he ordered on the strength of his great expectations an extra drink.

Meanwhile, Kelly went away, having marked this man as one to be watched.

When he heard from Tom Conquest, he would doubtless have a fair description of him. Still, the police officer had never had a good view of him, and could not give a very close description.

He must be very careful.

But as long as he kept quiet in Sydney, public attention would not be too strictly drawn towards him.

He determined to be very careful, and do nothing to excite suspicion.

He led a very quiet life, though he frequented saloons, and amused himself drinking and smoking.

Leaving Kelly, we return to Marie Franconnet and her other lovers.

CHAPTER CXIV.
THE THREE RIVALS.

MARIE FRANCONNET, by her quiet and reserved manner, quite won on the Earl and Countess of Belmont.

She was undoubtedly a very clever actress.

Two or three days after the circumstances related in our last chapter, she found herself in the evening seated next to a man who was a type of the superior Australian.

He was a squatter, and owner of some two hundred thousand sheep, besides having one of the largest stations on the Murray river.

He was a gentleman, highly educated and polished.

He was, moreover, a good-looking man, and had travelled in Europe.

His knowledge of the French language, acquired in a twelve months' stay in Paris, was not extensive, but he was just able to converse with Marie.

First he was drawn towards her simply to air his knowledge of the language, but soon he found himself interested.

He was attracted by her singular beauty and her charming simplicity of manner.

She knew how to fascinate all those who came within her influence.

Michael Eldred was about thirty-five, rich, and unmarried.

Here was a chance for her. In her heart of hearts, Marie did not believe that the Hon. Percy Boyd would dare to face the anger of his friends for her sake.

Still she would do nothing to repel him. Two strings to her bow might prove useful

She was, however, very careful not to let her intentions be guessed at.

The young secretary was watching her, and she knew it perfectly well.

Her manner was inimitable. She listened to Michael Eldred, answered his questions with apparent timidity, and then when Percy Boyd came to lead her to the piano she gave him a sweet smile and a curtsey that were charming.

The Australian squatter was delighted with the music, and went away charmed and desperately in love.

He knew she was only a governess, but she would not be received on the terms she was by his Excellency and his lady had not her character been perfect.

Percy Boyd had not been blind to the admiration of the squatter, one of the richest and most influential men in the colony.

He knew him to be impulsive and generous.

Next morning as usual he met Marie in the grounds.

There were a few lover-like endearments, and then he spoke.

"I wish you were not such a flirt," he said, half sulkily.

"I?" she cried, looking up with a glance of the most innocent and infantine surprise.

"Yes, *mademoiselle l'ingenue*," he went on, "don't pretend to have forgotten that big, handsome colonist."

"*Quelle horreur!*" lifting up her hands, "and monsieur is jealous."

"I am only joking," he went on, "but he is handsome, rich, and young."

"There is only one man in the world for me," she said sadly, "and yet he cannot be mine."

"Why?" he asked, looking somewhat puzzled.

"Your friends will never consent," she went on in a sweet plaintive voice. "I am noble, but I am poor."

"I shall have enough for both," he answered, "so cheer up, *cherie*, and all will be well."

She did cheer up considerably, and they chatted away pleasantly for the small time, when duty summoned him away.

Marie remained alone.

She was in deep thought. Should the colonist prove to be in earnest, should she accept him at once?

There is many a slip between the cup and the lip, and once married all would be well.

The colonist was young, handsome, and, Percy Boyd had assured her, rich, while the nephew of the Governor had only his pay and a rather liberal allowance.

This marriage with her would mortally offend his relatives and lose him his place.

She would temporise and act according to circumstances.

While on these thoughts intent, she heard footsteps, and looking up saw Kelly before her, accompanied by a curious looking Frenchman.

Marie rose as if to fly to the house.

"One moment, mademoiselle," said Jean Goujon respectfully, "my master only wants to say two words to you, in all honour."

Marie stood still. Despite herself there was something in Kelly's manner which impressed her.

"I am listening," she said coldly.

"Monsieur has only seen you once, but already he loves you. He is rich and ready to make you his wife."

Kelly, who knew the meaning of the word sa femme, nodded.

"Tell the gentleman," she answered in a dignified tone, "that I am honoured by his offer—but I cannot converse with a stranger. Let him obtain a proper introduction," she continued, "and I shall be happy to receive him—I mean an introduction to his excellency."

And with the air of a duchess she curtsied and left them.

"High and mighty," growled Kelly, as he repeated the incident to Zeph; "but I'll tame the she-cat. That young girl has a history. I'll find it out."

Kelly little thought how near he was speaking the truth of Marie, alias the petroleuse.

Still he must bide his time.

Kelly was careful not to remain too long at the bar kept by his sister, but he went in occasionally.

He did not stop long when the handsome captain was there in conversation with the attendant Hebe.

He continued, however, to have frequent conversations with the all-admired barmaid.

One morning the Captain spoke to the girl in an undertone.

"Any news?" she asked.

"Yes," replied the captain. "I have heard that Kelly is about. A man professed to have met him not long ago. He did not spot him at the time, he said, but, after thinking where he had seen the face before, he remembered."

"Ned Kelly in Sydney?" said the girl, with a hoarse laugh. "Impossible!"

"So they say," remarked the Captain, and walked off, leaving the brother and sister together.

"Nothing is impossible to that man," remarked a solitary bystander, a man of about five-and-twenty, very much of Kelly's build, and not unlike him in face, though much more refined in manner.

"Why so?" asked Kelly, secretly amused at the statement.

"Because he's got the pluck of the old one," replied the other, admiringly "You don't look half a bad one. Would you believe it," he whispered, "that, though not by the same mother, I'm his brother?"

Kelly looked at him in wild perplexity.

I ain't ashamed of it, neither," the other went on, "and would give anything to see him, if only once."

"Anybody in the den, Kate?" said Kelly to his sister.

"Nobody," she answered; "it is quite at your service."

"Send us in two goes," he cried. "If you've no objection I should like a chat."

The stranger nodded carelessly and followed his new acquaintance.

As soon as they were alone the redoubtable bushranger seated himself.

"I never heard as Ned Kelly ever had a brother," he remarked.

"He does not know it himself," was the answer. "Soon after my birth my mother had some money left her and went to England. She never saw my father again. It was only when dying she told me the truth. With all his faults and crimes she remained faithful to his memory."

"How did you come out here?" the bushranger asked curiously.

The man blushed slightly.

"I did not come of my own accord," said the other, who was no other than the man known to us as captain of the Kate, John Leary, but better known by his sobriquet of "Kit the Cruiser."

"You needn't be squeamish with me," replied the bushranger, "I ain't easily made such. You said just now you had a brother, and that you were not ashamed of him."

"I did," replied Kit Kelly, alias John Leary; "and I say it again. He's every inch a man, from sky-scraper to his lower stun'sails; and I like a fellow that's got the grit in him."

"Have you ever seen him?" said Ned.

"No, I haven't. No such luck! What a pal he'd make! By the living Jingo!—as the Yankees say—we'd sweep creation!"

"Would you like to see him?"

"I'd give the best haul I ever made to clap my two eyes on him!" said Kit, emphatically.

"Then just look before you, lad. I'm Ned Kelly, and ain't ashamed to own it to a man, for I see you are built of the stuff I like."

"You?" gasped the other.

"Yes," holding out his hand, "I'm the very fellow himself—your brother, as you say."

The younger man could scarcely believe the evidence of his senses.

"You are not joking?" he faltered.

(To be continued.)

THE CELEBRATED NOVELS,
BY W. STEPHENS HAYWARD.

Picture Boards. ※ Published at 2/-

NED KELLY THE IRONCLAD AUSTRALIAN BUSHRANGER

No 19,

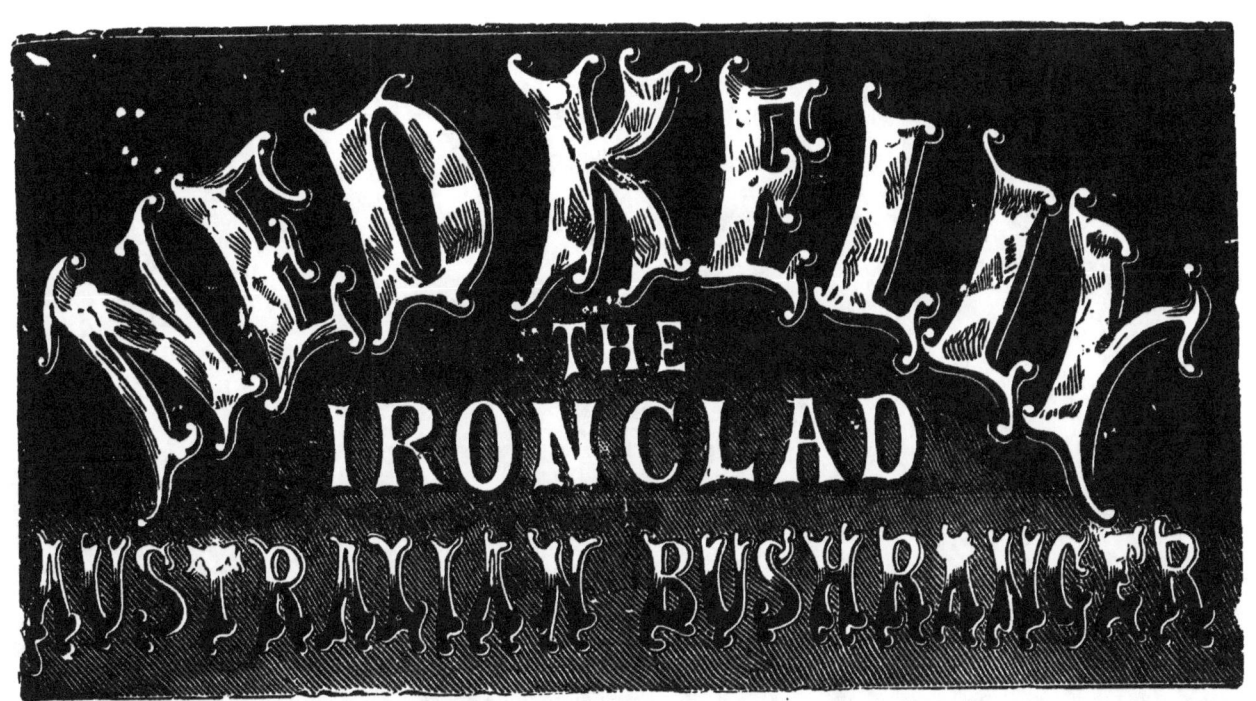

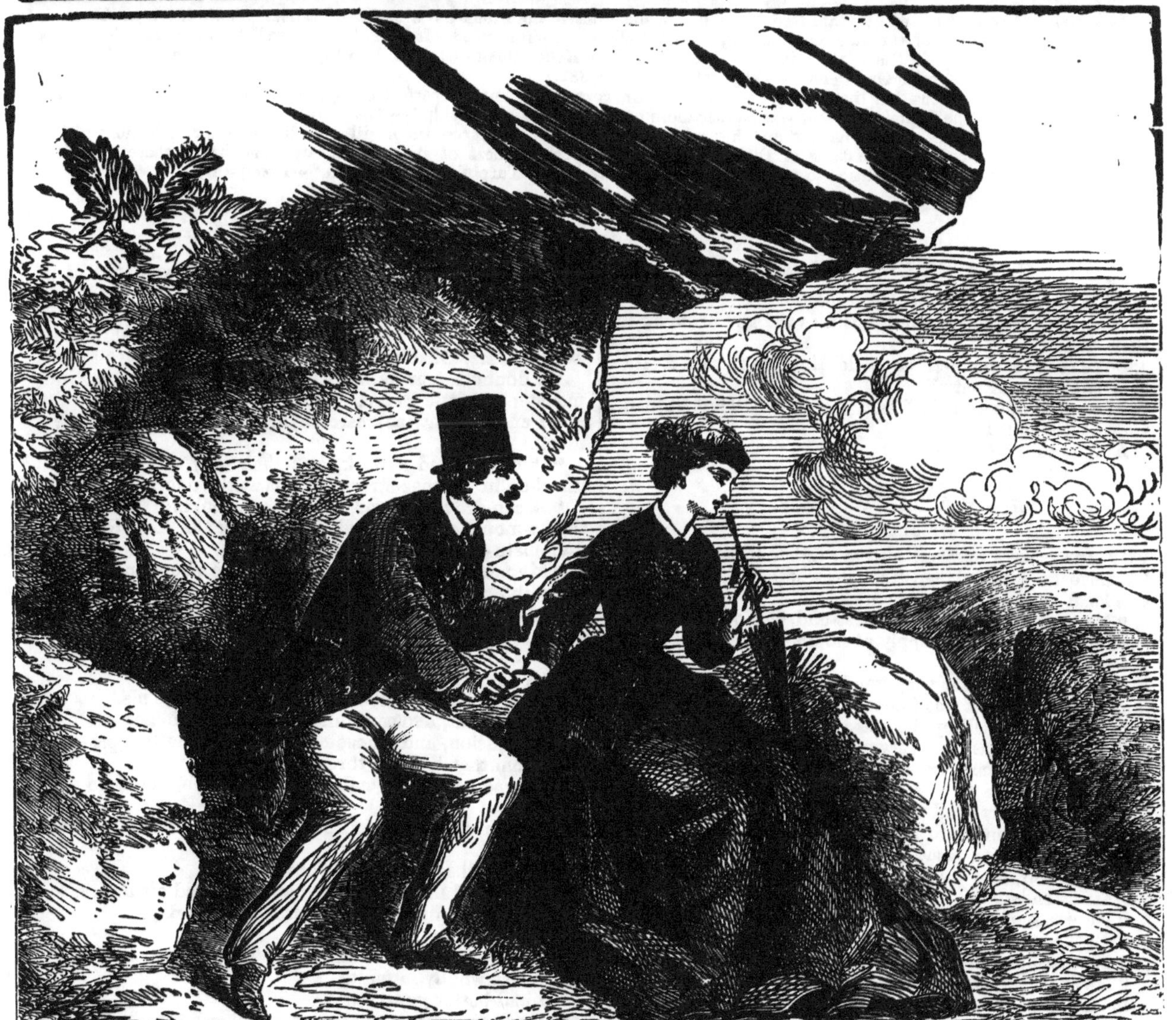

NED KELLY: IRONCLAD BUSHRANGER.

CHAPTER CXIV.—*Continued.*

"I'm no joker," was the dry response.

And the two shook hands again as the girl brought in their drinks.

"We're as snug here as a flea in a mat," said Kelly, "so spit out your yarn."

"I don't mind if I do," said the other; "but oh, lad, who'd a' thought it?"

And he told his story.

CHAPTER CXV.

KIT KELLY'S YARN.

"OF my mother's relations with our father I know nothing. I believe he married her, though, whether the marriage was legal or not, I cannot say.

"My mother lived in the East-end of London, where she kept a shop for the supply of sailors—a ship-chandler's it was called.

"She sent me to a very good school, and I went on fairly enough until I was fourteen. I was fond of reading, and improved myself by the better class of books.

"My mother was then very good-looking, but that mattered not. She was sure of plenty of sailors even if she had been ugly.

"She was very well-to-do; still for a long time she resisted all attempts to make her renew matrimonial relations. But there came one, Obadiah Helpmate, as he called himself, the pastor of a Little Bethel which my mother attended.

"He was a sleek, obsequious individual, with a snuffle, and all the usual pious jargon. He used to come to tea, and his consumption of food was wonderful.

"He was very kind to me, which helped him much with my mother. He always brought me presents, but though his books were rather too goody-goody for me, I never objected.

"I had no suspicion of his object; or, young as I was, I should have circumvented him, I believe.

"When I knew of it, it was too late. I was told of it only four days before the wedding.

"It was useless to object. So my mother, who had been the wife of Tom Kelly the renowned bushranger, became Mrs. Obadiah Helpmate.

"I doubt if our father was as bad as the hypocritical monster of Little Bethel.

"I and an aunt took care of the shop during the honey moon.

"It only lasted a week, and then they came home to the shop in Thames-street. I was at the door.

"A cab drove up, and my mother, looking years older than a month ago, alighted, followed by the Rev. Obadiah Helpmate—drunk.

"My mother walked straight into the shop, and kissed me with a sob.

"'Let that cub alone, woman,' said my pious step-father.

"'Who are you talking to like that?' I asked.

"'To my wife, you whelp.'

"He had been a sailor, and aimed a blow at me.

"I evaded it, and sent him sprawling. He got up in a furious passion, and a nose not at all suitable to a pastor.

"From that hour he threw off the mask.

"He had gained his end, and Little Bethel might go to a warm place.

"His brutality to my mother was excessive, but he feared me.

"I was tall and powerful for my age.

"I knocked him down twice and damaged his optics, so that he was confined to the house for some days.

"Then he changed his tactics.

"He became suave and bland, and persuaded my mother that I was wholly in fault.

"I had better go to sea.

"He had a friend, a shipping agent, who would get me a first-class berth as a midshipman bound for I——

"My   and gave him the m——

"Luckily her money was strictly tied up, and, though he had the run of the till, he could not touch anything else.

"He took me to an ill-looking place in the city, and there I signed.

"Two days later I bade my mother farewell, and went with my precious guardian to the docks.

"'I've a call to make,' said this amiable imitation of Stiggins. 'My brother is captain and part owner of a small vessel running between this and Newcastle.'

"I went on board innocently enough.

"It was a small, low-class collier, and the captain was a coarse imitation of his brother, profane and black-guardly.

"We went into the cabin, and soon I heard shouts of laughter.

"Then my stepfather, a little the worse for liquor, came on deck and prepared to land.

"I was about to follow.

"'Stop where you are, you whelp!' roared Captain Hetton—Helpmate was a false name—'you're bound to me for seven years.'

"I turned upon him, and plainly told him he was an infamous liar.

"Upon which I was floored by a handspike, and rendered insensible.

"When I came to, I was out at sea, and in the hands of as cruel a gang as ever lived.

"The captain, as they called him, was brutal, the mate was brutal, and the men, as a matter of course, followed suit.

"I was kicked, cuffed, swore at, half-stunned, and made the slave-of-all-work of the whole ship.

"My ferocious stepfather had kept the premium my mother had paid, and just given my master five pounds to take me away.

"His object was doubtless to drive me to some violent act.

"Well, I reached Newcastle, and here this brute was compelled to redouble his vigilance.

"He, of course, would not allow me to go on shore, but when night came, I swam ashore and escaped.

"It was easy enough to hide, as, unknown to Obadiah, my mother had given me money.

"I walked to Shields, and then I wrote to a trusty friend, who I knew would not fail me.

"I wrote a letter to my mother, enclosed in this, in which I told her all.

"As her precious husband spent nearly all his time at the public-house, she could easily receive the letter unknown to him.

"I told the whole story and begged her to send me money.

"I would go to sea, long voyages, and let her know how I got on. I would return home when he was dead, and not before.

"My mother sent me money.

"I came back several times, and communicated with my mother.

"She told me to be wary, as her husband and his brother were both on the look-out for me, determined on revenge.

"I laughed at them.

"Return to that vile slavery, I never would. That I was determined.

"When I was nineteen, I reached the port of London from China, and had some days leisure and plenty of money.

"I contrived to find that my stepfather was always out, at drinking-saloons, music-halls, &c.

"I was a man now, and feared him not, so I went home.

"My mother was very ill, nearly dying. The brute had ill-used her because she refused to make a will in his favour.

"She had left everything to me. I was furiously indignant, and spoke in no measured terms of his misconduct.

"'So,' said a malignant voice, that of the collier captain, as he touched my arm.

"I was eating some cold meat and bread my mother put before me.

"I had a knife in my hand, and struck at him, mechanically, meaning to knock him down and escape.

"But as ill-luck would have it, I know not how, the knife entered his body, and unintentionally I was a murderer.

"I was arrested after a fearful scene with my mother, and, after some days, committed for trial for wilful murder.

"At the trial, my stepfather swore hard and fast that I coolly and deliberately stabbed his brother, though he knew it was a pure accident.

"I was condemned to death, but my sentence, on account of my youth, was commuted to penal servitude for life.

"Ill though my mother was, she was allowed to see me before I was sent away.

"Then it was that, impelled by some impulse she could not restrain, she told me the secret of my birth.

"She told me something else.

"She could not make a will in my favour now, but she would transfer the money to a lawyer she believed in, in trust for John Morgan.

"If my sentence should be shortened, or if I escaped, the life of the convict, I believe I could claim the money.

"And so we parted. Before we left England I heard she was dead.

"We were taken to Norfolk Island, as you are aware, the worst of penal colonies.

"Why I should have been sent there is a matter beyond my comprehension.

"The place itself is charming, but man has made of it a hell upon earth."

Norfolk island was discovered by Captain Cook. It was then uninhabited, and it is believed that the well-known navigator and his people were the first who ever trod upon its soil.

It was and is a most beautiful region; but, nearly everywhere iron-bound.

From the top of Mount Pitt every acre of this land can be seen as on a map.

It seems strange in alluding to a penal settlement to speak of the magnificent Norfolk queen pine, with its sombre foliage, the pear tree with its softless green, the orange and lemon groves, and numerous gum-trees.

"I need not go into long details of my sufferings," continued Kit. "Let me shorten a horrible story.

"I was sent, after a time, with a gang some distance from the prison, to work at a small breakwater, which was being made in order to make a new port.

"For the convenience of the officers we slept on board a hulk moored about a hundred yards from shore.

"The intervening water was bright and beautiful, but beneath the waters were concealed some of the most dangerous and ravenous sharks known in those seas.

"A swim would not have been pleasant.

"The officer in command of this gang was a fellow named Captain Blood.

"If ever there was a fiend in human shape it was this villain.

"His power, of course, was despotic, and we poor devils were made to feel it.

"His cruelties were dreadful, some of them scarcely creditable.

"Blood was omnipotent.

"He could do what he liked, and to whom he liked.

"He always carried loaded pistols, as he knew how intensely he was hated, and that, given the opportunity, there wasn't a prisoner on the island who would not have murdered him in cold blood.

"The triangles ran with blood daily.

"Men were 'tied up' for a look, and Blood stood by gloating over the agony inflicted by the cat, which, if not laid on with a will, subjected the flogger (a convict) to the same punishment.

"Byron rails at 'Man's inhumanity to man.'

"He would have known what that could amount to if he had witnessed the 'bloody assize' daily held on an island which, for climate and natural beauty, is unequalled on the face of the earth.

"There was no appeal.

"We worked in gangs, watched by armed men, while outside of the hulk was an armed revenue cutter with her guns always run out and ready for action.

"But we felt that there must be an end to this.

"One of our men was a powerful Irishman, Dan Regan.

"He came in for more than his full share of punishment.

"How he cursed and threatened, and tried to induce his fellows to rebel, but for a long time in vain.

"We were forty unarmed wretches, while they were eight active, armed men.

"One morning Captain Blood, who, though not actually intoxicated, was always simmering with drink, was unusually abusive and scurrilous.

"He came aboard the hulk with several warders to take us off to the works.

"He cursed us all round—swore he'd flog the lot 'till our livers were bare,' and, just to show his brutal nature, violently kicked a man who was passing him to descend into the boat, when, with a yell and a bound like a tiger, Dan Regan roared out—

"'Take that!' and hit him on the head with a marling-spike.

"I saw at once that it was a planned thing, for the men flew at the warders, who were preparing to descend to the boats.

"Taken by surprise, they were hustled into the boats, and some disarmed.

"Then to work we all went to get rid of our bracelets. Though we knew the revenue cutter to be shorthanded, still she was well armed.

"Dan Regan had planned his rising with great sagacity.

"He had been off and on years on board that hulk.

"As soon as we were free he broke open a chest of carpenters' tools, and then attacked an arm chest, in which there was a supply of muskets for the use of our masters.

"There was not much ammunition, but still enough to suit desperate men.

"When we went on deck, where lay the dead body of Captain Blood, we found the revenue cutter within hailing distance.

"'Surrender!' shouted the manly voice of a young lieutenant, 'or I'll blow you out of the water!'

"'Blow away!' roared Dan Regan. 'Better go up than down among the sharks.'

"And he and the armed men fired a volley.

"This was answered by a broadside, which was kept up, while the boats put out with all the force they could make.

"They were fewer in number than ourselves, but well armed.

"Dan Regan and his intimates held a conference, and decided on a plan of action.

"It was communicated to us all."

It must be confessed the plan was both daring and ingenious as detailed by Kit, whose recital we must curtail by taking his story into our own hands.

It appears that a very strong current, running miles an hour, set in every day, and at the hour this melée took place, towards the shore, thus a very stout cable and anchor were necessary to hold even a light craft in that anchorage. Dan suggested, or rather decided, to cut the strong cable holding the hulk by four anchors, and let her drift bodily on to the Government cutter, and being a far heavier craft would either sink or fearfully damage that vessel, and give those on board enough to do to look out for their safety.

These forty desperadoes were determined when they "collided," or, rather came to "smash" on the cutter, to board her at once and master the crew, satisfied the awful confusion ensuing would divert the attention, if not paralyse the action of the crew.

Death awaited them under any circumstances, and Blood's death and the possession of the cutter were their only chances.

They worked with a will.

Axes soon severed the cables, and down before the insetting current came the hulk, increasing her speed every moment, and bearing down upon the devoted Government craft with the speed of a raft over the rapids.

Those on board soon saw the game that was up, and were appalled.

The sound of the heaving the anchor was heard, with the musical "heave ho!" which habit made the sailors indulge in even at this desperate moment.

But it was no use.

Long before the "bite" of the anchor was loosened, down came the huge hulk like an avalanche, and crash she came athwart the cutter.

The two guns discharged their contents into the hulk as she came on, but there was no time to reload, and the collision was followed by the forty convicts, headed by the Irishman, swarming over the side.

They were met by a murderous fire, and down went the leader, Dan Regan.

Kit was close beside him at that moment.

Dan's leg was broken.

"Don't let them take me, Kit," he said. "Shoot me first, alanna."

"Keep up your pluck, my boy, we'll soon settle this little business; be still till I'm back." And away he went to assist in mastering the crew of the cutter.

The fight, though against odds, was very desperate; but the forty desperadoes were too much for their eight opponents, who, being overpowered, were securely bound.

There was only one thing to do now: send Her Majesty's servants ashore, and use the cutter to reach more friendly shores.

Kit was a good seaman, and two of the captured crew offered to join him, provided he told the Government crew he was sending ashore, they went on compulsion.

The cutter was a good deal damaged, but not so as to render her unseaworthy.

Being in the Pacific Ocean, and no great distance from the Fiji Islands (then not colonised by Englishmen), they could easily send the cutter to the bottom and land in the long boat, whose name and colour would first be changed.

When they first landed they were in constant danger of being murdered by these savages, but by keeping together they were too strong to be molested.

Kit subsequently got off in a whaler.

His companions preferred to "chance it" with the natives rather than run the risk of the rope that awaited them elsewhere, if captured.

This accounts for the number of half-caste children existing in the island when recently annexed by the British Government.

It is quite possible the character of their progenitors was suspected, but the Paternal Government that emptied, on the sly, their jail-birds into the unsuspecting Australian Colonies, did not wish to be burdened with the cost of the support of forty criminals whom they would have been compelled to bring back to England, as the convict settlements in Australia had been abolished.

After relating this adventure, Kit (or Capt. Leary) continued—

"I went to England, and after some hesitation visited the lawyer. He proved to be an honest man.

"My mother had imbued him with a belief in my innocence and he paid me the money. I did not squander it, but still I spent some in travelling.

"I wished my personal appearance to change as much as possible, and so went to hot countries like Spain and Mexico.

"When I thought myself unrecognisable, I came over here and easily got to be captain of the smartest schooner I know, the Kate.

"I bought a third of her with my money, and by dint of industry and saving am now her master and owner."

"Got a craft of your own?" exclaimed Kelly, in a tone of delighted astonishment. "What do you do with her?"

Kit Kelly hesitated.

"I am not particular," he said, "to a bit of smuggling—perhaps worse; but since the day I shed blood unintentionally, I never lifted my hand against any man in that way. I'm proud of your pluck, Ned, and would place my schooner at your orders—but no bloodshed where I am."

"Who's a-going to kill anybody?" said Kelly, roughly. "Not me. I never made a stiff un, whatever fools say, except in self-defence."

"Glad to hear it," answered Kit, and fresh drinks were ordered in.

Ned Kelly became thoughtful for a time.

"Kit," he suddenly exclaimed.

"Well, what is it," answered the other.

"Would you, to oblige a pal and a brother, mind a little bit of kidnapping?" he asked.

"What do you mean?" said Kit.

"I'm spooney on a girl. She's a Frenchee, but she's a plucky sort," continued Ned. "I'd like to tame her."

"French?" said Kit, in a musing way. "I'd like to see her."

"So you shall," replied Ned. "Where do you put up?"

"Come and grub with me," remarked Kit; and the two went out.

Kit lived at a seaman's boarding-house in a quiet quarter, and had comfortable quarters enough.

Ned chuckled over this, as, in case of need, he might take shelter here, and, presumably, defy the police if it were necessary.

Ned spent the rest of the day with his brother, and then returned to his own place, after making an appointment with Kit for the morrow.

Kit was very anxious Ned should clear out of Australia. He had done enough to hang twenty men, but Kelly would not listen to any advice from any quarter.

He told Kit of the target he had been for bullets, and explained how his armour kept him bullet-proof.

Kit nevertheless was determined to get him away.

CHAPTER CXVI.

KELLY MEETS WITH A STRANGE ADVENTURE.

KATE KELLY, or Mary Meadows as she called herself, had a very good berth of it.

As she was very attractive, brought in customers and plenty of grist to the mill, she was not only well paid but had plenty of leisure.

Like all her class, she was very fond of finery and pleasure.

At her own request she did not lodge at the hotel, but had a small private lodging.

Here Kelly was able to visit her and hear the news.

Kate Kelly was proud of her figure, and liked, therefore, to show herself on horseback.

She bought a habit, and horses were easily hired.

Occasionally Ned, strictly made up for the occasion, would accompany her.

On these occasions he affected an elderly wig and spectacles, so that with a grey, short-cut beard and moustache, few would have suspected him for one moment.

It was a perfect metamorphosis.

One morning it had been arranged that they should take a ride, and Kelly had ordered the horses.

He then went to his sister's lodgings. It was early. She was not wanted until after twelve, when active business began.

He found her rather agitated.

"Anything up, wench?" he asked.

"Yes," she replied, "that lieutenant startled me last night."

And she told him what had passed. He came in elated and excited.

"Miss Meadows," he said in a whisper—he made a confidant of no one else—"I have certain news that Kelly is in Sydney."

"Indeed?" cried the girl, incredulously.

"Yes, he's been seen by two persons," was the answer; "one who was robbed and ill-used by him swears that next time he meets him he'll never leave him, but track him home."

"Why doesn't he catch him himself?" was Kate Kelly's contemptuous reply.

"He's afraid to," was the laughing answer; "he's no match for him and is afraid."

"Oh!" said Kate Kelly.

The gallant police officer then explained that the man meant in some way to worm himself into his confidence and then betray him.

"Scoundrel!" cried Kate Kelly, involuntarily.

"Why do you say so?" asked the surprised captain. "Kelly is a fearful vagabond."

"But I hate treachery," she replied, and so the subject dropped.

"Now, Ned," said the girl, "you must make yourself scarce—or keep close."

"I'm blowed if I does," replied Ned "I'm going to the races—and go I will."

"It an awful risk," urged his sister.

"I never harks back," cried the ruffian, "and I ain't a-going to begin."

"Remember, I'd be alone in the world," she said, mournfully. "Do be careful."

"I'm worth ten dead uns yet, Kate, darling," cried Kelly, and began to assume his disguise.

But to please Kate he took an unusual and less public direction for their ride.

They returned without any suspicious event occurring.

Before going to her business Kate again begged her brother to be very careful, and to leave Sydney for a while.

He bluntly declined.

"But tare an' 'oun's, Kate," he said, laughing, "I'll tell you a dodge. I'll ride side-saddle to the races. You'll lend me your habit—you're pretty plump."

"Get out with you!" she said, laughing; but so it was finally arranged.

Kelly then went to his lodging, and remained in all day, not showing himself in the streets at all—not even in the evening.

He explained all to Zeph and Salmon Roe, who blamed his foolhardiness.

But Kelly was obstinate.

"Only let me spot this bloke and I'll stop his jaw tackle," was his savage answer. "If I only could twig him, a knife 'ud be too good for him!"

He then recorded his determination to visit the races disguised as a woman.

They roared with laughter.

"Impossible!" said Zeph. "You would be spotted at once."

"Don't you make no blooming error," replied Kelly. "I'll do it."

As his friends were rather afraid of him they held their peace.

They would go to the races in any way they could. They were a recent experiment since the discovery of gold, and were doomed to lead to great things.

Next morning Kelly, after securing a horse well up to his weight and both powerful and swift, went round to his sister's, who had not been idle.

She had got him a wig with curls and a hat to suit his head, which was not exceptionally large.

She had procured a veil which would hide the coarseness of his face.

For the purposes of disguise he was always clean shaven.

He was dressed in a light tight-fitting suit, so that if he should have to throw off his female garb he might easily appear in another disguise.

Kate contrived to alter her habit to suit him, and as the skirt was very voluminous, there was no fear of detection.

The veil was tied under his chin, so that nothing was really visible but the mouth.

Kelly was in raptures. He so delighted in startling and dangerous adventures that he was in the highest spirits.

"Be careful, Ned," said the girl, in sorrowful alarm. "I dread that horrid Henshaw."

"Your young man," laughed Kelly.

He then kissed her heartily, and bade her be hospitable and bring out the whisky.

While she was getting this refreshment ready he secreted two pistols and a knife very much like a stilleto.

He then seated himself to await the arrival of the horse.

Kate warned him against any awkwardness in mounting. But Kelly was too good a mimic to fear detection.

Properly brought up, he might have proved a very good actor.

At half-past eleven the horse came round, and Kelly mounted.

He was very careful to act with becoming modesty.

Presently he, or she, was seated side saddle, and trotted off after throwing the man some money.

"He said the lady was a stout one," muttered the ostler, "faith, and she's a strapper."

Which was doubtless very true.

There was no difficulty about finding the way. Kelly had had it indicated to him, but the stream was guide enough.

Kelly had ladies brown gloves and a whip, and though one or two turned to look at the rather stout party, no one seemed to have the slightest inkling of the truth.

It was too audacious a thing to be suspected.

The number of persons going to the races were considerable.

All sorts of vehicles to be found in the colony, and they are very much the same as in England, were going.

There was the drag with the Government party, driven by the Hon. Percy Boyd, and among others on the roof was Marie Franconnet.

There were humbler vehicles, but not that exhibition of utter valgarity and poor horse flesh so often seen at popular races in England.

The distance from Sydney was not very great, and Kelly did not hurry.

When nearing the course, he turned to the left to where he saw the shelter of some trees.

Kelly had no intention of lunching on the ground. The act might betray him.

Reckless as he was he took every minute precaution not to be discovered.

As soon as he was alone in a secluded spot he examined himself keenly in a pocket-glass, and seeing that all was right, he again mounted and trotted gently to the race-course.

It was crowded, and most people had taken their places.

Kelly had no idea of entering the enclosures, and shook his head when offered tickets.

To a man of Kelly's tastes the scene was very attractive and delightful.

Only he would have liked to join in the fun of the affair. This however was denied him.

Several horsemen made pointed advances to him, which he coldly repulsed.

It was Kelly's game not to speak at all. He simply flicked his horse and moved away.

"Wife of the Great Mogul," said one.

"Queen of the Cannibal Islands," laughed another.

We have no intention of describing the races with which we have nothing to do.

One race is very much like another.

Kelly enjoyed it much and only wished he could have a refresher.

Just as one of the races was over, he saw Zeph and Salmon Roe looking anxiously around.

Kelly disengaged himself from the crowd and rode off to meet them.

"Off's the word," said Salmon Roe. "Captain Henshaw is looking for you everywhere, I have kept close to him all day. A man has just rushed to him, and declared you are in the disguise of a woman."

"—— him!" cried Kelly, with a fearful curse, and turned away quietly.

He did not, however, try his horse's speed at first.

He made for the road that led to Sydney. But he had not gone far when he heard shouts, and looking behind saw a confused mass of men, all mounted, following.

At their head, easily distinguished by his height and stalwart frame, was Captain Henshaw.

They were about a quarter-of-a-mile behind.

The whole question depended on the speed of his horse. It was bony and powerful, and Kelly had tolerable confidence in it.

Still the troopers, having to cope with such characters as they did, were well mounted.

On, on, on, sped Kelly, looking warily to the right and left.

He soon discovered that those in the rear were quite his equals.

They might prove his superiors. He knew nothing of the stamina of the horse when urged to a great pace.

Still he persevered. The road turned several times, and he lost sight of them several times.

But he could hear the unmistakable sound of pursuit, and again looked around.

After riding three miles, he came to a bridge over a stream of not very great width.

Instead of crossing the bridge, he swerved to the left and dashed towards a mass of thicket near which was a hut.

He had intended to leap the stream and take a cross cut.

But on reaching the hut, he found there was a plank over the river to serve the purpose of a bridge.

He at once dismounted, let his horse go loose, threw off his feminine habiliments, and dashed across, casting the plank into the water when he reached the other side.

He then hurried away.

When Captain Henshaw and his party came up, they found a hat, veil, habit, and a horse, but no sign of their owner.

Kelly took his whiskers and nose from his pocket, in which was also a cap.

Thus equipped, he followed a rough-beaten path until he came to an obscure shanty inn, where a few shepherds and stock-keepers were drinking.

Here he procured refreshments, and taking a supply of whisky and tobacco, took his way towards Sydney, which he entered in the dark.

He found Zeph and Salmon Roe smoking over their grog, and very anxious.

Captain Kit had been with them some time, but had gone away.

"Let us start at once," cried Zeph.

"No," said Kelly, "I'm hanged if I do until I've seen that there Frenchwoman.

It was useless reasoning with him; he must submit to his fate.

CHAPTER CXVII.

KIT'S POWER OVER MARIE.

AT ten o'clock the two met, and went in the direction of the Government grounds.

There was a turnstile by means of which the grounds could be both entered and left, but they were only for the use of those who lived in Government House.

No one ever ventured to break the rule; Kelly, of course, was an exception.

Prowling about in his usual cat-like way, he had discovered Marie's habit of meeting the governor's nephew of a morning.

Leading his brother to a thicket, he concealed himself to await the departure of the young man.

A moment after they were behind the trees, the lovers came in sight.

Captain Kit was very nearly whistling.

"Come away, Ned," he said, "there will be no kidnapping."

And he drew his astonished brother away. Not until they were in a retired place did the younger man speak.

"That girl's an escaped convict," he then said; "no one can do anything to her, but if her real charater was known she would be ruined

"Stark mad! that high-flyer a convict!" exclaimed Kelly; "it ain't likely."

"It is—and when we're at home, I'll tell you all about it," replied Kit.

Ned Kelly's astonishment when he heard the truth was something ludicrous to behold.

All the time he was listening, he was plotting. Greed and avarice were more powerful incentives to him than passion.

The girl was in his power, and in Government House there must be many valuables.

"Well—that is a start," he cried, when Kit's yarn was over; "did you pick up any *parley voo* in your travels?"

"A fair smattering," replied Kit.

"Then write and tell her ladyship she must come here, if she don't want the sack," said Kelly.

"What do you intend doing?" asked Kit.

"I mean to have that there girl under my thumb, to make her fetch and carry just as I pleases," he continued, brutally, "the wench shall be in my power—you'll see."

And he unfolded a plan, cunning and daring, by which she should join in a daring robbery.

"We'll take the swag on board your brig," he continued, "run to Adelaide, sell it, and come back when the kick-up is over."

Captain Kit, like a good many others, was easily ruled by a master mind and yielded his ready consent.

He had passed the Rubicon, and, though he looked with abhorrence on bloodshed, would probably in his brother's company learn to be less squeamish.

Captain Kit wrote a letter to Marie Franconnet in these words—

"A friend who knew Mlle. Marie Franconnet, but under another name, must see her on important business—this evening at eight. A guide will be in waiting outside the Government grounds, near the turnstile."

The consternation of the girl on receiving this laconic but alarming note may be conceived.

Of course she knew what it meant, and that she was in some man's power.

What should she do? Her first impulse was flight. She had money and jewels, presents from the family, and she knew that steamers were plying daily to every part of the colony.

But this meant ruin to all her hopes. She would go to the reading-room.

The countess was goodness itself. When Marie asked for her for leave to call on Madame Rabillard, permission was granted at once.

At eight she was outside the turnstile, plainly dressed and thickly veiled.

There Captain Kit awaited her. He bowed politely, but a cold grip went to her heart when she recognised the man who had aided her in her escape from New Caledonia.

She walked by his side in speechless terror. She could not have spoken if she had tried

They reached his house, and she was introduced into a sitting-room, where, to her increased surprise and alarm, she recognised her strange admirer.

"This is my brother," sait Kit, drily.

Marie sat down, more dead than alive, with fear and embarrassment.

Captain Kit then explained his views, or rather those of Ned Kelly.

His brother had wished to marry her.

Marie's eyes flashed eagerly.

"Don't be alarmed," said Kit, in a cynical tone, "no harm is meant you."

"A woman like you is after my own heart. One who could burn a town down is just the card I want to hold in my hand." said Ned; but the girl did not understand him.

"As she don t 'bite'" continued Ned, "just tell her if she won't marry me, she must help me.'"

Kit then explained that his brother was in want of money, had had severe losses at play, and must get gold somehow.

In Government House there must be plate and cash, the position of which she must know.

"You wish me to rob my employers," gasped the unhappy victim. "Never!"

"No—only to admit my brother when all are sleep," continued Kit, "and show him the place where the valuables are kept."

"They are under lock and key," said Marie, sobbing in utter consternation.

"Never you mind that," was the sardonic answer.

And, despite the girl's resistance, she was compelled ultimately to yield.

It was agreed that she should meet Kelly in the grounds.

There was a side door leading to an *escalier de service*, which was generally left open, to facilitate the exit and entrance of the servants who stopped out late.

Marie went away in a state of mind most truly pitiable.

What should she do? To tell the truth meant social ruin, and the end of all her hopes.

This, then, was not to be thought of. She must resign herself to her cruel fate.

It was long past midnight ere she entered the grounds.

Kelly was there dressed very plainly. He wore his favourite disguise of nose and whiskers.

Not a word was spoken. She led the way.

All was still. Presently they reached a retired part of the building.

She pointed to a door, and there would have moved away, but Kelly grasped a knife he wore in his belt, and looked at her with such fierce and menacing eyes that she trembled.

He then produced a bunch of strange keys, and soon had the door open.

He drew her in and closed the door.

The plate chest was not even locked, and Kelly easily filled a bag.

He however, after a long search, found no money.

Marie believed his Excellency kept his money in his study, which was next to his bedroom. This she faltered in broken English.

Kelly made no reply, but put his finger on his lips warningly, and went out.

Marie, more dead than alive, retired to her room.

Next morning, before the robbery was discovered, the Rate, Captain Kit, with Kelly and his pals on board, was far away.

The robbery was not discovered until late. There was to be a dinner-party that day, and in the afternoon the butler and his aide went to the strong-room.

Nothing seemed touched, but when the confidential servant opened the chest, he was taken with a kind of trembling fit.

The chest was empty.

"Great heavens!" the man cried, "whatever can I do? It is all gone."

"Put in the wrong chest, perhaps, Butler," observed his friend and aide.

"No!" gasped the unfortunate butler. "I must go and tell his Excellency."

The Earl of Belmont heard the news with great anger and annoyance. The intrinsic value of the plate was great, but it was also very unpleasant and awkward for it to disappear just as it was wanted.

Not the faintest suspicions occurred as to the means by which the robbery was effected. Because when Marie Franconnet appeared at breakfast, her eyes were heavy and her cheeks pale, no one thought of connecting that fact with the robbery.

Lady Belmont kindly asked what was the matter, and headache was given as an excuse.

There was nothing to be done but send for the police and set them on the track.

Such valuable plate with crests and other marks indicated its origin. But in all communities there are disreputable people who will buy anything without asking its origin.

Marks are not difficult to obliterate, and then the melting-pot does the rest.

Marie Franconnet was humiliated and terrified. That she should have conceived a passing admiration for a man of Kelly's character was humiliating.

But it was still more miserable for her to know herself to a certain extent in his power.

How could she get out of it? Not by remaining in Sydney, where he could always find her.

She must make a bold stroke for a husband, and yet even that would take time.

CHAPTER CXVIII.

MARIE MAKES A BOLD STROKE.

THE governor in a light and airy way spoke of his loss at dinner, apologising for the absence of the plate, but as that did not detract from the goodness of the dinner, everybody smiled and the dinner went on.

The young secretary and nephew of the governor could not very well pay marked attention to Marie before people. On the contrary he had to attend to others, and especially to his cousin Violet, who certainly looked upon him as very stiff and cold to what he had been.

Marie on this occasion was seated beside the wealthy squatter, who appeared to admire her more and more every time he saw her.

Marie's tactics were very clever. She was quiet and timid, doing nothing to draw out her lover and yet not repelling him.

Percy Boyd looked on with a frowning brow, though seeking to conceal his jealously and his infatuation.

Violet and her sister began to have a very slight inkling of the truth—at all events, that Percy admired the adventuress, as they then called her.

Not for one moment did they suppose it was anything but a young man's passing admiration for a pretty girl.

After dinner there was a reception and music, and the squatter, while Marie played, sat apart.

But there were professional players present on this occasion, and Marie's services were seldom required.

Percy Boyd scarcely ventured to speak, so that the squatter had it pretty well his own way.

The apartments were extensive, and during the time the orchestra was playing it was easy to find a corner where one was safe from interruption.

The colonist contrived a promenade with Marie when the music was rather loud and boisterous, and general attention was drawn off.

The girl instinctively knew that a crisis was coming. The man's manner was gauche and timid.

He was silent, too, as if trying to screw up his courage to the sticking place.

At last they reached a couch near a window, and sat down.

The squatter spoke about the country, asked her how she liked it, and carried on generally a commonplace style of conversation.

Then he paused again, and Marie, practised actress as she was, knew what was coming.

The state of the girl's heart, if she had one, was rather mixed.

Ned Kelly, by the exposure of his criminal tastes, had turned her utterly against him.

The Hon. Percy Boyd, she feared, was out of the question.

He was young handsome, well-born, and would be titled and rich, but, then, angling for him would take time.

And in the meantime she would remain in the power of Kelly, and this might lead to disastrous results.

"I am a very plain-spoken man," began the squatter. "I have travelled a good deal, and now mean finally to settle. My means are ample, and, should my good fortune continue, I may be probably able to sell off and buy property in England. But this would be useless unless I had a wife. Now I believe you are in every way suited to me. You have education and accomplishments, very welcome in the bush. I will strive to make you happy. Will you be my wife?"

"I am poor and obscure, and am penniless," she faltered in a low tone. "I have not a friend in the world!"

"More reason you should want one," was the hearty reply of the honest squatter. "Will you try to like me?"

"I like you already," she faltered, "but still my position is so beneath you."

"That is my lookout," he answered; "am I to consider you have accepted me?"

"Yes," she faintly ejaculated.

Well, we leave the ill-assorted lovers to their raptures awhile, and then resume the conversation.

"I shall ask permission of Lady Belmont—you can give up your situation, and be married at once," he said. "I know the earl well and will call to morrow."

"Monsieur," she began, timidly, really rather frightened, "I am a poor dependant—until you get her ladyship's consent, you had better not say I have accepted you——"

"Leave all to me," said the loyal colonial, "your feelings shall be held sacred."

And they returned to the crowd, not without notice from Percy Boyd, who however was tied hand and foot. He could not venture to find fault and expostulate.

Next morning, Marie took her usual walk in the grounds. She was rather more flushed than usual. Naturally she was paler, but had ventured on the use of cosmetics.

Percy Boyd came to the rendezvous in no very good humour. He was jealous, and he showed it.

"I was very much surprised, Marie," he said, "to notice how you went on with that horrid bush savage."

"He is a most agreeable gentleman," she answered.

"I dare say he is," he growled, "but I cannot let him come between the wind and my nobility."

"But you can never marry me," she went on, in a rather hard, sad, dry tone.

"In time," he replied, a little uneasy.

"I cannot wait," she exclaimed. "I am poor; my meeting you places me in a false position. It is sure to be found out. Our meetings must cease, our understanding must come to an end, unless you speak to your uncle and aunt at once."

"I cannot," he said, colouring highly. "I am expected to marry my cousin, Lady Violet Boyd—a mere schoolgirl. Were I to decline, I should be started off to England at a moment's notice—especially if I owned my love for you——"

"Then we must part," was the answer.

"You will give me time?" he asked, in despairing tones, he was really and truly infatuated, and would have married her, if he had been in a position to have done so, have married her at once.

"How long?" she asked, rather coldly.

"I cannot say," he urged earnestly, "but if you love me, you will wait."

"Consider my position—that of a forlorn girl—without any relatives—dependent on a few kind friends," she said, in tones of deep emotion, "and I fear me, I am behaving very ungratefully."

"Give me time," he begged.

"We will speak of it to-night again," she said, "if we can."

And she allowed him to take his departure.

Then she walked back to Government House and went to her room, where she made a seemingly simple, but really very elaborate costume.

As she expected, she received a summons to attend Lady Belmore in her boudoir.

Here, as she expected, she found the countess in conversation with the squatter.

"Sit down, mademoiselle," remarked the countess; "I have something very important to say to you."

Marie bowed low, and seated herself in the chair pointed out by the countess.

"This gentleman," began the countess, "has rather surprised me by informing me that, without having actually proposed, he has given you a hint as to his wish to make you his wife, and that you have referred him to me."

"Madame la Comtesse," said the girl, in accents which thrilled the listener's heart, they were so plaintive and sad, "I have no father, no mother; and, madame, I have dared to hope you would be my friend, to advise me, if I dared ask you."

"Certainly, my dear," was the answer of the kindly countess. "It is a serious step to take, and I shall be sorry to lose you. But you are poor and an orphan, and monsieur, who is a good man, rich, well known to my husband."

The squatter, at a sign from the countess, had moved away.

"And you think you can love him and be happy?" asked the countess, kindly.

"I know not much of love," she answered, with well-acted timidity—this Petroleuse, who had abandoned family and society, for a handsome Communist—"but I think him a good man, and will make me a good husband."

The countess laughed a sweet ripple of womanly laughter, and then turned to the squatter.

"You've won the day," she said, looking at her watch. "I'll give you five minutes to settle matters, as lunch will be ready, and then we can settle the particulars, as your return to the Murray river is to be so soon."

And she rose.

Marie could make no objection to an early marriage. She lived in constant dread of the re-appearance of Kelly, of whom by his real name of course she had never heard. He might expose her at any time.

When, therefore, the ardent lover spoke of an early marriage, she resigned herself into the arms of her lover and—the countess.

The news somehow spread before they met at lunch, and everyone was pleased except Percy Boyd.

It was with the greatest difficulty he kept down his indignation

But she was fair, fickle, and faithless. She had accepted another man, and he must learn to hate her.

That was his wish, but at twenty-two it is hard to feel that sentiment towards any woman, especially against the one you love.

Percy did not know much about drinking the waters of oblivion.

Only that he was—though slightly foolish—a perfect gentleman, he would have quarrelled with his father's friend.

After lunch the party dispersed, and there being no further fear of Marie proving a rival, Lady Violet and Lady Blanche were very gracious to Marie.

They hoped she would be happy; it was an excellent match; and, in the days to come, as the colony progressed, she would have a fine house and every luxury.

Besides she could always come for a short season to the capital.

Marie laughed in her sleeve. If they had only known!

And if she had only known in the time to come what it would produce to her!

The squatter, who was being pressed by his overseer to return to the station, proposed that the marriage should take place within a fortnight.

There was no opposition, as Percy Boyd, on finding that his sweetheart had finally jilted him and thrown him up, asked his uncle to send him on a mission to Melbourne.

Money of course was not wanting, and exactly a fortnight after she was wooed, Marie Franconnet became Mrs. Eldred.

Here we leave them. We shall find them again before long.

CHAPTER CXIX.
WHERE TO MELT IT.

CAPTAIN KIT knew those seas well, and as he was well aware that Ned Kelly would be the better for an absence of some duration from the colony, he proposed making a voyage to Hong-Kong.

There they could get rid of the plate.

Chinese and Jews were to be found ready and willing to buy everything and ask no questions.

At all events, in order to run no risk, it was decided to take out the crest.

This there was plenty of time to do.

Captain Kit had not a large crew. He was a cautious man and did not like to excite suspicion, but he had enough men for his purpose if he fell in with a moderate-sized ship.

As a rule there was little to be gained by assaulting small merchant vessels, as their cargo was bulky and of a kind which would not suit Kit the cruiser; while, as a rule, they had not much money.

So Kit trusted a little to chance and to something turning up.

Though he had plenty of arms on board, he had no cannon.

Captain Kit on board as a skipper was a very different man from what he was on shore.

When on his vessel he was every inch a sailor.

At Hong-Kong he had been more than once, but only in a legitimate way.

The voyage was not a very eventful one, for the weather was fine and nothing came in their way to excite their cupidity.

Either the vessels were too large to attack, or too small to be worth capturing.

In this way they arrived at Hong-Kong.

No one on board had any knowledge of Kelly, Zeph, or Salmon Roe, while Captain Kit had done nothing to bring down the vengeance of the authorities upon him.

So they performed the needed formalities, and went on shore to a lodging-house.

Now came getting the plate on shore. Once the ship was admitted to harbour, very little notice was taken of what was done.

Men went backwards and forwards without much questioning, but should any suspicion be excited, there would, of course, be a rare hue and cry.

The plate had been knocked out of shape and beaten into small pieces.

They made a great pretence of looking for a cargo, and so drew off suspicion.

In this way they contrived to take their plunder on shore and store it at their temporary residence.

Then Captain Kit, through an acquaintance of his in the settlement, found an introduction to a Chinese general merchant.

The man was a small innkeeper, who depended alto-

15

gether on sailors, and who assured them that Chi-he was not only trustworthy, but able to buy anything from a ship to a ship's anchor.

Like most of his countrymen he kept up no appearance; all he cared about was to make money.

The heathen Chinee acted with the most perfect coolness tested the precious metals, and then, weighing them, paid in notes and gold.

That he made a more than fair profit on them was not to be doubted.

Men selling under the circumstances seldom ask questions, being only too glad of the value for their swag.

It now became a question as to what should be done.

Kelly had no wish to return to Sydney at present. He knew that the suspicions of Lieutenant Henshaw might have been very seriously aroused.

He had vanity enough to think that the audacious robbery committed at Government House would be ascribed to him, and had no wish to run the chance of being accused of the crime.

Besides he knew not how far he could trust the French-woman. She might try and take time by the forelock and denounce him even at her own peril.

Women, he thought, were very artful, and she could easily make up some story to clear herself and implicate him.

At all events he did not think Sydney a safe place, neither was Melbourne, as he knew that Tom Conquest would never rest until he effected his capture.

He did not see much to be got by re-visiting his new friend the Wagga-Wagga butcher, as really and truly he did not believe in his story.

An arrant rogue himself Kelly was no fool, and could see discrepancies in the other's story which made him doubtful.

Kelly and Kit had a long talk as to what might be done, and could come to no conclusion, when a vessel, with a valuable cargo, put into port to refit.

She had passed through a severe storm, lost spars, had heavy leaks opened, and had several of her crew drowned.

She had a valuable cargo of silk, indigo, and tea.

Of course she would be of no use to the owner of Captain Kit's cruiser, even if they could capture her.

But Zeph hit upon a plan.

"Crews are scarce; men desert from here as else-where," he began; "let us ship as sailors."

"What's the use of going in for hard work when we've got the tin?" growled Kelly.

"You ain't half alive, Ned. I'll show you how we can make a pile. We ship aboard as able seamen. She starts for homeward voyage. Kit lies in her wake. She gets leaky. A few augur holes make her more so. She's abandoned by the crew. She's well insured, and the captain, nor, for the matter of that, the owners don't care if she sinks. Kit appears on the scene, repairs the damage—because he knows where the leaks are—saves the barque, and takes her into port and makes his claim for salvage. Now do you tumble to it?"

All this had to be explained to Ned Kelly, who naturally enough not understanding anything about the matter had to give way to the others.

The vessel in question would naturally take some time to repair.

There was therefore leisure enough to lay their plans.

After some further consideration, however, it was agreed that Kelly should go on board as a passenger. He would hear what was said in this way and communicate with his associates.

The Duncan was a very smart vessel. She had been driven out of her course and had gone through a good deal, but she had originally been well built.

The captain and chief officer believed she could be patched up to stand a voyage to England, and so orders were given to have her docked.

It was soon found that many of the sailors had bolted.

An offer from six   the diminished crew was gladly accep...

There was a state cabin vacant: although it was expensive Kelly did not care. The results would be, probably, very profitable.

All was settled, and the Duncan sailed on a fine day, with every hope of a prosperous voyage.

Kit Kelly's cruiser lay quiet in harbour for six hours after the Duncan started, and then departed also.

The Duncan, though she had a valuable cargo of indigo, silk, and tea, was not a large vessel. She had a moderate crew and only a few passengers.

There were only two state rooms, one of which had been secured by Kelly, the other by a rather saturnine individual who called himself a planter, and his name was entered on the ship books as Errol.

The passengers were all business men and numbered twelve.

Kelly, alias Bernard, made himself very agreeable. He had travelled, seen a good deal of the world, and could in his rough and ready way tell good stories.

In those days, when a large number of the travellers of the world consisted of the bagman class, coarseness went a long way for humour, and vulgarity for wit.

In such society as that Kelly could pass for a very smart and clever fellow.

He toned down his oaths to the finest point, he used as little slang as possible, and thus passed muster.

The individual who occupied the opposite state room to him, was somewhat of a mystery to him and to everybody else.

He was rather rough, but he had money. He appeared to possess a chronic cold and was always warmly wrapped up.

On the first occasion they met at dinner, the two eyed each other curiously.

There seemed to be something familiar to each in the expression of the face.

Both discarded the idea, and yet they were convinced somehow that they had met before.

Neither, however, made any remark, and after dinner smoked, drank, and played a game of dominoes without making the slightest allusion to their mutual suspicion.

The strange passenger, who called himself Rintoul, had also joined at Hong-Kong, where he had been remaining some time as an invalid.

It was only when the vessel offered him a rapid passage that Rintoul determined to start for England.

What was his other motive?

Certainly he had been for several nights in the company of Mr. Bernard (Kelly), and had noticed that he had plenty of money.

Whatever his ultimate motive was, this induced him to go on board the same ship.

Kelly's luggage consisted of just what an extempore traveller required, and a portmanteau for immediate use.

Kelly knew very well that any attempt to save his general luggage when the climax came would be useless.

He therefore decided to have merely what he required ready and no more.

The third evening out, Kit's cruiser well in sight, Zeph let him know that all was ready; that the plugs would all be out at the same time, and the signal be given a little before daylight.

Kelly went to his state room, but with no idea of finding much sleep.

He only partially undressed, and was in the act of putting some of his valuables in a small box, when the door of his state-room opened, and a stout, burly-looking fellow entered cautiously, as if expecting to find the other asleep.

Kelly had him by the collar of the coat in an instant.

He was as stout as himself, but a struggle under the circumstances would have been simply folly.

The captain's cabin was close at hand.

But there was no necessity.

The minute the stranger saw the occupant of the state-room in his déshabillé, he recognised him.

"Kelly !" he cried.

"Hush !" said our hero, "who are you, a-blurting out names like that ?'

"Why, Will Morgan, your old pal," the other retorted. "I've been dodging about these two years on my last stake, and things were getting warm for me in my last place, so I fished up another small pile, and took passage as a nob."

"But what did you want a-sneaking in here?" asked Kelly, who now recognised his old pal.

"Well," grinned Morgan, "I thought I'd just let you know—just for old acquaintance sake—that I spotted you, old man."

"All right," answered Ned. "You may be wanted, but not now my buck. When I'm asleep, none of your larks here."

"We'll have a jaw to-morrow," answered Morgan, who saw that his comrade was sulky-natured.

Kelly was not at all pleased with this meeting.

He did not like his personality to be known to too many people.

He finished his task, secured all he cared for in a kind of wallet, and then retired.

He slept heavily, nor awakened until a sudden uproar aroused him.

He hurried on deck, bag in hand, and found the captain and crew in a state of the utmost alarm.

The ship, which had been so sound the day before, had apparently opened her seams.

The men were working at the pumps, but from the first the captain and officers saw that it was a mere question of time.

She might float hours, but she must sink in the end.

She might even go down at any moment.

The captain determined to take to the boats.

They were numerous and well-appointed, and with such weather as they had, they had nothing to fear.

So they started for Hong-Kong, in their hurry not noticing a vessel hovering at some distance, nor the fact that Zeph and Salmon Roe were missing.

As soon as the boats were at some distance, Captain Kit hurried up and a gang went on board.

A number were put to the pumps, and then, as Zeph and Salmon Roe knew where the holes where, it was easy enough to plug them up.

In four hours after the ship was a derelict, she was clear of water and sailing back for Hong-Kong with what may be called a prize crew.

Meanwhile the officers, men, and passengers had reached Hong-Kong, and had reported their loss to Lloyd's agent and the British Consul.

Then all dispersed to await a chance of returning to England.

The vessel and its contents were fully insured, so, after all, only the underwriters would suffer.

Kelly and Morgan had struck up a certain kind of intimacy, though neither had full confidence in the other.

They had not met for some time.

Morgan after one of his feats, which consisted always of atrocious murders and robberies, had made a good haul.

To escape from pursuit he had sailed away and led a wandering life for more than two years.

His track had been marked by other crimes, and finding himself at Hong-Kong when the Duncan was in port, he had taken a passage.

The man never left himself without means. He was a cautious and calculating villain, as those who knew him will be well aware.

His object was to reach England and then work his way back to the colony.

Meanwhile Kelly and Morgan had returned to Hong-Kong with the passengers and crew of the Duncan, itself supposed to be at the bottom of the sea.

Morgan, having no idea of the nefarious trick that had been played, could not tell why Kelly kept such a sharp look-out seaward.

He expected every day to see the vessels appear in sight.

He was very fond of sitting for hours on the end of the jetty, talking to some of the old salts who usually hung about such spots.

Early one afternoon he took up his usual post and soon what he was looking for came in sight.

He had a glass, and peered through it with keen anxiety.

"If that ain't the Duncan," he suddenly cried, "then I'm a Dutchman."

The man whom he addressed was one of those men who are always to be seen hanging round such localities, peering through glasses without any or reasonable object that anyone knows of.

"You've good eyes, mate," he cried, "but it are the Duncan."

The news spread like wild-fire through the town Kelly modestly retired.

The Duncan was in company with the schooner Kate, which had left the harbour about the same time.

Soon the two came in, and the captain and Lloyd's agent went on board.

Captain Kit's story was simple. While pursuing his voyage, he had come upon the Duncan water-logged.

He had gone on board, and, knowing the vessel to be valuable, he had determined to save her.

He had put every man who could work at the pumps, while the carpenter had searched for the leaks.

Fortunately he found them and was able to stop them up.

They were strange leaks, being some small holes, under bales, which they had to remove to get at them.

They were however successfully stopped, and then the vessel brought into harbour.

The delight of the underwriters was great indeed.

Captain Kit, or John Leary as he was called on the ship's papers, was decidedly entitled, with his crew, to large salvage.

But Captain Leary objected to abide the decision of Courts of Law.

He had no time to waste.

The agent for Lloyd's said that he had a certain licence in the matter, and could pay him a sum down in draught on London, which any banker would cash.

Then after communications with the owners he could have the balance at a future time.

After some pretended hesitation Leary accepted, the draughts were signed by the captain and agent, cashed by the bankers, and the schooner Kate took her departure, to be seen no more in Hong-Kong.

It was now determined by the captain and the owner's agent to overhaul the Duncan.

A large part of her cargo was damaged. This was all sold at a rummage sale, the rest put in bond.

Then the secret came out. The vessel had been scuttled—but by whom?

They remarked that two of their crew had been missing when they took to their boats, while the two state-room passengers had also disappeared.

There could be but one explanation. They had been the victims of a foul conspiracy.

But it was too late to unmask the vile perpetrators of the cruel crime.

CHAPTER CXX.

KELLY MEETS AN OLD FRIEND.

NED KELLY had never been partial to the sea. On board a vessel, large or small, he was not king of the castle.

He therefore informed his brother of his desire to be put on shore at Adelaide, where once more he could take one of the flat bottomed steamers which go up the Murray river, and go in search of his horse.

Captain Kit agreed, but hoped that now they had met they would not entirely separate.

Kelly responded that his adventurous life would not

bably bring him to Sydney again, but that he should keep away from it for some time.

Kelly bade his brother keep up constant communication when in Sydney with the barmaid known as Mary Meadows, through whom, if he knew of any pal going to Sydney, he would send him messages.

This settled, the voyage was continued; and, finally, Kelly, Zeph, and Salmon Roe landed at Adelaide in sailors' dresses, and were soon lost in the crowd.

Captain Kit continued on his way.

The three confederates, having discovered the date of the departure of a flat-bottomed steamer, secured passages, and then kept quiet, going out for an hour or so in the evening.

They amused themselves on board in the usual way with cards, smoking, and drinking; and finally reached the landing-place.

Thence they made their way to the paddocks where they had left Marco Polo.

The owner of the paddocks was very much surprised to see Kelly after so long an absence, but on being paid all arrears readily gave up the animal.

He supplied the other two with horses; and the men, well-mounted, well-armed, and well-provided, started in search of further adventures.

It had been decided, however, to do nothing to draw immediate attention to their return. Their plunder had been chiefly turned into notes.

Spending money freely in the colony was too common a practice for anyone to notice it.

They would simply amuse themselves in their own way, until necessity and the prospect of a great *coup* made them yield to temptation.

At last they, after a night of gambling, in which they had been looked upon with suspicion, made up their minds to remove.

No bushman is ever encumbered with luggage.

They were now costumed as rough, but respectable diggers.

Their destination was a certain spot on the Murray river, where, while there were hiding-places enough, there were also scattered here and there inns, frequented by shearers, shepherds, and stock-keepers, where they could obtain all their requirements.

They could thus pass some time while planning some scheme by which to replenish their slowly, but surely vanishing purses.

Kelly did not know which he longed for most, to be at the head of his old gang again, or to be once more with his brother carrying out some daring plot.

They travelled slowly, as there was nothing to hurry for.

The country was thickly peopled for the colony, that is, they could safely depend on seeing a stock-keeper or shepherd's hut twice a day, where they could procure solids.

Thus they travelled until they came to the position they desired.

A large piece of bush, rough and thick with trees and scrub, was situated at no great distance from the Murray river.

In that district were some of the largest estates of the squatters scattered far and wide, and consequently rude inns existed for the use of their employés.

Kelly had no desire to draw attention, and so he and his companions found a safe hiding-place in the bush, where they could camp within a reasonable distance of the inn.

In these places no explanation was required, and no questions were asked.

They, therefore, after arranging their camp and securing their horses, walked down to the inn.

It was a rude one-storied building, with some rough tables and seats in front.

But rough and ready as it was, the accommodation was good. There was little that could not be procured there from rum to champagne, in which in their mad fits, even stockkeepers would indulge when in funds.

The inn was on a cross road, and was much frequented by bullock-drivers and others, so that the business was tolerably flourishing.

It was determined to move further on, as the neighbourhood did not seem to offer any inducements in their line.

Accordingly next day they mounted their horses after a late breakfast and made for the inn.

In front of the verandah were several waggons, harnessed with bullocks.

The drivers were inside.

Finding the bar crowded, Kelly and his party seated themselves at a table outside and called an attendant.

Their horses were attached to one of several posts that stood in the road.

They were close to an open window, near which several men were seated.

Presently Ned Kelly heard his own name mentioned.

"I tell you, mate, I ain't a-going for to say as that is Kelly, but I says as that is Kelly's horse; know'd him afore he stole him," the man was saying.

"What's your game?"

"Police-station ain't a mile off," the other answered "I'll step out at the back."

"Right you are," replied the other.

Kelly never moved a muscle.

The men spoke in a hoarse stage-whisper, but Kelly's ears were almost supernaturally keen.

He looked at his comrades, and then slowly turned his head just in time to see the men who had been at the window move away.

(To be continued.)

NED KELLY

THE
IRONCLAD
AUSTRALIAN BUSHRANGER

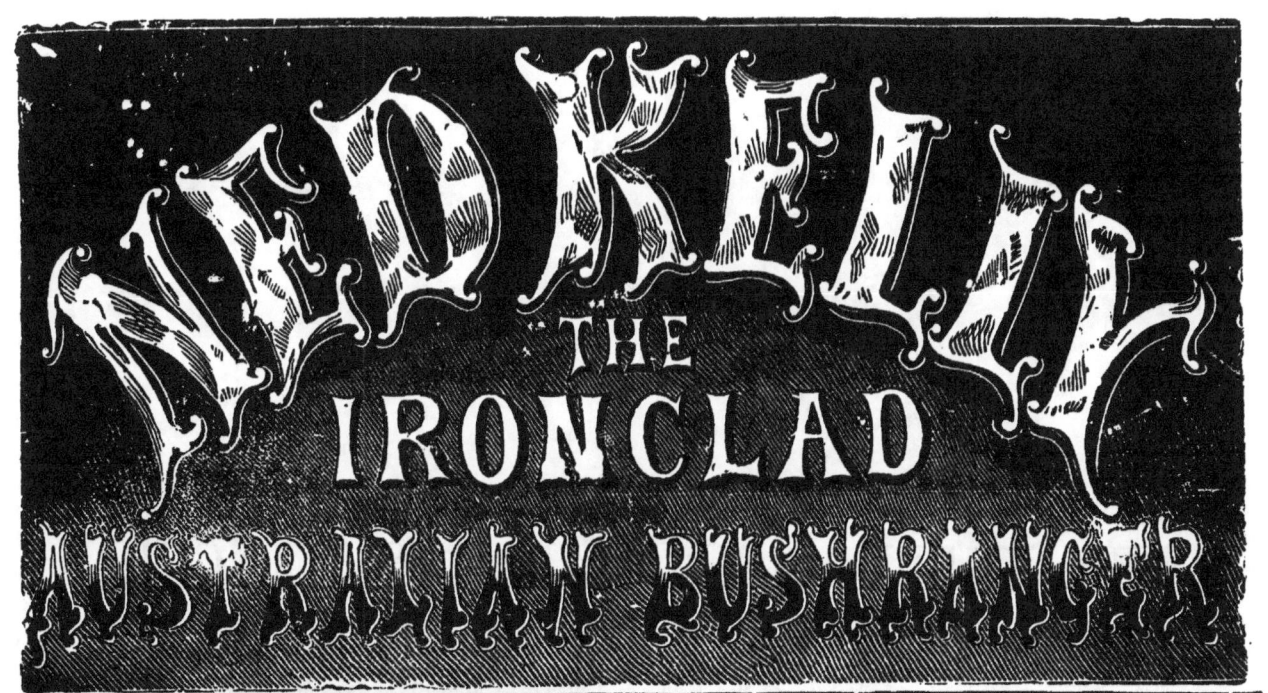

NO 20,

NED KELLY: IRONCLAD BUSHRANGER.

It is well known that for many years Ned Kelly had made himself notorious by a series of crimes wholly incompatible with the civilisation of the nineteenth century. Ned Kelly's celebrated steed, Marco Polo, is as well known at the Antipodes as Dick Turpin's Black Bess in these islands." *Ned Kelly*, illustrated, Nos. 1 to 11, already published at 4, Essex street, Strand, price One Penny.—*Telegraph*, 7th July, 1881.

'It is notorious that the robbery of Mr. Steward's corpse was mainly performed by the assistance of NED KELLY'S BROTHER, the Captain of what was neither more nor less than a pirate ship "—*Times*, July.

The history of NED KELLY and his celebrated black horse, Marco Polo, will ever live in the recollections of the Australian public. The deeds of Dick Turpin, and the performances of Black Bess, are tame beside those of 'NED AND HIS NAG;' in addition to which Ned's history is true, and Turpin's is pure fiction."—*Press*, July.

CHAPTER CXX.—*Continued.*

Not a moment was to be lost.

His comrades understood Kelly's warning look, and at once mounted.

At first they rode slowly, but when out of sight of the inn they hurried.

Kelly now told them what had induced him to leave so abruptly.

He determined to put a long distance between himself and that spot ere he halted.

Presently they came to a cross-road again, one being the main road, such as it was, to Geelong; the other had a bullock-track.

"They'll only squint at my beauty," said Kelly; "you've nothing to fear. I'll play 'possum for a day or two; you can spy, so that when we meet you'll have news."

They always obeyed Kelly. and so, after appointing a meeting in the first drinking-shop in the scattered village they were going to, he rode away.

The road he followed was a bullock-track, with many marks of wheels and also of horses.

Kelly knew he was going in the direction of a station.

He had no doubt that he might find some temporary shelter near it.

The traps would look for him the way his friends had taken, so that a few days might put them off the track.

As he went on he found all the signs of an extensive sheep-run.

At last, after a hard and heavy ride, he came in sight of the home station.

It was an extensive one, with the usual one-storied principal building, and out-buildings and paddocks for the horses.

In the verandah in front sat a lady, reclining in a rocking-chair, with a book in her hand.

She looked up at the sound of a horse stopping, and gave a faint shriek.

The recognition was mutual.

He knew her to be Marie.

She knew him to be the man who had saved her from the fire, but who held her secret.

What unlucky chance had brought him there?

It was a dreadful affair, but it must be faced.

Kelly alighted and approached her with an awkward pretence of politeness.

"Madam, we meet again," he said.

"Yes," she answered in good English, "how is it so, why do you come here?"

"Pure accident, ma'am," he went on. "I'm travelling—looking for a spot to settle on. Lost my way," he continued, laughing meaningly.

"My husband is out," she faltered, and then explained that he would soon be in to dinner—would he walk in and wait?

"Say I'm related—what you like—I wants a little shelter for a little time," said Kelly, thinking he would be as safe there as anywhere else

"I'll tell my husband," she said, "you saved my life from fire—that will be enough."

And Kelly entered after Marie had called a boy to take his horse to the paddock.

Marie desired another boy to show Kelly to a room, comfortable, though simply furnished.

She then retired to bemoan the cruel fate which had brought this man to her quiet and happy home.

Though love for her husband was out of the question, she was happy and contented to a certain extent.

He was kindness itself, and gave her every comfort and indulgence.

All that wealth could command was hers, and her room had been furnished regardless of expense.

She had a bullock load of things brought up, with a piano and other luxuries.

After her stormy and terrible career she had found repose.

She was alone, she had believed her crimes and sins could never find her.

And now this man by some fearful fatality had come like a ghost of the past.

That he was coarse and rough would be nothing to her husband.

He had saved her life under perilous circumstances.

He knew the whole story, and his gratitude was very great towards the man, who had really done a brave and gallant act.

Still she feared him.

He had committed to her knowledge one great robbery, and there was a fearful dread on her soul that he came there for no good purpose.

She did not believe in his having reached the station by accident.

She believed he had tracked her out to gain some end.

She was to a certain extent in his power, but she could only expose him, and force him to fly.

Did he betray his knowledge of her, it meant utter and hopeless ruin.

But she hoped that, whatever his object in coming, she might induce him to go away and leave her in peace.

Here she was told that her husband had come home and wanted dinner.

She ran down at once, looking bright and happy, and at once told him of her unexpected visitor.

He was delighted to welcome the man who had saved his darling.

"No matter if he is rough," he said, in answer to his wife, "he did a bold and gallant thing—and I thank him."

The wife kissed him.

Then she went and fetched Kelly, to whom he was profuse in his thanks.

He certainly did not like the look of him in any way, but he forced himself to hide his dislike and distrust.

"I ain't one of your polite swells," said Kelly, "and I want no thanks—so the least said is the soonest mended."

"Very good," replied the squatter, and led the way to the dining-room, which was amply supplied with luxuries.

Kelly from habit of imitation was able to just hold his own. Mr. Eldred, who was a gentleman, every inch of him, knew that the other had no pretensions that way, but he was polite and courteous all the same.

Kelly talked but very little, leaving the conversation to the wife and husband.

After dinner, however, Mr. Eldred proposed a smoke and a drink, hoping in some way to draw the other out.

But he totally failed. Kelly gave a very commonplace account of himself, al uded to London, briefly to Paris and Homburg—which did not surprise. The *nouveau riche* is found everywhere.

He was now looking about in the hope of settling. He had no taste for gold-digging. He had given that up when he had a legacy left him in England.

He was searching for a station, and when he found one to please him he believed he would settle.

Mr. Eldred politely hoped he might find one to suit him, but he devoutly wished that it would be a good distance off.

Two things struck the squatter. The man was too shifty about the eyes to be honest, while he clearly saw another thing.

Kelly admired his wife.

She, innocently enough, he thought, would not notice this, but he did.

He hoped Captain Higgins, as he called himself, would be a very distant neighbour, only to be seen on high days and holidays.

CHAPTER CXXI.

A STRANGE WOOING.

STRETCHED at full length in a Mexican hammock, slung beneath the creeper-shaded verandah running round her husband's dwelling-house, Marie Franconnet, now Marie Eldred, was musing on the good things of this life, and the advantages of virtue.

The girl was shrewd and clever, and had begun to appreciate the value of her new position.

As the honoured wife of one of the richest squatters of the district, to whom her lightest wish was law, there was no saying to what social eminence she might not aspire.

Eldred's wealth was increasing year by year, and it was his intention shortly to try for a seat in the colonial legislature.

Already in fancy she saw herself playing the part of one of the leaders of fashion in the capital of the colony, a part for which she felt she was in every way fitted.

Nay, in her dreams she even dared to look forward to the days when Eldred would realise his fortune, and return to Europe.

How she would queen it in London and Paris!

Paris! ah! how her heart thrilled at the word.

The past, with all its horrors, the frightful excesses of the Commune, the ghastly news of slaughter that had marked the entry of the Versailles troops into the devoted city, the agonies of imprisonment, the dreadful voyage to the Antipodes, the degrading tortures suffered at New Caledonia, were forgotten.

In seven or eight years, under a new name, as the wife of a rich Englishman, who would recognise her!

She was lost in the contemplation of a rapturous vision representing herself borne along the leafy avenues of the Bois de Boulogne, in an open carriage, drawn by a pair of the finest steppers that ever wore silver-plated harness.

A heavy step on the boarded floor of the verandah, and a whiff of coarse tobacco-smoke, puffed almost in her face, aroused her from her delightful reverie.

She looked up.

With his massy shoulders against one of the pillars of the verandah, his legs crossed, his hands thrust into his breeches-pockets, and his pipe sticking out of one corner of his mouth stood Captain Higgins, *alias* Ned Kelly.

For a moment their glances crossed in silence.

Then the bushranger took his pipe from his mouth, and broke into a chuckling laugh.

"You seem to find yourself pretty comfortable here," he remarked.

Since her marriage Marie had had plenty of practice in speaking English, and could now converse in that language fluently enough.

"Yes," she answered slowly, "I am very comfortable here."

"Yes, it's a decent crib, a very decent crib."

There was another interval of silence.

Marie looked up into Kelly's face to find his eye fixed on her with an evil, gloating look, the meaning of which she could read only too plainly.

Gradually she began to realise her position.

Her husband was away, the shepherds and stockmen were all far afield, and even if the women employed about the house were within call their presence was not likely to prove a check upon such a ruffian as she knew Kelly to be, if once his mind was made up.

"Look here, Marie," resumed Ned, "this is, as I was saying, a very decent crib, eh?"

"Yes," she replied.

"And you figure at the head of it very well, very well indeed. There's no denying," he continued in a meditative tone, "that you women do get the pull of us chaps there. Lord, now, anyone would think you'd been playing this here game ever since you were a kid, and didn't know the taste of Government rations," and he laughed again.

The woman did not want for pluck.

She had handled a revolver on the barricade of the Chateau d'Eau.

She saw that Kelly had some evil notion working in his head, and resolved to learn the worst.

"What is it you will?" she asked calmly, though all the while her heart throbbed violently at the thought of approaching peril.

"Well, yes," he said slowly, watching her as a tiger

does an antelope, "perhaps it will be just as well to have a bit of an explanation. Do you recollect how you and I first met at Sydney?"

"Yes."

"How I plucked you like a brand from the burning, as Holy Joe used to say, eh?"

"Well, I admit I owe you my life."

"Oh, you do? Well that gives us a fair ground to start on, anyway. Now don't you feel all a swelling and a bursting with feelings of gratitude towards me?"

"Gratitude? Yes; bad as I have been, I thank you from my heart for saving my life."

"Very good. Now I want a little practical proof of that gratitude."

"What do you mean?"

"Why, you see, I am thinking of shifting my quarters and lying close for a week or two on the upper waters of the Murray. I know one or two tidy little spots where one can lie snug and comfortable. But I am apt to feel lone-some at times, and I think I should feel all the better for your company."

"What!" she almost screamed, "you want me to—to—"

"To pass a pretty little honeymoon with yours truly, as the letter-writers put it," and he chuckled.

The woman was horror-stricken.

Bad as she had been, she was far from being utterly depraved.

Had Kelly merely asked her to betray her husband, she would have hesitated, for she had learned to respect Michael Eldred, if not to love him, and had besides a dawning consciousness of what was due to herself in her rehabilitated position to oppose to the powerful levers, fear and gratitude, by means of which the bushranger could work upon her feelings.

But to leave her home, to court shame and disgrace openly, to voluntarily abandon the high position she was beginning to realise, and all her dreams of future grandeur!

It was too much.

Self-interest is the strongest motive in the human heart, and self-interest told her to say "nay" to Kelly's proposition.

Only she was too wise to say "nay" openly.

Whilst she paused, seeking for a reply, the bushranger had kept his bloodshot eyes fixed on her steadily.

Coarse, brutal, and ignorant as Kelly was, he had a knack of reading human nature.

It was this that helped him to his supremacy over his comrades.

"Look here, my wench," he broke in, suddenly changing his tone from one of coarse banter to that of menace, "you know who I am. I am Ned Kelly, who never let man, woman, or child thwart him in any mortal thing he set his heart on. The day after to-morrow I start for the upper waters of the Murray, and you set out with me, either cantering by me on that pretty little grey mare of yours or strapped hand and foot across the pommel of Marco Polo's saddle like a sheep. And, by ——, if you don't behave yourself, you'll run a very fair chance of having your throat cut like a sheep's at the end of the journey."

Marie looked at him with a glance of horror.

The blood seemed to freeze in her veins as he hissed out these last words, with his face close to hers and his eyes riveted on her own.

At that moment the bushranger's keen ear caught the thud of approaching hoofs on the stretch of turf extending in front of the house.

"Look here," he continued hoarsely, as he thrust one hand into his pocket in search of his ever-ready knife, and laid the other on the woman's arm, "you'll swear now, by all you hold sacred, never to breathe a word of what I have said to a living soul, or I'll have that dainty neck of yours in half before you can count a dozen. Quick, now!"

"I swear, I swear by all that I hold sacred!" gasped Marie.

"And a precious good thing for you you did, young woman," muttered Ned, releasing her. "Ah! Mr. Eldred," he continued, addressing the squatter who had just ridden up and dismounted, "I hope you had a pleasant ride. Your good lady and me have been getting on famously."

Dinner was shortly served, and for the rest of the day Marie took care not to find herself alone with Kelly for a single instant.

She laughed and chatted and kept up a show of outward spirits, but all the while her heart was racked with rage and fear, and her mind scheming some method of releasing herself from her frightful position.

Tell her husband she dared not, for she knew his first impulse would be to attempt to seize Kelly, and the probable result of such an attempt was in her eyes not doubtful.

She was accustomed to reckon up a man's fighting-power, and rightly calculated that Ned would be a match for four like Michael Eldred.

At last she seemed to hit upon a plan that seemed to promise success.

She resolved to write a note to the nearest police station to inform the authorities of Kelly's presence on the station and meanwhile to feign acquiescence in the latter's plan.

Letters to or from the station were left to be called for at a small roadside public-house about five miles from the house, kept by a man named Gibson.

The difficulty was to get the letters there.

If she asked her husband to take it, he would naturally on seeing the address ask why she was in correspondence with the police, and an explanation, which she wished above all things to avoid, must ensue.

Moreover, she felt she could not trust any one of the hands to take it.

There was and is a widespread sympathy with what are called the dangerous classes in Australia, and the odds were that an epistle to the police would, if handed to one of the shepherds for transmission, be lost in transit.

Such things were continually happening.

Suddenly the bright idea crossed her of making use of a tame black, who used to hover about the station and pick up a living by tracking a lost sheep or any similar job.

He would be certain to come prowling about the kitchen-door some time the next morning.

So, before retiring to rest, she hastily scribbled a few lines to the police, and thrust them into an envelope in readiness.

Her spirits rose when this was done.

"Ah! Monsieur Kelly," she said to herself as she sought her couch, "you are very big, very brave, very strong, and I am only a little weak woman, but I think that I—that I—*enfin que je viens de mettre une punaise dans votre beurre.*".

CHAPTER CXXII.
THE LONE INN.

THE inn kept by Gibson was one of the class already described in this work.

It was rudely but strongly built of timber.

It stood by the roadside, but depended less upon the few chance customers travelling by that route than upon the station-hands who used to come flocking in for miles around after pay-day, in order to get rid of their six months' earnings with the utmost possible speed.

On such occasions a week of Pandemonium is the only comparison to be made with the scene presented.

But ordinarily the spot was dull and quiet enough, and it might be wondered how Gibson could pick up a living.

On the morning after his interview with Marie, Ned Kelly rose in a restless, unsettled humour.

Michael Eldred's station was Liberty Hall, as far as the guests were concerned, but the very odour of respectability had something in it irksome to Ned's nature.

He loathed it.

In company with Michael Eldred he felt ill at ea

was ronging for a pipe and glass of grog, and a hand at cards with some more congenial companions.

He resolved to ride over to Gibson's and see if his wishes could not be gratified.

With some notion in his head that Marco Polo might be recognised he left him in the stable, and, selecting a nice-looking chestnut of his host's, was soon slinging across the five miles of open country lying between the station and the inn.

Eldred had had to start at daybreak for one of the outlying huts in the opposite direction, and Kelly on leaving merely told Marie that he was going out for a canter to get an appetite for dinner.

She was only too thankful to see him off the premises.

No sooner was he gone than she sent for the black, and entrusted him with her letter.

He was to hand it to Gibson, with instructions for the latter to give it to the mail-cart, which would pass during the afternoon.

Meanwhile, Kelly had ridden up to the inn, and given a friendly hand to a red-faced, red-headed fellow who was lounging at the doorway.

This was Gibson himself.

Who or what he was, or whether Gibson was his real name or not, was a question about which none of his customers troubled themselves.

All they cared for was finding him at his post, ready and willing to supply bad liquor for safe cheques or genuine gold-dust.

Ned dismounted.

"Hi, Sam!" shouted Gibson.

A lean, wizzened old man, in a dilapidated stable-dress, with "lag" written on every line of his shrivelled parchment-like face, shambled round the corner of the house in obedience to this summons.

"Take his horse round to the stable," said Gibson, indicating the one Ned had ridden. "A tidy bit of horse-flesh, that chestnut of Eldred's?" he continued, as the old ostler led off the animal which he had recognised.

"A tidy bit? Ah, you should just see my Mar——" began Kelly, but suddenly checking himself from completing the name of his favourite steed.

"Your mare, is she such a ripper then?"

"Ripper? By goles! I believe you," said Ned, rejoicing at the other's misapprehension. "But come along inside, I want a quencher."

"All right. What'll you have?" cried Gibson, leading the way to the bar.

"Whisky," was the answer, "and fill one for yourself."

The two men drank and then stood looking at one another for a minute.

"Not much doing?" said Kelly.

"No, blow it!" was the reply. "Yours is the first face I've seen this morning, and I don't suppose anyone will look in before sundown."

"Then, mayhap you could find the time to sit down and take a quiet fist of cards?" said Kelly, in an insinuating tone.

"No only the time, but the cards," answered Gibson, with a grin.

And, after emptying and re-filling their tumblers, the two men sat down to a quiet game.

Ned had proposed this for the sake of amusement, and not for gain, so the stakes were kept moderate and both played fairly.

Whilst they were thus engaged, a shadow fell across the floor from the open doorway.

Both looked up.

The black fellow, Tiger as he was called, was standing on the threshold, with a look of enquiry on his face.

"Hullo! What is it?" asked Gibson.

The black advanced and handed him the letter, repeating the message about its safe delivery in the peculiar jargon that serves as a medium of communication between the English and the aborigines of Australia.

As Gibson took the letter into his hand, and glanced at the address a look of surprise passed over his face, and he uttered a low whistle.

"What's up?" asked Ned, seriously.

The bushranger had recognised the black, whom he had seen hanging about Eldred's station.

"Oh, nothing," answered Gibson, "only it seems a rum start for a lady to be writing to the police."

"To the police?" said Ned.

"Yes," said the other, holding out the letter so that the address was presented towards Kelly.

The bushranger could not read writing, but for the moment he resolved to keep that discovery to himself.

In daily and hourly peril, accustomed to read danger in a thousand things that to other men would have been so many unconsidered trifles, he divined at once that the letter was connected with himself.

Marie was the only lady at the station, and if she had written to the police it could only be to betray him.

It was necessary that, at all costs, he should become acquainted with the contents of the letter.

But how?

That was the question.

"I should just like to know what's inside that letter," he said, with the same air of jovial good humour that he had put on ever since he had entered the inn.

Gibson laughed, thinking he was only joking, and placed the document on a shelf behind the bar.

Then he resumed his place in front of Kelly, and took up the cards.

The bushranger was on thorns.

He was racking his brains for a method of learning what Marie had written.

It would have been easy enough to have hit upon a plan of filching the letter and destroying it, so as to prevent it from reaching its destination, but this was not enough for him.

He wanted to learn what was inside it, and he could only do this with another's help.

Despite his iron will, he could not help stealing a glance at it now and then from where he sat, and it needed all his power to keep his attention fixed on the game.

"Fill up again," he said, noticing the tumblers were emptied.

And as Gibson rose to do so, he followed him to the bar.

"Look here, mate," he said, leaning against the counter, "I'm blowed if I shouldn't like a squint into that bit of writing."

Gibson looked at him curiously.

"The deuce you would?" he answered, seeing that Kelly was in earnest.

"Yes."

The two men looked steadily at one another for half-a-minute.

Kelly was a good judge of character, and he read rogue written plainly on Gibson's face.

"Look here," he said bluntly, extending his arm and taking the letter, "I am going to find out what's inside there."

"Curse it! no," broke in the other; "I can't allow that. I am sworn to the Post Office, and should get into no end of a row."

"I'll make it worth your while if you choose to help me," said Kelly, with a tone of firmness that awed the other.

"Well, I'm not the man to refuse to lend a hand to a pal," he said, with a grin, as he noticed Kelly take out a bag, which he guessed contained gold.

"Now just listen," said the bushranger, untying the mouth of the bag and taking out a respectable-sized nugget, which he placed on the counter; "that's yours if I find out what's inside the letter."

"Stop a bit," said Gibson. "You only want to know what's inside it, do you?"

"That's all."

"Oh, well, we can soon fake that, and no harm done."

" What do you mean ? "

" Just you wait and see," said Gibson, with a chuckle.

As he spoke he went to the fireplace, where there was a pile of smouldering ashes.

Puffing at them for a few instants he brought them to a red glow, and unhooking a kettle slung above them, planted it in their midst.

In a few minutes the kettle began to sing, and a cloud of steam issued from the spout.

" Give me the letter," said Gibson.

Kelly obeyed, watching him closely.

He could not as yet divine the other's intention.

" If he means to burn it, I'll have his liver," he muttered, for he did not quite trust his companion.

But such an idea was very far from Gibson's mind.

After going to the door and glancing round so as to be sure that no new-comer was likely to interrupt them, he closed it and approached the fire.

He placed the envelope in the jet of steam issuing from the kettle.

In a few minutes the gum that held down the adhesive flap was moistened.

Then, removing it, he opened the envelope with ease.

This was done with an assurance and dexterity that were evidently the result of long practice.

It was obvious that it was not a first attempt at tampering with the correspondence that passed through his hands, and the ghost of Sir James Graham must have smiled approval at his skill

" Well, I'm blest," ejaculated Kelly in amazement.

Gibson held out the billet to him.

" There you are, mate," he said, with a grin.

Kelly took it and unfolded it.

Then fumbling in his pocket —

" Well, now, would you believe it?" said he, " I've mislaid my spectacles, so I must trouble you just to cast your eye over it and tell me what is written there." And he held out the open page towards Gibson.

So naturally was this said that Gibson, not dreaming that Kelly could not read writing, glanced down the page and repeated the contents aloud.

They were brief :—

" Sir,—A notorious robber hides himself at my husband's station. Have the kindness to send men to effect his arrest at once. He goes to-morrow.
"MARIE ELDRED.

" P.S.—He is very dangerous ; send six men."

Kelly's face was unmoved, but in his heart he vowed a bitter vengeance on Marie.

" The cursed French Jezebel !" he muttered to himself.
" I hope my hands may rot off at the wrists if she gets loose when once I have a grip of her."

Meanwhile Gibson had been quietly replacing the letter in the envelope and fastening it up again, but without losing sight of Kelly.

He was pretty well used to putting two and two together.

Kelly's eagerness to learn the contents of the letter and the paragraph about the "notorious robber," were two things that struck him.

Suddenly a thought flashed across him.

He had noticed Kelly's hand as they sat down to play.

He glanced at it again

Yes, there was the scar across the back.

He divined the truth at once.

It was Kelly who was before him !

Sharp as he was Kelly was sharper.

He noticed the other glance at his hand and guessed the very thoughts passing in his mind.

" You are right, my blooming swell," he said coolly, " I am Ned Kelly."

" Ned Kelly !" exclaimed Gibson, with feigned amazement.

" Ay, Ned Kelly, who never forgets an injury or forgives a traitor. You know me. Take a good look at me. I am worth looking at. This head of mine alone is worth ten thousand pounds at any police station. But," and as he spoke he gripped Gibson by the arm and placing his face close to the innkeeper's hissed out the words between his teeth, " the man who tries to earn that ten thousand pounds will never live to spend it. If I were lying in the condemned cell to-morrow with a hundredweight of iron on each wrist, he would not be safe from my vengeance. If I only lifted a finger he would have a dozen knives in him. And, by Jingo, if I was howling in eternal flames I'd come back to see it done, though all the devils in hell stood round to bar my way."

" Good Lord ! mate, no need to talk like that," said Gibson, confusedly, " I ain't the chap to think of peaching on a pal. So you are Ned Kelly, are you? Well, I've heerd a good deal about you and am glad to see you. Proud to have you in my crib. Come, let's have another nobbler. Here's luck to you."

As he rattled off these sentences, Kelly continued to watch him narrowly.

The bushranger could not get over the sense of mistrust inspired by his new friend.

They resumed their game however, and now Gibson was racking his mind how to betray Kelly with safety to himself.

He felt uncommonly nervous, but a man will do a good deal for the value of ten thousand pounds in the way of risk.

At last he hit upon a plan.

He would hocus Kelly.

It was not the first time he had played such a trick upon his customers, and the materials were at hand in the cellar.

" Look here, old pal," he began with a drunken air of confidence that was admirably put on, " such a regular ripper as you are, must have a mug of the best. I've got a bottle or two of the best stuff that ever trickled out of a still-worm stowed away below. I'm dashed if we won't have one in honour of this glorious occasion."

" What's the tipple ?" asked Kelly, with assumed carelessness.

" Whisky, man, whisky !" said Gibson, speaking thickly and with great verbosity, " real, genuine, hot, still with the true flavour of the turf clinging to it. Devil a drop could Roe or Jamieson turn out to match it. So I'll step down and get it at once."

As he spoke he advanced to one corner of the room, and after pulling a bolt, lifted a trap-door, along the top of a flight of steps.

Lighting a candle he prepared to descend.

Kelly was all on the alert for signs of treachery.

To him the change in Gibson's manner was suspicious and he had come to the resolve not to lose sight of him for a moment.

The thought occurred to him that there might be some other way of exit from the cellar by which Gibson meant to escape and make his way to the police station.

" No you don't, my tulip," he muttered to himself, and he staggered after the innkeeper, growling out—

" Let's have a squint into that underground den of yours, it might be a handy place to stow away a bit of swag."

Gibson had no objection, for the drugged liquor he was in search of was done up in bottles in a way to disarm all suspicion.

" Come along, then," he said, and descended the ladder, closely followed by Ned.

At the foot of the ladder was a sort of landing of earth. From this another short flight of steps led into the cellar itself.

Gibson raised the light, and Ned, looking down, saw that the cellar was a spacious place, but almost filled up with piles of rubbish, barrels, stacks of bottles, and the like.

Suddenly, as the two men were standing side by side the trap above their heads closed with a tremendous crash.

Then came the sound of the shooting of the bolt, followed by a chuckling laugh.

CHAPTER CXXIII.

THE CELLAR.

No sooner had the two men disappeared down the steps than the inner door of the room, in which they had been sitting, opened

A face peered cautiously round it.

Then a spare, lean figure glided cautiously across the floor.

It was that of Sam, the ostler.

He had been listening to their conversation, and had heard Kelly declare himself.

He felt the chance was too good a one to let slip.

Gliding across the floor he slammed down the trap and shot the bolt.

"I swear I'll go and draw ten thousand quid. They must settle matters down below there as they can," he muttered.

And, after locking the outer doors of the house and putting the keys in his pocket, he mounted Kelly's chestnut which was the only horse in the stable, and galloped off furiously towards the nearest police barracks.

As the trap slammed, Kelly turned fiercely on his companion

"You blooming scoundrel! what's your game?" he cried, seizing him by the shoulders.

"I don't know," gasped Gibson, who was himself equally bewildered.

Releasing him Kelly bounded past him up the steps and tried to raise the trap with the idea it might have fallen by accident.

But he at once discovered that it was fastened.

Mad with rage, he sprang down the ladder again and seized on Gibson.

"You cursed skunk, you mean, sneaking hound of a spy, so you think to trap Ned Kelly, do you? By all the holies, there won't be much of you left in five minutes to tell how you did it."

"Listen Kelly! hang it! it's not me, I'm square; hold on a bit!" gasped Gibson, striving to explain and at the same time to release himself.

But Kelly was far too maddened to listen to him.

"You miserable viper! I'll drink your blood, I'll rip your liver out," he foamed, grappling with Gibson and striving to throw him.

The innkeeper was a powerful man, and was, he felt, fighting for his life.

Like two maddened tigers they gripped one another.

Gibson had let the candle fall and they were in utter darkness.

For some moments nothing could be heard save their hoarse breathing, as they staggered to and fro on the narrow landing of slippery earth.

"You devil! I'll squeeze the life out of you," gasped Kelly, shifting his grip and grasping Gibson by the throat with one hand.

But the innkeeper had also got a hand loose and dashed it heavily into the bushranger's face, causing him to stagger.

As he reeled back without loosening his grasp, he felt the ground crumble away beneath his feet.

The next moment he fell backward from the landing into the cellar, dragging his adversary with him.

The descent was about four feet, and for a moment he was half stunned.

Profiting by this, Gibson tore himself loose and glided into the recesses of the cellar.

He knew every inch of it, and installed himself in a corner.

He remained in silence, listening for the movements of his adversary.

Ned rose to his feet a moment later.

"You murderous hound!" he yelled, with unconscious irony. "You rotten-hearted, red-headed fox, just wait till I get hold of you! You shall never see daylight again."

As he spoke he stretched out his arms and began groping in the darkness.

"A precious pretty tomb of a hole you've dragged me into. A tomb, yes—it shall be one for you before I have done with you."

As he spoke he stumbled against a barrel.

The next moment something whizzed by his ear, and the crash of broken glass against the wall followed.

Gibson, more artful than his adversary, had remained quiet in his corner.

Knowing every inch of the cellar, he could move about in the darkness almost as well as with a light.

He had selected a spot close to a pile of empty bottles

There, with neck outstretched, holding his very breath so as not to reveal his presence, he waited, a bottle in each hand.

When he heard Kelly stumble against the barrel, he hurled one of them in that direction.

It missed.

He sent the second.

The next instant Kelly felt something strike him a terrible blow on the top of the head, as he stooped forward.

The bottle splintered to fragments against his skull.

For a moment he was half-stunned, but the thick hair thatching his head in a great measure saved him, though he could feel the blood trickling down his face.

"You swine! I'll make you pay for this!" he yelled.

Crash!—another struck him on the jaw, almost knocking him backward, and inflicting a frightful gash in his chin.

This was too much.

Dropping on his knees, he began to crawl in search of shelter.

But every sound he made betrayed his presence, and served to guide Gibson's aim.

He sought to shelter his head as well as he could with his arms, but as the bottles broke, the splinters from time to time reached his face, whilst his hands also suffered severely.

From time to time, too, he would place them on the broken glass as he crawled along.

Suddenly his hand encountered a stack of bottles—full ones.

Seizing on them, he hurled a couple of score in rapid succession in the direction from which he had been attacked.

They crashed against the walls and pillars, covering the floor of the cellar in all directions with broken glass, whilst an almost overpowering odour arose from the spilt spirit they contained.

Gibson was, however, untouched.

No sooner had Kelly opened fire in his direction, than he threw himself flat on his stomach and crawled off into another corner, where he crouched down behind a barrel.

Having brought his bombardment to an end without any response, Kelly paused, exhausted, and began to wipe the mingled blood and sweat from his face.

There was a moment's silence.

Kelly listened, and Gibson, not quite sure of his enemy's exact whereabouts, remained quiet.

This puzzled Kelly.

"By gosh! I must have bowled the blooming cellar rat over," he chuckled.

A little prematurely, however.

No sooner were the words out of his mouth than a bottle caught him smash on the forehead, and rolled him over as if he had been shot.

"If I do get hold of you, my friend," he said almost calmly. "I'm blest it I don't tear your entrails out with my teeth before I've done with you."

The sense of the deadly peril in which himself, did more for Kelly than anything else.

It brought to him his senses.

He saw that passion was of no avail against an as cunning and clever as Gibson.

It would have to be a contest of skill, not brute force.

"Steady, Ned, my boy!" he said to himself, "you're not going to let this red-bearded Judas get the better of you. Not if you know it."

Acting on this resolve he lay quite quiet, though a bottle flew every now and then in his direction.

Gibson was discerned by this.

He knew by the noise of Ned's fall, that he had bowled him over, and came to the conclusion that he had stunned him.

He resolved to profit by this, bind him hand and foot before he recovered, and on the arrival of the police, for he guessed the line of conduct Sam had taken, to hand him over to them and claim the reward.

Cautiously and carefully he stole forward in the darkness.

Inch by inch, putting his feet down with the utmost caution, he advanced.

Suddenly he trod, as he thought, on a toad.

Something firm and elastic.

The next instant there was a mingled cry of pain and ferocious joy, and something gripped his ankle like a vice.

Before he could make an effort to free himself, his legs were jerked from under him, and he was thrown violently on his back.

He had stepped on to Kelly's outstretched hand.

A frightful struggle ensued as the two men rolled over and over amidst the fragments of broken glass, which tore their clothes and gashed their flesh.

"You may kill me," gasped Gibson, as Kelly at last succeeded in getting his antagonist undermost, "but you'll never get out of here alive without me."

Kelly made no answer.

One hand was occupied, despite the pain inflicted on his wounded fingers, in clutching Gibson's throat like a band of iron.

With the other he felt in his pockets for his knife, his only weapon.

He found it, and carrying it to his mouth opened it with his teeth.

Then he raised it.

Gibson could not follow his movements in the darkness, but he heard the click of the opening blade, and guessed the fate impending over him.

"Mercy! It was not me, Sam the ostler; I am innocent. Show the way out," he gurgled.

Thud.

Down came the knife.

There was a low groan, a convulsive jerk, the grip with which Gibson had striven to keep off his adversary relaxed, his arms fell to his sides, and he moaned some incoherent words.

Kelly staggered to his feet.

His head and face were terribly cut by the glass, but he had sustained no material injury.

"I must get out of this," he muttered.

Searching his pockets he found some matches, and lighting one of these staggered towards the steps.

Ascending the first flight he picked up the candle that Gibson had dropped, lit it, and sat down on the bottom rung of the ladder leading to the trap, to recover his wind and collect his thoughts.

Gibson, though frightfully wounded, was not dead.

As soon as Kelly left him, he managed to roll up his handkerchief, and held it with one hand against his wound, whilst he followed the bushranger with his glaring eyes.

Having recovered his breath, Kelly ascended the ladder and made an effort to lift the trap.

He soon recognised the impossibility of this.

He descended into the cave again, to see if there existed any other issue.

The last remarks of Gibson seemed to imply that there was, and for a moment he regretted not having listened to the innkeeper.

Glancing in his direction, he saw that Gibson was still alive, but presenting a horrible aspect.

His face, cut to pieces by the broken glass during their struggle, was one immense wound, and his whole figure was deluged with blood.

"Look here, mate," said Kelly, "perhaps I have been a bit hasty with you, after all. But I don't think there's much damage done, and if you'll tell me the way to get out of this infernal hole, why, I'll try and patch you up a bit, and no doubt you'll pull round."

Something like a smile flitted across the hideously-mangled face of Gibson.

He knew he was mortally wounded, and had not an hour to live.

"Come now, are you going to show me the way out?"

Still no answer.

"Curse you!" yelled Ned, seeing that persuasion was no use, "if you don't speak I'll treat you in such a way that, when you're in blazes, it shall seem a pleasant relief to you. I'll make your last moments on earth warm for you. Blowed if I won't roast you alive."

As he spoke the last words Gibson's glaring eyes seemed to light up.

"All right," he gasped, in an almost inaudible whisper.

"Is there a way out?" roared Ned.

"Yes," gasped the other.

"Will you show it me?"

"Yes. Lift me up."

Despite all Kelly's nerve, it was even to him a horrible task to raise the mangled form of his victim into a sitting position.

"Over there—by that—row of—barrels," continued the innkeeper.

Kelly understood him, and half-carried, half-dragged him to the spot in question.

"Start—the—bungs—of—those—two!" gasped Gibson, every one of whose words seemed to be forced out at the cost of a particle of his life.

Wonderingly, Kelly looked round, picked up a mallet, and drove in the bungs.

A rush of spirits followed, flooding the floor.

"What the devil is this?" asked the bushranger.

"All—right—now—carry—me—to—that—corner," and he pointed to where Kelly had left the light.

Wonderingly, Kelly obeyed.

"Now—over there—an iron—lever."

No sooner had he turned to go than Gibson, stretching out his hand, seized the light and held it over the pool of spirits.

"Kelly!" he gasped.

"Yes," said the bushranger, who had just laid his hand on the implement of which the other had spoken.

"You—said—I'd—burn - but - we - both!"

As he spoke the last words he sank forward, exhausted, whilst the spirits, catching light, lit up the whole cellar.

Kelly turned round.

The floor of the cellar was converted into a lake of liquid flame, in the midst of which Gibson was writhing convulsively.

Mad with rage at being tricked, Kelly dashed forward, and, in the excess of his passion, dealt his foe a blow with the lever that put an end to his existence.

The next moment he repented of what was really an act of mercy.

His own situation was a terrible one.

The heat and the terrible vapour of the burning spirit would in a few moments be fatal to him.

He rushed to the further end of the cellar, but the flames pursued him.

Another barrel burst, and the flood rose higher.

He glanced wildly around.

Suddenly he caught sight of a door in the opposite wall, now revealed for the first time by the light of the flames.

The only way to it, however, was through the lake of fire.

Maddened by the prospect of certain death, he dashed into it.

The flames leaped round him, burning his hair and beard, and singeing his garments, whilst the broken glass, amidst which he stumbled twice, cut his hands and knees.

He reached the door.

It was locked.

With all the fury of despair, he attacked it with his crowbar, and, wrenching off the lock, tore it open.

It merely led into an inner cellar.

Here, however, for a moment or so, was safety.

As he glanced round it, he perceived a kind of shutter in the upper part of the wall.

He tore this down.

Oh, blessed sight! The light of day streamed in upon him once more, through an opening about three feet square.

He staggered back, almost blinded by the light.

But oh, horror!—between him and light and air, and freedom and safety, there was a range of iron bars.

And through the open door behind him a stream of liquid flame, like a fiery serpent, had begun to steal into the room, and was spreading slowly and surely over the floor.

Inch by inch it crept towards him.

The iron bars were immovable, but the wooden frame in which they were embedded looked old and dilapidated.

Driving the claw end of his crowbar into this, he wrenched away splinter after splinter, till the lower ends of the bars were laid bare.

Then, seizing one of these, he tugged at it with all his might.

His strength, naturally Herculean, was tripled by the sense of danger.

The fiery flood had crept to his heels just as, by a superhuman effort, he bent two of the bars aside sufficiently to allow him to pass.

With his last remaining strength he dragged himself through the opening, and sank, scorched, blackened, and insensible, on the turf outside.

As he did so, a fresh sound of explosion was heard, and the cellar he had just left became one pit of raging flame.

CHAPTER CXXIV.

SWIFT VENGEANCE.

MEANWHILE the day had worn on at the squatter's station.

Dinner-time came, but, to Marie's surprise, neither Michael Eldred nor Kelly made their appearance.

She was not alarmed about the former, who was frequently detained at one of the outlying tents by some business connected with the station, but the latter's absence rendered her uneasy.

She augured that it meant mischief.

A sense of impending evil beset her, and seemed to increase as the hours went on.

At last she got so restless she felt she could not remain in the house any longer.

She had her horse saddled, and rode off in the direction of Gibson's inn.

She had merely intended the ride as a distraction to her thoughts, and had taken this direction almost unconsciously.

Suddenly she noticed a column of smoke on the horizon.

She was on the alert at once.

Michael Eldred had frequently spoken to her of the danger of bush fires, and warned her never to neglect any indication of them.

She was naturally brave, however, and was, besides, able to reason.

The air was quite calm, and she had learnt that the only danger to anyone mounted was when a strong wind was blowing.

So she resolved to push on a little further, and ascertain the cause of the conflagration.

After all it might only be an unusually large campfire.

She had to traverse a belt of scrub in order to reach her destination.

It grew in patches interspersed with tracks of sandy soil.

She had got halfway through it, when suddenly she heard a rustling sound some distance ahead.

She drew rein and listened.

Someone or something was evidently forcing its way in her direction.

Nearer and nearer came the sound.

Suddenly, through the parted brushwood, there broke upon her startled gaze a figure that froze her very soul with horror.

With hair and beard singed to a matted stubble, with face blackened with smoke and covered, as by a mask, with caked and clotted gore, with bloodshot eyes and parched, crackling lips, with garments hanging in scorched and tattered ribbons from his frame, Ned Kelly stood before her.

Less like a man at that moment than some fiend newly vomited from the lowest depths of Pandemonium.

As she gazed at him aghast, the gristly vision darted forward, and, with a hoarse and choking cry of recognition, seized her bridle.

For ten seconds or so he stood confronting her.

Then clutching her wrist with his disengaged hand he ejaculated the command.

"Get down!"

She remained motionless.

"Get down!" he roared, forcing the words with difficulty through his parched and blistered lips, and at the same time accentuating them with a jerk at her wrist that almost tore her from the saddle.

There was nothing to do but to comply with the invitation, for the grasp on wrist and bridle was one of iron.

Disengaging her foot from the stirrup and her leg from the pommel, she slid down and stood facing him

"You Jezebel! You spawn of hell!" he began, but even as he spoke he tottered and sank forward on his knees releasing her wrist as he did so.

His frightful struggle in the cellar, and his mad course on foot towards the station, had exhausted him.

Marie sprang back out of his reach.

In swift succession a train of ideas darted with lightning-like rapidity through her mind.

He had discovered her treachery, that was certain.

What was to be done to escape the fearful fate that only too certainly awaited her?

Flight was impossible, for in falling he had managed to slip his arms through the reins, and her horse was therefore in his power.

It was a moment in which it was no use recoiling before any extremity.

Marie carried a pistol, as she had been instructed by her husband to do on all occasions.

A woman riding alone in the bush is exposed to certain contingencies against which it is always well to be prepared.

She had had some experience in handling firearms during the fighting that marked the fall of the Commune, and since her marriage Michael Eldred had made her practise at a mark in the garden almost daily.

For, as he had told her, a woman had need to know how to defend both her life and her honour.

As Ned knelt before her, incapable for the moment of rising, she drew her weapon and levelled it full at his head.

"Villain!" she said, somewhat melodramatically, "release my horse and let me pass, or I will kill you."

Ned stared at her as though stupefied.

Then with a groan he sank forward on his hands with the reins still retained by his arm.

He moaned feebly, foamed at the mouth, and rolled his eyes wildly, as though about to have a fit.

Wretch as he was, the woman could not help feeling some pity for such a ghastly object.

She hesitated, despite his evil intentions towards herself, to shoot him down, as he lay, in cold blood.

Better for her and for many another had she done so there and then.

"Listen to me," she said, "if you can. Ah! do not move," she continued, as he seemed to be about to make an effort to rise, "or I will fire."

Her pistol cowed him and he sank down again.

"You had some talk with me the other day," she went on; "you told me I was to do certain things because it was your will. Now it is my turn. You are in my power. If I shoot you now everyone will say I do well. But I do not want to hurt you. No. Not if you will be wise. You will get up, you will let go my horse, I will ride home, and you will go to *au diable*, eh? And from this time we are strangers. Will that suit you?"

As she stood over him cutting him with each word like a whip-lash, he grovelled almost at her feet, his eyes now cast down as if in despair, now glancing wildly round as if in search of a chance of escape, his hands mechanically clutching and crushing the sandy soil.

"Do you agree?" she continued, with a stamp of her foot, and with the pistol still levelled straight at his head.

He looked up hopelessly, with his fingers still clutching and crumbling the sand, and gathered his legs under him.

"If—if you," he began falteringly, raising his hands, still full of soil, in a deprecating manner, like the paws of a dog who begs, "will only listen to—to reason a bit. Just look at it in a fair light. Now, how can I possibly —— "

Wish-ish.

His hands shot out straight before him and two handsfull of sand went smack into her face.

Brave as ever, blinded but undaunted, she realised her peril and fired.

But just as she pulled trigger he was flat on the ground again, and then up like a serpent springing from its coil. The next moment she was down on her back with one of his hands clenched round her throat, the other over her mouth, whilst one knee crushed her bosom, and the other pinned down her pistol arm.

"You serpent!" croaked Kelly in a voice scarcely human, as he bent over her; "you she-devil, you thought to send Ned Kelly to kingdom-come, did you, when you found your pretty little plot of selling him to the beaks was blowed? I know all that was written in that pretty little note you sent to Gibson's this morning. It was written plain enough, but I'll write my marks on you a sight plainer before I've done with you, you cursed frog-eating, double-tongued, black-hearted viper."

Over the scene of horror that followed, a veil had best be drawn.

Half-an-hour later, Kelly, mounted on Marie's grey mare, galloped up like a madman to the station.

There were only two women about the place, and his first care was to seize them, and, after binding them hand and foot, to lock them up in a room.

Then, after washing himself, changing his dress. patching up his wounds, and feeding, he proceeded quietly and systematically to go through the entire establishment.

There was not much money, for squatters are not in the habit of having large sums on the premises, lest these should tempt a visit from bushrangers; but one or two watches and the contents of Marie's jewel-case formed a very respectable prize.

With this swag carefully concealed about him. Ned took his pistols and made his way to the stable where Marco Polo was.

Leading him out he proceeded to saddle him, whilst the horse recognising his master, whinnied with joy, and thrust his velvet muzzle against Ned's chest.

Carefully the bushranger tightened the girth, and then ran eye and hand over strap and buckle.

He had a long ride before him, and he knew the importance of everything being in good trim.

Then he lit his pipe and swung himself into the saddle.

Just as he was about to start, a hail reached his ears.

He looked in the direction from which it came, and saw Michael Eldred advancing towards the station at a hand gallop.

"The devil!" said Ned to himself, "this is awkward."

"Hullo, captain," said Michael, as soon as he got within speaking distance, "where are you bound for?"

It was now late in the afternoon, and Eldred was somewhat surprised to see his guest apparently equipped for a journey.

"By gosh!" said Kelly, bluntly, "it's a jolly good thing you turned up. I've got no end of a yarn for you to listen to, so just range alongside."

It was important, above all things, to prevent Eldred from entering the house, where the captive women would soon have put him alive to the real state of affairs.

The unsuspecting squatter drew near.

For a moment Kelly debated whether to draw a pistol and shoot him down.

But he was afraid the shot might be heard.

He waited, therefore, till Eldred came right up to him, and, assuming a confidential air, began in a low voice.

"It's just the queerest thing you ever heard of, Mr Eldred, and if——"

"Great heavens!" said Eldred, as he ranged up alongside, and caught sight of the strapping adorning Ned's face, "what's the matter?"

No sooner were the words out of his mouth, than a sudden drive from Ned knocked him out of the saddle, utterly unprepared as he was for any such aggression.

Ned seized the horse's bridle to lead him off and turn him loose in the bush, so as to prevent immediate pursuit by Eldred, but whilst thus engaged the sound of approaching hoofs fell on his ear.

He looked up.

A group of horsemen were riding furiously towards the station from the same quarter from which he himself had last approached it.

Occupied with Eldred, he had failed to notice their approach, and now they were not more than fifty yards off.

He could plainly distinguish the uniform of the mounted police, and noticed that the foremost horse bore a double burden.

Supported in the rider's arms was a figure whose flowing garments were an obvious indication of its sex.

He recognised the grey riding-habit of his victim, Marie.

They had evidently found her when tracing him from the inn.

Such was the case, the new-comers being four troopers and a sergeant, whom the officer in command at the police barracks had despatched on learning from Sam the fact of Ned Kelly's presence at the inn.

On reaching Gibson's residence they had found it a pile of ashes, but the traces of Ned's escape were plainly visible.

Tracking him across the plain they had traversed the belt of scrub, and there discovered the senseless form of Marie, whom Sam had at once recognised as the wife of Michael Eldred.

They had pushed on to the station, and now arrived just as Ned was debating within himself whether he should add a new victim to the list in the person of the hapless squatter.

He judged, however, that in the present state of affairs flight was the best policy.

Dropping the senseless form of the squatter he sprang upon the back of Marco Polo.

A yell of execration from the troopers warned him that he was discovered.

Two of them pulled up and began to get their carbines ready, whilst the remainder galloped on at full speed.

Ned's position seemed somewhat critical.

To the right of him were the stables, and to the left the house.

In front was a kind of paddock of about a couple of acres, the further side of which was bounded by a stiff post and rail

The only method was to cross this, as the approaching troopers cut off all attempts to escape in the rear.

With a shake of the rein he got Marco Polo into motion, but, before the matchless steed could settle into his stride, the foremost trooper had considerably lessened the distance between them.

Whing, whing! a couple of carbine bullets whizzed harmlessly past his ears, for a sharp gallop was by no means a thing calculated to steady a man's aim.

Without looking back Ned headed Marco Polo straight at the fence, came steadily up to it, lifted his horse, rose in the air with a yell of defiance, and the next instant was scouring across the stretch of boundless plain extending towards the upper waters of the Murray.

CHAPTER CXXV.

THE PURSUIT.

THE troopers one and all paused at the fence and drew bridle.

A brief consultation took place amongst them.

" By all that's blue, the scoundrel is getting a long start of us!" said one of them, lifting his cap and mopping his forehead, as he watched the fast-receding form of Ned.

" All right, Casson," said the sergeant, a grim and grizzled looking fellow of forty whose face bore the marks of hard service, and whose wiry figure bespoke a man equal to any amount of fatigue ; " he hasn't got away yet. We're well on his trail, and if it goes right into the deepest pit of brimstone, I'll follow it!"

" The beasts are blown, though," said a young fellow named Anderson ; " and that clipper of his is as fresh as a daisy."

" Just so ; but I reckon there's no lack of fresh horseflesh in the stable yonder, and I don't think the boss of this show is the man to grudge the loan of it."

The three cantered back to the stable, where their two comrades who had halted to fire had by this time arrived, in company with Sam, who held in his arms the senseless form of Marie.

By the aid of a bucket or two of water and a nip of brandy, Michael Eldred was restored to his senses

He gazed wildly around him

" My head—the ruffian!—ah, sergeant!" he continued, as he caught sight of the trooper's uniform ; " you are just in time. I have been assaulted by a ruffian, a big bearded fellow calling himself Captain Higgins."

" And whose real name, sir," said the sergeant, " is Ned Kelly."

" Ned Kelly, the ironclad bushranger? Great heavens! to think I should not have suspected this!"

Even as he spoke his eye fell on the insensible form of his wife, which had been reverently laid on a couch improvised with straw and fodder.

" What—what is the meaning of this?" he gasped, staggering towards her

" More of that devil's work, sir," said the sergeant, who with his men had not lost their time during their colloquy, but had rapidly unsaddled their panting horses. " Now look here, sir, you can help us in this matter. Pick us out the five best animals you have in the stable, and I'll undertake to bring back Ned Kelly, dead or alive."

Eldred complied, and, by the help of a couple of his hands who rode up to the station during this colloquy, the troopers were mounted on five fresh horses.

" Look here, governor," said Sam ; " I put you on this lay, and I have a right to halve the swag. It's only fair and proper I should go along with you."

" Quite so," said the sergeant, who thought it would be just as well not to lose sight of such a slippery customer as Master Sam evidently was ; and accordingly a steed was provided for the ostler.

The two hands having helped Michael Eldred to convey Marie to the house, the little troop got under way,

Skirting the paddock in order to avoid the fence that had already baffled them, they struck out across the plain after Kelly, whose figure now appeared a mere dot on the horizon.

Meanwhile Ned, with a grim chuckle of satisfaction at the fact of the fence putting a temporary stopper on the pursuit, was sailing along merrily, Marco Polo having settled down into the long sweeping stride his rider knew so well.

Ever and anon, however, the fugitive turned his head to see whether the first check had sufficed to baffle his pursuers, or whether they were not yet shaken off.

" If they do try it, it will not make much difference," he muttered, " their 'prads' are pretty well blown, and a sharp burst will crack 'em up like so many tea-cups "

As he spoke he glanced back again, and his eye caught the moving gleam of the troopers' accoutrements, as they skirted the paddock.

" So you've not given it up, after all, have you? Well, I've a fancy for giving you a pretty little bit of a devil's dance! 1 guess some of you will be a trifle saddle-galled before I've done with you!"

With reckless bravado he slowed down Marco Polo, and suffered his pursuers to gain on him.

" It would be a blessed lark to string them, and pick them off one by one! If I did, it would be a lesson to them. None of the cursed traps would be in such a hurry to follow me after that!"

He continued at the same slackened pace, and every moment the pursuers gained ground.

" One, two, three, four, five, not six of them," thought Kelly " who is the chap in plain clothes? Old Eldred, I suppose. No, he ain't tall enough. By Gosh though! that's his grey gelding the first of them is on. Curse me for being a fool, but I never thought of that. The swine have changed horses at the station. I've a rougher job on hand than I thought for."

And so it soon proved.

Sergeant Whitewell had wondered at the foolhardiness of the bushranger, in thus allowing them to gain on him when he might have pushed on and ridden clear out of sight, but he was shrewd enough to profit by it.

He ran his eye over the little troop.

An excellent judge of horseflesh, he picked out at the glance the two worst horses of the five he and his men had appropriated.

" Attention!" he rang out. " Casson and Whitwell, ride on ahead as hard as ever you can pelt. Keep neck and neck, or the beggar may try to settle you singlehanded. But what you must do is to rattle after him till his horse is blown or yours are. We'll come slinging along steadily, and in the longrun are bound to land him."

Casson and Whitwell spurred their beasts, and, shooting ahead of their companions, came on with carbines ready, rushing like a pair of eagles about to pounce on their prey.

Neck and neck like jockeys at a finish, they swept on, and Ned had to wake up Marco Polo and keep him moving. Soon these three, the bushranger and his two foremost pursuers, were far ahead of the sergeant, Sam, and the two remaining troopers.

Ned, however, had divined the trick and was casting about for a means of defeating it.

" They don't quite know what Marco Polo's made of," he thought, " and they are not going to put their claws on me this journey."

But it was evident that even Marco Polo could not continue this mad gallop for long.

It is true he was nobly holding his own, and Ned was in no immediate danger

Still the steeds of the troopers seemed fleet and staunch, and if they could only continue to force the pace a little longer the ultimate success of their comrades would be assured.

Half-an-hour elapsed and the relative positions of pursuers and pursued were unchanged.

Ned kept about a quarter of a mile ahead of Casson and Whitwell, and the remainder of his foes were almost eight times that distance in the rear.

All around stretched the flat unbroken plain, save right ahead, where the crests of a line of timber were visible.

Towards these the bushranger was making his way.

"We must do the job before he gains cover," ejaculated Casson, in jesting tones to his comrade, "or he will be able to pick us off like parrots on a bough. Come, are you ready for a spurt?"

"Yes."

"Here you are then, ride every ha'p'orth you know."

Digging in their spurs, the two men urged their almost exhausted animals on at racing speed.

Ned glanced anxiously astern and ahead.

He noted the distance of the timber and the rate of his pursuers.

"Marco can live the pace and stay the distance," he thought, and in turn touched his horse with the spur.

He nursed and spared him as much as possible, bringing into use every trick by which a good rider helps and eases his horse.

A shout and a clatter behind warn him that the troopers are gaining.

"Now for it old man," and for ten minutes he urges Marco to the utmost.

The sounds of pursuit grow fainter again.

The wood is nearer and nearer.

It is a range of blue gums, and Ned guesses that they mark the course of a stream.

A faint cry far in the rear marks that his followers are distanced and that some mishap has befallen them.

A carbine-shot rings out as a parting salute, as he plunges beneath the sheltering timber.

But the bullet is wide, and in another instant he is swallowed up in the timber.

Twenty minutes or so later the sergeant and his companions, who have been riding steadily within themselves, come up with their advanced guard.

Casson is lying on the turf with his head bandaged, and his horse with dropped head and outstretched legs is standing by him the very embodiment of grogginess.

Whitwell is attending to his animal, whose heaving sides betray he is in little better plight.

"What's up?" asks the sergeant.

"Casson's horse dropped and threw him just as that fellow gained the timber," was the answer; "and I don't think mine can go any further yet awhile."

"Are you hurt, Casson?" was the next question.

"No, only a bit shaken."

"Well, you stay here with the horses till they come round, and then follow us. Jump down, you fellow," he continued, addressing Sam, who obeyed with no very good grace. "Get on his horse, Whitwell, and come on with us."

and the four continued their pursuit, leaving Sam to keep company with Casson.

The marks of Marco Polo's hoofs on the turf served to guide them even after entering the timber.

The trees were some distance apart as yet, and the light soil beneath them retained the impression distinctly.

The blue gums indicated water, and sure enough a short ride brought them in view of a rushing stream, a confluent of the Murray.

The track led down straight towards it.

The spot in which they found themselves was a kind of natural amphitheatre of some two hundred yards in diameter.

Across the centre of this the stream flowed.

The slope down towards it was covered with grass.

A similar growth fringed the opposite bank, but the further slope was covered with patches of bush.

The banks of the stream were low, and several tracks of hoofs, some old and some recent, proved that this spot was used as a ford.

To the right and the left the banks rose and were fringed with overhanging timber.

"Get your carbines ready and come on steadily," said the sergeant, "he may be waiting to have a pop at us from the cover yonder."

They reached the edge of the stream to which Kelly's tracks led.

"Halt!" commanded the sergeant, "this is just the place where such a varmint would try to double. Anderson, ride across and see if there are any traces of his getting out at the other side."

Anderson rode cautiously.

The water, however, did not come much above his horse's knees, for the stream broadened considerably.

"No," he reported from the other side, "there are several tracks leaving the water, but they are two days old at least."

"Just as I thought; he has doubled up or down stream. But we were just too cunning for him," and as he spoke he chuckled in his own conceit. "I'll unearth him yet."

He gave orders, and the party separated.

Entering the stream, two proceeded to follow its course upwards and two downwards.

With their eyes riveted on the banks and their carbines in readiness, they stole cautiously along scrutinising every twig and shrub, every inch of soil, for the trace of Kelly's passage.

(To be continued.)

NED KELLY
THE
IRONCLAD
AUSTRALIAN BUSHRANGER

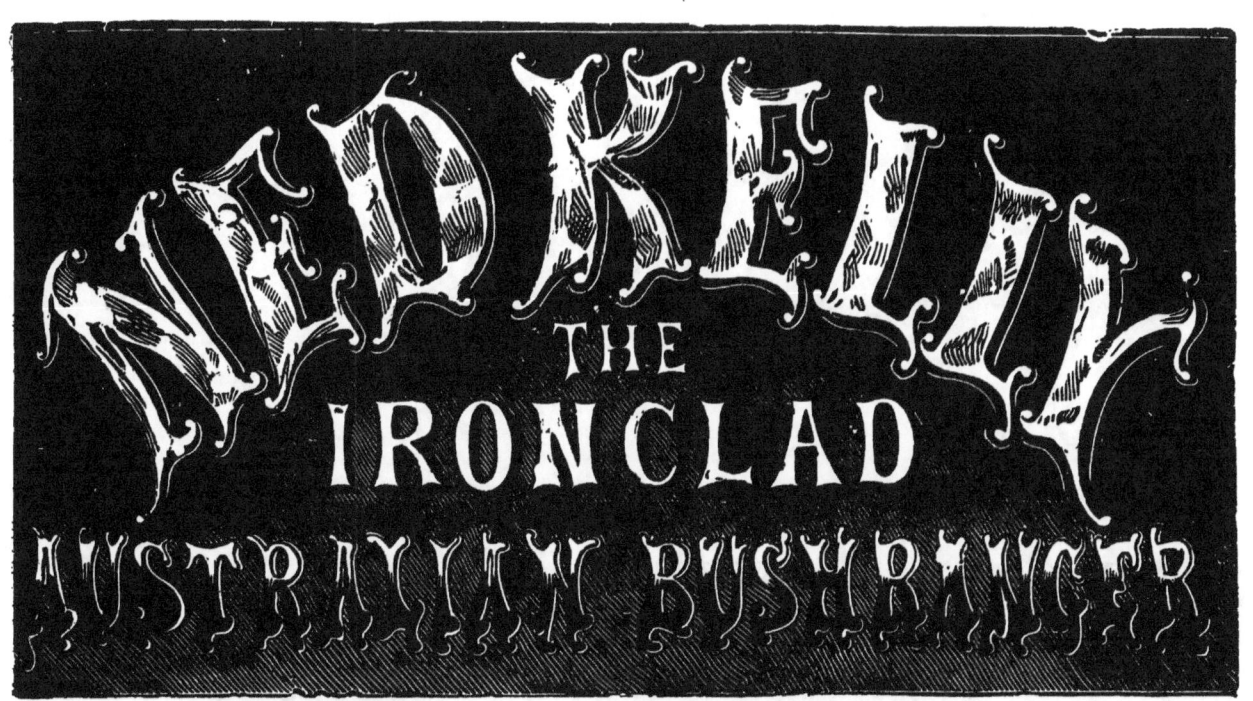

Nº 21,

NED KELLY: IRONCLAD BUSHRANGER.

"It is well known that for many years Ned Kelly had made himself notorious by a series of crimes wholly incompatible with the civilisation of the nineteenth century. Ned Kelly's celebrated steed, Marco Polo, is as well known at the Antipodes as Dick Turpin's Black Bess in these islands." *Ned Kelly*, illustrated, Nos. 1 to 11, already published at 4, Essex-street, Strand, price One Penny.—*Telegraph*, 7th July, 1881.

"It is notorious that the robbery of Mr. Steward's corpse was mainly performed by the assistance of NED KELLY'S BROTHER, the Captain of what was neither more nor less than a pirate ship."—*Times*, July.

"The history of NED KELLY and his celebrated black horse, Marco Polo, will ever live in the recollections of the Australian public. The deeds of Dick Turpin, and the performances of Black Bess, are tame beside those of 'NED AND HIS NAG;' in addition to which Ned's history is true, and Turpin's is pure fiction."—*Press*, July.

CHAPTER CXXV.—*Continued.*

Two hours later the party that had gone up stream returned.

They had failed to discover the slightest trace of Kelly's progress, and had found further advance barred by a cataract falling some ten feet over a shelf of rocks, up which it was impossible to scramble.

On either side the stream was bordered by walls of perpendicular rock, so it was quite impossible for Kelly to have escaped that way.

Ten minutes later the sergeant and Whitwell, who had ridden down stream, returned.

They had had no better luck.

A few hundred yards the stream broadened into a swamp, to traverse which was certain destruction.

Indeed, they had themselves had a narrow escape from being engulfed, and it was patent that the bushranger could not have gone that way.

But there were his marks plainly enough leading into the stream, and there was not the slightest trace of his having left it.

"I'm blessed!" growled the sergeant, "but unless he's been and dived into the mud like a turtle, or flown up into the air like a bird, I can't see where the deuce he can have vanished to."

The others were equally amazed.

Whilst they were debating, Casson and Sam, whose horses had recovered sufficiently for them to make a start, came slowly up.

The state of affairs was explained to them.

The ostler, who was an old bushranger, remained for some time lost in thought.

Then he rode into the stream. He crossed the ford, scrutinising the ground as he did so.

Arrived on the opposite bank, he halted for a moment.

Then suddenly he turned to them and yelled out—

"You infernal blind fools! don't you see how it is? He's crossed here and *backed* his horse out of the river!"

CHAPTER CXXVI.
TWO KINDRED SPIRITS.

SAM was right in his surmise.

Kelly had ridden into the stream, and, on nearing the opposite bank had turned Marco Polo, and backed him out of it.

By this device the track he left appeared to be the hoof-marks of a horse entering the stream from the farther side, and had been taken for such by Anderson.

The bushranger had continued to back his horse till he reached the dense patches of scrub dotting the further slope, in which it would be a work of time and difficulty to lift his trail.

Once arrived here he had turned Marco Polo round and galloped off, feeling sure of having gained a good start on his pursuers.

He had settled his destination in his own mind.

Some twenty miles off was a safe hiding-place.

It was a large ramshackle range of buildings, that had once been the residence of a squatter named Lomax.

Lomax had at one time been a well-to-do man, but a couple of dry seasons and the failure of a bank reduced him to beggary, after which he quietly proceeded to drink himself to death.

He had almost accomplished this when the thought probably occurred to him that there was a quicker method of leaving the world.

At any rate, he cut his throat during a fit of the horrors.

This brought the place into somewhat evil odour.

The run was gradually occupied by neighbouring squatters, and the house and buildings were falling into ruins, when they were taken possession of by a man named Appleby, who converted them into a kind of sly grog-shop, the general house of call for all the scoundrels of the district.

Only as the district happened to be rather sparsely populated, and the percentage of scoundrels not much above the average, he could not boast of a very extended custom.

Still, Appleby's was known far and near as one of those places where accommodation could be had, and "no questions asked," by any gentleman who might find it awkward to thrust his nose into an ordinary hostelry.

Night had closed as Ned rode up to Appleby's.

The long range of stables, woolsheds, shepherds' huts, and other outbuildings belonging to a station, presented a ghastly and desolate aspect in the moonlight.

Part of them had fallen into ruin, and their skeleton framework stood out gaunt and black against the sky-line

The dwelling house, which had once been a residence of some pretensions, was a large and strongly-built erection of timber, surrounded by a broad verandah, to which access was gained by a flight of steps.

At one time an attempt had evidently been made to render it a pleasant residence by the laying-out of a flower garden around it, but the beds had long since been trodden down, and a few stumps sticking out of the sun-baked ground were the only traces left of what had once been a tastefully-arranged cluster of flowering trees and shrubs.

The house itself, however, was externally in good repair, and it was evident that no slight attention had been paid to its external defences.

The door was securely fastened, and the windows secured by massively-constructed shutters.

As Ned drew rein in front of the verandah, he thought for a moment the place was uninhabited.

This was not an unusual occurrence, for Appleby was in the habit of starting off from time to time on secret expeditions, the object of which was only known to himself.

Only certain people of an objectionably prying disposition, and a disgusting knack of what is called "putting two and two together," were in the habit of maintaining that Appleby's disappearances always coincided with the disappearance of horses from somebody else's premises at a greater or less distance from his dwelling.

On looking closely, however, the bushranger marked a gleam of light stealing through the crack of one of the shutters.

He shouted loudly.

No notice, however, seemed taken of his hail.

"Hullo! house, Appleby!" he roared again.

Still there was no response.

After glancing round, lest there should be any sign of danger he alighted from Marco Polo's back, and, throwing the bridle reins over one of the posts always fringing the front of "publics" in town or country, ascended the steps and rapped loudly at the door.

Again with no result.

"Hi, Appleby, blow you! What's up, that you keep an old pal waiting like this? By gosh! if you're not slippy, I'll burn your cursed old dog-kennel about your ears."

"I don't think you will, sir," said a clear, ringing voice, close to his ear.

Ned glanced up in amazement.

A narrow slit had noiselessly opened a little to the right of the doorway, and through it protruded the barrel of a pistol which covered him completely.

But what still more surprised him, was to mark that the hand holding the weapon was that of a woman, whose voice it was that had addressed him.

"Now then," she continued, in undaunted tones, "perhaps you'll tell me who you are, and what you want."

This style of address pleased Ned.

With his usual recklessness he faced the speaker and replied—

"Well, my name happens to be Ned Kelly, and I want a roof, food, and fodder, not to mention the company of a pretty girl, if that's agreeable to you."

"Hold out your left hand," was the answer.

Ned complied, showing the scar.

"Yes," said the unknown, "you bear his brand, sure But you ought to have a password, I fancy, to

"True enough. Now, suppose I told you that we buried it to the south of the third gum tree on the left after crossing the creek?"

"That would be enough to get me to open the door to Old Nick."

The slit was closed, and next moment Ned heard the fastenings of the huge outer door being undone.

Then it swung back, revealing on the threshold the figure of a young girl holding a light in one hand and a pistol in the other.

"Welcome, Mr. Kelly," she said, in the same confident tone.

She was a girl about eighteen or twenty, whom nineteen men out of twenty would have styled handsome, and ninety-nine women out of a hundred a fright.

Hair of a reddish chestnut, falling in thick masses over a square forehead, a straight nose, a pale complexion, brightened now and again by a kindly flush, eyes greyish green in the light and black in the shade, a full pillar-like throat, square shoulders, and round and supple limbs, were the salient points of her personal appearance.

Ned ran his eyes over these points as he would over those of a horse, and nodded approval.

"You're a clipping wench," was his remark as he followed her into the hall, "but who the devil are you and what brings you here?"

The girl laughed.

"Well, I'm Appleby's daughter Jess, and I'm keeping house, you see."

"Ain't the governor at home?"

"No; he's off for a day or two on some lay or other."

"And left you here alone?"

"Why not? I reckon I can take care of the place and myself too," she said significantly.

Sooth to say Miss Jessie Appleby was in every way equal to the twofold task.

She had been dragged up, so to say, in the suburbs of Sydney, under the nominal care of an aunt whose ostensible occupation was keeping a "leaving shop," but who derived the chief part of her income from the purchase of stolen goods, and even less avowable transactions.

At sixteen Miss Jessie had emancipated herself from her aunt's care, and started life on her own account.

It is with deep regret we have to mention that in a very short time her career became of a somewhat prominent character, and led to her being brought into contact on several occasions with the Sydney police.

At length a little difficulty arising about a sailor who was found one morning on the pavement with his pockets turned out and his head caved in, led to her passing a twelvemonth in seclusion at the expense of Government.

On her release she judged a change of air advisable, and had accordingly come to act as housekeeper to her father at Lomax's old station.

"Well, you do seem a good plucked un," said Kelly in tones of unfeigned admiration.

"How about your horse?" asked the girl, paying no attention to the compliment. "There is very good shelter for him in the stable, it is better than it looks. Shall I light you to it?"

"No," answered Kelly with equal coolness, and an air as if the whole place belonged to him. "Marco Polo and I don't care about being separated, and I guess I can find him quarters here. Besides, I may want him sooner than you think—though I hope not, for he's done his work to-day—so I'll just bring him in here for a while. Lord love you, he's as quiet as a Christian, and a great deal better than most of them—gentle as a cat but as strong as a tiger."

Saying this he went out, and led the way up the steps into the large room which served as hall and dining and drawing room, all in one. Marco followed Ned like a pet dog, and seemed no way surprised at his new quarters.

"Oh, what a beauty!" cried the girl in admiration.

"Yes, there ain't two like him under the southern cross," said Kelly with equal enthusiasm.

"Get in there and make yourself comfortable," said Jessie, indicating a large room opening off the right of the hall.

"No, no! beast before man in a case like this," was the bushranger's answer. "Marco's heels may have to save my neck before daylight, and looking after him is only taking care of number one. Is there any fodder on the premises?"

"Plenty," answered Jess, leading the way to a back room.

Soon a corner of the hall was comfortably littered down for Marco Polo's reception, and, tired as he was, Ned proceeded to give the gallant animal a thorough rubbing down before leaving him to repose and the enjoyment of a feed of corn.

The girl aided him with approving eyes.

"You're the right sort," she observed, leading the way to the room she had already indicated.

It was roughly, but not uncomfortably furnished, and Ned casting his heavy frame into a huge American chair, and thrusting his feet out in front of him, heaved a grunt of satisfaction, for the day had been a terribly trying one to even his strength, and, in his own words, he felt " pretty well played out."

Jessie proceeded to set food and drink on the table and called on him to fall to.

As he cast aside his broad hat before commencing his meal, and revealed his scared and plaistered face and the burnt stubble of his hair and beard, the girl gave a start of surprise.

Ned laughed.

"I don't look much of a beauty, do I?" said he.

"No, you don't."

"Oh! you see me at my worst. Just wait a week or so, till my hair grows and I get rid of these scratches, and I'll astonish you."

"How? I always heard Ned Kelly was a very handsome fellow, but you can hardly pass muster as that."

"Just wait a bit, and you'll change your mind. But come, are you going to have a mouthful along with me?"

The girl sat down at the table, and the conversation between the pair soon became brisk and lively, rather too lively, perhaps, for good taste.

Each recognised in the other a congenial spirit, and the bond of sympathy between them grew stronger every minute.

Fatigue, a hearty meal, and two or three stiff tumblers began, however, after a while, to have their effect on Ned, and he nodded once or twice in the chair.

"Pretty well done up, eh?" said the girl.

"Rather!" was the rejoinder. "I've got through a fair job of work since sunrise."

"Well, you'd better roll yourself up in a rug and take a coil on the ground."

"And you?" he asked with a grin.

"Never you mind about me," she answered significantly.

Ned pondered for a minute.

His late experience with the Countess and Marie was of a nature to give him some right in feeling mistrustful as regarded the fair sex.

But on reflection he came to the conclusion that Jessie Appleby was a girl to be trusted.

"She knows me, and I don't think she'd go back on her father's pal," he muttered and, wrapping himself in the rug, stretched himself at full length on the floor, and was soon fast asleep, with his saddle under his head and his pistol gripped in his hand.

The girl sat watching him for some time, with a look of interest on her features.

To her, with her training, Ned Kelly was not a villain but a hero.

No young lady of High Church proclivities ever gazed more admiringly at a young curate; no feminine worshipper of lilies and sunflowers ever watched with greater interest the slumbers of an apostle of æstheticism.

Then she rose, and, passing into the hall, gave another to the comforts of Marco Polo.

Returning to the sitting-room, she resumed her silent vigil.

The hours passed on, the stars faded and the light of a new day began to steal over the plain, and still the robber slept and the girl watched over his slumbers.

Suddenly a shot, followed by a thundering noise at the outer door, made Ned spring to his feet, pistol in hand.

CHAPTER CXXVII.

"FIRST CATCH YOUR HARE."

WHEN Sergeant Whitwell found the trick that had been played on him by Kelly at the ford, his fury knew no bounds.

To be done in any way was bad enough, but to be made to look small in the eyes of those subordinates to whom he had been laying down the law, was unbearable.

In his heart he cursed Kelly, and vowed if ever he had the chance of a shot at him he would not hesitate.

After blowing off as much steam as he could in abusing Anderson, upon whom he laid the whole blame, and whom he threatened to put under arrest, he proceeded to resume pursuit.

It was a work of no small difficulty to find Ned's trail, and to follow it to the swamp.

"Is there a chance of getting hold of a black fellow hereabouts?" he enquired of Sam.

"Well, there are one or two hang about Eldred's station," replied that worthy. "There's a shepherd's hut somewhere about a couple of miles to the northward, and I fancy he might be able to help us."

Sam and one of the troopers were despatched in quest of this worthy, the rest of the party endeavouring to follow Ned's trail, which was by no means an easy job, as it was lost in the marshy ground.

Finally they had to give it up, and await the return of their messengers.

At length these made their appearance, accompanied by the shepherd and a black boy of about sixteen, and provided, moreover, with a lantern.

Night was indeed fast coming on.

The black, like all his tribe, had a great objection to be abroad in the dark, but threats, promises, the company of white men, and the light, helped to overcome his terror.

So soon as the black was made, with some difficulty, to comprehend the dodge Kelly had practised upon his pursuers, he directed the party to separate, and skirt the marshy swamp into which Kelly's tracks were followed. and thus find the spot at which he had debouched and started squarely on his journey. The black's advice was immediately followed, the sergeant imprecating his own stupidity in not having thought of this self-evident proceeding instead of being indebted to a "nigger" for the suggestion. The police divided their forces, each taking the half-circle skirt round the edge of the swamp. Keeping a good look-out (the moon shining as it only does shine in Australia, and illuminating the ground as clearly as an English sun) the said "nigger" was the first to detect the marks of Marco's hoofs, which important fact he heralded by loud guttural chuckles, and exclamations of " Yarrow-yarrow, quam by here !" (horse marks here).

"Got him at last, by Jingo!" shouted the sergeant, exultingly. "Now, my beauty, if I don't run you to earth and get a pile for your brush, why my head's only fit for cat's meat."

"I should say, sergeant," said Casson, "from the course he has evidently taken, that he's making his way to Lomax's old station. That chap Appleby, who's squatting there now, is a bad egg, if ever there was one, and would be sure to help him at a pinch."

"That's about it," answered Whitwell. Come, we can push on pretty smartly. There's no doubt but that's where he's making for."

They stuck to Marco's tracks, which the black followed like a beaten road.

Despite their hurry, however, it was broad daylight

before the old station stood revealed to them in all its desolation.

Before they approached it they halted, and a kind of council of war was held.

The black refused to advance any further.

In common with his tribe he firmly believed the spot haunted by the ghost of Lomax, and neither threats nor promises could induce him to venture within its clutches.

The shepherd was, he frankly admitted, a non-combatant, and Master Sam showed a decided reluctance to trusting his ugly carcase within pistol-shot of the man he had betrayed to the police, and whom he knew was a dead shot at twenty paces.

The five troopers resolved therefore to surround the house, after first riding round it in a wide circuit with the black, in order to verify the fact that there was no trail leading away from the station.

Dismounting and leaving their horses under the care of Sam and the shepherd, they stole cautiously forward to the main building.

Reconnoitring, they ascertained that there were only two entrances, one in front and one in the rear.

The sergeant stationed two of his men at the back of the house, with orders to shoot down Kelly if he attempted to break away in that direction, or if he sought to escape by the side windows.

Then with the other two he quietly ascended the steps of the verandah.

"If he's here," he observed, "we shall nab him to a certainty."

And placing the muzzle of his carbine to the keyhole he blew the lock to flinders.

After which, he and his comrades commenced a vigorous assault on the door with the but-ends of their carbines.

It might have been more in accordance with the laws of warfare to have summoned the garrison to surrender; but the sergeant, knowing from Marco's tracks up to the house that Ned was within, thought any such courtesy superfluous.

The bars held firm, however; and for some time the thundering din produced no response.

Suddenly a hoarse voice was heard within, demanding who the devil it was hammering at the door in that fashion.

"All right, Master Kelly," cried Whitwell. "Just open the door and let us in, or we'll find a way to smoke you out of your hole."

A laugh was the only answer.

"Hammer away, lads," cried the sergeant. "We'll have this door down in a brace of shakes, and then that joker'll laugh on the wrong side of his mouth"

Suddenly the panel in the shutter flew open, a pistol shot rang out, and with a low moan the sergeant dropped in his tracks.

Before the other two could well realise whence the attack came, a second shot was fired, the ball passing through Whitwell's arm, and, ere he and his companions could turn their carbines against their foe, the panel was re-closed.

A panic seized them, and, fairly turning tail, they trotted from the verandah like startled rabbits, and did not halt till they had gained the shelter of the ruined outbuildings.

Another shot, and a cry from their companions in the rear of the house warned them that they too were in equal peril, and next minute they saw them falling back.

Ere, however, they could gain shelter a fourth shot was fired from the house, and the bullet lodging in Casson's leg brought him to the ground.

Holmes, his companion, seized him in his arms, and, swinging him on to his shoulder, succeeded in bearing him out of range.

Matters were evidently critical.

With two of their number *hors de combat*, and a third wounded, their chance of capturing Kelly seemed farther off than ever.

Holmes and his wounded companion having rejoined them, they took counsel.

"Look here," said Whitwell, whose wound on examination was found not to be so serious as they had at first imagined, "we must turn this siege into a blockade. We can't storm the house, but the fellow inside is in an equally tight fix, for if he ventures into the open we can knock him over like a rabbit."

"That's so," said Holmes.

"Well, all we've got to do is to keep a sharp lookout, and, meanwhile, send back the shepherd for help."

"Yes, that's all very well," growled Anderson, whose temper had not been improved by the sergeant's rating concerning his oversight at the first, "but if the captain comes up with the rest of the police, he'll get the reward, and we sha'l run all the risk in the meantime."

"Something in that," remarked Holmes.

"I don't like this job over much," resumed Anderson. "If five of us couldn't come to the end of the fellow, I'm blessed if I see how two and a half, for that's all we are, can. How are we to keep watch on all sides of the house?"

"Oh, as to that," said Casson, pluckily, "I am not quite done for. My leg hurts awful, but I think I could manage to shoot straight, in spite of it. Only just let me have a fair crack at that beggar, and I'll lay odds he won't forget me."

"But how about the sergeant?" asked Whitwell. "I don't think he's dead."

"Ain't there a way of luring Kelly out into the open?" said Holmes. "If we could only manage that, we could bowl him over easily. He's got no horse."

"Where the devil has he hid his horse?" asked Anderson.

"Somewhere in these sheds, I expect. Hullo!"

This last remark was called forth by a startling incident.

About fifty yards intervened between the shed in which they had ensconced themselves and the dwelling-house.

Suddenly the door of the latter opened.

They sprang to their arms, expecting to see the form of the bushranger cross the threshold.

Instead of this, however, they merely saw a pole fitted at the end with a hook, thrust forth by some invisible hand.

Before they could advance, the hook was fastened in the garments of their fallen leader, the sergeant; he was jerked swiftly into the house, and the door was again closed.

Two minutes later, the same pole with a dirty white apron fastened at the end was thrust through the panel and waved in invitation.

"It's a flag of truce," said Holmes.

"Who's going to answer it?" asked Anderson.

"Why, I don't mind," said Whitwell, pluckily. "I am hit already, and it would be better for me to come to grief than one of you fellows. Besides, I believe Kelly will keep his word."

Fastening a hankerchief on the end of a stick, Whitwell advanced towards the door.

"Stop there!" yelled Ned, as soon as he was within ten yards of the door, "or I'll fire at you."

"What do you want?" asked the undaunted trooper.

"I want to know how long you fellows are going to keep loafing about the premises," was the jeering answer.

"Till you come out."

"If I do come out I'll give you a lesson you won't forget in a hurry. But I'm willing to do it."

"Oh!"

"Yes, if you'll give me a chance."

"What do you mean?"

"Why just this. In the first place, I've got your sergeant in here."

"Well?"

"Well, he ain't dead, but I tell you he blessed soon will be, unless you give me a chance of bolting. And I'll tell you something more, if you don't give me the chance I ask for, I'm blessed if I won't burn him alive over a slow fire before you get in this crib."

"Go on."

"It's just this. I'm not going to wait till you've sent off and roused the country, which will be your little game next, I guess."

"Oh, you're as deep as a lawyer, you are!"

"Right you are. Now, what I want is this. You and your mates shall fall back a hundred and fifty yards from the house. I don't think there's any chance of your hitting me at a hundred and fifty yards," he continued reflectively, "but to make matters quite safe we'll say two hundred."

"One of us is wounded and can't walk."

"Well! he can stay."

"What next?"

"Your horses must be tethered out of sight, so that they cannot be brought up to you before I get my start. Say yes or no. Sharp's the word. Neither Ned or the sergeant shall be taken alive."

"I will fall back and consult my comrades. I see nothing to disagree with, myself; and if they agree, I'll step out and wave this flag twice. You may trust me."

"I know I can. You are a brave fellow to trust yourself within pistol-shot of me, and I know you're the sort to keep your word."

Whitwell rejoined his comrades, and after a brief consultation it was agreed to accept Ned's terms.

It was evident he wanted to get a start, and trust to his fleetness of foot to escape into the neighbouring scrub.

But they felt sure of baffling him.

Holmes proceeded to the men in charge of the horses, which were grouped on a little knoll some five hundred yards to the left of the house.

In obedience to his orders Sam, the shepherd, and the black fellow picketed their chargers, and then fell back a hundred yards further.

Holmes rejoined his companions, and after Whitwell had stepped forward and waved his flag as a signal, the whole, with the exception of Casson, fell back to the distance indicated.

The position was then as follows:—

The troopers were two hundred yards in front but to the left of the house.

Their horses were five hundred yards behind them.

Consequently, they were about three hundred yards apart.

Kelly, on the other hand, was only two hundred from the advanced guard.

But then the shepherd, Sam, and the black fellow were only a hundred yards from the horses, and their orders were, directly the door opened to run like the wind to them and gallop off with them to the troopers, who would surely be able to overtake Kelly who, on foot, could not keep up racing-pace very long.

Meanwhile, Ned had been completing his preparations.

After despoiling the insensible sergeant of his uniform, he had locked him in the room in which he had himself passed the night.

Then saddling Marco Polo he led him quietly up to the front door.

He softly undid the bars.

Jessie was watching him with the utmost interest.

"Now, lass, it's your turn," he said.

She evidently understood him, for she stepped forward with a couple of silk handkerchiefs in her hand.

One of these he proceeded to tie over her mouth after bestowing upon her lips a hearty smack which she seemed by no means reluctant to receive.

With the other he tied her hands at the wrists, leaving, however, the fingers at full liberty.

Then he got into Marco Polo's saddle, cocked his revolver, that belonged to the sergeant, and crouched flat on the horse's neck.

"Now!" he said.

The would-be captors of Kelly were in an agony of expectation and excitement, expecting to see the redoubtable bushranger walk into the net, but they little knew the resource and ingenuity of the man they thought was within their grasp. They remembered that the fellow seemed to bear as charmed a life as that of Macbeth, who was to be slain by—

"No man of woman born!"

He had been shot at, but stood invulnerable, the bullets rattling off his body as harmless as peas off a crocodile's back. His enemies little knew that they wasted their pellets upon an "ironclad," for Kelly always wore in these encounters a suit of mail, hammered out of ploughshares, which rendered him bullet-proof. With open mouth and strained eyes they stared at the door by which they expected to see Ned escape. They were not long kept in suspense. Suddenly the door was rapidly thrown open, and disclosed Kelly mounted on Marco Polo, who the next moment was seen to clear the steps at a bound, with his tail as straight as a fence in a gale of wind, and his eyes as bright as lightning-flashes, as if he knew he bore Cæsar and his fortunes on his back. Whew! on he came, as Jonathan would say, like greased lightning, Kelly's loud defiant laugh ringing out clearly, while, waving his hat triumphantly, he chaffed his enemies with cutting sarcasm to "come and take him," to "get up behind," and promising to square up with Sam before many months were over that worthy's head.

Down and over the steps, as if he were taking a stream in his stride, the gallant animal answered the heel and hopes of his daring rider, who, with a pistol in his grasp cocked and ready for action, galloped to where the police horses were tethered, and drawing the policeman's sword, with which, as with his uniform, he was furnished, proceeded with a few furious slashes to hough—in other words, to hamstring—the unfortunate brutes, and thus render pursuit for the present impossible. The troopers looked on perfectly stupefied, and, if truth must be told, not a little dismayed. They knew that if able to come up with Kelly while engaged in his barbarous, but to him necessary, onslaught, the foremost arrivals would certainly be "dead meat," and Kelly's escape (being mounted) not prevented.

"Now, you blooming crawlers," he roared out, awakening the echoes of the forest, "such carrion as you will never put the darbies on Ned Kelly. Take my blessing before I show you a clean pair of heels!" and, with a devilish howl which he meant for laughter, he discharged the contents of his pistol amongst his astonished and, if the fact must be confessed, admiring opponents. They saw his retreating figure, and heard the departing sounds of Marco's thud, thud, as he flew over the ground with a swinging 20-foot stride, and looked at one another with something very like silent apprehension. As to Sam, he felt uncommonly uncomfortable, for he knew Kelly would never forget the little game he had played.

Kelly's onslaught on the troopers' horses had been witnessed, and its full significance understood.

A very crestfallen crew the troopers looked, and, knowing that the victory obtained by Kelly would find its way into the colonial papers, they feared something worse than the universal ridicule with which they were sure to be overwhelmed.

Pursuit was hopeless, for they were miles from any station where there was the slightest chance of obtaining horses, and the line of country Ned had selected was one calculated from its conformation to baffle all attempts at tracing him.

Disheartened and baffled, they returned to the house, in order to get something to eat.

Locked in one room they found the insensible form of Sergeant Whitwell.

In another, the key of which was lying in the passage, they found a young damsel bound and gagged, who, on being released, entertained them with a very voluble and highly-coloured account of how the preceding night she had gone to the door on hearing a knock, and had been seized and made secure in this manner by a black-bearded ruffian.

It was Miss Jessie Appleby, who, on Ned's departure, had retired to her room, and, on the troopers entering the house, had quietly turned the key with her bound hands, and then pushed it under the door into the passage, where they found it.

CHAPTER CXXVIII.

FATHER AND SON— THE LAST RESOURCE.

ARCHIBALD DOUGLAS KEITH ROTHSAY, seventh Earl of Stromness, in the peerage of Scotland, and a representative peer of that ancient kingdom in the Upper House of the British Legislature, was a nobleman better off as regards pedigree than possessions.

His blood was of the bluest, but his acres, on the other hand, were of the barest.

Indeed it was a paradox how such a spreading family-tree, with such an extent of roots, branches, and ramifications, could exist on such a scanty patch of soil, overgrown, too, as the latter was, with such a flourishing crop of mortgages.

He was the nominal possessor of two country seats with imposing titles.

But Dunstaffness Castle was a roofless tower, which had been uninhabitable for years, and the miles of moorland around, which annually let in August to southron sportsmen, formed no inconsiderable portion of the earl's revenue, whilst Kinlavorack Palace, on the shores of one of the Northern Isles, was merely a huge, rambling, dilapidated range of one-storey buildings, half of which were uninhabitable, whilst the other half served as a joint residence to Mr. John McCombie, the earl's "factor," his household, his cattle, and his pigs.

The earl himself, when not staying with or, as evil-disposed people who will not remember the golden rule of not speaking ill of a hereditary legislator used to style it, sponging upon his friends, was wont to occupy a first-floor in Clarges-street.

The Stromness family was one of those which bred with the rapidity and fecundity of an insect which enabled Dr. Johnson to direct one of his most pointed comparisons against Scotchmen, and Archibald Douglas Keith Rothsay had a number of brothers, sisters, uncles, and aunts, and a perfect army of cousins in the fifteenth degree.

But, strange to say, he had only had the honour of contributing two direct offshoots to the family tree—a son and a daughter

The latter, the Lady Sybella Malvina, was happily wedded to Leoni Schumacher, Esquire, a worthy millionaire of Hebrao-Germanic extraction and paltry presence, and the possessor, in addition to vast funded wealth, of a park in Surrey and a mansion at Queen's-gate.

The Earl had already learnt the value of an aristocratic title on the first page of the prospectus of a joint-stock company, and for some time he and his son-in-law were of great use to one another.

He figured as the director of upwards of a score of enterprises of a more or less speculative character, and pocketed guineas with praiseworthy regularity.

But after a time the British public, despite their proverbial love for a lord, began to weary of putting their hard-earned gains into enterprises whose only recommendation was a more or less skilled directorate, and the millionaire found he had no use for the Earl, and no longer cared to make those little financial advances at odd times for which, to tell the truth, the latter had parted with his daughter.

This was bad enough, but another sore thorn in the side of Archibald Douglas Keith Rothsay lay in the conduct and career of his son, who had been endowed with the names of Kenneth Shaw Ian and the title of the Master of Stromness.

Kenneth had been to Eton, where the high position he took in the boats was, in the eyes of his father and other prejudiced persons, a very poor compensation for the exceedingly low one he occupied in his form.

It was, moreover, a source of wonderment, even to such of his schoolfellows who were unversed in the hardening effect of the continual application of birch twigs to the human anatomy, how he could sit on the thwarts, considering the marked persistency with which his name figured week after week in the flogging-bill.

Till finally a letter which was nothing less than a politely-regretful, but at the same time unmistakable, sentence of excommunication, reached the badgered Earl from the head-master.

It detailed how Kenneth had committed the unheard-of crime of assaulting and battering his tutor, and had maintained that he considered his conduct was, under the circumstances, perfectly justifiable.

It was somewhat difficult to get him into Oxford after this, but he managed to scrape through a few terms, during which he distinguished himself by rowing stroke in his college eight, one fine May evening which saw the craft in question achieve the position of head of the river, running up rather more than the average amount of bills, driving tandem, and committing sundry other actions which, though venial in the eyes of everyday life, constitute dire offences to the proctorial vision, without incurring rustication.

Then he was sent to a cramming establishment, and thence duly gazetted to a cornetcy in the Princess's Own Rangers.

His cornetcy proved a very rapid act of horsemanship, yet even his comrades marvelled how he managed to live the pace anything like so long.

The Princess's Own was a crack regiment, and the holders of commissions in it managed to get through a great deal of money over bets, horses, balls, dinners, dress, cards, the drama, and similar objects of attraction, and in all these Kenneth took an interest not exceeded by any of his brother officers.

Till at length even the patience of the most obsequious of tradesmen and the purses of the most accommodating of bill-discounters seemed to be exhausted as far as he was concerned.

Under the old regulations it is probable that he would have had to sell his commission, but the memorable Royal Warrant, by means of which Gladstone checkmated the House of Lords, had put an end to that kind of transaction, and all that was left to him to "sell" was his creditors.

Things were in this state when a note from his father, requesting him to call the following morning to go into a matter of the highest moment, reached him at Hounslow, where the Princess's Own were quartered.

"Wonder what the deuce the governor means?" he mused, but as he had certainly nothing to lose, and it might be something to gain, by the interview thus suggested, he made up his mind to accept the invitation.

And then, as the warning blast of a trumpet fell on his ear, he roused himself from his reverie, and proceeded.

As he gazed at the fore-shortened reflection of his six feet of lithe, lean-flanked, broad-shouldered, hard-set thew and sinew in the handsome mess attire of the Princess's Own, a melancholy thought occurred to him that before long he would be forced to put aside that very becoming uniform for ever.

"Which will be a pity, for I think I can say, without vanity, we become each other," he muttered, as he took up his cap, blew out his candle, and descended.

The next morning saw him in presence of his father, a tall, grey-whiskered, hawk-nosed old aristocrat, with a wax-like complexion, a high shirt-collar, a starched necktie, and a pair of the most immaculate-looking hands ever seen out of a glass case.

"Kenneth," began the earl, with that easy, half-jovial air which some men always assume when talking of another's misfortune, "you are in an infernal mess—a most infernal mess."

"Quite so. If it was only to tell me that you sent for for me, I am afraid it was a piece of useless trouble on your part, for I was perfectly aware of it," was the cool answer.

" Certainly. certainly. No, what I wanted to speak to you about was to see if no way could be found of getting you out of it without—without—ahem!—scandal."

" I am afraid not."

" Look here, Kenneth, have you ever thought of matrimony ? "

" Only when suicide looked more than usually unpleasant."

' Come, come! a man with your rank, your position, your personal appearance, might choose anywhere."

And certainly there was some truth in the earl's remark

With his tall, erect, soldier-like figure, his neatly-set-on head, with its closely-cropped hair, his bright blue eyes now sparkling with merriment and anon glittering cold and keen as a rapier point in the face of peril, his haughty aquiline features with an expression at once reckless yet impassible, his firm red lips shaded by a long drooping moustache, and his mellow, ringing voice, he was fitted in all ways to catch a woman's eye and win his way to her heart.

Fitted for sterner work than that, however, as well.

There was a touch of the young eagle in the way in which he carried his head, and when those steel-blue eyes began at once to brighten and darken, that iron-clamp of a lower jaw to set, and those red lips to tighten to whiteness, those who knew him best recognised the waking of a spirit no earthly peril had power to daunt or check.

He was gifted with all the dour obstinacy, stern endurance, and native shrewdness derived from his ancestry on the father's side, but it had pleased Providence to temper these eminently useful but not always agreeable qualifications with the reckless daring, high spirits, love of fun, and genial, careless temperament that had formed almost the only dowery brought into the matrimonial parntership by his beautiful and graceful Irish mother.

" I must confess I don't like to regard myself in the light of a barber's doll," he answered.

" Look here, Kenneth, you might marry any amount of money to-morrow, if you wished."

" Perhaps so."

" There is Miss Rhys, the great Welsh heiress, with half a county of slate-quarries, a dozen coal-mines, and a couple of seaport towns."

" She has red hair and she squints."

" Miss Shortstaple, the Lancashire girl. Her father has three millions and——"

" Cannot write his name, and eats peas with his knife. Besides she's booked to Lugard of ours."

" Lady Emily Randolph. Her influence in a certain quarter would——"

" Obtain her second husband anything but the right of asking how much was due to his own merit and how much to the complaisance of his predecessor ! No, no; such a suggestion I should resent even from you, if I thought it made in seriousness."

" Well, there is the American girl, Daisy Vandipunt."

" I can't endure her "

" Come now, I'll tell you a girl you know as well as I do warts you to propose."

" Who ? "

" Miss Locatta, the daughter of that chum of Schumacher's. Won't she do ?"

" No more than the others. I won't marry."

" I was afraid not. Now, however, there is one way in which the Locatta girl can be of use."

" How ?"

" Why, you see, Schumacher wants her for himself."

" What ! does he mean to commit bigamy, or poison off Sybella ?"

" No, no. I mean, he wants her to marry his brother, and he looks upon you as a very dangerous rival. In fact, he has already spoken to me about the matter."

" Yes; go on."

" Well, the long and short of it is, he thinks if you were out of the way his brother would have a chance."

" And what does he propose, for I suppose the truth is that you have already a programme cut and dried ?"

" Schumacher is not, after all, a bad fellow, Kenneth. He has put certain things in my way, and I am sure he has behaved well to you. Now he offers to pay your debts if you will leave the country. You know I have not a penny, and you must smash if you go on as you are going at present."

" Very true."

" Well, I think I can get you an excellent appointment in the Australian police."

" In the what ?"

" In the police. Oh, I have learnt all about it, it is quite a different thing from what you fancy. Liberal pay, strictly military force, rank of a field officer. Surely you remember, some men of the best families in England have served in it."

" I'll think of it," said Kenneth.

Which he did ; and, seeing the thing was, so to say, inevitable, ultimately accepted it.

He resigned his commission, and quietly departed for few weeks to the Continent.

Schumacher then proceeded to fulfil his promise of paying his debts by buying up all his bills at about seventy-five per cent. discount, and offering his despairing tradesmen a composition of half-a-crown in the pound, which, seeing the seeming impossibility of ever getting their money, they thankfully accepted.

A week after, they read of the appointment of Kenneth to the command of the New South Wales police, and cursed their ready acquiescence.

CHAPTER CXXIX.
THE VOYAGE.

KENNETH ROTHSAY had elected to go to his future home in a clipper rounding the Cape, preferring the fresh breezes of the longer route to that premature acquaintance with the temperature of the infernal regions experienced by those whom the swift progress and luxurious accommodation of the P. and O. steamers lures into a trip through the Suez Canal and down the Red Sea.

So one fine morning saw the A1 clipper Compostella, bearing him and his fortunes, dropping down the Thames in the tow of a couple of snorting steam-tugs, on the top of the ebb.

Kenneth, standing on the poop, was watching the bustle and apparent confusion that mark the first day out of dock, and studying the appearance of his fellow-passengers, when the slight figure of a girl attired in deep mourning caught his attention.

He could not resist strolling with apparent carelessness in her direction, in order to get a better look at her.

The little journey in question was, in his opinion, fully justified by this closer inspection.

She was a young creature, slender and supple as a hazel-twig, pliant and graceful as a willow, with wide-open, arch, brown eyes, a delicate nose slightly aquiline, a sweet, womanly mouth, crimson and curved, sensitive, and with flickering dimples at the corners, a face of the true oval, and a profusion of chestnut hair lying in rings on the smooth, broad forehead and in soft clustering curls around the snowy white neck.

In five minutes Kenneth had contrived to render her one of the thousand little services a man can always find to do for a lady on shipboard, and in ten more he was chatting to her like an old acquaintance.

Before the Compostella reached Gravesend he was fully acquainted with her history, such as it was.

Muriel Lyndhurst was the orphan daughter of a poor curate, who had offended his family and lost a prospective living by marrying a young lady engaged as governess in a noble family to the sons of which he was engaged as tutor.

He might have, had he chosen, been the rector of Salt-combe-cum-Withersby, with an annual stipend of two thousand a year, and a population of six hundred parishioners to look after, had he only deigned to respond to the sheep's eyes which the Lady Jane Blenchester kept on casting at him, and to take that somewh't *passée* and mature beauty to his hearth and home.

Instead of which, he rashly persisted in marrying her younger sister's governess—pretty little Ada Craston, the daughter of a deceased naval officer; and, being from that time forward disowned by his own aristocratic connection, and disowned by old Lord Blenchester, who had fondly imagined that he saw a chance of getting rid of Jane, and was sorely disappointed, he obtained the post of curate in a London parish and within eighteen years was dead of hard work and heartbreak.

His wife had not the sorrow of witnessing this, for the poor thing had died in the third year of their marriage.

Muriel's only relation was a brother of her mother's a wild scapegrace, who, when a mere boy, had started off to earn his living in the colonies.

How he had fared she knew not, for he had not written to England more than twice since her mother's death.

However, she believed that he was living, and in New South Wales, and had accordingly resolved on setting out in search of him.

"I daresay it seems a wildgoose chase, Mr. Rothsay," she said to her new acquaintance; "but even if I do not find my uncle in a position to help me, or even if he be dead, I think I am doing well in going abroad. What could I do in England but try to get a situation as governess, and, after wearing out the best years of my life in teaching, have the workhouse before me for my old age? But I am sure in Australia I shall have a far better chance of getting on."

Kenneth could not help admiring the girl's pluck, and an intimacy soon sprang up between them.

There was a fair number of passengers on board the Compostella, and they exhibited a wide divergency of position and character.

Amongst them were several colonials of both sexes returning to Australia after a flying visit to the Old Country.

Kenneth had carefully kept back his real rank and the position awaiting him at Sydney.

He was simply Mr. Rothsay. and, as his manner and appearance betrayed, almost in spite of himself, his military training, was charitably set down by most of his fellow-passengers as a broken-down officer who, having found it impossible to exist by billiards and betting, varied by an occasional attempt at the wine trade in England, was about to try his luck, as so many of the like kidney have done before, in the colony.

It is true that his genial good nature, winning ways, perfect breeding, and superb personal appearance soon secured for him the suffrages of all but the most surly on board the ship.

Poor Miss Lyndhurst had a harder task

She was dangerously beautiful, and only a governess.

Consequently, some of the ladies regarded her as a rival to be extinguished as constantly and systematically as possible, and some of the gentlemen began to pay her compliments that at times became almost equivocal.

Kenneth's chivalrous nature suffered terribly at the slights to which the girl was subjected.

For him to have interfered in person would, of course, only have resulted in their names being coupled together.

But he got Mrs. Millington, the wife of a wealthy Melbourne merchant, and one of the most influential ladies on board, to take the girl under her wing, and gently hinted to a young snob named Hoskins, whose father had shipped him off to Australia with a couple of thousand pounds to start a station, and who, on the strength, gave himself the airs of a being able to buy up the entire colony, that he might feel compelled to drop him gently over the ship's side if he did not leave Miss Lyndhurst alone.

Muriel was deeply grateful for these services, which she quickly divined.

"Mr. Rothsay, she said to him one day, struggling between boldness and timidity as she spoke, "I know all you have done for me, and from the bottom of my heart I thank you. Some day it may lie in my power to prove my gratitude. At present I can only express it."

Under Mrs. Millington's wing Muriel was more at ease, and the good lady, who was a warm admirer of Kenneth, was by no means averse to allowing a fair amount of that flirtation without which existence on shipboard could hardly be carried on, between the handsome ex dragoon and her *protégée*.

So Kenneth and Muriel used to stand side by side, looking over the vessel's quarter, during those lonely moonlight nights that are only encountered in the tropics, and if at times a strong young arm did steal round a slim young waist, it was only natural as a precaution against those sudden dangerous lurches that will occur under such circumstances.

So the Compostella ploughed her way along day after day, meeting more than usually fine weather, and the feelings with which Kenneth had began to regard Miss Lyndhurst were very like those of a lover.

The Cape of Good Hope was safely doubled, and the Australian continent sighted.

The Compostella was bound for Sydney, and after passing through Bass's Strait she steered to the northward.

The commander looked anxious, for his keen eye detected unmistakable signs of a coming gale, and knew the dangerous nature of the coast, whilst a thick atmosphere prevented any observations from being taken.

At midnight the wind moved suddenly round to the east and lashed the sea to roughness during the whole of the following day, the sun, as during the preceding day, being obscured by clouds

At night the passengers were somewhat uneasy, but the skipper, Captain Parsons, assured them that there was not the slightest danger, as they had a good offing, and soon they were all in their bunks and the deck abandoned to the watch.

Suddenly the cry of "Breakers ahead!" rang out from the look-out man.

The captain sprang forward, but before an order could be given the Compostella struck on a reef with a mighty crash.

As the affrighted passengers, in hastily-assumed garments, rushed in terror to the deck, the billows sweeping over the ship, which lay on her starboard side, carried several of them overboard shrieking in mad despair.

Muriel had like to have met with a similar fate, when an arm of iron was cast around her, and, blinded and half-suffocated by the water, she was borne by Kenneth back to the companion-way.

"Have no fear," he said. "If I reach the shore alive, you shall."

Suddenly the stricken vessel heeled over to the other side and beat repeatedly on the rocks, as though writhing in mortal agony, whilst sea after sea swept over her.

"Cut away the masts," was the captain's order, and scarcely had the standing rigging been severed than the spars snapping off close to the deck plunged with a crash into the sea.

There was a cry for the boats.

Three had been swept away at the beginning of the wreck, and now a maddened throng flocked to the two remaining ones.

"It's not worth risking," said Kenneth to Muriel. "Do you think," he continued, "that you can keep up sufficient courage to stand here for a moment whilst I go below?"

The girl's face was very white, but she answered, "Yes" in a firm, if low, voice.

Darting below, Kenneth reappeared with a life-belt, which he proceeded to strap around Muriel.

"But yourself?" she said.

"Miss Lyndhurst," he answered, gravely, "if mortal effort can get you out of this peril you are as safe as if you were on shore ; and if," he continued in a livelier tone, for the very danger nerved and excited him, "mortal effort can't, why, it won't be for the want of hard trying."

Meanwhile the boats, with the frightened throng who had crowded into them, were, at what seemed a favourable moment, lowered into the water.

There was an awful interval of uncertainty.

Their fate was indistinguishable in the pitchy darkness.

Suddenly the appalling death-cry of the drowning rose out of the gloom to fill all who heard it with startled horror.

Too well did they realise the meaning of that sound, too well did they know that it denoted the foundering of the boats and the sinking of all who had sought safety in them.

Rapidly did the destruction of the Compostella follow.

A few minutes after the lowering of the boats she parted asunder, a confused mass of riven timbers, splintered planks, tangled spars, and writhing human beings.

In indiscriminate commingling the wreck and the wrecked, dead, half-dead, and desperately clinging to anything that promised support, were driven on to the reef.

Throughout the rest of that night of horrors Kenneth, who had never released Muriel from the moment the ship had broken up, and had enabled her to gain a place of comparative safety, did not quit her for a moment.

They had obtained a foothold on the rocks, which rose above water, though from time to time a wave larger than the rest threatened to tear them from the post.

Eagerly they longed for day.

As day approached the wind gradually sank, and their position became more tolerable.

Daybreak revealed a melancholy sight.

The Compostella had evidently deviated from her course, and come in much nearer shore than her captain had supposed.

She had struck on a reef extending parallel to the coast, which lay about a mile off.

Her fragments were seen extending for about the same distance along the reef, and bore melancholy witness to the tremendous shock the vessel had sustained.

Cabin doors, pieces of boats, casks, seats, cabin furniture, planks, beds, seamen's chests, and passengers' luggage formed a continuous ridge in places several feet high, whilst numerous drowned corpses added to the horrors of the sight.

A score of human beings, mostly sailors, clinging to the rocks, many half-submerged as the waves washed over them, were all that were left of the eighty souls on board the Compostella when she quitted the Thames

Amongst them was the chief officer, Mr. Sandilands, whom Kenneth at once hailed.

"What is our best way of reaching the shore?" he asked, cheerily.

"The sea is going down, and I think there is every chance that a raft will float us," was the answer.

The survivors, under Sandilands' direction, began to set to work to construct a raft, whilst Kenneth proceeded to break open one of the trunks washed on to the rock with a view of finding some clothing for Muriel.

The remains of one of the boats caught his eye.

"Do you think this could be patched up to carry us?" he asked of the chief officer.

Part of the planking had been stove in, and the little craft was quite unseaworthy, but Sandilands expressed an idea that it might be made to serve.

A copper bolt that might do at a pinch for a hammer was wrenched from a piece of timber, and a number of nails slowly collected from amongst the lumber.

Whilst one party continued to put the raft together, the remainder proceeded to patch up the boat as well as they could.

"Which do you think safest?" asked Kenneth of Sandilands.

The other stared at the question, coming as it did from one whom he had seen a moment before risking his life on the edge of the reef in the search for nails and the like, and he half smiled.

"You misunderstand me," said Kenneth. "I was thinking that there are women here."

"Well, they are patching up the boat pretty well, but I prefer rope to nails as a fastening."

And he glanced at the raft.

By noon the boat had been patched up and the raft completed, and preparations were made to leave the reef.

There were two ladies saved besides Muriel, and these took their places in the stern of the boat, and asked her to come with them.

"No," said Kenneth to her quickly. "Trust to me and come on the raft."

It had been arranged that the boat should tow the raft, and that the progress of both should be helped by improvised sails.

They were soon under way.

They found wind and current both serving their turn, and rapidly impelling them towards the coast, but a nearer view of this showed plainly that their perils were not yet over.

The sea swept in, in a succession of huge rollers, which broke with thundering sound on the strip of beach.

But between them and that beach were ranges of half-submerged rocks, amongst which the receding waves hissed and foamed and snorted in threatening whirlpools.

"We cannot risk a landing here," said the chief mate "We must pull along the shore till we find a better spot."

It was more easily said than done.

They found to their horror that wind and current were rapidly drawing them shoreward.

The men in the boat, thinking only of their own safety, cast off the tow-ropes, and began to try to gain an offing.

The raft, thus abandoned, was unmanageable in the current, and drifted each moment nearer shore.

Again Kenneth's arm was placed round Muriel.

"My darling," he murmured, "we will live or die together."

Even in that awful moment the girl evoked this indirect avowal of his love.

The next moment the raft was tossing madly in the surging sea of breakers.

There was a succession of desperate wrenches, the strong cords snapped like twine, and it fell asunder like a house of cards.

Muriel felt the seas go over her head, but the strong grip never loosened.

There was a desperate struggle of drowning men, seizing on one another.

A moment or so later, Kenneth, cut, bruised, and bleeding, felt himself dashed against the shore, still holding Muriel.

Digging his feet into the sand, he escaped the danger of the murderous undertow, and as it swept back, bearing off to death two hapless wretches who had pushed on as far as himself, he rose and staggered forward, out of reach of the waves, with his precious burden still clasped in his arms.

Then he fell again almost insensible.

"By Jove!" he muttered, rising to his feet and spitting out the salt water, "I have taken possession of my new territory like William the Conqueror. I wonder if my jurisdiction extends over this spot as chief of police?"

Muriel was insensible, and, before trying to revive her, he glanced seaward.

A few floating timbers amidst the breakers alone marked the spot where the raft had been engulfed, and it was plain that they were the only survivors of its crew who had reached shore.

The boat was still striving to gain an offing; but, even as he watched it, a succession of heavy rollers swept in quick succession down upon it, and the next instant it had disappeared, never to rise again.

Alone on that barren shore, Kenneth and Muriel stood, the sole survivors of all who had sailed in the good ship Compostella.

CHAPTER CXX.

AN ARISTOCRATIC SCOUNDREL.

AT this period, one of the most prominent, if not the most popular, characters in Sydney was a gentleman who bore the time-honoured name of Knatchbull—Captain Knatchbull, of the Royal Navy, brother to the esteemed and wealthy baronet of that name. From his childhood, George Knatchbull was like one possessed of the devil; as Tiberius said of Nero, "A thing of blood and mud." He belonged to one of the oldest and most influential families in the county of Kent, but from his childhood upwards behaved as if possessed of an evil spirit.

He was a liar and a thief, and was criminally and malevolently mischievous.

The old people who dwell about his ancestral hall will yet tell you how, when a mere lad, if he entered a poor man's orchard stealthily to rob an apple or pear tree, and found no fruit on it, he would take out his knife and bark the tree all round near the root, and thus kill it, for the sap could not ascend.

He would worry sheep with dogs, and chase cattle till they jumped into chalk-pits, and staked themselves in trying to clear fences.

To save him from the clutches of the law, his brother, Sir Edward Knatchbull, had annually to pay a large sum of money to people who would otherwise have prosecuted him.

At thirteen years of age, the only thing to be done for him was to send him out of the way to sea.

Accordingly, he was sent into the Royal Navy as a midshipman.

At nineteen he gazetted as lieutenant, and was appointed to a line-of-battle ship.

Interest had a great deal to do, no doubt, in bringing about his speedy promotion, for his uncle was a Lord of the Admiralty, but it would be unjust to dispute George Knatchbull's merit as either seaman or officer, for a smarter and more daring fellow never walked a quarterdeck.

But, at the same time, a crueller brute never wore the British uniform.

At the age of twenty-three he was appointed to the command of the Hecuba, one of the prettiest and fastest eighteen-gun brigs in the service, with orders to proceed to Staten Island.

The master, Mr. John Treadwell, was a skilful navigator, and an unusually scientific man; and not only was he specially required by the Admiralty to furnish a report on the swinging of the pendulum—a rather important question in those days—but to his care were entrusted several chronometers besides those required for the working of the ship, in order that he might test and report on their accuracy and value.

The Hecuba never got so far as Staten Island.

When she had been only three weeks at sea, Lieutenant, by courtesy Captain, Knatchbull discovered there was mutiny on board, mutiny fostered by his first lieutenant whose soul had sickened at the daily sights of horror to which he was exposed.

For Captain Knatchbull, finding himself for the first time in his life in absolute command of a vessel under orders for a foreign station, had thrown aside all restraint, and yielded to the fiendish impulses of his nature.

The gratings were constantly rigged, the cat was never out of the hands of the boatswain and his mates, and every night Knatchbull might have repeated the words of the captain who observed on coming ashore—"My ship's crew are at the present moment the happiest fellows in the world. I have just flogged half of them, who are delighted that it is over, whilst the other half are rejoicing that they have got off this time at any rate."

When, however, he found the officers could stand this no longer and were going to take an active part against him, he, one morning, suddenly gave the order to put the ship about, and returned to the Downs.

There was an investigation respecting the alleged mutiny, but the revelations concerning Knatchbull were so damaging that the matter was hushed up, and it merely ended in a recommendation that the Hecuba should be put out of commission and paid off, which was done accordingly.

In all there were seven chronometers on board her, in Mr. Treadwell's custody, but on the day on which he had to deliver them up only six could be found.

One had been abstracted from his cabin.

The old man, who had only his scanty pay to live on and a wife and three daughters to support, was unable to make the loss good, and inasmuch as Captain Knatchbull, when written to on the subject, falsely represented the old master as "a drunken fellow on whom no dependence could be placed," Mr. Treadwell was ordered to be dismissed from the service.

Numberless were the petitions addressed to the Lords of the Admiralty by the old man, setting forth the hardness of his case, and voluminous were the accompanying certificates signed by the various captains with whom he had sailed during the past thirty years, and bearing testimony to the honesty, sobriety, zeal, and skill of Mr. John Treadwell, late Master R.N.

They were of no avail, and at last the receipt of a petition from John Treadwell was not acknowledged by the officials, who looked upon the poor fellow as that greatest of all horrors in their eyes, namely, a man with a grievance.

As to Captain Knatchbull, six months after the Hecuba was paid off he was appointed to the command of a sloop of war, on the Mediterranean station.

Here he remained for two years, and then came home on sick leave in the hope of getting a larger vessel, a hope on the very eve of being realised, when an accident ordained it otherwise.

Poor old John Treadwell, in almost soleless shoes and rusty threadbare coat, was one morning walking down Holborn-hill, thinking of his grievance, when he stopped opposite the window of a pawnbroker's, and began abstractedly to look at all the various articles exposed to view.

Suddenly his eyes lighted on a chronometer, which he fancied he recognised as the one that had brought him into so much trouble—which, in fact, had ruined him.

To make sure he entered the shop.

"Is that chronometer for sale?" he asked.

"It is, sir," was the pawnbroker's reply.

"An unredeemed pledge?"

"Yes, sir."

"Its price?"

"A hundred and twenty guineas."

"May I have a look at it?"

"Certainly. You seem to know how to handle a chronometer," continued the pawnbroker, as Treadwell took the instrument in his trembling hands and rapidly examined every part of it.

"Yes, and I have handled this one before to-day, and a very bad one it is. Yes, this is the instrument," he said, solemnly.

"Indeed," said the pawnbroker, puzzled as to what his strange customer was driving at.

"It belongs to the Government. It was stolen from H.M ship Hecuba, in the Downs."

"I am sorry to hear that. It was pledged here more than two years ago by a man who said he was the captain of a merchant vessel in bad circumstances; and he certainly looked like a seafaring man. I advanced him fifty pounds on it."

"What sort of a man was he?" asked Treadwell eagerly

"Well. I could swear to him anywhere, for we were at least three-quarters of an hour higgling over the loan. He wanted seventy-five pounds, and I could not go beyond fifty. He was a shortish, thickset, broad-shouldered fellow. rather bow-legged; broad, flat face, black eyes, black as jet and very sparkling, with a cast in one of them which gave him a very strange expression of countenance and helped to impress his face on my memory. His lower jaw protruded rather, and the bridge of his nose had seemingly been broken.

"Good heavens!" exclaimed the old master, "you have described Captain Knatchbull."

"I have described the man who pawned that instrument."

"You must not part with it till I have seen you again. It will be to morrow perhaps this evening," and with these words the old man left the pawnbroker's shop.

He made the best of his way to the Admiralty, where he sent up his name and a note to the First Lord, whom he requested the honour of seeing on a very serious matter.

The First Lord sent back a verbal message to the effect that he would not see Mr. Treadwell, and the messenger when asked to take up a second note refused to do so.

"There is no help for it," sighed the old man; an from the Admiralty he wended his way to Bow-street Police-court.

The presiding functionary at the last-named institution, was not so difficult of access as the First Lord.

The old man's statement was taken down, his certificates. of which he always carried several about with him, carefully inspected a note made of the names of the pawn broker and of the famous chronometer-maker in Cornhill who had supplied the instrument, and certain instructions given to two of the most expert officers of the court.

Then old Mr. Treadwell was requested to be in attendance at the court at noon precisely on the following day.

How the officers obtained Captain Knatchbull's address, how, when, and where they found him, and how they placed him face to face with the man with whom he left the chronometer in pledge, need not be recapitulated here.

But the next day, when old John Treadwell made his appearance at Bow-street, he was informed that the prisoner was in custody, and that as soon as the night charges were disposed of, the case would be called on.

It was called on, and that very afternoon George Knatchbull, commander R.N., stood committed to take his trial at the Old Bailey.

It was too late for his relation at the Admiralty to think of devising means for averting a felon's doom from a scion of his ancient house.

A reporter's pen had been beforehand with him; the evening papers contained a full account of the transaction, and the public as one man were moved with sympathy with the poor old master who had been so cruelly treated, and with indignation at the conduct of his scoundrelly superior.

And old John Treadwell stoutly refused to be "bought out of the way," for the insult he had received at the Admiralty when he had last sought an interview with the First Lord rankled in his breast.

Captain Knatchbull was convicted, and sentenced to be transported for fourteen years, and in due course was landed in the colony of New South Wales.

At that time many men who were gentlemen of birth and education, and whose friends in England possessed sufficient influence with the authorities to bring about the result, were treated with great consideration on their arrival in the colony under sentence of transportation.

If they were not emancipated on arrival, they were suffered to be at large, sometimes without the formality of a ticket-of-leave.

Some of them, being amply supplied with funds from their relatives in England, lived in the most comfortable style, and, in more than one instance, shared the hospitality of Government House.

Knatchbull, however, soon forfeited all right to such treatment, and his career in the colony was one of vice and crime.

After suffering slight terms of imprisonment for various offences, he was arraigned before the Supreme Court of Sydney on the charge of forgery and sentenced to transportation to Norfolk Island.

What life in Norfolk Island was has already been spoken of.

So dreadful were the convicts' sufferings that gangs of them used to toss up which amongst them should be a murderer and which a victim.

The murderer would then put the other to death, and the remainder of the gang would come forward as witnesses with the sole object of being taken for a time from the scene of their daily miseries to appear in court at Sydney, and give evidence against their comrade, though they knew very well that after his execution they would be only remanded to their former haunt of wretchedness.

As to the murderer, he would frankly admit that he had no ill-feeling against the man whose brains he had dashed out, but simply wanted to bring about a happy release for them both.

So notorious did this fact become, that a Legislature enactment was made providing for the trial of criminals on the island by special commission, after which such occurrences became less frequent.

(To be continued.)

THE "ANONYMA" SERIES OF POPULAR NOVELS.
PICTURE BOARDS.　　　PUBLISHED AT 2/-

Anonyma, or Fair but Frail.
Skittles, a Tale of Female Life and Adventure.
Left her Home, a Tale of Female Life and Adventure.
Annie.
Delilah, or the Little House in Piccadilly.

Kate Hamilton.
Agnes Willoughby.
The Soiled Dove.
Skittles in Paris, a Biography of a Fascinating Woman.
Love Frolics of a Young Scamp.
Incognita, a Tale of Love and Passion.

Formosa, the Life of a Beautiful Woman.
The Beautiful Demon.
Revelations of a Lady Detective.
The Lady with the Camelias.
Paris Life at Twenty.

NED KELLY
THE IRONCLAD
AUSTRALIAN BUSHRANGER

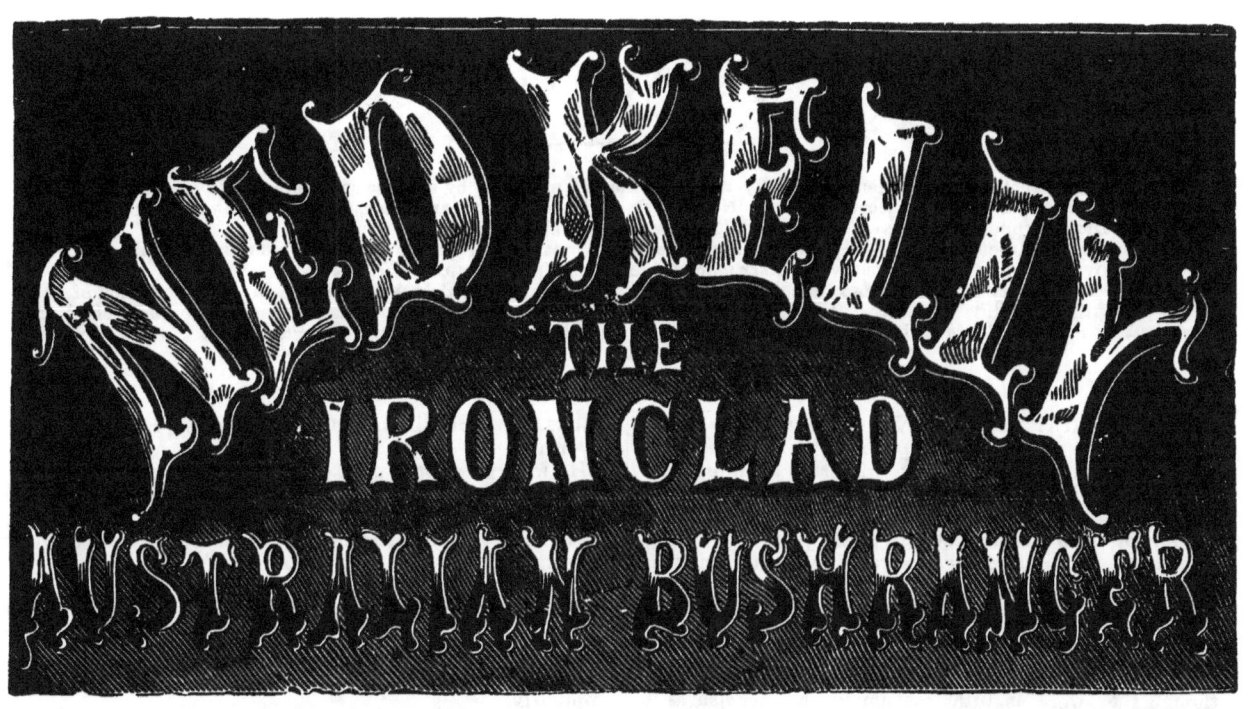

NO 22,

NED KELLY: IRONCLAD BUSHRANGER.

" It is well known that for many years Ned Kelly had made himself notorious by a series of crimes wholly incompatible with the civilisation of the nineteenth century. Ned Kelly's celebrated steed, Marco Polo, is as well known at the Antipodes as Dick Turpin's Black Bess in these islands."—*Telegraph*, 7th July, 1881.

" It is notorious that the robbery of Mr. Steward's corpse was mainly performed by the assistance of NED KELLY'S BROTHER, the Captain of what was neither more nor less than a pirate ship."—*Times*, July.

" The history of NED KELLY and his celebrated black horse, Marco Polo, will ever live in the recollection of the Australian public. The deeds of Dick Turpin, and the performances of Black Bess, are tame beside those of ' NED AND HIS NAG ;' in addition to which Ned's history is true, and Turpin's is pure fiction."—*Press*, July.

CHAPTER CXXX —*Continued.*

On one such occasion some prisoners were subpœnaed who could by no possibility have witnessed the crime, the only object being to give them a spell of absence from the island.

Some of them had been two or three years there, and, though all under thirty-five years of age, their sunken, glazed eyes, deadly pale faces, hollow, fleshless checks, and limbs shrivelled and withered up as if by premature old age, created a thrill of horror.

There was not one of them who had not from time to time undergone the punishment of a thousand lashes, though they were as little reclaimable by the lash as if so many drops of water had been poured on their backs.

As one of them said—

"When I landed here I had the heart of a man, but you have plucked it out, and planted the heart of a brute in its stead."

Two men named Champly and Shirley were convicted on circumstantial evidence of a burglary committed at the house of a Mr. Atkinson, at Oldburg, and sentenced to death, but the sentence was commuted to transportation for life to Norfolk Island.

They had been there a year when a bushranger, named Webber, was tried and capitally convicted.

The day before the one fixed for his execution Webber sent for the Attorney-General, and confessed to him that he alone had been engaged in the burglary for which Champly and Shirley had been convicted, and substantiated his statement by revealing a hiding-place known only to himself, in which the bulk of the property stolen was found hidden.

In consequence of this disclosure orders were at once given for the two men to be liberated, and an offer was made to Webber that, if he would disclose how he had disposed of the proceeds of the many robberies he had been for years engaged in, his life would be spared.

This suggestion was made to him after his death-warrant had been read to him, and when he had only four-and-twenty hours to live, but his reply was—

"I will disclose nothing. All I should gain by it would be to be sent to Norfolk Island, and I would rather be hanged than go there."

Such was the opinion generally held amongst the convict population of the place to which Capt. Knatchbull was now about to be shipped, on board a vessel chartered by the Government for the purpose of conveying convicts to the island.

She was a brig named the Wellington, and a few days later she sailed for her destination.

CHAPTER CXXXI.
ON BOARD THE WELLINGTON.

THE passengers, if such a term may be used, on board the Wellington consisted of fifty convicts, and twenty soldiers of the regiment of foot then quartered in the colony detailed to act as their guard.

The same official protection that Knatchbull enjoyed in the colony followed him on board ship, and would no doubt have mitigated even the iron severity of the discipline at Norfolk Island, had he ever reached that favoured spot.

He was, when once clear of the harbour, freed from his irons, and allowed, to a certain extent, the run of the ship.

Of this he resolved to avail himself, and began to concoct one of the most daring schemes of mutiny ever originated.

He was not of opinion that the more the merrier, but rather held that too many cooks spoil the broth, and resolved that the secret of the hell-broth he was going to brew should only be confided to a select few of his companions in crime and misfortune on whom he could rely implicitly.

For although a few years' decent behaviour in the colony would have secured him every privilege and a free pardon, his naturally base instincts led him to seek liberty in preference by crime.

Many of the convicts sailing with him had been his associates either in low debaucheries or in the numerous petty crimes he had perpetrated since his arrival in the colony.

Amongst them was a man named Crawford, who had been transported for forgery, committed under the most startling circumstances.

He had resorted to the ingenious device of putting a *living fly* into the mouth of a dead man, and then guiding his hand to trace his signature to a document purporting to be the will of the deceased.

When probate of this was disputed, he swore, with audacious assurance, " that he saw the testator sign the will with his own hand *whilst life was in him.*"

Crawford, since his arrival in the colony, had turned his legal knowledge to account by acting as a thieves' attorney, and in this way had become acquainted with all the leading scoundrels of Sydney.

Knatchbull resolved to turn this knowledge to account, and got him to pick out eight of the cleverest and most reckless of the convicts on board, to each of whom in turn the project of the mutiny was imparted.

They were ordered to hold themselves in readiness.

The Wellington was within two days' sail of Norfolk Island when Knatchbull found a chance of putting his plan into action.

The captain and first mate were working out the reckoning, the second mate being in charge of deck, and the officer in command of the troops in his cabin, when a message was sent aft requesting the surgeon to go forward and attend to one of the convicts who had a fit.

Hastily providing himself with some remedies he complied.

During his absence, Knatchbull managed to slip down the companion-way to enter the surgeon's cabin and abstract a large quantity of arsenic.

Carefully concealing this about him he regained the deck.

The meals for convicts, crew, and guard were all prepared by the ship's cook and his mate, with the assistance of a couple of convicts.

One of these latter was in the secret, and to him Knatchbull handed the arsenic with instructions how to use it.

The soup and burgoo for the whole of those on board was made in a huge kettle, and into this the next morning the convict slipped the deadly drug.

Dinner-time came, and the various messes had their allowances served out.

Knatchbull, Crawford, and their associates, either pleaded illness or made a pretext of eating, so as not to provoke suspicion.

The captain of the brig, one of the mates, the surgeon, the purser, and the officer in command of the guard, dined together in the cabin.

The meal was hardly over when a spasm of pain shot across the captain's face.

"I feel very queer," he remarked to the surgeon.

The mate also complained, and in a short time the whole party found themselves suddenly prostrate.

A voice was heard at the door, and the mate who had been left in charge of the deck entered the cabin.

"The man at the wheel has fallen down helpless," he gasped, "and one or two of the others are just as bad. I am in fearful pain myself, doctor; for heaven's sake give me something! I fancy it is cholera, for my inside is on fire."

The surgeon strove to rise in order to comply with this request, but sank back in his place with a damp sweat breaking out over his face, which was distorted with agony.

The mate dropped forward like a log and rolled on the cabin floor, whilst the remainder of the party, in equal pain, could only utter feeble moans for help, being powerless to move a finger.

Suddenly there was the sound of a scuffle on deck, followed by a loud plash into the water.

This was repeated several times.

Then after an interval the cabin-door slowly opened, and George Knatchbull, fully armed, stalked grimly in, followed by four other convicts.

No sooner had the poison begun to work, than Knatchbull had proceeded forward, and, having deprived the prostrate sentries of their muskets, had rapidly released the selected partners in his villainy.

Their comrades followed their movements with wondering eyes, and a volley of blasphemous requests to be freed in turn, to which, however, he paid no attention.

Aided by the same men he had selected, he proceeded to batten down the hatches, and then throw overboard the sentries and such of the crew as were on deck, they being quite unable to offer any resistance.

Then, after arming himself and his companions, and leaving Crawford and four others who knew a little seamanship, in charge of the vessel, he descended to the cabin.

The ghastly sight that met him might have appalled a demon, but he merely smiled.

"Good afternoon, gentlemen," he began, addressing the writhing officers. "I have called to pay you a little visit"

"Mutiny! help!" the captain, who guessed what was up, tried to shout, but the words only passed through his parched lips in a hoarse whisper.

"I think," said Knatchbull, "a little fresh air will revive you. Come, my hearties, bear a hand and get these gentlemen on deck," he continued to his companions.

And, in a very short time the captain, the two mates, the surgeon, the purser, and the officer commanding the troops, were ranged along the lee-bulwarks.

There was no need to bind them, for in their half-moribund condition they could neither move hand nor foot.

"Now," continued Knatchbull, chucklingly, "there is a delicate little question of etiquette to be settled—a question of precedence."

His comrades looked somewhat surprised.

"It is just this, whether the precedence in going over the ship's side belongs to the officer holding the Royal commission, or to the skipper standing, or, I should say, reclining on his own quarter-deck."

There was a hoarse laugh at this brutal joke.

"On second thought I think the soldier ought to go since it is the duty of the captain to remain to the last board in positions of danger. So now, mates, catch infernal lobster by the legs and arms and swing him over.

The fiends raised the unfortunate officer, who was too far gone to make any appeal for mercy as told.

"Now then, boys, watch her as she rolls. One, two, three, and over," and then the next moment a sudden plash to leeward announced the fate of the hapless soldier.

"Clear the deck of the idlers," laughed Knatchbull, "Now old Nipcheese, you'll never stint any more poor devils of their allowance in this world," he continued, as the men lifted the purser. "When you take your last drink alongside, perhaps you'll think of all the six-water grog you've served out."

"Water," moaned the sufferer, who was quite unconscious of what was passing around him, but whose ears had seized some of the last words.

"All right, my son, there's plenty of it alongside," and the next moment the purser was hurled over the side

"Doctor," Knatchbull went on, addressing the next victim, "I really must compliment you on your drugs. It's a case of the engineer hoist with his own petard, you know, but I'm sure such a testimonial to their efficiency as you could now give, would be invaluable to Apothecaries' Hall."

The doctor followed the purser, and the two mates were in turn committed to the deep.

The captain, who had partly recovered, moaned feebly for mercy.

"I—the only man—can navigate the ship," he gasped, in the hope of getting them to spare his life.

"Sir," said Knatchbull, with mock politeness, "I regret exceedingly being forced to deprive myself of your professional services for the rest of the voyage, but, at the same time, I would have you know," and here his tone changed to one of wolfish ferocity, "that I have held her Majesty's commission as commander in the Royal Navy, and know ten times more of seamanship and navigation than such a blind, old, mad, groping skipper of a rotten-timbered, coasting hooker as yourself. Over with him."

The skipper followed his companions, and then the hatches were taken off and attention turned to the guard and those of the crew who had been below at the moment of the seizure of the vessel.

Most of them were already dead, and the remainder in a dying condition.

Dead and dying were handed on deck and thrown over the side in quick succession.

Even Knatchbull felt the horrible nature of the massacre he had commenced, and had ceased to joke with his victims.

"And now the others!" he said, when the last redcoat had vanished over the side.

For a moment the men paused.

The soldiers and sailors were, so to say, their natural enemies, and had stood in their way to freedom.

But the convicts?

Their own pals?

"Curse you, you lily-livered swabs," roared Knatchbull; "do you mean to hang back now? Look here, I am the only man who can get you out of this mess, who can take this ship across the Pacific to a South American port, and make you free men and safe from all chance of recapture. Obey me, or, by thunder, I'll blow her up and you with her!"

"But," expostulated one of the men, "can't we give some of them a chance to get round? We are short-handed."

"There are quite enough of us, and as to giving them a chance of getting round, all who are not dead now will be in half-an-hour. So just rout them out sharp, and get it over."

A sudden thought seemed to strike Knatchbull as he

gazed upon the remaining portion of the crew and convicts whom he had resolved should feed the sharks

Whether he was sick of the murderous proceedings of the last hour or so it is impossible now to conjecture, but, telling them all to scuttle below, he called two or three of his ruffians to hold a council, and it was determined to land the half-dead or dying convicts, crew, and soldiers, left from the wholesale butchery, on a barren island close to Tristan D'Acuna, where they would soon perish from the absence of everything necessary to sustain life on this island rock.

This was done, and from that day to this no record of their fate ever reached human ears.

CHAPTER CXXXII.
SHARP PRACTICE.

FINDING himself in absolute command of the Wellington, George Knatchbull was not long in making up his mind what to do.

Indeed, his plan had been matured from the outset.

He had resolved to run across the Pacific, and, rounding Cape Horn, make for some South American port, where the brig could either be disposed of or fitted out as a privateer in the service of one of the incessantly-squabbling republics.

There was, however, one preliminary difficulty to be overcome.

The brig was amply provisioned, but the supply of water on board was not enough to allow of the carrying out of his scheme.

Accordingly he determined to bear up for New Zealand, and obtain the requisite amount of fresh water in the Bay of Islands.

As there was a chance, however, of the Wellington being recognised by someone on board the whaling vessels that frequented this spot, he set all hands to work to alter her appearance.

Her figurehead, representing the hook-nosed hero of Waterloo, was removed, and replaced by a piece of wood rudely carved into the semblance of a huge fish.

Her name was painted out, and the name of the Bonita substituted, and the streak along her sides changed from white to red.

An American flag was manufactured, and the crew set to work to practise speaking with a Yankee accent, it being Knatchbull's intention to represent himself as the skipper of one of those American trading craft which knock about from port to port in those latitudes.

So that when the brig cast anchor in the Bay of Islands any stranger would have sworn that she hailed from a port on the North Atlantic coast.

It happened, however, that a couple of whaling ships were lying at anchor in the bay when the Bonita put in.

The skipper of one of them, the Harriet, was a young sailor named Duke, who had for some time been in the employ of the firm that owned the Wellington, and had made several voyages on board her.

As she came to anchor, something in her appearance struck him as being familiar.

He had a boat lowered, and was pulled on board the new arrival.

Captain Fitch, as Knatchbull styled himself, received his visitor with great apparent cordiality, and thanked him for his proffers of service.

Duke kept his eyes open during the visit, and felt certain that the Bonita was neither more nor less than his old ship the Wellington.

On leaving her he proceeded back to the Harriet, but at nightfall his boat was again lowered, and he went on board the other whaler, the Sunflower, and communicated his suspicions to her captain, an old seaman named Clark.

The two took counsel together, and the following morning Clark went on shore, and had an interview with the missionaries who had established a settlement on the shores of the bay, and who had acquired great influence over the natives.

The missionaries at once summoned a couple of chiefs named Tau Tahi and Touma, and proceeded to concoct with them a plan for the recovery of the vessel.

Meanwhile Knatchbull and his crew had been actively engaged in getting water on board.

Such was the influence of the ex-commander over his followers that they had obeyed all his orders without hesitation, and had carefully refrained from any outbreak likely to arouse suspicion.

They had worked well during the day, and Knatchbull calculated that by noon the following day at the latest he would be able to set sail.

At night he was pacing the deck in company with Crawford.

Suddenly his eye caught sight of several boats putting off from the shore and pulling towards the brig.

"What is the meaning of this?" he thought.

The boats continued to approach rapidly, and he could make out that they were all full of men.

Stepping to the vessel's side he hailed them.

The answer was returned in the voice of Captain Duke.

"What is it you want?" asked Knatchbull.

The answer was unintelligible.

Knatchbull divined mischief, and gave Crawford hurried orders to quietly rouse and arm the crew.

But before these could be carried out, the boats had shot alongside the brig.

The next instant Duke and Clark with the greater part of their crew, accompanied by fifty armed New Zealanders, swarmed over her sides.

"What the devil do you mean by this?" asked Knatchbull, boldly.

"Captain Fitch," answered Duke, "this craft of yours is not the Bonita, but the Wellington, of Sydney. I know her well, although you have tried to disguise her. You have got hold of her by some act of piracy or other; so I call on you and your men to surrender her to me and go back to Sydney."

"Piracy!" blustered Knatchbull. "What do you call this but piracy, seizing on a vessel at night? I appeal to the laws of nations, and as he spoke he glanced round to see if there was any chance of an effectual resistance.

But the presence of the New Zealanders had cowed the spirits of his men, and they stood motionless.

Captain Duke proceeded to secure them, and then, after some little difficulty, got rid of his savage allies whom it was no easy task to restrain from plundering the ship throughout, but who carried off, as it was, a lot of booty.

An examination of her clearly established the fact that she was the Wellington, and Duke, after verifying this fact, put Knatchbull and his men in irons, and with the aid of a portion of the crews of the Harriet and Sunflower, succeeded in bringing her safely to Sydney.

During the voyage Knatchbull's mind was not idle, and he soon perceived a plan he thought could be put into execution for his own benefit.

He exerted all his eloquence to persuade his fellow-culprits that there was no direct evidence against them, and that, if they only remained true to one another, their acquittal on the capital charge was almost certain.

They fell into the trap.

On reaching Sydney, they firmly refused to give the slightest information as to the way in which the Wellington had been seized, or as to the fate of her crew, the guard, or their companions.

No one at first guessed the horrible tragedy that had taken place, and it was surmised that perhaps the remaining convicts had been put ashore to hide, and that it was the intention of the Bonita's crew to return and pick them up when she was watered.

Hopes, too, were entertained that the lives of the and the guard had been spared.

No sooner, however, were the convicts separated the thought occurred to Crawford that there might fair chance of driving a bargain with the authorities.

NED KELLY.

257

"If," he thought, "I turn Queen's evidence, I am pretty certain of a pardon."

Accordingly, the following morning he requested an interview with the governor of the jail.

That functionary made his appearance later in the day.

"I beg your pardon, sir," began the convict, with great mock humility, "but I believe you are very desirous of learning the true story of the mutiny."

"Well, yes, we were," was the answer.

"Oh," thought the convict, "this is feigned indifference, put on to deceive one. And he continued, "I suppose, sir, if anyone gave that information, it would be taken into consideration at his trial?"

"Yes, it might."

"He would be rendering a great service, sir?"

"Certainly."

"And in consideration of turning Queen's evidence, would have a chance of a pardon?"

"A very good chance."

"Well, sir, if that is the case I am ready to turn Queen's evidence, and give full particulars of the affair."

"It is a very kind offer on your part," said the governor, grimly, "but I regret to say that we cannot avail ourselves of it."

"Not avail yourselves of it."

"No."

"But you said that the man who would turn Queen's evidence would have a chance of pardon — a good chance?"

"Yes."

"Well, I am ready."

"Quite so—only you are too late."

"Too late?"

"Yes; one of your companions has already volunteered to be Queen's evidence."

"The sneaking hound! Who is it?"

"Knatchbull."

"The treacherous devil! Why it was he who tried to make us all promise to hold our tongues."

"Very probably."

"But he was the worst of us all, sir, the ringleader. I assure you, he planned the whole of it."

"So you say," said the governor, who imagined this outburst was merely a bit of spite on Crawford's part on finding himself forestalled in his revelation.

"But I assure you, sir, I swear to God," began the terrified wretch, who began to see the terrible trap into which he had fallen.

"It is no use, my good man," said the governor, "Knatchbull has been accepted as Queen's evidence, and one informer will be quite sufficient."

And so it proved.

The occult protection that shielded Knatchbull had led to his offer to play the part of informer being accepted without any demur.

At the trial he was allowed to give his own version of the mutiny.

According to him he had strenuously refused to take an active part in it, and would have been slain with the other convicts but for the fact of his skill in seamanship being known to his comrades.

It was this alone, he asserted, that led them to spare his life, and he insisted that, although nominally in charge of the Bonita, he had been in reality the mere slave of her crew.

Whether the authorities believed this story or not, they pretended to do so.

The consequence was that, despite all the recrimination of his companions, they were found guilty, and the whole nine were hanged.

Not only was Knatchbull pardoned for his share in the crime, but his original sentence of transportation to Norfolk Island was remitted.

He continued to live in Sydney, and had obtained the command of a small coasting craft, with a crew of five or six men.

CHAPTER CXXXIII
THE CANARY BIRD

THE Canary Bird was the name of an inn situate on the road from Sydney to Goulburn.

It had originally been a little shanty of a grogseller's, started by a crippled miner, and took its name from the fact that when it was first opened one of the chief attractions it offered to its few customers was the presence of a real live canary.

In the early days of the colony this was a rarity, and men came from a distance for the mere sake of hearing the bird that reminded them of home in the old country.

The landlord was offered sums comparatively enormous to part with it, but he knew better than to get rid of the goose that laid the golden eggs by listening to such offers.

Gradually, however, as the traffic on the road increased, the little shanty developed into a good-sized one, and was no longer dependent for custom on the canary.

Canaries too were getting common.

So when the bird which had brought him such luck died, instead of replacing it, old Bob Radley got a journeyman painter on tramp to daub twopennyworth of gamboge on to a square board, on which the departed favourite was rudely outlined in charcoal, and, writing underneath "The Canary Bird," hung it out as a sign.

It was just as well he put the name underneath it, for the picture might have been taken indifferently for a representation of a canary or of a gosling.

Late one afternoon, a few days after Kelly's escape from the police, a tolerably numerous gathering of a somewhat mixed character were assembled in the large room of the Canary Bird.

Miners, squatters, stockmen, travellers, and various other classes were represented, and a brisk conversation was going on about a score of subjects at once.

Glasses were being rapidly filled and emptied, and the lame landlord, and a couple of lathy youths who served him as waiters, had all their work cut out for them.

In the midst of the confusion, two stoutly-built but ill-looking fellows, dressed in a style partaking at once of the miner and the sailor, entered the room, and, selecting a table in one corner, sat down at it.

In accordance with their orders they were supplied with a bottle of brandy, and after filling their pipes, they stretched out their legs and remained with their eyes on the open door, in evident expectation of an arrival.

"I don't much like Ned fixing on this crib," said one of them, who was no other than our old acquaintance, Salmon Roe; "it's a precious sight too risky."

"You're about right there," said the other, who was no other than Zeph.

"Yes," pursued Salmon Roe, in an aggrieved tone; "it's what I call sheer tomfoolery, to choose a spot on a main road, where all kinds of people are popping in and out all day long, and where every minute a man runs a risk of being spotted."

"Well, as soon as he does turn up, I vote we make a move of it."

The pair had come to the Canary Bird in confidence, with a message from Ned, who had given them orders to meet him there.

Meanwhile, the conversation at the adjoining table, at which gold-digging, sheep, wool, stock-raising, and kindred topics had been exhausted, turned on bushrangers.

"Is it true," said a strongly-built fellow named Sam Smith, "that the police let Kelly slip through their fingers the other day, on the Murray?"

"Yes," said his neighbour, a Welshman named Owen, "they did, and it's not to be wondered at."

"Well, I'd only like to have a chance of getting hold of him," said Sam. "What do you say, Tom?" he continued, addressing his brother, who sat next to him; "he'd be a clever fellow to wriggle out of this."

And he held out a hand like a shoulder of mutton.

"Did you ever see him?" said Owen.

17

" No "

" Well, when you do, I'd advise you to leave him alone. He'd be a better man than you, Tom Smith, who can tackle Ned Kelly."

The other laughed

" Just listen to me," went on Owen, " and I'll give you some idea of what the joker is like. It was last autumn I was in the bush out Yanko Creek way. I had pulled up for a spell at a little out-of-the-way shanty, and the only other fellow there was a strapping chap with black whiskers. I had a nobbler with him and the landlord, and just let it drop that I was from the mines, which was, perhaps, an infernal foolish thing to do, for I had been doing a pretty good thing there, and had about sixty ounces of gold about me. It afterwards struck me that both he and the landlord had a hard look at my belt, but I never thought any more of it, especially as he got on one of the finest bits of horseflesh I ever saw, and rode off eastward, whilst I jogged along to the north where there was a station I counted on passing the night at."

" Well, was it Kelly?" asked Smith.

" Just wait a bit. I jogged on quietly till I got in a place about four miles from the inn, where the track narrowed, and was quite walled in by scrub. There was no news of bushrangers being about, but I kept my eyes open all the way, and what should I see but a hat full in the middle of the road?"

" A hat?"

" Yes, a felt hat. I was not going to get off to pick it up, but I slackened speed, and a voice says, a little way ahead of me to the right—

"'Hullo, mate! don't you hear what the hat's a-saying to you?'"

There was a laugh at this.

" Of course I guessed what was meant, and I felt pretty certain I was covered. So I pulled out a long bag I had with about ten ounces, and, undoing it, poured the lot into the hat. I thought that would satisfy whoever it was, for the deuce a soul could I see."

" I'm blowed," growled Smith, " if I'd have parted like that. Why didn't you try a bolt if it was impossible to show fight?"

" ' I've not done yet, mate,' says the voice. ' That ain't what the hat's a-saying.'

" ' What is it saying, then?' says I, and I was trying to make out where the voice came from.

" ' Why, it says just take off that belt of yours and drop it in the middle of the road, or you'll drop out of the saddle like a ripe plum.'"

" Oh, Lord!" laughed Smith.

" I felt this was a bit too much, and thought to chance it. My gun was strapped to the saddle, and I should not have had time to loosen it, so I stuck the spurs in and tried a bolt. Bang! came a shot. My horse went down, and I flew clean over his head. Before I had well got my senses again, out of the bush comes my friend of the inn, and holds a pistol to my head.

" ' It's devilish little use being polite with chaps like you," he said, " and for two pins I'd blow your stupid brains out. So just hand over that belt you were flashing about just now, without any bother.'"

" And you did?"

" And I had to. He meant what he said. I undid and handed over the belt, he covering me all the while, and then he gave a whistle, the bush parted again, and out there came, frisking and stepping like a dog that follows his master, the finest horse, as I said before, that I ever set eyes on."

" What was he like?"

" Black, with a white star on his forehead."

" Ay," said a man named Hill, " that's Kelly's Marco Polo, sure enough."

" I had a good look at him, and could swear to him in a thousand. Kelly put my belt into his pocket, made me pick up the hat, and put the gold-dust back into the bag, and hand that over—watching me all the time like a cat

watches a mouse—and then made me lift my hands and face round. As I stood with my back to him, I felt it was the longest moment in my life, for I did not know but what he might take it into his head to fire after all. But suddenly I heard his horse's hoofs clatter, and when I looked round he was vanishing in the bush, and before I could get my gun loose he was out of sight."

" I suspect he and the landlord were pals," said Tom Smith.

" Very likely."

" It was a very narrow squeak though," said Sam. " It was odd he didn't send you under when you obliged him to show you his face."

" Ned Kelly's not such a bad fellow, after all," said Hill. " He never robbed a man unless the fellow could pretty well afford it."

" Bravo, sir! that's so," said a hoarse voice at his elbow.

Hill looked round.

The man who had spoken was Salmon Roe.

Salmon Roe had listened with great interest to Owen's adventure, and, in order to listen the better, had remained silent.

But he had made up for his silence by quietly consuming more than his share of the liquor set before him and Zeph, and to this was to be ascribed his enthusiastic confirmation of Hill's words of praise.

" Do you know him?" asked Tom Smith, with a grin.

" No, I don't know him," said Salmon Roe, who saw that his remark might lead to awkward consequences : " but I'm sure more than one will bear me out that it's a commonly known thing that Ned Kelly only robs the rich and gives to the poor."

" And I suppose," said Owen, who had been watching him narrowly, " that you are one of the poor?"

" I'm none too well off, just now."

" Who are you, and where are you going?" asked Sam Smith.

" What the devil's that to you?" retorted Salmon Roe, who began to realise that he was in a fair way of raising a wasps' nest about his ears, and, not being able to see his way out of it, was losing his head.

" Hold your tongue, you fool!" said Zeph.

Some of the others in the room had been attracted by the story of Owen, and a man named Bassett had been watching Salmon Roe narrowly since he had spoken.

" I thought I knew your face, and now I have heard your voice, I am sure of it. Mates, this fellow is one of Kelly's gang. I will swear to him anywhere," he shouts.

There was a sensation at these words.

The guests sprang to their feet and crowded towards Salmon Roe and Zeph.

" You cursed fool!" said the latter in an undertone, " here's a precious mess you've got us into."

" Is this so?" asked a gentlemanly-looking man, a squatter, named Leath.

" Yes."

" Well, I'm a magistrate. If you are prepared to swear to the identity of this man, and he cannot disprove your statement, I will take upon myself to have him arrested."

Both Zeph and Salmon Roe knew that this would be fatal, since no lack of evidence would be brought against them from the police.

" It's a lie! you've no right to detain me," cried Salmon Roe.

" We shall see ; you had better give yourself up quietly," said Leath.

It was growing dusk and a couple of lamps had been lit to illuminate the room, the corners of which were almost in obscurity.

" We must fight for it," said Zeph.

" Right you are," was the answer. " Are you ready?"

" Yes."

" Now!"

Springing forward, the two men made a desperate effort to reach the door.

Zeph had armed himself with a bench, and a couple of blows from this stretched Sam Smith and Hill senseless.

Salmon Roe, close at his elbow, laid Owen's head open with a bottle and floored another antagonist.

So sudden had been their charge that for a moment it seemed as if they would succeed in getting away.

But fresh foes interposed, and the next moment they were forced to retreat to the wall.

Salmon Roe, caught up a stool, and so fiercely did the two fight that their antagonists drew back a little.

As yet no one had ventured to make use of firearms.

Suddenly the sound of hoofs was heard on the road without, over which darkness had stolen.

There was a pause, of which the two ruffians profited to place a heavy table in front of them.

"You had better surrender," said Mr. Leath. "Here are the police."

As he spoke a horse's head was thrust through the open doorway, and next moment its rider had crossed the threshold.

He was a strapping fellow in the uniform of the police.

"You are just in time," said Leath, "to help us to secure those two rascals," and he pointed to Zeph and Salmon Roe.

The stranger seemed to comprehend the whole business at a glance.

"All right, sir," was his answer, given in a hoarse voice, and he advanced into the room.

The eyes of Zeph and Salmon Roe had been fixed on the horse, and now they turned on the man.

They exchanged a glance of intelligence.

"Knife and pistol, mate," whispered Zeph to his companion, and the two thrust their hands into the pockets in which their arms were concealed.

The trooper drew a brace of pistols.

"If you don't surrender by the time I count three," he said, "I'll drop you. I know them both, sir," he continued to Mr. Leath.

"Now," he resumed, addressing Zeph and Salmon Roe, and levelling his weapons, "one, two, three!"

The surprise of Kelly's arrival was one of the most agreeable Zeph and Roe had ever experienced.

They felt their spirits rise, and their confidence in speedy delivery brightened their hitherto fear-drawn features.

"I'll take these scoundrels in charge myself, sir," said Kelly. "Just make out your warrant for their commitment, and I'll have them in the nearest gaol before dawn. In the absence of bracelets, just give me a pair of stirrup-leathers and I'll make them as tight and taut as the mainbrace in a gale of wind. They won't get away from me in a hurry, if they do it will be my fault."

With well-dissembled reluctance, the two ruffians allowed the novel "darbies" to be put on, and, with downcast looks accompanied the quasi-trooper, Ned Kelly, out of the Canary, and, as they hoped, out of danger.

But just as they left the house a man in the guise of a digger was observed to be eagerly conversing with the magistrate.

"I'll tell you it is him; no mistake about it. I ought to know when he robbed me of six months' work. I'd swear to him among a million;" and at once, as if despairing of convincing his auditor, roared out, "Don't let him slip through your hands, you darned idiots, that's Ned Kelly, he's worth £10,000 to any of you."

A rush, headed by the magistrate, instantly took place.

Kelly heard it, and so did his companions, who now thought the game was up

"Sharp to the right," cried Ned, as they rushed after him, and at the same time he unhooked Marco Polo's bridle from the fence where he had hung it up, whilst his assailants, recovering from their confusion in some degree, poured out after the fugitives.

He saw the impossibility of his comrades getting off on foot, and he had already hit upon a plan of escape.

To the right of the Canary Bird rose its stables, a large and strongly-built edifice formed of split logs.

It had only recently been put up, and replaced a number of ramshackle out-buildings that had formerly served to shelter the horses of travellers.

It was solidly constructed, because horses are amongst the most valuable and the most frequently stolen property that travellers are provided with, and hence it behoves a landlord to do all he can to secure them.

Into the stables the three darted.

An ostler, who was seated on a bucket repairing a saddle by the light of a horn lantern, sprang up at their entry.

Ned—who knew the place well, having several times visited it in disguise—caught him by the throat before he could utter a word.

"Pick out a couple of the best "prads," and mount for your lives," he said to his comrades.

But, before this direction could be carried out, the main body of their pursuers, who had followed as swiftly as the darkness allowed, were at hand.

Ned could have sprung on Marco Polo and galloped off safely, but he resolved to stand by Salmon Roe and Zeph.

Casting the half-strangled ostler to the ground, he pulled Marco Polo into the stable, and slammed the door.

It was a strong one, and was secured by a heavy bar.

Ned's next care was to tie the ostler hand and foot.

As he leant over him for this purpose, he burst into a laugh.

"What, Hopping Charley," he said, "is it you? I'm sorry I squoze your gullet so tightly. Here, take a sip of this to put it right again."

As he spoke, he held out his flask.

Hopping Charley was an ex-convict who, on more than one occasion, had been his partner in deeds of mischief.

An understanding was quickly come to with him, and, as he bore no malice for Ned's squeezing, he readily agreed to do all he could to further their escape, and even to accompany them.

"I am sick of this place, and had made up my mind to go off in a day or two," the truth being that he had been stealing and selling fodder, and was bound to bolt or to be found out.

Ned quickly reconnoitred the place in which he found himself.

The stable was a long, narrow building, with a high-pitched roof, the gable end being toward the road.

In the centre of this end wall was the door by which they had entered, and which formed the only means of ingress or egress.

Along each of the side-walls was a row of stalls.

Ventilation and light were given by a range of holes high up in the walls—and too small to allow the passage of a man—and by a window secured by a strong shutter at the further end.

In the stalls were sixteen or eighteen horses.

The four men listened for a moment in silence as Ned held up his hand and stepped softly to the further end of the stable.

"I thought so," he remarked, as he returned to his companions. "They have surrounded the place."

"The deuce!" said Zeph. "I was thinking we might have slipped out by that back window."

"We couldn't have got the horses through it," said Charley.

"Wait a bit," said Ned, "and listen to me. I think I see a way out of this."

"Bravo!" said Salmon Roe.

"Charley," began the bushranger, "do you remember when you were in quod how Holy Joe used to be dinning a lot of rot into your ears about those blessed old Jews that were always fighting with their neighbours?"

"Yes."

"Well, I'm blessed if ever I thought it would ever be

any good to me, but I think I can get a wrinkle that's going to fetch us out of this fix, tight as it seems."

"Don't jaw then, but let's have it."

"All right. Do you remember anything about a cove named Samson?"

"Samson!—Samson! Wasn't that the chap as pulled down a house with the jaw bone of an ass."

Zeph laughed at this.

"You're a strong fellow, Ned, but I'm blessed if I think you could pull a house down, even if you had a "moke" to help you; and if you did pull this one to bits I don't see what good it would do us."

"No, that's not it. Samson had a spite against a lot of fellows, and he just set fire to the tails of a lot of foxes and sent them scouting into the beggars' cornfields, and just played blue blazes with 'em. Now, that's my game."

"I think I see it," said Zeph, "but where's your foxes?"

"Here!" said Ned, pointing to the horses.

He then advanced to the end wall at the side by which they had entered.

"We're in luck," he muttered. "Have you got any tools here, Charley?"

"There are some picks and shovels."

"That'll do, first-rate."

Ned then proceeded to give his orders.

The end wall was constructed of longitudinally-arranged logs, and was secured to the side walls by iron clamps.

Armed with a pickaxe and lever, Zeph and Salmon Roe proceeded to loosen these clamps in such a way that a very slight effort would be needed to remove them altogether.

Ned meanwhile, with Charley's help, had picked out and saddled the three best horses in the stable, and had led them to the upper end.

Then he returned to assist the other two in their work of demolition, while Charley proceeded to arrange and tie up a number of small bundles of the dried fodder on which he could lay hands.

Meanwhile, the assailants, on finding the door closed in their faces, had retreated, and held a short council of war.

A detachment was posted in observation on each side of the building.

"By Jove!" roared Tom Smith, "I only wish I could get a fair smack at that devil of a trooper who made such a fool of us."

"Did any of you notice the trooper's horse?" asked Barrett.

"Yes," answered one or two.

"Well, wasn't it a black with a white star on its forehead?"

"Yes."

"Black with a white star on the forehead?" said Owen, who had been insensible when the false trooper had made his appearance. "Why, then it's no mistake. It is Ned Kelly!"

"Of course," exclaimed Hill. "By Jove, boys! the trooper is Kelly himself."

This announcement had a different effect upon his hearers according to their temperament.

Some were fired with the prospect of capturing and putting an end to the depredations of the bushranger, but others could not help thinking that discretion was the better part of valour.

Those, however, who had been hurt in the scuffle with the two ruffians were eager to revenge their injuries, and their outcries prevailed.

"Can't we make a rush at the door and carry it?" suggested Tom Smith.

"Or rig up a beam and batter her in," said Owen.

This plan was at once adopted.

A stout log was selected and a party advanced with it in their arms.

"By all that's lucky," said Ned, who discovered the manœuvre, "these fellows are going to do our work for us after all."

A couple of thundering blows shook the door, which, however, stood firm.

Encouraged, however, by the fact that no shots were fired from the stable, the assault was renewed.

"This won't quite do, after all," muttered Ned. "Look here, lads, shore up the door as strongly as you can."

This direction was obeyed. For a while the repeated strokes of the assailants were of no avail.

"I wonder they don't fire at us," said Mr. Leath.

"Perhaps they've no more powder."

"What a lark if they haven't."

"Stop a bit," said Leath, "the door stands firm, but it seems to me as if the whole of the wall is loosening bodily."

"That is so," said Owen, "it is getting loose all down the sides."

"Well, then, let's rig up a couple more rams and drive it in altogether."

"This advice was quickly taken, and soon, under the repeated blows, the whole of the wall began to sway and shake.

"What a lot of trouble they are saving us," chuckled Ned. "I meant to push it outwards, but they are going to drive it flat in. Look here, though, we must clear away the posts of the first three stalls so that it may fall flat."

This order was obeyed.

Next, by order of Ned, the horses were led from their stalls, and each had one of the bundles of dry fodder fastened to the crupper.

They then had their heads turned in the direction of the door.

Zeph and Salmon Roe, active as all sailors, each took his position on one of the cross beams running across the stable close to the end, and from this position proceeded to loosen the last of the clamps.

Ned mounted Marco Polo at the further end of the stable and took the bridles of the three other horses that had been chosen in hand.

Charley took his position in rear of the loosened horses, with a torch in either hand, and the lantern open before him.

"Are you quite ready?" said Ned, in a whisper

"Half a minute," said Zeph. "This cursed clamp still holds. There it goes."

As he spoke the whole of the wall forming the further end of the stable began to oscillate violently.

The blows of the battering rams were redoubled.

Suddenly it swayed inward, and fell with a tremendous crash.

A dense cloud of dust rose.

Suddenly from behind this there flashed a bright light.

Charley, at the signal, had lit both torches, and now applied them in swift succession to the bundles of fodder fastened to the horses.

Frightened by the light and maddened by the pain, these sprang forward in the only direction that lay open to them.

On they bounded like a living avalanche.

Before the assailants had time to realise their position, the maddened animals, urged on by shots and shouts from Ned and Charley, were upon them.

Some few managed to dart aside, but the majority were knocked down and trampled upon.

Kelly and his party took good care to be in the rush with the frightened and tortured animals, who came tearing on and through Kelly's enemies, scattering them like chaff before the wind. In the midst of the scared animals were to be seen the bushrangers with heads bent almost to the withers of their horses, urging with voice and heel the frightened brutes to racing pace, and quickly disappearing from the view of their would-be captors.

"Head westward," said Ned. "I am bound for Sydney, for it is just the last place they will think of looking for us after this little caper."

CHAPTER CXXXIV.
A WORTHY ALLY.

THREE weeks afterwards Ned was sitting in the parlour of a public-house at Sydney.

He had discarded his trooper's uniform, and was got up in tolerably decent style as a settler from up the country.

He had made up his mind to keep quiet for a day or two, and to see how the land lay, and not to venture into any haunt where he was known; still, as a measure of precaution, he had put on a wig and whiskers.

He felt a trifle lonely, and was not sorry to see a door open and a man enter the room.

The new-comer was a short, thickset man, with a broad intellectual-looking forehead, deep-set black eyes, a short nose that had at some period sustained severe damage, and was constantly moved by a nervous twitching, a long upper lip, good teeth, a mouth expressive of ferocity and daring, and a very prominent jaw and short neck.

He was dressed in a semi-nautical style, and, despite his somewhat unprepossessing appearance, was not without a certain fascination of manner.

He entered into conversation with Ned, and, after a few words, introduced himself as Captain Fitch, commanding a coasting schooner.

After their glasses had been replenished several times, their talk grew more confidential.

The stranger let out that he had been sent across the herring-pond at the expense of Government, and Ned, without revealing his real name, admitted having been guilty of several crimes that ought to have been rewarded with the Order of the Hempen Cravat.

"Fitch—Fitch!" said Kelly at last; "why, ain't you the fellow that helped to physic the lubbers on board the Wellington?"

"Yes," said the other, with a grin.

"By Jove, old pal! tip us your hand. Why, you must be one of the right kidney."

"I think so."

"But, stop a bit; if I remember right, Fitch ain't your right name."

"Perhaps it is not; but, as I don't know yours, we'll let it serve for the present."

"Mine!" said Ned, with his usual recklessness—"oh, you can read it on the wall of every police station in Sydney."

"Why, who are you?"

The bushranger caught him by the wrist with a grip of iron, and looked him full in the eyes.

"You'd like to know my name? Well, I'll tell it you. I'm Ned Kelly."

"Oh! that's it, is it?" said the other.

"Yes. Now, who are you?"

"I am the brother of an English baronet," was the answer, given with a certain pride; "and I once held a commission in the service. My real name is Knatchbull."

"Of course!" cried Ned; "I have heard all about you. You have got a ship?"

"A little coaster."

"What do you do with it?"

"Well, I've helped more than one fine fellow on the way to freedom, and I do a lot of smuggling."

"Do you want a couple of good hands?"

"I should not grumble at them."

"Good! I can find you a pair of beauties."

And Ned proceeded to recommend Zeph and Salmon Roe, in terms that decided Knatchbull to enrol them.

"But what are you thinking of doing yourself?" he asked.

"Well, I am going in for what I fancy is a clever dodge. Everyone thinks I have gone up country, and whilst they are scouring the country for me I mean to get to work here."

"What's the lay?"

"Burglary, I fancy."

"Good! I can put you up to a fine thing. I suppose you know we have got a new chief of police?"

"Yes; and the darned fool—he's a greenhorn from the old country—has gone up country after me. He'll find some few things wanting to be put straight."

This last statement of Ned's was a fact.

When Kenneth and Muriel had recovered from the effects of their struggle with the waters, they had started for the interior.

Fortunately they came across a party who had noticed the wreck, and were hastening down to the seashore.

The shipwrecked pair were at once taken to the nearest station, and received every attention.

Horses were provided to take them on to Sydney.

Arriving there a twofold surprise awaited them.

Muriel learnt that her uncle, instead of being a poor, struggling farmer, was in reality one of the richest squatters on the Murrumbridge, and had come in person to Sydney to receive his niece and destined heiress, and escort her to her future home.

Kenneth's surprise was not so pleasant.

He had no sooner assumed his new position than he was overwhelmed with accounts of Kelly's atrocities and outrages.

He saw that his post was likely to be a much more difficult one than he had perhaps anticipated, unless they were put a stop to.

Although ignorant of the bush, he was a thorough sportsman, and the prospect of a man-hunt, with all its attendant perils, seemed rather attractive.

So after roundly blaming the clumsiness of the troopers who had allowed Ned to slip through their fingers, he started in person for the scene of the bushranger's last exploit, vowing that he would either catch him or hunt him out of the colony.

"Now," said Ned," what's this scheme of yours?"

Knatchbull proceeded to unfold it.

At the corner of one of the streets of Sydney was a pawnbroker's shop, kept by an old fellow named Goodered.

He was, contrary to many of his class, a thoroughly honest man; and this fact had brought down on his head the enmity of several members of the criminal classes whom, to their great amazement, he had dared to hand over to the police when they had brought him stolen property to dispose of.

Several attempts had been made to rob him, in revenge; and, in consequence, he had not only fortified his house till it was as strong as a jail, but had a hired watchman to keep guard outside.

On the premises he allowed no one after nightfall, save himself and an old housekeeper.

Mr Knatchbull had taken a roomy but very dilapidated tenement, three doors higher up the street, in the name of a man called Hopkins, with a view of using it as a depot for smuggled goods, and to this he suggested Ned should accompany him, in order to unfold his plans.

Ned agreed; and the pair proceeded to the house, which was, ostensibly, that of a dealer in ships' stores in a small way.

The door was opened by Hopkins, a man of about fifty, with a grizzly beard fringing a forbidding countenance.

Ned and Knatchbull were soon seated at a table in the room behind the shop, with a bottle of whisky between them.

"I think you agree with me," said Knatchbull, "that old Goodered's crib is about as good a one to crack as any in Sydney?"

"That's so. Why, a sack wouldn't hold the haul in watches and jewellery alone."

"Well, do you see a way to do it?" and Knatchbull looked into the other's face with a grin.

"It'll be difficult," said Ned. "The crib is as strong as a jail, and there's no getting over the watchman; he's an old soldier, and true as steel. Besides, the police keep a special eye on it."

" And don't you see a way to outwit them ? "

" No, I don't," said Ned, surlily, for he began to dislike the other's chaffing manner.

" Well, I always heard you were so clever ! " and as he spoke, Knatchbull continued to grin.

" Just stow all that rot, and come to business if you mean it," cried Kelly, whose temper was getting roused.

" All right. But the reason I asked you—indeed, the very reason why I fancied you as a pal in the job, was because it can be best done by taking a leaf out of your own book "

" Out of my book ?"

" Yes. I remembered that plant of yours to rob the bank here. You'll have to handle the pick and shovel for a night or two."

" You don't mean to tunnel under the street, do you ? "

" No, there's an easier way than that. What do you say to starting a tunnel under my cellar wall, and ending it under old Goodered's ?"

" But there are two houses between."

" Yes, but they are untenanted and untenantable. The owner wants to sell them because he is too poor, he says, to pull them down and rebuild them, and can't get anyone to take them as they are."

" That alters the case," said Ned. " But does anyone ever visit your cellar ?"

" No ; for that is where I stow away the little odds and ends I don't care for the police to find lying about in case they put their prying noses into the shop. The only entrance is by a nicely-fitted trap, on which the four legs of my chair are resting at the present moment."

" Shall we have to tunnel the whole distance ?" enquired Kelly.

" No, we have only to make a passage large enough to crawl through under the three foundation walls."

" It looks pretty good. Do you mean to let anyone else into the secret ?"

" Only Hopkins."

" When shall we begin ?"

" What do you say to to-morrow ?"

" I don't care."

" Well, then, you had better stop here to-night. There's plenty of room. Then to-morrow, after breakfast, we'll set to work, whilst Hopkins minds the shop. At night, when we knock off, he can take a hand."

" All right."

Hopkins, who had been in the outer room during this conversation, was called in, and Kelly presented to him.

Such was the awe and reverence which the latter inspired amongst the class to which the man belonged that, despite the price set upon him, no thought of betraying him crossed the fellow's mind.

The three wound up the evening with a hand at cards and the relation of their former exploits and escapes from the hounds of the law, and then turned in.

CHAPTER CXXXV.
HOW THEY DID IT.

Two nights afterwards the weather was wet and drizzling.

At eleven o'clock, old Goodered, who had put up his shutters some three hours before, made a final round of his premises, to see that everything was securely fastened.

He and his housekeeper then ascended to their respective rooms.

After putting out his light, the old man looked out of the window to ascertain the state of the weather, and then retired to rest with a pistol beside him.

Three hours later—towards two o'clock—when all sleep the soundest, two figures crawled like huge vipers out of a hole tunnelled under the wall dividing Goodered's cellar from that of the adjoining house.

They rose to their feet, and one carefully removed the slide of a bull's-eye lantern, and by its aid the pair surveyed the place in which they found themselves.

Both were masked, but anyone acquainted with their voices would have had no difficulty in identifying them as Kelly and Knatchbull.

Hopkins had remained in the farther cellar.

" Here we are," said Knatchbull, " safe and sound, and the watchman outside knows no more of what is going on in here than you ever will of what is going on inside heaven."

" Hullo ! someone has been at work here lately," said Kelly, pointing to a heap of shavings and the ends of several newly-planed planks in one corner. " It was well he didn't hear us."

" Oh, that was four or five days back. The old boy had a carpenter in to fix up some shelves and partitions. But now the first thing is to get upstairs and find the keys of the safes. They'll be in the old man's room, I reckon."

" Do you know where he sleeps ?"

" Yes ; I know which is his room by watching the lights from the outside. I'll tackle him if you'll attend to the housekeeper."

" That's a bargain. Come on."

They stole up the cellar-stairs like cats.

The door at the head of the stairs was locked and the key was on the other side.

This, however, was no check to their progress.

With the aid of a convenient implement with which he was provided, Knatchbull turned the key almost as easily in the lock as if he had held the handle in his hand.

They were now on the ground floor, and after softly closing the door behind them stood without moving for a few minutes and listened.

" Shall we go through the lower premises now, or go up and make things safe at once ?" said Knatchbull, in a low whisper which lent a horrible significance to the word " safe."

" Go up," whispered Ned. " No ; stop a bit. Let's cast an eye over the premises so as to see the best way out in case we have to make a bolt of it."

A quick inspection showed the position of the back and front doors, and having ascertained this they with the same catlike stealthy tread slowly ascended the stairs and on the landing again halted to listen and reconnoitre.

" What is that ?" whispered Kelly, as his ear caught a faint voice.

There was a pause for a moment and then Knatchbull replied—

" It's the old man snoring, I do believe."

It was so !

The heavy breathing of the old man would have indicated to the prowling wretches the room he occupied had Knatchbull been unacquainted with it.

They listened again, and could in addition now detect the regular sound of the respiration of the housekeeper in the adjoining apartment.

" There lies your way, this is mine," said Knatchbull, to his companion.

The two separated, Knatchbull approaching the bedroom of the pawnbroker, and Kelly that of the housekeeper.

The doors of both were ajar, and before either entered they allowed a pencil of light from their almost closed bulls'-eyes to play over the floor, in order to show them where to step without falling over anything.

They were careful to only let this flash of light play over the ground, and to keep it thus low in order that it might not strike the eyes of the slumberers, and so arouse them.

It served, however, to point out the position of the beds.

Knatchbull stole quietly across the room, and drew near the bedside of the unconscious pawnbroker, who was sleeping even more quietly than when the burglar had first caught the sound of his breathing,

His mind was made up for every evil.

Had he so willed it, he might have merely sought to secure his victim and not to slay him.

But no ; death, he argued, was the only sure way.

But death with no outcry, no shrieks, no groans, no dying gasps.

He held the dark lantern in his left hand, and raised one of those tomahawks so common in colonial settlements in his right.

Then, allowing one flash of light to fall on the old man's silvery hair and guide his aim, he struck home heavily.

His aim was sure.

There was no struggling, no writhing, after that one dull, heavy thud with which his axe-blade had sunk into the old man's brain like a thunderbolt from a storm-cloud.

Satisfied that his victim was dead, the robber gathered up a few valuables that were lying within his reach, and then rummaged Goodered's garments for his keys.

With these in his possession he quitted the room, but he had scarcely crossed the threshold when a stifled shriek, followed by a gurgling sound and the noise of a scuffle, reached his ears.

He rushed into the room whither his comrade in this foul night's work had gone, and found him holding a pillow over the face of the housekeeper with one hand, and trying to strangle her with the other.

"Why, Ned, I thought you understood the business better. I'll show you the way to do it, that you may be better up to it next time."

And, raising the blood stained tomahawk, he struck the writhing woman a blow on the temple, which instantly deprived her of life.

"The old devil woke just as I was getting my knife out," said Ned, "and I had to drop it and stuff the pillow into her mouth, or she would have screeched out and ruined all."

"Well," said Knatchbull, "the worst of the job is over, and we're monarchs of all we survey."

"Speak lower," whispered Ned. "We might be heard outside. Have you got the key of the safe?"

"I've got a pretty big bunch of them, and if one doesn't fit, another will," was the reply.

"But we must get to work cautiously, and take care that the light from our lanterns does not play on the doors or shutters, for fear it should show through the cracks."

With this caution Knatchbull led the way downstairs to the business premises, and, placing a light under the counter, they set to work.

The large safe was first opened, and the contents—watches, jewellery, and other valuables—transferred to the bags with which they were provided.

A smaller safe yielded a similar store, and then they turned their attention to the drawers and cases containing silver and plated goods, packages of cutlery, pistols, nautical instruments, ornaments, and other articles of value.

All the silver was secured, and a hasty selection made of the choicest of the remaining things.

Several more bags were filled with this plunder and conveyed to the mouth of the tunnel by which the murderers had gained an entrance.

Knatchbull proceeded to turn the key of the cellar in the lock in the same fashion in which he had opened the door.

After a drink of brandy the two men approached the hole by which they had entered the cellar.

"Are you there, Hopkins?" whispered Knatchbull.

"Yes," was the reply.

Kelly produced several stout cords about eight or ten feet in length, and attached one to each bag.

Then, getting down on to his hands and knees, and taking the loose end of one of the cords, he dived into the hole, and on reaching the other side of the wall beneath which it was tunnelled, he drew his bag of plunder through after him.

Knatchbull followed his example.

The pair then returned, and the remaining bags were disposed of in the same way.

By the same means the stolen property was conveyed into the cellar of the second empty house, and from there again into the one below the premises tenanted by Hopkins.

It may be asked why this trouble to take the plunder through the tunnel instead of through the front door. The answer is—fear of the police, who, knowing Knatchbull well by sight, would have overhauled him at once. They had several times " had " Sir Edward, as they called him (after his brother the baronet), and looked upon him as one of the most dangerous ticket-of-leave holders out, game for anything—from robbing a church to murdering the incumbent—if anything was to be gained by it.

The job was not yet over, however.

The three men returned to the cellar adjoining the pawnbroker's premises and proceeded to push the earth back into the cavity leading into Goodered's cellar, striving to throw it as far forward as possible so as to fill up the hole on the other side.

Kelly and Knatchbull then returned to the cellar under the empty house adjoining the one in which the plunder was now stowed.

Then they, working on their side, and Hopkins, who had remained in the cellar next to Goodered's, on the other, removed all traces of the connection between the two by filling up the hole and levelling and beating down the earth.

Hopkins's retreat was apparently cut off; but this was pre-arranged.

Knatchbull then proceeded to pass into the cellar of the house rented by him; and, with Kelly working on the other side, this hole was filled up in a similar way.

Knatchbull then unfastened the shop-door, without opening it.

Kelly, left in the empty house, undid the dilapidated door, after first cautiously peering into the street to make sure no one was about, slipped out, pulled it to after him, and darted into Hopkins's dwelling.

Hopkins, observing similar precautions, followed him.

The next morning the watchman, who had been at the back of the premises during the half-minute required to accomplish this last feat, knocked at Goodered's door to rouse him, and help to take down the shutters before going off duty.

There was no answer.

He knocked, and knocked again, without result, and, getting anxious, started for the police-station.

He soon returned with a couple of policemen, and found several early customers wondering at the shutters not being taken down with the usual punctuality.

The police, after examining the outside of the building, rudely pounded at the shop-door for some time, but without result.

The back door was assailed in the same way, but no signs of life appeared.

"There is something wrong here," said one of them, and, whilst he kept guard with the watchman, the other returned to the station, and came back accompanied by the inspector and a couple more constables.

A fresh pounding at the door followed, and then the inspector gave orders to one of his men to fetch a locksmith.

In a few minutes a locksmith, furnished with keys and picklocks, made his appearance, and was ordered by the inspector to open the door of the shop.

The lock soon yielded to his skill, but not the door, which was barred on the other side.

The other door was then assailed, but with the same result—that, too, having fastenings on the inside which the locksmith could not reach.

The shutters were then tried, but it was found that they were so well secured that they could not be opened.

The inspector saw that the only means of effecting an entrance was to break down the doors.

An axe was procured, and, the back door having been broken in, an entrance was effected.

At a glance round the shop, the inspector saw that a robbery had been committed, and, from the state of the doors and shutters, he felt satisfied that the robbers could not have entered the house from the street.

Without permitting anything to be disturbed, he ascended with two of his men and the watchman to the sleeping room above.

The stillness of death prevailed, and, not one of those present did not instinctively divine that the shadow of a greater crime than that of robbery brooded over that silent dwelling.

On entering the housekeeper's room the sight of her corpse confirmed their worst suspicions.

Her head was almost split open by the blow from Knatchbull's tomahawk.

The room of the old pawnbroker revealed a similar sight of horror.

"Good Heavens!" exclaimed the inspector, "a more atrocious murder I never was called to look upon. How on earth did the murderers effect an entrance?" he continued, addressing the watchman.

"Certainly not from the outside," replied the man. "The only thing I can think of is that they hid themselves on the premises somewhere before they were closed."

"But how could they have escaped without my seeing them, and leave all the doors and windows locked and bolted behind them?"

"Perhaps they are still hidden here," suggested one of the police.

"That's an idea," said the inspector, and, after stationing a couple of men so that no one could leave the house unseen, he proceeded to the attics and commenced a thorough search.

The fact of the attic windows being fastened like those in all the other rooms on the inside, proved that the thieves had neither entered nor left the house by means of the adjoining roofs.

Every nook that might have afforded a hiding-place, cupboards, lofts, chimneys, were all peered into, without result.

A similar search on the first floor proved equally futile.

"It's evident that they have not only got off, but taken a tremendous amount of property with them," said the inspector, "but how they have managed it completely gravels me."

The door of the cellar now caught his eye.

"Where does that lead to?" he asked.

"To the cellar," answered the watchman.

The inspector darted forward but found the door locked and the key on his side.

"If they came in this way I don't see how they got out," he muttered.

On descending the steps, however, he began a careful examination of the walls, and the heavy trap-door of the side walls, which he found securely fastened on the inside.

At length the loose and broken appearance of the surface of the ground close to one of the walls caught his atten-

On examining it he found that it was soft, uneven, and had evidently been recently disturbed.

"Hullo! this looks like a clue," he said, and at once sent for spades and commenced to clear out the loose soil from the tunnel leading into the adjoining cellar.

In a short space of time the loose soil was cleared from the hastily-filled-up tunnel, and, passing through this, they found themselves, as they had anticipated, in the cellar of the empty house.

"This is how the entrance was made, and this is how the murderers got off," said the inspector.

A thorough search of the premises followed, but here again they were baffled.

The earth filling up the second tunnel had been levelled and beaten on the surface, in a way that defied detection without the closest investigation.

Some loose soil from the first excavation, too, had been scattered all over the surface of the cellar to add to the deceit.

Search, however, revealed the absence of any fastening to several of the windows and doors, and the conclusion come to was that the murderers had escaped by means of them into the street.

The only man not concerned was the watchman.

"I don't see how several men—for there must have been several to carry off all that swag—could have got into the street without my noticing them, especially if carrying bundles," he said to himself, and resolved to do a little search on his own account.

CHAPTER CXXXVI.
THE FENCE.

MEANWHILE the murderers had, after a few hours' sleep, been engaged in sorting out their plunder.

There was comparatively little ready-money, the bulk of the articles secured being watches, plate, and jewellery.

It was necessary to find some method of disposing of these.

Of course it would have been madness to have tried to have pledged them or to have offered them for sale at any respectable tradesmen's.

(To be continued.)

NED KELLY

THE
IRONCLAD
AUSTRALIAN BUSHRANGER

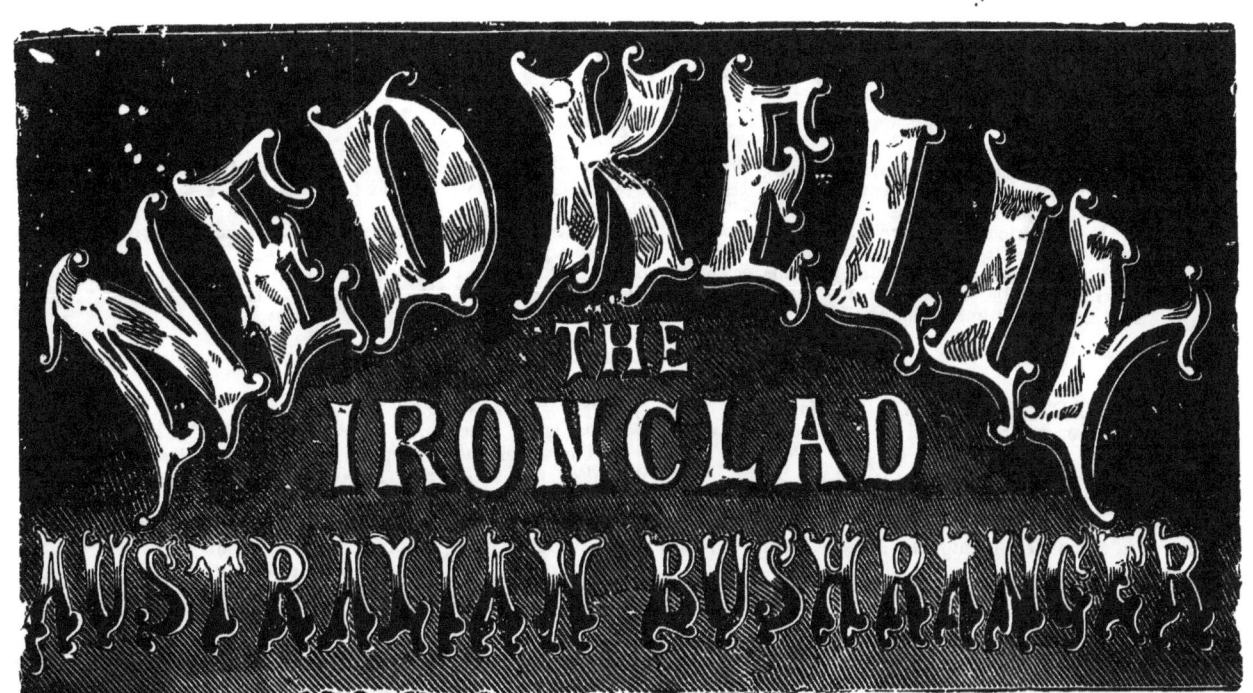

NO 23,

• It is well known that for many years Ned Kelly had made himself notorious by a series of crimes wholly incompatible with the civilisation of the nineteenth century. Ned Kelly's celebrated steed, Marco Polo, is as well known at the Antipodes as Dick Turpin's Black Bess in these islands."—*Telegraph*, 7th July, 1881.

" It is notorious that the robbery of Mr. Steward's corpse was mainly performed by the assistance of NED KELLY's BROTHER, the Captain of what was neither more nor less than a pirate ship."—*Times*, July.

" The history of NED KELLY and his celebrated black horse Marco Polo, will ever live in the recollection of the Australian public. The deeds of Dick Turpin, and the performances of Black Bess, are tame beside those of 'NED AND HIS NAG ;' in addition to which Ned's history is true, and Turpin's is pure fiction."—*Press*, July.

CHAPTER CXXXVI.—*Continued.*

The only plan was to get rid of them to a dealer in stolen goods or "fence"

Of these there was certainly no lack

At this period a traffic in stolen goods, on the largest possible scale, was carried on between England and Australia, and firms of the highest outward respectability were engaged in it.

Their dealings amounted to thousands and thousands of pounds per annum.

There is a perfectly authenticated story of an English officer quartered at Sydney recognising in the window of a leading jeweller of the town a magnificent jewelled comb, which had been stolen from his wife two years before in London.

He at once entered the shop, and gave the jeweller the choice of handing over the comb or of informing him of the name of the parties by whom it had been consigned to him from England.

The jeweller unhesitatingly accepted the former alternative.

He could not afford to betray his correspondents across the herring-pond.

Knatchbull's schooner had been actively employed in landing packages of a character that it was not desired should pass through the custom-house, and he was, therefore, well acquainted with most of the leading dealers in stolen goods.

One of these, to whom he had made up his mind to apply, was a Jew, passing under the name of Mendez.

He was a most mysterious being.

No one could exactly tell who or what he was, or where he lived.

But any one of his numerous customers having need of him, who knew how to set about it, had no difficulty in finding him out.

Accompanied by Ned, Knatchbull walked forth in the course of the forenoon.

A crowd was assembled in front of the old pawnbroker's house, for the news of the double murder had already spread through the town.

Avoiding this gathering, the two proceeded along several streets, till they reached a small watchmaker's shop with the name of Durlacher over the door.

They entered.

A stout, round-shouldered, heavily-built man, with a pale face, huge spectacles, and a mass of hay-coloured hair and beard, was sitting behind the counter, fitting a glass into a watch for a customer.

On the walls a number of clocks of all shapes and sizes were ticking away.

Conspicuous amongst them were several German cuckoo-clocks.

On one of these Knatchbull fixed his eye.

No sooner had the customer left the shop, than the watchmaker began to fumble in a drawer in the counter.

Directly he did so a little bird popped out of the front of one of the clocks, and his cry of "cuckoo" sounded.

"Have you any watch-keys in stock?" asked Knatchbull.

"Yaas," was the answer.

"I want a large one --a very large one."

The watchmaker stepped into a little glass den at one end of the shop, and began to look for the article required.

"Silver-gilt," continued Knatchbull, his eyes all the while being fixed on the row of clocks on the wall.

From the front of one of these another bird popped forth, and the cry of "cuckoo" sounded twice.

The hands of the clock began to revolve suddenly over the dial, and it struck ten.

The watchmaker came forward with a tray of keys, and Knatchbull, after selecting and paying for one, left the shop with Kelly, who was in a state of bewilderment.

"What did you want to go in there for?" asked the bushranger.

"To settle about getting rid of the swag," was the reply.

"Then why the devil didn't you do it?"

"I have done it."

"What do you mean?"

"I asked him if he had any watch-keys in stock."

"Yes."

"Well, that might mean I wanted a key; but it also meant that I had some stolen goods to dispose of."

"I see."

"I told him a large silver-gilt key, which meant a lot of gold and silver."

"That's all blessed fine, but how and when and where are the things to be got rid of?"

"At a crib in Pitt-street, at ten o'clock the night after to-morrow."

"But he never said that."

"No, but the clock did."

"What do you mean?"

"Why, directly we went in I spotted there was a customer. If it had been safe to speak before him the cuckoo on the first clock you heard would have popped out and sung. But it didn't, so I held my tongue till he was gone, and it gave the signal all was clear."

"But why didn't you speak out then?"

"Because you were with me, and, not knowing you, he might have refused to answer; so I spoke about the watch-key."

"Well, but how do you know when and where he will buy the swag?"

"The second clock is a house in Pitt-street, two cries of 'cuckoo' mean the night after to-morrow; and ten o'clock, striking the time."

"But, if it had not suited us, what then?"

"Why, I should have said 'this key won't fit; can you get me one by say eight o'clock to-morrow?' or whatever hour I wanted, and so on."

"All that's infernally artful. Of course the beggar never says a word to compromise himself, and you can't swear to what the clocks mean if you want to peach. Do you know how he works it?"

"Oh, there's some system of wires and springs, and electricity, I believe, but, of course, he keeps all that dark as possible."

Pitt-street was a thoroughfare running parallel to the one in which Durlacher's shop was situate.

The tenement inhabited by the old Jew Mendez was a tumble-down sort of a dwelling of one storey high, standing back some distance from the road, and having a tolerably spacious garden in front of it.

It was a relic of the early days, when many homes in the main streets were surrounded by a large patch of garden-ground, which has since, in most cases, been re-sold, at an enormous profit, for building upon.

But Mendez had firmly refused to part with his garden, or to rebuild his house on a larger scale, or let it.

Ostensibly he was a kind of pedlar, and was frequently accustomed to be absent for weeks together.

On such occasions his house would be closely shut up and left uninhabited.

Indeed he was not nominally at home more than a few weeks in the year, and very few of his neighbours had ever done more than catch a glimpse of him.

These described him as a tall old fellow, with a grey beard, usually wearing a long gabardine-like garment.

But it was a strange thing that, even when Mendez was supposed to be up country peddling, a man who knew the right way to work could always manage to see him by giving due notice to Durlacher.

At half-past nine on the night set apart for the interview between the receiver and the thieves, darkness and solitude reigned in the Jew's dwelling.

It was a strongly-built house, the windows being all secured by iron bars.

The back premises extended to the boundary-wall dividing it from the yard attached to the house occupied in the parallel street by Durlacher.

At the end of this yard was a deserted shed filled with lumber

As the clock tolled the half-hour, a figure glided along the yard and entered this shed, the door of which it carefully closed after it.

Five minutes later a creaking sound was heard in the cellar running under the Jew's house.

A portion of the wall swung aside, revealing a dark opening, through which stepped a figure, bearing a lantern in its hand with the bull's-eye almost closed.

Traversing the cellar, it approached a flight of steps, at the summit of which was a heavy trap-door securely bolted on the inside.

Removing the bolts and lifting the trap, the stranger stepped into a large room on the ground-floor, which was the only one, as already noted.

The aspect of this room was peculiar—not to say striking.

It was divided into two by a massive counter running right across it.

From this counter several stout wooden uprights ran up to the ceiling, and the spaces between them were filled with a strong network of brass wire.

In two places, however, the wire was arranged so as to leave a pigeonhole-shaped opening like that in a railway booking-office, about eighteen inches by fifteen.

On the further side of the counter there was simply a blank space, the only furniture of which consisted of a bench fastened against the wall.

The window, which was on this side, was not only defended by iron bars and thick and strongly-secured shutters, but by a species of padded mattress fixed over its whole surface, and the object of which was evidently to deaden sound.

On the other side of the counter was an iron safe, a tall desk, a large wardrobe with two upright wings, and an armchair.

The figure that had entered the room proceeded to light a couple of lamps fitted with semi-circular reflectors.

It placed these on the counter so that the light illumined the inner half of the room.

By this light the stranger stood revealed as the stolid, sleepy-looking German watchmaker.

The next act performed by this individual was to remove his huge goggles and reveal a pair of jet-black, piercing eyes strangely at variance with his lymphatic aspect and fair hair and beard.

A single twist of the hand, however, removed them, and displayed a closely-cropped head of jet black hair.

He then removed his coat and waistcoat, which were thickly and heavily wadded, and swung open one of the wings of the wardrobe, disclosing a recess filled up with a washing apparatus.

After sluicing his face with water, he turned round, and, instead of a hulking, clumsily built fair-haired, pasty-faced German, stood revealed as a square-shouldered, upright fellow of about forty, with sparkling black eyes, a dark complexion, and keen features of a Jewish type.

His next step was to open the other wing, the inside of the door of which was lined with looking-glass, and which contained a number of shelves fitted up with all the requisites for what is known in theatrical parlance as "making up."

He took a wig representing a bald forehead, fringed with scanty whisps of grey hair, and a long grey beard, and fitted these on.

A pair of bushy grey eyebrows were next attached.

Then, by the liberal application of paint, his complexion was converted to a sallow parchment-tint, and his countenance scored with innumerable lines and wrinkles

He looked a man of seventy at least, and when he assumed a long grey dressing-gown, and bent his back, rounded his shoulders, and hollowed his chest—the deception was perfect.

The various traces of this metamorphosis having been hidden away, Mendez unlocked the safe and took from it a couple of pairs of scales, weights, files, nippers, bottles of acid, and sundry other appliances, and ranged them on the counter together with a brace of pistols.

Then taking from his bag, he had brought with him a bundle of notes and some coin, he put them in a kind of till, turned the lamps so that the reflectors cast the light towards the outer side of the room, drew up his armchair, sat down in it, and waited.

At that moment three men were staggering down the street.

They were dressed as sailors, and each bore on their backs one of those canvas bags in which Jack is accustomed to convey his portable property about when on shore.

But either the men were very tired, or the bags were more than usually heavy, for the three lurched and stumbled along with apparent difficulty.

At last they arrived opposite Mendez's house.

After glancing around to make sure that no one was paying attention to their movements, they entered the garden.

At the front door they halted.

One of them, after groping about for some time, found a wire, which he pulled twice.

The door opened, and the three men entered.

They found themselves in utter darkness, and the next moment the door closed behind them.

"Well, I'm blowed!" grumbled one of them, who was no other than Ned Kelly, "but I don't like this game."

"It's all right," answered Knatchbull.

The three were in a narrow passage, as Kelly could tell by the feel of the walls.

"Who ish dere?" suddenly demanded a snuffling voice at some little distance.

"It's me; Fitch and two pals," answered Knatchbull.

"Very well. You know de rules. Vun at a time, if you pleash."

A door on their right opened a few inches.

Taking his bag in his hand, and dragging it after him, Knatchbull squeezed through the opening, which was immediately closed behind him.

Ned could hear the murmur of voices inside.

At last, after he had been for some time growing impatient, the door again opened, and Knatchbull slipped out.

"Who is de nexsht?" enquired the voice.

"Here, curse it! you'd better go, Ned," said Knatchbull. "and try if you can make any better terms for your bagful with the old hunks than I have."

Kelly slipped through the door, which was opened as before, and found himself in the outer half of the room already described.

The door which he found was worked by a system of rods and levers from within the grating.

He advanced towards the counter, and found himself confronted by Mendez, whose face, however, remained in the shade whilst the full glare of the light was turned towards the visitor.

"You will excushe all dis trouble," said the Jew, with an apologetic air. "I am a poor, weak old man, very ill and feeble, and I am very frightened of rough people."

The voice in which he spoke was an admirable imitation of the quavering tones of extreme old age.

"All right, mate," growled Ned.

"Vell, vot have you to sell?" enquired the Jew.

Ned hoisted his sack on to the counter, and displayed the contents to the other.

"Posh dem in vun by vun," said Mendez, taking his place at one of the wickets already mentioned.

One by one he took the articles of plate and jewellery handed in by Ned, and scrutinised each in rapid succession.

When he appeared in doubt as to the genuineness of any one of them, he tested it with a file and acid, and in the same way removed several of the stones from their settings and examined and weighed them apart.

Though this work was quickly done, it was done most conscientiously, yet all the while his eye never left Ned, whom he watched like a cat.

After weighing a few of the things, he took a certain sum in notes and gold from the till, and pushed it towards Kelly.

"What's this?" growled the latter.

"Vun hundred and dirty poundsh," was the reply.

"Here, but dang it all, the swag's worth a blessed sight more than that. There's a good twelve hundred pounds' worth of stuff, if there's a penny, or I'm a Dutchman."

"But dere is de rishk."

"Risk be blowed!"

"Oh, very vell. If you vant to blow de rishk, you shall open one shop in Sydney, and sell de goots acrosh de counter, and den perhapsh you vould get de twelve hundred poundsh, and perhaps not. Only it shtriketh me you vould not only blow de rishk, but blow de gaff ash well."

And he chuckled grimly.

"Come now, spring something more."

"Your friend will have told you dat I have only one prishe. Take it or leave it."

Knatchbull had, indeed, assured Ned of this beforehand, and the bushranger retired, growling like a bear with a sore head.

Hopkins was admitted in turn, and after an interval rejoined the others in the passage.

Then the outer door was opened by the same invisible means, and the three passed out into the garden.

On comparing notes the three found that the total sum they had received was a little over four hundred pounds.

"Curse it all!" roared Ned; "why there was a good three thousand pounds' worth of stuff. By Gosh! I don't wonder that the blasted old baboon keeps behind a wire cage. I felt blessedly inclined to try and tear his old heart out!"

"It is riling," said Knatchbull; "but there is no other way of getting rid of the stuff but through those fellows, and they know very well where they have the pull of us."

"He must be rich at that game," said Kelly.

"Not a doubt of it. I expect he has no end of coin invested."

"Do you think he keeps it stowed away?"

"No, no; he's too sharp for that."

"But he must always have a tidy stock of things on hand, not to mention the coin to do a deal with."

Knatchbull laughed.

"I believe you are hankering to have a go in him?"

"Do you feel that way inclined?" asked the bushranger.

"No, no; he's a bit too useful—and knows too much," he added to himself, and then said aloud, "But you?"

"Oh, I," said Kelly, "I'm blowed if I'll meddle with going after watches and spoons again. Give me a digger with a belt full of dust, or a squatter with a pocket-book full of notes. That's my style, and I ain't going to depart from it."

Nevertheless, Kelly separated from his comrades in an hour's time, under pretext of an appointment with a friend.

But instead of going where they thought, Ned was hurrying back to the house of Hopkins, muttering as he went—

"I've a good four hours before me, and I'll not sleep to-night till I've put matters straight with that Jewish ape, who thinks he has got the better of Ned Kelly!"

CHAPTER CXXXVII.
DIAMOND CUT DIAMOND.

IT was shortly after midnight and Mendez or Durlacher was peacefully sleeping the sleep of the just in a room over the watchmaker's shop.

After the departure of the three robbers he had reassumed the garb of the watchmaker, cleared away the scales and other paraphernalia, and stowed the articles purchased from his late visitors in a spot prepared for their reception.

Then he had returned to his dwelling, eaten a hearty supper of fried fish and salted cucumbers, sopped up by just a thimbleful of rum and shrub, and had turned in.

As he slumbered a little alarum suddenly rang out above his head.

He started up at once.

"Ah! someone trying the house. I had my idea it would be so," he muttered.

Hastily striking a light he glanced at the particular alarum which had sounded.

"So, so," he muttered, softly, "one of these fellows come back, I'll wager. I'll read him a lesson he won't forget in a hurry."

Hastily dressing himself he passed out of the back door, traversed the yard, entered the street at the end, and a few minutes later had noiselessly arrived at the room where the bargain had been concluded.

Noiselessly cocking a brace of pistols, with which he had come provided, he stood still and listened in the darkness, for he kept his lantern darkened.

Straining his ears he could catch a low grating sound.

"They are cutting through the window bars," he thought. "The idiots, they do not know that even a hand cannot be laid on shutter or door without warning me."

The faint grating sound ceased.

Then came a faint click and then another.

"Two bars sawn half through, and then snapped," thought Mendez.

A fresh noise of a grinding character followed.

It was that of a centre-bit at work on the shutter.

The ripping sound of a knife cutting away the mattress followed.

Then Mendez, whose ears were wonderfully sharpened, could make out that a hand had been thrust through the opening, and was groping for the bolts of the shutter.

"The fellow must have had a wonderfully sharp eye to have spotted the defences so well," thought the Jew. "Upon my word I want to see him."

Another hole was cut in the same way, so as to enable the unseen burglar to reach the second bolt.

When this was drawn the shutter was swung gently inwards, for there were no casements to the window of the room.

A huge figure slipped across the window-sill, pushed the shutter carefully to behind it, and then, facing round, began to withdraw the slide of a bull's-eye lantern.

"Very neatly done," said Mendez, in clear, ringing tones, very different from those in which he had hitherto spoken.

As he spoke he, in turn, drew the slide of his lantern aside and flashed the light full on the burglar, covering him with his pistol at the same time.

It was Ned Kelly.

Quick as thought Ned drew a pistol and fired in the direction of the voice and light.

But another report rang out simultaneously with his own and Kelly, after turning half-round, dropped heavily to the ground.

There was a pause.

Mendez kept the light of his lantern turned on the prostrate form of the burglar, but the latter never once stirred after his fall.

Then the receiver of stolen goods, advancing to one end of the counter, drew a bolt and pressed a spring.

A section of the counter swung inward on hinges, and Mendez, diving beneath the grating, passed through the opening with his lantern in one hand and his second pistol in the other.

Arriving close to the prostrate figure, he listened again, with a view of detecting if anyone without had been startled by the pistol-shot

There were, however, no signs of this.

Then, stooping down, he turned Kelly over.

The bushranger presented a most ghastly spectacle.

The bullet had struck him on the head, and his face was smothered in the blood that had flowed from his wound.

"I did not want to fire," muttered Mendez, "but there was no choice. The question now is, what the deuce I am to do with this carrion. That is just the awkward part of the question."

After thinking a few minutes, he took a large bag, with which he noticed Ned had come provided, and tied it round the corpse's head, with a view of stopping the flow of blood on to the floor as far as possible.

Then, taking Kelly by the legs, he dragged him through the opening in the counter, closed this, and, after some difficulty, succeeded in transporting the dead body, as he deemed it, to the cellar.

"I haven't time to settle what to do with it just now," he thought, and, passing through the aperture in the wall, he ascended a flight of steps leading to a trap-door, giving access to the shed at the end of Durlacher's yard, and again sought his bed.

For some time after the departure of the Jew Kelly remained motionless.

The truth was that the bullet, which, after striking the skull at an oblique angle, had glanced from the bone, and merely cut a long and deep gash in the scalp, had stunned him.

He had partly recovered consciousness when Mendez turned him over, but resolved on playing 'possum to the best of his ability.

He was dimly aware of his head being muffled, and then became partly insensible again.

When he came to himself, he was lying on his back on what seemed to be soft sand.

His head was still partly muffled up, and he could not very well see or hear anything.

He waited for some time, listening to the best of his ability.

All was quiet, and at length he ventured to raise his hand and remove the bag.

Then he managed, with some difficulty, for his head was aching and dizzy, and he was faint from the loss of blood, to raise himself in a sitting position.

He pulled out his handkerchief, and bound it tightly round his wounded head.

After which he succeeded in staggering to his feet, and examined the place in which he found himself, by the aid of some matches and a taper.

It was a large, dry cellar, with a soft sandy floor and brick walls.

A number of barrels and boxes of various shapes and sizes were scattered about it.

Ned had still his tools about him, and, after tapping the barrels until he discovered a full one, he speedily broached it with his centre bit.

A stream of spirits rewarded his exertions, and, after swallowing a little, caught in the hollow of his hands, he felt better

After bunging up the barrel, he began to cast his eye about in search of some way to escape from the cellar.

The only entrance he could discover was by the flight of steps leading to the trap down which he had been brought by Mendez.

Ascending the steps, he examined the trap-door, and found that it was secured by some catch that he was unable to fathom the secret of.

He resolved, therefore, to bore a hole with the centre-bit, and then cut away the wood with the saw.

The steps were awkward to work on, and he set to work to form a more commodious platform.

In order to do this he shifted several of the boxes and barrels.

On moving one of the latter his eye noticed a gleam of metal, and the next minute his toe had caught in a ring partly buried in the sand.

Stooping down he found that it was the ring of another trap.

In the hope that this might reveal some other mode of egress, he lifted it.

A square hole was revealed, and on holding the taper over it, the light was reflected back by a host of sparkling objects, amongst which Ned recognised the spoil they had disposed of that night.

It was one of Mendez's temporary hiding-places for valuables awaiting shipment.

It was a fearful job for Ned to stoop his wounded head over the hole, for the pain caused by the rush of blood upwards every time he leant forward was terrible.

But forgetting everything, even the fact of the peril in which he found himself, in his greed for gold, ignoring blindly the circumstance that Mendez might return at any moment, and that every second's delay might lessen his prospect of escape, he did not rest till he had completely emptied the cavity.

This done, he paused a little to recover himself.

The sight of all this wealth became, however, simply maddening, when he reflected suddenly that it would be impossible to carry it all away.

He began rapidly to sort it over, selecting from the glittering mass only the smaller and more valuable articles such as watches and articles of jewellery.

As there were a number of these, in addition to those he and his companions had brought, he managed to make a parcel less bulky, though of almost equal value, to those they had disposed of so cheaply.

He stowed this away in the bag, and then, changing his idea about the trap, shifted his platform, and set about attacking the boards which formed the ceiling of the cellar near the wall.

Thoroughly convinced that Kelly had been sent to his last account, the Jew felt altogether easier in his mind from the belief that one at least of the evidences of his receivership of stolen property was out of the way.

Full of this and other thoughts he retired to rest (?) after having hauled Kelly into the cellar, and closed the door leading thereto.

He even thought of searching Kelly before he retired.

Had he done so, the history of Ned might have been prematurely ended.

His mind was so agitated that he forgot, when closing the door to the cellar to shoot the bolt; and it was not until Kelly had bored a hole in its vicinity to enable him to draw back the bolt, that he discovered the omission, and that the door was simply on the latch, and that a good push from the shoulder would have opened the path to his release.

Overjoyed at the discovery, he quickly made his way out of the house, vowing to be the death of Mendez.

It was broad daylight, however, by the time he emerged from the window by which he had entered, and went staggering down the garden.

Fortunately for him, Mendez had neglected to re-fix the alarm communicating with the window in question.

The sight of an apparently drunken sailor staggering along, with a broken head and a decided air of having been up all night, was too common a one in Sydney to excite attention, and Kelly reached Hopkins's house unmolested.

Neither of the other two had returned.

Ned set about patching up his broken skull, and then, throwing himself on to a bed, fell into a sleep that was only broken by the arrival of his companions.

When asked how he came in that plight, he contented himself by spinning a yarn concerning a row he had got into in the street, resolving to keep his expedition a secret for the present.

The bag he had carefully hidden away.

As for Mendez, he postponed his visit to the cellar till the following night, when great was his horror to find the supposed dead man had not only come to life, but had carried off an amount of plunder the loss of which made the Jew almost frantic.

CHAPTER CXXXVIII.
FRIENDS IN THE ENEMY'S CAMP.

DURLACHER, alias Mendez, gave a howl like that of a trapped wild beast when he realised the loss that had befallen him.

His rage and anguish were unbounded.

Shylock suffered a great deal at the loss of his ducats and his daughter, but it is to be questioned whether Mendez did not suffer more at the loss of the money alone.

Moreover, he felt a twofold grievance against the robber.

In the first place, it was abominable, unnatural, detestable that he should have been robbed by one of a set of men whom he was continually in the habit of obliging, by buying stolen goods of them at only seventy-five per cent. below their value.

And, in the second, it was the unkindest cut of all to find he had been bested by a man whom he flattered himself he had so thoroughly got the better of as Ned.

Under ordinary circumstances, he would not have dreamed of betraying a customer, no matter what reward might have been offered by the police authorities.

But in this case he felt justified in using every effort to bring a villain who had pillaged his benefactor, as he considered himself, to justice.

He was, however, ignorant of one very important fact, and that was Ned's name, for he had never seen him before the bushranger had visited him in company with Knatchbull.

And at the same time he felt it would be rather a ticklish job to bring the matter directly under the notice of the police, who would be certain to make some very awkward enquiries as to the circumstances of his encounter with the burglar.

No, it would not do to say a word of that.

If his customers once learnt he had betrayed one of them, farewell to all future dealings.

Perhaps to life, for they might take it into their heads to avenge such a breach of confidence with a knife-blade or a bullet.

Still he might do something indirectly.

He had heard of the burglary and murder at Goodered's, and had divined that the goods offered to him by Ned and his accomplices had been plundered from the hapless pawnbroker's.

He resolved, therefore, to see if by any means the police could be quietly and unsuspiciously put upon the right track, careless whether he involved Knatchbull and Hopkins in the punishment he wished to have meted out to their companion.

Meanwhile Kelly had been somewhat troubled as to what he was to do with the plunder he had carried off from the receiver's.

As he had won it single-handed, he had come to the conclusion that he alone was entitled to its proceeds.

But for the time he was at a loss to whom to dispose of it with safety.

Accordingly he resolved to conceal it in a natural hiding-place he had noted in the rocks near the harbour.

Accordingly he hired a boat in the course of the afternoon, and managed to hide the treasure without exciting the suspicion of his companions, both of whom were bent on continuing the spree they had commenced overnight.

With his wounded head, Kelly was wise enough to see that a quiet life would be the best he could lead for a week or so.

Accordingly he took up his quarters with a widow who let lodgings at a short distance out of the town, and confined his excursions to an occasional visit to the tavern where his sister Kate was acting as barmaid.

Through her he was able to learn all the latest gossip, most of which turned on the terrible tragedy in which he had been engaged.

He was careful to keep the part he had taken in it a secret, even from Kate.

Knatchbull had started on a cruise, and, although Mendez was on the watch, he had failed as yet to run against the man who had despoiled him.

"I've a bit of news for you, Ned," said Kate to him one evening when he called in.

"What is it?"

"The new head of the police is back."

"I could have told you that. He turned up in Sydney yesterday."

"Ah! but he's been here this morning."

"What's he like?"

"Oh! awfully handsome, and no end of a swell. Almost as tall as you, straight as a ramrod, with a splendid moustache, and the whitest hand you ever saw in your life."

"Um! I reckon he'd better not try to clap those white hands on me, or he'll run a precious good chance of having them snapped off by the wrists," said Ned, with a toss of his head and a jerk back of his shoulders that meant that he was not over pleased at hearing his as yet unknown foe thus favourably spoken of.

"Perhaps not, but, by the look of his eye, he's the boy to try it, or anything besides."

"What! I suppose he's been telling you some foolery or other, eh?"

"Oh, you need not get in a flutter. He's the sort of man that has a pleasant word for any girl he comes across, but don't you suppose I'm going to listen to any foolery."

"I should hope not."

"Only, Ned, you might just remember one thing, that the more he says to me, the more I may have to tell you."

"That's true enough. It's a capital idea. Play up at him all you can, Kate, get all the information you can out of him, and between us we'll lead him such a devil's dance as will make him wish himself back in England before a month's out. That's the game, my girl."

"Well, I can't quite promise as much as that, but you may be sure I will try."

It was quite true that Kate Kelly had found Kenneth Rothsay a remarkably agreeable, not to say fascinating, individual, during the short visit he had paid that morning to the bar over which she presided.

But she was not the only one who entertained similar opinions by a long way.

During his expedition after Ned on the Upper Murray, Kenneth had halted at the abandoned station where the bushranger had so successfully defied the police, and had seen the girl who had aided him in this scheme. To her, also, the dashing ex light-cavalryman had done his best to render himself agreeable, though it is sad to relate that the innate perverseness of the convict's daughter led her to compare him unfavourably with the bushranger, over whose slumbers she had so tenderly watched.

Kenneth, returning from his fruitless chase, had been startled first with the news of Ned's exploit at the Canary Bird, and, secondly, with the horrible intelligence of the murder of Goodered.

A crime like the latter occurring in a city under his charge was, he felt, a serious blow to him, and he felt bound to spare no possible exertion to bring its perpetrators to justice.

He had ridden a few miles out of the city one evening and was returning in somewhat pensive mood, at a footpace, with his reins held loosely in his hand.

It was getting almost dusk, when he caught sight of a female figure some distance ahead.

There are some men who cannot see a woman walking along in front of them without being seized with an irrepressible wish to see her face.

The result is very often disappointing, but they persevere none the less.

Kenneth could not help scanning the fair unknown, and quickening his pace to overtake.

He could make out a tall elastic figure splendid shoulders, clean ankles, and a swinging, supple gait.

It only remained to be seen if the face corresponded with the decidedly promising outline.

Someone else, however, was bent on a similar investigation.

A fellow of a somewhat shabby appearance who had been sitting by the roadside had risen at the girl's approach, and had made some remark which Kenneth could not catch.

Neither could he make out the answer, which was evidently a sharp one.

The fellow, however, was clearly not to be shaken off easily, and he shambled alongside the girl, and continued to address her.

To tell the truth, the conversation had run something as follows:—

"What, Carroty Jess! you back again? Why, what brings you here, my girl?"

"Nothing that concerns you, Joe Hubbard."

"Oh, we're very high and mighty since we've been in the country for the benefit of our blooming health!"

"Just mind your own business. I don't want anything to do with the likes of you."

"The likes of me! I am good enough company for the daughter of an old lag any day. What d'ye mean by all your stuck-up airs? I'm not going to put up with it."

"Look here," said the girl, as he approached her, "if you lay a finger on me, s'elp me! I'll set my ten commandments in your face, and mark you so that none of your pals will know you."

"Oh, that be blowed for a tale! Come, give us a kiss for old friendship."

Whether the girl had caught sight of the horseman behind her or whether the hoofs of his steed had apprised her of his approach is doubtful, but it is certain that this last remark of Joe Hubbard's led her to utter a very nicely-modulated melodramatic scream that brought Kenneth up alongside her in double-quick time.

Meanwhile Mr. Joe Hubbard, exceedingly disgusted at what he considered a most ridiculous display of prudery on the part of a young lady who, during their former acquaintance, had been distinguished by anything except an excess of that quality, resolved—in his own words—to "take the blooming nonsense out of her."

With this view, he caught her very roughly round the waist, and was striving for the kiss he had spoken of.

But the girl continued to struggle and scream with surprising earnestness and not too much noise.

His lips had just touched hers when he received a gentle tap on the head with the butt-end of his riding-crop that caused him for a moment to imagine that one star had fallen on his head and that thirty thousand more were dancing before his eyes.

Only for a moment, however, for the next he was lying at full length in the road.

And the young lady was enthusiastically clasping the hand that held the riding-crop.

"Oh, sir! how can I thank you?" she exclaimed, looking up with a most candid and dove-like expression to her deliverer.

"What!" cried Kenneth, who, with a soldier's trained memory for faces, recognised her at once. "My little beauty of the Murray!"

"Dear me, Mr. —ah! Captain Rothsay, is it you?"

"Myself. But what, in the name of wonder, brings you to Sydney?"

Jess proceeded to explain at length.

She had been so terribly frightened by her adventure with Kelly that she no longer dared stay at the station.

She had, therefore, started off to Sydney, where she hoped to get some place.

She had come in a drag, which had broken down late one afternoon, and had resolved to hurry on on foot to reach the city before nightfall.

All of which in reality meant that she had guessed Ned Kelly would make for Sydney, and was determined to see him again.

Kenneth gazed on her with admiration.

It was a failing of his that he always did gaze on pretty girls with admiration.

"You want a place?" he said.

"Yes."

Probably if any disinterested person had asked Kenneth Rothsay when he started for his ride that afternoon if he knew of any vacant situation for a young woman, he would probably have answered "No," and with truth.

But, looking at Jess, it suddenly occurred to him that he had heard of a vacant situation.

He was living with a Mr. and Mrs. Fielding, since he had not yet had the leisure to start an establishment for himself, and he felt certain he had heard Mrs. Fielding express a desire for a nurse, or a governess, or a cook, or a housemaid—he was not quite sure which—a day or two before.

Here was a chance for Jess.

If Jess had been a dowdy looking wench it is probable that the remembrance of this chance would not have occurred to him, but he liked to see pretty faces about him; and, accordingly, he told the girl of the vacancy.

It was, he now recollected, a nursemaid.

He also mentioned that he was living in the same house as the lady who wanted the domestic in question.

And, after some further conversation as they strolled along, he at last felt bound to quicken his pace and leave her, for they were entering the outskirts of the city, and Sydney has its scandalmongers like every other spot where men do congregate.

As for Mr. Joe Hubbard, both had forgotten him, and he lay insensible till a passing teamster, finding he was in the way of the traffic, considerately drew him to the side of the road, and, after emptying his pockets, left him there to come to or not as it pleased him.

He came to, with a bump on his head like an ostrich-egg, and then managed to stagger home.

Meanwhile, Jess, on reaching the city, had gone straight to a venerable matron who had on more than one occasion befriended her.

This estimable old lay furnished her, after due consideration, not only with a suitable outfit but with three written testimonials of the highest character.

Armed with these, she went to Mrs. Fielding, and one of the testimonials, purporting to be signed by an eminent clergyman, impressed the good lady so favourably that she engaged the girl at once, despite her good looks.

Servants with good characters were scarce, and, with the head of the police staying at her house, it was impossible to be too particular.

But what was better than all was, that despite her good looks the girl evidently shunned, rather than courted, observation.

CHAPTER CXXXIX.
A TRAP.

MENDEZ found his task a more difficult one than he had anticipated.

Knatchbull being away, he had no chance of questioning him, and when he got hold of Hopkins and sounded him he found to his disgust that the latter either would not or could not give him any information as to the man who had been their companion on the night of the burglary.

Chance, however, at last did more for him than all his scheming had been able to bring about.

In the rather flashy get-up of the well-to-do middle Israelite of sporting tastes, he had been of late a constant visitor to hotel bars, gaming rooms, sporting publics, and the like, where he thought there might be a chance of running against the man who had robbed him.

Walking down one of the main thoroughfares during a breezy afternoon he saw the hat of a tall, broad-shouldered individual, striding along a few paces in front of him, carried off and whirled away.

The stranger turned with an oath to catch it.

Mendez noticed that one side of his head was done up with strips of sticking-plaister.

This, with the fact of the man's height and bulk, served to identify him, despite his change of dress and sundry other attempts at disguise.

Mendez was almost certain that he had the man whom he had seen but twice, and then in the dress of a sailor, before him.

But it was necessary to make sure of this.

He resolved to follow him quietly.

Ned Kelly—for the unknown was indeed he—had just paid his usual visit to Kate and was now on his way homeward.

As he strolled carelessly along the fancy took him to proceed by a roundabout route which, as chance would have it, led him past Mrs. Fielding's.

Just inside the fence stood a girl, in whom he had no difficulty in recognising Jess, with a couple of young children playing about her.

For the moment she did not recognise him, and, when he halted, leant his elbows on the fence and began to pass the time of day in a pleasant manner, put on an air of scorn and began to walk away, which said plainly enough as words that she was not going to have anything to do with loafers.

Ned saw she did not know him, and quickly called out in low but distinct tones—

"Jess, don't you know me? Don't you remember the night in the hut on the Murray?"

The girl started.

"I'm Ned, you know."

She did, and a wave of colour swept over her face as she came back to the fence.

Their conversation was brisk and animated.

"I cannot stay any longer," she said, at last, "or these kids will get talking to their mother about it. But I will meet you later on."

"When?"

"I will let you know."

"How?"

"Where are you living?"

Ned informed her of this and also of the alias under which he was known, and she promised to communicate with him.

Neither of the two paid much attention to the somewhat stylishly-dressed Jewish gentleman who had found it necessary to sit down on a pile of lumber at a short distance and remove his shoe in order to shake out a pebble that had got into it, and who continued to sit there till Ned moved off.

Nor did they pay much attention to a loafer coming along in the opposite direction, who paused to look at Jess as she moved up towards the house with her charges, and growled out something that was certainly not a blessing.

The Jew heard him, however, and said—

"Who's that girl, and what makes you swear at her?"

The fellow paused, and the answer which rose to the top of his tongue was —

"What the devil's that to you, you blooming Sheeney?"

But he thought better of it, and said—

"A blessed bit of stuck-up impertinence who got me a broken head the other night."

"Ah! how was that?"

"Oh, no matter. I'll be even with her."

"But who is she?"

"Who is she? A fine lot to be giving herself airs. She's the daughter of a wretched old swindler who keeps a grog-shop somewhere up country, and since she made Sydney too hot to hold her she's been stopping with him."

"But what's she doing here?"

"Blest if I know—playing the correct and proper. Though I've known the time when ——"

Here Mr. Joseph Hubbard—for it was he—gave some details respecting Jess's early career which were not of a particularly edifying character.

Perhaps, if it had not been for his indignation, he would not have been so communicative to a perfect stranger.

Mendez's shrewd mind guessed there was something to be made out of the connection with the man he was following and the girl."

He glanced after Ned, who was almost out of sight.

The road, however, was a straight one, and it would be easy to catch him up.

"Look here," he said to Hubbard, "do you want to earn a pound or two?"

"Rather."

"Well, just call at that address this afternoon, and ask for Mr. Simeon."

Having spoken, he handed Hubbard a paper, on which was the address in question, and walked on after Kelly.

He saw the latter enter a respectable-looking cottage-dwelling, and then, dropping into the nearest public, managed to learn that it was the residence of a widow named Bowles, who let lodgings.

Also, that the tall man living there was named Dawes.

Mendez then returned to the city to perfect his scheme.

His object was rather to frighten Ned into yielding up the property than to betray him to the authorities; or, if the truth must be told, he thought he might manage to terrify him into giving it up first, and could then, if he judged fit, hand him over at leisure afterwards.

If he had known that Dawes was Ned Kelly, with a big reward on his head, he would have denounced him.

Ned went into the city the next morning as usual, and was leaving Kate's bar, when a little red-headed Jew-boy stepped up to him.

"Mister Dawes?" said he.

"Yes," answered Ned.

"A young lady living at Mrs. Fielding's wants to see you," said the lad, blandly.

Ned started.

"Where is she?" he asked.

"At Hill-street."

Ned fell blindly into the trap in which chance served Mendez better than ever he had bargained for.

Jess had said she would let him know where he could meet her, and this was evidently her messenger.

It was rather habit than any sense of instinct that led him to ask—

"What young lady is it?"

"Miss Jessie—a tall young lady, with red hair."

"And how did you know me?"

"Miss Jessie said to me this morning, 'Go down to Mrs. Bowles', and tell the gentleman there, Mr. Dawes, that I shall be in Hill-street this afternoon.' When at last I got there, for I could not get away as early as I wanted, I found you were out. I had seen you two or three times before, and Mrs. Bowles said you were gone into Sydney. 'Well,' I said, 'I've got to go into Sydney myself, and I may run across him, but if he comes back in the day, tell him the message.'"

All this was rattled off so glibly that Ned was convinced.

"The young lady said this afternoon?" he asked.

"Yes."

"And what is the number in Hill-street?"

"Number fourteen."

Ned gave the lad something, and started off in the direction indicated.

Hill-street was not one of the cleanest or the most reputable in Sydney, but this very fact made it all the more likely to be the spot that Jess would select as a rendezvous.

Number fourteen was a dingy-looking dwelling of small size.

Ned knocked at the door, which was opened by a blear-eyed, slipshod hag.

"Is a young lady waiting here for Mr. Dawes?"

"Yes, sir; step this way—this; she'll be down in a minute, sir," mopped and mowed the old harridan, as she ushered him along a narrow passage.

At the end was a door, which she opened, revealing a spacious and tolerably clean-looking kitchen.

"Just sit down for a moment, sir," continued the hag.

Ned entered, and, throwing himself heavily into a chair, growled out—

"Now then, old Mother Brimstone, let the gal know I'm here."

The old woman passed out of the door, closing it after her, and the next moment Ned heard the sound of a bolt on the outside shot into its socket.

As the door clanged, and the sharp sound of the bolt fell on his ears, Ned jumped to his feet.

What was the meaning of this?

He glanced round the room in search of a way out.

It was a large and tolerably well-furnished kitchen, with a very fair-sized window, but his brows knit as he noted that the window was provided with a strong range of iron bars.

A jerk at one of them showed that a file or spring saw would be needed to overcome the obstacle they presented to flight.

The door was of unusual strength and as firm as a rock.

Escape being impossible, resistance was his next idea, and a howl of suppressed rage escaped him as he realised the fact that he was unarmed.

His eye fell on the heavy kitchen poker, resting on the oven-door, and he at once possessed himself of it.

The table-drawer, hurriedly ransacked, yielded him a long, sharp-bladed carving-knife.

Suddenly a gleam of anticipated triumph passed across his face as he noted a buttered cruet-stand upon the dresser.

He counted upon finding the most effective weapon of all there, nor was he disappointed, for the pepper-castor was almost full.

Filling his hands with the precious and pungent dust, he entrenched himself behind a barricade hastily constructed of chairs and tables, and awaited the result with perfect calmness.

"If it's the police," he thought, "they'll call on me to surrender, and I'll gammon them that I'm going to, and then try and bolt! But I don't think it is the police, for they'd

have been quicker over the job. And if it's not the police, but a bit of private spite, why I've all the more chance, since they will hardly dare use firearms in broad daylight, on account of the row."

There was no sign of the foe as yet, and Ned could not help feeling a little impatient.

"They'll never be such fools as to try to starve me out. If I set at that window seriously I can get those bars down in an hour with the knife. I wish they'd come, I feel equal to a brush with half-a-dozen," he muttered, still glancing round with quick, keen eye and pricked ears, and gathering his mighty limbs under him like a cat about to spring.

The sound of approaching voices and footsteps in the passage was now audible.

Suddenly he recognised the tones he had heard on the night Mendez had fired at him.

Yes, he could not be mistaken.

Instinctively he divined the whole affair.

He had been ensnared by the Jew in order that the latter might recover his property.

But he asked himself, was Jess an accomplice?

The bolt was withdrawn and the door fell back, revealing Mendez in the costume he had worn the previous morning, accompanied by three sturdy-looking fellows in the garb of labourers.

All four were equipped with bludgeons and cords.

Without giving his adversaries time to advance, Ned bounded over the barricade and dashed a handful of pepper, right and left, slap into the eyes of the two foremost of them, one being Mendez.

With shrieks of agony they dropped their weapons and clapped their hands to their faces.

Backing a step and snatching up the knife and poker, Ned advanced to the attack of the remaining couple.

The fellow on his right aimed a desperate blow at his head.

Holding the poker in the middle, Ned threw it upwards, caught and turned aside the descending bludgeon with it, and then dashed the knobbed end full in his adversary's face, knocking several of his teeth out and levelling him to the ground.

Almost simultaneously, the man to his left had also aimed a downward blow at him.

He could not quite avoid it, but managed to jerk his head aside, so that it only alighted on his shoulder, though with such stunning force that his left arm was for the time disabled, and the knife fell from his numbed fingers.

Raising his left foot, however, he gave his assailant a kick in the stomach that doubled him up in agony, and sprang through the doorway.

The outer door was closed, and the passage in darkness.

He slammed to the door behind him and, stooping down, sought for and shot the bolt.

As he did so he heard footsteps, and, before he could rise, had received a violent though ill-directed blow from a fifth man, who had been stationed as sentry just under the outer-door.

Rising to his feet, he struck in turn with the poker at this new assailant, but without effect.

Pushing forward he found himself grappled with at a disadvantage.

His left arm was still too numbed for him to make effectual use of it, indeed it hung almost useless by his side.

His adversary had caught him round the waist, and was striving to lift him and throw him on to his back.

At any other time Ned would have laughed at his effort, but with one arm the case was a little altered, and he had to do all he knew to keep up.

At length the bushranger brought his right arm across to the left side of his chest, and dashed the elbow smack aside the right side of the other's head just by the ear.

The fellow's grip slackened, and Ned repeating the blow with his fist caused him to leave go entirely, and to stagger back half stunned.

Then beating him down, he kicked him into insensibility, and stepping over his prostrate form gained the front door.

After some little groping he succeeded in opening it, and arranging his clothes as straight as possible, and picking up a hat lying in the passage, to replace his own, which had been lost in the first scuffle, he passed out into the street and made his way quickly but speedily in the direction of his abode.

By the time Mendez and his friends were released from the kitchen by the old woman, who had kept upstairs during the shindy, he had a good start.

CHAPTER CXL.
A CLOSE SHAVE

NED was resolved on having an explanation with Jess, and on his way home halted opposite Mrs. Fielding's.

The girl caught sight of him and managed to run out, told him to come to the boundary at nightfall, and appointed the trysting-place to be at the foot of a large tree, well known to both of them.

Accordingly, after going home and eating a hearty meal, Ned armed himself, lit a cigar, and strolled out to the appointed spot.

He had not been there long before Jess joined him.

He told her of the peril he had just escaped, and how her name had been used to lure him.

Jess indignantly denied all knowledge of the plot or the plotters, seemed greatly agitated at the news of Ned's danger, and it did not take long to make her confess that she had come to Sydney on purpose to renew her acquaintance with Ned.

"There's one thing that's rather comical," she said.

"What's that?" asked Kelly.

"I suppose you know that the new chief of the police is living here?"

"No; is it so?"

"Yes. And, do you know? he's a very nice young fellow indeed," she said, archly.

"I've heard that," growled Ned.

"And I really think he admires a pretty girl whenever he comes across her."

"What do you mean?" said the bushranger fiercely.

"Oh! don't get in a wax. He's got some ridiculous, old-fashioned idea that he ought not so much as to pay me a compliment because he happens to be under the same roof as myself, but there's a look in his eye which just says what he'd say if it wasn't for that stupid notion."

"Stop a bit, Jess," said Ned. "Do you think you could get him to be regular spoony on you?"

"Well, I won't say I couldn't."

"Then try it on, my gal, try it on."

"I don't quite see what you're driving at," said the girl, evidently hurt at the seeming want of all due and proper jealousy implied in Ned's remark."

"He's chief of police, isn't he?"

"Yes."

"Well, then, with you to wheedle all his little plans out of him, and me to thwart them, I will be able to carry on my little game without the chance of being "lagged.""

The girl laughed.

"Suppose," continued Ned, "we were to try something of the sort at once?"

"What?"

"Why, you see, I have robbed a good many people, but not a chief of police yet. It would be a fine feather in my cap to do it."

"Ah! Well, what is it you want me to do, for I suppose you are driving at something?"

"Right again. I want you to leave a window unfastened to-morrow night."

"Yes, I can manage that. The second from the left And on the ground floor."

"Good."

he after some further conversation that need not be repated, Ned took his leave

His last attempt at burglary single-handed had, though in the end successful, been attended with some peril, and he thought that on this occasion the services of a friend would be useful.

Accordingly he looked up Hopkins.

Hopkins did not seem overmuch pleased at the proposal, which offered a great deal of risk and not much prospective profit, as far as he could see.

But Kelly persuaded him, and he agreed to meet Ned the following night.

The following night Ned retired to rest at his usual hour.

His landlady, who was a quiet old soul and rather deaf, had already sought her pillow.

But, after remaining in his room about half-an-hour. Ned, who had not undressed, removed his shoes, and stole quietly downstairs with them in his hand, putting them on when he reached the door.

He opened the door and crept quietly out.

Having gained the gate and stepped into the road, he advanced a few steps to the left.

He halted, and, picking up a couple of stones, began to tap them smartly once or twice together.

The brushwood to his right rustled, and a figure emerge from it.

"Is it very late, mate?" said a voice he recognised as Hopkins's.

"All right," was his reply to this innocent sentence, which had been fixed on by them as a password.

The two quietly passed up the road.

Arrived opposite Mrs. Fielding's house, they halted for a moment to see whether the coast was clear.

Satisfied on this point, they got over the fence, and stole like two phantoms towards the house.

Here all was in readiness.

Mrs. Fielding was a woman who every night used to go round her premises in person, and satisfy herself, with her own eyes, that every bolt and bar was shot.

But Miss Jess was a very soft-footed young person, and after Mrs. Fielding had retired for the night, this young damsel stole out of her room, crept downstairs like a cat, and undid the window, as promised by her to Ned.

Consequently the two burglars had not any difficulty in effecting an entrance.

Once inside all was plain sailing, thanks to Jess's information, and they set to work at once.

The lower rooms were quickly ransacked, but they did not yield very much, for Ned's chief object was rather the glory of robbing the dwelling of the chief of the police, than actual plunder.

"The plate's in the old folks' room, ain't it?" said Hopkins.

"Yes. We can risk it if we're pretty quiet."

Accordingly the two stole upstairs, and went straight to the room occupied by Mr. and Mrs. Fielding.

Halting outside the door the burglars listened.

All was quiet within.

The door was not locked, and opening it, Hopkins, who was a far lighter man than Ned, stole in with noiseless tread.

With wonderful quietness and dexterity he appropriated a couple of watches, a small jewel-case, and the plate-basket, which it was Mrs. Fielding's habit to carry up to bed with her every night.

Ned meanwhile stood at the door, pistol in hand, prepared for any emergency.

The things secured, Hopkins rejoined his companion.

Ned was divided in opinion as to whether he should enter the room in which Kenneth was sleeping.

He wavered as to whether it would not be, as he put it, a very good move to go at once and cut the throat of a man who was no doubt destined to give him a great deal of future trouble.

A reflection came in time to stay his hand

The new chief of police, he argued, was young, was green, and was liable to be impressed by women.

Two women—Kate and Jess—had already said this.

"Therefore," argued Ned to himself, "it will be far better to spare a man whose secrets can be wheedled out of him by two girls who are devoted to me, than to kill him and make room for some hard-headed brute who doesn't care for the wenches."

He therefore signed to Hopkins to follow him, and the two stole silently downstairs again.

They had almost reached the bottom when Ned's foot slipped, and with a tremendous clatter he rolled at full length into the passage.

He was up again in a moment, but the mischief was already done.

Voices were heard in the upper part of the house, there was the scuffling of hurried steps, and the sound of lights being struck.

The two burglars hurried on to the window by which they had entered the house.

They reached it safely with their plunder, and swung themselves out of it.

Then they struck out swiftly across the lawn.

Suddenly they heard a sash go up behind them, and there was a hail to them to stop.

Bang! rang out a shot.

Hopkins staggered, and dropped his burden.

"Curse it! they have hit me," he gasped, as the pain tore on.

A couple more bullets whizzed over their heads but at that moment they gained the cover afforded by some trees.

"Come on quick to the road," cried Kelly, "we must cross it, and then make a bend to throw them off the track."

Hopkins's steps grew slower and slower as they reached the fence.

"Ned," he said, "give me a lift over. I'm pretty well done up."

Meanwhile the house was thoroughly aroused, and it was evident that in another minute the foes would be in hot pursuit.

It was lucky for them both that there was no dog, and that the night was a dark one, or they would have been almost certainly discovered.

Ned glanced as well as he could in the darkness at his companion.

"Hullo!" he said, "are you badly hurt?"

"Yes; lend me a hand to get over."

"And have dropped the swag?" continued the bush-ranger, as he helped him across the fence.

"Hang it! yes. I wish I'd never seen it."

"Look here," said Ned, "we'd better divide, and I'll try to draw them off, so that you can make the best of your way into Sydney."

There was something in the tone in which this remark was made that struck Hopkins.

"No, no," he cried; "I don't see that. You must stick by me, or I'll never be able to get along at all."

He spoke with difficulty.

All the while this conversation was going on, Ned had been helping Hopkins onwards.

He gave him a lift over the boundary running along the other side of the road.

"Now," he said, "you strike off that way."

"No, I'm hanged if I do," cried Hopkins. "If you leave me in the lurch like this and I'm nailed, I'm hanged if I don't——"

"Don't what?" hissed Ned, in tones that froze the other's blood. "'Don't split,' you meant to say, eh? By Jingo! you shan't get a chance of doing that," and as he spoke he drew a pistol.

"For God's sake—" began Hopkins, his voice rising to a scream.

But, clapping the pistol to his head, Ned pulled the trigger, and, as the wretched fellow sank to the ground a corpse, his murderer bounded off with the speed of a deer.

Guided by the pistol shot, Kenneth and Mr. Fielding were soon on the scene of this tragedy.

"It must be the fellow I fired at," exclaimed the former. "But what could that shot have meant?"

Meanwhile Ned, straining every muscle, had darted down the road, and then quitting it had made his way by a somewhat circuitous route to Mrs. Bowles's.

Here all was quiet, and opening the front door, he stole noiselessly up the stairs and gained his room.

Turning in, he was soon sound asleep. He had no conscience to trouble him.

CHAPTER CXLI.
A PRACTICAL JUDAS.

THE sensation which followed the attempted burglary at Mrs. Fielding's was tremendous.

Coming as it did after the similar crime which had ended in the murder of the old pawnbroker, people naturally maintained that there was a connection between the two offences, and that they must be the work of the same gang.

And they began to ask themselves, with an uneasy feeling, who was likely to be the next victim.

The death of Hopkins, too, was not without an element of mystery.

Kenneth, at the inquest, swore that he had fired at the burglars from the window of his room as they retreated from the house.

But the wound that had put an end to Hopkins was of such a nature that death must have instantaneously followed its infliction, and hence it was certain that he could not have proceeded to the spot where he was found, had he received it at the time Kenneth fired.

Further investigation, too, showed that the bullet that had put an end to his existence did not fit the bore of Kenneth's pistol, whilst both the latter and Mr. Fielding could swear that a shot was fired which helped to guide them to a spot where the body was found.

Both were certain of this.

The only conclusion, therefore, was that Hopkins had been accidentally shot, either by his own hand or by that of an accomplice, in endeavouring to scale the fence, for no one went so far as to imagine that his life had been purposely sacrificed to secure his comrade's safety.

His death led, however, to a somewhat important discovery.

He had been identified by several people as a man residing a few doors from the murdered pawnbroker, and, on his home being searched, a number of articles, the products of the former burglary, which it had not been thought worth while disposing of to Mendez, were found.

Some of these articles were identified, and led to a strict examination of his premises.

In clearing away the rubbish which filled the cellar, it was noticed that the earth along the wall separating his house from the abandoned tenement next door did not seem so solid as elsewhere.

On examination, it was found that it could be easily removed by a spade, and that the deeper they went the less compact it became.

The police proceeded to work at it, and soon traced the tunnel that had been opened into the adjoining house.

With this clue, the rest was easy, and it was soon perceived how the plunder had been removed and the searchers for the time thrown off the scent.

It was resolved to keep a sharp look-out on all who had visited Hopkins, but, as it turned out, no one had noticed Ned during his few visits, and he remained quite unsuspected.

A couple of days after the burglary Kenneth was at breakfast, when a card was brought in with the request that its owner, a Mr. Simeon, wanted to see him at once.

The young chief of the police had been pestered with visitors ever since the perpetration of the double murder, and had got disgusted with the countless number who had only come to bother his life out with suggestions of impossible plans for securing the offenders and bringing them to justice.

"Please ask him to send in word what he wants with me," he said to the servant who had brought the card, and added to Mr. Fielding, "If it's another of those fellows with a cock-and-bull scheme, I shall step quietly out of the house and down to the office. If he's got anything to say, he must say it there."

"Please, sir, he says he must see you in private on a most important matter of business," said the servant, returning.

"Tell him that if it's business, and he will name a time, I will see him at the police office. I'm hanged if I'll be worried out of my life like this. To be called before one has time to swallow one's breakfast, is too bad. Well, what is it now?" he continued to the servant, who had again re-entered the room.

"He says, sir, he must and will see you on a matter of the highest importance, and that if you refuse to receive him at once, the matter will not rest here."

"Confound his impudence! Tell him I'll join him in half a minute. By Jove, if he's come on any humbugging game, I'll give him a lesson he won't forget in a hurry."

This conversation had been carried on in such a manner as to reach the ears of Jess, who happened to be passing the open breakfast-room door.

The girl felt a strong desire to learn what this Mr. Simeon, who was so particularly anxious to see Kenneth, had to say.

Her sympathies, it is needless to remark, were with the criminal orders; and she thought that if Mr. Simeon's revelations were of a character to prove harmful to her friends, she could not do better than to make herself acquainted with them.

Nothing could be easier.

Mr. Simeon had been ushered to wait in a room with a window opening on to the verandah.

The window was open.

Jess slipped out, and, stealing round, placed herself conveniently outside it.

When Kenneth entered the room, Mr. Simeon rose to receive him.

He was a well-dressed, middle-aged Israelite, wearing one of the largest green shades that can be imagined over his eyes.

"Aha! a disguise," thought Kenneth; "wait a little bit, my fine fellow."

"Mr. Simeon?" he began interrogatively.

"That is my name," said the stranger.

"You wished to see me on business."

"Yes; if I am addressing Captain Rothsay, of the police?"

"At your service."

"You will pardon me," said Simeon, raising the shade and revealing two of the most inflamed-looking eyes ever seen outside an ophthalmic hospital, set in lids suggestive in appearance of raw beefsteak, "but I did not recognise your voice. I see it is you, Captain Rothsay. I have a very important communication to make to you."

"In connection with my official duties?"

"Yes."

"Ah! now I have you, my friend," thought Kenneth "I presume sir, you are aware," said he, putting on the red-tape air of a Foreign Office clerk, "that such communications are usually received by myself or by one of my representatives at the police office, where every attention is at once paid to them, and that your seeking me here at my residence, when half-an-hour later you would have found me at the office in question, has somewhat the air of an intrusion."

Kenneth paused, thinking to see Mr. Simeon, figuratively, bowled over.

But he was not.

"Sir," he replied, very politely, but very firmly, "you have, you will pardon me for reminding you of it, not held your present position very long, and are not perhaps thoroughly up in some of the peculiarities connected with it. This is not England, Captain Rothsay, and I may take it on myself to tell you that there is a very peculiar impediment which will at all times hinder men from crossing the threshold of the police-office in order to give you information. May I have the honour of mentioning it?"

"Certainly," said Kenneth, with a vague idea that his visitor was either a most covertly insolent scoundrel or a madman.

"It is that they run the risk of having their throats cut if they are seen coming out of it."

This answer rather confirmed Kenneth in his previous idea.

"You seem well acquainted with the little ways of the dangerous classes over here," he said.

"I am—so well that I am, with your permission, going to put one of the worst of them in your hands."

Kenneth started.

"Ah! an informer," he said, contemptuously.

"If it were not for informers, I don't think the police would reap much honour," was the answer.

Rothsay began to see that he was not likely to get the best of it at this game.

(To be continued.)

NED KELLY

THE
IRONCLAD
AUSTRALIAN BUSHRANGER

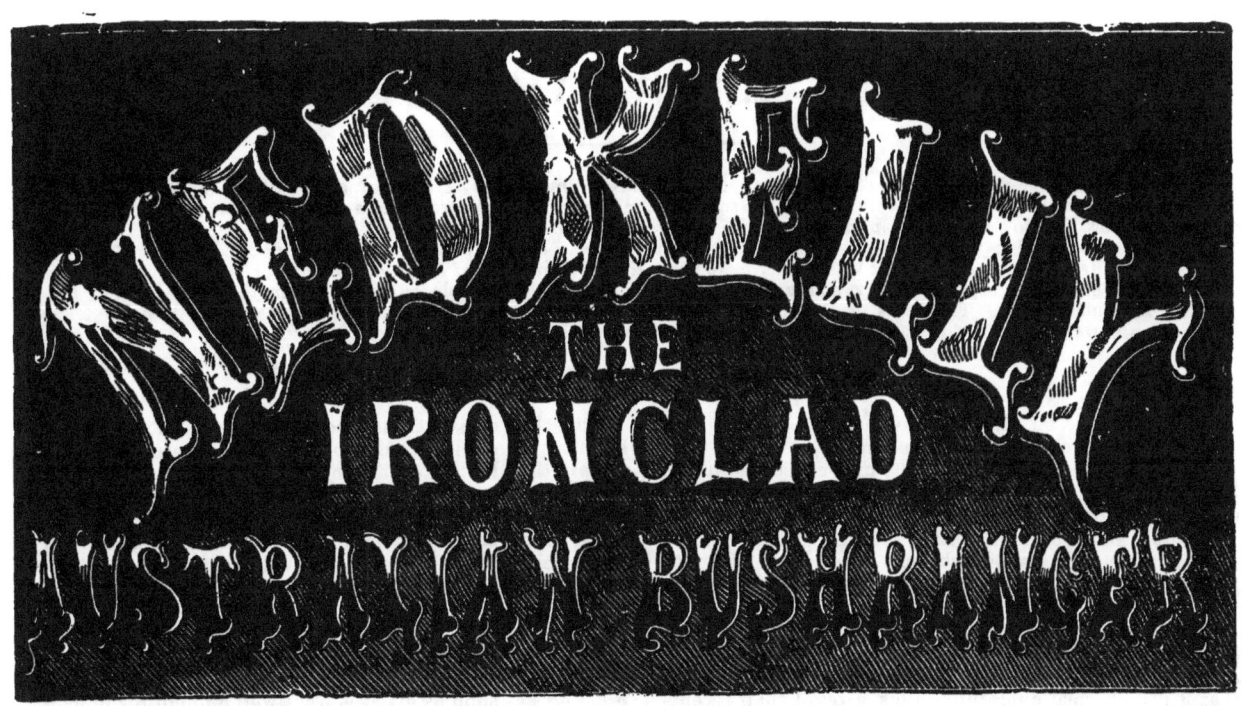

NO 24,

NED KELLY: IRONCLAD BUSHRANGER.

" It is well known that for many years Ned Kelly had made himself notorious by a series of crimes wholly incompatible with the civilisation of the nineteenth century. Ned Kelly's celebrated steed, Marco Polo, is as well known at the Antipodes as Dick Turpin's Black Bess in these islands."—*Telegraph*, 7th July, 1881.

" It is notorious that the robbery of Mr. Steward's corpse was mainly performed by the assistance of NED KELLY'S BROTHER, the Captain of what was neither more nor less than a pirate ship."—*Times*, July.

" The history of NED KELLY and his celebrated black horse Marco Polo, will ever live in the recollection of the Australian public. The deeds of Dick Turpin, and the performances of Black Bess, are tame beside those of 'NED AND HIS NAG;' in addition to which Ned's history is true, and Turpin's is pure fiction."—*Press*, July.

CHAPTER CXLI.—*Continued.*

" Well, sir," he said, " pray proceed."

" I am prepared to put one of the men concerned in the Goodered murder in your hands. There is a reward of five hundred pounds offered, I believe."

It would have been in better keeping for Mr. Simeon not to have made this remark, but he could not help it; he wanted to hear the fact officially stated.

" Yes," said Kenneth, " five hundred pounds."

" Well, I know I can trust to you, Captain Rothsay, and that you will forgive me if anything I have said has in any way annoyed you. I am willing, on your assurance that if my information results in his arrest I shall receive the reward, to put you in possession of his name and hiding place."

" Indeed."

" But, as I have said before, I cannot give you the information officially."

" Why not ?"

" You are new to this country, and cannot understand all its ways. The honestest man amongst us would hesitate before risking the enmity of such a powerful body as the criminal classes and their admirers are "

" Or the chance of losing their custom ?"

This was a mere guess shot of Kenneth's, but the other did not like it.

" You will perhaps more readily understand me when I tell you that the murderer is a man for whom an immense reward has already been offered, but who has evaded capture on account of the aid and sympathy he has received from almost all classes."

" Who is he ?"

Simeon rose and approached him.

" Ned Kelly," he said, in a low whisper.

" Ned Kelly!" repeated the other in amazement.

" Hush!" cried Simeon, looking round with an air of alarm.

" You say he did this murder ?"

" Yes."

" And you know his hiding-place ?"

" Yes."

" Then I call upon you to reveal it, sir."

" Exactly. I am going to do so; only I will venture first to remind you of the reward that has been offered for his apprehension, and which I claim, in addition to the five hundred offered for the Goodered murderer."

It was the fact of the large amount of this reward that had led Mendez to abandon the principle that had guided him throughout his career and give up a man to justice.

His first idea had been to secure the man who had robbed him and drive a bargain with him for his restoration to liberty.

This scheme had proved abortive.

He had unsuccessfully lured Ned into the house in Hill-street, but the bushranger had escaped.

Up to that time he had been quite unaware who his plunderer really was, and the men who had helped him, and who were mere ruffians he had hired for a few pounds, had merely thought the affair was a bit of kidnapping for private vengeance.

But when one of those who were knocked down in the kitchen picked himself up, his first words were—

" By thunder! that's a strong fellow; he's just the cut of Ned Kelly, too."

These words led Mendez to think. He mentally compared things together, and it flashed across him that, when he had purchased the stolen goods, he had noticed a scar on the left hand of their vendor.

No doubt it was Kelly.

And, if it were, why the reward would more than cover the value of the things Ned had carried off.

It was this argument that had brought him to Mrs. Fielding's as soon as his eyes were well enough for him to bear the light out of doors.

" That is true," said Kenneth, in reply to his last remark.

" Well then, sir, to earn me that reward, and yourself the reputation of ridding the colony of a most dangerous malefactor, you have only to proceed to Mrs. Bowles's, half-a-mile down this road, and you will find Ned Kelly, under the name of Mr. Dawes."

This statement startled Kenneth.

It startled another listener much more, however.

This listener was Jess, who had not lost a word of the conversation.

She was delighted she had made up her mind to listen to that interesting stranger, Mr. Simeon, and at once began to scheme how she should warn Ned.

Meanwhile Mendez and Kenneth had rapidly arranged the plan for Ned's capture.

The former was to loiter about the road, and keep watch at a distance over the cottage occupied by Mr. Dawes.

The latter was to ride at once into the town, and put himself at the head of a sufficient number of his men to render all resistance on the part of the bushranger futile.

With this agreement they separated, and Jess was left racking her brain for a chance of slipping away and giving Ned warning of this impending peril.

CHAPTER CXLII.
A SUDDEN ECLIPSE.

THE best-laid plans of mice and men, as we are informed by the poet Burns, often fail.

And usually by some unforeseen trifle.

So it was in the present instance

Mendez, sauntering out from Mrs. Fielding's residence, proceeded, with the air of a mere idler, towards that occupied by Ned Kelly.

Despite the green shade he could see pretty well, and he kept a close lookout as he went along, and carefully scrutinised everyone that passed him.

He met no one, however, resembling Ned.

Arriving in sight of the dwelling tenanted by the latter, he rubbed his hands joyfully.

" Aha!" he thought, " my fine fellow, you shall see if I won't give you cayenne in return for pepper."

Meanwhile, the girl Jess was in a terrible state of anxiety.

In vain she sought for a chance of getting away from the house for half-an-hour.

She knew it would be useless to ask the permission of her mistress.

As it happened, the housemaid had left in a great hurry the preceding evening, after what can only be styled a "row," and consequently Jess had to do more than her usual share of work.

It was impossible to slip away on the quiet, for Mrs. Fielding's eye was constantly on her.

For a moment she thought of breaking into open rebellion, and bolting; but a moment's reflection showed her that this would only arouse suspicion.

Almost at her wit's end, she scribbled a few words of warning to Ned on a piece of paper, and kept this in readiness to send by the first messenger who might present himself.

But time went on and no messenger presented himself at all.

As she looked from the front of the house towards the road, she saw Kenneth Rothsay pass by at a brisk trot, followed by four troopers.

She clenched her hands, and drove the nails into the palms with rage, as she watched them sweep on in the direction of Ned's abode.

Mendez, who had been waiting with equal anxiety on the road, felt a load lifted from his mind as he saw them approach.

They were soon alongside him.

"Well," asked Kenneth cheerily, "any sign of our friend yet?"

"No," answered the Jew, "he has not stirred."

"I suppose I must invest this place with all the forms and ceremonies of war?" said Kenneth with a smile.

"I assure you you cannot take too many precautions," replied Mendez earnestly; "the fellow is as strong as a lion, as slippery as an eel, and as cunning as a fox. He is a perfect demon."

"I should think he would be to slip through the fingers of five of us—eh, Gaskell?" and as he spoke Kenneth turned to one of his men.

"Yes, sir," was the answer, given with military promptitude and conciseness.

"Very good; so we will give the devil his due for cunning. Gaskell, ride up to the back of the house, and see no one escapes that way. Bell, you push on to the further end. Now trot."

Leaving the road the party made a sudden irruption into the little domain of Ned's landlady, the Widow Bowles.

Gaskell, taking up his position in the rear of the house, unslung his carbine, and covered the back door; Bell took up his position on the further flank of the building, and Kenneth, dismounting with one of his men, left their two horses in charge of the other, and rapped at the front door.

The Widow Bowles, in great alarm at this sudden irruption, hastened to open it.

"You have a lodger here named Mr. Dawes, madam?" said Kenneth politely.

"Yes, sir; but——" stammered the widow.

"I must see him at once, on matters of the utmost importance," continued the chief of police, advancing over the threshold.

"Really, sir, but I——" exclaimed the embarrassed woman, gazing up in his face in blank wonderment.

"Which is his room?"

Perfectly speechless, she could only point to the stairs in silence.

"The door in front?" asked Kenneth.

"Yes, sir; I—he—that is——"

"All right. Come on."

And, followed by his subordinate, Kenneth stepped up the stairs two at a time, and, without waiting to knock, threw open the door and stepped into the room.

His eye ran over it in a second.

It was empty.

"What the deuce is the meaning of this?" he cried;

and, darting out of the room again, sprang down the stairs, and faced the astonished landlady.

"Where is your lodger, madam?" he exclaimed. "In the Queen's name, I call upon you to answer me."

"He is gone out, sir," said the bewildered woman.

"Gone out?"

"Yes, sir."

"When? How long ago?"

"This morning."

"Early?"

"Yes, sir; quite early. I said to Mary, sir—Mary, you know, sir, is the girl that comes in to help me; she's the daughter of Mr. Jarvis, who used to keep the tobacconist's ——" and the woman, who was just recovering herself, was about to enter into one of those eternal rigmaroles in which her class delight, when Kenneth cut her short with——

"At what time did he go out?"

"Well, I think, sir—let me see—it was half-past seven, or, to be more exact, twenty-five minutes past seven; because, you see, I said to Mary, 'Now, Mary, it's quite time——'"

"Confound Mary! I beg your pardon, madam, but I am in a hurry, and this is a serious matter. Do you know where he went?"

"To Sydney, I think."

"And when will he be back?"

"Well, that, I'm sure, sir, I can't say. I said to him, said I, 'Mr. Dawes, shall I get you anything for dinner?'"

"Well, and what did he say?"

"Why, sir, he just said, 'Dinner be ——' you know what, sir, and went off."

"Confound it!" exclaimed Kenneth. "It seems as if the bird has flown. However, with your permission, I will just run an eye over the place."

"Certainly, sir," gasped the bewildered landlady; "but I'm an honest woman, sir, and should like to know what is the meaning of it all, sir?"

"The meaning of it is that your lodger, Mr. Dawes, is neither more nor less than Ned Kelly the ironclad bushranger."

"Ned Kelly!" screamed the affrighted woman. "Why, we might all have been murdered in our beds!" and she fell into a chair in a half-fainting condition.

Kenneth half regretted having mentioned the bushranger's name; though, as the interview progressed, he had grown more and more convinced of the woman's honesty.

A brief council of war followed the futile search, and it was decided that two of the troopers should remain in ambush at the cottage.

Followed by the remainder, Kenneth galloped back to Sydney, and a thrill of satisfaction shot through Jess's breast as she noticed that he was unaccompanied by any prisoner as he passed, and that his face did not wear the triumphant expression that denotes the return of a leader from a successful expedition.

The real reason of this failure was a very simple one.

Ned had taken it into his head to have a day's fishing in the harbour.

He had started off earlier than usual, hired a boat at Sydney, and, whilst his pursuers were wondering what had become of him, was sailing towards the Heads.

Towards evening he returned, well pleased with his sport.

Amongst the first persons he ran against on landing was Knatchbull, whose schooner had come in during the afternoon.

They greeted one another cordially; and, of course, "nobblers" were proposed.

Ned suggested that they should adjourn for this purpose to the hotel at which his sister was serving as barmaid, to which Knatchbull made no objection.

Accordingly they started in that direction.

Meanwhile the report that Ned Kelly was hiding in Sydney or its neighbourhood was rapidly spreading abroad.

Despite the almost piteous appeals of Mr. Mendez that he would keep the matter dark, Kenneth Rothsay had at once set all those acting under him at work to track the bushranger—a description of whose person had been forthwith circulated.

Mendez—who had gnashed his teeth with disappointment at the failure of the expedition of the morning—was still more enraged to find so many now engaged in a pursuit, the threads of which he wanted to keep in his own hands.

Kelly did not notice that, as he passed through the streets with Knatchbull, more than one passer stared a little hard at him, though such was the case, but, as it turned out, his disguise was so good that those whose attention had been caught by his height and figure came to the conclusion, on looking at his face, that they must have been mistaken in identifying this passing stranger with the notorious bushranger.

One man, however, seemed in doubt, and followed the pair at a distance, till he watched them enter the hotel bar.

He was a short, stout-built, red-bearded man, with a quick, keen eye.

After waiting for about a minute as if in doubt, he started off down the street at a brisk pace.

On entering the bar-room, Ned, somewhat to his surprise, saw that Kate was not at her place.

However, there was another girl there, and after being supplied with drinks, Kelly and Knatchbull stood conversing together.

They had been engaged in this manner for some minutes, Kelly being anxious to see Kate before leaving, when that young lady entered the bar.

At the sight of Ned she gave a start of surprise.

"Good heavens, Ned! You don't mean to say you are loafing about here?" she exclaimed.

"Why not?" was the answer.

"Don't you know the police are on your track, and that they are hunting for you high and low, all over Sydney?"

"No. How's that?"

"I don't know; but Captain Rothsay has been in here this morning, and several others, and it seems that the police have been warned to keep a lookout for you."

"That's very awkward"

"For goodness sake be off at once."

As the girl spoke the outer door opened and three men entered the room.

"By goles!" exclaimed Ned as he caught sight of them, "it strikes me your advice comes a little too late."

"What do you mean?" said the girl anxiously.

"Hush! don't do anything out of the way and likely to attract attention. But I know one of these three fellows, and, what is worse, he knows me."

"Confound it!" ejaculated Knatchbull, who began to feel uneasy on his own account, "so he does."

The first of the three new-comers was the red-bearded man who had watched Kelly and Knatchbull enter the hotel-bar.

The second was an individual of Jewish appearance, wearing a large green shade over his eyes, which were very much inflamed.

The third was a tall, stiff-looking, wooden-limbed individual, bearing that peculiar aspect of awkwardness, observable in the ordinary policeman when in plain clothes.

The first was a detective named Smithson.

He had never seen Ned Kelly, but when the latter passed him in the street, he could not help thinking that, making allowance for certain changes that could easily be produced by disguise, the latter would very well pass for the man of whom he was in quest.

Besides, the mere fact of the stranger being in company with Knatchbull, a ticket-of-leave-man, was in itself suspicious.

He watched the two enter the bar-room, and then set off in quest of someone able to clear up his doubts.

Chance favoured him.

He had not gone far up the street before he met Mendez, in company with the third man, a policeman named Cann.

Smithson knew from Kenneth that it was Mendez who had given the first information about Ned, and also that Cann had on one occasion met the bushranger face to face.

He told them of his suspicions, and they at once returned with him and entered the bar-room.

They took up their places near the door so as to cut off all retreat, and began to run their eyes quietly over those present.

"That's the man I mean," said Smithson; "the big fellow with the grey coat."

Mendez and Cann both glanced in the direction indicated.

It had grown dark by this time, but the gas in the bar had been lit.

"Yes," said the former, "that's him."

Cann remained silent for a minute.

"I don't know, I'm not quite sure; if it is, he has altered a great deal," he said at length, with an air of doubt. "The light is not very good."

"There's a way of settling that," cried Smithson, struck with a sudden inspiration "I'll go up in a minute and ask him to pass me a light for my weed, and I'll have a squint at his hand."

Having been boating Ned had omitted to put on gloves.

On his part, directly he saw these foes enter, Ned had set his wits to work to try and find a way of escape.

At first he thought of making a dash for it, but there were three powerful men against him, and amongst the other people present a number of respectable people who if called upon would probably help the officers.

The only way to get out would be by a trick.

"Look here Kate," he said, to the girl in as unconcerned a tone as if giving her an order or paying one of those trivial and impertinent compliments your bar-lounger delights in, "this is a tight fix, and I am not certain how we shall get out of it. You must lend us a hand."

"Very good."

"They don't suspect you. Can you leave the bar for a minute and slip out by the side door of the hotel?"

"Yes."

Slip out then, call a cab, and get the driver to draw up in the side street ready to bolt off at full gallop directly his fare comes. Tell him, by the way, his fare will be two gentlemen, one tall and the other short."

"Is that all?"

"Yes, for the present."

"All right, I'll do it."

A few minutes later Kate left the bar.

Smithson, Cann, and the Jew seemed to be in some hesitation as to what course they should pursue.

"It strikes me," said Kelly to his companion, "that these fellows are not quite certain after all whether they have got the right pig by the ear. I suppose the pepper I put in that chap's eyes has blinded him a bit and he can't see clear yet. That's it, and they do not care to kick up a shine by collaring the wrong man in a respectable place like this. Stand so as to keep between me and them as much as possible, whilst I try to work out a plan to fix them. Do you see any way yourself?"

"No, confound it! However uncertain they may be they don't take their eyes off us, and I can't see how to get out of this unless by breaking through."

"No good that," muttered Ned, "look at the crowd."

The evening frequenters of the place were now dropping in, and it was getting pretty full.

"I have it," said Ned, suddenly looking round.

The bar-room was oblong in shape and the only door giving access to it was situate in the centre of one of the longer sides.

It was by this door the police had taken up their position.

Ned and Knatchbull were standing together near the end of the room to the right of their enemies, and near a window looking on to the side street.

Leaving his companion Ned advanced towards the bar, as if to order another drink.

Smithson lounged towards him carelessly.

"Will you give me a light?" said he.

Ned complied, and the detective returned to his friends.

"There's no doubt of it," he said; "I spotted the fellow's hand."

Meanwhile, Kate had returned to the bar.

"Two more whiskies," said Ned, in a loud voice, to her, and then added in a low tone, "Is it all right?"

"Yes, the cab's outside."

In a whisper he gave her some further instructions.

"At once?" she enquired.

"At once," he said, and rejoined Knatchbull, whom he took by the arm, and hurriedly gave warning to hold himself in readiness.

"Shall we collar him off-hand?" asked Cann of Smithson.

"In a minute. Isn't the patrol due about this time?"

"Yes, they will be by in about a minute."

"Very good. You step to the door, and directly you catch sight of them signal them to come up. Then there will be no chance of a rescue, and, big as he is, he won't shake off the three of us."

Cann strolled to the door and looked out.

Half-a-minute had hardly elapsed and he stepped outside.

Then he re-entered.

"They are close here, and I have signalled them," he whispered to Smithson.

"Good. Now let us throw ourselves on him"

Carelessly, and with an affectation of indifference, the three men began to make their way towards the end of the room at which Kelly and Knatchbull were standing.

As they moved away from the door, it was pushed partly open, and the lights of the bar-room fell on the uniform of a couple of policemen.

Suddenly the bar-room was plunged in utter darkness.

There was a slight scuffle and a confusion of voices.

A rush of feet was heard, and a scrambling, tumbling, confused sound prevailed for a second or two.

A partial silence followed.

Surprise or apprehension seemed to produce this momentary quietude.

Then cries resounded on all sides.

"Helloa! what's up! Strike a light, and look sharp about it."

"Mind the door, men," shouted the detective; "don't let anyone out."

Matches were quickly struck, when it was explained that in moving some bottles the gas had been accidentally turned off at the main, the tap of which was behind the bar.

The jets were quickly relit, and Smithson cast his eyes round in search of his destined prey.

Neither Kelly nor Knatchbull was visible.

They had vanished from the room.

Smithson, careless of attracting notice, darted through the throng, and was soon satisfied that neither of the two men was there.

"Sold again by that infernal scoundrel. I have my suspicions that all is not square here," he muttered. "You are sure no one passed you in the dark?" he continued to one of the policemen at the door, who had recognised him.

"Certain, sir. We were here before the lights went out, and not even a mouse could have slipped between us."

CHAPTER CXLIII.
RUN TO EARTH.

KELLY's escape had been effected in the simplest manner possible.

The gas had been turned off purposely by Kate, in accordance with his whispered order.

No sooner was the room plunged into darkness than he seized Knatchbull by the arm and led him in the direction of the window, which, in consequence of the prevailing heat, was nearly always left open.

Through this aperture the two felons made their escape.

Both were active men, and it was only the effort of a moment to jump through the open window, a mode of egress they had both measured for some minutes before they availed themselves of such a means of escape.

"I'm hanged if it ain't quite providential! such a chance," grinned Kelly.

"You're lost in such a limited sphere, Kelly; your resources are marvellous. You are the Napoleon of 'fakers.' D—— me, but I almost respect you, my boy," said Knatchbull.

Kelly knew nothing about the great emperor, but felt his friend was paying him some compliment or other.

A cab was waiting in the side-street in readiness.

Ned and his companion jumped in, and, long before the fact of their absence had been ascertained, were driven out of sight of the hotel.

Dismissing the cab when they had gone some distance, and watching until it had driven off, Kelly and his friend separated.

The former, ignorant of the visit that had been paid to his domicile in the morning, and looking on his recognition by the Jew as a mere accident, resolved to return to his lodgings.

Walking rapidly and quietly along the road, he approached the widow's house.

Unfastening the gate, he entered the garden.

Everything seemed quiet, and he judged that, as usual, his landlady had retired to bed at an early hour.

He took the key with which he was provided from his pocket, and prepared to open the door.

He little thought that every movement was watched.

The two troopers who had been left in the house had passed the entire day on the look-out.

As evening drew near their eagerness increased.

The landlady had told them that when Ned went to Sydney and stayed beyond a certain time he very seldom returned till late.

Accordingly at dusk they installed themselves in a room on the ground-floor in the front of the house, with a window looking on to the garden.

They would thus be able to discern his approach, and to hold themselves in readiness to seize him the moment he entered the house.

It was a bright moonlight night, with only a few floating clouds; and, as Ned came up the garden, he was plainly visible to the two watchers.

They saw him pause before the door, and at once stole from the window and placed themselves at the door of the room which opened into the passage.

Their idea was to throw themselves on to him directly he had entered and closed the outer door behind him.

Just as Ned was about to put the key into the door a sound fell on his ear.

It was the neigh of a horse.

And coming from the rear of the house, too.

The events of the evening had roused his suspicions until he felt the most trivial event had a meaning.

He knew the widow had no horses.

What, then, was the meaning of the neigh he had heard, and which in reality came from one of the troopers' horses temporarily stabled in the woodshed at the back of the premises?

Instead of putting the key in the lock he turned away, and moved off in the direction of the gate, intending to proceed to the rear of the house and investigate the source of the noise that had startled him.

Hearing his retreating footsteps, the troopers judged that he had in some way learned their presence.

Throwing open the door they darted out.

At the sound of the opening door Ned turned his head.

He recognised the uniforms at once.

Hastening to the gate, he sprang out and darted down the road.

He turned to the left towards the town.

Without troubling themselves about their horses, the troopers dashed after him on foot.

In the moonlight he was clearly visible.

Ned was a splendid runner, and had no fear of being unable to distance his pursuers.

However, they proved better goers than he anticipated; and after a chase of about half-a-mile he found that, although he was gaining on them at every stride, they still kept up their pursuit.

He was preparing for a final spurt, prior to quitting the road and taking shelter to the right or left, when the noise of horses' hoofs approaching from Sydney caught his ear and caused him to pause.

A party of horsemen were evidently coming forward in such a way as to cut off his advance.

He could plainly discern the peculiar clank and jingle produced by a trooper's accoutrements.

The new-comers evidently belonged to the police as well.

Thus taken, as it were, between two fires, there was nothing to do but to quit the road and try and throw the pursuers off the scent.

A faint hail from behind showed that during the minute or two he had paused had enabled them to gain on him, and that they, too, heard the approaching horsemen, who were drawing nearer every moment.

Dashing at the fence to his right, he caught the bough of a large tree that projected over the road, and by its aid swung himself over.

This act had been marked; and in a few moments both parties of police had met at the point where he had quitted the road.

Leaving their horses to the care of two of their number, they pressed on in pursuit.

Ned had left the road just beyond Mr. Fielding's, and now, turning back, and, keeping a course parallel with the road, he found himself approaching that gentleman's premises.

In doing so, he was throwing himself into the very jaws of the lion.

Kenneth Rothsay was in the house, and there were several police about.

One of the two men left with the horses galloped along the road to the front of the house, and shouted to put them on the alert.

With Kenneth at their head, they turned out.

Ned, crushing through the belt of ornamental trees and shrubs that bordered Mr Fielding's garden, became aware of an unusual animation at the house.

Lights were flitting about from room to room, and soon Kenneth and his men began to search, spreading themselves out, so that it would be impossible for anyone to pass through their line.

Kelly found himself in a very ticklish position.

The party in his rear were getting nearer every minute, and to advance would be to fall into the hands of Kenneth and his men.

Flinging himself flat, he crawled over an open space, and gained a thick clump of trees and shrubs on the edge of the lawn and scaled a tree.

The two parties now united, and an active search began in all parts of the garden.

Glancing from his post of elevation across the lawn, towards the verandah, Ned noticed a female figure standing by an open window.

Even at the distance, he thought that he recognised Jess.

A bold idea struck him.

It was to hide, with her aid, in the house itself—provided he could only gain it unobserved.

The troopers were dispersed about the garden, and in a low tone Ned gave a signal with which the girl was familiar.

She heard it and looked up.

Ned pushed aside the branches.

She could not make him out, but she could discern a human figure in the tree, and, guessing whom it was, urged him to approach.

He was just about to comply, when suddenly a trooper, named Gaskell, appeared round the corner of the house.

For a few moments he stood as though uncertain which way to go.

Then, as though he had made up his mind to remain where he was, as a sentry, he took up his position on the lawn.

The girl drew back at once into the house without his noticing her.

"Curse him!" thought Ned, "is he going to stay there all night?"

The man kept pacing up and down, and casting keen glances around him, as though he thought it likely the fugitive would cross the open space.

He walked backwards and forwards, as on his beat, from the house to the edge of the lawn.

Every time he slightly lengthened his promenade, and at last it extended to the clump of trees amongst which the bushranger was concealed.

At length he paused at the end of one of these tramps, with his back to the trees.

At that moment a slight rustling sound in the tree behind him caught his ear.

He was on the point of turning round to discover its source, when all at once it seemed to him that a house had fallen on the top of him, and he dropped forward on his face perfectly senseless.

Ned had sprung from his perch, and alighted full on the top of him, almost breaking his neck.

Satisfied of the trooper's insensibility, the bushranger darted across the lawn to the house.

Jess met him at the window.

"I'm here," she whispered, "they are all at the back of the house, and no one will see you. Quick, take off your boots" she continued, as he entered the room.

Ned complied, and the girl led him cautiously upstairs to her bedroom.

"I am going to leave you here, and lock the door on the outside," she said, when about to quit him.

"What?" he cried, hoarsely, catching her by the arm.

"It is the best plan," she answered, "for then, if they search the house, they will never dream you are concealed here. Later on, I will join you, and arrange for your escape."

When the stunned trooper was discovered no further proof was needed that the fugitive was, or had been, close at hand.

But Gaskell could not tell in what direction Ned had gone, and the turf had not taken the imprint of his footsteps.

It was resolved to search the house, though Jess, like all the other inmates, vowed she had neither seen nor heard anyone.

As there was no reason to suspect her she was believed.

A search, however, took place, and in his place of concealment Ned heard the tramp of feet ascending the stairs.

He thrust his hand in his pocket to feel for the revolver that since his struggle with Mendez had never quitted him for a moment.

To his horror it was missing.

In his mad race through the timber he had lost it.

The footsteps paused outside the door, and the perspiration started from his forehead as he drew himself up prepared to dart out the moment the door opened.

But to his great relief a voice said, "He can't be here, the door is locked on the outside."

The next moment he heard the pursuers descend the stairs, and all was unbroken silence.

CHAPTER CXLIV.

THUNDER AND LIGHTNING.

NED, as the time went by, began to grow bitterly weary.

He had every confidence in Jess's devotion, but spite of this doubts would steal across his mind.

He kept wondering what had become of her, and why she had not returned.

The minutes went by like hours as he was occupied with these reflections, and the suspense began to grow intolerable.

A clock in the basement of the house struck midnight, and each stroke seemed to reverberate dolefully in his breast.

Almost immediately after, and, as if responding to the signal, a low muttered grumbling sound was heard in the distance and a flash of pale light lit up the darkness of the room for about a second.

Then all again was dark and silent.

The flash of lightning and the distant muttering were the forerunners of a storm on the point of bursting forth.

A sudden hope rose in Ned's breast, and he started to his feet.

"Thunder and lightning!" he muttered, "nothing could serve me better. The one will show me the way, and the other drown the noise I shall make in getting off. If the girl is only square, all is as right as a trivet. I wish she'd come. I've a good mind if she's not here in another quarter of an hour to risk it alone."

About ten minutes elapsed.

At the end of this time, Ned, whose ears were on the alert, caught the noise of approaching footsteps on the landing outside the door.

"I suppose it's her," he thought, "but it's as well to be prepared," and grasping a chair he held it in readiness to hurl at the intruder.

He heard the door open almost noiselessly and the dazzling light of another flash showed him a female figure standing on the threshold.

It was Jess.

She carried no light, and next instant darkness resumed its sway.

Where are you, Ned?" she asked, in an almost inaudible whisper.

"Here!" he growled.

Closing the door behind her, she advanced on tiptoe in the direction of his voice.

Another flash of lightning revealed that her hair was rather more disordered than it ought to have been, that her face was rather flushed, and that her bosom was heaving with the effects of past or present emotion.

She sat down by Ned, and the bushranger, despite the perils surrounding him, passed one arm around her waist and drew her towards him for a kiss.

"Stow that, Ned, there's a good fellow," said the girl, "I'm in an awful pucker how I'm to get you away, and we must manage it at once, somehow."

"How's it to be done?"

"Ah! that's just it."

"Can you let me out of the door below?"

"No, they are locked, and Mr. Fielding has the keys."

"And the windows?"

"No chance, the noise of opening them would arouse the sentinels."

"The sentinels?"

"Yes, we have a whole lot of the police here."

"The devil you have? Come, tell me all that has happened."

Jess rapidly narrated what had taken place since the search.

Kenneth Rothsay had not been able to get over his idea that Ned was hiding close at hand.

Accordingly he had resolved to keep the sergeant and the four troopers close at hand and to resume the search at daybreak.

"I am certain the fellow is somewhere about, Mr. Field-

ing," he said, "and if we have to unroof the house we'll have him."

With the fact of Ned's vicinity thus strongly put before him, Mr. Fielding was only too glad to have the police on the premises as a safeguard.

At ten o'clock, however, a change in the arrangements was necessitated by the arrival of a messenger from Sydney requiring the presence of Captain Rothsay at once at Government House.

He had been obliged to ride off, but left word that a strict watch must be kept, and that if he were not back by daybreak the search was to begin without him.

The sergeant left in command posted a sentry with instructions to keep a watch over the front of the premises and another in the rear.

Then, with the remainder of his command, he took up his quarters in the kitchen.

Here Jess did her best to render life agreeable to them.

She listened to their compliments, laughed at their jokes, and did not show too much anger when an arm was slid round her waist and a moustached lip pressed to her cheek.

Furthermore, she obeyed the orders that Mr. and Mrs. Fielding had given to look after their creature comforts with the utmost zeal.

Not only was an ample supply of cold provisions set before them, but she whispered to the sergeant—

"Look here, I can't do it before the cook, but as soon as she goes up to bed I'll bring you a bottle of whisky."

This was carried out.

The cook went up first, Jess saying she would follow her in a minute, but, instead of doing so, she produced not one, but two, bottles of the promised spirits and sat drinking with the troopers till close on midnight.

Then, when the sergeant rose to see after the sentries, she took advantage to slip off to Ned.

"Look here," said Ned to her, "can't I manage it out of this window? I won't stop here to be caught at last like a wild dog in a pitfall."

"That way won't do," said the girl. "This window opens, you know, on the front of the house. There's a sentinel there and you would be shot down to a certainty before you could cross the lawn."

"Can you get me into a room looking on to the back?"

"Yes, there is an empty lumber-room."

"Let's go there."

Ned stooped down and took off his boots, and the pair crept quietly into the room she had spoken of.

The thunder and lightning continued, and were coming nearer and nearer, though as yet no rain had fallen.

Ned opened the window with every possible precaution to prevent a sound being heard.

Putting his head carefully out, he could distinguish the top of the verandah that ran round the house.

"Where is the stable?" he asked.

"That building to the left," was the answer.

"Good," he replied, as a flash of lightning showed him the building in question standing about ten yards to the left of the house. "Are all the horses in it?" he added, drawing in his head.

"Yes."

"Is there a fence all round the garden?"

"Yes."

"Any way out except through the gate going on to the road?"

"No. Stop a bit; there is a gap in the further corner, beyond the stable there, it is only stopped up by bushes."

"Can a horse clear them?"

"Marco Polo could," said the girl, with a remembrance of Ned's former escape freshly before her.

"Yes, but I haven't got Marco under my hand just now," remarked the bushranger, grimly.

He looked up at the sky as he spoke.

The night was a strange one.

One half the heavens displayed a dome of burnished silver, studded with innumerable stars.

But across the other an inky veil, the edge of which was

as sharply defined as that of a knife, was being slowly drawn.

From time to time a flash of dazzling light leapt forth from its blackness.

"We shall have it in bucketfuls in three minutes," said Ned, "and then I'll try for it."

At that moment they heard the sound of steps below.

The sergeant having visited his sentry in the front of the house, had come to look after the one entrusted with the guard of the rear.

They heard the man's challenge, and the officer's response, which was almost drowned by another clap of thunder.

"It's going to be a rough night," said the sentry, who happened to be Gaskell, the trooper, whose neck Ned had almost broken.

"Yes," was the answer, "no chance of your falling asleep with that row going on overhead."

"Going to sleep," growled the other; "every blessed bone in my carcase is aching too much for there to be any chance of that. If I could only lay my hands on the fellow, I'd give him something to remember his little game of leapfrog by."

"Well, keep a sharp lookout, for there may be something in the captain's idea that he is hiding hereabouts. Fire at once, without challenging, if you see anything suspicious. Here, I have brought you out a nip of whisky in the bottom of this bottle; it'll serve to keep the damp out if the rain comes down."

Another dazzling flash of light and crash of thunder followed.

The next moment, as if this had been the signal, a blinding cataract of rain descended.

The sergeant darted into the house, and directly he had gone the soldier incontinently took shelter under the verandah, on the roof of which the rain was beating with a noise almost deafening.

Ned put his arms round Jess, and, hugging her close, pressed a dozen kisses on her willing lips.

Then he swung himself out through the window.

His feet touched the roof of the verandah.

There was another crash of thunder, and profiting by this, he let go.

The tremendous noise of the storm drowned the noise he made

For a moment he lay flat and motionless on the roof, which sloped slightly, but not enough to render his position a very difficult one.

Then slowly he began to edge himself inch by inch towards the corner of the house.

Crawling like some gigantic lizard, with the rain descending like a cataract from the eaves above him, on his back, he made his way along.

The faint, scraping sound of his progress was drowned by the torrent of falling water beating on the roof of the verandah like a succession of rapid blows from a gigantic drumstick.

Even to the sentry beneath its shelter, the sounds were indistinguishable.

At length Ned reached the corner.

The verandah continued along the side of the house, and he made his way till he had arrived at the centre of that portion of it running along the side.

Here he paused

"It's pretty well certain," he reflected, "that the sentry in front here has followed the example of the sentry at the back, and has taken shelter under the verandah. Now if one is at the front and the other at the back, neither can see me if I jump down from the centre of this part of the concern. The only danger will be from the lightning, as I make my way to the stable."

He watched and waited.

Another flash of lightning lit up the scene.

Another clap of thunder followed.

Profiting by the noise of this, Ned slipped down one of the pillars of the verandah.

But instead of making his way at once to the stable, he flung himself flat on to the ground amongst the climbing plants at the base of the pillar, and rolled himself close up to the supports of the wooden flooring.

It was as well he did so.

The tramp of feet sounded on the floor, and the sentry in the front of the house hailed his comrade.

"Gaskell."

"Yes," was the answer.

"Did you hear anything just then?"

"No, only the thunder."

"I don't know, but it seemed to me I heard something on this side of the house. Keep a sharp lookout for the next flash"

At the next flash the two men strained their eyes.

It revealed to them the garden with its drenched trees and the stable discernible through the falling sheets of rain.

"All right," said Gaskell, "I'll go round and have a look at the other side."

As soon as he heard them move off Ned darted noiselessly over the saturated earth in the direction of the stable.

The door was on the latch, and, unfastening it, he darted in and closed it behind him.

Upwards of half-a-dozen horses were in the stalls, and, to his great joy, the majority were saddled.

It was impossible in the darkness to make anything like a choice.

He unfastened the first that came under his hand from the manger, slipped the bit into its mouth, tightened the girths, and led it to the door.

Then waiting for the next flash, he threw open the door at the moment the interval of darkness commenced, led out the horse, jumped into the saddle, and darted off in the direction of the gap in the fence of which Jess had spoken.

The sound of the rain drowned the noise of the horse's hoofs.

The two sentries, after all, however, were not keeping a bad lookout.

Passing back and front along the verandah, they halted every time the lightning flashed, in order to glance around them.

Glancing in the direction of the stable, Gaskell fancied he could distinguish that the door was open.

Doubting for a moment the evidence of his senses, he resolved to make sure, and awaited with anxiety the second flash.

There could be no doubt of it.

The stable-door was open.

To jump from the balcony, and to tear across the garden to the stable was the work of a moment.

In less than that he verified the fact that one of the horses was missing.

Stepping to the stable-door, he fired his carbine into the air and shouted to his comrade, who at once began to thunder at the door of the house.

Before five minutes had elapsed the troopers had all turned out and had mounted in hot haste.

By the light of a stable-lantern Ned's tracks were plainly discernible, and, remembering the opening in the fence, they headed at once in that direction, since it was impossible that he could have passed out of the front gate unobserved.

Jess, who had been observing the whole affair from the lumber-room window, darted back into her bedroom directly the alarm was given, and presently emerged, half-dressed, as though aroused from sleep.

"I don't think they'll catch him, considering he has a fair five minutes' start on a night like this," she murmured to herself.

CHAPTER CXLV.
PLAYING 'POSSUM.

NED's start was, however, in reality, less than either the girl or his pursuers imagined.

He was, even in a country of daring riders, acknowledged by one and all to be one of the finest horsemen that ever crossed a saddle.

Confident in his skill, he urged his horse straight at the gap in the fence, feeling certain that he could lift the beast over the barricade of thorns and brushwood with which it was blocked.

The horse, however, on which he had laid hands, though a powerful beast, was a heavily-built, lumbering kind of animal, and had not recovered from the fatigue of the three preceding days.

Twice he refused the jump, and when the third time Ned, gripping his ribs like a vice and taking well hold of his head, rammed him at the obstacle, he rose, it is true, but only to jump short and come floundering down amongst the brushwood just as Gaskell's carbine rang out.

There was nothing for the bushranger to do but to spring from the saddle and clear a passage for the struggling animal, which took some time.

At last the breach was cleared, and Ned, to whom every sound from the house in his rear acted as a spur, sprang into the saddle again with the hope that he would distance his foes.

The road from Sydney lay before him, and along this he galloped furiously, intending to strike off across country as soon as he got well into the open, with no chance of finding his career suddenly checked by a fence or other enclosure.

But, to his horror, he found himself unable to get anything like a decent rate of speed out of the exhausted and lumbering animal he bestrode.

In vain, in the absence of spurs, he touched up the brute with his pocket-knife.

The poor beast did its best, but it was evident that it could not long continue even at the pace he was then getting out of it.

"Oh for an hour of Marco Polo!" thought Ned, "to ride clear away from those crawlers," as, on arriving at the summit of a somewhat steep ascent, he became aware that the troopers were following closely on his track.

The men had slackened speed, though the lightning still continued, and a gust of wind carried the sound of their advancing hoofs to his ears.

He listened, and became convinced that they were gaining on him almost at every stride.

To add to his misfortunes, his horse, who also heard it, and recognised without doubt the presence of its habitual companions, neighed loudly in reply.

Digging his knife furiously into the poor brute, he urged it, at the risk every moment of breaking their necks, down the further side of the hill.

Nothing but his almost marvellous horsemanship saved them from going a cropper at least half a dozen times during his frantic descent.

At the bottom of the hill he turned sharply to the right, left the road, and struck off straight across country, in the hope that his pursuers would ride straight on along the road.

His hope was, however, destined to be frustrated.

At the very moment that he thus strove to double on his pursuers, the lightning, which had ceased for a few minutes, in a succession of brilliant flashes lit up the scene as far as the horizon.

The troopers had just gained the summit of the hill down which Ned had galloped, and from it they could plainly discern the fugitive vainly urging his exhausted steed across the plain below, as plainly, indeed, as if it had been day.

They uttered a simultaneous cry of triumph, which sounded clearly and ominously on Ned's ears.

Then one of them quitting the road in turn, at the summit of the hill, tore like a madman down the rugged slope.

His horse seemed to skim over the broken surface like some gigantic night-bird, rather than a four-footed animal, and the rider seemed as reckless concerning his own neck as Ned himself.

In an incredibly short time he was at the bottom of the hill, and speeding across the plain.

This rider was no other than Gaskell, whose debt of vengeance against Ned had been yet further increased by the events of the night.

It happened that the horse on which the bushranger had laid his hands was no other than that of the trooper.

Consequently when the order of pursuit was given, the latter found himself at a loss to obey it.

But amongst the animals in the stable was a magnificent thoroughbred belonging to Kenneth.

Acting on the principle that necessity knows no law, and trusting that excess of zeal would be accepted as an excuse for his action, Gaskell clapped a saddle on this animal and mounted with his comrades.

Thanks to the superiority of his mount he was able, on catching sight of Ned, to ride right away from them, and by the time he had gained the plain, had secured an advance of about a quarter of a mile.

A few minutes more and he was within pistol-shot of Ned.

"I've got you at last, my lad!" he growled, unsheathing his sabre.

The bushranger glanced back.

The case seemed hopeless.

The lightning showed him that the thoroughbred was gaining at every stride, and flashed on the gleaming blade held in the hand of its excited rider.

Ned was unarmed save for his knife.

He felt that further flight was impossible, for his horse was ready to sink under him at every stride, whilst resistance against six men armed to the teeth seemed equally hopeless.

He began to wonder why Gaskell did not open fire on him at once.

"It looks like a case of all up," he thought; "but at any rate they shall only get my carcase."

And he resolved to fight tooth and nail like a wild beast until they killed him rather than surrender.

Suddenly his horse, winded and urged beyond its strength, fell under him so suddenly that it almost seemed as though one of the flashes of lightning that from time to time darted from the heavens had stricken it to the earth.

As it fell, Ned disengaged his feet from the stirrups, and, by a desperate effort, succeeded in preventing himself from being shot over the animal's head.

Nevertheless he was thrown forward in the saddle.

As he struggled to recover himself his hand encountered something cold and hard.

It was the butt of a pistol kept in the holster!

A cry of joy almost escaped him at this unlooked-for discovery.

Quick as lightning he plunged his hand into the other holster, which he found similarly provided.

This was the reason Gaskell had not fired.

He had left his pistols in the holster, and had not found time to reload the carbine with which he had given the alarm.

Ned was a man of quick resolutions and fertile in resource.

He at once hit on a plan which promised to ensure his escape.

It was "playing 'possum."

Taking a pistol in each hand, he disengaged himself from his horse and threw himself flat on his back beside the animal, which seemed unable or unwilling to rise.

Stretched thus upon the ground after a violent fall he appeared dead or stunned, and Gaskell, coming up at full gallop, did not doubt this for a moment, but exclaimed to himself with glee—

"Now I've got him!"

The trooper reined in his horse.

Springing to the ground, he slipped his left arm through

the reins and bent over the prostrate figure of Ned in order to ascertain whether the bushranger showed any signs of life.

Kelly had foreseen this movement, and was prepared for it accordingly.

As the trooper bent over him he raised his right arm with the speed of thought and pulled the trigger.

His aim had been a sure one, for the muzzle had almost touched his victim's head.

Shot through the brain the trooper fell forward upon the man whom a moment before he had considered so completely in his power, and whose face and garments he deluged with his blood.

Casting off the dead body with an exulting curse and triumphant chuckle, Ned sprang to his feet.

Then, disengaging the reins from the arm of the corpse, he sprang with one bound into the saddle of the thoroughbred.

The noble animal recognised the hand of a master, and, to Ned's reminders, darted off at a rate which promised soon to shake off all pursuit.

The sergeant at the head of the little troop had seen by the aid of the flashes of lightning the horse which Kelly was riding fall, and Gaskell come up with the dismounted fugitive.

He heard the shot, and, imagining it was the trooper who had fired, spurred furiously on, shouting at the top of his voice—

"Don't kill him—take him alive!"

What was his horror to find, on reaching the fallen horse, that the corpse stretched beside it was not that of Ned, but of Gaskell, and that the fugitive had obtained a start which, mounted as he was on a horse fresher and faster than those of any of his pursuers, rendered all hope of riding him down utterly futile.

CHAPTER CXLVI.
TEN THOUSAND POUNDS REWARD.

WHILST the troopers were gathered round the corpse of their unfortunate comrade, Ned, bending over his new mount's neck, continued to push onward at full speed, heedless of all obstacles.

His only idea was to distance his pursuers, and also put as great a distance as possible between himself and Sydney before daybreak.

For three hours he held on his way, until the heaving sides of his horse warned him that he was pushing the poor beast too far.

He saw that he must slacken his pace, or the same fate would again overtake him as had befallen him with the trooper's exhausted animal.

Besides, he reflected that the start he had now gained had put him out of all immediate danger.

Consequently, he gradually slackened his horse's pace to a walk.

Day broke and revealed around him a wide plain dotted with scattered clumps of timber, and bounded by a distant range of hills.

He strained his eyes in search of a dwelling, but in vain.

He saw something, however, infinitely less pleasant.

It was neither more nor less than what looked like a sheet of paper stuck up against a tree-trunk.

On riding up he found it to be one of the police handbills, offering a reward of ten thousand pounds for his apprehension.

Another and another soon met his eye.

The vast silent bush was filled with these mute denunciations of his crimes.

Even in this apparently trackless solitude, only occasionally traversed by shepherd, stockman, or teamster, his crimes had proclaimed him an outcast and a felon, had set a price on his head, and called on all good men and true to join in hunting him down like a wolf.

As he rode on, he saw on tree trunk after tree-trunk, posted up by the sides of those advertisements of "Holloway's Pills and Ointment," with which the whole Australian Continent has been so lavishly beplastered, the same white police-bill, with its terribly significant lines, "Murder! £10,000 Reward!"

And below a full description of himself.

"This is getting altogether too boiling," he muttered, and instinctively urged on his jaded horse.

Steering by the sun that had just risen, he continued to ride away from Sydney.

At length he caught sight of a column of smoke rising behind some trees, and pushed on cautiously in its direction.

He soon came in sight of a shepherd's hut.

Halting for a moment, he proceeded to reflect whether it would be safe to advance, since, with the exception of the undischarged pistol, he was without means of defence.

It behoved him, therefore, to be cautious, lest he should fall into the company of foes.

Watching the hut, he noticed a man come to the door, shake a rug, and then retire.

He came to the conclusion that this was the hut-keeper, and that the shepherd had probably already started to the ranges with his sheep.

After waiting a little longer, he resolved at all hazards, to put this surmise to the test, and pursued his way to the little dwelling.

As he drew near the same man that he had seen before, a sullen-looking, beetle-browed fellow of about thirty, with a face presenting a compound of imbecility and cunning, again come to the door with a pail in his hand.

He stepped across the threshold and advanced some steps, and then, suddenly catching sight of Ned—whose approach at a walking pace he had not heard, on account of the softness of the saturated turf—he started back, with a mingled look of surprise and terror.

It seemed as though he was about to bolt back into the house, but Kelly did not give him time.

"Hullo! mate," he cried, "whose place is this?"

"Mr. Morley's," was the answer, in a sullen tone.

"How far am I from Sydney?"

"Close on thirty miles."

"You can give me some grub, I suppose?" said Ned, dismounting, and feeling sure of that hospitality never refused to the wayfarer in the colonies.

The man continued to stare at him, and muttered some unintelligible answer.

"Hell and fury, mate!" cried Ned, his suspicions rapidly aroused by the man's manner, "what the devil makes you stare at me like that, man? Do you know me, eh?"

The fellow looked more confused than ever.

"That blood," he muttered.

"What blood?" thundered Ned, who had forgotten that, when he had shot Gaskell, the blood of his victim had spurted all over him.

"Why, your own, I should have thought," replied the other, with a look of suspicion. "Don't you know you're smothered in it, face and all?"

The recollection of the death-struggle of Gaskell recurred to Ned.

With an effort he recovered himself.

"Well, I daresay I do look something like a butcher in a slaughter-house, mate," he said with an attempt at joviality; "but you needn't be scared on my account. The blood's none of mine, but comes from as big a scoundrel as ever tried to plunder a poor chap of his hard-earned dibs. It comes from one of Ned Kelly's gang."

"Ned Kelly's gang!"

"Yes. Just give me a swig of something to clear my throat—for I am as dry as a lime-kiln—and I'll tell you all about it."

The curiosity of the other was excited by this, and he stepped into the hut, followed by Ned, to whom he at once handed a pannikin of tea.

The bushranger would have preferred something

stronger, but he swallowed it gratefully, being parched and exhausted.

"I suppose you wouldn't be sorry to get some of the blood off your face? You don't seem to know it, but it covers you like a mask," said the hut keeper.

"All right. Get me a bucket of water, mate, and I'll soon get rid of it Only I'll put my beast to rights first," answered Ned.

He passed out of the hut, followed by the hut-keeper —who continued to eye him with something like suspicion—and proceeded to rub down his horse, in which occupation the other lent him a hand with seeming willingness.

"It's a decent beast you've got there," said the hut-keeper.

"Yes," replied Kelly.

"But you must have taken something out of him last night to bring him into this state," continued the hut-keeper, critically scanning the animal, whose hair was matted with sweat, and its legs and belly caked with half-dried mud.

"I just think I did," responded Kelly, "considering I had to ride for my life."

"Ah! How was that?"

"I was bound for Sydney, and being in a bit of a hurry I pushed on through the night, thinking to reach a station I know, where I could get a fresh horse. I never thought of any dangers, when all at once in the darkness two fellows popped out of the bush and seized the bridle. There was a bit of a scuffle, and one of them pulled trigger at me, but, luckily, the cap had, I suppose, fallen off, and his pistol did not go off. However, they pulled me out of the saddle and got me down. One had got his knee on me, and the other was trying to check my horse from bolting, when I drew a pistol and shot the fellow holding me. He fell on me and deluged me in blood. I jumped up, knocked over the other, and got into the saddle. Just as I did so, two shots were fired from the bush, and not knowing how many more there might be, I was off like a shot."

"By Jove! a close shave," said the hut-keeper.

"I could hear horses' hoofs behind me, and drove ahead at top speed, till in the end my beast got the bit between his teeth and fairly bolted, and by the time I pulled him up, I'm hanged if I knew where I was."

"Ah! I see. I wondered how it was that you said you were bound for Sydney, when you rode up here turning your back on it," remarked the hut-keeper, with a grin. "I suppose they were some of Ned Kelly's gang?"

"Of course; no one else is about here now, is there?"

"No. Could you make out what sort of a fellow it was you bowled over?"

"Well, it was as dark as soot, but as far as I could judge he was a cross-built fellow with a beastly ugly mug."

"Hum, then it wouldn't be Kelly himself."

"Why not?" enquired the bushranger.

"Oh! Kelly's not at all a bad-looking chap, and I know his description by heart. I've got one of the police hand-bills in the hut, and I've studied it over often enough. They are stuck up over the bush, too, so that anyone may read."

"The deuce you have," thought Ned.

"I should know him if I set eyes on him, but I never ran across him yet, though I did meet one of his gang the other day."

"Oh, how was that?"

"I'll tell you. But you'd better give yourself a sluice, and come inside and wolf something."

The horse was rubbed down by this time, and Ned, after sluicing the blood off his face, entered the hut, and began to devour a meal of cold chops the other set before him.

The hut-keeper lit his pipe, and sat down on a stool.

He eyed his guest curiously and closely.

"Well," said Ned, between two mouthfuls, "how about your meeting with Kelly's gang?"

"Oh, it would take a long time in telling," replied the hut-keeper. "I had been down to the station to get the month's supply of flour and groceries, and was coming back through the bush with the load on the back of an old pony, when all at once a big fellow with an awful squint stepped right out in front of me. I kind of guessed what he was, but you know the bushrangers never meddle with us, so I just gave him good-day and was going on, when—

"'What have got there in that bag?' says he.

"'Flour and such like,' I said.

"'Well, just hand it over.'

"I said, 'It's too bad to want to take a poor chap's victuals like that. You'll get me in a blessed row with the boss; he'll never believe I've been stuck up.'

"'Oh, that be blowed!' says he. 'Hand over the bag, straight,' and he whips out a pistol, and covers me as if I'd been a parrot.

"There was nothing to be done, and I gives him the bag, and he was off into the bush without even a thank-you, before you could say knife.

"And a blessed fine row I got into with my mates when they found there was no damper, and with the boss, who stuck out that I ought to have kept the things at any cost. I'd have liked to have seen him risking his blessed neck for the sake of a few pounds of mouldy old flour."

And the hut-keeper puffed savagely at his pipe.

"A tall, squint-eyed fellow, did you say he was?" enquired Ned.

"Yes."

"Sandy beard?"

"Yes. Do you know him?"

"No; but it seems to me, as well as I could make out by the lightning, that the chap I sent to kingdom come last night was just about such another."

"And a very good job if it was," growled the hut-keeper, who all through the meal had been eyeing Ned with an attention that the latter could not help feeling uneasy about.

"I suppose," he said, "that since it is known Kelly's gang are about here, the police are on the alert after them?"

"Oh, the police are a pack of asses. No one cares a rap about them; they'll never do any good," said the hut-keeper, who probably at some period of his career had come into disagreeable contact with the authorities in question. "But a lot of the leading squatters have banded together to hunt the fellows out of the district, and they'll find it very difficult work trying to get away from men who know every inch of the country."

"Just so," said Ned.

"I only wish I could catch sight of the chap who boned my flour," continued the hut-keeper. "I'd bowl him over pretty quick." And as he spoke he glanced at a gun in one corner of the hut.

Then he turned his attention again on his guest, and continued his examination of his features.

Ned, having finished his repast, rose.

"Look here mate," he said; "my name is George Dawes, and I've got a little station up the Macquarie. If ever you are that way I won't forget the turn you've done me; but in case you don't, here's something for your trouble."

And he handed him a sovereign.

This very act of liberality served to confirm the other's suspicion.

A man who paid so high a price for an act of hospitality that would have been amply repaid by the gift of a fig of tobacco must be a queer customer.

As Ned got into the saddle and was about to ride off, the hut-keeper darted back into the hut, muttering—

"I am certain it's him. I can't be mistaken. But if it is I'll land him. The reward is too good to be lost. Ten thousand pounds! Oh, crikey! I'd be a swell for life; have my own shay, and lush for a dozen.

When he stepped outside his door again, his gun was in his hand.

Kelly had moved slowly away, and was about twenty paces off.

"Ned!" shouted the hut-keeper.

Mechanically, on hearing his name, Kelly checked his horse and turned in the saddle.

"Yes," he answered, unconsciously betraying himself.

"You've forgotten something."

"What?" said Ned, turning his horse round, and preparing to return to the hut.

"That you're worth a fortune, dead or alive."

And as he spoke, the hut-keeper raised his gun and fired straight at the bushranger.

CHAPTER CXLVII.
FAMILIAR FACES.

THE shot sped.

Ned felt the thoroughbred bound convulsively beneath him.

Uttering a fearful oath, Ned, his eyes blazing with anger and vengeance, sprung from his horse, but stuck to the reins, and drawing his pistol, dashed after the hut-keeper, who, having discharged his gun, was about to re-enter the hut.

Ned knew he now had the fellow at his mercy, and approaching the cowering dog with a ferocious expression in his firmly set teeth and glistening glances, roared out a volley of not very choice adjectives at the would-be murderer, who felt his attempt deserved and would meet with no mercy at the hands of Kelly.

He was livid with fear, and saw his only chance was to make a rush for it out of the hut.

Kelly felt he had no time to lose, even for vengeance, and sending the contents of his pistol into his enemy's body, quickly remounted and was off.

The traitor uttered a loud cry, and stumbled over the threshold.

The ball that had been destined for Kelly entered the animal's neck.

Ned had not noticed this; and when, after about ten minutes, the pace of the thoroughbred visibly slackened he attributed it to the fatigue of the preceding night, and urged the poor brute on in order to gain the shelter of a belt of woodland discernible at some distance.

Neither spur nor hand was able to get much more out of the gallant animal.

The noble creature made a last effort, and cleared the space separating them from the trees.

But no sooner did Ned draw rein in order to slacken his pace on entering their shelter than the poor brute fell.

A convulsive shudder shook his limbs, and, stretching them out in one final quiver, he lay motionless.

It was only then that Ned became fully aware of the extent of the mischief.

What he had taken for simple exhaustion was actually death.

A fearful oath burst from his lips, and, in his rage, he fiercely kicked the stiffening corpse of the creature who had served his end so well and to whom he owed his life.

He cursed the luck that deprived him of a horse at the moment when one was needed.

It was indeed necessary that he should put as great a distance between himself and the district in which he now found himself as soon as possible.

The hut-keeper had told him that the depredations of men whom, he had no doubt, belonged to his band had roused the country-side against them, and that, probably, they would be tracked like wild beasts.

And now the slaughter of the hut-keeper would inevitably lead to this result.

It was necessary to get away at all cost, since, if the hut-keeper were only wounded he could put the shepherds on the scent when they returned to hut; and, even if he were dead, there would be efforts made to track his murderer as soon as the body was discovered.

Ned determined to try to steal a horse from the next station he came across.

He took from the holsters of the saddle the pistols, now useless, since he had no means of re-loading them, and thrust them into a belt which he fashioned from the stirrup-leathers.

He was in hopes of coming across someone who would supply him with ammunition.

After glancing round to make certain that there were as yet no signs of pursuit, he plunged into the bush.

For two hours he made his way onwards, working in the direction of a range of hills he could perceive in the distance.

At length he reached the foot of the first slope, which he began to ascend, after first bathing his face and hands in a little stream that trickled at its base.

Despite the herculean strength with which he was gifted, and the terrible danger that kept spurring him on every moment to fresh exertions, fatigue and want of sleep had begun to tell upon his iron frame.

His legs seemed at times ready to give way under him, and the inequalities of the ascent caused him from time to time to stop and stagger like a drunken man.

A dozen times he was on the point of throwing himself down and taking the rest of which he was in such sore need.

(To be continued.)

NED KELLY
THE IRONCLAD
AUSTRALIAN BUSHRANGER

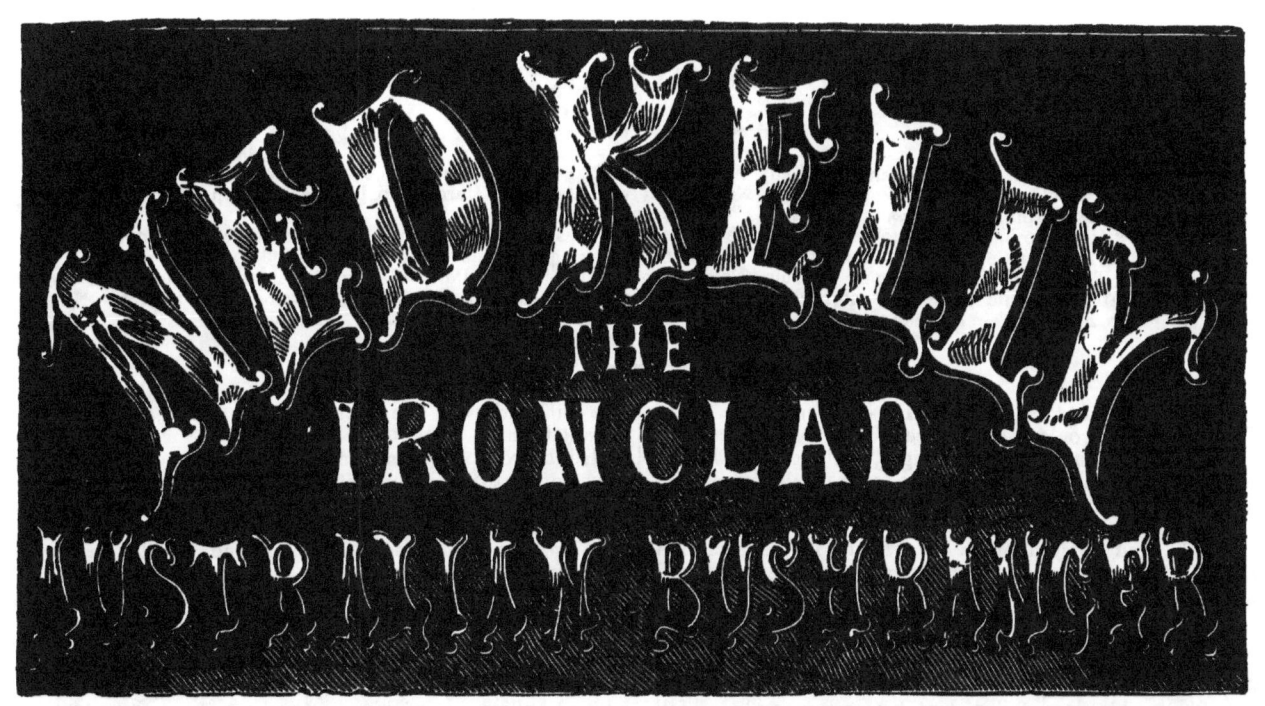

NO 25,

NED KELLY: IRONCLAD BUSHRANGER.

CHAPTER CXLVII.—*Continued.*

"No," he would mutter, resolutely trying to shake off the overpowering effects of fatigue, "I'll go on, I'll go on, till I find a safe landing-place to lie in till nightfall."

He made his way up the slope, though each moment his progress seemed more difficult.

His head swam, there was a ringing in his ears, and from time to time a mist passed before his eyes, and veiled the rocks and crags that he kept scanning as he advanced in the hope of discovering some hiding-place.

"There must be some hole about here that I can creep into, and the stones luckily will show no trace of my passage," he thought.

Twice his legs failed him altogether, and he fell heavily, but, game to the end, he rose again and staggered onward.

At length his expectations were realised.

On the right, beneath a projecting spur of rock, he caught sight of what appeared to be the entrance of a cave, partly veiled by brushwood.

He made his way to it with some difficulty, across the broken ground.

The opening was low and narrow, but, after crawling through it, he found himself in a kind of cave, some ten or twelve feet deep, and almost high enough for him to stand upright.

It was perfectly dry, the floor being of gravel, on which were strewn some large boulders, that had evidently fallen at some remote period from the summit.

Ned dragged himself into the cave, and, moving some of the stones, constructed a rude barricade just within the entrance.

This precaution taken, he stretched himself at full length on the gravel, and, despite the hardness of his couch, was soon fast asleep.

His was the heavy slumber of exhaustion, which a cannon-shot will hardly break.

When he awoke he was in utter darkness.

He moved to the mouth of the cave, and, after cautiously demolishing his barricade, sallied forth.

Night had come on, clear and starlit, and he at once glanced to the heavens in quest of the Southern cross, in order to steer his way by this Australian substitute for the Pole star.

Ned had recovered from his fatigue, but he felt fearfully hungry.

"Curse it all. I wish I'd got a bit of 'bacca, even," he growled.

He continued to make his way up the slope, which was evidently one of the bottom spurs of the range of hills.

The ascent became every moment more difficult in the darkness as the hours went on.

Several times he nearly missed his footing, and more than once was really puzzled as to how he should advance.

At length, after missing his footing and rolling down a steep incline, he lit upon what, as far as he could make out in the darkness, had some resemblance to a beaten track.

Its sides were bordered, however, by steep rocks, amongst which it wound.

Suddenly a new incident caused Ned to forget at once the difficulties of the route and the hunger that had assailed him.

He heard about ten paces off a sound which those accustomed to it have no difficulty in recognising.

It was the click of a gun-lock.

The next moment a tall figure stepped from behind a tree growing at the side of the path, and, levelling a gun, exclaimed in a hoarse voice—

"Halt, or I fire."

Ned's first thought was that he was in the presence of the men engaged in hunting out his followers.

"If there is a gang, luck's against me," he thought: "but if there's only one I'll try to funk the beggar."

And pulling one of his empty pistols from his belt, he cocked and levelled it with the speed of thought, shouting as he did so—

"Stow that. Drop your gun or you are a dead man, you blasted bushranger."

"Hi! hullo! stop, don't fire!" yelled the stranger, as soon as Ned had spoken.

"Drop your gun before I count three, or I'll drop you," said Kelly, advancing in order, if possible, to grapple with his foe before the latter was aware of his intention.

"All right, Ned, don't be in such a blessed hurry," replied the other, complying with the order. "Don't you know me?"

"What! Zeph?" exclaimed Ned.

"Yes, Ned, I and Salmon Roe are here; and, what I suppose will gladden your heart to know, we've got Marco Polo all right at hand."

"Yes," replied Ned, "and a pretty couple of fools you and Salmon Roe have been making of yourselves."

"What do you mean?"

"Hasn't it always been my standing order only to take from those who could afford it, and never to meddle with a poor man, eh?"

"Yes."

"Isn't that the only way to have friends and spies amongst all the hut-keepers and the shepherds and the like, so that one may be sure of help and information as to what the police are up to?"

"Yes," replied the other with a downcast air, for he began to see what Ned was driving at.

"Well, then, what do you mean by plundering such people? What the devil put you up to such a mean trick as to rob a poor, honest, hard-working hut-keeper of a few mouthfuls of victuals?"

Ned thundered out this moral lesson, as he considered it, in the most impressive fashion

Zeph continued to look downcast, and really began to feel ashamed.

Besides, he was tremendously puzzled as to how Ned had become acquainted in such an accurate fashion with his malpractices.

If he had only known that Kelly had just put a bullet into the "poor, honest, hard-working hut-keeper" in question, not only would his astonishment have ceased, but he might have been tempted to enquire whether robbing a man did him more harm than shooting him.

"Come," continued Ned, "I don't want to cut up rough

with such an old pal, but you must see that such a game can only end in rousing the whole country against us. What other devil's tricks have you been up to since we parted?"

"Why, the fact is that the country is pretty well roused against us as it is. Those cursed bills with the reward have set men's mouths watering, and neither Salmon Roe nor myself has dared to go into a hut or approach a station, lest we should be mistaken for you and shot down off-hand, or else collared as belonging to your gang."

"Yes," said Ned, meditatively, "you are right. Things are getting too hot in this quarter. I think we had either better knock off work altogether for a spell and lie close, or else cross the herring-pond."

Whilst they had been speaking, Zeph had been piloting his captain across the tolerably smooth track leading almost parallel to that by which he had ascended the hill.

It ended in a small natural basin almost entirely filled with trees.

Through their trunks the glow of a fire was discernible, but so steep were the sides of the hollow and so remote its situation, that the flames could only have been sighted by someone coming along the path they were traversing.

A figure lounging beside the fire started up at their approach and raised a gun.

It was Salmon Roe.

A whistle from Zeph assured him that they were friends approaching, and a minute later he was welcoming Ned.

A huge frying-pan was soon brought into requisition, and chops, cut from the carcase of a sheep hanging to the bough of a tree, were fried for supper.

Ned glanced at the sheep.

"Where did you get that mutton?"

"Why, to tell you truth," said Zeph, in an apologetic fashion, "we had to bone it off Morley's run the other day, we were so sharp set. We can't starve, and, as I told you before, we daren't show our faces."

Ned smoked in silence for a few minutes.

"Where's Marco Polo?" he asked, abruptly.

"Close handy, and your iron plates too. Shall I bring him?"

"Yes, and bring the armour, and give me some powder and bullets. You've raised such a hornets' nest about us that we may have to bolt at any moment."

After examining his horse, Ned reloaded the pistols of the dead trooper.

"I feel a little more able to take my own part than I did half-an-hour ago," he remarked, "when I tried to bully you with an empty pistol."

"An empty pistol!" cried Zeph.

"Yes," answered Ned. "You'll never have such another chance of getting rid of me, as you had then," and he laughed grimly.

Though he said this as if in jest he was not exactly easy in his mind, remembering the treachery of former comrades.

Tracked and harassed as they were, Zeph and Salmon Roe might be tempted to give him up to secure immunity for themselves.

"Look here, boys," he said, after a pause, "I've got a plan that I think we had better act on."

"Spit it out," said Salmon Roe.

"You two had better start to-morrow for the Murrumbidgee, where you are not known, and be quiet for a month or two. You must take Marco Polo with you and leave him there. Then get quietly down to the coast and ship for England."

"For England?"

"Yes. I am going there; this is too hot for me."

"Are you going with us?"

"No. I must get back to Sydney, despite the risk, because I have got a lot of plunder buried there. I shall lie by in the day-time, and travel at night. Once in the town I can disguise myself thoroughly, and take my passage before the very nose of the police."

After dividing the money he had about him with his two pals, and arranging for their meeting in England, Ned and Salmon Roe lay down beside the fire, leaving Zeph on the watch.

CHAPTER CXLVIII
CAPTURED.

THE following morning Zeph and Salmon Roe started, leaving Ned monarch of all he surveyed.

His idea was to keep quiet all day, and set out on his travels at nightfall.

If he saw a chance of doing so, he meant to procure a horse.

"Procure," to his mind, had a very elastic signification, like Shakespeare's "Convey."

It meant either to buy one, if he saw a chance of doing so without arousing any suspicion as to his identity, or to steal one, and after riding to the outskirts of the town to turn it loose.

As he meant to travel at night he judged that a good long nap in the afternoon would do him no harm.

The recollection of the cave in which he passed the preceding day occurred to him.

He resolved to take shelter in it.

He took up a gun which Salmon Roe had left him, and made his way towards it.

Creeping into it, he stretched himself on a rug with which his friends had also provided him, and, lighting his pipe, found himself exceedingly comfortable.

Meanwhile, things had been taking a very unfavourable turn as regarded his prospects of reaching Sydney.

The hut-keeper whom he had fired at was only wounded.

He was unable to leave the hut and give an alarm, but on the shepherds' returning home he informed them of the occurrence.

The police were at once communicated with, for the hut-keeper made out that Kelly had made a brutal and unprovoked attack on him, and thereby aroused a feeling of sympathy with himself, and disgust against the bushranger.

He was very careful not to say that he had fired first, with a view of gaining the reward.

The news reached Kenneth Rothsay.

The young chief of the police had begun to feel something like a personal animosity growing up against the daring ruffian who had so often foiled him.

On learning that Ned had been seen on Mr. Morley's station, he at once started for it.

Travelling through the night, he reached the shepherds' hut at daybreak the morning after the struggle.

A number of people were assembled there, for the most part settlers of the better class, who had reason to dread Ned's depredations.

Kenneth at once assumed the direction of operations.

The tracks by which Kelly had left the hut were so cut up by others as to be almost effaced, and to attempt to pick them out seemed hopeless.

At length it was suggested that a shepherd in the neighbourhood had a dog of wonderful skill and sagacity that might be of service.

A considerable time was lost in sending for the animal and its owner, but at length they arrived.

A fresh difficulty was to get the man to consent to take part in the chase; but at length he agreed to try.

It was in vain, however, that a handkerchief left behind by Ned was shown the dog, for he could not or would not track him.

At last someone explained the reason.

Kelly had left on horseback.

The case seemed hopeless again, when a scout who had been sent out returned with the news that a dead horse had been found just within the nearest timber.

Its description tallied with that given by the hut-keeper of the animal ridden by the bushranger.

A party headed by Kenneth at once rode off to the spot in question, but by this time it was getting late in the day.

The dog was again brought into requisition, and after some trouble was put on Ned's track.

Fortunately no one else had passed that way, and the animal, having at length made out what was required of him, went along steadily on the trail.

Kenneth followed close at hand.

At length the track led up into the hills, and the pursuers, on reaching the foot of the slope Ned had ascended, were obliged to abandon their horses.

They scrambled after the dog on foot, and Kenneth, in his eagerness, far outstripped the remainder.

Kenneth saw the dog dart with a growl into a hole beneath a projecting spur of rock.

Before he could follow it across the broken ground, a figure darted from the mouth of the cave, and, catching sight of the young chief of the police, turned and fled upwards along a narrow and broken path.

It was Ned, whose slumbers had been rudely disturbed by the sudden arrival of the dog, which had rushed into the cave when following the track taken by the bushranger the day before.

On seeing it, he guessed the purpose to which it had been put.

Not knowing how close the pursuers were at hand, he refrained from firing, lest he should guide them by the report, and, seizing a huge stone, dashed it bang on to the head of the unfortunate animal.

Then, seizing his gun, he rushed out as described.

Kenneth started in hot pursuit, and the remainder of the tracking party on reaching the spot found their leader had disappeared.

Their only guide as to the direction which he had taken was a distant shout, evidently given to guide them in the now thickening gloom.

Following in the direction from which this proceeded, they advanced some way at a slow rate, when suddenly the report of a gun at a considerable distance ahead inspired them to fresh exertions.

Meanwhile Kenneth had kept on in hot pursuit of Ned.

Young, active, agile, and accustomed in his youth to scramble over the hills and crags of Scotland, the chief of the police was perhaps a better mountaineer than the bushranger.

As regarded training they were both in very fair condition, for the sea voyage and the days since spent in the saddle by Kenneth had completely recovered him from the effects of his London life of frivolous dissipation.

But Ned knew he was running for life, and this made him put forth a pace that Kenneth had all his work cut out to equal.

Gradually, however, the bulk of the bushranger began to tell, and he began to find his progress more difficult as the ascent grew steeper.

The leap from rock to rock jarred his mighty frame.

Bitterly he longed for Marco Polo, and cursed the luck that had led him to separate himself from his gallant steed.

He saw, however, one chance.

It was rapidly getting dusk, and if he could only prolong the chase a little while longer, he would have a very fair prospect of getting off in the darkness, when pursuit amongst the hills would be quite out of the question.

He would have had no hesitation in stopping and grappling his pursuer, who would have been almost a child in his herculean hands, but he judged the duration of a struggle would have afforded his pursuers time to arrive on the scene, and by numbers overpower him.

From time to time he glanced back, and his hopes revived at seeing only one pursuer.

He wondered why Kenneth did not fire, but the latter had resolved not to do so if he could possibly avoid it, being desirous at all hazards to take Ned alive.

The track the two were now pursuing led between two precipitous walls of limestone.

A short distance ahead it turned abruptly to the right.

Ned put on a desperate spurt, hoping to get out of sight round this corner, and thus effect his escape.

Kenneth in turn redoubled his efforts.

He saw the bushranger turn the corner, and just at that moment his foot caught against a loose pebble and he almost fell.

When he recovered himself, Ned had disappeared round the angle.

He hastened onward.

Rounding it in turn, he found himself in face of a small natural amphitheatre, some forty feet across.

The bare limestone sides rose almost perpendicularly to a height of twenty feet.

The surface of the soil forming the floor was covered with smooth green turf, dotted here and there with a few dwarf shrubs.

Kenneth stood at the narrow opening which seemed the only way in, and gazed round him in amazement.

The perpendicular sides defied all attempts at further progress, the bushes would hardly have given shelter to a rabbit, and yet Kelly had vanished.

It was impossible that he could have scaled the rocks, and equally impossible that he could have hidden himself in the bushes.

Kenneth caught sight of something like a dark fissure in the rocks on the further side.

He stepped into the little amphitheatre, pistol in hand.

"If you move a step nearer you are a dead man," rang out the outlaw's challenge, and the barrel of a gun was protruded from the fissure that had attracted his attention.

Kenneth feared no single man on earth, and stalked onward.

"Go back," roared Ned, "go back. I've sworn to lay low the first man that steps over that strip of turf. Back, or I fire."

"Fire, then, for I have sworn to take you back to Sydney tied to my horse's tail, or wet the turf with my heart's blood. Fire then," he added, though at the same time he veered to one side instinctively.

A bright flash shot forth in reply from the fissure, but his aim for once failed him, and the bullet merely grazed Kenneth's cheek.

Thrusting his pistol almost contemptuously into his belt, and unsheathing the heavy sabre he had retained in his hand during the pursuit, Kenneth sprang forward.

As he did so a figure, looking gigantic in the dim light, bounded from the fissure with clubbed gun to meet him.

A fearful downward blow shivered his weapon in his grasp; but, darting forward, he dashed the hilt in Ned's face, and the next moment they were locked in deadly grapple.

Ned met his man boldly at this game, but found he had to do with an antagonist who was able apparently at one and the same time to convert himself into an eel, an india-rubber spring, a rod of elastic steel, and a bar of unwrought iron.

To and fro they wrestled over the turf.

"Curse your spurs!" snarled Ned, as the rowels of Kenneth's "persuaders" tore open his calf in an attempt to back-heel him.

"You're right," replied Rothsay, grimly, as they caught in a trailing bramble and almost brought their wearer to the ground.

Ned tried all he knew to get rid of his formidable foe, in the hope that if he could only accomplish this he might retrace his steps from the species of "no thoroughfare" in which he found himself, before the arrival of the remainder of his pursuers.

Twice in succession Ned lifted his man and swung him round, but each time Kenneth alighted like a cat on his outspread feet instead of upon the broad of his back as the bushranger had anticipated.

A third time Ned drew his opponent to his chest and whirled him round, and it looked all over with Kenneth, but just as he was falling he managed to click his adversary with one leg and make a step outwards with the other, so that the two foes came heavily to the ground side by side.

Before either could secure any further advantage there was a shout, and the remainder of the pursuers, rushing into the arena, threw themselves like a living avalanche upon the prostrate form of the bushranger.

Ned fought desperately, writhing and plunging like a snared beast, and striking out with fists and feet indiscriminately at his foes.

Twice he almost gained his feet, but only to be borne down again by weight of numbers.

With one hand he managed to seize one of his assailants by the throat, and had almost choked him into insensibility before a violent blow on the head from the butt of a pistol forced him to relax his grip as he fell back half-stunned.

Before he could recover himself a pair of handcuffs were slipped on to his wrists and his elbows pinioned behind him with a carbine-sling.

A cord was then attached to his ankles, so that he could not step more than a certain distance at a time.

" You had better put a bullet through me at once," he growled, when he had realised the impossibility of any further resistance.

" Not a bit of it," answered Kenneth, wiping his forehead, for he was almost as exhausted as his antagonist, " I prefer to take you alive to Sydney, and let the authorities settle your fate."

Ned relapsed into sullen silence, and, refusing to walk, was half-dragged, half-carried to the spot where the horses had been left.

Mounted on one of these, with his legs fastened beneath its belly, and escorted by Kenneth and the troopers, he was conveyed to Sydney, and, after a brief examination before a magistrate, committed to prison to await his trial.

CHAPTER CXLIX.

HOIST WITH HIS OWN PETARD.

ON the very day that Ned was committed for trial " Kit the Cruiser " put into Sydney.

On learning the position of his brother he resolved to leave no stone unturned to help him, and, being unknown, his efforts would not challenge attention.

The first thing he did was to hasten to the hotel where Kate was employed as barmaid.

From her he learned the full details of Ned's capture, and also that his condemnation to death would be the certain result of a trial.

" We must get him out of this fix somehow," he said to Kate, " but I'm hanged if I can see the way to do it just yet. Are any of his pals handy? they might put one up to a wrinkle."

" I don't think so," answered Kate, " I fancy they are all up country."

" That may be awkward if one wants a hand lent at any time. It doesn't do to trust everyone when there's such a bumping reward offered."

" Well, all that a woman can do, I will," said the barmaid, " I managed to get him off pretty cleverly a few days back," and, to Kit's great amusement, she related how she had baffled the detectives by turning out the gas.

" That's the sort of thing we must trust to. Dodgery, not violence," said Kit, " but the first thing is to get an interview with Ned and let him know we're going to work for him."

" I expect that will be rather a difficult matter ; you will have to get a magistrate's order."

The girl's anticipation was correct.

On Kit presenting himself at the door of the jail he was informed that under no circumstances could he be allowed an interview with Ned, unless furnished with an order signed by a magistrate and countersigned by the chief of police.

After another interview with Kate, he learned the name of the softest-hearted and most muddle-headed magistrate in Sydney.

The next day, got up in the most correct rig-out of a skipper ashore, he presented himself at the private residence of the gentleman in question.

He played his part to perfection.

He looked and acted the honest, upright British tar utterly befogged by all shore-going customs to the life.

He drew tears from the worthy magistrate's eyes by the little picture he sketched of his feelings on learning that his brother, whom, despite his crimes, he had never ceased to cherish, was a prisoner awaiting trial on such terrible charges.

" Many a time, sir, when I've been pacing the deck at night with the old barky quietly slipping through the water. I've looked up at the stars above and thought of the time when we two were lads at our mother's knee. And I've said to myself that, after all, it was as well that the poor old soul had gone aloft before one of her boys should turn out so badly as my unfortunate, misguided brother."

This was pitching it very strong, but, fortunately, the magistrate was unacquainted with the details of Ned's birth and parentage, and swallowed Kit's lies one after another like oysters.

But he would not at once give the order, whereupon Kit called upon the prison " parson," a young prig, who was as fit for the reclaiming of felons' souls as for reclaiming the Bog of Allan.

All his efforts would be about as successful in the one case as the other.

When Kit called, the pious pastor was reading a fast French novel, which are generally only one remove from the work of that worthy pair, Bradlaugh and Mrs. Besant, in their notorious " Fruits of Philosophy."

Kit could make no impression at first upon the young clerical, but the golden key apparently acts as powerfully upon these concierges of the portals of Heaven as upon the " Jeameses " of other establishments.

Offering to subscribe £10 in gold towards the charitable fund under the control of his youthful reverence, the application received his support, and the order was eventually obtained.

Furnished with this, he proceeded to the chief police office and obtained Kenneth Rothsay's signature to the document.

Thence he started for the prison.

Before applying for admission he walked round it twice, and examined the outside in detail.

At certain points he shook his head dolefully, but when he found that one side looked into a narrow and comparatively deserted lane, a smile of satisfaction crossed his features.

His survey completed, he presented himself at the entrance.

The officials, having such a desperate character as Ned under their care, were on their mettle.

Kit's order was examined and scrutinised by half-a-dozen in turn, and at length being satisfied of its genuineness, permission was given for him to be taken to Ned's cell, after he had first undergone a search, lest he should have come provided with any implement to aid the prisoner in effecting his escape.

" It's lucky I did not bring the stuff I thought of," he said to himself.

The regulations there were not so strict as at some places, and though, when Kit and Ned were placed face to face, there was an iron grating between them, so that it was impossible to pass anything to the prisoner, there were no warders to listen to their conversation.

After a brief greeting, Kit said—

" Look here, Ned—we mean to get you out of this. Are there any pals in the town who can lend a hand in the job?"

" I think not. Stop a bit. Do you think a girl would be any use?"

"I don't think so; besides, there's Kate."

"Well, if you should want one, there's a girl called Jess, at a Mr. Fielding's, whom you'll find as sharp as a needle and as true as steel. Don't forget the name, now!"

"All right. And now, do you know anything about this place you're in?"

"Anything about the place?"

"Yes; about the shape of it, the build of it, and such-like?"

Ned laughed.

"If I'd laid every blessed brick in the old caboose with my own hands I could hardly know it better. I've talked with old lags till I know the inside of every jail in the colony as well as you do the cabin of your ship."

"Capital! Now, on which side is the exercising-yard, east or west?"

"To the east."

"Just inside the high wall fronting the street?"

"Yes."

"Well, what is the range of buildings on the other side —the west?"

"The infirmary."

"Better and better. We shall fix it all right."

"But how?"

"Just have patience a minute. As you're only committed for trial, you're allowed to bring what you like to eat?"

"Yes."

"Where do you get your grub from?"

"Oh, there's a kind of a cookshop outside that serves as a canteen. But it's no use trying to send in files in loaves or any of those kind of dodges—they're certain to be smoked."

"Never fear; they won't smoke my dodge."

"But what is it?"

"Well, I'll tell you part of it. Let's see, to-day's Wednesday. Well, next Monday you order a roast duck—a cold one—for dinner."

"Well?"

"Eat the legs and wings, but don't touch the carcase. Take out the stuffing, tie it round your knee like a poultice and keep it there all night, and next day you'll be in the infirmary."

"I begin to see."

"On Wednesday or Thursday night you'll hear an organ playing 'Garryowen' outside the walls. Half-an-hour after it stops hold yourself in readiness to slip into the courtyard the infirmary looks on. Have you got a good nerve?"

"Yes, I guess I have."

"Well then, when blazes seems to have broken loose, slip out of the infirmary window, get into the left-hand corner of the courtyard, and when a stone comes over pick it up."

"Time's up," interrupted the warder, cutting short the interview.

Ned could not quite understand the plan of escape thus sketched by Kit, but he resolved to follow out his brother's instructions to the letter.

On leaving the prison, Kit strolled back to the hotel-bar.

"A girl has been here asking after you," said Kate.

"Do you know who she is?"

"Yes; her name is Jess, and she knows Ned. She has learnt somehow that you've had an order to see him given you, and she wants to know how he is."

"Where's she to be found? Ned spoke of her; and I think she'll come in handy."

Kate told him, and that very evening he managed to have an interview with Jess.

The girl expressed her perfect willingness to aid him in his schemes.

The next morning she had a tiff with Mrs. Fielding, and left her situation at a moment's notice—a thing so common in the colonies that it excited no suspicion.

She at once joined Kit, who had taken a small furnished house in the older part of the town.

The first care of Kit had been to remove a number of packages ashore from his schooner, and then send her round to the mouth of the Hawkesbury River.

He would not risk her in Sydney with the job he had in view.

His next task was to purchase a barrel organ which played "Garryowen" among other tunes, and to provide himself with a long, loose coat, peaked hat, and a grey wig and beard, by the aid of which he could completely disguise himself.

When these were on, his bronzed face aided the deception, and gave him the appearance of an old Italian organman.

Thus equipped and with Jess, disguised by means of dye applied to her face and hair and equipped with a tambourine, he began to play about the streets in the vicinity of the prison, so that people might get used to his presence.

On Saturday he sent Jess out to market to buy a duck.

This was duly plucked, stuffed with the sage and onions, and roasted by the girl the following day.

When it was cold Kit withdrew the skewer fastening the flap of the neck and took out the stuffing, which he placed on a plate.

Then taking a brown powder from a small box, evidently of Oriental manufacture, he sprinkled it over the stuffing, mixed it up thoroughly, and returned the sage and onions, thus flavoured, to its original place, and refastened the flap.

Jess looked on in wonderment; but a few words of explanation satisfied her.

Prisoners awaiting trial were allowed to purchase food at the canteen already spoken of, or to have it sent in from their homes.

In every case, however, it was subjected to a most careful examination by the authorities, and in Ned's case precautions were redoubled.

In order to break ground for Kit's plan, Kate had sent in several little delicacies for her brother, which had all been examined and found all right, and on Monday morning the duck was presented as if from her.

"Ah! it's well to be a fine-looking fellow, and have all the girls take an interest in you," said one of the warders who, like his comrades, fancied that Kate must be Ned's sweetheart and not his sister. "What a beautiful bird!"

"Well, I for one shouldn't care to change places with that fine-looking fellow. It's not many more ducks he'll have the eating of in this world," said his comrade.

"All the same it's a beautiful bird!" replied the other, eyeing it regretfully. "And to think that that chap inside will bolt the whole of it, like the shark he is."

"He has a devil of a twist! But come, let's have a look at the duck."

Taking it up, he pulled out all the skewers, examined the giblets, which were fixed beneath the wings, and then, taking up a knife, split the bird down the centre, and turned out the stuffing.

"Nothing there," he remarked.

"How nice that stuffing smells!" said the other.

A few minutes later the duck was placed before Ned.

He carefully followed the directions given him.

Pulling the bird to pieces, for he was not allowed the use of a knife or fork, he picked the legs and wings with great relish.

Then, taking out his handkerchief, he placed it on the table and folded it in the form of a bandage.

In the centre of this he placed the stuffing, and, rolling up one leg of his trousers, tied this novel poultice about his knee.

He had just pulled the trouser-leg down when the warder re-entered the cell to clear away.

"Hullo!" he said, noticing the carcase Ned had not touched, "off your feed to-day, eh?"

"Yes," answered Kelly, "I feel a bit seedy."

The man grinned.

"It is no use trying the malingering game, my boy, if that's what your up to," he thought.

Strictly following Kit's injunction, Ned kept on the poultice when he turned in.

After a time a kind of itching, tingling sensation began to manifest itself in his knee.

It was rather unpleasant, but not absolutely painful.

At the same time the knee seemed to swell, and several times in the night he slackened the bandage around it.

The first thing he did on awakening was to glance at his knee.

The sight that met his eye filled him with horror.

The joint had swollen to twice its normal size.

The skin, distended almost to bursting-point, was of a deep purple tone, verging here and there on a greenish black, with spots of whitish yellow.

"By ——, here's a pretty go!" gasped Ned. "What devil's trick has Kit been up to? I shan't be able to move for a week."

But, to his intense amazement, he found, on venturing to move the limb, that, despite its morbid appearance, the joint moved freely and without stiffness, or even pain of any kind.

He began to see the trick.

His first care was to get rid of the poultice, and then, returning to bed, he began to groan heavily.

Shortly afterwards the warder entered the cell.

"Phew! what a stink of sage and onions!" was his first remark. "Hullo, Kelly, ain't you up yet?"

Ned groaned in reply.

"What's up, man?"

"Oh, Lord, my knee!" groaned Ned.

"What's the matter?"

"My knee—oh, the awful pain!"

And Ned made a face that caused the man to start back in astonishment.

"Come, let's have a look at it," he said, half-incredulously.

"Gently, gently!" cried Ned, as the other laid his hand on the bed-clothes to draw them aside and inspect the seat of pain.

"Good heavens!" exclaimed the warder, as the knee appeared. "This is awful. Here, I'll go for the surgeon at once."

And he darted out and locked the door.

Ned continued to groan; and about a quarter of an hour later the warder made his reappearance, accompanied by the surgeon, a fussy, bustling little man, who, to tell the truth, did not appear particularly inclined to credit his subordinate's report.

"As big as a cannon-ball and as purple as a beetroot, you say?" were his words as he entered the cell. "Pooh! nonsense! Come, my man," he continued, addressing Kelly, "let's see this knee of yours."

But no sooner had he caught sight of it than he seemed absolutely dumbfounded.

"Why—why, what's this?" he gasped.

Approaching the bed, he laid his hand on the kneecap.

He did not hurt it in the least, but, no sooner had his fingers touched it, than Kelly uttered a roar that would have done credit to a prize bull.

"Is it painful?" asked the surgeon.

"Oh, oh! I should just like you to have it and see," groaned the bushranger.

The doctor bent over the afflicted limb.

"Most singular case—serious, too. We must have him in the infirmary at once."

"But, sir," remonstrated the warder, who was a slave to duty, "we have strict orders from the governor that he's not to leave his cell."

"Not leave his cell!" returned the peppery doctor, whose dignity was hurt at this answer. "Unless he leaves it at once, I'll answer that he'll only leave it in a coffin. Unless he's taken at once to the infirmary, I'll not answer for his life. Besides, how the devil do you think the man can

escape when he can't even put a foot to the ground? However, call the governor, if you like."

The governor was accordingly summoned, but, in presence of Ned's knee and with the doctor's assurance that he must be at once removed, he did not hesitate to give orders for him to be carried at once to the infirmary.

Ned played the part of an invalid, according to his lights, to perfection—not only by howling with feigned pain when lifted on to a stretcher, but by cursing the governor, the doctor, and the whole of the prison staff, in terms that made his hearers' blood run cold, at every jolt that occurred during the transit.

Placed on a bed in the infirmary, he lay back and closed his eyes, as though exhausted.

The doctor placed a hand upon his knee.

"Hold hard!" roared Kelly "It's as if you prodded me with a red-hot iron."

"When did the pain begin?" enquired the doctor.

"Ever since one of those cursed cowards who caught me kicked me, I've felt it," replied Ned.

"But why didn't you tell me?"

"Because I'm not a blessed milksop, to make a fuss over it. Only to-day I couldn't stand it any longer."

The doctor asked a few more questions, looked grave, and ordered the application of cooling lotions during the day.

At nightfall the swelling had not diminished, and next morning the knee looked, if anything, worse.

The doctor examined it, shook his head, and at noor sent a note to one of his colleagues, the most eminent surgeon in Sydney.

In course of the afternoon he arrived.

His colleague of the prison briefly explained the cause of the injury, and then together they examined the patient.

"Are you still in pain?" enquired the prison-surgeon.

"No, I feel a little easier," replied Ned, who was beginning to get tired of howling.

The doctors exchanged a significant look.

They then drew apart.

"Mortification?" said one.

"I'm afraid so."

A brief consultation followed.

Then certain orders were given to the two male nurses.

One of them left the ward, and returned with a case of instruments.

The other began to arrange sundry basins, towels, and the like.

Ned watched these preparations with a certain interest.

He had an idea they concerned him.

Nor was he wrong.

The prison-doctor approached him.

"My poor fellow," he began, "I know you are a man of courage, and I must tell you that you need it all now."

"What do you mean?"

"Why, from the appearance of your knee it is plain that mortification is setting in, and amputation is inevitable."

"Amputation! What the devil is amputation?" cried the patient.

"It means, my poor fellow," said the other doctor, advancing, "that in order to save your life we shall have to cut off your leg."

CHAPTER CL.

ESCAPE.

Cut off his leg to save his life!

Ned felt his blood run cold.

What an awful position he was in!

If he confessed that his illness was feigned, it would be guessed at once that it was meant to cover an attempt at escape, and he would in future be watched both night and day.

But then, on the other hand, if he did not confess, doctors would have his leg off.

Mentally, and with touching impartiality, he cursed hem and Kit. who, he felt, had led him into this hole.

He resolved to make an appeal.

"Do you think you need cut it off? It feels much easier this afternoon."

"Just so, my man. That's the worst possible sign; it means mortification."

Bitterly Ned regretted his lack of medical knowledge.

If he had only known that much, he thought, how he would have howled.

At that moment there was a knock at the door of the infirmary.

One of the attendants went to open it.

"A message from Government House for Dr. Philpott," he said, returning with a note.

"Give it me," said the prison-surgeon's colleague.

"Good heavens!" he exclaimed, on opening it. "Lady Belmont has been thrown from her carriage and is still insensible. I must be off at once."

"Certainly," said the other.

"It's a pity. This is such a curious case that I should certainly have liked to have performed the operation myself."

"Quite so. It is a curious case, and, to tell you the truth, I really don't like to undertake it single-handed. I do not think a few hours' delay will make any material difference. Suppose you come here the first thing to-morrow morning?"

"Well, after all, we may be mistaken about the mortification, for—to tell the truth—I never saw a limb present such an appearance before. Let it be as you say. I will call to-morrow morning at seven."

Ned watched him hurry off, and saw the basins, etc., put away.

"Don't you mean to cut it off?" he enquired anxiously of the prison surgeon.

"No; we are going to give you another chance. So good-night. Renew the dressings every other hour," he continued to the nurse, and then took his departure.

Kelly began to breathe more freely.

"That was a precious narrow squeak," he thought. "A very little more and I should have had to have blurted out the truth. I wonder what the devil kind of stuff Kit put in the stuffing that has bamboozled the doctors so."

Not even Kit could have answered that question.

The East has its medical secrets that have baffled the most skilful European enquirer, and he was ignorant of the very name of the drug which had been given him—together with instructions for its use—by an old Malay pirate whom he had once befriended.

As the afternoon approached, Ned began to grow anxious and to lift his head at the slightest sound.

A dozen times he fancied he could hear the strains of "Garryowen" rising in the air, but, after straining his ears for a minute or two, found that he had been self-deceived.

The suspense began to grow intolerable.

At last, just about dusk, he raised his head again.

Yes, it was the signal.

As the brisk and stirring notes of one of the liveliest fighting-tunes ever written rose in the air Ned's pulses began to throb in unison, and he felt tempted to fling himself from his bed.

Recovering himself he began to think matters out.

He would have half-an-hour in which to act from the moment at which the music ceased.

True; but the question to him was whether he would have one or two nurses to deal with when the moment came for escaping.

It was not that two men could stop him, but it is difficult for one man, however powerful, to get the better of two without making a noise.

And a noise was above all things to be avoided.

Chance again favoured him.

The nurses relieved each other at intervals during the

Ned happened to be the only patient in his ward, which was a small one especially set apart for cases requiring surgical operations that could not be well carried on before the other patients.

As he was to all appearances a complete cripple, only one man had been told off for the night watch, and he came on duty just as the organ ceased playing.

The day attendants whom he relieved quitted the ward a few minutes later.

Ned fixed his eyes on the clock at the end of the ward.

The hands seemed to him to creep with leaden slowness.

At length when they marked fifteen minutes after the music had stopped, he gave a low groan and called feebly to the attendant.

"What is it, mate?" enquired the latter.

"Just lift me up and give me something to drink," said Ned.

The attendant approached, and, passing his arm behind Ned's back, raised him up.

But no sooner was the bushranger in a sitting position than he suddenly threw both arms round the other with a jerk that almost drove the breath out of his body, hauled him on to the bed and threw himself on the top of him.

So sudden was the attack that the nurse had not even time to cry out before he was on his back.

Then he opened his mouth to do so, but before he could utter a sound Ned stuffed his cotton night-cap into it and stopped him.

He followed this up by squeezing the man's throat until he was almost strangled.

When he had choked the hapless wretch into insensibility, Ned tied a handkerchief over his mouth, which still contained the night-cap, and then bound him hand and foot with the bandages that had served for his own knee.

He then rose and was about to proceed towards the window.

Suddenly a very important want occurred to him, and one which unless it was supplied would render all further attempt at escape useless.

He had no clothes.

Patients were not allowed to have their garments in the ward, and though a flannel dressing-gown had been placed by his bedside. it was utterly impossible for him to make his appearance in public in such attire.

After a moment's reflection he returned to the attendant, and, temporarily slackening his bonds, peeled off his coat, waistcoat, and trousers.

Even with these he was not much better off.

The man he had despoiled was about five feet six, and though he was fortunately a very fat fellow, the coat would not button across Ned's chest, the waistcoat revealed six inches of shirt below it, and the trousers did not come much below his knees.

After forcing his feet in the shoes, he set about tearing the sheets into strips, which he fashioned into a rope.

With this in readiness, he approached the window.

The clock denoted the half-hour had elapsed.

Suddenly a bright flash illumined the sky, there was a roar like thunder, and a concussion that shook the prison to its foundation.

During the afternoon an old organman, who for several days had been favouring the neighbourhood with his music, had gone on his usual round.

He was—as well as could be judged from a stoop acquired by carrying his instrument—a tall old fellow of about sixty, with a bronzed face almost hidden by a thick, grey, bushy beard, and long grey hair streaming from under his pointed hat.

He seemed heavily and clumsily built, and moved stiffly and awkwardly under the weight of his organ, which was an uncommonly large one.

He had paused at the end of the lane running down the west side of the prison, and had played "Garryowen" for about ten minutes.

Then starting off again after two or three more halts, he

...d himself again in its neighbourhood some five-and-twenty minutes later.

But he seemed to have given up all idea of playing for the time being.

Indeed, the stock of tunes seemed very few, for, with the exception of "Garryowen" and a couple of slow, melancholy airs, he had played nothing that day.

The street running down the east side of the prison was not a very lively one.

On one side was the high, dead wall enclosing the place of punishment, on the other a row of small houses, the residents of which were for the most part employed during the day away from home.

Down this street the old man passed slowly.

When he had got about halfway down, he paused and glanced around.

Not a soul was about, except a couple of children playing in the gutter.

The old man stepped up to the prison wall, and, unslinging his organ from his back, rested it against the boundary.

Then striking a match, he proceeded to light his pipe, carefully turning his head away from the instrument as he did so.

But, his pipe alight, instead of throwing away the match, he applied it to a bit of greyish paper protruding from the side of the organ.

A fizzing, hissing sound followed, and the old man, striding rapidly away, turned the corner of the prison.

Hardly had he done so before a terrific explosion took place in the street he had left.

The dynamite efforts of the Fenians had thus found an imitator at the Antipodes.

The prison-yard wall was levelled with the ground for a distance of several feet.

The stones and splinters, hurled forward with incredible force, were dashed against the walls and windows of the building itself.

Doors were driven in and windows smashed, the splinters of broken glass inflicting serious injury on several of the prisoners who were engaged on that side of the building.

The houses on the other side of the street had suffered to a like extent.

Three of them were so injured that they collapsed as though built of cards, and the groans and cries of the people buried under their ruins were appalling.

The inhabitants of those adjoining them also suffered from falling or flying *débris*.

A cloud of smoke and dust served to partially veil, yet at the same time to heighten, the horrors of the scene.

A simultaneous rush took place in the prison towards the scene of the disaster.

The officials were inspired with a wish to learn the extent of the disaster, and the prisoners with a desire to escape.

Several of the latter succeeded in gaining the yard, and a desperate struggle took place to prevent their escape.

The very patients in the infirmary wards adjoining the one occupied by Ned had risen from their beds and striven to gain the staircase, under the impression that the prison was on fire, and no one kept watch on the courtyard.

Ned, though for a moment startled, did not lose his head.

He remembered his brother's words, and guessed that the noise he had heard was intended to favour his escape.

One end of his improvised rope was already secured to a bedstead drawn up to the window, and by its aid he quickly lowered himself into the yard.

He darted across it to the left-hand corner, and just as he reached it a stone flew over the wall, and fell at his feet.

He picked it up, and found it was attached to one end of a fine but strong cord, the other end of which disappeared over the wall.

He at once guessed what he had to do, and hauled at the cord.

Soon the further end of it came to view, with a knotted rope attached to it.

Meanwhile, the organ-grinder had darted round to the side of the prison on which the infirmary courtyard lay.

This side was bounded by a narrow lane, flanked on either side by dead walls, and seldom troubled with passengers.

The only occupant was a girl, who was at that moment engaged in freeing herself from a very singular kind of crinoline—neither more nor less than a coil of rope concealed beneath her petticoats.

After a glance at the new-comer, she continued her occupation.

Then, knotting one end of a cord she had in readiness to the coil, she threw the other, to which a stone was attached, over the wall.

"Bravo!" said the organman, "I never saw a girl cast the lead so well before."

Half-a-minute had hardly elapsed before the cord was pulled on the other side, and the two saw the end of the rope dragged after it over the wall.

"Now," said the organ-grinder, "catch hold of one end with me, and bear firm with all your weight."

As soon as Ned had the end of the knotted rope in his hand, and had satisfied himself by a steady pull that it was equal to his weight, he began to scale the wall by its aid.

This was not such an easy task as might be imagined.

His weight caused the rope to hang close to the wall, and his hands, knees, and knuckles were scraped and bruised considerably as he worked his way up.

The nearer he got to the summit the greater became the difficulty, and when he got his hands up to the level of the top of the wall they were almost crushed by the rope against the brickwork.

However, after a desperate effort, he managed to hook one leg sideways over the coping, and a few seconds later was seated astride it.

He looked down.

"Is that you, Kit?" he asked, on catching sight of the organ-grinder, whose disguise was perfect.

"Yes," was the whispered answer.

"Look here; how the devil am I to get down? It's too far to risk a jump, and there's nothing to fix the rope to."

"All right; haul up one end of it."

Ned complied, and found a large but light hook attached to the end of the rope.

Hooking this over the top of the wall, he slid down, and was soon by the side of Kit and Jess.

Whilst he was descending the former had pulled off his coat and turned the sleeves inside out.

When he had worn it, it had appeared a dirty drab garment, but, turned inside out, it was transformed into a tolerably smart coat of blue pilot-cloth.

He then divested himself with the rapidity of a "transformation dancer" of waistcoat and trousers.

The cause of his stiffness and awkwardness of gait was now apparent.

Underneath his organ-grinder's dress he wore a smart sailor's suit.

As he had laid aside his garments, Ned had assumed them, and found they fitted him to rights.

They had, indeed, been modelled on some of his own.

The organ-grinder's hat was double, a light grey felt with a low crown being concealed with it.

With this on his head over a fair wig, which, with a pair of false whiskers, was produced from Kit's pockets, the transformation was complete.

Kit, discarding his grey wig and whiskers, assumed a smart blue-cloth cap.

The clothes of the nurse whom Ned had stripped, together with the knotted rope that a jerk served to retach from the wall, were then made into a bundle of which Jess took charge.

The trio then separated, Jess proceeding in one direction and Ned and Kit in another.

The alarm in the prison gradually subsided, though for some time the officials were fully occupied in defending the breach in the wall from the prisoners attempting to break out, and the excited mob that had assembled without, and sought to surge through at intervals.

At length the arrival of the police restored order.

The roll was called, and it was found that three prisoners had escaped through the breach.

It was not till the excitement arising from this was allayed that any investigation was made in the infirmary.

An attendant, at length, entering Ned's ward, found his colleague lashed to the bed, and almost in the last stage of suffocation.

On being released he could only point to the window.

The rope formed of the bed-clothes, hanging from this, caught the eye of the attendant, and he at once raised the alarm.

The courtyard was reached, but without success.

The lower rooms and ward of the prison were then in turn examined, but no trace of Ned could be discovered.

The warders, one and all, swore that they had not seen him on the eastern side during the confusion; but, nevertheless, the only conclusion arrived at was that he had slipped through the breach during the excitement created by the explosion.

But how a man whom the doctor was willing to stake his professional reputation was a helpless cripple had managed to accomplish such a feat was a mystery none could fathom.

As to the idea of his having scaled the courtyard wall in his crippled state, it was so preposterous that no one even thought of it.

CHAPTER CLI
OFF AND AWAY.

THE sensation caused by Ned's escape was tremendous.

How it had been accomplished was a mystery.

A similar mystery enveloped the means by which the prison wall had been blown down.

At length one of the children who had been playing about when Kit had placed the organ against the wall, and who, like his companions, had been severely injured, recollected what he had seen.

The authorities kept a sharp look-out for the organman, and for the girl who had accompanied him on his rounds, but it is hardly necessary to state that neither of the pair ever appeared in public again in Sydney.

The way in which Kit had blown down the wall was simple enough.

Prior to starting on his rounds that morning, he had removed part of the works of the organ, and had replaced them with a package of dynamite.

The enormous power possessed by this terrible agent of destruction is well known.

A very small packet of it will wreak an amount of havoc appalling to contemplate, and Kit had not been sparing of it.

Ned had accompanied Kit to the latter's house, where Jess joined the pair later on.

The fugitive remained concealed in it all the next day.

But on the following morning Kit, who had sallied forth in quest of news, returned somewhat disheartened.

He had seen Kate, and she had told him that the suspicions of the authorities were aroused with regard to his visit to his brother, and that there was a strong possibility of his house being searched under a warrant, as the police were of opinion that Ned was still hidden somewhere in the town.

It was necessary, therefore, to get Kelly with all speed to the Hawkesbury river, where Kit's schooner was lying.

Kit blessed the forethought that had led him to send

her out there, for every craft leaving Sydney was so thoroughly overhauled that it would have been impossible to have got Ned off in her had she remained in the harbour, even had they succeeded in smuggling him on board of her.

How to get him to the Hawkesbury was the next question.

The police were scouring all the roads out of Sydney.

"I think I've hit it," said Ned, suddenly.

"What's your idea?" asked Kit.

"Well, what do you think is the slowest fashion a man would choose to travel?" was the reply.

"On foot, I suppose."

"Just so. But wouldn't he go even slower if he was pushing a wheelbarrow in front of him?"

"Bravo!" cried Kit and Jess, simultaneously.

Accordingly, that very afternoon Ned sallied out into the streets, got up as a labourer, and pushing a wheelbarrow, with some tools in it, in front of him.

The trick was successful.

No policeman dreamt of stopping a man who appeared to be on his way to some job a few hundred yards or so further on.

Ned got clear of Sydney, and took the road to the Hawkesbury, where the same impunity awaited him.

It never crossed the minds of the numerous lookers-out for Ned Kelly that a hunted fugitive would encumber himself with such an impediment to quick travelling as a wheelbarrow.

To one or two who exchanged a few words with him he simply said that he was going to a job of work he had on hand a little further on.

Before starting, he had revealed to Kit the marks and bearings of the spot where he had hidden the spoil he had taken from Mendez.

Accordingly, the skipper took a boat and made his way to the place indicated.

Having unearthed the swag, he returned with it to Sydney.

Jess, meanwhile, had not been idle.

She had hired a trap to drive to Hawkesbury, and was waiting for him with this on the wharf.

The spoil was transferred to the trap, and the pair drove off.

The sight of a sailor with a pretty girl beside him rattling along the road was too common a one to excite much attention.

Nevertheless, such was the vigilance exercised, that one policeman insisted that Kit must be Ned; and it was only after a long palaver, and an adjournment to a public-house and appeal to the company there, that the man was convinced of his error.

"If that chap's Ned Kelly, he has shrunk pretty considerably since he has been in Sydney jail," said the landlord. "Why, Ned is a head and shoulders taller, and far bigger altogether."

"He's devilish like the description though, anyway," said the policeman; and this was true, for there was a decided resemblance between the two brothers as regarded their features.

"Perhaps so; but it's very hard that because an honest man happens to resemble a scoundrel he's to be arrested," said Kit, in tones of great indignation.

"Just so," chimed in one of the bystanders. "Besides, the scar on the hand by which Ned Kelly has been recognised a score of times is wanting on this gentleman's fist."

The policeman was at length convinced by these arguments, and allowed Kit and Jess to resume their journey.

A considerable loss of time had, however, taken place from the delay, and it was almost nightfall when they overtook Ned, who was sturdily trudging along the road.

They drew up beside him, and a brief consultation followed.

It was arranged that he should join them the next morning at a certain point near the mouth of the river known to both.

They then drove on, and Ned, when night set in, drove his barrow as far as a thick clump of scrub at some distance from the road, and, turning it upside down, lay down on the turf, with it serving as a pillow.

Abandoning his shelter early next morning, he started for the appointed spot.

It was where a little creek emptied itself into the Hawkesbury.

As he approached a low whistle fell on his ear from the surrounding bush.

He looked round.

The brushwood parted a few paces off, and the face of Kit the Cruiser was revealed.

"Hush!" he exclaimed, in tones raised but little above a whisper; "come here quietly."

Ned complied, and found Jess with Kit.

"What is the matter?" he asked.

"Something very awkward," said Kit. "They evidently suspect the schooner, and she is being watched."

"Watched?"

Yes; there are police lurking in the trees on both sides of the river, and, what is worse, there is a Government whale-boat with four men cruising about.

"That's nice."

"Yes; I have not dared to signal her to send a boat ashore, for fear of arousing their suspicions, though I am sure the mate will begin to wonder why I have not turned up as arranged."

"Is the boat always about?" asked Ned.

"Yes; and I am afraid they'll have a revenue cutter round if they get very suspicious."

"And your schooner—is she ready for sea?"

"Quite. We could slip moorings in a moment if we were on board of her, but I'm hanged if I can see a way of getting there."

The three fugitives, concealed by the trees that bordered the stream, made their way to the water's edge, and peered cautiously forth.

The sight that met their eyes was tantalising in the extreme.

There lay the broad expanse of water, where the river met the ocean, and there lay the schooner, evidently ready to slip her moorings and hoist sail at a moment's notice.

But there, too, was the whale-boat, manned by five men, cruising up and down in such a way as to cut off all communication with the vessel and the shore.

"Could we swim it?" asked Ned.

"We might, but I don't see how the girl could," replied Kit; "and then our only chance would be at night. The police on the banks would spot us to a certainty, and signal us to the whale boat. Besides, we should have to give up all hope of getting the plunder on board."

"That's true. The police are watching it, you say—are you sure?"

"Sure! Keep still; why, there's one on the further bank now."

Ned plainly saw the sentinel in question.

"There's only one thing I can think," he said, after some time spent in reflection. "We must be as close as possible. It is not unlikely that the boat will put into shore some time or other. If the men land from her on this side of the river we must try to seize her and make for the schooner."

Kit agreed to this.

About an hour later the whale-boat pulled to shore, touching the bank about thirty yards from the spot where they were concealed.

Four of the crew landed, the fifth remaining as boat-keeper in the little craft, which was beached on a spot where the bank sloped.

The men who had landed proceeded to gather sticks and make preparations for lighting a fire.

Noiselessly making their way through the bushes, Ned and Kit, followed by Jess, reached a point not more than a dozen yards from the boat.

Beyond this point they could not expect to advance unseen.

Then, at a sign from Ned, both darted from their place of concealment, and raced towards the boat.

Before the sailor left in her had time to assume a defensive attitude they were upon him.

A blow from a stick carried by Ned laid him senseless.

"Hurry up, Jess," roared Ned.

The girl, who was encumbered with the bag containing the property plundered from Mendez, advanced but slowly.

"Hurry up," shouted the bushranger again, "or we shall have to leave you."

As he had been speaking, he and Kit—putting their shoulders to the boat—ran her off into deep water.

Kit, seeing how matters were with Jess, darted up to her and helped her onward.

As soon as she joined them, the three tumbled, with their plunder, into the boat and shoved off.

Ned and Kit seized a couple of oars, and began to pull like demons in the direction of the schooner.

Jess, who was at home on the water, acted as steersman.

Before the sailors, who had witnessed the capture of their craft, could gain the bank, the fugitives were several lengths on their way.

Heading the boat down stream, the pace they were enabled to put on would soon carry them out of all danger.

A new peril, however, awaited them.

A sentinel on the further bank a little lower down had his attention attracted by the shouts of the sailors.

Advancing to a point overlooking the water he awaited the passage of the boat.

As it came abreast of him he raised his gun and fired.

He had aimed at Ned, who was pulling the stroke oar.

Fortunately for the bushranger the marksman had not quite allowed for the speed got on the boat, and the bullet flew between him and Jess.

"A close shave!" said Kit.

The danger was not yet over.

Roused by the shot the other watchers sprang to their arms, and those within range opened fire.

A bullet tore its way from above through the planking, near the stern, just at the water line.

The water began to bubble through the hole.

Jess bent forward, and, while steering with one hand, thrust the fingers of the other into the aperture.

A few minutes later the little craft shot alongside the schooner.

The three fugitives were quickly on board, and everything being, as Kit had foretold, in readiness, the moorings were slipped and the sails set.

The breeze was fresh and favourable, and the tidy little craft was soon standing out to sea.

By the time the news reached Sydney and a Government vessel was got ready to pursue her, all prospect of such pursuit proving successful was quite hopeless.

By Ned's orders she was headed for Singapore, it being his intention to take the P. and O. steamer there for England.

After an exceedingly fair passage, the town in question was reached.

Ned went on shore and put up at one hotel, giving orders to Jess, who was to represent herself as a widow, to stay at another.

He had disguised himself, and was careful to behave with strict decorum.

A few days later the steamer he was expecting put in, and he and Jess went on board her, still pretending to be perfect strangers.

Several other passengers who embarked had landed at Singapore from a vessel which had arrived from Sydney.

Amongst them, to his amazement, Kelly recognised his old friend Count Anatole.

CHAPTER CLII.

THE CLAIMANT IN CLOVER—TWO OLD FRIENDS.

WHEN they were well under way Kelly went up to Count Anatole.

"Well, my lively Mounseer," he said, "what has made you turn back on Sydney, eh?"

The Frenchman started.

"Ah! Mistare, Mistare—" he began.

"Dawes," broke in Kelly.

"Mistare Dawes, yes; I am charm—I am enchant to see you, but, *ma foi*, I ask, in turn, what bring you here, away from your—how do you call it, your bush, *hein?*"

"I reckon my bush, as you call it, got a little too hot to hold me, thanks to the cursed simplicity of some of my pals, so I am going to try the old country a bit for a change. They want me back there. You see they have had a long spell from my little games. I shot a policeman there one night when he was rather in my way, and a fearful muss was made about the life of a bobby. My friend Peace, who put me up to a dodge or two, always cleared the way with his revolver; and the law says, you know, you may use firearms when you're afraid for your life. Now, if a 'copper' nabbed me, I should be uncommonly afraid for my life; therefore, in giving a bobby the contents of my *barrel-organ*, I only obey the law. Ha! ha! ha! But you, have you made your fortune in Sydney?"

"No, my friend, alas! no. Your colonies are too rude, barbarous, brutal, for a man of taste, of elegance, of fine feeling."

We do not give the conversation in the halting English of the count.

"You couldn't get on?"

"Ah, no! there was no scope for talent. Now, for instance, there is a very pretty little scheme of making a nice certain income that I have practised in Paris. It takes some time, some trouble, some thought, but, ah! it repays them all; it does *vraiment*."

"And what's the name of this pretty little game?"

"It is called by the police and other objectionable persons who interfere with its exercise *chantage*."

"And how do you carry it on?"

"Very simply! though, as I said before, it requires time and trouble. You spot—yes, that is the term—a man who is rich, honourable, in a good position. You make it your business to find out all about him. Perhaps he gained his riches dishonestly. Good. Perhaps he was not always honourable. Good. Perhaps he has relations who have suffered for some crime or of whom he is ashamed, or secret vices which he dare only indulge in private."

"Well, what then?"

"What then? Why, the richer, the more outwardly honourable, the higher placed he is, the more anxious he is that such things should not be known. You find them out after a great deal of trouble. You write to him a very pretty little letter informing him how grieved and shocked you are to learn of such things, and you deliberately hint at the time and expense this trouble has cost you. Do you see now?"

"No, I'm blowed if I do!"

"And yet it is as clear as day. He either takes no notice of your letter, or he requests an interview. In the first case, you write again, telling him you cannot think of keeping facts of such great importance from the public; in the second, you arrange an interview. And it ends by his making you a handsome present, as a return for your silence and discretion."

"Ah, I see."

"Not quite, I think. The secret lasts but the present does not. So you call on him regularly, twice, thrice, four times in the year, like a landlord for his rent. Do you see now?"

"Yes; but it's a pitiful business."

"Pitiful business!" cried the Frenchman, lifting up his hands in protestation. "Pitiful business! Why, there are hundreds of men in Paris, who move in good society, and draw handsome incomes from it. I did well myself, very well, till, *hélas!* I was forced to leave Paris by the police."

And he sighed.

"And you thought to try the same game on in Sydney, eh?" said Ned, with a grin.

"Of course. I said to myself, here is a nice field—superb! I begin to make enquiries. Magnificent! I learn that this public man's father was transported for forgery; that that fine lady's mother was a fish-fag. And I rejoice. I wait. I get all my facts, and then I go to the first on my list. He is a great man, a public man—a minister. I introduce myself, I tell my little history, and I say—

"'My dear sir, I have learned certain facts about your father which fill me with profound grief.'"

"And what did he do?" asked Ned.

"He stared at me like a wild beast. Yes; and then I went on delicately, very delicately, to hint that it would be a serious pity if such a thing was to be known to the leader of—what do you call the other party in the Chamber—the Opposition, *hein?*"

"Yes."

"When I have done, and he understands me, he bursts into one great roar of laughter."

(To be continued.)

NED KELLY

THE
IRONCLAD
AUSTRALIAN BUSHRANGER

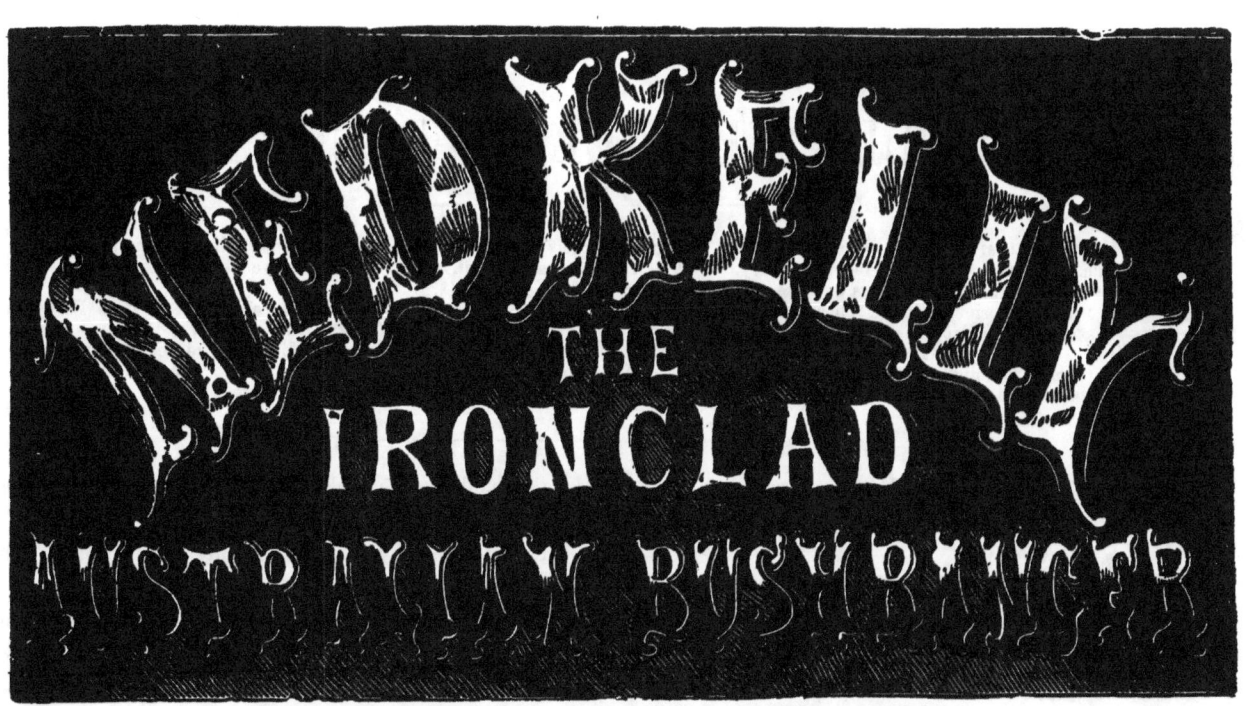

No 26,

NED KELLY: IRONCLAD BUSHRANGER.

"It is well known that for many years Ned Kelly had made himself notorious by a series of crimes wholly incompatible with the civilisation of the nineteenth century. Ned Kelly's celebrated steed, Marco Polo, is as well known at the Antipodes as Dick Turpin's Black Bess in these islands."—*Telegraph*, 7th July, 1881.

"It is notorious that the robbery of Mr. Steward's corpse was mainly performed by the assistance of NED KELLY'S BROTHER, the Captain of what was neither more nor less than a pirate ship."—*Times*, July.

"The history of NED KELLY and his celebrated black horse, Marco Polo, will ever live in the recollection of the Australian public. The deeds of Dick Turpin, and the performances of Black Bess, are tame beside those of 'NED AND HIS NAG;' in addition to which Ned's history is true, and Turpin's is pure fiction."—*Press*, July.

CHAPTER CII.—*Continued.*

" 'Ah!' he say, 'you are afraid that it will reach his ears that my father was transported for forgery!'

" 'Yes,' I say.

" 'Oh, you need not worry yourself then, for he knows it just as well as I and everybody else in Sydney knows that his grandfather was hanged for horse-stealing. But we don't trouble our heads about such matters here.' "

"And what did you do after that?" said Ned, with a roar of laughter.

"What did I do? Why, I went out like one very little dog with my tail between my legs. It was no use trying any appeal to the finer sentiments in such a barbarous country. No, my friend, for the man of genius there is only one place for the exercise of his talents, and that is Europe."

"Europe, eh? What do you mean to do when you get there?"

The Frenchman looked into Kelly's face.

"I have what you call more than one string to my bow," he said, with an air of mystery.

"Well, take care you don't find one of them twisted round your neck," growled Ned, who was offended at this seeming want of confidence.

"Oh, there is no chance of that. But, though you will excuse me saying that they are not all of a kind to interest you, there is one in which I should feel honoured by your distinguished co-operation."

As he spoke he bowed slightly.

"You grinning monkey!" grumbled the bushranger, "if you're chaffing me I'll smash your baboon face against the bulwarks."

"Oh! Mistare Kel—Dawes, I mean—how can you make such remarks when you know we have worked together like two gentlemen? Have you come to think I would insult you?" and, as he spoke, Count Anatole drew himself up with dignity.

"No; perhaps I'm wrong. But what's the job you have on hand that'll suit me?"

"Why," replied the other, in a voice scarcely raised above a whisper, "I want a man of pluck to help me to rob the Calais mail."

"The Calais mail?" echoed Ned.

"Yes. Oh, it is all arranged for!"

And Anatole proceeded to give Ned full details respecting the scheme in which he required his assistance.

During the remainder of the passage nothing particular ensued.

Kelly, keeping the character of a colonial who had made a fairish pile and was on his way home to spend it, freely engaged in all the games of chance and skill that are in vogue on shipboard, but, though he had both luck and address on his side, he was too wary to win too much.

With Kit and Jess he pretended to be on no better terms of acquaintance than with the rest of the passengers, concealing his intimacy even from Anatole.

At length the shores of England were sighted, and a few hours later saw the whole party in London.

Ned, in accordance with an agreement he had come to with Anatole, had resolved to take a quiet suburban lodging and live sedately for a week or two, until the time came for their great scheme.

He fixed upon the district of Peckham.

He got himself up as respectably as he could, and started in search of lodgings.

He was not long in finding a place that suited him, and having engaged rooms and paid a week's rent in advance in order to avoid giving references, he returned to the railway station and took his place in a train bound for Ludgate-hill, in order to fetch his luggage from the hotel he had put up at.

He was alone in a first-class carriage.

At one of the intermediate stations his train stopped.

At the same time, a train coming in the opposite direction, drew up also.

Kelly glanced mechanically into the carriage compartment parallel with his own.

It only had one occupant.

An enormously fat man, engaged like himself in smoking a cigar.

Kelly looked again.

Surely he had seen that face before.

And that figure! yes, there could be no mistaking that enormous corpulence.

It was Castro, *alias* Orton, the Wagga-Wagga butcher, looking fatter than ever, but, to Kelly's surprise, got up in a suit of superfine broadcloth and a glossy hat, and wearing a huge gold chain strong enough, apparently, to have held an ox, coiled across his prominent paunch.

"Hullo!" thought Ned, "what's the meaning of this? Castro in luck? No end of a swell. I wonder if there was any truth in that yarn of his."

He at once made up his mind to renew their acquaintance.

The only question was how to manage it.

Castro was in a train about to proceed he did not know where.

If Ned lost sight of him now it was perhaps a thousand to one against his ever catching sight of the ex-butcher again.

There would, he feared, be no time to leave his carriage, run round to the other platform, and enter the train conveying the man he wished to track.

Nevertheless he was about to attempt this, when suddenly another idea struck him.

A whistle and a snort announced that the train conveying Castro was about to start.

Before it could get under way, Ned sprang back from the door of his compartment opening on to the platform on to which he had just been about to step.

He jumped to the other door facing Orton's train, and threw it open.

Orton's train had just begun to move.

Like a cat Ned easily crossed the three feet or so of space intervening between the two trains, and alighted on the footboard of the carriage in which the hero of Wagga-Wagga was seated.

His hand caught the door-handle of the compartment.

So neatly and silently had this been done that no one noticed it.

Softly turning the handle, he stepped into the carriage and sat down in front of Castro.

The latter had been half dozing.

For a moment he took no notice of the entry of the new comer, whom he merely thought to be a passenger rather behind time.

He did not even notice the peculiarity of Ned's mode of entry.

It was not until the train was well in motion that he looked up, but without recognising Kelly.

Ned, sitting opposite him, stared him full in the face, and then calmly scrutinised his get-up from head to foot.

Castro had already acquired a certain notoriety, and had got accustomed to be stared at.

But he did not like the way in which Ned was regarding him.

The idea of an attempt to rob him flashed across his mind, and he glanced round to see if there was any means at hand for alarming the guard.

Kelly guessed his thoughts, and grinned

"You don't seem over-well pleased at meeting an old chum," he began.

"Old chum! what do you mean?" asked Castro with a very well put-on look of astonishment.

"Why, surely you're not going to say you don't know me?" said Ned.

"Know you, know you; ah! yes. Let me see, did you serve with me in the Carabineers, or was we at Stoneyhurst together?"

"What?"

"Or was it in South America? Or, stop a bit; how can I be so stupid as not to recollect an old Hampshire friend?" and he held out his hand with a look of enquiry.

"I don't know what the devil you mean," was the answer. "But I recollect very well the last time we two met in Australia."

"I am afraid there is some mistake," said Castro, with a wave of his fat hand, on which, Ned noticed, a fine diamond was sparkling. "You mistake me, I think, for someone else."

"Who are you, then?" asked Ned, ironically.

"I am Sir Roger Charles Doughty Tichborne, a barrowknight of the United Kingdom."

"*Alias* Tom Castro, the butcher of Wagga-Wagga; *alias* Morgan of Gippsland; *alias* Arthur Orton, the horse-stealer, and pal of Ballarat Harry," said Kelly, with a laugh.

The other sat dumbfounded for a moment; but, recovering himself, scanned Ned Kelly.

"You make a mistake. I have passed under the name of Castro, it is true, but I am Sir Roger Tichborne."

"Oh! that be blowed!" broke in Ned. "I heard all that yarn in Sydney; and how Bogle coached you there, and you were shipped off to England."

"Where I have been recognised by my mother, Lady Tichborne."

"An old idiot!"

"And by many hundred——"

"Fools or rogues—which, eh? Come, it won't do. I have heard your version of affairs, but in the bush I came across an old pal or two who could tell me all about that little mess of Reedy Creek and the rest, and when you first came to the colony."

"Who are you, then?"

"You ought to recognise me with that wonderful memory of yours, that recollects all about death's-head pipes and stripes on shirts."

"And so I do," suddenly cried the other; "you're Ned Kelly."

"Just so. You see, I know you."

The fat man began to recover his coolness.

"Look here, Ned," he began, "we did not do much truck together, but it was all right, eh?"

"Quite so."

"And it's not like you to put a spoke in the wheel of a pal."

"Not if that pal behaves as such."

"Well, of course I ain't come into my property—it's fifteen thousand a-year—yet, but when I do, I'll come down something handsome."

"I'd like something on account. You're a long way further from that property than you think for."

"Well, then, see here," said Castro, taking a thick pocket-book from his breast "I'll give you these."

And with the air of a millionaire he pulled forth a thick roll of papers, and selecting a score or so, handed them to Ned.

"Why, what are these?" ejaculated Kelly, as he tried to puzzle out the spelling of the documents in question: "they're not bank-notes."

"No," replied Castro, grandiloquently; "but they are worth as much. They are Tichborne bonds."

"Worth as much," roared Ned, in a rage; "why the infernal things ain't no more account than curl-papers."

"Oh! ain't they, though! You only keep your eyes open, and you can plant them at a good price, even if you are such a fool as not to stick to them."

"There's something in that," assented Ned; "though I'd rather have something else, that sparkler on your finger, for instance."

"Oh, come now, you can't expect that. And now. if you won't mind a word of business, Ned, I may just hint that, with a reward of ten thousand pounds on your head, you are hardly likely to go into court to swear anything about my affair."

"Right you are."

"Well, I hope you don't think of driving a great bargain with the other side; in fact I can't suspect you of such a thing."

"Such a thing as what?"

"As sending all you know to them in writing."

"No fear of that," answered Ned, who could not quite see what the other was driving at.

"Very well, then, I shan't, on my part, think of sending word to Scotland-yard that Ned Kelly is in London in disguise."

"If I thought——" and as Ned spoke he rose from his seat with a look that chilled the other villain, cool scoundrel though he was, to the marrow.

"But you don't. Here, Ned, here's the sparkler you fancied, as a token of friendship," and he pulled off the ring and handed it to him.

For a moment Kelly seemed to hesitate whether he should take the ring or seize Orton by the throat.

Next moment the train shot into the station.

"Here, take it. This is my station. Good day, old pal," and Castro bundled out of the carriage, shaking like a jellyfish, and muttering to himself, "By Jove! a lucky squeak—another moment and I believe he'd have strangled me."

Ned gazed after him with mingled rage and admiration.

"That's a clever beggar," he muttered, "and a plucky one. It would have been a pity, after all, to have choked him; he'll cut a fine shine before his little game is ended, and give the lawyers—curse them!—some trouble."

CHAPTER CLIII.
ALL HIS WAYS WERE "PEACE."

Ned took up his quarters at his new lodgings.

They were situated in a quiet street at Peckham.

As he had nothing particular to do, and had promised Anatole not to show himself abroad, time hung somewhat heavily on his hands.

He spent the greater part of the day indoors, and passed the evening either in taking a walk about the neighbourhood, or in the parlour of a quiet public.

Faute de mieux, he turned his attention to watching his neighbours.

He soon became, in spite of himself, interested in the occupant of the house on his right.

This was a very precise-looking, elderly little man, of about sixty, with a clean-shaven face and long white hair.

He was usually dressed in a black frock-coat and very white shirt and collar, and presented the perfect type of the retired small tradesman, with a dash of the dissenting minister.

Ned was particularly amused by his quiet, precise ways and intense respectability.

He saw very few visitors, though occasionally a friend or two would drop in of an evening to practise music, of which the old fellow was extremely fond.

A constant caller, however, was a friend with whom the stranger, who went by the name of Smith, was engaged in perfecting a scheme for the raising of sunken vessels.

The old fellow had a light trap and pony, which Ned's experienced eye set down at once as a capital bit of horse-flesh.

Sometimes his neighbours would borrow the turnout for the day, and amongst those making use of it in this way was Ned's landlord.

This led to a certain intimacy, which was fostered by the exchange of certain neighbourly services on both sides, such as are common in the suburbs.

At last one evening Smith asked Ned's landlord into his house to supper.

Mrs. Smith, a tall and not bad-looking, but nervous and careworn woman, and two other friends, were all who were present at the meal.

Smith delivered a very long and very formal grace before they began their repast.

Supper over, he and his friends betook themselves to music with great gusto.

Ned's landlord was amazed at the number of musical instruments lying about the room, and at the proficiency on many of them shown by his host.

Smith had half a dozen violins, and the same number of French horns and concertinas, not to mention trombones, oboes, flutes, ophicleides, and the like.

When Ned's landlord returned he told Kelly of the manner in which they had spent the evening, much to his lodger's amusement.

A few nights later, Kelly on going up to his room felt restless and unable to sleep.

After partially undressing, he put out the light and seated himself at his open window, pipe in mouth.

It was a bright moonlight night, and he could see everything almost as plainly as if it had been day.

The little street, however, was quite deserted, and not a light was seen in any of the houses.

Kelly sat and watched thus for some time.

Suddenly his attention was aroused by the sound of an opening door, rendered doubly audible by the prevailing silence of the night.

Putting down his pipe he looked cautiously forth.

It was Mr. Smith's door that had opened.

Presently Mr. Smith emerged from his house and closed the door behind him.

He was dressed in a rough tweed suit and soft felt hat, forming quite a contrast to his usual attire.

Then he went to his stable, which stood on the other side of the street, unfastened the door, and a few minutes later led out his pony and trap.

He got into the trap, touched up the pony, and soon disappeared at the end of the street.

Ned could not help thinking it strange that so quiet and methodistical a man as Smith appeared to be should choose such an hour for starting on a journey.

He thought, however, that he might have some business or other at a distance.

He turned in, and did not rise till ten o'clock.

Looking out at the back, however, he saw Mr. Smith pottering about in the garden amongst his flowers, in his usual orthodox get-up.

Ned could not help feeling a bit puzzled as to when he had got back.

The next night he resumed his watch.

Sure enough Mr. Smith left his home a little after midnight in the same fashion.

Ned remained watching at the window this time.

Several hours passed without anything fresh occurring, and he was just thinking of turning in, when the sound of approaching wheels caught his ear.

A few minutes later, Smith pulled up his pony before his door.

It was just getting light, and Ned could make out that the little animal was covered with sweat and foam.

It was evident that he had been driven far and furious.

Smith left the pony and cart, and, approaching his door, tapped at it softly.

It was evidently a signal.

The door was noiselessly opened in reply.

Smith returned to the cart and took from it in succession a variety of parcels and other objects of various shapes and sizes, some apparently very heavy.

These he handed in at the door, where they were received by someone whom Kelly could not see, but whom he guessed to be Mrs. Smith.

When the trap was unloaded, Smith led the pony with it into the stable, and after a space of time, evidently spent in unharnessing and rubbing down the animal, came out again and entered the house.

Kelly was more and more puzzled.

For a man of such strict outward respectability to go in for these midnight journeys began to strike him as suspicious in the extreme.

He recollected that on more than one occasion he had caught the sound of returning wheels in the small hours, and that they were in all probability those of Smith's trap.

Ned resolved to quietly investigate the mystery.

In the course of the day, he took the opportunity of examining the lock of Smith's stable on the quiet.

It was a perfectly ordinary one, and of a kind for which a key could be easily found.

His object in examining the stable was not quite clear to himself, but he had a kind of hazy idea that something might turn up.

He was not far wrong.

Lying on the ground near the trap was a scrap of printed paper. That paper had a heading, and under that heading was a bill for 3s. 6d., paid the evening before at the Falcon Inn, which was situate in the outskirts of Peckham.

"What's he up to?" thought Ned. "I saw one of them bills before. I'll find out, old bloke, what's your little game. Can't be a woman sure-ly. But them white-chokered codgers are so cunning. Blowed if I don't start off to the Falcon, and watch the old beggar. I should like to have the pull of his reverence—it might be useful to have his prayers if I get into trouble. Ha! ha! ha!" laughed the ruffian at the thought, for his instinct told him that Mr. Smith was, as he styled it, a "rum 'un."

He consequently started at once, and took up his position about two hundred yards from the Falcon, on the road he knew Smith would follow.

He soon heard wheels slowly approaching, and quickly recognised his saintly neighbour.

After a short pause he saw Smith alight.

Then the mysterious stranger took the pony's head and led it a short distance forward.

After proceeding for a few score yards Smith halted, after turning sharp round a corner.

As far as Kelly could judge, the last part of the journey had been performed over a very rutty road.

Smith drew the pony and trap close to a fence.

Then he got into the trap.

Kelly thought that he had only been leading the pony on account of the badness of the road, and that he would now drive on.

But, instead of that, the bushranger heard a kind of scraping sound, and saw the trap sway a bit to one side, and then grow lighter.

For a moment this puzzled him.

The next, he guessed at the solution.

Smith had evidently made use of the trap as a ladder to get over the fence by.

The bushranger could not help thinking that this was a very singular time and fashion for such a very respectable person as Smith to pay visits.

After waiting a few minutes, he became certain that Smith had got over the fence.

As far as he could make out in the darkness, he was in a narrow lane shaded with trees, turning out of a broader kind of road, but one equally rural-looking.

The pony and trap were drawn close up to what seemed to be a high wooden paling.

Kelly was a tall fellow, and reaching his hands up, managed to place them on the top of the paling.

It was garnished with spikes, but there was room enough between these for his fingers.

He drew himself up by his arms and looked over.

He could just discern the outline of a large house, separated from him by a lawn studded with trees and shrubs.

It was evident that Smith was paying a visit to the house, and a great desire to follow him stole over Ned at the thought.

What puzzled him was how the little man had managed to scramble across the palings without some damage to his skin, or, at any rate, to his outer-garments, from the spikes on the top.

By getting into the trap and examining the point where he had crossed, this was explained at a glance.

He had thrown the seat-cushion from the trap over the top of the fence, so that the spikes were neutralised.

Ned's ears were as keen as those of most men accustomed to hunting and being hunted in a wild country.

As he stood there in the trap, he detected the faint sound of splintering glass from the house.

"Oh!" he thought, "so my pious friend was not an expected guest there, after all."

Then came the faint click of a window-hasp being pushed back from without by a knife-blade; then the noise of a sash being quietly and cautiously raised.

Ned still listened.

A faint whirring noise denoted that a centre-bit was being employed to drill a hole in the shutters.

Then he heard the saw enlarging it, and then the low clank, as a hand was passed through this hole and the shutters unfastened.

The fact that a burglary was being committed flashed upon his mind.

"He's in now," he thought. "I wonder how long he'll be?"

He began to debate mentally as to the best course to take on his own account.

The artfully-played game of Smith filled him with great admiration for its player.

Who on earth would suspect a burglar in this quiet, respectable, outwardly-religious man, living in a modest but comfortable way in a suburban street, and devoting all his spare time to his music and his flowers?

It was all the more admirable to Ned as he felt it was so utterly out of his own line.

Indeed, he looked upon it as the lowest branch in the profession.

But, then, what an invaluable ally such a man was likely to prove, if he could secure him as such.

He resolved to make his acquaintance.

The question was, when?

Should he quietly introduce himself to Smith when the latter returned from his excursion over the paling, or suffer him to depart, and interview him at home on the morrow?

Whilst he was debating, his ear caught a fresh sound.

It was not, however, from the house this time, but from the main-road they had left.

Kelly had not been long in England, but he had heard it before in the watches of the night, and recognised it at once.

It was the peculiar tramping step of a policeman on night duty.

Ned debated for a moment what to do.

If he was caught by the policeman where he was he would certainly be arrested at once as an accomplice, and this would not suit his book at all.

Suddenly he thought of the mode of escape he had practised at Sydney when chased.

Stepping on to the summit of the fence from the trap he balanced himself for a moment and then caught hold of the bough of a tree.

With this he was about to swing into the garden, when, on second thoughts, he changed his mind.

His hunter's experience had taught him that a man is always looked for below rather than above.

So, instead of swinging himself to the ground, he made his way upwards into the tree.

He had not been long ensconced before a gleam of light caught his eye.

It proceeded from the bull's-eye of the policeman, who had arrived at the end of the lane.

He halted there for a short time.

He seemed to be hesitating whether to turn down the lane or to continue his way along the road.

At length he decided on the former.

He had advanced a few steps when he came to a sudden halt, in evident surprise.

He had caught sight of the pony and trap.

He at once took in the situation.

He again halted, after advancing a step or two.

Apparently he was unable to decide whether to advance to the house and give the alarm, or to try to capture the burglar, or burglars, on their retreat.

He was a plucky fellow, and decided on the latter course after but slight hesitation.

After glancing around for a place of concealment a thought seemed to strike him.

Bending down, he hid himself under the trap.

Several minutes elapsed.

At length Ned heard Smith approaching from the house across the lawn.

He was heavily laden.

After depositing his plunder at the foot of the fence on the inside, he returned for another load.

This was placed with the former, and then he returned for a third.

Then, by means of a garden chair which he placed against the fence and stood on, he passed the objects one by one over the boundary and let them fall into the cart.

The pony was evidently accustomed to this kind of work, for he stood like a rock.

This task accomplished, Smith stepped over the fence in turn, and, after arranging his spoil in the trap, got down to turn the pony's head and lead it back into the high road.

This was the moment for which the policeman had been waiting.

As Smith leaped from the trap the policeman darted from beneath it and seized him.

A desperate struggle ensued.

To Ned's astonishment, Smith, although far the smaller man and assailed at a disadvantage, was for some time able to hold his own with his intending captor

He twisted like an eel, and fought like a wild cat.

At last, by a desperate effort, he succeeded in freeing himself from the policeman's grasp.

He thrust his hand into his breast, evidently in search of some weapon concealed there.

Before he could draw it, however, the policeman had sprung at him again, with such violence as to bring him to the ground.

Ned saw that, if he was to interfere, now or never was the time to do so.

He advanced along his bough, dropped from it like an over-ripe pear into the road, and reached the combatants just as the policeman had planted a knee on his opponent's chest, and was choking him into a state of insensibility.

20

Ned clenched his fist, and caught the unfortunate fellow a blow with all his force just behind the ear.

He rolled over like a smitten ox.

Catching hold of Smith by the hand and pulling him to his feet, Ned tumbled him into the trap, pulled the pony's head round, and, jumping up, rattled away, heedless of ruts and jolts, towards the main road.

After driving a few score yards along this he slackened speed, and turned his attention to Smith, who was just recovering himself.

"Look here, old man," he began, "you'll understand I'm a pal by the way in which I have pulled you out of that little mess you were in with the bobby."

"Quite so," answered a voice which Ned would not have recognised as Smith's, and caused him to marvel at the fellow's resources of deception.

"I think you'll own up that, if it hadn't been for me, you'd have found yourself in a pretty tight fix?"

"Right," was the answer. "So now, what do you want for helping me? Name the price."

This answer almost disconcerted Ned.

He felt that a man he had saved from such peril in the colonies would hardly have assumed such a huxtering tone.

"No," he said, somewhat surlily, "that's not the point. I don't want any price for catching a bobby a clip under the ear and getting one of the right sort away from him."

"Well, what is it you do want? Before you tell me, however, you had better give me the reins. I know the road and the beast better than you do, and shall get more out of him."

"You're right there," said Ned, impressed by the other's business-like style. "But what struck me was that you seem a clever fellow and a plucky one. I have some little reputation in the same way myself, and I fancy we might get on together."

"No offence," was the reply, "but I prefer to work alone."

"You found it a bit awkward to-night, though," said Ned, with a grin that the night concealed from his companion.

"Yes; but I see how to avoid that in the future. I shall have a strap to fasten my barker to my wrist," he continued, half to himself, "then it will always be handy, and no time lost in feeling for it."

This business-like argument filled Ned with admiration for his companion's coolness and forethought.

"You wouldn't mind potting a bobby then?" he said.

"Nor anyone else," was the calm reply, given in a firm but quiet tone.

Ned saw that he had before him a man even more dangerous to society than himself, even as the serpent's bite is more dangerous than the tiger's claw.

In this cold, crafty, calculating villain he recognised a master hand.

But at the same time he determined to have the best of the game he meant to play.

"So you do not care about me for a pal?" he said.

"No: I am used to work by myself, and I believe that is why I have always got on. I treat matters from a strictly business point of view. But I should like to know what brought you to the spot so very conveniently for me just now."

Ned paused for a moment before replying.

Should he tell Smith that he knew him, and how he had followed, or rather accompanied, him all the way from his house?

He judged that, on the whole, he had better not.

He knew enough of his companion to guess that he would not hesitate at anything to get rid of anyone obnoxious to him, and that he carried a revolver and the road was deserted.

Not that he feared Smith, but he felt he would rather tame him than have to quarrel with him.

Besides, he might be useful.

Suppressing, therefore, with a great effort, his natural impulsiveness, he said—

"Well, to tell the truth, I was after the same game as yourself, but you were beforehand with me."

After proceeding a little further, Smith checked the pony, and said—

"I don't know where you are bound for, but I don't suppose our roads are quite the same. However, if it is anywhere near my way, I'll drop you, if you like."

"Oh, you artful fox!" thought Ned.

And he added aloud—

"Where are we now?"

"At Lee (a falsehood) on the main road to London."

"Oh, well, if you'll put me down a little further on, it will do for me."

This suited the other very well.

"Where shall we meet again?" asked he, "for I suppose I must pay you back the turn I owe you."

"Oh, where you like."

"Well, I'll be at the Elephant and Castle at nine to-morrow evening."

"All right, that'll suit."

At the top of the hill Ned got down.

"Remember, the Elephant and Castle at nine," called out Smith.

"Right, I'll be there," cried Ned. "Good-night!"

"Good-night!"

And Smith drove off, looking round from time to time to see that he was not followed.

Neither had the slightest intention of keeping the appointment, and Smith drove on at full speed, chuckling at the thought of how he had jockeyed his preserver.

As for Ned, he made his way quietly along the road, and, after several enquiries, made of the few wayfarers abroad at that early hour, succeeded in finding the way back to his dwelling.

All was silent, and he rightly judged that Smith had long since reached home.

Letting himself in, he stole upstairs, and, throwing himself on to his bed, was soon asleep.

CHAPTER CLIV.
THE HOLY ALLIANCE.

NED possessed the power of waking up almost at will.

At eight o'clock his eyes were open, and shortly afterwards he was down to breakfast.

After breakfast he took up a position commanding a view of the back gardens.

Before long he noticed Smith amongst his flowers.

In turn, he sauntered out into the garden.

Approaching the party wall dividing the gardens, he hailed the other.

Smith looked up.

"Can I have a word or two with you, Mr. Smith?" said Ned, as politely as he could and in a soft tone.

"Certainly," replied the other, somewhat astonished; for, although he knew Kelly by sight as his next-door neighbour's lodger, he had never spoken to him.

Consequently, he had not recognised him in the obscurity the night before.

"No time like the present, then," said Ned.

And, putting his hand on the top of the wall, he vaulted over.

"Really, sir!" began Smith.

"Listen to me," said Kelly, who had made up his mind what tack to pursue. "I've got a word or two I want to say to you on the quiet. So just come along to the bottom of the garden. I see you've got a summer-house there, and we'll talk things over."

Smith was puzzled.

"Suppose we step indoors," he said, feeling always on his guard, and thinking there would be a better chance of both escape and resistance, in case of any unpleasantness, in the house than out.

"No, you don't," said Ned, catching him by the wrist, with a grip of iron, "come where I said."

" If you don't release me, sir," said Smith, with dignity, after one effort to jerk his arm from Ned's clutch, " I shall call for assistance."

"Shut up, or I'll call for the police and give you into custody for the burglary committed last night at Lee. With the stolen plunder in the house, things would go rather hard with you."

"Who are you, then?" asked Smith, somewhat staggered.

" The man you flattered yourself you made such a fool of last night, but who wasn't inclined to go cooling his heels at the Elephant and Castle for nothing, old foxy."

Smith glared at him like a trapped wolf.

He was not used to being " bested."

"Look here," said Ned, " you've no need to cut up so shirty because other people are as smart as yourself. You are a very leary one, but I've had my peepers on you for some days past. I saw you start last night, and what's more, I saw you working."

Smith felt this was true.

He saw that Ned was not only as brave, but as cunning as himself

He resolved, therefore, to make a virtue of necessity.

" You are a smart fellow," he said, "what is it you really want of me, now?"

" I want you as a pal," said Ned.

" For what?"

" For a job or two in your own line. Oh, I know what you said about working alone, but there are jobs, and those of the best and biggest, that cannot be worked single-handed, be a man ever so much up to the knocker."

"Right you are."

" Well, I don't care for peddling work, I can tell you. I'm on the lookout for a job that will bring me in a lumping sum for my share, and the same for whoever works with me."

" A lumping sum in hard cash?" repeated Smith.

" Yes. It's not at all the first time I've landed a few thousand," said Ned, with a dash of swagger.

" Why, who are you then?"

" Who am I? I guess you've never been in the colonies or you would not need to put such a question. I'm Ned Kelly."

" Ned Kelly?"

" The same."

" Oh, I've heard of you."

" Very likely."

" Let's see, aren't you the man who has a wonderful horse, a sort of Black Bess? At least, so I read in those cursed newspapers that pull everything into the light—curse them!"

" Ay, Marco Polo, the finest bit of horseflesh that was ever foaled under the Southern Cross. But who the devil are you, and what's your real name, mate?"

" I haven't got one," said the other with a smile.

" What?" roared Ned, half angrily, at what he thought was chaff.

" It's quite true, I assure you. I am just the opposite of you. You have almost always gone for big things, and have done your best to attract attention. I, on the other hand, have been working for forty years in the quietest way that is possible, and under fifty different names."

" For forty years?"

" Yes."

" And haven't you been caught?"

" Not often."

" But sometimes?"

" Now and then."

" But then the police know you?"

" Not at all."

" But——"

" Let me explain. I have had twenty names and twenty different identities, twenty separate existences."

" Hang it, man, they must recognise your face."

" Do you think so?" said the other.

He turned away for a moment and then faced Ned, observing as he did so in an entirely different voice---

"Do you know me now?"

Ned started back in amazement.

By some marvellous power acquired over the facial muscles, Smith had transformed every feature.

If Kelly had not had him before his eyes the whole time he would have sworn it was a another man.

" But " continued Peace, for that was the real name of the musical burglar, "you haven't seen my Sunday School face, for I always perform my Sabbath duties to the Sunday School as regularly as either of our Lord Chancellors, or that simple-minded old cove, Lord Shaftesbury. I put the young 'uns through their facings, I can tell you. I make 'em shout the Old Hundreth with fifty parson-power, and I take good care the lot present hear my sweet voice chanting away like blue blazes. Oh! it's affecting; very. I'm looked up to, I am, and blowed if I don't deserve it! for I fulfil my Christian duties with regularity. I rest on the Sabbath; I never 'work' on the seventh day. I'm too conscientious, I am. Now you see the advantage of a good character and thorough respectability. It gives one such a pull when a job's up."

Kelly looked on with amused surprise.

" By Jingo, you are a whole team and two bullocks to spare, you are. You're the stuff I like to meet. Why, we could work together like a matched pair in the shafts."

Smith, or Peace, evidently appreciated the compliment.

" You're too flattering," he said, " but I ' do my best in that station of life to which God has called me,' as the prayerbook says," ejaculated Smith, with an affected exaggeration of the conventicle nasal twang, while his eyes twinkled mischievously.

He then dropped the clerical mask and turned his head aside once more, facing Kelly again with the appearance to which the latter was accustomed.

" But how the devil do you do it?" inquired Ned.

" It's mainly a natural gift, improved by years of practice. There are several men who give public entertainments, similarly gifted. I can knead my nose into any shape, like a piece of putty, screw up my eyes, bring wrinkles on any part of my face at will or smooth them away, alter the shape of my mouth and the slant of my eyebrows, and, what is the best trick of all, I can thrust out or draw back my lower jaw a couple of inches."

" Why is that the best of all?" asked Ned.

" Why, because I can do with it what is the most difficult thing, to alter one's profile and disguise the face, not only when seen frontways, which is comparatively easy, but when seen sideways. Now do you see what an advantage it is to me to work alone and have no pals to get me into scrapes and betray me, purposely or accidentally."

" True; but what is your real name?"

" As I have said, I hardly know. I suppose the one by which I shall be handed down to posterity—if I ever am to be handed down—will be the one under which I shall be scragged."

" Scragged?"

" Yes, for I am determined to put a bullet into any man who tries to take me as you saw the other night. For if I am nabbed its 'life,' so I say life for ' life.' "

This was a true prophecy, for it was for shooting a policeman that Smith, in whom our readers have recognised the burglar hanged under the name of Peace, was arrested.

" Well, I suppose, now, you won't object to join me?"

" No, you're a pal I believe any man would be proud to work with, and if you can put me on to a big thing that will bring in as much as you say, I am game to join you."

" All right," said Ned; " the man who is working the affair has not fixed it all through just yet, but as soon as he does he will let me know."

Peace remained pensive for a few moments.

" Look here," he said after a pause, " there is a job that I have been turning over in my head; but, fix it as I will, I can't see my way to bring it off single-handed. With you it might be pulled off, though, all right."

"What is it?"

"Well, it's a crib to be cracked in town. I usually prefer working in the suburbs, but in this case the swag is too tempting to be neglected if there's ever such a little chance of getting hold of it."

"What is it?"

"Why, the old fellow is a diamond merchant."

"A diamond merchant?"

"Yes, one of the old style. He was a lapidary before becoming a diamond dealer; lives down Hatton-garden way, and sleeps on the premises. I knows he keeps a large stock of stones in the house, and, once inside, it would be easy enough to lay one's hands on them if one only knew where they were."

"That's the rub, I suppose?"

"Yes. There's no getting a chance of a squint round the premises. If I could only get inside!"

"Well, you might tell me where it is, and I'll go and have a look at the outside, at any rate."

"It is Mr. Mallan, No. 21, —— Street, Hatton-garden. He's an old fellow, with a wife and one servant."

"Is there no chance of getting over her?"

"I'm afraid not. She's devotedly attached to her mistress; that much I do know."

"But a handsome young fellow might have a chance of talking her over?"

"Perhaps."

"At all events that game can be tried."

"I think," said Peace, "you and I have been talking together quite long enough for the present. People will begin to wonder what you have to say to me."

"Oh, blow 'em!" said Ned.

"Not at all, my dear friend. Come, get back over the wall at once."

"Well, when shall I meet you to go on talking over this job? None of your Elephant and Castle dodges this time."

"Do you know the Crown in —— Street? It's an old-fashioned sort of a place, and there's hardly any one there in the coffee-room of an evening. I'll meet you there to-night at nine."

And as Ned scrambled over the wall, and his landlord, who had stepped into the garden, stood in amazement at his return, Peace continued, raising his voice—

"I am truly thankful, sir, to have made your acquaintance, since it has enabled me to add my mite to this good work. Truly, it rejoices the heart to help the afflicted. Ah! Mr. Buttersby," he continued, pretending to catch sight of Kelly's landlord for the first time, "I am truly pleased to have made the acquaintance of your lodger. He has spoken to me of a great and good work, to the successful carrying out of which I shall, by the grace of Heaven, be only too glad to lend my slender aid."

'A born parson!" thought Ned as he heard him.

'How he must have soaped down the chaplain whenever he has been quodded. He's just the sort of fellow who shams sick and sorrowful, gets let off hard labour, and spends all his time lying on his back and guzzling boiled chicken and port wine in the infirmary. Oh! he's a downy card."

The same night saw Kelly and Peace seated cheek-by-jowl in one of the boxes in the large but deserted old-fashioned coffee-room of the Crown.

The contrast between the two was all the more striking by this proximity.

It would have been difficult to have found two more opposite types of humanity than the reckless, broad-shouldered, daring-looking bushranger in his somewhat rough attire, and the sanctimonious little white-haired burglar, something like a parson run to seed, in his black coat and hat encircled with a mourning-band.

At the same time it would have been difficult to have found two more thorough-paced villians.

The subject of conversation between them was the best method of effecting an entrance into the diamond merchant's, and it was not until this had been thoroughly discussed that the two separated, though without settling anything definite.

A few days later Ned started off to survey the house inhabited by Mr. Mallan.

Jess, who had joined him in London, accompanied him, though without being aware of what was passing in his mind, or the object of his stroll.

He paced slowly down the street with the girl on his arm, looking at the house on the opposite side of the way.

No. 21 was one of the old-fashioned, strongly-built houses to be found in the locality.

The lower floor evidently served as work-rooms and office, and the upper part as a dwelling-house.

As he looked, a butcher, with his tray on his shoulder, came up and rang the bell.

A middle-aged, decent-looking woman, dressed as a servant, opened the door in reply.

"Well, this is funny," said Jess.

"What?" asked Ned.

"You saw that girl who opened the door there?"

"Yes; what of her?"

"Why, would you believe it? she's a returned convict! She was in quod with me in Sydney; I knew her face at once."

"By Jove!" exclaimed Ned, "I've got it then. What's her name, Jess?" he continued to the astonished girl by his side

"Paramatta Sal."

"Hurrah!" cried Ned. "I see the way to do the trick."

CHAPTER CLV.
A SNAKE IN THE GRASS.

PARAMATTA SAL'S history up to a certain point was not at all an uncommon one.

The offspring of criminals, she had been brought up without ever having the difference between right and wrong pointed out to her.

She was of a dull, yet affectionate disposition, and looked up to and loved her wretched parents after a fashion.

They taught her to steal, and she stole without having the slightest idea she was doing evil.

Her intelligence was indeed remarkably limited, and the frequent ill-treatment she received did not do much to foster its development.

As she grew up she began to steal on her own account, and a little later became the slave of a man who used to thrash her and squander the product of her thefts, but to whom she displayed the dog-like affection that was part of her nature.

At last her lover, who was named Tom Hill, was shot in an attempted burglary, and she, being implicated in receiving stolen property, was sentenced to a rather long term of imprisonment.

She had already undergone several short sentences, but these had made no impression on her.

On this occasion, however, the death of her lover, and the admonition of the chaplain, who divined the poor woman's real nature, had a great effect on her.

It was a very difficult task for the chaplain to arouse in her stolid mind a sense of the difference between right and wrong, but, when he at length succeeded in doing so, her repentance was genuine and profound.

He saw, however, that on her release there was great danger of her returning to her old associates, and that the best thing to do would be to get her out of the colony.

Accordingly he found means to have her shipped to England, and received there in a house for training servants.

From this she had passed into the service of Mr. and Mrs. Mallan, to whom she had transferred all the devotion she was capable of.

She had gone so far as to tell them her story, and they

fully appreciated her evident wish to do right in all things.

Mr. Mahan was a man of about sixty, with a frank, open face, and a look of good nature which did not, however, detract from the shrewdness that had been acquired during some forty years devotion to business.

His bright eye and clear complexion denoted a sound constitution, and, despite his age, a life of sobriety and activity had rendered him, even at sixty, one of those men whom it is pleasanter to drink with than to fight with.

His wife, who was somewhat younger, was a house-wifely kind of body, stout and bustling, and occasionally given to scolding-fits, but at the bottom thoroughly good-natured.

Of this she had often given proofs, and one quite recently, in her treatment of poor Sal, whose true character she had guessed at and appreciated.

Sal one Saturday, a day or two after she had been recognised by Jess, was scrubbing away at her pots and pans till her face was as red as a peony.

She was hard at it when the kitchen door opened and her mistress came in.

"Ah, you are at it again?" said the new-comer.

Sue lifted up her head and look confused.

"But, ma'am," she said, twisting her apron with her hands in an embarrassed manner, "it's Saturday, and I felt bound to tidy things up."

"Nonsense, girl! I told you before to have a man in for this rough work. I don't want you to knock yourself up like this."

"No fear of that, ma'am; I'm too tough, and you can't think how pleased I am to be able to show how thankful I feel for your kindness by working with all my might and main."

"Pooh-pooh! my girl, there's no need of that; and besides, it would be a poor way of proving your gratitude to knock yourself up and give us the trouble of nursing you, eh?" And the good woman laughed at her own remark.

"Oh, ma'am!" said the poor creature, "I feel I never can repay all I owe to you. How few people would have taken in a poor girl like me, and treated me as you have done."

"Nonsense! Don't talk like that. I've just run down to tell you that I am going out for a couple of hours at least, in case anyone calls. I shall be in about teatime, tell your master when he comes in."

A few minutes later Sal heard the front door slam after her mistress.

"Ah!" she reflected, "the more I think of it the surer I am that no one else in the world would have treated me like they have. They know what I have been, and might always be thinking that I should let in some of my old friends, especially with all those diamonds in the place. But, God knows, I'd rather have my throat cut first."

At that moment the bell rang.

Wiping her hands on her apron she ran up and opened the door.

On the step was a tall young woman, plainly but comfortably dressed, and wearing a thick veil.

She stepped into the passage before Sal had time to utter any word of question as to her business.

"Who do you want, please, miss?" said Sal.

The new-comer raised her veil.

"Don't you know me, Sal?" she said in a pleasant voice.

A nervous tremor ran through poor Sal's frame.

"Jess Appleby!" she ejaculated, in agitated tones.

"Yes," said Jess, cheerfully; "but you don't seem over-pleased to meet an old friend, and I thought it would be such a treat for us to come together and have a talk about the Colony, and the jolly sprees we had there in poor Tom Hill's time."

"Be quiet—be quiet," said Sal, placing her hand almost fiercely on the girl's mouth. "Do not speak that name here. Say nothing more about those days, when I was a wretched, lost woman. Do not speak of it."

"What," said Jess, somewhat disconcerted, "not even a word about poor Tom Hill?"

A look from Sal checked her.

Although spoken in a sympathising tone, these words, instead of moving Sal as formerly they would have done, seemed rather to be repugnant to her.

"Tom Hill was a villain; may God forgive him as I do," she said at length.

"Oho Sal," thought Jess, "that cock won't fight. I see I must try another lay."

"Yes," resumed Sal; "now I have struggled out of the mud into which I had fallen, and live among honest folk, I see clearly and know what sort of companions I used to have."

"Do you mean that for me, Sal?" said Jess, in a tone of bitterness. "I suppose now you can afford to despise a poor motherless girl, who went to the bad when a mere child, not knowing right from wrong?"

Jess was closely watching Sal, and saw that this last remark had not been thrown away.

"It's true you were quite a kid, and did not know what you were up to," said Sal, meditatively.

"Oh! if you only knew how I have repented of the past and tried to break off with it," said Jess. "It is for that I have come to England. I saved enough for my passage, thinking to get rid of all my old wicked associates, but here in London there seems to be more wickedness than even in Sydney. If you only knew what I have had to fight against. Ah! how fortunate you have been to find honest people to look after you. I only wish I could get such a chance," and she almost sobbed.

"Have you been trying, Jess?" asked Sal.

"Yes, indeed I have, Sal, and I hope to get a place of some kind. I don't care how hard I work, as long as I can make a fresh start, and earn an honest crust."

Poor Sal was deeply touched by this experience, so like her own.

"I am glad you think of going straight, Jess," she said.

Jess suddenly staggered, and leant against the wall.

"What's the matter?" cried Sal alarmed.

"I feel a bit faint. I have not been living too well since I have been over here," was the answer, in a low voice.

"Poor girl. And to think of that—you, who never wanted anything. Come down into the kitchen, and I'll get you a cup of tea."

The pair descended into the kitchen, and Sal soon put a cup of tea and some thin bread and butter before her guest, who, however, assured her she was too faint to eat much.

She had, in fact, just dined with Ned.

However, the tea revived her, and they chatted rather pleasantly about the colony.

"And what sort of a place have you here now?" asked Jess, after a little time.

"Oh, a capital one!" said Sal, enthusiastically. "There is plenty to do, but I don't mind that, for the master and mistress are just bricks, they are."

"I don't know much about London houses," said Jess; "but there seems to be a sight more work to be done than at Sydney."

"Yes. And the beastly blacks and smuts makes things twice as hard to keep clean. There's a lot to do here, I can tell you."

"Do you mind letting me look over the place?" said Jess, in the most innocent tones.

"No. Come round and I'll show you. It's lucky there's no one in the house but me just now, both master and missus have gone out. Hark! there's the milkman. Just wait while I get the milk."

As soon as Sal left the kitchen, Jess drew from her pocket a small object which she began to knead in her hands, and then waited.

Her face had lost the meek and contrite expression it had worn during her interview with Sal.

In a minute the latter had returned.

"Come along," she said to Jess, whose physiognomy had resumed its subdued aspect on her reappearance, "and I will show you round the place."

She quitted the kitchen, followed by Jess, who smiled behind her back in a singular fashion.

The house occupied by Mr. Mallan was a tall, narrow building, of three storeys in height.

The kitchens were underground.

On the ground floor, the front room served as a kind of workshop, and the back room as Mr. Mallan's office.

The dining and drawing rooms were on the first floor.

Mr. Mallan's bedroom and a spare bedroom occupied the second floor.

The servants' room was on the third.

Jess and Sal first visited the upper part of the house.

The former praised the cleanliness and neatness of the bedrooms, and then they descended to the first floor.

With justifiable pride, Sal pulled back the table-cover to show the dining-table, shining like a mirror from a liberal application of elbow-grease.

"I declare I feel really a better girl, Sal, only to touch all these things that have all been honestly earned," said Jess, artfully.

"Well, I never! but that's just what I feel when I'm a-scrubbing of them. I says to myself, 'If ever there was an honest house, it's this,'" said Sal, quite charmed at this remark.

"Just so. And is this the drawing-room?"

"Yes. Isn't it fine? They have had these things some time, but missus is a rare tidy one, and they are as good as new."

"I am sure there's something in an honest house different from any other," cried Jess, enthusiastically.

Poor Sal was enchanted.

It was just the effect the place, with its air of honest hard work successfully wrought out, had had on herself, and she fully believed Jess was similarly impressed.

"And what is there on the ground floor?" enquired Jess.

"The office and the workshop. Do you want to see those too?"

"Oh! yes."

"Come along then."

After descending the stairs, Sal opened the workroom door, and ushered her companion into it.

The same order and cleanliness reigned here.

There was room for four men, and four stools were ranged along the two benches for their accommodation.

"So it's here the men work?" said Jess.

"Yes; from nine till five and six," was the answer.

"And the master?"

"Oh, that's his room," and she pointed to the door leading to the inner room.

"Can we have a peep in there?"

"Oh, yes; I dust it out every morning."

They entered the office. Jess holding in her hand the substance she had been kneading in the kitchen.

"Ah!" she said, glancing around, "that's the safe, I suppose?"

"Yes."

"Where the books are kept?"

"And something better than books."

"What?"

"The diamonds."

"Ah! of course. I had forgotten your master was a diamond merchant. There must be something worth having inside there. Four or five thousand pounds, perhaps."

Sal laughed.

"Twenty or thirty thousand would be nearer the mark sometimes," she said.

"Really? What a lot! I'd like to see twenty thousand pounds' worth of diamonds," she said, reflectively.

"It's not much of a sight after all," said Sal, innocently,

in a tone of consolation. "Master has shown me a lot sometimes."

After a few words more Jess took her leave, and hurried off to a quiet public where Ned, Peace, and Kit were waiting for her.

"Well?" said Ned.

"It's quite true, the man is a diamond merchant," said Jess.

"Good."

"And there are sometimes thirty thousand pounds' worth of sparklers on the premises at once."

"Thirty thousand pounds' worth!" echoed Peace.

"And a friend in the camp, eh, Jess?" said Ned.

"As to that, no. We can't count on Sal."

"What!"

"That's where the mischief is."

"Did you sound her?"

"Very carefully; and it was lucky I was cautious. She told me her story. She has gone in for virtue, fidelity, and a most devoted attachment to her master and mistress."

"Bosh!"

"Not a bit of it. All genuine."

"Well but, Jess," put in Kit, "you're a clever girl, couldn't you talk her over? Tell her we'll go snacks."

"You might as well try to persuade a Newfoundland dog to drown his master."

"Curse it!" said Ned.

"No swearing, my friends," exclaimed Peace, in his most sanctimonious tones, throwing up his eyes with an expression of holy horror.

"Perhaps this may be of some use to you," said Jess, with a smile, placing an object she had taken from her pocket on the table before them.

All bent forward to examine it.

"Yes," said Jess, "the locks of the workshop and of the office in which is a safe holding the diamonds."

"By all that's glorious, Jess, but you are a brick," cried Ned, enthusiastically.

"Besides, I know all the ins and outs of the place and shall call on Sal once or twice till I find out a good day to work on."

"Capital."

"Well, it is to be share and share alike between us, as arranged, I suppose?" said Peace.

"Stop a bit," remarked Ned. I'm expecting a friend who may have a word to say about that matter.

"Hullo!" said Peace, "what's the meaning of this?"

"I'll go and see if he's in the bar," said Ned, and, going out, he returned with our old friend, the Count.

"This is the pal who has the big job of which I spoke to you on hand," said Ned to Peace.

"I remember," replied the latter, gruffly, for he strongly objected to a number of people being mixed up in any affair in which he was concerned. "But can one patter before him?"

"Yes, freely."

"Oh, I will set you the example," said Anatole with a smile. "I know what you are up to now."

"Oh?" said Peace.

"Yes, the little matter of the diamond merchant, in which I wish to figure as your partner."

"Hum!" said Peace, "I think there are enough of us in it, as it is, to pull it off all right, and to share the dibs."

"The dibs? the dibs?" said Anatole in a perplexed tone of voice. "What are the dibs?"

"The plunder," said Ned, laughing.

"Well, suppose I show you how, in taking me as your partner, you can double, treble your share of the—how do you call it?—the dibs."

"Oh, bosh!" said Peace.

"Stop one little moment," said Anatole. "Suppose the little affair, the job, over, and the diamonds—the beautiful little diamonds—in your hands."

"Well?"

"Well, the diamonds are there—sparkling so prettily

ah, yes!—on that table, and you divide them into four lots, each representing—let us say—six thousand pounds."

"Certainly," said the three men simultaneously.

"Just so—and then?"

"And then?" repeated Peace.

"Yes, what do you do? You can't live on diamonds."

"No, but we can sell them."

"Exactly; that is what I wanted to come to."

"It's simple enough," said the old burglar.

"Perhaps. You have the diamonds in your pocket."

"And we sell them."

"To whom?"

There was a silence of a few moments.

Anatole went on—

"Could either of you three go to a Bond-street jeweller the day after a big robbery, and offer him six thousand pounds worth of diamonds?"

The three looked at one another.

"It's true," said Kit. "We might arouse his suspicions."

"And cause him to send for the police—eh?"

"That's so."

"Then it's no use thinking of Bond-street jewellers."

"I'm afraid not."

"But there are the wholesale diamond dealers."

"There are," said Kit, puzzled at what he was driving at.

"Only they are just as mistrustful as the others, and would be equally well aware of the robbery."

"Hang it all! cannot a man sell diamonds in a free country?" said Ned, who was getting impatient at all this talk.

"Yes, if he has a connection, gives a correct name and address to the buyer, and proves he has a right to them. But now to return to the point. To whom can you sell them?"

"Well, I suppose there are fences," said Peace.

"Fences! Ah, yes, the recéleur, the receiver of stolen goods. But, in the first place, where is the fence with such a sum as thirty thousand pounds at leisure to lay out in diamonds? And even if he had it—knowing the difficulty of getting rid of the stones, and accustomed to pay a shilling for what is well worth a pound—he would only offer you a thousand for the lot."

"A thousand!" cried Ned.

"Two, at the outside. You know it perfectly."

The three were silent.

"The result of this would be that, unless you succeeded in getting rid of your diamonds one by one to private buyers, and then only at a loss and with great difficulty and risk, your six thousand pounds apiece would mean five hundred, just enough to carry you on a few months."

"You're right," said Peace.

"Well, then, I am ready to give you cash down, half the value of the diamonds."

"Cash down?"

"Yes, I am willing to hand the money over on delivery of the goods, and I think our friend here," and he indicated Ned, "will tell you that I am a man of my word."

"And, now, when is the job to come off?" asked Peace.

"We cannot settle that just yet. Jess, however, will be on the lookout, and will let us know the best chance."

"How about the other affair?" enquired Ned of Anatole.

"Oh! that goes on slowly, but surely I think, and it promises very well," answered Anatole.

"This is the pal whom I meant to help us in it," said Kelly, indicating Peace.

A brief introduction followed, and then drinks round. The party separated in various directions.

Jess continued to visit Sal occasionally, feigning great virtue, and at length learned that Mr. Mallan was going to give a supper to celebrate the twenty-fifth anniversary of his wedding-day.

She told this to the others, and they came to the conclusion to attempt the robbery on this day, as it would be one on which such an attempt would be least looked for.

Furthermore, she got Sal to let her assist her in the preparations on the day in question, with the mistress's permission.

CHAPTER CLVI.
AT THE DIAMOND MERCHANT'S.

THE supper given by Mr. Mallan to celebrate the twenty-fifth anniversary of his wedding was a jovial gathering.

He was a man who had risen as it were from the ranks, having begun life as a working lapidary, and made no attempt at pretension since he had realised a fortune.

He had asked a score of friends and relations to a good, honest sit-down supper, to be followed by a song or two, a round game at cards and unlimited grog.

The cooking of the supper was done by Mrs. Mallan with the aid of Sal and Jess.

The guests began to drop in at about nine o'clock, and very soon a very merry and noisy party were gathered on the first floor.

Meanwhile, the intending burglars had not been idle.

Peace had had keys made which it was pretty certain would easily open the workshop and office doors, though the lock of the safe would probably present more difficulty.

At length, on the appointed evening, the three met at Kit's lodgings, which were situated near Holborn.

"Before we start," said Peace, "I should like to put in a word or two."

"Go it," said Ned.

"Why the first is this. It sometimes happens that at the last moment something unexpected crops up and spoils the best-laid plan."

"That's true, but I think we have foreseen everything."

"Quite so. But at the last moment we may be surprised by someone, and I know your temper and ways,' and as he spoke he addressed himself to Ned.

"What do you mean?"

"I mean that you are just the man to pull out your revolver, and blaze away, so as to rouse not only the house but the neighbourhood; such a game is all very well in the bush, but it won't do in London."

"You carry a revolver yourself."

"Yes, for country and suburban work, but not for this sort of job. If killing a man will get one clear off I'd shoot one like a cat, but it would be madness to use fire arms in a case like the present."

"But I'm not going to use them. What more do you want?" said Ned, savagely.

"I'll tell you what more I want," replied Peace, looking him straight in the face. "I want you to take your revolver out of your pocket and place it with mine on the table here."

"And if I won't?"

"Then I'll not stir another step in the matter."

"That is to say, you want to be cock of the walk in this affair," said Ned, swiftly slipping his hand into his pocket.

"I don't want to be cock of the walk, but I want you to agree to those conditions, returned the other, imitating him.

"You're a perky little sprat to talk about conditions," said Ned, pulling out his revolver and balancing it threateningly.

"We shall see about that," replied Peace, calmly producing a similar weapon and imitating him.

The two stood face to face for a moment.

There was a striking contrast between the coarsely-handsome and dashing, muscular ruffian and the precise-looking little old fellow in front of him.

At first sight it looked as if Ned could have eaten his adversary at a mouthful.

But the pale grey eye of the odd little burglar was full of that cold resolution that nought can quail.

"Here, hang it all, don't be a couple of fools," cried Kit, throwing himself between them. "This is not the way to do business. Peace is right after all, and for my part there is my revolver."

As he spoke he placed it on the table.

Growling like a bear with a sore head, and eyeing Peace in a manner that might have terrified a weaker minded man, Ned followed his example.

"Very well," he muttered as he did so, "but all the same, I think we are acting like a blessed pack of fools."

"You know your own tastes best, Ned," said Kit; "but for my part I don't care about making the acquaintance of the Newgate drop if I can help it."

"And suppose three or four of the people in the house catch us at the job, what are we to do then, eh?" asked Ned of Peace.

"Try and break through them and get clear," was the answer.

"All very fine," said Ned to himself; "but although I have given up my revolver, I'll stick to my knife, and I should not be surprised if it did not come in handy before the night was over."

"Come," said Peace, "it's about time t start. The supper was fixed for ten, and by eleven everything will be in full swing. They will be laughing and drinking and making noise enough to wake the dead, and we shall not be heard."

"It's a capital day to choose," even if they do hear a noise, a robbery with all the guests in the house will be the last thing they will dream of."

"How are we to get in?" asked Peace.

"Oh, I've arranged a signal with Jess," answered Ned.

Some twenty minutes later the three were standing outside the house of the diamond merchant.

It was close on eleven o'clock, and the street, the houses in which were mostly let out in offices, was completely deserted.

Very few of the houses had any lights in their windows. The night was a chilly one, and there was a slight drizzling rain.

The three waited for a few moments making their final arrangements.

It had been agreed that only Peace and Ned should enter the house, Kit remaining outside on the watch.

The last named retreated, therefore, to the opposite side of the street, while Ned gave a low but distinct coo-ee—the Australian cry—which was the signal to Jess.

The girl, who was in the kitchen, heard it, and held herself in readiness.

Accordingly, when a ring came at the bell a few minutes later she said—

"All right, Sal, I'll answer it," and started out of the kitchen before the other girl had thought of stirring.

Running upstairs she opened the door and admitted Ned and Peace into the passage

"Who is it?" suddenly called out Mrs. Mallan's voice from the landing above.

"A man wants to know if Mr. Thompson lives here, ma'am," was the ready answer.

At that moment the fun on the first floor had reached its height.

Supper was drawing to a close, and everyone's tongue having been set wagging, jokes were being bandied about on all sides, and all were trying to talk at once.

Corks popped, plates rattled, glasses jingled, and the combined din was almost deafening.

Jess pointed to the workshop door and darted down into the kitchen, where, as if inspired by the gaiety above, she began to sing in a loud voice, and to wash up plates and dishes with an accompanying amount of clattering that threatened every minute to demolish them.

Meanwhile Peace had drawn a set of skeleton keys from his pockets and applied one to the workshop door.

It opened easily, and the two men, slipping into the room, closed it quietly after them.

"Pretty neatly done, eh?" said Peace, with a chuckle.

"Yes," answered Ned, "but don't let us lose time."

The workshop was in total darkness, the shutter being closed, so Peace struck a match and lit a lantern.

By its light they approached the office door.

"There's one advantage in the closed shutter," said Peace, "and that is that no one outside can see the light.

He began to try the lock of the office.

"Confound it!" he said, after trying several keys one after another, "this is a more difficult job than I thought for. Hold the light closer."

Ned obeyed, and, after a careful examination, Peace selected another key.

"I think this one will settle it," he remarked.

His prophecy was correct, and next moment the office door was open.

The two stepped cautiously into the room.

The safe at once caught their eye.

It was a heavy but old-fashioned affair

"This will be the hardest nut of all to crack," said Peace as he surveyed it.

Selecting a fresh set of keys he began an attack on the lock, Ned eagerly watching him, and at the same time listening for the slightest sound from without.

(To be continued.)

NED KELLY THE IRONCLAD AUSTRALIAN BUSHRANGER

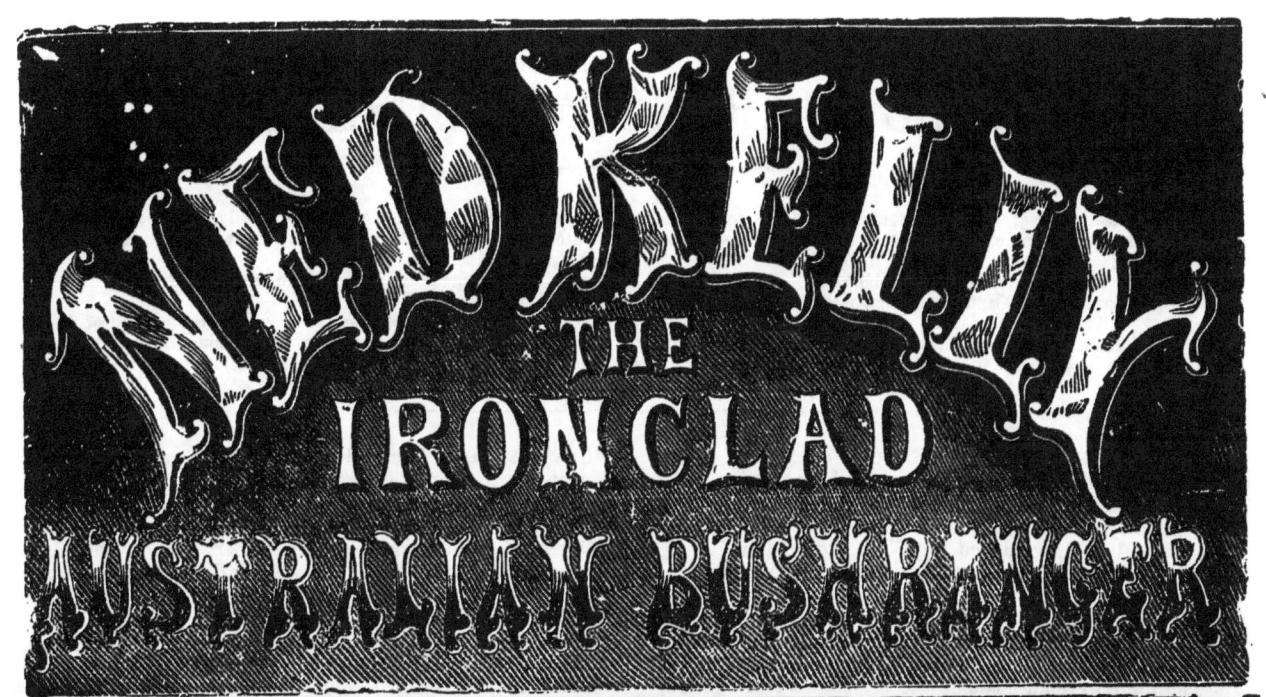

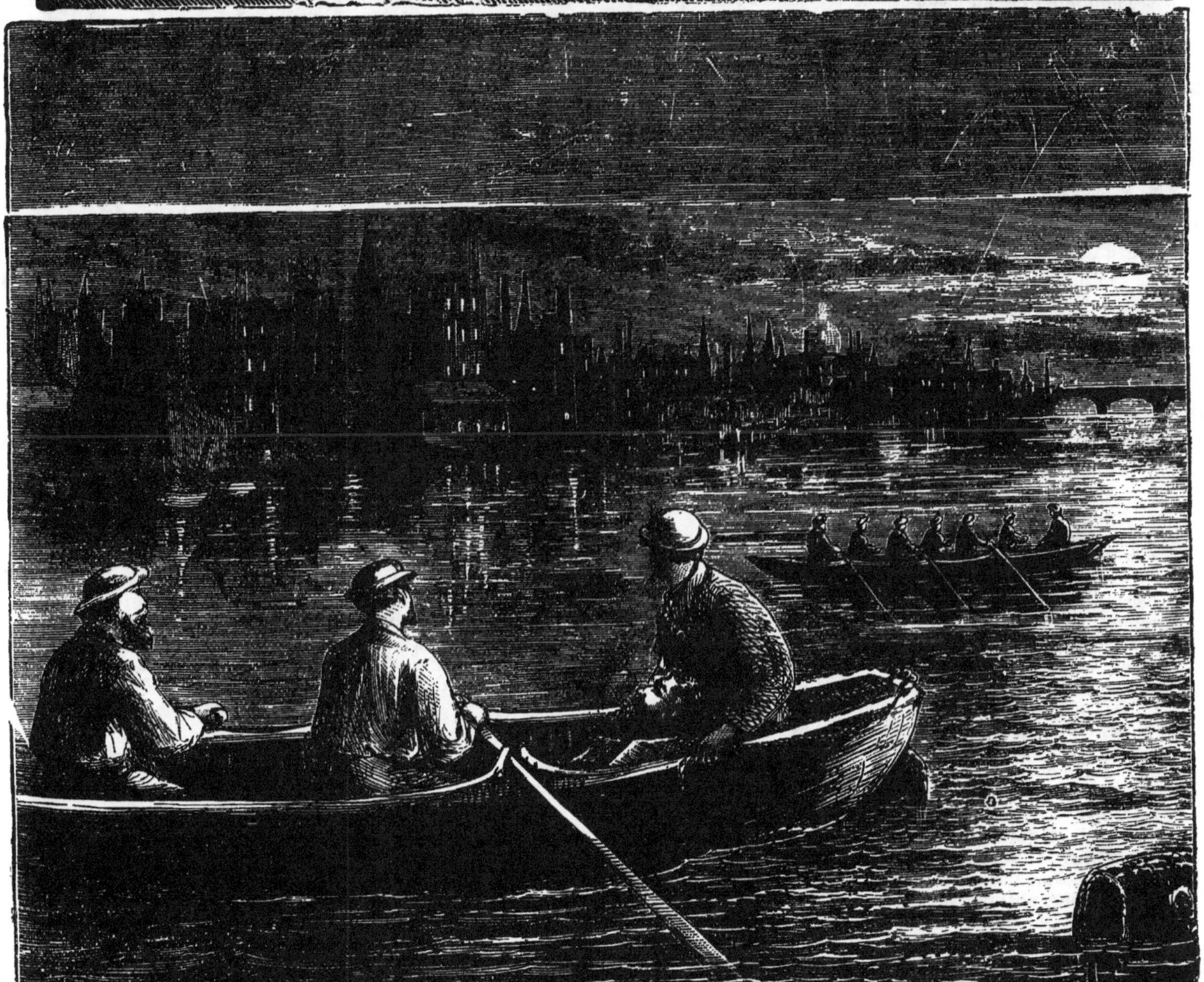

NO 27,

NED KELLY: IRONCLAD BUSHRANGER.

" It is well known that for many years Ned Kelly had made himself notorious by a series of crimes wholly incompatible with the civilisation of the nineteenth century. Ned Kelly's celebrated steed, Marco Polo, is as well known at the Antipodes as Dick Turpin's Black Bess in these islands."—*Telegraph*, 7th July, 1881.

" It is notorious that the robbery of Mr. Steward's corpse was mainly performed by the assistance of NED KELLY'S BROTHER, the Captain of what was neither more nor less than a pirate ship."—*Times*, July.

" The history of NED KELLY and his celebrated black horse, Marco Polo, will ever live in the recollection of the Australian public. The deeds of Dick Turpin, and the performances of Black Bess, are tame beside those of ' NED AND HIS NAG ;' in addition to which Ned's history is true, and Turpin's is pure fiction."—*Press*, July.

CHAPTER CLVI.—*Continued.*

A muttered oath from Peace caught his attention.

" What is it? " he asked.

" The keys are no good here," was the answer.

" Hang it all! " said Ned. " What's to be done ? "

" Oh, there are more ways of killing a dog than hanging him," replied Peace, " and I have not come out without all my tools."

From his pockets he produced several crowbars of different lengths, a number of wedges, and a hammer.

The tools were all made of the very finest steel, and the tops of the wedges and the head of the hammer were covered with leather.

" Shan't you make an infernal row with those ? " asked Ned in a somewhat uneasy tone.

" No," answered the other. " Just wait till you see me at work. I learnt this lesson from Casey, who so astonished all the big-wigs at his trial when he showed them that the strongest safe they could put together could be forced with 'a common councilman' (a wedge), 'an alderman' (a bigger wedge), and 'the chancellor' (the crowbar)."

Selecting an almost imperceptible crevice Peace succeeded in driving one end of a fine steel wedge into it.

Again the two paused for a while to see if the noise had been heard.

No; all was right, and the din above continued.

The wedge having once bitten, the rest was easy.

With a marvellous knowledge of the power and principle of the lever, Peace began to bring the crowbars into play, and, aided by Ned's immense strength, succeeded in wrenching open the door of the safe, with, however, a crash that it was impossible to avoid.

" That's awkward," said Ned.

" Sharp! let's clear it out," was the answer.

The diamonds were nowhere visible, till Peace hit upon a large, locked cashbox at the bottom of the safe.

" This must be it," he exclaimed, and seizing a crowbar, began to force the lid off, for the box was too bulky to remove.

" Quick—quick," said Ned, " I hear someone coming down the stairs."

" Curse this lid," said Peace, redoubling his efforts.

Ned bent over to see if he could help.

As he did so the lid flew open, and at the same moment a growl of pain and rage escaped him.

The crowbar, in slipping up, had caught him, in his bending position, a sharp blow on the ear, and cut it severely.

He fell forward on the box just as Peace had transferred the contents into a bag he had in readiness.

At the same instant a hand was laid on the second door of the office, opening into the passage close by the staircase.

Peace sprang up, and, darting into the workshop, opened its door, gained the passage, and began to unfasten the street-door.

Ned also rose, and was about to follow him.

But just as he gained his feet, the second door of the office was thrown open, and a man, dashing in, threw himself violently upon him and bore him to the ground, whilst shouting at the top of his voice—

" Help! murder! thieves! help !"

It was Mr. Mallan.

During the conclusion of the supper, despite the din going on all around him, the worthy diamond-merchant had fancied once or twice he heard some strange noises below.

The idea of burglars selecting such a moment for their attack seemed to him, however, so preposterous, that he had set the sounds down to mere fancy.

Still, as he had thirty thousand pounds' worth of diamonds in the house, he was naturally nervous.

At length the crash made when the safe was forced caught his ears, and he could no longer restrain himself.

He did not wish, however, to needlessly alarm his guests, and therefore slipped quietly away from the dining-room.

He descended the stairs, and listened for a moment at the second door of the office.

For a moment he thought he must have been mistaken, but the forcing of the cashbox-lid and Ned's growl of pain caught his ears.

Pulling the key from his pocket, he unlocked and opened the door.

Catching sight of Ned, he threw himself upon him, and bore him to the ground as described.

The struggle was a short one, however.

Mr. Mallan, though a powerful man for his age, was no match for Kelly.

It is true that, by the suddenness of his attack, he had succeeded in throwing Ned to the ground, and in planting his knee on his chest.

But Ned, hearing the noise of footsteps descending the stairs, understood that he was in fearful peril, and did not hesitate in having recourse to extreme measures.

Drawing his knife, he plunged it into his adversary's stomach, before the latter suspected his danger.

The unfortunate diamond-merchant fell back with a low groan, and Ned, springing to his feet, dashed out of the office, along the passage, and through the outer door, just as the first of the guests, whom the shouts of Mallan had aroused, reached the bottom of the staircase.

CHAPTER CLVII.

THE ACCUSATION.

SUDDENLY aroused from the festivities by the shouts of Mr. Mallan, the guests hurriedly quitted the supper-table in a body, and descended the stairs in time to see Ned just disappearing through the open doorway.

Whilst a portion of them rushed out into the street in pursuit, the rest flocked into the office, on the floor of which Mr. Mallan lay pale and bleeding.

" Help! robbery !" were the first words he ejaculated.

" Have mercy upon us! but he's bleeding to death !" suddenly exclaimed a voice.

And poor Sal threw herself on her knees by her master's side.

" Run for a doctor," cried someone.

" All right, I'll go," said another.

"My poor wife!" murmured Mallan, "where is she? And for it to happen to-day, too—our wedding-day!"

Mrs. Mallan at that moment made her way into the room, despite the efforts made to check her, and, at the spectacle presented, stood as if she were thunderstruck.

Then, kneeling down beside her husband, she raised his head and covered his face with tears and kisses.

"My poor old girl, it's nothing," he gasped, the sight of her grief making him forget even his own agony.

Sal, meanwhile, had recovered her senses sufficiently to descend to the kitchen, from which she returned with water and linen for bandages

With a resolution and nerve none of the others seemed to possess, she opened Mr. Mallan's garments, and, having discovered the wound, set to work to staunch the flow of blood as best she could.

Whilst she was thus engaged the doctor entered.

He at once proceeded to complete the task begun by Sal, to whose prompt action he stated the patient probably owed his life, and then ordered that he should have a bed improvised at once in the office, as he was afraid to have him moved.

Hardly had this been done, before a sergeant of police arrived, accompanied by a detective in plain clothes.

Notice of the robbery had been given at the station-house, and he had been sent round to take charge of the case, and see if any information was forthcoming.

Mrs. Mallan stepped out to meet him in the workshop.

"Good evening, ma'am," said the sergeant, drily. "As far as I can learn, this little job seems to have been a 'put-up' affair."

"What do you mean?" she replied.

"Why, to speak so as you can understand it, the thieves, whoever they were, had an accomplice in the house before they set to work."

"Impossible!"

"That's what people always say, ma'am," said the sergeant, with an air of superior sagacity, "but we are never far wrong. You have servants, ma'am?"

"Only one, the most faithful creature that ever breathed."

"Yes, ma'am, that's what they always are till they are found out."

"Oh, I can answer for mine."

"Well, I'd like to see her, if you've no objection."

"Certainly not."

And, going to the door, she called Sal.

The latter soon made her appearance.

"Here she is," said Mrs. Mallan. "Sarah, this gentleman wants to ask you some questions."

"I don't think there is much need of that," said the detective, who, for his part, had not hitherto spoken, but who had been watching everything that had been passing with quiet persistency,

"Ah, I thought you would tell what kind of a girl she was at a glance," observed Mrs. Mallan.

"Oh! yes, I know what sort of a girl she is," said the detective. "I never forget a face. She's a colonial convict named Sarah Benson, alias Paramatta Sal. Come, young woman, the best thing you can do will be to make a clean breast of it, or I shall take you into custody as an accomplice."

He had no right to make this threat, since he was rather bound to warn her not to criminate herself.

Poor Sal gazed at him with her mouth half-open, her features discomposed, and her eyes fixed.

It seemed as though her reason had left her, from some stupefying shock.

Mrs. Mallan looked on with amazement at the effect the detective's words had produced.

The fact was that the poor creature, who for so long past had been congratulating herself hourly on her escape from all the horrible associations of the past, was completely paralysed at once more being brought into contact with the dread and terror of her former existence—the police.

"Come along, my girl," continued the detective. "We shall want a word with you at the station-house."

"Oh, Lord! sir—no, sir!" cried   heart-broken tones, intermingled with sobs. "It can't be true. You don't believe it now, good gentlem——I'm sure you don't. Not to the station-house! Not me! No, you don't mean that you think I had a hand in helping the wretches who have robbed and murdered my poor master! Why, I would have been killed ten times over before a hair of his head should be injured."

"Stow all that," said the sergeant; "I've heard it all before, and it won't wash. So, come along, young woman."

The poor girl in despair threw herself at Mrs. Mallan's feet.

"Oh, missus! my dear, good missus! don't let them take me away. Don't believe what they say! You know, missus, I would have done anything rather than the slightest harm should have come to you. You know how grateful I am to you both. You believe me, missus, don't you?"

And seizing Mrs. Mallan's hands she kissed them frantically, whilst the tears ran down her face, which was utterly transfigured with grief and terror.

Her tones were so natural and heartrending that even the officers were shaken.

As to Mrs. Mallan, she was quite convinced of the poor creature's innocence.

"No, no, my poor girl," she said; "I don't suspect you."

As she spoke she raised Sal to her feet.

The detective, shaken for a moment, had already recovered himself, and, accustomed to such scenes being acted before him, was again becoming sceptical.

Besides, he knew Sal's antecedents and how seldom a convict's repentance is genuine.

"You won't let them take me, missus?" cried Sal, wildly clinging to Mrs. Mallan as if she had the power to protect her against the law.

"No, my poor girl."

"You're very kind, ma'am, I'm sure," remarked the detective, ironically, "but I suppose as you won't mind us putting a few questions to this young woman that will help to put us on the track of the thirty thousand pounds' worth of property that has just been stolen, I'm told, from this place?"

These words acted on Mrs. Mallan as though a bucket of cold water had been thrown over her.

They restored her to a sense of her actual position, and of the ruin that threatened her and her husband.

"Certainly," she said; "ask what you like."

"You say then," he said, turning abruptly to her, "that you have had no communication with the people who have carried out this robbery, and half-killed your master?"

"No—no, sir."

"Has there been anyone else in the house to-night, besides the guests invited?"

"No—yes—that is, only Jess."

"Who is Jess?"

"A young woman who came in to help me."

"With your mistress's leave?"

"Oh! yes, sir."

And Mrs. Mallan nodded in confirmation of this.

"Well, who is she?"

"A young woman, sir, I know."

"What's her other name?" continued the detective sternly; whilst the sergeant glanced at Mrs. Mallan in a way that plainly said—

"You see, ma'am, we're on the track."

"Jess Appleby. I think—I think she lives at Peckham," said Sal.

"But you don't know?"

"No," answered the girl, in evident trouble.

"When did you first know her?"

"In Australia. She was a poor lost girl like me, and now she has reformed, and come over here to try and earn an honest living ; and I spoke to my missus about her, and as she was doing very badly missus said I might give her the job of helping me to-night."

"A very pretty story. Where is she now ? "

"I don't know."

"Isn't she in the house ? "

"I haven't seen her since—since, let me see," said the girl, making a desperate effort to collect her thoughts, for she began to realise the peril in which she stood. "No, I have not seen her since I ran upstairs on the first alarm."

"Did she run up with you ? "

"I think so ; but I was so flurried, I can hardly tell. But she wasn't in the kitchen when I went down for the water and bandage for master."

"And she isn't in the house now, is she, ma'am ? " continued the man, addressing Mrs Mallan.

A brief search established the fact of Jess's absence.

"Well, ma'am, what do you say to that ? " asked the sergeant.

Mrs. Mallan was thunderstruck. She looked at Sal.

"Oh! missus," cried the latter, "do you think I should have had a word to say to her if I had not thought she was an honest girl? No, I swear I shouldn't."

"What did you say her name was ? " said the detective, who had been reflecting for a minute or two.

"Jess Appleby."

"I thought so. You knew her in Sydney ? "

"Yes."

"I heard of her too there, when I was in chase of a fraudulent bankrupt who had bolted there. And it is only the other day the news came that she was suspected of having aided the escape of the famous Ned Kelly, the ironclad bushranger, from Sydney Jail. If she be here it's most likely he is here too, and they have done the job together."

"Great heavens ! " cried Mrs. Mallan.

"That's it, and the girl here is their accomplice."

"Oh ! no, sir ! "

"I cannot believe it," said Mrs. Mallan, but this time with something of doubt in her tone.

"You must come along with us," repeated the sergeant.

"No, no," cried the girl, clutching her mistress's dress.

"Do you want to kick up a row, and oblige us to take you by force ? " observed the sergeant. "You know the master you pretend to make such a fuss about is lying in the next room, and that the least excitement, the doctor says, may kill him."

These words had a magical effect on the girl.

The kindness with which she had been treated by Mr. and Mrs. Mallan had produced a wonderful impression on her, and devotion to them had become the religion of her life.

Quitting hold of her mistress she stepped forward.

"I am quite ready to go, sir," she said simply.

Even the detective was touched at this sudden result of his appeal.

"Well, my girl, if you can clear things up, so much the better for you, but they look black enough just now."

"Missus," said the poor creature appealing to Mrs. Mallan, "you know what I owe to you, you who dragged me out of the depths of sin and misery, and gave me the chance of earning my bread as an honest woman. I can bear anything but your suspecting me. If the girl, Jess, has tricked me—oh, believe me, missus, in bringing her here, I only thought of trying to help a poor lost soul as you have helped me. Indeed I thought of nothing else. I can bear imprisonment—God knows I am used to it !—anything but your suspicions, anything but the thought that you imagine I am a vile wretch enough to have shammed all the respect and gratitude I have felt for you and master only to rob and plunder you the better in the end."

"I believe you, Sarah," said Mrs. Mallan.

"Thank you, ma'am—oh, thank you ! They throw my past at my head, but it is not my fault if I drew in vice and misery with my mother's milk, for she—God help her !—

was a thief, and I never had a chance of tasting honestly-earned bread till I came here, for I recollect how they used to joke about my being weaned on a stolen pound-cake. I knew no more of right and wrong, till the chaplain at Sydney taught me, than a brute beast. But oh ! when I once had learned the difference, how I suffered ! And when I found a new home, a new world, over here, and learned to love those who had held out a hand to save me from that horrid, shameful past, how grateful I was ! I tried to show it by working hard, by trying night and day to do my best to please you, and you know, ma'am, that ever since I have been here I have had no other thought."

"That's certainly true."

"Well, now, because of my past, I am looked upon as an accomplice of the treacherous girl I thought I was trying to save. I am ready to go with these gentlemen, but there is one thing I'll beg you'll do, ma'am, and that is to forgive me, and I ask it of you on my knees, for bringing all this misery on you, though the God above us knows it was innocently done."

"I forgive and believe in you, my poor girl," said Mrs. Mallan sobbing, and the next moment Sal was led away in custody.

CHAPTER CLVIII.
A RISKY REFUGE.

WHEN Ned bounded through the open doorway, he glanced hurriedly to the right and left.

Not a soul was in sight.

Peace had evidently got such a start of him as to have disappeared, though the bushranger fancied he caught the faint echo of flying footfalls to the left.

He turned sharply to the right, and dashed off at full speed, followed by the guests, who had devoted themselves to his pursuit and capture.

Ned was a splendid runner, and the majority of those in pursuit of him could have had no chance with him at the best of times.

And now, having just risen from a hearty supper, there should have been less prospect than ever of their catching a man, not only naturally fleeter of foot, but running for his life and aware of his peril.

Only they had the resource of calling others to their aid in the chase.

At the cry of "Stop thief ! stop thief !" raised by them, figures seemed to start out from all manner of unsuspected nooks and corners, and join in the pursuit.

However deserted a London street may seem to be, this cry is quite enough to gather a crowd at any hour.

A mob of about thirty or forty people were soon tearing along at Ned's heels, and their numbers increased every moment.

Twice he had been almost checked in his career by a figure darting out of a doorway, and trying to seize him as he passed, but in each instance the assailant had paid dearly for his temerity.

One he had knocked senseless by a blow with his fist, and his shoulder catching the other had hurled him into the middle of the street on the broad of his back.

But on each of these occasions Ned had nearly lost his own footing from the shock, and he realised well enough that if this should happen his fate was sealed.

The yelling mob behind him would, in such a case, be upon him before he had time to recover himself.

He laboured, too, under another terrible disadvantage.

He was profoundly ignorant of the neighbourhood in which he found himself at that moment.

It was his object to choose the darkest and least frequented streets, in order to get out of sight of his pursuers, if it were possible.

If he could once accomplish this feat he felt he was safe from them.

As he tore along his chest began to burn and his head to swim, from the tremendous pace he was putting on

He darted sharply down a dark and narrow street

The pursuers, among whom more than one policeman was now included, kept on his track.

The street was dark and narrow and seemed quite deserted, and he thought that if he could only put on a spurt and get a little way ahead, he could turn sharply to the right or left, out of sight, and thus put the pack off the scent.

The street curved somewhat, which was, he thought, a yet further advantage towards attempting this feat, though he could not as yet, in consequence of this, see the end of it.

Suddenly, on turning the curve, he saw its termination right ahead of him.

To his horror, he saw that the street led into a broad and brilliantly-lit thoroughfare, along which, despite the lateness of the hour, he could distinguish a constant succession of passengers and vehicles passing.

To go on would be madness.

To turn back and face his pursuers destruction.

He must turn off to the right or left.

He looked ahead.

Between him and the thoroughfare at the end of the street in which he found himself there was only one solitary turning visible.

It was a narrow street, narrower and darker even than the one in which he found himself, running off to the right.

He turned and plunged recklessly down it at full speed.

At the end of about fifty yards he pulled up suddenly, in horrible perplexity.

There was no thoroughfare! It was a *cul-de-sac.*

At the bottom of the street was a huge pair of wooden gates, evidently giving access to the yard of some factory or other, and securely fastened.

Indeed, behind them he could plainly distinguish the noise of work going on, and see the glare of lights waving and flickering.

His position was maddening.

Retreat was cut off, for he could hear his pursuers already at the upper end of the street down which he had just turned, and which had proved such a fatal trap.

He glanced around him.

His first idea was to scale the factory gates, but he noticed a kind of porter's lodge attached, and guessed that such an attempt would lead to certain detection from its occupant.

His pursuers were approaching every moment.

He could not only hear their voices but distinguish the dark outline of their advancing figures.

"We've got him now for certain," he heard one of them exclaim in jubilant tones. "There's no thoroughfare here."

"Look into each of the doorways carefully as you pass," said another voice, which evidently belonged to someone in command.

"That must be a police sergeant," thought Ned.

Suddenly another voice cried out eagerly—

"There he is; see, at the end of the street, close by the factory gates there."

And a rush forward followed these words.

It was all up, they had seen him.

At that moment Ned noticed that the door of the last house on the right hand of the street, a house, which, from its position, evidently had something to do with the factory, was open.

He darted through the doorway, but before he had time to do so his pursuers caught sight of this movement.

Swinging the door to almost in their faces Ned groped forward till he found a staircase and began rapidly to ascend it.

He was barely halfway up the first flight when a thundering knocking at the door announced that his pursuers were still closely on his track.

The house in question formed part of the factory, which was a tarpaulin-maker's.

There was a press of orders on hand, which accounted for the men working at night and for the door of the building in which the offices were situate being open.

At the knocking, a watchman who was making his rounds on the ground-floor, and whom Ned had narrowly escaped meeting, since it was he who had left the front door open a minute or two before, went to the door, the slamming of which had also reached his ears.

"Who is there? what is it?" he asked.

"The police," was the answer. "A murderer has just taken shelter in this house."

"A murderer! Oh, Lord!" and, terrified at the idea of being shut up in the house with one, the man at once threw the door open without further parley.

A flood of people poured in at once, despite the efforts of the police to check them.

Ned heard their voices in the hall.

The rooms on the first-floor landing were all fastened, as he found on trying them in swift succession.

He darted up to the second-floor with the same result.

At last he reached the landing of the third-floor.

It was the last.

And he distinctly heard his pursuers mounting the stairs

The watchman had briefly explained that it was impossible for anyone to have left the hall on the ground-floor without being seen by him unless by way of the stairs, and the police sergeant, after stationing a constable at the outer door and one at a back entrance giving on to the factory yard, began to ascend, followed by the rest of those who had gained admission into the house.

Standing on the landing of the third storey, Ned held his breath and listened to their approach.

By the faint light of the moon which had broken through the clouds and was streaming in from the landing window he made a new discovery.

His hands, his wristbands, and the front of his shirt and waistcoat were stained here and there with half-dried spots of blood.

The blood of Mr. Mallan which had spouted out over him as he stabbed the hapless diamond merchant.

This was awkward, since it took away his last hope of mingling somehow or other with the pursuing crowd and pretending to be one of them.

He drew nearer to the window in order to get a better view of the damning stains on his garments.

They were not many, but on his right wristband they showed very conspicuously.

He had already tried the door on this landing in quest of a hiding-place, and found that, like those below, they were fastened.

It would not do to break one open, as to do so would be only to leave another trace for his pursuers.

He looked out of the landing-window to see if there was any means of descent.

It looked on to the court-yard of the factory.

By the faint moonlight he distinguished a kind of cornice running along the whole of the side of the house, for some distance.

It was about a foot broad at the outside, and was situated some three feet or so below the level of the window-sill.

Flight was imperative at any price.

His pursuers had already reached the second floor, and were trying the doors, of which the watchman had the keys, and which were all found securely locked.

Ned noiselessly raised the window-sash, stepped out on to the cornice, and drew the sash down after him.

His situation was a fearfully perilous one.

Perched on a narrow shelf of masonry, some forty feet above the level of the ground, he felt that to look down might be fatal.

Owing to the narrowness of the ledge his foothold was difficult and insecure.

He slowly edged himself a few steps away from the window, the sill of which was level with his waist, and then remained motionless, listening with all his ears.

He was just in time.

The crowd, now somewhat lessened in number as the prospect of meeting a murderer at close quarters increased, flocked up the stairs to the landing he had just left, and the lights carried by them flashed across the window.

At that moment the moon, which had been feebly shining a few minutes before, disappeared behind a thick veil of clouds and all was dark as pitch without.

Ned heard an exclamation of surprise from the first who had ascended the stairs, and gained the landing.

"Not here! Why, where the devil can he have got to?" was his remark, in tones of astonishment.

"The staircase goes no further," said another.

"He must be in one of these rooms, then," said a voice which Ned recognised as that of the sergeant.

"Have you got the keys of them, watchman?"

"Yes, sir."

"Well, let's have a look inside. You are sure the fellow went upstairs?"

"Yes; he could not possibly get any other way without passing me in the hall."

"Then it strikes me he had some skeleton keys about him, and has let himself into one of the locked-up rooms either here or below, and refastened the door."

"That must be it," chimed in one of the police.

"Well, it's certain he's on either the first, second, or third floor. We'll give these rooms up here a thorough overhauling, and then work our way down in the same fashion. One thing is certain, he can't get out of the house, since all the doors are guarded."

The watchman handed the keys of the rooms to the sergeant, and retreated to a prudent distance like the bulk of the crowd.

They were evidently of opinion that the murderer might jump out suddenly on them like a jack-in-the-box from the room, directly the door opened.

The policeman smiled contemptuously as he suddenly threw open the first door.

The room, like those below, was used as a store-room; but on this occasion it happened to be empty of everything.

There was nothing to be seen but bare shelves, and not a place where even a rat could have hidden himself.

The sergeant looked up the chimney and retired.

The other rooms were searched with a similar result.

"Not a hole where he could hide; he must be below," said the sergeant, shaking his head.

All at once he caught sight of another door in an obscure corner.

"What is that?" he asked.

"Oh," replied the watchman, "it leads to a kind of cockloft up a few steps. No one ever goes there, and there is nothing but some lumber."

"By Jove! that's just the place for him," cried the sergeant eagerly. "Hullo! the door's locked too," he added, as he sprang forward and tried it. "Have you the key?"

On hearing these words a ray of hope shot across Ned's mind.

If they all went into the cock-loft he might have a chance of slipping back through the window and trying to make his escape from one of the lower rooms.

He heard the door opened, and the sergeant and several others ascend the stairs, and begin to rummage the lumber stowed away in the cock-loft.

He edged his way back towards the window, and risked a sidelong peep on to the landing.

Three or four figures, amongst them that of a woman, still were standing on the landing.

It was only a rapid glance he dared risk under the circumstances, but somehow or other the woman's figure seemed to strike him as a familiar one.

But second thoughts, however, convinced him that this must be impossible.

His plan of re-entering the house by the window was

Not only was there this group of people on the watch on the landing, but most of them had a lighted candle in their hands.

Yet he felt he must decide on something, for to remain where he was would be fatal, since daylight would at once reveal his situation.

An idea suddenly occurred to him.

It was to edge his way along the cornice as far as he could, in the hope of gaining some other window which might open on to it like the one he had passed through.

As far as he could make out in the darkness, the cornice extended for a considerable length.

It seemed to extend as far again as the width of the house on which he had found himself, and he judged that it must therefore run along one adjoining it.

If this were the case, it would probably have another window opening from that one on to it, and corresponding to the one through which he had passed.

If so, he was safe.

The task was a terribly perilous one, nevertheless.

He would have to edge himself along inch by inch on the verge of a precipice forty feet deep.

Still if he could once gain a window he was safe.

Suddenly he heard a fresh murmur of voices on the landing.

The police had returned from the cockloft and were consulting together afresh.

They might take it into their heads to look out of the window, and it was necessary above all things for him to move on beyond the range of their vision.

He no longer hesitated.

Moving inch by inch, and with every possible precaution, in order not to lose his balance, he slowly turned round so as to get his back to the wall and his face towards the courtyard.

Then he began to edge himself sideways along the cornice, holding on by each window-sill that presented itself to his wide-stretching reach.

In five minutes he had accomplished about twenty feet of the distance, when all at once, despite all his iron nerves and hardihood, a cold shiver ran through his frame.

Big drops of perspiration darted from his brow.

The cause of this shock was indeed terrible.

A portion of the cornice which he had just passed over slowly detached itself from the wall and fell crumbling into the courtyard below.

The cornice was not of solid stone, as he had imagined when he first set foot on it, but of stucco!

At any moment it might give way beneath his weight and precipitate him into space.

For a moment after making this alarming discovery, his very senses seemed about to leave him.

His head reeled, his eyes swam, his breath grew short, and it was only by a desperate effort of the will, that he saved himself from topling forward headlong from his perch.

CHAPTER CLIX.
A PERILOUS PASSAGE.

THE fragment of the cornice which had fallen was from the spot he had just quitted.

His eye involuntarily glanced down the gap it had left to his right hand.

He could distinguish the courtyard, and could make out that a little further onward in the direction in which he was advancing it was brilliantly lit up.

Making a desperate effort to recover his firmness, he leant slightly forward, and, risking vertigo, actually dared to look down over the cornice into the courtyard.

He saw that in advancing he would soon find himself right over a kind of large shed with a glass roof, whence the light proceeded.

The light came from the fire lit under several immense cauldrons, in which the composition for coating the tarpaulin was seething and bubbling.

A few steps more and he would be right over there.

"By ——! if the infernal thing gives way under my feet just there," was his sudden thought, "I shall be boiled alive."

At this idea reason again almost forsook him.

To fall from the height of a third storey through a glass roof into a huge cauldron of boiling pitch, was a prospect to appal anyone, however bold.

"I think I'd rather work back and face them," was his desperate idea on making this discovery.

But he found this idea impossible to carry out.

The portion of cornice that had fallen was not more than two feet in length.

But to clear this gap of two feet it would be necessary to bound sideways across the void.

Even if he succeeded in doing this without losing his balance the shock of alighting on the other side would infallibly carry away another section of the cornice, and himself with it.

Meanwhile, however, he reflected that every moment he remained in one spot increased the risk of the stucco giving way beneath him.

He continued, therefore, to edge himself on till he arrived at a spot immediately over the furnaces that had caught his attention below.

As he worked his way along this part of his journey he trod as gingerly as ever a cat did on hot bricks.

From time to time he glanced to his left, the direction in which he was going, to see if there were any signs of a window he had expected to find.

At length he fancied he could discern the sill of it in the darkness dimly and close at hand.

His heart gave a bound of satisfaction.

"Safe after all," he muttered, and quickened his advance as much as ever he dared along the cornice.

Suddenly the same deathly sense of despair that had before assailed him seized on him with redoubled vigour, and caused a bitter curse to pass out between his parched lips.

At the very moment of success the cup was dashed irrevocably from them.

He could, indeed, distinctly make out the window some twenty paces ahead at the most.

But between this harbour of refuge and himself the cornice was missing for a space of at least four or five feet in extent.

This was the severest blow of all.

To have a place of refuge before his very eyes, and to be divided from it by a gulf that nothing short of wings would have enabled him to traverse!

His situation was indeed a fearful one.

He could neither advance nor retreat.

And he was bound sooner or later to feel the section of cornice on which he was standing crumble away beneath his feet.

And then!

He would be precipitated headforemost into the seething, flaming gulf below.

Hardened ruffian as he was, and game to the backbone, the peril fairly appalled him.

His fate would be one of those horrible and inevitable deaths in which a man died about ten times over in the mere anticipation of them.

He set his teeth hard, and fixed his back against the wall, as if glued to it, striving to bear as little on the cornice as possible.

For a moment he had thoughts of ending this horrible suspense by one headlong leap forward.

Then all his thoughts turned on the strip of cornice on which he was standing.

"Will it hold?" he asked himself, though all the while he felt certain it could not.

With his ears straining, with every nerve in his body awake, he strove to tell whether he could hear it cracking, whether he could feel it loosening itself beneath his feet.

He remained like this for a couple of minutes, silent and attentive.

Then a fresh hope rose slowly in his breast.

"If I could only manage to lie down at full length," he thought, "my weight would be more spread out, and the cornice might hold out till I could call attention to myself, for even capture would be preferable to this. Besides, I might, after all, in daylight see some way of getting off."

As the cornice was fully twelve inches in width and Kelly had nerves of steel, or rather no nerves at all, the feat was not a difficult one.

With great difficulty, since every movement threatened to precipitate him into the abyss below, he succeeded, by degrees, in turning his legs sideways and sinking on to his knees.

Then he gradually lowered his body till he was stretched at full length, face sideways, on the cornice.

When he had succeeded in accomplishing this, the reaction was so violent that his figure shook, like a leaf in a breeze, with emotion and the prospect of safety, as well as the possibility of being smashed up by a fall.

With his hand, he felt carefully the line where the cornice started out from the wall.

The least gap or crack here would have been a sign that it was on the point of giving way.

He found no trace of this, however.

"Perhaps this bit is stronger-built than the rest," he thought. "There may very likely be stone bits here and there at intervals to stay the cornice, and this, perhaps, is one of them."

He felt again, and fancied the stucco seemed very hard at this point.

"It is stone, sure enough."

He passed one hand outside over the edge of the cornice, to feel if there was any support beneath, such as the head of a pilaster or a bracket.

"It seems very firm here, after all," he thought. "It feels quite as hard as stone, too. If it was stucco, it would already have given way. No, there must be some extra stay or other here, and I am safe. I can wait until——"

He was interrupted in this train of thought by a noise so slight that, at any other moment, it might have escaped him, but which at this critical juncture again caused a shiver to shoot through every limb.

It was simply, however, a kind of faint, rattling sound, like that produced by a shower of hail against the window-panes.

It came from below, and, faint though it was, it filled him once more with terrible anticipations.

"What's that?" he asked himself.

But, although he knew only too well, he dared not answer.

Yet he felt he must know the worst.

Again he passed his hand along the cornice close to the wall.

Yes, he was only too certain of the cause of the sound.

The cornice was slowly but surely crumbling away beneath his weight, and the sound he heard was produced by its fragments rattling as they fell against the glass roof of the shed below.

In another minute he would follow them!

Only, instead of rebounding against the glass, his mangled body would dash through it, bleeding and mutilated, into one of the seething cauldrons.

It was horrible, most horrible, to think of.

He felt again.

His groping fingers discovered a crack that he was sure had not existed a moment before, close to the wall.

It was, he felt, his death-warrant.

The cornice was parting from the wall.

A larger piece than had hitherto fallen rattled smartly on the roof below him.

It was to him as his death-knell.

And what a death!

To have fallen in free, fair fight, with his gallant steed beneath his knees, and the shots cracking fiercely around him, was a fate he had pictured to himself before now without terror, and at the present moment it rose before him by contrast like a vision of paradise.

Even the hangman and the scaffold appeared ten thousand times preferable, since that fate would give him, at any rate, the glory of dying game in presence of an admiring crowd.

"By Jingo! it's all over," he gasped.

Involuntarily he closed his eyes.

Helpless, hopeless, he set his teeth, and, with his heart full of blind rage and hatred against all things on earth and in heaven, doggedly awaited his fate.

"Game to the end," he said, repeating what, to him, was the creed of his whole life.

Suddenly he fancied that he heard his name.

He thought at first that it must be a delusion.

But, lo! again a voice fell on his astonished ears.

"Ned, Ned!" it seemed to say.

Was it a wild hallucination of his last hour?

"Ned, Ned, it's me—Jess," was repeated from above him in tones unmistakably human.

"Jess?" he gasped, hoarsely.

"Yes, I'm here, at a garret-window, just over you. Don't move, and you are all right."

The next moment a long waving object came dangling past his eyes.

It was a rope.

Seizing it with both hands, he transferred his weight to it just in time, for he felt the crack in the cornice enlarging as he did so.

"Hold on tight at your end," he called to Jess.

"No fear; it is fast, and, besides, I am not alone," was the encouraging answer.

Grasping the rope firmly, Ned began to hoist himself up hand over hand to a small window which he now perceived some twelve feet or so above the cornice.

This was a trick he had often before done, but, in the present case, the agonies through which he had passed had not been without their effect upon him, especially after the reaction.

After mounting about two-thirds of the distance he came to a stop, unable to proceed further.

"Come on!" cried Jess, anxiously watching him.

"I'm pretty well burst up!" he gasped faintly.

"Don't throw up the sponge, old man," cried the girl. "If you stop you're bound to leave go. Twice more hand over hand will do it, for then I can reach your collar and give you a lift."

Nerved by this appeal, Ned hoisted himself a couple of feet higher.

Then, blind and almost senseless, he felt himself seized by the collar and dragged through the garret window.

Ned sank partly insensible on the floor of the species of cockloft in which he now found himself, and which was the identical one which the police had already searched.

The moral and physical strain he had undergone had temporarily overcome him.

"He's going to faint, I think," said Jess.

"Enough to make him after such a narrow squeak as that," said another voice.

Ned opened his eyes and rose to his feet.

"Jess," he said, "you've saved my life again my girl—I shan't forget it."

"You are saved for a time, but you must pull yourself together, Ned, for you're not clear yet," was the reply.

"Where are we then?" he enquired.

"In the garret of the house where the police are still looking for you."

"But, how ever did you come here?"

"Why, when they started in pursuit of you, I thought the best thing I could do was to make a bolt too, as it would not have done for me to have stopped in the house any longer. I found that no one in the crowd knew me, for old Mallan's guests had not spotted me indoors, so I thought the very best thing I could do would be to follow and see if I could be of any use."

"You are a rare plucked one," said Ned admiringly.

"How you did vamimus!" continued the girl. "I had a hard job to keep up, though I am reckoned pretty smart on my pins; but I reached this place just as the door opened, and rushed in with the rest. I slipped upstairs with them, keeping my wits about me, and when the police searched this cockloft I came up too, and managed to hide and remain behind when they left it, on finding you were not here. Then I began to look about me, and going to the window saw you lying on the cornice just below."

"If you'd have been a minute longer you'd have seen me go flying head foremost into the courtyard. It was a lucky idea of yours, the rope."

"It was not my idea. I quite lost my nut, and could not even cry out to you at first."

"Not yours? Whose was it then?" asked Ned, in some amazement at this reply.

"Kit's," answered Jess.

"What! you here too?" said Ned, catching sight of Kit.

"Yes; I had got to the end of the street when you passed me, tearing along like a steam-engine. I joined in chase with Jess, in the hope of helping you at a pinch, and came on here. But, as the girl says, the job's not over yet. They are still hunting for you through the house," was Kit's reply.

Kit had entered the loft with the police and Jess, and, after they had left, he arranged to return and join the girl in her efforts, whatever they might be, for Ned's deliverance.

Had it not been for Kit's lending a hand to pull Ned in at the window, the bushranger's history would have been a trifle shorter; he would have tumbled into a boiling pit rather sooner than he anticipated, and vanished, like all demons, in a blaze of fire.

The sergeant of police felt certain, on comparing notes with his followers, that the culprit had, as the watchman asserted, gone upstairs.

But it was also evident that he had not gone down again, and, as a rigorous search in the rooms on the first and second floors revealed no trace of him, the officer began to entertain the idea that he might, after all, have got away somehow over the roof.

Once more he ascended to the third floor.

"Is there any chance that he got out of one of the windows?" suggested one of his followers.

"Three storeys high—impossible!" said another.

Nevertheless the sergeant advanced to the window and raised the sash.

"Nothing here," said he. "No ladder or anything to help him to get down."

Kit, Jess, and Ned, in the garret above, could plainly hear these words.

The situation was as critical as ever, as the sergeant might take it into his head to search the garret again.

The sergeant was going to draw his head in when he suddenly checked himself, and lowered the light he carried down towards the cornice.

"Hullo!" he exclaimed, "someone has been walking along outside here, I'll swear!"

He examined it further.

"Yes, there's no mistake about it; there are tracks of footsteps. It must be our man!"

"Blow it!" muttered Ned; and, glancing round the cockloft, which extended over the whole of the house, he caught sight of another window at the other end and went towards it, "he is on the right track!"

The sergeant thrust his body out of the window as far as he could, and held up his light.

"There's no doubt," he said. "The traces of footsteps are plain enough, but where they end the cornice ends too. There's a gap that, as far as I can make out from here, is freshly broken away."

"Then he must have fallen," said one of the others.

"No, for if he had we should have heard him crash through the glass down below there. He must have got beyond it just before it fell, for he can't have passed over it."

This logical reasoning sounded very unpleasant to the ears of the party in the cockloft.

"Are you sure he has gone on?" inquired a policeman.

"He could not have come back."

"Is there another window he could have got into further on?" suggested the other.

"That's an idea. No, there's only one in sight, and that's a good twelve feet above the cornice, so he could not reach it without wings, and he's not the sort of angel to have those," said the sergeant, who, even with the aid of the light, could not, from where he was, make out the window that Ned had originally striven to gain.

"Well, if he's not somewhere on the cornice still, or pitched into the courtyard, he must have got up to it somehow or other."

"Quite impossible!" said the sergeant; "but, still there's no harm in proving it. It must be the window of the cockloft we were in just now, by its position, so we'll go up and have another look round there."

Ned, Kit, and Jess, had heard all this conversation.

"It's all up," said Kit.

"They'll be here in half a minute," said the girl glancing around her wildly.

"It'll only take a quarter to save us," said Ned, who had been lost in thought for the last few moments.

Seizing a portion of an old grate that was lying in one corner of the cockloft, he stepped lightly but swiftly to the window through which he had been hauled a few moments before.

Next instant a most frightful crash was heard in the courtyard below.

It was the shock of the mass of iron, thrown out by Ned, crashing through the glass roof of the shed.

The sergeant and all the other policemen rushed at once to the window to look out.

"That's him, sure enough," cried the sergeant. "He had got further along the cornice, and this time it's given way beneath him and let him down."

The next moment he and the majority of those with him were hurrying downstairs, the rest remaining looking out of the window.

"Now," said Ned, "we've five minutes clear, and the way is open," and he pointed to the other window, which opened on to a narrow alley.

"But how are we to get down?" asked Jess.

"You by the rope, and me any way after we have lowered you."

As he spoke, he placed his hand on a water-pipe running down the wall.

CHAPTER CLX.
A BITTER SELL.—DIAMOND CUT DIAMOND.

A FEW moments sufficed to place the three in safety.

Jess was lowered by the rope, which was fortunately long enough for the purpose.

Ned followed her down it.

Then Kit, unfastening the end of the rope, in order not to betray the route they had taken, stepped in turn out of the window, and laying hold of the waterpipe running down the wall, slid down it with a sailor's agility.

The three found themselves in a narrow alley running between two houses.

It was closed at the end by a door.

This was locked, but, the lock being on their side, the two men had little difficulty in forcing back the catch.

Stepping out through the doorway, they found themselves in a street lying to the back of the one into which Ned had been chased.

They were now in safety from immediate pursuit.

Their great difficulty was, however, to tell where they were, and in what direction to make off.

However, they judged that by working to the south they should be certain at length to find themselves in Holborn, and in a short time this expectation was justified.

"I think we're all right now," said Kit.

"Hang it all," remarked Ned, but how am I to get along with all these bloodstains about me?"

A means was found of smoothing over this difficulty.

Ned borrowed Kit's large black sailor's neckerchief, and tied it round his neck, spreading out the ends so as to cover his shirt-front.

He buttoned his coat over his waistcoat, and tucked his wristbands well out of sight.

Then the three kept their eyes open till they found a drinking-fountain, at which he removed the blood that had dried on his hands.

This completed, he received directions as to the route he was to take from Kit, who knew London well, and, quitting the others, started off for Peckham.

Kit and Jess also separated.

Ned's first thought on waking the next morning was for Peace.

The idea crossed his mind that the latter, finding himself in possession of the whole of the booty, might be tempted to bolt with the lot.

It was with great satisfaction that he espied the little burglar make his appearance in his garden.

Peace had indeed been tempted to act as Ned had fancied.

Two things, however, had restrained him.

One was the fair value offered by Anatole for the diamonds, and the other the chance of losing his share in the other big robbery contemplated by Ned and the Frenchman.

He knew that Anatole, being a firm pal of Kelly's, would only plank down the coin under the original agreement, which included the whole party; also, that it would pay him better to get close on four thousand pounds for his share in a lump, than to try and get rid of the lot through other channels in detail.

Accordingly, he strolled close to his garden-wall on seeing Ned, and in a hurried whisper agreed to accompany the bushranger that same evening to the appointment made with the Frenchman.

This was at a little hotel frequented by foreigners, near Leicester-square, at which Anatole was temporarily sojourning.

They picked up Kit on their way, and, on arriving at the hotel and asking for Anatole, were shown to the billiard-room, where they found him engaged in executing a series of his favourite cannons, his opponent being a tall, black-bearded, and rather good-looking Frenchman.

As soon as the game was over, Anatole told a waiter to take some "grogs" up into his room, and invited the three visitors to follow him thither.

To their astonishment the black-bearded Frenchman was one of the party.

When they had entered the room, Anatole locked the door and requested them to sit down and help themselves to liquor.

Ned and Peace glanced at the stranger.

"And now, my friends, we will to business," said Anatole, with a bland smile.

He spoke in broken English, but it would weary the reader to give his peculiar English.

The three exchanged looks.

"What business?" said Peace, sharply.

"What business? Why, about the diamonds."

"Stop a bit," said Ned. "Before we go any further, I want to know who this other mounseer is, and what he has got to do with the matter in hand?"

"Aha! I see," said Anatole, gaily; "I have omitted to introduce you. I will remedy that. Gentlemen, let me introduce to you my friend Monsieur Chose, of Paris. Chose, mon ami, allow me to present to you Mistare Smeeth, Mistare Jones, and Mistare Brown," he added, with a great affectation of politeness.

"Chouse, Chouse," grumbled Ned, in an undertone. "I'll take deuced good care he don't chouse us."

He was not aware that Chose is the equivalent in French for Thingamy or Thingumbob.

"Gentlemen," said Chose, who spoke English like Anatole, "I am charmed to make your acquaintance."

"But what has Mr. Chose got to do with this affair?" said Peace, warily.

"My friends," said Anatole, facing them, with his shoulders shrugged up to his ears, and the palms of his hands turned outward, "when I say I will buy your diamonds, surely you did not imagine that I was going to buy them on my own account? I am not a millionaire nor a beautiful woman like Mees Jess," and he kissed his finger-tips; "and I do not see what I should do with thirty thousand pounds worth of diamonds. Do you see?"

"I'm hanged if I do," said Kit. "You promised to buy them, and what you mean to do with them after, is your affair."

"Exactly. I promise to buy them, but not for myself. I am the middle man. Where should I find five, ten, fifteen thousand pounds? I am but the agent of my friend Monsieur Chose."

"Oh! I see," remarked Ned, and he began to regard the black-bearded Frenchman with his scowling looks.

"Monsieur Chose is not only a capitalist but an expert. He knows the value of the diamonds and is accustomed to deal in them. And as you are all my friends he will give you a fair price."

"And what do you get, old Wide-O?" cried Ned.

Anatole smiled.

"Merely a little trifle of a commission, a bagatelle. Let us say ten per cent. on the sum paid you."

The truth was he was to receive twenty.

"Well then, let's settle things. Bring out the sparklers," said Ned to Peace.

The latter produced the bag from his breast pocket.

"How much do you reckon the diamonds to be worth?" remarked Chose, blandly, whilst Peace was unfastening the string securing the neck of the bag.

"The girl heard them say there were thirty thousand pounds' worth in the house," said Ned, "and we copped the lot."

"Copped the lot?" repeated the Frenchman, puzzled at the phrase.

"Yes, collared the whole biling, don't you twig?"

"Bagged the whole of them," explained Kit.

"Ah! Then I suppose I am to pay you from twelve to fourteen thousand pounds?"

"Fifteen."

"We shall see."

Peace had unfastened the string.

Taking a newspaper from a chair he spread it on the table and emptied the contents of the bag on to it.

The men held their breath as the diamonds rolled out in a glittering stream.

Then every eye became riveted on the dazzling pile flashing and glittering in the lamp-light.

The stones were none of them particularly large, but were apparently good medium-sized diamonds that a man in the trade could easily dispose of.

Chose's face lit up with professional satisfaction.

He took the newspaper by the edge and drew it towards him, the others keeping their eyes riveted on every movement of his fingers.

He picked up half-a-dozen of the stones and let them run through his fingers.

Then he produced a magnifying-glass from his pocket, and, placing three or four of the biggest diamonds on the palm of his hand, gazed at them through it.

Suddenly he gave a start.

The expression of his face changed.

He applied one of the stones to the tip of his tongue and uttered a grunt of surprise.

Throwing down those he held, he snatched another handful from the heap.

These he hastily scanned through the glass and then rapidly tested them with his tongue like the former one.

Then, casting them contemptuously on the paper, he rose to his feet, making a remark in a low tone, as he did so, to Anatole.

The other four regarded this proceeding in amazement.

"Impossible!" muttered Anatole, in reply to the remark of his companion.

"I give you my head to cut off if it is not so," said the latter, and both the Frenchmen began to cast black looks at the other three sharers in this strange scene.

"What the —— does all this mean?" demanded Ned, rising to his feet with a fierce glare in his eyes.

"There's something wrong with the sparklers," said Kit, who understood French and had partly caught the remark made by Chose to Anatole.

"What's that? What does he say about the diamonds?" cried Ned to Anatole. "Won't he buy?"

"Buy?" repeated the Frenchman, contemptuously, "buy? Do you take him for an ass, an idiot? Do you expect him to give fifteen thousand pounds for what is not worth so many pence? Bah!"

"What?" yelled Ned.

"Aren't the stones good diamonds?" asked Peace, feverishly.

"Diamonds?" answered Chose, with a laugh—"diamonds?"

"Curse your foolery! what's wrong with them? By ——, I'll make you stick to your bargain," exclaimed the bushranger.

"My bargain?" said Chose, with some dignity. "I am prepared to buy thirty thousand pounds' worth of diamonds whenever you like to produce them, but I did not think you could dream that a man of my experience would be taken in by such imitations as those."

"Imitations?" screeched Peace.

"Yes, there does not seem to be a genuine stone in the lot."

"It's a plant," cried Peace, in a bewildered fashion, after the three had recovered from the stupor in which this announcement had plunged them. "He wants to get the stones cheap."

"Cheap?" retorted Chose, ironically. "I have no wish to deprive you of them at any price."

And he pushed the lot contemptuously across the table towards him.

"This is worse than a crime—it is a blunder," quoted Anatole to Kelly, across the table. "You should not try such tricks on your friends, at any rate."

"Tricks on my friends?" cried Kelly, glaring round him like a maddened tiger. "It's on me the trick's played. By ——, and I think I see it, too."

And he laughed savagely.

"What do you mean, Ned?" asked Kit.

"Mean? Why, that this d——d white-faced, psalm-writing, double-faced skunk has changed the diamonds."

As he spoke, the bushranger turned fiercely on Peace and seized him by the throat.

Peace vainly strove to free himself from this terrible clutch.

For a moment he strove desperately to unclasp Ned's hands.

Then one of his own wandered to his pocket, but Ned saw this movement, and, removing one of his hands from his victim's throat, pinioned both the unhappy man's wrists with his iron fingers.

Peace was getting black in the face and his tongue was protruding, before the others, who when their first surprise was over had started forward, could succeed in freeing him from the grasp of his assailant.

For a moment it seemed as though Ned was about to assail the whole lot indiscriminately.

Peace, who had been laid back in a chair, was slowly recovering himself.

He cast a bitter look of malignity at Ned.

"Come, come, Ned," said Kit, "you're too hasty. There must be some explanation. Can you tell us anything about it?" he continued to Peace.

Only that I have been a precious fool to break through my rule of working single-handed," said the latter, gloomily.

"But the diamonds?"

"The diamonds are just as I took them out of the cashbox in Mallan's office," answered the other. "I had not even looked at them till now."

"This is all very strange," said Anatole.

"After the way in which I have just been treated," continued Peace. "I might with justice refuse to speak. But I want the affair cleared up, as well as you, and I think I can prove that I had nothing to do with changing these stones. In the first place, if I had chosen to bolt with the whole of them the night of the robbery, there was nothing to hinder me from getting clear off, and never facing any of you."

"That's true."

"In the second place, what opportunity have I had since then of procuring unset false diamonds to replace them? And, in the third, if I had changed them, should I have been fool enough to come here with you and risk discovery, for no one of us, I suppose, dreamt that these gentlemen would buy the stones without examination. I should have let you go on alone with my share, and quietly sloped."

He looked as if he regretted not having done the trick of which Ned had accused him.

"I suppose," said Kit to Chose, "all the stones are false?"

"All!" said the Frenchman, who had been carelessly picking them up and glancing at them during Peace's explanation. "Some are paste, some natural crystals. But there is not a single diamond in the lot, and no one who has ever handled precious stones would be deceived for more than a moment.

Ned advanced in silence to the table, and gathering up the glittering bits of mineral, restored them to the bag, and placed the latter in his pocket.

"You don't think I'm in this plant?" he asked of Anatole.

"No," said the other, who understood him.

"And I'm blessed if I can quite tell who is," continued Kelly, in a low tone.

"Stop a bit," said Peace. "I want to know something more about these stones. You say they are false, but how do I know, especially after the way in which I have been treated, whether all this is not a got-up affair, simply to do me out of my share, after I have had the hardest work, and all arranged beforehand between you and your pal the Frenchman?"

This assertion startled the others, and they looked at Peace in amazement.

"I demand to have the stones tested," he continued.

"That will not be so difficult," said Monsieur Chose, turning to a travelling-bag in one corner of the room. "Here is a book in English on precious stones, describing how to tell a true diamond. Here, too, are the materials for the various tests it mentions. If the stones are good, they will stand them, if false they will be destroyed."

Ned pulled out the bag, and the whole party began to assay the stones, and found Chose was correct.

As a further test they sallied out, and Peace and Chose entering a respectable jeweller's the latter introduced himself as a foreigner in the same line, and requested him to examine half-a-dozen of the stones, to decide a wager.

The man unhesitatingly pronounced them " duffers."

The party separated somewhat downcast.

Chose had lost the chance of a splendid bargain, Anatole his commission, and the other three the fruit of their labours.

But as Ned left Kit, he observed in a low tone of determination—

"Before I've done I'll find out who has rung the changes on us in this fashion. I am certain that little devil has jockeyed us somehow."

Mr. Mallan was evidently a cute customer and didn't even trust his household. The real diamonds were elsewhere. He rather ostentatiously let it be known where the "duffers" reposed.

CHAPTER CLXI.
A NIGHT ON THE THAMES.

THERE is a kind of "debatable land," on which the market-gardener and the "ferry-builder" contend for supremacy, stretching eastward between the Old Kent-road and the river.

It is a dreary region, the chief features of which are flat fields given up to the cultivation of vegetables for the London market, unfinished streets leading nowhere, and fringed by houses in every stage of construction, rows of builders' "carcases," immense cinder-heaps, and a network of interesting railway lines, chiefly devoted to the goods traffic.

At the side of the main thoroughfare, traversing it towards Rotherhithe, stands a quaint, old-fashioned roadside public, bearing the strange title of the Old Galley Wall.

It is an isolated house surrounded by vegetable-grounds, looking bare and desolate even in daylight.

Still more bare and desolate looking did they appear to a tall, powerfully-built man tramping along the road in question one evening at dusk, some three days after the scene described in the last chapter, and making his way eastward, and it was with a grunt of satisfaction that he marked the house and noticed the light shining from behind the old-fashioned red curtain of the bar.

"This must be the place," he muttered, "and job enough I have had to find it."

Crossing over the road he approached the house, and, as he did so, another man, who despite the lateness of the hour had been sitting on a bench just outside the door, rose and greeted him.

"I had got to wondering whether you were coming or not," he observed.

"I'm blessed if I could find the crib," replied the other. "I got blundering on down streets that ended in fields, and roads that finished up in market-gardens, till I fairly lost all bearings. It's worse than the bush, for there a track is pretty sure to end somewhere, and you've always got the sun or the stars to travel by, but in this cursed mulligatawny sky you've got nothing, day or night, to guide you. The beastly place! I'm dead sick of it, I am."

"Well, you're here at last, though a bit late. We'll have one drink, and I'll put you up to the business as we go along."

The two entered the bar, and, by the light, stood revealed as Kit and Ned.

After tossing off a glass of spirits and water a-piece, they set out together in the direction of Rotherhithe.

On their way Kit explained to Ned the service he wished him to join in.

Although the days of Will Watch and his followers are past and gone for ever, and it is no longer possible to run a cargo of smuggled goods ashore in the very teeth of the coastguard, and beat them off with the assistance of the entire countryside, there are still a number of men who devote a great deal of spare time to what is known as defrauding her Majesty's Revenue, an offence which, some how or other, is practised without compunction by gentle and simple.

Of course, now-a-days, ingenuity has replaced force, and countless are the dodges adopted.

Kit had become acquainted with some men engaged in this kind of enterprise, and had joined with them in a venture.

They had brought a quantity of tobacco over in a brig from Hamburg.

The Custom-house officers, however, had got scent of the scheme, and were on the lookout.

The tobacco, previously compressed to the smallest posable dimensi… by a hydraulic press, was so stowed away on board as to defy investigation, but the difficulty was to get it on shore.

"They're getting more fly to the dodges every day," said Kit, as he and Ned strode along the road, "though there have been some rare good ones played off on them in this very river."

"So I should think," assented Ned.

"There's an old chap in the swim who was telling me some of their little tricks the other night. Once he came across towards Christmas time with a whole lot of French walnuts. Whoppers they were, he said, and several score of bushel of them. But he said he felt devilish nervous at their looking so tempting, lest one of the tide waiters should fancy cracking a dozen."

"Why?"

"Because, barring a sprinkling on the top, all of them had been carefully emptied and the shells glued together again, with a small-sized kid glove rolled up inside each of them. The duty made it worth while then."

"Tobacco wouldn't do that way, it would smell too strong."

"Oh, he'd done tobacco lots of ways—in reams of printing paper with a square cut out of the middle of the inner sheets, and in plaster of Paris busts made hollow, only their breaking so easily made it risky."

"Ah! Anatole was telling me that that was the way they used to smuggle the pamphlets attacking the Emperor, into France"

"Ay, I've heard of that."

It was indeed in this way that Rochefort's famous *Lanterne* used to be brought across the Belgian frontier, the busts selected being those of the Emperor himself, as being less likely to arouse suspicion of such a thing.

"Anatole told me a pretty good yarn about a dodge he and a pal of his were working in Paris, when he was there last," remarked Ned.

"Let's hear it."

"Well, it seems that everything eatable or drinkable going into the city pays a duty, and that they've got a barrier all round, with gates, and custom-house officers at each."

"Yes, I know."

"Well, Anatole's chum used to live just outside the barrier, and used to drive in every morning in a light dog-cart. There was a rage for English turnouts just then; and he'd got a neat trap and a pretty stepper in the shafts, and a groom got up English fashion beside him, sitting bolt upright, as stiff as a post with his arms folded, and looking straight ahead at nothing."

"I know the style."

"Well, at first the custom-house people overhauled the turnout once or twice, just for form's sake, for they saw he was a respectable man driving up to his place of business regular as clockwork every day. But after that they used just to squint as he drove past, and nothing more, and in the end he used to go through and they would only nod and wish him good day, after their blessed bowing and scraping fashion."

"Well, and what came of it?"

"Wait a bit. Everyone used to envy him his turnout, especially the groom so awfully well-trained, sitting with his arms folded and never a smile on his face."

"Was he an Englishman?"

"I'll tell you. Well, one day just as he was driving in as usual, a runaway van came bolting down the street. He tried to clear it, but the gates were narrow and there were other traps in the way, and the end was they ran right into him, took off his wheel, and shot him and the groom and the trap clean over."

"Nice that."

"They picked up the master first and carried him into the custom-house, for he was cut about the head.

"The groom was lying quite still under the trap, for it had turned over on him, and the horse had fallen with it.

"There he lay, with a little pool of something spreading out round him, which they thought was the poor fellow's blood, and which kept growing larger every minute.

"They thought he must be dead, and that it was his blood; but directly they came close, they began to sniff a very strange smell, and when they laid hands on the carcase they twigged the dodge at once."

"But what was it?"

"Why, the groom was a dummy!"

"A dummy?"

"Yes, and filled from hat to boots with spirits. Of course, for the first week or so there had been a real groom, but directly the custom-house people got used to him, and did not stop the trap, the dummy was put up instead."

"What an artful dodge."

"Yes, but that wasn't all. It seems he used to empty the dummy at a crib inside the barrier, drive out by another gate, and come back again through that one with a fresh lot. In fact, he used to run three or four cargoes regularly through the day at different points."

"If the engine-rooms of some of the big river-steamers here could speak, they'd pitch some queer yarns," said Kit.

"They are the best hiding-places, for people don't like poking their noses too closely into furnaces and boilers at the risk of getting burnt, or scalded, or blowed up."

(To be continued.)

THE CELEBRATED NOVELS,
BY W. STEPHENS HAYWARD.

Picture Boards. ❈ Published at 2/-

NED KELLY THE IRONCLAD AUSTRALIAN BUSHRANGER

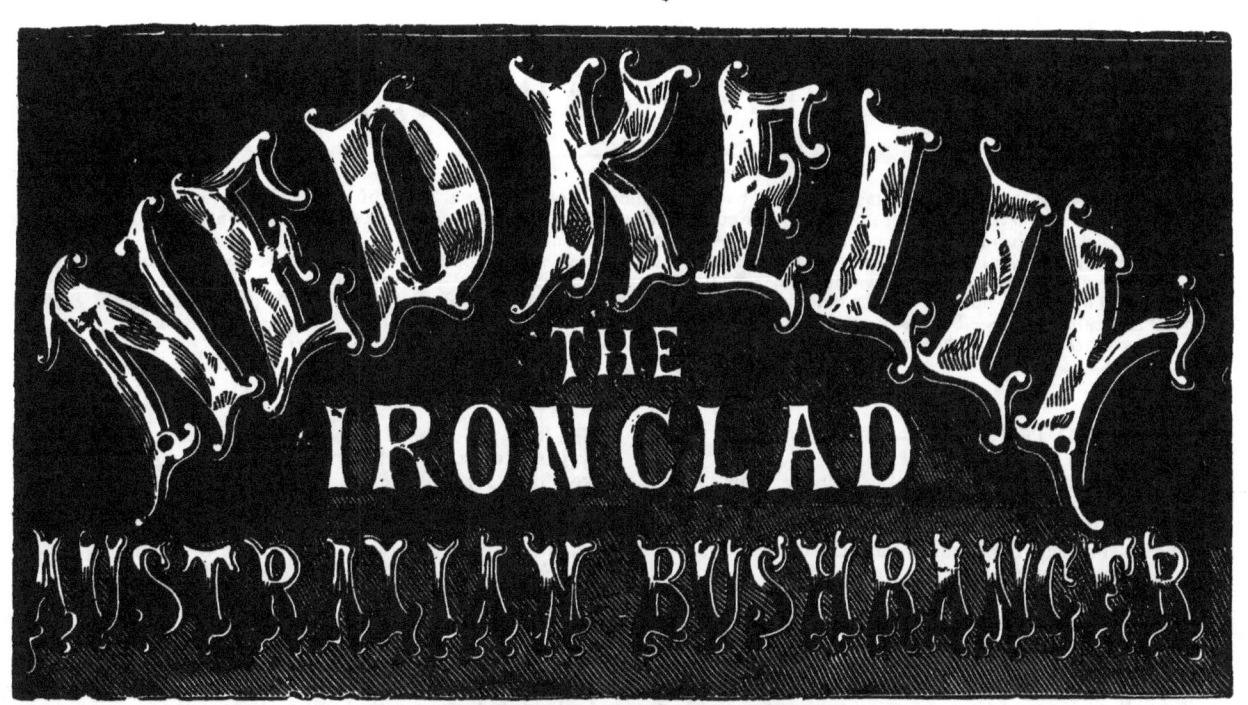

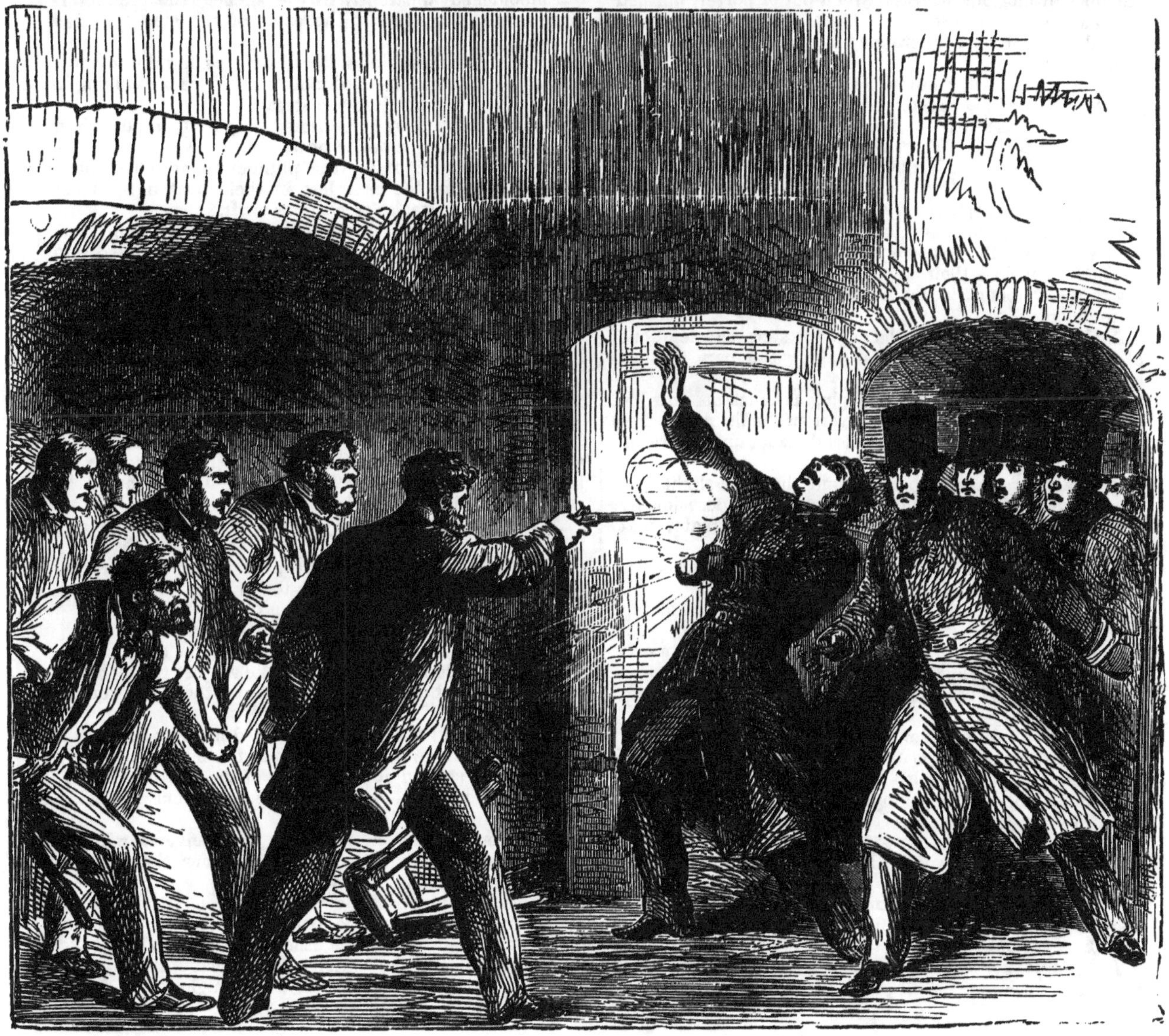

NO 28,

NED KELLY: IRONCLAD BUSHRANGER.

" It is well known that for many years Ned Kelly had made himself notorious by a series of crimes wholly incompatible with the civilisation of the nineteenth century. Ned Kelly's celebrated steed, Marco Polo, is as well known at the Antipodes as Dick Turpin's Black Bess in these islands."—*Telegraph*, 7th July, 1881.

" It is notorious that the robbery of Mr. Steward's corpse was mainly performed by the assistance of NED KELLY's BROTHER, the Captain of what was neither more nor less than a pirate ship."—*Times*, July.

" The history of NED KELLY and his celebrated black horse. Marco Polo, will ever live in the recollection of the Australian public. The deeds of Dick Turpin, and the performances of Black Bess, are tame beside those of ' NED AND HIS NAG ;' in addition to which Ned's history is true, and Turpin's is pure fiction."—*Press*, July.

CHAPTER CLXII.—*Continued.*

"Right you are."

"There's a big passenger-craft running now from London-bridge regular, that has every weight in her engine room made hollow, and it's not pounds, but tons, of tobacco that she has brought into the country during the years she has been plying."

Thus talking, the pair had gained Rotherhithe, and made their way to a little public near the church.

They simply entered the bar, had a drink, and went out again without a word, but a few minutes later a couple of longshore-men who had been loafing in front of the bar for half-an-hour at least, over a pot of porter, finished it up and went out also.

Ned and Kit were loitering at a corner when these two came up to them.

" Well," said Kit, " how are things looking ?"

" Not too well," answered one of the men, whose speech rather belied his dress. " They are keeping an eye on the craft, I am certain. There's a supervision-boat prowling about up and down in a way that shows there's something in the wind."

" Is your own craft ready ?"

" Ay, she's at the stairs close by."

" Well, then, the sooner we get afloat the better."

The four picked their way down a narrow turning leading to the waterside, at the bottom of which several boats were moored.

Ned and Kit took their places at the stern-sheets of one of these, and the two others, taking the oars, pushed quietly off.

Paddling softly along, and keeping as much as possible under the shadow cast by the various mills and warehouses, they made their way a short distance up the stream.

Then they paused in the shadow.

The night was a tolerably fine one, though a slight haze hung upon the water, and the moon only occasionally shone forth from the clouds that veiled the greater part of the sky overhead.

The tide was running up, and had almost reached its height.

Bringing themselves alongside a coal-barge and holding on to it, the four men looked out across the river.

Their attention turned chiefly on a brig moored towards the shore next to which they were keeping.

" Is that her ? " enquired Ned, in a low voice.

" Yes."

" Why don't we run alongside then ?"

" Because," said the man who was pulling stroke-oar, " there's that cursed police-boat dodging up and down, in and out that tier of shipping over there. Look, you can just make her out."

" Well, she's working down stream. We could slip out and be alongside without her spotting us, if she keeps on over there."

" Yes. But I lay any money there's another hiding behind something away on this side, and ready to pounce out like a cat on a mouse all the time."

A little longer they watched and waited till the tide turned.

The first police-boat had got so far down stream that they had almost agreed to adopt Ned's suggestion and make a dash for the brig.

All at once they noticed another boat creeping up against the ebb in the direction they had themselves pursued, and evidently striving to keep out of sight.

Watching it closely, they noticed it dodging amongst the tiers of different craft moored in the stream.

At length it ran alongside a vessel, and someone from it mounted the deck and was followed by another

" What's that ?" whispered Ned. " Police ?"

" Hush, no. Thieves at work. Be quiet."

Emboldened apparently by the silence, the plunderers were seen to descend into the cabin of the craft they had boarded.

Suddenly, from behind a tier of barges a few dozen yards above the point where Ned and his friends were lying, a boat shot swiftly out into the stream.

She was manned by three oarsmen pulling randan, and was unmistakeably a police boat.

She headed straight for the plunderers, and had made some way before the man left in their boat noticed her approach which was as stealthy as swift.

Directly he did so, however, he warned his comrades, and they came bolting up from below and tumbled into their craft.

Seizing their oars they pulled desperately, with the police boat in hot pursuit, the latter striving to cut them off from the Surrey shore, to which they were endeavouring to make their way.

" Now's our time," cried Kit, as pursuers and pursued were lost for a few moments behind some shipping.

" Yes," answered the man who had before spoken, " that boat was watching the Welcome, but now she's in for a good chase on the top of the ebb, and the other will probably help her, so we've got a clear field. They'll be some time working back."

A few minutes later and they were alongside the brig they had been watching.

They were evidently expected, for a low hail greeted them as the bow oar hooked on to her.

Several figures appeared moving on the deck.

" Are the things ready ?" asked Kit.

" Yes," was the answer. " Will you come aboard ?'

" No ; tumble them in sharp. We've just got a chance of getting clear before that beggar down there has time to work back again."

Several bulky packages were lowered in quick succession over the brig's side and received into the boat, where they were quickly stowed at the bottom of the little craft.

All went well till one of the last of them was being lowered.

Ned was standing in readiness to receive it with his arms outstretched, when somehow or other the rope by which it was being let down came loose.

The package struck Kelly full on the chest, knocking him to the bottom of the boat, rebounded on to the thwart, almost upsetting the other men by the shock, and thence rolled into the water with a heavy splash, that sounded distinctly in the silence of the night

It sank at once.

"Curse it all!" said the stroke-oarsman; "there's a pretty job. Who the devil hitched the rope round that lot in such a clumsy fashion?"

"Look out; that splash is bound to be heard," whispered a voice from the deck.

"Ned," said Kit, bending over Kelly, who still lay at the bottom of the boat, "Ned, are you hurt?"

There was no answer.

Kit stooped quite close to the prostrate form of his brother, and endeavoured to ascertain the extent of his injuries.

The moon was still behind the clouds, but as far as he could make out Kelly had been stunned by his head coming against one of the seats in his fall.

A couple more packages were lowered.

"Put off at once," said Kit.

Ned who was evidently insensible, was placed in the stern of the boat, and the two oarsmen pulled the boat out into the stream.

The haze was clearing, but it was still dark.

All at once the moon broke forth from behind the clouds and lit up the scene, making it appear almost as bright as daylight, by the contrast.

Kit stooped down once more in order to get another look at Ned, who continued insensible, by the improved light.

As he did so an exclamation of rage broke from the stroke-oarsman.

The moon had revealed to him a four-oared galley right astern of them, and evidently about to attempt to overhaul them.

"Here's that infernal supervision-boat astern of us," he exclaimed, fiercely.

"Does she see us?" said Kit, who had just dipped his handkerchief in the stream and was dashing the water from it over Ned's face.

"Yes, and she's after us."

A hail from the stranger confirmed this.

"Pull on like devils, then," said Kit, who had glanced round to measure the distance between them, "we may dodge her yet along the other shore."

A species of groan escaped Ned at this juncture. and he opened his eyes.

"Ned, Ned!" cried Kit.

"What is it?" he answered, sitting up.

"Can you take an oar?"

Making a desperate effort to shake off his giddiness, Ned answered in the affirmative.

He took the stroke-oar's place, the latter seizing on a pair of sculls with which the boat was furnished, so that there were now three to help her along.

But it was evident that the galley was equal, if not superior, in swiftness, despite the desperation with which she pursued were pulling.

The dead weight they were carrying told.

The man who had pulled stroke-oar turned a look on Kit.

"They must go over," he said.

"I'm afraid so," was the answer.

Pulling in his sculls, the other stooped, and, lifting a couple of packages from the bottom of the boat, tossed them overboard.

A couple more followed.

"Hold on at that!" suddenly cried Kit, "and pull away like mad I see a chance of doing it, after all."

The man resumed his sculls, and the boat, thus lightened, went considerably faster.

The tide had been running down some time, and several craft had profited by it to get under way.

Barges and sailing-vessels were slowly drifting down, and more than one big steamer, lying in mid-stream, had slipped her moorings, and was making her way along under easy steam

One of these was coming along behind them, taking a course almost parallel with that of their pursuer, but nearer to the Middlesex shore.

She was going at about the same rate as the police-galley, and both were gaining on the fugitives.

"If we keep straight on we are bound to run upon another police-boat," said Kit. "Our only chance is to double, and I mean to risk it."

First he began to edge a little towards the Surrey shore, as though intending to try to land there.

The police-galley followed his example to cut him off.

Then he steered once more out towards mid-stream, and straightened the boat's course.

The galley partly imitated this, and thus still kept a little nearer the Surrey shore than the smugglers' craft.

These little manœuvres had somewhat delayed the direct advance of the boats, and the steamer had gained on them considerably.

She was creeping up towards the port-quarter of the boat steered by Kit, her long, wall-like sides towering like a castle out of the water.

Kit began to edge a trifle towards her.

The steersman of the police-boat noticed this, and began to make sure of his prey.

The advance of the steamer would cut the smugglers off from all chance of gaining the Middlesex shore, except by going astern of her.

To gain the Surrey side, they must cross his bows.

By putting on a spurt he could, as it were, pin them between his craft and the steamer, in which case there would be no room for them to double, and they would be bound to give in.

Urging his men to a spurt, he succeeded in lessening the distance considerably.

Kit had continued to edge still further to the left.

The bows of the steamer were now some twenty feet astern of him on that side, and a like distance separated him from the police-galley, now creeping up on his right.

"Now!" he suddenly cried. "Pull every ounce you can for your lives!"

And, altering the boat's course, he headed her straight across the steamer's bows for the Middlesex shore.

There was a yell from the look-out man on board the steamer as the boat rushed, as it were, to certain destruction.

But Kit had judged speed and distance to a nicety.

There was no time to alter the steamer's course, and it was the nearest thing that he managed to clear her.

As it was, her cutwater missed his stern by about a yard.

The look-out man cursed him heartily, after the manner of his kind, for not getting swamped, as he deserved.

But once across, and with her bulk intervening between them and the police-galley, there was a chance of escape.

Heading for a tier of vessels moored near the shore, Kit pulled along behind them.

The galley had no chance of passing as he had done, but had to wait and go astern of the steamer

This caused a delay of some minutes, during which the chase was hidden from view by the hull of the huge craft she had so narrowly avoided.

When, at length, the galley passed across the steamer's wake, those on board her could discover no sign of the fugitives.

However, they pulled in towards shore, closely scrutinising every lurking-place.

Meanwhile, Kit had steered into the first stairs that presented themselves.

The boat was soon alongside.

"This is lucky. I think we can find shelter close by both for ourselves and the swag," said the oarsman.

Each man seized upon one of the remaining packages, hoisted it on his shoulder, and, abandoning the boat to its fate, set off up the lane.

As they approached the summit, the tramp of a heavy footstep caught their ears, and the next moment the light of a bull's-eye lantern flashed upon them.

CHAPTER CLXIII.

DOWN WAPPING WAY.

THE position of Ned and his companions was a ticklish one.

To go back and take to their boat again was to expose themselves to almost certain detection by the police on the river.

To go forward was apparently to run right into the lion's jaw, for there was evidently a policeman at the end of the alley in which they found themselves.

Perhaps more than one.

But an uncertain peril is always easier to confront than a certain one with the majority of mankind.

So, after a momentary hesitation, the party proceeded onwards up the alley.

Before they had gone many steps the light of a bull's-eye was flashed upon them, and a voice cried—

"What's your game?"

The presence of four men stealing up from the river, each with a sack on his shoulder, was in itself suspicious enough to cause this interrogation.

There was no time to stop and try to give a more or less plausible explanation.

The pursuers were too close behind.

"All right, bob —bob—by," hiccupped the rower, who was leading the way, staggering forward as he spoke with the voice and gait of a drunken man.

"It ain't all right. Stand where you are, or——"

The policeman had not time to complete the sentence.

Suddenly dropping his load, the other sprang forward on him like a panther on a goat.

The policeman was a powerful young fellow, and if he had had to do with this single antagonist he might have given a good account of him in spite of the sudden surprise caused by this unexpected attack.

Before, however, he could disengage himself, or even utter a cry for help, Ned, Kit, and their remaining companion had in turn dropped their burdens and joined in the ferocious and unequal assault.

There was a brief but desperate struggle.

A closely-interlaced group of human figures writhed and swayed to and fro in the blackness of the alley.

The hurried trampling of their feet, their hoarse breathing, a muttered oath, and a gasping cry for aid, choked back in the throat of the hapless bobby, who vainly strove to utter it, were the only sounds that rose out of the inky darkness.

Kit and the second rower had pinioned the policeman's arms whilst his first assailant was gripping his throat with one hand and thrusting a handkerchief into his mouth with the other.

Meanwhile Ned had possessed himself of the unfortunate fellow's truncheon, which he had withdrawn from the case.

Two crashing blows followed.

The thickness of the intended victim's helmet saved him, however, from their full effect, and, nerved to desperation by the peril in which he found himself, he succeeded in partly freeing himself from the grip of his assailants by one desperate effort.

"Help! mur——" he shrieked, as they again secured him.

There were hats, if not "wigs upon the green" in this melée, during which Ned kept a hold upon the safety-valve or throat of his antagonist, whose helmet, his only protection, now tumbled to the ground.

In the struggle the group had reached the end of the alley, and the rays of light from a neighbouring lamp partially lit up their figures.

These rays seemed to concentrate, as it were, on the white, horror-struck face of the doomed victim, which was revealed by them in all its ghastliness of aspect.

A wild look of despair flitted across his distorted features, as Ned raised the truncheon.

"Murder!" again broke in half-strangled tones from the terror-parched lips of the poor fellow.

Ned saw at once that unless the constable's voice was silenced, the career of himself and his companions would soon be decided by the tribunals of the country.

He thereupon struck the poor wretch in his grasp a heavy blow with the truncheon he had wrested from him. The man tumbled like a sack, and for a moment the ruffians paused, as if paralysed by the atrocity they had committed.

The poor bobby was a corpse, although of this fact the crew who were responsible for his death were not quite certain. Not that Kelly or Kit cared much for the crime, still that uncertainty of results which would follow rather perplexed and somewhat cowed them.

The four ruffians gazed at one another for a few seconds in silence and with half-furtive looks.

Ned and Kit were unmoved; both had seen too much blood in their time to trouble themselves about a little more or less spilt on their path through life.

But the other two were not so hardened.

A little smuggling they did not mind, but killing a man —even a policeman, the natural enemy of their class— was quite another matter.

Ned was the first to speak.

"Now, then, don't be chicken-hearted, my lads. It's done, and you're all in it, so let us slide, and be quick about it, if we mean to slope. Pick up the plunder, and don't stand staring like frightened calves."

The other two were more silent than Kelly liked.

The struggle had carried them to some distance from the spot where they had thrown down their loads, and in the darkness of the alley it was not easy to discern them, despite their bulk.

The policeman's bull's-eye had been extinguished in the scuffle to which he had fallen a victim, so they had to grope for a few moments in the darkness.

Just as they had managed to lay their hands on the packages, the sound of a boat running sharply to shore reached them from the bottom of the alley.

The noise of someone scrambling to land and of a voice exclaiming, "I'm certain they ran in here," also fell upon their ears with most unpleasant distinctness.

Hastily lifting their packages, they scuttled out of the alley into the main street.

As they stood for a moment and seemed to hesitate whether to turn to the right or the left, the noise of footsteps approaching from the latter direction decided them.

They turned sharply to the right.

Flitting cautiously onward as silently as possible past huge and gloomy warehouses, they made their way in an easterly direction, with eyes and ears on the alert.

"We must spread," suddenly observed the man who had pulled stroke-oar in the boat, and who answered to the name of Dick amongst his friends, and to that of Lomax on police summonses.

"Why?" inquired Kit.

"We shall get into the livelier streets in a minute or two in this direction, and four men carrying bundles are bound to be spotted by somebody or other and remembered."

"Besides," remarked his companion, "there is bound to be a bobby at the swing bridge just ahead, and he is sure to stop and question us like the other bloke."

A rapid council of war was held.

As Ned was a perfect stranger to the rendezvous to which they were all bound, and which was situate in Wapping, it was absolutely necessary that some one or other should guide him thither.

Kit was about to suggest that he should do so.

Before, however, he could open his mouth for this purpose, Ned said to him hastily and imperatively,—

"You and Dick Lomax both know your way to the meeting-place, and can get there separately. Let Bob here stay with me to show me the right road."

The others acquiesced, though Bob did not seem particularly well pleased at this little arrangement.

This feeling he strove as best he could to conceal.

His conduct, however, only served to confirm a suspicion that had been germinating in Ned's mind ever since the struggle with the policeman and its terrible termination.

He had watched the demeanour of his companions closely since that untoward event.

He read in Bob's bewildered, anxious glance a horror of the deed since it had been accomplished, and a sickening dread of discovery and its appalling consequences.

Ned, though utterly illiterate, was an accomplished reader of character and human nature.

Like a celebrated historical personage, he could say that his only books were men and cards.

It was to this faculty that he owed so much of his power over his associates on all occasions.

He detected that Bob was a man who looked upon smuggling and murder with very different eyes.

His conscience might be, and indeed was, perfectly callous about the former, but this was evidently not the case as regarded the latter crime.

The first excitement of a struggle into which he had been drawn, as it were despite himself, over, that very unpleasant feeling known as remorse began to make itself felt most obtrusively.

Remorse is, as a rule, a first step to atonement.

But atonement in such cases as the one under consideration only too often takes the shape of delivering up one's fellow-criminals to the anything but tender mercies of justice, and at the same time making the best possible bargain for the safety of one's own precious neck.

This artful little transaction, so eminently characteristic of our perverse and fallen human nature, is commonly known as turning Queen's evidence.

Ned plainly read that, if they were caught, Mr. Bob would be the first to peach.

Hence he thought it best to keep him under his own sharp eye, and to be prepared, in case of treachery, to twist his neck like a chicken's in an instant.

The faint sounds of pursuit in the rear now reached them as they sped onwards.

It was evident that the party from the police boat must have discovered the corpse of the policeman.

This was indeed the case.

As they had hastened up the alley one of the foremost had tripped and stumbled over the inanimate body.

Dragging it to the light they at once divined the cause of what they judged to be death.

The next thing to do was to find in which direction the murderers, whose identity they divined, had fled.

They had just decided to separate in two portions, to the right and left, when they too caught the sound of the approaching steps that had in the first instance led Ned and his companions to turn in the former direction.

Soon the men from whom the sound of these footsteps proceeded came in sight.

They were a couple of master lightermen, well known, as it happened, to the crew of the police boat as men of perfect honesty and integrity.

Their statement, when questioned, that no one had passed them coming from the alley was at once accepted as true.

Evidently the murderers had turned to the right.

All at once the inspector who had steered the boat was struck with an idea, which he put in practice.

Directing two of his men to hurry on to the right on the presumed track of the assassins, he stooped for a moment over the prostrate body.

Taking from the pocket of the murdered man his rattle, and directing two of the remainder to convey the body to the station, he hurried after his advanced guard, springing the implement vigorously as he went along.

By this means he counted on alarming the district and bringing the police on duty to his aid at once without delay.

The probabilities were that, in coming to join him, they, or some of them at any rate, would encounter the fugitives, who were speeding in the opposite direction.

As it happened, this plan had quite a contrary effect to what he anticipated as regarded Ned and his friends.

They were, as has been said, in a street bordered by huge and gloomy warehouses and running parallel with the river.

A short distance ahead it led over a swing-bridge crossing an inlet to one of the numerous docks of the locality.

Beyond this bridge there were several turnings leading from the street, by means of which the party could separate.

But between the spot in which they were and the bridge there was no such way of getting clear.

It was absolutely necessary that they should cross the swing-bridge, now some ninety or a hundred yards ahead.

But it was also pretty equally certain that a policeman would be found on duty at that very point.

The difficulty was how to avoid him.

Suddenly Ned's keen ear caught the sound of someone approaching from the direction in question.

The peculiar heavy clumping step of a man shod with the regulation police boots was unmistakable.

At the same instant the whir of the rattle sprung by the inspector sounded far in the rear.

Swift to conceive a plan, Ned dragged his companions into the dark archway of a warehouse door.

The result answered his expectations.

The policeman, who was the man on duty at the bridge, had been keeping himself warm by pacing up and down.

But directly he heard the rattle he darted off at full speed in the direction from whence it proceeded, in order to render the assistance it called for.

He bolted past the archway beneath which the four fugitives were lurking without glancing to the right or to the left, blundering along like a steam fire-engine.

Directly he had passed them they darted out in turn, and rushed in the opposite direction to that he had taken.

In another minute and a half they were over the bridge, and soon separated, making their way up the different streets beyond it.

The rendezvous to which the smuggled goods were to be conveyed was situate at Wapping.

According to the original plan, which had been interrupted by the appearance of the police boat, they were to have pulled down the river and landed in close proximity to it.

Now they had to make their way thither on foot.

Kit and Dick departed by different routes.

Bob, upon whom Ned's guidance now devolved, led the way in sulky silence, followed by Kelly.

Avoiding the main thoroughfare, he made his way through a series of streets so dark, narrow, and deserted, as to excite even Ned's astonishment.

Lights were few and far between, and several times Kelly stumbled over a pile of garbage lying in the roadway, and had a narrow escape of coming to the ground.

His companion, however, seemed to know every square inch of the district they were traversing, and never once made a false step.

Narrower grew the streets, darker the way, and fouler the stenches they had to encounter the further they advanced.

They were in a network of filthy little streets bordered by houses almost in ruins.

Suddenly Ned, for about the twentieth time, stumbled against a heap of some kind of filth or other, and the next instant measured his length in the roadway, which was, fortunately, tolerably clean.

Growling like thunder he rose to his feet, and, after picking up his burden, looked round for his companion.

Bob had vanished.

There was no sign of him anywhere.

For a moment Ned thought that he too might have fallen over something.

"Bob, are you down?" he asked softly.

There was no answer.

"Bob—Bob! where the devil are you?" he cried, in louder tones.

Still no reply.

"Bob, what's your little game?" yelled Ned, setting prudence at defiance.

Then a thought struck him.

There could be no doubt of it—Bob had bolted from him on purpose.

He recollected the peculiar look he had noted on his late companion's face, and which had led him to insist upon his company in order to watch him.

Bob had evidently profited by his fall to bolt up one of the side streets, and knowing the ground, as he clearly did, was long since out of reach.

But what had he bolted for?

Ned guessed only too well.

He stood still a moment to ponder on his next movement.

He knew his pal was off to hand the lot over to justice, and get the reward—for reward there certainly would be —for the capture of the policeman's murderer.

He ground his teeth with rage at not having removed this witness from the face of the earth when he had the chance he might never have again—no one near, night as dark as Erebus, the policeman's truncheon, everything so handy!

What a tender-hearted fool he was! It was losing the best chance he would ever have—it was a regular flying in the face of Providence, it was—at least, so thought Mr. Edward Kelly.

It was as Ned surmised.

Bob judged that the murder of the policeman was too serious a matter to be involved in, and had, therefore, made up his mind to secure immunity for himself by denouncing his comrades, on whom he intended to lay the lion's share of the deed at once.

CHAPTER CLXIV.

ORTON AS GUIDE, PHILOSOPHER, AND FRIEND.

Ned's situation was not a pleasant one.

He was in a neighbourhood with which he was utterly unacquainted, and which was not the pleasantest in the world for a stranger to be wandering about at night in.

He did not know in what direction he ought to proceed, and, moreover, there was no one to ask.

He knew that he was in a neighbourhood of wild beasts in the shape of men—that the place was about as safe to an unarmed man as the woods and wolves of Russia in winter.

But fear was an element of the human mind unknown to Kelly.

His courage was ferocious, brutal, and the reckless pluck of the unreflecting; it was the courage of the brigand, not of the soldier.

The great *peut être* had never yawned before him, and crime has lost half its atrocity when it has lost all its responsibility.

He knew that all was fish that came to the net of the human tigers who infest these quarters, and that, despite the Scotch proverb that "hawks will no' pick out hawks' een," they would plunder a bushranger as readily as a bishop.

With his bundle, too, he had something of the appearance of the favourite game of this district—the newly-landed sailor.

As to asking a policeman for guidance, if he could come across one, that would, in his idea, have been rather risky.

Bob had no doubt by this time lodged all particulars of the crime and its perpetrators with the police, and it was certain the hounds were on the scent.

He stumbled along, keeping a sharp look-out as he went, and carefully avoiding any human figure he saw or fancied he caught a glimpse of.

At last he found himself in a broader and more respect-able-looking, though equally-deserted, street, and began to breathe more freely.

He looked round about to see if there was anyone of whom he might venture to ask his way.

Suddenly he caught sight of an advancing figure.

Or was it two, walking arm-in-arm?

For one man could hardly have such a massy back as the object he could dimly make out approaching him.

He looked again.

His first impression had been right.

There was only one pair of legs, and therefore it was only one body that was advancing towards him.

But on these legs was a body big enough for two, and resembling that *lusus naturæ*, a turtle on castors.

The stranger was muffled up in a huge pea-coat, buttoned to the chin.

The lower part of his face was swathed in the folds of an immense woollen comforter.

The upper was hidden by a kind of travelling-cap, with a projecting peak that was pulled right down over his eyes.

Notwithstanding this, there was something in the vast globular rotundity and rolling movements of the newcomer, that struck Ned as being strangely familiar to him.

He could have sworn that it was not the first time he had set eyes on that "biggest circulation in the world."

The vast pendulous cheeks, like a couple of well-stuffed carpet-bags, that he could make out under the shadow of the cap, he felt certain he had some kind of acquaintance-ship with.

He stepped up to the moving flesh-mountain and asked the way to —— street.

"Fourth turnin' to the right and then the first to the left, and that'll take you hinto hit," was the reply.

If Ned had been in doubt as to the figure, the voice at once undeceived him.

"By the living Jingo!" he exclaimed, "it's Castro, Orton, or whatever you call yourself."

It was indeed the ex-butcher of Wagga-Wagga, the ex-horse-stealer of Reedy Creek, who was prowling about, muffled up to the very eyes, in the streets of Wapping.

"Hush!" exclaimed the other nervously. "Let's see, who hare you. Why, hit's Ned Kelly."

"The same. And now just bear a hand, and get me out of this blessed forest of houses; blowed if I couldn't get out of the Mallee scrub as easy—and there ain't no sky to travel by in this cussed country."

"You want to go to —— street, eh?" enquired Orton.

"Yes," replied Ned.

"Well, Hi think this 'ere 'll be the nearest way," said the fat one, giving a lead down a side-street.

"I say, mate, you seem to know this quarter as well as a rabbit does his warren," remarked Ned, as he stepped along beside him.

"Well, I dessay you do think it rum for a B. of B. K. to know 'is way habout 'ere so well."

"What the devil's a B. of B. K?" growled Ned.

"Why a Barrowknight of the British Kingdom, to be sure," was the reply.

"Oh! so you're a baronet now, are you? What's your lay?"

"Ain't Hi told you afore? Ain't Hi told you as 'ow my poor dear mother, Lady Felliseet, knowed me the very minute as she first clapped heyes on me?"

"Well, you are coming it strong, you are!"

"Yes. She was like a maniac with joy. Ah! Hi've got no hend of swells on my side, now; and hit won't be long afore Hi henter hinto my property, and live like Hi did when Hi was a horficer."

"What, a police officer?"

"No a horficer in the carabineers, a fine regiment, a thousand strong."

Ned's knowledge of the strength of a British cavalry regiment was on a par with that of his companion, and this statement did not strike him as peculiar.

"Not but what they were rather rough on my hat

tinues," continued Orton, shaking his head. "Hi recollects as 'ow they put a blessed moke—Hi mean a donkey—hinto my bed, and Hi took hit for the devil."

"Did you learn your way about this part so well when you were in the army?" said the shrewd Kelly, who put no faith in Orton's "blowing."

"No, the fact his, you see, that my wife, Lady Tichborne ——"

"Come, drop it! I ain't such a moke as to swallow that."

"My wife, Lady Tichborne, hain't hat hall a bad sort, but she wants a little polishing up. So Hi've just come down 'ere to 'ave a word with a young woman, a perfect lady—gold watch, silk stockings, and high heels, everything quite regular—as Hi'm beknown to, and who 'angs hout this 'ere quarter."

"Oh, I see," replied Kelly, laughing, "a real swell—diamond rings and everything to match?"

"I believe you. One of the haristocracy and no flies. Why, when we took a day out to Woolwich Gardings last Saturday, and I said I'd stand a glass o' ale, she started up like a fellow caught at the plate-basket, and said she'd be —— if she'd swaller anything under champagne. She was always accustomed to hact like a lady, and she'd be —— if she was going to change now. Oh, she's the real nugget, and no quartz, I can tell you."

"You're in luck," said Ned. "Mum's the word, I suppose?"

"Of course, her ladyship might be jealous, you know, at my getting a governess—ha, ha, ha!" laughed the "suffering nobleman." "But you'll come and have a shove in the mouth with me some day at the Waterloo, in Jermyn-street, where I hang out?"

"I don't mind if I do, old chap. I'll give you a look up about grub time," said Kelly.

"But, I say," observed Orton, who began to think, considering Kelly's peculiar habits, that there was plunder in a good hotel—"mind, no tricks."

"What are you driving at?" said Kelly. "Do you think I'm going on the fake for greatcoats and umbrellas? Ugh!" he uttered, in disgust.

"All right, old pal," said Orton. "And mind, if you sees anybody there, you never set eyes on me afore save onced when you saw me a-carving my hinitchials on a pipe—R. T. C. Are you down to it?"

"Like a knife. But I say, look here, my bloomer, what are you going to stand if I recollect all you want and forget all you wish—eh?"

"Oh, you mean business, then?" ejaculated the would-be Sir Roger.

"Business afore pleasure, as the cove said when he ordered his coffin afore he swallowed the pison," laughed Ned.

"Oh, I don't mind," said Blubberhead. "There's plenty as knows me here and in the colony—swells, all on 'em. I can get any amount o' hevidence."

"Yes," said Ned, "at a price."

"Well, what's your price?"

"I can't say yet, but I'll send my bill in before long."

The two had now reached a more brilliantly-lighted street, in which, despite the lateness of the hour, there were a fair number of people about.

A man, having the appearance of a foreign seaman, approached them.

"Pardon, monsieur," said he, addressing Orton, politely, "auriez-vous la bonté de me preter du feu?"

As he spoke he raised his hand in which he held the cigar for which he had requested a light.

"Helloa! what does the beggar want, Ned? Why can't he speak a lingo one can understand?" asked Orton.

The man repeated his request in the same terms, but to the person addressed it seemed still incomprehensible.

"He wants a light, I think," said Kelly, proffering his weed, which the stranger took, and, after lighting his own with it, returned to its owner with a polite—

"Je vous remercie bien, monsieur."

Then, raising his hat, he went on his way.

"Some blooming furriner hor hother," remarked Orton, in a contemptuous tone.

"Frenchman, I think," said Ned.

"No. Hi should say 'e was a Portugee now. Hi should 'ave hunderstood 'im hif 'e'd a spoke hin French, you know," was Orton's reply, "because I was foaled there."

"'Ere's your street," he said, indicating a turning a little way further on; "but afore you goes down hit you'd better step hin to this 'ere crib—Hi mean public-'ouse—and 'ave a drain."

Before going in, Orton peered into a little snuggery with the position of which he seemed fully acquainted, in order to be sure that there was no one there.

Then, pulling his cap still lower over his eyes and his comforter still higher up over his mouth, he stepped in, and, in a voice that Ned could tell was an assumed one, ordered their drinks.

A middle-aged woman behind the bar stared hard at him, but said nothing, after serving him.

"'Ow my helbow hitches," said Orton, rubbing the portion of his anatomy in question against the bar. "Hit's a sign, Hi should say, as we was a-goin' to 'ave rain tomorrer."

"How's the wind?" asked Ned.

"Nearly west; that's the heast that way."

And, as he spoke, he jerked his head towards one corner of the little compartment in which they were standing, whilst Ned speculated on the strangely perfect acquaintance shown by him of all his surroundings, including the points of the compass.

Orton's knowledge, in a room at night, of the points of the compass showed his familiarity with the locality.

No man ever lived who could enter a strange room and tell what was east or west, north or south.

Orton, being bred up in the locality, knew the four points of the compass there.

An old fellow, who stepped in that moment from putting up the shutters, took a long look at the fat stranger, who appeared uneasy at this scrutiny.

As the two men stepped out after drinking their liquor, he said to the woman behind the bar—

"If that fat chap ain't Arthur Orton as went out to Australia with a couple of ponies, I'm a blessed Dutchman—hang me if I ain't!"

"Right you are, Sam," said the woman behind the bar. "I've been puzzling ever since he came in as to who he was, and now you've been and hit it."

Meanwhile Orton had taken leave of Ned, and the latter proceeding down the street pointed out to him, halted in front of the number that had been appointed as the place of meeting by his late companions on the river.

Before knocking, he glanced carefully round to the right and left in order to be certain that no lurking spy was observing his movements.

He gave the peculiar knock at the door as he had been instructed by Kit.

There was no light in the front of the house.

After watching a few seconds he heard the shuffling approach of footsteps, and then the withdrawal of sundry bolts and bars, which had a very suspicious sound, as, from the appearance of the place, the idea that there was anything to rob would never enter the brain of the merest tyro in burglary.

The door was cautiously opened on the chain, and the head of an old man was protruded.

With its yellow skin, its skull as bald as a basin save for a couple of tufts of fluffy white hair above the temples, its sharp aquiline features and its huge hooked nose, it resembled rather the head of a baldheaded vulture than that of a human being.

"What do you want?" croaked this apparition.

Ned answered by repeating a password which he had received from the other companions of his late expedition.

The old man unfastened the chain. and silently beckoned with his skinny claw for Kelly to enter.

Carefully reclosing the door behind them, he took up a flaring, stinking paraffin-lamp, and led the way along a dirty dilapidated passage to the bend of a pair of stairs.

Down these he proceeded, followed by Ned, whose weight, increased as it was by the burden he carried, caused the rickety steps to creak and groan in an ominous fashion.

At the bottom of the steps was a strong oaken door, from behind which came the murmur of voices.

The old man threw it open and ushered Ned into a spacious underground apartment, half cellar, half kitchen.

In it about a dozen men were already assembled.

Amongst them were Kit and Dick Lomax.

The cellar was long and tolerably lofty.

The space near the door was taken up by a table, on which liquors of various kinds were set forth, and by the benches on which the men were seated.

The further end was encumbered by bales and packages of different shapes and sizes, piled up in some instances to the arched roof itself.

CHAPTER CLXV.
TAKING CARE OF NUMBER ONE.

KIT and Lomax advanced to meet Kelly.

" Where's Bob?" enquired the first-named.

" Blessed if I know," answered Ned. " I fetched a cropper over a pile of muck, and when I picked myself up Bob had clean mizzled."

" What's the meaning of this?" said Kit, looking a little scared, and turning to Lomax in an inquiring fashion.

" I suppose he must have gone on, thinking you were close behind him, and then, missing you, turned back, and somehow or other did not come across you," said Lomax.

" Yes, that must be it," remarked Kit. " Very likely he passed you without seeing you, and is hunting about for you now, near where you parted."

Ned beckoned Kit to come closer.

" No, no, that's not it," he said in a low voice. " The beggar bolted on purpose to peach."

" To round on us?"

" Yes; about the bobby that fell against his truncheon. I noticed the fellow's face, and I swear he was in a blue funk about this job directly it was over. Curse it all, what a lily-livered set the fellows are in this rotten old country. Why, the lads I'm used to would think no more of dropping a cursed copper than of cracking a clay-pipe."

" What's best to be done?" asked Kit.

" Why, the best thing to be done is to scatter out of this hole like shot. He is pretty sure to say we were coming on here, and I don't care about being pinned up like a rat in a hole."

" Don't fret your kidneys," said Kit; "it's not so easy to get in here as you may fancy, and I think I can show you a way to get out long before any bobby sets foot in this den."

" Can you? Then out with it."

" So you may as well have a glass with the rest of us, and listen to a song. There are one or two chaps here that can pipe a stave, and no mistake."

Ned complied, and after being informally presented to the company as Kit's brother, and a cove on the same lay as themselves, was accommodated with a seat at the table and a glass of grog.

The company mainly consisted of 'longshoremen and " lumpers," by no means particular as to how they picked up a living, and usually making use of the place in which they found themselves for the reception of smuggled or stolen property of various descriptions.

A song or two had been sung, but not in a very loud voice, and matters were pretty cheerful when a knock was heard at the outer door.

One or two pricked their ears for a moment, but on recognising the usual signal, paid no further attention.

Ned, however, could not help feeling uneasy.

He heard the old porter shuffle along the passage to the door above.

Then the sound of the bolts and bars being withdrawn, and a pause, during which the password was evidently demanded.

After which Ned heard the door reclosed.

" It's all right," he thought, " the old boy has let the cove, whoever he is, in."

Still, he fancied he could detect a confused rumbling, tusselling, scuffling sound in the passage.

A minute or two elapsed, but neither the old man nor the newcomer made their appearance in the cellar.

The noisy conversation again broke forth, but Ned, who could not restrain a feeling of uneasiness, felt all but certain that he heard the front-door softly open again.

He was not left long in suspense, for the tramp of feet sounded plainly overhead, and approaching the summit of the stairs.

Evidently more than those of two persons.

The next moment the turbulent noise of a number of men hastily descending the crazy staircase was plainly audible.

The men in the cellar glanced at one another as though demanding some explanation. They were as silent as if suddenly turned into stone. They stared with alarmed contenances towards the stairs.

The solution was furnished in a somewhat unpleasant fashion as it turned out.

The door of the cellar, which no one had thought of securing, was thrown wide open.

The light flashed on the uniforms and accoutrements of a number of policemen.

And one of these, stepping forward into the cellar, called upon the whole party to submit quietly.

Ned, with Kit and Dick, at once guessed how this had happened.

Bob, as Kelly had surmised, had been terrified at the thought of being arrested as one of the actors in the murder of the policeman.

On bolting from Ned he had hastened at once to the nearest police-station.

There he had given himself up and, as an earnest of his sincerity, had volunteered to guide the police at once to place where he assured them his accomplices had taken refuge, and, at the same time, to reveal the whereabouts of a large depôt for smuggled goods, the existence of which had long been suspected.

The inspector on duty had at once accepted his offer; but had refrained from telling him that the policeman was not dead after all, though severely injured by Ned's blow.

A party of the force were at once despatched under the guidance of the traitor to the house in Wapping.

Bob, stepping up to the door alone, had been let in by the old doorkeeper.

Once inside he had suddenly seized and pinioned the old ruffian, and re-opening the door admitted the police.

No sooner had these made their appearance at the door of the cellar than Ned sprang to his feet.

Drawing a pistol, he sighted the man who had called on them to surrender, and fired straight at him.

The effect of this shot was twofold.

The police were not accustomed to such a reception.

It was a little before the time of "the revolver epidemic," as it is styled, which has since set in with such severity, as far as they are concerned, and they were not used to " stand fire" unless in company of some friendly and amorous cook.

As a rule the dangerous classes, when cornered, would yield themselves without resistance and not make targets of their would-be captors.

So when their leader dropped with a bullet in his shoulder, for Kelly had sought to disable him, not to kill him outright, they remained for a minute or two quite stupefied.

But Kelly's companions, with the exception of Kit, were equally taken aback by his proceedings.

They did not mind "squashing a copper's head like a bug" with a brickbat when the opportunity presented itself, but firearms were rather out of their line at this epoch.

Hence the two parties gazed at one another for a moment in equal amazement.

Kit was the first to recover himself.

Just as Ned was about to throw himself forward and try and profit by the panic he had created to force his way through the police into the street, he laid a hand on his arm.

"Don't try that," he said, "there's a better way."

And at the top of his voice he gave the order that had long ago been arranged should such an event as the present intervene.

"Dowse the glims, my hearties, and lammus," shouted Kit, and, in a moment the place was in utter darkness.

The police held the door, but were afraid to move lest a way for escape should be left open.

Kelly knowing his herculean strength was for grasping the police and forcing his way out.

The thieves were the more numerous, and could certainly have carried the pass; but the undefinable something that surrounds the executors of the law quite cowed the vagabonds for some seconds.

"Blowed if I ain't got it," whispered Kelly to Kit. "Let's knock their blessed heads off. We know where they are, they don't know where to find us in the dark. Let's give 'em bricks and smash the lot. Don't give in without a fight. D—— it, let's have a shy at 'em before the job's ended."

"No, no, Ned; I know a better way—follow me, the other lot know the track they're to take—they'll slip off without being heard or seen—the bobbies will think they're simply funking."

Meanwhile a brisk movement went on.

Kelly found himself guided by Kit in the direction of one end of the cellar.

Passing behind a pile of goods, he felt himself conducted along a narrow passage in utter darkness.

At the end of it his feet struck against the bottom of a flight of steps.

Just as he began to ascend them, someone, who had preceded him, raised a trap at their summit.

It was one of those traps leading on to the pavement, such as may be seen by hundreds in the streets of London under shop-fronts and are generally used for the reception of heavy goods by tradesmen.

It opened on to a street running parallel with that by which they had entered the house, and which was apparently quite deserted.

Just as Ned began to ascend the steps, the police, who had guessed that their prey was escaping them, made a rush forward through the cellar, guided by the noise caused by the retreating ruffians.

They reached the beginning of the passage just as the rear guard of the gang were entering it.

A brief scuffle took place in the darkness.

The police laid about them furiously with their truncheons, hitting about indiscrimately, and more than one of their number had reason to bless the stoutness of his helmet, which alone saved him from a fractured skull at the hands of a comrade.

But some of their blows reached their intended destination, and consequently several of the 'longshoremen were struck down and captured.

The open trap let a little moonlight into the passage, and by its aid the state of things could be made out somewhat more distinctly.

The police saw that, by making a rush forward and gaining the steps, they could prevent the escape of several of the struggling throng.

But Ned also saw this fact.

He saw, moreover, that if once the police gained the steps and thence the street, they would be so closely on the fugitives' track that the chance of escape would be considerably lessened.

He rushed up the steps at the top of his speed.

Several of his companions were close behind him.

But, instead of waiting to allow them to come out, he deliberately slammed down the two flaps that closed the opening.

The trap, as is usual in such cases, consisted of two flaps, one opening to the right and the other to the left.

In the centre of each was a large iron ring serving as a handle to raise it.

Ned took in this at a glance.

Kit, who had preceded him up the steps, and was waiting for him, had cast down a heavy piece of wood with which he had covered himself on the arrival of the police.

It was about four feet long, and as thick as a man's wrist.

Seizing this, Ned slipped it through the two rings in the cellar flaps, rendering it impossible for anyone to open the trap from within.

A howl of despair from the men behind him announced this fact only too plainly.

Kit was the only one who witnessed this act of treachery, all of the others who had gained the street having already scuttled off at the top of their speed.

"Hang it all, Ned, what are you up to?" he cried.

"Look here, capture for those coves means quod for six months, but for us it means a morning picture in a white nightcap I don't care to make—at Newgate. If it was a fair fight, and with the rope round all our necks, I'd have stuck to my pals like wax," was the reply.

And whilst his unhappy companions, caged liked rats, were forced to yield to the police, who now had command of the only issue from the cellar—namely, the door by which they had first entered, he and Kit soon placed themselves in safety.

The trapped men never learnt to whose hand they were indebted to board and lodging at her Majesty's expense, but they had a shrewd suspicion.

CHAPTER CLXVI.
A GAME OF CROSS-PURPOSES.

OF course, the great diamond robbery in Hatton-garden created a tremendous sensation.

The papers were all full of it.

Innumerable callers, interested in various ways, or simply moved by curiosity, besieged Mr. Mallan's house.

For some time, however, they were unable to gain access to the master of the establishment.

The wounds inflicted by Kelly on the worthy diamond merchant were not fatal.

Though severe and for a short time dangerous, they had not reached any vital part.

When once the healing process had fairly set in, its progress, thanks to the wounded man's excellent constitution, was rapid and unchecked.

At length, the doctor was able to pronounce his patient in a fair way to recovery, and to withdraw his prohibition against anyone whatever entering the sick chamber, save Mrs. Mallan and the nurse.

He had given strict orders to Mrs. Mallan not to let his patient hear any news whatever of a nature likely to excite or distess him.

This order the poor woman had faithfully obeyed, though it needed a terrible effort to enable her to keep silent, as regarded the overwhelming loss that had befallen them in their old age.

At last, with the doctor's permission, she ventured to speak of it to her husband.

She touched first of all on the great danger which he had undergone from his injuries.

He admitted it.

She then enlarged on the joy she felt, and on the gratitude he ought to feel that his life had been spared, and in

834
NED KELLY.

this the poor woman was sincere enough, for she was deeply attached to her husband.

"My poor old man," she said, with the tears in her eyes, "you cannot think how grateful I am to have you still with me."

The sufferer pressed her hand without speaking.

"But, oh, John," she continued sadly, "I have some very sad news to tell you."

He looked at her inquiringly.

"You know that the villain who stabbed you managed to get clear off?"

"Did he?" he asked, for he had been kept in ignorance of this.

"Yes. He broke away from you and rushed out of the house."

"Did you—did you notice what he was doing when you discovered him?" she asked, hesitatingly.

"As far as I could make out," said the invalid, with some difficulty, "he was rifling the safe."

"Yes," sighed Mrs. Mallan, "he was."

There was a pause.

"He must have been at it some time before you heard him," she said, at length.

"Very possibly."

"And he had had time to pack up his plunder," she observed with a sigh.

"What?"

"Yes, dear. When we came to examine things, we found that not only the safe but the cash-box in it had been forced, and that the diamonds had disappeared altogether from the place."

There was a moment's silence.

Mr. Mallan, however, was not so terribly overwhelmed as she had anticipated by this intelligence. This his affectionate partner attributed to the strength of mind of her noble-minded husband.

He seemed to be making a strong effort to recover himself, and to succeed in doing so.

"The police, I suppose, are on the fellow's track? Have they got any clue, do you know?"

"They have been wanting to see you about it for some days past."

"Well, I suppose they had better."

"There's a man downstairs now who has something to do with it, and who wants to see you. Shall I fetch him up?"

"Certainly, my dear, I think I am strong enough for this interview."

There was almost a merry twinkle in the eye of the sufferer, but what it meant sorely puzzled the partner of his joys and sorrows.

After propping her husband up with pillows, Mrs. Mallan left the room and shortly afterwards returned with a little brisk man, whose appearance vaguely recalled that of a ferret, his face peeping out from a forest of hair of the most fiery red, with whiskers to match.

He was dressed in semi-clerical style, with a black coat and white choker.

He glanced from Mr. to Mrs. Mallan in a most significant manner.

"You can leave us, my dear," said the former, rightly interpreting his glance.

"Pray do not excite yourself too much, John," said the good woman to her spouse, as she prepared to leave the room. "You'll take care of that, won't you, sir?" she continued, appealingly to the visitor.

"Certainly, ma'am, certainly, we will take care not to bruise the shattered vessel," was the reply.

No sooner was the door closed on Mrs. Mallan, than he turned briskly towards the sick man.

"I am a detective."

"I presumed as much."

"Hush! Don't talk more than you can help. If you will just content yourself with answering yes and no to my questions it will do. You heard what your good lady said?"

Mr. Mallan smiled.

"My dear sir," resumed the little man, "you have, I believe, suffered, under Providence, from a severe affliction, you have been robbed of property representing a value of from twenty-five to thirty thousand pounds?"

"Yes," answered Mr Mallan, "that's it, property, representing a value of thirty thousand pounds."

"Don't say more than you can help. You would like to get it back, I suppose?"

"Yes," was the answer, given in a calm tone.

"Hum!" said the stranger, who seemed to have the habit of thinking aloud. "He does not seem to excite himself much about it. I think we may as well go into the business at once. My dear sir, I have mentioned before that I am a detective. A private detective."

"Ah."

"Yes, I am Mr. Tunstall, of Tunstall and Bigwood, Private Detective Office, 304, Little Smith-street. Enquirers in divorce, libel, loss, or any private case. Missing friends traced to any part of the world. Important cases personally conducted by the principals in the strictest confidence."

"But——"

"Exactly. I was merely repeating our advertisement. Matter of habit. But to resume. We devote ourselves especially to the recovery of stolen property."

"Indeed."

"Yes; and, under providence, I am glad to say that the Lord has usually blessed our labours. We have, I make bold to say to you—and, considering the loss under which you are suffering, I feel I can venture to speak openly—certain sources of information, certain connections which are, I flatter myself, not available to the first comers."

A smile passed over Mr. Mallan's shrewd features.

"We have I assure you, before this, been able, by a merciful dispensation, to recover very valuable property on its way to the melting-pot. Diamonds are rather difficult things to dispose of in large quantities, and I feel certain that if the thieves try to get rid of them we shall hear of it."

"Through your connection?" said the diamond merchant, somewhat drily.

"Yes, exactly; through the mysterious working of Providence and our connection," was the unabashed answer; "and I have no doubt that, with very little trouble, the lost property could be placed once more in your hands."

Mr. Mallan smiled once more, but somewhat ironically. rather than with the hopeful expression of a man anticipating the restoration of a lost treasure.

"Of course, this will entail trouble, not to say expense, and in such cases you, I know, will not dispute the fact that the labourer in the vineyard is worthy of his hire."

"I suppose so."

"Then you are prepared to offer a reward for the recovery, if it should be so decreed by Providence, of the lost property."

"I believe I must."

"My dear sir, let me assure you that there is not the slightest chance otherwise of getting it back. Not the slightest, let me assure you. The world, you know, my dear sir, the world is frail," and he sighed heavily, and then continued, "But what sum do you think of offering?"

"Well, as you have said, I have been deprived of property representing a value of thirty thousand pounds."

"Thirty thousand pounds!" repeated the other, rubbing his hands with anticipation.

"I think the best plan will be to offer a percentage."

"A percentage, my dear sir?—a most excellent idea."

"And, as you are experienced in such matters, I think I cannot do better than ask your advice as to the amount."

"Quite so, my dear sir, quite so. Your ideas are excellent, worthy of a chosen vessel, indeed they are. It is most singular, I was about to suggest a percentage on the amount recovered myself, and I have here already drawn up a little form of agreement, with just the figures left blank, which I trust you will sign. Thirty thousand pounds worth of diamonds, you say," he went on, producing the agreement and a pocket inkstand. " I will fill that amount in. And now for the percentage—I think we may say——"

" Ten per cent., eh ?"

" Oh ! my dear sir ; twenty-five at least. Consider the time, the trouble."

" Fifteen per cent. will repay them amply."

" Well, twenty—say twenty. There, that is filled in. And now, my dear sir, your signature here. Stop a minute, I will call the nurse and your good lady to witness it," and as he spoke he rang the bell.

A few minutes later the little man was rushing down the street with a paper in his coat-tail pocket, by which Mr. Mallan bound himself to pay twenty per cent. on the value of the diamonds recovered by his agency.

As he went along he muttered to himself—

" Any odds I get on the track of the diamonds at last. Whoever holds them ought to snap at fifteen per cent. of their value, and no questions asked, and with the other five per cent. I put fifteen hundred pounds into my pocket. There is only one puzzle to clear up, and that is, who has got them ? Well, whoever it is, they will hardly hesitate at my terms."

The private detective had scarcely left the house before the bell rang, and another visitor made a most pressing request for an immediate audience with Mr. Mallan.

The new-comer offered a striking contrast.

He was a very tall and powerfully-built man of somewhat portly outline, set off to advantage by a tightly-buttoned frock-coat of dark blue cloth.

His complexion was ruddy, his sleek and close-cropped hair iron grey, whilst his small side-whiskers, trimmed with military accuracy, were jet black.

He gave his name as Superintendent Smith, of the Metropolitan Police Force.

Mrs. Mallan was rather anxious at first not to admit him, fearing the two visits might excite her husband.

But her visitor was not to be checked.

" Madam," he remarked blandly but firmly, " I am especially entrusted with this affair by the authorities at Scotland-yard. I am willing to wait a little time to allow Mr. Mallan to recover himself from the interview you mention, but it is most necessary I should see him."

Mrs. Mallan was fain to agree.

The superintendent said that during the interval he should like to inspect the scene of the burglary.

He visited the workshop and office under Mrs. Mallan's guidance, inspected everything, looked awfully wise and impenetrably mysterious.

The London police are notoriously the most woodenheaded body of respectable men in the world. When on enquiries, " from information they have received," they appear pompous asses, and rarely, if ever, show any intelligence in detecting criminals.

But it must be admitted that for civility they are unequalled.

On this occasion the detective ejaculated with pomposity —" Hum ! " three times, and shook his head solemnly four. He certainly looked very wise.

He then went upstairs, slowly, solemnly, officially.

" Good-day, sir," was his greeting on entering the sickroom. " Glad to see you better, sir. Sad affair this."

" Yes," answered Mr. Mallan, in confirmation of the ' sadness.'

" Government has taken it up."

" Indeed ! Then they must think the affair one of some atrocity ?"

" Oh yes ! They offer twenty pounds reward for the murderous attack upon you. They offered one hundred pounds last week for the detection of a tax-gatherer who bolted with one hundred and fifty pounds he had received for taxes."

" Oh indeed ! Twenty pounds for attempted murder, five times that amount for stealing money ! Truly a paternal Government that thinks more of property than of life."

" We must respect the law, sir. A man may half or three-quarters murder his wife, and jump her inside out, kill her by accident on purpose, and get three months. But see how equal the law is. A starving child, who steals a growing turnip, gets the same. Oh, the law's uncommon equal, sir, it is. We're a humane people, we are, sir," said the detective, with a most reverent appreciation of that branch of science which has been called the " perfection of reason."

" Very considerate to offer any reward."

" Just so, sir. But the attack on you was not the only crime committed here, you see."

" How so ?"

" Offence against property as well as against the person. From information I received. I am given to understand you have been robbed of thirty thousand pounds worth of diamonds. Is that so, sir ?"

" Stones representing a value of thirty thousand pounds have certainly been carried off."

" Exactly. Now, sir, I suppose you would like the man who almost murdered you brought to justice, and punished according to his deserts ?"

" Certainly I should," answered Mr. Mallan energetically.

" And your property restored ?"

" Yes," was the reply, though in not quite such cordial tones.

" Well, sir, I think if you were to offer a decent reward for it, the men who have charge of the case would be likely to take a great deal more trouble about the matter than otherwise. You can quite understand that, sir ?" and the superintendent laid one finger against his nose.

" Quite so. I am quite ready to offer an additional reward."

" Ah, I thought you would, sir," and the superintendent smiled.

" Yes. Let me see, the Government offer twenty."

" Yes."

" Well, I don't mind putting another hundred to get hold of the ruffians."

" Yes ; but as regards the stolen property, sir, I should suggest——"

" Just so. I am coming to that. For the restoration of the stolen stones, I don't mind going as high as ——" and here he paused in mental calculation.

" Yes, sir, as high as ?" said the superintendent in an eager tone.

" Well, a hundred more," remarked Mr. Mallan quietly.

" A hundred more !" echoed the superintendent in a tone of amazement, and with a look at the invalid as if he began to entertain serious doubts of his sanity.

" A hundred more. I have reason to believe it will be sufficient," repeated the diamond merchant.

" Well, sir, you know best," said the police officer, with a somewhat disconcerted air, " but, as man to man, I may tell you I don't think there is much chance of your ever seeing your diamonds back again."

" Probably not," assented Mr. Mallan mildly.

" As regards the man who did the job, though, it may be another matter, and, with the clue we've got, I should not be surprised if we laid hold of him."

" Ah, what clue is that ?"

The superintendent looked as if he wished he had not said quite so much.

" Well, I think his accomplice will say something in the end, although she does keep precious quiet as yet."

" His accomplice ? Whom do you mean ?"

" Why, the girl."

" What girl ?"

" The girl you had here—Sal her name is."

" Good heavens ! Do you mean to say she is in custody. That explains it. I thought it strange she had not come into my room to see how I was, since she always professed such devotion to me."

"Or for your diamonds, sir."

"Nonsense, I know the girl too well. So she is in custody, eh? On what charge?"

"Being concerned in the robbery of thirty thousand pounds' worth of diamonds."

"Is that all? No other charge, eh?"

"No," replied the superintendent, who was fast getting somewhat bewildered.

"And who gave her in charge?"

"Your good lady, sir, I am told."

"At your instance, eh?"

"Yes; at least, at the instance of the police."

"Ring the bell for my wife."

The superintendent complied.

"My dear," said Mr. Mallan, when his wife entered, "I want you to withdraw at once this charge against poor Sarah, and have her released."

"Certainly, my dear," was the answer.

"Well, sir," said the thoroughly bewildered superintendent, "as you withdraw the charge, I don't see the good of opening it, and the bench will discharge the girl when next she comes up on remand, for want of evidence. But I must say that if you ever think of getting back the thirty thousand pounds' worth of diamonds, either through us officially or in any other way, you will be very much mistaken."

"I certainly don't expect to get them back through you, or in any other way."

"Ah," said the officer, in puzzled surprise.

"And I am really sorry you should have put yourself to so much trouble and taken such a trifling loss so seriously to heart," and Mr. Mallan smiled in that peculiar and enigmatical way that had already puzzled those about him.

CHAPTER CLXVII.
SOME NEEDFUL EXPLANATIONS.

His wife and the superintendent looked at one another.

There could be no doubt about it.

It must be the fever from his wound, rendering him utterly delirious, that made him talk like this.

Mrs. Mallan could not help bursting into tears.

Her husband saw this.

"Come, Mr Superintendent," he said, "let us have a clear explanation. You and I are playing at cross-purposes."

"In what way?"

"You would like to lay your hands on thirty thousand pounds' worth of diamonds belonging to me?"

"Yes," was the reply, in a very decided tone indeed.

"Well, if I chose I could grant you that pleasure in about ten minutes. They are all in the house now."

"In the house now?" exclaimed the other two simultaneously.

"Yes, and what's more, they never went out of it. Don't you see now, eh?" and Mr. Mallan fairly chuckled.

Then, as his wife and Superintendent Smith were too stupefied to answer, he went on—

"It is known that I am a diamond merchant, that I live here, and that I keep a large quantity of precious stones on the premises. What more natural than that some day or other an attempt should be made to rob me. But I was quite prepared for that attempt. I said to myself, Where will the robbers, when they do come, look for the diamonds? Why, naturally in the place where they are supposed to be kept. Is it not so, eh, Mr. Superintendent?"

The superintendent nodded grimly.

"And that is my safe. I tell a few people in the strictest confidence that I have stones representing a value of thirty thousand pounds in my safe. Do you see, eh?"

"Not quite," was the somewhat dazed answer.

"Well, I have there stones which represent, I say, a value of thirty thousand pounds, but which are in reality not worth thirty thousand pence."

The superintendent whistled in amazement, and regarded the invalid with admiration. He wouldn't be out of place in "the force."

"Now do you see? A thief enters the house. He looks first of all in the most natural place for valuables, the safe. He finds what he thinks is thirty thousand pounds' worth of diamonds, and he hurries out of the house without looking any further, eh?"

"That's so," remarked the superintendent, emphatically.

"If he is a bit cleverer than his fellows, he says to himself, 'What a fool this diamond merchant must be to keep all his diamonds down here on the ground floor in a back office.' But he does not, even in that case, think of looking any farther, and, meanwhile, the real diamonds are hidden away in a place known only to myself—not even to my wife—and which is so snug that you might pull the house three-parts down before you came on the slightest trace of their hiding-place."

"The devil you might!" exclaimed the superintendent, fiercely, starting to his feet. "Why, if——"

He checked himself.

His almost gigantic figure seemed to dilate as he glanced round the room, and, as his eye appeared to rest for a moment upon the fire burning in the grate, it's pupil seemed to grow too like a living coal of fire.

A grim smile curled his lip as he looked from Mr. to Mrs. Mallan, and drew near the latter.

(To be continued.)

NED KELLY

THE
IRONCLAD
AUSTRALIAN BUSHRANGER

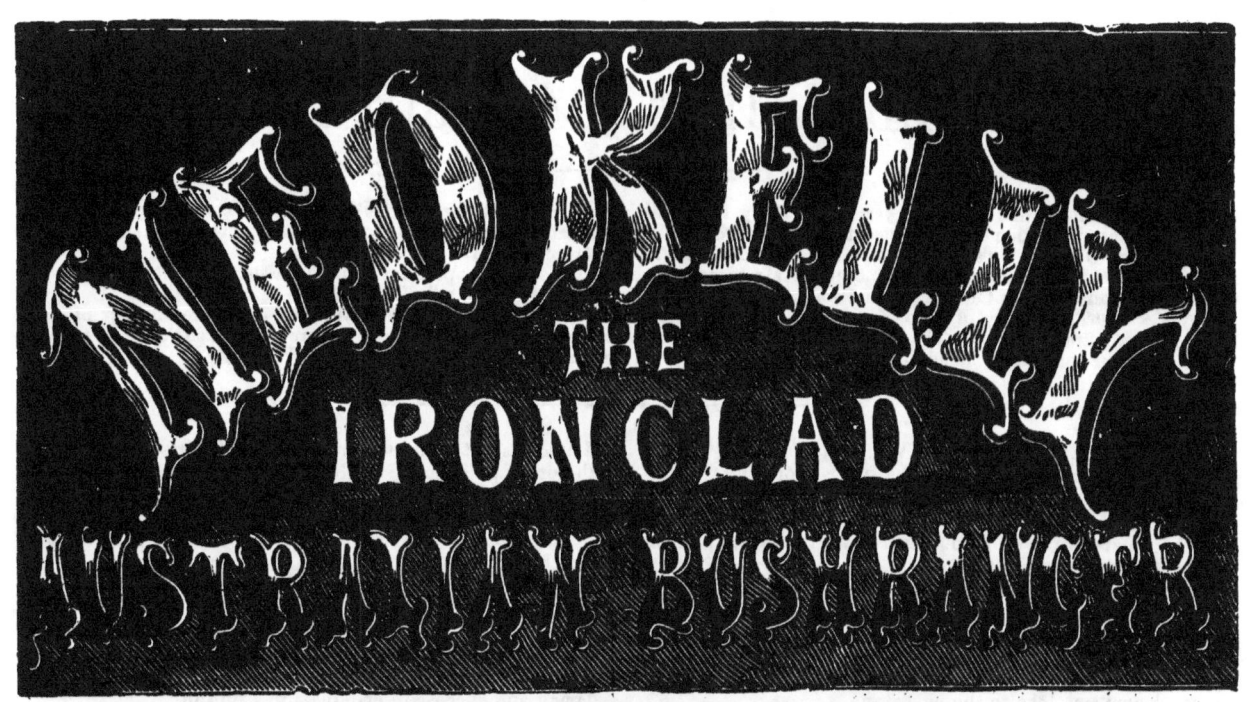

NO 29,

NED KELLY: IRONCLAD BUSHRANGER.

It is well known that for many years Ned Kelly had made himself notorious by a series of crimes wholly incompatible with the civilisation of the nineteenth century. Ned Kelly's celebrated steed, Marco Polo, is as well known at the Antipodes as Dick Turpin's Black Bess in these islands."—*Telegraph*, 7th July, 1881.

" It is notorious that the robbery of Mr. Steward's corpse was mainly performed by the assistance of NED KELLY'S BROTHER, the Captain of what was neither more nor less than a pirate ship."—*Times*, July.

"The history of NED KELLY and his celebrated black horse, Marco Polo, will ever live in the recollection of the Australian public. The deeds of Dick Turpin, and the performances of Black Bess, are tame beside those of ' NED AND HIS NAG ;' in addition to which Ned's history is true, and Turpin's is pure fiction."—*Press*, July

CHAPTER CLXVII.—*Continued.*

At that moment the bell of the front-door rang.

Mrs. Mallan stepped to the window and lifted the blind.

"Ah! Mr. Superintendent," she exclaimed, looking out, "there are two of your men down below at the door. Ah! and the doctor too."

"Damn——!" ejaculated the superintendent, and springing to the window by her side he glanced into the street in turn.

Two policemen in uniform were at the door, and the doctor's brougham, from which its owner was alighting, was drawn up close to the curbstone.

"Ah! two of my fellows, as you say, Mrs. Mallan," said the superintendent, recovering his coolness. "I will run down and see what they want. They must have come here after me."

He at once left the room, with the parting remark to Mr. Mallan—

"All right, I'll see about the girl being released."

Then swiftly descending the stairs he swept by the sergeant and constable standing in the hall, whither they had just been admitted by the nurse who had answered the bell, opened the door, passed into the street and walked rapidly away.

The constable and sergeant waited below till the doctor had seen his patient, whom he found suffering from excitement, consequent upon the two interviews just related, and for whom he prescribed absolute quiet.

They then sent up a request to see Mr. Mallan.

"Do you think it as well, doctor?" asked Mrs. Mallan.

"No, I think you had better not let him see anyone else to-day. If you like I'll step down with you myself and see what they want."

Accordingly the doctor and Mrs. Mallan went downstairs.

The two police officers, whom Mrs. Mallan recognised, stated that they were the men specially entrusted with the case, and that they wanted to know if Mr. Mallan had recovered enough to give any information likely to be of any service to them.

Mrs. Mallan replied that her husband had just had a long interview with Superintendent Smith.

Whereupon the two simultaneously asked who was Superintendent Smith.

They were told the tall man who had just come down and spoken to them in the hall.

"No one spoke to us," said the sergeant.

"A tall man! why he bolted past us like a rabbit without saying a word," cried the constable.

"Besides, there's not a Superintendent Smith in the force," they continued, simultaneously.

"Good heavens!" cried Mrs. Mallan, "it must have been one of the robbers themselves."

A little comparing of notes established this theory beyond all doubt, especially as the doctor had recognised in the stranger a gentleman who had called on or waylaid him several times with inquiries as to Mr. Mallan's health.

It was arranged that Mrs. Mallan and the doctor, with the sergeant, should at once proceed to Scotland-yard and explain everything, including the fact of the real

diamonds not being stolen, to the authorities there, whilst the other policeman should remain on guard in the house in case of a renewed visit from Superintendent Smith.

This plan was followed.

The Scotland-yard people, like the sham Superintendent Smith, were staggered when the trick by which the diamonds had been preserved from the robbers was revealed to them.

But they were still more staggered to learn of the impersonation of the sham superintendent.

Rapidly they ran over the names of some of the most daring and successful criminals in London.

Not one of them seemed to tally with the description given by the sergeant and Mrs. Mallan.

"There's only one man, I believe, in the world would have the pluck and cleverness to play such a trick," said an old detective, whose duty had led him at different times half over the globe, and who had just returned from an excursion to Australia, " and it does not seem quite clear, after all, whether he is in England just now."

"Who's that?" enquired one of the others.

"Oh, you know nothing about him, never heard of him. He was in full blaze in Melbourne when I went out there after a bolter last year. He was robbing every bank in the Colony, openly in broad daylight"

"Do you mean Kelly? He might be in London, for all we know. Is it like his work?"

"Yes, it is," replied the sergeant, "I saw a notice from the Australian authorities to the "Yard" that Kelly was supposed after his last crime to have quitted the colony, and it was thought for England or America, and we were to look out, as he would most likely give us a look in on his way. I'm blessed if it ain't like his work and himself too. We have his description, and the sham superintendent ain't very unlike him."

"Well, we shall soon hear of the beggar again if he is amongst us. We can only keep a sharp lookout until he turns up."

Another singular surprise also awaited the doctor and Mrs. Mallan in course of the day.

Knowing of the document that Mr. Mallan had signed, they thought it as well to call on Messrs. Tunstall and Bigwood at Little Smith-street, to explain to these gentlemen that is was not worth while for them to trouble themselves about the matter any further.

But what was their surprise on learning at the address indicated that the firm in question had only engaged a single room as an office the preceding day, paying a week's rent in advance, and that it appeared to consist of a single individual, a very pious old gentleman the landlord said, who stated that for the first few days he should only call in and see if there were any letters.

Strange to say he never did call for the expected correspondence.

The explanation of this was simple.

No sooner had Mr. Superintendent Smith got out of the diamond merchant's, than he darted into Holborn as fast as his legs could carry him.

He hailed a hansom to drive him to Waterloo Station, and there took a ticket for Clapham Junction, and got into a first-class compartment in which there were no other travellers.

En route he effected a number of changes in his personal appearance.

And this he did very simply and expeditiously. Firstly he pulled a false beard out of his pocket and became a second Abraham in a minute. He then took off his coat, which he turned inside out, revealing a white lining and, in fact, changing the black into a white overcoat. The metamorphose of his appearance was complete, and Kelly laughed to himself as he thought how he was selling what our Atalantic cousins would call "those dried up old cusses that haint no more life in 'em than the stuffed painter (panther) in Barnum's Museum."

From Clapham Junction he easily made his way by rail to Peckham.

Here he was once more Mr. Dawes, *alias* Ned Kelly.

On reaching his residence he kept a lookout till he spied his neighbour Smith, *alias* Peace, in the garden, pottering about in his usual style and humming a hymn-tune.

He at once sallied forth, and imperatively signalled to the other that he wanted to speak to him.

There had been a certain amount of ill-blood between the pair since the affair of the diamond robbery and the attempted sale of the spoil.

Ned had suspected Peace of having changed the stones between the night of the burglary and the visit to Anatole's hotel to dispose of them.

Peace could not resist the impression that by some sleight-of-hand the real stones had been replaced by false ones on that very evening with Ned's connivance.

Rapidly Ned related to his accomplice the particulars of his visit to Mr. Mallan in the character of a superintendent.

He had profited to do so by the information he had extracted from the doctor the day before, that Mr. Mallan was well enough to receive visitors, and had easily copied the bearing and manner of one of those police officials with whom he had such an extensive series of dealings.

He remarked, in conclusion, after describing Mr. Mallan's startling revelations as regarded the diamonds and their place of concealment—

"For a moment I was knocked all in a heap."

"I should think so," replied Peace, who himself was fairly staggered by Ned's revelation, the sincerity of which he felt sure of by the aid of a certain test only known to himself and unconsciously confirmed by the bushranger's story.

"But I pulled through. And when he said it would need to half pull the house down before anyone could find out where the diamonds really were, I thought to myself that there was a much easier way, which I was going to put in practice before the old fox was five minutes older."

"What was it?" asked Peace, curiously.

"Well, I don't mind telling you, though you are such a queer pal at times. He talked about pulling the infernal house down. That was all bosh. If we had not been led away by that Sal's yarn about the safe, where should we have looked for them first—eh? Answer me that, now, old tub-thumper."

Peace mused for a moment.

"In his room, of course," he said, with a sickly smile.

"Of course, artful old file. It wasn't a bad plant against having his shiners faked. I knew they were in his room, and in two minutes I could have bound and gagged the pair I could have done it in a minute. And after this I should have popped the old man's feet to the fire and grilled them there till he owned up where the stones were lodged. What a jolly lark it would have been! Ha, ha, ha!" laughed the ruffian.

"He is a tough old boy, even as the nether millstone. He might, under providence, have still held out."

"Don't you believe it. I'd another little dodge to open his mouth. I'd a-popped his old woman on the fire, and

I think that would have awoke the pair up pretty bright!"

And Ned chuckled at the thought.

"Truly, the only way to defeat the wiles of the artful man is to assail him with his own weapons," snuffled Peace, turning up his eyes.

"Perhaps after all, though, it was lucky," resumed Ned, "that the doctor and the police rang when they did, and not ten minutes later, or the blessed howling of the lot would have spoilt my little game, and got me into quod. They'd be sure to give tongue like a yelping pack."

"But how about the nurse?" inquired Peace, who, if pious, was eminently practical.

"Oh, I had thought of her, and meant to tie her up downstairs as soon as I had collared the other two, and before grilling them."

"What a valuable assistant in the vineyard," snuffled Peace, clasping his hands in veritable admiration.

"I'll tell you what it is, old patter-noster. I thought you'd grabbed all the grapes from that vineyard, and left none of the bunches for me; but now I see I was on the wrong track, and that you acted on the square."

"Oh, no, friend. 'Straight is the path and narrow is the way.' We should always pursue one path, my friend," ejaculated the pious one, exposing the whites of his eyes.

"You're better nor a dozen parsons, you are."

"I'll try and merit your favourable opinion," responded Peace, with a solemn twinkle in his eyes.

He did not, however, on his part tell Kelly that he also had visited Mr. Mallan that morning, disguised as a private detective, determined, if he could only get an inkling of the whereabouts of the diamonds, either to betray their possessors to justice, for the sake of the twenty per cent. reward, or to make a safe bargain for their restoration.

He did not mention how Mr. Mallan's conduct towards him, and the remark, "stones representing a value of thirty thousand pounds," confirmed Ned's statement.

And, above all, he took care never to return to the offices he had taken in Smith-street, where a real detective waited for several days in the hope of an explanatory interview with him, but waited in vain.

CHAPTER CLXVIII.
BACK HIM, YOU FOOL.

COUNT ANATOLE, as he delighted to style himself, had more than one string to his bow, and, pending the robbery of the mail on which he had set his heart, was gathering together as much spare cash as he could in various ways.

Chiefly, however, by cards.

Gambling, though not carried on in London to the which it reaches on the Continent, is pretty well prac nevertheless.

This has been especially the case ithin the last years.

Many men who used to risk their money on horses now prefer to stake it on a card, and not often on "the correct card."

The reason is, that, at cards, a man who chooses good company to play with is safe from being cheated, which, on the Turf, has become impossible, since horse-racing has ceased to be a sport and has become a matter of serious business to one and all engaged in it, and is in nineteen out of twenty cases, sheer swindling.

So openly is this swindling carried on that it almost ceases to be regarded as the device of blackleggism. An owner's horse is entered, he lays all the money he can against him, and then, at the last moment, scratches him. He never intended but to rob the public, and attempts to palliate his dishonesty by the poor excuse—"I don't run horses for the amusement of other people." A man might as well say, when cheating at cards, I don't play cards to amuse other people. With the exception of Lord Portland, Fred Johnstone, and one or two others, all runners of horses are blacklegs—pure and simple.

There are a number of clubs now existing in London

which, like the Parisian *cercles*, are wholly and solely devoted to gaming. and at which the committee sets no limit to the stakes.

Their degree of respectability varies.

The right of admission to some is exceedingly difficult to obtain, and the character, habit and social position of a candidate are scrutinised far more closely than if he were an aspirant for holy orders.

At these play is conducted in a style of solemn decorum that befits the gravity of the stakes, and the eminent respectability of the players.

Yet so far as the amounts wagered are concerned, there is but little change since the days when a Leader of the Opposition could lose fifty thousand pounds at a sitting, and go on playing forty-eight hours at a stretch till it became necessary for a waiter to stand by the party and tell each man when it was his turn to deal.

Other clubs are less strict, and willingly throw open their portals to any stranger who arrives with the reputation of a *beau joueur*.

It was by such that Lambri Pasha was so welcomed on his arrival there.

At one he succeeded in making a tremendous haul.

Of course fair play, it is presumed. prevails, and it is to be questioned whether the toleration accorded some years back to Lord de Roos would at present be met with. As the morality of the present is not an improvement on that of the past, it is not to be supposed that there is less cheating at cards than formerly. It is carried to an art in Paris, and has its professors, its Robert Hudins, here also.

The nobleman in question, a peer of the realm, was a notorious gambler

Only after a time people used to notice that he had the knack of dealing himself a fist-full of trumps at *écarté*, and of turning up a king at critical junctures of the game with unvarying good fortune.

Consequently some people began to get rather shy of playing with him.

Till one day a somewhat verdant youth, whose suspicions had been aroused, went to a mutual friend of maturer experience, and in the strictest confidence imparted his belief that Lord de Roos cheated.

"Very possibly," was the calm reply.

"I have watched him ; I am quite certain of it."

"I daresay you are right."

"But what am I to do?" gasped the bewildered greenhorn.

"Do?" repeated his mentor. "Why, do as I do, BACK HIM, you fool!"

And probably the greenhorn did so till another greenhorn of less prudent and more impulsive temperament detected his lordship at his usual tricks.

Whereupon he snatched a fork—they used steel forks in those days—from the adjoining buffet and pinned his lordship's hand to the table with the remark—

"If you have *not* got the king under your hand, my lord, I beg your pardon."

Only, when the fork was withdrawn, the king was found under his lordship's perforated palm, and this time the scandal was so great that the peccant peer was forced to retire for the remainder of his days to the Continent.

Besides the clubs, a great deal of private gambling goes on at different places.

The suburban villa at which some fascinating siren intoxicates youthful dupes with alternate doses of love and champagne in order that her accomplices may plunder them, is pretty well played out.

Men play for play's sake without any need of such allurements, and it is in bachelor chambers that the worship of the blind goddess is chiefly carried on.

Anatole was aware of this.

He had managed to gain admission to some of the minor clubs and had done pretty well. though taking the utmost care to play fair.

Still, the thought struck him that if he could have good

rooms of his own at which he could get a few men quietly together, he might do better.

Chance, he argued, might throw into his way one of those occasions with which she sometimes loves to tantalise her votaries.

She might dangle a golden prize before him, in which case, provided the prize was big enough to justify the risk, he meant to throw chance overboard, and trust to his ability to hoodwink his adversary.

Having taken a suite of rooms near Piccadilly, and furnished them with a combination of English comforts and French taste that made a pretty large hole in his recent winnings, he installed himself in them.

A few days later he sent a note to Kelly, requesting him to call and to be as well dressed as possible.

Kelly lost no time in complying.

His make-up was exactly the one that Anatole desired—namely, that of a wealthy, ostentatious, and perhaps somewhat vulgar, colonial, who had made his pile and come over to the Old Country to spend it, but who, if ignorant of certain points of social conduct, was by no means a fool to be tricked by the first comer.

His rough but determined way was equally removed from the polished blandness of the hawk, and the simplicity of the pigeon.

"By —— ! governor. but you've got a tidy crib here," he said, throwing his huge bulk into a magnificently upholstered chair, and glancing round approvingly at the fittings of the appartment.

"Yes, pretty well," said Anatole. "But, look here, I want to see you on business. I know you play a good game of cards."

"I think I do," answered Kelly, with truth.

"Very well. I want you to dine with me this evening, and then take a hand here."

"What at?"

"Oh, whatever they play—that is the others who may look in. It may be whist, or baccarat, or *écarté*, or Nap; I don't know."

"All right."

"Only look here, you must play perfectly fair. You understand me?"

"Yes," replied Ned. "But I don't see what you are driving at. Can't you open out a little more?"

"Well then—have you money?"

"Plenty for the time being. I have lived very quietly since I have been over here."

"Well, I want to introduce you to some rich men and good players, as a rich man and good player. Play well, back your luck when it is in, and don't make a fool of yourself when it is out ; and, above all, behave yourself."

Kelly complied, and that evening was introduced by Anatole to several rich men as Mr. Dawes, a rich squatter from Australia.

As he was a good player, a good-tempered loser when he had any object in view that caused him to keep a curb over his naturally infernal temper, and a jovial, if very unpolished companion, he was not unpopular.

For some time this game went on, Kelly neither winning nor losing much, but without his being any further enlightened as to Anatole's dodge.

One morning he called in, according to arrangement.

A small card-table, flanked by two large and comfortable armchairs, stood at one end of the room.

"Come," said Anatole, "take a hand with me for half-an-hour or so."

"What are you up to?" enquired Kelly, somewhat puzzled.

"Lock the door," remarked the Frenchman.

This done, the two seated themselves at the table.

"Comfortable sort of chair this," said Ned, as he stretched out his legs and leant back.

They settled to play *écarté*.

The stakes were not very large, but sufficient to give an interest to the game.

After they had been playing three or four games Kelly

began to suspect there was something wrong, but he could not tell what.

Three or four more convinced him that Anatole was cheating him in some way, but in what he could not determine.

He knew himself every dodge with the cards, and yet, watching his adversary's fingers with the utmost attention, he failed to detect any of the tricks.

Anatole neither turned up nor marked the king with unusual frequency, nor did he deal himself extra good cards.

Indeed, on the contrary, Ned had nothing to complain of on that score.

Luck, in fact, seemed to favour him in this respect, but still the Frenchman got the best of him.

He seemed to divine, as it were instinctively, whether to give or to refuse him cards.

If he had a bad hand and asked for cards, Anatole was certain to refuse.

If he had a tolerable one, and the Frenchman was equally unwilling to grant his petition, it always turned out that it was because he had a better.

Besides, Anatole seemed to know exactly what he was going to play.

Suddenly a thought struck Ned, and he held the cards up to the light, and then carefully scrutinised their backs to see if they were marked in any way.

When he looked up after this, Anatole was smiling.

"You suspect something?" said the Frenchman blandly.

"Yes, I'm d——d if I don't," answered Kelly, surlily.

"Play three games more, and if you can't spot it I'll show you this trick."

They resumed the game.

Kelly watched him, as a swimming nigger would a shark.

Once he fancied Anatole glanced over his shoulder at some object or other.

He sprang to his feet and looked round.

There was no one else in the room.

Neither was there a mirror on the wall behind him.

The three games ended, he confessed he was beat.

Anatole must have seen his cards.

"Look at the panel in the wall behind you," said Anatole.

Kelly turned round and fixed his eyes as directed. To his surprise—for he could not make out "what was up"—he saw the panel slide upwards and disclose a highly-polished piece of glass or mirror, which was so placed as to reflect the cards in the hand of any player who was not very careful to hold his hand on a level with the table.

The back of the chair was purposely made very low so as not to intercept the reflection, and a gas-light was placed on each side of the panel.

"Well, I'am blowed!" said Kelly, using an adjective of more florid character than it is prudent to reproduce. "You have cut your eye-teeth, you have, and no mistake."

The little piece of mechanism which produced this result was a communication between the floor where Anatole sat and the panel. The Frenchman pressed a button in the floor and the panel slid from its position, he removed the pressure and the panel slid back again.

It was by this means that Anatole had managed to get a sight of Ned's cards, and it was to frustrate such manœuvres that playing-card makers have taken to marking the value of each card in minute characters at the extreme corner, so that a player no longer need risk exposure by spreading his hand out at all.

The mechanism was simple, and removable at pleasure.

CHAPTER CLXIX.
A CLOSE SHAVE.

"WHERE did you get that dodge from?" inquired Ned.

"It's the latest Parisian novelty," answered Anatole, "and I had it direct from a friend there. What do you think of it?"

"It's clever, but risky if a man has his wits about him."

"Yet you, with all your suspicions, could not see how the trick was done. Besides, you are fresh and fasting, but a man after supper would be less wary, and I only reserve it for such occasions."

"You are up to a thing or two with the pasteboard."

"Yes; but, although I'm pretty sharp, I don't like trying such things except as a last resource. I had a very narrow shave in Paris the other day, which rather took the conceit out of me."

Anatole alluded to an adventure which had befallen him at a well-known gambling-house in the Rue de Helder.

He had been carrying on for some time a pretty successful campaign, under the name of the Marquis d'Albano, representing himself as an Italian nobleman who had emigrated to America, and returned with a fortune.

He played high, and, when his money ran short, was in the habit of staking unset precious stones, chiefly sapphires, a number of which he always carried about him, and which he said he had acquired during his travels.

Like all true gamblers he claimed to be extremely superstitious, and declared that these stones were so many fetishes for him, and that directly he staked them his luck would always turn.

This belief in a fetish is very common.

A bit of the rope with which a man has been hanged is considered on the Continent an infallible talisman in such cases.

A hunchback, too, is supposed to bring luck, and, if he wins, those about him will touch his hump in order to share it.

Whether the stones staked by Anatole were fetishes or not, it was observable that luck turned on his side directly he staked them.

The truth was, that they were simply very good imitations, and whenever he was forced by his losses to bring them out he at once began to cheat, since, if they had once parted into other hands, their worthlessness would have been discovered.

He had an accomplice in the shape of a little old fellow of foxy aspect and insinuating manners, who was known by the nickname of "The Counsellor."

The so-called Marquis d'Albano used to have recourse to the usual tricks of the professional card-sharper, packed cards and the like.

But his accomplice had a rather original dodge, which went far to help him.

He always had in his hands an immense silver snuffbox, which he polished till it shone like a mirror.

His habit was to stand behind the individual who was playing against the marquis, and, by the way, frequently changed, of tapping the box and taking snuff, telegraphed the cards of the marquis's opponent.

It happened one night that M. Claude, the celebrated chief of police under the Second Empire, was at the gambling-house of the Rue de Helder in disguise.

He had gone thither in search of information concerning a political plot, on the track of which he then was, and some of the men mixed up in which were in the habit of meeting there to play.

Fully versed in all the card-sharping tricks, he became convinced that the Marquis d'Albano, alias Anatole, was a cheat, and watched his play a little time.

The adversary of the so-called Marquis was a young fellow of two or three and twenty.

At first he was favoured by that luck which so often favours beginners, to their ultimate destruction.

He completely cleared the marquis of his ready-money, amounting to some forty thousand francs.

D'Albano pulled out his sapphires and emeralds and asked for his revenge.

The other consented.

From this moment luck turned to the side of the sharper.

In twenty minutes he had won back his forty thousand francs.

The other wanted to go on for higher stakes.

The marquis was perfectly willing, and continued to win.

A group soon gathered round the table at which the two were playing, attracted by the importance of the stakes.

M. Claude, who was standing in the front rank behind Anatole, watching every movement, not only detected his trickery, but also the manœuvre of the Counsellor with the snuffbox.

He had only to declare himself and arrest Anatole and his accomplice, as cheating at cards is an offence in France, but this was precisely what he did not want to do, for, by revealing that he was a police-officer, he would have lost all chance of observing the political conspirators.

So, when he noticed Anatole take a card from his sleeve and substitute it for one in his hand, in order to announce the king, he simply ejaculated sharply in a feigned voice—

"Sir, you are a cheat!"

This sudden exclamation breaking on the profound silence which had been observed during so important a match, acted like a bombshell.

None knew exactly to whom it was addressed.

The young man started up indignantly.

The marquis, quite taken aback and also at a loss as to where the accuser's voice had come from, lost his head.

He also jumped up hastily, leaving two kings of hearts on the table.

Evidently one of the two players was a sharper.

A cry of indignation broke from the lookers-on.

Claude thought that Anatole would be exposed, but he reckoned without the cleverness of the Counsellor and also of the mistress of the house, who was also their accomplice.

They profited by the confusion that prevailed.

The young man had darted forward and, accusing Anatole of being a cheat, aroused the greatest excitement.

The hostess and the Counsellor threw themselves between the two as if to prevent any violence, and the latter managed to withdraw the prepared cards from Anatole's sleeve, and to slily slip them into the pocket of the young fellow he had been victimising.

Anatole, thus relieved, loudly asked that they should be both searched on the spot.

The young man was equally anxious for this.

Nothing suspicious was found on the marquis; but, to the horror of the poor dupe, the false cards were drawn from his pockets.

He was at once kicked out of the place as a sharper.

Claude, who had not seen the manœuvre of the Counsellor to save his accomplice, only guessed it from this result; but, as stated, could not interfere.

However, he kept an eye on Anatole; and a few days later the latter received one of those quiet intimations, to the effect that a change of air would prove beneficial to his health, of which the Parisian police are wont to avail themselves when they want to get rid of anyone without scandal.

A few nights later Ned found himself at Anatole's rooms, in company with about a dozen others.

Everybody had come well furnished with money, and there was an evident intention on all hands of making a hot night of it.

Amongst the players was a stout, apoplectic-looking Belgian, who had figured at one or two of their parties of late, with varying success.

CHAPTER CLXX.
A DISINTERESTED FRIEND.

His name was Kint, and he was said to be a wealthy iron-founder.

Anatole had recently made his acquaintance, and he was known to a slight extent by most of those present.

Play began, and soon grew fast and furious.

Kint's luck was phenomenal, though there seemed no doubt but that he was playing fairly.

The company were all keen hands, and even Anatole would not have ventured on any tricks amongst them.

Baccarat was the game, and two or three men took the bank in succession; but Kint continued to make it money.

His eyes twinkled, and from time to time his face flushed, but beyond this he remained as cool and stolid as a Flemish ox; his hands, by which a man's nerves so often betray themselves, being firm as rocks.

His stakes grew higher and higher.

Some slight turns of fortune only seemed to spur him on to fresh exertions, and from a hundred he got to putting five hundred on a card.

At last he had won about four thousand pounds.

But even this did not content him.

It might have been better for him at that moment to have called a cab and departed with his winnings; but instead of this, he offered to take the bank.

Ned could not help glancing covetously at the heap of gold and notes the new banker had put in front of him, but his look was dull compared with that of Anatole.

The little Frenchman's eyes glittered like a cat's, his nostrils quivered, and his very moustache bristled with suppressed excitement.

Everyone now expected that Kint's luck would turn, and resolved to do their best to break him.

He proceeded to deal out the cards with the same ox-like placidity that had already characterised him all through the evening.

Contrary to expectation, his phenomenal good fortune continued.

If there was any foul play, no one could detect it.

At last, one by one, the other players gave up thoroughly cleared out, and the Belgian remained a winner of about eight thousand pounds.

At length, his success caused him to lose his head a little, and he swept up his gains in evident triumph, and stowed them away about him.

No one cared to go on at baccarat.

Anatole, who had been watching Kint with an expression in his eyes that was not nice to see, suggested an adjournment for supper, the materials for which were ready laid on a side table.

The proposition was gladly received, and the gambling party began to change into something like an orgie.

Anatole had a good cellar, and pressed its contents on his friends without stint.

The wine flowed freely, the losers drinking to console themselves for their losses, and not with impunity.

Ned took his share with the rest, but remained cool enough to keep an eye on Anatole.

The Frenchman's solicitude for the winner of the evening was admirable.

He placed him on his right hand, and took especial care that his plate was seldom empty, and his glass never.

He did his utmost to enliven the scene with jest and repartee, and succeeded in prolonging the repast considerably.

The result was that Kint became rapidly inebriated, in a quiet fashion, and most of the remaining guests did not remain much behind him in this.

His eyes shone more than ever, he grew more and more apoplectic-looking as the wine mounted to his head and his speech thickened considerably.

At last, when he deliberately put the lighted end of his cigar to his mouth, and tried to pour out wine from a bottle with the cork in, Anatole thought the time had come to strike a decisive blow, and poured him out a tumbler of brandy—a thing that only Ned noticed.

"What winesh ees dish?" spluttered the Belgian.

"Old Madeira," answered Anatole, calmly.

"Aha, ol reet," answered Kint, draining off a large gulp of the spirit.

He had a wonderful head, however, and even this failed for the moment to knock him over.

He would not have been able to perform on the tightrope, but he managed to gain his feet, and cross the room to the window, which he opened.

This was the worst thing he could have done.

The cold air at once overpowered him, and he toppled over senseless into the arms of Anatole, who had followed him, on charitable thoughts intent.

The rest of the guests by this time had all had quite enough of both supper and play, and rather too much wine, and began to take leave of their host.

Kint, however, was so helpless, that Anatole declared that it would be quite impossible for him to leave, and said that he would give up his bed to him, and sleep on the sofa.

When, however, the other guests had departed, the Frenchman found that this had already an occupant in the person of Ned Kelly.

Ned was very drunk.

The liquor he had taken seemed to have acted upon him precisely as that swallowed by Kint.

It had bowled him over all at once.

A few minutes before he had been one of the loudest and jolliest at the supper-table, and now he had collapsed, and lay as helpless as a log.

Anatole shook him roughly by the arm, and tried to rouse him, but in vain.

The Frenchman seemed annoyed at this.

But, after uttering two or three wicked words, he appeared to make up his mind to make the best of a bad job, and left Ned to his slumbers.

He passed into the inner room, where Kint had been placed on the bed, taking the light with him, and pulling to the folding doors behind him.

No sooner had he disappeared, than Ned opened his eyes.

Then he rose to his feet.

Huge as was his bulk, he could, at a pinch, step as softly as a cat, and, taking every precaution not to betray himself, he stole quietly across the room.

On reaching the folding doors, he applied his eye to the crack between them.

Kint was lying on his back on the bed, breathing stertorously.

Anatole was engaged in an operation, the bearing of which Ned entirely failed to comprehend.

His idea was that the Frenchman would probably abstract the Belgian's winnings, and bolt with them, and it was with this view that he had himself feigned drunkenness, in order to step in and claim snacks.

This belief was, at first, confirmed by seeing Anatole thrust his hand into the slumberer's pocket.

But, instead of pulling out his money, he contented himself with abstracting his handkerchief.

"Only faking," muttered Ned; "but what the deuce does he want with the cove's fogle?"

Anatole proceeded to pour some water into a basin.

In this he soaked the handkerchief.

"Blessed if I understand this," thought Ned.

He fancied he had the key of the puzzle the next moment.

When the handkerchief was thoroughly wet, the Frenchman took it up and laid it across Kint's face, carefully arranging the pleats about the nose and mouth.

A light broke on Ned.

Anatole was actually taking care of his friend. Blest if he could understand it.

And Ned quietly returned to the sofa, debating whether he should feign recovery from drunkenness, or play 'possum an hour or two longer, and then profit by the slumbers of Kint and Anatole to plunder the former and depart. £8,000 was a tempting prize.

He decided on the latter course.

He lay still a couple of hours.

Twice in the interval Anatole came out and looked at him with a light, remaining each time in intent contemplation for a few minutes, and seeming to be debating inwardly on some project.

As he turned to retire for the second time Ned risked opening an eye, and noticed that he carried a wet handkerchief in his hand.

"Ah," he thought, "he wants to see if I'm as bad as the other chap, but he judges that I don't need doctoring."

At the expiration of two hours Ned rose again and returned to his post of observation, still on robbing thoughts intent.

Anatole was not asleep, but was quietly seated in a chair, smoking a cigarette.

Kint lay in precisely the same attitude, with the handkerchief still over his face.

The sound of his breathing, however, had died away.

He lay still and silent as a corpse.

As a corpse!

A thought suddenly flashed across Ned's mind.

If he were one!

And then memory, shaken by the wine he had consumed, returned to him.

"The trick's done. Kint is a stiff 'un," he thought.

He remembered hearing of the manoeuvre which he had seen practised on the helpless Belgian.

The saturated handkerchief intercepted air, and suffocated as effectually as a feather-bed, and had, besides, an advantage over chloroform and ether, inasmuch as it left no smell to set doctors puzzling over. The features bore the expression of suffocation, but also of apoplexy.

"If Kint had been sober he might have thrown it off," thought Ned; "but he was drunk, and will never wake again."

And, as he recollected how Anatole had approached him a few minutes before with a handkerchief, he was glad that his own intoxication was feigned, as it was evidently a toss-up whether the Frenchman "cooked his goose," as he did that of the Belgian.

Ned reflected.

"His sparing me looks as if he meant to stop and brave it out; for if he had meant to bolt, one more corpse would not have mattered. But I'll settle the question."

Ned now always went armed.

Drawing his revolver, he pushed open the door of the room and stepped in.

Anatole looked up in amazement.

Levelling his pistol full at the Frenchman's head, and pointing with the forefinger of the other hand to the corpse, Ned uttered the single word—

"Snacks?"

The Frenchman saw that his trick was discovered.

Whatever his intention might have been as regarded Ned, originally, he at once put on his blandest manner.

"All right, my dear friend," he answered, calmly. "I mean to divide with you, since you have stayed to take half the risk."

The intention with which the last words were uttered rather cooled Ned's ardour.

He saw that, as far as he was concerned, his presence in any investigation that might arise would be awkward.

The prospect of being summoned as a witness before a coroner's jury was not a pleasant one.

Accordingly he fell in with Anatole's suggestion.

The Frenchman proposed that out of the eight thousand pounds in Kint's possession they should take only seven.

Ned agreed, and, having secured his share, left the house, without anyone noticing his departure.

The next morning Anatole aroused the household, stating that he had found his guest dead in his bed.

A doctor was summoned, and, on hearing the story of the supper and excitement of the night before, and looking at the corpse, did not hesitate to give a certificate of death from apoplexy, thereby doing away with all need for an inquest.

The thousand pounds found on the corpse did away with all idea of robbery, no one, except those playing with him the night before, having any idea that he had a larger sum.

This money was transmitted to Kint's heirs, who were distant cousins, and who, after sending instructions to London concerning his funeral, did not trouble themselves any more about him.

CHAPTER CLXXI.

A NEW FRIEND AND A FRESH PLAN.

WITH the money he had thus acquired Kelly, like all his class, who are utterly destitute of other resources for consuming time, simply indulged in the coarse dissipation that suited his temperament.

The fact that such men have no settled plan for the future, and that the excitement of crime is as necessary to them as drink to the drunkard, leads to their rapid capture.

Like the gambler who makes a good "coup," they cannot be content to even retire from "active service" until it is consumed. They weary from inactivity—they go in for another "coup," and so on, until the end comes.

In company more lively than select, he came across a certain Captain Montmorency Howard, a good-looking and well-got-up man, of about six or eight and thirty, who was the idol of a certain circle.

The captain was one of those men with no apparent means of livelihood, who contrive, nevertheless, to ruffle it with the best of the swells about town.

He picked up a certain amount at billiards and cards, and was said to be uncommonly lucky in backing winners at race-meetings.

After their first meeting, he attached himself wonderfully to Ned, who continued to keep up the character of the wealthy returned Australian.

Howard looked upon him as a vulgar beast—but then, the calf was a golden one.

Kelly grinned to himself, for he guessed that the fascinating captain was a swell sharper, and meant to get a good haul out of the man whom he took for an unsophisticated Colonial.

"You think, my fine fellow," thought Ned, "that you are going to get some pretty picking off me, but you'll find you'll break your grinders against my bones."

At length Ned received the invitation he had long been expecting, to come round to the captain's rooms and have a quiet weed.

He was quite prepared to hear his host suggest cards, and in this he was not disappointed.

He had scarcely lighted the aforesaid weed, when Howard suggested "the Devil's books," as our pious ancestors called them, "just to pass half-an-hour or so."

At first the play was fair, but when Ned began to play recklessly and double his stakes, he had no difficulty in guessing that his adversary was cheating.

It was admirably done, however, and, but for his thorough acquaintance with the trick, he would never have detected it.

He watched his opportunity, however, and suddenly sprang on the captain like a cat on a bird and caught him in the act.

The captain began to bluster.

Ned, however, held him in a grip like a vice, and quietly demonstrated the dodge of which the other had sought to make him the victim.

Somewhat to his amazement, the captain seemed relieved by this demonstration.

"If you know the dodge so well," he observed, "it must be because you have practised it yourself, and, therefore, I ought to have nothing to fear from you."

Ned thought there was some reason in that way of putting it.

It happened that a few days—or, rather, nights—before the pair had got into rather a disreputable row, in which Kelly's coolness, pluck, and strength had brought them clear, in spite of formidable odds.

The captain remembering this, and seeing that Ned was fly to his game, thought he might prove a valuable recruit, or rather companion-in-arms.

"Why, a smart fellow like you ought to make your fortune here in no time, if you haven't made it already. I suspect you're not what you seem."

"Go ahead," laughed Kelly; "spit it out. What the devil do you take me for—a greenhorn or a yokel, that you could pluck as easy as a dead goose?"

"No. I take you for as sharp a blade as ever I nearly cut my fingers with. Do you want money? I mean a blazing lump o' the coin, that will set us both up for the rest of our lives."

"Do I want coin! Ha! ha!" chuckled Kelly. "Do I want plenty of victuals and wine, and what will keep the life in my body, and tin in my pocket? What next will you ask, I wonder? I want this, and I'll tell you what more I want. I want something to do. I feel shrinking and drying up in this do-nothing life and beastly old country—I do. I shall have to break somebody's neck or rob the Bank of England, if I don't have something else to work at; but I can't go on with the card-sharping lay. That ain't my game. 'Taint big enough for me."

"Well, my lad, you're the fellow for my little game. You've got nerve, and pluck, and strength. All these are useful in our profession. I can show you how to use them all, and with profit, too."

"Is it a big thing?" said Kelly.

"A thumper, my boy! Make your mouth water. Worthy of your talents and of mine. Set us up for life. Think of that, my boy. But before we go any further, I'd like to be enlightened upon one little point."

"What's that?" said Kelly.

"Who the deuce are you, and what are you?"

"Never you mind who or what I am. I'm up to you, anyways, and if you mean business, out with it, and don't bother about me. What the —— is it to you who I am, if I'm fit for work? You're blooming curious—you are."

"Don't be offended, my friend. I think you're the right sort. You ain't too squeamish, I hope, when one's in a mess as to the way to get out of it?"

"If it's any satisfaction to you to know it, I may just as well tell you I'd cut your blessed wizzen or choke it, if there was no other way of clearing out of a mess."

"Much obliged to your candour! Charming frankness, I must admit, my friend; and as I know your ultimatum, I shall be as particular as ever in keeping the little life-protector, I always affectionately wear near my heart, in the best possible condition for the contingency you so graphically anticipate."

And the speaker laughingly produced a highly-finished six-shooter from the breast-pocket of his paletot.

"That popgun wouldn't serve you much, my lad, for I could chuck you and it out of any window in England, and would do it, too, if I had the least suspicion of foul play."

"I don't much fancy the dramatic tone of our friendly conversation, Mr. Dawes, and it would be quite as well under the circumstances of this amicable meeting if we refrained from discussing the effective methods by which we could indulge in mutual murder. I'll take the will for the deed, if you will be so good as to fall in with my views upon this head, and talk of something more profitable than making cold meat pies of one another."

"Oh, I'm agreeable, my tulip," laughed the other ruffian. "Now, then, uncover your plant, and let's see if it's worth anything."

"Well, the plant I have in view is risky—devilish risky but would bring a pile."

"If it's as good as that, put my name down, old man."

"I've been thinking of it a long time, but it needed a pal with lots of pluck."

"To keep you up to the sticking point?" broke in Ned, with a coarse laugh.

"Perhaps you've hit it," answered the other coolly.

"Very well. I'm game for anything from blowing up Windsor to burning down Westminster Abbey," said Ned recklessly, and with a string of oaths.

His manner impressed the other, who began—

"Do you know anything of bank-notes?"

"I know a good one when I see it."

"You're a wit, too, I see," said the captain, with a slight sneer

He rose, and went to a secretary, which he unlocked. From it he took out a travelling desk, and unlocked this also

Then, from a little secret recess in the desk opened by a spring, he took out a folded piece of paper, and handed it to Ned.

"What do you think of that?" he asked.

Ned unfolded it. It was a Bank of England note.

He held it up to the light and examined it carefully, scanning every line on it, and then rustling it between his fingers.

"It's a genuine flimsy, in my mind," was his comment.

"You think it would do?"

"Rather. It looks the real thing."

"Do you know what the difficulty has always been in imitating Bank of England notes?" enquired the captain.

Ned had made the acquaintance on the other side of the herring-pond of several gentleman who had got "into trouble" from attempting to infringe upon that monopoly of production claimed by the Old Lady in Threadneedle-street as regards the articles in question.

"The water-mark," he answered, without hesitation.

"Look at that again."

Ned did so.

"Well," he exclaimed, after a lengthy examination, "any living soul would swear that that is a real quid."

"Right you are. So it is," answered the other.

Ned looked at him with anger, and impatiently cried—

"Do you take me for a child or a fool, or what the deuce do you mean by this humbug?"

"You don't quite understand," answered the captain.

"Understand! All I understand is that you've been making a cursed lot of fun just to see whether I could tell a real from a flash note when I set eyes on it."

"Not at all. You said it was genuine Bank paper."

"Yes."

"And so it is. But it was a friend of mine printed it, and another who engraved the plate."

"Don't let's have any more blessed riddles," said Ned.

"We won't, then. Do you remember some years back that there was a robbery of paper at the mill at which the Bank paper is made?"

"I've heard something about it."

"The men who robbed the mill were caught, and some of the paper recovered. Some, however, passed into the hands of friends of mine, and they had a plate engraved and began to print. For a time all went swimmingly. The Bank had to pay the notes, for they were so well imitated that it dared not refuse them, for fear of discrediting its paper, as they reached it through honest holders. At last the scent got strong, and in the fright that seized on the parties, they destroyed the plates and most of the paper, being pretty well satisfied with the pots they had made."

"I guess one of the first that funked it was you, my friend," thought Ned; and added aloud, "Well, what's the game, then?"

"Why," answered the captain, in a low tone, "all the paper was not destroyed. I can lay my hands on a lot, and if we could only get a sure hand to touch up one of the plates I have also saved, we could start afresh."

"There's something in that," answered Ned.

And, after a little more conversation, he agreed to go into the scheme.

It happened that a night or two later, as he was pushing through the crowd on his way to the Criterion, Ned felt a hand softly insinuated into his coat-pocket.

Without apparently noticing it, he suddenly passed his own hand in that direction and seized the wrist of the intruding member.

He gripped it with all his force.

A stifled cry of pain sounded in his ear, and a voice exclaimed, in mournful tones—

"Oh, sir—please, sir, for mercy's sake, leave go of it."

He glanced round, and found that he was holding the wrist of a tall, pale, shabby-genteel looking young man of about five or six and twenty.

The pressure of the crowd was so great, that no one about them noticed their relative positions.

Still retaining his grip, Ned led his captive aside into a by-street.

"Now, then, what's your little game?" he demanded abruptly.

"Oh!" moaned the other, "for mercy's sake let me off, sir. I was starving, I assure you. I was driven to it by misfortune. I never tried such a thing before."

"So I should think, by your blessed clumsiness," was Kelly's grim remark.

"Indeed, I never did. I'm an honest, hardworking chap."

Kelly lifted the hand he had retained his hold of, and looked at it.

It was white and soft.

"That's not the hand of a hardworking man," he said.

"Indeed, it is, sir. I'm an engraver."

"An engraver?"

"Yes, sir."

"Where were you working last, and why did you leave your place?"

The fellow hung his head.

"I see how it is," said Kelly. "I can hand you over to the police for trying to pick my pocket, and as you are pretty well known to them it will go hard with you."

An "engraver" sounded most opportunely in Kelly's ears. He saw in the pickpocket the instrument he wanted.

A few minutes later he and his new protégé were seated at a table in one of the numerous cafés of the neighbourhood.

The only occupant of the next table was a quiet-looking little man, reading an evening newspaper.

"Now, listen to me," said Ned; "it's no good trying to pitch me any soft-sawdering yarn. I know your breed whenever I set my eyes on them What have you been up for?"

"What do you mean, sir?" was the answer.

"Stow that, my bird, and tell me how often you've been in quod, and what for; or I'll hand you over at once."

The style in which this question was put, reassured the other who had been, on his side, observing Ned.

"I had eighteen stretch," he replied.

"What for?"

The fact of Ned's understanding that eighteen stretch meant eighteen months, seemed to encourage his companion.

"They called it robbery with violence; but that was quite a mistake."

"Indeed?"

"The fact was that I was looking into a shop-window when, all at once—I don't know how it happened—but my sleeve-link caught in an old fellow's watch-chain."

"Accidentally, of course," said Kelly, laughing encouragingly.

"Of course. But before I could offer any explanation he began to cry out 'Thieves! police!'"

"That was very unkind, wasn't it?"

"Yes, especially in the street, before a number of people. So I thought the best thing I could do would be to clap my hand over his mouth to keep him from making any more noise till I had explained his mistake."

"I suppose your hand was closed?"

"Well, as well as I remember, it was." And the scamp smiled. "Appearances might have been against me, and, unfortunately, they were. I was laid hold of, and the old idiot swore that I had hold of his watch-chain in my hand, when I was only trying to unfasten it from my sleeve-link. But not only did he swear this, but also, that instead of just putting my hand to his mouth, I had given him a crack with my fist that sent two of his teeth down his throat. They must have been false ones, for I hardly touched him ; but the beak believed it. and ran me in."

Ned laughed, saying—

"You'll do, my chicken. Is it true that you are an engraver?"

"Yes. I served my time at one of the best firms of copperplate-printers in London."

"Why did you leave them?"

"All through a bit of professional vanity. I used to have some very hard work set me, and, instead of extra pay, all I got was the praise that I could imitate anything put before me. I thought that it really must be so, but resolved to test the matter fairly by the unbiassed judgment of others. But it turned out that it was difficult to meet with an unbiassed judgment. The thing I tried to copy was my master's signature, and his bankers were so biassed as to examine it a great deal more closely than there was any need to. In consideration of my youth and innocence, I suppose, the governor didn't prosecute, but I got the sack."

"And what is your name?"

"Samuel Higginthorpe."

"I suppose your present lay is not up to much?"

"Not very."

"Well, if you like, I can put you up to something handy."

"Blest if I didn't think it," chuckled the engraver, as he looked at Kelly. "Why, jiggered if you ain't one of us. Ain't I in luck, and no mistake!" and he laughed again and again with heartfelt satisfaction.

"Shut up your shark's jaws!" said Kelly, angrily, "and let's talk work. If you're game, I can put you on a tack that will bring you into harbour with a stunning cargo. Now listen to me." And, after a few more moments' conversation, the two new friends quitted the café.

The little old fellow who had been sitting at the next table, sauntered out after them.

A few words of their conversation only had reached him.

"It looks as if Slimy Sam had got hold of a mug," he soliloquised. "It won't be the first he has landed, and I think it will be just as well to keep an eye on him. The big fellow is evidently a yokel, and I should not be at all surprised if Mr. Sam wasn't going to land him with the confidence trick."

And, fully resolved to protect Ned from any such attempt, the stranger, who was a detective, followed the pair.

Ned was quite unconscious that, for the first time in his life, the police were playing the part of guardian angel to him.

CHAPTER CLXXII.
"I KNOW A BANK."

QUITE unconscious that he was the object of any such solicitude on the part of those whom he regarded as his natural enemies, Ned led Mr. Samuel Higginthorpe, *alias* Slimy Sam, into a neighbouring public, at which he had appointed to meet the captain.

They installed themselves in a compartment of the bar.

A few minutes later the old fellow of the café entered the adjoining compartment.

By getting close to the dividing partition, he found himself able to hear a great deal of what was going on on the other side of it.

Hardly had he taken up this position than someone entered the compartment occupied by Ned and his new acquaintance.

It was the captain.

Kelly began a kind of speech which was to serve as an introduction to the two.

As it turned out there was no need of it.

Captain Montmorency Howard and Mr. Samuel Higginthorpe were perfectly well acquainted with one another.

In company they had, like the old Scotch wedded pair, "climbed the hill together" in the form of a peculiarly-constructed rotating stair, with which some genius had endowed some of her Majesty's jails.

Their first meeting was not particularly cordial.

We do not like to meet with living reminders of our past misfortunes.

But when Ned had informed the captain of Mr. Higginthorpe's peculiar talents, that gentleman's manner perceptibly thawed.

In a little time the three were literally as "thick as thieves."

"Mr. Dawes," said the captain to Ned, "I know you will excuse the question, but have you ever come in contact, unpleasantly that is, with the London police?"

"No," answered Kelly, boldly, "but if I—I shouldn't mind if I did. It's my belief you could square any man in the force if you'd coin enough." Recent subsequent revelations have proved that Ned was not far out—*vide* Druscovitch and Company

"Well," observed the captain, "I think that if this affair goes on we had better arrange to meet at your diggings. I think less suspicion would be aroused."

Ned agreed, and after some further consultation it was arranged that he should hire a lodging in Soho, at which the others should meet, and where the work of planning out their programme should be gone into.

When he left the place the detective had considerably altered his opinion with regard to Ned.

"The big fellow seems to be boss of the show," he thought. "Who the deuce can he be, though? I don't recollect such a fellow mixed up in any case I've had the handling of. There's one thing, though. As I don't know him it's pretty sure that he doesn't know me, and he'll be the safest one of the three for me to keep watch on. I can always find the other two when I want them, they're old friends."

He had heard a great deal of their talk, but had not quite been able, as he phrased it, to spot their lay ; but that there was something up their eager whisperings and the reputation of the card-sharping captain and the engraver, convinced him.

He heard the word "bank" repeatedly used, and racked his brain to guess what was up. His face assumed that eager look a dog has when his nose is in a rabbit-hole.

After consulting with his superiors and with the bank authorities, it was decided for the present merely to keep as strict a watch as possible over the suspected parties.

The aim of the bank people was twofold.

They wanted to catch the rogues in some overt act that would ensure them a lengthy sentence.

They also wanted to lay their hands on the rest of the paper which had been stolen from their mills, and the actual thieves of which were undergoing their sentences at the time.

They felt that as long as this paper—a quantity of which had never been accounted for—was in dangerous hands they would always be menaced.

The imitation of the watermark and of the peculiar crisp paper of the bank has always been a stumbling-block to bank-note forgers, and here it lay all ready to their hands.

Accordingly, it was resolved to spare no trouble to bring matters to such a climax as was desired.

But, although a detective was keeping watch and ward over Ned, he never identified him, either as the famous bushranger or as one of the men engaged in the diamond robbery in Hatton-garden.

Ned was always prompt in action.

On leaving his new friends, he had gone home, and the following morning, after announcing to his landlord that he was going to spend a few days in the country, he packed up a portmanteau and came to town.

He called on the captain, and the pair sallied forth in quest of quarters.

They did not notice that they were followed by a

habby-looking fellow, who had been lounging about the street in which the captain resided all the morning.

The detective, knowing that he could always lay his hands on the captain, whose face, as a man always knocking about certa n quarters, was familiar to him, had changed his first notion of following Ned on the evening on which he had discovered the plot.

He resol ed instead to keep a watch over the captain's -esidence, where he divined Kelly would call, and to commence his espionage on the latter from that moment.

He saw Ned arrive, and the two new friends start on their lodging-hunting expedition, and stole after them.

After several enquiries, Ned found quarters that suited him very well in Soho.

A few hours later an elderly gentleman applied for apartments at the same address.

He was a very particular old gentleman.

He made minute enquiries as to what other lodgers were in the house, and the accommodation it afforded.

Then nothing would suit him but a room with a south aspect, and the only one vacant was one immediately adjoining Ned's sitting-room.

It was not very large, but the old fellow declared he preferred it to any other.

During the next day or two the captain and Mr. Higginthorpe made several calls on Ned.

Ned was not aware he had the old gentleman for a neighbour, and, indeed, it would not have mattered much if he had, for the room was separated by a good thick wall from Kelly, and nothing therefore could be overheard.

The little old gentleman was intensely interested in the arrival of these visitors, and would have given a great deal to have heard their conversation, but the fates were against him.

Several times he stole noiselessly from the room and applied his ear to the keyhole of Ned's door, which opened on to the same landing as his own.

But although his ears were quick enough to catch the sound of any approaching footstep, the noise of which made him bolt back into his room like a frightened rabbit, he was unable to seize on any part of the conversation carried on within.

After musing a little while he went out and made some purchases.

Then he descended and had a very long and important interview with the landlord, at the close of which the latter was considerably overcome with astonishment.

Well he might be on receiving the intelligence that one of his lodgers was a man contriving some fraud, and the other a detective engaged in preventing it.

The next day the detective entered Ned's room during his absence.

The first care was to see if there was any paper of a compromising character lying about.

In this respect he was doomed to disappointment.

Kelly being unable to write was consequently not in a position to make compromising memoranda.

To this very fact he owed much of his immunity.

He never sent or received letters, and as a natural result his correspondence never went astray or fell into the wrong hands.

Baffled in this respect, the detective turned his attention to the general arrangement of the room.

He seemed thoroughly puzzled and somewhat vexed at the absence of all clues.

He cast an almost despairing glance round the apartment. All at once his glance was arrested; his eyes brightened as he observed a picture which hung against the wall that divided his room from Kelly's.

By the aid of a two-foot rule he ascertained its exact position on the wall.

Then returning to his own room and measuring from the end wall and the floor, in order to be certain of the spot, he cut away a hole through the partition immediately behind it—taking care to do this work in Kelly's absence.

Over this, in order to mask it, he shifted one of the numerous works of art with which his wall was ornamented.

The next time Ned and his friends were in council the detective unhooked his own picture, revealing the hole

Then he put his ear to it, at the same time pushing the picture in Ned's room a trifle away from the wall.

So gently was this done that no one even actually engaged in closely watching the picture would have observed it.

By this means he was well able to overhear the whole conversation.

Matters were going on swimmingly.

Ned had hired a house at Hackney, that was to be the scene of their operations.

Higginthorpe had purchased a press and had it conveyed there, and had also given the requisite touches needed to complete the plate with which the captain had furnished him.

The captain had got hold of the bank-paper, which had been carefully packed up and warehoused under a false name for some time past.

He had arranged that it should be delivered at Ned's address at Soho that night, being too nervous to have it sent to his own quarters, a piece of attention for which Ned thanked by a look that caused him to feel somewhat uncomfortable.

It was finally arranged that Higginthorpe should return to Hackney, that the captain should call in at Ned's the first thing in the morning and take the paper on with him, and that Ned should follow a little later.

The detective had heard quite enough to settle on his course of action.

He had neither a warrant nor a sufficient force to secure the three, so he resolved to obtain the requisite authority without delay to secure the three at Hackney.

The following morning Mr. Higginthorpe being aroused by a ring at the bell opened the door and was immediately taken into custody by a couple of policemen in plain clothes, who were soon joined by several others.

A search of the house revealed the existence of a printing-press and plate concerning which this usual fluent individual was quite at a loss to give any satisfactory explanation.

A couple of hours later a cab drove up and a gentleman of gorgeous exterior stepped out, holding beneath his arm a parcel which appeared an object of intense solicitude to him.

On stepping into the house and into the arms of a detective-sergeant he was promptly relieved of it and was consigned in company with Samuel to a back room to curse his luck and lament ever having yielded to the temptation of engaging in this once so promising little "plant."

Time began to slip on and there were as yet no signs of the third party.

The detective, who knew the hour at which the bushranger had arranged to leave Soho, began to grow weary, and the prisoners, who possessed a similar knowledge, to indulge in anything but pleasant wishes towards the man who had apparently deserved the fate that had befallen them and resolved to steer clear of it.

The fact was that Ned had reflected that three bachelors could not well keep house together without inconvenience, and without exciting the suspicion of their neighbours.

It was absolutely necessary that they should have a woman of some kind to look after their domestic arrangements, though then there was the risk that she might discover things were wrong and unconsciously or intentionally betray them.

In this dilemma he thought of Jess.

He at once hunted her up, and got her to agree to keep house for them.

This, however, took time.

It was late in the afternoon when a hansom drove up to the house in Hackney.

A lady and gentleman alighted.

"Run up and let yourself in. Jess," said the latter, "whilst I settle with the cabman. Here's the key."

The girl complied.

She ran up the steps, opened the house-door, and went in.

The gentleman helped the cabman to get a couple of boxes from the top of the cab, and then was going to pay him

Whilst he was feeling in his pocket for some silver, and the man was carrying the boxes up the steps to the door, it was suddenly thrown open.

The girl appeared in the doorway.

Opening the door suddenly, she cried—

"Run, Ned! The coppers!" and banged to the door, which she quickly locked, and threw the key through the glass window into the street. She was soon collared by the police inside, who had witnessed her proceedings, but too late to frustrate them.

Ned took in the situation at a glance.

The police had been waiting for him in the house, ready to pounce on him.

Jess had discovered them, and, despite their efforts to restrain her, had succeeded in throwing the door open before they could lay hands on her, and, when in their grip, had shouted out those words of warning recorded above.

Simultaneously the bushranger saw his danger and his chance of escape.

With the quickness of a harlequin he bounded on to the driver's seat of the hansom, seized whip and reins, and, lashing the horse furiously, tore at full speed down the road.

The driver, in attempting to stop him, was knocked down and driven clean over.

The police started in pursuit, but in vain, as on foot they had no chance, and the locality was one in which vehicles do not abound, and are not to be had at a moment's notice.

Once under way, Ned took two or three turnings in succession, and, having secured a start, abandoned the cab.

He then made the best of his way to Kit's lodgings, and got him to provide the means of changing his appearance.

After which he took a fresh lodging, and, having communicated his new address to Anatole, awaited events.

CHAPTER CLXXIII.
HOW THE CALAIS MAIL WAS ROBBED.

A FEW days later Ned received notice from Anatole that the time had come for carrying out the plan he had so long been maturing—namely, that of robbing the Calais mail.

After a great deal of difficulty he had succeeded in getting a guard in the employ of the French railway to listen to his propositions.

Accordingly, it was settled that the affair should be brought off one night when this man, whose name was Henri Daudet, was on duty.

A few nights later saw Kelly and Anatole comfortably settled in a first-class compartment of the night mail-train bound from Charing-cross to Dover.

They were well provided with rugs, travelling-flasks, well-filled cigar-cases, and everything else they could think of to render their trip an agreeable one

Their luggage merely consisted of a couple of large Gladstone bags, stowed away under the seat of the compartment they occupied.

"Is this going to be a very big thing?" asked Kelly, when they were under way.

"It may be a fortune to both, and it may not. You see the job is, to a certain extent, a lottery It all depends on whether there has been a large amount of money sent across to-night or not, and, unfortunately, that is a thing which there is no means of ascertaining beforehand. At all events, there's sure to be money and valuables of some amount going. Be sure of that."

"Will there be much coin?" enquired Ned, whose notion of a mail robbery was rather Australian than European.

"No, there will be no money, but I daresay there will be a fair haul of English and French notes, amongst other things."

"But what will the rest of the swag be?"

"Securities, scrip, stock, coupons, and the like."

"Well, but what use will they be to us?"

"Why, there comes in the risky part of the job. What we have to do is to negotiate their restoration."

"On the risk of being nabbed?"

"No," answered the Frenchman. "I don't think there's much risk."

Ned remained in meditation for some time.

"Who's the fellow on the other side that is to help us?" he asked, after a pause.

"Ah, that is a curious thing," answered Anatole. "He is a man whose acquaintance I made under rather peculiar circumstances. The first time I set eyes on him I saw a great deal more of him than one usually sees on a first acquaintance."

As he made this remark the Frenchman laughed heartily.

"What's the joke?"

"I'll tell you," replied Anatole, and he went on to give the particulars of the circumstances under which he had first set eyes on Henri Daudet.

(To be continued.)

NED KELLY
THE IRONCLAD
AUSTRALIAN BUSHRANGER

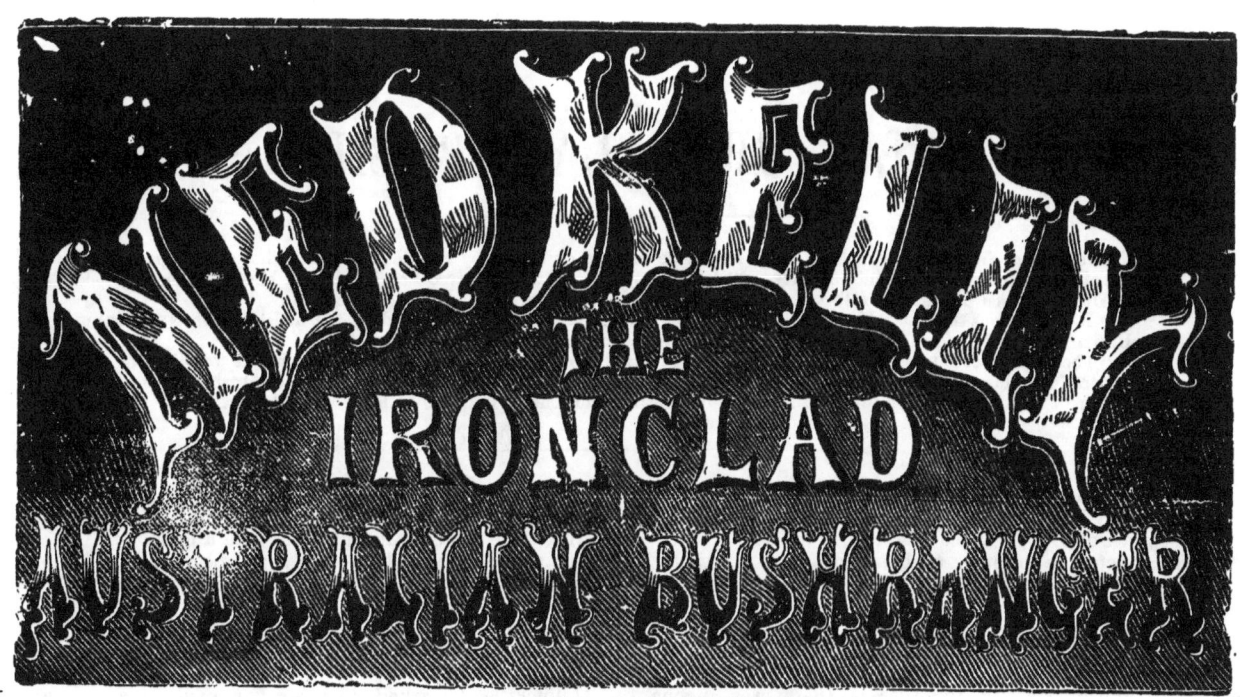

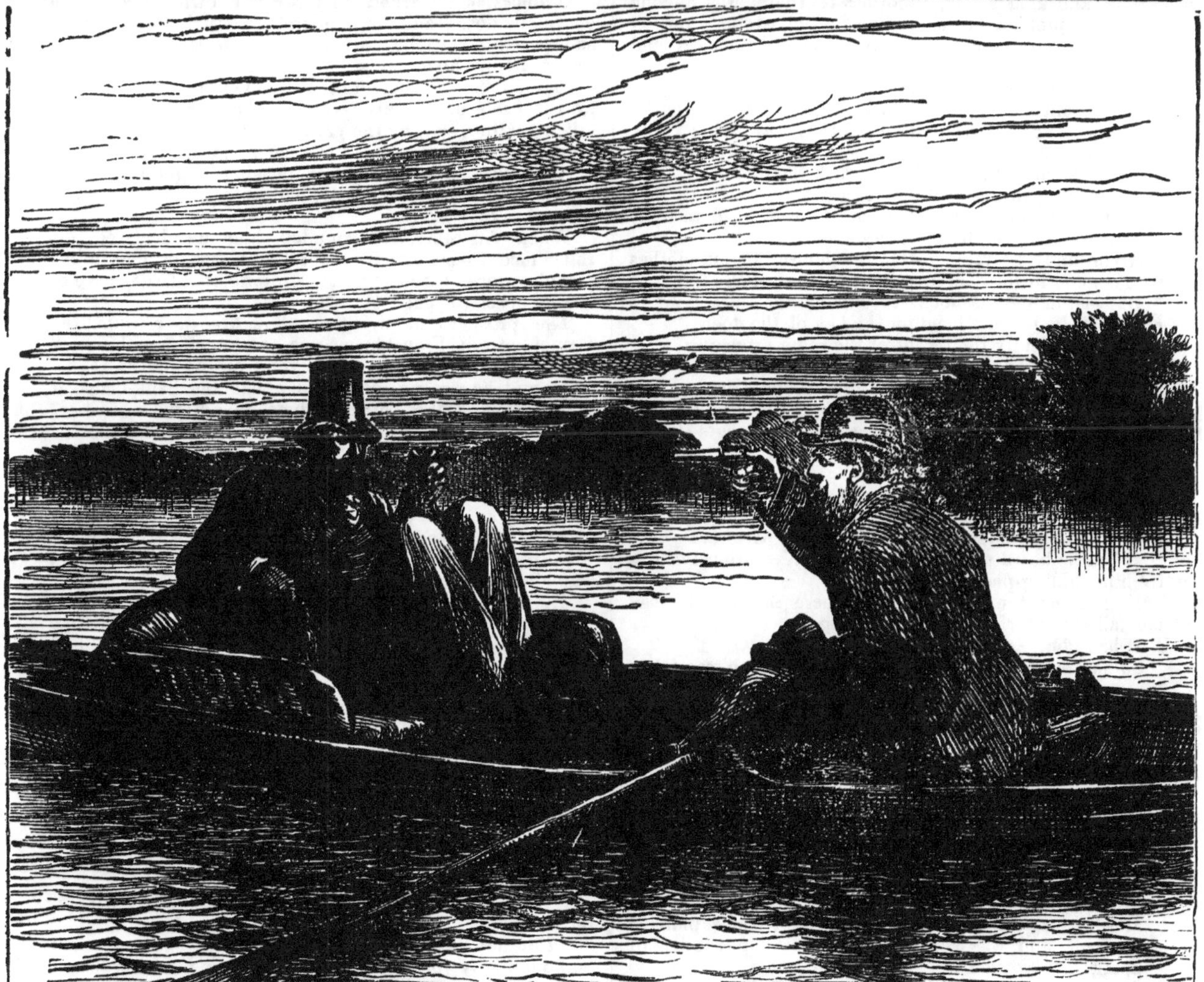

NO 30,

NED KELLY: IRONCLAD BUSHRANGER.

It is well known that for many years Ned Kelly had made himself notorious by a series of crimes wholly incompatible with the civilisation of the nineteenth century. Ned Kelly's celebrated steed, Marco Polo, is as well known at the Antipodes as Dick Turpin's Black Bess in these islands."—*Telegraph*, 7th July, 1881.

"It is notorious that the robbery of Mr. Steward's corpse was mainly performed by the assistance of NED KELLY's BROTHER, the Captain of what was neither more nor less than a pirate ship.—*Times*, July.

"The history of NED KELLY and his celebrated black horse, Marco Polo, will ever live in the recollection of the Australian public. The deeds of Dick Turpin, and the performances of Black Bess, are tame beside those of 'NED AND HIS NAG;' in addition to which Ned's history is true, and Turpin's is pure fiction."—*Press*, July.

CHAPTER CLXXIII.—*Continued.*

It appeared that Daudet in his younger days had taken to a species of robbery much practised in hotels.

It consisted in entering a room during its legitimate occupants' absence and walking off with whatever he could lay his hands on.

It happened on one occasion that in prowling about an hotel corridor, he noticed a room with the key in the lock on the outside.

After knocking softly, in order if there was anyone within to pretend he had called at the wrong room by mistake, and receiving no reply he turned the key and entered.

There was no one within.

The tenant had apparently been called away just as he was about to dress, for a suit of clothes was placed ready on a chair, and a clean shirt was spread out on the bed.

At the sight of these an idea struck the thief.

His own attire was of the shabbiest.

He resolved to change his garments from head to foot, in order to have the less to carry.

Accordingly he rapidly divested himself of his clothes till he stood in the condition of Adam before the fall.

But just as he was about to slip on the shirt, lying in readiness, he heard a hand on the key of the door.

It was evidently the tenant of the room returning.

What was he to do?

In desperation he slipped under the bed, trusting that the new-comer would dress and go out again, and above all that he would not notice the cast-off garments thrown down in one corner.

His expectations were realised.

The new-comer was evidently in a hurry

Daudet heard him rummage about the place, open several drawers, and then make a hasty departure.

When he heard the door close he stole cautiously forth from his hiding-place.

He glanced towards the place where the suit he had mentally appropriated had been lying.

It had gone.

So had the shirt, so had the garments he himself had thrown down.

A brief investigation convinced him that there was not an article of wearing apparel of any kind in the room.

The truth flashed across his mind.

The new-comer had been a thief bent on a similar errand to himself, but one who had set to work at once, without any hesitation, and stripped the room.

The wretched fellow was at his wit's end.

It would be impossible for him to leave the room in the war costume of a South Sea Islander.

Whilst he was racking his brains for some plan of getting off, and was speculating as to the possibility of slipping into some other untenanted room unperceived and appropriating a suit of clothes, the door suddenly opened.

This time it was really the tenant of the room.

His amazement at being confronted by a man in a condition better suited for a warm bath than on the Parisian Boulevards, was such as for the moment to render him speechless.

At first he thought he had to do with a madman.

But noticing how his room had been pillaged, he shouted for help, and soon the other inhabitants of the hotel flocked to the spot.

Amongst them was Anatole, who had a wonderful memory for faces, and the would-be thief had a remarkable one.

Ugliness had marked him for her own. He had an enormous nose; and a red splotch on his right cheek was, as he used to say, the only mark of affection he had ever received from his parents.

It was these peculiarities that enabled him to recognise, in the garb of a railway-guard, the man he had seen taken off in a cab, by the police, with a blanket wrapped around him to cover him, some ten years before.

As Daudet had really stolen nothing he got off with a reprimand, and, subsequently, had entered the service of the railway company.

When Anatole first sounded him he declared his reluctance to engage in the scheme, but at length his scruples were overcome by the promise of a large share of the prospective spoil.

The prospect of living as a *rentier en retraite*, the heaven of all Frenchmen, was too much for the poor devil. The temptation was beyond his power of resistance, and he was no more guilty than the bank manager and chairman (who between them govern their brother-directors) are, who are bribed by customers to make fabulous advances upon fabulous securities—only that the temptation is greater in the latter case—the thieves for a livelihood, the others for luxuries.

"So you see," concluded the Frenchman, in relating the matter to Ned, "I was quite right in saying I saw a great deal more of him than one usually does on a first acquaintance."

The train at length reached Dover.

Kelly and Anatole watched with interest the mail bags being transferred from the carriage in which they had been conveyed to the boat.

Then they embarked.

The night was a superb one.

The sea was so calm that even Anatole declared he preferred to remain on deck.

Accordingly he and Ned "lit up," and began to yarn about past accidents by flood and field.

Ned, who had hitherto been silent on the matter, gave him an account of his recent adventure in the cellar at Wapping.

The Frenchman listened with interest.

When Ned's story was done he gave a little shrug of the shoulders.

"I do not like adventures in cellars," he observed. "I had one in my younger days which gave me a shock that I was some time before I got over."

"Let's have it," asked Ned, who liked a yarn of the kind in prospect.

"It is no matter how many years ago," began Anatole. "when I was young—in fact, just beginning life

I was fresh from the provinces, where I had been brought up in that ignorance which some people hold to be bliss, and had just entered on a career in Paris.

"I was, as I said, green, not a bad-looking chap, and I had some tin

"I was always in love with someone or other—and always being in love is what I call the true *jeunesse dorée*. But you do not know what that means? Nothing like it—*vive l'amour!*" shouted the excitable Gaul, to the utter amazement of Ned, who holloed out—

"Damn your gibberish! Speak English, man. I don't know nothing about your John Dory or t'other fish you name!"

The Frenchman laughed at Ned's ignorance, and the words "*bête comme un bœuf*" escaped his lips.

"At that time, amongst the flower-girls on the boulevards who used to stroll from café to café with their baskets of posies, was a most charming creature," continued Anatole.

"In rags she would have looked beautiful, and in the coquettish Swiss-peasant kind of costume she had adopted she was perfectly ravishing.

"Her face, with its fair hair and blue eyes, was candour itself, resembling one of those delicious heads that Greuze had the secret of putting on to canvas—but *que diable*, what do you know about Greuze?"

"Don't you be so blooming conceited. Don't I know nothing about crews? I've seen a pretty job lot of them in my time, and you should just see the crews my brother Kit has shipped."

The poor ignoramus had no idea that the Frenchman was naming the celebrated French painter—Greuze.

Anatole looked at him for a moment, and his sides shook with suppressed laughter.

Shrugging his shoulders, he proceeded—

"Her actions, too, did not belie her looks, for she was modesty itself in her bearing, and used to repulse any customer who ventured to presume at all in the firmest manner.

"But when I looked at her I thought that she returned my glance, and I fancied at once I had made an impression, ass that I was. I need not detail how we became acquainted—you know as well as I do how that comes to pass.

"We had one or two brief interviews out of doors, and at last she consented to receive me at her residence, stipulating, however, the strictest secrecy.

"She lived, it seemed in the City, in a street long since swept away by Hausmann.

"I dressed myself with unusual care, and put on a quantity of jewellery, hoping to dazzle her eyes by the splendour of my appearance as I trusted to bewitch her ears with the charms of my eloquence.

"I half drowned myself in eau-de-Cologne, placed a fairly-filled purse in my pocket so as to be prepared for all emergencies, and then muffling all my splendour in a long cloak, for she had warned me not to come too conspicuously dressed, stole forth in the most mysterious manner.

"You must remember I was only a boy, and going to my first rendezvous.

"My heart thumped violently, and I alternately burned with a delirious fever and trembled violently like a culprit.

"Natalie—her name I should have said was Natalie—was punctual at our appointed meeting-place.

"Begging me not to take her arm, but to follow her at some distance lest it should excite attention, she led the way towards her abode.

"We traversed in this fashion several streets, fouler than at that time I had any conception streets could be, though I know more of such matters now.

"At length my guide halted in front of a low, gloomy-looking building.

"With a whisper to me to be silent, she entered a kind of alley closed by a swing-gate, and, greatly marvelling that so beautiful a creature should inhabit such a foul-looking den, I followed her.

"I thought of all the offers she must have refused to leave this hole, and that now for my sake she was going to do so.

"You see, I was very young.

"There was no porter, and I groped along after Natalie in a long, dark passage, till she took a lamp from a shelf, and lighting it began to descend a short flight of stone steps.

"I marvelled at our going down instead of up, but followed in silence as she desired.

"At the end of a second passage she, with a most inviting smile, swung open a ponderous door.

"She passed through it. I followed her, and found myself in a small vaulted chamber, and in the embraces—not of my charmer, but of three of the vilest-looking scoundrels I ever set my eyes on.

"I saw how I had been decoyed in an instant.

"I was young and strong, but the villains had sprung upon me before I had time to put myself on my guard, and Natalie quickly swinging-to the massy door cut off all hopes of my cries availing me.

"With the rapidity of lightning the fellows stripped me of watch, purse, pin, rings and studs, and caused them to disappear in a manner worthy of a conjuror.

"Since then I have seen the same business practised on others often enough, but never, I can assure you, more neatly.

"I was cool enough to see the futility of resistance, and thinking I should receive better treatment if I remained passive after my first effort to break loose, suffered them to strip me of my wealth without a struggle.

"But this operation completed, they dragged me towards an inner door, which I found, by the light still carried by Natalie, led to a vault somewhat larger than the first one.

"Two of them held me, and the third stepping forward opened a trap in the floor.

"The agony of that moment was intolerable, and I cannot recall it without a shudder.

"I could read murder plainly in the eyes of the fiends who held me, and hear below me the rush of waters which in a few minutes would be bearing away my corpse.

"The thought was maddening.

"To die like this, snared like a rat in a trap, with no chance or hope of being avenged, cut off in the prime of youth and enjoyment, when all things smiled upon me, in a vile den with gloating devils around me.

"I begged and prayed for mercy, I promised secrecy, ransom, anything they liked to name, but a given "It is safer" from the devil who had lured me thither, made the men who held me drag me yet closer to the horrible gulf.

"I bit and kicked, and tore and howled like a madman, to get loose, but all in vain.

"The villains held me in a grip of iron.

"One of them took a comforter from about his neck and passed it round mine.

"It was their intention to strangle me before throwing me down the trap.

"Natalie seized on one end of the comforter and one of her accomplices the other, and pulled it.

"I felt the cursed thing grow tighter and tighter, the blood rushed to my head, there was a singing in my ears, and sparks began to flash before my eyes.

"Suddenly there was a rush of moving figures, a scuffle, the arms that held me relaxed their grip, the cord slackened.

"For a moment I lost consciousness, but opening my eyes found my late assailants in the grip of a squad of police.

"The practices of my captors had for some time been suspected, owing to the mysterious disappearances of several young men, whose bodies turned up at the Morgue, and the police having obtained a clue had secretly entered the house and concealed themselves in order to catch the ruffians in the act.

"I got off with severe brain fever : I wonder I was not a madman for life ; and on my recovery learnt that Natalie and her accomplices, no murder be ng actually brought home to them, had been sentenced to a long term of penal servitude."

CHAPTER CLXXIV.
HOW THE PARIS MAIL WAS ROBBED.

As Anatole concluded his story, the boat entered Calais harbour.

The two travellers made their way at once to the station.

Despite the fineness of the night there had been but few travellers—a fact which helped their plan.

At a station Anatole pointed out to Ned a little dark fellow in the uniform of a railway guard, whose eyes were eagerly scanning the passengers who arrived.

"That is our man," he remarked.

Ned was about to advance towards him.

"No, no," said Anatole ; "we must not be seen in communication with him. He has seen us, and that is enough."

The time approached for the travellers to take their places.

"Everything favours us," said the Frenchman.

This remark was called forth by the fact that they were able to secure a compartment for themselves, usually a matter of difficulty on French lines, in the arrangements of which a paucity of accommodation, as regards the number of passengers carried, is conspicuous.

By a yet greater piece of good luck, the compartment was the end on of the carriage coupled next to the guard's van in which the mails were deposited.

The mails for Paris were placed in a separate locked-up compartment.

After this had been locked it was further secured by bands of linen with seals at the ends.

They were, of course, no extra security from actual violence, but they served for two purposes.

Firstly, to show if the compartment had been tampered with ; and secondly, to render even an unsuccessful attempt to rob the mails a criminal offence, breaking an official seal constituting one in France.

A few minutes later and the train steamed out of the station, and just as it started Daudet came to the carriage to look at their tickets.

"Now," said Anatole, consulting his watch, "we have a little under an hour for our job, which must be done between here and Amiens."

"Well, what have we got to do, and how are we to do it ?" said Ned, who was still in the dark.

"You saw our friend come to the window just now ?"

"Yes."

"You thought it was to look at the tickets ?"

"What else was it for, then ?"

"Why, to give me this."

As he spoke the Frenchman held up a key.

"What key is that ?" inquired Kelly.

"The key of the compartment in which the mails are locked. Now, do you understand ?"

"Yes, I think I do."

"You are a heavier man than myself," observed Anatole ; "but you are as active as a cat, and you are certainly stronger. I think that, with your permission, the lion's share of the work must fall on you."

"What is it I am to do ?"

"Pass from this carriage to the next, on the further side, and open the door of the compartment in which there are the mail-bags."

Ned whistled.

"That's an ugly job," was his remark.

"Exactly so. But, consider, success means a fortune. *Allons, mon cher.* Come, my dear boy ; time, as you English say, is on the wing."

After a few instructions from Anatole, Ned was ready to set out on his perilous expedition.

The door on the further side of the compartment was gently opened, and he stepped out on to the foot-board.

Standing there for a moment, he looked around him.

The train was tearing furiously through the dark night, seeming almost to sway from side to side in its velocity.

So swiftly was it moving, that the rush of air against him seemed to threaten every moment to make him leave go the rail outside the carriage to which his hands clung.

Anatole had closed the door, which Kelly had pulled-to after him.

After a little time Ned began to get accustomed to his novel position.

The rocking, jerking motion of the train, no longer threatened at every movement to wrench away his hold and hurl him down amidst the whirring, clattering wheels beneath him.

The rush of air became less awkward as he gradually grew accustomed to it.

The steps of the French railway-carriages are broader than those in England, it being the practise for the guards to pass from time to time along the whole length of the train in order to collect tickets.

To facilitate this, there is also a rail running along about head high, which the men lay hold of with their hands.

After a few minutes spent in standing on the steps and holding on to the rail, Ned grew acclimatised, as it were, to his novel situation.

He felt that he could have passed from one end of the train to the other with ease.

But this was not his task. He had but to pass along his one carriage, and to step from it to the next one while the train was in motion.

He had, firstly, to pass before the compartment holding the break, which intervened between him and the one containing the mails.

In this break-van was the guard, Henri Daudet.

But Ned was also aware that there was another guard as well sharing his vigil.

To pass in front of the window in an upright position was impossible.

He would be certain to be detected.

It was necessary, therefore, to crouch down and advance along the step in a creeping form.

Before stooping he paused for a moment.

The reflection of the lighted windows of the train was plainly visible on the side of the line as it flew by.

Kelly could make out the outline of the passengers in several instances, and could plainly recognise that of Anatole standing at the window.

There was no shadow cast from the guard's van.

All at once a shadow blocked the light that a moment before had been streaming full from the window.

The shadow of a man. From its outline it was evident that this individual either had his back or his face to the opening.

In the latter case he was bound to see Ned as the bushranger crept past, and it was useless to risk it.

But, in the former? All at once a thought crossed Kelly's mind.

Instinctively he divined the real state of affairs.

The guard Daudet knew that it was during this part of the journey that the robbery was to take place.

It must be he who was standing by the window in order to mask it from his colleague.

Stooping down, Ned crept cautiously along, helping himself onwards past the guard's compartment by the aid of the handle of the door.

Once past this compartment, he rose and continued his progress by the aid of the rail.

In a few moments more he had arrived opposite the door of the van containing the mails.

It was secured by the sealed bands already mentioned.

A few slits with his knife disposed of these.

Then, inserting the key Anatole had given him into the lock, he opened the door.

He plunged his hand in, and seized on the first bag he could lay hold of.

Holding this between his knees, in order to prevent it from being shaken from the step, he relocked the door and then commenced the return journey.

This was even more difficult than the former.

He had only one hand to help him, having to drag the bag along with the other.

The getting past the guards' van was exceedingly difficult for him.

But when he reached the end of the steps, further progress seemed impossible, encumbered as he was.

It had taken him all he knew to get across from one carriage to the other with his hands free, but the mail bag was a terrible impediment.

How was he to get it over?

At length an idea struck him.

Taking off his necktie, he managed with the aid of that and his handkerchief to secure the bag firmly to the end of the rail that had helped him along.

Then, crossing the gulf, he made his way to the compartment where Anatole was waiting.

The Frenchman did not utter a word till Kelly had entered the compartment again, lest their converse should be overheard.

" Where is the bag ?" was his remark.

Kelly explained the difficulty that had arisen.

He then by the aid of the straps that served to fasten their rugs, improvised a kind of rope.

With this he started again on his expedition.

Again he crossed the space between the carriages after fastening one end of his rope to the one he quitted.

The other end he attached to the bag.

Then he loosened the fastenings confining the bag to the rail, stepped back to his own carriage, and by the aid of his rope hauled the bag after him, and a minute later had swung it through the window to Anatole.

" Shall I go for another ?" he whispered, with his head thrust into the carriage so as not to be overheard.

" Yes, there is time," was the answer ; " but try to give back the key to Daudet."

" He's wide awake. I'll do that like a shot," said Ned.

Taking the rope with him this time, he set out again on his journey.

Practice was making perfect in his case, and he gained the door of the mail-van with comparative ease this time.

He noticed the shadow of the guard still blocking the window.

Securing another bag and relocking the door, he again commenced his retreat.

Then came the most difficult part of it, the stooping down and getting past the guards' compartment, encumbered as he was by the bag.

He stooped and began to crawl along.

All at once, just as he was right opposite the door and was taking every possible precaution not to make the least noise, he felt something touch him.

It was a hand !

For a moment the shock was great. Another man would have lost his balance and rolled, bag and all, beneath the wheels ; but his nerves of steel served him.

He looked up and could make out that the figure of someone was leaning with his back against the door, the glass of which was down.

One of this figure's hands was dangling into space outside the door ; and this was the dangling hand that had touched him.

But instead of the stranger trying to detain him or to give an alarm, he retained his position and remained motionless.

All but the hand, the fingers of which opened and closed several times in the air as though seeking to clutch something or other

Ned all at once guessed the enigma.

Daudet's hand was thrust out for the key.

By a miracle of balancing, Ned managed to maintain himself and the bag in position, whilst he drew forth the key from his pocket and placed it in the hand extended in anticipation of it.

Then he resumed his journey.

This time he had not so much trouble in completing his passage.

On arriving at the gap between the carriages, he fastened his rope to the bag.

Then he hitched it round the rail in such a fashion, that a sharp jerk from the loose end would at once unfix it.

With this loose end in hand he swung himself across, jerked the rope, freed the bag and hauled it after him.

Once more he regained his compartment.

During his absence Anatole had not been idle.

The first mail-bag had been ripped open by him, and the greater part of its contents was strewn about the floor of the carriage.

Half a dozen large envelopes and packages were, however, placed on one side.

" Good," exclaimed the Frenchman, " here we are again, as the clown says, eh ? I have pretty well sorted this lot."

A few more minutes and he had completed his task.

" Bundle all these books into the bag." he continued, adding two or three more envelopes to the selected lot, "and I will examine number two." Ned complied.

" Can I do anything else to quicken things ?" he then enquired.

" No," was the answer ; " all I can do is just to read hurriedly through the lot and spot the packets addressed to big banking firms. They are bound to contain money. There may be big remittances to private houses as well, but they will probably be in bills, and, besides, there is not time to look."

After the second bag had been ransacked like the first, the useless documents were returned to it.

The packets selected were then hurriedly opened by Anatole, and their contents subjected to a similar scrutiny

The securities that appeared negotiable were placed on one side.

The envelopes and everything of a compromising nature were returned to the bag.

After which these were quietly dropped out of the window.

The two travelling bags, with which the pair of rogues were equipped, were next taken in hand.

They had been expressly prepared for the occasion.

They had false bottoms, in which the stolen papers were readily hidden away.

A few minutes later the train reached Boulogne, and shortly afterwards resumed its journey without the loss being discovered.

It was not indeed found out till the train had nearly arrived at Paris, by which time several passengers had left it.

Hence the authorities were quite at a loss.

Ned and Anatole left the terminus without being suspected, and a short time afterwards the bushranger was seated by his accomplice in a café on the Boulevard. They wisely agreed that personal concealment in Paris would excite suspicion. They therefore frequented the most prominent café.

CHAPTER CLXXV.
HOW THE FRENCHMAN DID KELLY, AND HOW HE WAS FOUND OUT.

EVERY cock crows loudest on his own dunghill, but more especially the Gallic cock.

Anatole, with the asphalted pavement of his beloved Boulevards under his boot-soles, was a different being from the Anatole of the Colonies—or even London.

In these latter localities the little Frenchman had looked up to Kelly as one knowing the lay of the land as well as—if not better than—himself. He also had confidence in his courage.

23

But once in Paris, with, as Madame McGregor exclaimed, "My foot on my native heath," it was emphatically, in racing parlance, Anatole first and the rest nowhere.

The Frenchman had taken quarters for them both in a quiet, fourth-rate hotel in the Rue d'Amsterdam.

He had chosen it because it was chiefly frequented by travellers of a class amongst whom anything eccentric in manner on Kelly's part would not be likely to excite notice.

The frequenters of the hotel, which may be readily identified by some of our readers, consisted almost entirely of English acrobats, dancers, jugglers, music-hall singers, circus-riders, and the like, either engaged in Paris, or passing through that city.

The manners and customs of some of these "members of the profession," as they delight to style themselves, are often curious in the extreme, and their ignorance of the social amenities of life positively dumbfounding.

Hence Anatole felt sure that any awkwardness of Kelly's would pass unperceived, or, at any rate, unnoticed, either by the people of the hotel or by the other guests.

Another great point was that English was spoken and English fare provided, for Ned, in common with many of his kidney, had the firmest conviction that frogs and snails formed the basis of a Frenchman's diet, and that every dish that he did not recognise was composed of one or the other of these two things disguised in a more or less artful fashion.

At first Anatole tried to remove these impressions.

He took Ned to dinner at Brebant's, and devoted as much attention to the composition of the *menu*, or bill of fare, as ever the House of Commons did to a clause of the Land Bill.

But all in vain.

Kelly expressed an opinion that *supreme de volaille à la maréchale* was beastly rot, and left his stomach as empty as if he had been eating an old kid glove served up with butter sauce. It was a blessed kickshaw, and only fit food "for them blessed snakes that swallow their blankets."

He had evidently heard of the boa constrictor at "the Zoo" who had performed this operation.

He went through the *menu* from curiosity alone, and then swore he was more hungry than when he began.

Rumpsteak and onions and a bottle of gin was his idea of a first-rate *cuisine*. That was something to lie down on. French wines! Bah! disguised poison.

Anatole's first care on his arrival had been to rush, in swift succession, to tailors, hatters, boot-makers, shirt-makers, and hosiers, and to rig himself out from top to toe in the singular array of the Parisian dandy.

With cuffs reaching down to his knuckles, and shirt-collar rising above his ears, it was his delight to be driven in a victoria in the Bois de Boulogne, to sit sipping absinthe at some café on the Boulevards, and to pass the evening in one of the minor theatres, the Delassements-Comiques or the Folies-Marigny, where slang and indecency formed the staple of the entertainment; and the night at some gaming-table patronised by both sexes.

Ned's tastes were far too rowdy for this.

He did not care for being driven in a victoria; the only method of equine-travelling understood by him, being to have a good horse between his knees. He could not endure absinthe; he could not understand Parisian slang; and he did not, as he phrased it, "see the fun of playing with a lot of haggish-looking women hanging around you, and trying to wheedle you out of your winnings or else to grab 'em before your very eyes."

So Anatole, after shrugging his shoulders and vowing that it was impossible to act as bear-leader to "*un tel Ours*," began to leave him pretty much to his own devices.

Especially as a certain young lady rejoicing in the name of Tata Flandreheche, began to engross a great deal of his own attention at this juncture.

Ned for some time sought consolation in loafing about the streets, lounging of a night at the Folies-Bergère, where the members of a pantomime troupe he had struck up an acquaintance with at the hotel, were playing, or drinking at Jack Coney's.

But these pursuits began to pall on his active disposition.

Strange to say, Paris had no charms for the wild, rough nature of the bushranger.

The excitement of pleasure was to him as nothing compared to the excitement of peril, which was the very breath of his nostrils. He thought the life fearfully slow, and sighed for the Bush he had been compelled to quit. If ever he settled down (unless settled up with a hempen collar) he resolved to do so in the Bush. It was the only place where he felt he could breathe.

Mabille aroused first his curiosity and then his contempt.

His ignorance of the language irritated him.

If a woman laughed when she spoke to him, nothing could get the idea out his head that she was chaffing him, and he grew "riled" at not being able to answer her.

As to all the wondrous treasures of art enshrined in the French capital, all the monuments hallowed by association with the mighty dead, all the spots whose names are household words in history, he neither knew nor cared "a blessed rap about 'em."

They and their like were sealed books to him.

Anatole had taken care on their arrival to inscribe their names after a fashion of his own in the book which every French hotel-keeper is bound to keep for the information of the police.

Kelly he had set down as Mr. Tom Smith, of London. whilst he had given himself the title of baron, and the name of Isidore de Saint Phaar.

He felt certain that unless suspicion fell on them at once concerning the robbery of the mail, they would be quite safe, since it would be impossible to track out every one of the passengers by the train that had been plundered, and, unless this was done, there would really be no way of finding out the guilty parties.

Under these circumstances he began to weary of looking after Kelly, even to the extent he did.

He wished, too, to shift his quarters to a more fashionable neighbourhood, though, at the same time, he did not like to abandon his supervision of the bushranger.

In his heart he was ever afraid Kelly would get into some clumsy scrape or other with the authorities, or would manage to let the cat out of the bag, that is to say, the mail bag, in his cups.

So one afternoon he sounded Kelly as to the latter's returning to England.

Kelly expressed himself as "jolly glad" to clear out of Paris.

"I'm infernally sick of this blessed nest of jabbering monkeys," was his way of putting it.

"Well, my friend, we can, I think, arrange all that," said Anatole.

"The first thing to be fixed, though, is to share the swag."

"*Très bien*, very good. We will share it."

They adjourned at once to the double-bedded room they occupied.

The door having been carefully locked and a handkerchief hung over the keyhole, for the mere leaving the key in the lock was not considered a sufficient precaution, they set to work.

The plunder was spread out on the table.

It was, as has been stated, a very miscellaneous lot, consisting, for the most part, of those foreign stocks, shares, and bonds which are payable "to bearer," and are therefore easier to negociate than most of our own securities.

Ned gazed in silence at the heap of papers printed in black, red, blue, green, and mauve inks, with wonderfully elaborate headings, and long tails of attached coupons.

He knew an English "flimsy" well enough, and, since his sojourn in Paris, had learned to recognise the notes of different values issued by the bank of France, but the things before him were, one and all, as puzzling as a Chaldee manuscript would have been.

He stared his hardest, however, at them.

"I think I already have said to you," began the Frenchman, "that this little quantity of values, or, as you call them, securities, is to be divided in three."

"In three?" echoed Ned

"One for me, the head; one for you, the hand; and one for our good friend Henri Daudet, the eye—an eye which shut itself up when it is not wanted to see," and he grinned like a sick baboon.

"Quite correct, old fireworks," said Ned; "but drive along with your palaver, or I shall be as dry as a burnt gum-tree stump in a hot wind before you've done."

"Then I think the best plan will be to divide all these papers into three piles, heaps, is not that so?"

"Very good."

"Eh bien, come, let us set ourselves to the work."

So saying he pounced on a bundle of the securities, and began to deal them out in three heaps.

Ned looked on.

"Allons, come, my friend," said Anatole, "help me to divide them."

"How am I to divide 'em when I don't know a word of all the blessed scribble-scrabble," was the sullen answer.

"Of the blessed how do you say?" gasped the puzzled Frenchman.

"Of all the oughts and crosses and Lord knows what else that's stuck all over 'em," said Ned, in the same sulky tones.

"Cannot you read, my friend?" inquired Anatole, in his softest and oiliest tones.

"I can spell my way through a bit of honest print," said Ned, remembering how he had often managed to make out the bills offering a reward for his own apprehension; "but pen-writing beats me hollow. It's so different from the hand-bills that used to stick alongside of Holloway's Ointment all over the bush offering ever so many pounds for Ned Kelly, dead or alive. Oh, I could make that out easy enough, but them confounded snakes' tails you call writing is out of my course, I can tell you. No, I can't read these no how. Have you any more questions to ask?"

"No," remarked the Frenchman, meditatively, as he continued his sorting process in a swift but deliberate fashion.

His brain was working more quickly than his hands

Kelly's remark had suggested the germ of a scheme that a few minutes sufficed to think out in all its details.

"What do you think of doing with your share?" he at length said, carelessly.

"Well, I don't quite know. That's just where I want a word or two from you. I'm blowed if I quite know the use of these blessed things now we have got 'em, though you say they're worth a lot."

"I suppose you know that it will take some time and trouble to get rid of them?"

"Hum! I guessed as much. The same game as over those blessed diamonds—eh?"

"No, no! These are genuine. But, yes, in one thing you have reason. Like the diamonds, it is not everyone who can take them into the market for sale."

"Oh, curse the things!"

"Stop a bit. I'm up to a dodge here. I should like to start as a stockjobber on the Bourse, and then I can tell everybody that makes enquiries that the stuff I have on hand was received from my clients. D'ye see?"

"Not quite."

"I shall say I am in a large way of business as an agent for foreigners. After a time I bring these things into the market. If any are recognised, I say I receive them from my clients—my customers abroad, at Sydney, Rio, Hong Kong, where you will; and I show my books, all correct, to prove it."

"You're up to a thing or two."

"Only it will take time, and it will be necessary to spend a lot of tin in fixing myself in Paris. If I do it in three years I shall be lucky."

"Three years!"

"Three years. Now, I am willing to take your share and work it off in the same way for a little commission."

"Three years!"

"Hum, hum!" replied the Frenchman, very slowly, as though in doubt; "I do not see how it can be managed otherwise. No; to hurry faster would be to risk the loss of all."

There was a minute of silence.

"Listen to me," said Anatole at length. "You are a brave fellow, un bon enfant, and we have done well together. You are my friend, and I love to help my friends. I tell you what I will do. I will buy your share half-and-half—no, I mean out-and-out—as you say in England, now, and take all the risk."

"Ain't that a little bit too good to be true?" answered Kelly, whose suspicions were aroused by the other's manner.

"What do you say?"

"What's the worth of the whole lot of the swag?" asked Ned, doggedly.

"In English money, as near as I can make it, it is fifteen thousand pounds."

"Then my share is what?" asked Kelly, who could not even divide fifteen by three.

"Five thousand, naturally," replied the other, a little puzzled at such a question.

"Five thousand? Well, what will you give me for it?"

"Well, I will either give you four thousand by degrees as I dispose of the value of the securities, or I will pay you now two thousand and take all risk."

"Oh, that's the game, is it?"

"Take your choice—take it or leave it. I don't care which."

Ned mused a bit.

After all, the proposition seemed a fair one.

"Cash down?" he said.

"On the nail, as you say," was the answer.

"All right; fork over the tin, then."

Anatole had still the money stolen from Kint, and some more he had subsequently won in England.

He handed Ned the amount in French and English notes.

After some puzzling, Kelly was satisfied that the sum was right, and stowed it away about him.

"Come and wet down the bargain, Frenchy, won't you?" was his next observation.

"Not just yet," answered Anatole, who was restoring the securities to their hiding-place.

"All right. In forty-eight hours I slope out of these diggings," remarked Ned, as he left the room.

Left alone, Anatole could not conceal the exultation he had with difficulty suppressed in Kelly's presence.

"Ah, quel bonheur! quel coup de maître! what luck! Can I believe my eyes? Mais c'est incroyable! Nearly one hundred thousand pounds, and nearly the half of it for two! Anatole, mon vieux, you are a great strategist, greater than the great Napoleon. He crossed the Alps; so did Hanibal, and others before him. He had his luck—his coup; he lost it. I have had mine! I keep it, to enjoy it where one lives double the time of life anywhere else, surtout in that sad country, that triste pays, they call 'Merry England.' Merry—ha! ha! ha! Vive la France! vive la Bagatelle! vive Anatole! Tra, la, la! tra, la, la!" sang the excitable Gaul, as he danced a pas seul round the room, his face beaming with delight. "English dolt! ass! fool! idiot! I have avenged Waterloo!"

He struck a tragic air, and looked at himself in the glass.

He was almost choked with joy, and laughed at the way he had "done" Kelly, until the tears ran down his cheeks.

"*Allons!* let us see," he resumed. "I cannot hope for such luck with Daudet. He will want at least thirty thousand. That will leave me seventy. I go on the Bourse with that. In three years I realise, in three more I double it, in ten I retire with a magnificent and honourably-earned fortune."

Visions of a landed estate and a seat in the Chamber of Deputies here floated across his mind.

"Stop a moment, Anatole, *mon ami*," he resumed, as his thoughts flew back to the present. "You must keep a close watch on our friend whilst he remains in Paris. He has the money, and you have the securities, and if he took it into his thick head to denounce you that would be, *ma foi*, awkward. He may babble, too, in his cups, of his coin. He is naturally boastful, and suspicions may be aroused. No, you must not let him out of your sight till he leaves Paris; you must stick to him like his coat. He might even run against Daudet and have an explanation, which would be awkward."

Thus musing, he sallied forth in quest of Ned.

He did not find him in the hotel, but, knowing his haunts, went on to Coney's.

On the way, however he fell in with a friend, who detained him in conversation for some time, and it was upwards of half-an hour since he had parted from Ned before he again set eyes on that worthy.

He found Kelly seated at a little table in Coney's bar, drinking alone, a thing foreign to his habits.

His face was flushed almost to blackness, his eyes bloodshot, and his appearance that of a man labouring under some violently stifled emotion.

He was like a suppressed volcano.

Anatole set this down to hard drinking, consequent upon their recent haul.

Ned seemed to make an effort to recover himself at the sight of the Frenchman.

Anatole, faithful to his plan of not losing sight of Ned, proposed that they should go to the Alcazar that evening after dinner.

Ned consented readily, and the programme was carried out.

Anatole, seated in a fauteuil with the air of a conquering hero, shared his glances between the occupants of the stage and the fairer portion of the audience.

Ned, however, was more abstracted than usual, paid little or no attention to what was going on, and seemed to divide his attention between watching Anatole, and working out some mental problem.

After the performance the pair went into Peters' to sup, and Anatole found himself in such pleasant company, that he announced his intention of not coming home that night at all, a victory of pleasure over prudence that was only accomplished after a struggle.

Ned returned to the hotel alone.

He sat for a long time on the edge of his bed, evidently in deep meditation.

"What an infernal bit of luck," he growled to himself. "I made sure the little beast would have come home, and then I would have tried a dodge of his own on him. However, I'll fix him yet."

Whereupon he turned in, with the door carefully locked, and secured furthermore by a chair-back jammed up under the handle, for Ned was a man of precaution in such matters.

CHAPTER CLXXVI.
MEET ME BY MOONLIGHT ALONE.

ANATOLE came round the next morning.

"Look here," was Ned's greeting, "I've made up my mind to clear out of this crib to-morrow."

The Frenchman's look expressed his satisfaction.

"But I'd like to have a mouthful of fresh air before I start. Couldn't we just run out into the country for a few hours. I'm sick of being penned up here, like a wild bullock in the stock-yard."

He was only partially pleased with this proposal. Kelly's society was not very attractive, and as he had got all he could out of the acquaintance, he would have been glad, as Paddy says, to see "the full front of his back." Nevertheless, it would only be martyrdom for one day, and he would have the huge brute under his eye while he remained in France.

"I must not risk leaving him, as I did last night," was his thought. "I shall only breathe freely when he has left Paris."

Accordingly, after breakfasting together, the pair took their places in a train bound for St. Germain-en-Laye.

Anatole's proposition was that they should spend the afternoon in the forest, and dine in the evening at the Pavilion Henri Quatre.

Ned agreed, with every sign of satisfaction.

The Frenchman's idea of a forest excursion was, however, very different to Ned's.

He insisted, on their arrival at St. Germain, on hiring an open carriage for the purpose.

Ned had to consent, though this had not been his idea of the excursion, and the pair were driven to all the various spots of interest, which Kelly neither noticed nor understood. His thoughts were far from sylvan delights.

They then returned to the town, and were soon seated at dinner in the terraced garden of the Pavilion Henri Quatre, overlooking the Seine.

The evening was a magnificent one.

Ned did ample justice to the champagne, which was about the only wine he could drink, and after a time began to get noisy and opinionated.

At length he declared that nothing would suit him but a pull on the river, which lay like a streak of molten silver before them.

In vain Anatole argued that it was somewhat late.

"An hour's pull in the twilight will do us a world of good," insisted Ned, till his companion was obliged to yield.

There was indeed plenty of time, for the last train did not leave for Paris till half-past eleven.

Accordingly Ned lurched and staggered down to the riverside, followed by the Frenchman, who was more than ever apprehensive that some escapade on Kelly's part might attract the *gens d'armes*, and then who knew what might transpire.

There was not a very great choice of boats, and they had to content themselves with a somewhat cranky but heavy craft, with the oars working on a single thole-pin by an iron ring, such as abound on French rivers.

Anatole knew that Kelly was thoroughly at home in a boat, and too much of a waterman to play any foolish tricks, despite his apparent intoxication.

The result justified his impression.

Kelly took the oars, and, after a little growling at the way in which they were adjusted, began to urge the boat along with powerful strokes.

The mere action of taking them seemed to have sobered him.

He pulled up-stream in the direction of Bourgival.

His manner was glum and abstracted, though from time to time he glanced at the banks or across the surface of the river in an observant fashion.

The night had come on.

The air was heavy, and there seemed every prospect of a storm before morning.

Heavy isolated clouds were floating across the surface of the sky.

From time to time one of them would pass over the surface of the moon, which, round, full, and luminous, shone with a light almost rivalling that of day.

Then an interval of darkness, all the more intense by comparison, would occur.

All was profoundly silent save for the splash of Ned's oar-blades and the ripple of the waters against the side of the boat, which left astern of it that phosphorescent track observable on a hot night.

A short distance above St. Germain the Seine is divided

into two branches by a series of long islands which have been joined artificially.

The right hand arm of the river is a kind of watery no-thoroughfare, all progress after a certain distance being hindered by a dam stretching right across it, over which the stream flows in a miniature cataract.

Up this arm Ned went.

The sense of solitude and silence increased every moment.

On one side was the island fringed to the water's edge by a dense growth of alders and willows.

On the other side the main bank of the river, which here flowed past a stretch of cultivated fields, now quite solitary and deserted.

The spot was a terribly lonely one.

"Eh, my friend?" said Anatole, who, after one or two attempts to engage Ned in conversation, had given it up, and had leant back lazily in the stern of the boat, yielding himself to that pleasurable sense of half-drowsy enjoyment that is apt to steal over a man under such circumstances. "It is getting late. Is it not time to return?"

Ned pulled half a dozen more strokes, and then rested on his oars in silence.

In the still hush of the summer night the only sound that fell on their ears was the faint roar of the cataract, mellowed by distance.

The boat gradually lost the way that was on her, came to a stop, and then began to drift slowly back in the direction in which they had come, for the current was a strong one.

"Come, come," repeated Anatole; "it is getting late."

Ned raised his head and looked the other full in the face.

His own countenance showed white and set in the moonlight, and all traces of the intoxication, real or feigned, under which he had laboured, seemed to have disappeared.

"You needn't be in such an infernal hurry," was his reply. "You've a longer journey before you than you think for."

"What do you mean?"

"Where does this river go to?" asked Ned.

"To Havre," was the somewhat bewildered answer.

"How far is that?"

"I cannot say exactly, some hundred miles. *Allons,*" continued Anatole, who fancied Ned's questions were merely the freaks of a drunken imagination; "pull back quickly, or we shall never get to Paris."

"But you're not going to Paris," answered Ned, and, instead of turning the boat, he gave a stroke or two so as to keep her head up stream.

"What the devil do you mean, *hien?*" said Anatole, in an irritated tone.

"I mean you are going to Havre."

"To Havre! Are you off your head? How?"

"By water," answered Kelly.

"In this boat, monsieur? Come, pull back, and let us get the train," said the Frenchman, who began to feel bewildered.

"No, not in this boat; but by water all the same."

"Come, come, enough of this, monsieur. Explain yourself. What do you mean?" said Anatole, getting rather uneasy.

"I mean, you blasted viper!" yelled Kelly, in quite another tone, "that in two minutes I shall have wrung your neck and pitched you overboard."

Anatole was thunderstruck.

Then the idea suddenly occurred to him that Kelly must have lost his senses.

He knew that the bushranger had been of late leading a much more sedentary life than that which he was accustomed to in Australia, and had also been drinking hard, and he thought he must be in for an attack of d. t.

Half frightened, he resolved to try and humour him a bit.

"Come, Kelly, my boy," he said soothingly, "this is

some mistake. What has crabbed you like this? We're old friends, you know."

"A pretty friend you are, you sneaking thief."

"Me? What's up? What are you driving at?"

"What's up, indeed! Will you explain how it is that if the papers we bagged from the train were only worth fifteen thousand pounds, a reward of twenty thousand comes to be offered for the recovery of 'em?"

Frenchy began to feel rather uneasy. He would rather be out of that boat just then. He looked, as he really was, frightened to death.

"You're a blooming deep 'un," growled Kelly; "but this stretch you ain't a-going to have things quite your own way, as the hedgehog said to the snake when he tried to bolt him whole; not you, my bloomer."

The Frenchman stammered out with an effort, "I really do not understand."

"Stow that. You want to understand, do you. Well, you shall, and a good deal more before we part, you robbing hound. When I left you, feeling that you were not a bad sort to stump up the ready as you did, yesterday afternoon, I went straight round to Coney's. There were some chaps there talking about the railway robbery. 'Those chaps must have got a pretty good haul,' said one. 'Tidyish,' I thinks to myself. 'Over a hundred thousand,' says another. I pricks my ears at this. 'Is that true?' I says to him. 'See for yourself,' he says; 'here's the advertisement in the paper. Bonds to the value of a hundred and eight thousand pounds stolen, and twenty thousand reward for their recovery.' I felt for a moment knocked silly, just as if someone had landed me on the nut with a neddy, and I thought I was going to drop down in a fit."

"Aye, but consider," began Anatole, "the risk——"

"Risk be blowed! There was no risk," cried Ned "I got the fellow to read me the whole boilin'. They offered twenty thousand for the papers, and no questions asked. That, I worked out, would make my share about seven thousand. And you, you mean, pitiful, frog eating, soup-swilling, kangaroo-rat, tried to fob me off with two thousand. I swore I'd pay you out, and I mean to. It was a blessed lucky thing for you that you did not come home last night, or I should have served you the same way you did that foreign cove in London."

Kelly's tone and manner were so unmistakably ruffianly (more so than can be here depicted), that Anatole felt his last hour was come. Trembling in every limb, he abjectly implored Kelly to hear him.

"I'll give you the whole of the swag if you'll only give me a chance to show you what a mistake you've made," and he clasped his would-be executioner's knees.

"Hold off, you snivelling varmint. Do you think I'm going to give you another chance against Ned Kelly? Not for Joe, if I know it. A lot you'd fork up if you got safe ashore, wouldn't you? No," said Kelly, with brutal calmness, "I'm just going to send you to ——, where they're waiting for you, and hounds like you. Dead men tell no tales," and pulling out a pistol he levelled it at the Frenchman, who, in his frightened movements to escape the contents intended for him, nearly overbalanced the boat, which caused the bullet to fly wide of its mark.

Like a flash of lightning the Frenchman sprung over the side of the boat into the water, and dived like a duck, completely escaping from Kelly's view.

The report of the pistol was so loud, that even in his rage Kelly recognised the folly of waking the echoes of the night and alarming the police.

CHAPTER CLXXVII.
A NOVEL SWIMMING MATCH.

THE imminence of the peril, however, nerved him to immediate action.

"Well, I'm sold after all," cried Ned. "I opened my jaw a little too soon. I ought to have put my claws on him before giving him a bit of my mind. Can the swine swim, I wonder?"

He was not long without an answer to this question.

Ten paces or so from the boat down stream, the glittering expanse of the water was suddenly broken by a dark object rising to the surface.

It was the head of Anatole, who was swimming vigourously towards the shore in the moonlight.

Many Parisians are good swimmers, and he had acquired quite a good reputation as a crack practitioner amongst the frequenters of the large floating-baths of the French capital.

Aided by the current, he was making his way famously towards the shore of the island which was the nearest.

"Confound it! he swims like a shark after a nigger," said Ned; "but he's not clear yet."

A couple of powerful strokes shot the boat in the direction of the swimmer.

Just as it reached him Ned sprung up again. and, raising one of the oars, aimed a blow at his enemy's head.

The blow merely fell on the water, which flew up in a shower of glittering pearls.

Anatole had dived again as it descended.

The boat, with the impulse of Ned's strokes still on her, shot past the spot to some distance.

A minute elapsed before Ned could check her way, and bring her round to ascend the stream.

With eager eye he again scanned the surface of the water.

"If the moon goes in," he growled, "it's odds that the varmint gets off after all. It's that feeding on frogs, I shouldn't wonder now, that makes him so precious clever in the water."

The moon, however, continued to shine, though an approaching cloud threatened shortly to veil her glittering disc.

The surface of the stream was again broken about a dozen yards up stream, and Anatole reappeared.

He was striving to gain the yet distant shore, and, at the same time, to make headway against the current which threatened to carry him down towards the boat.

"This time, my bloomer," said Kelly, "I've got you as safe as a tree'd 'possum."

He began once more to urge the boat in the direction of the fugitive.

Anatole was getting spent.

He had managed to kick off his shoes, but he was heavily handicapped by his wet clothes, which were dragging him down, and the two long dives had told on him.

Again the boat came up with him, and Ned raised his oar.

Again he made a desperate effort and dived.

Ned uttered a tremendous oath.

"There's only one way of getting hold of this slippery eel," he muttered.

He felt that if the Frenchman escaped he was done for, as the police would be at once put on his track.

He kicked off his shoes, tore off his coat and waistcoat, and, opening his knife, thrust it in readiness in the waistband of his trousers.

His eye ranged over the expanse of water.

In a few seconds Anatole again emerged from the depths, this time half-suffocated, and breathing heavily.

He was not ten feet off.

Ned plunged into the stream in his turn.

Anatole made another attempt to dive, but before he could do so, Kelly's hand was on his collar.

But the Frenchman clung to Kelly, and dragged him under water; being the better swimmer, he got over Kelly, who was obliged to loose his hold to get to the surface to recover his breath.

Anatole, released for the moment, struck out for dear life. Kelly lost sight of him for a minute or two, but swiftly struck out for him when he discovered his whereabouts. The Frenchman, who was carried along by the current, threw himself on his back, and somewhat recovered from his exhausted and breathless condition.

Kelly rapidly approached him, and just had his grasp upon him when the agile foreigner allowed himself to sink under Kelly, whose feet he grasped, and thus pulled the monster under water, as an Indian would a duck.

The boat had drifted down with the combatants, and when the Frenchman, loosing his hold of his enemy's feet, rose to the surface, he found himself alongside of the boat. He clutched the gunwale and held on, but kept his head only level with the stream, and was thus effectually shielded from the observation of Kelly. who was on the port side.

Kelly, on coming up, looked around in vain for his intended victim, and, as certain people's children have a certain person's luck, just then the moon was obscured by a passing cloud, and, thrusting himself with a vigorous effort from the drifting boat, Anatole made for the shore.

Kelly looked round him in vain. He couldn't discern any object within two feet of him, so dark was the atmosphere at that moment. At this crisis the moon reappeared, and Kelly scanned the waters for his opponent, but saw no signs of the ruffian. With a muttered imprecation he caught the boat, which was drifting his way, and, grasping the tiller, allowed himself to be towed to shore.

"He's sunk to the bottom, and the weeds are settling his hash and saving me the trouble," thought Kelly, as he landed.

After resting on dry land for a few minutes he got into the craft again, and pulled back to look at the scene of the struggle, and for almost a quarter of an hour continued to scan the surface of the river.

There was no trace discernible of his adversary.

At length, fully convinced that Anatole was food for the fishes, he once more headed the boat down stream and began to pull for St. Germain.

After going a certain distance, however, he rested on his oars and began to reflect.

It would never do for him to take the boat back to the place where he had hired it.

His wet nether garments and the absence of his companion, were circumstances that would require to be explained.

His first idea was to pull on shore just above the town and make his way to the railway station, but on second thoughts, he reflected that although his coat and waistcoat had been preserved from the wet, his saturated trousers and the dilapidated condition of his shirt-front, which had suffered in his struggle with Anatole, could not fail to attract attention.

"Confound their lingo," he growled; "if it was England I could easily hash up a yarn to stall 'em off."

Another plan presented itself to his mind, which seemed more appropriate to the situation.

Like many men accustomed to find their way about a scantily settled country, he was a naturally trained topographer.

As if by instinct, he could divine the bearings of one spot in relation to another.

He had marked the direction of the main road to Paris, and resolved to gain this and make his way back to the capital on foot.

In this way all awkward enquiries would be avoided.

Accordingly he resumed his work at the oars and ran the boat ashore on a deserted spot on the further bank, some distance above the town.

After landing, he pushed the little craft out into the stream as far as he could.

A few minutes later he struck the main road, and heading in the direction of Paris, set off at a round pace towards the capital.

CHAPTER CLXXVIII.

ALMOST CAUGHT—A RESURRECTION.

ALTHOUGH the night was young when Ned left St. Germain, and he had only some sixteen miles to cover, the morning was pretty far advanced before he reached the Rue d'Amsterdam.

He had taken his time pretty leisurely over the journey for one thing, and had halted near the fortifications, at a tavern open for carters and market people.

But the delay had been chiefly caused by the fact that though it was very easy for him to find Paris, it was a very different matter for him to make his way to the street of which he was in quest.

Several people to whom he addressed himself could not understand him, and he on his part was equally at a loss as regarded the instructions given him in French.

Hence he wandered about at haphazard for some hours, till he recognised certain landmarks with which he was familiar, and by their aid made his way to the hotel.

He was not over pleased at this delay, as his idea had been to pack up and leave at once with the whole of the stolen bonds before any news of Anatole's "misfortunes" arrived.

He felt under the circumstances that a cautious approach might be advisable.

Just as he was nearing the door he noticed an official-looking person in plain clothes, accompanied by a couple of police in uniform, approaching at a brisk rate in the opposite direction.

He at once faced round towards the nearest shop-front, and became intensely interested in a very elaborate display of marvellously embroidered baby-linen in its windows.

A woman behind the counter, who caught sight of him, took him for a newly-married man, intent upon the purchase of a *layette*, or a benevolent godfather in quest of a christening-robe, and smiled towards him in the blandest fashion.

But whilst pretending to admire the embroidery, Ned was watching the policemen out of the corners of his eyes, and waiting for them to pass by.

He was, however, disagreeably startled to see the official-looking individual enter his hotel, and the two *gardiens* take their stand at the door.

At the same moment two Englishmen were coming out of the hotel, laughing heartily at the enquiry they had heard made, by the official before named, for "Monsieur Tome Smid, of London."

The words acted like an electric shock upon their auditor, who immediately made tracks for the St. Lazare Railway, as he thought the enquiry boded him not much good.

He never thought of his traps in the hotel, and, as he always carried his capital on his person, he was prepared for a start from the post. This said capital he had invested in his own bank, as he styled the leathern waist-belt.

The Gare St. Lazare, the terminus of the Western Railway line, was close at hand.

Entering an outfitter's close by the station, where the announcement, "English spoken," denoted that travellers of that nation could hear their language murdered, on condition of paying about forty per cent. more than a Frenchman would have to pay, Ned bought a travelling rug, a comforter, and a few other necessaries.

He then made his way to the station.

In previous conversations with Anatole, the latter had once explained why he had, when bolting from Paris, chosen the Havre line. It was a less suspected route than the direct one to England *via* Boulogne. Kelly subsequently studied this line, should his visit to the gay capital be suddenly abridged. He had a first rate memory —especially where it was likely to be of importance to his future movements.

He did not feel at all easy in his mind. The police could only have wanted him upon one plea, and that plea could only be advanced by Anatole; and yet Anatole dared say nothing, as he might be caught in the same net. What the deuce they wanted with him, puzzled him sorely. He little suspected that Scotland-yard was in communication with the Paris police, and that his real and assumed names were well known within the last twelve hours.

The police had been hunting every hotel in succession for Tom Smith, and had found several. Indeed, the lists of arrivals are always in the hands of the police shortly after the appearance of the newcomers. The police found plenty of Tom Smiths, and underwent many delays in following up the track of such of our countrymen of that name as bore no resemblance to the personal description in their hands of the real culprit. Thus Kelly only escaped by the skin of his teeth.

Amongst the visitors to the hotel at which he had been staying, was a gentleman whose goings and comings were at one time a matter of considerable interest to the British police.

This was Stephens, the eminent Fenian head-centre, who might sometimes be seen consuming a modest cutlet like any other ordinary mortal, in the little *salle à manger*.

He seemed to be in clover, was well dressed, and generally had two or three "patriots" in his wake. These gentlemen were very outspoken, and the sanguinary Saxon was denounced with an affluence of adjectives more forcible than elegant.

Kelly was sitting rather moodily and anxiously in their vicinity, and happened to ask "whin the staymer started?" with a brogue that instantly recommended him to his listeners.

The violent denunciations continued to pour from the Fenians' lips like lava, and nearly as hot, as from Vesuvius.

Warmed with the few goes of brandy he, like the rest, had imbibed, he exclaimed—

"Why the divil don't you give 'em an ounce of lead?"

It was an instantaneous letter of introduction—he was warmly shaken by the hand—all round.

The whole party retired to the head-centre's room, more glasses were drunk to the good cause, and, before five o'clock in the morning, Kelly was in possession of the Fenian "pass" for Ireland, and was duly sworn in.

But the scoundrel entered the confederacy for two reasons:—firstly, he would be out of danger from detectives; and secondly, if big enough reward was offered— why, he'd think about it. He should like to make another haul before he returned to the bush, which he felt was his natural home.

But to return to Anatole,

After striking out from the boat, as before-mentioned, he managed, half-drowned and wholly exhausted, to reach the shore. Keeping Kelly well in sight, he watched his catching the boat and pulling himself up out of the water, to take another survey of the surface in search of his slippery friend.

Under the shadow of the neighbouring trees, which threw a dark shade over the spot he had reached, he kept perfectly quiet, and at last had the satisfaction of seeing Kelly drift on behind the craft to land. He observed that he again entered the boat and pulled off.

Anatole congratulated himself upon his "narrow squeak," but made up his mind for a due revenge, even if he left Europe and wrote an anonymous letter to the authorities, giving particulars of Ned's hand in the mail robbery, and other items, that would be sure to lead to his apprehension.

But he was not quite sure that Kelly might not contrive to have him arrested with part of the stolen bonds in his possession. This thought made him pause. If he went back to Paris Ned might find him out, and in his hate and desire for vengeance smash him where and whenever he set eyes on him.

He knew the man's savage and reckless character, and trembled when he contemplated their meeting. Would it not be well to go to the police and give information at once against him? He would be handed over, in pursuance of the Extradition Treaty, to the English authorities, and this would not only remove a pressing danger, but give him time to get rid of the bonds, and mature his plans for the future.

Kelly and he could not exist in the same hemisphere. However, his next move was to return to Paris; but this must be done cautiously, and he must reach his quarters unknown to Kelly.

He knew his whereabouts perfectly, and felt that before he could walk to Paris, his clothes would be dry. But then, the walk just at that moment was more than his exhausted powers could accomplish.

He consequently entered a fifth rate *cabaret*, a low drinking shop, boldly said he had swam across the river for a wager, and offered the garçon two francs to enable him to dry his clothes, and provide him with a *chambre à coucher* while that operation was performing.

The wet vestments were soon baked dry on the stove, and in an hour Anatole started off for the Poissy railway, *en route* to Paris.

As he reached it Kelly's train was rolling in an opposite direction slowly through the same station.

A number of passengers were waiting on the platform for the up train to Paris.

Ned was looking out of the window.

He suddenly started to his feet with a very unparliamentary exclamation.

Was it possible? or was it his ghost? No, it could not be. He would never show until his body rose, swollen and distorted, to the surface.

Nevertheless, Anatole it was.

He, at all events, little guessed he had been recognised. He imagined Kelly would think of him as food for the fishes.

Meanwhile Ned was speeding onwards to Havre, and the police were patiently awaiting him at his hotel.

When they got tired of this, they began to suspect he had bolted, and made enquiries at the railway station.

They thought it most probable that he would have gone by Calais and Boulogne, or, at any rate, Dieppe, and hardly thought of Havre.

The arrival in Paris of Anatole, who walked blindly into their clutches, helped to draw off their attention.

Consequently Ned reached that port safely, and, to his great satisfaction, primed by his recent "patriot" friends, took the Southampton steamer.

On arriving there, he found he could go direct to Ireland by sea, and a few hours later was on board the Shamrock, commanded by that most genial of navigators, Captain Murphy, bound for the city of Cork.

Kelly now felt tolerably secure, and smiled as he thought how the gendarmes were "sold."

They were, no doubt, still waiting at the hotel for the return of M. Smid, and would, no doubt, be doing their duty there until they got sick of it.

CHAPTER CLXXIX.
IN IRELAND—THE WARNING.

A patch of wild heath, dotted with furze and thorn bushes, and here and there a pool of black peat water.

All around stretched a bleak and desolate expanse of bog and moorland, bounded by ranges of black hills.

The sun had set.

Daylight was fast fading from the sky, and earth and heaven wore the same grey tint of desolation, whilst the wind came sweeping fiercely down the hillsides, and whistling through the skeleton thorn bushes, full in the teeth of the small party of men making their way in the direction of the hills.

They were four in number.

"Sure, an' it's a mighty fine night for the little matther we have in hand," said one of the foremost, as strapping a young fellow as ever handled a bit of blackthorn, named Micky Linahan.

"Troth, an' it is entirely, Mick," replied one of his comrades; "the laste taste of live coal under the thatch in a wind like this, and the blaze will be illigant."

"Under the thatch, Andy, ye gander? Is it thatch now that the colonel, bad cess to him, has covered his roof with?" broke in a third, with conscious superiority of knowledge.

"Aisy now, aisy, Larry, avick," was the answer; "slate or thatch it'll be all one whin a light's put to it."

"Ah! yondther was the blaze that must have warmed the boys' hearts to see," said Mick, pointing to the crumbling walls of a ruined dwelling on the spur of the hill, towards which they were directing their course.

"'Deed, an' it was so," acquiesced Larry O'Shane.

"When was that?" asked the fourth member of the party, who had not yet spoken.

"Ah, captain, it's forgettin' we are ye're a stranger in these parts. 'Twas the house of the colonel's uncle, and a black and bloody tyrant he was, like all his kin," said Andy Mulvany.

"And who burnt it?" enquired the man addressed as captain, who was no other than Ned Kelly.

"'Twas the Whiteboys, in '98," was the reply. "Many a time I've heard my father tell how they broke down the great door with sledges and axes, and how the wicked colonel—for he was in the army, like his nephew—stood and fought for his life at the head of the stairs. He stood there all alone—for not one of his people would lift a finger to help him—in his scarlet coat, with his sword in his hand, and his long white hair floating behind him. Four of the boys he struck down, and it seemed as if neither steel nor lead could reach him, till his own foster-brother drove a pike into him, and then he fell, and they cut and hacked him till the blood ran from his black heart down into the hall below. An' then the boys fired the place, and it became what you see."

(To be continued.)

NED KELLY
THE IRONCLAD
AUSTRALIAN BUSHRANGER

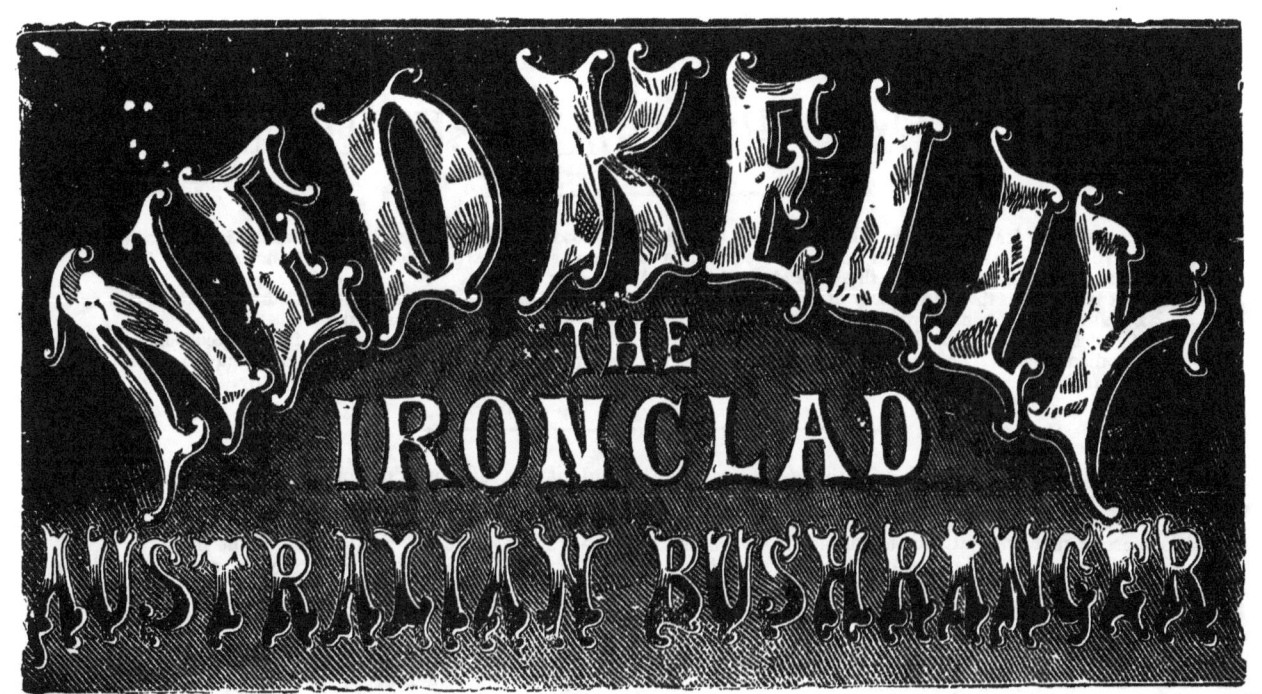

NO 31,

NED KELLY: IRONCLAD BUSHRANGER.

It is well known that for many years Ned Kelly had made himself notorious by a series of crimes wholly incompatible with the civilisation of the nineteenth century. Ned Kelly's celebrated steed, Marco Polo, is as well known at the Antipodes as Dick Turpin's Black Bess in these islands."—*Telegraph*, 7th July, 1881.

"It is notorious that the robbery of Mr. Steward's corpse was mainly performed by the assistance of NED KELLY'S BROTHER, the Captain of what was neither more nor less than a pirate ship."—*Times*, July.

"The history of NED KELLY and his celebrated black horse, Marco Polo, will ever live in the recollection of the Australian public. The deeds of Dick Turpin, and the performances of Black Bess, are tame beside those of 'NED AND HIS NAG;' in addition to which Ned's history is true, and Turpin's is pure fiction."—*Press*, July.

CHAPTER CLXXX.—*Continued.*

About twenty minutes more brisk walking brought them to the scene of the tragedy just narrated.

Half a score of men were already assembled in the ruins.

Amongst them was a sullen looking fellow with fiery red hair, who stood somewhat apart from the rest, leaning his back against the crumbling wall, and scowling on the new comers.

"What is it ails Martin Freeny now?" inquired Linahan of one of the men, who had advanced to meet him.

"Whist! it's just out of all consate with himself, he is. Sure, an' he thought he was goin' to play first fiddle in this matther o' the colonel's, and now here's Captain Kelly sent by the Head Centher to put his purty nose out of joint intirely, the red-headed nagur!"

"The saints be praised! He's been tryin' to crow over the whole bilin' of us for a long time, and his heart's every bit as black as a kitchen chimley that hasn't been swept since the Battle o' the Boyne."

Kelly advanced into the centre of the ruins, and the men, with the exception of Freeny, gathered round him.

"Are the arms all ready?" he asked.

"Yes, captain, jewel," was the answer.

And in a few minutes a number of weapons, produced from a hiding-place in the wall, were distributed amongst the party.

"And now, who amongst you knows the way to the colonel's hut?" inquired the bushranger.

A loud and sneering laugh broke from Freeny at this remark.

"What are you sniggering at?" asked Ned, fiercely, for he guessed that he had, in some way, provoked the other's mirth.

"Och, sure now, and mayn't a man laugh when he likes?" was the sneering reply, at which several of the other men grinned.

"None of your chaff to me, you Murphy-faced moke, or I'll welt that ugly mug of yours until it's as flat as a new shilling," said Kelly, with a ferocity of tone and manner that clearly showed very little would make him put his threat into execution.

Mr. Freeny looked at the powerful frame of the spokesman, and felt it would be more prudent to sing small.

"Come," said Ned, "if the job's to be done, let's do it."

"Maybe ye know the way, and don't want my 'chaff to show you. I suppose, if you're the captain, you'll lade the way?" sneered Freeny.

"Shut up you pot-faced, moth-eaten looking sneak!"

"Howld your whist, Freeny, sure it's the captain you're bothering entirely."

"Och, thin, it's a pity they didn't send someone that knew more about the work he's got in hand. It's a quate thing, now, that the captain shouldn't know his way to the scene of action, when there's not another boy amongst us who could not find his road there blindfolded."

Ere his words had died away, he was lying sprawling on his back from the effect of a heavy "planter" from Kelly on his jaw.

"Pick him up, or kick him up, some of you," said Ned;

"and let me tell you I'm not going to stand any of that sort of game. How long will it take us to get to the colonel's?"

"A good half-hour," replied one of the men.

"Very well," said Ned, consulting his watch; "a friend, you know, has promised to meet us there half an hour after midnight. It's only half-past ten, so we've got nearly an hour and a half to wait. We may as well settle down and have a drop of whisky."

Accordingly the men made themselves comfortable.

"It's an illigant fist the captain has," observed O'Shane to Mulvany.

"Indeed, an' it is, and the saints presarve my face from being better acquainted with it," was the reply.

Colonel Townshend, to whom Ned and his friends purposed to pay an uninvited visit that night, was a wealthy landed proprietor of the district.

He was a man of about fifty, slightly severe in manner, but frank, open, and entirely unprejudiced, save as regarded his dealing with his tenants.

The terrible fate of his uncle had had an effect upon him, which nothing could remove.

He had grown to regard his Irish tenants as a set of bloodthirsty and vindictive savages, whom it was no earthly use in striving to conciliate.

For eleven months or so out of the year he was an absentee, and during this period they were delivered over to the tender mercies of his agent, a rasping, blue-nosed Presbyterian from the "Black North," named M'Guire.

The tender mercies of the wicked are, we know, cruel, but it is to be doubted, after all, if they are not preferable to the tender mercies of one of the "unco' guid," and such was M'Guire, who, as one of the "elect," seemed to hold it his bounden duty to make earth as much like a hell as possible for all he was brought into contact with.

His argument was, that as nine thousand nine hundred and ninety men out of ten thousand are doomed by predestination to perdition, such a course of action is a positive kindness to them, as it prepares them for their future state, and, as it were, serves to let them down by degrees.

Between him and the colonel, who put perfect trust in him, the tenants had rather a hard time of it, and compared their situation to that of the man between the devil and the deep sea.

At first they had tried shooting M'Guire, but three successive attempts had only resulted in putting a bullet through his hat, blowing off one of his sandy side-whiskers, and killing his horse.

And, as the three men who had made the successive attempts had all been caught, they began to think that, after all, the providence he was so fond of canting about must really watch over him, or that he had sold himself to the devil for a charm to render his carcase bullet-proof.

In the secret council presided over by "Rory of the Hills," or "Captain Moonlight," or "Molly Maguire," or whoever else presided over the Agrarian Inquisition, the colonel had been tried, and sentenced as a bad landlord; and "justice to Ireland" was to be propitiated by his death. Lots had been drawn, and the party now on the way to his house, were the assassins chosen, and bound, under pain of assassination themselves, to carry out the murderous decree.

The colonel, however, only came to his Irish estate to shoot for a month or so every year.

He had always refused to rebuild the manor house which had been burnt on the night of his uncle's murder, and contented himself with a small stone building, which he had furnished as a shooting-box, and which stood at some little distance from the ruins of the former dwelling.

He was sitting in the parlour in company with his nephew and son-in-law, about an hour after Ned's arrival at the ruins, and just thinking of going to bed, when his nephew's valet entered the room, and announced that a man wanted to see him on very important business.

"What is it, Simmons?" he asked.

"He won't say, sir," was the reply; "except that he must see you at onct."

"Go and ask him what he wants. It is just like these Irish fellows to come pestering one at this time of night, with some cock-and-bull story of a grievance against M'Guire," he continued.

After a few minutes' absence the valet returned.

"He won't say what he wants, sir; all I can get from him is that he must see you yourself, sir, and that it's a matter of life and death."

"Perhaps you'd better see him," suggested the colonel's son-in-law, Mr. Blamire; "it may be something to do with the Fenian business we hear so much of."

"Hum—yes; well, show him in, Simmons."

"He won't come inside the house, sir; he's standing outside the door, and says he'll speak to you if you'll come down to him."

"Confound his impudence! let him go to the devil, then!" cried the exasperated colonel; "does he think I'm at his beck and call?"

"I'll go and see what he wants," said Harold Townshend, the colonel's nephew.

The colonel gave a gruff assent, and the young man went to the front door, his uncle calling after him as he went along the passage—

"Look out you don't get shot, Harold!"

Harold started when he saw the strange guest who was standing about four paces from the door.

His hat was pulled down over his brows, and a handkerchief tied about the lower part of his face, so as to entirely hide his features.

"What is it you want?" asked Harold, keeping a wary eye on the fellow, lest he should draw a weapon.

"Are ye the colonel?" was the reply, in a voice evidently feigned.

"I am his nephew; but I represent him. What is your errand?"

"My errand is, to warn you and yours that in about half an hour's time those will be here who will serve him and all who are of his kin, as his uncle was served."

"Thanks for the warning," replied the young man, who half suspected some hoax; "but we have strong bolts and bars, and plenty of powder, and your friends may reckon on a warm reception."

"Look well to both, for there's bitther treachery amongst ye," was the reply, and, as he spoke, the stranger turned to go.

"Treachery, how?"

"That ye must find out for yourself. You've had the warning, so you can't complain."

"But, who are you? Why do you warn us?"

"No friend of yours, but an enemy of your enemies," and, turning abruptly, the stranger strode off without further parley, and was soon lost sight of in the darkness.

On Harold returning to his uncle, and communicating this intelligence to him, the colonel was at first inclined to treat the matter as a joke, a mere attempt to scare him.

"The fellows could not, however, have chosen a better night," observed Mr. Blamire, "since most of the servants are away at the fair."

"You are right; there may be something in that," replied Harold.

In fact, all the servants employed about the place indoors—namely, the butler who acted as the general's valet, the cook and two girls, together with Mr. Blamire's man and the grooms, had started off at nightfall, by permission, to a fair and a dance held in the neighbourhood.

Simmons and a scullion were the only attendants left in the house.

"If you'll just give an eye to the fastenings, Harold," said Blamire, "I will have a look at the fire-arms."

The house was of stone, and very solidly built.

The lower windows, in addition to thick shutters, were protected by iron bars of immense strength, and the upper ones were also grated.

The front door, which was plated inside with sheet-iron, was almost as strong as that of a jail.

That in the rear of the house, however, though of massy construction, was not quite so impenetrable.

After making an inspection of the upper story, Harold descended to the lower part of the dwelling.

The windows were all secured, as was the front door.

To his astonishment, however, he found that, although the back door was locked, the bolts were not shot, neither was the key in the lock.

He asked the scullery maid the meaning of this.

"Sure," said the girl, who was almost half-witted, "Mr. Rooney tuck it wid him to the dance to let himself in wid the rest of 'em when they came back."

The answer was satisfactory enough, but after sending the girl to bed at the top of the house, and locking her in her room, Harold took care to shoot the bolts of the back door.

"When Rooney and the rest come back they must knock," he observed. "I wish he had not gone, though."

Rooney the butler was an old servant, greatly trusted and esteemed by the colonel.

When Harold returned from his tour of inspection to the sitting-room, he found his uncle and Blamire looking far more serious than when he had left them.

"Have you any cartridges in your room, Harold?" asked the latter, somewhat anxiously.

"Yes."

"Will you go and get them?"

"Are there not plenty in the gun-room with the guns?" said Harold, rather astonished.

"Go and see about yours, there's a good fellow."

Harold was absent some time on this errand, and they heard him call Simmons.

At length he returned to the sitting-room.

"I can't make it out," he said. "I had a lot of cartridges in my drawers, both for my gun and revolver, and I can't find one of them. Simmons declares he saw them in the drawer only this morning."

The colonel and Blamire exchanged glances.

"This is a nastier affair than I thought for, Harold," said the former, gravely.

"What is the matter?"

"We have no ammunition in the house!"

"What?"

"Every cartridge in the gun-room and in Blamire's room, has disappeared!"

"But there is a lot of powder. Can't we make up some at once?"

"There's not an ounce of it fit for use. Some treacherous devil has wetted the lot."

Harold stood quite appalled at this statement.

"The fellow was right about treachery; but who the devil can it be? Simmons is an Englishman and there is no one else in the house, excepted that half-witted girl, Aileen."

"It must be one of the others."

"But who? Blamire's man is English, and Rooney I would trust with my life ten times over. He is one of those old family retainers who continue the tradition of

Caleb Balderstone and who look upon the head of the house as a kind of deity."

"Yes," assented the colonel, "he is a regular servant of the old school."

"It must be one of the womenfolk," said Blamire, "who has been talked over by a Fenian sweetheart."

"But is there not a bit of ammunition fit for use in the place?" cried Harold.

"Not a charge," replied his uncle, gravely; "even the guns in the gun-room have all been unloaded."

"Good heavens!" gasped Blamire. "are we to be butchered here like rats in a trap? Can't we get away?"

"Impossible! They would track us, and shoot us down like rabbits."

"There is only one thing," said the colonel, "to die as my uncle died—firm to the last amongst these treacherous devils. We must trust to cold steel, not to save, but to avenge us ere we fall, on some of the scoundrels at least."

At that moment Simmons entered the room.

"I fancied, as I was putting away your things, sir," he said, with the bland manner of a well-trained domestic, and as though quite oblivious of the peril in which they one and all stood, "that I felt some loose cartridges in the pocket of your grey jacket."

As he spoke, he placed half a dozen oblong rolls on the table.

"Bravo!" exclaimed the colonel, with a flash of youthful energy; "six shots are six men's lives. There's a chance of beating them off, after all. Out with the lights, and let us hold ourselves in readiness. Hark! I think I hear the tramp of footsteps!"

CHAPTER CLXXXI.
THE NIGHT ATTACK—THE TRAITOR'S FATE.

SHORTLY before midnight Ned gave the signal to his followers to assemble.

"It's about time to start," he remarked; "but before we are moving. I may as well see if we are all to the fore. Helloa! where's Martin Freeny?" repeated Ned. "Have any of you seen Martin Freeny?"

The men glanced at one another.

"Faith! the last time I set eyes on him," said Linahan, "he was sitting just beyant the bit o' wall there, with his jaw in his hand, cursing to himself, and looking just as black as a crow on a coffin."

"Martin Freeny!" shouted Ned again.

"Well, here I am," said that individual, stepping from behind a wall into the centre of the group.

"Why didn't you answer?"

"Answer! it's no aisy matter to answer at all, whin me jaw works as stiffly as a gun-spring that's been lying buried in a bog for a twelvemonth. But I had just stepped down to the little brook beyond to dip my handkercher in water, and tie round it to ease the swellin' that's murderin' me intirely."

Freeny's handkerchief was, in fact, tied round the lower part of his face, so as to conceal it.

"Well, are we all ready now?" asked Ned.

"Yes—all."

"It's too easy work for me," said Ned; "it's like knocking down a bullock tied up in a stockyard. Well, no matter; it will soon be over, as the arms have been made snug. Push along, and finish it!"

Bent on their murderous errand, the little troop swiftly and silently made their way onwards along the hillside, to the home of Colonel Townshend.

They approached it from the rear, moving across the ground as noiselessly as ghosts.

A short distance from the house a figure rose suddenly from the earth, and advanced to meet them.

"Is that you, Darby?" said Mulvany, who was acting as guide to the party.

"Yes, Andy; is the captain wid you?" was the reply.

"Here I am," said Ned; "is it all right?"

"I think we'd better wait a little bit, captain: sure they have not long gone to bed. I have been watchin' and waitin' here the last half-hour. I could not get away from the dance before, and the lights have only just been put out in the house."

"Did you notice anything at all?"

"Well, when I first got here, the lights seemed to be moving about upstairs and downstairs as if they were a bit uneasy. We'd better give 'em time to get fast asleep."

After waiting the time indicated, the party resumed their advance towards the house, which was all dark and silent.

Like shadows they glided softly up to the back door.

"You've got the key?" whispered Ned, to the man who had met them.

"Yes," answered Darby, "and the lock is greased like Micky Oulaghan's head on Sunday."

As he spoke he inserted the key in the lock.

The well-oiled wards obeyed its pressure, and yielded without resistance, and the bolt of the lock shot back with only the faintest possible click.

Darby pushed the door gently.

It was immovable.

He pushed harder, with the same result.

"Oh! murther!" he muttered. in amazement.

"What is it?" whispered Ned.

"Sure, some murtherin' fool—it must be that pryin idiot of a Simmons—has been and shot the doorbolts."

Kelly looked simply disgusted.

"What's to be done?" asked Linahan.

"Let us burst the door in," suggested O'Shane.

"And rouse 'em up, that they may be pepperin' at us all the time out of the window," protested Mulvany.

"No fear of that at all," chuckled Darby; "the devil an ounce of powther have they to pepper with. I took care of that."

"Sure and you're a born giniral, Darby," was the reply whispered at this encouraging announcement.

"There's a quieter way than that," said Ned, and as he spoke he produced an implement from his pocket. "Look here, here is a centre-bit that will go through oak as a knife goes through a pat of butter."

And he held up one of the finest implements of the kind that the virtuous town of Birmingham ever supplied a burglar with.

"Is the door lined with iron?" he asked Darby.

"No, glory be to God!"

"Where are the bolts?"

"One at the top and the other at the bottom."

"Then I'll cut two holes, and you can slip your hand through and draw them back."

Ned set to work to cut the lower hole, whilst the others stood round in silent admiration at the device which was new to them.

The instrument made very little noise while biting its way into the wood.

It was a considerable time before the hole near the bottom, which was the first selected, was completed.

Those inside, in perfect darkness, divined what was going on, and were fully prepared to frustrate it. They at first feared fire, but that was not an easy weapon to employ upon stone walls and oak doors The working of the drill was perfectly audible. The sound could not be mistaken. The colonel's nephew quickly withdrew and returned with a lantern covered with a cloth to conceal the light He had also a slip-knot rope. With terrible anxiety they listened to the progress that was made and the suppressed whisperings outside.

At last it was done.

"Put your hand through and pull the bolt," said Ned to Darby, "you know best where to feel for it."

He put his hand carefully through the hole, and began to grope for the bolt.

The light from the lantern was turned close on the opening. And there was a hand wobbling about in search of the bolt. While thus engaged, the slip-knot, which was greased to make it run easily, was quietly and quickly thrown over and pulled tightly with a sudden jerk, round the intruding wrist. A loud cry of pain and alarm followed, with frantic efforts to pull the hand away from the hole. So furious and reckless were those attempts that the flesh was almost cut to the bone. Tight hold was maintained by the rope-holder, who even pressed his foot upon the knot to keep it from slacking in the least.

"Holy Vargin!" he gasped, in low, horror-stricken tones, "what's this now?"

"What is it?" said Ned.

"My hand's caught," replied **Darby**, forcing the words with an effort through his white and quivering lips.

"Well, pull it out, you omadhaun."

"But I can't, they've got it in a slip-knot. Och, I'm murdhered intirely, that's what I am. Och, masther, jewel, colonel, agrah! Sure it's Darby Rooney that's being forced into this by the blackguards, yur honer. Sure you'll let me go an' loose the rope. Don't I know the family since you were a gossoon, and it's not Darby that would harm one of them."

"You infernal scoundrel," echoed the voice of the enraged colonel, "I wouldn't remove it if it was round your neck, and I'll take good care you shall feel it there yet."

"Arrah, don't be hard on a poor boy, colonel. Sure they pushed my hand through the hole, bad luck to them. Oh, wirrasthrue! wirrasthrue, and the masther, too, I'd die for," whimpered and whined the frightened villain.

"Let him go, colonel," cried a strange but steady voice outside, "and we will leave you at once. You've fairly won the game, and I'm ——— if I don't like one who's real grit."

"You vagabond," was the answer, "we've got a witness against you and your gang, and intend to keep him dead or alive."

"He can't be much of a witness, I'm thinking," replied one of the gang, "if we stop here much longer." There was a significant threat in this remark that made Darby's knees knock together.

"Tell him you'll burn the stables and farm-buildings, if he won't act like a Christian, and let me go," whispered Darby in agonised tones to Ned.

Ned cried out, "He's not worth the cost of the outbuildings, colonel. I'll fire then, if he's not free in five minutes."

"Fire and be ———," shouted the colonel, "the blaze will be a beacon to the police; I wish to heavens you would. I'd sacrifice every brick in the place to see you devils with the handcuffs on."

"Arrah, don't be so like a haythen, masther, dear," groaned Darby. "Let me go for the love o' God, and I pray for you every night an' mornin'."

"Come, come," said Kelly, impatiently, "we've had enough of this. One way or the other, we must finish this little job."

"Oh, thin," cried another, "I'm afeered Darby's prayers are like the judge's, when he puts on the black cap—they won't do any poor boy much good."

The Irish would enjoy a joke in the jaws of death.

At this moment a shot rang out from an upper window and one of the Fenians dropped with a low groan.

Ned and his followers opened a scattering and random fire in reply, but without the least effect, while Rooney shivered and shook, and moaned as he cowered down by the back door, his hand as fast as if in Milo's oak.

Another shot from the house hit its mark, the victim this time being Freeny, who thus paid dearly for the warning he had given Harold.

Freeny would not have been present, but he feared the penalty of absence.

Doubly unnerved by this reception, after the assurance they had had that there was no powder whatever in the house, the panic-stricken assailants broke, and the majority retreated, carrying their wounded, and sought shelter behind some outbuildings from further shots.

Ned, however, remained close to the door, where, owing to the projection of the porch, it was impossible for a shot to reach him from the windows.

He had caught hold of the arms of Linahan and Mulvany, and obliged them to remain with him.

"Look here," he said, hurriedly, "there's no chance of this job being done to-night; but there's one thing we must do—we must take care of our necks, and to do so we can't leave a witness behind us, and especially this one, who'd sell us like pigs to the butcher."

"What d'ye mane?" said Mulvany, with a frightened, awe-struck air. "Is it murdher you'd be afther doing upon a poor innocent boy? Howly mother! have yis no conscience?"

"I've a neck which is a blooming sight to me more than anybody's conscience, and, if you don't care for your carcase swinging in the morning air, I do, that's all."

Mulvany seemed struck with the force of Ned's logic. He scratched his head in his perplexity, and quietly said to Rooney—

"Darby, jewel, as yis can't have a priest, maybe ye remeraber a bit of a prayer that's handy to ye."

"Oh! praying to the colonel, is it? You might as well pray to the rock o' Cashel, an' you'd move it just as soon."

"Haven't you ne'er a patrynoster convanient?"

"What for?"

"Because, you see, Darby avick, your present position is neither convanient for you nor for us, and we'll relave you of it as soon as you're ready and willin'," said Mulvany, in tones intended to be soothing and tender.

"Then be quick about it, Jimmy Mulvany, for the hand is nearly cut off me, and I'm dying with pain. Oh! don't leave me here behind."

"'Deed an' we won't, Darby, no fear. We won't leave you behind—alive."

"Mother o' Mercy! what d'ye mane?" was the frightened reply, gasped out with difficulty.

"In the name of all the saints in the calendar, Darby, try the laste taste of a bit of a prayer."

"Let me out, ye brute bastes!" roared Rooney, now guessing the dreadful intention of his associates. "If you don't take me wid ye I shout out all your names, this blessed minute, to the colonel!" roared the frightened wretch.

Ned and the others now clearly saw there was no time to be lost.

He looked at Mulvany and nodded.

"What's that ye're saying?" said Darby, whose ears, sharpened by terror, had caught some of their words.

"Whist! whist! never mind!" said Mulvany, and he added to Kelly, "Must it be done?"

"Of course; there's no other way."

"I suppose not; poor craythur."

"What are you whispering about?" said Darby; "why don't you cut another hole in the door and set me free?"

"Faix, Darby darlin', I'm afeard that same's impossible," said Linahan, gravely.

"But you're not going to leave me here?" said the prisoner, "to be caught by the murtherin' colonel?"

"Oh! have no fear, you'll not be caught alive."

Darby made a desperate effort to free himself, but had to leave off, moaning with pain.

"The rope has cut to the bone," he groaned.

"Are ye sure ye can't get loose at all?" said Linahan, "make another try for it."

"Darby, ye know the oath you swore when you joined us, that you'd give yourself up body and sowl to the cause?"

"Yes, but not be caught like a hare in a trap."

"Well, you are caught, and it won't do for your own sowl's sake, let alone for our necks, to risk breaking that oath. You might be tempted to do it if the colonel talked to you to-morrow; and where wud your sowl go to then?"

"The devil a word they'd ever get out of me, if you'll

just be off and let the colonel take me inside. Say the word, Mulvany, or I'll give your names out now."

"Settled the job?" growled Kelly. "Do you think I'm going to trust my neck to that hound?"

"Captain, jewel," almost screamed the unfortunate villain, making a last effort for his life, his eyes starting from their sockets, his hair on end, and perspiration bursting from every pore, "for the sake of the mother that bore ye, spare me, and I'll kiss the Book and swear that the devil a word they'll ever get from the lips of Darby Rooney, but a blessing upon you, captain, dear."

"You'd better make your pace up there," said Mulvany, with that strange perversion of thought which belongs alike to the Irish and Italian lower classes. An Italian brigand robs and murders with an image of the Virgin in his hat, and often a crucifix on his breast

"It's no use," said Kelly. "Go to work, or I will."

Seeing the hopelessness of the situation, and thinking as a last chance to scare the marauders from the scene, Darby roared out the names of the gang.

His cries rang through the silent night.

"Help, help! Save me, colonel, darlint! They're goin' to murther me out o' the world entirely! For pity's sake, for mercy's sake!—Andy, avick! Micky, jewel! Spare me—spare me! Bad luck to the word I'll even breathe! Oh, you won't, ye murthering villyans!"

And he repeated the names of the gang for the information of the besieged.

He sealed his fate at once.

Still his screams rang out with fearful distinctness in the night, scaring the night-birds on the hill, and causing the blood of the little garrison inside the house to run cold in their veins with horror.

To sally forth, however, in order to attempt to rescue the poor wretch from his fate would have only been fatal to themselves, as they would have had an overwhelming force, with only four shots left amongst them.

One shrill cry, more wild and despairing than the rest, pealed forth and pierced their ears.

There was a loud report from a pistol, which was fired by the bushranger, then the sound of retreating footsteps.

A faint, dripping sound, like the plash of falling water on the stone door-sill without, followed.

After being fully satisfied of the retreat of the gang, the door was opened, and lying stone dead, weltering in his blood, with his brains scattered over the doorsteps, and trickling down them, lay the corpse of the trusted butler, Darby Rooney.

CHAPTER CLXXXII.
THE MIDNIGHT STRUGGLE.

IT was past midnight, and most of the streets of the little town of Clanturk was wrapped in silence and darkness.

The sky was starless and threatening, the air heavy and oppressive as if laden with a coming storm.

The majority of the inhabitants had long since retired to rest, and were probably dreaming of some happy future when potatoes should grow spontaneously and rent be a thing unknown.

A light, however, streamed through the open door of a little public house, situate near the outskirts of the town, and fell upon a small group of people gathered in the roadway around the prostrate figure of a man.

"It's his change he has, sure," observed one of the bystanders, scrutinising the fallen man, who was apparently insensible, with an enquiring look.

"Faix, an' he has that same," said a second. "It's yerself that has basted him finely, Rory," he continued, addressing a powerful young fellow, who was putting to rights such of his clothes as had been disarranged in the struggle that had evidently just taken place between himself and the overthrown champion.

"If he hasn't enough, I can just stretch a point and oblige him with a little taste more," answered Rory, grimly.

A young girl who was standing beside him said in a somewhat compassionate tone—

"Sure, ye're not goin' to let the poor crathure lie tnere now, are ye?"

"Oh! make yerself aisy," replied Rory: "divil a bit o' harm will he come to, by slapin' out o' doors in this hot weather. It's mighty fine for ye to be consarnin' yerself with his comfort, when it's thanks to yer airs that he's got the dressin' he has."

"But, Rory, darlin,' sure ——"

"Sure, an' if I hadn't had my eyes on ye all the time. It it hadn't been for yer deludherin' ways, I misdoubt me if this had ever happened this night. But come away home at wunst, Ally, I'm not goin' to sthand coolin' my heels here till some murtherin' peeler lays me by them. Good night to all of ye."

So saying, he took the girl by the arm and hastened off, whilst the others raising the fallen man carried him indoors and strove to restore him to his senses.

Rory and Ally O'Hara were brother and sister, and occupied a small holding some distance from the town.

The injured man, Terence Reardon, was a neighbour of theirs in a somewhat better position.

For some time past an ill feeling had been growing up between the two men, originating out of an act of trespass committed by Reardon's cattle, and since fostered by various trifles.

On the present occasion they had met at a quiet bit of merrymaking given by the landlord of the public, and had remained with a few other guests somewhat late.

Terence had taken upon himself to pay a little attention to Ally, which the girl, from sheer coquetry, had rather encouraged than otherwise, and the result had been a furious quarrel between the two men, and a struggle in which he had got the worst of it.

Hardly had Rory and Ally moved away than Reardon recovered himself and opened his eyes.

"The black-hearted thraitor, where is he?" was his first remark, as he glanced around him fiercely.

"Aisy, Terry, aisy now," exclaimed old Peter Driscoll, the landlord; "sure an' he's gone long since."

"Gone, gone, the coward, after strikin' me down before I had time to be on my guard. Give me a sup of whisky, Peter, and I'll be after him, the mane thafe, in a twinklin'."

"It's mad ye must be, Terry, to think o' runnin' after him with a rap on the head like that he gave ye, and a storm comin' on every minute."

As he spoke, a bright flash of lightning leaped from the sky, and was followed by a peal of thunder.

"Devil a bit will a storm stay me. Quick, a taste o' the crather now," and, hastily draining the glass offered him, Reardon darted out of the house, and was soon lost in the darkness that enwrapped everything.

Meanwhile Rory and Ally had proceeded some distance on their way home.

They had left the town and had advanced some distance along the road leading towards their dwelling.

They were approaching a bridge crossing a broad, deep, and rapid stream.

Suddenly Rory halted and listened.

"Who can it be runnin' along after us?" he said, and turning round he peered into the darkness.

At that moment the storm that had been threatening suddenly burst upon them, and the rain began to come down in torrents.

"Come along, Rory, come along now," cried Ally, "it's drenched to the skin we'll be, an' ye sthandin' there like a fool in the middle o' the road."

"Hold yer tongue now," cried Rory, as a sudden flash of lightning revealed a figure rapidly approaching in the direction from which they had come.

Rory advanced a few steps towards it, and, when some ten paces separated them, cried out:

"Who are ye, and what is it ye want?"

"I want to end the little matther ye began at Pether

Driscoll's, ye villain," was the answer, in a voice hoarse from rage and exertion.

"Terry!" cried Rory and Ally, simultaneously, and the former added in a threatening tone—

"So it's a bit more ye want, do ye? So much the worse for ye, my jewil."

As he spoke he gave his stick a scientific twirl.

"Ye're a black-hearted coward, Rory O'Hara," said Reardon, slowly, as he paused to recover himself before advancing to attack his foe, "and sthruck me down unfair. It's payin' ye out I mane this time."

"If ye come within reach o' my stick, I'll settle ye entirely, and now ye're warned," replied Rory.

"We'll see that same. I give ye lave to break ivery bone in me skin if ye can, for I'm not goin' to spare yours."

"Come on, and don't sthand pratin' thin."

The two men rushed upon each other.

The rain was coming down in a perfect deluge, and save for the flashes of lightning, which lit up the scene at rare intervals, the darkness was Egyptian.

From out this darkness came the sounds of the bitter struggle, the sharp clatter of the blackthorns as they met one another in a parry, the duller sound of wood alighting on flesh and bone that marked when a blow had gone home, and an occasional exclamation of pain, or rage, or triumph from one of the combatants.

Both men were expert stick players, but the darkness rendered their skill of little use, and it was by chance that each got home from time to time.

Ally, standing at a little distance, in vain strove to make out which of the two was getting the best of it in this strange encounter.

"Holy mother, look down on us," she murmured.

All at once the sticks met in full swing with such violence that Rory's was sent flying from his hand some yards away into the darkness.

Before Reardon, however, could profit by this to deal a finishing blow, his foe sprang upon him and clutched him fiercely by the throat.

He gripped it with all the energy of desperation.

In a few seconds Reardon was half choked, but, by a violent effort, he shook off his adversary, as a bull shakes off a dog, and drew back a step or two to recover the breath that had been squeezed out of him by the other's fingers.

O'Hara had almost lost his footing from the jerk with which his opponent had freed himself from his clutch, but, recovering himself, glanced round in search of his stick or some similar weapon, but in vain.

Ally suddenly seized him by the arm.

"Run for it, Rory, darlint!" she exclaimed, pulling him towards the bridge. "It's aither murtherin' ye he is, the gandther-faced desaver! Run for it!"

O'Hara followed her advice.

"Come on, ye dirty spalpeen," shouted Reardon, who, in the darkness, did not at first notice the other's retreat, covered as it was by the roar of the tempest.

Rory and Ally had gained the beginning of the bridge, a long and narrow wooden structure, protected only by a handrail.

"Come on," cried Ally; "he is close behind."

"Ah! ye're runnin', are ye, ye coward?" cried Terry, who now perceived their flight. "Just wait till I come up with ye, that's all."

And, bounding after the fugitives, he overtook them on the centre of the bridge.

Pushing Ally behind him, O'Hara awaited his attack, since it was impossible for him to avoid it.

Dashing furiously onward in the darkness, with upraised hand, Terry rather overshot the mark.

Before he could well recover himself, Rory had seized him sharply by the arm, and had torn his stick from his grasp by a sudden wrench.

Ere he could himself make use of it, however, he was gripped in turn by Reardon, and another struggle ensued.

Each man strove his very utmost to gain possession of the weighty blackthorn.

The rain continued to pour down, and it was with difficulty that they could keep their footing on the wet planks of the bridge.

"I'll smash ye to smithereens before I've done with ye, ye black-avized murtherer!" cried Terry.

"Plaze God, I'll fit ye for yer coffin first," was the defiant reply of O'Hara.

Reardon made a tremendous jerk at the stick, and tore it from his adversary's grasp, the shock at the same time causing Rory to fall forward on his knees.

Clutching O'Hara by the collar and holding him in that position with one hand, and raising the weapon with the other, Terry cried, in triumphant tones—

"By the powers! it's a pity the night's so black, for it's the colour of yer blood I'm goin' to find out now."

For a moment Rory thought himself lost.

All at once an idea struck him, and he threw his arms round Terry's knees with a vigorous jerk.

Taken by surprise, Reardon lost his balance, released Rory's collar, and fell heavily backwards across the parapet of the bridge, which he seized with one hand, and strove to raise himself.

O'Hara felt that his life depended upon the events of the next moment.

Assembling all his strength in one mighty effort, he succeeded in hoisting his opponent clean over the parapet of the bridge.

"Mother of Heaven, have mercy!" gasped Reardon, as he swung above the roaring torrent of the river, clutching the parapet with his hands, from which the stick had fallen into the water.

The parapet consisted of a top rail about waist high, supported by a row of uprights some six feet apart, between each of which two other beams were placed diagonally, so as to cross each other in the form of a letter X.

It was one of these crosses that Reardon had managed to lay hold of.

His hands could hardly retain their hold on the wet and slippery wood, and he strove in vain to dig his nails into it as the wind seized his body and swung him, like the corpse of a hanged man, over the dreadful gulf below.

He was strong, however, and the danger in which he found himself gave him additional strength.

After a terrible effort, he succeeded in clasping both his hands round one of the diagonal beams, and in joining them in a firm grasp.

Grasping the beam like a vice he strove to hoist himself up again.

O'Hara, exhausted by the struggle, leant for a minute or two in a breathless state against the parapet over which he had cast his adversary.

The reaction was so great that for a short time he almost lost consciousness.

Suddenly Ally's voice falling on his ear aroused him from his semi-stupor.

"The saints in heaven be praised! Ye're safe, Rory. Come home at once, darlin'! For mercy's sake, come home!"

CHAPTER CLXXXIII.
A MOST WELCOME VISITOR.

IN the darkness of the night neither Rory nor his sister saw that Reardon was still clinging desperately to the parapet of the bridge just below them.

Amidst the wild tumult created by the wind and rain they thought that he had fallen headlong into the stream.

Rory uttered a sigh, half of relief and half of horror, and was about to move away.

All at once he staggered.

Reardon had been able to make out that his foe had not changed his position.

Summoning all his energies, and nerved to exertion by a wild hope of revenge, he hung for a moment by one hand.

and, thrusting the other through the interstices of the parapet, gripped Rory by the leg, round which he succeeded in throwing his arm.

Thus assailed, Rory clutched the hand-rail firmly with one of his hands, and struck at his enemy to make him leave go with the other.

"Ye'll either have to pull me up or go down with me," gasped Reardon, tightening his grip.

The frightful struggle recommenced with all its terrible accompaniments.

The rain descending in hissing showers drove into the faces of the combatants with such force as almost to blind them; the wind threatened at times to tear them both from the bridge and plunge them into the stream, and the flashes of lightning from time to time shewed the situation in all its horrors.

Reardon still clung despairingly to Rory's leg, which, jammed as it was by his weight hanging to it against the cross-beams, was in danger of snapping like a pipe stem at any moment.

Maddened by this peril and by the pain he suffered, O'Hara leaned over the parapet as far as he dared and kept striking at the top of his adversary's head in order to make him relinquish his grasp.

Reardon's scull, however, was a thick one, and had undergone a pretty good training for such a state of things in the shape of a long series of raps with a stick in many a faction fight, and Rory began by experience to learn the truth of that axiom, known to every old ring-goer, that "the hand is softer than the head."

Moreover, jammed as he was against the parapet, O'Hara could not lean over far enough to make his blows tell with good effect.

Ally was roused to action by her brother's peril.

She had taken part in more than one fight and did not shrink now.

Kneeling down on the bridge, she struck fiercely at the hand with which Terry gripped the cross-beam with the heel of one of her heavy brogues, which she had taken off for the purpose.

A groan of mingled pain and horror escaped the poor wretch at this fresh assault.

The sight revealed by the flashes of lightning was a horrible one.

Rory's face was white with passion, save where it was stained with the blood that his exertions had caused to flow from his nose, and his collar was rent away, and displayed his bare chest similarly stained, despite the torrent of rain with which he was inundated, as he continued to lean over the parapet and strike at his foe.

Ally, on her knees by his side, her hair unbound, and hanging in tresses like wet serpents about her face, her eyes aglow, and her teeth gleaming between her parted lips, hammered away at Reardon's hand with her shoe.

On the other side of the parapet Reardon hung, his saturated clothes giving him the aspect of a drowned corpse, suspended some fifteen feet above the inky waters that rushed furiously beneath the bridge.

As he felt his grasp failing under Ally's blows, and realised that in a few more seconds he would be forced to leave go his hold, his eyes began to start from their sockets, his hair to bristle on end with horror, and already he seemed to feel the rush of the waters, which were so soon to engulf him, sweeping over his head.

Instinctively he clutched Rory's leg harder than ever.

"Ally!" groaned O'Hara, in tones of agony; "the murtherin' thief is breakin' my leg! Oh!"

Drawn tight up to the parapet as he was, by Reardon's weight, he could not himself stoop down in order to remove the other's grasp.

The girl, abandoning her attack on the hand that clutched the beam, strove to force asunder the grip on her brother's leg.

"I'll break his fingers but I'll make him lave go!" she said savagely; "have ye yer knife, Rory. I niver thought of it before."

Reardon's agony at this remark was fearful. All seemed lost.

"Mercy! for the love of heaven—mercy!" he gasped. "Spare me, for yer sowl's sake!"

"Whisht, ye scoundrel!" cried Rory; "it's no use yer pratin', divil mend it, but I've lost my knife in the scrimmage, anyhow," he added, after a rapid search in his pockets. "Feel on the ground for it, Ally, machree, it must be lyin' close handy, and we'll settle this spalpeen. No, niver mind the knife; go back to the road, and bring a big sthone, and we'll fix him with that."

These words, which Reardon could plainly hear, uttered as they were during a lull in the storm, fell on his ears like a sentence of death.

He heard the girl depart on her murderous quest.

"Help! murther! help!" he yelled, despairingly, though help at that hour there could be none.

"Screech away, screech away, ye nagur!" answered Rory, ironically. "It's little more breath ye'll ever need to cool your porridge with."

"Help, help!" cried Reardon.

And his shrieks rang out even above the noise of the storm, which had again burst forth upon them in all its fury.

He succeeded in shifting his hand a little higher along the cross-piece, and, still retaining his clutch on Rory, made an attempt to hoist himself up, so as to get a hold for his feet, being nerved by the fact that, unless he could manage to do so before the girl's return, he was indeed lost.

But he only brought his face by so doing within better reach of O'Hara's fist, and sank back again, half blinded by the shower of blows rained down upon it by his ferocious enemy.

"Help—help—help!" his cry again rang out.

And then he listened in the vain hope of an answer to this appeal.

His strained ears caught the hurried sound of footsteps on the bridge again.

It must be Ally returning with the stone.

In a few minutes it would be all over.

He closed his eyes and began to repeat a prayer.

"What in the devil's name are you up to here?" suddenly thundered a rough voice immediately over his head, in stentorian tones.

It was the voice of a stranger.

A ray of hope sprang once more in Terry's breast.

"Help! murther! help!—save me!—for the love of heaven, save me!" he cried.

"What's up? Curse you, can't you answer?" cried the voice.

And at the same moment a sharp cry of pain broke from O'Hara, and Reardon felt the leg he held on to almost jerked from his grip.

"Och! lave go, lave go, and I'll tell ye," cried Rory. "Sure, if ye shake me like that, with this divil below here hanging on to my leg, it'll snap like a twig anyway. Och, aisy, for mercy's sake!"

A sudden flash of lightning revealed to Terry a stranger whose face appeared almost gigantic, standing close by Rory, with his hand on the latter's collar.

The same flash also enabled the stranger to gauge the state of affairs.

He was evidently a man of quick decision.

"Can you hoist yourself up, mate, if I keep this beggar quiet, eh?" he said to Reardon.

"I'll try," answered the latter, whom the chance of escape had given fresh strength to.

Shifting his grip from Rory's leg to the cross-piece, he succeeded, after one or two attempts, in swinging one foot up and hooking on with it, and then in getting his knee on to the edge of the bridge.

He then hoisted himself up a bit.

Suddenly he felt himself seized by the collar, and hauled upwards with a force that seemed almost gigantic by the stranger.

The next moment he was standing on the bridge, faint and dizzy from the reaction, which, as was only natural, had set in after the awful peril which he had just undergone·

The stranger who had thus unceremoniously hoisted him up on to the bridge, had continued to maintain his hold all the time on Rory.

Ally now approached the group.

"Who are ye?" demanded Rory, "are ye one o' the polis?"

The stranger laughed.

"Not quite, though I'm pretty well up to the dodge they have of clapping their claws on a chap," and as he spoke he gave Rory's collar a most scientific twist.

"Who are ye, thin? Lave go my collar, or 'twill be the worse for ye," said O'Hara, fiercely.

"It seems to me, now, that if I hadn't clapped my hand on your neck when I did, the next person who would have had a chance of fingering it would have been the hangman. Don't you think you ought to feel kind of thankful, mate, that I stopped you just in time from running the risk of having to dance a jig on nothing for the murder you were up to?"

"Murder!" repeated Rory indignantly; "it was a fair fight, sure now. Ask the spalpeen there; bad luck to him if it wasn't thin. Ask him."

"Well, if that's your style of fair fighting, I should like just to have a squint at the other kind out of curiosity, as the pig said when he poked his nose into the sausage machine," said the stranger, releasing him as he spoke.

"'Twas no fair fight, Rory O'Hara, as well ye know," said Reardon, "but, plaze God, I'll meet ye in a day or two in the light o' day, and then we'll just see which of us is best man."

"Save ye till thin. Come, Ally," and as he spoke O'Hara began to move off.

"Stop a bit," cried the stranger, "I've gone a bit astray, I reckon, in this cursed storm. Is this the right road to Clonturk."

"Yes," answered the two men, simultaniously.

"Well, where will I find a place hereabouts called Teernabeg?"

"Sure an' it's close at hand," ejaculated Ally, "an' the——"

"Whist!" cried her brother, impatiently, cutting her short, whilst Reardon said in somewhat distrustful tones—

"An' might I be so bowld as to ask ye what ye want at Teernabeg now?"

"I want a man named Terence Reardon."

There was a moment's pause.

O'Hara was Reardon's bitter enemy, and a moment before had done his very best to murder him.

But with the rooted aversion of all his class to lend the slightest aid to anyone they think in authority, he would have bitten his tongue out before mentioning Reardon's identity in presence of one whom he still suspected of being a policeman.

Terry at length spoke.

"Ye saved my life anyway," he said to the stranger; "an' it's not for the likes of one who's done me such a good turn to be after hiding myself. I'm Terry Reardon."

"The devil you are," replied the other, "then I've killed two birds with one stone. I've saved you from feeding the fish in that stream down there and pitched on the very man I wanted."

Then pulling Terry on one side he whispered in his ear—

"Do you know Andy Mulvany?"

"Faix an' I don't say I don't."

"Well, he's sent me to you to say," and the stranger rapidly uttered a sentence serving as a pass word.

Terry replied in a similar fashion, and then sundry signs were exchanged between the two men.

"So that's it, is it now? He's a friend sure enough, Rory," he cried to his late adversary, who had stood ready to waive their private quarrel, and to join him in any onslaught that might be found necessary or advisable in case the stranger had turned out to be an emissary of the law.

Then as Rory and his sister disappeared in the darkness, he turned to the stranger and asked him to follow him.

The storm had lulled considerably, and after they had been walking some twenty minutes, it ceased.

By this time they had arrived opposite a fairly comfortable looking farm-house.

Crossing the strip of ground dividing it from the road, they approached the door.

As they did so a dog began to bay furiously.

"Quiet, you cur, quiet! Don't ye know your friends?" said Reardon. "Faix," he added, reflectively, "but if I'd have had ye with me this blessed night, it's very littl chance Rory O'Hara would have had of getting off with whole skin."

"Is your dog such a devil then?" asked the stranger.

"Wait till ye see him."

At the sound of Terry's voice, the animal had relapsed into silence.

But on his master's opening the door, he appeared on the threshold, like a sentry.

He was an enormously powerful brute, a cross between a bull-dog and a mastiff, with deep-set, fiery eyes, a broad wrinkled forehead, and a pendulous jowl, which revealed a formidable array of teeth.

"Aisy, Jowler, boy; sure, it's a friend," said Reardon. And at his voice the animal fell back, and suffered the pair to advance across the threshold.

They found themselves in a large, and rather comfortable kitchen, with a peat fire smouldering on the hearth.

"An' so ye're the new captain?" said Reardon. "Sure, an' I've heard of your doins' up beyant there; an' it's welcome ye are to this roof."

"Thank you. And now just see if you can't fish out a drop of whiskey. I'm as wet as if I'd been lying under a pump-hole for the last six hours."

As he spoke, the stranger threw aside his saturated hat, and revealed the features of Ned Kelly.

CHAPTER CLXXXIV.
TEETH INSERTED GRATIS.

On the following evening, a number of men assembled in an upper room of a large house in the town.

They were the members of the Fenian local council.

The majority were the frieze-coated farmers and peasants of the district, mixed with whom were a sprinkling of the townspeople.

There were, however, several exceptions.

There was a tall, slender, excitable-looking man, with long hair brushed back from his forehead, and very prominent light blue eyes, who at that time sat on the bench of the British House of Commons as member for an Irish borough, but who has since found it necessary to cross the broad Atlantic, with little hope of returning.

There was a little dark, natty man, with an upright figure, and small black moustache.

He was known by the name of Colonel A.*, and was nominally one of the European correspondents of a leading New York Journal, which at that time had its temporary offices in London, at the Queen's Hotel, St. Martin-le-grand.

But to this function he united that of a leading organiser of the Fenian conspiracy.

On one occasion, he left London to pass a week in Paris, leaving an English journalist as his *locum tenens*.

To the latter's great surprise, Colonel A. turned up within twenty-four hours of his departure, looking terribly agitated.

He did not explain the reason of his sudden return, but

---

* Correspondent of the *New York Herald.*

after a little conversation, asked his substitute whether, during his absence, he had had occasion to open a certain drawer in the room.

The other answered that he had not.

Colonel A., with a sigh of relief, took a key from his pocket and locked the drawer.

He had recollected on his arrival in Paris that he had left it unlocked, and without losing a moment, had caught the first train back to London to repair this oversight on his part.

It was not till many years after, when the two men renewed acquaintance in America, that the Englishman learnt that the drawer in question had held papers for which the British Government would have given almost any sum, containing, as they did, the secrets of the entire conspiracy.

The majority of the meeting had taken their seats when some new comers were heard coming upstairs.

Their progress was accompanied by a bumping, scuffling sound, and by something that ominously resembled the rattling of a chain.

Several of those present started to their feet, and more than one turned pale.

Visions of the police, dragging along some unwilling guide and jingling handcuffs prepared for all of them, flashed across their minds.

They heard, however, a short but quiet parley with the sentry stationed on the landing outside.

This parley reassured them.

Then the door opened, and the new comers entered.

The first head that thrust across the door-sill was that of Terence Reardon's bull-dog, Jowler.

He was tugging hard at a huge chain, the other end of which was in the hands of his master.

Behind the latter appeared the massive bulk of Ned Kelly.

The laugh that had escaped several present on discovering the real cause of their alarm in the person of Jowler died away and was replaced by a look of enquiry and suspicion as their eyes rested on Ned.

He was, with one exception, quite unknown to any of those present, save his introducer.

The exception was a cadaverous-looking fellow, of about fifty, named O'Reilly, who had come back from "foreign parts," a year or two previously, and had established himself in a small way in the town.

The precise locality of the "foreign parts" in which Mr. O'Reilly had passed the last few years was a matter of some mystery, for he was a man of cantankerous disposition and could not bear being questioned on the subject.

Spiteful people said they were a penal settlement.

Even he was not quite certain that he knew Ned, though, at the same time having a very strong impression that he had seen the bushranger's face before.

"I shall remember where, presently," he thought.

"Who is this with you, Reardon?" asked the M.P., severely.

"Sure, yer honour, it's just one of ourselves, God save us," answered Reardon; whilst Jowler, still tugging at the chain, stretched out his nose and sniffed at the calves of several of those in his immediate neighbourhood in a way that caused them to retire as far as possible.

"He's quite right," said Ned, "I'm one of you, and if the boss of the show will just step this way, I think I can show him I'm one of the right sort."

The M.P. and the American advanced, and in a few words Ned convinced them of his being a member of their brotherhood, and showed certain credentials.

"An' what is it made ye bring that baste of a dog along with ye, Terry?" enquired a farmer, named Martin Flynn, of Reardon.

"Yes," broke in another, "what in the name of all the saints, Terry, makes ye drag that devil after ye here?"

"Faix an' its draggin' me after him, he is, rather," replied Reardon, with a grin.

"But why, sure?"

"Oh," returned Terry, in dolorous tones. "it's sickenin' that the poor crathur is, I'm afeard."

"Sickenin'?"

"Yes. It's not himself that he is at all at all, so I just brought him along into the town, that ould Con Duffy, the cow docthor, might have a look at him."

"And what did he say, now?"

"Sure, and he says he's feared entirely that the baste is just sickenin' with some disase that has a—— "

"And what was it?" enquired a man, named Mat McGrath.

"Well, it puzzled me so that it's clane gone out of my mind, but he says for sartin sure that if the baste won't dhrink wather, he's got it."

"Bad luck to ye, Terry," cried Flynn, but it's the hydriphobee the dog has got."

"The hydriphoby, that s it, sure enough."

"Devil mend yer manners, but don't ye know that if he wunst bites one o' us we shall all be taken raving mad and run away from wather," cried Mat McGrath.

"Och, murder, and is it so!" exclaimed a third, whose rubicond nose and moist eye indicated a toper.

"Faix, an' if it's the dread of wather that means madness, Mickey, there must be as mad as a March hare—for the devil a drop of anything wayker than whisky I ever heard of his taking."

A laugh followed this, and Reardon proceeded to drag the dog, who seemed perfectly passive, to the farther end of the room, where he secured him by his chain to the leg of a table.

The others clustered together and began to relate experiences, each more horrible than the preceding one, of deaths by dydrophobia, and to enlarge on the awful sufferings of victims stifled between feather beds by their friends, or cut in a vein and left to bleed slowly to death, as was for a long time the practice in the rural districts of Ireland.

The conversation between Ned, the M.P., and the American, had been of a more satisfactory character.

The two leaders recognised that they had before them a ruffian capable of any act of atrocity, but at the same time cool, collected, and with presence of mind to extricate himself and those with him out of any scrape.

To them he made no secret of his identity, and though they did not feel exactly flattered at having to associate with a man who was avowedly a robber, they could not help feeling that he was a capital instrument for the cause.

The cause to them meant a handsome annual income from the pockets of others.

"It's just as well not to let these fellows know exactly who you are," observed the M.P., in a low tone. "You see they've got certain prejudices that it's as well not to rub the wrong way, as matters stand at present."

"What d'ye mean?" asked Ned.

"Why, do you see, my friend," said the American, "there are prejudices, as our worthy senator here says, in this rotten, measly old country which must be respected. In other words, any one of these gentlemen about us would think no more of shooting a landlord or a process-server than a treed coon; but, at the same time, would no more dream of rifling his pocket afterwards than a New York hackman would of giving change, or a Chinaman of cutting off his pigtail."

"In other words," said the M.P., "it's just as well for you not to drop a word about your colonial adventures. My friends here don't mind paying their rent from the barrel of a gun, but robbery or any other form they have a prejudice against—at present."

Kelly sneeringly replied, "They're mighty honest, no doubt, when there is nothing to take."

Soon the whole of the ministers of the secret council met and the proceedings commenced. As usual, it was to consult about the assassination of an unpopular landlord living in a distant county—for it was always arranged that the avenger in such a case should be drawn from a region remote from the scene of crime—was put upon his trial behind his back, as it were.

He was accused of certain offences, which were stated by the president, and which evidence was brought forward to establish with the grim and ghastly mockery of a court of justice.

The impromptu jury were called upon for their verdict. Of course it was "guilty," and the sentence—death.

That had already been fixed beforehand.

It was the same in all such cases—death.

Despite the proverbially excitable nature of the Irish, these proceedings had been conducted in a stolid, business-like fashion that would have gladdened the heart of a British tradesman.

This gathering might very well, indeed, have passed for a vestry meeting.

There was little speechifying on the part of the majority.

The only attempts at eloquence were displayed by the American and the M.P., who felt bound, perhaps, to show off a little, and by a young fellow named Mahoney, who indulged in a little rhapsody about "98."

There was, besides, no outward display such as is usually associated with a conspiracy.

Neither flags, masks, daggers, or any other of the symbols and paraphernalia popularly associated with such proceedings as those in progress, were displayed.

Nothing was recorded in writing, though the American nominally filled the post of secretary.

Mahony, who wanted to display his business-like talents, proposed that the "minutes" of the meeting should be made, and expressed his surprise to the Yankee colonel at the absence of such "matayrials."

"My friend," was the reply, "if language was given to man to conceal his thoughts, writing was invented to enable him to find out other people's. Pen and ink are dangerous things to meddle with unless you have all your wits about you, as a friend of mine found out in New York the other day."

"How was that?" asked the M.P.

"Well, he had been lunching pretty heavily down town, and, perhaps, he could not walk in straight along the sidewalk as he ought. Anyway, he ran right into the arms of a perfect stranger to him."

"Who boned his watch, I suppose, under the pretence of helping him along? I know the dodge."

"Not a bit of it. The stranger was a perfect good Samaritan. He was a young man from the Far West—the home of rural simplicity—and a model of temperance. He took my friend into a temperance hotel, and told him, in the most feeling manner, how sad he felt at the sight of a respectable man in his condition; and he set to work to sober him, and read him such an eloquent and touching lesson on the evils of drink, and so worked on his feelings, that he then and there put his name across the temperance pledge offered to him. It turned up, that pledge did, a month later in the shape of his acceptance for a thousand dollars. As he didn't like to face the music of exposure, he paid the bill, but he warned one or two friends on the quiet of that virtuous young Western man."

"By gorrah! look now—there's a power in education, ye see."

After this little digression, business was proceeded with.

It was that of selecting the men upon whom was to devolve the execution of the court's decree.

This was settled by lot.

The number of chances corresponded with that of the men present, with the exception of the president and secretary.

It was a rule that the assassin should always be selected from a district lying at a distance from the spot where the murder was to be committed.

The reason was that they would be personally unknown to their intended victim, and that, if he survived his injuries, he would have greater difficulty in describing or identifying his assailants.

The lots fell on Kelly and on a young excitable looking fellow, with a slender frame, pallid face, and flashing eyes, named Brian Mahony, who had already spoken at some length on the matter.

He was one of the most ardently patriotic of the assembly, and was rather a favourite with most of his companions, from his evident sincerity and "spouting" propensities. He talked a fearful amount of fluent rubbish ever in praise of everything Irish, especially of the "foinest pisanthry in the wurrld," and of the "nation rising in its might," whatever that might mean, and was eloquent about the time when "Malachi wore a chain of gold," (which, by-the-bye, would not have been very safe wearing when the quotation was made), so that he was "a big spaker entirely," and looked upon as another Meagher of the Sword.

It is curious to note the resemblance in this respect between the Irish and the French.

Tallyrand said of the latter, " *Ils sont toujours sous l'Empire de la phrase!* "—they are always under the influence of happy phraseology. The Irish are likewise as malleable as wax in the hands of mob or other orators.

Old O'Reilly had been watching Ned very closely for some time past, and had at last made up his mind as to his identity.

No sooner had the lot fallen on Kelly and Mahony, than he turned to the latter, next to whom he was seated, and whispered something in his ear.

"You're draimin', man!" exclaimed Mahony, with a look of indignation at his neighbour.

"Divil a lie in it," was the reply.

"Ask him yerself, if ye doubt me; but I'll swear to him anywhere."

"If it is, thin," cried the other, in indignant tones, "I'll do the job single-handed before I'll collogue with the likes of him."

"What is it, Mahoney?" said the M.P., noticing the young man's excitement.

"Are we thaves and rapparees, yer honour; or are we patriots, inspired by the glorious memories of '98?" was the answer.

"Patriots, I trust."

"Is it right then that a murtherer and a horse-stealer should come sneaking into our midst and be evened with honest men?" cried Mahoney, with the air of a sucking Emmett.

"What do you mean?"

"Mane. Why, I want to know if it's true, as O'Reilly here says, that Misther Kelly there is neither more or less than a horse-stealer, thafe, and robber from Australey."

A dead silence followed this announcement for a moment.

These men, who would not have shrunk at murder, had a horror of theft.

Ned looked astounded at this revelation of his career. He had no reason to fear this biographical sketch of his Antipodean life, and he avowedly wished he was safe in the scrub at that moment. However, there was only one thing to do. Face the foe boldly as he had often done before. He, however, was furious, and we know he was revengeful. He knew that unless he cleared out of that his danger would commence, so he simply launched a bottle of whisky at the head of his accuser, striking him full in the face, which was instantly covered with blood. It was the only reply he could make. Drawing his revolver, he stood in his defence, as the favourite's friends rushed towards him with threats of lynching the "spy."

"Are you mad, you fools; do you want to be jail-birds, all of you?" cried the M.P., in an agitated tone.

"Dry up, there," said the American, "hold hard."

"Pitch him out o' the window."

"Murther him," and similar outcries were heard on every side, for the word spy acted on one and all like a red rag on a bull.

In vain the American and the M.P. strove to restore order; their voices were drowned in the general uproar.

As is always the case, under such circumstances, the more peaceably disposed of the party added to the din by their loud appeals for silence.

Amidst the confusion, the door of the room suddenly opened, and the face of the sentry, which wore an expression of alarm, was thrust inside.

This incident attracted their notice, and stilled the uproar.

"Whisht, boys!" he ejaculated; "the rucktion ye're makin' will be heard all over the town, and the polis will be here in no time."

There was a temporary lull at these words.

Kelly, backing to the wall, stood in a defiant attitude, revolver in hand, facing his opponents.

Excited by the tumult around him, the dog Jowler had begun to tug furiously at his chain, and he now uttered a most fearful howl.

Another and another followed.

"To hell with the spy!" cried Flynn all at once; and a rush towards Kelly took place.

Kelly met the rush with a force and quickness that astonished his assailant. He floored the foremost attackers like bowling over ninepins.

They were no match for his Herculean power. Like Perry, the celebrated black pugilist (transported by the backers of Spring, who placed a flash £5 note in his pocket the day before the fight), he could kill a man with a blow, or smash his jaw like glass—and he knew it. The conspirators drew back in amazement.

"He's the devil entirely, boys; by gorrah, he's charmed!"

All this time the dog howled furiously, and under the pretext of soothing him, Reardon stepped up to him.

He muttered as he did so.

"Spy I'll niver belave he is! and thafe or no thafe, he saved my life last night, and by dad I'll pay the debt!"

As he finished the sentence he placed his hand on Jowler's collar.

Meanwhile, with the wolfish glare of murder in their eyes, the maddened throng pressed round Kelly, who had drawn his revolver.

He would himself have probably been shot down ere this, had it not been for the fear of the sound of firearms attracting the police, situate, as the house was, in the centre of the town.

His foes were evidently nerving themselves for one overwhelming rush, in which he would be borne down, and in all likelihood torn limb from limb.

In vain the M.P. and the American strove to obtain a hearing on his behalf.

"Sure, we may as well betray ourselves as be sold by the horse-stealing, murdering spy!"

"It's a spy he is, and we'll have the heart's blood of him!" was the reply of those they addressed, and who, in their blind rage, had quite forgotten the real cause of quarrel

The idea of a spy once started, nothing could shake it.

"Down with him, boys!" cried M'Grath; and, with faces aglow with fiendish passion, the others prepared to throw themselves on their victim.

Suddenly a yell broke from Reardon.

"The dog's loose—the hydriphobee!" he screeched at the top of his voice, in tones of panic clearly heard above the tumult.

The words struck terror to the hearts of the boldest of those present.

Men who were about to rush boldly on Ned's levelled revolver, shrank from this peril.

The frightful stories they had been telling about hydrophobia flashed across their minds.

And as Jowler, with eyes ablaze, and hair bristling down the whole length of his back, bounded towards them, his open mouth displaying his array of white and glistening fangs, the effect was magical.

One and all turned to flee, the fallen men springing from the floor like acrobats.

It was literally a case of the devil—for as such they regarded him—take the hindmost.

Cursing, swearing, scrambling, fighting, they made their way in frantic confusion towards the door of the room.

Excited almost to madness on his part, the dog made his teeth meet in the calves of several of the hindmost as they were jammed in the door.

Maddened with pain and fear, they kicked and struggled till the whole mass rolled down the stairs like a torrent and never paused till they had gained the street.

In less than a minute none were left in the room but Ned, the M.P., and Reardon, who was joyously waving the dog-chain in exultation at the success of his stratagem.

Thus the meeting was dissolved.

CHAPTER CLXXXV.
OUT OF THE FRYING-PAN INTO THE FIRE.

THE three men gazed at one another for a few moments after the room had been thus unceremoniously cleared.

Then the American and the M.P. broke into a fit of laughter in which Kelly joined.

"Well, I reckon there ain't been such a skedaddle since Bull's Run," observed the first. "It was a caution to snakes to see the way those fellows slid."

(To be continued.)

NED KELLY
THE
IRONCLAD
AUSTRALIAN BUSHRANGER

NO 32,

NED KELLY: IRONCLAD BUSHRANGER.

It is well known that for many years Ned Kelly had made himself notorious by a series of crimes wholly incompatible with the civilisation of the nineteenth century. Ned Kelly's celebrated steed, Marco Polo, is as well known at the Antipodes as Dick Turpin's Black Bess in these islands."—*Telegraph*, 7th July, 1881.

"It is notorious that the robbery of Mr. Steward's corpse was mainly performed by the assistance of NED KELLY's BROTHER, the Captain of what was neither more nor less than a pirate ship."—*Times*, July.

"The history of NED KELLY and his celebrated black horse, Marco Polo, will ever live in the recollection of the Australian public. The deeds of Dick Turpin, and the performances of Black Bess, are tame beside those of 'NED AND HIS NAG;' in addition to which Ned's history is true, and Turpin's is pure fiction."—*Press*, July.

CHAPTER CLXXXVI.—*Continued.*

"YES," remarked the M.P., "it was a clear case of devil take the hindmost. It was a deuced lucky thing too. Reardon, that your dog got loose just when he did. 'Pon my word, I believe our friend here would have been a dead man in another minute but for that."

Reardon grinned.

"Yes," said the American, "I don't think anything else could have saved him. How was it the brute got loose?"

"Faix, an' I'm not quite sartin how 'twas, yer honour. Sure, I was just tryin' to quiet him, the crathur, and I had my hand on his collar just to see if it might be chokin' of him, and thin, mebbe, my fingers slipped," said Reardon, with that sly, comical affectation of innocence assumed by Pat when launching a "thumper."

"And the collar came undone, eh?" said the M.P., who perfectly understood the meaning of this rigmarole.

"Sure, your honour's a witch!" was the answer.

"Well, Kelly, it strikes me that if it had not been for the cuteness of our friend here, you'd have been down among the dead men, as the saying is, long ago."

"There would have been more down with me. I wouldn't have gone under alone, no fear," rejoined Ned, with a grim emphasis; "but all the same, I thank you, mate, for the dodge."

As he spoke, he held out his hand to Reardon.

"Faix, and is it more than payin' back my debts that I've been doin'? When I was hangin' like a ripe pear on Father Flaherty's garden wall, over the black waters, with that divil hammerin' at my hands, who was it but you that pulled me up again, and saved me?" answered Terry, with some emotion.

"Oh! you two have a little private account between you, eh?" said the M.P. "But now to the main business. After your squabble with Mahoney, Kelly, I'm afraid it's impossible for you to work together."

"So am I," replied Ned.

"Well, what's to be done? The only thing that I can see is for the lots to be drawn afresh; and, meanwhile, we must get it out of these fellows' thick heads that you're a spy, though, till this is done, perhaps you'd better keep out of all chance of meeting them anywhere."

"Devil a bit will I keep out of their way," replied Ned. "I'm not a chicken-hearted chap of that sort. And, what's more, if that sneaking hound I bashed over the mug thinks himself too fine to work along with me, I'm blest if I won't show him the stuff I'm made of."

"What do you mean?" enquired the M.P.

"I mean I'll do the job single-handed."

"Bravo!" exclaimed the American. "You're the right sort, true grit, a regular ring-tailed screamer, I reckon."

"Do you mean it?" asked the M.P.

"I always mean what I say. Just tell me straight the particulars, and I'll go to work at once."

"Then hurry up," chimed in the American, "or we shall have those fellows who were hoppin' around just now like so many bob-tailed bulls in fly-time, come sneaking back to see how the land lies."

As he spoke, there was a scuffling, bumping noise on the stairs, followed by a scratching at the door.

"There they are!" exclaimed the M.P.

"No, sure," answered Reardon, stepping towards the door; "it's just Jowler, the baste. I know the noise of him. He'd be equal to any Christian—if he liked a drop!"

As he spoke, he opened the door and admitted the dog.

Jowler limped a little with one leg, and sundry marks on his body showed that he had not come off quite scot-free, though he had sustained no material damage in his recent encounter.

Reardon called to him gently to advance, but on his doing so, both the American and the M.P. showed signs of mental perturbation and alarm.

The former retreated at once to the further end of the room, and the latter hopped up on to a table with all the agility of a professed acrobat.

Ned quietly fingered his revolver and kept a wary eye upon the formidable brute.

The dog at first seemed a little reluctant to join his master, but at last did so.

Reardon began to examine whether the animal had been much hurt in the fray, though Jowler did not seem to particularly desire such handling.

"For heaven's sake, look out, man," exclaimed the M.P., "consider if he should bite you."

"He knows me too well, yer honour, he won't harm me at all, at all," was the reply.

"But you can't be certain, there's no trusting these brutes, and especially in a case of rabies."

"A case of what, your honour?"

"Of rabies, madness, hydrophobia."

"Hydrophoby, is it; hydrophoby! Oh, sure now?"

And the fellow broke into a roar of laughter.

"What do you mean. Hasn't he got it?"

"The devil a bit, that I know of."

"But didn't you say he had?"

"Sorrah a word. I just mentioned that the cow-docthor had towld me that if the baste refused to drink wather, it was a sign of hydriphobee, but up till now I'll go bail that he's not shewn the laste avarsion to it."

"Well, I never saw a mad dog, if yours isn't a trifle off his head, for he charged those coons like a runaway engine."

"By Gorrah, if he hadn't charged the vagabones, I'd a thought him mad enough—but that proved the sinse o' the crathur."

Then he looked up with a droll twinkle in his eye.

"Sure the poor baste had his rasins. Whin my hand happened to slip on his collar, I just whispered to him to go for them into one ear, and somehow I managed just to drop the red-hot ashes from my pipe into the other."

This quite accounted for Jowler's frenzy.

After a little more conversation, during which Kelly who convinced the others of his determination to carry out the job single-handed, received full instructions as to the best way in which to set about it, the parley separated.

It had been arranged that Ned should remain for the night at Reardon's, and start on his expedition early the following morning.

Accordingly he set forth, bent from mere reckless

bravado, on the slaughter of a man he had never even seen.

His route had been carefully mapped out for him, and various stopping places at which he might halt in safety had been also indicated.

It nevertheless happened that the first day he got rather out of his road, and, just before sunset, was surprised in a heavy storm of wind and rain.

After pushing on through this for some miles—for his path lay through a lonely and desolate district—with a keen and cutting wind blowing full in his teeth, and without a trace of human habitation to take shelter in from the stinging shafts of the shower, he struck the high road he had been in search of, and, proceeding a little distance along it, came in sight of an inn.

It was not a very pretentious place, but signs of comfort were not lacking, and, drenched as he was, it was a sight more than welcome.

The walls, it is true, were of mud, and those serving to partition off the apartments into which it was divided only reached the spring of the roof, so that warmth and air, not to mention the cackling of fowls, the grunting of pigs, and other domestic sounds, were equally diffused throughout the tenement.

But there was an ample chimney, on each side of which was a stone bench.

In the centre of the hearth a large fire of turf and bog wood was burning briskly, and over it, by a chain, swung a huge iron pot, from which ascended a by no means unsavoury odour.

Ned entered, and greeted the host and hostess, who told him that supper would be ready in half an hour or so.

After draining a stiff dose of whiskey and water, he seated himself on one side of the fireplace, and, stretching out his legs to the fire, leant back against the wall and inhaled the fragrant steam from the pot, which contained a stew intended for supper.

The soothing murmur of the bubbling pot, the comfortable seat, the warmth of the fire acting with double effect on him in his chilled and wet condition, his fatigue, and it may be the extra dose of the "rale thing" he had just swallowed, had their effect on him, as might be expected.

The host and hostess were busy with their domestic affairs, and there was no one to talk to him and distract his attention at all.

So gradually his eyes closed, his breathing grew more and more even, and his head sank on one shoulder as he dozed off.

At length, after one or two spasmodic grunts, he sank down sideways on the bench, and was soon as sound asleep as a top.

No sooner was he asleep than two new comers entered the inn with the usual greeting.

They were both strapping young fellows, in the neat uniform of the Irish Constabulary.

"A nasty storm, Pat," observed one to the host, after he and his companion had been supplied with drink, as they seated themselves on the bench opposite Ned.

"Indade, an' it is," was the reply. "I nivir seed it come down so sharp. The gintleman by the fire there, was just like a drowndthed rat whin he came."

"Not many travellers about on a day like this?"

"Arrah, no; sure he's the only one that has crossed the door this blissed day."

"Where's he bound to?" enquired the other constable, in a low voice.

"Sure an' it's not myself that can answer ye that anyway. Divil a word has he said since he came in."

There was a lull in the conversation, during which Ned's snores were plainly audible above the bubbling of the pot.

The bushranger was, as a rule, a light sleeper, like all men accustomed to peril; but on the present occasion the

warmth and the whiskey had exerted a marked soporific effect upon him, which, singular enough, the arrival of the two constables, and their conversation, had quite failed to dissipate in any degree.

He continued to sleep the sleep of the just, and to snore with the force and regularity of a blacksmith's bellows in full play.

"Good lungs that chap's got anyway, Daly," said one of the constables to his companion.

"Yes, if his lungs are in his nose, he has."

"Maybe it would be as well to take a squint at him before he wakes. He might think it a liberty if one stared too hard at him when awake," said the first constable, whose name was Purcell.

"It might be as well," replied the other.

Rising from his seat, he stepped noiselessly round to the side of the fireplace where Ned was stretched at ease upon his bench.

He stared hard at Kelly's features.

If he had been an Australian bobby, he would have had no difficulty in identifying the man before him as the iron-clad bushranger.

Ned's description had been so extensively circulated throughout the colony, that there was not a member of the force there, down to the latest joined recruit, that did not know it by heart a deuced sight better than ever he knew his catechism.

But as Kelly's presence was unsuspected in Ireland, no particulars of his personal appearance had as yet been supplied by the authorities.

The constable scanned his face, and even glanced at the scar on his hand, but failed to identify him with anyone who might be "wanted" to his knowledge.

He was just about to return to his comrade, when all at once he started.

Ned had unbuttoned his coat, and in his slumbers it had fallen aside.

Peering out from the breast of his waistcoat, where he had thrust it as the dryest place at his command during the storm, was the butt of his revolver.

The constable began to smell a rat.

Moreover, it was his duty in any case to make an enquiry into the matter, the carrying of firearms of any kind in Ireland being strictly prohibited, unless a license had first been specially obtained.

Daly beckoned to his comrade, who joined him in his contemplation of Ned's slumbers, and to whom he pointed out the weapon.

He took in the situation at a glance.

Ned was not a bad-looking fellow, and if the police who were now looking at him had met him in good company, in broad daylight, and well-dressed, very likely they would have been the first to swear that he was as respectable a looking fellow, if a little unpolished in aspect, as they would meet with on the longest summer day.

But lying there, unkempt and storm-beaten, in the coarse garments he had assumed for his errand, and with a pistol peeping from his breast, he at once, in their eyes, assumed the appearance of a most desperate-looking ruffian, ready for any deed.

The two policemen arrived at this conclusion with that wonderful unanimity which distinguishes the force in all things, especially in hard swearing.

The slumbering stranger was evidently a very ugly customer.

With a quiet dexterity that the cleverest of Fagan's pickpocket pupils (who were trained to pick a handkerchief from a lay figure hung with bells) might have envied, Daly clasped his fingers round the butt of Ned's revolver and drew it from its hiding-place with a gentleness that would not have scared a fly.

So artistically was this little feat done that the bushranger never felt it in the least.

The two then withdrew to their own side of the fire to await events.

CHAPTER CLXXXVII

KELLY'S PATENT DYNAMITE.

SUPPER being cooked, the landlady hastened to dish it up, and the bustle of this operation and the clattering of the platters effectually aroused Ned.

He yawned, uncoiled his lengthy herculean proportions, and sat up on the bench.

At the sight of the constables he could not repress a slight start, which did not escape their watchful eyes, though they affected not to perceive it.

It confirmed their suspicion that he was a dangerous customer, and they resolved to act accordingly.

They did not, however, quite see their way to lay hands on him and arrest him at once without further enquiry, and began to reflect that by depriving him of his weapon they had perhaps put it out of their power to find a legitimate pretext for securing him.

Nevertheless, they made up their minds to subject him to due enquiry after supper.

"A wet evening," said Daly, as they sat down at table.

"How did you find that out? The cursed country's nothing but a bog," growled Kelly.

"Have you come far through the rain? I see you've got pretty well sprinkled," went on the other in a genial tone, for he did not at first want to rouse Kelly's suspicions by his questioning.

"Yes, a pretty fair step," answered Ned.

"From Ballyturin, maybe?"

"No."

"Ah, from the south, then?"

Ned did not answer.

"And how does the country look down your way?" went on the constable, with an amiable air.

"Looks pretty much the same, I suppose, as it always does—dull, dirty, and dismal."

"What part, now, might you hail from?" put in the other constable, insidiously, not minding Kelly's growl.

"Oh, I'm a stranger in Ireland," returned Ned, who saw it was no use trying to hoodwink them with any story of his being a native. "I have not been in the country long, and have had no time to look about me."

"And what do you think of it?"

"I think some people are a blooming sight more inquisitive than they had any need to be," was the answer.

Daly laughed.

"Mayhap it's our duty to be so. There's such a lot of queer customers about just now, you see. You're not a native of Ireland, you say, now. You come from America, I suppose?" he went on, as he scanned Ned keenly.

"Yes," answered Kelly, recklessly; for he wished, at any rate, to keep his interlocutors off the scent as to who he really was, and thought this a good dodge.

"I thought as much."

And as he spoke Daly exchanged a significant glance with Purcell.

They at once set Ned down as a Fenian emissary from the United States.

The repast proceeded and at its close Purcell at length remarked—

"If it's all the same to you, I think you'd better come a step or two on the road to our barracks, and have a word or two with the inspector."

"What for?" said Ned fiercely.

"Why I don't think your answers quite satisfactory, and in fact you must consider yourself in custody."

Ned sprang to his feet, and glared at his interrogators as a wounded tiger at a "Shekarry."

"You say you've only been a little time in the country," said Purcell.

"What's your game? I've a right to come here, ain't I?"

"Well, perhaps you may be ignorant of the laws. Perhaps you don't know that there's one against the carrying of arms."

Ned thrust his hand into the pocket in which he usually kept his revolver.

It was missing.

He recollected placing it in his waistcoat pocket, and, simultaneously with that recollection, realised the fact of its absence from its hiding place.

"Was this what you were feeling for?" said Purcell, holding out Ned's revolver as he spoke with a grin.

The bushranger understood the situation at once.

Like a general surveying the country over which an engagement is to be fought, he glanced round the place to calculate its chances of aiding him in either flight or resistance, as might prove most advisable.

The huge fireplace occupied one end of the room, and was faced at the other by a rude dresser.

In the centre of the wall on the right hand was the door leading on to the road.

It was open, though the shutters securing the two windows flanking it had been fastened.

On the opposite wall was another door, also ajar, apparently leading into the back premises, and thence through the yard to the waste land extending in rear of the house.

If Ned understood the situation, the police were equally on the alert.

Daly rose and placed himself before the open door with his rifle, which he had kept during the meal in his hand.

Purcell held Ned's revolver, with the muzzle pointed in an unpleasantly straight fashion towards its legitimate owner's figure.

Knowing to an ounce the lightness of pull of the trigger of his favourite weapon, Kelly felt somewhat uncomfortable at the little circumstance.

"Come, we don't want to have any unpleasantness," said Purcell, "but it's our duty to take you before a magistrate as a suspicious character carrying arms in a proclaimed district. If you can explain matters, so much the better for you; but it's not for us to decide the question—so come along quietly."

Ned glared at him for a moment like a trapped wolf.

Then he retreated a step towards the fireplace, whilst the landlady simultaneously retired in alarm to the further end of the room.

Again Ned glanced around him, this time all but despairingly, in quest of either a means of escape or a weapon.

There was nothing.

"Look here, what the devil d'ye want to nab me for?" he began. "What do you take me for?"

"A Fenian, if you must know."

"A Fenian?"

"Yes, so you had better cave in quietly."

Ned had made up his mind not to be taken alive.

A desperate resolution suddenly lit up his face.

He was close to the fireplace.

Thrusting his hand into his pocket he drew out a largish square packet.

It was done up in white paper.

He stretched forth his hand, and held the packet over the fire.

"A Fenian, you say? Then since it is so, I'll show you a Fenian trick before I've done with you."

"Do you think you're going to quod me for nothing? Just come two steps towards me, and I'll Fenian you both. Do you see this?" roared Ned, hoarse with rage. It's your death-warrant, and mine too, for the matter of that; but no jail shall hold me, and none of your blooming beaks stop my gallop. Do you see this, I say, you Irish blood-suckers?"

The two constables gazed with surprise at the roaring ruffian, but had no idea of what he meant. Purcell replied—

"Come, my man, draw it mild; you don't think you've got a couple of babies to deal with, do you? What have you got in your fist there?"

"Dynamite enough to make this house and all in it jump into——"

"Dynamite!" exclaimed the now alarmed officers of the law.

"Yes. I guess you've heard of it? There's enough here to blow every stock and stone of this infernal caboose into smithereens; and by ——, I'll do it before one of you lays hands on me."

At this epoch the first dynamite scare was in full force through the United Kingdom.

The Clerkenwell explosion was fresh in the minds of all.

The landlord turned white as a ghost, and fell back against the dresser, too paralysed by terror to try to flee.

His wife dropped on her knees, and throwing her apron over her head, began to pray aloud to all the saints in paradise to lend her their aid.

Even the two policemen were daunted.

With his giant form standing beside the fire, its smoke curling around him, his face, with its grim expression of set determination lit up by the lurid glow of the smouldering peat, over which he held the fatal packet, there was something in Ned's aspect to appal the stoutest heart.

In that red glare he resembled a fiend newly risen from the pit of Tophet.

"Now, my blooming swaddies," he cried, with a laugh that was appalling to hearken to, "another step, and by —— I'll blow every soul of you to ——; and there won't be a bit of your carcasses left big enough to feed a flea. Move a hand towards me, an' I'll give you a journey quicker and further than you've h. d yet."

"Och murther!" gasped the landlord.

"The saints presarve us all!" ejaculated his wife.

Purcell made an effort to recover himself.

"Drop that packet, or I'll fire," he said, levelling the revolver at Ned.

"Drop it?" echoed the bushranger, sneeringly. "If I do, you'll find yourself the other side of the moon. Alive or dead, you shall come with me; for even if you pull trigger, it falls into the fire."

The policemen realised that even if they shot Ned down, the explosion would avenge him by shattering the place to pieces, as it fell from his dying grasp into the fire.

Setting aside the risk, they did not quite feel justified, even under the circumstances, in shooting a man down like a rabbit. Besides which, they knew they had no power to kill the man, or even wound him.

Coroner's juries in Ireland are apt to take a very different view when a man is shot by the police, to that which they entertain when his death has been compassed by a private individual, and the verdict, in case there were sufficient fragments of Ned left to hold an inquest on, was certain to be "Wilful Murder."

Ned saw they were shaken, but he saw more than this. He saw by a sign the landlord made to him, that he was a Fenian, which considerably eased Ned's apprehensions from that quarter.

"Will you or won't you clear out?" roared Ned to the police. "If you don't before I count five, I'll clear you out pretty sharply, with the contents of this," showing the packet. The men hesitated, but there was that in Ned's face that confirmed this belief in his recklessness.

"Arrah, boys," said the landlord to the police, "is he worth all our lives, if he was the biggest Rapparee that ever shot a priest? Sure you know he'll murther us all, an' what profit will we get out o' that?"

Ned shouted, "One, two!" but ere "three" sounded, the police had left the premises.

"Now then, avick!" said the landlord, when the officers had withdrawn; "the blackguards have taken your revolver with them; but sure I've got one of the same family, that ye can have in the mane time. It's as dark as the bottom of the Devil's Punchbowl at Mangerton, and nearly as cold. The Peelers won't be able to see three yards beyant their noses, and you can't slip out off to the hills."

Kelly here indulged in, to him, the rare amusement of a hearty laugh. He said something to the landlord which sent him off too. Indeed, he seemed highly tickled for some time after Ned's departure.

Kelly darted through the back premises, and was soon scoring away in the darkness, feeling quite safe as regarded the police, as they could hardly see an inch before them.

Ere he started, he returned to his pocket the half-pound packet of "Limerick twist," which he had purchased that morning to smoke on his journey, and which had enabled him to play his little comedy in so successful a fashion.

Kelly's dynamite was tobacco.

CHAPTER CLXXXVIII.
HOW TO DEAL WITH A LANDLORD.

ON leaving the little inn, Kelly made the best of his way up the hillside at a good round pace.

He had little fear of the policemen overhauling him; but at the same time he judged it prudent to increase as much as possible the distance between himself and them.

As he stumbled along over the rough and broken ground, he anathematised it with a fluency of language and a fertility of epithet that few could have equalled who have no learned the art in a British colony. The vocabulary of an Australian bullock driver is *sui generis*. Oaths of every form and grotesque awfulness come rushing from his lips, like bullets from a *mitrailleuse*, in showers of profanity of the nature of which it is to be hoped he is ignorant. De Quincey has spoken of murder as a fine art, the Australian bullock driver has done the same for swearing.

The rain had ceased, but the air was damp and misty, a circumstance which, however much it might serve to favour his departure unobserved, by no means conduced to his comfort.

Vigorously he censured—to use a very mild phrase—the wretched climate of the Emerald Isle, the "melancholy island" of D'Israeli, the wet sponge of creation. After the gorgeous atmosphere of Australia, he could not but detest the land of perpetual downpour, which to him was misery, but to the inhabitants only "soft weather."

"I can't stand this any longer," he growled; "it's always raining in this beastly bog-hole of a country, that's only fit for wild duck and mud turtle. I wonder how the devil anyone better than a frog, and with any coin at all, can live in it; no wonder the swells clear out!"

Two more steps and he suddenly plumped up to his knees in a hole full of water.

After having gone a certain distance from the inn he halted, in order to reconnoitre the position.

It was not a very enchanting one.

He was alone on a bleak hillside, with, as far as he knew, not another shelter save the one he had so abruptly quitted, within miles of him.

The darkness and mist not only rendered his progress difficult and dangerous, but threatened to hinder all success in his attempts to find a shelter.

After a little deliberation, he decided to push on, as far as he could judge, in the direction in which he had originally been making his way.

Even if the police were still lurking about, there was but scant chance of his running against them.

Accustomed to steer through the bush at all hours of the day and night, Ned headed almost by instinct to the quarter to which he was bound, resolved, if necessary, to tramp on steadily through the night.

Fortune saved him this task.

He had not been tramping more than half-an-hour when he caught sight of a light glimmering from what he took at first to be a mere mound of earth, but which, on a closer approach, he made out to be a mud cabin.

He saw through the chinks in what was figuratively called a door. He knocked loudly.

With the natural hospitality of the people, the knock was answered with an invitation to "come in, in the name of God."

Kelly pushed in the two or three planks slightly nailed together, doing duty for a door, and found himself in a dwelling-place scarcely a shade superior to the cave of an ancient Briton, and certainly not so dry.

The cabin consisted of a single room measuring some eight feet by ten.

The walls were n...d and so was the floor, in which puddles of water had formed in different places.

The furniture comprised a ricketty table and a broken bench, bedstead and bedding being alike conspicuous by their absence.

A sickle hung from a beam in the roof, and a spade stood in one corner; the remaining household utensils consisting of two or three tea-cups, a couple of cracked plates, a jug, with a broken spout and without a handle; a griddle and a kettle swung by a chain over a scrap of turf-fire that might have been put into a pint pot.

Two ghastly scarecrows in tatters and rags were crouching on either side of the fire, the glow from which had caught Ned's eye through the hole serving as a window and the slits in the door.

After some difficulty, owing to the dimness of the light, he made out that they were a man and woman.

Ned had not had much experience of what is termed high life, and had been no stranger to poverty, but, accustomed as he was to the rude plenty of the colonies, the ghastly squalor of the scene before him forcibly astounded him.

For a moment he hesitated about revealing his real position, lest his hosts should be tempted to betray him.

On second thoughts he decided otherwise, and boldly stated that the police were after him.

This was enough to ensure him the warmest welcome.

"It isn't a mighty power o' food we've got to offer you, but before the mayzles tuk the praties we had plenty of them anyway and a welcome to give, but now what we have you're as welcome to as the flowers o' May, though *male* isn't much to keep the little spark of life that's left burnin'. If it wasn't for a drop o' comfort we git from a friend, the exciseman—bad luck to him!—hasn't yet found out, we'd all be as dead as Cromwell."

Ned thanked them in his rough way, and said that a taste of whiskey to dry up the wet was all he wanted.

This was soon produced, and then, on the reiterated assurance of his host that there was no chance of the police coming in quest of him there, he stretched himself, in his clothes, on a little straw that had been spread for him on the dryest spot of the floor.

The master of the house and his wife took up their quarters for the night in similar fashion, whilst a donkey, who formed the rest of the family, was also accommodated in a like manner close to the door, serving, as was explained, as a kind of living barricade to prevent its being blown down in windy weather.

If there had been a pig he would probably have shared the general couch; but that indispensable adjunct to an Irish cotter's existence, had just been parted with in order to pay the rent, for at that time the Land League was in embryo, and rent was still paid—when found convenient.

The next morning at daybreak, Ned resumed his journey, after rewarding his host with the greater part of the tobacco that had enabled him so successfully to scare the policemen in the little inn.

The scene of action to which he was bound, was in the county Mayo.

His destined victim was a gentleman named Mountclare, who resided in a house situate on the slope of one of the hills overlooking the beautiful expanse of Lough Corrib and its multitude of picturesque islands.

Mr. Mountclare was a gentleman of ancient family, but impoverished estate.

His rent-roll numbered under a score of tenants, and these mostly of small holdings; his whole income from the land he owned in Mayo not reaching £400 a year.

He had been considered a kind and indulgent landlord, especially when contrasted with some of his neighbours, by whom whole districts had been depopulated, as on the the estate of the Marquis of Sligo, in the neighbourhood of Westport, where hillside after hillside may be passed on which not a head of cattle or a single sheep can be seen to-day, though ten years ago cottages might be counted by the hundred.

But for all this, Mr. Mountclare had incurred the enmity of the Fenians, and so sentence of death had been pronounced by them against him.

The way in which the sentence had been notified, was, so to say, grimly ludicrous.

He had received a letter one morning, calling his attention to a certain spot on his estate.

On proceeding there he found a grave had been dug, at the heap of which was a notice placed in a cleft stick, to the effect that he had better make the best of the time left to him to prepare for its occupation.

Such a warning was not to be neglected, and Mr. Mountclare applied to the government for a police escort.

The Marquis of Sligo's agent never stirs without a couple of armed policemen, who follow him like shadows. This number is sometimes exceeded, as in the case of Mr. Nicholson, of Balrath, in Meath.

After an attempt made to shoot this gentleman at Kells, a post of police was established in his home, and in such a state of terror did he live, that he rarely ventured outside his own park, about which he promenaded around with a loaded rifle, and escorted by no less than four constables with their carbines at full cock.

Policemen guarded the approaches and entrance to the mansion; there were constables on the gravel walks, in the shrubberies, on the lawn and in the stable-yard, and no strangers were admitted into Mr. Nicholson's presence, or even inside the house, which was barricaded and guarded more like a fortress than a country gentleman's mansion.

When visiting the Marquis of Headfort, whose seat was only a short distance off, he thought it safer to go on foot than in a vehicle, the procession, which recalled that of the Lord Mayor's Show, consisting of an armed constable acting as a scout, then a couple of others abreast, then two more with Mr. Nicholson and his son, all parties armed to the teeth between them, and finally, another *posse* of police in a car, with a ladder slung at the side of it to enable them to scale any wall from behind which an assassin might fire.

Mr. Mountclare was duly furnished with an escort of constables, two being detached to accompany him everywhere.

After a time, however, he began to feel more secure, and contented himself with one of these guardian angels in uniform.

Of this fancied security his enemies had resolved to avail themselves.

Accordingly Ned and the young fellow who had so bitterly objected at being associated with him, had been told off to carry out the sentence.

On the evening of the day following his adventure at the inn, Ned arrived at the little hamlet of Clonbur.

He at once proceeded to the house of a man named Brennan, who had been indicated by those from whom he had received his instructions.

At first Brennan was inclined to look at him with suspicion, all strangers in the district being set down by the police as Fenian agents, and by the peasantry as detectives in disguise; but on matters being explained to him, he placed himself at Kelly's orders.

The bushranger was speedily made aware of the habits of his intended victim.

He learned that the following day Mr. Mountclare would be certain to drive into Clonbur to attend a magistrates' meeting, and that he would be pretty certain not to leave the hamlet before nightfall.

"Could one drop him on the road home?" asked Ned.

"Faix, yes; the road runs mighty convenient for that same," answered Brennan; "only there'll be one if not two of them murtherin' polis along with him in the car."

"Will there be a driver?"

"No, here he droives himself."

"Well, if there is only one bobby, it won't make any difference to me. I don't funk any brace of men ever whelped. Only I want something better than I've got to do the job as it ought to be done."

"What d'ye mean now?"

"I mean that though this revolver of mine is a very good one, it's not quite the right sort of tool for a snap-shot at a man driving by on a car."

"What is't ye want thin?"

"A double gun with a good load of swan shot in each barrel."

Brennan chuckled.

"Oh, make yerself aisy then," was his reply. "Sure an' it's the beauty of the world that I have close at hand now. Just wait a bit."

Stepping out of his cabin, Brennan glanced round to make sure that no prying eyes were following his movements.

Satisfied on this score, he stepped up to a huge pile of turf in the rear of his dwelling.

Thrusting his hand into this, he pulled out a long object swathed in hay bands, with which he returned to the cabin where Ned was awaiting him, and closed the door.

On the hay bands being removed, there stood revealed a short but heavy double-barrel gun.

"Sure and there's a beauty now," was Brennan's remark as he displayed the weapon.

Ned stretched out his hand for it.

"Be careful, captain, darlin'," ejaculated Brennan; "sure an' she's loaded."

"Loaded!" cried Ned, "then the best thing will be to fire her off and re-load her. I always mistrust an old charge, and the damp may have got to it lying in that old peat stack."

"Divil a bit of it. Just look at all the hay bands. Besides, it'll nivir do to fire her off here, or them nagurs the polis will be hearin' it."

"That's true, but still I always like to load a gun that I've got to handle."

"Och, make yer mind aisy. I loaded her myself, and there's two baccy pipe fulls of shot well rammed down in each barrel."

Ned had to accept this assurance.

The following forenoon, at an early hour, armed with the gun, and accompanied by Brennan, he started off to inspect the road, witness the passage of his intended victim to the town, in order to be able to identify him, and to select the exact spot for the scene of the crime.

Not that he had any particular fancy for this sort of profitless work.

It would bring him nothing, and might cut short his career, but he knew the consequences of refusal, and the dangerous secrets he was in possession of; also that he was watched, and that the least suspicion of treachery would be his death-warrant.

But he resolved to "cut it," and profitably too, at the first opportunity.

He carried the stock of the gun in one of the pockets of a long frieze coat, like that worn by most of the peasants, and the barrel, which had been purposely shortened some six inches or so, in the other.

His coat, together with a hat to correspond, caused him to resemble a small tenant farmer.

As he left the outskirts of Clonbur, in company with Brennan, a car was rapidly approaching the little hamlet.

"Whist, this is him!" ejaculated his guide; "I can see the glint of the sun on the peeler's gun. Take a good look at him as he goes by, the black-hearted thafe of the world, bad luck to him."

The car was driven by a firm yet mild-looking elderly man, in the dress of a country gentleman.

An armed policeman accompanied him.

As the vehicle passed them Brennan saluted the driver, who acknowledged it graciously.

"Ah, ye murtherin' ould villin!" muttered Brennan, in a bitter tone, as soon as the car and its occupants were out of earshot, "the curse of Cromwell be on ye. Plaze God, it'll be a cowld bed ye'll be slapin' in this night."

"Have you got any spite against the old buffer," asked Ned, somewhat surprised at his companion's vehemence, "for any ill turn he has done you?"

"Divil a ha'porth," was the frank answer, "but isn't he one of the bloodsuckers of the country? Isn't he a hathen protestant? Isn't he a Saxon tyrant that's thramplin' the very life of his poor tinantry?" was the reply, in a tone which plainly implied that the speaker was deeply surprised that anyone could be ignorant of the facts for a single moment.

To tell the truth, Mr. Mountclare was a man of old Irish family, and one of the mildest landlords in the district.

If Brennan had taken the trouble to reason out the state of affairs, he would possibly have come to this conclusion, but he preferred to accept the dictum of the Fenian emissaries, who denounced the poor gentleman as a Saxon tyrant, to taxing his own brain on the subject.

The road they were travelling along was bounded on either side by uneven stone walls, and ran between low hills and broken rocky ground, affording more than one convenient lurking-place.

At an eminence about a mile from the hamlet, Ned halted and looked round.

He felt very sick of the job. His heart was not in it.

He didn't care a pinch of salt whether all the peasantry in Ireland were starving or not; still he must now go on.

A range of hills rose about a quarter of a mile from the road on the one hand, whilst on the other a stretch of rocky, undulating ground swept down to the shores of Lough Corrib.

Ned scanned the surroundings approvingly.

"There's a boat down yondther, by that bit of rock ye see sticking up beyant," said Brennan, "so that if a man wanted to get off by wather he could do it aisy"

"Yes," assented Ned, as he continued to look round, "it's a handy place. There's firstrate cover behind the wall, and he must slacken pace a bit up the rise of the hill. Why, it will be as easy to bring him down as a tame goose. Hang it, it's almost mean to pot a poor devil like that. But, hilloa! we'll be spotted here—look at that crib, there," pointing to a comfortable-looking thatched cabin, about two hundred yards distant.

"Arrah, what matther, sure they are all for the 'cause.'"

"Oh, —— your cause, if my neck's to pay for it. Suppose they split?"

Brennan stared.

"What is it ye mane now?" he asked, in wondering tones.

"Why the people there will be sure to twig the job and spot me," replied Ned; "I mean they'll be bound to see what I'm about."

"Do you think they're dirty protestants and would risk their sowls by breaking the oath they've sworn by all the Saints' to keep?" and Brennan crossed himself devoutly.

"And if they do, sure——" was the answer.

"Well, for all that, if a reward was offered, they might blow the gaff."

"An' what's that now?"

"Why to peach, to let on to the police."

"Divil a word, ye may rest yer sowl on it. Not a finger will anyone hereaway be after lifting to hindther yer, and sorra a worrud will the blood-thirsty palers be able to git out o' them."

"That's good news, anyway," said Ned.

After a brief consultation the plan of action was arranged.

It was settled that Ned should make his way to a clump of woodland, lying on the hillside, at a short distance, and pass the rest of the day there; Brennan undertaking to bring or send some food, and to arrange means of flight when the deed had been done.

CHAPTER CLXXXIX.
KELLY AS A PRACTICAL LAND LAW REFORMER.

THIS programme was carried out.

Ned retreated to the wood, and throwing himself on the ground, began to smoke his pipe.

If he had been a lover of nature, bent upon a morning of tranquil enjoyment, instead of a cold-blooded murderer awaiting the hour of crime, he could not have taken things more coolly.

But he was body and soul a man of iron.

Not a spark of pity for his intended victim stirred in his adamantine breast.

He had not long been lying *perdu*, when he noticed a girl coming across the "bit o' plough," lying between the road and the wood.

She carried a basket in her hand and was evidently making her way towards the wood.

Ned showed himself for a moment, and she came straight up to him.

She handed him the basket and said—

"Misther Brennan bid me tell ye, sir, that there will be a man waitin' for ye in the boat he pointed out, and that he thinks that the safest way for ye."

So saying, she left; leaving Ned in a state of comical wonderment, at the cool and open manner in which the details of a murder were planned in Ireland.

After feeding off the contents of the basket and smoking several more pipes, Ned thought it time to make the final preparations.

He had been warned by Brennan, that Mr. Mountclare would hardly leave Clonbur before dusk; he thought it as well to be a little in advance.

The road was bordered on either side by walls, composed of stones roughly piled together.

The height of these walls varied according to the holdings they enclosed, in some instances being only a couple of feet high and in others four or five.

Other walls, serving to separate the different fields, ran off at right angles to those bordering the road.

At the point which Ned had selected, just at the top of a rise in the road, some two hundred yards beyond the cabin, already mentioned, the wall bordering the road was nearly six feet in height.

Ned took up his position in the angle where one of the walls dividing the fields started.

He began to pull down two or three stones, in order to form a convenient loophole through which to fire.

Whilst so engaged a couple of men passed along the road.

He was so closely occupied that he did not notice them till they were close abreast of him.

Designedly or unintentionally, however, they did not speak to him, neither did they pay the least attention to the somewhat singular task on which he was at that moment engaged.

They passed on, and he saw them enter the cabin.

"I don't much like that," he thought, "but I suppose it's some of the same pack."

Glancing around him, he could make out that there was more than one labourer at work on the hillside.

From the studied indifference to his work exhibited by the people about, he knew they were sympathisers, and that he was as safe as the Pope of Rome.

Still, the work had nothing in it to attract or stimulate him.

If it was to protect himself, all right; but "the cause" and all the tenantry and Fenians in Ireland might go to the bottomless pit for what he cared. In fact, he wished them all there at this moment.

For some time longer he remained at his post, watchful and observant, his eye "skinned" and his ear alert for the slightest sound.

He had completed his loophole, and had now sank down behind the wall completely out of sight, so far as anyone passing along the road, either on foot or on a car, was concerned.

He had arranged the loophole so that through it he could command a pretty fair extent of road, and now he sat on a stone close to the wall, with his eye glancing through the aperture in question.

A few peasants had passed along the road, and once he had pricked his ears at the sound of wheels, but only to find that they were those of a turf-cart.

Dusk was fast coming on, and the road, as far as he could see, was utterly deserted.

At length his strained ears caught the sound of some vehicle approaching from Clonbur at a sound pace.

He glanced in that direction.

At first he could only make out a dark object rapidly advancing from the hamlet.

In a few moments more he could discern that it was a car conveying two people.

He had no doubt that it was the one he was awaiting, and, indeed, he was soon certain of this fact.

The colour of the horse and the uniform of the policeman were easily recognised.

A momentary hesitation crossed his mind.

It was not whether he should abandon his attack, for such an idea as that never entered his head.

What he was in doubt was, which he should fire at first, Mr. Mountclare or the policeman.

The former was the most important to dispose of, but the latter was the most dangerous, besides which his very calling made Kelly feel inclined to give him the preference.

He hated a policeman with the furious antipathy of a London rough.

He evidently had his gun in readiness, and was no doubt a fair shot and a formidable antagonist.

Ned's mind was one of those which are soon made up in an emergency like the one now presenting itself.

"I'll down the bobby first," was his decision. "It won't take much trouble to pick off the other old cove before he can get away."

Withdrawing his head from the loophole, through which he had been observing the approach of the car, he replaced it by the barrel of his gun, taking care, however, not to thrust it too far forward, least it should be observed from the road.

Then dropping on one knee, and glancing along the weapon, he prepared for his right and left shot.

As he had anticipated, the horse was compelled to slacken speed a little in breasting the rise, but nevertheless he came up at a fair pace.

For all this Ned felt confident of his aim.

In a few seconds more the car was almost abreast of his loophole, and he had a fair view of it.

With the speed of thought he sighted the unfortunate policeman, and pulled the trigger of the right hand barrel.

A bright flash seemed to leap from out the stone wall, there was a loud report echoed back by the hills, and the hapless policeman, toppling forward from his seat, pitched headlong from the car into the roadway.

He was stone dead.

The muzzle of the gun had been scarcely six feet from him when Ned pulled the trigger, and the swanshot had acted like a bullet, and knocked a regular hole in him.

Before the report had died away, Ned shifted his aim, and, levelling at Mr. Mountclare, pulled the second trigger.

But, instead of toppling him over in turn as he anticipated, he found quite a different result.

No flash burst from the barrel, no shot whizzed forth on his death-dealing errand.

The ruffian had been right, and Mr. Brennan wrong, as to the propriety of stowing away a loaded gun in a peat stock.

The charge in the left-hand barrel had somehow or other got damp, and the result was that the cap snapped, but that no explosion followed.

Mr. Mountclare realised the position directly the first shot was fired.

He had been living in hourly anticipation of such an occurrence for the past three months, and when it thus came it did not find him unprepared.

He realised simultaneously the death of the policeman and his own peril.

For aught he knew half-a-dozen assassins might be lurking behind the wall from which the shot had been fired with such fatal effect as regarded his companion.

Flight was the best and only thing.

Hastily ramming down powder and slugs into the discharged gun, Kelly deliberately took aim at the unfortunate gentleman, and lodged a couple of slugs in his right arm, which, when struck, was in the act of gently applying the whip to the mare to increase her pace at this ugly corner of the road.

Immediately on hearing the report of the gun, and frightened by the flash, the animal sprung forward, but not before the driver leaped from his seat, with a pistol in his left hand (having instantly seized a revolver which lay handy on the seat beside him), and, being a powerful and very active man, rushed for Kelly.

He felt his right arm was done for and helpless, and the blood oozing rather rapidly from the wound. He was perfectly collected, and was soon within a few yards of the would-be assassin, who, afraid of nothing on the earth or out of it, awaited, in the consciousness of his great strength what he thought would be a very feeble attack.

But when he saw Mr. Mountclare clear at a bound the space that separated them, pistol in hand, and felt the whiz past his ear of the bullet that was discharged at his head, he made tracks to enable him to get another shot at his pursuer.

He soon put a respectable distance between himself and his enemy, at the same time succeeding in reloading his piece (which was not a breechloader) hastily, and without being able to ram down the charge.

Having, as he now judged, sufficient power to kill, or at least disable, Mr. Mountclare, he calmly awaited the approach of his panting pursuer, into whose body he poured charge No. 2, but only inflicted flesh-wounds.

Astounded at the apparent unwounded condition of his enemy, and aware that he had a foe not easily shaken off, he clubbed his gun, and, striking the unfortunate man a powerful blow on the right ankle, brought him to the ground.

Before he was struck he unfortunately exclaimed—

" I'd swear to you, you scoundrel, amongst a million ! "

Down came the sweeping blow, and no sooner was he prostrate than the barrel, wielded by the ruffian's powerful arms, crashed through the skull of Fenian vengeance.

So exhausted was Kelly with the chase and the excitement that he deliberately sat down upon a large stone near him, none of the people looking on taking the least notice of the fray, and inwardly sympathising with this mode of petitioning for " Justice to Ireland."

Fearing his victim might still survive, Kelly quietly reloaded his gun.

" Be quick wid your b'essed work, agrah ! " suggested a bystander, who guessed what the assassin was about. "Sure the music o' them shots may invite the peelers to the dance, and, maybe, they'd choose you for a partner, and be so tuk wid you that they wouldn't give up your company for a bit. The poor craythur's best out of his misery, and a bit of lead, more or less, when he's got so much of it, may be convainient for yiz both."

Kelly never opened his lips, but he followed the advice, and effectually prevented the probability of Mr. Mountclare's ever swearing to him amongst a million. His corpse was some distance from that of the policeman, for according to the *Times* he had jumped two ditches, and with his broken bleeding arm, ran one hundred and fourteen yards !

His body lay exposed, where it fell, for some two hours.

The horse, which had been frightened by the report of the firearms, and suddenly finding itself loose from the usual curb of the reins, bolted, and, with the instinct of its kind, made straight home at a rattling pace to its stables. Hearing the rapid approach of the horse and car —the pace being greatly in excess of the ordinary one—the inmates rushed out to see w at was the cause of this unusual speed, when the vehicle was observed to be empty and the condition of the animal obviously unusual.

The worst fears were immediately entertained, and a neighbouring gentleman, accompanied by police, proceeded along the road taken by the unhappy victim.

They soon were at the fatal spot. Horror was stamped on the countenances of the party. They reverently lifted the body and made for the snug neighbouring cabin, whose contiguity had first of all discouraged Kelly. It was tenanted by a man named Flanagan.

The body was at once taken there, but Flanagan obstinately refused it admission under the plea that if it was admitted nothing belonging to him would be alive that day twelvemonths.

He even refused to allow it to be taken into an outhouse, and nothing could be done but to place it on a car and convey it back to Clonbur, though before this was accomplished the doctor was satisfied that life was totally extinct.

And here the police, or rather, the masters, showed their usual folly. Why not have forcibly used the fellow's premises? They manage these little affairs better in France. The idea of perilling a man's life out of deference to fantastic " rights " is not only foolish but illogical.

A policeman can call upon a passer-by to assist him in a capture, but he can call upon a householder to receive in his outhouse a half-murdered man, whose removal might produce death. This is the abuse, not the use, of the law.

The police, employed in the exercise of these onerous duties, are openly refused the use of vehicles for transport. In any other country in the globe they could be taken. A man's property is taken when such an act is for the public good ; but a licensed car is sacred though needful to those employed in suppressing rebellion, and the fire, blood, and misery that accompanies it.

Well might Madame Roland exclaim when under the guillotine—" Oh, liberty, what deeds are done in thy name."

The liberty acceded in this instance by the authorities to the sympathisers with anarchy and rebellion is opposed to common-sense, and only possible under a timid and vacillating government.

As to evidence, Flanagan and his family at the inquest swore they had not heard any shots, and, neither he, nor the friend who had seen Ned making his loophole, dreamed of mentioning that fact.

The peasants working on the hill-side, who must have actually witnessed the struggle, one and all declared they had seen nothing, nothing whatever.

As in the *Critic*, " their unanimity was wonderful."

Neither threats, bribes, or snares on the part of the police were of the slightest use towards obtaining testimony, and the Government reward was equally fruitless.

The bills offering it were pasted up in all directions, and were spelled over by the peasantry, but there their effect began and ended, since not a soul troubled himself, or herself, about earning the sum promised for the revelation of the name of Mr. Mountclare's murderer.

CHAPTER CXC.
NED INTERVIEWS A HIGH OFFICIAL.

OWING to the excellent organisation under which the business of assassination is carried on in Ireland Ned's escape was an easy one to accomplish.

A man was waiting for him with a boat at the spot indicated to carry him some distance down the lake to a point where a guide was stationed to direct him on his way.

He soon found the nearest railway for Dublin, receiving the Fenian sign *en route* from half of the railway subordinate employés on the line

But in course of this journey he began to realise a very unpleasant fact.

He was no longer his own master.

He was nothing more nor less than the bond slave of the Fenian Brotherhood, since he had to halt where they decided and to journey as they wished.

To a man accustomed as he was to the widest possible personal liberty, the mere suspicion of a chain was irritating in the extreme.

This circumstance and the climate combined to render him extremely savage and discontented.

"I've had about enough of this beastly country," he soliloquised. "It's nothing but like living in a marsh. The confounded drizzle, drizzle, all day long is enough to turn a man's blood to water. The sun, when it does shine, is like a tallow-tap in a scooped-out turnip. Blowed if I wouldn't do six months on the mill than stop here for half that time. I'll hook it. I'm not going to be shunted about all over the country like a bag of wool. If these blokes think they're going to have me as tame as a bull-pup to their call, they'll find out their mistake before long."

But he found that to get clear of the toils into which he had thrust himself was no easy matter.

He soon realised that every movement he made was watched, and he was furthermore told that he must hold himself in readiness to do his duty to the cause at any moment's notice and without hesitation.

He was also given to understand that he was under surveillance like the rest, and that the slightest suspicion of his loyalty would be followed by deadly vengeance. This turned his blood to gall; and he resolved, not only to put the ocean between himself and the brotherhood, but to sell the lot, if he could make anything out of the sale.

Arrived in Dublin, he fell in with a Yankee Fenian, with whom he "liquored up" to a fearful extent, and whom he agreed to accompany to America.

The two villians soon understood one another upon one point, and that was to sell their party, or any one of them, to the authorities, provided the price was tempting and silence could be secured.

Having concluded this compact, Kelly, in one of the subsequent drinking bouts, let out his possession of a considerable sum of money, and at the same time slapping his waistband, said that was *his* blooming bank.

It was enough for his friend. At the next bout, he simply hocussed Kelly, and while the latter was insensible, plundered him of his ill-gotten gains. On coming to himself, he discovered his loss and knew the thief.

The reader can imagine the fury, and, at the same time, the consternation, the stranded rascal felt.

He guessed at once the bird had flown, and that he was powerless. But he was a man of action. Money he must have, and only one way remained open to him to accomplish that end.

He quickly made up his mind.

One fine morning he presented himself at the Castle and demanded an interview with the secretary.

After half-a-dozen understrappers had tried, firstly to choke him off altogether, secondly to snub him into imbecility, and thirdly to learn all about the business that brought him there, he was at length admitted to the presence of the official he desired to see.

As soon as he had broached the subject of his visit, the secretary put on the bland official smile in use in such cases.

"My good fellow," he began, in a patronising manner, "I can assure you that you are rather late in the day. We have already been placed in possession of full details of the Fenian agitation."

Ned saw through his game.

"Oh! you have, have you?" he replied. "Then why don't you go and cop the blessed lot?"

"There are reasons of State which it is quite impossible to discuss here," said the secretary, with a dignified wave of his hand.

"What are you offering those rewards for, then, if you know all about it? Perhaps you know, too, that you are spotted, and that your gov'nor is marked down too?" said Kelly, with cool audacity.

The official looked somewhat scared, as he knew the brotherhood would hesitate very little to carry out such a purpose if practicable.

Having already, from other sources, the thread of the conspiracy in his hands, he was able, by adroit questions, to discover that Kelly was behind the scenes, he listened to the tempter with more interest.

"Look here," said Ned, "you say you know all about the Fenian business. Well, I daresay you've had a lot of peddling little sneaks come to you and offer to tell you this, that, and the other for a price."

The other smiled and nodded assent.

"But did any one of 'em name the day next week that's been fixed for cutting your throat and that of every other man Jack in this old building?" retorted Ned, with an earnestness that went far to convince the other of his sincerity.

"Perhaps you had better explain yourself a little more fully," observed the secretary.

"Very well, in the first place there's a plot to seize on this place."

"We know that already—that's no news."

"But you don't know when or how it is to come off, or who are to take part in it. Now let us come to the point. For a hundred pounds cash down and a free passage to the colonies I'll put you in the way to bag the whole lot—say the word."

"Really, the suddenness of the offer renders it quite impossible for me to accept it. I will consult the home authorities, and, if, after due consideration, we find——"

"Oh, stow all that—it won't wash! You've got the power to settle the job and plank down the coin. I'm not a fellow to shilly-shally, and I tell you straight, that if once I walk out of this old caboose of yours, you'll be sorry for it."

"But suppose, mind I only say suppose," said the secretary, with a smile, "that we do not care to part with a gentleman possessed of such very valuable information as you claim to be?"

"You mean you'll clap me in quod, eh? unless I'll speak out; is that it?" cried Ned.

"Precisely."

"Well, then, you'd have to keep me here till I rotted, before you'd get a word out of me."

The secretary saw that such was the case; he also knew that if he carried his threat into execution, he would effectually stop all future sources of information from the class to which his informant belonged—and thus stop up all sources of information from the best quarters—and to which the Government was already indebted for many important particulars of the plot they desired to unravel.

"Well, sir," he remarked with his most official air, "it may be as well, after all, to entertain your application.

"You say you are in possession of certain information of great importance, which you are willing to impart for a consideration, namely, the sum of one hundred pounds."

"In gold, mind," broke in Ned. "None of your cheques. I've seen that dodge played more than once, and none of your flimsies either. Gold is my price, take it or leave it, as the coster said to the old woman when she told him that his fish stank."

"I think if you will show me you are in a position to give the information you promise, that I can recommend the payment of the sum you wish," said the secretary.

The fact was that the authorities were perfectly aware that a plot was hatching at that time for the seizure of the castle, but were utterly at a loss as to its details, and for some weeks had been living in hourly fear of an outbreak.

Hence, after a little more discussion, the secretary agreed to the terms.

The money having been handed over, for Kelly refused to open his lips till that had been done, Ned proceeded to unfold the plot then in progress for the seizure of the castle.

Of the fact of such a plot having been formed, most people are aware, though the exact circumstances under which it was revealed to Government have hitherto been kept a secret.

At that time the political situation rendered it necessary, before all things, that matters should be kept as quiet as possible in Ireland.

It was a knowledge of this kind of forbearance that encouraged the Fenians to go as far as they did.

It was only at their direst extremity that anything like decisive measures were taken against them.

Hence, even when in possession of the information given by Kelly they hesitated about making full use of it.

Political trials of any kind are unpopular.

They contented themselves, therefore, with taking measures to secure the castle from attack, and even went so far as to warn the intending rebels a few days later, that their plot was found out.

There was little need of this latter step, however.

The excitement prevailing amongst the officials, the coming and going of messengers, the doubling of sentries, and the hasty convocation of the authorities, were sufficient warning to the Fenian leaders that something was up.

By means of their spies they learnt, that without a doubt, they had been betrayed, though by whom was at first a profound mystery.

At length the fact of Ned's visit to the castle became known to them. The fact was, that one of the castle servants, a red-hot Fenian, had seen Kelly call several times at the Chief Secretary's office, and communicated that fact to the conspirators.

They at once resolved to take summary vengeance upon him for his treachery.

The task of putting him quietly out of the way was at once delegated to a member of the brotherhood.

But when he proceeded to the quarters occupied by Kelly in order to learn the most feasible way of setting about the task, he found the bird had flown.

Ned had seen quite enough of the Fenians to know the danger to which he was exposing himself by betraying them.

He resolved, therefore, to clear out from Dublin directly he had completed his revelations.

On quitting the castle with his blood-money, he had returned to his lodgings

After stowing away the cash in a belt which he had bought on the way, he buckled this round him, packed up his traps, and that same evening went on board the Lady Clive, bound for London, there being no chance just then of a direct passage from Dublin to the colonies.

It did not take long for the Fenians to find this out, and the boat that left the following night for Holyhead, bore with it a dwarfish-looking, red-headed fellow, answering to the name of Mike Hefferman, to whom the task of avenging them on Kelly had been entrusted.

CHAPTER CXCI.
DONE ON BOTH SIDES.

THE reasons that prompted Ned to take the boat to London, instead of proceeding thither by way of that conglomeration of public-house, and dissenting-chapels, known as the town of Holyhead, were two in number.

He judged that if any of his late friends wished to make enquiries as to his destination, they would be less likely to suspect his departure by this route, and, consequently, that there was a chance of them losing the scent.

Although he had a hundred pounds, Ned judged that if a chance of doing a little bit of business on the way, in order just to cover his travelling expenses, did arise he would certainly not neglect it."

board the boat, and occupying one of the berths in the same cabin as himself, was a highly respectable-looking, elderly gentleman.

Amongst his goods and chattels, was a fair-sized black travelling-bag, concerning the safety of which he seemed more than usually anxious.

It was placed in his berth, though it did not seem to contain any travelling requisites, and was never opened by him.

He profited by the old fellow's absence from the cabin, to lift it, and was at once struck by its weight.

He tried to get in conversation with the owner, but did not succeed very well, for the stranger was, to Ned's idea, a "dry old stick," and was not inclined to chum with such a rough and ready style of customer as the bushranger.

In course of the day, he heard the stranger mentioning, in the course of conversation, that he always insured his luggage, which struck Ned as somewhat singular, unless there was something more than mere wearing-apparel to insure. It increased his suspicions that the black bag was valuable. He resolved that he and that bag should be better acquainted, but the question was how to manage it.

The old man evidently kept a close watch over his property, and had even gone so far as to ask the steward to have any eye to it.

It was locked too, though Ned judged that it would be easy enough to cut it open with a knife, provided he could arrange to decamp unobserved with its contents.

He puzzled in his mind as to whether there was any chance of slipping ashore with it at any of the places at which the boat stopped on her way to London, but he could not hit upon one.

Especially as he noticed that the old fellow was on the alert, and that there would be little prospect of quitting the boat with the bag unnoticed.

They had touched at Falmouth and were nearing Plymouth when he hit upon the germ of a plan.

He went down into the main cabin, and then passed into the smaller one in which was his berth, leaving the door open on purpose, so that if the steward chose to look in he would see that he was not up to any tricks.

Then he sat down, and for about ten minutes stared his hardest at the bag.

It was as though he desired to imprint a mental photograph of it on his mind, and such was his object.

When he felt certain that the shape and size were stamped upon his memory, he rose and left the cabin.

On reaching Plymouth, where a stay of several hours was made, he went on shore and visited several outfitting shops in succession.

It was some time before he could get what he wanted, but at last he became the owner of a bag in all respects like the one on board.

But this did not satisfy him.

He seemed to have a decided fancy for bags, for at another establishment he purchased the largest carpet bag he could find.

In this he placed the first one he had bought, together with several articles of ironmongery, small but weighty, of which he had also become the proprietor.

He then returned on board, and slipping down into the cabin again, proceeded to rub and discolour the new bag until it was an exact copy of the one belonging to the stranger.

He then placed the articles of ironmongery in it, and stuffed it over with old newspapers and odd articles of wearing apparel, till it was a tolerably exact reproduction of the other, as regarded size and weight.

Then he replaced it in the huge carpet-bag, and waited till the fitting time arrived to carry out his plan.

"This, I fancy, will be a pretty neat job," he thought; "the old fellow would not be so precious anxious about it unless it was something jolly well worth laying hands on. Rum old cubby he is. Blessed if I can make out his lingo He was jabbering away about 'talks' and 'sacks,' I'm sure I caught something about bracelets and necklaces, too."

The next halting-place was Southampton, but this did not quite suit Ned's plans.

Portsmouth, at which they would also stop, was close at hand, and if he discovered his loss, the old man could land there

But on leaving Portsmouth the boat did not stop again till she reached London, so Ned resolved to carry out his plan at the seaport immortalised by Marryat

He told the steward that he should be delighted to go on shore at Portsmouth, instead of proceeding to London.

When they got into harbour he stepped down to get his traps together.

In a moment he had opened the carpet-bag, pulled out the dummy, placed it in the old man's berth, and thrust the coveted prize in its place.

No sooner was the transfer effected, than the steward sauntered in in a careless way.

He leant against the berth, and in a half unconscious way lifted the bag Ned had just placed there.

"By Gosh!" thought the latter; "it was a lucky thing I thought of making the weight all right!"

It was evident that the steward was keeping a watch over the old man's property.

"Rum old cock; the chap that has that berth, steward," said Ned.

"Yes, sir," answered the steward, with great civility, for he could not help respecting a customer like Ned, who had drunk about three times as much as any other man on board, and had tipped him with colonial liberality. "Very respectable old gent. sir, though, and as rich as the Bank of England. Isn't he?"

"Don't know, I'm sure. sir; but he travels by our boat two or three times a year regular, and is always liberal to us, sir."

"I'm right," thought Kelly. "That's what he is—the partner in a jewellery firm."

After bidding the steward good day, Ned made his way to shore, having taken care to delay doing so till just before the ship resumed her journey.

His luggage only consisted of a small portmanteau in addition to the carpet-bag.

He consigned the former to a porter to carry, but retained the latter in his hand.

The custom-house people merely asked him if he had anything liable to pay duty, but did not trouble to examine his luggage.

Having engaged a fly, he was driven to the station, and found that a train was on the point of starting for London, and that, to his great satisfaction, it was an express.

He tipped the guard, and, with his precious bag, was soon seated in a first-class compartment, and flying towards the metropolis at full speed.

By this time he felt sure that the Lady Olive was well on her way, and that even if the old fellow he had plundered discovered his loss, he would have great difficulty in getting on shore.

Ned felt in a great good humour.

In his own opinion, he had done the little trick very neatly and cleverly, and he rather began to look on the bag in the light of the reward of merit.

"Now," he mused, "I'll just overhaul this little collection, whatever it is."

There was no prospect of the train stopping for at least three-quarters of an hour, so he had plenty of time for his delightful task.

He opened the carpet bag, and drew forth the other with due deliberation.

He poised it for a moment in his hand.

"It's jolly heavy," he muttered, approvingly. "Even if they're only gold fakements inside, they ought to be worth a good lot. They must be, or the old buffer would never half looked after them so sharp. How his blooming old chops will fall when he goes to open the bag I left him, and finds all his swag changed into flatirons and trivits."

And Ned broke into a roar of laughter at the picture he thus conjured up.

The bag was locked, but this offered no impediment.

Pulling out his knife, he opened it, and cut a gash right along the side of his prize.

Into this he thrust his hand and pulled out an object carefully enveloped in soft white tissue paper.

It was evidently of metal.

Carefully he undid it.

To his amazement, instead of some article wrought in gold or silver, what to him appeared a shapeless lump of dingy metal, almost eaten away by corrosion, made its appearance.

Ned was dumbfounded.

In swift succession he pulled out half-a-dozen packages of different sizes, and undid them.

The result was in every case the same.

The objects revealed were of different shapes and sizes, and in various stages of dilapidation, but one and all appeared to be composed of the same dingy corroded metal.

The bulk of them were to him mere shapeless lumps, but in one or two he fancied he could trace a faint resemblance to such ornaments as some of the savages he had met in his wanderings had worn.

Rapidly he emptied the bag in the hope of perhaps finding a grain of wheat in all this chaff, but in this he was disappointed.

(To be continued.)

NED KELLY

THE
IRONCLAD
AUSTRALIAN BUSHRANGER

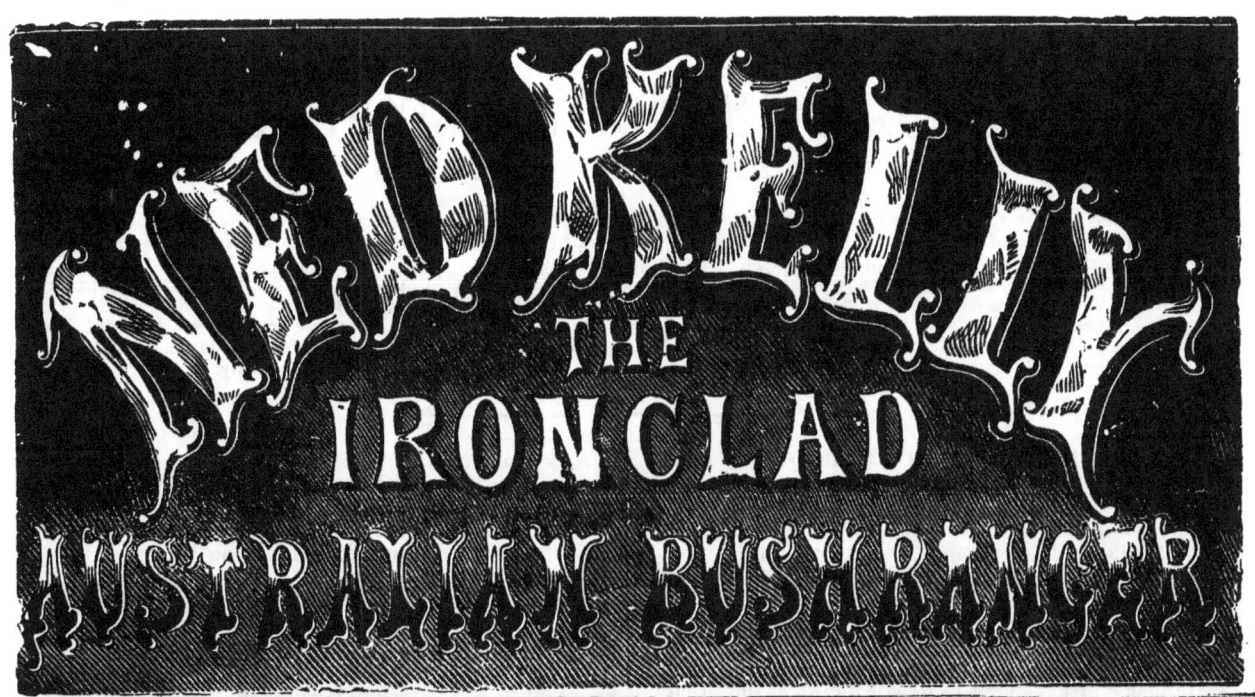

NO 33,

NED KELLY: IRONCLAD BUSHRANGER.

It is well known that for many years Ned Kelly had made himself notorious by a series of crimes wholly incompatible with the civilisation of the nineteenth century. Ned Kelly's celebrated steed, Marco Polo, is as well known at the Antipodes as Dick Turpin's Black Bess in these islands."—*Telegraph*, 7th July, 1881.

"It is notorious that the robbery of Mr. Steward's corpse was mainly performed by the assistance of NED KELLY'S BROTHER, the Captain of what was neither more nor less than a pirate ship."—*Times*, July.

"The history of NED KELLY and his celebrated black horse, Marco Polo, will ever live in the recollection of the Australian public. The deeds of Dick Turpin, and the performances of Black Bess, are tame beside those of 'NED AND HIS NAG;' in addition to which Ned's history is true, and Turpin's is pure fiction."—*Press*, July.

CHAPTER CXCII.—*Continued*.

Then he relieved his feelings by swearing a string of oaths, that almost splintered the window-panes.

" By ——, I was chuckling just now at the thought of the old fellow's face when he set eyes on my flat-irons. The laugh would be on his side if he could only spot my being sold over his filthy, rotten verdigris."

Ned, however, was quite wrong in this conjecture.

The gentleman in question was a very earnest and very wealthy antiquarian.

He took a great interest in what is known as the Bronze Periods, and his collection of weapons, utensils, and ornaments belonging to that epoch was one of the most extensive in the United Kingdom.

Hearing that an extensive " find " had lately been made in Ireland, he had hastened to secure it at great expense, and had supplemented it with several other purchases.

In addition to the sceax and torques, that to Ned had sounded as "sacks and talks," there were celts axe and spear heads, sword blades, armlets, necklaces, brooches, shield-bosses, and numerous similar objects which it required all the enthusiastic zeal and wonderfully credulous perception of an antiquary to identify.

No doubt there were a few bits of modern copper tea-kettles and the like mixed up with the lot.

Nevertheless the entire collection was one which an appreciator of such things would almost go down on his knees and worship.

Only Ned was not at all an appreciator of such things, which to him were simply dirty bits of metal.

Gathering the lot together, he hurled them by handfuls out of the window.

The train at that moment was passing a range of disused gravel pits, into which most of the relics pitched.

Here the bulk of them were discovered scattered some months afterwards, and formed the staple for several papers read at archeological societies, meetings in which it was conclusively established that an extensive settlement must have existed on the spot during the bronze period.

The bag was also thrown out, and was appropriated by a thrifty farm-labourer, who got his wife to sew up the hole in it.

This accomplished, Ned relieved his feelings by another burst of highly seasoned adjectives. When he had done so he lit his pipe and smoked doggedly till he arrived at Waterloo Station.

CHAPTER CXCIII.

AN AVENGER ON THE TRAIL.

NED took up his quarters in a respectable private hotel in a street off the Strand.

He resolved to " play possum " a bit.

The recollection of his late exploits in London, was, he guessed, pretty fresh in the recollection of the police, and he resolved to avoid appearing in any of his former haunts.

Kit had gone to sea again, and Jess, who had been released after Ned's escape from capture in the matter of the intended banknote forgeries, in consequence of there being no case against her, returned to the colonies.

As to Peace, Ned did not care about renewing his connection with that sanctimonious scoundrel, and he judged it prudent not to hunt up any of the gambling set into which he had been introduced by Anatole.

Time therefore hung a little heavy on his hands in the evenings.

He did not like to sail by the P. & O. boats, but made enquiries as to when a sailing ship would leave for Australia.

He found that none would clear out of dock for at least four or five days, and that the first to sail was bound for the little frequented port of Perth, on the Swan river in Western Australia.

He was quite ignorant of this district, but thought he should have no difficulty in getting on to Adelaide or Sydney from there, so took his passage on board her.

He was pretty busy for the next day or so in buying a small outfit for the voyage, but his evenings were dull.

He had a little touch of dulness on him which led him to feel somewhat inclined for company.

All company was, in his mind, pretty much alike, provided there was a certain amount of noise, fun, and liquor ; so he took to visiting the minor music halls and to drinking at a public till closing time.

Although his chief anxiety was to keep out of the ken of the police, he was equally desirous of evading any contact with his recent acquaintances, the Fenians.

Hence he shunned those establishments where the Irish element was likely to muster to the fore.

On the morning before that fixed for his departure, the servant mentioned to him that, during his absence the evening before, a gentleman, who had declined to leave any name, had called to see him.

He did not like this, but the morning passed without anything suspicious happening.

Towards noon he sallied forth, having taken it into his head to visit the Crystal Palace, where a popular *fête* was to take place, and where, if "wanted," the police would scarcely look for him.

As he passed up his street into the Strand, he noticed a little, cross-built, ugly-looking fellow with red hair, lounging on the other side of the way, but paid no further attention to him.

On reaching the Strand, he hailed a hansom to take him to Ludgate Station.

If he had thought of looking round he would have seen the stranger get into another and follow him.

The train was very full, and he had some difficulty in getting a place.

At the Palace, too, not only did he pass the day in the thick of the crowd, but happened to run against some men whose acquaintance he had made when in London before, and to whom he stuck throughout the day, standing drinks with a freedom that charmed them.

Once or twice he was seized with the impression that someone was watching him, and, glancing round, caught sight of a pair of eyes glaring at him from behind a pillar.

However, he soon succeeded in shaking off this impression.

His friends, as evening drew on, closed round him like

a body-guard, and it was decided that they should all return to town and finish the evening together.

Here again, Ned could not help fancying that someone was observing all his movements, nor was he mistaken.

The man Heffernan, to whom had been entrusted the mission of avenging Ned's betrayal of the Fenian plot, was indeed on his track.

It was an emissary of his who had called the night before at Ned's residence, which the Fenians had only just succeeded in discovering; for his dodge of leaving the boat at Portsmouth, had for the time thrown the Fenian police quite off his track.

Indeed, had he not been accidentally spotted in the streets of London by a Fenian acquainted with his person, who tracked him home, and told Heffernan of his whereabouts, he would have probably got out of the country unknown to any of them.

Heffernan's agent had learnt from the people at Kelly's hotel that he was preparing to leave immediately, and, therefore, there was no time to be lost.

Accordingly, he set himself to follow Ned like his shadow.

But the entire day had passed away without his being able to get the chance he sought.

Ned was either surrounded by people, or mixed up in a crowd.

As the time sped on, Heffernan grew more and more desperate as to the feasability of his attempt.

He was one of those reckless fanatics, who when worked up to a certain pitch, count life as nothing compared to the accomplishment of the object on which their souls are set.

He had sworn to slay Ned, and he had made up his mind to do this, even if his own life paid the forfeit.

Escape was a secondary consideration.

Ned had gone to the Hoxton theatre, and taken his place in the back of the pit, to escape as much as possible, general observation. Heffernan was not far off.

His hand thrust into his breast, gripped the hilt of a long, double-edged knife, ground to the sharpness of a razor, with which he had armed himself in preference to firearms, as being likely to do the job without making a noise.

He left the theatre shortly before the fall of the curtain, and took up his position in the passage amongst the crowd who were pouring out from the pit.

The crowd was a dense one, and being a little man he had great difficulty in trying to work his way through it towards Ned.

Just too, as he was getting near him, a man who had been indulging in several drinks between the acts, pitched forward and completely cut off his approach from his victim.

Kelly noticed him, however, and as he left the theatre the recollection of having seen the same face in the morning crossed his mind.

Heffernan resolved to follow and do his work without a witness.

Kelly strode along at a brisk pace with his enemy following stealthily in his rear.

CHAPTER CXCIV.
NED SETTLES THE FENIAN EMISSARY.

THEIR route at first, however, lay along a thoroughfare so lively and well-lighted, that Heffernan resolved to defer striking his blow till a somewhat fairer opportunity presented itself.

He did not want to be checked in his work by the interference of some officious bystander.

Suddenly Ned turned into a huge gin-palace, the lavishly decorated bar of which was blazing with light.

Heffernan followed him.

A very motley lot of individuals were collected in front of the long pewter counter, behind which half a dozen sturdy, white-shirt-sleeved barmen were hard at work attending to the wants of their numerous customers.

These chiefly consisted of costermongers, labourers, small traders and the like, with a sprinkling of thieves and cadgers.

Ned shouldered his way to the bar and called for a drink.

His appearance being rather better than that of many present, drew some attention from the cadging portion of the assembly.

A cripple, all tongue and wooden leg, like the sign of the Magpie and Stump, began badgering him in a hissing, husky voice, sounding like chronic-catarrh, but in reality due to the "blue ruin," to "buy er box o' lights."

Another old wretch whose scalp, save for three or four long grey hairs on the top of it, was as smooth as a new-born baby's, and whose skeleton frame was so wrapped in an old brown overcoat which looked as if at some former period it had seen hard service on a scarecrow in a cornfield, requested to be refreshed at his expense.

Ned, being in a reckless, generous humour, complied with this modest request, and extended his hospitality to several others of the company, who gathered round him in a way which prevented Heffernan from getting near him

He only bided his time, however.

Ned liked to be the king of the company, and, when "half-cock," was apt at times to "blow" somewhat.

He took it into his head to extol the beauties of colonial life, and sketched Australia as a land overflowing, if not with milk and honey, at least with rum and mutton.

His hearers listened with some attention, for there are no people sharper to guage a man than the lower classes in London, and they could see that, though generously inclined, he was not a "mug."

"Are the wages good there?" enquired a respectable mechanic.

"Good! I believe you. A chap like you could get a pound a day easily."

"What's the use of giving a man a pound a day if he won't work for it?" said a one-eyed cadger, with a grin, a remark which caused the other to toy with a peculiar and meaning playfulness with the heavy pewter measure on the counter before him.

"Shut hup, boss-heye!" growled a hulking costermonger, in a blue jersey, with a species of white bolster swathed around his bull neck.

"Who are yer a-callin' 'boss-eye'?" retorted the other. "Some coves with one eye can see a sight better than them as has two."

"Just so," remarked another of the company; "we all know as how you can spot a likely-lookin' old lady or gentleman with half an eye, and keep the other half for the copper as is a watching on yer."

From Australia Ned turned his attention to Ireland, the climate and the loss of his money combined having given him a deep grudge against that country, despite his descent.

He wound up a scathing denunciation of it by calling it—

"A fifty bog-hole full of squabbling swine living in styes, and only fit to be dug in the ground to manure their own potato patches with."

This gave a chance, for which Heffernan was waiting.

"That's a loie, sor!" he exclaimed in a loud voice, which at once attracted Kelly's notice.

"Hilloa!" cried Ned. "Here's one of the swine. Who are you, you pig-faced bog-trotter?"

"Only an Oirishman, sor, who's not going to say his down-throdden counthree abused by the loikes of yeself," said Heffernan, pushing his way forward towards Ned, his eyes gleaming with fury and revenge.

Heffernan had gained a position in front of Ned, and gave a wave of his arms to keep the rest of those around from crowding in on him.

"It's a loiar, sor, that ye are!" he continued, with the evident intention of provoking Ned to some commencement of violence, in order to find an excuse for using his knife.

"Stand back, you monkey-faced hound!" said Ned, as he all at once recognised the man who had been dogging his footsteps all day, and whose face he had caught a glimpse of.

The thought that the stranger might be a police-spy crossed his mind.

"Never mind, old pal," put in a bystander, "it's not worth rowing over."

"Will ye come outside and setthle the matther?" cried Heffernan, wishing to lure Ned into some by-street.

"D'ye think I'd strangle a shrimp like you, you hump-backed crab?"

A laugh followed these words.

"Order there!" cried one of the barmen, sharply.

"Ye're a murtherin' loiar and a big blackguard of a coward!" yelled Heffernan, striving to provoke him. "Ye daren't fight me!"

"No fighting here," cried the barman.

"Shut up, you blathering fool!" said Ned to Heffernan. "I could wring your neck if I'd a mind to in a jiffey. Here, have a drink and end this shindy."

This was exactly what Heffernan did not want.

"Be easy, now, dear," observed a lady, whose own face and bonnet bore evidence that she had engaged in personal conflict in course of the evening, "or you'll get chucked."

Heffernan glared at Kelly with his red, ferret-like eyes.

Finding that he could not provoke Ned to an attack, and seeing that if he persisted in kicking up a noise he would get himself turned out of the house, he resolved to end the matter at all risks.

He had sworn to have Kelly's life.

He thrust his hand into his bosom, whilst a look of fiendish hatred distorted his naturally hideous features.

Ned was standing with his elbow on the counter, at a distance of about four feet or so from him.

The contrast between the two men as they thus stood facing one another—the tall, bulky bushranger, with his reckless air and dark, coarsely handsome features, and his dwarfish enemy, whose cocoanut-shaped scull was thatched with a thick felt of red hair, and whose thickly freckled face was of a type to be met with in the highest development in the monkey-house at the Zoological Gardens—was most marked.

Suddenly clearing the intervening space at a bound, and simultaneously unsheathing his knife, Heffernan threw himself on Kelly.

Twice the bright blade flashed in the air, and twice to all seeming was buried in Ned's body, the latter astounded at the suddeness of the onslaught had time neither to escape or to defend himself.

So swift had been the attack that the bystanders had had no chance to interfere.

They gave Kelly up for lost.

Heffernan had aimed his blows with deadly intent at the lower part of the bushranger's body.

Ned's hand tightened round the handle of a quart pot from which he was drinking.

He threw his mighty arm high above his head.

The next instant he brought it down with a swing, like that of a trip-hammer, full on his assailant's scull.

Heffernan dropped to the ground as though smitten by lightening itself.

His scull was fractured.

A convulsive quiver ran through his limbs, he drew up his knees and crossed his arms over his stomach.

"The knifing coward."

"The scoundrel."

"That's right, mate."

And a chorus of similar cries broke forth.

The crowd had all an Englishman's love of fair play.

In a fight between Ned and Heffernan, their sympathies would have been all on the side of the latter, as the smaller man, but this dastardly attempt at assassination had thoroughly disgusted them.

The knife they held in abhorrence.

One of them bent over Heffernan.

He then rose and stepped quietly up to Ned.

"Mate, I'm afeered you've killed him," he said, in a low tone. "Are you hurt, 'yourself?'"

"That's so," added a companion. "You'd better bolt, or the coppers 'll nail you."

"Oh! we can all swear he put a knife into you first," said the first.

"Hook it at once," cried a third, "if you are able. It's the best way."

The advice was too good not to be taken, and Ned moved swiftly towards the door, no one making the slightest attempt to check or detain him.

The whole affair, indeed, had taken place so quickly that many had hardly had time to realise the event, and others had not yet recovered from the stupor into which it had plunged them.

"Hi, there, stop that man!" cried one of the barmen, recovering from his confusion just as Ned reached the door.

But no one paid the least attention, and before he could get over the counter Ned had passed out through the swing doors.

By the time the barman had managed to get there, the bushranger had vanished.

The police were sent for, and Heffernan was conveyed to the nearest hospital, where the house surgeon pronounced life extinct.

The greatest puzzle to those who had witnessed the matter was the ease with which Kelly had been able to kill his assailant, and then walk off after the fearful stabs he had received.

They could not make it out.

The solution of the mystery was a very simple one.

Ned had placed the hundred sovereigns received from the Government in a broad belt buckled round the lower part of his body, and divided into a number of little compartments, each filled with coin.

Each time the knife had struck against this novel armour, which it had failed to penetrate.

It was a strange irony that the very money that had been paid to him for betraying the Fenians should have saved his life from the knife of the man deputed by them as their avenger.

CHAPTER CXCV.
NED IN LONDON HAS THE LUCK OF LEFROY AT BRIGHTON WITH THE POLICE.

NED thought that the sooner he cleared out of London after this little incident the better.

However, the adventures of the night were not yet over for him, and he was destined to undergo a peril as dangerous as the one from which he had so luckily escaped.

On quitting the public-house he had walked sharply along a little way, and turned down the nearest side street.

Then, after making a detour, he had regained a main thoroughfare, and made his way homewards.

By this time the public-houses were just closing, and a number of drunken people, disgorged from them, were beginning to reel about the streets, as is customary.

Ned could not help turning into one of them again to obtain a final glass.

He seemed predestined to get into rows that night.

A strong-built, bandy-legged, bull-necked fellow, in sportingly-cut tweed suit, with a pot-hat on his head, a silk scarf, fastened by a huge horse-shoe pin, round his neck, and a big cigar in his mouth, was standing in the bar.

He was one of that peculiar class who earn their living by "travelling the meetings," or, in other words, attending races throughout the country.

He was, ostensibly, a bookmaker, but really picked up a livelihood by welshing, "lumbering," "brief snatching," and the like pursuits.

Like all his kidney, he could use his hands a bit, and was always ready to "take it out" of any "mug" who might cut up rough after being "gone through."

He happened to be in a very bad temper on the evening on which Ned for the first time set eyes on him.

A very promising little "plant," in which he was especially interested, had gone wrong.

He was just in that state of mind in which a man is ready to quarrel with his own shadow for following him about.

He hardly noticed Ned's entry into the little compartment labelled "private bar," of which he was the sole occupant, and seemed lost in bitter meditation.

Ned stepped up to the counter and demanded a brandy and soda.

In taking it up, his arm accidentally touched that of the stranger.

"What are you shoving for?" exclaimed the latter, jerking his arm in such a fashion that his elbow struck Ned's so sharply as to cause him to spill a considerable portion of the liquor he was conveying to his mouth on to the floor.

"Just look out what you're up to!" replied Ned.

And he showed his half-empty glass.

"Oh, rot! What's the good of cackling about a drop of spilt liquor?"

"Well, you're blooming civil any way, you are."

"Civil be blowed," returned the other. "If you don't like it you can do the other thing."

This was more than Ned's temper could stand.

"If you don't want me to drink it, you shall——"

And raising his glass as he spoke, he sent the rest of its contents slap into the other's face.

The fellow burst into a white rage.

As soon as he had wiped the liquor from his eyes with his sleeve, he drew back and prepared to attack Ned.

The latter, in anticipation of this, had already got his hands up.

The bookmaker, for the first time, realised the formidable customer he was about to tackle; but he had perfect confidence in his abilities.

He jumped in boldly at his man.

Ned met him with a straight left-hander, shot out with force enough to fell an ox.

But, quick as his hand had shot out, the other's duck had been quicker, and the blow, instead of alighting between his eyes, slipped over his head like a pat of butter across a hot frying-pan.

Simultaneously Ned felt the bookmaker's fist in the neighbourhood of his ribs like the kick of a horse.

The belt here again proved of service, for the blow alighted on it, and hurt the striker's knuckles far more than it did Ned.

The bookmaker broke ground, feinted, and succeeded in putting in a small clip on Ned's jowl, without any return, and in landing another body blow.

At out-fighting he had clearly the best of it, and, had they been in a ring, would perhaps have come off conqueror.

But Ned succeeded in working him into a corner of the bar, and plunged in on him like an avalanche.

The other hit out, but failed to stall off the bushranger's rush, and, once at close quarters, Ned's weight and strength completely demolished his adversary's preconceived notions of artistic in-fighting.

A flash hit on the forehead sent him all abroad, and before he could recover another on the jaw knocked him completely out of time.

The whole affair had not taken a minute.

But there had been time for the landlord, who had witnessed the scrimmage, to take certain measures.

The potman had closed and fastened the door by which Ned had entered directly he had passed its threshold, it being close on half-past twelve.

The only way out of the compartment of the bar was by passing through a couple of other divisions.

But when Ned turned to make his exit he was most disagreeably surprised.

A sergeant of police and a couple of constables were just making their appearance at the door leading into the next of these divisions.

They had looked in presumably to see that the house was being cleared, but in reality to have a sly drink just before closing time.

The landlord would probably have preferred no scandal at all, but, seeing he was in for it, played a virtuous part.

The bookmaker was a constant and a very good customer, whilst Ned was a stranger.

Consequently, he felt bound to take the former's part in the difficulty, since he was for the moment quite unable to take it himself, being stretched as limp as a damp rag amongst the sawdust on the floor.

The landlord charged Ned with creating a disturbance in his house, and asked the police to remove him.

Of course they never took the trouble to enquire as to who had begun the row.

For a moment Ned calculated the chances of trying to force his way through them and gain the street.

He felt inclined to risk it, and it certainly was not fear of the struggle that checked him.

It was a kind of superstition resembling inspiration.

He had got off once that evening, and, somehow, the proverb of the pitcher going to the well occurred to him.

Then an idea, based on a tolerably intimate acquaintance with the police, occurred to him.

In a few hours the particulars of the fatal affray in which he had been engaged would be circulated amongst the police, accompanied probably by a rough description of himself.

They would be on the look-out for him.

But of all places in the world the least likely to harbour him would be one of their own station-houses.

Accordingly he quietly submitted to be taken into custody.

His appearance, which was respectable, was in his favour, and also the fact that the bookmaker, on being picked up, was found to have sustained no material damage.

If Ned had seen a good chance of making a bolt of it, as he was conducted through the streets, he would have tried this, but, as it turned out, the station-house was only a few doors from the public in which the row had occurred.

He was searched in the usual preparatory way, just to see whether he had a knife, and congratulated himself that, by the merest accident, he had left his revolver at his lodgings that morning, packed up with some traps.

The man who searched him just put his hands into his pockets, and never noticed the cuts in his waistcoat made by Heffernan's knife, or the money-belt around his body.

He did not show any extraordinary want of common sense observation in this when compared with the run of his comrades.

The detective of the London and Brighton railway, who lately displayed such a singular lack of the commonest inductive power in his dealings with Lefroy had previously graduated in the Metropolitan Police, and was reckoned a smartish hand.

The Turf Frauds amongst other things would seem to establish the theory that when a detective is honest he is a fool, and when he is clever he is a rogue, were it not that, more recent evelations go to prove that some manage to be both rogues and fools at the same time.

Ned after being searched and asked his name, which he gave as Donelly, was consigned to a cell.

He did not feel downcast as to the result.

Shortly after he had been incarcerated, he heard a bit of conversation extremely interesting to him.

"Case of murder up at the Red Lion, —— Street," said a constable, entering the corridor into which the cells opened.

"What is it?" replied one of those on duty there.

"Man had his head smashed with a quart pot."

"Ah! Any particulars?"

"Seems the other fellow had been abusing Ireland, and that he stuck a knife into him, and got a lick over the head, that smashed his scull in for his trouble."

"Anything known about the fellow who did it?"

"As far as can be made out, he was a big man, with a beard, rather well-dressed."

"An Irish landlord, riled because he can't get any rent," said the other, with a laugh.

"Perhaps. But the beggar's pretty well sure to be spotted, for the Paddy almost ripped him up before he settled him."

"Ah! then we're pretty sure to nail him. What time did it happen?"

"A little before closing time."

"Why, we've got something of the same kind, only not so hot, in there," said the other, indicating the cell occupied by Ned. "It's another Irishman whose been scrapping in a pub close handy, and has bashed up a cross cove."

"Who?"

"Jerry George, the welsher; so for once he's found the boot on the other leg. The sergeant knew him, and I don't think he'd have collared the chap that gave him the doing once, if it hadn't been that old Croskey, the landlord, charged him."

This news was pleasant in the extreme to Ned.

It was evident, as he had thought, that the last place in the world where the police would dream of looking for Heffernan's murderer, was their own cells.

It was almost, if not quite, as good as an alibi.

He also felt perfectly safe in the results of his appearance before the magistrate in the morning.

As to any one having the least suspicion of his identity with Ned Kelly, the bushranger, he was quite at ease on that score.

The next morning Ned was allowed to send out for some breakfast, after partaking of which he was removed to the police-court, with the remainder of the night-charges.

"Don't see your man amongst this lot, eh, Hackett?" observed one of the police to a somewhat stupid-looking member of the force who was waiting to be called.

"No," answered Hackett, somewhat sulkily, whilst a grin spread over the face of several of his comrades.

Hackett, as Ned subsequently learnt, had had a bit of experience, of which he was not fond of talking about, and did not care to be reminded of.

The preceding winter he had been on duty in Oxford-street, and was passing a furrier's, when he noticed a light through the chinks in the shutters.

Thinking it not quite right he rapped.

"Is that you, policeman?" said a voice within.

"Yes," answered Hackett.

"All right, it's only me. Cold outside, isn't it?"

"Thought so. I'm trying to get the fire to light. Good-night."

Hackett said good-night, and passed on.

On his next round he noticed the light still burning.

It did not seem right, and he banged at the door again.

"Hullo, is it you, policeman?" said the voice within.

"Yes."

"All right. Will you step inside a minute and warm yourself. It must be a bitter night outside."

The door was opened, and Hackett stepped into the shop, the only inmate of which was a very respectable-looking man with a long apron on.

"Come up to the fire. Excuse me a minute."

And, leaving the shop, he stepped into the back room, from which he returned with a shovel of coals.

"Chilly, isn't it?" he went on; "cold outside and dull in. I've got a pretty job on; here's a lot of winter stock just come in, and it must be looked through and sorted over at once, for it looks as if the moth had got into some of the packages. Will you have a drain?"

And he procured a bottle and glass.

Hackett had a drain, and having wiped his lips and given his hands a rub before the fire, resumed his beat, satisfied that all was right at the furrier's.

Morning, however, altered his opinion.

On the shop boy coming the next morning to take down the shutters, it was found that the place had been pillaged of upwards of a thousand pounds' worth of goods, and though Hackett had carried away an impression on his mind of the clever rascal who had done him, he had never set eyes on him in the flesh since.

As he said, "It was the beggar's coolness in fiddling over the fire that put me off my guard."

The night charges were disposed of in quick succession, and on Ned being placed before the magistrate the result proved to be as he had anticipated.

The landlord did not appear in support of the charge, and Mr. Jerry George took care not to show his nose in court.

Consequently, after the magistrate had heard the statement of the police, he read Ned, whose name of Donnelly had stamped him in his opinion as a native of the Emerald Isle, one of those lectures that all police-magistrates seem to think it their duty to deliver.

In set terms he gravely assured Ned that he was in some degree inclined to make allowance for him as a stranger, coming from a portion of the Queen's dominions only too unhappily known from the frequent recurrence of broils.

Ned had not the slightest notion what he meant, but had the good sense to hold his tongue.

"It is only too apparent," continued his worship, "that you, despite your respectable appearance, are imbued from your associations doubtless with that anarchical and turbulent spirit that has wrought such havoc on the other side of St. George's Channel. Doubtless such conduct of yours would be held as venial there. But in London such brawling cannot be for a moment tolerated, and to mark my opinion of it, and taking into consideration that, from your apparent station in life, you seem a person well able to pay a fine, I feel bound to inflict upon you no less a penalty——"

Here he made a little artful pause.

"By all that's blue," thought Ned, "he could not pile it on hotter if he was going to put on the black cap! What an old scorcher! It looks as if he's going to quod me after all."

"Than that of fining you twenty shillings," continued his worship blandly.

"Next case," said the clerk, and Ned, after parting with a sovereign, was again a free man.

He walked a short distance from the court, jumped into a cab, drove to his lodgings, collected his traps, paid his bill, and then proceeded to the docks.

He was in ample time, since the ship he had taken his passage in did not clear out till the afternoon.

Once on board he was quite safe; and as the vessel dropped down the river indulged in a grim chuckle at the police, who, having actually had Ned Kelly red-handed in their custody, had suffered him to slip through their fingers, as their Brighton confreres did Lefroy.

CHAPTER CXCVI.

HOW TO CURE SCANDAL-MONGERS.

In embarking on board the Atalanta for Perth, Ned had been moved by two reasons.

One was that she was the first ship leaving for the Australian colonies—and the other, that her port of destination was one at which there was little chance of his being recognised on landing.

Like many royal personages, Ned had a fancy for travelling incognito.

He had gone so far as to book his passage under the prosaic name of Brown.

He had also resolved to behave properly on board, so as to land at Perth with a good character from those who had sailed with him.

As his language was apt, when he got a little excited, to be more vigorous than elegant, he made up his mind to hold his tongue as much as possible, and acquired the reputation with those on board, of a decent, but rather taciturn, sort of fellow.

Indeed, one or two of them began to speculate as to who and what he was, and Ned, when they had been about a fortnight out, heard a gentleman named Cathcart—who was himself returning to the colony—observe to a companion——

"I am almost certain I have seen our friend Brown before, but I can't for the life of me say where."

"Perhaps you are deceived by some likeness," answered his friend, whose name was Evans.

"No," insisted the other, "I am certain I have seen him. Like the royal family, I have a capital memory for faces. I can't quite make out when or where it was, but I'm certain that directly I get the clue I spot him in a moment."

"I don't think the affair is worth troubling your head over," was the reply. "The best thing would be to ask Brown if he ever remembers meeting you, or whether there was any place he has visited at which you were likely to come across each other."

"No, no," replied Cathcart; "I don't think he's the man who would stand much questioning. I have only got to wait a bit, I am sure one day a chance word will give me the clue I want.

"Do you," thought Ned to himself, as the pair strolled away from the spot where he had been an unseen listener to their conversation. "Well then, I'll take jolly good care that you don't hear that word from me."

From this time forward his guard on his tongue increased, and he was careful to abstain from drink to any great extent, lest under its influence he should be tempted to talk too freely.

He began to realise the German proverb, that "Speech is silvern, but silence is golden."

When places that he knew, were mentioned before him, he was careful not to betray any acquaintance with them; and, whilst acknowledging he had been a bit of a traveller, studiously avoided mentioning he had been in the colonies.

One day, when they were about six weeks out, a little celebration took place in the cabin in honour of some anniversary at which a wager of a case of champagne was laid.

The bet being decided, the wine was at once put on the table, and under its influence conversation grew brisk and Ned forgot his reserve.

He had become interested in a dispute between two of his neighbours as to the situation of a certain hotel in Sydney, and suddenly blurted out—

"Why, any fool knows it is on the right hand side of the street as you come up from the wharf."

On hearing this remark, Cathcart nudged his friend Evans.

"Our silent friend," he said, in a low tone, "has been in the colony. I guess if he only lets on a little more, I shall recollect where I have seen him."

"All right," said Evans, "I'll draw the badger."

After letting a certain time pass, so as not to excite suspicion, Evans purposely appealed to Ned on some other question connected with Sydney.

Ned saw that his former remark was an acknowledgement that he knew something of the place, and that it was too late to plead ignorance of it.

He therefore made the best of the job, and answered as briefly as he could with decency.

But Evans, not to be choked off, began to chat with him on all kinds of colonial matters, and at last drew him out a little more, with the help of a glass or two.

Ned came out of his shell, and told a tale or two.

The conversation turned on horses, and the usual lot of lies as to wonderful distances coursed, and leaps made by favourite steeds, were told.

"Well," said Ned, after one of the party had given the particulars of a jump, he was pleased to consider miraculous, "I recollect taking the creek at Tarramea, and that's a good three-and-twenty feet."

No sooner had the words escaped his mouth, than Evans felt Cathcart, who was sitting beside him, start, and softly murmur—

"Tarramea!"

"Aye," went on Ned, slightly excited from having more drink aboard than usual; "and there was only one beggar that followed me."

"What was it," inquired one of the company, "a steeplechase?"

"Yes," answered Ned, who had now lost his prudence, and was indulging in that reckless way of talking that had more than once brought him into trouble; "a match between me and a chap named Conquest."

The name slipped out.

Just as he had spoken these words he happened to cast a look towards Cathcart.

A sudden gleam of recognition, which the latter could not conceal, lit up his countenance, which became flushed and anxious.

Ned felt that he had let out too much for prudence.

Cathcart had, as it happened, been one of those present on the occasion on which Ned had cleared the creek at Tarramea, after riding up to the station, disguised as a mounted policeman, and shooting M'Pherson.

Ned's words had supplied the missing link in his memory, and he now felt certain of his identity with the bushranger, for whose reward such a large sum had been offered by the authorites.

He was in such a state of excitement, that he could scarcely contain himself.

A fortune was in view.

Cathcart was a greedy man, and his thoughts at once turned to this reward, and to the chances of securing it all to himself.

Here was independence in his grasp.

The thought set his heart beating with anticipated joy.

It might have been better for him if he had quietly imparted his suspicions, or rather his convictions as to Ned's identity to Captain Dunn, the commander of the Atalanta.

But a twofold reason restrained him.

He was not only greedy, but suspicious.

In the first case Captain Dunn, he thought, might refuse to believe him, and even go so far as to acquaint Kelly with his accusation, in which case he felt sure the bushranger would find some means of avenging himself before the voyage was over.

Kelly instinctively felt that the man recognised him, or at all events had suspicions which might prove dangerous.

In the vessel he might either at once arrest Ned on his own authority, clap him in irons and hand him over to the authorities, or profit by his position not to allow anybody to go on shore before himself, and on landing go straight to them, and, announcing that Kelly was on board, claim the reward for this information.

Cathcart resolved, therefore, to pretend ignorance of Ned.

When, in course of the evening, Evans said to him—

"I felt you nudge me; have you spotted the fellow?"

He answered in the negative, and added—

"I'm afraid it's no use puzzling my head about him any longer. He's not the man I thought, after all."

Kelly, for his part, felt sure that Cathcart had spotted him, and was fully alive to his peril.

From this time forward a curious game began between the two men.

The bushranger was rather anxious to pass a quiet quarter-of-an-hour alone with the other—and a very *mauvais quart d'heure* it would have turned out for his friend.

But this was exactly what Cathcart was particularly careful to avoid giving him a chance of.

He religiously avoided leaning over the ship's side, or

standing near an open hatchway, when Kelly was any-where about.

He met Kelly's glance rather too often to make him feel easy.

Accidents do happen so easily on ship-board, and he had no fancy for becoming food for the fishes, or breaking his neck from a tumble down a hatchway—accidentally, of course.

Ned felt his fate hung on the life of this man.

They were approaching their destination, and Ned felt that every hour the peril was more imminent.

We have already shown that such a villain did not value human life beyond that of a sheep, if its sacrifice served his purpose. He had no more compunction in this respect than one of the aboriginal blacks, or, in fact, any of the savages of the creation.

Poets talk of—

> " When wild in woods
> The noble savage ran,"

but if any of our readers happened to roam unprotected amongst the noble savages of Australia, or of Solomon, or Tonga Islands, they would form a more prosaic idea of the poet's description.

No bushranger ever yet spared human life if there was the least advantage in taking it, and very often they murdered out of sheer wantonness

The writer once saw a bushranger named Fogarty deliberately potting a (West Indian) shepherd, who was all the time begging for his life.

Kelly began to rack his brain as to the possibility of getting on shore unobserved, and to realise the truth of that well-known definition which sets down a ship as a prison in which a man has a chance of being drowned.

"If I could only get clear of this infernal craft," he thought, "I would soon show them a clean pair of heels."

And he continued to watch for a chance of putting Cathcart out of the way, and to run over in his mind all the stories of undetected murders he had heard in the course of his career from the lips of his extensive criminal acquaintance

It happened one evening in the cabin that the conversation turned on such topics.

One of the passengers mentioned the way in which the convicts at Toulon used to get rid of an obnoxious warder, namely, by striking him across the back of the neck with an eelskin filled with sand, which left no mark.

Ned sighed at the thought of how far they were at that moment from sandy shores and eel-ponds.

Another told the old story of the widow of Lambeth, who got rid of six husbands by pouring a little molten lead in their ears whilst they slept.

Ned pricked his own ears at this.

For some time he sat in thought, as though trying to solve a mental problem.

At length a gleam of satisfaction flitted across his face.

In course of the following afternoon he strolled forward to where the sail-maker was engaged in repairing some of the lighter sails.

He was pretty well liked by the crew, with whom he often exchanged a word or two, and to whom he stood a drink sometimes, despite all regulations to the contrary.

He made up his mind to remove all he felt was a spy on his actions. If he did not, he himself would be removed; and this armed him with determination.

He passed the time of day with the sailmaker, who was seated at his work with his implements around him, and after a time went aft again.

Though Cathcart avoided being in Kelly's company when no one else was about on deck, he did not scruple at finding himself alone with him below.

He knew that if any murderous attack was made on him there he could easily summon assistance, and guessed that Kelly would not risk such a step.

He was in the habit of lying down of an afternoon in the cabin, and generally managed to doze off.

The heat was intense; 114 degrees in the cabin, and a dead calm.

Three days after the conversation noted he went down below and threw himself on a couch.

After a time he was left the sole inmate of the cabin, and his breathing announced that he was fast asleep.

A short interval elapsed, and the door of Ned's room was opened stealthily.

The bushranger, who had slipped into it just after dinner, stole cautiously forth in his stocking feet.

An opportunity for which he had been on the alert for three days past had presented itself.

As carefully as though stepping on egg-shells, he crossed the cabin floor, and approached the sleeper.

He glanced all round to make sure that there was no one about, and was satisfied on this point.

He could hear the steward busy in his pantry, but felt safe from interruption from that quarter.

Stooping over the prostrate form of Cathcart, he drew from his pocket a small implement, which he held partly concealed.

His left hand was ready to fall on the sleeper's mouth, in case necessity arose.

A sharp movement on his part followed.

A faint sound, between a sob and a moan escaped from the lips of Cathcart.

He moved slightly in a convulsive fashion, and a spasm of some kind shot across his features.

Then they resumed their former immobility.

He lay perfectly still.

Ned swiftly retreated to his state-room, from which he again emerged, but this time with his boots on.

He passed through the cabin and gained the deck.

By-and-by one or two of the passengers descended, and the steward began to make preparations for tea.

The noise failed to arouse Cathcart.

Tea was got ready, but neither the noisy summons of the gong announcing it, or the influx of those who floated in in response, awakened him.

"Hullo, Cathcart," cried one of his friends.

"Hi! rouse up, man," said Evans, advancing to give him a shake.

No sooner had he laid his hand on the sleeper's arm than his face changed.

A look of bewilderment stole across it, as though he doubted the evidence of his own senses.

He shook the sleeper's arm a second time, but in a nervously hesitating fashion.

Then the look of astonishment changed to one of downright positive horror.

"Good heavens!" he gasped, "the man's dead! How sudden! It must be apoplexy."

A panic followed these words.

Some of the passengers shrank back horror-stricken, several ladies fainted, and the rest fled from the cabin; whilst a few of the bolder spirits, amongst whom was the captain, approached the sofa on which Cathcart's figure lay.

The captain in turn placed his hand on the motionless figure before him.

"It's true," he exclaimed. "He's dead, sure enough."

The Atalanta was not an emigrant ship, and had not more than six or eight passengers on board in all, and did not carry a surgeon.

The captain, as is usual in such cases, acted as doctor, and in this case was possessed of a little more medical knowledge than the skipper, who went to sea with a medicine chest and a book of instructions, and who, finding that one of his crew developed symptoms, for which two spoonfuls from bottle No. 15 were prescribed, and being out of that picture, gave him one of No. 7 and one of No. 8, which he urged must amount to the same thing, and killed him as dead as a door-nail.

One of the passengers, too, had a smattering of surgery, and he at once confirmed the captain's assertion as regarded Cathcart.

The cabin was at once cleared, and the captain and the chief officer, aided by the passenger, proceeded to make an examination of the corpse.

The cause of death was a perfect mystery.

The features were hardly convulsed, and there was not the slightest external sign to excite suspicion that death had been other than natural.

Such a suspicion, however, did not occur to anyone.

A kind of inquest was held, but nothing was elucidated —save the fact that Cathcart had lain down on the sofa some hours before, and that nothing had occurred to disturb him in his supposed slumbers.

The steward and some of the passengers had noticed him lying there, but had thought he was asleep.

Kelly was amongst these witnesses, and stated that he had retired for a short time to his room, and that he had seen Cathcart on the sofa, when passing through the cabin on his way to the deck.

The conclusion arrived at was that the unfortunate fellow must have succumbed to heart-disease or apoplexy.

As it was impossible to preserve his body till they made their port—even if the sailors would have consented to such an arrangement—it was launched into the deep.

With it went all hopes of the grim mystery ever being elucidated satisfactorily, for the instrument of death had preceded it, and was already lying at the bottom of the ocean.

Ned had cast it overboard, within a few minutes of the perpretration of his crime.

It consisted of a needle which he had stolen, unobserved and unsuspected, from the sailmaker.

He had mounted it in a wooden handle, and plunged it in the ear of the sleeping man, and so into his brain.

There was no sign of violence, and nothing but a *post-mortem* examination of the head would have revealed the cause of death.

CHAPTER CXCVII.
AT HOME AGAIN.

A FEW days later the Atalanta cast anchor at Freemouth, a place at the mouth of the Swan river, serving as the port of the town of Perth, the capital of the colony, which is built some miles higher up the stream in question.

Ned was one of the first to hurry on shore.

His idea was to get a horse and strike across country to the Murrumbridge, whither he had despatched Marco Polo, under the care of Zeph and Salmon Roe.

Once in possession of his matchless steed, his plan was to get together a band, and start afresh on his career of plundering.

"I guess I'll wake the country up again a bit, and make some of those police see snakes," was his reflection.

He thought he had better go on to Perth, in order to learn the best way of getting to the Murrumbridge.

Although profoundly ignorant of geography, he was a splendid bushman, and felt sure, that if once he had his bearings given, he could steer by sun, stars and compass, to the point he wished to reach.

He was not likely to make the blunder of a shepherd, who got lost on the Stony Rises; a singular desert tract, bounded on one side by the ocean, and on all others by the most fertile portions of Adelaide; on which it encroaches to the extent of some hundred of square miles.

As its name implies, it is a mass of stone; the surface being broken and irregular, and strewn with boulders.

From the crevices of these, and the scanty soil formed by their decomposition, grows a forest of small trees of sombre and dreary aspect, gnarled and stunted by the arid nature of the rocky region in which they have taken root; and displaying a depressing monotony in their brown trunks, metallic-looking foliage, and rigid uniformity of outline.

The shepherd had come to his station, which extended for many miles along the border of the stony rises, straight from the ship that brought him to the colonies; but had never been in them, his flock being stationed out on the plains in another direction.

For some reason or other he resolved to leave the service of the squatter; and, after settling with him and receiving his wages, determined to go on to the ranges to see if he could discover any trace of a horse belonging to him, which had strayed some weeks before.

Unluckily for himself he communicated his intention to no one which led to his neither being missed nor sought for, it being supposed he had gone on to get some other berth.

He entered the stony district, taking his gun and accompanied by a dog, and wandered about without any thought but that of finding the missing animal, till late in the afternoon, when, on glancing round on a landscape of unvarying sameness, the thought that he was lost occurred to him.

He concluded that by walking straight on in one direction he would get out of the labyrinth; and, after eating some provisions he carried, pushed on therefore till darkness came on; when he lay down, suffering greatly from thirst—for it was summer—and no rain had fallen for weeks.

The second day was passed in a like manner in incessant walking, and night found him in a state of great suffering.

The third day he resolved, in his own words, to "steer by the sun."

A storm of rain came on, and he drank out of the pools it made, and this awakening his hunger, he shot his dog, and roasted part of him.

All that day he steered by the sun, and the fourth and fifth days also, by which time the heat had dried up all the pools, and his sufferings from thirst became dreadful.

Several times he was tempted to put an end to himself with the gun; but on the afternoon of the seventh day he shot a parrot, and moistened his mouth with its blood.

On the eighth and ninth days he was delirious, and late on the afternoon on the latter, was seen by one of a gang of splitters, engaged in procuring timber from a belt of trees growing on a plain bordering the rise, who had strolled a short distance into the arid desert.

The shepherd at first took his rescuer for one of the visions that had haunted him in his fever; and could not believe that he was flesh and blood, till he laid hold of him.

"But," said his rescuer, when he had taken him to the hut tenanted by his companions, what do you mean by saying that you steered by the sun? If you had done so, you would not have been more than nine hours, instead of nine days on the rises."

"Indeed," he replied, "from the third day I always went by the sun."

"But how?"

"Sure I followed it. I heard the boss at the station say that he always followed the sun as a guide, and I thought I had better do the same."

Incredible as it may appear, the man, not knowing the compass, had interpreted "steering by the sun" to mean "following it;" and facing it in the morning when it rose, had kept it always before him till it sank in the west.

He had thus wandered in a circle, and in all probability was never more than a few miles from the edge of the rises, that so nearly proved his burial place.

Kelly was not one of this sort, but in some respects he was equally at sea as regarded conformation of the Australian continent.

His idea was, that a good horse would take him anywhere.

But when he entered a public-house at Perth, and began to ask the landlord as to the best means of getting an animal to carry him to the Murrumbridge, he was surprised to see a look of blank amazement on the man's face, and on those of three or four others who were drinking in the bar.

One of them even laughed right out, and the landlord's expression of astonishment changed to one of indignation as he said, with due gravity—

"Look here, mate, I'm quite ready to serve a drink or to answer a civil question ; but you've come to the wrong shop for trying on any of that kind of chaff."

"What's your lay?" answered Ned, quite in a fog as to what the man was driving at. "I didn't ask you to help me to steal a horse, but to tell me where I can best buy one."

"I reckon you're a new chum in these parts?" observed one of the company. "Fresh from the Old Country, perhaps?"

"You're about right," answered Ned. "But before I went there I spent a few years Sydney side, and I can pick my way through the bush as well as a bandicoot."

"And you really think of riding from here to the Murrumbridge?"

"Why not?"

"Bravo! you seem a good plucked 'en; but do you know what you've got to get through, to find your way from here to Sydney?"

"No."

"Why, the Mallee Scrub."

"The Mallee Scrub?"

"Yes. Don't you know there's a belt of it a couple of hundred miles broad, run right across, and that no single man, however well-mounted, could struggle through it? There's neither grub for man nor horse, and no water."

"I'll tell you what there is, though," broke in another of the company, "there a lot of warrigal blacks, who'll have your kidney's out to grease their hair with, before you could say knife."

This was true.

The Mallee is a small species of Eucalyptus, from ten to fifteen feet high, growing together so closely as to just allow a horseman to make his way through it ; and covering a district of several hundreds of miles, almost cutting off Western from Eastern Australia.

The dense scrub is, however, relieved by openings, which only serve to lure men who have once entered the labrynith to destruction.

The sensation produced by being pent up in this dense scrub, able only to see the sky overhead, with no air circulating, and nothing visible but the same monstrous brown items that the traveller keeps pacing through hour after hour, is so intolerable, that the first glimpse of light showing an opening promising deliverance is hailed with joy.

It requires resolution few men possess, to resist the temptation and keep in due east, which if adhered to will at last bring the traveller out of the scrub, provided he only sticks to it long enough.

If a man turns inside to the south, and enters the plain which may be miles in circumference, or perhaps the front of a series of similar openings, he is safe to be tempted further and further on into the heart of the wilderness ; and, in this case, if his knowledge of the country is only local, his doom is sealed.

Again he enters the scrub, and again is tempted from it by the same fatal snare.

"That scrub's a caution and no mistake," said one of the party to Ned. "I once helped to look for a man lost in a patch, not more than fifteen miles in length by ten in breadth ; and we found his body after the blacks had tracked him for scores of weary miles, not more than a mile and a half from the hut he had left ten days before, and from which he had never, at any time, been more than a few miles away."

Nor was the statement about the blacks exaggerated.

Amongst their customs there is none more deeply rooted than that of cutting out the kidneys of anyone they slaughter, and of using it instead of Rowland's Macassar.

Ned began to realise the responsibility of his projected attempt, and to cast about as to whether there was not another method of getting to his destination.

He soon found there was a chance of getting a passage in a small coaster to Adelaide, and of that he resolved to avail himself, and make his way from the capital of South Australia to the Murrumbridgee.

Before quitting Perth he purchased some garments of a style more suited to the character he intended to assume, which was that of a shearer.

This done, he embarked on board the coaster, and reached his destination without anything of moment happening during the voyage.

CHAPTER CXCVIII.
NED PUTS THE SADDLE ON THE RIGHT HORSE.

MARCO POLO had been left in the charge of a Scotch squatter named M'Vittie, whose station was on the Murrumbridge, at a place called Garoona.

He was a man who had started as a shepherd on the very station which now belonged to him.

His first master had been a careless, thoughtless, happy-go-lucky chap, named Willoughby, who, after a somewhat dissipated career in England, had realised the remnants of a once large fortune, and had come out in the hope of retrieving his affairs.

At first he had done pretty well.

He got a good run, and his sheep increased and multiplied in a very encouraging fashion, whilst the healthy open-air life he was leading made him feel ten years younger.

But after a time its monotony began to pall on him.

He took to running down to Melbourne, or up to Sydney, whenever there was a race-meeting or any other kind of excitement on, and to dropping his money over bets or cards.

Gradually he became a confirmed gambler and sot.

His affairs became more and more involved, and their control drifted from his hands into those of M'Vittie, who had gradually risen from the position of shepherd to that of superintendent of the station.

Mr. Willoughby had several attacks of delirium tremens, during which he was nursed by M'Vittie.

At last, after a hard bout of drinking at Melbourne, in course of which he squandered and gambled away a large sum, he returned to his station—but only to die.

M'Vittie and an old hut-keeper named Wilson were the only persons present at his death-bed.

After his death the former produced a number of documents, going to prove that for a long time past he had been, though nominally Mr. Willoughby's superintendent, in reality his partner, having, he alleged, began by advancing him a sum of ready-money at a time when the deceased was in great need of it.

He also produced a will leaving him everything.

There was some astonishment expressed at this, but, as Mr. Willoughby had no relations in the colony whose claims might have been put forward, and, as all his outstanding debts were settled out of the estate, it blew over.

Ned, however, knew a little more of the transaction than did the general public.

The man Wilson, who had been a convict, was an old acquaintance of his, and one day let out to him in confidence that he and M'Vittie had made the will in question, and had got Willoughby to sign it and the other papers when in a state of intoxication and quite oblivious of his action. He also complained that M'Vittie had not acted on the square, that he got nothing, M'Vittie everything. While the latter was rich, he was as poor as a wild dog.

A few weeks after he had made this revelation Wilson was found drowned in a water-hole.

How he got there there was no evidence to show, but Ned had a shrewd suspicion that he had been put out of the way by the bigger villain, who was his partner in crime.

He kept, however, this suspicion to himself, and merely hinted to M'Vittie that he knew some facts, the disclosure of which might prove very awkward to him.

It was this knowledge that had made the squatter willingly agree to take charge of Marco Polo in Kelly's absence.

M'Vittie was a tall, lean Scotchman, of about sixty, with a gaunt, angular figure, a freckled face, and hair, the original sandy colour of which was now changing to that grizzly tint, styled a dandy grey russet.

He set up, like Peace, for being one of the "unco guid."

If there had been a kirk near at hand no doubt he would have been an elder; but, for lack of this, he contented himself with inflicting long prayers on all with whom he came in contact, especially his household.

He professed an intense veneration for the "Sabbath," and devoted all his spare time on that day to what he styled "guidly meditation," but what was in reality quiet scheming as to the best way of getting the advantage of his neighbours in business.

Ned had resolved to make his way towards the Murrumbridge, by taking the river steamers up the Murray, and then scobble a strange horse until within reach of his destination, after which he could turn the animal loose, and no one be a bit the wiser. A bit of a rope often in the hands of tramps, does duty upon a quiet horse for a bridle, and his jacket taken off and made to do duty for a saddle, enables the rider to get along for many a long journey. The horse, when done with, is turned out in the bush, and in nine out of ten cases, finds his way back to the station he was breed in. Working bullocks have been known, when lost in the road, to find their way home a distance of 500 miles.

He knew something of the place, and he made his way in the first instance to an outlying shepherd's hut situate near the boundaries of the run which he reached shortly before mid-day.

On tramping up to the door he found the hut was untenanted.

The door, however, was open, and he stepped inside and sat down to rest himself a bit—for he had started before daybreak from the spot where he had passed the night; and the day was a hot one, even for the colony, and the hundred sovereigns he carried were no light weight.

He knew the free and easy habits of the district too well to dream of being called to account, for what in England would be looked upon as a liberty.

He went so far as to help himself to some cold mutton and damper, and then mix himself a panakin of grog out of the flask he carried—for there were no spirits in the hut —filled his pipe, for a quiet smoke.

As he sat with his back against the wall of the hut and his pipe between his teeth, placidly smoking and digesting, his eye fell on some tiny object glittering in a ray of sunlight, streaming through the half-closed door.

The object in question lay on the floor about three yards off, and he could not at first make out what it was.

He glanced at it several times without caring to take the trouble to get up to examine it.

At last when he had finished his pipe, his curiosity prevailed over laziness, and he rose, and approaching the little object, stooped down and picked it up.

It was not a nugget as he had half fancied, but simply a metal button.

He was about to send it spinning away out of the door, when he suddenly paused and examined it closely.

It was a uniform button, and this fact at once set him thinking, for like all men accustomed to hunt and be hunted, he had learned to attach importance to the merest trifles.

It was evidently from the uniform of one of the mounted police.

From its very position it had evidently only fallen a little time previously, or it would have got tramped into the floor or kicked on one side.

Hence it was evident that a mounted policeman had called at that hut a few hours before.

Now there was nothing very unusual in this, but Kelly could not help fancying that such a visit might possibly have some reference to matters interesting himself.

He went so far as to regard it as a warning.

"It proves those traps are loafing around in this quarter, and I must keep my eyes open in order not to tumble onto some of 'em," was his reflection.

He made up his mind, after a little consideration, to set out in search of the shepherd inhabiting the hut, and to try and learn from him what the police were hunting for in the neighbourhood, if it were possible.

He started forth on this errand, and in a little time came across the shepherd who was sitting under a tree.

Ned pushed up to him and bid him good-day.

After a little chat he sat down beside him, the shepherd being very glad of the chance of a gossip, leading the lonely life that he did.

"Things pretty quiet just now about here?" Ned asked.

"Yes," was the answer.

"No chance of a chap getting stuck up, I suppose?"

"No, you're all right there's no one playing that game in this part of the country."

"Well, I'm precious glad to hear it. I've had to work blessed hard for my pile and I shouldn't like to have to hand it over, though it ain't much."

"What's your lay?" inquired the shepherd.

"I'm on a shearing job."

"Oh! I thought you shearers were such blooming swells that you never went about on shank's mare, but always on a bit of horseflesh."

An idea occurred to Ned.

Since he had seen the button in the hut he had come to the conclusion that it was necessary for him to get a horse at all costs as soon as possible, in case the police should come across him and oblige him to fly for his life.

He put on a half-sheepish air.

"Well, to tell the truth, I started with one, but, like a blessed fool, I got drunk at the last township, and matched him against a grey yelding, a fellow was bragging about. We agreed to go three miles across country, owners up, the horses being stakes. I'd have won easily, though I rode two stone heavier than he did, if I'd been sober; but somehow I blundered at a bit of fallen timber, and the beast fell under me and broke his back."

"Well, if you lost the other fellow didn't gain much," said the shepherd, with a grin.

"No; but he insisted on having the hide and the saddle."

"That was smart."

"Yes; but I'm on the look-out for a horse. Have you got one to spare? I thought I saw one grazing as I came along?"

"Aye, that's the boss's mare. But she's dead lame."

"How's that?"

"Why, he rode out to the hut yesterday to meet one of the police, and the mare fell dead lame just as he reached it. So he had to tramp all the way back again, and a pretty growling he made over the job, I can tell you."

"Yes, I daresay. It must have sweated him a bit to hump his saddle along this weather."

"Oh, he didn't trouble himself to do that. He left it in my hut, to be fetched back by the store cart that comes over next week."

"Oh," thought Ned, "it'll come in handy if I lay hands on it."

And then he continued aloud—

"But what did he want to meet the police for?"

"Why," answered the shepherd, "that's quite a yarn."

"Fire away with it, then."

"Well, you know, you asked me if there was any chance of your getting stuck up in this quarter."

"Yes."

"There ain't just now, as I said, but one of these days we expect a visit from a regular out-and-outer in the bailing-up line."

"Who is it?"

"Just guess."

Ned ran through the names of half-a-dozen well-known bushrangers.

"No," said the shepherd, "it ain't one of them, but a chap as'll give anyone of them a stone and a beating over any course they like to name."

"Who is it?" said Ned.

"Why, that villain, Ned Kelly, the Ironclad, as they call him, to be sure!"

Kelly was not prepared for this.

He was electrified.

How was it that just at this moment his whereabouts should spring to the point?

He had not given anyone but the dead man a clue to his movements.

It appeared, however, that the scent was discovered in a most singular way.

Cathcart had some days before his death written a letter addressed to a friend in Melbourne disclosing his suspicions as to Kelly, and giving his personal description most minutely, and also expressing his determination to hunt him down and bag the reward.

As this letter was found amongst his effects it was forwarded to its destination by post, and, on the arrival of the particulars of Cathcart's death, his friend communicated his letter to the police.

Kelly, of course, knew nothing of this.

M'Vittie, now a magistrate, had received a communication with the county authorities of the expected reappearance of the Kelly plague, and resolved to rid himself as quickly as possible of a man who knew too much.

"Oh!" replied Ned, "but what the devil makes you think he'll turn up here?"

"Why, I'll tell you. I suppose you've heard of his horse, Marco Polo, eh?"

"Yes."

"He's a regular clipper. Well, he was left in the guv'nor's care some time back, and it stands to reason that his master will come for him some day."

"I shouldn't wonder if he did," answered Ned, with a grin.

"The guv'nor gave me a hint of this a fortnight ago. He knows all about Kelly, I'm thinking. He's as sharp as Old Nick, himself, has been in communication with the police, and has arranged that directly Kelly shows his nose about the place, he shall be smartly nabbed."

"Oh! that's it, is it?"

"That's just it, my bloomer!"

The expression of Kelly's face was not very amiable.

His compressed lips, and the savage gleam of his eyes, spoke a little volcanic commotion within.

His determination, whatever it was, seemed taken, and he strode off in the direction of M'Vittie's home station.

To go straight on there was not, however, his intention.

As soon as he got out of sight of the shepherd, he turned and doubled back in the direction of the hut.

Making a circuit, he succeeded in reaching it unseen.

It was deserted, as when he had visited it some hours before.

Entering it, he glanced round in quest of the saddle, of which the shepherd had spoken.

At first he could not discover it.

At last he found it, with the bridle, stowed away in a corner of the hut.

The shepherd would not be back until sundown, and then be too tired to notice whether the saddle and bridle were missing or not.

Putting it on his head, and the bridle in his pocket, he started off for the main station at Garoona.

He could not hope to reach there that evening, and had to take up his quarters at another hut.

Here he represented himself as a shearer on his way to a job, and pitched the same yarn of the death of his horse.

He did not say anything about buying another, however, as he thought he was near enough to Marco Polo now not to bother himself about any other animal.

He started off the next morning, and arrived in sight of Garoona early in the afternoon.

Instead of going straight up to the station, he concealed himself in a belt of timber, and waited for the approach of nightfall.

He noticed M'Vittie ride up, and remarked with disgust that the old fellow was mounted on no less a steed than Marco Polo himself.

"Jee-rusalem!" mentally ejaculated Kelly. "You'll never cross such a piece of stuff as Marco again, my bloomer. You'll sell Ned Kelly, will you? I'll teach you a lesson that will last you longer than a plate of porridge for your breakfast, you Scotch hound! Wait till I'm on your track, Mr. M'Vittie."

Evening gradually came on, the men on the home station came in, the horses were turned into the paddock, and preparations for supper made.

Ned had brought some provisions with him, so this last operation did not tantalise him as it might otherwise have done.

At last, as darkness came on, all signs of human life about the station began to disappear.

The men had withdrawn into their huts, which were close to the main dwelling inhabited by M'Vittie.

People who have to be out by sunrise are not usually given to sit up late, and in a very short time the gleams of light that had shown through the cracks in the closed shutters faded away.

(To be continued.)

NED KELLY THE IRONCLAD AUSTRALIAN BUSHRANGER

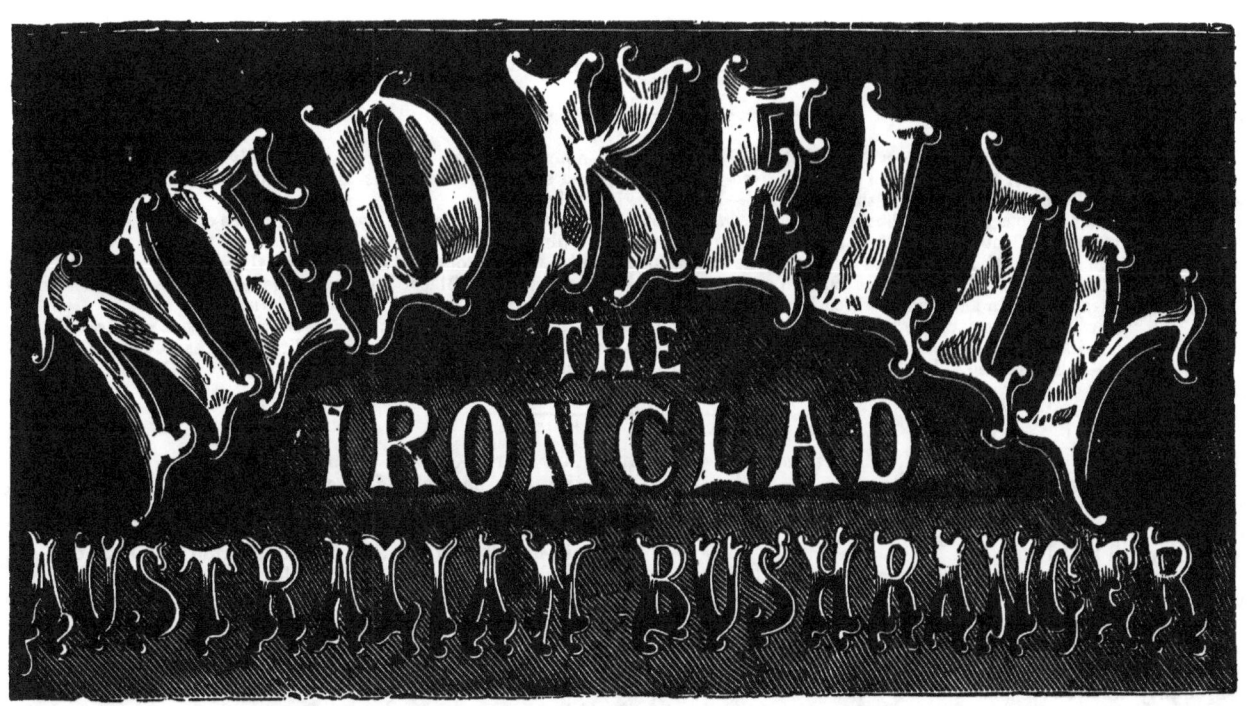

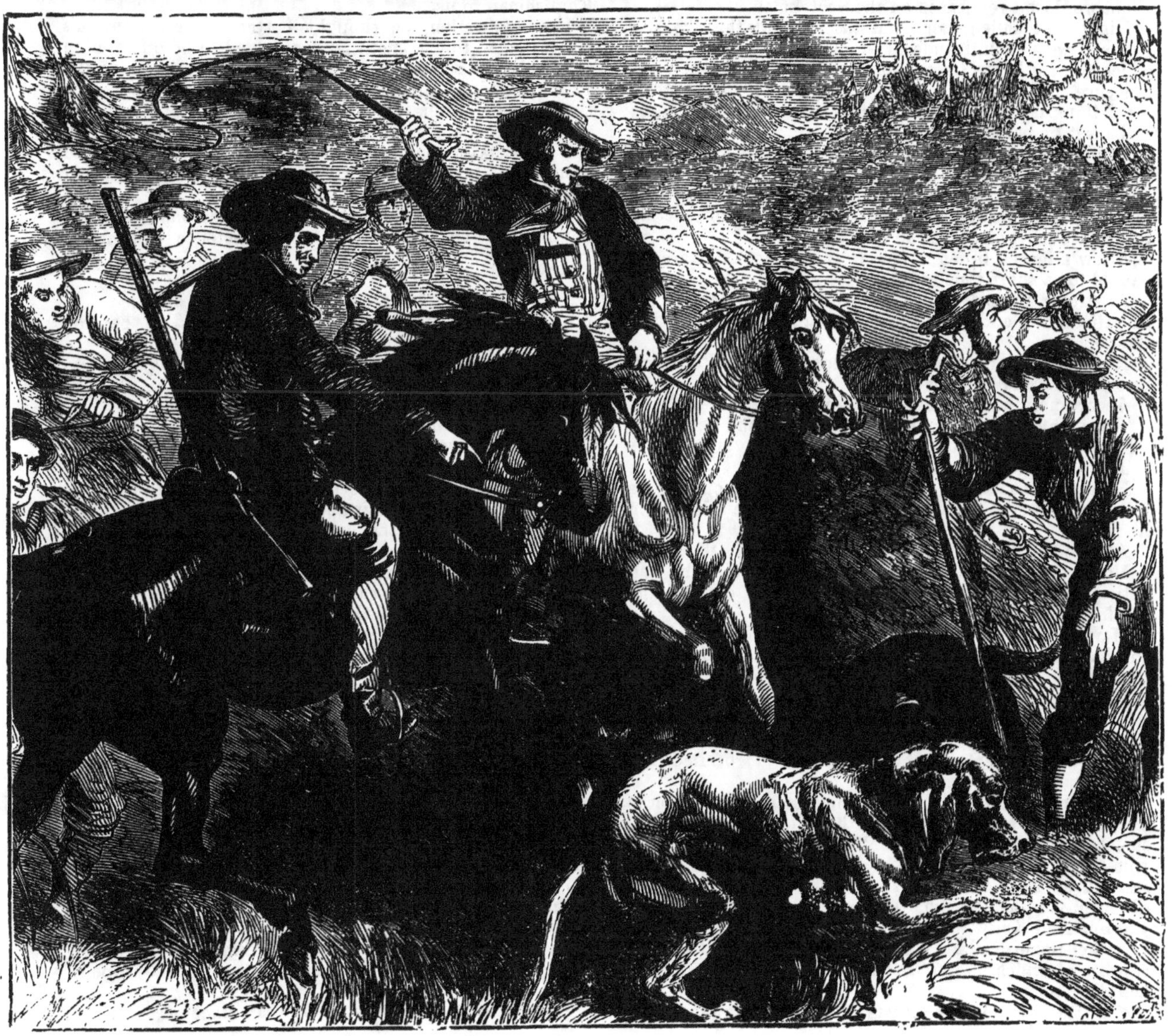

NO 34,

NED KELLY: IRONCLAD BUSHRANGER.

"It is well known that for many years Ned Kelly had made himself notorious by a series of crimes wholly incompatible with the civilisation of the nineteenth century. Ned Kelly's celebrated steed, Marco Polo, is as well known at the Antipodes as Dick Turpin's Black Bess in these islands."—*Telegraph*, 7th July, 1881

"It is notorious that the robbery of Mr. Steward's corpse was mainly performed by the assistance of NED KELLY'S BROTHER, the Captain of what was neither more nor less than a pirate ship."—*Times*, July.

"The history of NED KELLY and his celebrated black horse, Marco Polo, will ever live in the recollection of the Australian public. The deeds of Dick Turpin, and the performances of Black Bess, are tame beside those of ' NED AND HIS NAG ;' in addition to which Ned's history is true, and Turpin's is pure fiction."—*Press*, July.

"The stirring story of NED KELLY, the Australian Bushranger ("Illustrated London Novelette" Office, 280, Strand), pursues its way with unabated vigour. Full of incident, it should suit those who like their literature as they do their cigars—full-flavoured. It is published in weekly numbers."—*South London Press*, November.

CHAPTER CXCVIII.—*Continued.*

Still Ned resolved to be cautious.

He knew that the soundest slumber is that which comes after midnight, and had made up his mind not to approach the station till that hour.

He, therefore, sat patiently under a tree speculating as what means he could employ to get M'Vittie into his power, and running over all the various punishments his ingenuity could devise as best fitted for that venerable hypocrite.

Mentally he vowed that the first task he would set about would be vengeance on the Scotchman.

Night had fallen calm and placid, and the sky was gemmed with a multitude of stars, conspicuous amongst which the Lutheran Cross shone in all its refulgent magnificence.

"I think it's safe to make a move now," thought Ned ; "It must be past midnight."

Rising, he took up the saddle, and stealthily approached the station.

"If there are any dogs prowling around there may be a bit of a muss," he meditated ; and, with a view of meeting this emergency, he looked to his knife.

A few minutes brought him to the paddock. Here he paused for a short time to reconnoitre.

A strong temptation stole over him to knock at M'Vittie's hut, and shoot the old ruffian as he appeared at the door.

It was necessary, however, to secure Marco Polo first in order to carry out this scheme.

Accordingly he proceeded to the paddock.

The night was a clear and brilliant one, and he had no difficulty in making out his horse amongst the others.

The next question was how to catch him.

He could not expect that the animal would come to his call any more than a bird would wait to have salt put on its tail.

A sieve full of oats might have proved handy though.

However, the task proved an easier one than he had anticipated when he slipped the bar and entered the paddock.

Marco Polo was evidently in the habit of being ridden, and had been turned out with a trail rope attached to him, to facilitate catching.

Ned profited by this to effect his capture.

"Steady, old man, steady," he whispered, as he laid his hand on Marco's mane.

With rapid dexterity he saddled and bridled the animal.

"By Jove!" he exclaimed, as he noted certain marks on the horse's withers, "so that herring-gutted old skeleton of split-shingle couldn't ride you without getting you saddle-galled, whilst I, big and heavy as I am, never scraped an inch off your skin, my beauty. Never mind, old man, it's the last time any one will throw a leg over you but Ned Kelly."

As he spoke, Ned led the horse out of the paddock, the slip-bar of which he purposely omitted to replace after he had done so.

"If the old devil's beasts have strayed away a few miles by morning, why so much the better," was his reflection, as he hoisted himself into the saddle and marked with satisfaction that, owing to the exercise to which he had been put, Marco was in capital condition.

Again he debated whether he should ride up to the old fellow's door, and try to lure him forth so as to shoot him down.

No, that would be letting him off too easy.

"I'll make him remember Ned Kelly, if I don't, I——"

What he was we need not mention, but the adjective he used is historically given as the birthright of every Englishman to use.

Upon reflection, he thought better of assuaging his vengeance at this moment, and resolved to be off to more agreeable and safer regions in the neighbourhood of the Murrumbridgee River, make a good pile, and then quit the colony for ever.

He had heard a good deal about South America, its free and easy style of morality, and there he resolved to "pull up," but to do so comfortably, he would have to replenish his purse, and pretty heavily too.

His ideas upon this subject were rather vague, and he never calmly considered what a "competence" meant.

CHAPTER CXCIX.

MR. VITTIE STARTS ON A WILD GOOSE CHASE.

MR. M'VITTIE's slumbers were not destined to be prolonged to a very late out that night.

Just after daybreak he was aroused by hearing someone pounding away at the door of his dwelling.

"Ech, wha's there?" was his response.

"Get up, gov'nor ; there's a blessed fine go," was the answer, in the voice of his overseer.

"Andrew, my mon," was his reply, "how often must I tell ye to lay aside the profane and ungodly habit o' blasphemin which is a sair abomination baith in the sight o' the Lord and in the lugs o' a decent douce mon like mysel.'"

"Confound it all, it's enough to make an angel swear. Some fool or other left the slip panel open and everyone of the horses are out of the paddock.

"D——" began M'Vittie; but he checked himself just in time, with a gulp that almost made him bite his tongue off.

"Ech now," he ejaculated, as soon as he had got his breath, "but this is sair tidings, sair tidings, it's eneuch to drive a decent body clean daft to have to deal wi' sic a pack o' blaitherin boobies as I hae aroun me. Let's see wha's the gowk that has done this."

Hurrying on his garments he sallied forth, and soon a general muster of the men took place.

On being interrogated each and all stoutly declares that the slip rail had been in its place when they had last set eyes on it.

Further cross-examination showed that three of the hands who had been the last to leave the paddock had done so in company, and that, according to their united testimony, the rail had been carefully replaced by one of them.

"Ye must one and all start awa' at aince in search o'

the beasties," exclaimed M'Vittie; and the men at once bestirred themselves to carry out this order.

"Hadn't we better send down to the black camp by the river for a fellow or two to help to track them," suggested Andrew.

"That's no bad notion," said M'Vittie; "aye ye can just going and tell them that they shall hae the carcass o' the sheep that deed yestreen for the job."

Andrew hastened away and in a short time returned with a couple of black fellows.

After carefully examining the paddock and its surroundings, and jabbering away amongst themselves, they turned to Andrew, who had explained to them the state of things.

On hearing their report he at once hastened to his master.

"The blackfellows say that whoever left the slip rail down rode off on one of the horses," he said.

"What mon?" exclaimed M'Vittie.

Andrew repeated his remark, and in confirmation the blacks pointed out the tracks and signs which, to their eyes, revealed that a horse had been led out of the paddock and mounted, including its trail rope left on the ground.

They declared that the animal had been halted just in front of M'Vittie's house, and had then been galloped off in a straight line, its trail widely differing from that of the other animals.

"Wha would hae dreamt o' sic a thing?" wailed M'Vittie. "'Tis some hellicate reiver o' a house thief that has done this trick. To think that sic things should be dune aneath the vary nebs o' a pack of feckless loons that hae na mair thocht o' their maister's gear than o' their ain salvation."

"I wonder which horse the fellow boned?" said Andrew.

"The best, the vara best, ye may be certain," answered his employer. "My mind sair misgives me but it's the beastie left here a few months sinsyne. Ye ken the one I mean?"

"What, Marco Polo?" said Andrew, who knew to whom the animal really belonged. "Well, that's all the better, since it was not one of your own, and the real owner is never likely to turn up and claim it, or, if he does, can't well kick up a row about it."

M'Vittie pulled a long face.

He had not informed Andrew that he had long since began to look upon Marco Polo as his own, and that he had determined to secure Ned whenever he put foot on the station to claim the animal from him.

And now all his hopes of the ten thousand pounds offered for the capture of the bushranger had galloped off on Marco's four legs.

For if once Ned learnt that the horse had been stolen, it was not very likely that he would take into his head to pay M'Vittie a visit.

"By my saul, but it's euch to drive a mon distracted," groaned the squatter, when later in the day the men returned with all the rest of the horses, thereby conclusively proving that Marco Polo had been carried off; "there goes the growden opportunity o' putting ten thousand p'unds o' sill'er in my pouch, and riddin' the country-side at the same time o' as great as rogue as ever supped prison-porridge. My certie, but I wad gi'e somethin' for the chance o' settin' my e'en on the mon that stole you' horse, the de'il tak' him for a greedy gled."

This wish came from the M'Vittie's heart, though he hardly imagined how soon it was to be realised.

For on reflection, the idea occured to him of starting at once, endeavouring to trace the stolen horse, with the view, if no other means of repossessing himself of it arose, of ransoming it from its present possessor, or of shooting him down.

It was a decided wild-goose chase; but the old fellow had been brooding so long on the delightful prospect of luring Ned to his station and their ensnaring him, that it really seemed to him that the disappearance of Marco Polo

meant nothing less than a loss of the ten thousand offered for the capture of the bushranger, and on which he had counted with certainty.

He was not only a determined, but, when roused by avarice, a truly desperate man, and he resolved to set out in pursuit.

If the horse had been sold by the thief, he would claim it, and to facilitate matters would go so far, he thought, as to recoup the purchaser in the sum he gave tor it, since ten thousand pounds would be worth such a sacrifice.

Accordingly he started well-mounted and armed.

The route selected by Ned had led him into the steep and rugged district in which the Murrambridgee rises.

Deep and precipitous ravines, and stupendous chasms, enclosed between walls of rock, mark this region, which is seldom visited owing to its sterility, though bordering on a rich range of pasture land.

The M'Vittie was a capital bushman and tracker, and, as Ned had taken no trouble to conceal his trail, he was able to follow it with ease, for as luck would have it, the ground was like the weather, soft, and the track so far lay distinct.

He was rather astonished, however, to find it leading towards the desolate region in question, instead of to some settlement.

Nevertheless, the thought of getting the representation of £6,000 into his hands again nerved his efforts.

He pushed on, though after a time he began to experience great difficulty in tracking the horse, owing to the stony nature of the soil.

On the second afternoon after quitting the station he found himself in a narrow valley or ravine, paved with broken fragments of stone.

To the right and left rose two ridges of brown and splintered rock, from the crevices in which sprung a few stunted trees.

A short distance ahead the ravine apparently took an abrupt turn to the right.

As he had tracked Marco Polo to the entrance of the gorge in which he found himself, and as there was no means of a horse getting away either to the right or to the left without wings, he did not trouble himself to look for hoof-marks, but pushed steadily forward.

Suddenly the report of a pistol rang out from behind a rock, standing a little in advance of the angle he was approaching, and abreast of which he was about to pass.

The aim of the unseen marksman was a good one, to judge by the result.

Struck by the bullet, M'Vittie's horse staggered and dropped in its tracks as dead as a doornail, pitching its rider, who had not time to recover himself, clean over its head on to his own.

The shock with which his skull came into contact with the ground was so sharp a one, that he lost all consciousness for some time.

When he recovered, it was several minutes before he could exactly realise the state of things.

At length he began to do so.

He was lying on his back with his head, which seemed to him to have swollen to double its usual size, supported by a stone.

It was aching intolerably, and after just opening his eyes he closed them again, and almost relapsed into insensibility.

On reopening them, he recognised that he was still in the same place.

Drawing a long breath he made an effort to rise.

To his astonishment he found he could not do so.

His limbs refused all movement.

For a moment he fancied that they had been temporarily paralysed by the shock.

He waited a little and then made another effort, but with same result.

Things, however, were growing clearer to him.

The reason of his inability to move became apparent.

He was securely fastened, hand and foot.

The sense of peril arising from this discovery completely aroused him from his state of semi-stupor.

He raised himself after some exertion into a sitting position, and looked first at his bonds and then at the spot in which he found himself.

As regarded the former, he was secured like a trussed fowl.

His hands had been tied together, and his elbows fastened to his sides, whilst a stout lashing had been passed round his ankles.

As to his whereabouts, he was lying a pace or two from the spot on which he had originally fallen, beside the dead body of his horse.

But who the deuce, he thought, could have secured him in such a fashion, so different to the customary style of the Australian bushranger, who generally covers his victim, and then summons him to bail up?

For some moments he fancied himself alone. But then these bonds. Who pinioned him? What did it all mean? Turning his eyes to the left he saw a form sitting quietly smoking on a block of stone, that sent all the blood in his body into his head and back again. He was almost choked with surprise and alarm.

CHAPTER CC.
A COMPANION FOR JOSS.

THE bushranger glared down on the prostrate figure of the squatter, who had sank back in mingled terror and amazement at his appearance, with a look of ferocious joy.

"Well, Mr. M'Vittie," he repeated, "how do you find yourself?"

For a moment M'Vittie's senses seemed on the point of leaving him from mingled fear and astonishment.

He managed, however, to pull himself together again.

"What, Ned Kelly!" he ejaculated. "Ech, mon, but this is a strange meetin'. Sakes alive, what garred ye shoot the puir beastie and lap me in bonds like to a sucklin' babe in its swaddlin' claithes?"

"Can't you guess?" said Ned.

"De'il a bit, mon; de'il a bit, unless ye tuik me for anither. But joost loosen these tows ye have cast aboot me if it's a bit crack ye're wushin' for."

"You didn't think to meet me hereabouts, eh?"

"Na, I didna, I didna even ken that ye were bock agin in the colony, and it's little I thocht to foregather wi' ye in sic a fashion."

Ned looked at him for a little time in silence.

"What brought you here, M'Vittie?"

"'Deed, it was joost a wee bit service I was doin' yer animal, Ned. Ye ken the browny beastie, it's Marco Polo ye ca'ed him, that ye left in my care sinsyne?"

"Yes."

"Weel, some hellicate loon has stolen him fra' the station, and I was trackin' the villian. Sae if ye'll undo the bonds we'll just set out after him together. But I misdoubt me. Surely if ye have been lurkin' here ye must have seen him pass, the reevin rogue."

"I've only seen one rogue to-day," said Ned with a grim earnestness; "and he's about as black-hearted a traitor as ever broke bread or swallowed porridge."

"What d'ye mean?" asked M'Vittie, who, for all his coolness, began to grow terribly uneasy.

At that moment the neigh of a horse sounded from behind the angle of the ravine.

"Why, 'tis the neigh o' the beastie himself," said M'Vittie, somewhat reasured. "Ah, I'd ken it amangst a thousand. I see how it is. Ye came across the reiver, who was walkin' off wi' him."

"No," shouted Ned, throwing off all disguise, "but I have come across the scoundrel who was going to use him as bait to draw me into the hands of the traps, and by—— I'm not going to leave go of him in a hurry, now I've got him. You didn't expect to drop on an old friend so soon again did you? you blood-thirsty Scotch whelp! ain't you glad? You look it."

And Kelly burst into a loud laugh.

The terror of his quondam associate would have been ludicrous if it had not been despairing.

"Out with it, old man. Why have you taken such a fancy to Ned Kelly that you must track him like a spy? Yes, like a spy! D'ye hear—a spy? And you know, Mac, how Ned pays spies!—eh? You've mistaken Kelly."

"Fac or neath, I thocht it was some reovin thief that had lifted your bonnie beast, my lad; and I was just——"

"Yes, I know, you were just seeing if you could see whether Kelly was handy to fill a cellar or jail I know ye, Andy. I'm fly to it all, and your little game too. But you havn't won the trick yet, my laddie. No, you've got a little performance to go through before them cards turn up trumps. Just get up and follow me."

"What do you want me to get up for—I may as well be where I am when I've no horse."

"Why, you don't think I'd be so cruel as to let you lie here until the crows picked your liver out?" laughed Kelly. "Oh, dear, no, Mac, I mean to provide a lodging for you for life."

"What the diel are ye at mon?" said M'Vittie, looking rather anxiously at Kelly, but still ignorant that his enemy was aware of his treacherous intentions.

"Up you sneaking hound—you shall never lap my blood. D'ye think I'm not fly to your police jabberings; do you think I don't know your game for the Reward? You've come for it, and my government oath, you'll have something that will show such vermin as you are what it is to meddle with Ned Kelly.

"I know your little game. I know how you plotted to keep the horse till I came for it, so as to hand me over to the traps. I know all about your meeting the police at the out-station. The man who stole the horse you talk of! Why, the man who stole the horse was me, and as I stood by your blooming shanty I felt a devilish mind to put a light to the roof, and to shoot you down as you came out, like the dog you are."

He paused for a moment, half choked with fury.

Then he resumed in more solemn tones—

"Only I'm very glad I didn't, for then I should have lost the chance of teaching you the very pretty little lesson of how Ned Kelly repays treachery, which I mean to do before you're an hour older."

"But, Ned——" began M'Vittie, feebly.

"Stow it!" thundered the bushranger. "Don't try any of your gibberish with me. I ain't been very particular in my line about knocking a fellow on the head if he stood in my way, or when the Californey was to be turned up; but if I did a trifle more, I never put a pal's life in my pocket and drunk out his heart's blood in the nearest pub. No; Ned Kelly never sold a pal or sneaked a swag. He always went straight at his work, whether it was a man or a bank. No; he'd stand or fall like a man, not like a cur that would bite you in your sleep, and sell your wisen to the rope as he would a bale of wool or a cask of tallow."

Thoroughly alarmed, Andrew tremulously cried—

"I dinna ken what ye are bletherin' aboot me betrayin ye; it's a'together a mistake on your pairt. I'm yer freend, and I can prove it. Let me gang, and I'll gie ye any sum in reason ye could name."

"There's only one thing I mean to take from you," replied Ned.

"And what's that?"

"Every drop of blood in your body, and every ounce of meat on your bones."

As he spoke, Ned stooped over the prostrate figure of squatter, and hoisted it to its feet.

Then throwing it on to his shoulder, he carried it to the spot beyond the angle where Marco Polo was tethered.

The Scotchman roared loud and long, hoping, but in vain, to attract succour.

A few minutes later, and M'Vittie was balancing like a sack, across the saddle of the gallant animal, which Ned took by the bridle. Andrew threw himself off the animal, and fell on his face, and lay there howling and imploring for mercy, and asking wildly what Kelly was going to do?

"If you don't lie quiet in the saddle, I'm hanged if I don't drag you by this tether-rope to the lodging I'm going to give you for the night, at all events."

Groan upon groan flowed from M'Vittie's throat. He realised his prospects, and he knew his man; he also knew his man knew him. White despair enshrouded his face, the features of which were working with dread. He ceased to plead, for hope had fled. Kelly threw him again across the saddle, face downwards, like a sack, saying—

"Tumble again, and you'll know more of the stones than you ever yet felt."

After travelling for half-an-hour, they arrived at the foot of a small, isolated peak, on the flat summit of which was a solitary tree, forming a conspicuous landmark.

Here Ned halted, and laughed and chuckled, while his his eyes gleamed revenge.

He removed M'Vittie—whose sufferings, mental and physical, had reduced him to almost a state of imbecility—from the back of Marco Polo.

Placing him on his own shoulder, he commenced the ascent of the peak, which was not high, merely prominent.

The ground led very gradually up to it, and Marco Polo had carried the burden up to the foot of the rock.

At length they reached the summit of the peak, which formed a small plateau.

Ned threw himself down, utterly exhausted by the side of M'Vittie, whom bruises and terror had by this time reduced to a condition of almost imbecility.

The plateau was about eight or ten feet square, and from its summit an extensive view could be obtained.

The tree rooted in it was a small but strong one.

As soon as he had recovered himself, Ned rose and lifted M'Vittie to his feet.

He placed the squatter against the tree, and lashed him to it securely.

A look of frozen terror spread over the squatter's face.

He turned his eyes to Ned, his blue lips parted and in a husky whisper he gasped—

"What is it ye mean to do wi' me?"

Without vouchsafing him any reply, Ned drew his knife.

"For mercy's sake, for pity's sake, spare me, I'm no fit to dee. I'm a miserable sinner," screamed M'Vittie.

Still in silence Ned raised his knife, but instead of plunging it into M'Vittie's breast as he had anticipated, he deliberately set to work to cut away every shred of clothing the unhappy man wore, taking care at the same time not to sever his bonds.

When this was completed, and M'Vittie stood as naked as Adam before the fall, Ned returned his knife to its sheath, and said—

"I told you I meant to have every drop of blood from your body, and every ounce of flesh from your bones. I give the first to the insects and the last to the birds."

"For God's sake," yelled M'Vittie, who began to realise the awful fate awaiting him, "put your knife into me."

"No," answered Ned," my knife for a man who fights me, and not for a sneak, who wanted to earn my blood-money, like you."

"Help, mercy, mercy, help, murder," yelled the squatter, almost mad with fear.

"It's no use howling M'Vittie, there's not a living soul within fifty miles of us."

The squatter made a desperate effort to free himself.

He tugged at his bonds till they buried themselves in his flesh, and then heedless of the agony he inflicted on himself he endeavoured to snap them by a series of jerks.

At length he paused exhausted and bleeding from a dozen places where they had cut through his skin.

'You won't get loose, those fastenings would hold a couple of working bullocks.'

'Ye coward, ye fause-hearted coward, I spit at ye, ye

dare na snub me, ye dare na," howled M'Vittie, in the hope of taunting Ned into using his knife.

"That cove won't fight," replied Kelly calmly.

"Kill me in mercy, mon, it's the only thing I ask o' ye, if ye've got a human heart in ye kill me."

With his eyes protruding from his head, and his hair standing on end, M'Vitie forced this frantic appeal from between his lips, from which blood and froth were running down to his chest, that panted and heaved with his recent exertions and his present terror.

"No," answered Ned. "Good bye. I mean to leave you as a warning to others not to play tricks on Ned Kelly."

With these words he turned away and began to descend the peak heedless of the wild string of prayers, blasphemies, curses, and entreaties that pealed forth from the lips of the doomed wretch at its summit.

As he descended the sounds grew fainter and fainter.

On reaching the bottom he looked up.

The figure of M'Vittie lashed to the tree trunk was plainly visible against the sky, across which clouds that indicated a storm were floating.

Ned fancied he could discern it struggling to get loose.

After gazing at it for some time he remounted Marco Polo and rode onward.

As he did so one last wild despairing yell reached his ears.

Before nightfall a terrible storm of wind and rain broke over the mountains.

This weather lasted for several days and its effects extended over a large area.

When, after waiting a week without hearing anything of M'Vittie, his overseer made an attempt to track him, the faintest hope of doing so had vanished.

It was not till months afterwards that a shepherd who had strayed into the mountainous district was attracted by the singular object he observed on the summit of one of the peaks.

On reaching this he found himself in the presence of skeleton securely fastened to a tree trunk.

The birds of prey had long since stripped it of every particle of flesh, and nothing remained to identify this victim of Ned Kelly's vengeance.

CHAPTER CCI.
NED ENTERS THE GOVERNMENT SERVICE.

AFTER disposing of the treacherous squatter in the fashion described, Ned had to look ahead.

From what he had gathered on his journey up country, it was evident that, thanks to the information given by the Scotchman, the police were on the alert for his return.

The presence of Marco Polo at Garoona had evidently converted that station into a kind of honey-pot, round which they had been continually buzzing like so many flies.

Ned argued that with Marco Polo away, however, they would no longer think that there was any certainty of the horse's owner making his appearance in the district, and would therefore gradually relax their vigilance.

"They'll hear the horse has been boned," he thought; "but they'll never dream of such a thing as a fellow stealing his own horse, when he'd only got to go straight up to the station and ask for it."

He determined therefore to remain quiet for a few months longer, until the police had given up all hopes of his putting in an appearance in that quarter, and left him a clear field for future action.

There would, no doubt, be some fuss made over the Scotchman's disappearance; but Ned judged that it would, after a time, be set down to one of the countless accidents of the bush.

The body might not be found for months, or even years; and, even then, its identification would probably be a matter of difficulty.

At any rate there would be no evidence to connect him

with it, since he had not been recognised since his return to the colony.

"That's the dodge," he said to himself. "I'll put Marco Polo in sure hands this time, lie up a bit longer, and then, when they least expect it, I'll just wake snakes amongst some of those police buffers. Just when they've given up all chance of seeing me, and fancy I'm lying somewhere with my toes turned up to the roots of the daisies, I'll just streak slick across the colony like a bush fire, and warm 'em up all round."

In pursuance of this plan he travelled for some days, till he reached a spot where he thought his horse would be safe.

After journeying for a week, he came upon the outstation of a cattle run, the owner of which was in England, and the station, as is often the case, in charge of a working overseer.

As the stock is all branded with the owner's initials, and no sales are to take place except through the master's Melbourne agents' cattle brokers, there is little or no chance of robbery by those in charge.

Of course, the overseer's small herd of cattle, allowed to depasture in the run, increases in a miraculous manner.

Every cow belonging to him has two calves, and none of them ever die.

Here Kelly soon agreed with the overseer to take Marco Polo in, and let him run with the mob of horses in the station.

He was to be hobbled for the first month, to get him accustomed to the locality and his new associates, from which he would not stray.

Having left him there, he worked his way down to the Murray, and obtained a passage on a flat boat conveying wool to Adelaide.

Here he learnt that an expedition was on the point of starting with a view of surveying a line of country for the railway proposed to run right across the Australian continent from south to north, a distance of 1,200 miles, in a straight line.

There is no country in the world better suited for the laying out of railway lines than Australia.

It seems as if nature, anticipating the appliances of steam, had prepared the land for the locomotive. It is almost a dead level throughout the vast continent, and engineering difficulties are consequently minimised.

A company is now in formation to lay the rail from Adelaide to the North Coast. The land is as level as a billiard board.

The expedition was organised by the Government, and the idea occurred to Ned that the very last place of all others in which he would be likely to be sought would be in the Government service.

Accordingly he joined the expedition, and very glad the leader was to obtain "a hand" of such splendid physique.

Of course he did not give his real name, and selected that of Tom Smith, as one easily remembered and not uncommon.

The expedition started, and for some weeks no event of importance took place till they had entered the Northern part of the Continent.

One day, however, one of the blacks attached to it in the capacity of tracker declared that amongst the trail left by a party of blacks they had come across, was the unmistakable print of a white woman's foot.

This created some astonishment, not unmixed with unbelief.

Mr. Jackson, the leader of the party, closely questioned the black, whose name was Tiger, but the fellow persisted that the tracks were unmistakably those of a "white Mary," as he styled her.

There had been several rumours in the colony of white women carried off by the blacks and kept as captives, and this discovery led to their being discussed again.

It was determined to come up with the blacks and rescue the "white women."

One strong argument against this lay, however, in the fact of the somewhat crippled condition in which the explorers found themselves, owing to their provisions running short.

For several days past they had been making their way over low stony ridges, with peaks rising here and there, and tracts of bare red sandy soil dotted with patches of prickly trio-dia.

They had run out of meat, and the chief occupations of the day were stalking parrots, catching kangaroo rats, and digging for water in the sandy beds of dry creeks.

The parrots, which fed on the blossoms of the bloodwood trees, were pretty plentiful, but after a time they palled on the appetite. They fell in with kangaroo, and were soon so far in clover.

It was known that there were several stations lying in a north-westerly direction, and Mr. Jackson resolved to dispatch a man in that direction with a view of obtaining provisions. What they chiefly missed was bread.

"We are pretty lucky as regards water," he observed, "though in a few more days we shall find it without having the trouble of digging for it."

"Time we did," observed the second; "for if this sort of thing goes on much longer, we shall have the horses taking a shovel and going down to the creek to dig for themselves. It's very rum the way in which they hang about for a water-hole to be opened for them, they know as well as we do what the digging is for."

"Yes, it may be laughable to see that, but I question if the diggers think it is, especially when they have to go down so deep that every drop for the horses has to be bailed out into an artificial water-hole made by a waterproof spread on the sand. That is why I want to push on out of this region into the grass country, and why I do not like turning aside to follow the track of the blacks."

"Right you are."

"I intend to send that fellow, Tom Smith, with Tiger, on ahead towards the north-west, in order to get one of the squatters up there to send some beef and mutton walking down to us."

The party had indeed got over the worst part of their journey, and were approaching the grassy plains met with in approaching the Gulf of Carpentaria.

Here boundless plains, richly grassed, stretched away to the horizon, and were intersected by magnificent lagoons, promising a never-failing supply of water.

It was arranged that Ned and the black should start off at dawn the next morning, and push on as far as they could.

When morning arrived, however, the black was missing.

No one could give the slightest clue to his whereabouts, but it was supposed that with the carelessness of his race, he had forgotten all about the mission he had been informed of, and had started off on a hunt of some kind on his own account.

Seeing that Mr. Jackson was seriously annoyed at the delay, Ned volunteered to push on alone.

"Give me my bearings," he said, "and I'll steer as straight as a bee line to the station."

During the journey, Mr. Jackson had had ample opportunities of testing Kelly's skill as a bushman, and was in no apprehension on that score.

Indeed, it was on account of these very qualities that he had selected him for the mission.

"It's not so much that," he answered, "that I am in doubt about, but on account of the blacks."

"The blacks?" echoed Ned.

"Yes. They are very fierce and dangerous up here. I know that they are continually spearing sheep and cattle on the runs, especially during the rainy season, and that the squatters have all their work cut out to keep them under."

"Oh! that's it, is it?"

"Yes, and the main reason I wanted to go with you, was in order to keep a look-out. You know what cunning devils they are at hiding, and you might have half-a dozen spears through you before you sighted the tip of an ear."

"Oh! never fear for that. I'll keep a sharp enough look-out," said Ned, "the spear ain't sharpened that's to drill a hole in my hide, I feel certain."

As he spoke he could not help thinking how handy his armour would be under the circumstances, for the northern blacks are a fierce race, and their spears are thrown with a force and precision that sends them through a man's body like a skewer through a fowl.

After repeated warnings and instructions, Kelly cantered off with the understanding that if Tiger turned up in time he should be despatched on his trail.

As Kelly rode along, the warnings respecting the blacks were uppermost in his mind, but armed as he was with rifle and revolver, he felt equal to facing a score of them.

By noon he had got to the edge of the barren region, and halted to give his horse a rest, and eat some mutton and damper with which he had been furnished. Nor was the comfort of a pipe denied him.

Remounting he continued his journey at a swinging canter across the level plain now stretching before him. He was mounted on a Government horse, and didn't spur him more than was necessary. But like a good bushman he pulled up more than once to give his animal a spell and a bite of grass, while he loitered on the greensward, and tranquilly blew a cloud. We say tranquilly—for he began to appreciate the feeling of security and rest which he experienced from the utter absence of any kind of apprehension. He felt that he was acquiring capital for future adventures.

Mile after mile did they speed along with nothing in view to break the monotonous expanse of verdure.

Thirty miles were at length covered, and the shades of evening began to settle on the landscape, which was now varied by belts of small timber and low shrubs.

The sun set, and darkness came rapidly on.

Ned was just about to select a soft spot for the night, when a single spark of fire glittering through the darkness drew his attention to a dense scrub some three or four hundred yards from where he stood.

At first he thought he might have been deceived by fancy or by a falling star low down on the horizon.

Whilst still in doubt, and hesitating whether to ride forward or wait, a second spark, for such it evidently was, floated out from the same spot.

That there was a fire in the scrub was beyond question, and that it must be either an abandoned fire or one made by natives, was at once apparent to Ned, who was well versed in the ways of the aborigines.

He had no doubt that it was one made by natives for the simple reason that no smoke or glare was visible over head.

Had it been an encampment of white men there would have been a roaring fire and the tops of the surrounding trees would have been lit up by the blaze.

Kelly determined to ascertain the number of those assembled, and to find out if it were merely an ordinary camp, or whether the myalls or male blacks were out on some essentially warlike errand.

In the former case they would be accompanied by their guns or wives or piccanennies, but in the latter like the North American Indians on the war path, they would be alone.

Having decided on his course of action Ned dismounted, and leading his horse as near to the camp of the blacks as prudence admitted, he hitched the bridle over a broken branch.

Patting the animal gently as an admonition to remain quiet till he was wanted, he moved noiselessly onwards towards a spot whence he could obtain a view of the fire and its makers.

The chief danger of discovery lay in the fact of the natives being always accompanied by a pack of curs, whose yelping serves to give notice of the approach of any stranger to the camp.

By the exercise of the utmost caution Kelly managed to crawl near enough through the scrub to obtain a view of the occupants.

CHAPTER CCI.

THE NATIVE CAMP AND THE PILLAGED DRAYS.

THESE he speedily discovered to consist merely of old men, useless as warriors, women and children, who were sheltered by the usual "miamis," composed of sheets of bark placed on end and overlapping each other, forming merely sloping screens between the wind and the fires.

The adult males were evidently absent on some predatory expedition.

Satisfied with his survey, Ned retreated as quietly as he had come to the spot where had left his horse.

Mounting him he made for another patch of scrub at some half-a-mile distance from the natives.

Here he unsaddled, hobbled his horse, and lay down for a few hours' sleep.

He rose at daybreak and rode forward for some hours, when it occurred to him that he had started without breakfasting, and that it might be as well to repair that omission.

He was just on the point of alighting in order to do so, when he heard the peculiar jingle-jangle so familiar to the bushman's ear—the sound of the bullock yoke—he pricked up his ears, knowing now that a white man was close at hand. He followed the sound, and came upon a pair of working bullocks feeding in their yokes. Hence the noise.

It at once occurred to him that the dray must be bound to the station of which he himself was in quest, and he started at full speed to find it.

As he drew near, however, he noticed to his surprise that there was no smoke about to indicate that white people were encamping anywhere about.

Doubts began to arise in his mind as he recollected the character of the blacks, and the fact of the absence of the men from the camp he had seen the evening before.

There was, it occurred to him, just a possibility that these men had surprised the teamsters and rifled the dray.

He was well armed and felt that, provided he kept out of any ambush, he could easily get near enough to the spot to reconnoitre the state of affairs.

Riding slowly, and sheltering himself as much as possible behind the narrow belts of scrubby timber, he gradually advanced until he could plainly distinguish two drays between the openings in the bushes.

A nearer approach gave a full view of the waggons themselves, but there was no sign of human life near them.

He began to fear the worst, though perhaps the bullocks might have strayed and the drivers were away searching for them.

Determined to neglect no precautions, he satisfied himself that the coast was clear before advancing to the waggons.

When he did so he realised what had happened.

A glance at the drays sufficed to show him that they had been ransacked of their contents, and that everything eatable or useful, in a black fellow's estimation, had been carried off.

Lying beneath one of them was the mutilated body of one of the drivers and an elderly woman.

Their heads were beaten in with nullah-nullahs, their hands and feet had been cut off and probably devoured, and their bodies hacked and hewed in a revolting fashion.

The tracks of a large mob of blacks were plainly visible, and it was evident that after their murderous work they had departed with their plunder in a body.

But to Ned's astonishment he noticed amongst their tracks the unmistakable footprint of a white woman.

There could be no mistake about it.

The ground was soft, and, amidst the traces left by the bare feet of the natives, that of a woman's small boot was plainly discernable.

But where was the other driver.

Either he had been killed at a distance from the camp

or had succeeded in making his escape, in which case he would probably make his way to the nearest station and return with a search party.

"It's pretty certain," thought Ned, "that the blacks who have stuck up the drays are the myalls of the lot I came across last night. The tracks are fresh, and the job was done this morning so they can't have got much of a start. It's pretty certain, too, that there was a girl with the drays, and they've carted her off along with them.

"The tarnation vermin! I'm after them, and if I don't make 'em hand over that white woman why I don't know the crack of a rifle. The niggers can never get within fifty yards of me. I can down 'em before they know where the bullet comes from; and I don't know but a little black practice won't keep my hand in. Besides I'm getting tired of this here work—nothing to wake one up day after day. This will put a spurt into work, and be such a jolly lark too."

Anything was a lark to Kelly that smelt of blood and danger.

He forgot all about the mission with which he had been entrusted by Mr. Jackson, and started in pursuit of the white woman.

The excitement suited him.

He was a man of ready action, but his anxiety did not lead him into the error of headlong haste.

He did not know how far he might have to travel, and proceeded to rummage the drays in quest of anything eatable that might have escaped the notice of the natives.

The blacks had cleared out everything eatable.

So Kelly fell back on his own commissariat of cold mutton and damper, which he carried with him.

The proximity of the two murdered people seemed to have little effect upon him.

Nevertheless, he resolved, if he got the chance, to thin the ranks of the niggers.

The meal dispatched, he started on the track of the blacks, which led—though of course he was unaware of this—in the direction of some large lagoons, beyond which was a stretch of broken country, affording a safe retreat to such marauding hordes as the one he was following.

The mob he was tracking were indeed bent on crossing the lagoon, and gaining this fastness where any attempt at pursuit would be hopeless.

After some hours' riding Ned came in sight of a belt of oak scrub, fringing the head of the lagoon, or rather lake.

The track of the blacks ran along its shore.

Stopping for a few moments to breathe and water his horse, Ned began to think matters over.

It would soon be dusk, and, from the freshness of their tracks, it was plain that the blacks had but a very slight advance on him, thanks to the speed at which he had been travelling.

It was also plain that they would camp on the borders of the lake.

Ned resolved to come up with them at nightfall, and make an attempt to rescue the girl, if he could see his way to it.

Wishing to time his arrival, as well as to spare his horse, he rode slowly along the western borders of the water, which lay placid and smiling in the midst of a vast plain.

Splendid pink and white lilies reared their wax-like heads above their broad leaves, with which its mirror-like surface was thickly studded to a distance of twenty yards from the bank.

Amongst these leaves water rails chased each other in sport, and ever and anon a red-legged crane would stalk from its cover in the tall reeds, or a stately black swan sail by.

Flocks of wild ducks swam slowly about, diving from time to time beneath the surface of the water, and now and then a crocodile would slide noiselessly from the bank and vanish with hardly a ripple.

As the shades grew longer and darkness fell, the task of the lonely tracker grew more and more difficult, since he dared not strike a light.

At length, on turning the head of the lake, he caught sight of smoke, and, advancing a few steps further, could plainly hear the mob of natives.

The time for action had come.

Selecting a secluded spot some distance from the black camp, he fastened his horse to a tree in such a manner that the animal would remain, if required, but in case of the prolonged absence of his master, or of a surprise by the blacks, could break away without much struggling.

Having disposed of his horse, Ned looked to his revolver, and taking his rifle, cautiously made his way through the oaks towards the spot whence the talking and shouting of the natives reached him.

This time he had no fear of the dogs, as he knew that when on one of their murderous expeditions the men left their dogs with their wives and children.

The noise made by the blacks themselves, who concluded they were safe from pursuit, helped to cover his advance, made as it was under the dense shade of the oaks which grew thickly together.

He was not long in gaining a spot whence he could see and hear all that went on.

The blacks, whose number he roughly guessed at fifty, were busily engaged.

Some were disposing of the provisions and articles stolen from the drays, and others were cutting down branches of the oaks to make a slight shelter for the camp to windward and making up small fires.

By the light of these he could plainly distinguish the prisoner, a white girl sitting on the ground with her face buried in her hands.

She was unbound but was guarded by three or four young men, to whom the duty of watching her had evidently been assigned.

Kelly having satisfied himself as to the number and disposition of the men, turned his attention to the surroundings.

The spot chosen for the native camp, was a natural clearing of about a quarter of an acre.

It was washed on one side by the waters of the lake, where a narrow passage had been cut through the reeds, and bounded in every other direction by the oak scrub.

Glancing towards the lake Ned noticed, to his surprise, that a number of canoes were lying up in the shallow water close to the shore.

It at once occurred to him that the blacks intended to make use of these to continue their flight.

It was doubtless their intention to embark in them the following morning.

The sight of the canoes gave Ned a fresh idea.

Two days' hard riding with his weight on its back had told on his horse, and it was doubtful whether the beast would be equal to carrying off him and the girl, whilst a flight on foot would be almost certainly fatal with such keen trackers to deal with as the blacks.

But it was absolutely necessary to rescue the girl that very night, and once embarked it would be impossible to follow her.

Water, too, he reflected, would leave no trail by which their own flight could be traced.

CHAPTER CCIII.
THE WHITE CAPTIVE AND THE BLACK TIGER.

He resolved therefore to try and carry her off by means of one of the canoes.

As however some hours must elapse before the attempt could be made, he drew back through the bushes with the intention of examining the shores of the lake for a little distance.

It would be as well he thought, to make sure that no treacherous sand or mud bank existed in the neighbourhood, that might interrupt his flight and render him and the girl a mark for the unerring spears of the natives.

The sky, which had hitherto been clear, was now charged with heavy clouds, and a strong breeze had got up—two things both favourable to his desperate enterprize.

As soon as he had got some distance from the camp he entered the water, and waded out beyond the fringe of reeds.

He felt somewhat uneasy, remembering the crocodiles he had seen; but in reality there was no cause of alarm on this score, as these animals, though numerous in the inland lakes and lagoons of North Australia, are not dangerous.

They rarely attain a greater length than six feet, and, unlike their congeners, the alligators on the coast, never attack human beings.

Feeling, as has been remarked, somewhat nervous on this score, he waded slowly and cautiously towards the camp, the water barely reaching above his knees.

He found no obstruction, and a less depth of water even would have sufficed for the light native canoes.

In his anxiety to avoid the crocodiles, he had incautiously approached so near the passage cut in the reeds to the camp, that before he was aware of it, he found himself within five yards of a couple of blacks, who were searching for some article they had dropped into the water.

For a moment Ned thought he was discovered, and stood in readiness to shoot the first who should give the alarm.

He had presence of mind to cock the weapon noiselessly, by pressing the trigger as he raised the hammer; as otherwise the click would have betrayed him.

Finding that he had not been observed—and if he had, even had he escaped himself, the fate of the woman he was scheming to rescue, would have been sealed—he drew back again into the reeds, and from there watched the proceedings going on ashore.

The sight was a strange one.

Amongst the other goods which the drays had contained, were a case of brandy and a small keg of rum.

These were being broached, and it was evident would, in a few hours, render a large majority of the savages helpless.

The very guards appointed to look after the prisoners were not likely to resist this temptation, though there was some danger that in their banbanaban orgies the hapless girl might be brained in mere drunken fury or sport.

The two savages who had alarmed him, having rejoined their companions, Ned examined the canoes, and selected the one he thought best suited to his purpose.

Bending low, and keeping well out of the glow of the fires, he placed the best paddles he could find in it, and then returned to his cover in the oaks.

As he was emerging from the water a hand was laid on his arm, and a voice he thought he recognised, whispered—

"All right, marmy (master), Tiger come along."

Kelly's first impulse at seeing a naked black before him was to shin him with a blow of his foot, but on hearing the voice he recognised Tiger, the black, who was to have accompanied him on his expedition.

Tiger had evidently followed him, but was he a friend of the blacks in camp before him?

Might he not be an accomplice in their outrages, and had he not merely hastened thither to join them?"

Ned felt a bit suspicious.

"How did you know I was here, Tiger?" he whispered.

"Tiger yan along a track. Plenty track sit down. Yarraman baal all same like it."

A little more questioning showed Ned that Tiger had followed him shortly after he had left camp, but had been unable to get up with him before, owing to an accident to his "yarraman" or horse, which he had finally abandoned, pursuing the rest of his way on foot.

"Marmy," observed the black, "White Mary sit down belongin' myall camp" (there is a white woman in the black's camp).

"Your" (yes), answered Ned.

"My word! You want 'em, marmy?"

"Mine want 'em, and mine get 'em bimeby; 'spose altogether kill 'em, myall nigger," growled Ned, implying that he would rescue the captive even if he had to slaughter the whole of her captors.

"Plenty canoe sit down, take canoe," suggested Tiger.

"Canoe all right," answered Ned. "Plenty grog sit down, too long a camp, Tiger," he added, imprudently.

"My word! plenty rum, eh?"

And the darkey's eyeballs glistened at the thought of unlimited rum.

Ned noticed this, and saw his mistake.

He feared for the success of his plan.

He knew the inveterate craving of the blacks for rum, and he saw that he must at once check this desire in the breast of Tiger, or simply kill him on the spot.

"Look here, Tiger," he said, "mine want white Mary to-night. S'pose you help me mine give it you plenty rum and baccy long a station. Every day some rum. S'pose baal (no) get Mary, mine shoot plenty black fellow. Shoot Tiger first. You see?"

The myall had wisdom to see the odds would be considerably against him in a fight, so he at once made up his mind to accept the compromise of "rum every day," and from that moment his whole energies were devoted to the rescue of the white woman.

"Marmy," he said after a pause, during which the blacks in camp had commenced a corroboree, and were howling in a manner which was in itself a sufficient indication that the liquor had been tapped, "you 'top here. Tiger yan (go) look out. Baal (don't) walk about."

His dark form was soon lost in the oak shadows.

In a few moments Ned began to regret having trusted him so far.

What if the sight and smell of the liquor should prove too much for his good resolutions?

What if he betrayed him, and brought a horde of drunken savages down on him?

Even to a man of Ned's iron nerve such a prospect was not a pleasant one, and as the minutes flew by he grew more and more uneasy.

"Urra!" said a voice behind him, in the opposite direction to that in which the black had disappeared from sight.

Ned wheeled round with his rifle ready, but only to confront Tiger in person.

"Baal shoot marmy," whispered the black, with a grin.

"By gosh, Tiger! hanged if you didn't give me a start. What news? Is the woman all right? Are the myalls drunk?"

"White Mary all right," answered Tiger. "That fellow patter (eats) damper. Blackfellow plenty drink it grog. Mine been bring canoe. Canoe sit down," and he pointed to a spot close to where they were standing.

It was very fortunate for Ned that Tiger had been well treated during the expedition.

Mr. Jackson, knowing that their very lives might at times depend upon the skill of the blacks accompanying them in tracking strayed horses or discovering water, had made it a strict rule to earn their good will, and had insisted on one and all of those under him acting up to it.

By this he had secured Tiger's devotion.

It was well for Ned that such was the case, as, otherwise, the temptation to join in the orgies before him would very likely have been too strong for the black.

But he regarded the bushranger as his friend, and extended to him the feeling of gratitude he entertained towards Mr. Jackson, his leader.

The possession of the canoe was a great point in their favour, but it would never do to allow the blacks to retain possession of the others.

If they did they would naturally start in pursuit, and, by their superior numbers, would soon tire out two men encumbered with a woman in their little craft.

Tiger, on being questioned, explained that he had waded round into the passage, and, selecting the canoe to which Ned had already transferred the paddles, had gently withdrawn it from the others.

The feat he had accomplished, unseen by the drunken blacks, who had now scarcely a thought for anything save the unexpected and plentiful supply of liquor.

The success of this manœuvre decided Ned to attempt the removal of the other canoes.

As Tiger was quite sure that there was no watch kept over them, he was dispatched to bring them away.

This feat he successfully accomplished in a very short time.

The two then set to work to damage all, except the one they had chosen, beyond repair.

With crafts of such fragile build this was easy enough.

A long consultation followed, as soon as pursuit by water had been thus rendered impossible.

Ned found out that Tiger was thoroughly well acquainted with the district in which they were and with the situation of the stations, to one of which he was to have guided his present companion.

He questioned him as to the size and shape of the lake, and the best spot to which to make in order to land.

Tiger enlightened Ned to the best of his ability, and the line of flight was decided upon.

Kelly arranged with Tiger that the latter should attract the attention of the savages when the white woman was prepared to make for the boats, and thus draw off their watchfulness.

When this had been settled, Ned thought it was time to set about the most hazardous and arduous portion of his task.

That of rescuing the captive girl from the maddened horde of savages by whom she was surrounded.

CHAPTER CCIV.
KELLY RESCUES THE WHITE GIRL.

TIGER was instructed in the dusk of the evening to get near the captive girl and convey the intelligence to her that aid was near.

Stripped to the buff like a native he would be mistaken, if seen, for one of themselves.

When the savages were engaged in their drinking bout, he crawled through the grass within earshot of the girl, and, as instructed by Kelly, said—

"A friend, look out."

The sound startled the captive at first, but, after the first surprise, she sat as still as death, eyes and ears open.

Kelly being informed that she had been thus made aware that a friend was near, soon crawled up the edge of the clearing and again reconnoitred the condition of affairs.

He found to his great satisfaction that he could approach so near to the spot where the girl was seated as to be able to make himself heard by her without attracting attention.

Accordingly he made his way, with the utmost caution, to a spot immediately in the rear of where she was seated.

In order to accomplish this, he wormed himself along like a serpent, taking every imaginable cover, that not the slightest sound should betray his presence.

He had purposely deferred this moment until the night had commenced to fall, as he knew daylight would be most unfavourable to his plans.

A fresh trouble now occurred to him.

This was the likelihood of a cry of joy or surprise breaking from the girl directly he made his presence known.

If this took place both would be lost.

"I wonder if she's got the gumption to know when to hold her tongue," he thought; "it's precious few of her breed that have. She seems taking things pretty coolly though, and looks like a wide-awake one too."

She was a slightly made girl, of about eighteen or nineteen, with black hair and large grey eyes.

Ned noticed that those eyes were full of spirit, and that they glanced round her from time to time as though she was looking for an opportunity of escape on her own account.

Her features, too, though pale, wore a resolute expression, and there were no traces of tears on her cheeks.

"Now or never," thought Ned.

Choosing a moment when the corroboree was at its highest, when the savages were jumping and yelling like maniacs, their keen perceptions deadened by drink, he whispered—

"Missie."

The effect of the single word was instantaneous.

The girl started half up, but checked herself by a violent effort.

She resumed her former attitude, and in tones even lower than his own said—

"Who's there?"

"A friend," answered Ned, pleased with her evident courage and coolness. "I think I can get you out of this, but it'll be a risky job, for I'm single-handed. Can you run a bit?"

"Yes; I'll do anything to get away from these beasts."

At this moment a black came up to the girl and looked about him.

He even went to the edge of the scrub and peered into the darkness.

Ned, however, had drawn noiselessly back on his approach, and the girl, who guessed that the myall's keen ear had caught the sound of voices, clasped her hands and began to pray aloud in a low tone.

This satisfied the black, and he returned to the fire.

Ned had noticed the girl's presence of mind, and concluded she was of the right sort.

As soon as she was again alone—for her guards had been unable to resist the temptation of the general debauch—Kelly crawled up again within hail.

"Look here, missus; I think I see a way out of this muck if you've got pluck enough to try it."

"I'm ready for anything," said the girl. "Only tell me what I'm to do and I promise not to flinch."

"That's your sort. I've got a canoe close handy, and I've smashed up all the others. It's about a quarter of a mile from here, and, once in it, we can soon get clear of these herring-gutted devils," said Ned.

"How am I to get to the canoe?" asked the girl, who, with great coolness, kept her position unchanged.

Ned reflected for a moment.

The spot at which the girl was seated was at the edge of the clearing but at some distance from the shore of the lake.

"The blacks seem pretty far gone," said Kelly after a pause, during which he had elaborated his plan of action, "and don't seem to be keeping much of a watch on you, so you can get up in a minute or two as if you wanted to change your seat. Stroll about a bit near the fire and then edge down towards that dead tree near the water's edge. Do you see the one I mean?"

"Yes," answered the girl.

"When you get to the tree wait, and be ready to slip into the oaks directly I give a sign. You may have to run for it pretty smartly, so pull yourself together and keep your wits about you."

"Yes, I promise. But before I start I want you to promise one thing, too," said the girl, in a solemn and appealing tone, but in the suppressed tone necessary.

"What is it? Be quick."

"I don't know you, but, from your risking your life to get me off, you are surely no ordinary man. Risk one thing more. If they—if they lay hands on me before I can get clear, or if there is no hope of my getting away unseen, shoot me down as I stand, and with my dying breath I'll bless you."

Hardened ruffian as he was, Ned was moved by this terrible request so plainly put.

Even in his barren heart there was one vein of gold, one chord that throbbed responsive to this piteous appeal of a woman in her helplessness.

No one would have believed it, and Ned himself less, perhaps, than anyone else, but he was strangely stirred.

He had in the first place attempted the girl's rescue out of sheer recklessness and a feeling of indignation at the blacks for daring to lay hands on a white woman.

"All right, my lass," he answered, "I promise."

And he really meant it, though, to carry out his promise, might only expose his own life uselessly.

For, if it was evident that the girl was too closely watched to render her escape feasible, nothing would be easier than for him to abandon all further attempts at rescuing her and to silently withdraw; but he was essentially a brave man; it was about the only redeeming quality he possessed.

He determined, at all risks, to stick by her to the very end.

The orgie of the blacks was now becoming every minute faster and more furious.

Howling and yelling they poured the fiery liquor down their throats, every fresh draught render them more fiendishly hideous in their aspect.

In pursuance of her instructions, the girl rose and sauntered towards the tree as agreed.

As she moved past the fire no particular attention was paid to her until one of the least drunken of the blacks held out a panakin of liquor to her.

With great presence of mind the girl accepted it.

She knew that it would help her in the desperate task before her, and did not hesitate to taste its contents.

"My word, you budgeree, Mary," hiccoughed the owner of the pannikin as she returned it to him.

Strolling on the girl gradually approached the dead tree, and at length gained it and sat down at its foot.

"All right," said Ned, whose voice came from behind the tree; "are you ready?"

The girl was about to reply, when a sudden stir took place amongst the blacks.

The most sober amongst them had started to their feet, and seizing spears and firesticks had darted into the scrub, in the opposite direction to that in which Ned was lurking.

Something had evidently alarmed them.

The whole attention of those who had not gone off, and who were still sober enough to keep their eyes open, was fixed on the spot whence the alarm had come.

The opportunity was too good not to be profited by.

"Now, my girl," whispered Ned, "slip round the tree; sharp's the word."

Swiftly the girl slipped round the tree trunk and joined him.

"No time for palavering," said Ned. "Push on after me in silence."

A few seconds later, and the girl and he were speeding in the direction of the canoe.

They were not, however, to reach it unmolested.

The quick eye of one of the young niggers had noted the girl's departure from the clearing.

At once he started in pursuit.

Knowing nothing of the presence of a white man, and thinking that the girl was trying to escape on her own hook, he did not trouble himself to call his companions to his aid.

He did not anticipate any difficulty in recapturing the fugitive singlehanded.

Following on their tracks he caught sight of the girl's dress, and at once bounded forward and seized her by the arm.

She had the presence of mind to repress a scream.

The black at first had not noted the presence of Ned.

The latter, however, had marked his pursuit.

It was not until he had clutched the girl that the myall became aware of the proximity of the bushranger.

Before he could utter a cry or raise his nulah-nulah or war-club, a tremendous blow on the head from Kelly's sledge-hammer fist, in which there was a large stone, dashed him senseless to the ground.

Ned had abstained from using firearms, so as to delay giving an alarm as long as possible.

"Quick!" he exclaimed, as a few minutes later they gained the water's edge at the spot where he had placed the canoe. "Quick! into the canoe! That fellow I bowled over's sure to bring a swarm of them down on us."

The girl obeyed him, and stepped quickly but carefully into the frail craft.

Her bearing throughout these trying moments had shown her to be full of courage and resolution.

Kelly was lost in admiration.

What a mate she'd make. Why, she'd be just the Poll to pot a policeman! Couldn't they work together? He'd almost give Marco Polo for her, bless'd if he wouldn't.

"Tiger!" said Ned, noticing for the first time the absence of the black from the spot where he had left him.

"Tiger!" he repeated, in louder tones, but there was no response.

The idea of treachery crossed his mind, but, as he thought it over, he guessed that the sudden alarm amongst the blacks must have been produced by a ruse of Tiger's.

It was evident that the faithful nigger had attracted the attention of the natives to the opposite direction to that in which the projected escape was to be effected, and thus had probably saved Ned and the girl, perhaps, the former thought, at the expense of his own life.

Whilst these thoughts were passing through Ned's mind he had not been idle, but had seated himself in the canoe, and had set about forcing it through the reeds.

This he at last effected, and for the moment felt in comparative safety.

He knew it was no use waiting about for the return of Tiger, if indeed that devoted myall were still in existence.

The route to be taken had been arranged beforehand between him and the black, and in the event of the latter having escaped he would probably turn up at some point of the journey.

To tell the truth, Ned did not particularly care whether he did or not.

Gratitude was by no means one of his strong points, and the very notion of gratitude towards a black would have seemed ridiculous to him.

Still the idea did cross his mind that the black might yet be useful in case any further difficulties had to be overcome.

"The beggar was a smart varmint and no mistake," he thought, "and we may find ourselves in a tight fix yet."

Without delay he began to urge the canoe towards the northern end of the vast lagoon.

There was a station Tiger had informed him in that direction, and the homestead overlooked the lake.

This once reached, they would be of course safe from attack, but the distance to be traversed was somewhat over forty miles, and there was no knowing what accidents might happen on the way.

There was one point especially on the journey where they were likely to have some trouble.

Ten miles from their destination, as Tiger had explained, a sand bank, nearly a mile broad, stretched across the lake.

The only way of passing it was to paddle close to the western shore, where a passage existed, or to get out of the canoe and carry it across the strip of sand.

It was just possible, too, that the blacks might discover the direction they had taken, especially as the fellow Ned had knocked down and whose skull, like that of all his fellows, was as thick as a bullock's, had scrambled to his feet as soon as he felt that it was safe to do so.

He was seen standing on an eminence. looking out for the canoe.

Their destination once known, the blacks would do their utmost to reach a spot where they might intercept the fugitives and recover their prey.

All this passed through Kelly's mind as he paddled vigorously and urged the light craft onward over the rippled water.

To the yells of the savages on shore had now succeeded a death-like silence.

From this he augured that Tiger was either killed or had succeeded in effecting his escape. in which case he would, no doubt, pick them up somewhere on the journey.

CHAPTER CCV.

THE CAPTIVE'S STORY. THE FLIGHT ON THE LAKE.

Up to the moment of pushing out into the lake there had been no time for the girl to mention her name or to narrate the circumstances which had led to her capture, and the murder of the unfortunate bullock-driver.

Now, however, that immediate pursuit was not likely, Ned thought he would like to have a little information on those points.

"Well, now we seem pretty well out of this blessed mess," he began, "perhaps you could manage to give me some idea how you tumbled into it? There must have been a precious bad look-out kept. it strikes me."

"I better begin at the beginning," said the girl; "and then you will understand it all better."

"All right. fire away. I can listen and paddle, too," answered Ned.

The girl explained that her name was Bella Bolton.

Her father was established in Melbourne, but a brother of his, who had settled in Queensland, was at one time a rather well-to-do squatter.

He had originally settled in the Logan district; but as the population increased, and the squatters began to find themselves hemmed in by land selectors and farmers, had resolved to go yet farther afield and take up a run in the far north, where he would not be likely to be disturbed for many years to come.

Accordingly he had pushed on, and after a long and fruitless search, during which he sustained severe losses, had made his way to the district in which they now found themselves, where he discovered a stretch of country that would have suited the most fastidious and grasping of his class.

Richly grassed plains intersected by extensive lagoons, promising over ample supply of water abounded.

Satisfied with the spot, he started a mob of cattle for the new country and formed a station.

Things went on very satisfactorily in all respects, save for the continued hostility of the natives, who were very troublesome.

The chief drawback, however. lay in the distance from any settlement, the drags employed to bring up stores taking months on the journey.

After a time Bolton the squatter who was a bachelor, wrote to his brother at Melbourne, asking him if he could

spare one of his sons to help him on the station, with a view of ultimately succeeding him there as his heir.

The offer was gladly accepted, and Philip the second son joined his uncle, whose affairs soon began to flourish again, thanks to his energetic aid.

As their comfort increased, so did the wish to have the civilising influence of a woman about the house.

Accordingly Philip Bolton wrote to his father and after some discussion it was agreed that his sister Bella, with whom he was a great favourite, should join him and keep house for him and her uncle.

The girl had started, accompanied by her nurse, on her long and wearisome journey.

All had gone well up to the night preceeding the attack, which had resulted in her captivity.

On that evening the bullocks had strayed, and one of the two drivers had started in search of them.

He had not returned at nine o'clock. at which hour Bella had retired to the shelter fitted up for her under the tilt of one of the waggons.

The second driver instead of keeping awake as he should have done till his mate returned, lay down under the other drag and fell asleep.

Just before dawn the girl was awakened by the sound of a scuffle, in which she could distinguish the voice of the imprudent driver, exclaiming—

"My God! I'm done for."

In an agony of terror she heard the horrid sound of the blows that completed his murder, and the fiendish yells of his assailants. Her nurse also lay a mangled corpse; but at some distance from her—she had been brained in her sleep.

As a bright wood fire was burning during the attack. the savages distinguished the form and features of the young girl, whom they resolved to domesticate amongst their tribe.

Several nullah-nullahs were raised to despatch her, when some of the savages interposed in her favour.

She was placed in the charge of four or five of the younger men, whilst the rest proceeded to ransack the drays.

The blacks, having loaded themselves with their plunder, started, with the girl in their midst, to the lake.

(To be continued.)

NED KELLY

THE
IRONCLAD
AUSTRALIAN BUSHRANGER

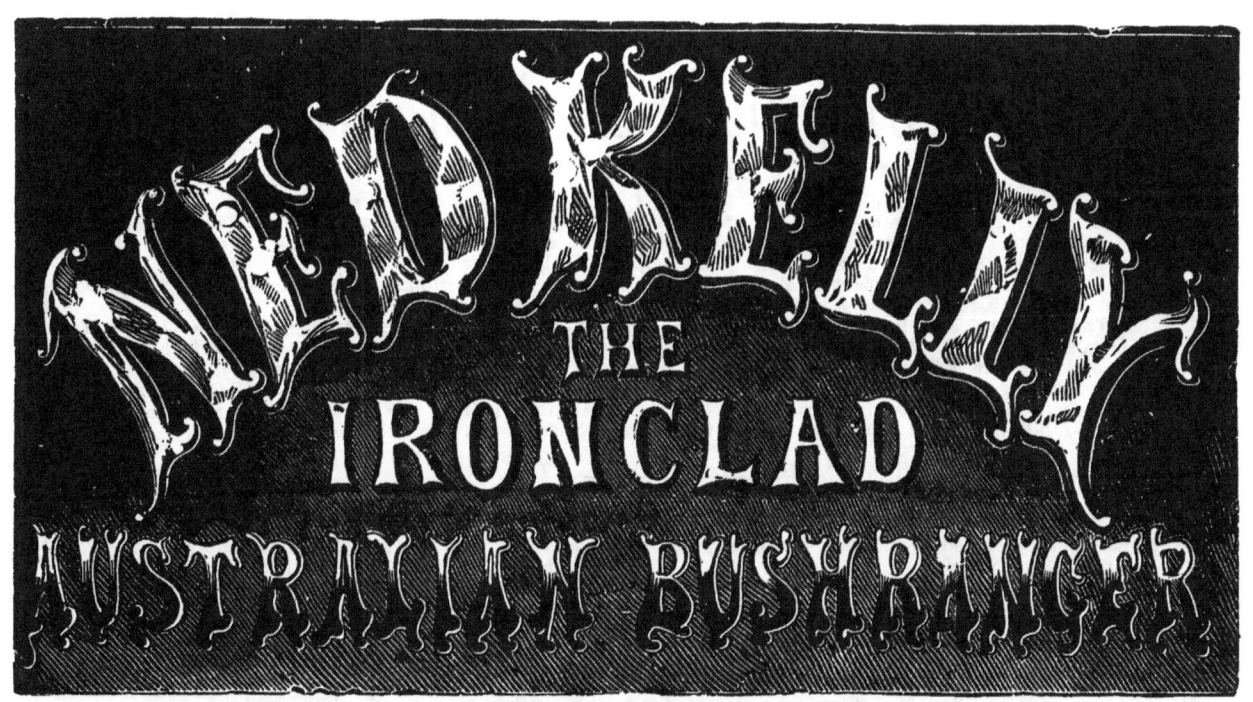

THE PLAN TO ROB THE GOLD CRUSHING MILL.

NO 35,

NED KELLY: IRONCLAD BUSHRANGER.

CHAPTER CCV.—*Continued.*

"I suppose," she concluded, "you saw my letter, and that is what made you follow me."

"What letter?" asked Ned.

"I took advantage of the confusion to scribble a few words on a piece of paper, saying that the blacks had killed the driver and carried me off, and dropped it by the waggon."

"No, I didn't see it," replied Ned, though he refrained from adding that if he had it would not have advanced matters much, since he would not have been able to make out a word of it.

Still he could not help admiring the presence of mind thereon by the girl in writing.

"Did you come across the blacks by accident, then?" inquired the girl.

"No," answered Kelly; "I didn't see your letter, but I spotted your footprints among the nigger-tracks, and I said to myself, 'There's a white girl there, and if I don't have her out of the hands of those beggars in the shake of a bull's tail, why I'm not——'"

He was just going to blurt out his name but he checked himself in time, and added—

"A chap that does know how to work a thing or two."

"You are a brave and clever fellow," said the girl, "and I owe a debt to you I can never repay. How sorry I am my poor nurse had no such deliverer as you. Why they murdered her I can't imagine. You have saved me from worse than death. What is your name?"

"Tom Smith," answered Ned, and added, "Bolton you say yours is?"

"Yes."

"And your father lives at Melbourne. It's very odd I can't call to mind any one of that name I know, but somehow I'm quite certain I've heard of Bolton of Melbourne before. Yes, I'm sure of it."

The girl smiled, and said—

"My father is pretty well known there, and there are a good many who are perfectly familiar with his name but who have not the slightest wish to make his acquaintance."

"What do you mean?" exclaimed Kelly.

"Simply that he happens to be the keeper of Melbourne jail."

His mind was quick to grasp the situation.

"By gosh," he thought, "here's a young woman who may do me a good turn some of these fine days, if I pal up with her properly. This is a streak of luck."

And he added aloud—

"Yes, I see. I've met a chum or two knocking about who thinks your guv'nor the last man in the colony he'd care to drop in and take pot-luck with. But I don't suppose you think I'm one of that sort?"

"No," answered the girl; "and I am sure my father would make no one more truly welcome than his daughter's preserver. There is no one in the colony he would esteem more highly."

"Quite so," thought Ned, "considering my head's worth just ten thousand pounds to him or any other man who can shoot a bolt on me."

"Or cherish more closely," continued the girl.

"Exactly," was Ned's mental commentary. "He would 'cherish' me, as you call it, my dear, so closely that he would lock me up in the very strongest bedroom in that ugly stone jug, and never let me out for fear I should catch cold till I stepped abroad at eight o'clock some Monday morning to do a little jig in a white night-cap. I don't think he'll get a chance though yet awhile."

"It strikes me," resumed Ned, aloud, after a pause, "that your uncle's station must be the one I was originally pushing on for when I came across the drays."

And he proceeded to describe how he had been sent on in advance of Mr. Jackson's party.

On comparing notes, it was evident that this was the case, as there was no other station in the direction in which she had been proceeding, a fact of which her brother's letters had informed Bella, who knew a good deal about Millaroora, as it was styled.

"There's a chance, perhaps, that the other driver escaped, in which case he would push on to the station, and they would send out a scouting party," suggested the girl.

"Yes, there is that, but it's a dicky one," answered Kelly. "I guess we've a better chance in pushing on to this Wirriba station, at the end of the lake that Tiger spoke of."

At that moment the canoe was passing a small islet covered with rushes, and a sudden cry from Bella caused Ned to look up from his paddling.

Plainly visible in the moonlight on the islet was a naked black fellow, standing up, and apparently only awaiting a chance th throw his spear.

Ned dropped the paddle at once and seized his rifle.

Before, however, he had time to fire, the black fellow had evidently come to the conclusion that the odds were against him, and had ducked down out of sight.

"That's cruelly awkward, miss," said Ned. "That black brute has spotted where we're bound to, and we shall have the whole tribe of 'em round to cut us off."

"Can't we pass round the other side of the lake?" suggested the girl, who kept up her spirits wonderfully.

"No," answered Ned; "the sand-bank starts from that side and runs right across to this. The only chance is to keep on along this shore and through the channel, and that's just where I reckon the niggers will try to nail us—for it narrows to a kind of gut—or else to land and try to tramp it."

"Well," said Bella, "I really think I'd rather try it on foot than be cramped up in this wretched little canoe after all. Besides, if the blacks are trying to stop us at the point you say, it strikes me that we shall be more at their mercy at such close quarters than if we could hide in the scrub."

"I don't know but what you may be right, girl," replied Kelly; "but we won't give up the canoe till we're bound to. I guess you'll find being cramped up in it easier work than tramping mile after mile through the bush. If we must take the shore we'll do it as near as we can to Wirriba station. I wish, though, I'd had time to put that black devil on the island. He's sure to carry the news the rest of the beggars. But it can't be helped now, as the hangman said when he found he'd tucked up the wrong 'un."

Bella could not help thinking this last remark a rather strange one, nor from noticing that, despite the gallantry that Ned had shown on her behalf, his manner and speech were decidedly lacking in polish; for she was a girl of keen observation, and had all her wits about her.

But this did not in the least detract from the overwhelming sense of admiration and gratitude that had sprung up in her breast for the stranger who was so generously risking his life on her behalf.

Even he seemed influenced by her presence in a way he could not account for. It made him, not more refined, but less brutal.

She could not help regarding Ned, whose cool courage was most conspicuous, as the greatest hero she had ever seen, and would not suffer these little solecisms to lower him in her eyes.

All this time the light canoe had been skimming the surface of the lake.

Ned was not in the least fatigued, and declared that he could go on all next day.

But he thought it better not to risk travelling by daylight.

Accordingly at the first streak of dawn he pushed the canoe amongst a dense mass of reeds stretching out from the shore.

In the centre was a small islet large enough to afford Bella a short promenade and a more luxurious couch than she would have found in the canoe.

Provisions they had none, but up to the present the excitement of their escape had made them forget the pangs of hunger.

Now, however, they began to be keenly felt, but it was useless to wish for food.

There were several water-fowl within range, but though Ned's mouth watered for them, he dared not risk disclosing their situation by firing a shot, nor could he have ventured to have lit a fire to cook them by.

Having landed the girl, and moored the canoe to the island, he waded through the reeds towards their inner margin, from whence he could examine the shore, the water being shallow enough to allow of this.

The oaks at this point lay back some distance from the edge of the lake, and he could get an uninterrupted view of a tolerably wide extent of country.

Nothing suspicious was in sight.

Returning to Bella, he assured her that she might lay down and take some rest, in perfect confidence.

"I'm used to keep a pretty smart look-out," he said; "and even if I wasn't, the lesson those black devils taught your driver ain't going to be thrown away on me. I don't mean to be woke up by a tap on the head with a nullah-nullah, so you can go to sleep in comfort, as the schoolboy said when he put the hedgehog into the master's bed."

CHAPTER CCVI.

THE ISLET.—TIGER'S PLAN OF ESCAPE.

THE girl had the sense to see that sleep would do her good and help her to stand the fatigues in store for her, and complied with Ned's wish.

Ned waded back to the shore and took up a position amongst the reeds, from which he could command any approach from that side, the only one whence an attack was to be dreaded.

He had kept watch for about four hours when the scrub opposite his post parted, and a black face protruded cautiously through the opening.

From the spot where he was, he could have planted a rifle-bullet between the eyes of the intruder.

He decided, however, to wait, and to be guided by circumstances.

It would be better not to fire till the last moment, lest he should bring down the whole mob on him.

After some minutes spent in reconnoitering the ground, the black fellow probably concluded that he might safely emerge from his cover.

On his doing so, Ned, to his astonishment and delight, recognised Tiger.

A slight motion imparted to a branch of a shrub rising amongst the reeds by Ned's hand, was sufficient to attract the attention of the myall.

But, instead of advancing to discover its origin, he took to a tree with the agility of a monkey, directly he noticed it.

The habitual caution of the black would probably have resulted in half a day of manœuvring before he could have been made to understand that a friend was at hand.

Kelly, after cursing his black hide once or twice, took the bold course of showing himself for a few seconds in the open.

Five minutes later Tiger stood beside him.

"White Mary sit down canoe," remarked the black, pointing in the direction of the islet, and speaking in a low voice.

"Why, how the devil could you know that, you son of a burnt gum-tree?" said Kelly, in a tone of surprise.

"Quiet marney, you plenty yabber (make a lot of noise), black fellow sit down all together," whispered Tiger, indicating the surrounding scrub and implying that it swarmed with their enemies.

"Do you mean to say those myalls are here already?" asked Ned.

"Yowi (yes) myall. Plenty black fellow. Black fellow look out for white Mary. Black fellow want white Mary yakka waddy, dig yam, carry piccaninny, my word." And Tiger grinned as he added, "Baal (not) got um Mary though, eh marney?"

"Here's a pretty kittle-of-fish, as the chap said when he boiled the jelly fish. What's to be done?"

"White Mary got patter (food)?" abruptly asked Tiger.

"No, Tiger. Baal damper, baal bullocky (beef), baal tea," replied Kelly.

"You wait," said the other.

And he disappeared again amongst the oaks.

In a few minutes he returned with a parcel securely done up in the thin silvery bark of the tea-tree.

"Come on," he said.

Without another word he led the way through the water to the islet with an undeviating step, which showed that he must have been aware of the exact whereabouts of the canoe.

Kelly followed in silence.

On reaching the islet they found Bella asleep, but she started up as they drew near, and an expression of terror spread over her face at the sight of Tiger.

However, Ned's presence reassured her, and it was soon explained to her who the black was.

Tiger's parcel, on being opened, proved most acceptable.

There were several large cakes of flour and water, some pieces of beef boiled on the wood pine, some tea and sugar, and nearly half a pound of tobacco.

The fastidious might have objected that all these were packed up indiscriminately, but neither Kelly or Miss Bolton could afford to be fastidious just then.

Kelly however could not help looking suspiciously at the black.

"Where did you get all this, Tiger?" he asked.

"Myall blackfellow run away; leave 'em long a camp Tiger look out patter (food)," he answered.

"Then it was you," said Bella, "who drew off the blacks whilst we escaped?"

"Yes," said Ned, who had explained to her the part played by Tiger.

"White Mary patter bullocky (eat beef)," observed the black. "Bimeby talk."

The advice was good and the three made a hearty meal, after which Kelly and the black filled their pipes.

"Mine think it, yan now," said the latter, after they had puffed for some minutes in silence, implying that in his opinion it was about time they made a start.

"It's all very well to say go, my lovely blacking bottle," replied Ned, "but how about the myalls seeing us?"

"S'pose myall see budgeree," said Tiger, "Myall say bimeby canoe come close : 'spear whitefellow ; catch Mary. Myall altogether yan catch canoe. Canoe baal yan. Canoe 'top bimeby."

"What does he mean?" asked Miss Bolton, who was quite at a loss as to the meaning of this gibberish.

"He means that it'll be all the better if they do see the canoe for it will make 'em think we're heading for the gut I spoke of, and they'll all hurry on ahead there to catch us. But instead of going on all the way by water Tiger means us to land before we get to the gut. That's it, Tiger, isn't it? Baal yan to Werriba long a canoe, eh? (No going to Wirriba in the canoe?)"

"Baal, baal," replied the black, "canoe good one, two, tree hour, then altogether walk about."

"I see, I see," said Ned, "off she goes, missie. Get in with you and with Tiger to help I reckon we'll spin her along like the winner of a four mile heat at Paramatta. Jump in Tiger."

But the black held back.

"What! aint you coming with us?" cried Ned.

"Baal Tiger yan long a canoe. Mine look out black-fellow. S'pose look out bimeby see Tiger. Then canoe no good."

"He means he'll look out for the blacks on shore and that we're to keep a watch for him and to land when we catch sight of him," explained Ned, adding, "a first-rate plant Tiger, we'll look out for you, but don't go and get a waddy about your nut."

Tiger grinned at the idea of such a piece of stupidity on his part being possible and waded to shore again.

With a vigourous shove or two Ned forced the canoe through the reeds, and once more they were on the open lake and in full view of their enemies if they were about, as there was every reason to believe they were.

But this mattered little as it was their intention to allow the blacks to see them.

"Tiger is certainly a most valuable ally," said Miss Bolton. "I do not know how we should manage without him."

"That's true," said Ned; "the beggar has shown real grit all through this muss. I question if we'd have managed that bolt so cleanly last night if he hadn't sneaked round and drawn the beggars to the other side of the camp."

"It's a pity he's so awfully ugly," said the girl.

"'Handsome is as handsome does,' as the fellow said when he gave the waiter the bad sovereign to keep for himself. It's not everyone can have such a pretty mug as yours on 'em. But just keep those eyes of yours, and a fine pair they are, on the shore, so that we mayn't miss any signs. Tiger's watching us as well as the blacks, for certain.'

They coasted along for over an hour without seeing any sign of friend or foe.

The sun had come out from behind the clouds, and its pure rays beat down on their unsheltered heads.

Despite her courage, the heat and her cramped position were evidently beginning to tell on Bella Bolton.

"Cheer up, missie," said Ned, who although she would not complain, could not help noting her uneasiness. "It can't be long now before Tiger makes a sign. I can make out that blessed sandbank plainly, stretching away there to the north."

Sure enough they could make out the long, narrow peninsula which, starting from the eastern shore ran right across the lake almost to the western bank.

They were rapidly nearing the point of danger, and unless warned by their faithful ally on shore, another hour and a half would see them running the gauntlet of the narrow straight at the head of the peninsula.

But they were spared this ordeal.

The girl, who in obedience to Ned's request had been keeping a sharp look out, now uttered an exclamation of surprise.

"Look, Mr. Smith," she cried, "there is a column of smoke rising from the shore, just opposite the head of the sandbank. Yes, and there's another I can see over the trees nearer here. What does it mean?"

Ned took a look in the direction indicated.

"It means that the beggars have spotted us," he growled savagely. "Those five lines of smoke are signals made by the myalls near us to those at the passage. They think we are going to try it, and now the whole mob will be hurrying on there to be in at the death, curse 'em."

The girl could not repress a little shudder.

"Oh, don't be scared, my lass," said Ned more cheerfully, on seeing the effect his words had produced. "I reckon they'll find themselves sold as far as that goes. There are one or two little capers they've got to be up to before they'll get a chance of planting a spear in my carcase, or yours either."

"How do they make their signals?" said the girl, recovering herself, and desirous of showing that she was equal to emergency. "I should have thought that the smoke from a fire on the ground instead of going straight up like that above the trees would have got lost and scattered amongst the branches."

"So it would," explained Ned, who was pretty well acquainted with the manners and customs of the aborigines, "but when the beggars want to make signals they just manage to pitch on a hollow tree. Then they cut a hole in the lower part, and make a fire with damp leaves and sticks inside it. The hollow stem serves as a chimney and takes the smoke right bang away straight into the air. You can spot it miles off sometimes."

"Could we manage to cross the sandbank," suggested the girl, "instead of trying the passage? The canoe is not so heavy. Couldn't we drag it across?"

"No go," answered Kelly. "The sandbank, Tiger says, is a mile broad at least. Besides, you may bet your boots there's a gang of them have swam across the gut on to it, in order to nail us on both sides as we come through. Hullo, there goes another smoke on the eastern side of the lake."

Bella looked in the direction in question.

"That must be from the mob of old men and gins I spotted the night before last. They mean to come along the sandbank to cross the lake," said Ned.

"They are not so dangerous, though?" said the girl.

"I don't know about that ; those gins are perfect devils to fight with their yam-sticks."

"What are they?"

"Pointed sticks they use to dig up yams with, and ain't they blessed smart in handling them. I've seen men that fancied themselves a bit with the sticks—old soldiers, mounted police, and the like—cut away at an old gin for half-an-hour at a time, without once reaching her hide, and she standing as cool as a water melon, just stopping and never troubling to hit back."

"Worse than that," continued Ned. "In a scrimmage they keep on encouraging the men with songs, and yells, and chaff, that makes 'em regular mad. The niggers hereaway, I know, are a sight harder to drive off when their gins are about, than when they are alone. Oh! the blacks up here in the north are a deuced sight worse than the southern ones, they're a bloodthirsty set of devils, and always on the look to catch a stray white man, or woman either."

A few minutes later the bushranger suddenly cried—

"Hullo! what's that away under that snag?"

The girl looked in the direction indicated, and saw a black head seemingly resting on the water.

A second glance showed the grinning face of Tiger, who beckoned them to come ashore.

Ned quickly paddled to the bank, and helped the girl to land.

" Well, Tiger, what's in the wind now ? " he asked.

" Baal wind," said Tiger. " Make canoe go bong; no good canoe."

By this he meant they were to destroy the craft.

" Can we manage to get away by land from here ? " asked Bella, somewhat uneasily.

" Yes, missie," replied Tiger. " Blackfellow altogether sit down long way."

" He means the whole tribe are squatting together at a distance," said Ned. " Are there many, Tiger ? " he added.

" Penty myall, my word," answered the black, holding up his two hands, with the fingers extended, to indicate more than he could count.

" Then the quicker we're off the better, as the cook said to her sweetheart, when they sat down together on the red-hot stove. Here, lend a hand, Tiger, to smash up this rotten old bark concern."

Tiger understood Ned's action, if the words were unintelligible to him.

His tomahawk and the bushranger's knife soon reduced the little craft they had travelled in, to a useless sheet of damaged bark.

" Now, come on," said Tiger. " Baal yabber (don't talk.)"

Taking the lead, he started off at a pace which, though swift, admitted of the girl keeping up with him.

Miss Bolton followed close in his tracks, and Ned, with his rifle ready for action, brought up the rear.

" Now, missie," said Ned, as they started, " make up your mind, and pull yourself together for a final spurt. We're on the home stretch now. A ten mile spin from here will land us safely at the Wirriba station."

" Never fear for me; I'll do it," answered the girl, pluckily.

CHAPTER CCVII.
THE BATTLE WITH THE BLACKS.

THE party led by Tiger moved rapidly away with the intention of making a circuitous course round the point of danger, where the blacks were assembled waiting for them to make their appearance in the canoe.

They had walked on for about an hour and a half, and had accomplished perhaps four miles, for their progress was hampered by the scrub, when Miss Bolton began to show evident signs of distress.

Despite her courage, the cramped position in the canoe, and the heat of the sun had told on her severely, and now her boots were being cut to pieces and her feet blistering from the broken nature of the ground they had to traverse.

Once or twice she staggered and almost fell.

Ned took her by the arm; but, though she would not complain, it was evident that, despite the mental excitement that in some degree kept her up, she was sinking with fatigue.

At length a moan of pain escaped her.

" Courage, missie," said Ned. " A little more and we shall have broken the back of the journey. Come, I know you're a good plucked 'un. Lean on me as heavy as you like, and I'll help you along."

" I'll try, I'll try," gasped the girl, though her drawn face, quivering lips, and wild eyes indicated the sufferings she was enduring plainly enough.

She staggered a little farther with the help of Ned's arm, and then again paused, half-fainting.

This was mainly due to the glare of the sun on her head in the boat.

She had hardly noticed its effects at the time beyond feeling a headache, but now she was walking they began to develop themselves.

It seemed to her that a thousand fiery needles were being plunged into her brain, and consciousness was fast deserting her at intervals.

It was evident that she was fast sinking, but what was to be done ?

To stop where they were was to linger in the very neighbourhood of danger.

They were about opposite the strait at the head of the sandbank, and about a mile from it in a direct line, and it was quite possible that while waiting for the canoe's arrival a party of the blacks might be out hunting in their very direction.

" By gosh, Tiger ! I'm afraid the only way to take the girl along will be to carry her. She's quite done up," said Ned.

" No good 'top here," growled Tiger. " S'pose missie no walk 'top here. Bimeby myall come. Missie go bong."

This last remark meant that she would be destroyed.

Again the girl's energy, roused by these, words carried her forward a few paces.

" That's your style," said Ned, encouragingly; " Keep on like that and we'll be in the parlour at Wirriba in a couple of hours, all safe and snug as a joey in its mother's pouch."

They had now reached a more open tract.

The trees were larger and at further distances apart, so that progress was less difficult amongst them.

It was evident they were at the outskirts of the timber bordering the lake, and at a little distance they could see that the ground was rocky and broken.

Miss Bolton managed to get on a little better as the ground improved.

All at once they found themselves confronted by six blacks, who suddenly seemed to spring up before them, like demons in a Christmas pantomime.

At the sight of their gaunt, naked figures, mop-like heads of hair, fiercely gleaming eyes, and glittering teeth, Bella Bolton recovered some of her energy.

Her's was one of those natures which rise in presence of actual and deadly peril.

Instead of being overcome by terror she was roused to exertion by the sight of the wretches from whose clutches she had been so miraculously delivered by Ned.

Tiger had already jumped behind a tree.

Ned jerked the girl behind another, and also hastened to interpose some three feet diameter of growing timber between his carcase and the weapons of the blacks.

He was only just in time.

A shower of spears was hurled by their enemies, but fortunately the fugitives had all by this time got sheltered, and there was no damage down.

Ned raised his rifle. He covered a gigantic savage evidently the " boss " of the roaring, screaming brutes. A bright, fierce flame sprung from the mouth of his piece, and the yelling monster sprung five feet into the air and fell flat on his face, to the great astonishment and terror of his party. The latter had evidently never heard this " report " before, nor witnessed the effect. They turned over the corpse and stared at the blood pouring from the body.

Another " ping " from the same rifle potted the sable gentleman who was holding this amateur inquest over the remains of his friend, which so frightened the rest of the " black watch " that they took to their heels with a rapidity which has never signalised the movement of that celebrated regiment in face of the enemy.

Kelly could not help laughing loudly when he saw the racing pace at which the niggers scuttled off.

Ned had slipped yet another cartridge into his rifle, and managed to get a snap shot at another of the gang, who pitched forward in his flight with a yell of agony and a bullet in his hip.

Shooting a black has never cost any squatter much repentance, as the Government always protect the black from any retaliation for murdering a white man.

When that awful imbecile Charles Joseph La Trobe was superintendent of Victoria, he officially offered a reward of £100 for the conviction of a white man who had shot a black, and £50 for the conviction of a black who potted a European !

"That's scared 'em a bit," said Kelly, "but the whole gang will be on us before half-an-hour is over. It's no use trying to push on, they'll pick us off to a certainty. We must try and find a place where we can make a standing fight of it."

Tiger uttered a grunt of assent, though if the two men had been alone he would doubtless have counselled their pushing onward.

"That broken ground out there looks about the best chance for us. Head for that rock, Tiger."

Bella Bolton had partially recovered under the new excitement, and managed to advance at a tolerably brisk pace by Ned's side in the direction indicated.

The rock he had indicated was an almost square mass of basalt, rising some twelve or fifteen feet above the surrounding surface.

The sides, on arriving close to it, they found to be almost perpendicular, save at one point, where Tiger quickly scaled it.

He signalled his companions to follow him, with evident glee.

With some difficulty Ned succeeded in hoisting his own bulk and helping Bella to the summit, which he found to be almost level.

Such a formation is not uncommon in the north-eastern districts of Australia, which exhibit many signs of volcanic origin.

Ned noticed that there were several loose boulders on the top which might, with but little difficulty, be arranged to form a kind of shelter from spears, and even as missiles to roll down on the foe.

He expressed his opinion to Tiger, and the two set to work.

In a short time all further ascent at the point where they had scaled the rock was blocked by a huge mass of basalt, and the others had been carefully disposed.

"Ouf," said Kelly, drawing a long breath, for the exertion had taxed even his herculean strength to the utmost; "I reckon we've fixed all that lot up ship-shape. It's like the game the kids play at, called 'King o' the castle,' this start is; and I'll bet odds we'll pepper the hides of a tidy few of those lanky devils if they come sneaking up here."

Indeed the boulders as arranged would form a complete shelter from the spears in case of their being attacked.

Starvation and thirst were, however, the two enemies they had to dread far more than the weapons of their inhuman antagonists.

Their best chance was that a scouting party might have been sent out from Bolton's station, and might yet arrive in time.

"This looks a tight fix," muttered Ned, "and it's a rum start for me to have put my carcase in danger for the sake of a girl I never set eyes on before. Tiger," he added aloud, "black fellow patter white fellow, eh?"

"Your, nyam nyam," was the sententious answer.

"Well," ejaculated Ned, as he glanced at his bulky figure, "a nice square meal I should make for a few of 'em, too. They'll have to eat me with gunpowder sauce though this time."

"Mr. Smith," said Bella, "would you mind letting me have your revolver?"

"Can you use it?" said Ned, in surprise.

"Yes, I assure you I have often practised, and am a fair shot. I will take it while you handle the rifle."

"All right," observed Kelly, handing her the weapon.

He had a shrewd guess at her intentions, and, ruffian as he was, he could not help admiring, almost loving her.

As the girl took it she said aloud—

"At least, I shall know what to do with the last charge. There is no danger of my missing that."

She had made up her mind to use it on herself if escape or rescue became hopeless.

An exclamation from Tiger, who was standing like a statue of bronze, with his eyes fixed on the quarter from which danger was anticipated, drew their attention.

The black extended his hand towards the timber.

The figures of several myalls could be seen flitting like dusky ghosts among the trees.

Twice Ned raised his rifle with the idea of trying a shot, but the distance and the dim shadows of the trees rendered his chance of hitting a mark doubtful; so he refrained from firing.

"D'ye think they know where we got to?" he inquired of the black, who stood by his side.

Tiger looked at him in wonderment.

"Plenty track sit down. Blackfellow yan along track," was the answer by which he denoted that there had been no difficulty for the natives to follow their trail.

A horrible yelling now broke from the blacks, of whom about fifty had assembled on the outskirts of the timber.

"The beggars are going to rush on in a minute," observed Ned.

Miss Bolton stepped to his side, revolver in hand.

"Look out for their blessed spears," said the bushranger. "They'll go slick through you like a stone through a window, and the devils barb 'em with bits of fish-bones and the like, so that they tear at your flesh like fifty antipedes."

The rush Ned had anticipated took place.

Like a horde of yelling fiends the blacks advanced across the open to the base of the rock.

The job before them, however, was a harder one than they had anticipated, the only path to the summit being securely blocked.

A cloud of spears came whizzing and bristling through the air, and many of them dropped upon the rock.

These were seized upon by Tiger, who hurled them back at their owners, and in one or two cases with effect.

The almost miraculous dexterity in avoiding and parrying which the myalls possess stood them in good stead, however, and the majority of these weapons were thrown by him in vain.

Ned was more fortunate.

It is more difficult to dodge a bullet than a spear, and twice his rifle rang out with fatal effect.

Two of the yelling pack dropped in their tracks.

They broke, and retreated to the shelter of the timber, carrying their wounded with them.

Ned managed to bowl over another of them before they could get into cover.

A lull now followed.

Ned guessed that there was not the slightest fear of the myalls exposing themselves again to such a destructive fire.

They would take the surer and more successful way of starving out their enemies.

The chances of their succeeding in doing so were ominously in their favour.

The little party on the rock had a few mouthfuls of provisions, the remains of their breakfast, but these would not go far; and, besides, a yet more terrible foe than hunger was to be dreaded in the shape of thirst.

The heat of the sun darting down on the rock, and their own exertions, had increased the feeling till it had become almost unbearable.

In vain they sought to obtain some shelter from the sun's rays by crouching close to the boulders they had piled up together.

The sun had rendered the rock so hot that its contact almost blistered them.

All the while they kept a keen look-out on the myalls.

Thrice Ned got the chance of a shot at them as they skulked in the timber, and succeeded in putting a couple more out of the hunt.

But after that they kept perfectly close.

A couple of hours had passed since the last attack.

"I don't like this," muttered Ned. "The scaly vermin are up to some dodge or other, and they'll come sneaking on the top of us before you can say knife, when we least think of it. Keep a good look out, Tiger, or we'll be stuck as full of spears as a porcupine is with quills."

CHAPTER CCVIII.
THE RESCUE.

ALL at once a strange and unexpected sound fell on the watchers' ears.

It was the discharge of firearms.

With every sense on the alert, the besieged looked forth from their rocky fortalice.

The shots continued, and evidently came from the timber in the rear of the blacks.

A wild confusion was observable amongst the latter.

They were running about in evident consternation.

It was plain that a brisk attack was being made upon them from the rear.

In a few minutes a mob of them broke from the corner and rushed, helter-skelter, across the open towards the broken and hilly country of which the rock, where the fugitives had taken refuge, was one of the outskirts.

As they tore along past the rock their exposed bodies offered a splendid mark to both Ned and Tiger, who sent bullets and spears amongst them with deadly effect.

"Hurroo!" shouted the bushranger. "That's the style."

A party of mounted white men were now to be seen advancing through the scattered timber, and shouting words of encouragement to the party on the rock.

"There's my brother; I see him, and Carter the bullock-driver, too," screamed Miss Bolton.

At this time the scene was a singular one. Several mounted men, armed to the teeth, were riding furiously after the flying devils that were flying for bare life.

Crack, crack, was heard on all sides, but the crack was accompanied by another crack, but of a different character. The crack of the stockwhip—a dreadful instrument, to which the Russian knout is a feather in severity.

The Australian stockwhip has attached to a handle one foot long an eighteen feet leather lash, all made of bullock hide, and the belly or thick part loaded with lead. This lash, whirled round the head by a practised hand, can be brought down upon the victim's hide with a force that cuts through the skin of a bullock and to the bone of a human being.

The thong at the end of the last is a solid slip, or strip, of bullock hide. The report of each cut is like the crack of a rifle.

Rounding up the mob of flying savages who yelled as the lash fell upon their naked bodies, they were kept well together like a mob of cattle, for they dreaded this "cut" more even than the bullets of their enemies. They presented a compact body as a target, and down they went like partridges.

Kelly lent his aid, too, and a wholesome lesson was taught the bloodthirsty cannibals.

"Wire in, boys," shouted one of the rescue party, "and knock the beggars over."

Crack, crack, went their rifles, and down went the myalls, till, completely routed, they scampered like deer into the broken country, leaving almost a score of their number on the field, dead or dying.

Two or three of the rescuers had been slightly wounded with spears; but this was the extent of the damage sustained.

The party consisted of the two Boltons, and several other squatters and stock-keepers.

It turned out that the bullock driver, Carter, had escaped the blacks.

On his return to the drays, he had found his comrade slaughtered and Miss Bolton carried off.

He had at once hastened on to the station to give the alarm.

It fortunately happened that rather a large party were assembled there.

These at once armed themselves, mounted, and started in pursuit.

They had several dogs with them, which they judged might be available in tracking.

As soon as they arrived at the scene of slaughter these animals rushed to a heap of leaves and dry grass.

Carter, the driver, hastened at once to the spot, and, pushing them away with the butt of his gun, called on the others to help him in keeping the animals off.

This heap of grass he had hastily piled over the murdered and mutilated body of his comrade before starting to give the alarm.

"Help me to keep the brutes off," he exclaimed," and lend a hand to give poor Jim a decent burial."

Despite the impatience felt by some of the party to continue the pursuit, this request was complied with, and the remains of the murdered driver hurriedly but decently interred.

Whilst this was being done some of the party searched the ransacked drays, and the surrounding bush for traces of Miss Bolton.

One of them was fortunate enough to come upon the note dropped by her, stating that she had been carried off by natives, which Ned had overlooked.

This at once increased their anxiety to come up with the plunderers.

The track left by the retreating mob of natives was so plain that the assistance of the dogs was hardly needed, especially as the marks of Miss Bolton's shod feet were conspicuous amongst the naked footprints of the blacks.

They had accordingly pushed on, and were somewhat puzzled at the appearance of the hoof tracks of Ned's horse evidently following the party of which they were in search.

The discovery of the animal itself, tethered to the tree where Ned had left it, only served to increase the mystery.

However, they could plainly distinguish the footprints of Miss Bolton in the camp that had been made by the natives at the side of the lake.

Yet they were greatly perplexed, on following up the route taken by the blacks from this point, to find no further signs of her presence amongst them.

The dogs were of no use to clear up this matter, for no one had brought any little object, especially belonging to the young lady for the animals to be made to smell, and thereby understand that they were to follow her especially.

Even if they had, it would only have increased the puzzle, since the brutes would have only been able to trace her to the water's edge, where she took the canoe.

The rescue party were puzzled.

Their hesitation in consequence of this caused some delay, but at length they decided to push on and come up with the natives at all hazards.

Consequently they tracked them firstly to the spot opposite the head of the sandbank, where they had lain in ambush for the canoe, and thence to the position they had taken up in front of the rock.

On arriving here, they guessed at once the real state of affairs, and commenced a sudden and vigorous onslaught on the assembled myalls, with the result already narrated.

For Ned and his companions to quit their rocky fortress was the work of a moment, and soon rescued and rescuers were united.

Bella described the way in which Kelly had saved her, and the two Boltons were profuse in their expressions of gratitude to the bushranger, whom she introduced under his assumed name of Tom Smith.

"I can never sufficiently repay you, old fellow," said the elder Bolton. "You're a man every inch of you. Not one in a thousand would have ventured his carcase after such a mob of blacks, single-handed."

"You're a thundering brick," chimed in his nephew, "and whatever fix you may ever get into, remember you have a firm friend at Nullaroora. If the devil himself came to fetch you I'd go bail for the man who risked his life, as you have done, to save my sister."

Tiger too came in for his share of praise, and was assured that "big one plour, big one sugar, plenty baccy, and drink him rum," should be the least of his engagements for the rest of his natural life.

Ned was somewhat (for him) moved at Bolton's thanks,

he did not fail to see the advantage the squatter's gratitude might possibly be to him on some future occasion.

He was far more interested, however, as regarded the impression he had made on Bella, for whom he had some idea of "going in." Not the only instance of "Beauty and the Beast."

He thought it as well to inform Mr. Bolton of the mission on which he had been despatched by Jackson, as by this time his late comrades must be getting into a pretty tight fix as regarded provisions.

He did so, and it was at once decided that as they were now only a few miles from Wirriba station, the whole party should push on there, and that fresh horses being obtained, a relief party should be organised to join Jackson.

"These niggers up here in the north," observed Ned, to Mr. Bolton, "are a very different set to those down south."

"Yes," replied the old squatter; "and it's quite another queer sort of work having to deal with them. We've given them some pretty sharp lessons from time to time, but it hasn't taken all the blazes out of them yet."

"I guess they won't digest this little scrimmage in a hurry," remarked Phil Bolton.

"It'll be precious nasty for anyone who tries to ride through this part of the country single-handed," replied his uncle. "They're a revengeful set of devils, and will be as keen after a white man's blood as a cat after cream."

In a couple of hours or so the party reached Wirriba, where they were hospitably received.

The necessary preparations were very rapidly made, and the relief party prepared to start.

Before it left Bella found an opportunity of speaking a few words to Ned as they stood on the verandah.

"Mr. Smith," she said, "you have saved me from a fate so awful that I shudder to contemplate it. I owe you, I know, more than life itself. I do not suppose I shall ever have an opportunity of repaying this debt, but if ever I do, trust me it shall be done ten-fold."

What a strange compound is even the worst of men! The worst of murderers exhibit affection for somebody. Lefroy, the cold-blooded assassin, wept over his nephew; Marat loved flowers, Robespierre music. The most bloodthirsty have "one virtue linked with a thousand crimes." Somebody placed flowers over Nero's grave.

Perhaps there are none so utterly depraved as not to feel at odd moments a touch of human sympathy.

It was so in this case.

Whether it was that something in the girl reminded him of Rose, he knew not; but Ned felt strangely softened in his feelings towards her.

The iron-hearted bushranger, who had shed blood a score of times in sheer wantonness, and who had stained his soul with countless crimes, could not help feeling a tender interest in the girl he had rescued from the blacks.

Such a feeling was, however, decidedly exceptional on his part, and it by no means followed that he always would play the part of a rescuer of distressed damsels.

Indeed, even in this instance had he encountered Bella Bolton under other circumstances, it is probable that he would have been far more likely to have captured her on his own account than to have rescued her.

"No need to come it so strong, my girl," was his answer, given with a certain bluntness that sounded hearty and genuine. "I'm jolly glad to be able to do you a good turn, for any man can see you're just built up with right sort of wattle and dab, and no mistake. It does a fellow good to come across your sort—it does."

Ned fixed his eyes on the girl as he spoke with open admiration.

A sudden idea crossed his mind.

He would test the sincerity of the girl's avowal.

"You think you're in debt to me, eh?" he said.

"I do," was her answer.

"And you say you'll cry quits if ever you get a chance, that's it, isn't it?"

"It is, I swear," exclaimed the girl excitedly, "that I will spare nothing to show you my gratitude."

"Well," said Ned gravely, "it's as well you should know who you're making promises to. For one thing, you may happen to change your mind when you hear my name, and for another, you may after all have a chance of doing me service since your father must be hand and glove with the traps, The police you know."

"The police! What do you mean?"

"I mean that you may be able some of these fine days to send me a bit of a warning that'll come in useful."

"I don't quite understand you."

"Oh, I'll soon make matters plain. You say I've saved you from worse than death, and that if ever you can help me you will. Now I believe you, and I'm going to give you a proof that I do by putting my neck in your hands."

"Your neck?"

"Yes. Give me your hand."

"Now, you've taken me by the hand and you're looking me friendly-like in the eyes. You think, may be, that I'm a bit rough in my ways and nothing more, and you feel you are grateful to me for what I've done. You don't mind the roughness I can see, and you don't think altogether that I'm as rough in heart as in talk and look, at least not rough so far as I feel towards you."

The girl blushed a little and dropped her eyes.

"Well, now I've only got to say half-a-dozen words," Kelly went on, "and it's odds that you don't drop my hand as if it was a diamond snake, and bolt away into the house like a wombat into his hole."

He felt her hand shake a little in his.

That little speech rather startled her, but she recovered herself.

"Tell me what you will," she answered, "I will be firm and true."

"I believe you are true as death," he exclaimed. "Well, you know when I first popped on you in the camp of those black devils, there wasn't much time for an introduction, and that afterwards I told you my name was Tom Smith?"

"Yes."

"Well, it is Tom Smith for the present and in these parts, but away down south, where it's posted up on the walls of every police-station, it reads different. It's Ned Kelly."

For a moment the girl was too puzzled to speak.

Then a light broke on her as to her companion's identity.

"Ned Kelly, the—the——"

"The bushranger, whose head is worth ten thousand pounds! Yes, that's me. I'm the cerrolian (swell)."

Miss Bolton remained silent for a few seconds.

The shock of the discovery overwhelmed her.

She was not exempt from the terror that the mere mention of Kelly's name inspired.

But she called all her firmness to her aid, and, though her blood ran cold at the thought of how completely at his mercy she had been, the recollection of how generously he had acted on her behalf, overpowered every other feeling.

"I said I owed you a debt," she remarked, speaking with some difficulty; "and, surely, that debt remains the same. I cannot forget that, whatever evil may be attached to your name, you treated me in a fashion the noblest man on earth could not excel. I repeat, I shall never forget it, and shall miss no opportunity of repaying it. And now—and now," she concluded, somewhat emotionally, "I don't feel very well; I must go indoors and lie down."

And, bursting into tears, she darted away from Ned, and hurried to the room set apart for her.

"Women are rum creatures, but this one is up to my measure. She's the best of the lot I've seen as yet," thought Kelly.

He stood musing for some time. Who shall say what humanising thoughts occupied his reflections?

Did the softening presence of this graceful young girl conjure up wishes, that appeared like bubbles on the surface of his life, to burst and disappear in a moment? Was it a vista of what might have been, that coloured his thoughts, and softened the ruggedness of his features at that moment?

"Bah!" he ejaculated, suddenly. "All bosh—just now, at all events. When I make another haul, perhaps I'll ask her."

Half-an-hour later the arrangements of the relief party were completed, and they set out.

After a toilsome journey they came on Jackson and his followers, who had been pushing on with great difficulty, and were in a deplorable plight.

The relief was warmly welcomed, and when the cause of Ned's delay was explained, his seeming negligence was excused.

After making his report to Mr. Jackson, he joined his mates.

Two of them who had been talking apart in a confidential manner, suddenly became silent on his approach.

Ned was certain, however, he had caught a bit of their conversation.

It was only a name, but it produced a very strong sense of uneasiness on his part.

For he could swear that one of the two had distinctly uttered to his companion, the word—

"Bushranger."

CHAPTER CCIX.
A FATAL LEAP.

DURING Ned's absence there had been plenty of talk going on in the camp about him.

The men naturally took to speculating as to when he was likely to return with the expected succour.

From this they got to discussing his peculiarities.

All at once it occurred to one of them named Matthews that he had seen or heard of some one answering Ned's description.

The more he thought the matter over the more certain of this he became, though the puzzle as to when and where continued to rest unsolved.

One afternoon, however, the conversation happened to turn on bushrangers and their exploits, and the deeds of many of those heroes were discussed.

A light broke on Matthews.

He had recollected where he had seen the description of a man closely resembling the one he knew as Tom Smith.

It was outside a police-station; but the name on the bill was not Tom Smith, but Ned Kelly.

If the stranger were Ned Kelly he was worth a fortune. The question was how to grab this reward.

It would not do to proclaim the discovery he had made to his comrades, for if the whole of them took the matter up the reward would have to be divided.

Matthews didn't see it at all in this light.

But, on the other hand, he could not, situated as they were, take Kelly single-handed and convey him to Port Darwin, their ultimate destination and the proposed terminus of the railway.

He determined to enlist a partner, and arrange with him to pounce on Kelly as soon as they got near enough to Port Darwin, and to hand the bushranger over to the authorities there.

He selected a man named Shirley, and imparted his suspicions and his plan.

Shirley readily agreed that it would be a very good day's work to capture Ned, but thought that the identity of the so-called Tom Smith with the bushranger was by no means clearly established.

The two were talking of their plan when Ned returned to the camp, and it was this that caused him to catch the word, "Bushranger."

These words were quite enough for Ned. He knew at once that mischief was in the wind.

The two talkers changed the subject as soon as they noticed him, and did not know they had already betrayed themselves. They were inartistic in the way they suddenly pulled up and stared at him.

People don't suddenly cease talking when a third person approaches, unless they don't want their conversation overheard.

In doing so their manner on the approach of the unwished-for party becomes suddenly constrained, silent, and awkward, betraying the fact they wished to conceal.

Kelly saw this at a glance, and the word "bushranger" settled the matter with him.

"Here's a pretty go," thought Ned to himself. "If I'd only twigged this, I'd have sloped quietly off without saying a word to the Bolton's about the fix these lubbers were in. But then what would have become of the girl, and she's worth the whole lot of these lubbers put together. One can't do a decent job without being spotted by some hound or other."

He made up his mind, however, to try and get off unobserved as soon as they were near enough to their destination to allow him to do so with safety, for it was evident that natives were about, and that for a single man to attempt to make his way to the coast would be madness.

Already one poor fellow who had wandered from the rest, had been discovered speared to death.

They had left Powell Creek where they had made a halt for the purpose of recruiting men and horses, and were pushing on for Daly Waters, where there was a small settlement.

When they were within two days' ride from this, Ned determined to abandon the rest of the party and push on.

This purpose he carried out early one morning.

Matthews and Shirley were the first to notice his absence.

The others thought he had merely galloped on a few miles ahead, and though this was to a certain extent a breach of duty, no particular attention was paid to it.

"I shouldn't have thought Smith was such a flat as to risk riding off like that, after poor Collins' death and the brush he himself had with the natives the other day," said Mr. Jackson, when he heard of Ned's departure.

Like the rest, however, with the exception of Matthews and Shirley, he never imagined that there was more than a temporary absence.

These two, however, judged otherwise.

They came to the conclusion that Ned had made up his mind to slope. He had been unable to conceal his hatred and suspicions of them. They knew he had spotted them and their desire to nab him.

"Even if he hasn't," said Matthews, "here's a chance we shan't get again in a hurry."

"What way?" enquired Shirley.

"Why, snapping him up quietly. What we had better do will be to ride after him. He'll let us come alongside without suspicion, and then all we've got to do will be to grab him before he knows what we're up to."

"And you don't think he'd be fly to us?"

"He'll never dream what we're up to. We can swear Jackson was uneasy and sent us on scouting after him."

"He's a thundering powerful chap though, do you think the two of us can tackle him?"

"Of course we can," observed Matthew, who was a powerful fellow, "even without the surprise surely we'd be able to scrag him?"

The two had quickly arranged their plan.

They left their companions, and pushed on ahead during the mid-day heat.

As they jogged along, Shirley said—

"Why do you think the fellow, whatever his name is, has bolted?"

"Oh! that's simple enough. He wanted to get across the Continent, and, of course, he couldn't do it single-

27

handed; so he joined on to our party. But now's he getting up to the northern coast he means to sneak away on his own hook."

"Well, but are you sure we shall come up with him?"

"Sure. Well, he's bound to funk on Daly Waters, and we can manage to track him from there."

The two were indeed close on Kelly's track.

Resolving not to spare their horses, they urged them on to the utmost speed that was consistent with safety.

They camped out in the open, and next day resumed their journey.

They had hoped by pushing on to reach Daly Waters by nightfall.

However, darkness obliged them to camp within a few miles of it, much to their disgust.

At daybreak they were once more in the saddle, urging their jaded beasts towards the settlement.

They entered it some hours later, and learned to their disgust that Ned had passed the night there, and had started early that morning on a horse he had obtained in exchange for his own somewhat exhausted animal.

With some difficulty they succeeded in following his example, and in swapping their weary nags for a couple of fresh mounts, though they had to plank down a fair sum in addition to equalise the bargain.

This done, they pushed on after Ned, who they ascertained was bound for Yam Creek.

Their way lay across a series of plains of eight or ten miles in diameter, divided by belts and patches of timber and scrub, and here and there intersected by water courses, now generally dry, but at certain seasons evidently torrents.

The horse Ned had obtained was a powerful animal, with a wicked look about its eye that might have rendered a less skilful rider than the Bushranger doubtful about mounting him.

But Ned could sit anything that ever bore a saddle, and was only too glad to get a beast up to his weight to feel uneasy.

As he had anticipated, the brute made one or two attempts to get rid of him, but had to give in to his master.

Ned halted at midday for a feed and a pipe, having taken the precaution to hobble his new purchase; but on his going to mount him, a little trouble ensued.

The horse backed, sidled, and played sundry other capers, till Ned settled him by flinging his blanket over his head, and then terrifying him into submission.

But a certain amount of time had been cut to waste, and on his looking round as soon as he gained the saddle, he could distinguish two horsemen coming towards him across the plain at a great pace.

They were evidently in a hurry to overtake him, and he was by no means over well pleased at this.

People did not ride as they were doing for nothing.

He began to wonder what they could want with him, and resolved to let them come a little nearer before he took any decided steps.

At last they got sufficiently close for him to recognise Matthews and Shirley.

The two had ridden on in the hope of capturing him, since the words he had heard in camp plainly proved that they had recognised him.

Ned debated quietly for a moment whether he should fight or fly.

They were it is true two to one, but such odds did not daunt him.

He reflected at the last moment that he could fight at any moment, but that, if he intended to fly he had better set about doing it at once.

Accordingly he gave his new horse the spur, and was extremely pleased to find that the animal, when once he had settled into his stride, apparently forgot all his little tricks and was a very good goer indeed.

His pursuers on seeing him dart off, at once guessed that he was intentionally avoiding them.

"The beggar has smoked the trick," said Shirley.

"I'm afraid he has," answered Matthews. "He must have got an inkling after all that we suspected him, and that's what made him cut his lucky."

"Well, it's plain it's no use whistling him back to have salt put on his tail; the only thing is to go after him."

"All right," answered the other, and, touching up their animals with the spur, they started in hot pursuit.

"Do those two pumpkin-headed fools think they're going to collar me as easily as a more-pock swallows a midge?" thought Ned, as he marked the way in which the others settled down to work. "If they do, they'll find themselves off the track. They'll be precious sick of this job before they've done with it."

Ned could not tell how his pursuers were mounted, but he found he had got a capital bit of horseflesh between his knees, and that the animal carried him gallantly.

"Bravo, old boy," he muttered, as he patted the animal's neck, "you're not up to Marco Polo by a long chalk, but you're a devilish good 'un, and you make up for those little tricks of yours now you're once settled to work."

But if Ned's horse was a good one, his pursuers were almost as well mounted.

It is true their horses had not had the advantage of a noonday halt, for they had pushed right on till they came in sight of Ned.

But this was in some degree compensated for by the lighter weight the animals had to carry.

The chase continued for about an hour in this fashion.

Matthews and Shirley could not tell whether Ned was riding his hardest, but he seemed able to maintain his advance without much difficulty.

The bushranger did not even turn his head to see if his foes were gaining on him.

"The beggar is taking it easy," said Shirley.

"Rather," replied Matthews; "it's a tidy beast he's got, but weight is bound to tell in the end. We'll nail him to a certainty."

After a little time a line of trees appeared ahead like a fringe along the horizon.

"There's water there, for a hundred!" cried Matthews.

Sure enough, in a few more strides, the gleam of water could be distinguished now and again through the foliage.

"I guess we'll have him now if he can't clear it. Be ready to go off to the left if he turns and tries to double," said Shirley.

The two separated, and rode in a parallel line some twenty yards apart.

As the trees grew larger and nearer, and as the water flashed back the sunlight, it was evident that Ned would have a difficulty in getting over.

The water course swept in a curve, and he was heading straight for the centre of this, so that escape either to the right or left would be impossible, unless he faced one or both of his pursuers.

The water course was between two steep, rocky banks. There was no path down to the water.

The sides were as sudden as those of a canal. So he must either turn or jump it.

"Blowed if he ain't going to try it," cried Matthews, as he saw Ned swerve slightly from the course he had hitherto been pursuing, in order to head his horse for a point which seemed to offer the best chance for a leap.

"Then blaze away at him," cried his companion. "Try and nobble his nag, at any rate."

The two saw that there was a chance of their prey escaping them, and began to urge their beasts furiously onward, in order to get within sure pistol range.

Before they could succeed in accomplishing this, Ned had put his horse at the chasm.

Aiding the animal with hand and heel, he lifted it across, and though sparks flashed from the rock on which it alighted from its efforts to save itself from falling by half-frantic hoof beats, it at length recovered itself, and was soon sailing away on the other side.

"After him!" yelled Matthews, excitedly, putting his steed in turn at the gulf.

The horse rose bravely to the leap, but, whether from fear or over-anxiety, the rider embarrassed rather than helped it, and it jumped short.

Shirley saw the forefeet hang, as it were, for a moment to a jutting bit of stone; a mad, wild effort by horse and rider; a moment's interval, and then the banks were clear and peaceful as ever.

The tragedy was down below, where Matthews lay stretched upon the rocks beside his broken-backed horse, with his skull fractured.

CHAPTER CCX.
NED TRIES HIS LUCK ON THE ETHERIDGE.

NED chuckled as he looked back and noticed that one of his pursuers was missing, and that the other had reined up his horse at the edge of the chasm and was gazing down with an expression of horror into the depths below.

"I reckon that chap has saved me the trouble of cracking his cocoanut," was his comment, "and that the other's got a sickener of the job by this time."

This surmise was correct.

Shirley had a sickener of the job, and, after dismounting and scrambling down to the bottom of the water bed only to find that Matthews was as dead as a door nail—his horse having fallen back on him and smashed his spine as well as his head—came to the conclusion that the only thing to do was to give it up and to ride back to Daly Waters in quest of help to bury his comrade.

He resolved, however, not to let out that they had been in quest of Kelly, lest it might be asked why he had not given information to the authorities and obtained their help, but to continue on Kelly's track in the hopes of coming up with him unawares at some future time.

As to going back to Mr. Jackson and his party, that would never do; as awkward questions might be asked, touching the reason of his sudden desertion.

Meanwhile Ned had made the best of his way on to Yam Creek, and thence to Port Darwin.

Here he was lucky enough to find a coasting schooner on the point of starting.

She was bound for the small settlements at the mouths of the rivers emptying themselves into the Gulf of Carpentaria, settlements which have considerably increased in importance during the last few years, owing to the development of Northern Queensland.

Ned landed at the mouth of the Gilbert, and determined to make his way up to the Etheridge district, where he heard there was a recently discovered gold field, and where he thought he might have a chance of picking up something.

He found the latest and most successful rush was at a place called Warramot.

A little was being done in getting coarse gold from some alluvial workings, but most of the gold raised was got from the quartz reefs.

The quartz when raised was conveyed to a crushing mill, erected by a company, and was crushed and its gold retorted.

Ned, after surveying the ground, decided that the only big haul likely to be obtained would be got from the crushing mill.

The company to which it belonged had a claim of their own, which was yielding a good percentage of gold, averaging about five ounces to the ton, and had plenty of work to do besides for their neighbours.

The mill had been erected in a somewhat solitary spot.

It stood against a mass of rock cropping out from the ground, and from the roots of which a constant supply of water trickled.

It was this circumstance that had led to the choice of site, water being required for the crushing process

In this the quartz is pounded up by huge stampers into a kind of paste; which is then washed until all the powdered stone is carried away, and nothing but the precious metal is left.

The mining camp and the reefs that were being worked were situate on the other side of a small range about half a mile in breadth, and the quartz to be crushed was brought to the mill in waggons drawn by oxen.

The mill was worked by steam power, and the staff was a small one, consisting merely of the manager, a young fellow named Douglas, the engineer, and the feeder, as he was styled, whose duty it was to supply the stampers.

These three slept on the premises.

It was customary for the gold, crushed and retorted during the week, to be delivered to its owners on Saturday afternoon and Sunday morning.

On the latter day a representative of the company used generally to drive over in a buggy from the township, and take their share to the bank there.

Ned by a little judicious loafing about became acquainted with these facts.

He began to think over the best chance of making a haul.

Singlehanded he thought it was impossible, and kept his eyes open for a suitable pal.

He found loafing around rather expensive work, for provisions were at the usual high rates which they rule at a goldfield, yet he could not quite hit on a satisfactory method of bringing off the job he had set his mind on.

He got in the habit of strolling across the range which lay between the diggers' camp and the crushing mill, and reconnoitering the latter at all hours from the shelter of a patch of timber.

He got thoroughly acquainted with the hours of work, and of meals, the habits of the residents of the mill, the amount of stuff they managed to crush in a day, and could even make a fair guess at the number of ounces they had in store at the end of the week, but he got no further to success.

In a little time, however, he got to notice that he was not the only one engaged in the contemplation of the Warramot crushing mill at all times and seasons.

An old man seemed to have the same interest in it as he did himself.

The old man was a queer-looking customer Ned could not help thinking to himself.

He was a little chap, hardly more than five feet high, and so lean, dried up, and fragile-looking, that it seemed a wonder that he did not snap in two at any moment like a dry twig.

He looked as if in a strong wind he would be blown away like a leaf.

His features, which were as sharp as a razor edge, were full of keen intelligence, and his black, bird-like eyes twinkled like two needle-points.

His hair was gray and worn somewhat long, and when he lifted his hat it revealed a high, but narrow forehead, as bald as a billiard ball.

As to his dress it was decidedly the worse for wear.

After a time Ned began to puzzle over this queer old stick.

He could not help noticing that the same object seemed to interest both of them.

Both were continually crossing the range to see what was going on at the crushing mill, and despite their mutual caution, they kept meeting at odd times.

Ned speculated as to the reason of the other's presence.

"I wonder if he's a trap paid by the company to keep watch over their place. If I felt certain of that, I'd take him by the scruff of the neck some dark night and drop him quietly down a shaft. I could do it as easily as I could lift a kitten. Surely though, he can't be a fellow on the same lay as myself."

The stranger observed Ned for some time in a like manner.

He, however, seemed to have easily come to a decision

as to the bushranger's object in lurking about the crushing mill.

Accordingly one day, whilst Ned was at the usual post of observation, the little old fellow strolled up and sat down beside him.

"You're quite right," he began suddenly as though they had been in the midst of a conversation. "It only wants a little patience and a pal who knows what he's about, and the thing's done as slick as butter."

"Out with your meaning!" growled Ned.

"I mean you've been hankering for a couple of weeks to put your pickers and stealers on a crushing or two out of the mill there, only you don't quite see your way to do it."

"Look here," said Kelly, trying to come the virtuously indignant, "if you don't dry up that sort of lying non-sense, I'll just take you up and snap you over my knee like a dry mimosa twig. What d'ye mean by saying such things to an honest man, you old varmint. Can't you tell an honest man when you see one?" said Ned with a twinkle in his eye.

"Oh, you're too blessed honest to live. I know all about it, we're all honest men till we're bowled out. Come, I've twigged your little game for some time past. You want to nail that gold and you don't know how."

There was an ugly look in Ned's eyes as he suddenly seized the little man by the collar.

"You know a sight too much for your post," he said significantly.

"Don't be a fool," exclaimed the other without dis-playing any symptoms of alarm. "I'm on the same lay myself, and like you, I want a pal to help me."

Ned grinned encouragingly.

"A pretty sort of chap you'd be at that game. Who the devil would think of picking out a wretched little shrimp like you for a pal."

The other met his look unflinchingly.

"I'm quite right. If you've got muscle enough for two, I've brains and pluck too, for three. By jingo, if I'd only your strength, I'd have done the job single-handed by this time."

Ned looked at him curiously.

Despite his unpleasant position, the old fellow was as cool as a cucumber.

"Look here, old bag of bones," observed the bush-ranger, "it strikes me you're neither more nor less than a trap."

"A trap! why if I'd been one of them sort I should have let you go in with your plant until I nobbled you in the act. I knew what your lay was, and I had only to wait. Haven't you brains to see that?" His tone was jeering, he certainly showed no signs of fear in taunting his gigantic acquaintance. Kelly somehow felt he had his equal in nerve, and his superior in brains.

This argument was to a certain extent unanswerable.

Ned released his hold of the old fellow's collar.

"Suppose you just tell me how you think the job can be fixed?" he said, reflectively.

"On one condition," was the answer.

"What's that?"

"That we work it together."

This was the first man he had met with since he had been in Etheridge who seemed likely to answer his pur-pose.

It was true he was not much to look at, but he evidently was "a good 'un to go."

"All right, mate," he growled, "I'm there."

The old fellow pointed to a delapidated shanty at about fifty yards from the crushing mill.

"You see that crib?" he said.

"Yes," answered Ned.

"Have you got a few ounces to spare?"

"Why, what the deuce do you want 'em for?"

"If you've got them, say so," said the other, impera-tively.

"Well, I might find them at a pinch."

"Let's have your 'pinch' then. The first thing to do with your 'pinch' is to start that shanty as a grog-shop."

"Why?"

"Because it'll give us an excuse to be on the spot, and to always have an eye on the mill. Besides, it strikes me that the engineer does not mind a glass, and we might get something out of him."

"Won't it look queer starting a grog-shop in this out-of-the-way hole, where there are no customers?"

"No; it'll look as if we started it for the chaps who come with the quartz. Besides, don't you go to think there'll be no customers. A grog-shop'll draw customers as a honey-pot will flies. I believe if you set up one in the middle of the Mallee Scrub you'd have as many cus-tomers as a rotting carcase would flies."

"But now, mate, what's your name? I like to know them as I work with."

"Oh," replied the other, "Avery."

"Very good, Avery. I suppose as you've been marking me down over this little matter, you know already that my name's Tom Smith?"

"All right. We're in for the job together as close as bullocks in a yoke. But work square with me, or, downy as you may be, you'd better have shoved your nut under one of the mill-stamps yonder first."

And the two proceeded to settle the details of their plan.

(To be continued.)

NED KELLY

THE
IRONCLAD
AUSTRALIAN BUSHRANGER

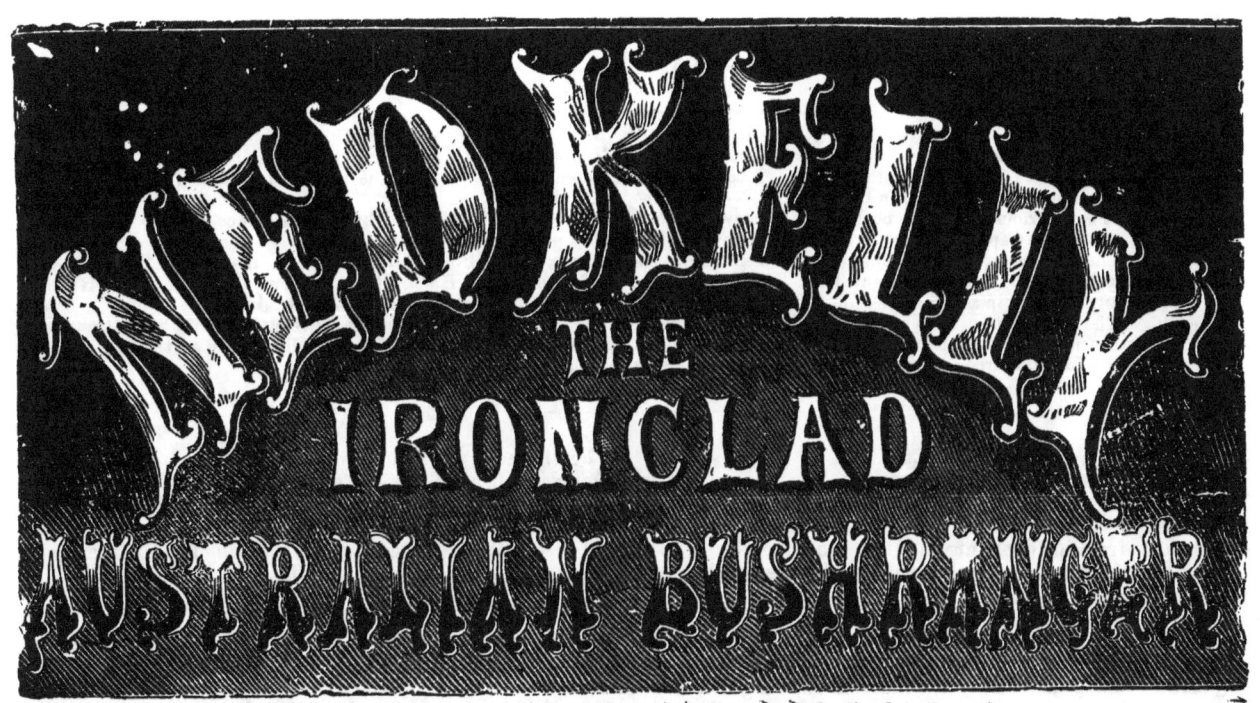

NO 36,

NED KELLY: IRONCLAD BUSHRANGER.

CHAPTER CCXI.
SCREWING OUT A SECRET.

MR. DOUGLAS, the manager of the crushing-mill, was rather surprised to see the dilapidated shanty a few dozen yards from his door turned into a grog-shop.

Like Ned, he was very much puzzled at first as to where the customers were to come from.

He found, however, that they were not lacking.

The carters who brought in the quartz, and the miners who came for gold, would halt and take a nobbler there, and of an evening men would stroll across the range from the camp.

The place, somewhat to his surprise, was well conducted, too, for a place of its class.

One of the proprietors, a big man named Smith, had a knack of slinging anyone who made himself offensive out of the place in such an effective style that a second lesson was seldom needed.

Douglas had only one objection to the shanty.

He began to notice that his engineer, whose name was Hicks, began to call there rather often.

The man was a capital workman, but was rather fond of a drop, and when he had one, was given to talk.

He did not get drunk in the daytime, but sometimes when he turned in at night it was evident that he had had a skin-full, fresh proof of which would appear in his shaky state the next morning.

As to the feeder, Barry, he was a somewhat stolid, disappointed-looking sort of a man, who had a habit of roving about the ranges when he had nothing else to do, as though he expected to come across a big nugget by accident.

One Saturday they knocked off work at noon.

Mr. Douglas could not help feeling a little uneasy, though he could hardly tell why.

For one thing, the gold belonging to the company had not been taken to the bank the preceding Sunday.

Hence he had almost double the usual amount in his care.

Some men had called in the morning for their crushings, but altogether he had nearly five hundred ounces of the precious metal in his safe.

Of this three hundred and fifty were in the shape of a big ingot.

Barry strolled away over the range in his usual fashion after they had knocked off.

Hicks was engaged in some task of hammering and filing in the machine-room.

After completing this, he retired to his quarters and changed some of his clothes.

He lounged for a moment or two at the door of the little office in which Douglas was sitting making his accounts up.

Are you going off?" asked the manager.

" Yes, I'm going down to the camp. There's a bit of a spree on. Can I bring back anything for you?"

" No, I don't think so. When d' you think you'll be back?"

" A little after dark, I suppose."

" All right."

The engineer strolled off.

Douglas felt a bit anxious at his departure.

He did not like to ask him to stop, but yet he felt half inclined to do so.

He rose with this intention, but checking himself, merely stood at the door, and watched Hicks' retreating figure.

To his surprise the man, instead of striking direct across the range lounged down to the grog shop.

" I wonder what the deuce he wants to go up there for ?" was Douglas's comment. For one thing though I'd rather he stuck there, for he's close handy."

He would have been considerably edified if he had followed the engineer to the place in question.

Ned and Avery were the only two occupants of the place when he arrived.

After a word or two of greeting, a nobbler of whiskey was filled by the latter for Hicks.

He drank it off, and a few minutes later, was nodding in a half-stupefied state on his seat.

" Another drop, mate," said Avery.

" Right you are," ejaculated the engineer, with some difficulty.

The second lot completed the job, and he pitched forward with his head on the table in a state of stupor.

" You're sure you ain't given him too much ?" said Ned.

" No," answered his companion, " I've mixed that sort of stuff too often to make a mistake. I knew to a drop what would settle him. He's gone to doss for twelve hours, and by the time he opens his peepers again, we shall be ' over the hills and far away,' as the song says."

" Well, the job's only began, it won't do to crow too early."

" Oh! I'm not one to count my chickens before they're hatched. But everything goes to help us, and we shouldn't get a chance like this again in a twelvemonth."

" That's it. Only think of them having a fortnight's gold on hand, as the butcher there let out."

" Yes, and no chance of any one coming over from the camp. There's a bruising match to come off this afternoon there, and I guess we shan't see a soul."

" When had we better set to work ?"

" As soon as I come back with the buggy. Meanwhile, let's stow this beggar away out of sight."

They lifted the hocussed engineer, and stowed him away on one of their beds in the inner room.

Avery then started off in the direction of the camp, and in about an hour returned with a light cart that had been retained in readiness for this occasion.

The pair then sauntered up towards the mill.

Douglas was sitting under the verandah of his quarters which adjoined the main building.

His uneasiness had not diminished.

Still he did not attach any particular importance to this visit from his two neighbours.

" Mr. Douglas! Mr. Douglas!" began Avery, as soon as they got within hearing.

Douglas rose and advanced to them.

" Will you step down to our place, your engineer looked in, and he's fallen down in a sort of——"

Whilst Douglas was listening to this statement Ned suddenly threw himself upon him and bore him to the ground.

The manager was a fine active young fellow, but even had he not been taken unawares, he would have been no match for Kelly.

"Quick! clap the gag into his mouth," exclaimed the bushranger, planting his knee on his victim's chest.

As Avery knelt down for this purpose, Douglas gave a loud cry for help.

"Look sharp, man," exclaimed Ned, clapping his hand over the mouth of the prostrate man. Douglas in his desperation made his teeth almost meet in it. "The swine's bitten me to the bone."

In his rage he seized his victim by the throat with the other hand.

"Gently, gently does it," said Avery. "If you choke him he won't be able to answer any questions. I'll make him leave go in a minute."

As he spoke, the little scoundrel placed a thumb on each side of Douglas's face just by the ear.

"I didn't take my diploma for nothing," he said in a half-bitter, half-exultant tone, as the prostrate man's mouth opened in spite of himself.

The next moment the gag was thrust into his mouth, and he was secured by the bonds with which the two had come provided.

"Now then for the key," exclaimed Ned.

With rapid dexterity, Avery searched the prostrate man.

"Confound it," he ejaculated when he had finished; "I'm hanged if he's got it about him."

The two accomplices looked at one another.

"We must get it out of him somehow, said Avery.

"Of course," said Ned. "Where's the key of the safe, you biting bandicoot?" he added, fiercely shaking Douglas.

Avery gave a laugh that sounded like dry bones rattling together.

"What are you sniggering at, you old skeleton," cried Ned, looking up at him.

"Can't you see he can't answer," was the reply, "with his mouth corked up like that.

"True," said Kelly, and he was about to remove the gag.

"Stop a bit," cried Avery, "let's take him inside the mill where there'll be less chance of any rumpus being heard."

Kelly obeyed, and, lifting up the helpless form of the manager, carried him to the door of the mill, which was only latched.

Entering, they found themselves in the crushing room, the machinery of which was grim and silent.

Avery advanced to the door of the little office.

It was locked.

"I'll soon settle that," observed Ned, and, selecting a bar of iron, he quickly prised the door open.

The safe met their view within.

The two stepped up and examined it.

"It's a tough one, a devilish tough one," observed Kelly, looking at the same with a half-admiring, half-doubting air, like a connoisseur scrutinising a picture.

"That's so," said Avery.

"Even with proper tools it would be a long job to tackle, and there's neither iron bars nor wedges tempered to the right pitch amongst these tools here."

"Well, then, we'd better try and squeeze the key out of our friend in the next room," remarked the older villain.

They returned to the crushing room.

"Look here," began Avery to Douglas, "will you promise not to howl if I take that gag out, but to answer a question or two civilly?"

Douglas made no sign in reply.

"Well, I suppose I must trust you," went on Avery, and as he spoke he removed the gag. "Now will you tell us——"

"Help, murder, help," yelled Douglas.

"Curse you, you squealing pig," cried Kelly, and the

two threw themselves upon their captive and forced the gag into his mouth again.

"What's to be done with the beggar?" asked Kelly.

Avery remained silent, as if lost in thought.

The bushranger repeated his question.

"Yes, I've got it," replied the other, with a malignant smile stealing over his harsh skeleton features. "Bolt the outer door."

As he spoke he passed into the portion of the building that served Hicks as a workshop, and was fitted up as such with bench, vice, &c.

He made a sign to Kelly to bring his victim along and put him on the bench.

No sooner understood than done.

Avery went out for a minute and then returned, bearing a pen and ink and a sheet of paper, which he placed by the prisoner, who appeared as though perfectly indifferent to what was going on around him.

"A bird that can sing and won't sing must be made to sing," chuckled Avery to Ned, who continued to regard these preparations with some amazement.

Avery, addressing Douglas, said—

"You've stowed away the key of the safe—turn it up."

"Now no rubbish, my friend! You're going to do it, and that pretty sharp, too. Do you think you're going to play with two men like us? If you don't write the word I want on that paper I'll make you, that's all."

There was the same immobility on the part of Douglas, who lay where Ned had placed him, apparently quite insensible to the remarks addressed to him.

With diabolical deliberation Avery proceeded to loosen one of the arms of the prisoner, and, grasping his hand, placed his thumb in the bite of the screw.

"Blessed if it ain't as good as a play!" roared Kelly, apparently enjoying the cruelty. "What a thing it is to be a doctor."

Avery gave the vice a turn, and a deep groan issued from the unfortunate man.

The ruffians saw the test was sufficient, and loosening the man's right arm placed ink and paper before him.

He knew it was useless to hold out against such merciless villains, and that human nature would at length be obliged to yield.

He therefore wrote the desired information, and in a few minutes the treasure was in the possession of Avery.

"Let's get it down at once to the trap," said Avery. "I'll just look out and see if the coast's clear."

As he spoke, he moved to the outer door and looked out.

An exclamation of deep disappointment broke from him—

"There's a trap and a couple of fellows in it driving straight for the mill. They've come to take the gold to the bank. I know the turn-out as well as I do my own face."

CHAPTER CCXII.
GOLD IN BUCKETSFUL.

THEY resolved to brazen it out to the new-comers. Both of them stowed Douglas away, gagged, in an inside room, and were prepared to represent themselves as workmen employed about the mill, and for this purpose smudged their faces and clothes with a trifle of grease and smut. A gunny-bag was carefully thrown over the gold in the corner.

They would inform the new arrivals that Douglas had gone over to the camp, and would return in an hour.

They opened the bolts of the outer door of the mill, so as to make everything look open and usual.

The next moment the buggy drew up in front of the crushing mill.

It contained Mr. Staples, the shareholder, who usually took the gold into the bank, and a friend.

The former sprang down, and stepping to the door, pushed it open.

Ned met him as he crossed the threshold.

The bushranger held a short but heavy engineer's hammer in his hand.

Avery noticed that his fingers gripped the handle convulsively.

"Stow that, mate," he whispered, anxiously in a low tone.

"Hallo," said Mr. Slater, as he stepped across the threshhold and caught sight of Ned and Avery, "where's Douglas?"

"Gone over to camp, back in an hour, he said."

"Hum, hum," said Slater, who was a red-faced, fussy fellow. "Is Hicks about?"

"No, there's no one here but me."

"Ah! Who are you? I don't think I've seen your face here before," and as he spoke Slater stared hard at Ned.

"Hicks has got a couple of days off, he's a bit queer, and I'm taking his place. Mr. Douglas told me to stop here while he went to camp, and said that if you called you would wait in his house. The door is open, there ain't a soul about but myself and this gentleman, who just come up from the shanty to see Mr. Douglas," said Ned, indicating Avery.

Just as Ned uttered these words, there was a crash from the workshop in which Douglas was lying.

It was reached from the crushing-room, in which they were, through an open doorway.

"What's that?" exclaimed Slater, suspiciously.

"I expect it's that cat of Hicks."

Slater hesitated a moment.

He turned on his heels and faced the doorway leading into the workshop.

He seemed to be debating whether or not to enter it.

Kelly's grasp tightened on the hammer.

After a few moments hesitation, which seemed to be an age to the two ruffians, Slater turned away.

In answer to his enquiry, he was informed that the office was locked, and that Mr. Douglas would not be back before an hour.

"I say, Brent," said Slater to his companion, who was seated in the trap, "Douglas is away, and won't be back for an hour. We're to wait. Would you like to have a look over the mill?"

No sooner had the two moved away to the stables than Ned darted into the workshop.

Douglas had heard Slater's arrival, and by a desperate exertion managed to get one arm sufficiently free to knock an oil can, the only thing within reach, on to the floor with his elbow. He was so tightly gagged that he could make no other noise.

This had caused the noise they had heard.

He was now making desperate struggles to free himself from his bonds.

Kelly saw his efforts, and quickly re-adjusted the bonds of the unfortunate manager in such a way that all chances of his freeing himself was hopeless.

"Look here, if you start loose again," he muttered, "I'll light up the fires, get up steam, set the mill a-going, and run you through the stampers."

The new comers had taken up their quarters in the verandah, and Kelly would be compelled to pass their front carrying the bucket which contained the stolen gold. The weight was considerable, but Kelly steadily trotted along as if carrying a bucket of water.

"That's well over. Fill me a nobbler," was his first remark on his arrival.

The precious ingots were soon removed from their hiding place in the buckets, and after being done up in a couple of blankets, were transferred to the trap.

"I think there's nothing left but to start," said Avery.

"Those fellows are still on the verandah," said Ned, "and they can spot us easy."

"Let 'em watch, whatever they think they can't follow. I've taken care to spoil that game, their nag has got a nail in his foot that won't make him travel very far."

In a few minutes more the pair were *en route*.

Their plan was a simple one.

They had agreed to halt at a spot known to Avery, and plant the gold there.

This done they were to separate, and either make their way to mining camps, or get a job as hut-keeper or the like, for a short time, in some pretty, remote spot, where they were not likely to get hunted up.

Could this precious pair of villains have read the thoughts that simultaneously sprung to their minds, they would have flown at one another's throats like bull dogs. The fact was, that each was thinking of "disposing" of the other at the first convenient opportunity and grabbing the gold.

We regret that we cannot dignify the infamous pair with the interesting qualities usually decorating the character of highwaymen, such as Paul Clifford, Dick Turpin, or Claude Duval, to say nothing of Robin ("Robbing?") Hood; but our history is a true one, not like those alluded to, pure fiction. We "show vice its own feature," the authors of the other named works, show vice the feature of virtue, and make infamy romantic; we make it hideous.

There are some readers who may think the representation of Kelly's atrocities are overdrawn. They are much mistaken; and Colonial records exhibit bushrangers whose villanies would make men of Kelly's stamp, almost blush.

When the excitement of the gold robbery had died away, the two thieves were to come back and dig up the gold, which they would then dispose of.

As they drove along, Kelly could not help looking with some admiration at his companion.

The old fellow's daring and ingenuity, his coolness and fertility in resource, had impressed him.

His observation about the hocussing, and the way in which he had opened Douglas's mouth.

"Haven't you been a bit of a doctor?" he remarked.

The old fellow smiled a little scornfully.

"A bit of a doctor. I am a fully qualified practitioner, if you know what that means?"

This was Greek to Ned, but he guessed its meaning.

"Regular license to kill or cure, eh?"

"Yes."

"And how did you get out of it. Lushing, I suppose?"

"No, I'll tell you if you like, if you're ready for a yarn," and on being told by Kelly to "shove a-head," he began.

CHAPTER CCXIII.
AVERY'S STORY—THE CHAPEL VAULT.

"My father was a swell in the Midland counties, with a fair estate and a large family.

"He managed, however, to give all a fair start in the world; and after I had taken my diploma, which means a ticket-of-leave in the doctoring line, bought me a fresh practice in a London suburb.

"I had been doing pretty well for about a year, when one night I was called up to a very rum case.

"It was late in the morning before I could leave it.

"I had been too busy to think of eating, but when I got into the street I began to feel a bit empty, and turned into the first tavern I came across to get something to wolf. A man named Vaughan was with me.

"It was not much of a place, though it was clean and decent.

"I noticed a man sitting in another box, who caught my attention at once.

"'Who's that man, Vaughan?' I said.

"'Don't you really know?' he asked.

"'No.'

"'Well, he's the owner of the Baal Peor Chapel close by that's let to the Grimstonians, followers of the Reverend Jabez Grimstone. His name is Judkins.'

"'How do you come to know him, Vaughan?'

"'Well, you're a decent fellow, and I don't mind telling you. Under the chapel is a vault, and in that vault are placed the mortal remains of that very eccentric congregation. Now, Judkins manages that part of the business, and a very good thing he makes of it, too.'

"'Still, I don't quite see.'

"'What's that to do with it? Well, if you must know, Judkins doesn't mind disposing of a body now and then.'

"I was a bit startled at this.

"But, mind you, many years ago body-snatching was pretty lively.

"'And you're a regular customer of his?' I said to Vaughan.

"'Yes. There's a young subject to be put into the vault to-day, and he has promised, as young subjects are scarce, to let me have it. It's not from mere curiosity either. The fact is, I was called in to see the girl, though too late to do any good, and though I wanted to make a *post mortem* the parents refused. It is a very singular case of disease of long standing, and I was determined to find out something more about it.'

"'How do you get the bodies?' I asked.

"'He delivers them to me at his own house, which is next door to the chapel. My coachman is a steady fellow whom I can trust, and I fetch them away in my carriage. Once or twice when I have only wanted to make a brief examination Judkins has accommodated me with his kitchen.'

"I felt rather disgusted at this Mr. Judkins, who sold protection to the dead in the shape of his vault, and then broke faith, but at the same time my curiosity was roused.

"After a little trouble I got Vaughan to promise to call on me that same evening and to take me with him.

"Punctual to his time he called, and we were soon on our way in his carriage to Baal Peor Chapel.

"We stopped opposite the court, at the end of which the chapel was built, and alighted.

"We dived into the court, and stopped at a house next to the chapel.

"Vaughan gave a peculiar knock, which convinced me that, from time to time, he must have been a regular customer of Judkins.

"The door opened, and there was Judkins with a candle in his hand.

"He did not look particularly pleased at seeing mn.

"However, when Vaughan had explained that I was a doctor like himself, he cleared up.

"'Very glad ter see yer, sir,' he began; 'and any time as yer wants anything in my line I shall be very glad ter serve yer out of the jam-pot.'

"'Out of the what?' I said.

"'Oh,' said Vaughan, 'that's an old joke of Judkins' He calls the vault the jam-pot because his friends are not only preserved there but jammed in pretty tightly.'

"'Have you any objection to my seeing your "preserves"?'

"'No; you're one of us,' said the fellow.

"As we followed Judkins down the stairs leading to the kitchen, Vaughan looked rather fidgety.

"'Remember, this is all confidential,' he whispered to me, as a reminder, as we groped our way down.

"We reached a large kitchen, in the grate of which a bright wood fire was burning cheerfully, whilst a pile of fuel was stacked ready to hand. It was composed of broken coffins.

"Judkins opened a cupboard in one corner of the kitchen, and, to any ordinary observer, there would certainly not have appeared anything peculiar about it.

"The shelves contained the ordinary crockery. There was something, however, behind them. Deftly lifting the whole shelf out, a door was apparent in the wall. The lock of this was quickly turned, the door swung back on its hinges, and Judkins proudly exclaimed—

"'There's my diggin's; preserver and all!'

"I shrank back a moment, and felt uncomfortable.

"'Lor', there ain't nothing to be afeard on,' he said. And added, 'The Grimstonians is all put in down a trap in the chapel floor, and if I has a customer for 'em why they comes out this way through my kitchen.'

"'But you don't sell them all?'

"'Dear no, sir. I wishes as I could'

"He led the way into the vault.

"Hardened to the presence of mortality, as my professional training had rendered me, I felt really horrified at this profanation.

"'It's all the same,' said Mr. Judkins, as though divining my thoughts. 'Some folks lives on their neighbours when they're alive and kicking. I lives on 'em when they isn't. And mine is the best way, too, for I don't take what they want. They don't feel that I'm living on them as if they was alive. I does them no harm, and me a sight o' good.'

"I had had enough of this, and made my way back into the kitchen again, for I felt a little queer.

"Vaughan said to Judkins—

"'Well, where's the lot I have come for?'

"'Here yer are,' said Judkins, pointing to a sack in the corner.

"Vaughan saw I was rather disgusted, and said, after settling up with Judkins—

"'Let's clear out at once.'

"'All right,' said Judkins. 'Lumpy—here, Lumpy, where are yer?'

"In reply to this call there appeared a hideous old fellow in a shabby great coat and very little else.

"As I looked in his face I saw he was evidently somewhat idiotic, a fit person to help Judkins in his dreadful trade.

"'Now, Lumpy,' said Judkins, 'carry out that sack for the doctor, and I shouldn't wonder if he won't stand yer a pot.'

"Lumpy did not hesitate, but with Judkin's help got the sack containing the body on to his shoulders, and preceded us to the court and then down to the carriage, where the sack was duly placed.

"Vaughan gave him a trifle, and we drove off with our ghastly load.

"We reached Vaughan's house, and stopped at a side door leading to his surgery, which he opened with a key.

"We carried the body in through the surgery into a small room fitted up as a laboratory and dissecting room.

"The sack was removed, and the subject placed on the table.

"It was that of a girl of sixteen or seventeen, of very emaciated appearance.

CHAPTER CCXIV.

AVERY'S STORY CONTINUED.—THE DEAD ALIVE.

"VAUGHAN had just given me some explanation as to the symptoms of the disease the girl had succumbed to and the points he wanted to clear up, when there was a knock at the door.

"'What is that?' he said, somewhat angrily, for he could not bear to be disturbed at his work, and it was a standing order that no one should rout him out of this den of his.

"'Please, sir,' answered his servant's voice, 'it's Mr. Finch, and he must see you at once.'

"'Why the deuce didn't you say I was out?'

"'He caught sight of the light in the surgery, sir.'

"'Confound it! I suppose I must go,' said Vaughan to me. 'He's a crotchety fellow, and one of my best patients. Wait here; I shan't be more than a quarter of an hour.'

"He went out, and I was left alone with the body.

"There was nothing unusual in this; it was a situation in which I had found myself scores of times.

"Still, I felt more uncomfortable than I ever had before under such circumstances.

"The ghastly disclosures of Judkins oppressed my mind.

"I could not help a feeling of horror every time my thoughts wandered to that profaned vault and its hideous revelations.

"The very fact of the body having come from it increased this feeling.

"Vaughan seemed a long time gone.

" i began to get impatient.

" Anything was better than this sickening inaction and its accompaniment of troubled idea.

" I felt I must do something. or I should go mad.

" I resolved to begin operations myself.

" I took up a knife and bared the corpse.

" Even now I can hardly tell what followed.

" No sooner had the knife cut into the flesh than the subject's eyes opened, and fixed themselves upon me.

" I gave a shriek, to which she responded, as she slowly rose into a sitting position.

" I lost all command over myself, and with wild cries for help, threw open the door and fell into the passage.

" Vaughan, his patient, and the servants came flocking up to find me stretched insensible on the floor, and the girl sitting on the dissecting table, with the blood streaming from her breast, gibbering like a maniac.

" Of course it was evident that she had been buried in a state of catlepsy.

" The result of all this was my ruin.

" The girl's parents had to be sent for, and instead of being pleased at her restoration, their only thought was that of taking some vengeance on those who had profaned her tomb.

" The news soon spread, and the next afternoon the Grimstonians, in a body, made an examination of their vault, and, instead of finding their deceased relatives snugly reposing therein, they only found Mr. Lumpy unconsciously drunk.

" Worse than this, the unfortunate girl only survived a few days.

" The shock may have accelerated her death, though at the inquest held it was clearly proved that she was suffering from a disease that must have ended fatally in a few days at the farthest, and I narrowly escaped a trial for manslaughter.

" But the scandal was so great that neither Vaughan nor I could hope to face it.

" I had to cut away.

" For months my nerves were utterly shattered.

" I bolted to the colonies.

" On the way out I took to drinking, and—here I am.

" Perhaps the strangest part of my tale is to be told.

" It was just before I embarked that I was down at the East end of London where I had been down to the docks.

" There is no lack of squalid scarecrows there, but my eye was caught all at once by one of the most ghastly and tattered objects it is possible to conceive.

" Looking at it closely, I recognised Lumpy, though it looked as if ten years instead of ten months had passed over his head since I had last seen him

" He was crawling along in the last stage of exhaustion and distress.

" As he paused to beg a copper he recognised me.

" I had always wondered what had become of Judkins; and I resolved now to find out.

" ' Ah! doctor,' he said; ' spare us a copper.'

" 'I'll give you five shillings if you'll tell me anything you know about Judkins.'

" He stared at me in a half vacant, idiotic way.

" ' All right,' he said at last; ' but give us a drop of drink first.'

" I took him into a public-house and gave him a quartern of gin, which he tossed off at once.

" ' Ah,' he said, ' I don't care for wittles. I live on drink. A stunning drop o' summat like that does wake you up.'

" ' Well, he got to hear of there bein' summat wrong. He had gone out early, and he comes boltin' back as white as a sheet. 'Lumpy,' he says, says he, 'it's all up; the gaff's blowed, and we're just about bust up in our little game.' He began to rummage about a bit, and he says, 'There's half a quid for yer. Go and try yer luck at summat else.' 'What,' says I, 'half a quid.' 'Yes,' says he, and he chucks it down on the table '

" ' I looks at it,' continued Lumpy, ' and says, ' Mr Judkins, if it's all up, you aint made a bad thing o' the business. Give us five quid and I'm off.' Well, doctor, he wouldn't, but away he went out.

" ' Now I knew as how he had money hid somewheres, but I never nicked where he kep' it. However, thinks I, he'll get it now and be off, so I kep' a good watch on him, and I see him go into the chapel, and then I knew he had all his money hid away there. And my pockets as empty as this here pewter.'

" I understood the hint, and had the quartern refilled.

" After a pull, Lumpy went on—

" ' I was in the vault, you must know, for I'd gone in there to listen, and I could hear him trampin' about overhead, when the idea all of a sudden came acrost me that he might as well come down below. So I jest undid the two bolts as held up the trap door in the chapel floor, down which they used to put the bodies, and in about half a minute Judkins treads on it, and down he comes.'

" ' Was he killed ?'

" ' Not quite, I think. He was only stunned a bit, I fancy, so I got a hundred sovereigns out of his pocket and into mine, and then I pops him into an empty coffin. It was the one as had held the young girl, as there was all the row about, I found out arterwards.'

" ' And then ?' I gasped.

" ' I'll tell you,' and he lowered his voice confidentially. ' I went into the kitchen, and I broke open the cupboard where old Judkins kep' his sperrits, and mixed myself a drain. Perhaps I overdid it, but all at once some idea came acrost me that I'd better make old Judkins snug, so I just went into the vault again and screwed him down all proper.'

" ' In the coffin ?'

" ' Rather.'

" ' And what happened then ?'

" ' Well, I hardly know. I set there a-drinkin' till a lot of people came and punched me all round and turned me out, and since then I've spent all my tin, and come down to what you see me. But if so be as you wants Judkins very particular, you'll find him there now,' and the fellow chuckled at the thought.

" I felt as if I could have annihilated the monster, who related the horrible fate of his former master as he would that of a trapped rat or reptile."

" How jolly nice you are all at once," said Kelly, with a diabolical sneer.

" Oh, I forgot. Birds of a feather, you know," retorted Avery, with a look that spoke of contempt and dislike. " However funny as it may seem to you I was disgusted with the brute, and throwing him his five bob, motioned him to be off, which he was not long in doing."

CHAPTER CCXV.
NED PLANTS THE SWAG AND HIS PAL.

THUS ended Avery's " strange, eventful history."

On the pair drove for some considerable time.

Avery appeared to know every inch of the way, as well as if he had been " prospecting " there all his life.

" Pull up," at last he cried; " here's the spot (at the foot of a large tree) where the plunder can be hidden until we come and get it."

Each of the parties had their own idea of which would be the successful " digger."

Avery meant treachery, not death Kelly meant the latter.

Ned drew the rein.

It was a dreary flat, the horizon only broken in one direction by a dim line of rock and tree.

" Are you sure we are right ? " he asked almost incredulously.

" Quite," answered Avery; " yonder lies the river."

He pointed, and Ned, following the direction of his finger, could distinguish its course, marked by the sullen water-holes lying between its banks like a string of irregular beads, as it swept away to the horizon like a writhing snake in alternate articulations of sand, and sedge, and pool.

"Should we drive up to it? asked Kelly.

"No," replied Avery, "we mustn't bring the wheel tracks any further."

The two men alighted and secured the horse.

Ned pulled out the blanket containing the gold, and with some difficulty hoisted it on to his broad shoulders.

"Come, show the way," he said to his companion.

Taking a spade, Avery stepped off in front.

They were making their way to an elbow in the river at some distance ahead.

Nevertheless despite the weight Kelly had to carry, he appeared to be the fresher of the two when they gained the banks of the stream.

His fragile companion seemed utterly exhausted as he cast himself upon the turf.

The bushranger proceeded to spread out the blankets in which the gold had been wrapped.

Then with great skill he trimmed round three sides of an oblong of turf, and rolled it back so as to lay bare the soil beneath it.

This he began to dig out, casting the loose earth as he threw it out into the blanket.

Avery stretched upon his stomach, with his chin supported by his hands, watched him in silence for a few moments.

"You'll excuse me helping you, I'm sure," he at length remarked, in a tone of old world politeness, strangely at variance with his appearance, and his usual style of address towards Ned.

"All right," ejaculated the latter.

Avery took up a handful of earth, and let it dribble through his fingers, with his gaze fixed on the far away horizon.

In the hush of the night, the only sounds were those of Ned's hard breathing, and the grating made by his spade.

Avery continued to look across the plain to the horizon now dying out in dimness against the darkening sky.

"Yes," he resumed, as though speaking to himself, "this is the safest bank, a bank that holds more secrets than gold".

Ned had all but completed the hole to his satisfaction, and straightening himself as he stood in it, bent on his spade.

"I reckon that's deep enough," he said.

"You're right, deep enough and strong enough. The turf will keep it better than three-inch iron could. You've been in quod, mate?" he continued abruptly, changing his tone to his usual one of familiarity.

"Yes," replied Kelly in some astonishment.

"Then I suppose you've heard the chaplain preach there, if you never did anywhere else. Do you recollect the text about laying up treasures where moth and rust corrupt, and thieves break through and steal?" he continued in his sneering manner.

"No," said Ned sullenly; "I think you're a bit overhead from the way your e jabbering."

"I almost think so, too."

The bushranger had by this time finished the hole to his liking.

Stepping out of it, he knelt by its side, and taking up the smaller ingots began to throw them in one by one.

Kelly had thrown all the smaller ingots in, and only the big one remained.

The bushranger rose to his feet with this held in both his hands.

Avery was again staring aimlessly into the night

Just as this moment a spear came whizzing past Kelly's head, and the two men sprang to their feet. The view that met their astonished glances was not very encouraging. Some fifty Aborigines, laden with spears, seemed to spring like ants from the ground, and a shower of spears fell amongst the two white men, making a noise like the rustling of bird's wings. Kelly shouted out—

"It's all up!" and bolted like mad for where the horse was tethered.

He unharnessed the animal, took a saddle he had brought with him, in case they wanted to take up a stray mount, and clapped it on the horse with the speed of a practised hand.

As he looked round he saw Avery down with a spear through his body, and being smashed up under the murderous blows of the waddys wielded by the savages. The bushranger was soon on the back of the horse and was off, the fate of Avery not causing him the least concern. He muttered something about being saved the trouble, and looked forward to subsequently exhuming the buried gold, and having no claimant for a share of it.

CHAPTER CCXVI
BLACKS AND WHITES.

NED judged that the best thing would be for him to shift his quarters for a few months, and get a berth at a convenient distance from his late exploits.

He could there lie *perdu* till the robbery had blown over, and come back to unearth the gold.

He heard that a hut-keeper was wanted at an out-station on the Flinder's river; and, after an interview with the owner's overseer, undertook the berth, and started for the out-station.

As he approached it, laden with the saddle of a knocked-up horse, a rough but anxious voice rang out—

"Who's there?"

Ned was some yards from the door, walking on the grass and, as he judged, making very little noise.

However it was evident that he had been either seen or heard, for the voice continued—

"What cheer, mate?"

He soon enlightened his interviewer, giving his name as Smith.

A door was unbarred, and he was asked in, and when he had entered the bars were at once replaced.

He found himself in the presence of three men.

One who had just refastened the bars was putting back his gun into a kind of rack, the other two were watching suspiciously.

"You seem precious skeary of strangers, mates," said Ned. "I've been sent up here by Mr. Calthorpe, and have been on the road since Monday."

"Oh! you're the new hut-keeper, are you," replied one of the men who was the shepherd. "There's the billy, the damper's on the table. Our mutton is rather high."

Ned began to eat his supper.

The other two men were sawyers, stout, broad-chested fellows, who appeared to have lived so long in the wilderness as to have got to regard speech as almost a superfluity.

"And what did old Calthorpe say about the Warrekerro station?" asked the shepherd, when Ned had satisfied his hunger.

"Didn't he pitch it to you that this was the healthiest spot in the colony, that there was next to nothing to do, and that the blacks had given over troubling us."

"Yes," answered Ned; "he said the blacks had bolted."

The shepherd laughed grimly.

"Bolted. They're all round here as thick as sheep tracks, and it's as much as one risk one's nose outside without the chance of a spear in his liver."

"Lively that," said Ned.

"We were bailed up in this very hut, two of us were, last year for a week, and were pretty well dead with thirst before a party came up and drove the beggars off. We'd got some rum, but hardly any water, and the hut-keeper got so mad from thirst and liquor, that I had all my work cut out to keep him from opening the door and bolting out into the middle of 'em."

"Why didn't they burn you out?"

"It's an awful sight a fired station," meditatively put in one of the hitherto silent sawyers, an elderly man. "I mind one down on the Murray, years and years ago, and the sight of the poor old squatter, lying with his white hair dabbled in blood, and his daughter, a likely lass of seventeen, stuck as full of spears as ever the poor lassie had stuck a pincushion of pins, will be before me to my dying day."

"The fighting blacks are all wiped out there now," said the shepherd

"Yes; we didn't leave many after that. The settlers mustered every man they could, and in two months there wasn't a black fellow in the district."

"Were you in the hunt, old 'un?" enquired Ned.

"Yes," replied the old fellow, "and we didn't much care how we destroyed them. One time, I mind we got hold of an old four pounder gun that some naval officer had brought up country with him as an ornament. That was a fine lark," and the old boy chuckled at the reminiscence.

"How did it work?" asked the shepherd.

"Oh! beautifully, beautifully. We got scent of a big mob, who were pretty well driven into a corner, and were going to make a stand for it So we just sent a few fellows forward with the gun to tempt 'em out. They didn't twig it, but made a rush and then it was blazed off at 'em at close quarters."

"What was in it, slugs?"

"Slugs, no; we'd crammed it to the muzzle with broken glass and old nails. A lot of us came up and then we had a little more fun, for we lighted a big fire and clapped all the howlers we could lay hands on on the top of it.

There was one old beggar, I mind me, who was extra cunning and shammed dead, thinking that we'd respect his corpse."

"Respect a black fellow's corpse," laughed Kelly. "That's a good 'un."

"He didn't play 'possum quite well enough, for he couldn't help shaking a bit, may-be he was scared, so we chucked him on the top of the fire with the rest. He tried to wriggle out again from the burning logs like a snake, but we twigged it and chucked him back again along with a snake that the fire had drawn from a hollow log."

"Two reptiles got rid of at the same time," said the shepherd sententiously.

After one or two more brushes they were quite settled, though to my mind if I'd have been one of them I'd rather have been wiped out that way than served as a mob were by a canny Scotch squatter on the Murrumbidgee."

"What's the yarn?"

"Why, he just let them help themselves to as much poisoned flour as they could lay hands on. He'd got a lot of arsenic up for dressing the sheep and he mixed it up with flour so that the beggars poured down on it and carried it off to their camp. I didn't see that myself, but a chap as did told me that the sight in that camp, when a visit was paid to it, was enough to make a fellow feel a bit creepy. Men, women, and children all stiffened out with their faces twisted up in their agony, their teeth bare, their lips drawn back, and the whites of their eyes showing as they had rolled back in their sockets."*

"Well," remarked Kelly, "I only came across your northern blacks for the first time the other day, and I shouldn't mind if the whole blessed boiling were served in that fashion. I had spears and clubs whistling round my head till I got sick of the music."

He proceeded to relate his adventures with Bella.

"Ah," remarked the old sawyer whose name was Bailey, "all that nonsense has been pretty well knocked out of 'em in the south."

And so it had and by a summary process.

When the squatters of a district used to find that their lives and those of their families and servants were in danger and that no assistance was to be obtained from the

Colonial Government, they used to take the law into their own hands.

They and their most trusted stockmen on whose fidelity they could rely, used to meet at an appointed spot and hunt up the tribe of blacks against whom their vengeance was aimed.

Now and again a white man drops from the saddle with a spear in his body, or a horse darts off, maddened by pain; but as a rule, those engaged are old fighters and know how to avoid these hurling shafts.

As the spears whiz past them they manage to catch and break them, so as to prevent their being used again.

At length the ammunition of the blacks gives out.

Then their foes tighten the fatal circle, till those enclosed in it are driven into the marsh or the water-hole.

This object attained, fire is opened on them from the revolvers of the horsemen.

One by one they are bowled over as they "squatter" like young wild ducks on the pool, and then the whites ride back with the knowledge that that district will be safe for a time at least.

The Government, it is true, regard the proceedings in another light.

But then, thanks to the influence of Exeter Hall, they have peculiar views as to the relative value of a black and a white man's life.

In the north the Government has taken a view more in accordance with that of the settlers.

The Queensland Commissioner of Police, in his report for 1878, wrote as follows—

"The complaints of cattle killing and hut robbing by the blacks along the northern coast, from Cairns to Crooktown are never-ending, and will never cease as long as there are blacks there."

The whole coast is studded with timber-getters and settlers, by whom the blacks are disturbed, and prevented from getting their natural food in that direction; whilst further inland the country is occupied by small cattle stations, which again cut them off from their hunting and fresh water fishing grounds.

The intervening scrub is small, affording but a scanty supply of fruits in their seasons, and hence the natives take advantage of the cover it affords, to make sudden raids on the cattle and huts, which are rendered more easy by the nature of the ground.

Hence the bitter feeling between the settlers in the north and the blacks, from whose assaults they are never safe; and hence the terrible thoroughness of the vengeance they have from time to time taken.

On one occasion, in Northern Queensland, two white men were speared.

The rest met and determined, as a measure of precaution, and to ensure their future safety, to hunt the blacks out of the district.

A party was organised, and well mounted and equipped, they set out on their expedition.

They were not desirous of making captures, and set to work in the usual fashion.

Dividing, so as to effect a surround, they came upon a tribe of blacks encamped near a water-hole.

Fearful of reprisals, or apprehensive of danger, most of the blacks took to the water, and diving like dab-chicks, tried to elude the bullets of their foes.

It was a vain hope, however, for the whites surrounded the water-hole, and succeeded in "potting" no less than fifty of the unfortunate wretches as they swam about in wild terror.

Near Crooktown, almost within gun-shot of a popular town, the murder of some white men was similarly avenged, by the destruction of a whole tribe by the police.

Several of the blacks in this case swam out to sea, to escape the bullets of the police, and never returned to shore.

Out of a party of thirty-five men, women, and children, only three women and a child escaped the triple perils of

---

* These details (the cannon, burning the black and the poisoned flour) will be found detailed in an Australian journal, Melbourne. 1868.

the revolvers of the police, the waves of the ocean, and the jaws of the sharks, with which that portion of the coast abounds.*

A writer in the *Australian Magazine* has asserted that the policy of the Queensland Government has much to do with keeping up the chronic ill-feeling between black and white.

He represents the superintendent of an absentee squatter getting instructions, if he anticipates annoyance from the blacks, to send for the native police.

A travelling tribe crosses the run and startles the cattle.

Perhaps they spear a few, or wantonly chase them, and in the season when the beasts are "topping up" such a scare may take from off the fat "mob" of say three hundred beasts a certain percentage of weight, which in the aggregate represents a fair sum.

Brown, the superintendent, writes to the officer in charge of the district at once.

The lieutenant and his party ride up a few days later.

Each of the troopers has one spur only; consequently one side of the horse goes faster than the other, the result being a peculiar amble styled the "policeman's jog."

Next morning after their arrival at the station they take a circuit of ten miles and quarter the ground backward and forward till they hit on a solitary track.

They run this track with a speed and certainty which the trained bloodhound alone can equal.

No impress on the soil, no bent blade of grass escapes them.

Presently more tracks join, all going in the same direction, and it is evident that they have struck the main trail of the blacks.

The party dismount and hobble their horses in a hollow.

Two of them peel themselves of every rag of uniform and glide on ahead, crawling and dodging.

In about an hour they come back with the report that there is a camp of blacks on the edge of a scrub some two miles off.

The party stay where they are all night, but at the first streak of day they mount and push quietly but rapidly over the ground.

When they catch sight of the fires of the black camp they rush on at a gallop.

The alarm is given, the camp is empty in a few seconds, but the troopers are off their horses and into the scrub, carbine in hand, throwing off their clothes as they go in hot pursuit.

The lieutenant waits outside smoking his pipe and meditating over the prospects of a deal for a colt that has caught his eye at the station.

Shots are heard in the scrub, and the troopers come back after an interval.

They have cut off some half-dozen of the last of the fugitives, whose dead bodies are lying in nameless gullies under bush and thicket.

The leading men of the tribe have of course escaped, and, with broken-hearted women and wailing children, shriek to heaven for vengeance against the horrible "whitefellow," to whom they ascribe all this.

It is as likely as not that Brown, the superintendent, never pulled trigger on a black, and does not even hear of how the lieutenant and his men carried out their "duty."

Only, if Brown's horse does come home riderless some evening, and his owner's carcase is discovered riddled like a sieve with spears, it is hardly to be wondered at.

As to his superiors, they, of course, never know anything about the matter, being merely business speculators working the station with bank money.

Questions of policy or humanity to the blacks have nothing to do with them.

---

* Inglis—Our Australian Cousins—1880.

"Blacks on our premises? Why then, they were trespassing. It's clearly the business of the authorities to turn them off."

That is all they know or understand about it.

Their concern with the Gondary station is simply one of pounds shillings and pence, and, as long as the money comes out right, what more is wanted?

Meanwhile, half-a-dozen black corpses lie in their blood in the scrub, because the tribe they belong to, or some other tribe unknown, is suspected of having gone near the Gondary cattle camp.

CHAPTER CCXVII.
AN ATTACK ON THE HUT BY SAVAGES.

NED found a hutkeeper's life fearfully wearying. The silence all day until the return of the shepherd at sundown left him without resource.

He resolved to "cut it" at once; but he had a little experience to go through before he carried out his intention, which was not altogether unpleasing to a man of his active habits.

He soon had an opportunity of becoming practically acquainted with the dangers of the spot.

It was five or six mornings after his arrival.

The shepherd was away on his rounds, and the bushranger was alone.

He was sitting in his usual place, and before him hung a little circular mirror resting on two nails.

He threw a careless glance at this, and all at once his attention became fixed on it.

Across its face were reflected two small straight sticks.

He usually sat in that position, and knew every bough outside that the mirror reflected; but these two sticks were new to him.

He was about to go to the window and put out his head, when a sudden reflection caused him to change his mind.

He leaned forward instead, and slightly shifted the position of the mirror so as to take in a wider field.

He was partially successful in this.

He could see a little more of the sticks, and also make out the slender fingers and muscular forearm of the native who held one of them.

It was evident that they were a couple of spears, and it was odds that one of them did not come flying through the open window of the hut and into his body.

The position was a ticklish one, and Ned knew it.

He felt that the black outside was watching him, and that if he gave the slightest sign that he was aware of the enemy's presence it would be the immediate signal for an attack.

He looked round.

His gun was in the rack, but if he stepped up to get it, no doubt the spear would at once be thrown.

"Curse that black snake!" he muttered; "he's got his eye on me for a certainty."

The door of the hut as well as the window, was open, and, for aught he knew, a black might be lurking by that, too.

The window could be closed by a shutter now swung back against the wall, but to step up to it for that purpose would be to receive the black's spear in his chest.

At length he made up his mind what to do.

He rose and took up a pail as though about to leave the hut.

His eye was on the mirror, and he noticed that the position of the spear shifted.

It was evident that the savage was watching every movement he was making.

"He'll think he's got a better chance of nailing me outside," muttered Ned, and moved to the door.

But instead of passing the threshold he swung the door to, shot the bolt, and jumped back at once into an angle of the hut formed by the walls, in which the door and window were.

It was well he did so, for even as he moved away a spear came flying through the window and struck the door, just where he had been standing, and was followed by another.

In his angle he was comparatively safe.

The wall in which the door was lay to his left, and that in which the window opened to his right.

Hence he was out of reach of any spears, unless the thrower thrust his head into the hut.

But with only one opening to guard instead of two, Ned felt pretty safe.

The next job was to shut the window.

If the shutter had swung back towards him as he stood, this would have been easy enough.

But, unfortunately, it swung back against the further half of the wall, so that to get to it, it was absolutely necessary to pass before the window.

His gun, and also his revolver, which he had not dared to seize for fear of drawing the fire of his enemies by this action, were also beyond the window.

A clumsy-looking, old-fashioned pistol of the shepherd's, was, however, hanging on a nail on the wall near him.

He unhitched it, and examined it.

It was loaded, but had evidently been charged a long time before.

"Just the sort of thing to miss fire when a chap's life rests on it," he thought, "I must get mine at any risk. Here goes."

It was absolutely necessary to cross the window to get to his arms.

The only plan to do so without being seen, was to crawl along the floor of the hut in a stooping position.

But could he be certain of doing this unseen?

How did he know but that the blacks had not found some crevice or knot hole, through which they were observing his movements.

He could not tell how many foes he had outside.

More than one he was certain, by the way in which the two spears had been thrown.

After reflecting, he decided to crawl along past the window, keeping as close to the wall as possible.

He lay down, not on his face, but on his back, so that he could watch the window all the while.

As noiselessly as possible he worked himself along.

His eyes were fixed on the square of sunlight opening in the wall, as inch by inch he edged himself along.

At length he was abreast of the window, which his glances had never left.

A moment more and he would be past it, out of reach of arms, and with weapons to his hand.

All at once the patch of sunlight was darkened.

A hideous shadow obscured it.

A face appeared at the opening.

A black, repulsive face with gleaming teeth, and eyes aglow with the fire of savage vengeance.

A woolly head was thrust boldly through the opening simultaneously with a lean, but muscular arm, holding a short, sharp spear.

Ned's movements had evidently been guessed.

A grin of triumph spread over the face of the black as he marked the position of his prostrate foe.

He poised the spear just over Ned's chest.

A look of anticipated enjoyment rendered his features positively demoniacal.

For a moment even Ned's blood ran cold.

There was no way of avoiding the coming stroke, by jerking or rolling himself to one side.

Accustomed to spear fish in the rivers, the black's arm is a sure one.

The bushranger glanced up at the grinning face above him, and read in it a desire to prolong the agony of anticipation he was enduring.

The black did not notice the pistol, and thought that his enemy was quite unarmed.

"If this old pistol is a duffer, I'm a gone coon."

Raising the weapon in question, he took a swift aim at the hideous face bending over his own, and before the black had even time to realise that his foe was armed, pulled the trigger.

As he did so he jerked his body towards the middle of the floor.

There was a flash and a report followed by a cloud of smoke.

Ned heard the spear feebly strike the floor, and simultaneously the thud of a heavy body falling across the window-ledge.

Then came a pattering sound, like a gentle rain.

By this time he had secured his gun and revolver, and advanced to close the window by closing the shutter.

There was an obstacle to this.

As the smoke cleared away he saw the body of the black hanging as limply as a damp rag over the window-sill, with the blood pattering on the floor from a ghastly wound in the face.

"I reckon you'll never come trying to spear white fellows again, you crawling black viper," was Ned's only comment.

Grasping the body with one powerful arm, and pulling it into the hut, Ned peered round the edge of the shutter.

He caught sight of another black stealing off towards the nearest shelter.

He raised his gun.

The steady barrel flashed out, and the second native seemed to sink peacefully down.

Ned glanced around.

There were no more signs of natives in that quarter.

A noise from the side of the hut in which the door was, attracted his attention.

Fastening the shutter he stepped towards the door.

As he neared it a blow was struck against it, and a voice without feebly cried—

"Open quick, mate."

Ned withdrew the bar, and cautiously opened the door to the extent of a couple of feet or so.

The shepherd staggered in and sank on to the nearest seat.

"Hullo," said Ned, seeing him sway from side to side, "are you hit, mate?"

"Yes," moaned the other feebly; "a spear under the shoulder. There are a gang of the devils gone down to the river to surprise the sawyers. Can you get down there in time to warn them?"

Ruffian though he was, Kelly was by no means the man to let such a tragedy be perpetrated without trying to prevent it, even at the risk of his own skin.

After fixing up the shepherd's wound as well as he could he left the hut, which the other barricaded after him, and started for the sawyers' camp on the river.

Scanning the ground as he advanced, he noticed a swaying of the grass some distance ahead.

Presently he noticed the upper part of a native's head rise above it, and the thought of an ambush occurred to him.

If there was only one, he judged the best plan would be to advance, risk a spear, and boldly rout the lurker out.

Again the grass moved, and again the black fellow's head rose above it as Ned drew quietly nearer.

A couple of bounds would place him at Ned's mercy before he had time to raise a weapon.

Clutching his gun, Ned jumped forward.

The head was again lifted and the eyes looked straight into his, with the perplexed, wild look of a trapped animal.

The face was drawn with pain, the lower lip had fallen and the brow was damp with sweat.

As the wild, clouded eyes rested on Ned, the wretched creature held up first one hand and then the other, to show that he was unarmed.

It was the native he had fired at from the hut.

Ned's bullet had struck the black fellow's spine, rendering his lower limbs dead and useless.

Behind him the grass lay broken down in a long furrow.

where he had dragged himself along by the mere strength of his hands and arms, in the hopes of gaining the river.

Ned looked at the wretched creature, and, raising his gun, hesitated as to whether he should put an end to his sufferings.

He reflected, however, that the shot might attract other blacks who might be prowling about, and passed on.

It was not long before the blacks showed themselves in a party of about a score, headed by a fellow of gigantic size.

Ned saw at once he was the leader, and resolved to shoot him down.

Just as he raised the gun, a long, faint "Cooey" fell on his ear from the direction of the sawyers' camp.

As soon as they heard it the blacks plunged into the scrub, and disappeared with the quickness of lightning.

Ned cooeyed in reply, and made his way in the direction of the sound.

As he pushed through the thick scrub he could not help thinking how easy it would be for the blacks to send a dozen spears through him before he caught a glimpse of them, but at the same time he guessed pretty well that the danger for the day was pretty well over, as far as he was concerned.

CHAPTER CCXVIII.
THE MASSACRE OF THE SAWYERS.

THE melancholy tone in which his "cooeys" were answered from the sawyers' camp told him that mischief had been done there, and he had no doubt that it was the party he had just sighted who had done it, and who, having accomplished their murderous work, were wriggling back to their holes like snakes.

The sawyers whom he had seen at the hut, had told him that the blacks were ever on the alert for mischief, and that whenever they left their huts for any time to look for timber they were down on them like hawks.

Not a bit of flour or a rag of clothing could they keep, and, on several occasions, they had come home tired and hungry, to find their bark "humpies" burnt down, and every bite and stitch carried off.

As he drew nearer he caught sight of the man who was cooeying.

It was one of the sawyers, a man named Jem Holt, who was sitting on a dead log with his hands and face covered with blood.

At his feet lay his brother, Bill, a fine young fellow of about twenty, stretched on his back with the blood bubbling in crimson froth bells from between his lips every time he breathed.

"Hullo, mate," cried Ned, "here's a precious lively game on. What's up, and where are the rest?"

"Done for, I think," gasped Holt. "Leastways, Raikes and Bolton are; I don't know about Bailey."

"How did it come about?"

"I'll tell you. You know we five were in a gang, and had come up stream some way above any of the other lots who are working along the river?"

"Yes, I know."

"We kept our camp on the banks instead of building a hut close to our sawpit, because we'd got a boat to look after, and knowing that the blacks had been plundering the other gangs directly their backs were turned, we settled that one of us should always remain in camp and look after the boat."

"That's just what's made the blacks so darned spiteful towards you," said Ned. "They saw there was no way of robbing you without a fight, and they've gone in for it. If they could have sneaked your swag on the quiet they would."

"I guess that was it. Well, this morning my brother, Raikes, and Bolton, left the hut with me, and Bailey stayed in camp. We saw nothing of the blacks, and after awhile we had all got to work. Bill and I were at the pit, and the other two were cross-cutting a big cedar-tree we'd cut down yesterday."

"Hadn't you your guns?"

"Yes, they were close handy, but we hadn't no time to use 'em. As I said, Bill and I were at the pit—he on the top, and I at the bottom—and the saw was going merrily, when all of a sudden I felt it stop in my hands. Before I had time to look up to see what was the matter, there was a loud cry from poor Bill, and a screech from twenty black devils. It told me all at once what was up."

"Aye, there's no mistaking when the brutes do give tongue."

"I scrambled out of the pit, and the first thing I saw was my brother lying bleeding just where he had fallen after jumping off the log. Before I had time to see any more, a whack from a waddy tumbled me back into the pit. I was stunned, and the fellow who hit me thought he'd settled my hash at one swipe; and I don't wonder at it, for he was the biggest black I ever set eyes on."

"A big black?"

"Yes, a whopper--nearly seven foot high, I should think."

"That must be the same chap I saw just now, heading a party. I wish I'd have had a chance of a shot at him, I've got a fancy for that fellow. Well, what happened next?" said Ned.

"I lay stunned for some time, as I guessed by the sun, and when I came to myself all was quiet. I got out of the pit, and there was poor Bill, lying where I saw him before, with a pool of blood round him. He had five spear-wounds in the breast, but, for a wonder, not a blow on the head; and he just gasped out to me that the tall black had the chief hand in it."

"Curse that black! we owe him one."

"Owe him one, aye, and I'll pay him," said Holt, with flashing eyes. "I'll never rest till I've had his blood."

"And the other two men, what about them?" asked Ned.

"Raikes and Bolton. They were lying a few yards away quite dead, with their sculls and faces battered in, and their arms and legs broken by waddies. I was hardly able to hold up, but I managed to get poor Bill on my back, and I brought him on as far as this, till I felt clear knocked up, and obliged to sit down. So then I began to cooey, in the hope the shepherd might be this way, or that Bailey might hear me from the camp by the river."

"Perhaps they've done for him too," suggested Ned.

"I think not; he's an artful old fox, and up to all their dodges. But come, mate, I feel up to moving now; so lend me a hand to get poor Bill down to the river. There may be a chance of his pulling through after all."

Ned looked at the prostrate man.

He was no surgeon, but he saw at a glance, from the blood coming from his mouth, that the poor fellow had been speared through the lungs, and that his case was hopeless.

Even as they looked, the eyes of the dying man were turned upwards till nothing but the whites were visible, and a thrill shot through his frame.

In another minute all was over.

Even Ned was moved, as they stood in the lonely scrub with the corpse at their feet.

An Australian thicket is a dull place at all time, and now it was doubly gloomy.

The two brothers, though rough fellows, had been very fond of each other, and had gone through many dangers in company.

They had been sailors, and had run from their ship together, and intended as soon as they had got some money, to go back to England, where their mother was.

Jem suddenly threw himself down on the ground beside his brother's corpse.

He seized the clay-cold hands in his.

"I know what'll make the earth lie lighter on you, Bill, and by ——, I'll do it! If ever I set hands on that big black—and I'll not rest night or day till I've done so—I'll put him across the pit alive and cross-cut him with the saw."

There were no means of digging a grave for the murdered man, so they broke off some boughs to rudely cover him, after Jem had cut off a lock of hair with his knife.

After a brief consultation, they settled that they would first push on to the camp by the river and ascertain Bailey's fate.

They found him stretched on the grass, pinned to the earth with a spear, and with his head and face mutilated out of all knowledge.

Close at hand lay the body of a gaunt native, slain by an axe blow, and two more black corpses announced that the old fellow had sold his life dearly.

His murderers had probably been alarmed at something, for the hut had only been partially pillaged, and, to the great satisfaction of Ned and Jem, the boat had apparently escaped their notice, and was neither staved nor stolen.

Ned bound up the wound on Jem's head, which was fortunately not serious, and another consultation followed.

Night was approaching, and they decided to remain where they were until the next day, and then to start for Ned's hut, get out the wounded shepherd if he was still alive, and then make their way down stream in the boat.

Jem insisted that they should also bury his brother's body before they started, being resolute not to leave it to the mercies of the native dogs, and Ned agreed that this should be done.

All at once they heard a sound from the river that roused them to attention.

It was like the stroke of oars.

Listening again they felt sure they could not have been mistaken, for they heard a voice sing out, "In bow," followed by the crushing of brushwood, that showed that a boat had shot into the bank.

Ned and Jem hastened down the track made by rolling timber to the river, and found a large ship's boat containing five and twenty men, sailors and sawyers, and all well armed.

A few words sufficed to explain matters.

The boat belonged to a little trading schooner that was moored a short distance up the river.

For greater convenience, a tent had been pitched ashore and used as a storehouse; but one morning, about fifty black fellows had darted from the woods, murdered the two men in charge of the tent, seized everything they could lay hands on in a hurry, and set fire to the rest.

Before the remainder of the crew could get on shore, they were off with their prey, shouting and waving their weapons in defiance.

The captain of the schooner was a determined fellow, and made up his mind for revenge.

The next morning early, he started off in his boat, calling at all the saw pits on the river, and beating up for volunteers.

The sawyers were ready enough to join, and, with them and his own men, he had got a pretty strong muster.

"Our hut was robbed and burnt down yesterday," said one of a gang working down the river to Jem, "and we were just thinking of coming up and asking you and your mates to join us in giving the devils a lesson on our own account, when the skipper here came alongside."

"Aye," said one of his mates, "and it's that big brute of a Cobawn Jack who is at the bottom of it all."

"Who's Cobawn Jack?" asked the captain.

"A great bulking beast of a black as big as a bullock," was the answer. "He's had a hand in stirring up all the devilry on this river, from the very beginning."

"An awfully big fellow, did you say?" said the captain.

"Yes; tall as a gum tree."

"Why, that's the very chap then who headed the lot who killed my two men. If I only get a chance of a shot at him he'll never spear another."

"Mates," said Jem, with a solemn earnestness that touched even the rough fellows with whom he was surrounded; "I've just got one favour I'd like to ask of you all."

"What is it, Jem, old man?" said several of the sawyers.

"It's about that Cobawn Jack."

"Fire away, boy."

Jem glanced round at his auditors.

"It was him who headed the mob who burnt your tent, captain?"

"Yes."

"Then you and your men will know him again directly you set eyes on him?"

"Just so; and if ever I do set eyes on him, I'll——"

"Stop a bit, captain. Now you say, Banks, he was with the lot who burned your hut."

"I'm certain of it."

"Well, mates, Cobawn Jack gave me this crack on the head you see, though I don't count that for much; but he did more than that for me. He struck down my poor brother."

Then he went on.

"Ah! I see," said the captain. "You want to kill him yourself."

"No," answered Jem, simply, "I want to take him alive; so on second thoughts, if you can blaze at his legs and cripple him, I'll be much obliged to you."

There was plenty of talk that night about their plans, and it was agreed that all hands should keep close on the spot where they were till the next evening, when they would start and give the blacks a lesson.

(To be continued.)

NED KELLY

THE
IRONCLAD
AUSTRALIAN BUSHRANGER

NO 37,

NED KELLY: IRONCLAD BUSHRANGER.

CHAPTER CCXVIII.—*Continued.*

Jem Holt was like a madman, and could hardly rest a minute, but kept starting up to see if it was time to rise, and fingering his gun.

All were glad when daylight came, and a party set off to fetch in the wounded shepherd from the hut from which Ned had started, and another to bury the dead.

The shepherd was found alive, and his wounds were judged not to be mortal by those of the party who had the best knowledge of surgery.

Poor Bill Holt had not been touched by the wild dogs, though the other two men had been shockingly torn by them, and those deputed to bury them had not much heart for dinner when they came back from the job.

The rest of the day was spent in cleaning firearms, casting bullets, and making up cartridges.

Some blankets were torn up to muffle the oars, and by nightfall all was in readiness.

The blacks, it had been ascertained, were in the habit of encamping on an island in the river.

One of the arms of the stream divided by the island was broad and deep, but the other was narrow and comparatively shallow, forming a kind of ford, across which the blacks were accustomed to wade to reach the shore.

The attacking party mustered twenty-seven in all, and it was arranged that the captain and half-a-dozen men should take the boat belonging to the sawyers' camp and pull up the broad arm of the river abreast of the island.

Here they were to land, crawl up to the blacks' camp, and fire a volley.

Naturally all who were not hindered from further flight by bullet or buckshot, would at once bolt across the shallow arm of the river, in the hope of escaping into the scrub on the mainland.

But here they would find the other boat containing Kelly and the rest of the sawyers and sailors waiting to pepper them on their retreat.

The white men had altogether about forty guns, besides pistols and revolvers, and counted on making a terrible slaughter.

It was a bright starlight night when they pushed off, and dropped down the river, hardly dipping the oars into the water, and keeping close in under the shade of the scrub.

In about a couple of hours they reached the end of the island, and here the boats separated.

Holt, who knew the place well, had gone in the captain's boat to serve as a guide.

Kelly, with the rest, pulled up the other arm of the river, carefully sounding as they went in order to discover the shallow.

When they found it, two-thirds of the party landed on the island, leaving the rest in the boat, which pulled out a little way again.

However, as time went by, and there was no sign of the expected attack from the other side, some of the men began to get impatient.

Kelly, who had, to a certain extent, assumed the command, suggested that they should themselves push on and make an attack.

"There's enough of us to tackle five hundred black fellows," he said, "so let's go in and have a slap at 'em at once, like bulldogs. Is that the sort of game, mates?"

Some of the rest were tempted to listen to his suggestion, but more prudent counsels prevailed, though doubts were expressed as to whether the captain's party, instead of surprising the natives, had not been themselves surprised and cut off.

"No," said one of the number, "we should have at least heard one or two shots in that case."

It afterwards turned out that the captain was puzzled to find a good place to land, without making too much noise with the crackling of the dry reeds and branches which stretched right out into the river.

All at once Ned's party heard a shout, evidently from a black fellow, followed by a general hooting and yelling, and the discharge of firearms.

It was evident the attack had commenced.

"Steady, mates, we shall have 'em here in a minute," observed Ned.

The party with him stood to their arms, as the howling and hooting came nearer and nearer.

Presently the blacks came pouring over a little ridge, near which Ned and his companions were lying in ambush, and began to leap into the river at the shallow place.

"Now's the time," cried Kelly, and the volley rang out with deadly effect.

Surprised and staggered by this discharge, the blacks turned tail and met a whole lot more of their fellows coming over the ridge.

Whilst the two lots of blacks were in confusion, the one party striving to make their way down to the water, and the other to fly back into the island for shelter, the whites had time to reload.

Advancing from their ambush before their foes had time to get out of each other's way, they poured another volley into them.

It was as equally destructive as the former, as the groans and yells amply testified.

The whites got behind shelter to load again.

But their big stroke of work was done.

Such a formidable camp of fighting blacks were not going to be frightened very easily.

Their numbers were higher than had been supposed.

They had been taken by surprise, and would have been glad enough to get away, but now that they were "bailed up," like rats in a trap, and could not turn away without facing the guns, they showed fight like devils.

There were no women or children amongst them, but only the warriors of their tribe.

They left off their wild screaming and yelling for a steady cry of

"Wah! Wah! Wah!"

"I know that screech," said one of the sawyers. "That is as much as to say they mean to face the music and see it out."

"That's so," replied one of his companions. "Heads below, and look out for squalls. We'll have spears and sticks whizzing round us like bees in a minute."

His prophecy was correct.

A shower of spears and nullah-nullahs flew through the air, and the fight began in earnest.

It raged for upwards of an hour.

The blacks kept so well under cover that their adversaries could no longer inflict anything like the preceding amount of damage upon them.

The whites were too strong to be in much danger, but they fired away almost at random, for when once the blacks had got amongst the trees it became almost impossible to get a fair aim at them.

Big as he was, Ned had also managed to get very fair cover for his carcase, and the sawyers, all pretty well broken to such fighting, were equally lucky.

The sailors, however, were unused to bush work, and four of them were lying wounded, though not mortally, and there was a prospect of using up all their ammunition.

"We had better get back to the boat," suggested the mate of the schooner, but this was found to be no easy matter.

The ground was more open nearer shore, and, as Ned's party began to attempt a retreat, they were exposed to the fire of the blacks.

One of the sawyers dropped with a spear in the thigh, and the mate of the schooner had the top of his ear cut off.

The whites retreated back to their cover again.

"All we can do is to keep close under shelter, pop away, and take care of the wounded," said the sawyer.

"It'll never do; our powder will give out in time, and then they will rush us. We must get to the boat."

They were preparing to move down in a body at all risks, when a thought occurred to Ned.

He communicated it to the others.

It was that he should slip down to the six men left in the boat, and get them to land and fire a volley.

Under cover of this the retreat could be effected.

It was agreed to, and, with some difficulty, Ned managed to crawl down unobserved to the water's edge, and to signal the boat.

Alarmed at this, and thinking that the captain's party, which had first surprised their camp, had come round to the help of the others, the blacks took to their heels, and retreated towards the middle of the island.

There was no time to be lost, so the whites picked up their wounded and hurried at once to the boat.

Just as they had got afloat the blacks made a final charge, dashing into the shallow water and hurling a cloud of spears, several of which got home, for the men were too closely packed in the boat to be able to dodge them.

But their own black bodies standing out above the shining stream also afforded capital marks, and a succession of shots from the boat dropped several of them into the water to rise no more.

The boat was pulled down stream after this parting salute, and the blacks could be distinguished crossing in a body from the island which had witnessed this scene of slaughter, to the mainland.

"I reckon a few of the devils have stopped behind for the night," observed one of the sawyers grimly.

Such indeed was the case, and from that day forward the natives have shunned a spot so fatal to their race.

Just as Ned and his companions reached the end of the island they met the other boat.

It had been arranged that, after starting up and scaring the blacks, the captain and his party should wait a bit on their side of the island, in case the natives sought to escape on that side, and then pull round to Ned's party.

"We'd have been here before," said the captain, in explanation of the delay, "only we'd got a prisoner."

"A prisoner? What did you want with a prisoner?" said the mate.

It was a black who had had his kneecap broken at the first shot, who was lying, tied neck and heels, at the bottom of the boat.

By his side, looking at him with a look of bitter exultation, never suffering his glance to stray for a moment from his face, was Jem Holt.

As to the prisoner's identification, it was easy enough to all who had once seen his gigantic figure.

It was Cobawn Jack.

The next morning, at the request of Holt, the prisoner was left in his hands, and, with the exception of himself and Kelly, the rest of the party separated.

The exact fate of Cobawn Jack is a mystery which will never be fully solved.

Change of air occurred to Ned as being again advisable.

A report of the atrocity in which he had been engaged might, he thought, possibly reach the ears of someone in authority, and lead to an investigation and to his ultimate identification.

In reality he need not have been alarmed.

The authorities in Northern Australia take very good care to close their ears when any such reports are flying about.

The black question, in any shape or form, they utterly abominate; and they would be only too glad to hear of the utter extinction of the troublous race.

The schooner was still at the mouth of the river, and he resolved to offer his services to the captain.

As the skipper was very short-handed, Ned's proposal was readily agreed to by him.

After touching at a number of places she worked her way, by coasting via Torres Strait, down to Brisbane, and here Ned abandoned her.

He resolved to make his way from here over-land to the neighbourhood of Melbourne, and recommence his old career in the south.

He had heard of a capital haunt in the neighbourhood of the head of the King River.

He had entered the territory of Victoria, and all went well till one afternoon, when, after traversing an undulating and somewhat sparsely inhabited tract, he resolved to halt and camp for the night.

Although if he had chosen to push on, he might have obtained shelter either at an inn or a station, he had avoided doing so, and also shunned the more beaten tracks as much as possible.

He had hobbled his horse, lit a fire, and prepared to make himself comfortable for the evening, when he observed two horsemen coming in his direction.

A glance at them showed him that they were both armed, but in ordinary civilian costume.

"As long as they're not any of those cursed traps, I don't care who they are," thought he, but at the same time he felt it just as well to be cautious, and placed his gun convenient to his hand.

The two men rode straight up to him, and the bigger of the pair, a tall, red-headed fellow, ranged his horse alongside him, and began, with a hand at his holster:

"Hullo mate! I'll trouble you——"

Before he could get any further Kelly was on his feet, and had covered him with his gun exclaiming:

"Trouble me for what, you lubber? by —— if you move your fist an inch nearer your holster I'll drop you out of the saddle before you can wink an eyelash."

The fellow stared at him in a somewhat bewildered way.

Kelly kept his eye on him and also on his mate who was gazing at the bushranger in something the same fashion.

"I'm hanged," ejaculated the latter, a swarthy, ill-looking ruffian, "but it's Ned Kelly."

Ned recognised this man directly he had spoken.

He had been a member of his old gang.

"Hullo Briggs!" he exclaimed in turn, "what the devil are you cruising about here for?"

"The old lay, boss;" replied Briggs, "we're just doing a bit of toll collecting in these parts. We thought you were a stranger hereaway, and were going to make you take out a travelling license."

"Catch a weasel asleep," grinned Ned

"Just so. But what brings you out here, squattin' under a tree, for all the world like a blessed mushroom a springin' up, or like the pannakin in the wilderness that Holy Joe, the devil dodger, used to sport about in Pentridge jail on a Sunday?"

"Pelikin, not pannakin, you fool," growled his mate, who had remained all the while like a statue without daring to move a finger covered as he was by Ned's gun.

"Oh! it's all the same This here is a pal, Tom Spurrell, boss. I don't think he knows you, but you'll get on well enough. But what have you been a doing of all these long months?"

Ned after telling Spurrell that he was welcome, and requesting the two men to join him in his evening meal gave a brief account of his adventures, which were loudly applauded.

"S'elp me, but you are a stunner, and no mistake," cried Briggs. "There ain't a man like you in shoe leather. If you're goin' to start the old game I'm with you, and so is Spurrell here."

"Yes," said Spurrell, somewhat sulkily.

Kelly told them his ideas, which were to get the old band together again.

In course of the evening the two men found themselves alone for a few minutes, and Spurrell said to his companion:

"Look here, Briggs; I suppose when a good chance does come in your way you're not such a fool as to let it slip, are you?"

"Not me, I reckon, but what are you driving at?"

"You wouldn't mind a little risk for the sake of picking up five thousand pounds to your own cheek, eh?"

"Rather think not."

"Well, if you'd only have been of that mind an hour ago, and had had your pistol handy, you might have earned it."

"How?"

"How? Why, isn't there a reward of ten thousand pounds for Ned Kelly, and couldn't we have gone snacks?"

Briggs was somewhat staggered at this.

He had served under Kelly, and had yielded to that peculiar and marked influence which the bushranger exerted over all whom he was brought in contact with, that moral as well as physical ascendency which stamped him, all illiterate as he was, as a born leader of men.

Spurrell, who only knew Ned by reputation, had not had time to fall under such influence.

"Look here," he went on, "here's a chance we shall never get again, if Kelly's going to get a gang together. It's now or never. Five thousand quid and a free pardon, or say a year's knocking about, with such scraps as we can pick up, seasoned with Kelly's bullying, and death in your shoes at the end of it."

Briggs was rather staggered by these arguments.

Still he had an awe of Kelly.

"It's all very well to talk about, but you don't seem to think what a job it'll be," he said.

"Ain't we two to one?"

"Yes; but you don't know what sort of a customer you've got to tackle. I'd sooner take hold of a five-year-old bull than grip Ned Kelly when his monkey's up. Why he'd catch hold of us and bash our heads together like a couple of cokernuts."

"Couldn't we serve him as Mike Howe, the Van Dieman's Land bushranger, was served by his two pals?" suggested Spurrell.

"How was that?"

"Why, they got him to stoop down and blow the fire up with his mouth, and then the pair of 'em jumped on his back and tied him up."

"Yes; but with Kelly you'd first of all have to kid him into blowing the fire up, which wouldn't be so blessed easy as you may think for, and in the second, if you jumped on his back, you'd get a hoist that would send you as high as the top of that gum tree before you could say knife."

"Well, then, knife let it be. Let's stick a knife into him."

"No, that'll never do. If we did, the blessed traps would swear we found him dead in the bush from their shots, in order to do us out of the reward. If we want the cash and the free pardon, we must take him in and hand him over alive."

The temptation had staggered Briggs, and he was now quite willing to enter into a scheme for Kelly's capture.

"We shan't have far to go for the traps, if once we get him," he observed.

This was true, for the two men were themselves being pursued by the police, and knew where to find these latter.

In a few more words they briefly matured their plan.

Ned returned to the camp a minute or so later.

He had no particular suspicion of Briggs or his companion, but habit had rendered him cautious in such company.

He kept his gun beside him, and his revolver ready to his hand.

The two traitors began to think their plan would not be such an easy one, after all, to carry out.

It was agreed that they should watch in turns through the night.

Briggs and Spurrell thought that there might be a chance of surprising Ned in his sleep, but he lay with his hand on the stock of his revolver, and when one of them, whose watch it was, accidentally approached him, started up in a way which showed he slept with one eye open.

Next morning they gathered round the fire.

Spurrell brought up some wood to feed it.

He threw on two or three boughs, and then laid hold of one about four feet long and as thick as a man's wrist.

He raised it, but, instead of pitching it into the fire, brought it down, with the swiftness of a crack-stick player, smack on to the top of Ned's head.

The blow was a tremendous one.

It would have cracked the skull of nine men out of ten like an egg-shell.

But Ned's skull was almost as thick as a bull's, and was almost as hard to damage, as though he had his iron helmet on.

The blow, too, was deadened by the thick felt of hair with which his nut was thatched, and by his hat.

It was hard enough, however, to make him imagine that a procession of thirty-six thousand lighted candles was passing before his eyes, and to knock him backwards in a semi-stunned condition.

Simultaneously with the blow, Briggs gave the bushranger's gun, which was lying beside him, a lift with his foot that sent it flying ten paces off, and, at the same time, slipped a noose, he had in readiness, round his arms.

Spurrell dealt him a second blow with the stick that stunned him, and, after snatching Ned's revolver from his breast, joined Briggs in the task of securing him.

Before this was entirely completed, Ned partially recovered.

But Spurrell held his own revolver within a foot of his head.

"Now, just see here, Kelly," he said, "we're playing life and death, and I hold the ace of trumps here in my fist. It's no time for joking. If you make a single move to wriggle loose, by the Eternal, I'll manure this strip of turf with your brains."

Ned was too stunned to make much resistance, either mentally or physically, and Briggs rapidly finished securing him.

He roped him as strongly with the horse hobbles, and tethered his limbs as though he had been a young elephant.

He had too often seen the bushranger exert his Herculean strength not to use every precaution.

Ned, when the pinioning was completed, rose to his feet.

His senses had returned to him.

He glared at his captors with the blood-shot eye of an enraged tiger.

His face became almost black as the blood rushed to his head from the excess of passion; his eyes glowed like live coals, his brows met, and his nostrils dilated.

The corded muscles on his massy limbs writhed and swelled like serpents, and as he stood there in his might, like the bound Samson before the Philistines, it seemed as though he had but to make an effort to break his bonds, "as a thread of tow is broken when it toucheth fire," like the Hebrew champion ere his locks were shorn.

Spurrell read this danger.

"I swear to ——," he said, "if you loosen a single knot it'll be a dead man the rest will be tied round. It's our life or yours, and we can't throw a chance away."

"You mean, canting, white-livered, treacherous skunk!" said Ned, "what's your game? What d'ye want to do with me now you've tied me up like a wool-bale?"

"Well, we're going to hand you over to the traps, and I reckon they'll cart you off slick to Melbourne."

Melbourne.

The word fell on Kelly's ear as one of hope.

It was a good distance to the capital of Victoria, and, for aught he knew, a dozen opportunities of escape might turn up on the road.

"You're a cursed set of hounds to try this game on! A nice pal you've got hold of, Briggs."

"Well, you see," said Briggs, apologetically, "the traps were getting precious inquisitive after us, and we ran a devilish close chance of being nabbed. And when it was a question of that or of earning five thousand quid, a free pardon, and what the blessed newspapers call the gratitude of the entire community, why we couldn't resist it."

Ned was not only bound, but, as an additional precaution, was made to walk on foot between the other two, who were mounted, with a rope from each side secured to his captors' saddles.

Such was the awe with which he inspired them, even in his bound condition, that they rode revolver in hand, and warned him that at the faintest sign of an attempt at escape they would shoot him down without mercy.

The almost miraculous escape of Mike Howe was fresh in their minds.

After his capture, as related, this miscreant was marched off strongly bound, one of his captors going in front of him and the other behind.

Both were armed with loaded muskets.

Suddenly Howe, by a miraculous effort of strength, snapped his bonds like pack-thread, faced the man in his rear, disabled him by a kick in the stomach, sprang on the foe in front, tore away his knife and musket, stabbed him to death, and then fired at, and mortally wounded, his companion.

Briggs and Spurrell were determined to allow no such tricks to be played upon them by Kelly.

Towards noon they arrived in sight of a station, to which they conducted Ned.

To their great satisfaction, some of the police engaged in their own pursuit were at hand.

Kelly was promptly given over into their care.

The sergeant in command replaced some of the bonds by handcuffs, and somewhat slackened the others, besides allowing him a horse.

His party was strong enough to admit of this.

It was, of course, settled that Spurrell and Briggs should accompany the party to Melbourne.

Ned's eye never quitted the traitors.

On the second day, when they were about to start, he managed to edge up within reach of them.

All of a sudden he shot out one leg with the speed and viciousness of a kicking horse.

The iron-bound toe of his heavy riding-boot alighted just where he meant it to—on the tip of Spurrell's knee.

With a yell of agony the traitor sank to the ground.

His knee-cap was smashed, and he was lamed for life.

"You'll have to limp to blazes now!" roared Ned, darting forward at Briggs.

His hands were bound, but he dashed the top of his cast-iron-like head full in the man's face, smashing his nose and sending half his teeth down his throat.

It was a trick like this, in the days when butting was allowed in the ring, that alone won young Dutch Sam his fight with Tom Gaynor.

Briggs was picked up insensible, and fearfully disfigured.

This manœuvre caused the sergeant to keep a closer look out on Ned than he would perhaps otherwise have done, and hence he had no chance of escape on the road.

But the bushranger kept up his spirits, counting on finding friends in Melbourne.

CHAPTER CCXIX.
NED ESCAPES FROM MELBOURNE JAIL.

THE news of Kelly's capture spread like wildfire through the colonies. His daily progress towards the capital was duly telegraphed to the papers. The liveliest interest in his movements was evinced by all parties, especially by the Government he had baffled and bamboozled so often.

He felt almost proud of the notice he attracted. All great, that is, notorious criminals, luxuriate in the infamous *eclat* they produce.

Kelly was the object *en route* of almost ovations from the lower classes. His air was jaunty, and he had that "don't care a button" demeanour, which was remarkable in the launching into eternity of the convict criminals during the reign of convictism in Van Dieman's Land.

Many of these wretches, at the last moment, kicked off their shoes and danced. It was a dance of death that never entered Holbein's brain when he painted his celebrated picture under that title.

The mob threw themselves in his path as he approached his goal. He was a celebrity; that made him with them a god. A bad eminence excites as much attention as a good one.

Many were the cries from the sympathising crowd to "keep up his pecker," &c.

Thousands would have walked miles to see Lefroy who would not cross the street to look at the saintly Earl of Shaftesbury.

Besides, there were plenty in the colony who looked upon Kelly rather as a hero than what he was—namely, a villain.

Brute courage will always have its worshippers amongst the English race, and no heroes are so popular as those who display it.

Two powerfully-built fellows, dressed as diggers, made themselves conspicuous by pushing their way roughly through the crowd until they got quite close to the front.

They did not, however, seem to be very ardent admirers of Ned.

On the contrary, one of them shook his fist at the captive bushranger and roared out—

"Ah! you black-muzzled bandicoot, so they'd laid you by the heels at last. If they'd only have done it a bit earlier, I'd have been a few ounces the better off in this world."

Ned recognised the voice.

It was that of Zeph.

He glanced at the speaker, whose disguise was so perfect that but for his voice he would have been unable to penetrate it, and then at his companion, who roared out in turn—

"Yes, the greedy sarpint. You won't get another chance of plundering honest diggers again in a hurry. As old Mother Flannigan in Hell-street said to me last night, Old Nick'll have a partner before the month's out."

This time Ned recognised Salmon Roe.

He knew, of course, that all this abuse merely meant

that they were on the alert to help him, and guessed that Salmon Roe's mention of Mother Flannigan meant that they could be communicated with through her.

He was careful, however, not to exchange the slightest sign of recognition with the pair of ruffians, who, after blackguarding him a little longer, fell back amongst the crowd and related to whoever chose to listen to them, how they had been stuck up "and eased of a considerable amount of gold dust by Ned" some months before.

"Well," he thought, ' I've got friends outside the jail, at all events. This child don't mean to dance on nothing this time."

On arriving at the jail there was a regular assemblage to meet the modern Dick Turpin. Curiosity was abroad, and no tickets on a Patti night at the opera could have commanded a higher price than a "pass" to see Kelly had they been obtainable for money.

Every old lag in the colony—and Van Dieman's Land had emptied her jail birds into the colony—trooped to the jail as Ned approached and gave him a regular reception.

Amongst those who regarded the Herculean ruffian with more than ordinary interest was a young girl. In coolly scanning the crowd, Kelly's glance fell on the girl; he started nervously, and looked at her in a marked and meaning manner.

The girl almost screamed, then trembled, and a flush rose to her face.

Ned had recognised Bella as the daughter of the head jailer at Melbourne, and who had returned from her visit to the north.

She too had recognised in the person of Ned Kelly, the bushranger, the so-called Tom Smith, who had preserved her life and honour from the blacks.

Ned felt still more pleased at recognising her than at his meeting with Salmon Roe and Zeph.

"She ought to prove a friend at court at all events," he thought, and it was with a somewhat jubilant feeling that he crossed the threshold of the prison.

But when the massive door of his cell had clanged to behind him, and he was left in solitude and silence, matters did not wear quite such a rosy hue to his imagination.

He seated himself on the edge of his bed and began to rack his brains as to the best means of opening up a communication with his friends outside.

He knew that his former escape from Sydney would lead to his being closely watched, and that unless he had an ally within the jail as well, he would not have much chance of giving his captors leg bail.

Meanwhile Bella Bolton was in a far more agitated condition than Ned himself.

She had recognised in him the man who had rescued her from captivity amongst the blacks.

Ned's courage and consideration, as displayed on that occasion, had greatly impressed her.

He was not the man to inspire love in the heart of a cultivated woman, but nevertheless there was much that was essentially fascinating to a girl in his reckless daring.

She felt she ought not to rest while the man to whom she owed so much was languishing as a captive.

Ned was aroused from his reverie by the appearance of one of the warders.

He looked hard at the man, but could not remember ever having set eyes on him before.

On the fellow opening his mouth, however, he at once detected, from his brogue, that he was an Irishman.

An idea struck Ned.

He made the Fenian sign.

To his great satisfaction, it was at once answered.

The man was one of the brotherhood.

There was nothing astonishing in this.

In Ireland itself the bulk of the staff of some of Her Majesty's jails were Fenians.

The escape of Head Centre Stephens, who walked out of Richmond Bridewell, Dublin, as he would have walked out of his own house, is a proof of this.

A similar state of things prevailed in the Antipodes.

In April, 1876, it will be remembered the whole of the Fenian convicts in Western Australia were able to effect their escape in a vessel specially chartered by their brethren in America, thanks to the concurrence of some of those appointed to look after them.

Neither will the attempted assassination of the Duke of Edinburgh in Australia be forgotten, though it is maintained by many that private vengeance for a wrong of personal character, and not Fenianism, was the motive that prompted this deed.

The story they tell is a curious one, and some day may be printed at full length.

If Ned had been a headcentre, or any similar great gun, he would simply have ordered the man to arrange his escape when he saw his sign responded to.

But he thought he could not go quite so far as that, and merely asked him if he could bring about an interview with Bella Bolton.

Ned would have written to the girl had he been able; but, as it was, he had to content himself with a verbal request for an interview.

The warder was somewhat puzzled, but consented to carry Ned's communication without much demur.

The next day, Bella, by the connivance of the warder, paid a visit to Ned unobserved.

The interview was necessarily a brief one.

Miss Bolton could not help feeling greatly moved at Ned's unpleasant situation.

"I will tell my father all I owe to you," she said, "and I feel sure he will do everything in his power to render your position tolerable. He would do a great deal, I am sure, for the man but for whose courage he would never have set eyes on his daughter again."

"Begging your pardon, miss," said Ned, who had already framed some notions of a plan of escape, "but I'd rather your father didn't show me any too much outward kindness. If, though, he could just manage to shut those eyes you spoke of for about half-an-hour or so when the time comes, it would help me more than a little bit."

"I can hardly pledge him to that," said the girl, "but I will do my best."

Ned briefly instructed her how to enter into communication with Zeph and Salmon, and this duty she willingly undertook.

Several days elapsed, and, thanks to the system of communication established through Bella and the warder, Ned was kept fully acquainted with all the measures in progress for his escape.

Still, as time slipped on, and the hour for him to make his appearance in court drew near, he could not help feeling a little anxious, though he did not lose his trust in his friends.

He was quite the lion of the hour, and would have had as many visitors as Jack Sheppard had in Newgate, had it been allowed.

At length the assizes commenced.

The calendar was a very heavy one, and Ned's name was somewhat low down on the list.

Mr. Bolton, the head jailor, and his second in command—a somewhat scatterbrained young fellow, named Hammond, whose chief characteristic was a habit of falling in love with one pretty girl after another, and who, at this moment, was a helpless captive to the charms of Bella, held a brief consultation overnight.

"It's pretty nearly certain," said the former, "that Kelly's trial won't come on till the day after to-morrow, for there are ten cases to be settled first. I'll go down with those ten to court and leave you to keep a watch over our iron-clad friend,"

"All right, sir."

"Of course, if the trials are got over quicker than we think for, I'll send down to you to bring him along."

Bella was present at this interview.

She saw a splendid chance of carrying out the plan that had already been partially agreed on, and at once sent a note containing full particulars, and also another document, of which more hereafter, to Zeph and Salmon Roe.

The next morning Mr. Bolton marched off with the ten prisoners whose names were first on the list, for trial to the court house.

Hammond, feeling his responsibility as regarded Ned, passed most of the day in the lodge of the prison-gate.

Shortly before half-past three o'clock, Bella came that way, equipped for a walk.

He gallantly came forward to see her let out, and began to talk to her.

Contrary to her custom, instead of snubbing him she became very amiable; and, consequently, he fell in the seventh heaven of delight.

While they were so engaged, a squad of four of the fort police marched up to the door of the jail.

Their leader saluted Hammond, and handed him a letter.

It ran as follows—

"DEAR HAMMOND,—Send Kelly along at once, under the escort of bearer. No evidence was offered by the prosecution in two of the cases I took up this morning, and the other fellow pleaded guilty; so it is settled they will take on Kelly's case, and open pleadings at once.—Yours truly,
"PETER BOLTON."

Hammond glanced over the document.

It was, he had no doubt, in Mr. Bolton's handwriting.

He at once gave an order for Kelly to be brought from his cell, and handed over to the policemen.

"I suppose you four will be enough to take care of him?" he said.

"Oh, yes, sir," observed the leader. "We're to take him up in a cab, Mr. Bolton says. Nobody thinks that his trial's coming on to-day, and there's not many people about."

"Very good."

One of the policemen had been sent for the cab, and by the time he returned with it, Kelly had been brought to the lodge.

He was handed over to the custody of the police, three of whom got into the vehicle with him, whilst the fourth mounted the box by the side of the driver.

Just as they were going to drive off, Hammond, who did not seem quite at ease in his mind, made a motion for them to stop.

He was about to put some questions to them.

But Bella Bolton began to chatter to him, and in answering her, he quite lost sight of what he had been going to say, and just waved to the cab to continue on its way.

It drove off, and was lost to sight round a corner.

Miss Bolton, after a little more conversation, during which she expressed her regret that duty hindered Mr. Hammond from accompanying her on her walk, also left the prison.

Left alone, Hammond lounged about the place.

He had pulled out Bolton's letter, and was reading it for the second time, when the head jailor returned with several of the prisoners he had taken away in the morning.

Hammond glanced over the ranks.

"Hullo!" he said. "Where have you left Kelly?"

"Kelly?" repeated Bolton. "Why, you must be wool-gathering. I left him with you this morning. A nice fellow you are to leave in charge of a jail, when you forget all about the most important prisoner in it."

"Don't humbug," said Hammond, nervously; "you know you sent for him."

"Sent for him! Why, what the deuce do you mean?"

"Why, this," replied Hammond.

As he spoke he held out Bolton's letter.

The head jailer took it and glanced at it.

As he did so he became white as a sheet.

"Great heavens!" he gasped, "I never wrote that."

"What!" yelled Hammond.

"I never wrote that. It—it's a forgery."

"I could have sworn it was your handwriting."

"It is awfully like it. And do you mean to say you have given up Kelly?"

"Yes, to an escort of four policemen who brought your note."

"Four policemen? Four bushranging devils in disguise."

"That was the only thing that made me at all suspicious. I did not recognise any of their faces as belonging to the force, and thought they were hardly well set up. But it was your handwriting clenched the matter, or I should have questioned them."

He omitted to mention how much his attention had been taken up by Bella.

That young lady shortly afterwards returned, and expressed the utmost amazement at what had taken place.

She, of course, carefully avoided mentioning the fact that the letter by which Ned's release had been obtained had been forged by her.

Nor did her father even suspect this; or, if he did, he kept his suspicions to himself, no blame attaching to him in the matter.

CHAPTER CCXX.

NED GIVES A POLICEMAN A LESSON IN SURGERY.

IT is hardly necessary to state that the supposed police escort consisted of Zeph, Salmon Roe, and a couple more of Ned's friends, and that the cab-driver was also a confederate.

As soon as they were out of sight of the prison the policeman on the box jumped down and hurried away.

There was nothing left to attract attention to the cab, those inside it sitting well back with the windows up, so that their uniforms might not be seen.

After sundry twistings and turnings it stopped at the door of a small house in the suburbs.

The four men alighted and hurried into this.

Fresh disguises were hastily assumed, and they then left the house one by one, a rendezvous having been previously arranged.

This rendezvous was at a lonely hut situate at a spot known as Eleven Mile Creek, between Winton and Greta.

It was tenanted by a young fellow a namesake of Ned's named Dan Kelly, and by two old women, named Wright and Mulligan, and bore by no means a good reputation.

Ned was pleased to learn that Marco Polo was in safety, and that Zeph and Salmon Roe had given orders that he should be taken to the projected rendezvous so as to be in readiness for his master.

Ned having been dressed and "made up" with as much care as if he had been a leading tragedian about to step on to the stage, started on his journey, and was clear of Melbourne before Bolton's return to the jail had led to the discovery of his escape.

He travelled for several days without let or hindrance, and the nearer he got to his destination the more at home he began to feel.

Not only was the country a wild and broken one, affording capital cover in case of pursuit, but the sympathies of the populace were decidedly not on the side of law and order.

At several out-of-the-way spots Ned encountered men who recognised him, but whom he found had not the slightest idea of betraying him to the authorities.

It was almost nightfall when he reached the hut on Eleven Mile Creek that had been appointed for the rendezvous.

It was a dilapidated-looking erection of timber, serving as a kind of sly grog-shop and meeting place for horse and cattle stealers.

Kelly approached it with great caution.

He dismounted on reaching the shed serving as a stable, and looked in.

To his astonishment he saw a horse which, from its accoutrements, he at once guessed to be that of a trooper of the mounted police.

Taking his revolver in one hand, and retaining a hold on the reins with the other, he crept to a window giving him a view of the interior of the hut.

The table was spread for supper, and at it were seated four persons, the women Wright and Mulligan, Dan Kelly, and a trooper of the mounted police.

For a moment the ruffian thought that he was betrayed, and that this was a plot to ensnare him.

He debated for a moment whether he should not fire through the window and shoot down the whole party, and then ride away.

When an Irishman is bloodthirsty, he's a human tiger.

He resolved to wait, and a few scraps of conversation convinced him of his error.

The facts were that the constable, whose name was Fitzpatrick, had ridden over that afternoon from Bennala with a warrant for the arrest of Dan Kelly.

He had made his appearance so suddenly, that the latter, who was unarmed, was compelled to surrender, and had the handcuffs put on him.

Instead of riding away at once with his prisoner, Fitzpatrick, who was a good-hearted, jovial fellow, consented to stop and have some supper, to which the others invited him.

Their object was of course to gain time for the arrival of friends, or to make Fitzpatrick drunk.

The latter sat opposite his prisoner with his revolver handy for use.

He kept a keen eye on Dan, and was surprised to see his face suddenly assume a jubilant look.

The truth was that Dan had just caught sight of Ned's well-known face at the window behind Fitzpatrick.

Fitzpatrick's suspicions were aroused, and the noise made by Ned, who proceeded to open the window, confirmed him in the idea that something was up.

He seized his revolver and faced round.

As he did so Ned fired at him point blank.

The suddenness of Fitzpatrick's movement saved his life, for Ned's bullet, instead of entering his body, struck him in the right arm, causing him to drop his revolver.

One of the women snatched this up and flung it into a corner of the hut, and the two then threw themselves on to the unfortunate policeman and bore him to the ground.

So closely were they mixed up that Ned dared not fire again but entered the hut.

At the sight of his levelled pistol Fitzpatrick offered to surrender.

Dan was freed at once from the handcuffs.

A sudden notion struck Ned.

The trooper had not recognised him as Ned Kelly, and if he at any future time turned the tables on him, could only charge him with shooting at himself. The proceedings of Kelly to frustrate future evidence against him, as far as the production of the bullet was concerned, are historical and well known in the colony. He simply compelled the unfortunate trooper to cut out the bullet from the wound (fortunately it was not very intricately buried in the muscles) and hand to him.

Kelly grinned at the pain and humiliation inflicted on the constable, saying as he removed the lead—

"No fitting this to the barrel to prove I used it."

The woman pitied the poor wretch, and gave him some brandy, bound up his arm, and helped him to mount his horse.

The man was only too glad to escape with his life.

No sooner had he left than the sound of horses' hoofs were heard.

Kelly sprung to the door.

"He's bringing back the traps," he yelled.

However, a brief examination proved to him that the newcomers were in reality friends.

To his delight, Zeph and Salmon Roe, under the names of Byrne and Hart, made their appearance.

Kelly related with great glee the surgical operation performed on the constable, at which Zeph grinned grimly, saying—

"You didn't perform the operation as I'd have done. It would have been much safer when you had him to have kept him. He'll bring the traps on you."

"By jingo! you're right. But, you see, I was on the bolt myself, and did intend to wait for them. However let's stop his gallop."

The three mounted and started off at a break-neck pace towards Bennala on the trail of Fitzpatrick.

The poor fellow had been riding slowly on account of his wounds, but was roused when he heard the noise of his pursuers, who, feeling sure of their prey, came tearing along at the top of their speed, yelling like demons.

Fitzpatrick put spurs to his horse and rode for his life.

He guessed the bloodhounds were on his track.

Fortunately for him his horse was fresher than those of his pursuers, and had had a good rest in the inn shed.

Once, nevertheless, they got near enough to fire at him, though without effect.

This, however, was a final effort, and they had to give over the chase, for their animals were fairly distanced.

CHAPTER CCXXI.
THE STRINGYBARK CREEK ENCOUNTER.

[The rest of this eventful history is taken from the Colonial press. Our Melbourne contributor has, in the foregoing, supplied us with Kelly's history up to the time his deeds became public records.—ED.]

On Fitzpatrick reaching Bennala, and stating what had happened, the authorities had no difficulty in guessing that the perpetrator of the outrage had been no other than Kelly.

The entire police force of the district began to scour the country.

It was known he had taken up his quarters somewhere near the head waters of the King River, where the ground, cut up into numerous deep and narrow gullies, and covered with luxuriously growing vegetation, afforded splendid cover.

At the close of September 1878, a party of four policemen, who were in quest of him, pitched their camp at a lonely spot known as Stringybark Gully, about twenty miles from Manfield.

They comprised a sergeant, named Kennedy, and three constables, named Scanlan, Lonigan, and M'Intyre.

They had a shrewd idea that Ned and his gang were hovering somewhere in the vicinity, but they had the greatest difficulty in obtaining the least information as to his movements.

Numerous sympathisers kept him fully posted in every movement of the police.

The men boasted of doing so at drinking bars and other gatherings.

The movements of the little party of police, already spoken of, were well known to Kelly.

He was under the impression that they included two men, named Steel and Flood, against whom he had registered a vow of vengeance, and full of this idea, resolved to pay them a visit, and, in his own words, to "wipe the lot out."

The police had a tent with them, and had pitched it near the creek, between the ruins of two deserted huts, in a spot where the reeds and long grass grew thick and tall.

On the morning of September 25th, Kennedy and Scanlan left the camp, and went scouting across the ranges.

M'Intyre and Lonigan remained in camp, and in the course of the morning, the former fired at some parrots.

The sound of the shots reached the ears of the bushrangers, who were already stealing on their prey.

"I reckon that's the last shot some of those beggars 'll fire," observed Ned.

The two policemen left in camp were quite unsuspicious of any danger.

M'Intyre, who had left his revolvers in the hut was

sitting on a log, whilst Lonigan was standing at a short distance from him.

All at once there was a slight rustling in the dry reeds near them.

The two policemen turned their heads.

The bushrangers, gliding like serpents through the grass, had crawled up on their hands and knees, till they had gained the camp.

Springing as one man to their feet, at the first movement of the police, they levelled their guns at them, and called upon them to surrender.

"Bail up, or we'll let daylight through you," roared Ned.

At the sight of the four outlaws rising from the ground, like pantomime demons from a trap, the police were for a moment paralysed.

M'Intyre, who was unarmed, felt that the situation was helpless, and threw up his hands at once.

His companion, however, was a brave fellow.

He drew his revolver and darted towards a tree for shelter.

He was not quick enough.

Ere he could gain the tree, Kelly, who had covered him from the commencement, glanced along the barrel of the Spencer rifle with which he was armed, and pulled the trigger.

As the echoes of the shot died away, Lonigan was seen to throw up his arms and pitch heavily forward on his face.

"Who are the other two with you?" enquired Ned.

M'Intyre hesitated to answer.

"It's no good playing any tomfoolery with me," said Ned, holding the muzzle of his rifle within an inch of his prisoner's head." "I know there are two more of you who left camp this morning, who are they? Give me an an answer or I'll drop you."

"Kennedy and Scanlan," replied M'Intyre, who saw it was no use hesitating as his life was at Kelly's mercy.

"I was hoping it was Flood and Steel," observed Ned.

M'Intyre shuddered at a threat that was uttered by Ned.

Burning alive was an atrocity not unknown in bush-ranging annals.

Two well-known Tasmanian outlaws had once captured a bullock from a run and had just slain and skinned it, when they were surprised by the owner.

Without a moment's hesitation they seized him, rolled him up in the yet reeking hide of the slain animal, and threw him into the large fire they had kindled to cook their plunder at.

The hide contracting with the heat held the unhappy wretch as in a vice, till he was roasted alive.

One of the pair confessed this atrocity when under sentence of death for other crimes.

Ned's rage against Flood and Steel was based on a perfectly legitimate feeling.

His sister Kate had shortly before left Sydney, and was residing in the Mansfield district.

The two policemen in question had ridden up to her house one day, and under pretext of searching for a clue as to Ned's whereabouts, had not only ransacked the place but had grossly insulted and ill-used her.

Kelly's intention was to cut off the whole four policemen, and thus strike terror into all future pursuers. Only that he subsequently confessed as much, such silly atrocity would be incredible.

Under his direction the party set to work to arrange what was destined to be a death trap for the unfortunate sergeant and his comrade.

The body of Lonigan was removed from the spot where it had fallen, and concealed in the tent, where Ned also retreated.

The other three bushrangers retired into the long grass.

M'Intyre, whom they had kept covered with their rifles all this time, was forced to resume his seat on the log, and warned that if he gave the least warning by word or gesture to his returning comrades, his death would be the immediate penalty.

The hapless constable's feelings as he took his post on the log may be more easily imagined than described.

To sit in feigned unconsciousness that four deadly muzzles were levelled at him, and that twice that number of ferocious eyes were watching his every movement, required no slight effort.

The minutes seemed hours as he sat there

Ned had announced that he intended to bag the whole lot, and M'Intyre, believing this, felt the full horror of the part he had to play.

Some time elapsed, and M'Intyre felt as though he should go mad with suspense.

At last his straining ears caught the clank and jingle of accoutrements and the beat of hoofs.

A few minutes later Kennedy and Scanlan rode up to the front of the tent.

With an effort M'Intyre found his voice.

"Sergeant," he said, "you'd better bail up at once. You're surrounded by bushrangers."

Kennedy hesitated, thinking he was joking.

"Bail up," shouted Kelly from the hut.

Kennedy still thought a joke was intended, and that it was Lonigan who was speaking from the tent.

He merely laughed, and carelessly advanced his hand to his holster.

"For heaven's sake don't resist," cried M'Intyre, who knew the fearfully dangerous position in which his comrade stood.

At the same moment one of the hidden bushrangers, seeing Kennedy's movement, fired at him, but only hit his horse, which he slightly wounded.

Kennedy instantly threw himself from the wounded animal, and jumped behind a tree.

Scanlan, who was armed with a Spencer rifle, also dismounted, and attempted to follow his example, but was shot down before he could reach cover.

Kennedy opened fire in turn from his revolver on Ned, who had stepped out from the tent.

One of his shots actually passed through the fellow's whiskers, and another tore the sleeve of his coat.

Seeing he was in danger of being surrounded, Kennedy made an attempt to gain another tree, in order to effect a gradual retreat.

As he was trying this move, Kelly fired again, the bullet striking him in the side, just as he reached the wished-for cover.

The sting of the bullet caused him to throw up his right hand in token of surrender, an action which Kelly thought was for the purpose of getting another shot at himself.

Accordingly he fired again, and this time with fatal effect, his shot stretching the unfortunate sergeant dead on the ground.

Meanwhile M'Intyre had become alive to the true state of affairs.

He saw that the death of his unfortunate comrades was resolved on, and that he would in all probability share their fate.

Profiting by the confusion, he managed to spring on to Kennedy's horse, which was only slightly wounded, and to gallop off at full speed.

He was pursued by a volley of shots and oaths by the bushrangers.

Riding for his life, he tore along at a breakneck pace, urging his half-maddened animal over ground which the boldest steeplechase rider might have been justified in hesitating to cross in cold blood.

The pursuit was somewhat slack.

The bushrangers had left their horses at some distance, when they stole up to surprise the camp.

Of the animals belonging to the police, that of Scanlan had dashed off, alarmed at the firing, and the other two had been unsaddled.

Hence, by the time these were in readiness, M'Intyre had got a good start.

Dan Kelly and one of the others mounted and rode a short way after him, but abandoned the pursuit on seeing the hazardous line of country taken by M'Intyre.

When they returned to Ned he was greatly enraged at this fact.

"I bowled over two out of these three single-handed. I don't know which of you hit Scanlan, but I mean the whole of us to be tarred with the same brush in this matter. Every man jack of you must put a bullet into each of them.

The others were surprised at this, but thought it as well to comply with Ned's whim.

The arms of the slain men were then collected, and after securing them and some other articles that took their fancy, the bushrangers set the tent on fire and departed.

Meanwhile M'Intyre continued his ride for life.

Before he got much further his horse fell, throwing him heavily.

On recovering from the shock, he found that the animal was on the point of death, and unable to carry him further.

He made his way some distance onward, and in the anticipation of pursuit, concealed himself in a wombat hole.

Finding no signs of the bushrangers being on his track, he stole out again, and at length arrived at a station on the outskirts of Mansfield.

Utterly exhausted by his tramp, he had sunk down insensible amongst some reeds in a patch of swampy ground, when he was discovered by one of the ladies of the station who had ridden out on some errand.

CHAPTER CCXXII.
NED VISITS FAITHFUL CREEK STATION.

THE sensation created when the news of this outrage reached Melbourne was indescribable.

People could scarcely believe it possible that even Kelly would have ventured on such a thing as an unprovoked attack on the police.

Bushranging was not unknown in the colony, but it had been fondly supposed by the authorities that it was becoming as much a thing of the past as the exploits of Robin Hood in Sherwood Forest and Rob Roy in the Highlands.

Since Ned's former exploits, matters had been pretty quiet in Victoria.

Power, the most notorious of his predecessors, had carefully avoided taking human life, and when he was captured in 1870, was only sentenced to fifteen years penal servitude in Pentridge jail, which he is still undergoing.

But here was a man reviving the worst exploits of the bloody and relentless Morgan and the reckless Thunderbolt.

The authorities resolved to spare no pains to capture the daring outlaw, whose exploits were even brought before the Legislature in course of a debate, owing to a letter being put forward as having been written by Ned to one of its members detailing the particulars of the attack on the police at Stringybark Creek, and corroborating some on of M'Intyre's statements.

The entire police force of the colony was despatched in pursuit of Ned, and was supplemented by a number of artillerymen drawn from those in garrison at Melbourne.

The departure of these men resembled that of troops proceeding to the seat of war, and to the encounter of a formidable army rather than a gang of bushrangers.

In a short time no less than two hundred and fifty police and artillerymen were scouring the Strathbogie ranges in which Ned was supposed to be lurking.

Several armed parties of volunteers joined in the pursuit, but the bulk of the inhabitants of the district, many of whom were related to Dan Kelly, displayed far more sympathy with the bushranger than with the authorities.

Kelly received timely warnings of all the movements of his pursuers, and was enabled to baffle them with ease, though fifteen years imprisonment was proclaimed as the penalty of all who sheltered him.

In vain they beat up the head waters of King's River and the Mansfield Range, amidst the dense vegetation of which Ned had been lurking, and in vain they strategetically surrounded a lonely hut on the Wombat Ranges, where it was reported he had been seen.

In every case the bird had flown before their arrival.

They began to suppose that he had worked his way north into New South Wales, going round by the head of the Upper Murray and thence to Gippsland.

All at once news reached them of a fresh outrage.

On the afternoon of the 9th of December, one of the station hands of the Faithful Creek Station, named Fitzgerald, was standing at the door of the homestead, when he observed someone approaching on foot.

The new-comer was a tall, powerfully-built fellow, with a heavy beard.

"Good-day, mate," he began. "Is Mr. Macauley in?"

"No, not just now."

"When d'ye think he'll be back?"

"Well, we expect him in this evening; but if it's anything particular, maybe I could help you?"

"Oh, it don't matter," replied the stranger, turning on his heel.

He walked away for a short distance, and suddenly halted, waving his hand as a signal.

At this, three mounted men, whom Fitzgerald had not noticed, rode up at a swift rate, one of them holding the rein of a led horse.

The first stranger vaulted into this, and rode up to the front door with his companions.

Alighting, he boldly marched into the house, into which Fitzgerald had already retreated in some alarm, chiefly on account of his wife, who was its only other inmate.

"How many men have you got about the place?" demanded the stranger. "You'd better tell the truth, or we'll make it hot for the lot of you."

"There's only myself here now," answered Fitzgerald, "and a young fellow working at the back."

"Well, look here," observed the stranger; "you'll have to bail up. We don't want to hurt you, but we must have some grub, and some feed for our horses."

"But who are you?" gasped Mrs. Fitzgerald.

"Ned Kelly," was the answer; at which the poor woman almost fainted away.

Ned was wise enough in his present position not to meddle with station hands and the like, amongst whom he might pick up plenty of valuable information.

Still, he thought it was as well to take certain precautions.

"You're quite welcome, I'm sure, to grub and horse-feed, as far as I'm concerned," replied Fitzgerald.

"Of course, I knew I should be. But see here now, I think you may just as well wait in that slab hut yonder, while we rest a bit. Your wife shall wait on us, but I promise you she'll not come to any harm."

There was no help for it.

Fitzgerald had to proceed to the slab hut, over which Dan Kelly was posted as a sentry.

Zeph and Salmon Roe went in search of the young fellow he had spoken of, and consigned him to durance vile in his company.

The bushrangers then proceeded to feed their horses, and to partake of refreshments, insisting that Mrs. Fitzgerald should first taste everything put before them.

"I'm not going to be poisoned by you, you old cat, if I can help it," observed Ned, when the poor woman—who was half-choked with terror—showed some reluctance to comply with the request.

"No," echoed Zeph, "we know that trick; so just shove your grinders into a slice of that mutton, lest you've been making a mistake and sprinkling it with arsenic instead of salt, as I've heard has been done."

There was nothing to be done but to comply, and the poor woman, with great difficulty, managed to gulp down a few mouthfuls.

Whilst partaking of their repast, the bushrangers did not neglect to keep a good look-out.

Four of the men employed on the station, who came up to the homestead in the course of the afternoon, were promptly seized on and bundled into the slab hut, to keep company with Fitzgerald and his companion.

"If I catch one of you as much as poking the tip of his nose outside," said Zeph, who had replaced Dan Kelly as sentry, "I'll blow your heads off."

About half-past four the owner of the station, Mr. Macauley, came riding home.

On crossing a bridge leading to the cottages, it struck him that the place presented a somewhat deserted look.

Being under no apprehension of danger, however, he rode on, and drew rein in front of the door.

Fitzgerald appeared at the window of the slab hut.

"Mr. Macauley," he exclaimed, "for the Lord's sake, be careful! The Kellys are here, and if anything goes wrong the lives of the whole lot of us 'll have to pay for it."

At the same moment Ned stepped through the door, and made his appearance on the verandah, revolver in hand.

"You'd best go slow and behave yourself," he said; "it's not the least use kicking up a row."

"But who are you?" said the bewildered overseer.

"Ned Kelly," was the reply, in an undaunted manner.

"Who?" he repeated, for, like almost every one else in the district, he imagined Ned was scores of miles away.

"I'm Ned Kelly; so just get off that horse of yours without any more nonsense."

Macauley complied, and at that moment Dan Kelly, whom he knew by sight, made his appearance, and convinced him as to the hands he had fallen into.

"I don't want to shut you up with the rest, since it'll never do for a boss and his hands to be put on the same footing," said Ned, whose dinner had put him into a good humour, "so Dan can just keep an eye on you."

The overseer was tolerably satisfied with this arrangement.

"I don't want to shoot any one unless I'm forced to, and I only want to use this station as a camping-ground to rest ourselves and our horses," continued Ned.

The overseer was struck with the appearance of their horses, and especially with that of Marco Polo.

"You've got a pretty valuable lot of beasts there," he observed; "and they don't look as if they wanted much feeding either."

"No," replied Ned; "we can always lay our hands on good horses when we want 'em."

After a short interval a cart was seen approaching the station.

It belonged to a hawker named Gloster, who had a place of business at Seymour, and was in the habit of travelling about the district, vending clothes and fancy goods.

He was a pretty frequent visitor to the station, and, in accordance with his usual custom, he drew up his cart and unharnessed his horse within a stone's throw of the homestead.

Leaving a boy who assisted him in charge of his cart, he stepped up to the kitchen to get some hot water for his tea.

Mrs. Fitzpatrick met him there.

"For goodness' sake, be careful," she said; "the Kellys are in the place."

Like Macauley, the man was incredulous, and simply laughed at her.

"It is so, I assure you," she said.

"Nonsense," was the answer. "I ain't a-going to be gammoned in that way."

Mr. Macauley, who was sitting in front of the house, knowing Gloster to be a plucky fellow, grew terribly anxious at his advent.

He felt almost certain that he would show fight, and feared, in this event, that the life of every one in the station would be sacrificed without mercy.

Gloster was about to return to his cart when Ned called out after him—

"Stop."

The hawkers, who thought it part of a joke, paid no attention to this command.

Dan Kelly levelled his gun and was about to fire, but refrained at Macauley's entreaties.

Meanwhile Gloster had gained his cart and mounted it.

Ned, however, had stridden after him, and clapping a revolver to his cheek, ordered him to descend.

"What d'ye mean?" replied the other.

"What do I mean, you infernal fool," cried Ned; "why I mean you to bail up, to be sure."

Still Gloster seemed unable to realise the fact that he was stuck up by bushrangers.

"Who are you, with your airs?" he said sneeringly.

"I'm Ned Kelly."

"Go to blazes, I ain't a-going to swallow that yarn."

"Oh, you ain't. Then it strikes me you'll never wait to swallow anything else in this world."

Ned's finger was on the trigger, and probably in another minute he would have fired, when Mr. Macauley, who had come up, interfered.

"Don't fire, Kelly, for heaven's sake. Gloster, this is Ned Kelly; and the lives of the whole of us are at his mercy."

"I'd like to have met him, Ned Kelly or no Ned Kelly, with one no else to look on," said the undaunted hawker, "I'd have cut his work out for him."

"I'll blow the top of your skull off, and see whether you've got any brains at all inside, if you say another word," shouted Kelly, who was losing all control over his temper.

Again Macauley interposed.

"I've a devilish good mind to put a bullet in him; there's not one man in a hundred would have dared to cheek me in that fashion," grumbled Kelly.

Gloster began to realise his peril, and reluctantly consented to join the other prisoners under Zeph's charge in the hut.

The two Kellys and Salmon Roe proceeded to ransack his cart.

The find was a capital one, the man's stock consisting of clothes.

Each of the four desperadoes in turn selected a complete rig out.

"This is a bully find," said Salmon Roe, strutting about like a peacock.

"Smartens one up a-bit," said Kelly as he inundated his beard and garments with a bottle of scent from the hawker's stock of perfumery.

"It'll be just the thing for our visit to Euroa to-morrow," said Zeph.

"Right you are," said Ned; "why, we look so respectable, I guess the bank clerks won't be able to refuse us anything."

"What are we to do with the old duds?" asked Dan Kelly.

"Oh, leave 'em about," replied Salmon Roe.

"Not a bit of it," broke in Zeph; "we must burn every stitch of 'em right off."

"Why?" enquired Ned.

"So that they may never be used as a means of tracking us. Suppose they were used to give a blood-hound to smell, in order to put him on our trail?"

Their toilettes completed, the bushrangers sat down to supper.

Mr. Macauley had the honour of sharing their meal, but only as a precautionary measure.

As with Mrs. Fitzpatrick, he had to partake of every dish in turn, before they ventured on a mouthful, lest they should be drugged or poisoned.

Ned showed himself in rather a jovial mood at supper.

He conversed freely with Macauley, and related with exultation the manner in which he had surprised the police camp at Stringybark Creek.

"It's not the last job I'll do either," he said. "I'll send a hundred of 'em to kingdom come in a bunch, one fine day."

It was afterwards known that he had referred to a plan he was hatching, for pulling up the sleepers on the railway line.

The gang watched their prisoners turn and turn about throughout the night.

CHAPTER CCXXIII.
HOW NED STUCK UP THE BANK AT EUROA.

THE next morning the bushrangers appeared in high spirits.

They had a risky, but, as they judged, a prosperous day's work before them.

They carefully cleaned their arms and looked to their horses.

The spot at which they found themselves, the homestead of Faithful Creek station, was situate some four miles from Euroa, on the road to Violet Town.

The North Eastern railway from Melbourne ran right past the homestead, so close, in fact, that with a field glass a passenger in the train might be easily recognised.

This fact will serve to show Kelly's audacity in selecting such a spot for a temporary resting-place.

He did not neglect precautions, however; for, at the passage of every train, he compelled his prisoners to keep under cover, lest they should strive to draw attention by means of signals.

It must appear almost incredible that four men should hold possession of a house only four miles from a town and within a stone's throw of a railway-line running direct to the capital of the colony; but, daring as was the act, it was subsequently far outdone.

A number of trains passed during the morning, and amongst them a special one conveying a cricketing eleven to Melbourne, which town was about ninety miles off.

Struck by a sudden idea, Ned ordered Salmon Roe to disconnect the telegraph wires running along the line.

Salmon Roe succeeded in uprooting or beating down several of the telegraph posts, disconnecting the wires, breaking the insulators, and practically cutting off all communication.

Noticing the state of the wires, several of the trains stopped on the way, and in some instances the guard alighted to inspect the damage, which was set down to accident.

It never for one moment crossed the minds of any one that it was the work of the Kellys.

On its being reported at the nearest railway station that the telegraph poles were injured, two navvies were dispatched to repair them.

Whilst engaged in this task, Salmon Roe and Dan Kelly marched down, surprised the men, and made them walk up to the homestead, where they were locked up with the rest of the prisoners.

It may hardly be credited, but by no less than two-and-twenty captives at the

"I reckon we'd better be making a move," said Zeph.

"That's so," replied Ned.

"But what are we to do with all these prisoners?" observed the other. "If we leave 'em here they're bound to get loose, and come running after us into the town."

"That's awkward. They'd rouse the place on us."

A counsel of war was held.

"Suppose we cut all their blessed throats," suggested Ned, half in jest.

"No, that won't do; it'll only rile people. Look here, we're coming back this way. Let one remain to keep guard over 'em, and the rest pick him up as they come back."

Lots were cast for the awkward, if onerous, post of sentry, and the duty fell to Zeph.

He was left single-handed, if well armed, in charge of nearly two dozen people.

Daring as this might be, it pales before the enterprise on which Kelly and the other two set out.

The hawker's cart and a spring cart were brought out and horses put to them.

Ned got into one, Dan Kelly into the other, and Salmon Roe mounted his horse.

On reaching Euroa they separated for a time, and Salmon Roe, riding boldly up to the North-Eastern Hotel, ordered dinner.

At the conclusion of his repast, he sallied out, and rejoined his two companions.

The three made their way to the local branch of the National Bank.

Ned drove up to the front door, and Dan into the backyard, whilst Salmon Roe rode up to the front of an adjacent public-house, and fastened his horse there.

Ned knocked at the door of the bank, which was opened by the accountant, whose name was Bradley.

"What is your business, if you please? he enquired politely.

"I'll just trouble you for the cash for this," replied Ned, pulling out a cheque, bearing the signature of Mr. Macauley, which he had exacted before leaving Faithful Creek from his involuntary host.

(To be continued.)

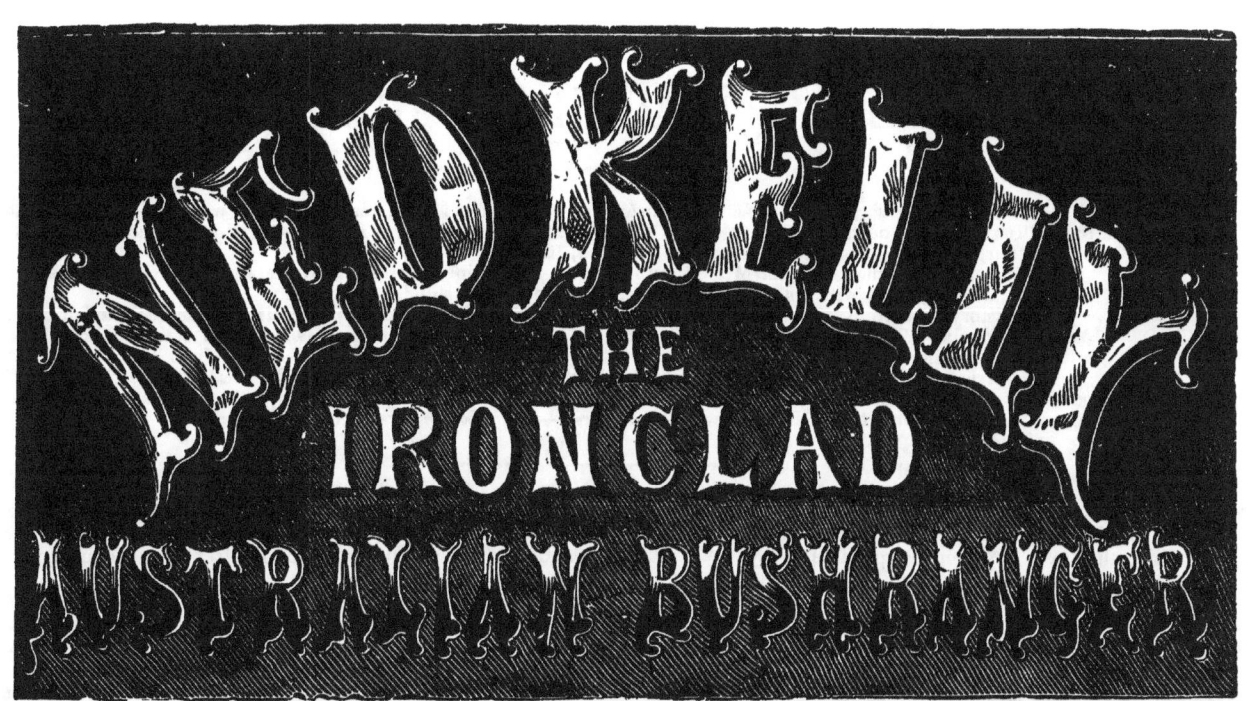

NED KELLY
THE
IRONCLAD
AUSTRALIAN BUSHRANGER

NO 38,

NED KELLY: IRONCLAD BUSHRANGER.

CHAPTER CCXXIII.—*Continued.*

Bradley smiled that bland smile, peculiar to bank clerks when they have anything disagreeable to say.

"It is past banking hours," he said.

"What!" cried Ned, "can't you cash it?"

"It is past four o'clock—the bank has closed for the day."

"Can't I see the manager?"

"Hum! I'm afraid it is no use."

"Oh! you know Mr. Macauley's all right, and I've got to start up country to-night," pleaded Ned, with well-assumed anxiety.

The accountant thought that there might be some truth in this story, little dreaming that Ned had purposely put off his visit until the bank was closed, in order to be secure from interruption from any customer.

"Perhaps you'd better see Mr. Scott," he said.

He ushered Ned into the bank, where the manager and two clerks were engaged in making up the day's accounts, and balancing the books.

"A man who will insist on seeing you about a cheque of Mr. Macauley's," said Bradley to Scott, who was busily writing.

Ned stood in front of him with his hands in his pockets, and the downcast, sheepish air, of a countryman who has come to ask a favour, and does not quite see his way how to do it.

"Well, sir, what can I do for you?" said Scott, looking up from his desk.

At that moment, a door at the other end of the room softly opened.

A man entered with noiseless step.

It was Salmon Roe, who had quietly managed to gain admission into the rear of the bank.

At the sight of him, Ned's bearing and appearance changed as if by magic.

He drew himself up to his full height.

Whipping his hands from his pockets, he displayed a brace of levelled revolvers.

Covering Scott and his companion with them, he replied to the former query.

"Do for me? why throw your hands up, every mother's son of you, in double quick time."

Salmon Roe advancing in turn, displayed a brace of similar weapons, which he pointed at the clerks.

"What is this? Who are you?" exclaimed Scott in the wildest bewilderment.

"Bail up, without any blasted cackling, or by —— I'll blow a hole through you," was the reply, "as sure as my name's Ned Kelly."

The very name of the ruffian had a paralysing effect upon his hearers, in whose memory his late terrible exploit was fresh enough to need no recalling.

They threw up their hands above their heads.

"That's pretty now," said Ned, "I see you know who you've got to deal with."

They did, only too well.

"Now I warn you that the first one that tries any tricks on, I'll bowl over," continued Ned, "and that I've got half-a-dozen fellows outside to help me."

The prisoners were obliged to stand in a row in the centre of the room, whilst Ned searched them; Salmon Roe and Dan Kelly, who had come in after him, keeping guard over them.

"Now where's the way?" said Ned.

Scott, who was a courageous man, had by this time recovered himself.

"I can't, perhaps, prevent you from taking whatever you may lay your hands on, but I'm hanged if I'll help you to a single farthing," he said.

Ned glared at him with unmistakable ferocity, and began to search the place.

He succeeded in laying his hands on £300 in gold, notes, and silver.

"This ain't enough," he said. "Keep a close look-out over these beggars, whilst I overhaul the rest of the crib."

As he spoke he moved towards the door, leading to Scott's private residence, which adjoined the bank.

The manager, heedless of his peril, stepped forward with flashing eyes and clenched hands towards him.

"If you come an inch nearer I'll drop you," said Ned, with a stern look.

"Listen a minute, Kelly," said the other, in excited tones, "my wife and children are in there, and you will frighten them to death. If you'll only let me go first to reassure them by a word, I promise I'll not try to give the alarm. But if you hurt a hair of their heads, I'll avenge them even if my life's the forfeit."

"All right," said Kelly, surlily, "I don't want to harm your blessed kids."

Scott advanced to the door of the room, in which his family, consisting of his wife, her mother and seven children, were, and implored them to remain quiet and not be alarmed

He then broke to them the news that they were in Kelly's power.

The ladies took his advice and did not betray any outward alarm, though they felt anything but at ease.

Ned, after rummaging about, discovered the door of the strong-room, and fitted one of the keys found on Scott, to it.

On opening it he discovered upwards of £2,000 in gold, silver, gold-dust and notes.

He also came across a couple of revolvers, and some cartridges, which he secured.

The plunder having been placed in a strong sack, preparations were made for an immediate departure.

Dan Kelly was sent to get out Mr. Scott's buggy and harness his horse to it.

"What are you going to do with us?" said Scott.

"Well we're just going to take you for a little jaunt into the country along with us," replied Ned.

"And my wife?" cried the manager.

"Oh, we'll bring her and the kids along too. Don't be skeary, we're not going to hurt any of you."

With the vague idea of putting off the departure as long as possible, in the hope that help might turn up in some way or other, Scott said—

"Will you have a drink before you go?"

"I don't mind one," was the reply.

A bottle of whiskey was produced from the dwelling house, and a stiff dose poured out.

"Now, then, bottom that," said Ned to Scott.

"But I don't care about it."

"Whether you do or not, you'll just lap it up before I swallow a drop. I am not to be dosed."

Scott swallowed the whiskey in order not to arouse Ned's suspicions any further, and then the bushrangers each took a glass.

"Now then," exclaimed Ned, "off we go."

The procession that started from the bank was one of the most singular ever witnessed.

Indeed, the whole of the details of this daring robbery are of so startling a character as to be almost incredible.

First came the hawker's cart, driven by Dan Kelly, and containing the three bank clerks and a female servant.

Next came the buggy with Mrs. Scott, Mr. Scott's mother, and the children, seven in number, packed into it.

This was followed by the spring cart, in which the sack containing the money had been placed, and which was driven by Ned himself, his companions being Mr. Scott and a female servant.

Salmon Roe brought up the rear on horseback.

"Just listen to me, one and all of you," said Ned, when they were on the point of starting. "If any one of you —man, woman, or child—raises the least alarm as we go through the town, or does the least thing to call attention to us, I swear I'll shoot you down on the spot."

The way in which this threat was delivered was enough.

It is one of the peculiar features of the affair that this motley party of fifteen prisoners and three guardians, failed to attract the least notice when passing out of the township.

This was all the more strange as the bank was only a few yards from the railway station, and was only separated from the other houses in the vicinity by a small, vacant allotment.

The party drove straight for Faithful Creek Station, Ned consulting Lonigan's watch, which he wore in order to ascertain the progress they were making.

The only incident on the road was the falling of the horse Ned was driving, which caused a temporary delay.

Faithful Creek being reached, the whole fifteen were placed in the hut with the twenty-two people already in custody, this making a total of thirty-seven prisoners.

The gang then began to make preparations for departure.

"Hang it," said Zeph, "you're always flashing that blooming tuber. I'm dashed if I don't have one, too !" exclaimed Zeph, and stepping up to Mr. Scott, he coolly appropriated his watch and chain.

"Now listen to me," said Ned, addressing the prisoners. "It's now half-past eight. We're going to start, but we're going to leave one of our pals behind here to watch the hut for three hours. It'll be done, and the first of you that puts his nose outside before that time is up will be shot down. So you'd better keep close 'if you value your skins.'"

Mounting Marco Polo, to whose saddle the sack containing the money had been attached, Ned rode off in company with his three companions.

Such was the terror he had succeeded in inspiring, that not one of the captives dared venture outside the hut till the three hours were up.

At the expiration of that time they started for Euroa, and gave information to the police there, who were thunderstruck at the occurrence.

CHAPTER CCXXIV.

NED VISITS NEW SOUTH WALES, AND DRAWS HIS DIVIDENDS FROM THE JERILDERIE BANK.

This feat of Ned's was the signal for the commencement of something very like a reign of terror amongst the banks of Victoria.

The managers of the local branches kept flocking into Melbourne to escape being served like Mr. Scott.

The police on their part kept dancing about fruitlessly for months, and it was proposed to call in the aid of the black trackers from Queensland, and of bloodhounds from Tasmania to aid them.

Whilst the authorities were utterly at a loss to guess where Kelly and his friends had got to, Ned suddenly took it on himself to reveal his whereabouts in a most startling way.

He had quietly crossed the Murray into New South Wales.

At midnight on Saturday, February 8th, he, with Dan Kelly, Zeph, and Salmon, rode into the town of Jerilderie, situate some forty miles across the border.

They first proceeded to the local police barracks, in which two constables were quartered.

They alighted from their horses and began to knock at the door.

"Who's there ?" demanded one of the bobbies, in a drowsy tone.

"Hi, rouse up !" was the reply. "There's a — of a shindy going on at a public down town, and you're wanted there."

The two policemen, whose names were Richards and Devine, unsuspiciously came out and were confronted by four levelled revolvers.

Resistance was useless, and they were instantly made prisoners.

The gang remained in quiet possession of the police-station during the whole of the following day. which was Sunday.

Zeph and Dan Kelly remained in the barracks, keeping watch over one of the policemen they had captured.

Ned and Salmon Roe, both got up in police uniform. which they had found in the barracks, walked through the streets with their other captive, and compelled him to point out the bank they intended to rob the following day, and to give them all the information they required as to the best means of carrying out the projected robbery.

He did not dare reveal who his companions were, and none of those who saw the trio guessed that the tall, full-bearded fellow, whose stalwart figure was set off to such advantage by his uniform, was Ned Kelly in person.

Early on Monday morning, Zeph took the whole of their horses to the blacksmith's to be shod, and Salmon Roe sauntered into the town and purchased some provisions.

At ten o'clock the gang left the barracks, leaving one of the constables bound within the building and taking Richards the other with them.

The two Kellys walked with their prisoner between them, Zeph and Salmon Roe following on horseback.

Ned, Dan, and their captive proceed straight to the Royal Hotel, which they entered.

The landlord advanced to meet them.

"Mr. Cox," said Richards, addressing him, "this is Ned Kelly."

"Don't be flurried, old bladder chops," said Ned. "I'm Ned Kelly sure enough, and I want to use your crib whilst I rob the bank; but I'm not going to hurt any one if they'll only be quiet."

The cool audacity of this statement was nothing to what followed.

Zeph and Salmon Roe rode up, and dismounting, stationed themselves in front of the hotel.

As fast as customers came up to get a drink they were seized and compelled to enter a room where Dan Kelly stood as sentinel.

Ned then actually proceeded alone to the bank, which he entered from the rear.

Suddenly making his appearance with a revolver in each hand, he called on the manager and his clerks to surrender.

"Bail up, every one of you; I'm Ned Kelly," he shouted.

The order came on them like a thunderbolt, for they had not the slightest notion that Ned was in Jerilderie.

He had reckoned, however, that the mere mention of his name would be enough, and so it proved, for his order was instantly complied with.

After locking up the staff of the bank in an inner room, Ned set to work to ransack the premises.

Whilst he was engaged in this pleasing task, three gentlemen entered the bank on business.

To their amazement the building seemed deserted.

Suddenly Ned popped out of the manager's room, revolver in hand.

The three stood petrified.

Then one of them turned to flee.

"Stop," roared Ned. "If you pass the doorway I'll drop you like a dingo."

The three saw that escape and resistance were equally out of the question, and having surrendered were compelled to join the bank clerks in their confinement.

Dan now joined Ned, leaving the other two bushrangers to look after the prisoner at the hotel, and the pair, after getting together upwards of £2,000 from the bank coffers, amused themselves by destroying a lot of the books.

The four robbers then began to disport themselves about the town like the soldiers of a conquering army.

Incredible as it may seem, they went from hotel to hotel drinking and standing treat to everyone they met with with great apparent civility, but keeping Richards in their company.

At one hotel, in sheer bravado, Ned placed both his revolvers on the bar, and swaggered up and down the room with his hands in his pockets.

So universal was the terror that he inspired, that not a man present dared attempt to seize his weapons and shoot him down.

The bushrangers then "stuck up" the telegraph office, destroyed the wires, and compelled a number of residents to cut down several of the telegraph poles.

At seven o'clock they left the town in triumph, with their plunder and two splendid horses belonging to the police, and recrossed the Victorian boundary.

"What are you going to do with all that money?" inquired one of the townspeople to Ned before he rode off.

"Oh, I'm going round robbing banks to get a pile for my sister to marry on," was the jesting answer, though, if the truth be known, it was to the judicious distribution of some of the stolen money by Kate Kelly that much of the sympathy and assistance received by the bushranger were due.

There is no doubt that the police had their share of it.

As soon as they heard of this inroad into their territory the New South Wales Government added three thousand pounds to the reward already offered by the Victorian authorities, but with no result.

Neither were the Queensland black trackers, who were now employed, and who could follow a man's trail at full gallop, in any way successful.

For some time Ned and his gang lay hid on an island of the Murray, whilst no fewer than three hundred mounted police were being employed in their search at a cost of no less than five thousand pounds a month beyond the usual expenditure.

A local writer was very bitter on this, declaring that all the police officers did was to do "a quiet cigar in the police stables after breakfast, a stroll to the hotel for lunch, another stable inspection with the aid of a fragrant weed, another walk to dinner, and then cigars and billiards for the rest of the evening."

About nine hundred pounds were collected for a memorial to the police shot at Mansfield, towards which two banks, inspired probably by a lively apprehension of a visit from Kelly if they showed themselves too liberal, contributed the insignificant sum of half-a-crown apiece.

As to the men who were arrested from time to time as sympathisers with Kelly, not only were the police unable to secure convictions, but several of the parties accused, on their release, began actions for damages against the magistrates who had remanded them, whilst, owing to the withdrawal of a large body of the Melbourne police to join in the hunt for Ned, crime of all kinds began to become rife in that capital.

In the Legislature it was admitted that this hunt had already cost the colony twenty thousand pounds, but that there was no better prospect of success than at the outset, and, after some time, most of the police were withdrawn to their usual posts.

A singular proof of the terror universally inspired took place at Lancefield.

Two men entered the Commercial bank there, just after it had opened in the morning, gagged the accountant, placed him in an inner room, and made off with six hundred and fifty pounds.

A customer who came in while they were there to deposit two hundred pounds, saved his cash by the ruse of calling their attention to the fact of the blinds being up, which enabled people to see what was going on from outside.

The robbers turned to the windows to pull down the blinds, and the man profited by this to slip his money, which was in notes, under the hearthrug before they searched him.

But this was all he dared do.

The singular part of the story is, that when both men were captured, which occurred the following day, neither of them were found to be armed.

The mere fact of their being supposed to belong to Kelly's gang, and the presentation, by one of them, of a pipe case which terror magnified into a a pistol, had been sufficient for both bank clerk and customer.

Meanwhile, Ned and his friends were quiet and comfortable.

After a time they quitted their island retreat and led a pleasant nomadic life, being well informed of all the movements of their pursuers beforehand, and well supplied with necessaries by their friends.

It was during this period that Ned caused suits of armour, similar to his own, to be forged by a blacksmith out of boiler iron for the rest of the gang.

"I'm blessed if I don't ride into Melbourne and stick up the governor himself one of these days," he said, "rigged up as we are we could lick the whole colony."

From time to time they were reported as having been seen and the police bolted off after them, but in vain, till the old doggrel rhyme made when Sir Frederick Pottinger was Superintendent of Police in New South Wales and spent his time in fruitlessly chasing Frank Gardiner, the bushranger, and beginning "Sir Frederick Pott shut his eyes for a shot, and missed in the usual way," began to be applied to them by one and all.

Kelly's example led to similar deeds in New South Wales.

A man named Scott who took the alias of Captain Moonlight, and who had already served a term of imprisonment in Penbridge jail for highway robbery, got a gang of half-a-dozen together and began to plunder on the Murrumbidgee.

On the 16th November, 1879, he stuck up the inn at Wantabadgery, twenty-five miles from Wagga-Wagga, where Orton used to live.

Information reached this latter place and four police started for the scene of the outrage.

They came up with the bushrangers, six in number, near the inn.

After a sharp encounter, the police being outnumbered were forced to retreat into a swamp.

As they had previously hitched their horses to a fence, these were seized and carried off by the bushrangers.

Being reinforced by five mounted and two foot constables from Gundagai with a vehicle containing extra arms and ammunition, the police again started in pursuit

They proceeded to Wantabadgery station, where they found the bushrangers had bailed up thirty people from the Saturday night till the Monday morning.

No one however had been ill-treated, except the overseer, whom Moonlight had commenced to hang but had released from the noose on account of the screams of the women for whom the bushranger professed a chivalrous respect.

When the police reached the station they found Moonlight and his gang had left, intending to rob the Gundagai bank, but they succeeded in coming up with them at the farm of a selector named McGlede, where they had a number of people bailed up.

On being summoned to surrender, the bushrangers refused.

Some sharp firing took place for half-an-hour, during which two of the bushrangers—one of them being Nesbit, the second in command—were killed, and one wounded, after which the rest surrendered.

One of the police, named Bowen, was shot in the neck by Moonlight, and died of his wounds.

Moonlight was tried at Sydney, and hanged, in company with another of his gang, on the 20th of January following.

Notwithstanding this, Ned's capture seemed as far off as ever, though the hour was approaching when he, too, was to pay the penalty of his crimes.

CHAPTER CCXXV.
KELLY TEARS UP THE RAILWAY LINES.

FOR some time Ned remained so quiet that a local writer observed that "the Kellys are being forgotten, and may be enjoying themselves in London for aught we know."

The truth was that he was still lurking in the north-eastern part of the colony, where the hilly and rugged nature of the country, with every inch of which he was familiar, and the information freely imparted to him by his sympathisers in the district enabled him to set all pursuit at defiance.

Of all outlaws the Australian bushranger is, perhaps, the most difficult to catch.

Native and to the manner born, he knows every lurking-place and fastness of the wilderness, over which his sway extends.

Riding like a Comanchee, he is usually mounted on a horse, in whose veins run the purest blood in the stud book, and who would fetch a "monkey" at Tattersall's any day.

Hence he has little difficulty in showing his heels to the police if they do catch sight of him.

Only this does not often happen, for he has, in the broken and mountainous country, a host of scouts of unrivalled keenness and dexterity.

These form the "bush telegraph."

The brown-faced urchin, lounging after his father's cows on a three-legged screw, with a ragged saddle and green hide-girth, fixes his watchful eyes on the troopers as they enter the forest and disappear up the winding, slate-strewn ravine.

They wear rough, tweed suits and old felt hats, and are riding in stockmen's saddles, with rusty stirrup-irons.

But he knows them for all that, and marks them down.

So the bare-legged girl, tending a flock of sheep or racing after the milkers' calves, meets them camped by a creek, and demurely answers all the questions they put to her about the strayed bullocks they pretend they are in search of.

But, all the time, she knows the "traps" by a dozen signs known to the initiated.

And before midnight the news of their presence has been conveyed to the outlaw in the lonely hut or sylvan den that is his lurking-place, and when his pursuers arrive and surround the spot it is only to find that he has flown on, silently as the night-hawk.

The King River, which is a tributary of the Murray, was Ned's favourite lurking-place at the time, and here

he had selected an unassailable position, from which—as it was afterwards admitted by the authorities—a hundred armed men could not have dislodged him.

As to the sympathy and support he then drew eeci district, it may be judged from one simple fact.

A State school-teacher—a profession one would have thought to be above all others calculated to inspire its follower with a respect for law, and a love of morality,—at Hurdle Creek was dismissed by the Minister of Education, for his partisanship of the outlaws.

Nor can it be denied that much of Ned's immunity was due to the blundering inefficiency of some of the police.

A Royal commission, appointed to enquire into the reasons which enabled Kelly and his followers to set the authorities at open defiance, declared that the administration of the police in the north-eastern part of the colony had been anything but satisfactory.

The conduct of Captain Standish, the Chief Commissioner, was not characterised either by good judgment, or by zeal for the interests of the public service; and though Mr. Nicholson, the assistant commissioner, showed himself to be a capable and zealous officer, he laboured under great difficulties, through the undue interference of the captain, and the jealousy occasioned by the latter's favouritism towards Superintendent Hare.

Inspector Brook Smith, for having neglected a favourable opportunity of capturing the outlaws, in November, 1878, was recommended to retire.

The Commission also, amongst other things, recommended that Superintendent Sadleir should be placed at the bottom of the list of Superintendents, for errors of judgment whilst assisting in pursuit of the gang, that Sergeant Steele should be reduced to the ranks, for having failed to take advantage of the opportunity of capturing the gang, thrown away by Inspector Brook Smith; and that Detective Ward should be disrated, for having misled his superior officer on several occasions.

Such a state of things as is revealed by these recommendations, plainly establishes a good reason for the length and success of Kelly's predatory career.

It is a fact worthy of note, that very many, if not most of the leading bushrangers of the Australian colonies, were shot or captured by private individuals, and not by the police.

Ned continued to have his imitators throughout the colonies, though, it must be confessed that their success was not equal to his.

On November 5th, 1879, two brothers, named Shank, young men of twenty-one and twenty-two, attempted to stick up the Bank of Australasia, at Moe, in South Gippesland, but were beaten off by Mr. Munro, the manager, and subsequently captured.

A man named Wills, stuck up the Queensland National Bank, at Cunamulla, the following January, and secured £170, after shooting a local store-keeper, who came to the assistance of the bank managers.

He left the building, and would have got clear off, had not his horse, which was a magnificent one, broken away before he could reach it.

Owing to this, Police Sergeant Byrnes and some of the townspeople were enabled to secure him.

On the other hand, Ned's freedom from arrest during this period, was ascribed by the local journals, to the assistance afforded by sympathisers.

As a writer in the *Argus* remarked, "A large proportion of the inhabitants of the 'Kelly country' was favorable to the outlaws, whilst the remainder was kept quiet by a system of terrorism."

What this system was, may be judged from a letter written by Zeph, under the name of Byrne, to one of the police, and stating that if the gang could lay hands on him, they would "place him in a hollow log and burn him alive."

No wonder that the police felt chary of facing such foes; though, so disgusted were the authorities of the colony at the supineness or inefficiency of the force, that ir April they had announced that, if the Kelly's were not captured by the beginning of July, the reward offered for their apprehension would be entirely withdrawn.

To maintain the system of terrorism in all its efficiency and at the same time deal a crushing and, in all probability, final blow at the police, Ned resolved on a master stroke.

"I'm going to set a little trap for some of the big bugs amongst 'em that'll open their eyes a bit," was his remark.

In obedience to his orders, his three associates got ready, and, on the evening of Saturday, June 26th, the four bush-rangers, well mounted and armed to the teeth, swept like a dark thunder-cloud down the ranges towards the little township of Glenrowan.

Glenrowan, which is in Moira county, is situated about 136 miles from Melbourne, in a gap of the Futter's Ranges, which bound it to the north-west and to the south-east.

To the north-east, in the direction of Wangaratta, is an extensive plain, whilst to the south-west the ground is low, flat, and swampy.

At a short distance from the town stood the hut of a young man named Aaron Sherritt, who had at one time been an acquaintance of Ned's, but who had recently married and had settled down to hard work.

Ned had received information, which was correct, that Sherritt was in communication with the police.

Indeed, at the very moment of the outlaw's arrival there were four members of the force in the hut.

The gang became aware of this on inspecting the stables.

"What do you mean to do, Ned?" asked Dan Kelly.

"Do? Why, try and snap up the whole blessed lot of 'em, since luck has thrown 'em in our way. We're a match for ten times as many in our armour."

"All right," was the reply.

"But, first and foremost, we must settle up square with the sneak who wants to sell our necks. I'm not going to miss him at any rate, to-night."

"We'd better 'tice him outside then," said Zeph.

"Yes. He don't know your voice, so you'll be the best to do it, but, mind, I'm going to have first crack at the crawling skunk."

"Very good; we'll not fire unless you miss," said Salmon Roe.

"That's not very likely," was Ned's grim remark.

Advancing softly, Zeph knocked at the door of the hut.

"Hi, Sherritt!" he called out.

The unsuspecting man opened the door.

At first he did not recognise his visitors.

"Just step out a minute, I want a word with you," continued Zeph.

Sherritt stepped across the threshhold, and, as he did so, Ned strode forward and confronted him, revolver in hand.

The unhappy man realised his peril.

He guessed Ned's terrible errand only too well.

Fear, however, paralysed his movements.

His tongue refused to utter a word, and, before he could try to flee, Kelly had covered him.

"You know what I'm here for, you sneaking blood-sucker," cried Ned. "You thought to handle the pile that's offered for me, only, like one or two more in their time, you'll find that it's lead not gold you'll be paid in."

As he spoke he pulled the trigger, and Sherritt dropped a corpse.

"Shot down as though he were a dog," to quote the words in which this outrage was recorded.

One of the police within the hut had risen, on hearing what sounded like an altercation outside the hut, and reached the door.

On hearing the shot fired, he thought discretion the best part of valour, and, careless of Sherritt's fate, at once banged to the door and secured it with the bar.

This, probably, saved the lives of himself and his comrades, though they were subsequently severely censured by the royal commissioners for not making any attempt to avenge the poor fellow whose fate they had witnessed.

Kelly ordered an attack on the hut, but without effect.

The door was too strong to be forced, and the bush-rangers were exposed to the fire of their adversaries, which but for the protection afforded by their armour would probably have thinned their ranks.

Nor was an attempt at firing the hut more successful, the tough iron-bark shingles of the roof, and many logs which formed the walls, defying the flame.

"Never mind that lot of cowards in there," said Ned, as he withdrew his forces, "they'll do their work for us as well alive as dead."

"How do you mean?" inquired Zeph.

"Why, as soon as news of this gets to Melbourne they'll send down all the police big-bugs, and Inspector O'Connor from Queensland, with those cursed black trackers of his that they've got there. Those are the beggars above all others I want to wipe out, for as to the Victoria police they're the biggest set of duffers that ever straddled a saddle."

"You're right there," said Dan Kelly; but what is your dodge when they do come?"

"Why, I'm going to pull up the rails at Glenrowan. They'll send the traps on from Melbourne to Beechworth in a special train, that'll come scooting along twenty miles an hour. Only instead of Beechworth being the end of their trip, they'll just find themselves in ——"

Kelly's surmise was correct, for on the news of the outrage at Shirrell's reaching Melbourne, a special train was despatched, containing police officers and trackers, shortly after 10 o'clock, for Beechworth, the capital of the district, situate some miles beyond Glenrowan, through which the railway runs.

Meanwhile, however, the gang had made arrangements for its reception.

At about three o'clock on the Sunday morning Mr. Stanistreet, the station-master at Glenrowan, was roused from his slumbers by a knock at the door of the station.

Huddling on some clothes he went to the door, but before he could reach it it was burst in.

"Who are you? What's this mean?" cried the bewildered official, as several men entered the passage.

A tall man clad in a long overcoat stepped forward.

"I'm Ned Kelly, and you'll have to come along with me and pull up some of the rails."

Stanistreet, having finished dressing, followed the bush-ranger out on to the railway line, where six or eight of the inhabitants of the township were standing, under the guard of Salmon Roe alias Stephen Hart.

"Now then," roared Kelly, "tell those beggars how to get the rails up. We're expecting a special directly."

The unfortunate station-master felt his blood run cold.

"I know nothing about lifting the rails," he gasped.

"Who does then, you thick-headed fool?"

"The platelayers."

"Where are they?"

"In their hut, about a quarter of a mile down the line."

Leaving Salmon Roe in charge of the station-master, Ned proceeded to the hut occupied by the platelayers, whom he roused from their slumbers, and obliged to return with him to the station.

"Now then," said Salmon Roe, giving Stanistreet a prod in the ribs with his gun, "where are the tools to rip rails up."

"I haven't got the key," was the reply.

"Where are they?"

Stanistreet had to point out the place where the tools were stored, which was in a shed near the station, the lock of which was promptly forced.

Forcing the two platelayers to equip themselves with the necessary implements, Ned started off with them to a spot a little beyond Glenrowan towards Wangaratta.

Here, under his direction, the rails were torn up and a trench cut across the line.

"I guess if they once get into that hole they'll not wriggle out in a hurry," muttered Ned, as he surveyed the result of two hours' labour on the part of the platelayers.

This task accomplished, he returned to the tool-house, where the station-master and six or eight others had remained prisoners, in charge of Salmon Roe.

Ned proceeded to question Stanistreet as to the method of signalling.

The other gave some explanation.

"But there's a way of stopping a train with a lamp, ain't there?" said Kelly.

The station-master admitted there was.

"Well, now, you just mark my words. There's a special train coming, and it's just going to run on clean through past this station. If you try to stop it by your lamps or flags, or other devilments, you'll be a dead man the next minute. Watch his face," and here Ned turned to Salmon Roe, "and if he gives any sign shoot him down."

The station-master and his companions were marched back to his dwelling, and left under the charge of Salmon Roe.

Other persons were made prisoners and lodged in the same building, to the number of seventeen.

They remained locked up all day on Sunday, but in the evening were allowed to go over to Jones' Hotel, situate close to the station, where Ned and the other two bushrangers had taken up their quarters, with several other captives, Salmon Roe occupying the station-master's house, and continuing his watch over that functionary.

Ned's plan was diabolically ingenious.

He counted that the train would pass through Glenrowan without stopping, and would come to grief just beyond the town, where he had torn the rails up.

He had, therefore, settled with his mates that, as soon as it had passed the station, they were to mount their horses, gallop on to the scene of the inevitable accident, and, in his own words—

"Rake the whole concern with shot till not a beggar was left alive on it!"

Sunday night came on, and it was evident that the train could not be much longer in arriving.

With their rifles in their hands, three out of the four outlaws gathered on the verandah in front of the hotel, listening in anxious expectation for the signs of its approach.

Every ear was on the alert; but the hours rolled on and there was no sign.

At last, towards three o'clock on Monday morning, a faint noise was heard away to the southward.

"Is that it?" whispered Dan.

"Hush! I'm not sure."

A few moments elapsed.

The noise was louder and nearer.

"That's it, I'm certain," cried Zeph, exultingly.

"That's so," echoed Dan. "My eye! what a jolly fine smash-up there'll be in a minute or so."

"All ready for a start, boys?" inquired Ned.

"Yes," was the reply.

"Cut across to Salmon Roe," ordered Ned, "and tell him to keep his eyes open, and see that that cursed station-master isn't up to any tricks to stop the train, and then to come on with us directly it has passed the station."

Zeph darted off on this errand, and soon returned.

Louder and louder grew the noise of the approaching train.

A few minutes more would decide the fate of all on board it, for, once past Glenrowan signals, it would rush unchecked into the pit prepared for it.

Soon its lights became visible as it drew nearer.

"It's going a blessed sight slower than I care for," he muttered. "By —— it looks as if it was going to pull up at the station! No!"

As he spoke, a dark mass was visible on the line, and rolled slowly past the station.

"It's all right!" cried Ned, "let's be off. But what a short train!"

Zeph had his hand on his arm.

"Look!" he exclaimed, and Ned glanced in the direction indicated.

Behind the dark object appeared another.

"What the devil's this?" cried Kelly, "another train?"

As the words left his lips the second object rolled alongside the station platform and came to a halt.

A host of dark figures leaping from it advanced towards the hotel.

CHAPTER CCXXVI.
THE ATTACK ON JONES' HOTEL AT GLENROWAN.

THE fact was that the attacking party had availed themselves of a measure which Ned had not foreseen.

The train had reached Benalla at half-past one o'clock, having Inspector O'Connor and his black trackers aboard, and was there joined by eight troopers and their horses, under the command of Superintendent Hare.

As they were now about to enter the Kelly country it occurred to the authorities that it would be as well not only to keep an extra sharp look out, but to send on a pilot engine in advance.

This was accordingly done, and the train resumed its journey at two o'clock.

It was travelling at a rapid pace, and had arrived within a mile and a quarter of Glenrowan, when it was stopped by the pilot engine, owing to the following circumstances.

Amongst the people captured by Ned at Glenrowan was the schoolmaster, a man named Curnow, who was seized in company with his wife and sister.

Ned, however, allowed him to go home with these ladies, at the same time warning him "to go quietly to bed and not dream too loud," or he might get shot.

Curnow had heard the outlaws mention the plan of lying in ambush for the train, and resolved to foil it.

He went home quietly, but got ready a scarlet woollen scarf to serve as a danger signal, and a candle and matches.

With these he started from his house during the small hours, and met the pilot engine a little way from Glenrowan.

On reaching a straight part of the line, where he judged those on the train would be able to see the signal at some distance, he lit the candle and held it up behind the red scarf.

This was observed by the people on the pilot engine, who at once pulled up.

Curnow came forward and told them that the Kellys were in Glenrowan, and that the rails had been torn up just beyond the town.

The pilot engine halted, and warned the train when it came up.

Superintendent Hare ordered the carriage doors on each side to be unlocked, and his men to get in readiness.

The lights on the train were then extinguished, and following close behind the pilot engine it advanced on Glenrowan.

It was the pilot engine that Ned had mistaken for the train, but he was quickly undeceived, for whilst it passed through the station and then halted, the train itself drew up alongside the platform and the police leaped out.

The next moment Salmon Roe came rushing up from the station to the verandah of the hotel, where Ned and the other two were still standing in amazement.

"The traps, the traps!" he gasped. "They're on us thick as wasps—a whole train full—trooper and black trackers."

The words had hardly escaped his lips, when the dark mass of men was seen advancing from the station towards the hotel.

The police on alighting from the train had at once been told of Kelly's whereabouts.

Hare at the head of his troopers, followed by Connor and his blacks, advanced on the hotel building, the outlines of which they could discern in the darkness.

"Come on," shouted the former, charging almost up to the verandah.

"I'll take the crow out of that cock," said Ned; "leave him to me. Now blaze away, boys."

A fringe of fire broke out along the verandah in obedience to this order, and lit up the black darkness beyond.

A groan escaped Hare as Ned's bullet struck him on the left wrist and shattered it.

Nothing daunted, however, he continued to fire with one hand, till he became exhausted from loss of blood.

The police fired a volley, and a bullet struck Ned on the left foot.

"Curse it, I'd like to have my hand on the neck of the skunk who fired that shot," he growled. "It's so dark that there is no chance of spotting the man who hits you, or even of shooting straight."

This was indeed the case, and to it must be ascribed the slight loss sustained by the attacking party, who, after their first rush, had sought cover behind trees and palings, sheltered by which they continued to pour in their fire.

The first brush was exceedingly hot, but, for some time, there was more powder burnt than mischief done.

The police and the bushrangers blazed away at each other furiously in the darkness for about a quarter of an hour, during which the reports of their weapons and the screams of the terrified women, kept as prisoners in the hotel, made in combination a deafening uproar.

"I'm hit again, curse it," said Ned, who was fearlessly facing it all.

"Where?" asked Zeph.

"In the left arm. It aint much though. They've rapped my carcase half-a-dozen times, but its no use their trying that game when I've ninety-seven pounds of iron-plating on me."

"It strikes me," said Salmon Roe, "that we're in a tightish fix."

"We'd better get inside the hotel, or they'll be sneaking round and getting into the back," suggested Zeph.

This advice was adopted.

A lull followed, though nothing could be distinguished for a moment on account of the smoke.

The police driving their adversaries more, and determining to cut off their retreat, scattered and surrounded the building.

Hare had retreated to the railway station with a shattered wrist, bleeding profusely; but after Carrington, the artist of the *Australian Sketcher* who had accompanied the expedition, had bound the wound up with a handkerchief, he returned to the scene of action, and cheered his men as best he could, and urged them to keep a good look out.

At length he became exhausted from loss of blood and had to retire.

Inspector Connor and Constable Kenny took command and kept pelting away—the former, with his black trackers, having taken up their position in a little creek running along the front of the hotel, the banks affording them capital cover.

"We've only one chance," said Ned, "and that is to break through their lines whilst it is still dark. By daylight we shall have fifty more of the vipers round the place."

"We might get through singly, but they'd spot and rush us if we tried to do it in a lump," said Salmon Roe, "and if they bowled over our horses, what chance would we have."

At these words a chance of escape flashed across Ned's mind.

His horse was not in the hotel.

He had hidden Marco Polo in the bush, a few hundred yards from the building, on the way to the spot where the railway lines had been torn up.

That few hundred yards covered, and he would be on the back of the fleetest horse in Australia, and could defy pursuit.

A momentary struggle stirred him at the thought of abandoning his companions.

They had stuck to him faithfully and well.

But, on the other hand, it was evident that all could not

escape, and it was better, he thought, that one at least should be saved.

Still he felt angry and ashamed of himself.

He was in a rage, and naturally wanted to vent it upon some one.

A respectable old fellow, named Martin Cherry, who was one of the hostages the bushrangers held as prisoners in the hotel, was standing near him.

"Pull aside that blind," said Ned, indicating one that hung before a window through which he wished to reconnoitre the ground.

The old man hesitated, as well he might, since to do so would probably be to draw a shot from the watchers without.

"Pull aside that blind." repeated Kelly, "or I'll blow your brains out, you old bandicoot"

And as Cherry stood bewildered with fear, he raised his revolver, and sent a bullet through the old man's body.

Up to this time the prisoners, amongst whom were several who were in reality active sympathisers with the Kellys, had been well treated.

This unprovoked act of brutality filled them with horror. Ned saw this, and it fairly maddened him.

Suddenly quitting the room, he darted down the verandah steps and was soon swallowed up in the darkness.

No sound reached those within indicating that he had been spotted by their foes.

"By all that's lively." exclaimed Zeph, "I believe Ned has got through them."

And so, indeed, he had.

Of all the miraculous escapes that marked Ned's career, there is not one more wonderful than that from the beleaguered hotel at Glenrowan

Stealing noiselessly as a ghost across the ground, he advanced unperceived towards the cordon of police by whom it was surrounded.

As soon as he was close upon them he threw himself on his face.

They did not see him.

Wriggling along like a snake, he passed between a couple of them, and had soon gained the cover of the bush and broken ground extending in their rear.

He made his way in silence towards the spot where he had tethered his horse.

In a few moments more he stood beside Marco Polo, who joyfully pressed his velvet muzzle to his master's shoulder in greeting.

In a few moments Ned could be free from all danger.

He had but to spring on Marco Polo's back and give the noble beast the rein, and he had seen the last of his perils for many a day to come.

Yet something seemed to weigh heavy on Ned's mind as he stood in silent thought with his hand upon his horse's bridle.

CHAPTER CCXXVII
NED KELLY IS CAPTURED.

MEANWHILE the siege continued, the hotel being surrounded, and a vigilant watch being kept up through the dark hours.

Firing went on intermittently, as occasion served, and bullets were continually heard whizzing through the air.

Several fired from the hotel lodged in the station building, and some struck the train ; but the police had found admirable cover amongst the trees and palings, and were not hurt.

All at once, about five in the morning, a heart-rending wail, issuing from the beleaguered hotel, chilled the blood of all who heard it.

It was the voice of a mother mourning for her firstborn ; of Rachel weeping for her children and refusing to be comforted.

The son of the landlady, Mrs. Jones, had been accidentally struck in the back by one of the besieger's bullets, and it was supposed fatally wounded.

The distracted mother came out of the hotel crying

bitterly and wringing her hands, and then returned in despair to its shelter.

She ultimately succeeded in removing the wounded boy from the building, with the aid of the released prisoners, whose escape is referred to further on.

Another bullet from without, flew, though also by accident, to a fitter mark.

At half past five, Dan Kelly was standing in the bar room.

"I'm sick of lugging about this hundredweight of iron," he grunted, as he temporarily relieved himself of his armour. "It's all very useful when you're in the open. but, cooped up here as we are, all it does is to tire a chap and hinder him from jumping about as spry as he might."

"Don't make a fool of yourself, Dan," said Zeph. "You'd better stick to your plating to the end."

"I wish," said Salmon Roe, half to himself, "that the chap who first hit on the plating dodge had stuck to us as well as it does."

"What d'ye mean?" cried Zeph, "d'ye think Ned's bolted for good and all?"

"Well, it looks something like it."

"Not a bit of it. He's working some dodge to pull us all through, I'll swear. Ned Kelly's not the cove to go back on a pal," cried Zeph, whose faith in their leader was of the most robust character and who firmly believed Ned was absent on some scheme that was to free them all.

"Yes," exclaimed Dan, who had filled himself a glass of whiskey at the bar and was in the act of raising it to his lips, "Ned's a rare good 'un, and we've not seen the last of him yet."

Even as he spoke a random bullet entered the bar-room window.

The glass he held dropped from his fingers with a crash on to the floor, and the next instant he had sunk down beside it as though paralysed.

Zeph and Salmon Roe advanced to raise him, but he was already a corpse.

"If Ned doesn't pull us out of this," exclaimed the former, "we're in a trap for certain."

"If it is one I'm not coming out of it alive," was the reply, given with despairing energy.

"Will you shake hands on that, mate?"

"Yes, if I can't walk out of here scot free, I'd rather lie alongside Dan there than give Gateley a job."

Gateley was the Victoria hangman, a vicious and depraved fellow who passed most of his time in prison for misdemeanour, and when free was generally drunk.

"I'm with you then," said Zeph, and the pair shook hands on the bargain to die rather than surrender.

Then they turned their attention to external matters watching for the flash of their assailants' guns and sending a shot in answer.

At daybreak police reinforcements arrived from Benalla, Beechworth, and Wangaratta, raising the number of the attacking party to thirty men, of whom Superintendent Foster now took command.

On the new comers dispersing, to take up the best positions they could around the building, numerous shots were fired at them from the hotel, most of them striking the fences or burying themselves in the turf.

"I expect they'll make a sally and try to break through us as soon as it is fairly daylight and they can see where they are going to, and once in those cursed ranges we'd have all our work to do over again; so be on the alert, boys," was the superintendent's order.

"I can make out some horses in the little yard at the back, sir," remarked a constable named Dwyer. "Hadn't we better pepper away at them, and try to cripple 'em? That'll stop their bolting."

"Bravo! a capital dodge!" cried the superintendent.

This brutal but far-sighted plan was promptly carried out, and soon the sickening screams of the wounded and maddened horses were added to the other infernal sounds of warfare.

"They've hit the horses," said Salmon Roe to his pal.

"Yes, and what's more they mean to," replied the other, who had guessed the plan. "The fellow who is bossing this show has got his head on the right way, and our chance looks devilish dickey."

Nevertheless, the two bushrangers had no thought of flinching, but continued to load and fire steadily.

"Hullo, here they come at last! Stand firm, boys," cried the superintendent.

The door had opened, and several figures appeared in front of the hotel.

"Hold on, don't fire," yelled Connor, whose keen-sighted blacks had detected who these were; "they are women and children."

They were, indeed, the women and children who had been made prisoners in the hotel, but who were now suffered to depart.

"Let 'em through one by one," was Foster's order, "and see there are no tricks on travellers. I don't want to have Master Ned go sneaking off under our very nose under cover of a petticoat."

Accordingly the women were challenged individually as they approached the police lines, and were carefully examined before they were allowed to pass through them.

Close attention was paid to the hotel, it still being taken for granted that the whole of the gang was there, for Ned's departure and Dan's death were unknown to the women who had left.

Before daylight a revolving rifle and a cap had been found about a hundred yards from the hotel, in a pool of blood.

They were Ned's, who had found that the wound in his arm was more troublesome than he had thought, and who had consequently abandoned his rifle.

Suddenly, whilst every eye of the attacking force was fixed on the hotel, a series of shots rang sharply out in their rear.

They turned, half panic-stricken, nor was the sight that met their eyes, one calculated to re-assure them.

A weird, unearthly-looking figure could be distinguished, gliding towards them through the trees.

Its stature approached the gigantic, and its bulk seemed still further magnified by the grey light of early morn, whilst its outline was startling and fantastic.

The head was covered with a strange and hideous mask of iron, and a long grey garment floated down to the knees.

"It's a madman!" exclaimed one of the constables.

"It's the devil!" cried a second.

"Holy saints! it's a bunyip," ejaculated a third, named Murdoch, in accents of unfeigned terror.

The bunyip is a mysterious and destructive creature, on which no white man in Australia has yet set eyes, but which the natives, who profess the deepest dread of it, assert to have a semi-human shape, and phenomenal strength and rapacity.

Then a voice rang out—

"Steady, boys, it's no bunyip; it's Ned Kelly himself."

A brief glance showed that it was indeed Ned, who had made up his mind to free his comrades at any cost.

The police at once opened fire on him.

His wound prevented him from using a rifle, but he carried a revolver, and walked coolly from tree to tree, receiving the fire of the police with the utmost indifference, and returning a shot whenever a good opportunity presented itself.

Their bullets rattled off him like rain-drops from a window-pane.

"It's charmed he is," cried Murdoch. "Nothing but a silver bullet will ever bring him down."

"Deuce take me, if I can make it out," said a steady old trooper. "I sighted fair at his chest, and I swear I saw my bullet pop off him like a parched pea."

Shot after shot was fired without effect, and the men were fast getting demoralised by their seemingly supernatural antagonist, who bade their bullets defiance.

Ned passed further along the line, and found himself confronted by Sergeant Steele, of Wangaratta, Constable Kenny, and a railway guard, named Dowsett.

They too opened fire on him persistently, but, to their surprise, with no effect.

" His hide's bullet-proof," said Kenny.

" No," suddenly exclaimed Steele, " he has got armour on. Blaze away for your lives at his legs."

Steele set the example.

His first shot aimed at Ned's legs made the bushranger stagger, and a second brought him to the ground, with a cry of—

" I'm done! I'm done! '

Steele and Kenny rushed up, followed by some others.

The former threw himself on Ned and grappled with him, escaping by the closest shave, a ball from the outlaw's revolver.

Ned howled like a wild beast at bay, and strove to strangle his determined antagonist.

The others threw themselves on him, and a desperate struggle ensued.

He kicked, bit, tore and yelled, till at last numbers and the loss of blood prevailed over his Herculean might, and he was disarmed and secured.

" Curse you all, I wish I'd have shot myself," he ejaculated as he lay bound and panting. " You think you've done a precious fine thing, you cowards, when I'd only one arm and couldn't handle my rifle. I could have got away last night if I'd have liked, for I got into the bush with my horse and lay there safe and snug all night. Yes, I could have got off, but when I saw them all pounding away I thought I would wait and see it over."

At this moment a woman dressed in a black riding habit, red underskirt and white Gainsborough hat, galloped recklessly up, despite the warnings of the police for her to keep back.

On seeing Ned she sprang from her horse and threw herself down beside him.

It was his sister Kate.

" Oh! Ned, Ned," she cried, " have they got you? "

" Yes, through no cleverness of theirs, though. I got into the bush with Marco Polo and could have rushed away, but I wanted to see the thing out, and remained."

Ned was almost fainting from loss of blood.

He was at once carried down to the station and attended to by Dr. Nicholson, of Benalla.

His face was smeared with blood, and his body literally covered with wounds.

He had been shot in the left foot, left leg, left arm, right hand, and twice in the region of the groin, but no bullet had penetrated the armour that had protected the vital parts of his body.

His wounds having been dressed, the doctor declared that he was in no danger from them, and arrangements were made to convey him to Melbourne in course of the day.

CHAPTER CCXXVIII.
DESTRUCTION OF THE GANG.

THE siege had all this while been maintained without intermission.

The fact that the other three outlaws were in the place was confirmed by Ned, who was ignorant of Dan's fate, and they could be heard shouting and rapping their armour.

The interest and excitement heightened every moment.

The Kelly gang were at last within reach of the hand of the law they had so often defied.

Only before that hand could tighten its grip on them, it was very probable that there would be a siege on the green.

Zeph and Salmon Roe had witnessed Kelly's attack on the police, which they judged was intended to release them.

They marked his fall, and knowing that he had vowed not to be taken alive, held that he was slain.

" Ned's gone under," exclaimed Salmon Roe.

" Yes," said Zeph, " didn't I tell you he'd not desert his pals while there was life in him."

" You were right. He was a game one."

" A game one. The pluckiest bit of man flesh that ever trod in shoe leather."

The two continued to keep up a steady fire from the rear of the building where they had barricaded themselves after Dan's death.

From time to time they exposed themselves recklessly to the police, shouting defiantly as they did so.

It was the mad recklessness of despair, for it was impossible for them to hold out for ever, despite the mail made out of ploughshares with which they were covered, and which at least a dozen times saved them from what would have otherwise been a deadly bullet.

It struck Foster that the police would act with still more vigour if the persons whom he knew were confined in the hotel were allowed to make their escape.

At ten o'clock in the forenoon he gave orders to cease firing, and called on all prisoners to make their escape.

As soon as word to that effect was passed on by the police lying nearest to the front of the building, a white handkerchief was held out as a flag of truce at the front door.

Immediately afterwards there was a rush of about thirty men out of the building, all holding up their hands above their heads in token of their harmlessness.

" By Jove, there are a lot more than I thought for," said Foster. " We must take care and see if there is any wheat in all this chaff."

The police levelled their guns at the advancing crowd, and called upon them to stand.

They at once did so, and then, in obedience to a further order, threw themselves down on the ground, a precaution highly necessary, as the outlaws might have been amongst them.

The scene presented, as they all lay on the ground attempting to verbally demonstrate their respectability of character, was unique.

" This is shameful! I'm a respectable citizen," cried one.

" I'm Smith—John Smith, of Glenrowan."

" I've lived here twenty years," shouted another.

" Good heavens! do I look like a bushranger? I'm a barber," yelled a third.

" I'm a storekeeper from Benalla," exclaimed a fourth.

" It don't matter, darlins, who the divil ye are!" exclaimed an Irish constable, in answer to these appeals. " It's only what ye aren't, we're after seekin', and if ye aren't Kelly's lot, we've no consarn wid ye."

Nevertheless they were all examined, and passed beyond the police lines one at a time, two brothers, named McAnliffe, suspected as Kelly sympathisers, being detained in custody.

The police now heard of Dan's death, and that there were only two of the desperadoes left alive.

The siege was kept up till three o'clock in the afternoon, by which time the fire from the hotel had grown considerably slacker.

The police were so sheltered that Salmon Roe and Zeph had resolved not to throw away any ammunition on them unless with certainty.

They thought that by playing 'possum a bit they might tempt them into the open.

The assailants, though sticking to their cover, began to grow impatient.

The best part of the day was over, and things seemed very little advanced.

" Mayn't we rush the place, sir?" was an appeal made by them to their leader several times.

" No," was the reply, " I can't risk your lives. There are several hours daylight yet, and we're bound to get the best of them."

" But there are only two—or, mebbe, one—left. We could do them easily," expostulated Kenny.

"Yes, and how many of yourselves at the same time? A rush in the house could not be supported from the outside, as there is a long narrow passage, and we don't know in what part of the house they are. You know you can't knock 'em over till you've actually got your hands on em, because of their armour."

"But their powder must be running out. They're not firing at all," pleaded the pertinacious subordinate.

"Don't trust that; they've lots of ammunition. Their final capture is a certainty, for there is a cannon on the way from Melbourne. I have a telegram to say so. They'll soon be at the end of their tether, but meanwhile I won't waste life."

A cannon was actually on its way as stated, though the affair was ended before its arrival.

Moreover, such an importance had the siege assumed in the eyes of the authorities, that preparations were also being made to despatch an electrical lighting apparatus to Glenrowan in case the conflict should be prolonged into the hours of darkness.

Nevertheless, after a little more importunity Foster consented to another plan.

The fire from the hotel had slackened to such a degree that he began to surmise that, after all, the inmates might be dead or crippled.

By his orders they were formally called upon to surrender, but still no reply was returned.

A short consultation was held.

Constable Charles Johnson of Violet-town, volunteered to fire the building.

Foster accepted his offer.

A strong body of the assailants was massed in front of the hotel and another on the west side, both approaching as closely as they could, though keeping well under cover.

"What's this mean?" said Salmon Roe to Zeph as he marked this disposition of the attacking force.

"Blamed if I know, but we'd better keep our eyes open," was the reply.

"Well, if they're going to try to rush us up by a rush, I guess one or two won't see the inside of this caboose."

The two then separated, in order for each to look after one of the threatened frontages.

Suddenly each of the two parties of assailants poured in a tremendous volley.

Under cover of the smoke Johnson dashed boldly forward towards the house.

He carried a large bundle of straw, which, having fired, he placed on the ground on the west side of the building.

It broke into flames.

Salmon Roe fired twice at the daring fellow, but without effect.

"Devil smother them all," he muttered, "but they mean to burn us alive, the cowards."

There was a moment of intense excitement, and the hearts of all without the building were relieved when the daring fellow, who had accomplished this feat, was seen to regain, uninjured, the shelter he had left.

In the meantime the straw, which had burnt fiercely at first, had all been consumed, and doubts began to be entertained as to whether Johnson's exploit had been successful.

Not many minutes elapsed, however, before smoke was seen coming out of the roof.

Flames were then discerned through the front windows on the western side.

"By the hookey, the crib's ablaze, and if those beggars don't come out now they'll be roasted in that armour of theirs like lobsters in their shells," exclaimed a policeman.

A light easterly wind was blowing at the time, and this had carried the flames from the straw underneath the house, which was built a little way from the ground on piles as is the custom.

As the building was all wood, when once these flames reached the floor, and this caught, they spread rapidly.

The house began to fill with smoke, which rolled in stifling clouds along the passages.

Flickering tongues of flames leaped up here and there from the floor, and darted up the walls which they attacked.

To the sharp crackling sound of blazing timber, was joined a muffled roar like that of a furnace in full blast.

The fire had got well hold of the house.

Zeph and Salmon Roe retreating before the flames gained a room in the rear.

"What's to be done?" said the latter, "it seems to me that this time the game is up."

"I'm afraid so."

"Well, shall we bolt out of this infernal blazing hole. We'll be roasted if we stop much longer."

"I don't much see the good of bolting out," remarked Zeph calmly.

"Have you got a fancy to be grilled?"

"If the parsons are right, we shall both be grilled to all eternity, so a little more or less won't matter. Besides, I'd as soon be grilled as hanged."

"So'd I, for the matter of that."

"Well, see here. If we get out, we can't get clear. They'll fire at us, and as they can't kill us through our armour, they'll cripple and capture us to hang us at Melbourne."

"I'd blow my brains out first."

"That's just what I was thinking of. Only I'd as soon die by a pal's hand."

Salmon Roe understood him.

"You're right there," he answered.

The two men so strangely united by the bond of long continued common crime held out each a hand.

They gave one another a firm grip to bind the strange bargain they had concluded.

Then each laid aside his breast armour.

Standing face to face and levelling their revolvers at each other's chest they paused for a moment.

"At the word three," said Zeph.

In unison they counted "One! two! three!"

Then there was a loud report.

"What is that?" cried one of the assailants.

"It must be the fire got to some cartridges," said a comrade.

It was the death-knell of Salmon Roe, alias Stephen Hart, and Zeph, alias Byrne, who had fallen, shot to the breast each by the other's hand.

Several more explosions followed from the burning building.

Still no signs of life appeared, despite repeated calls addressed to the inmates to surrender.

All eyes were fixed on the blazing and now silent pile, and the besiegers began to close in rapidly on it, some dodging from tree to tree, and others, persuaded that everyone in the hotel must be dead or *hors de combat*, advancing boldly into the open.

Father Gibney, a priest, who had already started for the house, and had been checked by the police, was the first to enter.

At much personal risk from the flames, he hurried into a room to the left, and saw two bodies lying on their backs.

From their position it was evident that they had shot each other.

He touched them, but only to find that life was extinct, and had barely time to ascertain this, before the flames forced him and those who followed him, to leave the room without venturing to risk attempting to remove the bodies.

They were those of Zeph and Salmon Roe.

They certainly were not "lovely in their lives," but it could be truly said of them that "in their deaths they were not divided."

The corpse of Dan Kelly, which lay at the entrance to the bar-room at the eastern side of the house, was recovered, but not until it had been dreadfully scorched.

Hardly had this been done than the roof fell in.

In a few minutes all that was left of the hotel was a lamp-post with a signboard bearing the following inscription:—"The Glenrowan Hotel. Ann Jones. Best accommodation," swinging in mockery above the pile of smoking ashes, that had formed the funeral pyre of the "Kelly Gang."

CHAPTER CCXXVIII.
CONCLUSION.

NED, after having had his wounds seen to by Dr. Nicholson and Dr. Ryan, was placed in a railway van and sent off to Melbourne, where the excitement during the "Battle of Glenrowan" had been indescribable.

The newspapers had been publishing fresh editions concerning it every hour.

When it was known Kelly was *en route*, this excitement increased, but the authorities did all they could to keep the time and place of his intended arrival dark.

Crowds assembled at the Spencer Street Station, but the train halted at North Melbourne, where he was removed, prostrate and helpless, from the van on a stretcher, transferred to a covered waggon, and driven to Melbourne jail, where another dense crowd was assembled.

As soon as he had been sufficiently doctored up, he was taken to Beechworth, the chief town of the Murray River and Ovens districts, by special train on August 6th, and placed at the bar of the police-court charged with the murder of Constables Lonigan and Scanlan.

Being committed for trial, he was brought up at the Beechworth Circuit Court on August 11th, and sentenced to death.

The excitement in Melbourne continued to be immense and a strong feeling of sympathy manifested itself in his favour.

"Flying Scud" was put on at one of the theatres, in order to introduce Ned's horse, which was loudly cheered every evening.

A monster meeting, presided over by no less a person than David Gaunan, Chairman of Committees in the Legislative Assembly, was held at the Hippodrome, and the 4,000 persons who obtained admission, and the 2,000 more for whom there was no room, passed unanimous resolutions in favour of a petition for a reprieve for Ned.

It was signed by no less than 32,424 people.

Nevertheless the law took its course, and on the 11th November the Victorian Jack Ketch fitted the fatal noose round the neck of Ned Kelly, the Ironclad Bushranger of Australia.

THE END.

The crowd fought amongst themselves like hungry dogs over the bones of the fifty years buried outlaw. They turned them up with the steamshovel during alterations to the old Melbourne Jail, also Deeming's body. The latter was scrambled for by women, above all!

COLLECTOR'S NOTE

May 20/29

This most
interesting account
was sent to me by
Mr. J.P. Quaine, of
South Yarra,
Melbourne,
Australia, and it
seemed but fitting
to stick it in
this copy of "Ned
Kelly", for future
readers or
museums to ponder.
An Australian's
point of view,
lurid language and
all. BARRY ONO.

I must confess that the Australians are a race of bloody savages. The scholars from the adjoining building - The Working Mens College - joined in the scramble and all that was saved was Kelly's skull. From this all the teeth were knocked out before the contractor saved it!

This is a fitting end to the great Kelly story, and, as the year 1928 was the fiftieth anniversary of the outbreak, it should make a pretty chapter in future Australian history. The nasty part of it is that Kelly's surviving brother is a respectable farmer in the district which his outlaw brothers gave the historic name of the "Kelly Country" to. Mrs Kelly, the mother died only three years ago, and was known for a long time as a very decent old body. She was nearly ninety when she passed out.

The only son of Kate Kelly, Ned's sister and the heroine of the old days, was killed at the great war and the husbands of her two daughters won a certain degree of distinction at the front as well.